NO MORE TOMORROWS

Penny Merrington

ARTHUR H. STOCKWELL LTD
Torrs Park   Ilfracombe   Devon
Established 1898
www.ahstockwell.co.uk

This is an entirely fictional story,
and no conscious attempt has been made
to accurately record or recreate
any real-life events.

ISBN 978-0-7223-3931-2
Printed in Great Britain by
Arthur H. Stockwell Ltd
Torrs Park   Ilfracombe
Devon

CHAPTER 1

Glencree Castle stood like a sentinel silhouetted against the Highland mountains, its regal splendour reflecting the brilliant early morning sun in the loch below. The peal of the ancient doorbell rang more persistently than it had ever done before, startling Elena, who was crossing the hall on her way upstairs.

She called to Jamie, "Whoever is ringing the bell so furiously? It is far too early for Lawrie, the postman!"

"I am hastening to see, Lady Elena," Jamie replied. He was as alarmed as she.

She waited impatiently on the stairs, a puzzled expression on her usually serene face, as he went to open the door. Jamie pulled back the huge bolts on the massive oak door and peered out.

"It is Lawrie!" he exclaimed.

"So early?" she replied, a pensive look on her face.

"He has a telegram for Sir Bruce!" he exclaimed with dismay.

"A telegram?" she gasped. "Oh, no!" She clutched at her throat. "Surely not now!"

After all they had been through over these past years!

"No, no, it cannot be."

The colour drained from her face as she clung to the banister rail for support. Her thoughts shot back to his previous letter: 'I am now convalescent. I wasn't seriously wounded.' Had he just said that to allay any fears they would have? 'Now', she thought, 'he must surely be dead. No, no, it just cannot be,' she told herself.

Jamie's hand shook with anxiety as he reached out to take the telegram. 'Is it good news or bad?' he thought to himself, but the smiling face of Lawrie soon began to allay his fears.

"I am sure it is good news for the master!" Lawrie exclaimed excitedly, as he saw the anxious look on Jamie's face.

At the sound of his excited voice, and his utterance of "good news", Elena's eyes lit up, and a faint smile crossed her face. She rushed to the door and flung it wide open, much to the astonishment of both men.

"Please give it to me, Jamie!" she exclaimed excitedly.

She snatched it from his grasp and ran as quickly as she could down the long hall. The two men watched her hurry away, both happy to see the evident joy on her face.

"I just know it is good news at last for the master," Lawrie repeated. "I just know it, Jamie. I have already taken some good news to other families in the village, Jamie."

He had, he told himself, brought enough bad news to nearly every home in the village over these past years. Now, surely, it was time for only good news to be coming. Even so, he still dreaded the sight of these small buff-coloured envelopes. He could never be quite sure it would be good news he would be bringing. Daily as he had wended his way through the village, he had felt every mother's eyes on him as he approached, and he saw the fear, anxiety and dread on their faces.

If he passed them by, they still never took their eyes off him as he bade them a sombre good day with no smile on his usually happy face. They would breathe a sigh of relief as he went on his way. He had passed them by today but there was always tomorrow. Some of them had already had more than one telegram, and, even now, with the Armistice signed, so many were dying of wounds. Not until every one of their loved ones were back safely in their arms again would the dread of the small envelopes in Lawrie's hand cease.

Lawrie had told himself over and over again, as he approached the castle that morning, "Oh, how glad I shall be when I have no more of these so dreaded envelopes to deliver! But this one, I feel sure, is good news for the master."

"You will let me know, Jamie, if it is good news that I have brought today?"

"Surely," Jamie replied. "Come in and wait. Sit here and I will get you some tea. You have had such a long walk from the village."

Jamie closed the door and hurried to the kitchen. He told Sarah, the maid, to take Lawrie some tea, and hurried to the lounge, where Elena had gone. He too wanted to hear if this really was good news that had been brought today. As he reached the half-open door of the lounge, he could hear the excited voices of Elena and Harriet.

"Do hurry, Bruce dear!" exclaimed Elena and Harriet, almost together. "Open the envelope quickly, and tell us what it contains."

Bruce, with an anxious look on his face, hurriedly tore it open and unfolded the brief note inside.

"Oh, what does it say?" Elena kept demanding. "Hurry, Bruce dear, hurry!"

His hand was shaking visibly. He somehow dreaded what it might contain, in spite of Elena's assurance that she was sure it was good news. 'Oh, how I hope so!' he told himself.

"Do hurry, dear brother!" Harriet exclaimed.

"Give me time, dear sisters, give me time," he said, but Elena was already holding on to one corner of it.

'ARRIVING HOME TUESDAY EVENING. LOVE, CRAIG.'

He couldn't read the last words. "My son – my son, arriving home at last," he whispered. "At last!"

"Why, that's tomorrow, Bruce dear!" Elena exclaimed, almost screaming with delight. "Harriet dear, our boy will be home tomorrow."

"Thanks be to God," said Harriet, as always taking the good news in a more matter-of-fact way than Elena.

Bruce was rereading the telegram over and over again.

"Is it really true, Harriet?" he asked.

"Yes, dear Bruce, it is true at long last – the day we have longed for, for so long."

His voice faltered with emotion and he clung to them both, wiping tears of joy from their faces. Nothing else mattered to the three of them, only the fact that their darling Craig was on his way. Bruce buried his face in their hair as they clung to one another.

"To think, dear sister, he will already be on his way!"

Bruce was the first to raise his head, and, as he glanced up, he saw Jamie standing at the half-open door. He too had tears in his eyes, and he quickly reached for his handkerchief as Bruce caught his eye. Bruce knew only too well what the news meant to Jamie.

"Jamie, our boy, my son, will be home tomorrow. All must be ready for him. Make sure, Jamie, everything is ready."

"Yes, to be sure, Sir Bruce, everything will be ready."

He hurried out and closed the door and he went to tell Lawrie the good news.

"You were right, Lawrie," he said. "Young Master Craig will be home at last tomorrow."

"Oh, the Good Lord be praised!" he exclaimed. "Now, I must be off to tell the rest of the village. What a happy day this is, to be sure!"

Jamie waved him off down the long drive, closed the door and wended his way to the kitchen, muttering to himself as he went.

"Of course, all will be ready for the young master's homecoming. Haven't I been getting things ready ever since he went away? Of course I have," he reassured himself. He, like the rest of them, had dreaded every day that the news would come that the young master and heir of Glencree Castle would never again enter the door of his home, but now he was coming home at last.

He disappeared into the kitchen, but he knew by the smiling faces and gay laughter that they had already heard the good news. Laughter in Glencree could only mean one thing: the young master was on his way home. No one had laughed in this household since he went away.

"Well," he asked, "how did you get the news?"

"Well," Cook said, "Shona was coming down the stairs and heard you telling Lawrie. Tomorrow, I believe! The Good Lord be praised!" she exclaimed, and she wiped a tear from her eye with the corner of her apron. "Now we will have to hurry to be ready on time. Lady Harriet will be along soon to tell us what she wants doing. Now, Shona, hurry and take some tea to the lounge. They will surely want some."

"We will have our morning tea before we do anything," said Harriet as Shona entered the room with the tray.

'Oh, how like Harriet to be so placid when we have had such exciting news!' Elena thought to herself.

"I am so thrilled, Shona, I hardly know what to do next," she said. "Shona, have you been crying?"

"Yes, Lady Elena, and so have Cook and Sarah – tears of happiness at the good news."

"Now, come and sit down, Bruce," said Elena.

"I won't join you at the table. I will sit in my chair," he replied.

They both watched as he gazed up at the large picture of Isabelle over the fireplace. They knew full well what he was thinking. Never, they knew, would he ever get over her death, and his longing and need for her. Oh, why oh why had that dreadful day to be always with him – a day that had dawned as bright and beautiful as all their days had been since they first met? He, the handsome young 11th Earl and laird of Glencree Castle, with every girl in the village wanting to be his wife and the next Mistress of Glencree! No one had ever caught his eye, until one day, whilst visiting his friend, Lady Margot Emslie, at her home, Harrison Hall. All the villagers had thought she would be the one he would finally choose, but his eyes rested on the beautiful Lady Isabelle, visiting from England. From that moment on, he was bewitched, and they were inseparable. Within two months, they were married. The birth of their son, Craig, a year later, was to complete their heaven. Then, it was always just the three of them, riding, fishing, or visiting the villagers and crofters scattered over his estate. They were occasionally joined by Craig's favourite childhood playmate, Fiona, but it was really only the three of them, always together.

The villagers, as they passed, would comment to each other: "Never have we seen our dear laird as happy as he is now."

Then, suddenly, it had only been the two of them.

'Why had it all changed?' Bruce thought with a sigh. 'Why is she not here by my side waiting for our son? Why? Why?' A deep sigh escaped his lips and he was startled by the rattle of the teacups.

He looked up to see Elena by his side.

"Bruce dear, you haven't drunk your tea."

"I must have fallen asleep. So sorry, my dear. I will have some later."

Harriet was always the first to take hold of any situation: "Come, Elena – we have a lot to do before our dear Craig arrives. I will go and tell Cook to get his favourite dinner ready for tomorrow night, and to get all his favourite dishes back on the menus. And you, Elena, can tell Sarah to get his room ready."

"Well," said Elena, "I daresay Jamie will have seen that everything has been left just as it was when Craig went away."

"Really, Harriet, I can hardly believe it is true after all this time."

"Well, it is true, but we must hurry."

As they turned to go, Bruce called after them: "Please tell Jamie to come to me. I want to go down to the wine cellar."

After they had gone, he walked over to the large window overlooking the loch.

"To think my darling son will be arriving on our small pier tomorrow night, never to leave my side ever again!"

He read and reread the telegram, hardly daring to believe its short but so happy message. Jamie's knock on the door broke in on his thoughts.

"Come in, Jamie," he called. "Are all the lamps ready to be lit?"

"Yes, sir. I got fresh supplies from the village a few days ago. I knew Master Craig would soon be coming home."

"Yes, Jamie, you always seemed to know, in your own canny Scots way, the young master's every move. Sometimes I think you know him as well as I do. Now, we will go down to the wine cellar and choose the wine for his dinner tomorrow, and also bring up the special whisky I have been saving for this our special celebration."

Flint, the dog, rose to accompany them.

"No, boy, you stay."

The dog looked up at him with a questioning look in his large brown eyes. He, like everyone else, was so excited. He had felt the happiness all around him as he heard his master's name mentioned over and over again, and that he was coming home. To be told to stay in the room by himself was not at all to his liking.

"Only for a short while, boy," Bruce assured him with a pat on the head as they passed.

Jamie closed the door as they went out, and Flint flung himself into the corner, his head between his paws, thoroughly dejected. But after a brief moment he was on his feet again. He shot to the window. 'They said my master was coming home. Where is he? Where is he?' He stood as high as he could on his hind legs, and his keen gaze took in the great expanse of the loch. He could see nothing stirring. He hurried to whine and scratch at the door as he heard Bruce's step outside.

"Come on, boy," Bruce called to him, as he bobbed his head round the door. "Let us take our usual stroll."

He strode off with a firmer, sprightlier step than ever before. A beaming smile, not seen for many years, lit up his handsome face. He picked up his gold-handled cane from the hallstand.

Jamie watched them out of sight as they wended their way to the glen, down the long drive, bidding a cheery good day to Dougal as they passed through the tall iron gates. Flint raced off to and fro between the trees and shrubs, then back again to Bruce's side. Then, off he would go again.

"You won't find your master today," Bruce called to him, "but he will be home tomorrow."

Harriet and Elena greeted Bruce anxiously on his return.

"We were getting most alarmed!" exclaimed Elena.

"Yes, I am so sorry!" Bruce exclaimed. "I walked further than intended, and so many of the villagers kept me talking about Craig's arrival."

"We are having an early dinner tonight," said Harriet. "You just have time to change – it is almost ready."

"Good! I am famished after my long walk, and I am sure this young rascal is too."

They spent very little time in the library after dinner. They all agreed to get an early night.

"I don't think", said Elena, "that I will sleep a wink. I am far too excited."

They both watched as Bruce downed far more whisky than his usual nightcap. Then he rose to bid them goodnight. He kissed them both fondly on the cheek, a beaming smile on his face.

"I shall rise extra-early tomorrow."

"As we all shall!" exclaimed Harriet. "We still have a lot to do."

"How happy he is! It is a joy to behold," said Elena.

"Come, Elena," said Harriet: "we must hurry and get some sleep too."

'Unruffled as always!' thought Elena. 'Nothing will stop Harriet getting to sleep.'

"You go, Elena. I just want a word with Jamie before I retire. Goodnight, dear – and do try to sleep. It won't bring our boy home any quicker, you lying awake all night."

"I will try, Harriet dear, to do as you say."

Soon all was silent in the big house. Bruce stood at the window for a long time after he retired to his room, as he knew that sleep would evade him. The news that he had waited for for so long had now come at last. The wretched war was over, and his son had been spared to return to him.

'If only – if only', he told himself with a deep sigh, 'his darling mother had been spared to savour this wonderful time with me!'

He gazed out over his beloved loch, which had always given him so much happiness. He still loved it, but in a way, since that dreadful day, he hated it.

Never, as long as he lived, would he ever forget that dreadful day.

He watched the silvery moon casting its silvery streaks across the loch, and he was pensive and sad as the thought of it all clouded his tired mind. Once more he recalled that day and the events that followed.

CHAPTER 2

The day had dawned as usual: so beautiful for the three of them, as every day was, alive with laughter and song and music. No one surely could have been as happy as these three always were.

They left the castle that morning, Isabelle and Craig in the small carriage, Bruce, as always, riding alongside. They parted at the small crossroads, he heading off to view the estates after kissing her goodbye.

"I shall be a little later today," she called out to him. "I am going to visit the dressmaker after I have visited the crofters."

Craig called out to several of his friends as they passed them, before he too dismounted to join them in the small village school. After kissing his mother goodbye, he watched as she waved a farewell until she was out of sight.

Bruce hated every minute he was separated from her and his son, and he was always anxious to get the affairs of the estate settled as soon as he could with his ghillie. Today was no exception.

At last, he was able to get away and await her arrival. Craig, who was already at home, was just waving goodbye to his music teacher, Mr Ritchie.

"How is my son doing with his music?" he asked.

"Very well indeed. He is doing advanced work for his age," the music teacher assured him.

"Well, I am well pleased," replied Bruce. "See you keep it up, my son. Mama will be delighted too when I tell her."

They both said their farewells to Mr Ritchie as they watched him ride off.

"How long will Mama be?" enquired Craig. "I thought she would be home waiting for me when she didn't meet me out of school as she usually does."

"I too thought she would be home!" exclaimed Bruce. "She said she would be going to the dressmaker's on her way home, but she shouldn't be too long now. I am sure she will be back in time for tea with us, as she always is," Bruce reassured him.

"Will Mama be much longer, Papa?" he asked anxiously yet again.

"No, my son, she should be here any minute."

They both waited despondently, but tonight there was no carriage at the door, no panting horses breathless after their long pull up the hill from the village. Always at a gallop she came, in case she was late, arriving by the time tea was be served; and Jamie would rush to open the door for her when he heard the clatter of the horses' hoofs on the cobbled forecourt.

But the day that was not like any other day had dawned. In her haste to get home to her loved ones and to escape the threatening mist, which she could see descending far too quickly all around her, she misjudged the turn in the road which would take her safely to the castle, and she rode straight on to the narrow road round the loch. The mist now completely enveloped her. The carriage wheel struck a boulder and over it turned, flinging her face down into the water.

Bruce was getting more and more anxious because of her delay, and because of the mist, which had descended so suddenly. He tried to hide his anxiety from Craig, but he could see him glancing repeatedly at the clock.

The rest of the household were anxious too.

"It's so unlike madam to be so late!" Cook exclaimed to Sarah.

"Yes, it is, but I daresay she has got delayed at the dressmaker's."

"But", said Cook, "she would not let herself get delayed and so keep the master and young Master Craig waiting. She would call again another day."

"I know she would normally, Cook!" Sarah exclaimed, "but she was most anxious to get her new dress finished in time for Master Craig's birthday."

"Oh, so she was – so maybe you are right, Sarah. But I wish she was home. All the griddle cakes are getting cold; and you know only too well how the master likes his tea on time, and the griddle cakes warm."

But they did get cold. In fact, nothing was eaten again for days afterwards. Never again was Isabelle's carriage, with her sitting in it with the regality of a queen, seen at the open door of the castle.

Bruce, beside himself with anxiety, sent the men to the village to ask if anyone had seen her, or if she was still at the dressmaker's. He set off to follow them with Craig and Jamie, lanterns lit to show the way more clearly. They met the men coming back from the village with most of the villagers. They were all carrying lanterns.

No one had seen her since she drove away from the dressmaker's that afternoon. Soon there was only the road round the loch to search. Suddenly, they heard the whinny of the horses and a cry went up.

"Sir, sir, here is the carriage overturned."

Bruce and Craig and Jamie leaped from their carriage. Bruce frantically searched his wife's carriage while Craig raced on ahead.

Bruce heard his son's scream: "Papa, Papa, she is in the water! Papa, Papa."

Bruce raced to his side and into the loch, knee-deep. He dragged her sodden lifeless body to his carriage, and a deathly silence fell.

Jamie gathered up Craig in his arms and gave him to one of the village ladies, who wrapped him in a large shawl. He raced back to his master's side in the carriage, and bade the woman bring Master Craig along. He gathered up the reins as Bruce cradled his wife in his arms and cried her name over and over again, his head buried in her wet hair. Alas! their darkest night, laden with the heavy mist, had fallen.

After the funeral, Bruce went daily to kneel and pray, and to place her favourite flowers beside the vault where she lay. His sisters, Harriet and Elena, left their home to come and look after them, and decided that they would stay for good.

"We just cannot leave them alone," said Elena. "Bruce will never get over his loss and Craig – poor child! – neither will he."

"I agree," said Harriet. "Our property must be put up for sale as soon as possible."

Bruce, not caring one way or the other, nodded his approval. They were beside themselves with anxiety as he wandered over the glens and hillsides with only the dog, Cam, for company.

Jamie daily would hand Bruce his cane as he departed. He spoke to no one and never said when he would return. He would bang his cane against his thigh as he went, in deep sorrowful mood. In fine weather or foul, he would be gone for most of the day.

The villagers, too, would watch as their beloved laird and his dog daily wended their way. He only nodded in response to their morning greetings.

"How much longer?" they whispered to one another. "How much longer has our poor master to suffer in his sorrow and loneliness? And where is his son? Where is young Master Craig?"

No one had seen him since the funeral. Craig had never left his bed since then. A constant stream of tempting food, prepared by Cook, was taken by Elena to his bedside, as they tried in vain to tempt him to eat.

"Really, Harriet, whatever are we going to do? Neither of them will eat anything. The master is strong," said Cook, "but the wee bairn—" She shook her head.

All three looked at one another, but none had the answer.

Then one day, as he was passing the kitchen, Bruce overheard Cook's remark to Sarah. He stopped to listen in disbelief to what she was saying.

"You mark my words, my girl, it will soon be true what all the villagers are saying. You mark my words."

"What is that, Cook?" Sarah asked.

"That is, my dear girl, that the family vault will soon be reopened – to receive Master Craig, and then our dear laird."

"Oh no, it cannot be!" exclaimed Sarah.

Bruce heard the anguished cry from Sarah's lips.

"That is what they are saying, my girl, and I can see what they mean," she said emphatically.

"Do Lady Harriet and Lady Elena know what the villagers are saying?" Sarah asked.

"Well, Lady Elena was in the village one day in the library and Miss Stuart mentioned that Master Craig had not called for the books he had asked her to order from the mainland for him. Lady Elena told her he wasn't reading very much at present. Miss Stuart said she thought that very strange, as he was always coming in for books, and he had told her he was very keen on reading.

"The grocer's wife mentioned to me what all the villagers were saying about the vault being reopened very soon, and Jamie and Lady Elena must have heard what she said to me as they were standing only a few feet away. They were both strangely quiet on the way home – especially Lady Elena, and you know what a chatterbox she always is."

Bruce stood rigid and frozen to the spot.

'Oh no! It cannot be true. It just cannot,' he said to himself. He thought back to his walks in the glens, and recalled how Merry-Berry had waylaid him more and more persistently to ask about the boy. He had brusquely pushed her aside and never answered. This kind old lady loved Craig so dearly, and always took so much care of him when he played in the woods. 'No, no,' he told himself over and over again, it's just idle village gossip.

He hastened to the library and closed the door, then stood with his back to it for several minutes in deep contemplation. A deep concern welled up inside him for his son, and he realised he had scarcely given a thought to him.

"Oh no, not my darling son – not my dear Isabelle's son!" He was filled with remorse. "What is happening to us?"

He rang for Jamie, and told him to tell Lady Elena to come at once.

Elena knocked nervously on the door, not knowing what mood he was in or what awaited her.

"Tell me, Elena: is it true that the villagers are saying that soon the vault will be reopened again?"

"Yes, it is true, dear Bruce, and we must do something very soon to stop it from coming to pass. We have had the doctor to Craig, but he says he has no cure for such inward sorrow. The shock has been too much for such a small boy. You, Bruce, were so wrapped up in your own sorrow you were never here, even when the doctor called so many times. The doctor also wanted to see you, as everyone is so concerned for your health too."

"Oh, I am all right. I just wanted to be alone."

"Margot has called daily, and so have the General and his wife and almost all of your old friends. So many came to call on you. Craig will not even speak to Fiona, and you know how much they mean to each other."

"All these people called, you say? But I never saw anyone. How often did they come?"

"Very, very often, but you were never here. You were out on the moors with the dog, and they had gone before you came back."

"But they never left their cards!" he exclaimed, feeling more and more guilty at his lack of concern for his son, and his discourtesy to his lifelong friends.

"Yes, dear Bruce, they did leave their cards, but you just tore them up without looking at them."

"Did I really? I cannot remember anything – only that dreadful, dreadful day."

"They all understood and invited you and Craig to call on them whenever you liked."

"And now, of course, all the villagers are saying I am going to lose my son."

"You must do something, Bruce dear. He cannot go on like this, pining away, or it will, as they say, surely come to pass."

Bruce stood a long time silently overlooking the loch and gave a deep sigh as she finished speaking.

At last he spoke: "I have put my own grief above everything else, and everyone else. To think that my dear son is pining away before our very eyes! I must look after him better in future, Elena."

"There have been days and days when you have never been in to see him."

"I have, Elena, but he has always been asleep."

"No, not asleep, Bruce dear, just lying there, not eating, speaking or moving – like one in a dream."

"I must go to him at once, Elena. It is as you say. The loss of his dear mother is too much for such a young child to bear."

'Whatever would my darling Isabelle think of me for allowing this to happen?' he thought.

"Come, Elena – we will go and see him together."

"No, Bruce, you must go alone and talk to him."

The sight of that small, frail boy, lost in the huge bed, as white as the sheets upon it, shocked him to distraction.

"My God! My God! It is true what they are saying. I am going to lose him too. Oh no! Please, God, do not let me lose him too.' He sank by the bed in prayer.

Every day, for what seemed to Bruce an eternity, he sat watching Craig quietly by the hour, as he tossed and turned, in and out of his delirium.

"My poor wee boy!" he would whisper over and over to himself. "It is all my fault – all my fault."

It was as if there was a dagger in his heart, being twisted over and over, each time Craig called out in anguish, as he lived and relived that fateful night.

"Mama, Mama, where are you? Where are you?" He would scream out in terror and put his thin, small, frail hands over his eyes. "I cannot find you. Where are you? Where are you? I cannot find you in the mist, Mama." Then another scream: "Papa, she is in the water! Papa, Mama is in the water!"

Then he would sit up, his hands over his face, weeping bitterly. He would reach out, as if to suddenly find her there, and then discover it was all a dream.

On one of these days, as he reached out, he felt the strong hands of his father.

"Is that you, Papa?"

"Yes, my son, it is. There, there, my son! Papa is here."

He gathered Craig in his arms, and Craig wept on his shoulder as Bruce stroked his hair, which was wet with perspiration.

"I thought I had lost you also, Papa. I couldn't find you anywhere. I looked everywhere for you."

"Well, Papa is here now, my son, to take care of you. I will never ever leave you again."

"Nor I you, Papa. I will never ever leave you."

"We will have to look after each other from now on!" exclaimed Bruce.

"Yes, dear Papa. I will look after you too. Dear Mama would like that, wouldn't she?"

Bruce felt the knife turn in his heart as he spoke: "Yes, my son, dear Mama would like that." Never again, he vowed, would they ever be parted, and he hugged his son closer. "All will be well now, my son."

The feel of his father's hand on his forehead told him all he wanted to know.

"Rest now and get well and strong."

"Yes, Papa, I will do as you say. Then we can go over the moors and mountains again, as we did before, riding and fishing, just the two of us. Maybe Fiona will come with us also."

"Oh, I am sure she will be only too delighted. She has called to see you several times, but you were asleep."

"Was I really, Papa? Fancy my being asleep when my favourite playmate came to call on me!"

"Well, you rest now, my boy. I will send word to her parents as soon as I can."

Then Craig dropped back on his pillow exhausted.

"My poor wee boy! Your twelfth birthday has just gone, and there's no dear mother to share it with you this time. Sleep now, my son."

Soon Craig's breathing became more restful, and a look of tranquillity appeared on his so thin face.

"I will see no harm ever comes to you, my son," he whispered as he kissed him goodnight.

After that, the two of them were rarely apart. Craig's strength grew daily, and they were often to be seen together in the glens with their dogs beside them. The fresh Highland air brought back the colour to Craig's once pale face.

As he got older, boarding school was mentioned from time to time.

"It is time he went!" Harriet would exclaim. "He should not spend so much time with his father. It is not good for him." Time and time again, she would argue with Bruce, but to no avail. "He needs boys his own age," she would complain to Elena. "He shouldn't spend every day with his father."

"Yes, I agree, Harriet dear," Elena would venture now and again, but she was not as emphatic as Harriet.

Craig had mixed feelings on the matter. He did miss his friends from the small village school, who had left for boarding school, but he told himself, "I would miss Papa too much. If I went, I couldn't join him in fishing in the loch, sailing, climbing these mountains, and walking and riding in the glens. No, no, I just cannot be away from my dear mountains and Papa. They are more to me than life itself."

"No, Papa," he told him one day, after he had given it more thought, "I will stay here with you."

Bruce decided he would have a private tutor from the mainland, and the matter was settled. Both sisters knew Bruce, as always, would have his way. No further arguments would be of any use.

"I can teach him all he needs to know about the running of the estate, the rights of the crofters and the upkeep of the church. He will have first-hand knowledge of all that if he accompanies me, as he does now. He has got to know all about his heritage and the responsibilities it entails in order to be able to pass it on to his future heirs."

"Yes, we know all that," Harriet told him, "but he should also study other things."

So the laird and his heir would be seen side by side, riding in the glens, climbing the mountains and sailing on the loch, smiling and laughing most of the time. Merry-Berry always greeted them with a jolly smile as they passed. Now and again a dark cloud crossed her countenance, as if she too thought father and son were too attached for their own good.

Craig always rode with Flint, the dog given to him as a small puppy by a villager to aid his recovery after the death of his mother.

Bruce missed Craig terribly after he had left for Sandhurst, and he became more and more anxious as the war news worsened. He tried all he could to prevent him from volunteering, but to no avail. His son had inherited his own streak of stubbornness. He knew it was his duty to fight for his country, to defend this, his motherland. There was no waiting to be conscripted. The family motto was firmly entrenched in his mind: 'All is lost if thou art not true.' Well, he had been true and he had gone. A short leave was granted and then he was sent to the front.

Bruce knew he could not deter him from going. Craig would never have forgiven himself if he was seen to be a coward in the eyes of his clan and the villagers. He was Bruce's son, and, like many other people's sons, he had answered the call. It would, he knew, have been his mother's wish too. She had come from a family of soldiers serving in famous regiments, as his father had. Bruce knew he would have to do as Isabelle wished, no matter how lonely he would be after Craig left.

"God knows how I have missed you, my boy." He felt once more for the telegram in his pocket, and he took it out to read it once more. "Yes, it is true," he called out to the loch below: "my son will be home tomorrow. But why, my darling Isabelle, could you not be here to greet him with me? Why?"

The dark eerie water seemed to re-echo his longing sigh.

CHAPTER 3

"Home, home, I shall be home tomorrow."

Try as he might, he could not refrain from repeating it, over and over again. His heart was so full of longing for home and his yearning was now almost unbearable. The choking feeling of joy welled up inside him again and again. Could it really be true at last that he was on his way home? Home! The word seared into his mind. A smile of happiness crossed his handsome face, as his dark, piercing eyes continued to scan the distant horizon ahead. Behind him were the war-torn battlefields of France and Belgium.

He stood tall, proud and erect as befitting his proud name, proud heritage and proud Scottish regiment. Captain Craig Alisdair Bruce Stuart McNair, the only son and heir of his father, the 11th Earl and laird of Glencree Castle, was at last on his way home. His increasing smile at the thought of it brought a devilish twinkle to his dark-brown flashing eyes. His even white teeth were in sharp contrast with the close-cropped black moustache which outlined his top lip. He tilted his cap a little further back, and swept the dark, unruly, black waves of hair away from his forehead. Then he put his cap back at its correct angle.

"I shall be home tomorrow," he muttered aloud, unaware of the questioning look of his fellow officer, who stood beside him.

"Yes, Craig, we are all on our way home. Blighty to all of us means home."

Craig turned to face him.

"I am sorry, Ian. I didn't hear you approach. I was daydreaming and I was back in my beloved Highlands with my father by my side."

"Well, we are at last on our way, none more gladly than the lads here below us. The dreams we have all had over these past years are at last coming true," said Ian. "I am going down below, Craig, to see our boys in the sickbay."

"Yes, do, Ian. I will come down to see them later."

Craig watched him go, then turned his gaze to the men grouped on the deck below him.

'Yes, they too are going home. I wonder how each of them will fare when they reach there. At last we are going back to our loved ones aboard the troopship for home. None deserves it more than these.'

The thought of his own dear father waiting for him with outstretched arms gave him a feeling of being safe and secure for the first time since he had sailed away so many years ago.

'To me, it feels like a lifetime. It must also seem so to these gallant men below.'

He looked down on them, his smile now gone. A deep sadness crossed his countenance as he thought of the ones left behind in Flanders Fields.

'What has it all achieved?' he asked himself over and over again. 'What has it achieved? What? What?'

He turned once more towards the coast of France and leaned over the side of the large troopship. He gazed into the dark swirling water below him, but it only reflected back his sorrowful expression, adding to the deep, restless turmoil within him.

The jolly laughter of the men below him could not release him from the anguish he felt within. Once more, he was back with the men he had left behind, back in the trenches. He thought of the men who were not there with him, and who would never return to their loved ones, or the homeland they had fought and died so gallantly for. Only their lives the warlord would accept, it seemed, and he had had his way.

A deep, deep sigh escaped from his lips as the thought of it all swept over him again and again – the suffering horror, the agony of it all, week after week, month after month, year after year. At times it had seemed as if it would go on for ever. Hadn't it been said it would all be over by Christmas? But, which Christmas? It was left to the men on the battlefields, and many of them would never see Christmas again. Fine, stalwart young men were blown to bits or drowned in the deep squelching mud, the never-ending mud, or choked and blinded by the dreaded gas.

'I shall never, ever forget you all, my gallant men. Never, till the day I die.'

They had died in their thousands to save mankind. Let no man ever forget them. Some of them had died in no-man's-land. What a place to die! They had given their all for their loved ones and their homeland.

Joyful shouts of "Hurray! Hurray!" brought Craig out of his sad, thoughtful reverie.

'At least I have got some of my men with me,' he told himself: 'Not all, but some.'

He knew that the happiness of the men shouting "Hurray!" now they were going home was mingled with sorrow at the thought of the comrades they were leaving behind. However, none felt it so deeply as their own commanding officer, Captain Craig McNair. He was not just leaving his men behind, he was leaving part of himself.

The shouting of the men continued, and he looked at them fondly. Like them, he watched as the final ropes anchoring the ship to the huge bollards on the quayside of France were released and flung back to the ship.

"Hurry up, Frenchie!" they had been calling. "Throw the damn ropes."

At last they were dragged aboard.

'Those,' Craig told himself, 'were the final ties holding us back from the motherland.'

More hurrays echoed and re-echoed over the ship. "We are away, boys," they called to one another as they felt the first lurch of the ship from the quayside. With a 'toot-toot' and sirens blasting she moved further and further away. The swirling puffs of black smoke from her funnels seemed to be signalling a thankful farewell.

There were more loud cheers from the troops, now all grinning broadly at one another. These oh, so war-weary men threw their caps into the air, not knowing or caring where they would fall. Some waved gaily at the seamen on the quay, who waved back at them and called out, *"Bon voyage!"*

"Sure, it will be the best trip we have ever made," one called out.

Craig looked at them fondly: 'We are all so proud of you, our wonderful gallant men, and so is your motherland,' he said to himself.

He turned again and raised his fine, dark eyes to the now disappearing coastline of France. His thoughts once more were back with the men he was leaving behind.

"They say, sir—" said a young soldier, who had stood by his side for several minutes.

"What do they say, my boy?"

"That this Great War we have just fought was the war to end all wars."

"Well, let us hope so, after all the sacrifices that have been made by so many of our comrades."

"Yes, sir, so many."

He turned to go as he could see his officer was in no mood for further conversation on the topic.

'So many!' Craig thought to himself again. 'Their lives had gone like a sigh passing on the wind.'

He seemed to hear their families calling to them: "Come home, my son. Come home, my son. Come home."

He held his head in anguish. The nightmare of it all! He could almost see them as he remembered the anguished cries and sobbing whispers of "Mother, Mother" escaping from their dying lips.

The familiar tunes, 'Home, Sweet Home' and 'Take Me Back to Dear Old Blighty', winged their way over his melancholy thoughts as the men sang and played on their old mouth organs. Some sang, some played cards, some idly chatted, and some sat silent and thoughtful. Some, now and again, would get wearily to their feet and peer out anxiously, looking for the coastline of home; then, seeing nothing, they would sink back wearily on deck.

Craig still gazed back the way they had come, and the fact that someone was standing close beside him did not cause him to alter his gaze or thoughts. Captain Ian Fraser stood beside him for several minutes, gazing out with him, his thoughts also of the men left behind. He also pondered long on the friend by his side – this fine, brave, daring man, a holder of a medal for gallantry in battle, who showed no fear as he launched assault after assault at the head of his men in the fight for freedom.

Ian turned slightly to cast a sidelong glance at Craig before speaking. He saw the sad anguish on Craig's face, and it troubled him greatly to see how deeply affected he had been by the loss of so many of his men. He knew only too well how deeply sensitive Craig was – a sensitivity which his fine, stalwart physique and his usually so happy and mischievous nature and countenance belied.

Craig had within him the fiery streak of his father combined with the gentler streak of his mother, and this sometimes puzzled all around him. Sometimes he would be a fiery Scot, like his father, and then, to the consternation of all around him, the gentleness of his mother would suddenly strike through, completely overpowering the fiery nature, and the fury which had welled within him only minutes before.

Ian had known him far too long to ever be surprised by any change in his moods. He was now deeply troubled for the dear friend by his side. He stood a few moments longer, pondering, wondering whether or not to speak and so break his friend's train of thought, or go away as quickly and quietly as he had come.

He decided on the former, but when would be the right moment? The suffering and horror they had gone through together had sunk into the depths of his own mind, but for the friend beside him it was a totally different matter. He knew the thought of it all would never leave this brave, gallant, yet gentle, man by his side.

At last he put his hand on Craig's shoulder and spoke: "Think, now, dear friend, only of the future. That is all we can do now."

"Yes, Ian, my dear friend, we can think of our futures, but they have no future," and he waved his hand towards the coast of France. "What future have they got?"

"I know, my dear friend, what you are going through and what you're suffering. We are all suffering, and what we have suffered will be with each and every one of us for ever, but we must now think of the future. We will always remember our comrades. What is done is done, and cannot be undone, try as we might. All we can do now is to help one another to adapt to the future awaiting us."

Craig turned to face the men once more.

"Yes, Ian, we can be optimistic about our own future, but what of these poor men? How are they going to face the future? They have been promised by those in higher spheres that, when they return, England will be a land fit for heroes to live in. We will have to wait and see," he said bitterly.

Ian remained silent. He watched Craig whose thoughts wandered away, again and again. At last Craig spoke:

"Yes, Ian, it is as you say – rightly so. Now we must think of the future. Tell me: how are the men in the sickbay?"

"They have settled quite well. The naval personnel are looking after them very well."

"Oh, good! I will go and see them soon. There is so much to be done for them, especially the permanently sick ones. God, give us the strength to help them all."

"Well now, my dear friend, let us drink to the future!" Ian exclaimed, as brightly as he could. He wanted somehow to get Craig out of his melancholy frame of mind.

He pulled a small flask from inside his tunic.

"How on earth did you manage to get hold of this, Ian?" A faint flicker of a smile crossed his face as he looked at Ian in disbelief.

"I saved it especially for this, our departure-for-home day," he replied, laughing.

"Well," Craig said, "you have saved it a mighty long time, then. I am sure you must have often thought that day would never come."

"Well, I did sometimes have my doubts, but now it is here, so now is the time to celebrate. Drink up, my friend!"

Craig watched as Ian undid the cap of the flask and offered it to him. He took it and hesitated.

"Tell me, Ian; why is it I haven't thought so much before of all the suffering and misery that we have all gone through these past years, and why are my thoughts dwelling so much on the men who will never return home again? Why now, when all my thoughts should be happy ones, when we are all on our way home at last? My heart is so sad, so lost, so desolate, in spite of all these happy men around me."

"Now, my dear friend," replied Ian, "you have the time to ponder. Before there was no time to think. Our time was spent in planning and scheming how to win battles without losing men. Now we have time to think of these other things."

"Yes, you are so right, Ian. We now must only dwell on the future, so here is a first drink to the future, whatever it might hold." He smelt the sweet aroma.

"Ah, only one drink in the world could smell like this," he said, and his eyes twinkled at the thought of the many drinks of this famous Scottish elixir he would soon be relishing with his father.

He tilted his head back, and, with a wide grin, downed a fair measure of it, before handing it back to Ian.

"The Captain of the ship says there is a ration of rum for the men," said Craig.

"Yes, I believe so," replied Ian. "There is the Captain on the bridge now, about to make the announcement."

The Captain looked down from the deck above to the men below, and called for a moment's silence. The men looked at each other questioningly.

"Oh, not more bloody orders!" one whispered to his comrade.

"I hope not," his pal replied. "We have had enough of those to last us a lifetime."

Barely had the Captain finished the first line of his statement, than a loud cheer of delight filled the air. 'For He's a Jolly Good Fellow' was sung over and over again. The navy boys filled their old tin mugs with a good measure of rum.

"Could you not fill the bugger to the top?" exclaimed one.

"Well, this will have to do for noo," they all agreed " – there'll be more when we get to bonnie Scotland."

There were no elegant crystal glasses for them, but never did a tot of rum taste as sweet. There was a stilled silence for the first time since they came on board.

Craig and Ian stood watching them fondly.

"They all deserve the very best of everything in the future, every damned one of them!" exclaimed Ian. "Their country should never cease to honour them for the hardship they have endured, and the sacrifice they have made. I suppose your father will be waiting eagerly for your arrival," said Ian.

"He will," replied Craig. "He is probably waiting by the side of the loch at the moment, yet he will have had my message stating the time and day of my arrival. Major Sinclair, who left for England a few days ago, said he would get a telegram to him as soon as he could, so that should have reached him by now."

"How he must have missed you!" commented Ian. "You are so close, the two of you – such good pals. That's something I have never been able to enjoy with my own father. As you know, he died soon after I was born."

"What a great loss it was for you to never have known the closeness and comradeship of a father!" said Craig, as he heard his friend sigh.

"Yes, dear Mama did her best to fill both roles, but it never really worked out. However, as we have said, I must not dwell on days gone by, now. I must look to the future. Tell me, Craig: will your lovely Fiona be awaiting you also?"

"I hope so," replied Craig. "She last wrote to me when she was staying with a friend. She said she would be returning to her parents' home very soon, and she should arrive almost as soon as I do. She has been very busy doing voluntary work for the war effort."

"Yes, the war seems to have involved everyone in one way or another," said Ian. "I daresay," he continued with a grin, "you will both be getting married as soon as you can."

"Yes, most certainly – later in the year. And you, of course, Ian, will be my best man. You do remember the promises we made to each other (although only jokingly at the time) when we left for the front. We said that if we both survived the war, we would each be best man at the other's wedding."

"Yes, I remember," said Ian. "I know you and Fiona will be first, as I haven't as yet even met my future wife."

"Well, dear friend," Craig laughed as he held the flask of whisky, "here's to you finding the right girl very soon."

He took another little gulp from the flask before handing it back to Ian, who drained off the last drop.

"How I am longing to see my darling Fiona again, and my dear father!" said Craig.

The whisky had made him more relaxed, and now and again he broke into a little laugh as he spotted some of the amusing antics of the men on deck. They too were now more light-hearted. Mouth organs were playing, and men started to sing, hum or whistle, as was their wont. Then the singing became louder and louder, and the men sang with greater gusto. The tot of rum was having the desired effect, and caps were waved in time to all the old familiar songs the men had sung in the trenches. Tin mugs were tapped on the rails of the ship. Such happy songs they seemed now, whereas before they had often been rendered with a deep melancholy by men who couldn't know whether or not they would ever see dear old Blighty, home sweet home or the faces of their loved ones ever again.

Private Dunbar, standing in the middle of them all and using his cap as a baton, was singing louder than anyone else. He was trying to do a jig at the same time, but he had too little room. He knew every song by heart. Some of the others watched him closely and tried to pick up the words as they went along.

Well, now the war was over, they could sing them to their hearts' content. Several of the naval boys joined in with their accordions, and added to the gaiety.

The two officers still stood watching them. They sang softly to themselves, along with the men.

"Isn't it just wonderful to see them all smiling again?" said Craig. "None of them ought to have a sad face ever again after what they have been through."

"Let us hope the future is good to them," Ian said.

"Come, Ian – I will go and see our men in sickbay if you will go and collect our landing orders."

They wended their way between the men on deck, picking their way carefully so as not to disturb the ones sleeping. Some were so exhausted for want of sleep that they were oblivious to the sing-song going on around them.

Craig entered the sickbay with a heavy heart. How he hated the sight of suffering. Many of these wonderful men were badly wounded; some were blind.

'My God! My God! What have they done to deserve all this?' he asked himself over and over again.

"Are we really on our way, sir?" one asked.

"Yes, laddie, we are on our way at last. The French coast is finally out of sight."

"Thanks be to God," he replied, as he dropped back on his pillow with a sigh of relief.

"Now you must all rest. We still have a long way to go before we are home, boys. I will send one of your comrades to come and tell you the minute we spot the coast of England."

"You won't forget, will you, sir?"

"No, laddie, I won't forget – never fear."

Craig stopped to speak to one of the naval men as he was leaving: "They seem to have travelled well in spite of their injuries."

"Yes, but only one thing will make them happy now, and that is the sight of home. The coast should be sighted soon."

Craig wended his way back and stood watching the men, his feet tapping to the music.

'It must be the whisky,' he told himself wryly.

He turned once more towards the sea and gazed out over the blue-grey water. He leaned heavily on the ship's rail.

'How tired I am, but oh, so happy! Home tomorrow!' he thought.

The early morning mist had lifted. He raised his glasses and gazed out longingly to the distant horizon, then lowered them again.

"Not a sign, not a sign!" he exclaimed almost angrily to himself as he gazed at the huge ship cleaving its way through the water, and flicking aside the white frothy foam. It seemed to be creaking along to the melodies, as if adding its own little message: "I am taking you home, I am taking you home – as fast as I can, as fast as I can."

Craig watched as Captain Ian Fraser and Lieutenant Alex McGregor threaded their way back along the deck, stepping carefully between the sleeping men. Now more and more men leaned over the side of the ship, scanning the distant horizon, some still singing, but now more softly as tiredness crept up on them.

"I see we disembark first," said Craig, as he read his landing orders.

"Yes. I shall leave later with the severely wounded from the sickbay," said Ian.

"Then we shall be ready to receive you at the other end," replied Craig.

"I will be staying on deck to liaise between you and the naval staff," said Alex.

"Well, that's all clear. All we want now is to get there," said Craig. Once again he turned towards the sea, staring fixedly into the distance. "Oh, Blighty, where are you? Where are you? You should know your sons are on their way."

"Did you say something, Craig?" Ian asked.

"I did, but as usual I was talking to myself. I was saying, 'Blighty, where the devil are you?' but as usual I got no reply."

"Oh, I see. It seems to be taking a long time on this homeward journey. I am sure it did not take us as long to get to France," said Ian.

"How right you are! The ship is making good speed, but not speed enough. The boys are now getting very restive," said Craig.

Craig raised his glasses once more and then: 'Yes, surely, there is something there at last,' he told himself, being careful not to raise false hopes in the boys, who stared up at him every time he raised his glasses and looked disappointed whenever he lowered them again. 'Yes, surely now,' Craig thought, 'a shaft of sunlight just caught the whiteness of the cliffs.' He lowered his glasses again for a fleeting moment to relieve his tired eyes. 'Have I really seen them at last?' he asked himself. He looked once more, and a slow smile crossed his face and tilted the corners of his mouth.

"What is it, Craig?" asked Ian, who had been watching him intently and noted his smile. He looked happier than Ian had seen him since leaving France. His face was now beaming.

"It is the view we have all been waiting for!" he exclaimed excitedly.

"Are you sure?" Ian said.

"Take my glasses and tell me what you see. Tell me I am not dreaming it all."

Ian scanned the far horizon in a wide sweep and then stared fixedly ahead, a smile breaking over his face too. He handed the glasses to Alex.

"No, you are not dreaming, Craig. Those are the white cliffs of home."

He handed the glasses back. He could see Craig's impatience. The men, noting their officers' every move and expression, looked up at them from their crouched position on the deck. The singing now stopped as one by one they wended their way to the side of the ship.

"What is it, sir?" asked the one nearest to him. "What is it, sir?" the excited voice repeated. "What do you see?"

"Here, soldier, take these and tell me what you see."

Ian took the glasses from around his neck and slipped them over the head of the soldier. Private Dunbar looked out to where his officer was pointing, his hand trembling with emotion. Dunbar's face broke into a relieved smile, though like the others he scarcely believed what he saw.

He let out a yell of delight: "It's the white cliffs, boys, at last – at last!" Tears ran down his face unashamedly.

All the boys were now quiet as the good news sank in. Tears welled up inside them, and some let them flow.

"We are nearly home, boys, nearly home!" Private Dunbar kept exclaiming.

A roar of joy rent the air as more and more pressed closer to the rails of the ship. Only those who were unable to get there remained where they were on the deck. Craig took the glasses back and watched as Private Dunbar wiped away a tear. 'This soldier', he thought, 'showed no emotion or fear on the battlefield, and he is the possessor of a medal for gallantry. Now he sheds a tear at the sight of the white cliffs of Blighty.'

Blighty meant home to one and all.

"What a wonderful sight, sir!"

"Yes, laddie, a truly wonderful sight!" Craig replied. "None better!"

"Let me see, let me see," several of them chorused.

"Look more closely over there, boys. You can see them now without glasses," said Craig.

"Yes, yes!" they all exclaimed. "We are nearly home."

"There they are, boys," they yelled to one another as they pointed into the distance. "We are really home."

Caps once more were flung into the air. Some were hastily caught, but others dropped at the feet of their comrades and were lost in the milling crowd. Nothing mattered any more. They had had enough of uniforms and caps.

"Corporal Emslie," Craig called, "take one of your comrades to the sickbay and tell the boys there what we have in view."

"I will go along also!" exclaimed Ian.

"You, Sergeant, tell the boys to start getting ready now."

"Yes, sir," the Sergeant replied.

"Ian," Craig called after him, "tell the two who have gone to sickbay to return as soon as possible."

"I will," he replied.

The mist had now finally cleared and all was shining bright, as though a heavy veil had lifted so as to let them see the motherland in all her glory.

The ship now seemed to be going faster as it drew closer and closer to the quay. Its hooter blew in glee. The strains of a well-known tune came from a band on the quayside.

"Listen to that band playing just for us, lads!" exclaimed Private Dunbar. "Play up, lads," he called to them. "We are home at last. Now, come on, lads – let's show them how we can sing," and he stood with his back to the rails of the ship, using his cap as a baton as before.

Craig had once again turned to face the way they had come. His thoughts wandered back as before – back to the men he had left behind.

The yell of the men once more broke in on his thoughts as they called to the men on the quay: "Hurry up, you dozy lot! Tie her up and make sure she is fast to the motherland. We don't want to be sailing back to where we have come from."

"No bloody fear!" yelled one.

The deck was now alive with laughter, as never before.

Captain McNair and the Lieutenant tried to converse, but it was hopeless, as they soon realised, above the tumult. Their beaming faces were as bright as their men's. The singing grew louder and louder.

The atmosphere heaved with emotion as the men gathered up their belongings, tied their kitbags more tightly, and sought high and low for their caps.

"That's my cap," chorused several.

"No, it's mine," came the reply.

"That's not your cap – look at the badge, mate. You are not in the artillery," said one.

"We wouldn't have you in our regiment," one retorted, laughing. "Get back to the Pioneers where you belong. Here is your cap. Get it on your big, thick skull if it will fit, which I doubt. Stay with your own bloody breed, *s'il vous plait*."

"What jollity and good humour amongst them!" exclaimed Craig. "It's so wonderful to behold."

"It certainly is," replied Alex.

They watched as a Scot, just for fun, handed a cap he had found to one of his friends, who looked at it with disdain.

"And how long have I been in a bloody Welsh regiment?" he said, and he threw it into a crowd of Welsh soldiers, who were still searching.

The ones who were ready to disembark were getting quite impatient as they stood by the ship's rail. Some, in spite of the laughter all around them, had tears running unashamedly down their faces. They were tears of joy at being home at last, and tears of sadness for the friends they had left behind.

Ian, who had rejoined them, watched as Craig turned once more to look back, and said aloud, "We will never, ever forget you, our gallant comrades – never as long as we live."

"I will go now, Craig, back to the sickbay. Then we will be ready to disembark when you have all left the ship. The stretcher parties are all assembled."

Craig watched him go, silently pondering on the lines running through his head:

Envelop me, envelop me
Ever in thy open arms, oh motherland,
Never more to leave thy succour for others' foreign lands
No more to wander, or to roam.
Now we are safe at last,
Now we are home.

He was suddenly aware of his sergeant by his side.

"The men are all ready, sir."

"Good!" he replied. He put his cap more squarely on his head and slung his kitbag on his shoulder, as he proceeded to the exit and waited eagerly for the sailors to secure the gangplank more securely. Every second seemed like hours, and his impatience grew every minute. The men too were restless. They waited behind him, muttering under their breath.

"How much longer have we to wait?" said one, as he tapped his feet with impatience.

They wanted their feet on the motherland.

At last it was ready. The small chain was removed. Craig tucked his folder with the landing orders in more securely under his arm and, with a final glance round to see all was in order, he hurried quickly down the narrow, rickety gangplank. It creaked alarmingly as he sped down at a furious pace to meet the RTO (railway transport officer) awaiting him at the bottom. He was followed just as quickly by Sergeant Ritchie.

They waited eagerly at the bottom for the men to descend.

Corporal Sterling, at the top of the gangplank, ticked off their names as each in turn descended. He studied his list carefully, but he could be sure no one would be missing for this happy event.

The men straightened their tunics and caps and slung their kitbags over their shoulders and started down the rickety stairway to home. It now swung and creaked more violently with the added weight.

Private Dunbar, his usual clowning self, was thoroughly enjoying himself, as only he knew how. He tripped and danced down the gangplank in time to the music which wafted up to them from below. Suddenly the band struck up his favourite tune and he started to dance a very intricate dance step to the Scottish reel being played. The confusion and chaos it caused was a joy to behold as the men following him fell backwards one by one.

The very regimental Corporal McTavish behind him almost fell through the ropes they were using as a handrail. In trying to save himself, his kitbag (which contained his all, and which, like the others, he was guarding practically with his life) slipped from his grasp. He scrambled to his feet out of the confusion of legs and arms surrounding him, and he was just in time to see his kitbag sinking unceremoniously between the ship and the quay.

His fury knew no bounds. He hastily reached for his cap from one of the others and put it firmly on his head, then he tried to regain his composure and continued down.

Private Dunbar, unaware of the very angry man behind him, had now reached the bottom. He was still dancing gaily and humming the tune. Suddenly the angry corporal caught hold of his collar.

"You, you, you bloody clown! Did you not see what happened? My kitbag, thanks to your stupidity, is now lying in the drink," he shouted at him.

"Well, I am truly very sorry. I had no idea, but you should be thankful it's not yourself in the drink."

This statement did nothing to alleviate his friend's anger.

Private Dunbar still continued to hum and dance. Nothing on earth was going to spoil this moment for him, now that his feet were firmly planted on the soil of home. Even his captain could not restrain his faint smile at what had happened. He buried his face in his folder of orders to hide his amusement and pushed Dunbar into the milling crowd now gathered on the quayside.

Craig and the RTO compared their notes, and he called out to his sergeant to carry on with the disembarkation.

"Corporal McTavish, you follow me. We are going to the convoy of trucks."

They wended their way through the throng with great difficulty. At last the long convoy of trucks came into view.

'Another stepping stone nearer home,' Craig said to himself.

"Are all these trucks for us?" he asked the RTO.

"Yes," he replied, "all the drivers will be ready when all your men are aboard."

"Right then. You, Corporal, go and tell the Sergeant to get the men assembled as soon as they have all left the ship – only the mobile ones, not any from the sickbay. They will follow later with Captain Fraser. I am going with the first truck of men."

The Sergeant tried to get the men into the trucks, but they had scattered far and wide, chattering to old comrades they had not been able to see on board ship. The Sergeant's and the Corporal's orders for them to make their way to the trucks were rendered almost inaudible by loud bursts of laughter and song.

Meanwhile, Private Dunbar was still more full of glee than anyone else, if that was possible. He was always so eager to bring a smile to his comrades' faces in their darkest hours, and this had endeared him to all his fellow men. He had seemed not to care that every hour could be his last as the battles raged about him. He chatted gaily to a group of soldiers who stood nearby.

"Hold on to my kitbag," he yelled to one of them.

"Hi, give it to me, Jock," one of them said as he took it from him.

Then Private Dunbar took off his cap, bowed very low to the ground and said, in a loud voice, "Good earth of Mother England, here we are at last." As he straightened up, still in tune to the music, he flung his cap in the air, raised his arms and started to twirl around as fast as he could, exclaiming as loudly as he could, "To the good earth of bonnie Scotland: we are on our way, och aye, och aye!"

Although small in stature, he was a fine figure of a man – broad and strong – an expert exponent of his country's reels, and a delight to behold. He yelled with glee in his broad Scottish accent as he proceeded to dance a mock sword dance. The men surrounded him, drawing closer and closer, to watch his antics, and one or two tried to copy him.

His hat, which he had so joyfully flung in the air, was picked up by one of the onlookers, who now tried to place it on his head as he continued to dance around. After a long struggle, he succeeded, but it was at a rakish angle. It had fallen over his left eye, and they all roared with laughter. This was the first good laugh many of them had had, and a large dose of medicine could not have done them more good.

The Sergeant called to the Corporal: "Are all the trucks full yet?"

The men had, one by one, been leaving the gathering as their names were called.

"Only one man is missing," came the reply.

"I know who that will be," said the Sergeant. "You go and get these other trucks away. I will wait in this last one."

The occupants of the last truck were getting very angry at their delay.

"He would be missing! It's always him! Where the hell can he be?" the Sergeant exclaimed over and over again.

He stood on tiptoe, hanging on to the canvas roof of the truck. He could tell by the extra-loud laughter in one area that the missing man must be nearby. There was so much noise and commotion. The band was still playing, and orders were being called to other regiments. The Sergeant was getting quite frantic.

"I suppose he is right in the middle of that crowd somewhere. Why is he so damn short?"

He called his name over and over again, getting more and more angry at the delay. The driver had already asked twice how much longer he had to wait. The Sergeant turned his head to see the last of the other trucks almost out of sight.

"Why are all these guardsmen so damn tall? I can't see a damn thing over their heads."

Just then, during a lull in the music, Private Dunbar heard his name being called, and, on looking round the faces surrounding him, he suddenly realised that none of them were from his regiment. He stopped dancing, snatched his kitbag from the soldier holding it, and put his cap on at its proper angle.

He yelled out to them all: "Ach! I must be away to yon bonnie Scotland of mine."

As he struggled to get away, he could still hear the Sergeant calling his name.

"Oh, it would be yon mon, bawling his head off!" he exclaimed, but he was not perturbed. Nothing or no one was going to spoil his homecoming.

The driver said he had had orders to move off at once, and proceeded to pull up the back of the truck.

"Wait a bit longer!" several exclaimed.

"No, I cannot," he said, and he clamped in the last peg.

At last Private Dunbar ran up to him, exhausted.

"Hi! Hi there!" he shouted to the driver. "Let the back down. I want to get aboard."

The Sergeant looked at him anxiously as the driver yelled at him: "No, no! You are too bloody late. I am already late. The other trucks left long ago. You will have to catch the next convoy. Besides, my truck is too full as it is," he said, and he proceeded to the front and climbed in.

Dunbar looked after him in disbelief. He couldn't believe what the driver had said, and anger now spread across his usually so happy face.

"Wait for the next convoy? Not bloody likely, mate," he yelled after him.

He flung his kitbag into the truck with as much strength as he could muster, and it caught several of his comrades on the head and knocked them off the small, rickety form along the back of the truck. Then he jumped up as high as he could to try to catch the edge of it, but he missed it by inches. Several pairs of arms reached down to him. They were not going to leave him behind.

He hung on precariously, his short legs dangling in mid-air as the truck started to move away. The driver was unaware of what was going on. The hurried grasp of his friends had almost dragged his tunic over his head. Then with a final heave-ho they dragged him aboard with such gusto that he and some of the others collapsed in a heap on the floor – he on top of them – amidst curses and laughter.

He stood up as quickly as he could and waved his success to the men watching on the quay.

They waved their caps back at him with glee and shouted: "Hurray! Hurray!" until the truck was finally out of sight.

CHAPTER 4

Captain McNair and Lieutenant McGregor stood on the dark, dismal platform comparing travel documents with Captain Carey, the railway transport officer. They were all awaiting Captain Fraser's convoy. A band was playing on the platform opposite. Nothing, it seemed, had been spared to give the men the welcome home they so richly deserved.

"Thanks be to God we have got so far – every mile brings us nearer to home!" exclaimed Craig. "Thank God this wretched war is over at last."

"Yes, over at last and on our way home – something we never thought would ever be," remarked Alex. "To think we are nearly home!"

Craig stood tapping his feet with impatience, gazing into the distance.

"What time do you expect to reach your home, Craig?" he asked. "Is it a long way to the far north of Scotland?"

"Yes, it is," Craig replied, "but I shall be home sometime tomorrow evening."

'I shall be home tomorrow – home tomorrow,' he told himself over and over again.

"Yes, Alex, we have been away from home and our loved ones for far too long, as have all these poor blighters waiting so patiently." He glanced over and over again towards the station entrance. "The platform is filling up more quickly now, Alex. The convoys seem to be arriving, thank God."

Craig readjusted the cap on his proud, dark head and stroked a wayward curl back underneath. His flashing dark eyes tried to penetrate the smoky gloom of the dimly lit station. His tall, broad-shouldered frame stood out above most of the rest and he had no difficulty seeing all around him. He watched the worn-out, war-weary men wending their eager way onto the platform, searching for their comrades. His steely eyes darted here and there, viewing each batch of the crippled men now arriving from the ship.

Captain Carey took his leave of Craig: "I will see you again before your train departs."

"Very well," Craig remarked as he glanced over to the other platform, where another train was waiting to load up.

'I wonder where they are heading for?' he asked himself.

A soldier broke in on his thoughts: "Is this train going to Scotland, sir?"

"Yes, it is."

"Oh, thanks be to God!" he exclaimed. "Thank you, sir," and he rushed back to his comrades, shouting with glee. "Yes, lads, that is our train, going to bonnie Scotland at last."

"I daresay", said Craig to Alex, "that he has asked his friends time and time again the same question, but he must have felt the need to clarify it by asking me."

"Yes, they can only think of home, and the sooner we all arrive home the better."

Craig's face clouded as he glanced once more to the station entrance.

"Well, here is Ian now with the boys from the sickbay!" he exclaimed.

A wave of anger and desolation swept over him as once again his thoughts winged their way back to all they had been through.

"Bloody, bloody war!" he exclaimed. "I hope mankind has once and for all learned its lesson. These poor men, and those we have left behind for ever, have paid the price." His voice choked with emotion.

Alex looked at him anxiously, his thoughts the same.

They watched as the men approached. One by one they linked up with their fitter comrades. Some had one eye bandaged, some had both, but their friends' hands were held out to them to guide them to their sides. Others followed with arms and legs missing, struggling on crutches they thought they would never need. As they struggled along, their fitter comrades were as steady as rocks in their support.

Cups of tea and sandwiches were being handed out by the Salvation Army girls and the Voluntary Aid Detachments (VAD) – these wonderful helpers of mankind when in dire trouble. What a wonderful sight they were to these so war-weary men! The men chatted gaily with them. No matter what they had gone through, somehow their smiles always broke through. Some were still standing, and some were sitting on their kitbags as they sipped their hot tea. Some, having finished, were singing or playing mouth organs, in tune with the band opposite. They made no move to get on the train standing in the station waiting for them.

They were all patiently waiting. Waiting for what, and whom? In spite of their eagerness to get home, they were prepared to wait patiently still.

Suddenly the gaze of the men turned toward the barriers, which now had been fully opened by the station porters. The ambulances had arrived at last.

Craig saw Captain Fraser heading towards him and went to meet him.

"I have got the other chaps away now to the various hospitals, Craig. These arrivals are for our train to Scotland and the north."

They both compared their lists, having now been rejoined by the RTO.

"Are you satisfied all is in order, Captain McNair? If so, I will go and get the other trains' travelling arrangements sorted."

"Yes," Craig answered, "we can carry on from here."

They headed towards the train.

The groups of soldiers, their long wait now at an end, went in organised groups to help the stretcher-bearers as they rested their precious loads on the station. So many of the injured would never walk again, but their faces lit up as they met up with their comrades once more.

The station, even by dim gaslight did not seem gloomy to them. It was a glorious palace of hope, a haven of peace and happiness at last. The smell of the engine after the smell of the dreaded gas grenades and gun smoke, was as welcome as the smell of the may blossom in the dewy morning down a country lane. The sound of the steam hissing from the engine was music to their ears. The train was waiting oh so patiently to take them all to home sweet home at last.

There were tears of joy and sorrow on their faces – never would any of them forget the friends who had not survived to make this journey home with them. Some of them were fearfully injured, but to have survived at all was a blessing.

Now they too were served with tea and sandwiches and their friends lit up cigarettes for them. Now they must all get on their way. The stretcher-bearers once more picked up their pals and headed for the train, parting columns of soldiers as they went. But to board the train was no easy task. Welcoming hands of comrades, missed in the melee, reached out to them as they passed, calling out greetings and reassurances.

"You'll be all right now, lads – you are heading for home," someone called.

Cigarettes and chocolates for the journey were stuffed in their pockets by the helpers. Ladies in neat grey dresses, some of them of noble birth, who before the war had never as much as washed a cup, were washing tin mugs and pouring tea. They coaxed badly injured men to sip hot tea, or to eat cakes made with their own hands. Any noble lady who still had lily-white hands, or who refused to do voluntary work to help the fighting men back from the front, was now a social outcast.

Craig's transfixed gaze followed their every move. Every moment he was getting more and more despondent at the sight of them all, as they moved past him into the train.

"War, war, war!" he muttered between clenched teeth. "What has it done to these fine brave men? What has it all achieved? Nothing! Nothing but misery and sorrow. What has mankind done to itself?"

No one answered him. Once more he was back at the front with his men.

"Man must never go to war again. Something must be done for all these now returning," he muttered aloud to himself. "Something will have to be done. This I will do. Yes, Aunt Elena will help me to organise something for them. She knows so many people who can help."

"What were you saying, Craig?" asked Ian, who was standing beside him.

Craig had forgotten he was there.

"Oh, I was just saying to myself what a waste of life and limb the war has been – and for what, Ian? Just look at them! There are so many of them. There seems to be no end to the column. We must arrange some help for them as soon as we can. There must be no delay."

Ian nodded his head in agreement.

Army Nursing Sisters and the VAD were waiting for them eagerly as they boarded the train.

"There doesn't seem to be as many as we had on board ship, Ian," Craig remarked.

"Well, maybe you have forgotten, Craig: some were too badly injured to travel home as yet, so they have gone to the nearest military hospital. I left Lieutenant Saunders to accompany them."

"Yes, I had forgotten for the moment, with so much going on all around me."

They were rejoined by the RTO.

"Are all the ambulances away now?" Craig asked.

"Yes, all away. I can now concentrate on the rail transport."

The three officers checked their lists with one another as Sergeant Ritchie, saluting them as smartly as ever, approached.

"All the stretchers are settled now, sir," he said, looking straight at Craig.

"Good work, Sergeant. Now the rest of the men can entrain."

"Right away, sir."

The rest of the men proceeded towards the train in orderly columns. Their progress was slow, but sure.

It had been considered at one time, when the officers were planning the journey, that the men for certain destinations should be accommodated in certain sections of the train, but the men, on hearing of this proposed plan, decided otherwise.

"No, no," they had chorused, "we will not be parted from our comrades any sooner than necessary," so Craig had told the RTO that the men's wishes must be granted.

Some of the men with only one leg were having difficulty with their crutches. They leaned on their comrades for support and, as they reached the door of the train, eager arms reached out to them. Blind men also hung on to their comrades grimly, wondering, no doubt, how long it would be before they had to cope alone in their darkness once they had all gone their separate ways. Their fumbling attempts to get up the steps of the train were pitiful to behold. Craig watched them, his anger mounting and he tapped his cane against his thigh.

'To think that such fine, stalwart men, so strong and upright when they left these shores, should be reduced to such pitiful states!' he thought.

These men were now groping like babies taking their first faltering steps. Their comrades called to one another for more assistance for them as they groped their way.

"This way, Bill" or "A little to your right, Jock – that's the idea, laddie" could be heard time and time again as they entered the train. At last they sank, weary and exhausted, into their seats.

"I wonder, Craig," remarked Ian, "if there will always be such willing arms outstretched to help them?" He held his head in despair. "I wonder."

"We must never let them down, Ian, whatever happens. We must never, ever forsake them – they who have given so much."

"No, I agree. We must all assist them. It must be one of the first things we do when we get home."

Craig's pensive gaze swept over them like that of a protective father until the last one had disappeared into the dim corridor of the train. The train had been specially altered for such as these.

"You go on, Ian. I will follow shortly."

Craig turned his gaze towards the other platform. It too was almost deserted.

"I will go and say farewell to Captain Catterall before his train pulls out. It is due out before ours."

"Wish him all the best from me," remarked Ian as he clambered aboard the train.

Craig rushed off, in spite of his weariness, so as not to delay their train.

"Goodbye, Catterall – keep in touch."

"Yes, I will – you also. Come and spend some time with me whenever you are down south."

"Thank you. I will. And you must visit me in Scotland sometime."

He nodded his acceptance, and, with a final shake of hands, they parted and Captain Catterall's train pulled away.

Ian was awaiting Craig eagerly.

"We are due out any minute now," he said, but Craig stood gazing out over the platform, his eyes anxiously looking to the now closing barrier doors of the station, as though waiting for more men to appear. Ian watched him anxiously.

"Come, Craig – all the men are on the train. There are no more to come."

But Craig still stood there, as though he could not accept the fact. Once more he was back on the Western Front. The faces of his fallen men flashed before his eyes.

"No, Ian, there are no more to come."

He looked up to see Ian and the RTO.

"No, no more to come," replied the RTO. "Yours is the last train for the day."

Craig bent down dejectedly and picked up the kitbag containing all his worldly goods. He hauled himself up to his full height and slung it onto the train. The transport officer closed the door after him and, after a final handshake Craig and Ian turned to watch him go to await another convoy of boys going home another day.

"I daresay he is a very happy man, as he sends every train on its way home," remarked Craig, as he continued to gaze from the window.

The hissing of the train seemed to him to say, "Let's be on our way with these our gallant men."

He leaned out of the window as far as he could. Every door was closed. With a whistle and a wave of the porter's flag, they were on the move. The band put down their instruments, and all the helpers left till another day. The station was now strangely quiet.

Craig continued to stare fixedly at the porters, who now drew huge bolts across the barrier gates. Each bolt that shot across was like a dagger in his heart. It was to him as if they were bolting his men out for ever.

'You will never be shut out, my gallant men. I will remember your sacrifice for ever, as will your motherland,' he thought.

He watched as the porters took off their caps to wave them on their way and the soldiers' faces disappeared one by one from view.

CHAPTER 5

Craig pulled the window shut and, stepping over the exhausted men in the corridors, he wended his weary way to where Ian was. He slung his kitbag on to the floor.

"Come, Ian – we will check if the men are all right before we, too, try to rest."

The train was full to overflowing. Nursing sisters and RAMC orderlies and VADs hurried and scurried about the injured men, readjusting dressings which had come adrift with all the handling on the journey from France, and making pillows more comfortable.

"Real pillows at last!" remarked one, as he leaned back, thankful for rest at last.

The rest of the not so badly injured men were with their comrades in the ordinary carriages, all of which were packed far too tightly for comfort. But what did comfort matter now? – they were on the train for home, in the Blighty they thought they would never see again. Here they were in Blighty, and that meant home to one and all.

Craig and Ian, after walking the whole length of the corridors and entering all the compartments, to ensure that all was well with the men and all was going to plan, arrived back at the spot in the corridor where they had flung down their kitbags. They flung themselves beside them on to the floor, almost too weary to speak or stand any longer.

The train thundered on into the darkening night, as the men nodded off into exhausted sleep, rocked in the vibrating coaches, seemingly in tune with the fast-rolling wheels, speeding on and on. 'Dudra-da, dudra-da, dudra-da' went the train as it shot over the rails, on and on like a soothing lullaby of the night. Silence fell in the compartments as the battle-worn, weary men sank, one by one, into restless slumber.

In spite of their discomfort, cramped positions, and makeshift pillows of shoulders and kitbags, no one stirred.

The two captains were leaning heavily against the sides of the carriage, legs outstretched into the corridor, not sleeping, just resting their weary backs on their kitbags, but their men were sleeping and that was all that mattered to them.

Suddenly, the roar of a passing train broke the deep silence. The men stirred uneasily, and some were startled into an upright position. A scream of terror rent the air.

Craig and Ian shot to their feet simultaneously and raced to the area from where it came. A blind, badly wounded soldier was holding his head and screaming.

"The guns! The guns! Will they never stop firing? Oh, God, will they never stop?"

A nursing sister was already by his side, trying to comfort him.

"I will take over, Sister!" Craig exclaimed, as he cradled the nerve-shattered lad in his arms. "It's all right, son. It's all right, son," he whispered to him softly as he held him close.

A memory came flooding back to him of the night his father had held him close to comfort him after the death of his mother. He recalled the warm succour and strength it gave him to hear those words: "It's all right, son, I am here by your side." Somehow, to him, this boy felt like a son. He was so young, and yet he himself was not much older than this boy who trusted him and clung to him, and was so in need of him.

"Ian, go and check if the rest of the men are well. I will stay with this boy for a while." Craig heard himself saying, "Yes, my boy, the guns have all stopped firing now. No more firing, no more shells – all is now quiet on the front."

He felt the boy relax a little as he spoke to him.

"What was it, then, if it wasn't the guns?" the boy asked.

"It was only a passing train," Craig replied. "All is well, all is well."

He rubbed the boy's damp hair, wet with sweat, with his handkerchief, but the Sister handed him a dampened sponge with which to wipe the sweat from the boy's brow.

"A passing train, sir?" the boy queried in disbelief. "A passing train? Are we really on our way home at last?" he asked. "Are you sure, sir?"

"Yes, I am sure," replied Craig.

"Is this you, Captain McNair?" he asked, as he moved his thin, frail arms along his shoulder and felt the three pips.

"Yes, it's me," he reassured him. "Now, get some rest – we still have a long way to go."

"Yes, I will, sir. Thank you, sir."

Before he leaned back, the Sister turned his sweat-drenched pillow, and he sank wearily against it, a tired, grateful smile on his face. Craig's words had given him comfort and relief. He knew that his officer's word was true; he could rest now. All was quiet on the front. He released his grip from his captain's arm, and closed his sightless eyes to the night.

"Stay close to him, Sister," Craig said, and she nodded as she watched him go.

He wended his way back, treading warily over the outstretched legs of the men resting in the corridors. Most of them were awake now. Some had tried in vain to get to sleep again, but it was not possible. Several sat up and stretched their cramped, weary limbs. Some stood in the corridors to do the same, rubbing their limbs to get back the circulation.

As Captain McNair passed them, several asked, "How is our comrade now, sir?"

"Resting now, resting now," he called to Corporal Sterling as he passed: "How about some music for the rest of the men? I don't think there will be any more sleep tonight."

"Yes, by all means, sir. There's nothing like a tune to pass the time away and lighten the heart. We will play very softly, sir, so as not to waken any who want to sleep."

By now, more and more of them were fully awake.

"Ian, go and see if you can drum up some tea for them. They will need it if they get singing and playing for any length of time, and it is almost due anyway."

"I agree. I will go and see how long it might be."

He hurried off to the rear of the train.

They started to play and hum, very softly. The first ones, as always, were 'Home Sweet Home' and 'Shenandoah'. It didn't matter what they sang now – wrong words, right words or, as more often, their own made-up ones.

Several of them went to see their other comrades. Sergeant Ritchie, on the instructions of his captain, had gone to see the soldier who had screamed out. The Sergeant looked at him sadly as he stood there cursing to himself the horror of the war and all they had been through.

'This comrade's war will never be over,' he thought to himself. 'Never, never!'

He touched him lightly on the arm.

The soldier reached out to him. "Who is it?"

"It is I, Sergeant Ritchie. Are you feeling better now, laddie?"

"Yes, Sergeant. I am all right. How are all our other comrades? I am sorry if I disturbed their rest."

"That's all right, mate – think nothing of it. We are all on our way home. That is the only thing that's important now. Can you hear the boys singing?"

"Yes, it is a joy to listen to. How happily they sing now, Sergeant! It sounds so different to when we were in the line. We always tried to sing them happily, didn't we, Sergeant? It wasn't easy – was it, Sarge? – but we did it."

"No, laddie, it wasn't easy, but, as you say, we managed it. Now, you must not talk any more. You must rest. We still have a long journey ahead."

"Have you any idea, Sarge, where we are?"

"No, laddie, but we are in Blighty so what does it matter? I will come again later to see you; then I may know our whereabouts."

He patted him lightly on the hand as he left.

"How is the soldier now?" asked Captain McNair on his return.

"Quite calm and restful, sir; and all in the sickbay are enjoying the singing."

"That is good, then."

Suddenly above the sound of their singing came the loud shout: "Tea up! Tea up! That's right, lads, let's drum up the char," and immediately out came their battered old tin mugs, followed by the mess tins.

Then the call came through. "Grub up! Grub up! Clear the gangways, lads! Clear the gangways!" The men from the Catering Corps were coming through with trays of sandwiches on their heads, stepping as deftly as only they knew how between the men's feet, still calling as they went: "Clear the gangways! Clear the gangways, if you please!"

On and on the eager train flew through the night. Home was getting closer with every mile. The train seemed to be singing a message as it sped over the tracks: "Soon be home, soon be home, soon be home. Won't be long, won't be long. As fast as I can, as fast as I can, as fast as I can." Then, a slackening of speed and an alteration in the rhythm roused one or two of the restless men, who eased themselves up and wondered if they had dreamed it. Had the rhythm altered? Had the train changed speed? They eased themselves up a little more, with questioning looks on their faces, and in doing so they disturbed their sleeping comrades.

"What's wrong now, you bloody nuisances? Keep still and let a fellow sleep, can't you?"

Some sat up, now wide awake: "What is it?" asked several. They looked up to see Captain McNair. "What is it, sir?" they asked, almost in chorus.

"I am not sure. I don't think we are anywhere near any of our destinations as yet," he said, as puzzled as they.

Some of them got to their feet, and, trying not to tread on their less able-bodied friends, they raced eagerly to the carriage windows. Some who tried to join them found they couldn't move quickly enough, if at all, or even stand. They cursed as they found their shoelaces tied together, or to one another's shoes.

"Hellfire! If I find the sod who did this, I will throw him off the damn train, to be sure I will," said Private Jock McKay.

They all looked in one direction, but not a smirk on the face of the guilty one could they see. Fury and anger and laughter were all mingled up together as they rushed to the windows.

Then there was a loud howl of dismay from Private Dunbar, who was first to open the window and feel the cold night air on his face. He bobbed his head back in again quickly. He had been drenched to the skin with ice-cold water. The train raced on and on, having filled its gaping mouth with its ration of water.

"You damn black monster!" he screamed at it. "You damn sod!"

He hastily dried his face and neck, cursing still as he did so, much to the amusement of all around him.

"That will teach you a lesson. I am damn glad!" exclaimed Corporal McTavish. "It serves you right for causing my kitbag to fall in the water."

At every opportunity he had wailed loud and long at Private Dunbar for causing him to lose all his worldly possessions in the dock.

"Come on, men – settle down again!" exclaimed the Captain. He too was trying not to smile. "We have a long way to go yet."

CHAPTER 6

The two captains started to sort out their labels and documents from their kitbags as some of the men once more tried to settle. But most were far too restless and, at the thought of the nearness of home, they remained on their feet. They wanted to be ready. Just as they had been ready for battle, now they were ready for home. They straightened their tunics, tied their laces and combed their hair. They tried to part it straight, brushing it with their hands if they couldn't find their combs.

"How's that mate?" one of them asked his comrade as he stood in front of him.

"*Très bon, très bon*," one of them muttered through half-opened eyes.

"Now, now! We are in dear old Blighty now, so no more of this '*Parlez-vous Français*', *si'l vous plait*."

"Have any of you dozy buggers got a mirror?" asked Private Miller.

"I have, Jock," called one from down the train.

"Loan it to me for a moment, then, Jock."

He pulled from his pocket a small pocket mirror, cracked down the middle, only held together by its shabby leatherette backing.

"I look a funny devil in this," he commented as he viewed himself from the side.

"Well, what do you expect? You are a funny-looking sod at the best of times, anyway. If it wasn't already cracked, you would crack it with your funny dial."

"Now, less of your wisecracks! You are no oil painting. Here's your mirror back. I will bring you a new one when we meet at our reunion."

"Right. I will hold you to that."

The two captains disappeared once more down the corridors towards the sickbay, and commenced, with the nursing sisters, to check and recheck names and addresses. They then gave the stretcher-bearers the order of movement from the train when they reached their eagerly awaited station.

Those who would be alighting first were busy putting their few precious things in their kitbags and making sure they were securely tied.

All the men able to walk were now helping their more disabled pals pack their kitbags. They adjusted their scarves and caps, and buttoned up their coats against the cold night air they would encounter.

"Well," said one to the friend by his side, "I won't be wearing this damn rig-out after today."

"No, me neither," his friend replied. "Once I take the buggering thing off, it stays off."

"And that goes for all of us," one called out.

"We have all done it proud. It will be civvy suits from now on."

The train slackened speed and the men looked at each other excitedly.

"This time for sure, this time for sure!" exclaimed Private McKinley. "I'm sure we are arriving at someone's destination."

"But whose?" they chorused.

"Where are we, where are we?" one impatient voice called out. "I hope the bugger doesn't forget to stop. I am sure it's my stop – I can feel it in my bones."

"So can I," replied several more, all tapping their feet with impatience.

Several were straining their necks out of the carriage windows as the train drew to a standstill.

"I can't see the damn station's name. These damn gaslights are so poor. Shut up, some of you, then I can hear what station the porter is calling out."

But his plea for silence fell on deaf ears.

"Yes, yes," shouted one, "it is our stop – the one we have all been waiting for." The name of the station was heard and repeated over and over again.

"That's us, boys. We are home at last. At last we are home."

Captain McNair and Captain Fraser scrambled as best they could through the excited men.

"Make way for the Captain!" called out Sergeant Ritchie. "Make way, boys!"

At once they lined up as the captains sped past them. Craig tucked his movement orders more firmly under his arm, and held his hand firmly on the handle of the door, waiting for the train to come to a final halt. When it did so, he leaped straight out on to the platform.

"Now, one at a time, boys," he called to them.

The Sergeant ticked them off one by one as they too leaped on to their platform of home.

CHAPTER 7

Little huddled masses of people, who had stood hour after hour in the chill dark night, were now approaching the train. The longed-for train had at last arrived. Several hurried along, calling their sons' names over and over again, only falling silent when the dear son fell into their eager arms.

The crippled ones were being helped by the VADs and other men from the train. Their loved ones, too, hurried to meet them, seeming to know them at once in spite of the dim lights. Some suddenly stopped in their haste, to hesitate and look again. 'Is this really the fine splendid boy, so perfect in limb when he went away? Is he now returning to us a cripple?' they thought as they saw their sons approaching on their crutches, helped by their friends. Some could hardly believe it was really true what they were seeing. They shed tears of joy at seeing them home at last, and tears of sadness at their sorry plight. All tried not to show their anguish at their pitiable state, and tried to laugh with them, showing their joy that they were home for good.

Other groups stood watching with tears in their eyes. 'But where are our boys?' they thought, lost in a maze of anxious looks. 'Where are our boys? What is the delay? Why are they not off the train?' Mothers looked anxiously at fathers, and wives looked anxiously at their children. 'Where are our beloved ones? Where are they?' their eyes seemed to be asking one another. 'Please let them be with us soon! Surely they are on this train?' their anxious looks seemed to be saying.

The soldiers shook hands with one another over and over again, all sad to be leaving comrades with whom they had shared so much. The parting of the ways had finally come.

This was what they had all dreamed about, sung about, even cried about alongside one another. They were more like brothers than just pals. They had eased one another's pains and suffering when all before them was death and destruction.

The able ones raced off the train, their kitbags dangling over shoulders.

"See you at the reunion. So long, Jock." The words clung to their lips as they gripped their pals in a last, long farewell, patting each other on the back. With jolly banter and parting jests they leaped from the train, and then they were out of sight in the arms of their loved ones.

Captains McNair and Fraser had been joined by the station RTO as they checked and rechecked their lists with the sergeants. The ambulances arrived and the stretcher-bearers alighted and made their way to the train with the nursing sisters. The RAMC officer made his way to where Craig was standing. He knew how anxious the men still on the train were to see the loved ones waiting for them.

"Ian, go and tell the relatives still waiting over there that their loved ones will soon be with them."

One by one off the train they came. They too were anxious to see their loved ones, but they were sorry to be leaving their many friends behind. At last they were all on the platform, being carried away to the waiting ambulances. Their loved ones walked beside them, overcome with joy. Fathers had tears streaming down their faces and wives and mothers put their arms around the necks of their husbands and sons, determined never to let them out of their sight ever again.

It became difficult for the stretcher-bearers to proceed on their way. The sisters gently extricated their loved ones' arms from around their necks.

"We must be getting along. They are home to stay now," they were heard to say so many times.

Finally, the last one was through the barrier. Craig stood on the steps of the train and watched them go with deep despair.

"What is to become of them?" he sighed – but at least they were now home and with their loved ones.

Then through the barriers came the Salvation Army girls, pushing their trolleys loaded with home-made buns and steaming hot tea for the men still aboard the train. The more able ones could clamber down to stretch their weary limbs as they stood in their little groups chatting and joking, and teasing these so loved and welcome friends. The chink of their old tin mugs was now the only sound on the dimly lit station. The buns and hot tea were like ambrosia and nectar to them as they recalled the hard biscuits they had at the front.

The two captains also stepped down from the train. They had seen that all inside had eaten.

At last the men were ready to get back on the train. The sergeants and corporals told them to hurry and get aboard, and they waved goodbye to the so welcome providers. Craig and Ian stood watching them.

"Well, Ian," Craig said, "a good part of our journey is now over. Every mile has brought us all nearer home."

"More tea, Captain?" a voice called to him, and he turned to see a very young slip of a girl in her army uniform. A big bow under her chin almost hid her tiny features from view. Her frail appearance startled him.

"No, thank you, my dear. My, you are very young to be out in the early hours of this chilly morning."

"Oh, sir, we have all got our duty to do."

"Well," Craig declared, "you all do it very well. We could not manage without your wonderful help. These buns are delicious, aren't they, Ian?"

"They certainly are, but I cannot eat any more buns or drink more of your delicious tea," replied Ian. "Thank you all the same."

"I will bid you goodbye. Good luck to all of you," she called as she turned to go.

Ian and Craig turned to board the train. The station was now practically empty, but a commotion at the recently vacated barrier caused Craig to hesitate. He watched as the small figure of a very frail old lady, dressed in clogs and with a grey thin shawl covering her head, came hurrying as fast as she could towards the train. A porter followed in hot pursuit. She flung herself at Craig's feet.

"Please, sir," she cried, "where is my son? I have searched all the ambulances out there and watched the others go. He should be home today, Captain. Please tell me where he is. He said he would be home today."

"Well, Mother," said Craig, "if he said he would be home today, he will come."

"Well, he hasn't come yet. Is he on your train?"

She was sobbing bitterly and Craig bent down and gently raised her to her feet.

"What is his name, Mother. I will try to find him for you." He glanced down at his long list, then he called to Ian. "Will you please bring the other list you have. These lights are so poor that I can't see. I want to check if this mother's son is still on our train. Please hold the lantern."

Ian took the lantern off the porter and held it as Craig tried to read.

As they perused the long lists, the tiny lass from the Salvation Army came to the old lady's side.

"Take this warm drink, Mother dear," she said. "The Captain will find your son if he can."

She took the drink readily; it was as if she had not had a drink or meal all day. The pinched, hungry, anxious look on her face told of her pitiful state.

"No, Mother, your son is not on our train," commented Craig at last. "He would have been put off already if he had travelled with us. I repeat, Mother dear, he is not with us," he said as he noted her disbelieving look.

"Please, please, Captain, look again," she pleaded. "I beg of you, sir, look again. Let me see inside the train. You do not know my son, Captain."

Craig looked at Ian. The men in the train were getting more and more restive at the delay. Several peered out of the windows, and in the gloom could see the old lady talking and gesticulating to the Captain. They didn't know why they were having to wait, and the delay for them was getting too long. The engine's whistle had blown several times. The porter tried to reason with the old lady, but Craig could see that it was impossible to convince her.

"Very well, Mother dear, come inside and look."

He led her gently by the arm through the carriages and corridors. She stood peering closely at a group of them before passing to the next. Several of them touched her lightly on the arm as she passed by. They didn't ask why she was looking at them with such a lost look in her eyes. They knew only too well. Now and again she would peer more closely at some, and ask, "Was my son with you? Have you seen my boy anywhere?"

All shook their heads sadly, full of distress at seeing the anguished longing in the old lady's eyes. Fresh tears fell on top of already dried ones and she wiped them away with her shawl.

"Now, there are only the ones in the sickbay, Mother dear. Follow me," said Craig, and he walked slowly towards the front of the train as she followed behind.

"How ill they all are!" she muttered frequently as she passed. "How their dear mothers must have missed them so, waiting like me for them to come home." She looked hard and long at the ones with bandaged faces, and whispered to them, "God bless you, my son."

The men were anxious to get on their way, but not for one moment would they let her see their impatience. At last, she had seen the last one.

"I am sorry, Mother, there are no more," said Craig.

"Yes, sir, so I see," she whispered despondently, her sad eyes once more filling with tears. "Thank you, sir, for helping me look for my son. I shall never forget your kindness."

She wended her way slowly back to the door of the train, calling to the soldiers as she passed: "Goodbye. God bless you all."

"Goodbye and God bless you too, Mother dear," they called after her.

Craig stepped down from the train to help her off.

"Where can he be, sir? Where can he be?"

"There are more trains to come, Mother dear. They are nearly all home now." He felt a catch in his throat as he said it.

'Not all will be coming home,' he reminded himself.

"I am sure he will be home with you soon," he said.

"Do you think so, sir?"

"Yes, Mother, I am sure he will soon be home."

The RTO hastened down the platform to ask the cause of the delay of the departure of the train. He stopped to speak to the guard, who pointed to where Craig and the old lady were leaving the carriage.

"Oh, dear me! Not Mother again!" he exclaimed.

"Yes, it certainly is," the guard replied.

They watched as the waiting girl took her gently by the arm, and led her away.

Craig stood gazing after her, his heart too full of pity for words. The girl pulled the old lady's shawl further round her shoulders to protect her from the chill night air. Her clogs were far too big for her tiny feet, and they clattered on the silent platform. The anguish Craig had seen in her eyes, her pinched little face and her thin little body emphasised the malnutrition she was a victim of and the sight tore at his heart.

'What can I do to help such as these? I must do something,' he thought. 'Yes, I will get Aunt Elena to help me to assist them. But I must first get home.'

He suddenly realised that the train must get on its way. He mustn't stand here any longer. The RTO's voice broke in on his thoughts.

"She meets every train, Captain. Her son was killed months ago."

"Is that so?" exclaimed Craig. "He, like others, died in no-man's-land, I daresay," he muttered angrily.

He climbed wearily back into the train. The RTO shook hands with him through the window as the guard's whistle blew and, with a wave of his flag, the train was once again on its way. He pulled the window up to the top, pulled the green blind down, and wended his way back to where Ian was.

"I will go and see how the men are settling."

"Is everything all right, Captain?" asked Private Dunbar. He could see that his captain was troubled by the old lady's visit.

"Yes, yes, everything is all right, so tell the boys to settle down. We still have a long way to go, and the next stop, I am sure, will be in our bonnie Scotland."

"Yippee, yippee!" several yelled.

"Now, you heard what the Captain said. Silence, please, and settle down!" the Sergeant commanded. "We have a long way to go."

They were all thankful for the extra room, and the men stretched out their cramped limbs with relief. A deep depression had descended on all of them at the parting from their friends, and they were saddened by the anguished look on the little old lady's face as she had gazed at each one of them in turn. A hushed silence fell. They tried to pull their kitbag-pillows into less neck-aching positions, and soon they all dropped off into restless, worn-out sleep.

The train sped on through the night.

The two captains were now able to move into a compartment, and they too fell into restless slumber.

CHAPTER 8

The dawn broke over the horizon in long streaks of gold and crimson between the dark low-slung clouds. The night of yesterday slipped quietly away and a new day dawned. At last, here was today! Today! Today!

Craig had hardly closed his eyes on the long journey, and he was the first to see the chink of light heralding the new day.

"Dawn, at last!" he muttered. "I shall be home today. I shall be home today. No more tomorrows to wait for – I shall be home today."

He rose to his feet just as one of his men woke, and he too blinked at the brilliant light of dawn.

"Is it dawn out there, sir?"

"It is, laddie," Craig replied.

The soldier scrambled to his feet like lightning, and rubbed his cramped limbs. "At last! At last!" he exclaimed. He scrambled to the window and, in doing so, trampled on several of his comrades. With anguished yells of "You bloody clumsy bugger, sit down and go to sleep!" ringing in his ears, he shot up the blind, pulled down the window, and hung his head out as far as he could to get the blast of the fresh Scottish air into his lungs.

"Hey, lads," he yelled out excitedly, "we are in our bonnie Scotland. We have crossed the Border. We are home."

There was a huge roar of exultation and excitement. "Let's see! Let's see!" they shouted as they scrambled to the windows.

"We have crossed the Border and are in bonnie Scotland, and we had to be bloody well asleep!" said Private Dunbar.

He had managed, as usual, to get a good view. The train had left the lovely Lake District far behind.

"All of us fast asleep! Our bonnie Scotland will never forgive us," he said.

By now, general pandemonium had broken out. Some of the soldiers raced down the corridors to tell their pals in the sickbay.

"It's true at last, lads: we are home. Glasgow here we come!"

They started to sing and play all the Scottish melodies they knew. Private Dunbar sang and danced a reel as best he could.

"This is the land we have fought for. None of us will ever leave you again. And so say all of us," they choroused.

Now came the hustle and bustle of packing final oddments into their kitbags. Some belongings had become mixed up with their friends', and these were hastily exchanged. Boots that had been slipped off to relieve tired war-weary travellers' feet were being hastily retrieved and swopped over. There were curses galore when soldiers tried to claim other people's boots, but the fumblings and sortings-out were hampered by haste and the excitement of being home at last.

Tears of joy fell down many of their faces. Private Dunbar danced a jig, despite several of his comrades pushing him out of their way. At last he sat down quite breathless.

"Now, lads," he said, "how about a last real sing-song before we part? First one, then – come on, musicians!" he yelled. "Keep those mouth organs out a bit longer whilst we sing. Now, all together, 'These Are My Mountains' – they are, aren't they, lads? They sure are, and these are our glens."

He had stood up again and was again using his cap as a baton.

At last, the train started to slow down as a station came into view. Caps fell on to the lines as heads were strained out of the windows to get a better view. The men were now all ready, kitbags tied securely and packed to overflowing. Their old tin mugs, so precious to them not so long ago, were flung out of the train and landed on the hard surface of the station with a loud clatter. Some missed the station staff by inches; others were not so lucky. However, they all joined in the laughter of the boys, now tumbling out of the windows before anyone could open the doors. Private Dunbar, as expected, was the first one out. Before the train had stopped, he knelt on the floor and kissed the ground.

"At last, at last! Bonnie Scotland, your lads are home."

Their anxious relatives, who had waited night after night and day after day, gazed eagerly over the barrier. The two captains stepped down.

"The boys in the sickbay are all ready, Craig."

"Right, we will get them away first. We can't keep these boys waiting too long."

Craig called them all to attention. At once they obeyed and were once more the disciplined soldiers of their proud regiment, although the sight of their loved ones straining their necks over the station barriers was almost more than they could bear. They stood still, and all turmoil ceased, as they lined up to hear their captain's last orders.

They all stood in one long line as their pals from the sickbay were brought out of the train, and they all said their last farewells with tears in their eyes.

"Try and come to the reunion," they kept calling to them.

"We will, we will," they cried, but it was doubtful if many of them would ever be fit enough.

The two captains shook hands with all the men before they were dismissed, and they watched as the men raced off to join their loved ones. Then both went with the RTO to the waiting ambulances.

"Captain McNair! Captain, sir," cried out a voice from one of the stretchers.

"Yes, my boy," he replied, bending low over his chest to hear what he had to say.

"Will we ever meet again, you and me and all our comrades?"

"Yes, my son, we will. Captain Fraser and I will call to see you all in a few weeks' time. We will not forget you ever. We will all meet again in far happier gatherings than we have in the past. Just get well soon," Craig said, and, with a final handshake to them all, he watched them till they were all out of sight.

Craig knew he would never forget the pathetic look on the faces of their relatives as they saw for the first time the extent of their loved ones' injuries.

At last, the words had come true of the song that had never been far from the hearts of either the men or their loved ones: the dark clouds were at last turned inside out. The boys were home, and the home fires would be burning.

All was now silent and desolate on the station as only Craig and Ian were left. They sat side by side.

"How long will you have to wait for your train, Craig?" Ian asked.

"I am not sure yet. They were very infrequent before the war, so goodness knows now. I will ask the RTO, if and when he reappears."

"Shall I stay and talk with you whilst you wait?"

"No, thank you, Ian. You too must get away to the ones waiting for you. I know they will be as anxious as the loved ones who are waiting for me."

"I will get a cab outside. I haven't far to travel, as you know. I will contact you soon, and then we can visit the men together."

With a final handshake and wave, he was gone.

CHAPTER 9

Craig was now at last on his own. He could see that no one else was going as far north as himself. He felt suddenly empty without any of his men by his side. They had all now gone their various ways – all except the ones they had left behind. Once more his thoughts drifted back to them. He sat on the cold and isolated platform, sad and weary. 'I must not be sad,' he told himself. 'I am, like my men, on Scottish soil once more, and I will be home tonight. What a wonderful feeling after all this time! I am so tired, but I am longing to be home. Dear, dear, Papa will be waiting to greet me with outstretched arms, and soon I shall see my darling Fiona again. How I have missed her and my dear aunts, Elena and Harriet! God knows how much I have missed you all!'

He knew Aunt Elena would help him in his efforts to help his men, all of whom were so badly in need of help. She with all her contacts everywhere could and would help him the most. She loved him dearly, and she had tried so hard to fill the gap left, like a deep ravine in his heart, when his darling mother had died. Of course a mother's place can never ever be filled by another, no matter how anyone tries, but Aunt Elena did understand Craig, and she was closer to him than anyone else.

His father had been too wrapped up in his own grief to try to help and understand him till it was almost too late.

Dear Aunt Harriet was good to him in many ways, but she was far too severe in her approach and too much like his father to understand his sensitive nature.

'But that was all so long ago,' he thought, as his thoughts drifted on and on. 'My dear dog, Flint, will be waiting for me too. I bet he is sitting by the loch this very minute.'

"Oh, how I missed you all!" he exclaimed aloud.

His thoughts raced on and on, as he sat getting more and more stiff with the cold. He had forgotten how cold it could get in his beloved Scotland.

'But what does it matter?' he told himself. 'I shall soon be home.'

At last he clambered into the small train, which the stationmaster assured him was the connection he had waited so long for.

"Yes, sir, this is your train for the Highlands and Glencree."

When he heard the name of his home station, a sharp thrill of joy leaped through him, but he still could not believe it was true.

"I must still be dreaming," he told himself, and, to make doubly sure of what the stationmaster had said, he sped to the front of the train to ask the driver. "Are you sure this train stops at Glencree?"

"Yes, Captain, you have my word for it. This is the train you have been waiting for."

"You will be sure to stop?" he queried.

"Yes, my son, I will be sure to stop. Just get aboard and then we will be away."

Craig flung himself wearily on to a seat.

'How cold and weary and hungry I am!' he thought as he flung the kitbag containing his possessions on to the seat opposite.

He knew he would be alone on this little-frequented train to the Highlands, especially with the war just being over. Normal travelling had not been re-established. So much was in turmoil up and down the country.

'But soon, no doubt,' he told himself, as if to try to cheer himself up, 'all will be as before. Soon all the fishing and shooting parties will be coming to Glencree Castle, like the ones I took part in before I went away – but no more shooting for me! I have seen enough killing and heard far too much gunfire to last me for life.'

He felt the train lurch forward.

"Thank God!" he exclaimed. "We're away on the last mile home."

He stood up and lowered the window and felt the cool, fresh mountain air rush in on him as the train left the station. As they steamed through the built-up area of the city, he gazed out at the huddled houses.

'They're all too close together,' he told himself.

Here in the city were people who asked little of life, but who had given so much when the call came. How many times he had witnessed their selflessness! They gave themselves unstintingly, no matter what the cost.

Swirls of smoke rose from the chimneys of the small houses in street after street. Yes, the home fires would be burning as they had never done before, to welcome the boys home at last. What awaited them now – especially the wounded ones? Craig's thoughts dwelt long on them, all now back beside their own hearths at last, with the grim facts of the aftermath of the war to face head-on. The brave limbless ones would have to explain to their children how their injuries had happened. They would tell them of the bravery they had witnessed alongside their comrades. He imagined how proud the children would be of their fathers.

"Oh, what a brave father we have! Surely he must have won the war all by himself. Surely no one could have such a brave father as us."

He imagined their eyes wide open with wonder and pride, and their father raising his eyes above their heads to meet the proud look of their mother – so loving, but so anxious too.

He imagined them asking, "How are we to feed these children of ours?" with a look shared just between them; and most had the faith to say, "We shall manage somehow. God will help us provide."

Craig could visualise the ones with badly gassed lungs, who would never get any relief until their final breath, trying between each painful gasp to tell their stories too, not for one moment letting their loved ones know how much pain it caused.

And the blind ones, who would never again see the faces of their loved ones – what would they be saying to their families?

Over and over again the faces of his men criss-crossed his mind. His mind was in a whirl as he imagined their plight.

'Well, at last they are home – the precious few. My God, I will help them! That is my vow. Dear Aunt Elena will help me, I know.'

He gave a last look at the fast-disappearing city covered in its smoke shroud.

'How will they adjust to life now they are back, or how will I?' he thought.

Weary as he was, he was still reluctant to move from the window. The cool mountain air of this his homeland sank into every fibre of his being. He leaned out as far as he could, inhaling the clear, bracing air.

'Oh, how wonderful it all feels! Is it really all true at last, or am I dreaming? It has to be true. Where else would I see such green, green grass?'

The sheep, grazing so peacefully on the slopes and crags and in the gullies, looked up with their soulful eyes at him as the train passed by.

Now the sun catching the tops of the snow-covered mountains in the distance caught his eye and, although almost too tired to stand, he gazed out.

'Yes, these are my mountains. Now I know I am really back in my bonnie Scotland. Never again will I leave you, land of my fathers – never again. I will be home tonight with my dear, dear father.'

He reluctantly drew the window to the top and turned away from the scene outside. He sank wearily on the seat, his thoughts now only of home and all his loved ones awaiting him with open arms.

'Well, no more tomorrows! I shall be home tonight.'

He sat and recalled once more how he had felt as he waved his final goodbye to his father – the feeling of utter loneliness and emptiness. It was the first time they had been separated since the loss of his darling mother. He thought how lonely his father must have felt as he watched Magnus row him away from the small jetty on the loch. He had wondered if he would ever see him again, or his dear aunts or his darling Fiona. He could still see his dog, Flint, straining at the leash as his father held on to him firmly. As the mountains had faded away in the distance he had wondered if he would ever see them again, and now here they were, just as before.

"Oh, how I have missed you all!" he sighed.

The rhythm of the train lulled him into exhausted, restless sleep. His head rested uneasily on his makeshift pillow as he tried time and time again to adjust his kitbag more comfortably. His head constantly slipped off and roused him again and again out of his troubled dreams. Heavy rain was now pounding the windows. Suddenly, the crash of thunder woke him with a fearful jolt, which flung him on to the floor between the seats. He made a vain attempt to save himself by trying to catch the seat opposite, but he was too slow and landed with a loud thud. Another loud crash of thunder made him wince.

"Oh, my God! My God! Will the guns never cease their bombardment? Will they never stop?" He held his head in his hands, as if to squeeze out the sound for ever.

He groped around in the eerie light of the darkening afternoon. The train lights were not yet on.

"Sergeant, Sergeant, where are my men? Where are my men?" he demanded. "Answer me, damn you, man! Answer me!"

But all was silent. Not a voice answered his frantic call.

Another crash of thunder made him once again wince in anguish, and then the eerie silence set his thoughts in turmoil. The flashes of lightning – the only light – reminded him of the Very lights he thought he had left behind for good.

'Are my men still here?' he asked himself.

Never had he felt so alone. He had always had his beloved men by his side. Where were they?

"Where am I? Where am I?" he called out, over and over again.

Only another crash of thunder answered his plaintive cry.

He searched for his handkerchief and wiped the beads of cold, clammy sweat from his forehead as they started to run into his eyes. He tried to raise himself to his feet, but in his weariness he only managed to get to his knees. He buried his face in his hands as he rested against the seat. He was shaking with cold.

"God, how exhausted I am – and how alone! I feel as though the whole world has deserted me."

He shakily drew his knees up to his chest and sank his head on to them. He prayed over and over again. "My God! My God, will this nightmare never leave me?"

At last, he lowered his hands from his face and looked round the small compartment. The realisation at last dawned on him that he had mistaken the thunder for gunfire.

"No wonder!" he muttered to himself.

He sat there – how long, he neither knew nor cared. Every minute seemed like an hour; every hour of his journey seemed like a week. His thoughts were filled with tangled memories of the horrors he had left behind. He seemed to hear again the whine of the horses and the shrieking bullets, which had filled the air night and day, shattering all their nerves to shreds.

The horses had suffered alongside the men. They too had been flung into the holocaust. Instead of being left to graze peacefully in some lush, green meadow, as was their right, they sank alongside the men in the never-ending mud, never to be seen again. Death waited for everyone. He could still hear the sound of his own voice and the whistles blowing.

"Those damn whistles!" he heard himself saying, and, "Over the top, over the top! Your turn now to die!"

Fine young men, who were too young to die, had fallen all around him, and for what? For God's sake, for what?

He clambered wearily back on to his seat. His head had caught the edge of the door as he fell, and he pressed his handkerchief against the cut to stem the blood. Then he flopped back on to his makeshift pillow.

'Oh, how tired I am – so damn tired! I cannot think straight.'

After a few moments of exhausted contemplation he raised himself wearily on one elbow. He tried to peer out into the dark, stormy night. He cleared the condensation from the window with his sleeve. The rain now fell more heavily and the strong wind was thrashing it against the glass and making the carriage door rattle furiously.

'I am going to get drenched sailing over the loch, but what will that matter after all I have been through? This storm is nothing. I shall be home tonight. No more tomorrows! I shall be home tonight.'

At last his eyes closed in sleep.

CHAPTER 10

Bruce was awake long before Jamie came in to bring him his morning tea.

"Well, Jamie, today is the day. No more tomorrows to wait for now! My son, the young master, will be home today."

"We have all waited so long for this day, master, and now at last it is here. He has been away far too long, but now he is on his way," said Jamie.

"Go now, Jamie – I hear Lady Harriet calling you."

This old castle, sitting so serenely by the large loch of Glencree in its splendid isolation, had been the family seat of the Earls of Glencree for hundreds of years. Situated in one of the wildest and most isolated parts of the far north of Scotland, it stood like a tall sentinel amongst the tall pine forests and deep valleys and glens. In the distance, the mountains overlooked it, as if to remind everyone that they were the real monarchs of the Highlands. The mountains had been there longer than any people.

The castle was built by the 1st Earl of Glencree as a retreat. He was a man noted for his love of solitude, and also for ruling his family with a rod of iron. To him, only the family name mattered and he believed the clan of which he was head must always be upheld: no one must ever shirk the duty of carrying on the family name. He decreed that all future lairds of Glencree must be born and married there, and be buried in the special family crypt in the church grounds. The church he had had built in the village. Almost all the land belonged to the Earl of Glencree, apart from one or two large mansions, which were owned by families that had been there almost as long as the McNairs themselves.

They also owned land on the other side of the loch, which they visited frequently, and the Earl had his own ferryman to carry him across. Only the laird and his family and special guests were allowed to cross over to the castle using the ferry. Everyone else had to travel further on, by the longer route round the bend of the loch to the small village. This laird had insisted that as long as there was a laird of Glencree there would always be a ferryman to carry him over. Only the finest boatmen were chosen, and to be the Earl's ferryman was considered the highest honour that could be bestowed on a boatman.

Magnus, the present ferryman, had had the job for many years and was the best there was. Every week he would row over to bring supplies to the castle and then on to the village, which lay round the bend a few miles away.

Bruce told himself over and over again, 'Magnus will never carry as precious a load as he will carry today.'

He would trust his son to none but Magnus. Today his son and heir would be home.

It was late afternoon, and a deep calm had settled on the castle. What a day it had been since early morn! The house had been a hive of activity since the cock crowed, with everyone racing about, their happy smiling faces a joy to behold.

"What a difference that telegram has made!" said Elena.

She sang everywhere she went, preparing everything needed. Even dour Harriet had now and again managed a little hum to herself, which one could hear if one listened very carefully. She was never one to show her true feelings.

However, no one was so happy and restless as the master.

Bruce called constantly to Jamie: "Jamie, are you sure all the lamps are filled ready for lighting? Are you sure?"

"Yes, Sir Bruce, they will be lit as soon as dusk falls – almost any time now!" he exclaimed.

Jamie had spent most of the day polishing the large brass lamps, which now proudly sat in their deep bases in the window alcoves in the turrets of the castle. They could be seen for miles around. Today, he had polished them as never before, as well as the large glass bowls around them.

"Jamie," Elena called to him, "are all the lamps lit? Surely it is time."

"Yes," he replied to Lady Elena, who had come into the room, "this is the first one," and he turned up the wick. "I won't be long now with the rest."

She noticed the halo of happiness that enveloped his countenance as the round bright bowl of golden light came to life with the heightened flame.

"What a wonderful night this is going to be for us all, Jamie! – especially for Sir Bruce. I, too, can hardly wait to greet him."

"Me too, Lady Elena. I cannot settle to any job properly. Cook was saying that the master has hardly eaten a thing today."

"Yes, that is so," she replied, "and I know he didn't sleep at all last night. I was awake too, and I heard him pacing the floor."

She looked out over the loch to the ferryman's cottage on the other side.

"The castle will look so lovely tonight from the loch when night falls. All the lamps will be shining forth, and all the villagers' bonfires will be lit when they spot the boat coming. Tonight is the night we have waited for for so long. The night we feared might never come is here at last, Jamie," she said, and she tripped out of the room humming an old Scottish tune. 'To think,' she told herself, 'he must only be a few miles away now!'

Jamie lit the last lamp and stood gazing out over the loch. He whispered aloud to himself: "Where are you now, my wee bonnie bairn?"

He had never got used to the idea of his young Master Craig ever growing up to be a man. 'To think', he told himself, 'he has been to war! Thanks be to God, it is over at last!' and he hurried out of the room.

Sir Bruce Craig Lindsay Alisdair McNair, 11th Earl and laird of Glencree Castle, sitting in his favourite chair was hardly visible in its great depth. He rested his hands on the high, wide arms and sat gazing into the burning log fire. He sat there every night, but tonight he was dressed in his full clan tartan. His fine, dark head was held high, as always. This was the night he had waited for for so long, and now it was here. Tonight his precious son would be home. He could hardly grasp the fact as his thoughts wandered on and on. No more tomorrows to wait for! His son was nearly home at last; his dearest wish was coming true.

'Is it really true?' he asked himself. 'Yes, it must be true,' he told himself again and again.

'Hasn't everyone been busy all day preparing for his arrival? Of course! My precious son has been spared from the terrible war to come home to me and his heritage. Of course he has!' Bruce looked down at his full highland dress. 'I have not dressed like this since he went away,' he thought.

Still pondering, but in doubt no more, he rested his elbows on the beautiful, highly polished antique table. Night after night he sat like this, but tonight was different. He poured another drink into the priceless crystal glass in his hand and held it up to the flickering firelight glow. The mature whisky in it looked even more scintillating with the added amber glow as he turned the glass round and round slowly. His full generous lips pursed together in his deep contemplation. His eyes came to rest on the family crest, which had been engraved for his family so many generations ago. It had been cut by the finest Scottish craftsman of his day. His intent gaze weighed up every precious cut in the engraving of the family motto surrounding the crest: 'All is lost if thou art not true.' The family honour and proud name mattered immensely to him. That was why his precious son and heir had been spared to come home to him. Of course it was, and nothing would convince him otherwise. The proud name of the McNairs would live on for evermore. His son was spared and would be home tonight.

'Yes,' he thought, 'now everything will be as it was before he went away. All my plans can be fulfilled. We will go fishing, riding, shooting and sailing as before. We will take long walks over the glens. Everything will be as before – as if he has never been away. Nothing now can separate us again. Nothing will mar our peace and happiness.'

His face softened into a faint smile of utter contentment. Already some of the deep furrows on his brow were less deeply etched. Some were almost imperceptible. His dark eyes, luminous with the light from the fire, were softened by his mellow reflections. He had now lost the restless fear and anxiety of the past years.

Unintentionally – but it was an old habit of his – he uttered his thoughts aloud: "Craig Alisdair, you will be home tonight where you belong, never to leave my side ever again."

He drained his glass, reached once more for the decanter and refilled it. Both clinked together musically in perfect unison.

Harriet and Elena, sitting in the far corner of the large sitting room which overlooked the loch, looked up at each other and smiled happily. Elena, busy putting the finishing touches to her latest landscape painting, stopped to look at Bruce. Harriet put down her sewing, and her gaze too came to rest on her brother's face. Neither of them could concentrate on anything tonight. Not for many years had they seen Bruce so at peace. All the long years of loneliness and longing that had passed since Craig left for the front were forgotten – the long heartbreaking years of not knowing when, if ever, he would return. Even they themselves had hardly existed since he went away. Craig was their reason for living too.

Harriet often exclaimed to Elena, when discussing him (which had been daily),

"It seems wrong to think so much of our darling Craig!"

"But we have only him!" Elena would exclaim again and again.

"Thanks be to God, he has been spared to return to us, Harriet," Elena said. "How lucky we are, when so many have fallen! So many of his friends have fallen; so many he will never see again. It will be hard for him to bear."

Bruce raised his eyes from his glass as he heard their chatter. For a moment he had forgotten they were there.

"Yes, dear sister, he will be with us tonight."

Bruce glanced up at the old carved clock on the broad mantelpiece above his head.

'Oh, how slowly time moves!' he told himself.

Then, out loud, he repeated, his irritation showing for the first time since he woke that morning, "How slowly time is passing!"

He rose to his feet, a tall, handsome man, his back as straight as a ramrod. His jet-black hair, brushed back loosely from his forehead, fell in soft, deep waves. His finely arched brows were a perfect frame for his dark, piercing eyes. He had full, perfectly shaped lips beneath a fine black moustache, which extended almost to his high cheekbones, and which he twisted round and round until the ends were like long darning needles. His finely chiselled aristocratic features were tanned by the bracing Highland air, in sharp contrast to the snow-white jabot at his throat. His tailored jacket fitted his broad shoulders perfectly. His own specially woven tartan kilt and matching socks were worn to perfection, as only he knew how. His handmade buckled shoes had never shone as they did that night, and they reflected the sparkling silver handle of his skean-dhu, which was tucked in his sock. Never had he dressed as carefully as this. Jamie, his valet, had done him proud.

"Seldom", declared Elena to Harriet as they looked at him, "have I seen him look so elegant – not since his wedding to our darling Isabelle. Just look at him Harriet. Do you not think so too?"

Harriet nodded her head in agreement.

Yes, here was the proud 11th Earl and laird of Glencree Castle in all his splendour, and tonight his son and heir, the future 12th Earl, would be home.

"Hasten home, dear boy," said Bruce.

Again and again he looked at the clock anxiously, tapping his fingers restlessly on the mantelpiece as he gazed at it. He felt sure the hands kept stopping.

"How time is dragging!" he exclaimed, the impatience in his voice now more pronounced than before. "My God! My God! Will the time never move on?"

He ran his fingers along the mantel, following the finely etched old carving. He momentarily admired the superb craftsmanship as he outlined every little scroll and twist.

The huge logs in the open fireplace beneath it had been burning fiercely for several hours, and they were now like bright-orange sticks of amber. They grew smaller, dropping lower and lower in the gaping mouth of the old grate; and as the fire burned low, the beaten-copper surround reflected less and less of the firelight's glow, which had danced so brightly before.

Bruce's gaze travelled upwards, and his eyes came to rest on the huge, carved, gold-framed picture, which was almost as wide as the fireplace itself. He gazed at the lovely face of his wife, Isabelle. She looked more radiant tonight than ever before, he thought. Her beautiful, long auburn hair seemed to fall in softer, longer ringlets. Little wisps of hair fell forward on to her white forehead. Her beautiful eyes were almost the colour of the emerald-green velvet dress which graced her lovely figure; it was the colour he always wanted her to be dressed in.

Tonight her eyes were more compelling even than usual, as though she was trying to tell him something. What was the message she was trying to convey?

"What are you trying to say, my darling?" he whispered, over and over to himself as he looked longingly at her lovely face and beckoning beautiful eyes.

His gaze wandered to the ruffle of snow-white lace round her tiny wrist and along her long elegant fingers to rest on the exquisite ring of rubies and diamonds and the plain gold wedding ring beneath it. The rubies seemed to be glowing defiantly and the diamonds shone with an extra brilliance.

He gazed up at her adoringly, with a look of deep, deep sadness and despair, and a deep sigh escaped his lips from deep within his soul. His broad frame shook with emotion.

'Why, why, my darling, couldn't you be here tonight? Why? Why could you not be here to greet our son with me? Why? Why? My darling, our son will be back with us once more. Only you, my darling, will be missing.'

The huge, flickering candlesticks glowed brilliantly, lightening up her large, luminous eyes, and golden tints flashed across her hair like a halo. Her eyes seemed to be conveying a message to him as he was drawn once more to her wistful gaze: 'But I am with you. I am with you, my darling. I am with you.'

He lowered his eyes from her compelling gaze with a deep heart-rending sigh. In vain he tried to overcome his intense feeling of grief, and his longing to have her at his side once again.

'No, no, I must not be sad tonight,' he told himself. 'Not tonight! Tonight our son will be home and she would want me to be happy.'

His gaze left her eyes reluctantly, and, as he lowered his eyes, he caught sight of the long tassel of the fireside bell. He gave it an impatient, frantic pull to summon Jamie.

The sudden movement startled the sisters, and they looked at each other in alarm. They had been watching him for several minutes, and they knew only too well what had been going through his mind as he gazed at the picture. They knew he would never get over Isabelle's death, and the memory of the upturned carriage and his darling Isabelle lying face down in the water would never leave his mind. The loch up to that time had brought them only happiness – so much happiness – but then had come so much sorrow.

'Tonight it will once again bring me happiness,' he told himself. 'My darling son will be brought across the loch tonight to my waiting arms. Surely I am the luckiest father in the land tonight. Why, even at this very minute he could be very nearly home.'

"Will this clock never ever move its hands?" he called out angrily. "And where has Jamie got to?" He pulled again frantically on the bell. "Where is he? Where has he got to?" He turned quickly to his sisters. "Tonight! Tonight of all nights!" he yelled at them. "And the fire is nearly out – on the night my son comes home."

He continued to yell at them, and they looked at each other, neither wishing to answer him. They knew he was always quick to raise his voice in anger when displeased on the slightest pretext, but as the years had rolled on, his angry outbursts, caused by anxiety about his son, had increased. Over the past years no day had dawned when he had not dreaded what news it might bring; and each night he sighed with relief that another day had passed and no messenger had come with bad news.

"Where is Jamie? Does anyone know?"

"Oh, he cannot be far away, Bruce dear!" Elena exclaimed.

She was always first to step in to appease him when his anger was aroused. Only she, apart from his darling wife, had ever been able to calm him down.

She got up and said, "I will try to locate him," but she sat down again when a loud knock on the door heralded Jamie's arrival at last.

"Come in, come in!" Bruce yelled at him as he appeared in the doorway.

"You rang, master?"

"Yes, of course I rang!" Bruce exclaimed angrily. "Put more logs on the fire. Do you want Master Craig to freeze tonight, on his first night home?"

"No, master."

"Well, then, man, get those logs as soon as you can. Where were you? Why were you so long answering the bell?"

Jamie bent down to pick up the huge basket for the logs, and stood up to his full height, tall and proud. Like so many of the servants serving this old household he had been born in the Highlands and his only wish was to serve his beloved master, as his father and his father before him had served the other lairds of Glencree Castle.

Bruce turned to him as he prepared to go.

"Now, Jamie, where were you?"

"I was down by the loch. I went to see if Master Craig's boat was in sight. I was on the jetty."

Bruce had known where he would be.

"Now, Jamie, you know as well as we do that his train won't get into Glencree Station until late afternoon. The time varies, and it is always later rather than earlier."

"Yes, I know, master," he replied, "but I thought tonight it might just be early. Tonight is so important to us, and we have waited so long for this day."

"But you also know", Bruce continued, "that Magnus has to row him over the loch and that will take time." His tone of voice grew softer and kinder.

"Yes, master, I know all this."

"It may be just wishful thinking, Jamie, but I am sure it won't be long now before he is home."

Harriet and Elena looked at them both and smiled at each other.

"Now, Jamie, just get those logs cracking. We want a nice bright fire crackling tonight."

Bruce could not really be angry with him. He knew how much he loved the young master. He had watched over him like a guardian angel from the moment he had been born, and had been such a tower of strength to all of them when his mother had died, even though his own heart was broken at her death.

Flint, the dog, had bounded into the room as Jamie had entered and had flung himself into the corner. He, too, was restless tonight. He, more than anyone, felt the expectancy in the air, and his ears pricked up again and again at the sound of Craig's name. The master he had not seen for so long – the one he thought was dead – was now being spoken of more and more. But where was he? Why wasn't he here with all of them as before? A sharp whimper escaped from him as he looked up longingly at Bruce. He turned from him to Elena and Harriet, and back again to Bruce, a puzzled look on his face, as if asking, "When? When will he be here?"

"All right, Flint, my boy. There's not long to wait now. Soon he will be home with all of us. Now, lie down, boy."

The dog did as he was bid, in spite of his need for closer human contact. Although Bruce had taken him everywhere with him after Craig's departure for the front, Flint had fretted a great deal for him and had never left Bruce's side. It was as if he thought that one day they would find him on their long walks. His whimpering continued. This night, he knew, was different from all the other nights of the past year. He knew his master was on his way. But where was he? Why wasn't he here? He got to his feet once more, ambled over to where the sisters were sitting, and lay down at the feet of Elena. He looked up at her and Harriet for an answer. Elena leaned over and patted him affectionately on the head.

"Good boy, Flint! Your master won't be long now. Soon, soon! Now go and lie in your corner. Good boy!"

They all knew he would be the first to sense Craig's nearness. He ambled back to his corner, and Bruce patted him on the head as he passed.

"Not long now to wait, boy – not long!" Bruce's eyes lit up with happiness as he said it.

He poured himself another drink, leaned back in his chair and sipped it slowly.

The door opened and Jamie trundled in with his heavy load of logs. He knelt down and placed them, one by one, in a huge stack on the fire. Soon they were blazing away. He rose to his feet.

"That's more like it, Jamie!" Bruce exclaimed. "Refill the basket, Jamie. Master Craig and I will have a lot to talk about tonight."

"Yes, master, you will," Jamie replied.

"Oh, I think he will be far too tired to talk much tonight, Bruce dear!" exclaimed Elena. "Yes – far too tired, I should think!"

"Yes, you are right as always, Elena. You are always so right," said Bruce. "Yes, my poor boy will be so very tired, but at least he will be home and that is all we want. If only the time would go a little faster! Surely it must be almost time for his train to arrive."

CHAPTER 11

As Jamie closed the door behind him, several of the shutters on the huge windows blew together with a loud bang, and the French windows started to rattle ominously.

Bruce shot up out of the depths of his chair. His face, which had only minutes before been so happy and peaceful, had changed practically out of recognition. He looked over his glass towards the window in disbelief. Then he looked at his sisters. They had lowered their work and they looked across at him as the rattling of the windows became more and more persistent. He put down his glass with a thud which startled them both – he was always so careful with these glasses he prized so much.

He hurried over to the window. Harriet and Elena looked again at each other, and again at Bruce. They were both too alarmed to speak. Anxiously they watched as he flung back the long, dark-green velvet curtains and looked out into the night. All was dark now, except where the pools of light from the lanterns were reflected in the loch.

Jamie had hung them as dusk had fallen, so that his beloved young master could see his way home. 'That is what tonight is all about,' he had told himself as he lit them, one by one, and he had hummed a coming-home song.

Bruce watched as the huge trees close by shook vigorously. They creaked and groaned, as they always did when the wind was in this direction. He could hear the vicious thud-thud of the water lapping against the jetty steps as he drew the heavy curtains together.

"Hell! Hell!" he yelled as he stood with his back to the window in angry contemplation.

Then he strode quickly back to the small table and poured out another drink. He sat down, quickly drained the glass, and hastily picked up the bottle again and poured another one out. Elena, who had looked at her sister with alarm, moved quickly to his side.

"Bruce dear," she said as she put her hand gently on his shoulder. "Bruce dear," she repeated, "please do not drink any more tonight. Maybe it is only a slight change in the wind's direction. It might not develop into a more severe storm. It doesn't always." She disguised the anxiety in her voice to allay his fears and, deep down, her own. "Just you see! It will pass over as they have done before. You'll see."

He remained silent and morose and did not reply, but he lifted the whisky bottle again and drank another glass as he sat gazing into the blazing log fire. His anger mounted as he listened to the storm's increasing violence and sipped his whisky.

Elena glanced anxiously across at Harriet, who looked back at her, perplexed. Thoughts raced through her troubled mind.

'Dear Craig must get home tonight. He must!' she thought, anxiously looking towards the rattling windows.

Tonight meant so much to them and to Bruce. The strain during the years his son was away had been more than Bruce could bear. His son was his principal reason for living. The years of Craig's absence had taken their toll and Bruce had found it hard to adjust to life without Craig by his side.

'He is so keyed up for Craig's arrival tonight – surely the storm will not be so cruel as to prevent it,' Elena thought as she looked across again to Harriet.

"No, Bruce dear," Harriet agreed, "I am sure the wind will change direction soon. You'll see."

Suddenly Bruce got to his feet again. He shook Elena's hand off his shoulder and strode once more to the window. He flung the heavy curtains aside so violently that they almost came off the rail. He peered out again in disbelief at the now violently swinging lanterns. His gaze wandered from them to the high turrets overlooking the loch. Each turret window was ablaze with light, especially for this night. The dreariness of the past years and the darkness would soon be over. They were all looking forward to returning to a life full of light, peace and happiness.

Bruce flung open the tall French windows to peer out further over the loch. The violent wind howled and whined into the room as if it was glad to be in out of the blackening night. In its blast the priceless crystal chandeliers trembled violently, as if the clinking of the droplets were playing some angry concerto. Myriads of sparks from the blazing logs shot up the chimney as the heaving gusts of wind made the crackling fire crackle more wildly. The heavy velvet curtains were flung aside by the wind as if they were tissue paper and the priceless paintings and plaques were almost swept off the walls.

Harriet and Elena gasped with shock. Never had they seen the like of it before, or Bruce in such a rage as now. Both looked at him in desperation, not daring to speak. They were horrified that this change in the wind and the heavier rain could change him so quickly into a rage as wild as the storm.

He slammed the windows shut, and drew the curtains together in one fell swoop. He stood leaning against them, his hands gripping them tightly. His knuckles were white. He glanced towards his sisters as if he had only just realised they were there.

"Why? Why, of all nights, have we to have a storm tonight?" he yelled at them. Then he murmured, less angrily, "We have known stronger winds than this." It was as if he was trying to find some consolation from somewhere. "At least the mist hasn't descended – that is one consolation. I can still see the villagers waiting on the jetty."

"Oh, bless them all!" Elena exclaimed. "Waiting all this time and getting so wet and cold! After his arrival they must all come in for a warm drink before they go home. Some of them have come so far. They are talking to Jamie. He won't come in, no matter how heavy the rain."

This night, for them too, was special. The young master was coming home, and his homecoming was as important to them as if it was their own son's homecoming. In a sense, he was theirs.

"I can still see the bonfires on the hillsides. They are quite clear, so the mists are not descending, thanks be to God," said Bruce.

But he knew, as did the sisters, that the mist could drop suddenly.

"Oh, I am sure the mists won't come tonight!" exclaimed Elena, looking at Harriet as if for some reassurance.

However, Harriet's replying look was not at all reassuring.

"Well, we can at least be thankful for that," she said, "but even if the mist doesn't descend, I doubt whether Magnus would bring him over in this storm, with the wind increasing as it is."

She bit her lip in consternation as she suddenly realised she had said the wrong thing. Elena looked at her in anguish. Bruce had once more gone to the table and poured himself another drink.

"Not bring him over?" he exploded in anger. "Not bring him over? And why not, pray? Why not?" he roared. "He has crossed over in worse storms than this."

He banged his fist on to the table with such force that his decanter toppled over and the whisky trickled over the table in an amber-coloured rivulet, staining the wood as it went. This in itself, at any other time, would have been enough to put him in a rage, but now he was thinking only of Craig. Nothing else mattered.

Elena rushed with her handkerchief to try to stem the flow. For a long time Bruce had been expecting his son to come home on this night, and now nothing would convince him to give up hope – storm or no storm. 'Craig will be home tonight,' – that was his one thought, and woe betide anyone who suggested otherwise.

He strode over to the wall and selected a cane from the many which hung under a huge stag's head. He yelled frantically to Flint to follow him.

"Come on boy!" he roared, in a raging, impatient voice.

The dog was already on his feet. He had felt the atmosphere change and, although he didn't know the reason why, he knew by his master's voice that something was wrong. All had been so quiet and peaceful only a short time ago, but now there was an air of despondency all around him. What was it?

Bruce tapped his cane against his thigh, his furious temper rising more and more. He strode out with the dog at his heels and slammed the door behind him.

Elena called out to him: "Bruce dear, Bruce dear, don't go out in this storm and cold wind, I beg of you."

She followed him out into the hall, but he paid her no heed and he slammed the outer door too.

"I do wish he had stopped to put his cloak on," said Harriet. "You know he would not listen to anyone except Isabelle. She was the only one that could make him do anything against his will."

"Yes, I know," Elena agreed, as she glanced up at Isabelle's picture. "She was the only one."

CHAPTER 12

Craig roused once more from his restless nap with a start as the heavy rain and now increasing wind beat heavily against the window of the train. He forced his eyes to stay open. He knew that he must be nearly home, but his weariness threatened to engulf him. The incessant rhythm of the train made his head whirl. He sat up wearily, stretching and yawning. He was so tired and dazed that he hardly seemed to know what day it was.

Slowly the rhythmical ditty of the train started to falter.

"Surely", he told himself, "the rhythm is slower. Surely I am not dreaming this time."

He sat further back on his seat and listened more carefully.

"It is! It is!"

He bounded to his feet, staggered as he did so and steadied himself against the rack above. He strained his head towards the window to listen more intently.

"It is! It is! Please, God, let it be so," he pleaded. "Please let it be so. Please let it be stopping for home. I just know I shall be home tonight."

He could now see by the dim carriage lights.

'Home at last!' he thought.

He reached across to get his kitbag, and tightened the straps to secure its contents. He ruffled his fingers through his hair, too excited now to search for his comb; he searched anxiously on the floor for his cap, and put it firmly on his unruly curls.

The train slowed and almost came to a standstill. By now he could hear a human voice.

"Home at last! Thanks be to God!" he muttered aloud.

The incessant repetition of the name 'Glencree' in his native dialect became more and more clear.

"I must be home – I must!"

He did not wait for the train to stop. He pulled down the window, opened the carriage door and flung out his kitbag on to the platform. He watched as it bowled alongside the train. He pulled his cap on more firmly as the sudden wind caught him, and he stumbled out after it.

"Home at last! I can't believe it," he said.

The small limping figure coming towards him calling out "Glencree, Glencree" in a lilting Scottish voice told him all he wanted to know. The only light came from the dimly lit carriage and the small lantern in the man's hand. Craig pulled up the collar of his greatcoat to ward off some of the driving rain. His cap was pulled down well over his eyes.

The small figure couldn't believe his eyes. No one had got off at Glencree for a long time, and here was a soldier. Surely he must have got off at the wrong station, he told himself. He had called out "Glencree" as the train was stopping, as sometimes the driver left the mail and stores for the castle and village. But no mail had been dropped on this night.

He went close to the soldier, raised his lantern a little higher and gazed up at him, still not speaking.

"Hello there," the voice called out of the hardly visible face from within the protection of the upturned collar. "Do you not remember me?"

Again the old man looked up at him, trying to raise himself to see and with a puzzled look on his face.

"Hi there, Robbie. Have you forgotten me?" Craig called out to him.

Then it finally dawned on the man who it was. He gave a shriek of delight.

"Why, it's Master Craig, I do believe – home at long last! I do declare!" He shook Craig by the hand, as if he would never let him go again. "The Good Lord be praised! Is it really you, Master Craig? No one told me you were expected home. I am sure Magnus does not know either."

"Yes, Robbie, it is I – home on my own soil at last."

"Yes, my bonnie wee laddie, it is still as you left it."

"But I'm not a wee laddie any more," Craig replied.

"No – but my, how you have grown since you went away!" said Peggoty, and he tried to hug Craig as if he was his own son. "Welcome home, laddie! Welcome home!"

He was so overcome with joy and emotion that he had forgotten the train was still standing at the station. A shrill, piercing, high-pitched 'toot-toot' jerked him back to reality. 'Toot-toot-toot' it kept on, as if it also was welcoming the soldier home before it went on its way.

"Oh dear!" exclaimed Robbie. "I had forgotten about the train."

"So had I!" exclaimed Craig, and they both started to laugh.

Peggoty released his hold on Craig. "I will just get the train away, Master Craig."

He picked up his lamp and raced off as fast as he could on his one good leg, his wooden leg clomping along as best it could in his haste. Craig followed him, pulling his collar higher and his cap further down against the worsening storm. The chill wind made him shudder. He rubbed his hands together. Robbie closed the carriage door and hastened to the front of the train with Craig close on his heels.

The driver, seeing them coming, stepped down from his cab and held out his hand to Craig.

"Welcome home, boy! Welcome home!"

Craig shook his hand.

"Thank you. Thank you also for my safe journey home."

"It is an honour to bring any of our brave soldiers home. I am glad you are safe."

He climbed back into his cab and, as Robbie waved him away with his lantern, the train, with a loud hiss and shriek and 'toot-toot', chuffed away. The two figures were only just visible as the driver leaned out once more to wave them a last farewell, and Craig continued to wave him on into the night.

Robbie picked up Craig's kitbag and slung it over his shoulder. He carried it towards the little gate of the station.

"To think, my dear boy, you are home at last, and I have the honour to be the first to greet you! What a delight, to be sure!"

"Yes, Robbie, it's great to be on my own soil at last; and oh, how I have longed for this day! Never again will I leave it. No, never again as long as I live!"

"Yes, laddie, I know how you feel. It's the best land God ever made. I felt the same as you, Master Craig, when I arrived home from the Boer War. I too vowed never to leave it again, and I never have. I couldn't get very far, minus one leg. I went to war with two good legs and came back minus one. That's how it goes." He glanced up at Craig. "I am so glad to see you have come back all in one piece."

"Yes, but I am not the same person that went away, Robbie. I don't think anyone who goes to war is ever the same again. Wars, wars, wars! What do they ever achieve? Nothing. Nothing!"

Robbie could sense that the young master's thoughts were back with all the horror he had left behind. No, he was not the same boy as when he went away.

"Yes, begorra," he said, as he slung the kitbag further over his shoulder. He marched off at a stomping pace, up and down on his wooden leg, at which Craig started to laugh, just as Robbie intended.

'This young sir must start to laugh again,' he thought. He knew Craig had been through enough hell.

Craig could not remember the last time he had laughed and here he was, tired, weary, chilled to the bone and drenching wet, enjoying the antics of this poor old man.

"I am sure my kitbag is far too heavy for you, Robbie. Please give it to me."

"No, begging your pardon, young sir, it is an honour for me. Please do not deny an old soldier his bit of fun," and he started to sing a little song: 'Marching to Georgia'.

They reached the small gate.

"My, what a wild night, to be sure, Robbie!" Craig exclaimed. "I had forgotten how violent the storms can be in bonnie Scotland."

"Yes, that is because you have been away far too long, Master Craig."

"Yes, that must be it," he replied. "But I will soon be home."

"Well, here we are, my boy," Robbie said, and he bent down to undo the small latch.

Craig took his kitbag from him and shook him by the hand.

"Thank you, Robbie. I shall see you again soon."

"Yes, laddie, it is wonderful to see you back. No doubt your father is waiting for you on the jetty."

"Oh yes, he will be," he called back. "I told him I was coming tonight."

Craig bade him goodnight and heaved his kitbag on to his shoulder. It knocked his cap to one side, so he put it back on straight, and shuddered as the rain fell down his neck.

"Oh, how I wish I was home, out of this storm! It won't be long now. Now I must find Magnus and get over the loch."

Robbie watched Craig out of sight, fastened the gate and turned to go to his little room, which had been given to him by the laird.

"No more trains tonight!" he said aloud.

Craig hurried on through the blinding rain towards the small jetty at the edge of the loch in search of Magnus, the ferryman. The rain was heavier now, and it ran down his neck in spite of his efforts to keep it out. The wind was buffeting him from side to side.

"My, my, what a wild night for my homecoming!" he told himself yet again. "But what is a storm after what my men and I have gone through? Now, I wonder where Magnus is – that is, if he is still here after all the time I have been away."

He strode to the end of the jetty and looked out over the loch.

"My, how wild it looks tonight! But it's so wonderful to be beside it once more."

He turned back and could see, underneath the broken planks of wood, two dimly lit lanterns swinging to and fro. He could hardly hear the sound of his own footsteps above the roar of the wind and the furious lapping of the water against the jetty. He looked anxiously around. Everywhere seemed so desolate.

'Where can Magnus be, I wonder?' he thought as he retraced his steps back and forth, looking for some sign of life. A feeling of despair welled up inside him. "I must get home tonight, but where is he? Only Magnus can take a boat out in such a storm."

Suddenly, he spotted another dim lantern further along the jetty. He was sure it wasn't there when he first walked over the jetty. He put his kitbag down and leaned wearily over the side to peer underneath. Then he spotted a darkly clad figure bending over the boats and making them secure.

"Magnus, Magnus!" he called. "Is that you, Magnus?" He raised his voice over the sound of the wind.

At last the man rose to his feet. Whoever could be calling his name on such a night as this? He raised his lantern as Craig approached.

"Yes, it is I – Magnus," he replied. "But who are you, out on such a night as this?"

He was quite startled to see it was a soldier.

"It is I – Craig. Home from the war at last."

"Oh, the Good Lord be praised! Home on your Scottish soil at last! Thanks be to God, you have been spared to come safely back to us all again." He could hardly speak in his excitement and joy at seeing Craig. "My, how tall you have grown! His Lordship, your father, has longed for the day of your return."

"Yes, I too have waited far too long."

"But I must hurry and get you out of this storm. I will soon fix the boats safely. Did you travel up north alone, Master Craig?" he asked. "Have you seen anything of my son – although you would hardly remember him?"

"No, Magnus, I have not seen any other soldier come so far north. I was the only one on the train, but they are nearly all on their way now. The final battalions have all left. Only a few rearguard companies are left. I am sure your son, too, will be home soon."

"I hope so, Master Craig. He, like yourself, has been away far too long."

'Oh, I know he will return soon," Craig replied, as he flung his kitbag into one of the boats and proceeded to haul himself in after it. "Come, Magnus – my father is expecting me home tonight, and only you can manage to cross on a night like this."

He continued to settle himself in the boat, and he wedged his kitbag in firmly. Craig, in his excitement and exuberance, had chattered on incessantly and he failed to notice that Magnus had gone strangely quiet.

"Oh no, Master Craig, it is not possible to take you across tonight. We couldn't go across in this wind and heavy rain, and the mountain mist will soon descend."

"But, Magnus, you have sailed the loch in far worse storms than this," Craig shouted angrily.

"No, my boy. In worse storms, maybe, but not when the wind is in this direction. The mist will fall very soon – certainly before we could get halfway across."

"But, Magnus, I have to get home tonight. Papa is waiting for me. It must be possible somehow. You have to take me home tonight," he demanded.

"No, Master Craig, it's not possible. If it was, nothing would stop me." He took hold of Craig's arm to try to comfort him. "I fully understand, my boy, how you feel and what your dear father will feel if you don't arrive home tonight."

"Yes, I daresay you do, Magnus. Your own boy is not yet home, so if anyone understands, it is you."

The look of utter dejection on Craig's face touched Magnus deeply. 'How I wish it were possible to take him home tonight!' he thought.

"I know your dear father is anxious for you to get home safely, but *safely*, Master Craig, *safely*," he repeated with emphasis. "I couldn't risk your life now. You have been spared from this dreadful war and you have reached your home soil safely."

Craig got out of the boat when he realised Magnus was not joining him and stood, utterly dejected, gazing out over the dark, eerie loch. He stood at the edge of the water, silent and morose. Even the rain didn't seem to matter now. He kicked furiously at the pebbles on the shore and kicked them viciously into the raging water. The discomfort he had felt, so cold and tired and so drenched, was nothing to the misery he felt now.

"But, Magnus," he said, still hoping for a change of heart, "I am sure we could still make it."

"No, Master Craig, nothing on earth would prevent me from taking you if it were possible to get you to your father – but not tonight. At first light tomorrow I will get the boat away."

Craig knew in his bitter disappointment that Magnus was right.

"Always tomorrow! Always tomorrow!" Craig exclaimed angrily. "Is there never any end to these tomorrows?"

He reached into the boat and heaved his kitbag out and on to his shoulder.

"We will send up the flares," said Magnus, "to tell them on the other side that you have arrived on your home soil. I am sure that Jamie will be keeping a lookout for you."

"Yes, he will, and so will Papa," said Craig, "so let's hurry, Magnus. We can at least send up the flares so Papa will know I have arrived – but oh, how I wish I could have got home!"

He stood looking over the loch, oblivious of the drenching rain, lost in his despair.

"Come, Master Craig," Magnus called to him, "let us not delay any longer. The mist will soon be down."

He finished tying up the boat and wended his way to a small cupboard which stood at the side of the jetty on four tall legs. This held his flares and matches. He brought them back to the edge of the jetty, with Craig close on his heels, guided only by the light of his swinging lantern. They cast eerie shadows as they walked along. They both struggled against the wind. Craig bent down beside Magnus as he assembled the flares.

"You light the flares, Master Craig. It will be like sending a personal message to your father that you have arrived back on Scottish soil. I will hold them steady and shield them from the wind as you strike the match."

They both straightened up as they watched the first flare soar away into the turbulent sky. A shower of sparks fell, like sparkling glow-worms, before disappearing in the darkness.

"We will send others just in case that one has not been seen. The mist may have fallen on the other side."

"Yes, we must," agreed Craig, "although I am sure Papa, with his keen eyesight, will have seen it. Here goes the second one!" he exclaimed.

"Come – we will shelter under the jetty and await their answering flares. They won't be long. Then we can send our final one in reply," said Magnus.

CHAPTER 13

Harriet and Elena went over to the window.

"Yes," said Elena, still carrying on the conversation as before, "if only his darling Isabelle could have been spared to have been with us tonight, for her son's homecoming, what a wonderful time it would have been for all of us – especially Bruce and Craig!"

"Ah, well, it was not to be," said Harriet, "so it is no good talking."

They pulled back the heavy curtains a little and peered out over the loch at the increasingly storm-tossed night. Bruce and Flint came into view, hastening towards the jetty. Bruce was walking at such a furious pace that it seemed as if Flint could hardly keep up with him.

"Magnus, I feel sure, will never venture out in a storm like this," said Harriet.

Elena, however, was always more optimistic than Harriet: "If Bruce can will it so, Magnus will attempt it – storm or no storm. Anyway, the storm may abate soon," she continued. "Let us still hope."

She was hoping for Bruce's sake that it would be so.

"The wind might still change direction," said Elena. "As you see, the mist has not come down as yet. The lantern lights are still clear."

"They are too attached to each other – father and son," Harriet declared. This was a statement she had often made when Craig was small. "It is not good for either of them. I have said so time and again. At least Craig has Fiona to think about. Bruce has only Craig, so it is worse for him. You saw how he behaved tonight. It is not a good sign. It's as if he is willing Craig to be beside him always, as if he wants Craig to be his darling Isabelle. I tell you, Elena, it is not a good sign."

"Oh," declared Elena, "that anger was because of the storm. He will be all right when Craig gets home, and they are together once more. He has been so lonely since Craig went away. He will be all right once he is home – you'll see."

"Soon all will be as before he went away. All his own friends will be back, and Craig's also – and Fiona. You know Bruce thinks of her as a daughter. All Craig's friends will be visiting again. That is, if he has any of his old friends left," Harriet adjoined.

Bruce hastened along the jetty, and as Flint caught up with him at last, he bent down to pat him on the head. He knew what Flint was suffering, and how excited he had been, like himself, only a short time ago. In spite of his own sadness and his anger at the wild storm, the sight of this sodden, whimpering animal by his side, this dog that had stayed by his side all the time Craig, his master, had been away, softened his heart.

"There, there, boy! Maybe the storm will soon abate and our darling boy will soon be with us again."

The villagers bade him, "Good evening, sir," and he returned their greeting. They also were most concerned that he was out without his cloak on, and they muttered amongst themselves.

Flint kept closer as Bruce edged nearer to the end of the jetty, where Jamie was still looking out anxiously over the loch.

Bruce tapped his cane time and time again against his thigh and, to all who knew him well, this was a sign that he was very angry. He too gazed over the loch towards the ferryman's cottage.

"There's not a sign of anything yet, master," Jamie ventured to say. "It's a bad sign having the wind in this direction. I am sure the evening train will have arrived some time ago, and I am sure the mist will be down soon. I don't think Magnus will put the boat out in this storm. I don't think he will come till tomorrow."

Jamie waited with bated breath for his master's reply.

"Tomorrow, tomorrow! How many more tomorrows must I wait? It's always tomorrow. I am sick and tired of waiting for tomorrow," Bruce yelled angrily.

The villagers looked at one another and started to drift away.

"We will be back tomorrow, master," they said, as they bade them goodnight.

"Call into the house before you depart for home," Bruce called after them, "and get some refreshments. You have all stood far too long in this wet, cold night."

They thanked him and wended their way towards the castle.

Only he, Jamie and the dog were left, shuddering in the chill night air. Bruce peered out over the loch as if, by doing so, he hoped to will the boat over, but he only became more and more morose.

"Shall I prepare the flares, Sir Bruce, just in case we need them?"

"Do as you wish, Jamie," he replied, lost in despair.

"I do wish Bruce had put on his cloak!" exclaimed Elena, again and again, as she and Harriet both still watched from the window.

"The storm is getting worse – don't you think so, Harriet? I hope Bruce doesn't get a chill staying out on a night like this."

"Oh, he won't get a chill," Harriet replied. "He is far too robust for that. You worry far too much about his health, Elena."

Harriet, like Bruce, mainly worried about one thing: the family name. Their heritage and the clan were of great importance to them. She was like Bruce in so many ways. A real dour Scotswoman, she had never had any time for any sentiment in her life, and as long as she got her wee dram now and again, and the family line was assured, she was quite happy.

"The lamps are swinging much more now," Elena said with alarm, "and the villagers are leaving. I do hope Bruce told them to come in here first, before leaving for home. Yes, he must have done. I can hear Cook calling to Sarah to come down from the gallery. She will have been up there, waiting to see if the boat came. The poor people will all be so disappointed, but they will be back tomorrow."

"Yes, I can make out just Bruce, Jamie and Flint on the jetty now. Dear old Flint! He will be fretting and whining all night now, I daresay. I am sure the train will have arrived, so if Magnus cannot bring him over, maybe we will see the flares before long; otherwise the mist will come and we won't even see those. Oh dear! What a night, to be sure! It is as if everything is against his getting back home to us."

Only the heavier rain on the window panes answered her.

"The flares will be the only consolation for Bruce. Dear Bruce! He can't take much more anxiety."

They both knew he would be in a furious mood when at last he came in, and their spirits sank more and more as time went by.

On the jetty, Flint sat looking up at Bruce, as if at any moment he would tell him what he wanted to hear: that his beloved master was coming.

Flint had been very upset by his master's going away. He would roam over the hills for days on end looking for Craig, without food or rest. When he returned, he was so very thin, bedraggled and ill with exhaustion, but he would bound into the lounge, always hoping his master might have returned in his absence. Then, after looking all around, he would drag himself up the stairs to Craig's room and lie in front of his door, whimpering and whining. But he would only stay a few days; then he would be off again, hardly touching a morsel of the tempting food Elena tried to encourage him to eat.

Elena and Bruce would often go in search of Flint, but they always returned empty-handed. The villagers too were always on the lookout, until, eventually, Bruce decided to keep him chained up. To gain his confidence, Bruce took him for long walks, always now on the chain, till Bruce became his new master and they had become inseparable. He had accepted that Craig might never return, and his and Bruce's mutual loss and loneliness had strengthened the bond between them.

Until today he had accepted it all, but now his master's name was on everyone's lips and there was an air of expectancy. He knew, by all the excitement, that his beloved master was coming. Then, just as suddenly, all was different again: there was a sudden sense of sadness everywhere. It was as if his master was not coming after all. He snuggled up closer to Bruce as if to get an answer, but none came.

Jamie repeated again, "Shall I prepare the flares, Sir Bruce?"

"Yes, Jamie, you might as well."

Suddenly, Bruce's excited cry caused Jamie to straighten up and look to where he was pointing.

"There! There! Craig's flares!"

"Yes, yes, I see them. He is with Magnus. I just know it!" exclaimed Jamie.

"But, my boy will have lit those, Jamie – I know he will."

"Yes, master, he will have lit those."

The excitement in their voices rose.

"There is the second one. Quick, Jamie – I must light ours in reply. I must send three in reply, then they will know we have seen theirs."

Suddenly, the black, eerie loch was ablaze with stars of light falling down as if from heaven itself.

"The flares! The flares at last! My darling boy has arrived on his beloved Scottish soil, never again to leave it."

"No, master, he never will."

"See, Jamie – there is their final one to say they have seen ours. Oh, my boy, my boy! Home at last!" he said, and Jamie watched as he wiped away a tear.

"Oh, Harriet, Harriet!" exclaimed Elena, "what is that light shooting over the loch? Surely you can see! Hurry before it disappears. Now two more! They are the flares from Bruce to Magnus. How we missed Magnus's flares to Bruce I'll never know! They must have fallen too far out in the loch. Oh, Harriet, it can only mean one thing: our darling Craig has arrived safely on the other side. At last, he is almost home, but Magnus has decided that he cannot bring him tonight."

She hugged Harriet. She was laughing and crying at the same time.

"The Good Lord be praised! He will be home tomorrow. Tomorrow he will be home. Now I must go and tell Cook," she said, and she rushed to the kitchen. "Cook, Sarah," she exclaimed breathlessly, "the flares have gone up!"

"Praise the Lord!" exclaimed Cook. "I have got some hot soup ready for the master and Jamie. Fair chilled to the bone the master will be. He won't eat dinner tonight; he will be too upset at Master Craig not being here to join him. He was so looking forward to his coming tonight."

"Well," said Elena, "Harriet and I will have some later on. It is such a lovely dinner you have cooked for him. But first, Harriet," she said, "I must go down to the loch to Bruce and take his cloak."

Bruce stared hard and long towards the cottage on the other side of the loch. The mist was falling now.

"Only the loch divides us now, my boy, only the loch."

The gentle voice of Elena broke in on his thoughts: "Bruce dear, you must come in out of the storm. There is nothing more you can do tonight."

She reached up to try to put his cloak round his shoulders.

"Let me!" Jamie exclaimed. "You are far too tiny, Lady Elena."

He took the cloak off her and put it round Bruce's shoulders.

"Fancy, Elena, our boy on the other side of the loch! He will no doubt be still standing there."

"Well, I hope Magnus does not keep him out too long in this storm," she replied.

Jamie picked up his lantern and the three of them, Flint walking at their side as drenched as they, wended their way back to the castle.

"He will be home early in the morning," said Elena.

"But why have I always to wait for tomorrow, Elena?"

"Well, never mind, dear – tomorrow will soon be here. Tonight will soon pass."

"Harriet dear, did you see the flares?" he asked, as soon as he saw her.

"Yes, of course I did. Now you must eat this hot broth."

"Yes, I will. I cannot eat any dinner tonight. We must all retire early and be ready to greet Craig in the morning. Oh, what a happy day awaits us tomorrow! But first, I must have a last drink before I retire. Goodnight, my dearest sisters. I could not have borne this anguish today without you both by my side."

They bade him goodnight as they left the room.

He walked over to the small table and poured out a drink. A soothing warmth swept over him, and, as he refilled his glass, he glanced up at the picture of Isabelle again. He looked lovingly at her beautiful eyes. They seemed to convey a message to him, and he whispered to her as if in reply:

"Yes, my darling, our son is almost home. He will soon be home."

He slowly put down his glass on the table, looked ruefully at the stain which he had caused and went slowly out, turning once more to bid Isabelle goodnight. The dying embers of the fire gave a last splutter of flame and lit up the eyes of Isabelle. He thought he saw her gaze follow him out of the room.

Elena was waiting for him in the hall.

"I can't get Flint to eat anything. Jamie has tried," she said. "He will no doubt eat twice as much tomorrow when our boy is here."

"He, like us, has not long to wait now," said Bruce. "Thank God we were able to see the flares! The mist is falling. If only he could have been with us tonight, as it should have been!"

He sighed heavily. Only when he could lovingly clasp his son in his arms would he know that at last he was with him for good. Only the two of them could understand the tie that bound them so close. It all went back to when Craig was small boy, fretting and pining for a beloved mother, and the vow that Bruce had made to him then: that never would they be parted from each other – all their lives would be spent helping each other to overcome their great loss.

They had thought that nothing would part them, until the war had decreed otherwise. But now it was over and Craig had been spared. He was nearly back home amongst them again. Nothing, Bruce vowed, would ever take Craig from his side again.

The whimper of Flint by his side reminded him that the dog was still trying in vain to disentangle the events of the day.

"Come, my boy – you, too, have to wait only until tomorrow."

Elena followed Bruce upstairs and heard his door close. She passed Flint, who was lying, as he always did at nights, at Craig's door. She patted him lovingly on the head.

"Your master will be home tomorrow, my boy."

He whimpered back, as if he understood.

Harriet was standing at her bedroom door.

"I have told Jamie to leave all the lamps lit in the turrets tonight, and every night from now on."

"As they should be!" Elena exclaimed. "What a day this has been, to be sure!"

They bade each other goodnight.

The castle was now all quiet. Bruce stood a long time by the window overlooking the loch. He gazed towards the ferryman's cottage, then sank down on his knees and prayed silently in true gratitude for his son's safety. He rose to his feet slowly, all his anguish now over. He was calm and serene for the first time for many years. All his anger at the storm which had kept them apart for yet another night melted away now within his heart.

'God's will be done,' he told himself. He still gazed out. 'No sleep for me tonight!' he told himself. 'But sleep well, my son, sleep well! Soon it will be our tomorrow.'

He took his watch from his pocket and studied it closely. He was barely able to see it in the dim light of the room. Suddenly the village clock struck midnight. He gave a sudden gasp.

"We will have no more waiting for tomorrows. It is already our today."

CHAPTER 14

Magnus and Craig stood looking intently over the loch after they had sent their final flare.

"I am so glad we were able to see all their flares before the mist finally came, Magnus," said Craig.

"Yes," he replied, "the mist will soon be down."

"My, what a night, to be sure! Of all the nights to get a storm such as this! Still, Papa will have lit those flares so this is the closest we have been for a long time. You know, Magnus, I never ever thought I would see my beloved loch again, and to see the flares shimmering so brightly over it, announcing my safe arrival, is unbelievable. Time after time on the battlefield, when the sparks from the Very lights shot into the sky, I wished and wished they could have been the flares of home, and now I have really seen them. They are the flares of home, Magnus. Please, tell me I am not dreaming."

"No, Master Craig, you are not dreaming. Now we must go and get out of the storm."

Magnus made the boats secure under the jetty and picked up his lantern to light the way up the narrow path to the cottage.

"As you know, Master Craig, my cottage is very small and humble, but the door is always open to any traveller, and none are more welcome than you and your family."

"Yes, Magnus, it is indeed very kind of you. I am most grateful for your offer of refuge for the night. I am so exhausted."

"Yes, I can see that, my boy, but after a good night's sleep you will soon feel better."

They struggled towards the door, with the wind almost sweeping them off their feet. Craig pulled his saturated scarf further round his face, and Magnus, carrying his kitbag, could hardly keep his balance in the wind. The lantern in his hand swung to and fro as he walked in front to try to shelter Craig as he led the way up the cobbled path.

Craig turned once more to look at the loch.

"Oh, how I wish I could have got home to Papa tonight!"

He looked up as Magnus called to him: "Come, Master Craig – don't delay in this storm."

The stream of light from the cottage lit their way.

'It seems bigger than I remember,' Craig told himself.

It was two storeys high, built high on the bank overlooking the loch.

"Do many people stay at the cottage now, Magnus?" he asked. "I used to remember my father saying many years ago that it used to be full of travellers, and was used very often."

"Not any more, but many years ago it was the only place people could stay the night, when coaches and horses were used, long before the railway was built by your ancestors. The travellers were usually members of shooting and fishing parties on their way to the Highlands."

"Ah yes!" Craig exclaimed. "Now I recall."

Magnus lifted the huge latch, flung the door wide, and put the kitbag inside.

"Come inside, laddie. Later on I will see if the animals are safe for the night."

Craig stepped inside, glad to be indoors at last. The huge paraffin lamp over the table spluttered violently as the wild wind swept in. The dying fire in the huge black grate sprang to life again. The large stewpot hanging over it swung to and fro across the dancing flames.

'Oh, what a welcome sight, to be sure!' thought Craig.

The smell of the broth and home-made bread and cakes in the kitchen floated out to him. It reminded him that such smells would have been coming from the kitchen in his own home.

'Ah well,' he told himself, 'I must not dwell too much on home tonight. I should be thankful for this humble cottage refuge. It is so welcome, to be sure.'

The savoury smell of the broth from the swinging pot on its iron hook made him realise how very hungry he was. He couldn't remember the last time he had eaten a decent meal.

'Gosh!' he exclaimed to himself. 'It must have been when I was in France. I only ate a bun on the train. This small cottage', he thought, 'is really as good as a castle in its welcome.'

He stood gazing round the room, and his eyes grew more used to the light. He stood with his back to the door, taking in the homely scene. "Welcome, welcome," everything seemed to be saying. The flames in the old brightly polished brass lamp over the table and another lamp in the window settled down after the sudden gust, and the fire settled once more in the grate.

'This is a home. This is what it is all about. This is what all the fighting was for: home and all the loved ones therein – the loved ones who were waiting for the soldiers to come home. God speed all of them home, wherever they may be,' he thought to himself. 'The quiet, humble people who live in cottages such as this deserve peace and contentment.'

The small, bent figure of Magnus's wife, Martha, gave the stew a final stir. She straightened up as she heard the door latch click and the wild wind swept in. She turned to face Magnus, and she gave a gasp of dismay as she saw the two men inside the door. For a fleeting moment, she thought it was her son, who was also due home from the front. Craig stood straight and tall beside the older man, just as her son used to stand, but, with a true mother's instinct, she knew at once that the tall boy standing there was not her son.

'Who is he?' she wondered. 'Who could it be at this hour? And the state of him!' she thought. (There was dried blood still on his forehead.)

Craig took off his cap and scarf and struggled to get out of his greatcoat with the help of Magnus.

'Who is he?' she asked herself, over and over again. 'Whatever has brought this strange young soldier to my home?' However, as he stepped further into the room, the flickering lamp's beam caught him full in the face. She gave a gasp of delight as she suddenly recognised him in the lamp's bright glow.

"Why, it is Master Craig, I do declare!" she exclaimed, and she dropped him a little curtsy. "Welcome to our humble home! It certainly is an honour to have you under our roof. Thanks be to God you are saved from this dreadful war and soon to be back with your father after all these years."

"Yes, Martha, it is wonderful to be back on home soil once more and so near to my father, but I am very disappointed not to get home tonight as I expected."

"But the storm is so bad, Master Craig. If Magnus could have taken the boat out tonight, he would have done so."

"Yes, I realise that, but I will be home tomorrow," he said. "I believe your son too, Martha, will soon be home. Thanks be to God, he too has been spared."

"Yes," she replied, "we expect him home very soon now."

Magnus's voice broke in on her chatter: "Take care of his wet clothing, Martha. Can't you see how wet, tired and chilled he is? Don't keep the boy starving whilst you chatter away. I must go and see if the animals are safe for the night," he said, and he disappeared into the stormy night.

"Yes, yes, how thoughtless of me! Please forgive me, Master Craig, for prattling on so much."

"There's nothing to forgive, Martha!" Craig exclaimed.

"Now, Master Craig, give me those wet clothes and I will get them dry. You sit here by the fire and rest in this comfortable rocking chair."

She pulled the chair closer to the fire and fluffed up the large feather cushion a little more. Then she reached for another one from the other chair and placed it behind his head.

"That wound on your head is still oozing blood. I will bathe it and put a bandage on it."

Craig was past bothering about such a small cut, but he let her do as she wished.

"People will really think I have got badly injured if they see me bandaged like this, Martha."

"Oh, it will be healed by morning," she reassured him. "Now rest back my boy and I will soon have a hot meal ready for you."

She took his clothing away and came back to take the pot of broth from the fire. Then she disappeared into the kitchen.

"Oh, how weary I am! I'm so thankful to be a little warmer. How good these people are!" he murmured, as he gazed into the flickering fire and snuggled back into the depths of the chair.

His eyes kept closing; no matter how hard he tried to keep them open, it was all to no avail. The rocking of the old chair lulled him into a deep slumber. As the chair rocked to and fro, it seemed to be saying to him, "Home tomorrow, home tomorrow."

Suddenly the sound of a door opening upstairs roused him momentarily from his fitful slumber, but he did not raise his eyes from the flickering fire. He was far too exhausted to question why a door was opening above him. The floorboards creaked and feet pattered hastily along the passage above. He looked up pensively and raised himself a little further out of his chair.

Then he heard the sound of a young, excited voice calling repeatedly: "Roddy, Roddy, you are home at last. At last you are home."

He raised his eyes from the flickering fire to the staircase, and gave a gasp of disbelief. He raised himself higher, his eyes resting unbelievingly on the vision now starting to descend the stairs. The light from the candle she was holding made a dancing shadow on the wall and surrounded her in a luminous aura of misty gold and silver. It reflected the pure whiteness of her gown, with its layer upon layer of snow-white lace, which fell in numerous froths of frills at her throat. Her long golden hair, transformed into silver by the light, hung in a glorious array of sleep-ruffled ringlets and framed a face of such exquisite beauty that Craig rubbed his eyes in disbelief.

The small, dainty figure descended further and further down the stairs, still calling, "Roddy, Roddy."

"Surely, I must be dreaming," he told himself.

Many times he had been close to death and visions such as this had flitted before his eyes, and then they were gone. He had seen many visions of angels, like the one he was seeing now. Was this another one come to haunt him? Had he not, after all, left the dreadful battlefields? Had he not reached his beloved Scotland?

"No, no, fate could not be so cruel to me," he murmured over and over to himself. "But apparitions like this only appear when people are on the brink of death. I know I am exhausted, but, hopefully, I'm not on the brink of death. Besides, angels don't make mistakes and they don't call people by name," he told himself.

The vision sped down a few more steps, still puzzled by Craig's silence. She peered over the bannister rail and lifted her candle a little higher.

"Roddy, Roddy," she called out excitedly in a soft voice. "Roddy, why do you not answer me? Are you playing your old tricks on me again? Please answer me."

She peered further over the rail.

'Why isn't he as excited as I am at his being home with me again?' she thought.

Her eyes came to rest on the silent soldier, sitting rocking himself to and fro. Craig turned towards the table slowly. Her hand grasped her throat in dismay as she saw the bandage round his head.

"Roddy, Roddy, you are wounded, but you did not tell us that in your last letter," she admonished him.

Craig was reluctant to rush to turn the light a little higher in case he startled her. He turned the wick of the lamp up and tilted it slightly so that it shone fully on his face. He gazed at her entranced, a faint smile now crinkling up his eyes and the corners of his mouth.

She held his gaze for a fleeting moment and stood several seconds gazing at him in disbelief. The young soldier sitting there was not her darling after all – the brother she loved so dearly and had missed so terribly after he had left for the front.

'It's not possible,' she told herself. 'He said he would be home soon, but who is this?' she asked herself.

Her thoughts raced on in dismay, and a puzzled look appeared on her pretty face. She dropped her eyes in bitter disappointment that this handsome young soldier, sitting rocking himself to and fro so nonchalantly, was not Roddy. He seemed to pay no heed to her disappointment. She dropped her eyes disconsolately, and her eyes came to rest on her long, white nightgown. She gave a gasp of dismay and horror. Whatever was she thinking about, standing here in front of a total stranger in her nightgown? Whatever would her mother say if she found her?

His face now had a broad grin across it, as he looked her up and down. The situation filled her with shame. What if her father came in? Oh, the embarrassment of it all!

'I must hurry and get away,' she told herself.

She turned swiftly in her haste to get up the stairs, and the candle she was holding spluttered and almost went out. She sped away up the stairs and along the passage, the dancing light casting an aura around her. She reminded Craig of a fairy with dragonfly wings. The shimmering silver light only enhanced the delightful apparition she was, and left a lasting impression in the mind of the soldier watching from below.

"She's like the Lady with the Lamp," he told himself.

Then the golden-silvery angel, with its dancing light, vanished. He heard a door close and darkness fell above.

"Well, at least she is real: angels don't close doors after themselves. Thank goodness I am not dreaming!" he muttered aloud.

Although the faint smile on his face had come about through her mistake, he was sorry to see her so dismayed.

'Who is this Roddy?' he wondered. 'Maybe he is her betrothed? Her husband? Oh yes, that must be it. I wonder what her name is?' He was acutely sorry to be the cause of her embarrassment, but he knew that now he would always think of her as a glorious real-life angel.

He lowered the wick of the lamp and flung himself once more wearily back into the depths of the rocking chair. Tired as he was, he tried to rack his brains to recall bygone days and to remember what he could of this area, this house and its occupants. He thought back to his childhood, when he used to sail over the loch with his parents. They used to come to catch the train to the city, to visit his aunts. He vaguely recalled seeing a boy similar to his own age. A small girl was sometimes with him. They used to play at the side of the loch, but then they disappeared so he thought they must have been visiting. He couldn't recall his parents ever mentioning them.

"Oh, I am too tired to think any more!" he exclaimed.

"Were you saying something, Master Craig?" Martha's voice broke in on his murmuring.

He was quite startled for a moment.

"No, no, Martha, I think I was talking in my sleep," he replied.

"You are so tired, my boy, but here is some broth and warm griddle cakes. Now, just you turn your chair round to the table and get some of this warm broth into you. It will take some of the chill out of your bones."

She set the table with more food than he had seen since he left home.

'These poor people', he thought, 'are giving me their finest food. It must surely have been saved for their precious son's homecoming, not mine. I do hope they have saved some for him.'

It was so typical of these poor, needy folk to give their last to anyone who came to their door, and now they were doing what they could for Craig, the laird's son and heir.

'I must see that Papa repays them in some way,' he told himself.

"Now, Master Craig, you must eat your fill, and I shall go and prepare a room for you."

He watched as she slowly ascended the stairs, lighting her way along the passage with a candle. The floorboards creaked as she went.

At last Magnus came in out of the wild night, shaking his wet clothing.

"Is the storm not abating as yet, Magnus?" Craig asked.

"No, Master Craig, it is one of the wildest I have seen for a long time."

Martha descended the stairs and hurried to help Magnus with his clothes. "Now come into the kitchen and get out of those wet clothes. I have dry ones waiting for you and I have the young master's drying for tomorrow."

'How I hate that word *tomorrow*,' said Craig to himself.

"Martha," Craig said, "this meal has been fit for a king. Thank you so much."

"Are you sure you have eaten enough, my boy?"

"Yes, yes, I couldn't possibly eat any more."

"Now, a good night's sleep is what you need," she said. "It will make you feel like a new man. Come – I will show you to your room. The storm will have gone by morning and the day will break fine for your crossing."

"I hope so, Martha!" Craig exclaimed.

"Oh, it will, Master Craig – have no fear about that," said Magnus, now clad in dry clothes.

"Well, no one knows the loch or these storms as well as you do, Magnus," Craig said as he bade him goodnight.

He followed Martha wearily up the stairs. He was almost too weary to climb them. He watched the flickering candlelight outlining the two of them as they wended their way.

'The light seems so different to the angel's vision I have just seen,' he told himself. 'How I wish I could see her once more to make sure I wasn't dreaming!'

Martha's voice broke in on his musings: "It is only a small room, Master Craig. I hope you will be comfortable."

"Anywhere will be more comfortable than the train!" he exclaimed.

"I have put out some nightclothes for you. I will wake you early. Then, after a good breakfast, you will be ready to sail over to your dear father at long last."

"Yes, Martha, it has been so long. I am longing to see all of them, especially my dear father and home once more."

"Yes, I am sure you are, my dear boy. Now rest well. I have put some hot water in the bowl for you to wash yourself." She bade him goodnight and, with a Gaelic blessing, closed the door.

"Thank you, Martha. You are so kind. Goodnight."

He sank wearily on top of the bed.

"My, my, real white sheets at last! My, what a treat, to be sure!"

He picked up the pyjamas at the foot of the bed. They, like the sheets, were beautifully patched.

'They are Roddy's, no doubt.' Craig thought.

He put the small lantern she had left for him on the small table beside his bed, and his gaze wandered all around the room.

'What a cosy little room this is!' he thought. 'I wonder if this wall divides me from the angel. And that window, I think, must look out over the loch.'

He clambered off the bed, walked to the window and peered out into the inky blackness of the storm-tossed night over the eerie loch.

The wind was still howling relentlessly. He could hear the waves lashing against the small landing stage, and he gazed out towards the high castle outlined against the night sky. He made a bigger clearing on the window. He could still see the lighted turrets, though they were now mere pinpoints against the pitch-black clouds that scudded across the top of it as if to engulf it. He could see the mist now falling, and the turret lights disappeared one by one.

"Home sweet home!" he muttered aloud. "Oh, how I have missed you and all my loved ones!" He could see, in his mind's eye, his father still looking out over the loch, as he himself was doing now. "He must be as bitterly disappointed as I am. But for this dratted storm I would be home in my own bed," he sighed. He swept the curtains together against the stormy night. "However, I must be thankful to have come so far, and to be safe with these kind people."

He plunged his face in the now cool water and reached for the towel. He ran his fingers through his unruly hair – he was far too tired to search for his comb. He clambered into the pyjamas, sat on the bed and smiled ruefully as he viewed the large patches.

"Yes, dear Roddy's, I do declare. I do hope he gets home soon to his waiting angel."

Craig padded over to the window once more, as if to reassure himself that Magnus was right about the impossibility of crossing the loch that night. He lifted up the corner of the curtain and saw that the mist had finally fallen. He clambered between the sheets.

'What a joy', he told himself, 'after all those grey army blankets! This is a lot better than lying on the old duckboards and sheltering in a bivvy.'

He sank his head into the soft pillow and closed his eyes. The warm bedding enveloped him like a large, soft Shetland shawl. There was a strange, dark feeling of stillness around him as he heard Martha and Magnus pass his door.

He tossed and turned, unable to get the thought of his men out of his mind. The horror of all they had been through came back to him again and again.

"Oh, I must clear my mind. I must get rid of this nightmare. I must, I must. But how? How?" he asked himself.

CHAPTER 15

Craig woke next morning to a gentle tapping on the door. He opened his eyes and gazed slowly round the room, wondering where he was, as the gentle knocking continued.

'That's not the banging of the guns,' he told himself. He looked at the snow-white sheets. 'We didn't have these over there.'

"Master Craig, Master Craig!" The call was louder now, and Craig was fully awake.

"Come in, come in."

He glanced at the door as Martha entered with a cup of tea.

"Good morning, Master Craig."

"Good morning, Martha."

She put the tea on the bedside table, went to the window and drew back the curtains. A sudden shaft of brilliant sunlight flooded the room.

"It's a lovely day, to be sure, for your crossing."

"My, my, it is, to be sure, Martha!"

"Did you sleep well, my boy?"

"Yes, very well, thank you, Martha."

"Now, drink your tea. I will be up presently with fresh water."

"Thank you, Martha," he called as she closed the door. He rested back enjoying the peace of it all. Suddenly, he sat bolt upright. "Now it is today. No more tomorrows to await!"

He leaped out of bed to the window and flung it wide open. The bracing mountain air rushed in, almost taking his breath away.

"Oh, what a glorious morning, and what a sight it is to see the loch shimmering in the morning sun! My home, my loch, my mountains! No more roving for me ever again!"

He hummed a little Scottish tune as he gazed out. Now he could see his castle home high on the hill.

"Come in, Martha."

She poured the water into his basin and joined him at the window.

"Yes, my dear boy, there is your home. Now, don't be too long. Your father will be getting impatient."

"I daresay he is standing at the edge of the jetty already."

"I daresay!" she replied as she softly closed the door.

He washed and shaved as quickly as he could, flung his shaving tackle in his kitbag and searched for his comb. When he didn't find it he swept his hair back quickly and put on his dried uniform, which Martha had laid neatly over the back of the chair.

"My, my! Martha must have been up since dawn pressing this to make me look smart for my father. How good these people are! I will never forget their kindness."

He stood for several seconds in front of the mirror and viewed himself.

'I must admit, you do look in better shape to greet your kinsfolk than last night.'

He dashed down the stairs like a young colt, humming a gay Scottish melody. Martha, standing at the kitchen door, laughed at his exuberance.

"I am here, Martha. Oh, it's so good to be alive."

"Now, sit down, my boy. I am bringing in your breakfast straight away," she called from the kitchen.

"Goodness, Martha! I can hardly eat anything. I am so excited."

"But you need the nourishment, my boy. The crossing will make you hungry."

"Martha, this is the nicest porridge and these are the best griddle cakes I have ever tasted." He indicated the running butter and syrup.

'These poor people have really done me proud,' he thought.

"Magnus is away fixing the boat. He will be here soon to collect your things."

Craig looked aghast at her as she insisted on piling more griddle cakes on to his plate.

"Really, Martha, I cannot eat any more. The meal has been fit for a king."

"Well, it is not every day we have the honour of having the heir of Glencree under our humble roof – and you just home from that dreadful war."

"Yes, it was dreadful, Martha. They say it was the war to end all wars, so let us hope so."

"I am sure they are right," she agreed.

"Have you heard recently from your son, Martha? Magnus said he should be home soon."

"We expect his telegram any day now. Yes, we can hardly wait for our dear Roddy to return."

The sound of the name *Roddy* rang in his ears. The 'angel' had called Craig *Roddy*.

'She must have been real,' he thought. 'I wasn't dreaming, after all.'

As Craig stood in a deep reverie going over the previous night's events in his mind, he didn't hear the door open and Magnus calling his name.

"The boat is ready, Master Craig. Master Craig!"

Martha and Magnus looked at him, puzzled.

"Are you all right, Master Craig?" Martha asked.

She touched him on the arm.

"Yes, yes, Martha, I am all right. I am sorry – I wasn't listening."

She offered him his cap.

"Will you be putting on your coat?"

"No, Martha. I want to feel the wind of home through my hair. It has been denied me for too long." He took the cap from her and threw the coat nonchalantly over his shoulder.

"But you will find it very chilly in the morning air."

"I shall be all right, Martha. Thank you for all your kindness."

He clasped her hand as he bade her goodbye, and she dropped him a little curtsy.

"Shall I take your kitbag?" Magnus said, as he noted Craig still hesitating.

Martha also felt that Craig wasn't listening to them. She noted the puzzled look on his face, and that he kept glancing towards the stairs.

"Have you forgotten anything? I will go and look in your room."

"Oh, no, Martha, but as I sat by the fire last night, I thought I saw a young girl at the top of the stairs. Tell me: was I dreaming? I thought I saw an angel?"

She looked at him and smiled. "No, Master Craig, it was not an angel. That would have been our daughter. She should not have been there. She knows it is forbidden. She has been ill and confined to her bed, but she is getting overexcited about Roddy's return. They are very attached to each other. I do hope she didn't disturb you."

"Oh, no, Martha. I am sorry to hear she is not well. I hope she is better soon."

"She is much improved now, thank you, and will be more so when Roddy gets home."

Magnus had now returned to see the cause of the delay.

"Martha," he exclaimed, "do not delay the young master any longer! His father will be waiting anxiously for him."

"I am ready now, Magnus," said Craig.

He ran down to the boat and flung in his cap and coat.

"I will hoist the flag now, Magnus, then Papa will know I am on my way. What a sign that will be for him, Magnus!"

He turned to wave again to Martha, and, in his haste to get aboard, he fell headlong into the boat, much to Martha and Magnus's concern. But the golden-haired girl watching from her bedroom window let out a peal of laughter. She then quickly stifled it in case her mother should hear and chastise her for laughing at someone's embarrassment – someone who had been a guest in their home.

"I wonder who he is?" she mused. "I am glad he stumbled. It serves him right for pretending to be my darling Roddy, and also for shining the light full on me when I was only in my nightgown."

The thought of it made her shudder.

The boat now drew away. Magnus was proud to be taking his master's son and heir back to him. Craig stood up in the boat to wave a last farewell to Martha, who was still standing at the cottage door. He glanced up at the window above just in time to see the lace curtain flutter across the window, and he knew she was there.

Elizabeth Dawn Angeline Ingrid Anderson had awakened that bright sunny morning to hear her father in a raised voice telling her mother not to delay 'the young master' any longer. The term puzzled and intrigued her. 'The master? The master? Master of what? What did it all mean?' she wondered.

She had raised the curtain just in time to see 'the young master' fall headlong into the boat.

Who was he? She racked her brain trying to think. She had met most of the young men from the village since they had returned from the front. Some had rejoined the church choir, but she couldn't recall seeing this man before. She heard her mother close the door.

"Mama, Mama."

"What is it, my child?"

"Please come and talk to me."

Martha smiled to herself.

"Yes, yes, young miss, you want to know all about the young master. I shall be up directly."

She cleared the crockery away, and at last she mounted the stairs.

"Now, now, my child, why all the haste to talk to me?" she said as she joined her daughter at the window.

The boat was now well on its way across the loch.

"Mama, who is the soldier who has just left with Papa? Does he live nearby? I have never seen him before. Who is he?" she asked.

"He, my dear child, will one day be the 12th Earl and laird of Glencree Castle. He is Craig, the only son and heir of the master, Lord Bruce McNair."

Elizabeth pondered awhile.

"But I have never seen him before," she said.

"Well, like so many others, including our dear Roddy, he has been away at the front. His father owns all the land as far as the eye can see and far beyond that, all the property on it and all the boats. His ancestors many many years ago had the railway built to serve the people.

"Can you not remember, my dear, the laird and his lovely wife and their small son? Your father used to row them over to catch the train when they went to visit the city. The three were always together. The boy was about Roddy's age, but you were only a young child. You probably don't remember."

Elizabeth still looked puzzled. "Yes, Mama, I think I recall. Wasn't there sometimes a little girl with them – always very prettily dressed?"

"Yes, that would be Lady Fiona. It is said she is soon to be betrothed to him.

When you and Roddy were young, you used to play together beside the loch, until Aunt Ingrid took you both to live with her.

"How I wish", her mother continued, "that his dear mother could be waiting for him on the other side to welcome him home."

"But why won't she be waiting for him?" Elizabeth asked.

"Did your aunt never tell you? It's a wonder she didn't. She was friendly with Lady Margot, who is a great friend of Craig's family."

Once again a puzzled look crossed Elizabeth's face.

"No, I can't recall. Why, what happened?"

"His mother – God rest her sweet soul – drowned in the loch when her carriage overturned one night after a thick mist came down as she was on her way home from the village. What a dear lady she was! If only she could have lived to see this happy day!"

The small boat was now almost out of sight. Martha saw Elizabeth give a shudder again. She didn't know the reason why, but Elizabeth had been thinking once more of her encounter on the stairs.

"Now, come, my child – back into bed before you get a fresh chill!"

She obeyed her mother at once and got hastily into bed.

"Tell me again, Mama: why did Roddy and I have to go and live with Aunt Ingrid?"

"Well, dear, she was very lonely after her husband died, and as she was very rich she said she would pay for you to go to the music academy near where she lives. She recognised your talent for music and your lovely voice. She herself was at one time a well-known music teacher. She knew you would go nowhere without Roddy, so she agreed to take him also to keep you company and to give him a good education. He went to the college, and you went to the music academy."

"But why couldn't we have stayed with you and Papa? We both missed you so."

"Well, we could never afford to give you the education that we wanted you to have. At one time, your poor father owned a large fishing fleet in the islands, but, through no fault of his own, it all came to grief when you were both babes in arms. Aunt Ingrid was godmother to you both, and she wanted to help us in this way when you got a little older. So that's why we let you go, my dear. It was a dreadful decision we had to make, and your going left a big space in our hearts and home." She paused for a moment as she thought of her sister. "Yes, dear Ingrid and I sang many a duet together when she used to visit us. Now I hope you realise how happy your father and I are to have you back again so close to us. It was so nice of Lady Margot to give you that position at Harrison Hall. We are deeply grateful to Her Ladyship since Aunt Ingrid's death."

Martha saw a look of deep sadness come over Elizabeth. She sighed and a faraway look came into her eye.

"Well," she exclaimed at last, "Roddy will soon be back from this dreadful war!"

"Then, as soon as he comes," Elizabeth said with a pout, "I shall have to leave you all and go to Harrison Hall."

"Well," replied her mother, "it was very kind of Lady Margot to accept you for the position of assistant and companion to her mother. It was only because she was such an old friend of your aunt's that she accepted you. There are such a lot of girls looking for positions like that. I think you have been very lucky, and she has been very kind to allow you to come home whilst you have been ill, and now to allow you to stay till Roddy comes home. At least you will be on the island. We will see you at church every Sunday, and your father calls every week at Harrison Hall and the village with their supplies. Of course, when Roddy comes, he will come over every day to visit those of his friends who are now back home."

"But, when is Roddy coming home? Everyone seems to have come home but him. He should have been home by now!" Elizabeth exclaimed impatiently, once again remembering her encounter with the laughing soldier.

'If Roddy had been home, I wouldn't have had to suffer the indignity of being in front of him in only my nightgown,' she thought angrily.

"All we know is that he is back in England. We have to await his telegram or letter, which will tell us his time of arrival. Maybe we will get it tomorrow."

"Oh, it always seems to be tomorrow. It has been such a long time, Mama, for me."

"Yes, my child, I know that. It has also been a long time for your father and me."

"Yes, Mama, I realise that."

"Now you, my girl, must rest, or else you will not be well enough to go to the station to meet him, and I must go and prepare for his homecoming. I am sure it won't be too long now. Your father will be back soon."

"I think I will read a little to pass the time away."

"Yes, you do that, my girl, and I will bring up your breakfast soon."

"Oh, yes, I had quite forgotten that I haven't had breakfast."

Her mother closed the door, and Elizabeth heard her steps fading along the passage. She hurried once more to the window but could see nothing and so she got back into bed. She rested against her pillows and tried to read, but she soon closed her book and sighed. Soon her dear Roddy would be home and soon, too, the laughing soldier would be home. Her eyes once more strayed to the window.

'I wonder if his girl is waiting for him,' she mused.

CHAPTER 16

Craig's thoughts wandered to and fro as he sat back, trailing his fingers in the loch. His thoughts returned to the small cottage as he looked at Magnus:

'What a pretty daughter he has! I do hope she didn't see me stumble in the boat – but no matter, I don't suppose I shall see her again. I am going home to Papa and my lovely Fiona and that is all that matters now.'

He watched as Magnus skilfully avoided the jutting boulders, some only just visible beneath the surface of the clear water. He recalled the times when Magnus would take him rowing in his small rowing boat. Magnus had always reminded him to watch out for them.

"Do you know every current and dangerous boulder in our lovely loch, Magnus?"

"Yes, almost. I have sailed the loch so often and for so long."

"Look, Magnus!" Craig exclaimed excitedly. "Can you see the bonfires on the hills?"

Magnus turned round to where he was pointing, and smiled at Craig's excitement.

"Yes, I see them. They are all for your homecoming. It means they have seen the flag you hoisted. The last time they were lit, my boy, was the day you were born. What a happy day that was for your mother and father!"

"Yes, it is deeply sad that my darling mother will not be alongside Papa waiting for me." Craig sighed and lapsed into silence.

"Yes, my dear boy, that is a very deep regret felt by us all."

"Yes, Magnus, I know how much everyone loved her."

"What a lovely day it is, to be sure!" said Magnus, hastily changing the subject as he noted Craig's crestfallen face.

"Yes, Magnus, it is, to be sure, in spite of everything not being as we would wish. I can already smell the pine forests on the breeze. What a wonderful feeling to be once more on the loch, and to see the mountains and the trees! You know, Magnus, all the trees were blasted away on the front and the birds stopped singing. They had all flown away – frightened by the noise."

"Yes, I daresay. Mankind is always destroying God's wonderful world."

"Yes, we had to leave this beautiful world and our bonnie Scotland to fight for what was right. But, Magnus, let us hope it was the war to end all wars; let us hope no one has to go to war ever again."

Magnus looked at Craig anxiously. 'I must get his mind off the war,' he thought.

He pointed out to Craig the higher peaks now coming into view.

"How good the Lord has been to me, Magnus, to spare me to see them all again!"

Magnus rowed on, watching Craig intently. He knew every thought passing through Craig's troubled mind.

"I can see more of the crofters' cottages now, and the spire of the village church, and there, Magnus – " he said, as he scanned all around him, "there is my music teacher's old cottage."

He raised his glasses again as he spotted the small inlet where he and his friends used to go fishing. After their day's fishing, they would tell their tall tales of the fish they had caught.

"My dear friends! I wonder how many of you have been spared to come home, like me. I must find out as soon as I can. It does seem to be taking a long time today, Magnus."

"Not far now, my boy!"

"Are you quite sure?" Craig asked doubtfully.

'How silly of me!' he thought. 'Of course Magnus is sure.'

Magnus looked at him and smiled. "Yes, Master Craig, I am sure."

Suddenly, as Craig looked through his glasses, he sat bolt upright, gazing towards the shore.

"See, Magnus, over there by the water's edge! Surely it is not who I think it is? Yes, yes, to be sure, dear old Merry-Berry. How wonderful to see her! I wonder how she knew I would be home today."

"Ah, she knows everything long before it happens."

"Of course she does – I had forgotten for the moment."

Suddenly he rose to his feet, steadying himself as the boat rocked. Never had he seen his home, Glencree Castle, looking so magnificent. The sun caught it in all its splendour.

"I can now see the turrets, Magnus."

He smiled to himself as he remembered how, as a child, he had been forbidden to go up to them after he was caught climbing out on to one of the parapets.

"I can see the flag."

"We'll soon be at the jetty," Magnus assured him.

CHAPTER 17

An early morning shaft of sunlight woke Bruce from his restless sleep, and he hastened to the window to look out over the loch. He flung the window wide open in spite of the chill wind from the mountains. A beautiful clear blue sky met his eager gaze. The stillness over the loch augured well. Shafts of early morning sunlight on the still water caused shimmering silvery ripples on its surface.

"Oh, what a lovely day for my dear son's homecoming at last! He will be home today. No more waiting for tomorrow. Today – today has come."

Jamie knocked on the door.

"Well, Jamie, today has arrived at last!" exclaimed Bruce as he entered.

"Yes, Sir Bruce. I have brought your tea and your other dress suit. Your other one is still not dry."

"Come – we must hurry to the loch as soon as we can. Have you seen the flag flying yet, Jamie?"

"No, but it might be by the time we reach the jetty. I have just come from there."

Bruce shaved and dressed hurriedly with the help of Jamie. He was humming a tune to himself.

"Oh, what a happy day this is, to be sure, Jamie! Do hurry and fasten my buckles."

All the household had been astir since dawn. Harriet met Bruce at the foot of the stairs.

"Breakfast is on the table, Bruce," she said, noticing his haste to get to the front door.

"I haven't time for breakfast, woman!" he exclaimed. "Do you not know what day this is?"

"But you must eat something. The boat won't be here yet."

He paid no heed to her persistent calling. He was gone, with Jamie by his side and Flint at his heels. Flint too had sensed the joy and expectancy in everyone's mood and he had been whimpering at the foot of the stairs, ready to go as soon as he heard Bruce's tread on the stairs.

Bruce stopped to look into the hall mirror on his way out, to see that his attire was just as he expected.

Jamie stopped to pick up his gold-handled cane and Flint's lead, and then he hurried to catch up with both of them. The dog bounded on ahead, then bounded back again to make sure they were following. Then he raced to the edge of the jetty, as if he realised that at last his true master was on his way. If that was so, Flint was determined to be the first to greet him. Time and time again, Bruce called him back.

"You must have your lead on, boy. You get far too excited."

It was some time before the dog would stop moving for long enough for Bruce to put the lead on, and Bruce's laughing rebukes did nothing to calm the dog. The trio stood on the jetty, Bruce nervously tapping his cane against his thigh.

Flint kept looking up at him with his large brown eyes, as if saying, "Where is my master? Where is he?" and Bruce, knowing all his expressions, kept telling him, "Not long now, boy! Not long now! He will be here soon – the one we are all waiting for."

"It is a grand morning to be sure, Jamie," he said, and he raised his glasses again. Then suddenly he gave a shout of delight. "Jamie, Jamie, the flag is out. It's flying at last. Thanks be to God. Hoist ours, Jamie. I want to make sure that Craig sees it."

The bonfires were now well alight as the villagers too had seen the flag. Elena, watching from the library window, screamed out to all within earshot: "The flag has been hoisted. Come and see, Harriet. Come – let us hurry to welcome him with Bruce."

They hurriedly put on their cloaks to join the ones now waiting on the jetty. All the villagers from miles around came down from the hillsides. Some were already standing beside the loch. Some on the jetty stood aside to let Harriet and Elena pass, and, as they did so, the women dropped them little curtsies and the men doffed their caps.

Bruce's own piper stood close beside Bruce in his full tartan dress, with his son by his side. He too was only recently back from the front. He had been chosen to be 'Master Craig's Piper' – an honour greatly coveted by all the young pipers on the island. Their tartan attire vied with that of their master, but no-one could surpass him when he was in full tartan dress. None was so resplendent as he was today.

As the ferry approached the jetty, Craig rose to his feet so suddenly in his excitement that he startled Magnus.

"Be careful, Master Craig," he beseeched him. "We don't want the boat to overturn."

"Oh, it won't overturn, Magnus," said Craig, and he started to laugh at the thought of it. "Don't worry so, Magnus. We won't tip over."

Magnus was not quite as sure as the young soldier, who, in his excitement, was making the boat rock alarmingly. He was oblivious to all Magnus's protestations.

"Oh dear!" exclaimed Elena. "See how the boat is rocking. I do hope it doesn't go over."

"Of course it won't tip over," said Bruce. "Magnus has full control over it."

Craig was waving frantically to his father, who was waving just as frantically back. The occasion was almost too much for him to bear.

"Look, Harriet. Look, Elena. Can you see my fine bonnie boy – my fine bonnie boy?"

"Yes, we see our fine boy!" they both exclaimed.

Elena was too overcome with joy to speak. Tears ran down her cheeks, and she patted them away with her damp handkerchief.

"Craig, Craig," Bruce called out to him, and the eager breeze flung his name out on the silvery ripples of the loch.

"Papa, Papa," came back the excited cry, and, at the sound of his young master's voice over the water, Flint gave one joyful whine and an excited tug and lunge.

In spite of Elena's quick reaction as she tried to grab his lead, the dog almost pulled Bruce off his feet. With the lead trailing after him, he disappeared over the edge of the wooden jetty and hit the water with a plop. Then he swam for all he was worth out to the boat, frantic with excitement.

Craig saw him coming and called out to him: "Flint, Flint, come on, boy. Come on, boy."

Craig knelt down in the boat as the dog drew nearer, and reached out to him. He dragged the sopping, happy dog over the side and into his arms.

"Well done, bonnie boy! Well done! You are the first one from home to greet me."

The dog licked Craig's face and barked with joy. He looked so bedraggled, and Craig and Magnus were beside themselves with laughter, as were several on the jetty. Craig was saturated as the dog constantly jumped up to him and shook himself from time to time. Magnus did not escape the drenching either.

'But what does it matter,' Magnus told himself, 'when there is so much happiness around me.'

"All right, boy, I am home to stay now, so don't get so excited. I won't ever leave you again, boy – never again. Quiet now, boy!"

Flint sat down as he was bid and nuzzled close to Craig as though he understood that at last his beloved master was home to stay. Magnus looked at them both, with pride welling up inside him.

"Oh, what a happy day this is, to be sure! To think that I am the one to be bringing the young master home at last to his father! Soon my own bonnie boy will be home too. What a happy day that will be for us!"

He hastened his stroke as best he could, watching the boat carefully as it tilted from side to side, again and again. Craig waved more and more enthusiastically as he spotted more and more familiar faces.

Bruce, looking through his glasses, could hardly contain himself with the joy of it all.

"What a fine boy he is, to be sure! Jamie, can you see my bonnie boy?"

"Yes, Sir Bruce, I see him," Jamie replied, wiping away a tear.

"See, Harriet and Elena – can you see him?"

"My word, how tall he has grown!" said Elena.

Now more and more of the household staff left the work they were doing as news of the boat coming into view reached them. More and more of the villagers had arrived, streaming up the country lanes from the village and down from the hillsides.

Cook made sure everything was left simmering. Then she and the maids dried their hands on their aprons and headed towards the jetty.

"Play his music, pipers!" Bruce exclaimed, and they struck up one of Craig's favourite tunes.

"Magnus, can you hear the pipers? They are playing one of my favourite tunes. Just listen, Magnus."

"I am listening, Master Craig."

"Nothing is as wonderful as the skirl of the pipes over the loch. Do you agree, Magnus? Isn't it a wonderful homecoming for me, Magnus?"

"Yes, my young master, it is. The only worthwhile thing is to be coming home to all one's loved ones."

The music now became louder and louder as the boat drew closer. Flint, now standing beside Craig, barked louder than ever before as he rushed to the front of the boat and looked towards all of them on the jetty. It seemed to Bruce as if Flint was telling him, "Look – look who I am bringing home at last. I am bringing him home to you."

Craig could see his aunts and Jamie more clearly now. As usual, they were by his father's side.

"I can recognise just about everyone now, Magnus," he said.

Then his face suddenly took on a look of bewilderment as he raised his glasses once more. Magnus noted the change in him.

"Is anything wrong, Master Craig?" he asked anxiously.

"I cannot see Fiona anywhere. She should be standing next to Papa. It is not possible that she would not want to be here to await my homecoming. Where can she be?"

"Maybe she is just delayed," said Magnus, trying to soften Craig's obvious disappointment.

"Look, Harriet!" exclaimed Elena as she dried her eyes once more. "Just look at our darling boy. I can see him so clearly now. His lovely dark hair is blowing in the breeze. Those tiny waves drop over one eye as they did when he was a child."

"Oh, Elena, how you do go on and on!"

"But don't you agree how like Bruce he is when Bruce was his age? Such a handsome boy he was also," she said, and she sighed. "How like his father he is!"

"Yes, too much like him in every way, I'll be bound – more so now he is a grown man," replied Harriet.

"Oh, how I wish his dear mother could be with us to see our boy's homecoming!"

"Now, be quiet, Elena. You will upset Bruce if he hears you talk like that."

With a resounding thud the boat hit the jetty. Craig did not wait for it to stop and steady itself. He shot up the wooden steps, two and three at a time, and, with a flying leap, he was in his father's arms. He clasped him to him as if he would never ever let him go again.

"Papa, Papa, I am home at last."

Bruce was speechless with the joy of it all, but at last he managed to whisper, "Yes, home at last, my son! Home at last!"

"Aunts, I am home," he called to them as he rushed to clasp them in his arms.

They pressed their heads to his as they held him in their arms. Elena, as usual, was weeping tears of joy; Harriet, as always, was much more composed.

"The Good Lord be praised! Home at last!"

"How we have all longed for this day!" Elena whispered.

"But, Aunt Elena, where is Fiona? I felt sure she would be here with you!" he exclaimed, a look of disappointment on his face.

"Well, she doesn't arrive home herself till tomorrow, and so of course does not as yet know of your arrival."

Elena looked at Bruce and noticed he looked a little crestfallen. She knew only too well that he did not want to share his son with anyone – not even Fiona.

"Well, I shall just have to wait until she arrives, then. But I am with you, dear Papa, and that is all that matters. I am where I have longed to be for so long."

"Yes, nothing ever again will separate us, my son."

"No, Papa, nothing ever again."

The four of them stood holding one another, and, as Craig glanced up, he saw all the others close by smiling and happy at his safe return. There were tears on some of their faces, and this made him realise how much he meant to them. As they started towards the house, Craig suddenly gave a gasp of dismay.

"What is it, my son?" Bruce exclaimed.

"In my haste to see you, Papa, I have forgotten to thank Magnus for bringing me safely home."

He released himself from his father's grasp and hastily ran back to the edge of the jetty. Magnus had been watching the laird greet his son. He had stood, cap in hand, with a deep longing in his eyes as he thought of his own son. Roddy was soon to be home too, amongst his loved ones. There would not be as many people as this to welcome him home, but it would be just as joyful a reunion, he told himself. Roddy was just as eagerly awaited and longed for as this, the laird's son.

'My son also has been away far too long,' he thought.

He walked back to board his boat and was climbing aboard when he saw Craig flying down the steps, calling to him, "Magnus, Magnus, thank you for bringing me safely over the loch; and please thank your dear wife for all her kindness to me. I do hope your son gets home soon. I hope too that your daughter gets well soon."

"Thank you, Master Craig. It has been an honour and given us much pleasure. Now go to your father – he is awaiting you."

Bruce was waiting for him at the top of the steps, and he gave Magnus a wave as he watched him climb into the boat. Craig stood for several minutes watching as the boat headed out into the centre of the loch. Craig waved him away and Magnus gave him a final wave as he headed for home.

'How like my dear son the young master is!' he thought.

Craig hurried back up the steps to rejoin his father, who was getting quite anxious at his delay in returning.

"Magnus's son is expected home any day now, Papa," he said.

"Oh, I am so glad he has been spared from the dreadful war to return to his father, like you. Now, let there be no more talk of war. That was the war to end all wars, it is said. Home is all that matters now, my son."

"Yes, home sweet home at last!"

He bent down to pat Flint once more. The dog was now feeling rejected and dismayed that so many people wanted his master for themselves. Wasn't he *his* master? Hadn't he waited so long for his return?

"All right, boy," Craig said, "I haven't forgotten you."

Suddenly Craig felt a tug at his arm and he saw Jamie, one of his closest and dearest friends, looking up at him with tears in his eyes.

"Dear, dear Jamie, thank you for taking such care of Papa whilst I have been away," he said, clasping Jamie to him.

"You are home now, my wee bonnie boy. That is all that matters now."

"Yes, Jamie, home to stay – and not such a wee boy now."

"No, Master Craig. You have certainly grown a lot whilst you have been away."

Bruce and Craig walked arm in arm with Elena and Harriet hanging on to Craig's other arm.

"Thank you, dear aunts, for looking after Papa so well."

"Well," exclaimed Harriet, "it has been quite a hard job at times, hasn't it, Elena? You know how stubborn he can be."

"But all will be well now that you are back," replied Elena.

"Tell me," said Craig: "how is my darling Fiona?"

"Well, she is still as beautiful as ever," said Elena. "She visited us a few weeks ago – just before she went back to her hospital duties. She has done such a lot of voluntary work whilst you have been away. She wrote and said she would be home tomorrow, so you will see her soon."

"Ah, well," he said, "I will have to wait until tomorrow. I must be satisfied. I cannot have everything at once. I must save something for another day."

"Yes, yes," exclaimed Bruce with a touch of satisfaction, Elena thought, in his voice. "Yes, I can have you all to myself for a while."

Elena looked at Bruce again as he spoke. She knew that no matter how much Bruce loved Fiona – almost as a daughter – he did not like the idea of Craig spending too much time away from his side with her.

'He forgets', she told herself, 'that he could never tear himself away from his darling Isabelle. But then,' she added after a little thought, 'Craig is the only reason he went on living after Isabelle had gone. Dear Bruce! He will have to get used to the idea of Craig being more at Fiona's side than his. Well, that will all come in due course,' she reminded herself.

"Yes, Papa. You will have me for always. You can rest assured I will not be roving from your side or leaving this dear home of mine ever again."

Craig went over to greet the other members of the household who were still waiting to greet him. The ladies dropped him curtsies and the men doffed their caps as he shook each one by the hand. Then they hurried back to the kitchen, stables and gardens, from where they had come.

The villagers too were still waiting to greet Craig before wending their way back to the village. There was old Angus, the saddler, whose embossed leatherwork was surely the best in Scotland. He had eagerly been awaiting Craig's return and now presented him with a new embossed saddle for the horse his father had bought him at the sales recently. He had made the young master's first saddle when Craig was a child.

Douglas was also there. He had taught Craig to fish and sail, and he had helped his father choose a new boat for him, ready for his return.

Rory had taught him many riding skills.

Mr Ritchie, his old music teacher, was also there.

"How I have longed for this day!" he told Craig.

"So have we all," said Rory. "We will bid you good day, Master Craig."

Craig watched them out of sight, then he turned to go back to his father, who was waiting rather impatiently. Suddenly he spotted, in the corner of the shrubbery, a small colourfully clad figure, whom he recognised at once. He went over to greet her.

"Merry-Berry, fancy you being here also! How happy it makes me to see you! Who told you I would be home today?"

"All the birds told me," she replied.

"Ah, yes, now I remember – all your friends, the birds, tell you all you want to know. You must have walked many miles to come here today."

"Master Craig, I just had to come and greet you. Now, go to your father. He is anxious for you to rejoin him, so go, my dear boy, with my blessing." She repeated it in Gaelic. "You have been away from him far too long," she said.

She picked up her basket of sticks, nodded her head and glided silently away.

He hastened to rejoin his father and his aunts.

"Come, son – " Bruce said, "we still have someone else who is waiting to see you."

"Who is it, Papa?"

"Now, wait and see," he said.

Flint was still jumping up and down and following Craig wherever he went.

Craig kept patting him on the head and reminding him, "All right, boy, I am home now."

Craig put his hand on his father's shoulder as they strolled on behind the pipers.

"Oh, it is so good to hear the pipers playing again in the Highlands. Thank you, Papa, for my own piper. It is a great honour you do me."

"You are worthy of more, my son. You will see, now you are home to stay."

Harriet and Elena walked on ahead, then stopped and turned.

"Now, see who we have here, Craig dear!" exclaimed Harriet.

He gave a gasp of dismay as he saw her – a small, bent figure, with hair now silvery grey, and a coloured shawl over her bent shoulders and around her knees. She had been brought in specially to greet Craig.

"My dear old Nanny," Craig exclaimed, hardly able to believe it. He sat at her feet and clasped both her small wizened hands in his and kissed them. "Dear, dear Nan," he whispered over and over again.

"Let me try to see you more clearly, my son. I cannot see as well as I could."

He bent lower and kissed her on the forehead and she lovingly fingered his face.

"Have you come to scold me today?" he laughed gaily.

"I shall if you misbehave," she replied, and he laughed louder than before.

He kissed her lovingly on the cheek. "Thank you, Nan, for coming to greet me," he said. Then he reluctantly let go of her hands. "I shall call and see you when I come into the village."

Still more of the villagers stood to greet him. Many of them remembered him as a happy little boy riding wild over the glens with his father and mother, until that fateful day, after which they saw him change in to a solemn little boy. No more did he ride over the glens in happy, gay mood. He would be seen only with his father, just bidding them a polite good day as he passed by.

He had not seen any of them since he had sailed away to the front.

CHAPTER 18

He had not been home since he had sailed away that morning. Even when wounded he had spent the time in convalescence at the home of Fiona's aunt in the south of England.

His father, Aunt Elena and Fiona had gone down to spend some time with him. It was there that an unofficial engagement between himself and Fiona had taken place, much to the satisfaction of both families. But as soon as he was well enough, he was back at the front with his men.

"Now, all inside for warm griddle cakes and hot toddies to take the chill out of your bones," exclaimed Harriet.

For this they were all truly grateful.

Craig had turned once more, with his father and Flint beside him, to look out over the loch to the rolling countryside at the foothills of the mountains in the distance and the pine forest catching the early morning sun.

"It's truly a wonderful sight, Papa. How often I have dreamt of standing here with you, admiring it all! So often I thought I would never see you or it again." He stood in silent thought for several minutes. "Yes, these are my mountains and I really am home," he said.

He turned to look at the old church in the distance, which had been ringing out a special peal of welcome for him.

Bruce touched his arm.

"Come, my son – you are really home now."

They both turned to face the castle and they slowly walked towards it. He looked up to see his bedroom window, overlooking the loch. All the windows were open to the bracing air. The morning sun cast its bright light over the castle. He again gripped his father's arm, as if to reassure himself that he was not dreaming.

They reached the ornamental fountain, filled with goldfish, which his father had had built for him as a boy. Craig dipped his fingers in the still water and paused to peer into its depths to see if he could see any of his old fish lurking below. As if by magic, the surface of the water rippled and broke, and the oldest inhabitant popped up, almost as fat and bright-eyed as before. Craig thought he did look a little more faded.

"Even you, old fella, have come to welcome me home," he said, and he laughed gaily. "Now, Papa, what do you think of that for a welcome?"

"Just as you deserve, my son."

"Aunt Elena did say that Fiona was expected home tomorrow, Papa."

"Yes, my son, she did. The General and Lady Cleveland said so also when they visited us a few weeks ago. They said how much they had missed her."

"Yes, I too have missed her, Papa. It will be wonderful to see her again."

"They said how much she was missing you too, dear boy, and how alone she felt without you for so long – just as we have felt so lonely."

"Well, I am back now, Papa. You will never be lonely again, ever."

Elena and Harriet had now gone on ahead to complete the tasks they had so hurriedly left. They knew father and son would not need anyone else now they were together at last – only themselves. No one must intrude on their today. Tomorrow would be soon enough for Craig and Bruce to share with others, but not today. They walked slowly up the stone steps and Craig gave a playful pat to the two large lions guarding the main entrance.

"These two are still here, I see, Papa, as strong and upright as ever."

"Yes, my son. They will be here for ever, just like us. Here is the door of your home. We purposely left it closed so that you could have the pleasure of opening it yourself at last."

Craig stood looking at the huge oak door, before he turned the handle and went inside.

"Yes, Papa, it is a beautiful home."

"Yes, my son. It was built to last for ever by our forefathers to hand down to our sons. It is part of that great heritage handed down to me to pass on to you and to your sons."

"I make a pledge to you, Papa, at the doorway of our ancestral home, that my sons and their sons will enter this doorway just as I am entering it today. I shall never leave this, my home, or you or my bonnie Scotland again."

He smiled broadly to his father as he listened to his father's quote:

> The McNairs were here yesterday;
> The McNairs are here today;
> The McNairs will be here tomorrow.

"I haven't heard you say that, Papa, for so many years."

They both turned to listen to the farewell tune of the pipers as they stood at the doorway and, as they finished playing, Craig called to them:

"Thank you, pipers. I am so glad Papa has chosen you, Rory, to be my very own piper." He shook his hand as he bade them both farewell.

"It is an honour for me, Master Craig."

"Now," exclaimed Bruce to both pipers, "before you go home you must go to Jamie for a wee dram and tell Cook I say to prepare a meal for you."

After they had gone, Bruce turned to Craig.

"And you, my son," he said gaily, "now you have entered this, your home, I can guess the first thing you will do. I will just wait and see if I am right."

When they entered the Great Hall, Craig, with a smile on his face, did as his father suspected: he flung his cap on to the antlers of one of the huge stag's heads – one of many that adorned the castle, trophies from bygone days, relics of the many hunting parties that were once held there.

They both laughed gaily when he missed, and he ran to pick it up and try again. Again he missed.

"Soon, Papa, I shall, as I always used to, get it first time."

At last it landed on the antlers and his father gave him a playful pat on the back.

Harriet and Elena, hearing their laughter, joined them in the hall.

"Up to your old tricks so soon!" said Harriet.

"Yes, dear aunt, I'm afraid so," he replied, "but I got it the third time."

"Yes, Bruce, our boy is well and truly home!" she exclaimed laughingly – and Harriet was not one to smile very often, especially at Craig's mischievous tricks.

Craig was spellbound as he stood with the three of them at the bottom of the long, winding gilt-and-wrought-iron staircase. He looked up to the magnificent carved ceiling above.

"Yes, everything is just the same as when I left; all the deer heads on the walls remind me of the days we spent shooting on the moors."

'No more shooting for me!' he told himself. 'No more guns, no more gunfire!'

"Well, my son," said Bruce, "nothing has changed whilst you have been away. Soon we will pick up where we left off."

Craig ran up a few of the stairs and pointed to the large stained-glass window at the end of the first landing. He marvelled at it, as he had always done, sometimes in awe. The window depicted the imposing figure of the first laird of Glencree Castle, who had built and procured all that Bruce now owned. The morning sun streaming through the coloured glass reminded Craig of a rainbow. The purple of the thistle; the various shades of green of the Scottish countryside; the snow-white tips of the mountains in the background; the mauves and pinks of the heather; the red, blue and gold of the scrolled names of his ancestors; and the family crest in stark relief above them. 'Everything seems to be dancing with delight today,' he thought.

"The old chieftain is still here in all his glory, Papa, I see."

"Yes, like you and me. You are home to carry on your heritage," Bruce replied.

Jamie had now rejoined them and was looking at Craig with pride and joy as he watched him taking in all his familiar surroundings. Flint still watched his every move and followed him wherever he went, and Craig bent down now and again to pat him on the head.

Jamie put his kitbag in the corner, and Craig looked at him and grimaced.

"I won't ever be needing that again, Jamie!" he exclaimed with relief. "Never again! Please take it to my room. I will sort it out later. I will keep only the things I treasure – small keepsakes from my men. Keepsakes from my men! My men! My men!"

He was overcome again at the thought of the ones he had left behind. They would never again enjoy life as he was now, back in his beloved home and with all his loved ones round him.

"I will never forget you, my wonderful men – never."

His father looked at him anxiously. "Are you all right, my son?"

"Yes, Papa," he replied, "I am all right."

He looked up and spotted Cook and others from the kitchen, who stood watching him closely. He hurried over to greet them again.

"Well, Cook, here I am, back again to sample your wonderful cooking, which I have missed so much."

"We have missed you too, Master Craig," Cook replied. "My, how you have grown since you went away!"

"Well," he replied, "I could not stay a small boy for ever – much as you and Jamie would have liked me to, no doubt."

"As long as you are home, that is all we want," Cook replied.

"Now, how about some hot griddle cakes? I know they are the best in bonnie Scotland."

"Yes, all is prepared. Come along, Sarah," she said, and they hurried away.

As old Ben turned to go, Craig called him back.

"Yes, Master Craig?" he answered.

"Please tell Alex that I shall want some flowers later in the day." He turned to his father. "I want to go to Mama's grave as soon as I can."

"Yes, my son, as soon as you are ready."

"Now," said Elena, "both of you go into the lounge and stay there until we bring you something to eat and drink. In the meantime, Harriet and I will finish what we were doing before you arrived."

Craig hurried on ahead of his father, and Bruce knew why he was anxious to get there. He hung back to tell Ben to bring the horses round later. Bruce proceeded to the lounge and stood in the doorway, looking at his son.

"Oh, how I have longed for this moment, my dear son!"

He watched silently as Craig gazed up lovingly at his mother's portrait. Bruce knew what thoughts were going through his mind.

He heard Craig whisper, "Here I am, Mama, home at last with dear Papa and you. We are all together again, just the three of us."

He turned as he sensed his father's presence.

"Yes, my son, just the three of us – never to part again."

Craig wandered over to the window overlooking the loch, as if to try and hide from his father his deep sadness and yearning for his mother. Her absence was the only thing marring his enjoyment of the day. His thoughts drifted out to the loch. He dearly loved it, but it had cruelly taken from them the one they so adored.

Bruce joined him at the window, knowing he must try to break his son's trend of thought.

"Soon we will go sailing and fishing on the loch as we did before, my boy."

"Yes, Papa, it will be so peaceful."

He knew his father was trying to break his trend of thought.

"Yes, it will be so quiet and peaceful after the holocaust of the war."

"Well, my boy," – Bruce put his hand firmly on his shoulder – "there will be no more wars. That was the war to end all wars – they all say so."

"Let us hope so, Papa, after all the suffering it has caused!" he exclaimed bitterly.

"Now, you two, no more talk of war!" said Elena, who had entered the room just in time to hear the conversation about the war.

"That word must never ever be mentioned in this house again and, I hope, nowhere else either."

"Yes, you are so right, as always, Aunt Elena."

"We will eat here today. Harriet will join us very soon."

She joined them at the window after she had put some flowers on the table and put her arm on Craig's.

"Well, my dear boy," she asked happily, "how does the loch look to you?"

"Just too wonderful for words, Aunt Elena – just too wonderful. I am only now starting to believe I am really home at last."

They were joined by Harriet, and the four of them stood looking out to the mountains in the distance.

Craig was the first to break the silence: "I never really thought I should ever see this view again when I was away."

"Well, we too", declared Harriet, "had those fears but somehow they always disappeared as quickly as they came. We knew – didn't we, Bruce? – that it was just not possible that our boy would never return and carry on his heritage."

"Yes," replied Bruce. "We sat for hours gazing at this view, never doubting that Glencree Castle and the McNair family name would carry on with your safe return. Now you are home, son, we know that will now happen."

Elena looked at them both as Craig peered out, lost in the beauty of the scene. She recalled the talks Harriet and Bruce had often had regarding the importance of carrying on the family name. If Craig did not return, Harriet was most emphatic that Bruce would have to marry again. However, Bruce had been adamant that if Craig did not return, the title would die with him. Elena could still hear in her thoughts the raging voice of Bruce as he roared at Harriet:

"No, no! Only the son of my darling Isabelle will ever hold the title of 12th Earl and laird of Glencree Castle. Only he will carry on the direct line. No one else will ever take my Isabelle's place or that of her son. No, Harriet, I shall never marry again."

There the matter had rested until news of battles raised fresh anxieties.

Now at last Craig was home. Now all was well. They had no more doubts or fears. They all had a glorious future to look forward to.

The smell of the hot griddle cakes wafted into the room, and Craig turned sharply from the window.

"Oh, what a glorious smell, to be sure! Dear, dear Cook! Give her my thanks and tell her, Shona, that I shall be in to see her and thank her myself soon."

"I will, Master Craig," Shona replied.

"Please tell Cook to send in some more. I am so hungry after my journey over the loch in the fresh mountain air."

"Now, come – let us all enjoy them whilst they are warm," said Elena.

"How wonderful it all is – the four of us round the table, just like old times!" said Craig. "Soon everything will be back to normal. All Papa's friends will come to visit, and all my friends will be here again. We'll have dances and parties, as before. All my friends must be back by now."

He was too lost in his joy and happy thoughts to note the look pass between Elena and Harriet. They knew that many of Craig's friends would never visit them again, and that he would find that out soon enough when he visited the village.

"Yes, yes!" exclaimed Elena. "It will be grand to have your friends round again, won't it, Harriet?"

"It certainly will," she replied. "We have missed you all so much. It has been quiet here for so long."

Craig pondered a moment in deep thought.

"I wonder if they have all got home yet," he said. "I shall go to visit them all very soon. But first I must go and see my darling Fiona. I shall go first thing in the morning, Papa."

"Yes, my boy. I shall ride over with you. I haven't given my dear friend, the General, a game of chess for a long time. Maybe tomorrow we shall have time to have a game."

"It will be wonderful arranging all the parties to celebrate your homecoming and, of course, your official engagement to Fiona. All the invitations will need to be sent to our friends, and Fiona's relatives and friends in the south of England. How busy we are going to be, Harriet! This is just what we need after all the dismal times we have had with the war on," said Elena. "I can hardly wait for the engagement party at last."

"Yes, yes!" exclaimed Craig. "That will be the best party of all. It is all I dreamt about whilst I was away. Oh, how I am longing to see her! Tomorrow cannot come soon enough."

"It will be good to hear this old house ring with laughter again – and none too soon," replied Harriet.

Flint had realised that at last his beloved master was home to stay. After a request from Craig, he had finally gone to sit in his usual corner near the door, but his soulful trusting eyes never left his master's face.

Bruce now sat in his favourite chair and listened quietly to the plans being made all around him. He was deep in thought, and his mood was one of peace and happiness. The excitement of the past two days had been almost too much for him.

He was the kind of man who did things with gusto and excelled at everything, be it shooting, fishing, riding, climbing or hunting; and he was renowned for the keenness of his mind when dealing with the business of his estate. Lately he had bought more and more land for his son and heir, and the sons and heirs that followed him.

Elena looked at him anxiously. "Are you all right, Bruce?" she asked.

Craig too looked at him with deep concern.

"Yes, yes, I am fine – just fine."

"We were only saying the other day, Bruce, how much we missed all Craig's friends, and the parties we used to have. His friends used to stay for days, and sometimes weeks, at a time. Some of them never wanted to go. Do you recall, Bruce? Bruce dear?" Elena repeated.

But Bruce, with a happy smile on his face, had closed his eyes and he was enjoying his first restful sleep since his son had sailed away.

"Poor Papa!" said Craig. "It has all been too much for him – all this waiting and anxiety."

"Yes," said Elena, "he didn't sleep much last night. I could hear him pacing the floor, just waiting for today. Well, his day is here."

"No waiting for tomorrow for him or you, dear aunts. I will go to my room and rest now; then I will change before we ride over to the church."

He got up to go and immediately Flint was upon his feet also. Never again would he ever let his beloved master go anywhere without him. Craig kissed both his aunts.

"Thank you both for my wonderful homecoming. You are both so wonderfully dear to me."

He glanced up longingly at his mother's portrait and whispered to her: "It's so good to be home with all I love."

Then he quickly left the room, too overcome with emotion to say another word. Harriet got to her feet as he left.

"Come, Elena – we still have a lot to do before evening. I will see how Cook is getting on with the preparations."

"Yes," said Elena, "I will get some flowers from the greenhouse for the dinner table. I want everything to look just right tonight."

They both paused and looked at Bruce as they passed him on their way out of the room.

"Dear, dear Bruce! How he deserves this long-awaited contented sleep!"

CHAPTER 19

Craig bounded up the long, winding staircase two stairs at a time, with Flint close on his heels.

"Now, Flint, you know you are not allowed up the stairs. Down! Good boy!"

The dog shrank back on his haunches, watching Craig go, with a look of pathetic dejection on his eager, loving face.

Craig stopped to look at his mother's portrait. It was one of the last ones she had sat for before that dreadful day. She was dressed in full riding habit, a lovely smile as always on her beautiful, tranquil face. Everywhere he went in this great house, a picture of her was always looking down at him.

He paused and whispered, "You are always with us, Mama dear – always," and she seemed to smile back at him in agreement.

He carried on up the stairs. He could hear Flint whimpering below, and he looked lovingly at him over the rail. The dog, so well trained, sat obediently gazing up at him. However, as soon as Craig disappeared into his room along the corridor, and Flint heard the door close, he rose to his feet and bounded up the stairs. He flopped down on the sheepskin mat outside Craig's door, utterly contented. He was determined that his beloved master would go nowhere else without him.

Craig stood with his back to the door for several minutes, taking in all the familiar surroundings.

"Oh, what a happy, happy day! Please, God, let it be real. Don't let me be dreaming all this. I have dreamt it so often – let it be real."

He gazed lovingly round the room. Not an inch of it did his happy eyes miss. Everything was the same as when he left it: every picture on the wall, every ornament and all his books were just where he had left them so long ago. His mother's picture was still in its silver frame on one side of his bed, and on the other bedside table was a picture in a matching frame of a beautiful dark-haired girl.

Her eyes seemed to be looking straight into Craig's and she seemed to be whispering, "Darling, I love you. I love you."

He wandered over and picked it up lovingly.

"My darling, Fiona, oh, how I have missed you! I am longing to see you, my love. I will see you tomorrow, my darling. How beautiful you are!" He kissed her picture over and over again. "Soon I will hold you in my arms, never to let you go. Everything here is just the same as the morning I rose to go to that dreadful war." The mere thought sent a shudder down his spine. "That useless, useless war!"

He wandered over to the large window overlooking the loch. The vista always filled him with a deep feeling of love and pride.

'Did I go to war to save all this for all who follow me?'

He pictured in his mind every season waiting its turn to appear as if by magic. He pictured the dawn of spring, then the brightness of the flowers in summer, followed by gold-amber autumn. The colours of autumn were like a blazing fire waiting to be quenched, as soon they would be by the snows of winter. Then everywhere would be decked in snow, from the tallest pine to the grass in the glens. Then, as if by magic, the cycle would start all over again, and the snow would hurtle down the slopes into the glens below.

'Yes, these are my mountains and these are my glens – my Scotland, my home for evermore. Yes, this is what we fought for. But for all this, as truly magnificent as it is, the price that was paid was too, too high. Unlike me, those who have gone will never again see the glory of the seasons.'

Suddenly his face darkened and he realised that his thoughts were back where he never wanted to be again.

'No, no, I must now only think of the future.'

His eyes wandered away to the small village in the distance and the small scattered crofts. He could see the village school he used to attend, and he pictured his parents waiting for him when his day was finished – his mother in the small trap and his father alongside. Then he would tell them of his busy day, as he clambered in beside his mother. His eyes rested on the tall steeple of the village church.

"I must go there as soon as Papa has rested enough."

He could see the cottages of his old music teacher and his nanny close by, and, in the distance, he could just see the chimneys of the Academy for Young Ladies, which most of the village maidens went to after they left the small village school. Then some, luckier than the rest, would proceed to universities or finishing schools. However, the poorer girls of the village would go back to the farms and crofts.

'My, how they will have all grown since I went away! I daresay I won't recognise most of them when I see them. I wonder how many of my old friends have returned from the front. I must go and visit them all as soon as I can.'

His gaze wandered on to the small bay and the anchorage for the small boats, some of which were still there.

'Oh, how I am longing to sail my boat again on the loch!'

Jamie's knock on the door broke his trend of thought.

"The master is waiting for you, Master Craig," he called.

"Tell Papa I will join him in a few minutes, please, Jamie."

Craig hadn't had time to change, as he had intended. He hurried from the room and rushed down the stairs two at a time, with Flint close on his heels.

"Here I am, Papa."

He slipped his arm through his father's as they made their way towards the door. They called their goodbyes to Harriet and Elena, who stood in the hall to see them go.

"Now, don't stay too long talking to all you meet along the way," said Harriet.

"No, today you must get more rest. There will be lots of time for visiting and talking another day," said Elena.

"No, I promise we won't," replied Craig, and he kissed them both.

"Come, my dear boy – we want to return before dark," Bruce said.

The sisters followed them to the door and watched as they hurried down the broad steps and across the cobbled courtyard towards the stable boys holding their horses. Craig stroked both horses lovingly.

"Fancy, the same two we have ridden before so often!" he exclaimed.

"Yes, my son, the same two. One day we will ride over to Giles' Stable and see about adding to our stable. I thought I should wait until you returned, then we can choose together. Our two dear horses here are due a well-earned rest."

Craig's horse snuggled up to him at the sound of his voice.

As they mounted, Craig looked up to see Alex approaching, carrying a huge bunch of his mother's favourite flowers, which were always grown in the greenhouse in memory of Isabelle. Craig bent down to take them from him.

"You knew which flowers to bring, Alex, I see," said Craig.

"Yes, Master Craig. I never forget the mistress's favourite flowers."

"Yes, I know that," Craig replied as he laid them gently across his saddle. He turned to give a final wave to the aunts, and to Jamie who stood close by, looking at him so proudly. His bonnie wee lad was home.

Craig and Bruce cantered off down the long driveway, and Dougal came to greet them and to open the tall, wrought-iron gates. He lived in the small gatekeeper's cottage close by. He had lived there since before Craig was born. He had proudly opened the gates to let Bruce and Isabelle through after their marriage and also a year later when they took their newborn son to be christened. He had also opened the gates with a very heavy heart to let Isabelle's carriage through, followed by Bruce and Craig in such deep sorrow. But this day was a happy day. The young master was home again – back where he belonged.

They both smiled as they wished Dougal good day, and Craig turned to wave to him as he closed the gates behind them.

They rode on in silence, both deep in their own thoughts, till they reached the small gateway of the church. They gazed around for several minutes.

"I cannot see anyone from the vicarage," said Craig.

"Well, we won't go to the vicarage today," said Bruce. "We will call another day for a chat."

This day was his and his son's alone. Neither of them felt the need for anyone else – not on this day.

They dismounted, tied their horses to a nearby tree and proceeded on foot along the narrow path leading to the family tomb. It lay on a high rise by the side of the old church, underneath the old oak tree, overlooking the loch, with the snow-crested mountains in the distance.

The silence was only broken by the song of the birds – a late winter lament, it seemed to Craig as he stood there lost in thought. The late afternoon sunlight shone on them both and also caught the inscription on the tomb, which stood out in brilliant gold relief against the black marble.

Craig knelt down and placed the flowers into a vase next to the one his father filled daily with flowers.

"Dearest Mama," he whispered with a catch in his throat, "I am home. We are all together at last."

He wiped away a tear quickly, but Bruce had seen it and turned quickly away. He himself had done the same.

Craig reached out to caress her name in the ice-cold marble. He read to himself the inscription as he traced and retraced her name with his finger over and over again:

Isabelle Constance McNair,
Darling Wife of Bruce (11th Earl of Glencree),
Darling Mother of Craig Alisdair.
Loved for ever.

He got slowly to his feet, still caressing her name as he did so. Bruce stood silently watching him, and a look of utter loss passed between them. Neither of them spoke. Their eyes said all that they felt. The perfect silence of their surroundings added to their complete unison. Now once more only the birds broke the silence.

At the sound of their names being called, they both turned to see the Reverend Corwell hastening towards them.

"Ah, Your Lordship and Master Craig, home again at last. I was so sorry not to be able to greet you. Pressing church matters kept me away too long. But what a delight to see you safely home once more and back amongst us!"

"Yes, it is good to be home," Craig replied. "Tell me: is Charles home yet?"

"No, not yet, but we expect him soon. How we are longing for the day. We have missed him so, just as your father has so longed for your return. Have you time to join us for tea? I know how much Mrs Corwell and Emma and the boys would love to see you."

"No, not today, thank you, Vicar," Bruce replied. "We promised we would be back before dusk."

"Another day, then, perhaps?"

"Yes, another day, thank you. Please convey our good wishes to your wife and family – and especially to Tony. How is he now?" asked Bruce.

"Much better in himself, thank you, Sir Bruce."

"Oh, good! I am very pleased to hear that. Good day!"

The Reverend Corwell watched as they retraced their steps and mounted their horses, and, with a final wave, they were gone.

"Has Tony not been well?" Craig asked.

"No, he has been very ill; he has lost a leg," Bruce replied.

"Poor, poor Tony – and him so fond of sport! This war seems to have affected everyone."

Not another word passed between them as they rode home.

CHAPTER 20

Jamie was at the door to greet them as soon as he heard the clatter of the horses' hoofs on the cobbled courtyard, and the stable boys came hurrying to take the horses.

"Will you join me for a drink, my son?"

"No, not just now, Papa. I will join you after I have changed for dinner."

"Very well, then, but don't be too long," Bruce called after him as he watched him race up the steps – as always, two at a time.

Flint waited till he heard Craig's door close, then he followed. Jamie came up behind him and stepped over him on the mat. Jamie gave Flint a smiling scolding, and then Craig called out to tell Jamie to enter. Craig had flung himself on his bed, sad and depressed.

"I have prepared your bath and laid out your clothes for dinner, but you have grown so much since you went away: I doubt if any of them will fit you now."

Craig rose slowly from the bed. "Oh, I am sure they will, Jamie, thank you, but I shall soon be going into the village to see Sanders and get measured for a whole new wardrobe."

Craig revelled a long time in his first real bath for years. He lingered in its luxurious warmth and tried to recall the last time.

'Yes, it would be when I was in the convalescent home down south that I had the joy of such a bath as this. How thankful, too, am I that I have not been too badly wounded and wasn't affected too much by the gas!'

He was not in a hurry to get out of the soothing water.

As he dressed in his best Highland dress, he viewed himself ruefully in the long mirror. He tried to pull the now too short sleeves further over his wrists. The collar was far too tight, and the kilt was far too short.

"It will have to do for the time being. It is just too wonderful to be able to put my Highland dress on at long last."

He combed his unruly waves, and decided that he looked just the same as when he went away – but a sadder, wiser man.

He opened the door to find Flint standing there. His tail was wagging furiously, and there was a look of patient longing in his eager brown eyes. Craig looked at him with a deep affection. He hadn't realised how much he had missed his faithful dog. He knelt down and cupped his face in his hands and hugged him to him.

"How I have missed you, my dear friend! Come now, old faithful – let us away."

They both hurried along the passage and Craig stopped to look at the stained-glass window, caught now in the flickering lights of the chandelier. The colours had taken on a different hue since he saw it in the morning light. He gazed at the swirls of purple and white heather entwined around the border like a long ribbon, the family motto in bold gold letters at the bottom of it, and the bright scarlet of the Highland dress of the first laird in the middle of it.

'He too,' thought Craig, 'seems to have a special smile of welcome for me.'

"Yes, I am back," he called out to his ancestor, and he smiled up at the figure, who seemed to be smiling down at him. "Everyone seems to be happy today. I could even smile at the man in the moon without batting an eyelid at my stupidity." He looked again at the picture. "Oh, you are not such a bad old devil really – is he, Flint?"

When he heard his name, the dog gazed up at his master questioningly. Craig was still looking at the picture, his mind flooding back to his childhood. He thought of the times when he had committed some minor misdemeanour and was sent to his room by his father. It was a picture he had always hated then. As he passed it dejectedly to do his father's bidding, this figure always seemed to be chastising him also. He would hurry past it as fast as he could. Craig's thoughts wandered on and on. He imagined he could still hear the sound of Aunt Harriet (she was visiting at the time) exclaiming to his mother: "Oh, that boy! A good boarding school is what that boy needs. It will curb all his mischievous pranks and high spirits. The furious way he rides that pony of his all over the glens, fishing and sailing on the loch with the boys from the village when he should be studying more about his inheritance! He is so like his father – so wilful."

How like him *she* was, he used to tell himself. She always wanted him to grow up too soon and to be too serious for his age. She was always worrying about his being thoroughly educated and learning about managing the estates. She wanted him to spend his time with his father, learning about the problems of the crofters and the buying of stock and all the other things he would need to know as heir to the estate and the future 12th Earl of Glencree.

"He does forget he has a duty to all this. And, Isabelle, you must see to it that he never does forget it," she once said.

'How she did go on and on!' he thought.

He remembered the sweet voice of his mother, above his aunt's: "But, my dear Harriet, how ever will I get used to the idea of my small boy going so far away from his father and me to some strange boarding school?"

"Yes, me too," agreed Aunt Elena. "I couldn't bear the thought of our darling boy so far away and not here when we come visiting. These little pranks are only childish games, and he is only a child."

He could still see his mother sitting doing her embroidery, listening to both of them, now and again smiling at the way they carried on, but Aunt Harriet would still keep on and on.

"There's no time for games in this life – especially for him. He must always be preparing for his future tasks."

Then Aunt Elena's voice could be heard again: "All in good time, Harriet. He is only a child. There is plenty of time for that serious business."

'Dear, dear Aunt Elena,' he thought. 'She could always be relied on to take my side, no matter what I had done.'

Craig could always get round her. She always seemed so quiet and unassuming, but she spent a great deal of her time tending the villagers when they were sick, and she saw to the education of their children and the welfare of the families, always accompanied by his mother. They would take produce and gifts from the estate to the outlying crofters, who always worked so hard tending their crofts, which often yielded so little for all their efforts.

The church also, and the missionary work connected to it, was her very life and devout passion. Often she would go overseas for long visits. He remembered how much he missed her visits to the castle when she was away. Her absence seemed to him, child that he was, to last a lifetime. Then, suddenly, she would be back with them again. He would sit on a small pouffe at her feet in front of the roaring log fire, listening in awe to the tales she had to tell of strange places and people. The long winter evenings were made shorter as he sat spellbound. He remembered her telling him of the natives she had seen: women with long necks stretched by the many necklaces they wore, men with coins in their ears and some even in their top lips. He hoped one day to go with her and see them for himself. She told him of the poverty and the strange sicknesses, and the many strange animals she had seen. He knew she would only be home long enough to raise more money to help those people. Yes, of his two aunts she was his favourite, and, next to his parents, he loved her best.

'Aunt Harriet is good to me also,' he told himself, 'but she is so stern. Sometimes she frightened me.'

Harriet was capable, staunch and immovable; everything had to be done correctly and quickly; she had never seemed satisfied with anything Craig tried to do. She had never forgiven fate for the death of her husband.

One day they were climbing in the mountains and she slipped on some loose shale. Robert, her husband, struggled to reach her, but he overbalanced and fell crashing to the rocks below. She watched in horror as he hurtled down. In an effort to save him, she stumbled, permanently damaging her leg so that now she walked with a limp. They had married only the month before.

Craig recalled how his mother had tenderly nursed her through it all. Then he recalled, as he still stood there, that after his mother died the aunts had come back to the castle to care for him and his father. But, even then, Harriet still kept on about him being sent to a boarding school instead of wasting time playing with the village boys. She wanted him to be educated properly.

'Ah, yes,' he told himself as he ceased staring at the first laird in the window, 'the glad days, the sad days! But what am I doing dwelling on the past like this? Today is a happy day for us all – the happiest of days. I am home at last to stay.'

He rushed to the top of the stairs, lifted Flint up in his arms and threw one kilted knee over the bannister rail. He gripped the dog tightly and commenced his swift descent below. Flint remembering this trick from his puppy days, knew he was quite safe in his master's arms and he enjoyed it as much as Craig did. At the bottom, Flint tumbled out of Craig's arms as they parted company with the rail and landed on the soft mat. A wild "Whoopee!" heralded their coming.

Harriet, Elena and Jamie were standing talking in the hall, and they looked up as they heard the familiar yell. Harriet looked at Craig askance as he landed. There was a look of disbelief on her face.

"Now, don't say it, Aunt Harriet!" Craig exclaimed.

"Say what, my dear boy?"

He laughed joyfully as he sat there. "You surely haven't forgotten, dear Aunt?"

"No, I haven't forgotten."

She stood as she did in days gone by, with her hands on her hips, as if in dismay

"That boy is once again up to his old tricks," she said.

They all laughed heartily together as Jamie helped Craig to his feet. Then Elena and Harriet went into the dining room. His father was in the lounge, standing gazing into the blazing log fire.

"Oh, out of your uniform at long last, I see!" he said as Craig entered.

"Yes, Papa, at long last, thank goodness."

"The dress hardly fits you now, my boy. The sleeves are too short and so is the kilt."

"Yes, it is," replied Craig. "I shall have to have a complete new wardrobe."

"And that you will surely have, my son."

"But, however badly this fits, it is wonderful to be wearing it."

Craig moved over to the small table and poured himself a drink.

"One also for you, Papa?" he asked, holding the bottle high. "To celebrate my homecoming and the end of the war to end all wars, as the saying goes! Surely, Papa, there just couldn't be anything so dreadful ever again." He sighed deeply.

"Now, my son, let us not talk of it or dwell ever again on such a disastrous affair."

He put his arm round Craig's shoulders, and they both stood gazing into the fire.

"We will have to see that the boys who have returned home get some work and help financially. It will take a lot of our time, but it will have to be done. I will have a lot of visiting to do, Papa, to make sure none of them want for anything which it is in my power to give them."

"Yes, I know that, my son. Elena and I have already visited most of them, but there are still some to be seen who have only just got back – like yourself."

How alike they were! Craig was now as tall as his father, and their proud, dark heads were level with each other. Father and son at the same moment instinctively raised their eyes to the one who was never far from their thoughts, and they both stood lost in contemplation of bygone days that would never ever return. They stood silently for several minutes, both seemingly on his own, yet both felt that the three of them were together at last.

Bruce went to the small table and brought back the half-empty whisky decanter. He filled Craig's glass and his own.

"Now we must drink to our being together at last," he said. "Nothing now will ever part us again."

"To us!" they both exclaimed, as they clinked their glasses together and emptied them.

CHAPTER 21

"How are things on the estate now, Papa?" Craig asked.

"Oh, not too bad, in spite of so many of the men being away at the front for so long. We can go ahead now with a lot of new plans. There are alterations to be done, and we need to buy more stock, now things are getting back to normal everywhere. I have bought more land from Lady Roxburgh, who was telling me the other day that, due to her advancing years and poor health, it is all too much for her now. Margot, as you know, came over from India to stay with her during her serious illness. She is anxious to return now that her mother's health has improved, and the war is now over. I am constantly visiting the old dear and Margot. It seems the old dear wants to sell the house and go and stay with her sister up north when Margot returns to India. The house should be up for sale pretty soon, I should think, as Margot is desperately anxious to return to see her own daughter, who now has twin girls. She is anxious to see them all and, of course, get back to her mission work and school.

"Fiona's father has already shown some interest in it and some of the adjoining land as a wedding present for you both, so you will see how much extra property and land you and Fiona will possess when you eventually marry. Both the General and Fiona think that it will be an ideal place for you to live after you marry."

Craig exclaimed angrily, "Oh, no, Papa, I would not, under any circumstances, live anywhere else but at Glencree Castle. It is my home and my sons, as you know, have all got to be born here. No, no! I would not agree to that plan."

"Well, I did explain to Fiona and her parents that it might not be possible. However, nothing has finally been decided, so do not worry about it, my son. It is, as you say, quite out of the question."

"I shall never leave this, my home, ever again. I shall tell the General and Fiona that when we marry I will stay here and have the West Wing altered to suit Fiona in any way she wishes. The aunts can have Harrison Hall."

"Yes, I am sure the aunts would like that; then they would not be too far away from us. I will discuss the sale with Lady Roxburgh and Margot," said Bruce.

Bruce could still see that Craig was perturbed.

Craig continued: "Papa, you know what this old house means to me. It holds everything I hold dear in life; my happiness is woven into its very being. For instance, I can't even consider leaving the garden Mama used to tend so lovingly. However, it was very kind of Fiona's father to make the offer to buy the property for us. I shall tell him so tomorrow when I visit. You did say, Papa, that Fiona would have arrived by tomorrow, didn't you?"

"Yes, my son," Bruce replied, "her father said so when I last saw him."

"We must leave very early in the morning, Papa. I am so longing to see her. I can't wait to see her again."

"And she you! The General was saying how busy she has been with all her voluntary work all these years."

Bruce was glad Craig had dropped their previous topic.

The dinner gong sounded loud and clear.

"Oh, what a lovely sound that is!" said Craig. "It's so much better than the old bugle call of 'Come to the Cookhouse Door, Boys'."

They both laughed heartily. Neither saw Harriet and Elena enter the room.

"Just look at the two of them, Harriet," Elena whispered to Harriet, "together at last after all this long waiting. It's been such a long time. I could weep with joy just to see them standing side by side, as they did in days gone by, with the picture of dear Isabelle between them. How happy they would be if she was only here with them! Don't you agree, Harriet?"

"Yes," she said, never very generous with remarks of praise or delight.

"They sure are a delight to behold. Craig is now as tall as his father," Elena continued. "How like Bruce he is when he was his age! Do you recall, Harriet?"

"Yes, I recall, but Bruce was always much more serious than Craig is," she remarked.

"Yes," continued Elena. "Craig has a lot of dear Isabelle's wit and charm, gaiety and spontaneous laughter. She had such a love for living every moment. Do you remember her joy when she danced? She certainly was a delight. Do you remember those little tricks she used to play on Bruce to tease him so?"

"Yes, yes, I agree," said Harriet. "He is much more like his mother in that respect, but he, like Bruce, can be so unpredictable at times."

Craig overheard their subdued conversation and turned to greet them.

"Now then, you two little chatter-birds, what are all these secrets you are sharing?"

"We were just deciding which of you was the most handsome," declared Elena, "but we agree how wonderful you both look tonight in your tartan."

"Now, come, dear aunts – let me pour you a drink to celebrate my homecoming. Now, what will it be, Aunt Harriet? Sherry tonight?" he asked, although he knew she hated it. "Why not try a tot of whisky for a change?" He was only teasing her, as he knew she was especially fond of a wee dram. "And you, Aunt Elena – have one too."

"Well, only a medicinal tot," she said, "to soothe my excited nerves."

She was normally against drink, but tonight she felt that a little medicinal tot was quite in order for this happy occasion.

"Now, Craig dear," she repeated, "only a medicinal tot."

He laughed gaily at her insistence as he poured out far more than a medicinal amount.

"Just a little more medicine tonight, dear Aunt Elena! And yours, Aunt Harriet – is yours only a medicinal amount also?"

"Now, now, my dear boy, you are already starting your teasing. You know as well as I that I am no stranger to the whisky, so a little more for me, if you please."

Yes, he knew she was no stranger to it: it was a habit she had acquired after the shock of her husband's death. She would shut herself up in her room sometimes, drinking far too much.

"Here's to my safe return home," said Craig, "and to this happiest of days. No more waiting for tomorrow!"

They all drained their glasses of the soothing amber liquid.

"The vicar will certainly approve of your celebration drink tonight, Aunt Elena," said Craig, laughing.

"The dinner will be ruined – tonight of all nights!" exclaimed Cook. "Sarah, go and sound the dinner gong again and announce yourself at the door."

The maid hastened to do her bidding. The dinner gong sounded again and

Sarah announced that dinner was served. They all turned towards the door as she made her announcement.

"We're coming," said Harriet.

"Yes, I am ready for my first dinner at home!" exclaimed Craig. "I am hungry."

"Is your appetite improving already, now you are back in the glens?" asked Bruce.

"Yes, Papa – no more bully beef and dried biscuits from now on!"

They proceeded to the dining room. Bruce took the arm of Lady Harriet and led the way, followed closely by Craig with Lady Elena, all laughing gaily as they went. The effects of the whisky were now starting to show. The laughter could be heard in the kitchen.

"The Good Lord be praised", Cook said, "for the joy and laughter once more back in this house. The young master is back to stay for ever. There will be no more tears in this old house ever again."

Sarah reappeared at Cook's elbow.

"Oh, how happy everyone is, Cook!"

"Well, of course, my girl. The young master is home. Everyone will be happy now – and none more so than Sir Bruce himself, after all he has gone through. He has waited so long," said Cook. "Now, hurry and take in the soup, or it will be too cold."

She watched as Sarah and Shona hurried away before she turned again to the big ovens, which tonight had given her rosy-hued face an extra glow. She opened the door once more to give the dish an extra turn.

"That is just right!" she exclaimed to herself. "What a happy day it is, to be sure! It is good to be preparing Master Craig's favourite meal once more. I can hardly believe it's true after all this time."

She had never known a happier day since the day he was born.

"Fancy him being old enough to go to war, war, war!" she said, and she shuddered as she uttered the words. "How his poor mother would have hated him having to go. However, glory be to God, he is back with us."

She wiped away tears of gladness and sadness from her eyes with the corner of her apron.

Harriet and Elena stood back as they reached the dining-room door. Jamie was standing there waiting for them, his face, too, beaming with smiles. In his own mind he echoed Cook's sentiments. There would be non-stop laughter now that Craig was back. He opened the door wide and Bruce stood at one side to let Craig in first.

Craig stood spellbound with amazement at the sight that met his eyes. He stared at it all in disbelief. The old mahogany furniture glistened in the bright ruby glow from the flickering firelight, and Craig could see all its fine carving, done by their own wonderful craftsmen so many years ago. The beautiful oak panelling around the walls gave to him a wonderful feeling of warmth and homeliness as he entered. The glittering chandeliers, which hung over the long family dining table, were fully lit. The gleaming crystals looked like huge glistening raindrops, suspended in mid-air. Two silver candlesticks, each holding eight candles, stood at each end of the table, and in the centre was a huge arrangement of glorious flowers. The old family crested silver and priceless glasses were laid out at each place setting.

Two pipers at the head of the table started to play the moment Craig entered. The last time he had seen the dining room laid out like this was when his mother was alive. He looked at his father, who was also taken aback at the splendour of it all. Craig glanced at both the aunts, who had followed him in, and they both smiled at him when they saw his pleasure. He turned to them.

"Oh, dear, dear Aunts, how wonderful you both are to me! Thank you so much," he said, and he kissed them on the cheeks. "Everything is just so perfect."

He helped them both to their seats, as did Bruce, and Jamie busily poured out the table wine.

"Oh, I see, Papa," Craig said, "that you have brought up the special vintage from the cellar."

"Why, of course, my son – especially for your homecoming: your favourite."

"Also we are having venison, and the special pudding you always insisted on as a small boy," said Elena.

"I have dreamed of this day, never thinking I would ever again be sitting here amongst you all," said Craig.

He glanced up at the large picture of his mother. She, as always, was dressed to perfection. Her beautiful satin gown seemed to be shimmering as it caught the reflected lights from the chandeliers.

"I must remind the vicar," said Bruce: "we must hold a special service of thanksgiving for the ending of the war and the safe return of our brave men to their homes."

"And a special service to honour our brave men who will never return," said Elena.

"They will never be forgotten, dear Aunt, as long as we live," replied Craig.

CHAPTER 22

As they left the room, Craig suddenly exclaimed, "Papa, I must go and thank Cook and all her staff for this wonderful meal, and I must get them some wine and whisky from the cellar. Sarah, please tell Jamie to come here as soon as he can."

"Yes, Master Craig," she replied, and she hastened away to do his bidding.

"They must all celebrate my homecoming, Papa."

"Just as you wish, my son," Bruce replied.

Jamie soon appeared.

"We are going to the wine cellar," Bruce said. "Will you arrange the lights?"

Jamie needed no second telling. Of all the rooms in this large house, this was his favourite haunt.

"Elena and I will go to the lounge for coffee. Join us there when you return," said Harriet.

Bruce and Craig followed Jamie down the long corridor to the door of the wine cellar and waited whilst Jamie opened it with a heavy key, which he then put safely away in his pocket. Jamie proceeded down the old stone steps, lighting the flares on the wall one by one as he descended into the dark depths below. Bruce and Craig followed on behind, holding on to the iron rail of the twisting stairway. It was cool and dark, even with the lighted flares.

It was a place Craig, as a child, had viewed with an intense dislike because of the darkness. Jamie would try to coax him to follow him down, but he always declined, as it filled him with foreboding.

"I daresay, Jamie," Craig called to him, "you could find your way down here without the flares." His voice re-echoed in the vastness of the vault.

Craig had only just been getting used to the vastness of the cellar before he left for the front, and now it seemed as though they would never reach the bottom.

"Are we nearly there, Jamie?" he called.

"Yes, nearly there now, Master Craig," he said, and his words were repeated by the chill echo of his voice.

At last they reached the bottom and proceeded along the rows of old casks of mellowed wood – row upon row of the finest old wines and whiskies of the homeland. The McNairs' own special blend had been produced and labelled with the family crest. The racks were full to overflowing.

"My goodness!" exclaimed Craig. "Papa, it is about time we started to celebrate and so reduce this stock."

"Yes, it is, my son, I know, but we have had nothing to celebrate for so long – no parties or gatherings."

"But now I am home, Papa, we can have parties again."

"We certainly can, my son. Our home has been so dull for too long."

"Oh, I will soon remedy that", Craig said, "when all my friends join me here."

"How well I realise that!" said Bruce. "We have missed you and all your friends so much."

"That we have, Master Craig," rejoined Jamie.

Jamie knew off by heart which wines and whiskies the staff preferred, and after a short discussion the bottles were selected.

"Now, Jamie, pick your own bottle," Craig instructed.

Jamie made his own choice and placed it in a large wicker basket along with the rest. Before they wended their way back, Craig chose a bottle for himself also. He carefully put it under his arm.

"Jamie," said Bruce, "can you return later to put out the flares? Also, you must return for a further supply for all if needed – and don't forget the pipers," he said, laughing.

"As if I would dare forget them, Sir Bruce!" Jamie replied. "They wouldn't let me forget them. It would be more than my life is worth," he continued. "Piping is thirsty work."

"Now, Craig, you carry on with Jamie. I am going to join Elena and Harriet. Join me there when you return."

"I will, Papa. I won't be long."

"Jamie, don't go into the kitchen for a moment."

"Very well, Master Craig."

Craig hurried down the steps to the kitchen and kicked playfully at the door.

"Cook, Cook, let me in," he pleaded.

The kitchen was always a favourite haunt of Craig's as a child. Sarah, who had been cleaning up in the kitchen after dinner, looked up anxiously at Cook.

"Who is that, Cook?" she exclaimed.

"Why, that will be the young master, I daresay, up to his old tricks so soon. I am coming, Master Craig, I am coming!" she exclaimed in mock alarm, hurrying to open the door. "I couldn't think for a moment who it might be," she teased.

"Yes, dear Cook, it is me as of old, knocking once more on your kitchen door."

"Well, you are now back for good and just as welcome in my kitchen as before."

"Now, Jamie, put the basket down here," said Craig.

He proceeded to lift the bottles out, one by one, and he placed them on the table – the same old table he used to lean against when, as a child, he watched her at work. However, Cook's kitchen was always forbidden territory. His father and, more so, Aunt Harriet, would scold him if he was seen there.

"I have brought you all a drink to celebrate my homecoming and to thank you for the splendid dinner tonight. It was just like old times. I can hardly believe it is true. Now I must hurry and rejoin my father. Goodnight," he called as he left.

"Goodnight, Master Craig," they called to him.

"And thank you," Cook called again, as she followed him to the door and watched fondly as he raced up the steps two at a time.

Shona and Sarah curtsied as he passed.

Cook closed the door after him, feeling very pleased with the praise Craig had showered upon her. The girls were pleased to see her so happy. They had had such a busy, tiring day, but it was all worth it, they agreed.

"Now, we can all relax and enjoy the master's gift," said Cook, and the girls knew only too well how fond she was of a wee dram.

CHAPTER 23

Elena poured out Bruce's coffee as soon as he entered the room. He sat down in his favourite chair, from which he could see Isabelle's picture. His eyes hardly ever left her face when he was sitting there, especially when he was alone. But now things would be different, he told himself. Now he was at peace with the world. All would be well.

"I have never seen him look so contented and happy and peaceful," said Elena. "He deserves it so much and he has waited so long."

"Well, the boy is home now. He has so many plans set aside for both of them to do," said Harriet.

Craig entered the room like a gust of wind, talking and laughing excitedly. "Now then, Aunt Elena, are you going to sing for me?" He went over to the piano. "I wonder if I can still play as well as I used to?" he muttered as he sat down.

"Oh, I am sure you can," murmured Elena, "after all the lessons you had. You always play well. Here is your coffee. Drink it before it gets too cold."

'How like old times!' Craig thought.

When the aunts visited, they would all gather round as his mother played the piano and his father the violin, and he, as a child, would stand turning the pages of the music for his mother as the aunts sang a duet.

"What shall I play for you, Papa?" Craig asked.

"Oh, anything, my dear son, anything. Some of our Scottish melodies would be fine."

"I will try any that I can recall, although I doubt if I can remember all I was so carefully taught."

As he commenced to play it was evident that he had lost his touch and would have a lot of practising to do before he was up to the standard he was before he went away.

Harriet and Elena looked at each other and smiled. Their smiles said it all: 'He is back with us: what else matters?'

"No, no, it is no use!" he exclaimed. "I cannot find my touch. Maybe another night, Papa! I am too tense and excited about being home, and I am very tired after all my travelling."

"Come and sit by your father. More coffee?" Elena asked.

"No, thank you, dear Aunt, I will, as you say, just sit here beside Papa."

"Elena will play tonight, won't you?" suggested Harriet.

"Of course I will," she replied.

She sat down to play, and the others leaned back in their chairs, lost in the beautiful Scottish melodies.

Craig was the first to break the silence: "Do you remember, Aunt Elena," he called out to her, "when you and mother used to sing such lovely duets with Papa playing for you?"

"Yes, I remember all those lovely evenings we had so long ago."

She looked across at Harriet, who was searching for more music, she wondered if she should continue playing if it brought back so many memories. She knew how it always upset Bruce.

Craig had closed his eyes as he listened, and now he reopened them. He glanced across at his father and noticed that he was gazing up at Isabelle's picture. Craig's eyes followed his gaze.

"How beautiful Mama was, Papa! So beautiful!" he repeated.

Bruce looked across at him as he broke into his thoughts. "Yes, so beautiful in all she did!" He gave a deep sigh. "If only she could be here with us now!"

"Yes," replied Craig. "If only she could be with us again!"

Harriet stopped looking for more music when she overheard the two men. She and Elena looked at each other anxiously.

"Well," Elena said as she jumped up from the stool and closed the lid of the piano, "what shall we do now?"

"We could play cards," Harriet suggested.

She was as anxious as Elena to get the four of them involved in something to get the men's thoughts away from Isabelle, tonight of all nights.

"Yes, of course," said Elena as she went to get the cards out of the drawer. "We haven't played for such a long time."

"Oh, yes," said Craig. "I haven't played cards in such ideal company for years. The last time I played was in the trenches between spells of waiting for further orders to come through."

The games continued in gay abandon until Bruce exclaimed: "That's enough for me, for tonight at least! I will take Flint for his evening stroll."

Flint, who was lying at Craig's feet, pricked up his ears as he heard his name, but made no move to get to his feet when he heard the word 'stroll'. Tonight he was staying put.

"Ah, I see!" Bruce exclaimed, as he looked down at him. "You have got your own master back with you now, so you don't want me."

"Fancy that, now!" exclaimed Elena. "All these years Bruce has taken him for his evening stroll, and now Flint is deserting him. What do you think of him, Harriet?"

She was busy putting the cards away and only grunted a reply: "I am not surprised really."

Craig bent down to pat Flint's head.

"There, there, my boy! We will all go for a stroll."

"Not for me tonight!" said Harriet.

"Or me," said Elena. "We have had such a busy, exciting, wonderful day. Harriet and I will retire."

"Thank you, dear aunts, for such a lovely welcome home and a wonderful dinner. It has been such a wonderful day."

He kissed them both before they mounted the stairs.

On the landing they turned to call out a final goodnight. "We will rise early tomorrow," Harriet called down to them.

"Yes, call us early. We are riding out to see the General and I know someone wants to see his Fiona," said Bruce.

"How right you are, Papa! I can hardly wait for tomorrow to arrive, but first we must take this faithful friend of ours for his evening stroll."

As they went along the hall, Bruce reached for one of his canes hanging on the wall.

"I see, Papa, you still carry your cane."

"Yes, my boy, I never travel without one."

The sound of music and gay laughter and chatter floated up to them from the kitchen below.

"They're all enjoying their celebration tonight – just about finishing their dinner, I think!" exclaimed Craig.

"It will be the first of many celebrations, my son," said Bruce.

The two men crossed the main courtyard and Flint disappeared into the shadowy moonlight. Bruce and Craig stood side by side, gazing across to the mountains in the distance.

Elena, gazing out over the loch from her bedroom window, could see the two men she loved so dearly, silhouetted in the moonlight.

"What a wonderful sight to behold! They are together at last. Oh, how I have prayed for this day! Nothing will ever part them again. All is well," she whispered to herself as she drew the heavy curtains together. Then she knelt beside her bed in silent prayer.

As Bruce and Craig stood there, looking out over the loch, Craig said, "How calm and peaceful the loch is tonight, Papa! It is so different from last night."

"Yes, it was the night of the storm, to be sure," replied Bruce.

The stillness of the night was broken by the chimes of the old church clock.

"How wonderful, Papa," Craig exclaimed, "to hear once again the old chimes! I never thought I should ever hear them again."

"Well, my son, they are there for you at last. I often thought you might never return to hear them again, but at last you are home. Now, where has Flint got to, I wonder?"

"Not far, I warrant," said Craig, and, as if by magic, the dog was by his side. "Ah, there you are, you rascal." Craig bent down to pat him. "Come, my old faithful friend – it is time for us all to retire."

They wended their way back into the house. Jamie was closing the shutters one by one as they passed him on their way up the stairs.

"The last job of the day, Jamie?" Craig called to him.

"Yes, Master Craig. It has been the happiest of days."

"We are travelling early tomorrow, Jamie. Wake me at seven sharp."

"Just as you say, Master Craig. Goodnight."

"Goodnight, Papa. Thank you for such a wonderful day."

"Goodnight, my dear boy. I shall rest peacefully now you are safely home."

Craig watched his father's door close behind him and entered his own room. He flung himself on to his bed.

"Oh, how weary I am!" he exclaimed aloud. "I'm so weary but oh, so happy. I still can't believe it: I am really home at last."

He rose and went over to the window and flung it wide open to breathe in the fresh mountain air.

"Yes, yes, these are my mountains and I am really home."

His gaze wandered over to the far side of the loch, and to the dear family who had sheltered him from the storm. He closed the window, pulled the curtains together, and so ended his own perfect day.

CHAPTER 24

The following day dawned clear and fine. The early morning sun glinted through the small chink in his curtains.

"Another joyous day has dawned for me," mused Craig as he wakened to the persistent knocking of Jamie, who had come with his early morning cup of tea.

Craig had wakened refreshed after a peaceful night in his own bed, but he was still unbelieving as he gazed slowly round his room.

Jamie's voice called, "Master Craig, Master Craig."

'Is that really Jamie's voice?' he asked himself.

"Come in, come in, Jamie," he called.

"What a grand morning it is, to be sure, Master Craig!"

As soon as the door was opened, in rushed Flint, who had sat outside his door all night and had been waiting patiently for such a moment. He jumped straight onto the bed, but, as soon as he saw him coming, Craig pulled the pile of bedclothes over his head. The dog immediately started digging as frantically as he could, whimpering as he did so, to find his beloved master.

At last Craig emerged, to the delight of the dog. He hugged him close.

"Here I am, old pal. I won't ever leave you again."

Jamie drew back the curtains and called to the dog: "Come down, Flint. You know you are not allowed on the beds."

"Oh, he is all right," said Craig and laughingly rolled Flint over and over in the bedding.

The bed was a shambles, much to Jamie's consternation. Flint was trying to free himself, his tail flailing around. He let out yelps of joy when he reappeared from the blanket and found his master again. Craig laughed wholeheartedly. Never had he enjoyed an awakening so much.

The noise and commotion brought his father to the door and he stood watching the rumpus for a few minutes. No one knew he was there. He was dressed in full riding habit, his jodhpurs finely tailored, and his snow-white silk shirt outlined his magnificent physique. His coat was slung over his arm. He tapped his riding crop idly against his thigh as he stood laughing at the antics of Craig and Flint enjoying themselves so much. He was loath to intervene. How wonderful to see at last so much happiness! Craig and his dog were just as they were before he went away. Craig was already up to his old tricks. Yes, it was so good to hear all this laughter in this fine old house. It had seen enough of sorrow, partings and silence. Now there would be young people around again, and parties as before.

'Of course,' Bruce thought, 'the first party will be Craig's official engagement to Fiona.'

As her name crossed his mind, he suddenly remembered that they must be on their way with no more delay.

"Now, Flint," he called, "that is enough."

The dog, as obedient as ever at the sound of his voice, looked up at him as if to heed him. Then, to Bruce's consternation, he carried on as before. He had not had a good romp since Craig went away, and he was reluctant to stop.

"Craig, we have a long journey ahead. Have you forgotten how far away Fiona's house is?"

"No, Papa, I have not forgotten. I will soon be ready. Down, boy! Down, boy!" he called to Flint.

The dog obeyed at once, with a look as if to say, 'Must it really end?' Craig gave him a final pat on the head.

"The homecoming romp must cease now, but we will spend all our time together from now on."

As Bruce turned to go, Flint followed him out.

"I will be in at breakfast, my son."

"I won't be long, Papa," Craig called after him. "Are all my things ready, Jamie?"

"Yes, Master Craig."

"Well then, I must hurry."

Harriet and Elena were already at the breakfast table as Bruce entered.

"It sounded like old times with those two upstairs romping about," said Elena. "And hearing your laughter too – ah, it is so good to have him home. I still can't believe it."

A sudden thud came from the hall, followed by a cry of anguish and fright from Sarah, who was coming from the kitchen with their breakfasts. The three of them hurried out to see what the commotion was all about. Craig was in a heap on the floor.

"One day", declared his father with a laugh, "you will grow up and leave sliding down that rail to your children."

"Yes, I agree; I am really out of practice," he told the four of them.

They looked at him with amusement – all except Sarah, who had almost dropped the tray she was carrying in her alarm. She put down her tray and rushed over to help him to his feet.

"Don't bother, Sarah. He does it all the time!" exclaimed Harriet.

"I am all right, Sarah. Thank you for your concern. I can see these others are not a bit concerned."

They all laughed as they proceeded to have breakfast.

"What time will you be back?" asked Elena.

"I don't know," said Bruce. "Craig will want to stay as long as possible with Fiona."

"I most certainly will," Craig said.

Jamie passed him his riding crop as they prepared to leave.

"We will be back for dinner, Harriet," Bruce called to her.

"Invite them over to stay," Harriet called after him.

"I most certainly will," Bruce replied.

"Come then, Elena – as soon as they have gone we will go and tell Shona to prepare the West Wing for them."

"Craig," Harriet called after him, "tell them they can stay as long as they wish."

"Thank you, dear aunts. I daresay you, Aunt Harriet, will be making all the preparations for their visit?"

"I most certainly will, my boy."

"And you, Aunt Elena?" Craig asked. "What will you be doing today?"

"Well, first I will go to the vicarage, then on to see Margot, to discuss with her and the vicar's wife our plans for helping our missions. Our work has been interrupted so much due to the war, but I know Margot is anxious to get things moving again as soon as possible. She means to return to India, and I shall, of course, be visiting her there."

"I see," said Craig. "You are already making plans to travel overseas as soon as possible, but I hope you will help me get some aid to our boys back from the front. You know so many people who can help me."

"Yes, my boy, that is my first priority."

"Come, my son," Bruce called to him: "we have a long way to go."

They were soon on their way, waving a cheery goodbye as they sped down the drive. Jamie was as crestfallen as Flint, who he was holding on his lead, as they watched Bruce and Craig out of sight.

"It is too far for you today, Flint, your master said, but soon you will be running over the glens with him as before."

Jamie realised Craig might frequently be away from Glencree Castle visiting Fiona.

"Ah well, I daresay he will be more at Fiona's home than ours now. Come, Flint – I have work to do."

The journey exhilarated Craig as they sped along the narrow, winding paths, rich with young spring foliage. The pure mountain air cleansed his lungs of the foul gases he had inhaled at the front.

"How good this lovely clean air is, Papa!"

"Yes, my son, you will soon feel as fit and strong as you did before you left."

They reined their horses to a halt and viewed the vista before them: the mountains in the distance, which seemed to stretch on for ever, the valleys and glens and rushing waterfalls, the blueness of the tall pines on the hillsides and the shining silver loch below them. The silence was broken only by the shrill shriek of a startled bird in the hedgerow.

Craig started to hum a favourite tune and said to his father, "Yes, these are my mountains. Now I know I am really home."

They carried on along paths that would only allow one at a time and his father, ahead of him, kept turning round as Craig constantly stopped to admire the scenery.

"Come, my son – we have a long way to go."

They hurried along, skirting the edge of the loch for several miles. Ahead Corrie, an old fisherman, was standing watching them approach. This bridle path was not often used, especially so early in the morning. Corrie soon recognised the laird.

'Is that Master Craig with him?' he asked himself as they got closer. 'Yes, begorra, it is. The bonnie wee laddie is home at last.'

His face lit up in a huge grin as he recognised Craig.

"Good morning, Corrie. How are the fish biting today?" asked Craig.

"Quite well, Master Craig," he replied. "It's a delight to see you safely back."

"Yes, it is good to be riding the trails again with my father," he replied.

They bade Corrie good day and he raised his cap as they sped away. He shaded his eyes from the early morning sun as he watched them out of sight.

'That's just as it should be – just like old times – father and son riding side by side at long last,' he thought to himself as he turned back to his line.

Craig and Bruce quickened their pace.

"We are now on the land I have bought off Lady Roxburgh and Margot," said Bruce. "They have decided they cannot manage it any longer and, as I explained before, they will be selling the house eventually. If you recall, Craig, Margot had to return from India to care for her mother some years ago, but her mother's illness lasted longer than she anticipated. Margot has decided to stay until her mother is well enough to travel to her sister up north. She is most anxious to get back to her mission station – more so now the war is over. As you see, my son, the land is very extensive."

"And how is Lady Roxburgh now?" Craig asked.

"Well, one day she seems quite well and then another day not too well at all. That's what puts Margot in such a quandary. She is also practically blind."

"Oh, I am so sorry to hear that," said Craig. "She is such a very sweet lady."

"Yes, she is," his father continued. "It seems Margot has now got a companion for her, and the companion also helps Margot with all her correspondence, so that has helped a great deal. Also, she is hoping to get a nurse soon."

"I am sure that will help a great deal," said Craig. "Margot must have much more correspondence now that things are getting back to normal. I must go and visit them very soon."

"Yes, you must, my son. They are both very fond of you."

The paths had now widened and they were able to ride side by side, resting their horses now and again.

"Nearly all this land will be yours one day," said Bruce proudly. "The General will own the rest, so you can see that, when you and Fiona marry, you will have a very big estate to hand on to your sons."

"Well, Papa," said Craig, "what with all this and my mother's property too, I shall certainly have to get down to my studies on estate management, which were so rudely interrupted by the war."

"All in good time!" said Bruce. "You must first have a good rest and visit all your friends and invite them all to stay, as they used to do. There will be your wedding to arrange and all the accompanying celebrations. Also, we have to have a Highland gathering. It will be the first one since before the war. I foresee such a lot of good times for us before you start to manage the estates. Until then, Dunby and his son can manage, now he is old enough."

"Dunby's son, Papa – how old is he now?"

"About sixteen," Bruce replied.

"My goodness!" exclaimed Craig. "How quickly time flies! He was quite a small boy the last time I saw him."

They had now reached a small croft in a clearing in the woods. They reined their horses to a halt and alighted.

"We will rest here awhile," said Bruce.

"Still the same old resting place!" remarked Craig.

"Yes, and here is Mac and Ian to greet us, as always."

"Greetings and good day to you, Your Lordship and Master Craig. Welcome home."

"Thank you both," replied Craig. "It's good to see you all again."

They walked towards the small homestead as Mac called to his wife: "Katy, Katy, here is His Lordship and Master Craig."

She rushed in from the kitchen and dropped them a small curtsy as she exclaimed, "Welcome! Welcome to our small home. The young master is lucky today: I have got some warm griddle cakes ready, and I know how much the young master likes those."

"Yes, I do like them," said Craig. "Oh, I had them so often here when I used to call on you. Has your son, Lawrie, returned yet from the front?"

"Yes, he is visiting his sister in Glasgow at present," she replied.

"I must see him as soon as he returns," said Craig. "Was he wounded at all?"

"Just shrapnel wounds in his leg," said Mac, "but he is doing well now."

"Now we must be going," said Bruce after they had eaten the cakes and enjoyed a long conversation. "Thank you for your hospitality."

"It is an honour, Your Lordship."

"Ian will bring round your horses now. They are rested and fed," said Mac.

They waved their goodbyes and set off at a gallop. The family watched till Bruce and Craig were out of sight.

Craig had taken his coat off at Mac's home. The sun had risen higher and he was warm with the effort of galloping alongside his father. Their dress was alike in every detail, except that his white silk shirt was too small; it clung to his broad shoulders and slim waist. His black wavy hair was blown back from his high, proud forehead by the breeze. His dark-brown eyes glistened with the thrill of it all.

The sheep, grazing peacefully on the high moorland, raised their sleepy eyes and watched as the two raced past. In the distance were the scattered crofts, isolated and yet so closely connected with the closely knit village in the bay. That was where everyone met to discuss the land problems and collect their supplies from the local grocery store when they knew Magnus had arrived with them.

Bruce was a father figure to them all, and he thought of them as his family. He knew them all by their Christian names, as did Elena and Harriet. Isabelle had known them too. Craig knew that, given time, he too would get to know all their names.

Bruce stopped once again and Craig drew alongside him. Both were now a little breathless with the exhilaration of their gallop. In the distance, Craig could see the tall turrets of Lady Roxburgh's Harrison Hall, and the small bridge over the stream was visible, as the trees were only just starting to sprout their canopy of green. Bruce was the first to break the silence.

"Yes, my son, as you can see, everything is just as you left it. We have left everything in its place." There was a lilting laugh in his voice as he spoke.

"Yes, so I see," said Craig, laughing back at him.

"I must call and see Margot and her mother soon," said Bruce, "to finalise the purchase of her land. Now, my son, what do you think of it all up to now?" Bruce asked.

"It is just perfect, Papa – too perfect for words! There is such peace and serenity. It is unbelievable after all the noise and melee I have had to endure all those years along with the rest."

"Well, my son, this will, like our family line and heritage, last for ever. Nothing can ever take it away."

They urged their horses forward once more and, for several miles, rode side by side, laughing and chatting.

"It seems a long way today, Papa," Craig said.

"I daresay it does, my son. That is because you are so anxious to set eyes on your lovely Fiona."

"Yes, you are so right as usual, Papa."

They broke into a gallop, Craig following his father as the lane narrowed. Again Bruce came to a halt and Craig drew alongside.

"We are now entering the General's land, and just round the bend you will see the house you know so well: Ravenswood Hall. Ah yes, there it is," said Bruce, "but there are still quite a few miles to go."

"Then we must hurry, Papa," said Craig and he set off at a gallop, his hair blowing wildly in his face, his father close behind him.

Suddenly, across his path shot an excited dog, barking furiously at his heels, followed by another one. He reined his horse to a halt and his father drew alongside.

"It is only Prince and Royal, the General's dogs. They are always together, so he too won't be far away, I warrant."

The General suddenly came into view, hurrying to see why the dogs were barking. He called the dogs off and rushed over to greet the two men with a happy smile on his face. Craig dismounted to greet him.

"My son, my son, how wonderful to have you home again," the General said, and he hugged Craig close. "You have been away such a long time."

"Yes, but now I'm back home for good," Craig said.

"No more leaving us again! I know what you are waiting to hear."

"Yes, sir. Tell me, is my darling Fiona home?"

"Yes, my son, she arrived only last night and I know she is longing to see you. So hurry on, my boy, whilst your father and I follow on at a more leisurely pace. We have a lot to talk about. We were not too sure when you would arrive."

"I only arrived yesterday."

The two men stood aside, watching Craig remount, and, with a grin and a wave of his riding crop, he was away like the wind in a cloud of dust up the long drive to the house.

"My word, Bruce!" the General exclaimed. "What a fine bonnie boy he is!"

"Yes, to be sure," Bruce replied. "I am blessed with a wonderful son."

"He's soon to be my son too," the General reminded him.

"And your lovely Fiona is to be my daughter as soon as their wedding can be arranged."

"Yes, I know Fiona is longing for the day. This war has caused such a long delay, but it is all over now and everything can get back to normal."

They walked side by side, Bruce leading his horse, as they went slowly up the long drive. Craig was now out of sight.

"Fiona will be the perfect mistress for Glencree Castle," her father said.

"Yes, I agree," said Bruce. "They will make a delightful couple."

"They will, no doubt, marry very soon," commented the General.

"There's no reason why not," said Bruce, "now he is back home."

"He has also come of age for his mother's inheritance. She also owned property and land. Of course, he will be very busy attending to the business of selling it all. He will have enough land here to take care of, especially with all the extra land I am buying from Margot."

The General nodded his head in full agreement. He was most anxious for the wedding to be as soon as possible. He had set his heart a long time ago on his daughter becoming mistress of Glencree Castle and his grandsons eventually owning all this land.

Fiona was sitting at her dressing table tying a ribbon in her hair. Her maid, who was unpacking, glanced towards the window as she went towards the wardrobe to put her mistress's gowns away.

"Mistress, mistress!" she exclaimed startled. "A rider is approaching at a mad gallop up the driveway."

"Well, who is it, girl?" Fiona asked sharply.

"He is too far away for me to see who it is, Lady Fiona."

"Oh!" exclaimed Fiona. "I do hope Papa has not met with an accident."

She started to rise out of her seat in alarm.

"No, mistress, it is not one of our estate boys. I can see him more clearly now."

Fiona stepped out onto the verandah overlooking the drive to look for herself, and she screamed with delight. Her excitement was almost uncontrollable.

"It's Craig! My darling Craig, home at last!"

She ran quickly across her bedroom, along the long passage and down the long winding stairs. She stopped only for a fleeting moment to make sure her appearance was just right, but, as always with Fiona, it was just perfect. She always had to reassure herself, but then she was off again, her long, dark hair tied back with a ribbon that matched her yellow dress. She ran across the hallway and out through the huge doorway, turning quickly to the right to the steps leading to the garden – the way he always came. At the top of the steps she stopped a moment to regain her breath and rearrange her hair.

Craig had already reached the bottom, and he looked up and called to her: "Fiona darling!"

She gazed down at him, still unbelieving that at long last he was here. When she reached the bottom of the steps he leaped from his horse and gathered her up in his arms as if he would never let her go again. He swung her round and round, laughing gaily, and, as he put her dizzily back on the ground, he smothered her with kisses. He whispered her name over and over again as he buried his face in her long, dark hair, which shone like a raven's plumage.

"Oh, how I have longed for this moment!" he sighed. "I dreaded your not being here when I arrived." He was kissing her hair and her ears, over and over again. "Darling, I love you so."

As she opened her lips to speak, he gripped her in a breathless hug and his lips closed over hers.

"We are together at last – the day I thought I would never see. We shall always be together now, just as before. Nothing will ever separate us again."

He released his tight hold of her slim waist and looked down into her lovely hazel eyes, which sparkled with love and ecstasy. She was gasping for breath as she looked up at him adoringly.

"My darling, darling, I am quite breathless but so very happy."

She put a wisp of her hair back into place and reached for the ribbon, which was now on her shoulder. It had fallen there when Craig had untied it to bury his lips in her hair.

"Come – we must go inside. You must be quite thirsty after your long ride."

"My thirst is only for you," he replied, as he kissed her again and again.

He held her gently by the waist as she tried to tie back her hair with the ribbon and he, as quickly, untied it again and again.

"Oh, my darling, you are just as big a tease as ever you were," she laughed.

"And," he replied, "I shall be more of a tease now that I am back. Then you will know that I am really home."

He took the ribbon from her and playfully wound it round both their wrists as they climbed the steps. They were both quite breathless with gaiety and laughter. They looked up to see both fathers looking down at them adoringly. Bruce hugged Fiona to him and kissed her fondly on the cheek.

"See, Papa," she called to him, as he hugged them both together, "we cannot now be separated ever again. Craig has tied us together."

"So I see!" her father exclaimed. "It is so good to have you home at last, Craig, my boy. You both have been separated for far too long."

The four of them stood for several minutes, taking in the superb view from the terrace.

"We hope to see you married very soon. That will make us two fathers very happy – the laird with Fiona as his daughter, and me with his fine boy as my son," continued the General.

He had longed for a son and heir ever since his only son had died at birth. His overriding concern now was the marriage of these two, so that his daughter's sons would one day inherit the earldom and all that went with it.

Lady Cleveland almost swooned with delight when she was informed of their arrival by Kirsty.

"Now all will be well!" she exclaimed aloud. "Now he is home at last."

At last her two principal aims could be fulfilled. She was determined to achieve both as soon as possible. The first was Fiona's coming out: her presentation at court and the London Season; and the second was her marriage to Craig.

'To think', she told herself, 'it could have happened a long time ago but for that dreadful war!'

She hastened outside to greet them.

"Lady Cleveland!" exclaimed Craig. "How wonderful to see you again! It's been so long."

"Far too long, my dear boy. My, how you have changed! You are so much taller and even more handsome than before you went away – don't you think so, Fiona?"

"Oh, Mama," she said, "he is the most handsome man I have ever seen."

She looked up at him adoringly and he kissed her tenderly. Both of them were oblivious of the ones beside them, who were looking at them with parental delight.

"Now, we must all go inside. You must be quite exhausted after your long ride," Lady Cleveland said, turning to Craig and Fiona. "Now, you two children come along," she called to them, as they still stood, too enraptured with each other to heed her calling.

"Children?" exclaimed Craig.

"Oh, Mama still thinks of us as two small children – as if we have never grown up. Only when she has her grandchildren around her will she ever stop thinking of us as children." Fiona looked up at Craig as she spoke. "That won't be too far off now, will it, my precious one?"

"No, my darling," Craig replied, looking deep into her lovely questioning eyes. "I still haven't got used to the idea that I am at last really home."

"But you are back home now, my darling."

"I know I am, but sometimes I still cannot believe it is true."

"Now, come – we must go inside. Your mother is calling."

At that moment the lunch bell sounded. "My, my, how quickly time is flying!" exclaimed Craig. "It's already gone midday."

"Well," said Fiona when they were all seated, "we must first all toast your homecoming. Papa has been saving a special champagne just for this occasion."

As soon as the meal was finished, Fiona rose to her feet.

"Craig and I are going for a stroll in the garden, Mama. We have so much to talk about."

"Now, take your wrap, dear," her mother called after her. "The afternoon air can be quite chilly. Kirsty, hurry and get Miss Fiona's shawl."

"Yes, ma'am," she said, and she hurried away upstairs.

Craig put the shawl lovingly round Fiona's shoulders and led her out to the garden.

"Shall we have a game of chess, Bruce," suggested the General.

"Yes, it is a long time since we last played," replied Bruce.

"Well," said Lady Cleveland, "if you are all going to be occupied, I will go and lie down for a spell. All this excitement has been too much for me today: Fiona arriving home and Craig here at long last." The pleasure was evident in her voice as she thought what Craig's safe return would mean to them all in the future.

"Very well, my dear," the General called after his wife as she prepared to go.

Craig and Fiona ran swiftly down the steps to the garden. They stopped to kiss and then strolled across the lawn hand in hand.

"Mama says I cannot possibly be married until I have done the London Season with my cousins, and that won't be until next year. No arrangements could be made for us this year as we didn't know when the war would finish and preparations take such a long time. There will be all the balls to go to and dresses to be made. To think," she exclaimed petulantly, "if the war had ended sooner, this would have been the year of my coming out and our marriage, my darling."

Craig looked at her pensively, turning over in his head the words she had spoken.

"Yes," he said a little sadly, "yes, my dear. It would have been better if the war had never happened in the first place."

He noticed she was completely oblivious to the sarcasm in his voice.

She continued: "But we can still go to London in the summer, and stay with my cousins in the country. Mama and Papa and I will be going down this year. Will you come with me, my darling?"

"You know I couldn't possibly stay away from you. I could take the opportunity, whilst I am there, to visit a lot of my old comrades, to see how things are going for them."

"Oh, you can't possibly, my darling," she said. "We will have so many of my friends to meet and invite to our wedding. We cannot possibly find the time, unless whilst you are visiting your men, as you call them, I shall have to visit my friends without you by my side. It will look too ridiculous for words."

"Well, I shall do as I have said, otherwise I shall not go."

She looked up at him in disbelief for a fleeting moment, but really she knew that he meant it. She remembered several instances in their childhood when she had tried to get the better of him: she always failed.

'But', she thought to herself, 'if he is with me in London, I shall see that he has as little time as possible to visit his men. He speaks of them as though he is the father of them all.'

"How long are you proposing to stay in London, my darling?" he asked.

"About two months, but certainly not less than six weeks," she replied.

"But, darling," he said, "I cannot possibly be away so long – not even a month. I have been away from West Wing far too long as it is, and now I am of age I have to attend to the inheritance from my mother. It will take most of the summer to attend to it all."

"Yes, my darling, I had quite forgotten about all the time it will take you to sort all those things out."

'Yes,' she told herself, 'I had forgotten he is now of age to claim his mother's estates and add those to our children's inheritance. Of course, I shall have to let him get all those things settled first.'

"Yes, my darling, forgive me. I am so excited at your being here with me again," she said demurely, "that I just don't know what I am saying." She looked up at him and said, "Kiss me. Kiss me again and again, then I will know I am not dreaming."

"How can I keep kissing you when you chatter on so much?" he teased. "It's so wonderful to have you in my arms once more. We will always be together now, my darling," he said. "Nothing now can ever keep us apart."

"How safe I feel here in your arms! Hold me very close, darling," she whispered, "and never let me go."

"I will never let you go," he replied, "but we must now part for a short while. The afternoon is getting late and you are quite chilled."

"But darling, I am never chilled when I am with you. Kiss me again before we go inside."

He pulled her shawl closer round her shoulders and kissed her again and again. Then they ran quickly up the steps, laughing like the two happy lovers they were. Her shawl fell on the steps as they ran and Craig almost fell over it. He bent to pick it up, and she stood laughing down at him from the top of the steps. She reached out both arms to grasp him to her, and his lips found hers as he slid the shawl round her shoulders. "Come – we must go inside. Papa and I have a long journey home."

The two fathers were watching them from the library window.

"What a beautiful couple they make!" exclaimed the General, and Bruce nodded in agreement. "They are so perfectly matched in every way," he continued. "They will join our two families together for ever."

"Yes," agreed Bruce, "that is the day I long for also. I realise how much you will miss her when she comes to Glencree Castle to stay after they are married, but you will always be able to stay as long as you like."

"I know that, my dear friend, but I think my wife and I will spend more time in London. She misses it so and also longs to see more of her sisters."

Craig and Fiona waved gaily to their fathers and ran into the library to join them. Craig stood next to the chessboard and exclaimed: "Ah, his queen has you in check, I see, Papa."

"Yes, my son, the General is beating me today. I cannot concentrate. Your homecoming has caused me too much happiness."

"That goes for us all," said Lady Cleveland as she entered the room.

"Now then, my dear boy," Bruce said to Craig, "I know you are still reluctant to leave Fiona's side, but we have a long way to go and must be back for dinner."

"What a pity!" said Fiona's mother. "Another day, perhaps?"

"Why can't you stay the night?" said Fiona. "The aunts will know where you are. It's not fair that your stay is so short. I have hardly seen my darling Craig."

Her bottom lip dropped in disappointment. She, who usually had every whim immediately granted, did not wish to be disappointed this time.

Bruce looked at her a little anxiously. He knew how possessive she could be and he had no intention of letting his son stay away from his side yet.

"Now, we will be waiting patiently for you all to join us soon at Glencree Castle in a few days," said Bruce.

"But why a few days?" exclaimed Craig. "Why not tomorrow?"

He looked lovingly at Fiona.

"Because, my dear son," said Bruce, "Lady Cleveland's brother is coming to stay with them for a few days. He too has only just got back from the front."

Craig whispered to Fiona, "It is just as well it is only for a few days or I would be riding over every day."

"Well," she said, "couldn't you still?"

"No, I have lots of visiting to do with Papa, and I know he would disapprove of my intruding on your uncle's visit here."

Craig had noticed the look on his father's face. He wanted his son all to himself for a while.

They all followed Bruce and Craig to their horses, which had been waiting there for some time. Craig and Fiona trailed behind, reluctant to part. Before mounting his horse, Craig kissed her passionately; then he swung himself into the saddle. Fiona hung on to his hand for as long as she could as their goodbyes were said. Then Bruce and Craig were finally away. Craig turned to give a final wave before they were out of sight. He had eyes only for Fiona. When he blew her a kiss, she returned it almost in tears.

She watched several minutes after they had disappeared from view, as if she was willing him to reappear.

"Oh, how I have missed you, my darling!" she murmured. "I love you so much."

"Come now, my dear," her father called to her. "It is far too cold for you to stay out any longer."

"All right, Papa, I'm coming." Sad and forlorn, she rejoined her parents. Papa," she said, "I can't really believe he is here at long last. It is like a lovely dream come true."

"Well, no more dreams, my dear!" exclaimed her mother. "He is home for good. Nothing will ever separate the two of you ever again. Now," she said with glee, "we can start to make all our plans for the London Season and your wedding next year. What a shame there isn't time to arrange it for this year. That dratted war has spoiled everything. I can hardly wait for it all to take place. My plans have had to wait so long," she said, and she tut-tutted to herself. "However, this year will soon pass. We've got plans to make and then our darling daughter will be Craig's wife at last."

But Fiona had gone to her room quite disconsolate.

"Do you hear me?" Lady Cleveland said to the General, who was idly putting away his chessmen.

"Yes, my dear, I hear you."

CHAPTER 25

As Magnus rowed over the loch he grew more and more pensive. His thoughts were only on one thing: when would his beloved son be home? A week had passed since he had taken the young master of Glencree Castle home.

'Surely,' he thought, 'our dear boy should be on his way by now? They should all be home by now, surely – well, all except the ones who will never come home again. I must be more patient. At last we do know that our son has been spared. I wish he was here,' he sighed.

Daily, as he returned from the village after taking the stores over, he would call at the little post office or accost Lawrie, the postman, on his rounds.

"Any mail for us today?" he would say, but he already knew the answer when he saw their sad faces.

"Maybe tomorrow," Lawrie would say.

"Yes, maybe," the postmistress would add. "Yes, maybe tomorrow," she would agree.

"Yes, maybe tomorrow," he would reply.

'How many more tomorrows must we wait?' he asked himself.

Martha would be anxiously waiting at the side of the loch for Magnus's return, and he would look up at Elizabeth's window, from where she always looked out when she knew Martha was going to greet him. But when she saw him shake his head, she would sadly let the lace curtain flutter back in place.

Every day Martha asked him as he stepped ashore, "But when is our Roddy coming home?"

And every day he put on a brave face and told her, "It will be soon. It will be very soon now, it can't be much longer."

Magnus delivered all the goods he had to that day before calling into the post office to see if there was any mail. But he didn't want just any mail. He only wanted one bit of news. He spotted Lawrie with his head in the big bag that held the mail.

"Hi there, Magnus," he called to him. "This has just arrived for you," and he held out to him the small buff-coloured envelope. "I just know it is good news for you. Didn't I take good news to the master at Glencree Castle a week ago?"

Magnus took the envelope from him.

"Well, I hope this is the same news that His Lordship received."

"Oh, I am sure it will be. I just know it," said Lawrie. "Open it and see."

Magnus's hand shook slightly as he opened it, and a big smile crossed his face as he read the letter.

"Yes, Lawrie, it is good news. Now, this will bring a smile to Martha and Elizabeth's faces."

"How is dear Elizabeth now? I believe she was quite ill," asked the postmistress with concern.

"Oh, much improved now, thank you. She will be better still when I get home today with this," he said, and he waved the letter gaily in the air before slipping it safely in his pocket. He bade them good day.

He sailed back that morning with a much happier heart, and he was surprised to see that Martha was not at the edge of the loch awaiting him.

'Ah well, she must be busy in the kitchen,' he told himself as he tied up the boat.

"Martha, Martha, we have good news at last," he called excitedly.

She came hurrying out of the kitchen, wiping her hands on her apron. Elizabeth, hearing the excited voices below, jumped out of bed, hastened to the top of the stairs and started to descend.

"Mama, Papa, what is it? Do hurry and tell me," she demanded.

"Now don't you dare come down those stairs without your gown on," her mother said. "You don't realise, my child, how ill you have been."

She pulled a wry face and hastened back to get it, and she almost fell down the stairs in her haste.

"Yes, my dears," Magnus declared. "He is on his way and will be home – well, now, let me see? – two days from today."

"Oh, my darling Roddy home in two days!" shrieked Elizabeth, and she danced round the room, waving the precious letter in her hand.

"The Good Lord be praised," said Martha as she sat in the big chair by the fire, wiping her tears of joy away on her apron.

"Two days!" exclaimed Elizabeth, rather glumly. "Two more days! It's so far away, Papa. Are you sure we have to wait so long?"

"Read the letter, my angel."

"Yes, you are right, Papa," she said forlornly. "But, Mama, it seems such a long time." She went and knelt at her mother's knee to hug her.

Martha dried her eyes. "My darling child, we must be thankful our Roddy has been spared to come home to us – so many of them have not."

"I am sorry, Mama, I mustn't be selfish and impatient, but I have missed him and I know you and Papa have also."

She kissed them both on the cheeks.

"It's not too long, my child, after all our waiting," said Magnus.

"I must come to the station to greet him, Mama."

"Well, if you are well enough," said her mother.

"Of course I am well enough, Mama," she pouted.

"Well, if you are wrapped up warmly, maybe it will be all right."

"Mama, I have got to go and meet my darling Roddy."

"Now you must get back to bed, then you won't get another chill. Don't get too excited!" she exclaimed.

"All right, Mama, just as you say; but I will be well enough, you'll see. I am so much better now."

"I know, my child, but you still have to take care," her mother replied.

After she had gone, Martha and Magnus clasped each other and both wept silent tears of joy.

"Now I have such a lot to do," Martha said. "Oh, what a joy it will be!"

"I will go and tell Peggoty to come and join us for a cup of tea whilst we tell him the good news. I will also tell him it will be something stronger when Roddy does arrive home," said Magnus.

Martha, Magnus and Peggoty sat round the table talking. Peggoty, who had no family, was always made most welcome. He had missed Roddy and Elizabeth a great deal when they had been sent away to reside with their Aunt Ingrid, but now they would both be back to stay and they could all enjoy being together again.

"Yes, nearly everyone is back home now!" exclaimed Peggoty, "– and about time too. There will be lots of parties to celebrate their homecoming."

"There will be so much gladness; but there has been so much sadness in the homes of the ones who will never return. God help them to bear their great loss," said Martha, and she sighed a deep sigh.

"Now I must be away," said Peggoty, and he closed the door on another happy home, waiting for their soldier son's return.

Elizabeth returned to her room and grabbed a pillow from her bed.

"I just cannot go back to bed," she said. "This is such good news. My darling Roddy is coming home at last."

She danced round the room, singing one of his favourite melodies. Round and round she went, lost in her own delight.

Her parents looked up at the ceiling in dismay as though expecting it to come crashing down on them.

"How happy our little girl is – and what a beautiful songbird she is!" said Magnus.

"Nothing will stop her singing now," said Martha. "Go and tell her to stop jumping around so much and to get into bed. Take her the letter. She may want to read it again, just to make sure it is really true. I will be up directly. I have some work to finish."

When Magnus entered Elizabeth's room (after she bade him enter) she was gazing out of the window.

"I have brought you the letter to keep, my angel," he said.

To her adoring father she was always his angel. He watched as she gazed out of the window, and he thought back to the day she was born. She had been born just as dawn was breaking, the silver streaks of the sun striking the tops of the mountains in the distance. He had waited patiently for her birth, always declaring to Martha that it would be a girl. When he saw that Martha had borne him his dearest wish, his happiness knew no bounds.

"Ingrid," he said to his sister, who had come to visit them specially for the event, "have you ever seen such a beautiful angel? Isn't she just too wonderful?"

"I suppose," Ingrid replied, "you have already named her?"

"Well, she is certainly a heaven-sent gift, and she was born just as dawn was breaking, so she is called Dawn Angeline," he had declared emphatically.

"What does Martha say about that?" she'd replied.

Well, Martha had said all along that if it was a girl, he could have his wish, as she had chosen Roddy's name. However, she had made it clear to him that their daughter should also be called Elizabeth, after her own mother. She was also given the name Ingrid, after her aunt. So the matter was settled, or so Martha thought.

"I shall always think of her as my dawn angel," said Magnus.

"Well," said Martha, "Elizabeth will be the name she will be known by. What do you think, Ingrid?"

"Yes, I agree. It is a lovely name and more suitable for everyday use," said Ingrid, solidly behind Martha.

But Magnus was quite adamant about his choice of names, and so she was duly christened, Elizabeth Dawn Angeline Ingrid.

"Well," he said as he handed her the note, "and what does my Dawn Angel think of the good news I brought her today?"

"It is just too wonderful, Papa. I can hardly believe it's true after all this time."

"Yes, we also!" exclaimed her mother, as she entered the room. "Why, my child, are you still standing at the window? Come – get into bed before you get another chill."

"I am feeling so well now, Mama, and I'm too excited to stay in bed, but I will do as you say, Mama. I just know I will be well enough to meet him."

She clambered into bed, and Martha and Magnus sat on the bed beside her, reading and rereading the letter over and over again.

"Well, we will have to go now, dear. Your father and I have so much to do before he comes."

After they left, she gathered the bedclothes round her shoulders and hugged the letter to her.

'Dear, dear Roddy, coming home at last! Now, let me see: how long is it since I last saw him? I just know it's years and years. Now I recall: it was when I went to stay with Aunt Ingrid before I went to the music academy. Yes, yes, now I remember. Roddy had joined a junior corps and he came to spend some leave with us. Then he was sent off to the war, and I haven't seen him since. I wonder how tall he has grown. I just know he will be as handsome and as tall as the soldier who recently spent the night here.'

She shuddered as she thought of the indignity she had felt as she stood there in the full light in her nightgown with Craig laughing at her. She pulled the bedclothes further round her shoulders as if to blot the memory out.

'He had no right', she told herself, 'to pretend to be my Roddy. Why, to think he was a total stranger and he still had the audacity to turn the light up higher and laugh. Oh, he had no right!' She pouted indignantly. 'But I won't give him another thought. My darling Roddy is coming home and that is all that matters.'

She slid lower and lower down the bed, hugging the good news to herself.

CHAPTER 26

The happy day dawned at last. Elizabeth woke to the early morning sun streaming in through her window. She hastily flung back the bedclothes and gazed out over the loch.

"Oh, what a beautiful, beautiful day!" she exclaimed with delight. "Now I must hurry and dress."

She could see her father by the side of the loch, tying up the boat.

'Papa must have been up very early. He must have already been to the village with supplies.'

She could also hear her mother busy downstairs, singing a song.

"Oh, what a happy day, to be sure! Such a happy day! I must hurry and get ready for Roddy's homecoming," she said, and she started to sing a happy song.

After washing, she sat at her dressing table, brushing her long, blonde hair, which she had inherited, her father had told her, from a distant Nordic ancestor, along with her sapphire-blue eyes.

"Well, I feel much better today," she told her reflection in the mirror. "Don't you think I look quite well?" she laughingly asked herself in the mirror. "Of course I do," she added, as if her reflection had said something to the contrary.

She burst into a happy song as she busied herself getting ready.

The day since the letter arrived had seemed like a week to her. She had tried to help her mother but somehow only succeeded in getting in the way. Martha had told her repeatedly to go and play the piano and sing. ("You have missed so much practice lately.") But somehow she couldn't settle to anything for more than a few minutes. She was far too excited. She had watched her father sail over the loch to take supplies to the village, but her mother had refused her request to accompany him, saying it was too chill a wind and she was only just getting well.

Martha had spent all day in the kitchen, baking and cooking for her son's return – replenishing the stock after Craig's visit. Everywhere one looked there were batches of home-made bread and cakes and tarts – everything her dear son loved. As a small boy, he had raided her cake tins as often as he dared. How angry she got when, to her dismay, she found the cake tin empty and she had very little to offer visitors; but how often she had wished, when Roddy was at the front, that he was back raiding her tins again. She had carefully stored everything that she knew stored well. Now they had all been taken out of their storage places, and the baking was complete.

"But what can I do?" Elizabeth kept on asking.

"Well, as you cannot settle to playing anything, you can come and help me prepare Roddy's room."

That gave her some pleasure, but the day had gone far too slowly for all of them.

Now at last it was the day when Roddy would be home. She was bursting with happiness as she looked at herself in the glass, her eyes dancing with the sparkling happiness she felt. Her black eyelashes were in sharp contrast to her fine porcelain skin, which was still too pale after her recent illness.

"I must hurry or I won't be ready in time."

Magnus had come indoors after tying up the boat and attending to the animals.

"That is the only trip I am making over the loch today. Today is my son's day.

Like the Earl of Glencree, I have waited for far too long. Now it is the day to welcome my son home."

He came over to Martha, and gave her a fond hug as she placed his breakfast on the table.

"You made good time from the village today!" she exclaimed. "I very nearly hadn't got your breakfast done in time."

"Well, have you forgotten what day this is?" he said teasingly. "The Good Lord has been more than good to us in more ways than one," he said. "Just hearken to our little angel singing. Doesn't she sing like a nightingale?"

"She has never stopped singing since she rose this morning," Martha said. "I don't think I have ever heard her sing so sweetly before."

"It is because she is so happy," replied Magnus, "and, like us, she has not been truly happy for years.

"It was so kind of Ingrid to pay for her to have her voice trained at that expensive music academy and, of course, for Roddy's fine education too. We could never have afforded it, although it has been such a sacrifice not to have them with us for all those years when they were growing up. Then Roddy had to go to the front for such a long time, and now our dear girl has to go to Harrison Hall as companion to Lady Roxburgh, so we shall see far too little of her."

"Now, do hush, Magnus dear, and hearken to our little nightingale. She's almost a grown woman now."

They both stood for several seconds listening. Then suddenly she came running down the stairs.

"Papa, Mama," she exclaimed in surprise, "are you not ready yet? Do you not know what day it is?"

They all three let out peals of laughter.

"Do hurry," she continued, "or we will miss seeing Roddy get off the train."

"All right," said her father. "It won't take long for us to change."

"Now, come, my child," said Martha, " – you must eat something before we go."

"But I am too excited to eat, Mama," she replied.

"Nevertheless you must," insisted her father.

"Well, just a little, then. I will eat more, I promise, when my darling Roddy arrives. You'll see."

"Always her Roddy!" her father exclaimed to Martha as they ascended the stairs. "The two of them will be inseparable once he gets home. I can see Roddy spending more time visiting her at Harrison Hall than ever he will spend with us. Are you ready, my angel?" her father called to her, as he came down the stairs.

"Yes, Papa, I have only to get my coat and bonnet," she said, and she rushed upstairs.

For the first time she had chosen her own clothes, with some money her Aunt Ingrid had bequeathed to her. The remainder of her inheritance, as with Roddy, would come to her when she married. She slipped into her lovely coat of pale blue with matching bonnet and muff, all edged with white fur. Her button-up shoes were the very latest fashion – and, owing to her excitement she had had a job buttoning them up that morning with her new buttonhook.

She glanced once more in the mirror to make sure her bonnet was on straight. A wisp of her golden hair peeped out entrancingly over her eyes. The rest of her hair, tied back with a blue ribbon, hung in ringlets almost halfway down her back.

What a picture she made! If only she knew how pretty a picture she made, which was doubtful, it never dawned on her to give it a moment's thought. Her aunt and her parents never set a great deal of store with such frivolities as looking as pretty as a picture.

As her aunt would exclaim: "One isn't put on earth to be just a pretty ornament. One has to achieve something worthwhile in life."

When she realised what a lovely voice her niece and goddaughter had, she had decided to offer her the chance to go to the music academy. She had already taught Elizabeth to play the piano, and she had satisfied her aunt in her ability to play well. To sing was an added bonus.

Elizabeth hurried down the stairs to join her parents waiting below. "My word, my angel, what a pretty picture you make! Don't you think so, Martha?"

Martha just nodded her approval.

"We are ready, then," he said, as he proudly led them to the door.

They wended their way past the small landing stage and up the path to the little white gate of the station. Peggoty heard the latch go and knew who it would be. He too had waited patiently for this day. He hurried to meet them, arms outstretched.

"My dear little girl!" he exclaimed as soon as he saw Elizabeth.

"But I am not a little girl any longer," she replied. "I am nearly eighteen."

"No, I know that, my child, but to me, as well as your parents, you will always be a very special sweet little girl. What a day, to be sure, Martha, after all this time!"

"Yes, I can hardly believe it is true. Our son is almost home."

Peggoty and Magnus stood idly waiting and talking, and Martha stood looking into space. Only another mother can understand how she must have felt. Elizabeth couldn't keep still. Her tiny hands were clasped in her muff to keep out the chill morning air, but her feet were dancing and tapping with impatience. Now and again she twirled round in circles.

"Oh, how much longer do we have to wait for the train, Papa?" she asked.

"Oh, do keep still," her mother said. "I am sure it won't be long now."

Her mother was getting quite exasperated with her, but she tried not to show it.

"Oh, when? When, Papa?" she continued to ask.

"Not long now, dear one," he called.

Just then she heard a noise behind her, and she turned to find Peggoty re-approaching. He had gone to check the signals.

"Peggoty, please, how much longer will it be before the train comes?" Elizabeth asked, still dancing up and down.

He took her by the arm, reached inside his waistcoat pocket and pulled out his treasured gold watch – the most valuable thing he possessed. He peered at it.

"Now, let me see," he said, pretending to her that he couldn't quite make out the correct time. "Oh, my pretty one, I should think at least another two hours," he teased. He already knew that it had passed its final signal and he had already seen it in the distance.

She looked at him askance, then she noted a slight smile on all their faces.

"Oh, Peggoty, please tell me. Don't tease me so. I just know you are teasing me."

He relented at last and turned her round by her shoulders.

"If you look far away over yonder in the distance, you will see a puff of smoke."

She looked to where he was pointing and she could just see the outline of the train. She gave a shriek of delight, and hastily ran to tell her parents.

"Can you see the train, Papa and Mama?" she called to them excitedly.

"Yes, yes, child, we see it," her father replied.

Martha, like her daughter, could now hardly keep still with excitement. Her own happiness was only marred by the thought of many of her friends, who would never know the happiness she was feeling now. She said a little prayer of thankfulness that soon her dear son would be home. The thought overwhelmed her. She hastily reached for her handkerchief and dabbed her eyes.

Magnus put his arm through hers and hugged her close.

"There, there, my dear! We must not have tears today of all days – even tears of joy. Now he is almost here. We have waited so long for this day."

The train was now slowing down.

"Can you see him, Papa?" Elizabeth called to him.

"Yes, I see him," he said, and they all waved frantically to the soldier, who was waving his cap in the air as he leaned out as far as he could from the carriage window.

The massive frame of the engine pulled into the station, and its billowing smoke seemed to be everywhere. The noise, like thunder, drowned their happy voices, as its squealing brakes brought it to a grinding halt.

Elizabeth let go of her father's arm and ran up the platform beside the train, frantically calling, "Roddy, Roddy!" She caught his cap as he flung it out, and she kissed it gaily as she ran to meet him. He had jumped from the train before it had stopped, and now he flung his kitbag to one side as he clasped her in his arms and kissed her over and over again.

"My darling little sister! My, how you have grown!"

He picked her up and swung her round and round before putting her firmly on her feet. By now she was quite dizzy.

Martha and Magnus hurried to meet him and he hugged them both. All of them were close to tears. Martha, at last, was overcome and her tears flowed freely. Roddy wiped them away and kissed her tenderly.

"I am home now, Mama – home to stay. It has been such a long, long time, Papa."

"Yes, it has, my son. How are you, my boy?"

"Just fine – just fine, but tired and hungry."

'Well,' thought Martha as she looked at him proudly, 'he always was hungry.'

Peggoty waved the train away and came over to greet Roddy.

"Welcome home, my bonnie boy!" he exclaimed. "My, how good it is to see you after all this time!"

"Dear, dear Peggoty! Yes, I am back to tease you again."

Peggoty laughed as he recalled all the childish pranks this young man used to play on him.

"Thank the Good Lord you are home with your loved ones."

He watched as they wended their way through the little gate where all of them turned to give him a final wave.

"Don't forget, Peggoty, to come to our celebration," Magnus called to him.

"No, I won't," he replied as he locked the little gate. "There's no more trains today."

They wended their way to the side of the loch and, to Roddy, it was the most beautiful sight he had ever seen. Never had he seen it as it was now, its shimmering stillness reflecting the distant mountains in its crystal-clear water. As he looked towards the mountains in the distance he could see the tall turrets of Glencree Castle.

"The young master came home the other day," said Magnus.

"Oh, I am so glad that he too has been spared to come home to his father."

"Yes, he was away for far too long, as you were, my son. We had the honour of putting him up for the night in your room as, owing to a storm, he couldn't get across the loch."

Roddy, as of old, threw pebbles as far as he could into the loch.

"What a fine boy Craig has grown into!" remarked Martha.

"Oh, and what did my pretty little sister think of him?" asked Roddy, as he playfully tugged her ringlets.

"Oh, I didn't speak to him," she replied, a little disconcertedly.

She dare not let it be known that she had appeared in her nightgown halfway down the stairs.

"Oh, what a shame," he teased, "that the young master should not have had the pleasure of seeing my pretty little sister."

Elizabeth was anxious that none of them should notice her discomfort and wonder why, but Martha attributed her heightened colour to her recent illness.

"Come – we must all go inside now out of this chill air. Elizabeth has had a severe chill recently and it is too cold for her to be standing here too long."

"Oh, I am so sorry," said Roddy. "I had no idea."

He hugged her to him. "We cannot have you ill again now I am home. Come – we must hurry."

They wended their way to the cottage, all chatting gaily.

"Have many of my friends arrived back, Papa?" Roddy asked.

"Nearly all of those who have been spared to return," he said sadly. "Some have returned badly wounded."

Roddy looked at his father grimly.

"Wars, wars! Why? Why? What good has it done?" he remarked bitterly. "I must go and see them as soon as I can, Papa."

Elizabeth ran on ahead to open the cottage door after pestering her mother persistently to allow her to be first to welcome Roddy into the house. She flung the door open wide.

"Welcome home, darling Roddy! Welcome home!"

She stood aside and Roddy allowed his mother to enter before he followed her in. He clasped her to him.

"Dearest, dearest Mama, nothing has changed," he said, looking round the room with his back to the door when they were all inside.

"Mama, all I dreamed about whilst at the front was this precious moment. I hoped against hope that one day it would be true."

"Well, it is true at last, my precious son," Magnus replied as he hugged him close.

"Now, I must hurry and get you something to eat. You must be famished," said Martha.

"Yes, Mama, I cannot remember the last time I ate."

The smell of home-baking coming from the kitchen drifted to him, and he hugged his mother to him once more.

"Thank you all for my wonderful homecoming."

He tossed his cap in the corner and followed his mother into the kitchen. He playfully untied her apron strings, and he put a strong arm round her waist as he slyly reached out to take one of the warm griddle cakes.

"Now, now, you saucy boy," she called to him, "up to your old tricks so soon!" She playfully tapped him on the hand with her wooden spoon. "Now go and talk to your sister."

Elizabeth was now standing at the door watching him. 'How like old times this is,' she thought. 'Dear, dear Roddy is back home again and up to his old tricks as if he had never been away.'

"Yes, do come and talk to me," she said, with a playful pout.

They went to sit by the bright log fire and put Jimbo the cat down between them.

"You have missed him also, haven't you?" she said to the cat.

The cat seemed to purr back his answer as Roddy stroked him fondly.

"Oh, it is so good to be home again and not have to worry that I might not see you all and my dear home and bonnie Scotland. Now that is all behind me. They say, Papa, that it was the war to end all wars, so let us hope so. Surely nothing like that could ever happen again?"

"Well, let's have no more talk of war," his father replied. "It is all over now."

Magnus was sitting in his favourite chair next to them, and they all gazed into the fire.

"Come now, little sister," Roddy suddenly exclaimed. "Help me sort out my kitbag and you shall see what I brought back from Paris. I had a few days leave there."

"Paris!" she exclaimed. "Paris! You are not teasing me, Roddy, are you?"

"No, I am not teasing. I really spent a few days leave in Paris."

She watched, fascinated as he untied the cord and dug deep down inside the bag. She gasped in dismay as he brought out his old battered tin mug and several old pairs of socks. "This," he said, holding something aloft, "is my housewife."

"Housewife!" she exclaimed as she took it from him. "Why do they call it that?"

"Because it contains needles and thread."

Then he pulled out an old bugle. He put it to his lips and blew a note on it, which frightened Martha as she entered the room.

"Oh, Mama, I am so sorry. I didn't mean to startle you so."

Martha sat down in a chair, pretending to faint.

"Such a shock it gave me!" she said smilingly as she looked at him with a mother's love all over her face.

"But, Roddy dear," Elizabeth said, a look of disappointment on her face, "I thought you had something pretty to show me?"

He glanced up at her and laughed. He dug deeper and pulled out a pretty shawl. Her eyes lit up.

"Now, that is for Mama, and this pipe is for Papa." Elizabeth took them off him and gave the pipe to her father, who smiled broadly. She draped the shawl round her mother's shoulders.

"My, how pretty it looks, Mama!" she exclaimed. "It's such a lovely colour too."

Roddy continued to dig deeper in his bag, pretending he couldn't find anything else.

"No," he declared, "I think I must have left it behind."

He watched as her smile faded; then he started to laugh and she realised he was teasing her.

'I wish he would stop teasing me,' she thought, 'and show me what he has brought me from Paris.'

"At last!" he exclaimed in mock surprise. "This, my pretty little sister, is for you."

"Oh, what is it?" she exclaimed excitedly. "What is it, Roddy dear? Please don't tease me so."

"Well, close your eyes and hold out your hands," he demanded.

She did so, and he placed a small gold chain and locket and a small bottle of perfume in her hands, and closed his hand over hers.

"Now you can open your eyes."

He smiled at the delight in her face as she looked at them.

"Oh, dear, dear Roddy, my very first bottle of perfume!"

In her haste to smell it, she had difficulty in opening it. At last she managed it and held the bottle under her nose.

"Oh, it is wonderful – real perfume. I can hardly believe it. Thank you, thank you. I shall save it for my very first dance with you, whenever that might be. Surely we will be having dances soon in the village now the war is over."

"I daresay!" Roddy exclaimed.

"Please put my chain on for me. I cannot manage the fastener."

She was so excited. He did as she asked and he hugged her close.

"See, Papa, what Roddy has brought me from Paris. Do you like it? Just smell my perfume."

Magnus did as she asked. Never had he smelt anything like it before, but he agreed it was beautiful.

"And my chain and locket! Oh, Papa!" she said as she went closer to him.

"Yes, my child, they are both very nice."

"Do you like the pipe he brought for you? Mama simply loves her shawl."

"Well," declared her father, "as long as our dear Roddy is home, that is all that matters."

"It truly is," said Martha as she entered the room to lay the table.

"Your meal won't be long now, my son," she said as she went back in the kitchen.

"Well, my son, your homecoming is not as grand as the laird's son's homecoming. They had lights in every turret window and a flag flying and bonfires burning on the hillside as soon as the boat was sighted, and pipers playing him ashore. Yes, he now has his very own piper. Such a homecoming I have never seen the like of – and will never see again, I'll be bound."

"Now, Papa," Roddy said, "nothing could be finer than my homecoming. It's the happiest day of my life. And he hasn't got a sister as beautiful as mine waiting to welcome him home with a big kiss, now, has he?"

He tugged her close and planted a loving kiss on her forehead. He led her to the piano and sat her down.

"Now, my dear Elizabeth Dawn Angeline, play something for me and sing to me while I rest."

He slid into the warm, welcoming comfort of the rocking chair beside the fire, and he closed his eyes and rocked to and fro to the music as she burst into song.

He opened his eyes and gazed in her direction, marvelling at her lovely voice, so clear and sweet.

'How beautiful she has grown,' he thought.

He closed his eyes again, revelling in the peace and serenity of it all.

'This is what we fought for,' he told himself, and his face saddened as he thought of those who had been left behind. 'They died to make such as this possible.'

As Elizabeth came to the last few notes she glanced towards him.

'My, how he does resemble Master Craig!' she thought to herself. 'Anyone could have made the same mistake I did the other night.'

Once again a shudder went through her at the shame she felt.

Roddy was now fast asleep. Elizabeth rose from the piano and closed the lid softly. She crept to his side, and he stirred in his restless sleep. She playfully tickled his nose with the ribbon from her hair and laughed softly to herself as he raised a weary hand to remove it. As he caught it, he opened his eyes.

"Oh, you little minx!" he exclaimed with a start. "You're still as playful as when you were a little girl – just like a little kitten. Ah, how good it is to be home with you all again, in spite of you teasing this very weary soldier."

"I am singing to you," she said, pretending to be vexed, "and you fall asleep." She pouted.

He looked around the room. "Where is Papa?" he asked.

"He has gone to tend the animals," she replied.

"Now, tell me, little sister: what do you do all day? Play with your dolls, I daresay," he teased.

"Ah, but I am not at home all day," she exclaimed, still trying to tickle his nose with her ribbon. "I spend my days at Harrison Hall."

"Doing what?" he asked in dismay, thinking she might be employed there as a servant.

"I help Lady Margot with her correspondence for the missions, and I am a companion to her mother, Lady Roxburgh. I also sing to her. Do you not recall Lady Margot – Emslie, that is?" she corrected herself. "She was a great friend of Aunt Ingrid's. She used to visit her sometimes."

"Yes, now I recall the lady."

"Well, when Aunt Ingrid died and I had to leave the music academy, Lady Margot offered me the post of companion to her mother and asked if I could also help her with correspondence. I have been there for some months now."

"Ah, now I remember. Mama wrote to me about Aunt Ingrid's sudden death. What a dear aunt she was! I am so grateful to her for sending me to college." He suddenly noted the look of sadness on his sister's face and hurriedly changed the subject. "So are you there now?"

"Yes," she replied. "I will be going back soon now you are home and now that I have got over the chill I had. She very kindly allowed me to stay until your arrival."

"Well, that was very kind of her. I am very grateful."

"Come, now, all of you," said Martha. "We can all sit by the fire after we have eaten and talk."

"How my little sister has grown, Mama, since I went away!" Roddy exclaimed. "Now I will be able to take her to all the celebrations and dances."

"Oh, will you, Roddy?" She screamed with delight. "Oh, will you, my darling

Roddy? To think, Mama, I am now old enough to go to dances and Roddy can be my partner! Will you keep your promise, Roddy?"

"Yes, I promise."

She gave him a big hug and danced round and round the table, smelling her perfume.

"Do sit down at the table and eat!" her mother exclaimed. "You will get overtired and be ill again. Roddy is eager to eat after his long journey."

"Yes, let us all eat," said her father, who had been watching her dancing around and singing ever since he entered the room. "That's a sure sign she is better, don't you agree, Martha?"

"And the way she chatters on so! She hardly stops for breath," replied Martha.

"Well," Elizabeth said, "I haven't had anyone to talk to and I haven't seen my brother for years and years and years."

"I am really famished," said Roddy. "I don't think I have eaten for years and years and years," he mimicked back at her. "What have you cooked for my homecoming meal, Mama dear?"

"All your old favourites: soup, and we have some venison."

"Venison!" Roddy exclaimed.

"Yes, Marcus saved us some specially for today."

"A tot of whisky, my son?" said Magnus. "This too has been given to us for today."

"How kind everyone is to think of me."

"Now," said Magnus, "we must have grace."

They all sat down.

"That was a feast fit for a king," said Roddy, as he leaned back in his chair after he had finished eating. "I bet you and Mama have been going without proper meals for months, saving up all these nice things specially for today."

His father put his arm on his shoulder.

"Now, my son, don't you worry about all that. We thank the Good Lord you have been spared to return to our home."

"Come," said Martha: "we will all sit round the fire as we did when you were children – just the four of us. Let us all enjoy our evening."

She rocked to and fro with her soldier son at her feet, and his sister sat beside him at her father's feet, humming a little tune to herself.

"What a perfect day!" Magnus said. He reached out and took Martha's hand and whispered, "Our children back home!"

They looked fondly at each other and then gazed lovingly at the two sitting at their feet gazing into the blazing log fire.

"Yes, it has been such a perfect day for all of us," said Martha.

She rocked to and fro and her eyes finally closed on a mother's perfect day.

CHAPTER 27

The day for Elizabeth's departure to Harrison Hall dawned clear and bright. It had come far too soon for all of them. She had almost finished packing her case. She held up a long black skirt and pulled a wry face as she glowered at it.

"Such a lot of black to wear!" she exclaimed, as she laid it on top of the two already packed. She placed her three snow-white blouses on top and carefully straightened the pretty lace edging on the collars and cuffs.

'Well,' she sighed, 'if I wear the pretty brooch Aunt Ingrid gave me, and the chain from Roddy, I will feel a little gayer. Even my ribbons are nearly all black.' She sighed as she closed the lid. 'At least,' she told herself reassuringly, 'I can travel in my blue coat and bonnet.'

She tied the blue ribbon in her hair and glanced in the mirror as she put her bonnet on. Then she heard Roddy's feet pounding up the stairs, and his voice calling her name.

"Are you ready? Papa is waiting to put your cases in the boat."

"Roddy!" She was almost in tears as he came bounding into the room.

As he glanced at her he noticed a tear trickle down her face.

"Now, now, little sister – no tears!" he pulled a snow-white handkerchief from his pocket and lifted up her chin. He dried her eyes and kissed her on the forehead as he hugged her close.

"But, Roddy," she sobbed, "I have only seen you for such a short time. You were away so long in that dreadful war, and we never knew if you would get killed."

"Well, I didn't get killed, and now I'm home for good. I will be helping Papa with the boats and then I'll get my own croft, so I shall never be too far away from you all."

"Now, you two," called Martha, "your father is waiting."

"Yes, Mama, we are coming. Now dry your eyes. Don't let Mama see you have been crying."

He picked up her suitcase and hurried out.

Elizabeth dabbed her eyes, picked up her small bag and muff, and took a last took in the mirror. She pushed a stray ringlet back under her bonnet, and, with a final glance round her small room, closed the door and ran quickly down the stairs to join Magnus and Roddy at the boat. They waited as she kissed her mother goodbye.

"I am going to miss you all so much, Mama," she said, on the verge of tears.

"Oh, my child," her mother replied, "we will be over every Sunday to church, and your father and Roddy will be over every day to take supplies to the castle and the village; and twice a week they will take supplies to the ladies at Harrison Hall."

"I know, Mama, but it won't be the same as being at home with you and Papa and Roddy. Goodbye, Mama," she called as the boat pulled away from the jetty.

She kept waving her small, wet handkerchief until her mother was out of sight. Her mother's final words rang in her ears:

"Now, my child, you must keep up with your singing and playing. It means so much to us, and also to dear Aunt Ingrid."

"I will, Mama, I will."

"I will take the oars on our way back, Papa," Roddy said. "I am not as quick as you, and you know the loch better than I do. It will take me some time to get to know all its twists and turns, but I know I shall never know it as well as you."

"Just as you say, my son," Magnus replied.

The loch was calm and serene, and Elizabeth leaned over to gaze into the crystal-clear water. She trailed her fingers in it.

"How calm the loch can be at times, and yet how violent when the wind changes suddenly!" she mused.

"How beautiful the mountains and pine trees are!" Roddy called out to her. "Just look over there, my little sister. Isn't it just beautiful? Tell me: is there anywhere else on earth quite like it?"

Her gaze followed to where he was pointing.

"No, Roddy dear, nowhere else in the world is as beautiful as this, our Bonnie Scotland, so I have heard tell. I have never been anywhere else, so I cannot say."

"How tall the pines have grown, Papa, whilst I have been away! They are just like sentinels standing so straight and tall and so proud. Oh, how I missed all this whilst I was away. There'll be no more roving for me now."

Magnus rowed on with a happy smile on his face.

'What a lucky man I am,' he thought.

As they sailed past the private jetty of Glencree Castle, Elizabeth glanced in its direction.

'Am I hoping for a glance of the tall young master?' she asked herself. 'I have passed this jetty before and never given it a thought or glance. Well, maybe I am,' she thought. 'Isn't he just like my darling Roddy? Of course he is.'

She failed to see that Roddy was looking at her closely with a questioning look in his eye.

"Elizabeth, what are you staring at so intently? Is there something of interest on the jetty? I cannot see anything," he said, and he stood up to take a closer look.

"Sit down, Roddy!" Magnus exclaimed. "Can't you see you are making the boat unsteady?"

"Yes, Papa, I am so sorry." He hastily sat down, but he continued to tease Elizabeth. "Maybe it's the young master himself you are hoping to see," he joked laughingly.

She remained silent as he laughed, but she could feel the colour rising in her cheeks. She hoped neither of them would notice it. She was quite cross to think that he had read her thoughts so clearly, but, well, he was Roddy, and didn't he know her thoughts better than anyone else?

"No," said Roddy, still teasing her, "the young master and his kind are not to be stared at by the likes of us. You should know that, my pretty little sister."

"But I wasn't staring or hoping to see anyone!" she exclaimed indignantly.

"Oh, but I think you were," Roddy insisted.

"No, I wasn't," she replied, now getting more and more angry.

"Now, you two, stop arguing. Roddy, stop teasing her," Magnus rebuked.

By now the castle was well out of sight round a bend in the loch and the village landing stage came into view. Mac, the old fisherman, came hurrying to meet them as they stepped ashore.

"Roddy! Roddy, my boy! Home at last, thanks be to God! Another one back!"

"Yes, Mac," Roddy said, delighted to see him. "Yes, I am back at last. It is so good to see you and our dear land again."

"Magnus, how is Martha? Well, I hope," asked Mac.

"She is fine now that both the children are home. She is very, very happy, as we all are – in spite of Elizabeth not living at home now."

"I see Elizabeth is now well enough to return. She will be quite all right with the ladies at Harrison Hall," remarked Mac.

By now, the horse and trap had been loaded with her cases and the provisions ordered by Elizabeth's mistress. The village, although boasting a general store/ post office, a dressmaker's, a small library and old Mrs Eddy's home-made bread-and-cake shop, some things had to be brought over from further afield. Magnus was able to bring most of them over, but larger items had to travel further on by train, then go on a lengthy trip by carriage round the loch to reach the village.

"How are you and your family, Mr Mac?" Elizabeth asked.

"We are all well, thank you," he replied.

Roddy helped her into the small trap, and gave her a rug that his mother had insisted he take to wrap round her.

"I don't need the rug, Roddy," she said.

"We must do as Mama has requested. We cannot have you ill again."

He clambered up beside her and they were away. Magnus sat in front with Mac, who began to tell him all the local news. Magnus told Mac to take the road to the vicarage.

"I have a small package to leave for the vicar," he said.

"Oh, then I shall be able to see Emma!" Elizabeth exclaimed with glee.

"And I will drop off there also to see the boys," Roddy said.

At last they turned into the driveway of the vicarage and, at the door, the horses' hoofs clattered to a halt on the cobbles. Emma, who was playing the piano, heard them arrive and dashed to the lounge window to see who it was. She knew it might be Magnus with something for her father, but when she saw Elizabeth and Roddy she screamed out with delight. Her father, who had been listening intently to her playing, looked at her in dismay.

"Whatever is it, my child?" he asked.

"Oh, Papa, it is Elizabeth returning – and Roddy, too, is home."

She rushed out to greet them. She was so happy and excited that she was almost in tears, as was Elizabeth. Roddy stood aside to let them greet each other after he had lifted her out of the trap. 'They are more like sisters than friends,' he thought. 'My, how pretty Emma has become!' he thought, as he looked at her intently. His memory of her was of a freckled, pigtailed little girl with a turned-up nose. 'She is almost as pretty as my little sister, now – almost,' he told himself.

She turned to him and exclaimed, "My dear, dear Roddy! Thanks to the Lord, you have been spared from that dreadful war. Do come inside and see Anthony. He is the only one at home at present. Charles and Donald are away visiting friends in Glasgow, but they will be home soon."

Magnus had returned after handing the package to the vicar.

"Come, Elizabeth – we are already late."

He knew that when these two got together they could be talking for hours.

Roddy and Emma stood on one side as they prepared to depart.

Emma called out to her, "I will see you at choir practice."

"Yes, I will be there if Lady Margot allows it," she replied. "Roddy, Roddy," she called to him, leaning over the side of the carriage, "when shall I see you again?"

"I will be coming over with Papa to bring the provisions, so I will see you quite often."

"I am going to miss you so much," she said, almost in tears as she waved goodbye.

"Papa," Roddy called after him. "I will meet you at the jetty."

"Well, don't be too long," his father replied as he turned the carriage back up the driveway.

Elizabeth stood up in the carriage and waved to them till they were out of sight; then she sat down and busied herself, tying her bonnet strings and straightening her dress and coat. She pulled the rug closer round her herself.

'My, how chilled I feel since Roddy left my side!' she thought.

Mac had already alighted at his little cottage and he bade them good day.

At last Harrison Hall came into view, and Elizabeth felt a chill come over her. She tugged the rug more over her knees. Mama was right about her feeling the chill, but then Mama was always right. Already Elizabeth was missing her so much.

'It's such a big house,' she sighed, 'that sometimes I feel quite lost in it.'

She retied the ribbons of her bonnet more firmly under her chin. She was feeling more and more apprehensive as they neared the house and she tried to stem the flutter in her heart. Her only thought now was of the sadness she would feel once her father had left her. Soon she would be on her own, with people she hardly knew.

They crossed the small bridge over the stream and passed under the ivy-clad archway. Then they clattered along the cobbled driveway and came to rest at the foot of the steps. Two small dogs came bounding out to greet her and her face lit up at once. They were closely followed by Charles, the footman. The dogs were yelping with excitement, and the horse, not liking the encounter one little bit, hastily moved his feet from side to side to avoid them.

Lady Margot knew by the noise of the dogs that Elizabeth was back. They only ever got so excited when she was around.

'Thank goodness she is back,' she told herself. 'This house is always so much happier when she is in it with her gay youthful laughter and singing and playing.'

Magnus helped Elizabeth alight, and, as she stepped down, she picked the dogs up, one under each arm. As she went up the broad steps, both tried to lick her face in greeting. When she reached the top, she put them down, and she turned to watch her father and Charles get her luggage out of the carriage. They followed her up the steps and put it in the hallway.

"Welcome back, Elizabeth!" Charles exclaimed. "It is so nice to have you back again and to see you looking so well."

"Thank you, Charles. It is so nice to see you. Are you keeping well?"

"Yes, miss, very well."

She stood watching as her father clambered back into the carriage.

"I will take the supplies round to the entrance at the back, Charles," he said.

Then she suddenly ran down the steps to the front of the carriage.

"Papa, Papa, I am going to miss you all so much."

She was almost in tears as she hugged and kissed him goodbye as he leaned over the side.

"Well, my little girl, I am going to miss you also, but I shall see you when I call with supplies for Lady Margot."

"Only twice a week!" she called out in dismay. "But you will bring Roddy with you?"

"Yes, I will."

"And you will come over to church on Sundays with Mama?"

"Yes, my child, if it is safe on the loch. Now go, dear, and do as your mother said: keep up with your music and singing."

"Yes, I will, Papa."

"Now, hurry, my child. You must not keep your mistress waiting."

She hurried back up the steps and waved to him as he turned the corner. Charles closed the door after her.

"Lady Margot is awaiting you in the morning room," he said, and he stood aside as she crossed the huge hall, straightening her dress as she went.

Charles had already put the dogs in the conservatory, and she could hear their excited yelps as they tried to rejoin her. She knocked on the door and heard Lady Margot's voice bid her enter.

"Welcome back, dear Elizabeth," she greeted her warmly. "I do hope you are much better and happier now Roddy is home. Is he well?"

"Yes, he is very well, thank you," she replied.

"Now, come and sit down and take off your bonnet. I will ring for some tea."

She summoned Clara, the maid, with a small bell on the table, and Clara exclaimed her delight as she put down the tea tray.

"We have all missed you so much, Elizabeth. We have missed your singing and playing, and I know their Ladyships have too."

"Clara," Lady Margot said, "tell Charles to take Elizabeth's cases to her room. She will wish to unpack as soon as possible."

"Very good, milady," she replied, with a little curtsy, before she left the room.

"Mama is resting, but she will be delighted to know you are back. She has missed you so much. We will go and visit her as soon as we have had our tea. I will see if she is ready to receive us."

"Mama," said Margot, "here is Elizabeth back with us once more. I know how much you have missed her."

"Yes, that is so, my child. Do sit down. You are now quite well, I hope, and much happier now that your brother is home. And your parents – are they keeping well too?"

"Yes, milady, they are all well, and they send you their good wishes."

"Now," said Margot, "Elizabeth must go and change and unpack; then she can come and help with all my correspondence, which has been mounting daily. After dinner she can come and sing and play for you."

"I shall look forward to that very much," the old lady replied.

Lady Margot left Elizabeth at the foot of the huge winding staircase. "Join me in the study when you are ready, Elizabeth."

"Yes, milady."

She dropped her a little curtsy and hurried up the stairs to her room and closed the door. She hurried over to the window and looked out over the loch. She was just in time to see her father's boat setting off for home.

"Dear Papa and dear, dear Roddy," she whispered aloud, "how I am going to miss you so! Please hurry back as soon as you can."

She unpacked her cases and changed into the long black skirt and white blouse that Lady Margot had instructed her to wear whilst she was working.

'I don't like this outfit one little bit,' she thought as she viewed herself in the full-length mirror. 'At least my white blouse takes some of the drabness away.'

She pinned on the brooch her aunt had left her and put the locket and chain from Roddy round her neck. She brushed her hair and tied her ringlets back with the black ribbon, pulling her face in rueful displeasure at it. When she had assured herself that she looked as Lady Margot would wish, she hurried down the stairs.

"Well, my dear Elizabeth, I have done very little work since you went away. Mama did not stay very long at her cousin's up north as she was feeling ill again, so I had to go and collect her."

"Oh, I am so sorry," said Elizabeth. "I do hope she is now improved once again."

"Yes, she is much better, but it has thrown my correspondence regarding the mission stations very far behind. However, now you are back, we can get busy and catch up. I have hired a permanent nurse for Mama as she will need a lot more nursing care from now on. It will give me a chance to carry on with my plans and correspondence. You will, of course, relieve the nurse from time to time, and sing as usual for her after dinner before she retires."

Elizabeth sat silent as Lady Margot listed her duties.

"I believe," Madam continued, "the choir practices are held on Tuesdays and Fridays, so you will be free both those afternoons – also Sunday afternoons. I always dine at Glencree Castle with Lady Harriet and Lady Elena on Sundays. As you will remember, your Aunt Ingrid and Lady Elena and myself have always worked for the missions."

"Yes, Aunt Ingrid did tell me."

"I remember, dear, after I met your aunt she mentioned you and your interest in music and how well you were doing at the music academy. When I went to visit her during her last illness, she asked me if I would assist you; when she passed away I decided it would be nice to have you help me here."

"It is very kind of you, milady."

'How I wish', she thought to herself, 'she would not speak of my dear aunt,' but Lady Margot had noticed how deeply affected she was at the mention of her aunt, so she changed the subject.

"Dear me, dear me!" exclaimed Lady Margot. "How quickly time flies! It is almost time to change for dinner. We have done enough for today. The dinner gong will sound at seven o'clock. Join us in the dining room."

"Thank you, milady," Elizabeth replied, and she dropped her a small curtsy before she hurried from the room.

Elizabeth sped swiftly up the stairs to her room. She flung herself onto her bed.

"Madam has not stopped talking since I arrived," she sighed.

The mention of her aunt's death had deeply upset her, and she was almost on the verge of tears.

"I must get over her loss," she said.

She rose and rinsed her face in the bowl of cool water.

'Now what shall I wear tonight?' she pondered. 'I need something bright to cheer me, so it will have to be my tartan dress, in spite of it being so old.'

She looked in the mirror as she tied the tartan ribbon in her hair and pulled the locket Roddy had given her more to the front.

'This will shine and make me feel a little brighter – plus a little of my perfume.' She took a long deep breath as she took the cap off. 'Oh, how lovely it smells! I do hope Lady Margot does not object.'

She knocked timidly on the door as she entered the large dining room. The loch was not visible tonight as the deep-red velvet curtains were drawn. A log fire was burning in the huge grate, spluttering and crackling as if to welcome her in. The long white-clothed table was set with the most exquisite china and crystal glasses, and the tall silver candlesticks catching the light quite took her breath away.

Her mistress was standing looking into the fire, and she turned to greet her.

"Come in, Elizabeth. We are waiting for Mama. She will join us soon with Nurse Cameron. You haven't met her yet."

As she spoke, the huge door opened and Charles entered pushing Lady Roxburgh, accompanied by her nurse dressed in a stiff grey calico dress with starched apron and cuffs. She wore a flowing stiff triangular square of fine muslin on her closely cropped head.

"I must apologise for my attire, milady," she said as she curtsied. "I was late returning from the village and didn't have time to change."

"It doesn't matter for tonight, Margot. I have told Nurse not to worry so."

"No, Mama, it's quite all right. Elizabeth, this is Miss Cameron."

They greeted each other warmly.

"I have heard so much about you," Nurse Cameron said.

"And soon you will hear her sing. She plays delightfully also."

Elizabeth felt her colour rising as she started to blush.

"That is, when I can spare her. Of course, she will be singing for Mama nearly every night before she retires."

"I shall look forward to that," Nurse Cameron replied.

"Do you mind, milady," she continued, "if Elizabeth calls me by my Christian name – Faye?"

"No, do so by all means. You are both in the family, as it were," Margot replied.

"Now," said Lady Roxburgh, "we will take coffee in the music room. Then Elizabeth can sing and play for us."

Elizabeth, after searching for the music Lady Roxburgh had requested, seated herself at the piano and sang. The others all relaxed and began to enjoy it.

"Ah, that one is my favourite one of all," the old lady said as she came to the end. "Never have I heard it played or sung so beautifully."

"Thank you, milady. I shall sing it as often as you wish."

"Now, Nurse, it is way past my bedtime."

As they prepared to leave, Elizabeth dropped Lady Roxburgh a little curtsy and bade her goodnight. Then she hastened down the corridor in front of them to open the door of her room. It was a large room overlooking the loch, and it had been converted into a bedroom for her since she became too weak to mount the stairs.

Margot stood at the door and watched them go after kissing her mother goodnight. Elizabeth rejoined her.

"We must retire now. Join me in the library tomorrow at ten o'clock. Goodnight, Elizabeth."

"Goodnight, milady," she replied, as she dropped her a small curtsy.

She waited till Lady Margot had closed the door of her bedroom before she entered her own room. She flung herself on her bed, untied her hair ribbons and let her long flowing locks cascade round her shoulders. She idly twisted one of her ringlets round and round her finger, exclaiming, "What a day! What a day!"

CHAPTER 28

"Aunt Elena, Aunt Elena," called Craig excitedly.

"What is it, my boy?" she asked, although she guessed what was making him so deliriously happy.

"A messenger has arrived with a message: Fiona and her parents will be arriving this weekend."

He ran up the stairs two at a time, with Flint, as always, close on his heels.

"Have you told Harriet yet?" Elena called after him. "She likes everything to be ready on time."

"No, I haven't seen her yet to tell her the good news. Please, Aunt, tell her for me. I am in a hurry to go visiting with Papa, and I have yet to change."

"Very well, then, my boy, I will tell her. Where are you and your father riding today?" she asked.

He stood for a moment pondering, then leaned over the bannister rail. "We are riding over the estates first, then Papa is calling in to see the vicar and I am going on to see some of my friends. Then I will join Papa at the vicarage."

"Well then, you had better hurry. Your father will be waiting, and you know how he hates any delay."

"Yes, I most certainly do!" he exclaimed, and then he ran off laughing to his room.

"Craig's happiness is complete now he knows the day of his darling Fiona's visit," said Elena when she had passed the good news on to Harriet.

"How wonderful it will be to see them both together after all this time! Did he say how long they would be staying?" asked Harriet.

"No, but it will be quite a few weeks, as it always was before," said Elena.

They both stood at an upstairs window watching as father and son left, riding side by side as always.

"If only our dear Isabelle could be riding with them!" said Elena with a sigh. "Just as before!" She sighed again with a longing for the old days.

"Well, that can never be. We must be thankful that Craig has been spared to return and carry on the family heritage," said Harriet.

"Yes, so many of the boys are never going to return, and there is so much to do for the relatives they have left behind. The boys who were badly injured and gassed also need our help. Margot and Becky and myself have already had discussions as to what is the best thing we can do for them," replied Elena.

They watched till the two were out of sight, the two dogs bounding beside them.

"Come, Elena – we have a lot to do before our visitors come."

Craig and Bruce rode side by side, chattering gaily. Craig stopped to admire the view.

"Come, my son – it won't go away. It will, like your heritage, be here for evermore. We must hurry. We have lots of calls to make."

"I will join you for the rest of the day, Papa, and make my other calls another day. As you say, we have many to call on."

At last they were at the vicarage. Tony, sitting in his wheelchair gazing out of the window, spotted them as they came to a halt.

"Papa, Mama, come quickly. Here is the laird and Master Craig."

They both hastened outside to greet them and welcome them inside.

"Well, how are things with you all?" exclaimed Craig.

"Well, I cannot get around very well with only one leg," said Tony, with a faint ironic smile, "but I try very hard not to let it worry me too much. You know how much I used to ride and climb a few years ago, but now look at me. However, I am always being told that I am better than most."

Craig looked at him with despair in his heart. He recalled how agile Tony used to be.

"When did you arrive home?" he asked, trying not to let Tony see how much the sight of him so maimed had upset him.

"Nearly a year now. I'm improving all the time, aren't I, Papa?"

His father nodded his head.

"Ah, here are Charles and Donny just back from their ride. As you see, Master Craig, all my boys are safely home," said Becky. "Magnus and his son Roddy called to see us the other day," she said.

'So, Elizabeth's dear brother is back,' Craig told himself. 'But why should I be thinking of her? It must have been the name Roddy that brought her to mind.'

"Have you seen anything of Ian Cameron, any of you?" Craig asked.

"His mother called only the other day," said Becky. "She said she had heard the date of his arrival. He too will be home now."

"We must all get together for a reunion as soon as we can," said Craig, " – all our friends of bygone days."

"Yes," they all chorused, "but our numbers will be much reduced, more's the pity. So many of them will never return," said Charles.

"But we will never, ever forget them as long as we live," said Craig.

They stood, all lost in their own silent thoughts. "Now, my dear boys," Becky said at last, "these constant sad thoughts which haunt us all must not be allowed to spoil today. Just sit down all of you whilst I go and see about some tea."

At that moment Emma rushed in after her visit to the village. She was all agog with news of someone she had seen. Then she spotted Craig sitting in the corner and curtsied.

"Now then, why are you all so sad in the presence of such a lovely girl?" said the laird, as he entered, followed by the vicar.

"We were just thinking of all our old friends who will never return," explained Craig as he rose to greet her. After she had curtsied to the laird, Craig continued: "My, how you have grown, Emma – and into such a lovely lady! I hardly recognised you."

"And you have changed too, Master Craig. How tall you are now! I could hardly recognise my brothers when they returned either," she said, trying to hide her blushes at his previous compliment to her.

'I daresay', thought Craig to himself, 'all the village girls will have grown into young ladies whilst we have been away. I know I won't be able to remember all their names when I meet up with them.'

"Now," said Becky, as Rhona (the maid) put down the tea tray, "we must all have some tea. Your father has had a long talk with the laird and it is agreed."

"What is that?" asked Craig, looking as puzzled as the rest.

"Now all the boys are back, there is going to be a special thanksgiving service, several social events and dances. The ladies of the church will make all the arrangements."

"The choir will need to have rehearsals for the service," said Emma.

"Well, Mr and Mrs Knowell will arrange all that," her father said.

At this, Emma pulled a face of displeasure behind her brother's back. Her grimace did not go unnoticed by Craig, and he gave her a smile of understanding. He knew, from his very early days of unwillingly being a choir member, that Mr and Mrs Knowell were not at all popular with the younger members of the choir. But then, he had to admit that it was he who had been the instigator of many of the tricks which had so displeased both Mr and Mrs Knowell, though they never dared to complain to his father or aunts.

Then the laird spoke: "We have also to arrange a Highland gathering later in the year. None has been held during the war, so we must make it the grandest one ever."

"Yes," said Tony, "we must all make it so. It will be wonderful to get back to normal – as near as we can, anyway. Nothing will ever be quite the same again, but we must all do our best to help the boys who have returned and support the families of those who have not returned."

"Tony has expressed all our feelings about that," said Bruce, and the others nodded in agreement. "It will take a long time to get everyone settled and adjusted with some kind of work, but, with God's help, all will be accomplished."

"We have lost some of our finest young men," Craig continued: "the Brady and Eckersley boys, to name just a few. Grieving children and widows have been left without the help and support of their fathers and husbands."

"Yes," continued the vicar, "the Ladies' Circle will be arranging other events to raise funds for the orphan children and widows. Lady Elena, Lady Margot and my dear wife, Becky here, are taking care of all that."

"Yes, that is so," Becky remarked. "Everything is going along smoothly."

"We must, Papa, visit them all as soon as we can and see to all their needs," said Craig. "Have you got the full list yet, Vicar?"

"Yes, I have news of most of them. I shall bring you the names of the rest as soon as possible."

With thanks to all and goodbyes all round, they took their leave.

On their way home, they stopped at the home of Craig's old music teacher. His son, Rory, had been blinded in one eye and could now only use one arm. Craig tried not to show how deeply moved he was by what he saw.

'To think', he told himself, 'Rory's musical career is gone for good!'

He sighed deeply with despair and all his thoughts of the front surfaced once more.

"Master Craig," said Rory, "will you be able to come and play chess with me as you used to, or will you now be too busy with the affairs of your estates? I realise how busy you will be."

Craig was suddenly jolted out of his sad reflective reverie.

"My dear Rory, of course I will come. I shall never be too busy to call on you. I'll come as often as I can. I must have more music lessons from your father, so I shall come often."

"Thank you, my dear friend. It will mean so much to me," Rory said.

"And to me," his father commented to him as they departed.

"The poor devil!" Craig commented to his father as they rode side by side in deep thought. "What does the future hold for him now? He was such a brilliant musician on the violin and piano! Maybe he could try composing. I cannot see anything else for him. And what is available for all the others, Papa?"

"I don't know as yet, my son. We must see about encouraging some light industries of some kind, but I don't hold much hope."

"Well, Papa," Craig said, in between the long silences on the way home, "with your help and Aunt Elena's I shall spend all my life caring for their welfare."

"And I too will do all I can," replied Bruce, still in a sad, thoughtful mood. "We will get the best possible advice on every aspect of the help they need."

They rode on, each with his own thoughts. Bruce realised more and more how lucky he was that his own son had been spared.

Craig, as usual, stopped now and again to gaze into the distance. He knew that he was one of the lucky ones: his future was secure. He knew that one day all the land, as far as he could see, would belong to him and he would be the custodian of it for all the sons that would follow him. His father, who had ridden on a little way, returned to join him. He followed Craig's gaze and guessed his every thought.

"Yes, my son," he said, "all you survey will be yours one day."

"We will, I think, Papa," he replied, "divide some of the extra land you are buying from Lady Margot into crofts for the boys to farm."

"Whatever you wish, my son, will be done. There will be still enough left for the sons that follow when you and Fiona marry. And there's no reason to delay that day either," said his father emphatically, "now you are home."

"None whatsoever, Papa – and there is home. I bet my horse can beat yours home."

"I don't think so," his father replied, and he spurred his horse forward in a mad gallop, closely followed by Craig.

The dogs knew they would have to make their own way home.

Elena laughed gaily as Bruce and Craig arrived in a flurry of clattering hoofs. Craig was only inches behind his father. Craig waved to her from the courtyard when he spotted her leaning from an upstairs window.

'Dear Aunt Elena', he thought, 'always seems to be watching for our return.'

She was first, as always, to greet them as they dismounted, both out of breath.

'Craig', she thought, 'is panting a little more than Bruce. It must be the effect of the gas attacks he endured at the front, but he will soon be fit and strong with our pure mountain air in his lungs.'

Jamie, too, rushed out when he heard the clatter of hoofs. He called the stable boys to take care of the horses, and then he followed Bruce, Craig and Elena inside.

CHAPTER 29

The day had dawned. A cool wind but bright sunny sky above boded well for their journey. The household was alight with happiness. Everyone seemed to be humming a tune of some kind as they busied themselves for Fiona and her parents' arrival.

"It will be noon, I daresay," said Cook, "so everything must be ready by then. It is just like old times. They will be the first of many visitors we will have now the young master is back!" she exclaimed to Shona and Sarah, who were finding it hard to keep up with Cook's orders. "Now, Shona, hurry and finish the job you are doing; then you can start on the preparations for the second course. And you, Sarah – are all the vegetables prepared?"

"Yes, Cook, I have almost finished."

"Well, hurry, my girl. We have such a lot to do in the time."

'But we have been up since before the cock crowed,' Sarah told herself, 'and we have been hurrying all morning. How much more of a hurry does Cook expect? I shall be glad when they arrive: then we can all relax.'

"Now, come, my girl, don't get daydreaming," said Cook, and Sarah hastened away to do her bidding.

Craig had been smiling happily all morning in between singing a little love ditty over and over again. 'Oh, I am so happy! It's the happiest day of my life,' he told himself. He heard Elena and Harriet pass his door as he was fastening his lace jabot at his throat. For the first time since his arrival he was wearing full Highland dress. This suit of clothes had been rushed through by his tailor in the village specially for this day.

"Hurry, Craig dear – the carriage is approaching," Harriet called to him.

"I am ready," he replied as he hastily closed the door of his room.

On the landing he stumbled over Flint, who would not move for anyone except his master.

"Come, boy! We must hurry."

Bruce was already on the steps taking the cool mountain air as the sisters joined him.

"The carriage has entered the long drive," Elena said, "so they will be here any moment now."

They all three turned to welcome Craig.

"Good morning, everyone. Isn't it the most joyful and lovely of days? I can hardly believe it is true!" Craig exclaimed.

"My dear boy, how splendid you look today!" exclaimed Bruce. "The tailor has done you proud as always."

"Yes, Papa, I am very pleased. It was such a rush job for him."

"Don't you agree, Harriet and Elena?" Bruce continued.

Harriet, as usual, gave just a nod of approval, but Elena was quite ecstatic.

Craig was the first to run down the steps as the carriage clattered to a halt opposite the great door, and, as Jamie opened the carriage door, Craig leapt inside to kiss Fiona. He sat beside her as his father helped her parents alight.

"Come, you two," Bruce called to them. "The horses have had a long journey and must be attended to."

Craig alighted and helped Fiona down, laughing gaily at her pleas for him to release her. "I shall never release you ever," he whispered in her ear. "I must apologise for not riding out to accompany you on the drive over. I wanted to greet you properly dressed, as I am now, not in my jodhpurs and shirt, as would have been the case if I had ridden over to join you."

"You look so splendid, my darling. I have never seen you looking so elegant. How tall and handsome you are! You look so fit and well with our fresh mountain air. Come – we must go inside. The rest of the family are out of sight already."

"How long can you stay?" he asked. "I wish it was for ever."

"So do I, my darling, but soon it will be. Papa has to return soon, and Mama and I have some visits to make, but we will be staying for a short time at least."

"Oh well, I guess I shall have to be content with that," Craig said, looking a little crestfallen as he replied.

CHAPTER 30

The church bells had been ringing since very early morn, calling everyone to this special service of thanksgiving. The bright sun shone in a cloudless sky, the loch had a shimmer of silvery ripples on its blue-green water.

All the villagers from every croft and hamlet were wending their way down the hillsides and along the narrow country lanes, greeting each other with open arms as they chatted excitedly in little groups. Soldiers home from the war were greeted with outstretched arms and exclamations of thankfulness for their safe return, though some fathers pushed their once strapping sons along in wheelchairs, and some doting mothers, wives and sweethearts led their blinded, limping, loved ones. All were wondering about the hard future ahead of them, but their families were determined that a future they would have, no matter what sacrifices they had to make.

Suddenly, the sound of horse-drawn carriages could be heard echoing along the narrow lanes. As the carriages came into sight, all the villagers stepped to one side; the women dropped curtsies and the men doffed their caps as the laird's carriage passed. Bruce, accompanied by the General and his wife, nodded his head in acknowledgement.

Craig was delighted to see so many old friends, and he stood up to acknowledge their greeting. It was the first time most of them had caught a glimpse of the young master since his return, and it was evident by the enthusiasm of their greeting that they were overjoyed at seeing him.

The islanders could never have borne the situation of their dearly loved laird's son never returning to them.

Fiona, as was her wont, barely glanced in their direction as they passed – a point which Elena noted with dissatisfaction as she sat beside Harriet in the following carriage.

"The church will be filled to overflowing today, Harriet. It will be wonderful to see so many of our old friends," Elena remarked as she continued to wave until their carriage was out of sight.

The beautiful old church had been specially decorated by the ladies and choirgirls. Every type of spring flower had been specially arranged by the Misses Gibson from the florists. Everyone took up their places after being greeted by the vicar and his wife.

The laird and his party sat in their special seats in the Laird's Gallery. The organist played a beautiful rendering of a well-known Scottish hymn. Special hymns and prayers were said for the bereaved families, and special thanksgiving prayers were said for the boys safely returned.

The choir stood up to sing, all dressed in their new red cassocks edged with white ruffles at wrists and throats, which had been presented to them some weeks before by Lady Elena as a gift from the laird.

Then a tiny figure proceeded to the front of the altar. She was dwarfed by the tall pulpit on her right, which was surrounded by flowers at its base.

Craig and Fiona were engrossed with each other. Fiona gazed up at him adoringly and he smiled into her bright adoring eyes. Both were completely oblivious to all around them.

Suddenly, a beautiful, clear, young voice began to sing 'Ave Maria'. Craig looked away from the beautiful eyes of Fiona to see who was the owner of such an exquisite voice, the like of which he had never heard before. Then, as his eyes came to rest on the small, dainty figure, he became transfixed with wonder and amazement. He couldn't believe his eyes. He stared at her in disbelief.

It was the beautiful angel he had seen that night at Magnus's house. She was certainly beautiful the last time he saw her, in the reflection of the candlelight, but in this setting, with the sun slanting through the stained-glass window behind her and the glorious array of flowers practically surrounding her, she looked even more exquisite. His eyes never left her till she sat down beside Emma.

'Truly an angel!' he exclaimed to himself.

"What did you say, Craig dear?"

He felt the pressure of a hand on his arm and looked down to see Fiona looking up at him with a puzzled frown on her face.

"Oh, nothing, my dear. I was just thinking what a beautiful tune that is," he whispered to her as he jerked back to reality. His heart was racing at the sudden sight of the angel.

Everyone was enthralled by Elizabeth's singing.

Fiona's mother commented in a whisper to Elena, "I do hope she sings for us again."

"I don't think so today, my dear," Elena replied, "but we shall all hear her quite often in future."

"We certainly must," the General commented approvingly.

As the congregation stood to sing the next hymn, Craig tried to locate some of his friends. Some soldiers in tartan caught his eye, but he could not make out who they were amongst so many people. There was row upon row of sombre black, navy and grey apparel – so many sad faces. Some, he noted, were finding it difficult to open their mouths to sing.

'There has been far too much sorrow, far too much sacrifice,' he thought.

He felt a nudge on his arm.

"Darling, you have not sung one verse of the hymn as yet," Fiona remarked, angry at his woeful expression.

He glanced down at her but did not answer. They sat down as the hymn finished.

Elena, too, had been watching him closely and had followed his gaze along the rows. She marvelled at the effort all the villagers had made. The ladies wore broad-brimmed hats, remodelled out of their old ones, newly trimmed with fresh ribbons; the men were in well-brushed suits, which probably had not seen the light of day since their wedding days – or maybe longer. In some cases, suits had been handed down from long-gone relatives.

The choir stood once more to sing their special anthem. Craig strained his neck to catch a glimpse of Elizabeth, but all he could see was her long golden hair.

'Who is that tall girl next to her? Why can't she shrink a little? It's Emma – today she seems ten feet tall.'

Suddenly, the choir turned to face the congregation and Craig's interest knew no bounds. Elizabeth started to sing with the choir, but her mind was in turmoil as she perused each row, trying to spot her parents and Roddy.

'They must be here. They said they would come. They did promise,' she told herself. 'The weather is fine. Where are they? The loch is still and should be calm enough to cross,' she reassured herself time and time again. 'But where are they?'

She searched every row, getting more and more anxious as she failed to spot them. Suddenly she raised her eyes and her gaze met the piercing, faintly smiling eyes of Master Craig, who, unbeknown to her, had been watching her intently and had secretly guessed whom she was searching for.

She was so startled by the intensity of his gaze that she almost dropped her hymn book in her panic and confusion.

'Oh, why is it?' she asked herself angrily. 'Why, why? When I am looking for my dear Roddy, *he* appears – and smirking too!'

She turned her head away sharply and met the disapproving glare of the choirmaster. She hastily tried to hide behind Emma as she frantically searched for the line of the anthem they were singing.

Emma, who had noticed her dilemma, pointed to the line. Elizabeth breathed a sigh of relief but the line was almost ending, and she was only just in time to sing the amen. She closed her book and sat down. She was trembling slightly – partly with annoyance at Craig's piercing stare and partly because she had been unable to continue to peruse the rest of the rows in search of her loved ones.

Then there was the choirmaster's wrath. She knew he had spotted Emma helping her find her place in the hymn book, so she had got Emma in trouble also. She knew she would have to stay behind to make her apologies to him, and that filled her with more alarm. What if he detained her so long that her parents and Roddy sailed back without seeing her? The very thought of it all made her knees go weak. Oh, that dratted man!

"Elizabeth, Elizabeth!" It was Emma whispering to her. "Are you all right? You are quite flushed and you are trembling. Are you feeling ill again?"

"No, no, Emma. I am quite all right, thank you. I have just mislaid my handkerchief."

She searched frantically in her cloak pocket.

'Any excuse will do', she told herself, 'to give me time to compose myself.'

She suddenly felt a firm prod in her back and, as she and Emma turned round, they met the angry glare of Mrs Knowell, the choirmaster's wife.

'Oh, not her as well!' sighed Elizabeth to herself.

Emma, ignoring the angry glare of Mrs Knowell, carried on whispering: "Oh, the laird is about to speak. He is going to join Papa in the pulpit."

The vicar told the congregation to remain seated as the laird had some special announcements to make.

A hushed murmuring came from the congregation as they wondered what he would say.

Then Bruce started to speak. He told them that several events would be taking place in the coming months to raise funds to help anyone who was suffering because of the war. There would be, in the autumn, the Highland Gathering and also the Church Fayre, but first of all he was giving a banquet and grand ball at Glencree Castle. It was to be a huge gathering and everyone was invited to attend. It was to welcome back the soldiers from the front.

The people, after the last hymn, began filing out of the church, all happy and agog with the news they had just heard and heartened by the thought of happier times ahead.

'Thank goodness we can all go home now,' Elizabeth told herself.

Emma asked her once more, "Are you sure you are all right? You look so flushed."

'Well, let Emma think I am flushed with the fever and not with embarrassment because of that man,' Elizabeth said to herself. 'Even now I cannot look up to see where they are because of him.'

Craig still kept his gaze on her. He was entranced by the thrill of her voice and the sight of her Dresden figure as she stood at the foot of the altar.

'It was as though', he told himself, 'she was waiting for a golden crown or a halo for her lovely head. She is truly an angelic angel. Why, why, does the sight of her disturb me so?' he asked himself. 'Why, when I have the darling girl I adore by my side?'

Fiona, he suddenly realised, was tugging his arm impatiently.

"My dearest one!" she exclaimed impatiently with a pout. "Why are you gazing around? Everyone is waiting for us."

"I am so sorry, my dearest one. Come – we must hurry, as you say."

He was angry with himself for distressing her so, and they hastily rejoined their parents outside the church.

The congregation all gathered outside, talking with their friends and neighbours while the laird's party said their goodbyes to the vicar and his wife and other churchgoers. At last they had bid everyone goodbye and entered their carriages. The village men doffed their caps, and their wives and other members of their families dropped them curtsies as they left. Some of the women commented on the beauty of Fiona and their delight at seeing her and Craig together at last. Their wedding will take place before very long was the general opinion.

"What a lovely pair they make!" said Margot as she seated herself next to Elena in the carriage.

"Yes, it is wonderful to have him home at last," said Harriet.

"And when might their engagement be announced?" continued Margot.

"Oh, very soon now!" exclaimed Harriet as the carriage pulled away.

"And," said Elena, "we shall have the most wonderful wedding seen on the island since his father's."

Elena smiled at her happy thoughts as the three carriages pulled away with cheerful waves from the occupants to all.

"Mama, Mama!" exclaimed Emma. "I am going to walk a little way with Elizabeth before I come home."

"Very well, my dear, but don't be too late."

"No, Mama, I promise."

The choirmaster had told her he would speak to her about her misdemeanour at the next choir practice. He dare not detain her then as she must be by her parents' side to bid the laird's party goodbye.

However, with Elizabeth it was a different matter. She came running up to Emma breathlessly, still smarting from the reprimand of the choirmaster, who had told her to stay behind after the others had left, though he had not dared keep her too long as he also had to say his farewells.

"It's just as well for that young lady," exploded Mrs Knowell. "She has got off very lightly today!" she exclaimed to her husband as they took their places outside the church before the laird left.

Elizabeth was just in time to hear the villagers' remarks about the forthcoming wedding of Craig and Fiona as the lovely couple drove out of sight.

'Well,' she thought to herself, 'the sooner his marriage takes place, the better. Then maybe he will stop staring at me as though I am still wearing my nightgown – the bold-faced cad! I don't care if he is the laird's son and the young master of Glencree Castle. Because of him I am in disgrace with the choirmaster and his wife and I have got Emma in trouble also.'

"Emma dear," she panted, "have you seen my parents and my dear Roddy anywhere?"

But before she had finished asking, Roddy was by her side, laughing gaily as usual.

"Why so glum, little sister?" he exclaimed teasingly. "There must be no sad faces on such a day as this – don't you agree, Emma?"

Emma smiled back at him in agreement, but did not reply. She knew why Elizabeth was upset.

"Where are Mama and Papa?" Elizabeth demanded. "I have been looking for them and you everywhere. I couldn't see any of you in church. I looked and looked." She pouted, still smarting at all she had gone through.

"We are here, my dear," her mother said. "You sang so beautifully – didn't she, Papa?"

"You did, my little dawn angel – superbly. I have never heard you sing as well as you did today. We are so proud of you."

"I am so glad you enjoyed my singing," she replied.

She was feeling much happier now, but she glanced sideways just in time to see the three Crawford sisters glaring at her in annoyance. Their mother looked annoyed too, but she was deep in conversation with the choirmaster's wife.

'Well,' she asked herself, 'what have I done, I wonder, to warrant their displeasure? But then, they have never liked me.'

She tugged Emma to one side.

"Emma," she said, rather puzzled, "why are the three Crawford girls looking at me with such displeasure?"

"I cannot think why," Emma replied, "unless it is because Mama decided with the other ladies of the church to choose you to sing solo, instead of Ruby. One of the three is usually chosen from the choir to sing solo for any special occasion like this one, and Ruby is always the main one. Yes, that must be the reason," she continued.

"Yes, that must be why," agreed Elizabeth.

"I did hear at one of the meetings," Emma continued, "that Ruby was chosen; then suddenly the ladies changed their minds – quite right too! You are a much better singer than any one of Mrs Crawford's precious daughters will ever be – her precious jewels, as she calls them."

Elizabeth looked aghast at Emma. Never had she ever heard her say a wrong word of anyone before.

"She must be really incensed about it all."

"Come now, you two chatterboxes," said Magnus. "We have a long walk to the landing stage."

"Yes, Papa, we are coming."

The two hastened to rejoin them, both of them walking demurely with Roddy in between.

"How lucky I am," he exclaimed, "to have the two prettiest girls on the island walking with me!"

They all laughed gaily.

"Now, Roddy, you can let go of my pretty girl," declared Stuart Roberts, Emma's boyfriend, as he caught up with them.

"Very well then," said Roddy, pretending to be peeved.

"And Roy and Madge have decided they too would like to walk as far as we go."

"Oh, the more the merrier," said Roddy.

"Roddy, you did hear the announcement about the ball, didn't you?" Elizabeth ventured. "You will take me, as you promised when you arrived home – do you remember?"

"Yes, I remember. I shall take you."

He pulled her ringlets playfully.

"Oh, what a jolly crowd we shall be altogether, Emma, I can hardly wait for the day to arrive."

Then she held her breath for a second or two. A devastating thought had crossed her mind: 'But I have no dress to go in,' she told herself. 'I have no dress for the ball. What am I going to do?'

"Why so quiet, my little sister?" remarked Roddy, a little perturbed at her sudden change.

But she could hardly bear to think of it herself, let alone tell anyone else – no, not even Roddy – what was going through her mind.

"Oh, nothing really. I just remembered to ask Mama for something before she leaves. I will go and speak to her now."

"All right then," Roddy replied. "Hurry on. They are just round the bend."

She sped along after them and was quite breathless when she reached her mother's side.

"Why, my child, you are quite out of breath. Whatever is wrong?"

"Well, Mama, about the ball: Roddy is going to take me and I have no ball gown. What am I going to do?" She looked up at her mother's face anxiously. "I must have a new dress. It is my very first ball."

"I know it is, my child, and I agree you should have a new gown, but it is impossible. We have no money to buy a new gown. You will have to make do with your white Scottish-dancing dress. Quite a lot of the girls will be wearing theirs, and you will have to do likewise."

"But Mama," she said with a pout, "that isn't a real ball gown. How can I go in that old dress?"

"You will look just as nice as any of the other girls," her mother said. "That dress will just have to do."

Elizabeth knew that that was the end of the matter. 'How can I possibly go to a ball in such a plain dress?' she told herself disconsolately. She lowered her face dejectedly and dropped behind them looking very crestfallen.

"Another sad face!" Roddy exclaimed when he and the others reached her side. "That's the second one today. What is it this time?"

"Mama says I shall have to go to the ball in my old white Scottish-dancing dress and I know everyone else there will have a new ball gown."

"But you will look just as pretty in that dress," Roddy said, trying to appease her and bring a smile to her face. "I will buy you a new tartan sash."

"Of course he will," Emma agreed.

"I know," Elizabeth pouted, "I shall be the only one there dressed like that."

"Oh, I don't think so," Emma said, she too trying to make her closest friend feel a little happier. However, she knew as well as Elizabeth that a new dress would be the order of the day for this, the very first ball for most of the girls. For all the girls from the academy for young ladies, all of whom had been in church that morning, it would be their first ball, and, as they were the daughters of rich landowners, a new dress would be worn by all of them. Emma knew only too well how Elizabeth would feel without a new dress. "But, Elizabeth," she continued, "you will look much prettier than all the others, I just know you will." Emma tried to reassure her, but to no avail. Elizabeth's disappointment could not be appeased.

The small group chatted for a while before her parents and Roddy clambered aboard the ferry.

"I will row back, Papa. I am so out of practice."

"Very well, my son, just as you wish."

They all kissed Elizabeth goodbye, and her mother's final words as always rang in her ears: "Now, my dear, do as Lady Margot wishes at all times and keep up your singing and music practice."

"Yes, Mama, I promise," she replied disconsolately.

Her mother looked at her a little anxiously, wishing in her heart that she could get her the new dress she so badly wanted.

"I will call with Papa when he brings the provisions to Lady Margot," Roddy called, as he started to row away.

"Don't be too long, Roddy dear," she called to him as she waved them goodbye.

Roddy rowed on in silence, still watching her on the jetty. At last he spoke: "Mama, is there no way at all that we could get her a new dress for the ball? It is so important, a first ball."

"No, my son, it just isn't possible. Maybe some time, in a few years, when the croft is improving."

"Maybe I could give some money from the legacy Aunt Ingrid left me."

"No," Martha insisted, "that money is yours and not to be given away. It is for your wedding day or when you reach the age of twenty-five, and Elizabeth's legacy has the same conditions. Elizabeth has just got to realise that she cannot have everything she wants."

Magnus sat quietly pondering, smoking his pipe as he watched his son with the oars, now and again reminding him to avoid the rocks in the loch. He too wished that he could grant his darling daughter's wish. He secretly cursed the ill luck many years before which had caused his fishing business to crumble. As a result he was unable to provide his darling daughter with the dress she so badly wanted.

'But there is nothing we can do about it in our plight,' he thought.

Elizabeth stood waving to them until they were out of sight; then she rejoined the rest standing chatting a little distance away. She tucked her small white handkerchief in her pocket. How alone she always felt when they were not by her side – more so today, when everything had gone wrong!

First, being stared at by Master Craig had brought to mind the night when she had stood before him on the stairs in her nightgown; then she had displeased the choirmaster; then she had aroused the envy of the Crawford sisters; and now she had to go to her very first ball in an old dress.

She stared out, not really seeing or hearing anything. Emma called to her several times, then she touched her lightly on the arm.

"Come, Elizabeth, we must be going before the mists come down."

"Oh yes, Emma, forgive me, yes, we must hurry."

At last they reached the crossroads. Emma and Stuart took the road to the vicarage, Roy and Madge took the path to the village, and Elizabeth took the path to Harrison Hall.

"Would you like us to come a little further with you, Elizabeth?" asked Stuart, a little concerned at her being alone.

"No, thank you, Stuart. I am quite all right, but thank you for your concern," she replied. She wanted to be alone for a while before she reached the Hall.

"I will see you at choir practice," Emma called to her as they turned to go.

After she had waved them a last farewell, she proceeded along the small path that would take her beside the loch; it was much longer, but she wanted time to think. She had much to think about. She walked slowly beside the loch, kicking pebbles as she went. Her thoughts were on only one thing: a new dress for the ball.

'Where am I going to get a new dress from?' she asked herself.

She had spent her allowance left her by her aunt to buy clothes for Roddy's homecoming and new clothes for commencing her duties with Lady Margot. Her legacy from the estate of her aunt she couldn't have until she was twenty-five, or until her wedding day.

'Oh, why can't I be twenty-five now, instead of silly eighteen?' she said with a pout. 'And who is going to marry me, or even look at me at the ball, in that silly old white dress?' (Until now that silly old dress had been her pride and joy.)

She stopped beside the loch, looking into the lovely clear water at her reflection.

"Where, oh where, am I going to get a new ball gown from?" she demanded of the reflection. "Where, oh where?"

She received no reply, just a gurgle as she threw a stone into its midst and watched it swirl around, as if chuckling at her.

"Oh, you are no help."

The Hall was silent, as was usual on Sunday afternoons. Lady Margot, as always, was dining at the castle and spending the rest of the day there, talking to Elena and Harriet. There would be much more to talk about today, with all the plans for the future events to be arranged.

Lady Roxburgh, still not too well, was having her afternoon nap with her nurse beside her. The rest of the servants had the afternoon off and had gone their various ways. Flora (the cook) and Clara (the housemaid) had gone to their homes in the village after morning service. Charles was out with the two dogs – his chore every afternoon. He wouldn't be back until dusk.

Cook had left Elizabeth a cold lunch. Today she didn't mind the silence of the big house. All she wanted was to be alone with her miserable thoughts. She didn't feel like eating anything, so she wended her way to the library and sat down at the piano and played several of her favourite melodies. But today she felt no happiness and peace of mind, as she usually did when she played, so she closed the lid and climbed the stairs to her room.

It was quite late when she heard voices in the hall below. She heard Lady Margot passing her door. Charles bade her goodnight and a carriage drove away.

Sleep eluded her as she thought of the ball. She visualised all the girls dancing in their new ball gowns. She shuddered as she thought once again of that old white dress.

CHAPTER 31

It was the custom at Glencree Castle to entertain friends after the morning service, but many had been invited today to plan the events for the coming year.

"It's like old times," remarked Bruce to Craig and Fiona as they stood holding hands, looking out over the loch.

They turned to greet their guests as they returned from the dining room.

Fiona's parents and Harriet were the first to join them. Elena followed with the vicar and Becky, his wife; Doctor Robertson and his wife came next, with their daughter, Sybil. The others were Professor Roberts and his wife, who were in deep conversation with the principal of the academy for young ladies and her son, Robin, Craig's old tutor and his sons, Rory and Andrew, two of Craig's oldest friends, and Lady Margot Emslie, always a regular visitor to Glencree.

"Now we are all here," said Harriet, "I will ring for coffee, and Jamie can serve the men with drinks if they so desire."

"When are we going to see you two happily married?" asked Doctor Robertson, looking at Craig and Fiona. "Very soon, I hope, after all the years you have been kept apart by the war."

"All in good time, Doctor, all in good time," Craig replied nonchalantly.

Fiona was a little peeved at the seemingly dismissive retort from Craig. She looked up at him as if to rebuke him, but decided against doing so in front of their friends.

"Our engagement has to be announced and published in the London papers. So many of my friends and relatives are yearning for the news," said Fiona. "We will marry next year after our return from London, after I have been presented at court and we have done the London Season. What a wonderful time ahead for me!" she exclaimed rapturously.

"It will be for both of you," said her mother, "and such a busy and exciting time for me. How we will fit it all in I really don't know, but it will all be done to perfection." She looked deliriously happy as she gazed around at the group.

Several nodded their heads in approval.

"It will be a glorious wedding," enthused Margot. "I do hope it takes place before I return to India to rejoin Davinia. That is my intention as soon as Mama is well enough to rejoin her sister up north, but I am determined to attend your wedding."

"Oh yes, Margot, it is unthinkable that you would not be at our wedding, wouldn't it, my darling?" exclaimed Fiona, turning to Craig, who was gazing over the loch. "Craig! Craig dearest, you are not listening to me," she said with a pout.

"I'm so sorry, my dearest," he replied as he hurried to her side. He grasped her hand in his and kissed her lightly. "I was so engrossed, looking at the mountains. Of course Margot must be at our wedding. She cannot possibly leave before – so you see, my darling, I was listening."

"Oh, what a tease you are, my darling! We shall be making our engagement official soon. I wish it was today, Margot," she sighed. She looked at Craig adoringly as he crossed the room to rejoin Rory and Andrew.

"Well, why not today?" exclaimed her father eagerly.

"Yes, why not?" reiterated her mother. "All our friends are anxiously waiting and most of them are here."

"And we have the two most important people present," said Bruce. "I also have the family engagement ring in this very room."

"Have you?" Fiona exclaimed excitedly. "Please show it to me, Papa Bruce, please!" She looked up at him pleadingly as she released her hand from her father and tugged Bruce's arm.

"All right, my dear daughter, just give me time to get it out of the safe. I have only the ring and the Luckenbooth brooch here. The rest of the matching collection is kept in the vault in the city. Only the ring can be worn on your engagement; the rest on your wedding day. You can see the complete set on Isabelle's picture."

Fiona and Sybil wandered over to the picture. "How beautiful they are! I shall long for the day to see you wearing them, Fiona."

"It will be wonderful to be wearing such a priceless collection and to be married to my darling Craig." In her excitement she had forgotten about him, but her parents had joined her beneath the portrait.

"It certainly will be a joy to us all!" her mother exclaimed. "Won't it, my dear?" she asked, looking at her husband with a glint of satisfaction.

"It certainly will, my dears." Her father was just as enthusiastic as she to see their daughter as the next Mistress of Glencree Castle at the earliest possible moment.

"You will let me try the ring on today, Papa Bruce?" she pleaded.

"Of course, my dear. You know, my dear," Bruce continued, "the ring has never yet not fitted the next Mistress of Glencree Castle."

"Well, Papa Bruce," she said, "I know I shall not be the exception."

"Of course you won't – the very idea! Don't you agree?" said Fiona's mother, looking at her husband to confirm it.

He nodded his head in total agreement.

"I am sure you won't be either," agreed Bruce as he went over to the safe, which was hidden by a large picture.

Craig, who was in deep conversation with the vicar, Rory and Andrew, glanced up to see his father opening the safe and bringing out the huge jewel boxes.

'Why the red jewels? I haven't asked for them, so why?' Craig wondered.

He watched as his father laid them on the table.

"Please hurry, Papa Bruce, and let me see my ring," pleaded Fiona.

He noted his father's haste to appease her, and he cast her a glance of surprise and annoyance. Suddenly he realised that the conversation at the table must have led almost to an announcement of their engagement without his consent. Surely this should have been just between themselves, and he alone should have produced the ring before anyone else was informed.

'Fiona knew I wanted to choose a special time and place,' he said to himself.

He knew she would expect him to spend all his time with her discussing the alterations to the West Wing before they left for London, but he was determined to have more time with his father, to attend to matters of the estate. He had also promised his men that he would make their welfare his priority before attending to his own and Fiona's desires. He knew too well that she would resent anything or anyone occupying his time. Why was she being so insistent about the red box? His thoughts were in turmoil.

The guests were watching Bruce and Fiona, but Elena was looking at Craig. She knew instinctively what he was thinking. She knew it would be his wish that all the villagers knew of their betrothal at the same time as these few friends here.

'Surely,' she thought, 'Bruce should have realised that also.'

She could see Craig's anger mounting as Fiona clapped her hands in delight and told Bruce not to keep her in suspense. She pleaded with him to show her the engagement ring and some of the other jewellery which would be hers on her wedding day.

Elena's anger was mounting also as she saw how upset Craig was getting. Fiona, she thought, was not considering his feelings at all. She knew Fiona was most anxious to be Mistress of Glencree Castle at the earliest possible moment. She was not looking forward to that day dawning, in spite of Harriet's assurance that all would be well. She had always had misgivings as to how Fiona would treat them when she did become mistress of the house. Harriet, she noticed, even seemed to be egging Bruce on to hurry and open the boxes.

At last Bruce sat down, surrounded by several of the jewellery boxes. He was determined to open the red velvet box last. He, himself, had suddenly felt that what he was doing was not quite right. The last time he had touched the red box was when he had put it away after his darling Isabelle's death. Suddenly, the thought had crossed his mind he would be losing his darling son after his marriage: he knew how possessive Fiona was. However, he realised that with the clamour of voices around him he could not put the boxes away unopened.

All heads were now bent over the table, all waiting to see some of the McNairs' spectacular gems. It was a well-known fact that they were the possessors of a fabulous collection of jewellery from their ancestors' travels abroad and the diamond mines owned by Isabelle's parents. Fiona knew the jewels would belong to Craig on their wedding day, and so they would be hers and hers alone. Her father had often told her of the McNairs' wealth – Bruce had always been her father's closest friend and confidant. Fiona knew also that the sisters were well provided for. Elena had already given most of her wealth away to the overseas missions, and she could never imagine Harriet ever wearing any kind of jewellery, except her wedding ring – certainly never any of these jewels.

Gasps of delight and astonishment came from all of them as they gazed at the gems: sapphires, emeralds, amethysts, diamonds.

"Oh, they are all exquisite!" exclaimed Fiona. "But, Papa Bruce, do hurry and let me see my ring in the red box."

'It's the only thing she is interested in,' thought Elena, growing more and more annoyed at Fiona's lack of concern for Craig's feelings.

As Bruce raised the lid, she couldn't hide her delight. Neither could her parents and the friends present. The ring consisted of a beautiful red ruby surrounded by two circles of diamonds, the likes of which they had never seen before. Even those who remembered Isabelle wearing it were amazed at the size and brilliance of it. They had forgotten how beautiful it was.

Bruce felt a shudder pass through him as he gazed into the depth of the blood-red stone. For a moment he wished he had not been so anxious to please Fiona, but he had been so happy at Craig's safe return from the front that he wanted everyone near him to be happy too.

Craig now seated himself next to Fiona, and he too looked at it. His face saddened at the thought of the last time he had seen it on his darling mother's tiny hand as she lay on the bed on that fateful night. He, as a small boy, had clung to her hand as Elena and Harriet tried desperately to pull him from her side.

Now he heard Fiona's voice whispering to him: "My darling Craig, isn't it just too beautiful for words?" but he did not answer.

"Well now, my dear boy, it seems a pity to have such a beautiful ring like this hidden away in a box in the safe. A beautiful ring is meant to be worn by a beautiful lady, and where could we find a more beautiful one than our Fiona? In fact, we have a lot of beautiful ladies with us today. This ring has been hidden away far too long." Bruce opened the lid wider. "My son, why not slip it on Fiona's finger?"

"Yes, yes, why not? What a splendid idea!" exclaimed her father.

"Indeed, why not?" her mother replied.

Elena was getting more and more concerned about Craig. She could see he was ill at ease. It was not at all to his liking to be rushed into anything like this. Whatever was Bruce thinking about to let such a thing happen?

'He must have lost his senses since the boy came home,' she told herself.

"Now that we are all assembled," said Fiona's father, "we can all drink to your engagement."

"Well, my son, what do you think?" Bruce said, as he at last looked up at him.

"Well," said Craig, "I thought Fiona would have preferred us to be alone when we became betrothed."

"Maybe you are right, my son."

Bruce commenced to close the lid.

"But Craig, my darling," Fiona said with a pout, "I have waited so long and we have been parted so long because of that dreadful war. Please, my darling!"

Well, what could he do with Fiona's plaintive cry and her mother's shrill voice begging him in just as doleful a voice not to delay any longer?

"I don't mind all our friends being around us," said Fiona excitedly.

"Well then, it might just as well be now as later," he agreed.

He took the ring out of the box and closed the lid slowly. Then he looked at her and smiled.

A smile of satisfaction crossed her face. She knew she had won the day. She extended her left hand towards him.

"Well, if it is your wish, my darling, why should I disappoint my lovely girl who has waited so long?"

He kissed her hand lightly, then slid the ring as far as he could. A slight look of consternation crossed his countenance.

"Fiona darling, it won't fit."

"Of course it will," she replied crossly. "Let me try."

But all her efforts were to no avail. She got angrier by the minute. Craig was at a loss for words as he tried to appease her.

"Well, it can soon be made to fit," her mother retorted, most displeased. All she ever wanted was to see her daughter wearing the engagement ring of the McNairs – to be able, at last, to write to her dear sister that soon Fiona would be Craig's wife and the Mistress of Glencree Castle.

"I will take it to our jeweller's tomorrow," said Craig.

"But I don't want to wait so long," Fiona said, almost in tears.

"Well," Bruce suggested, "Craig, you could try the diamond one from your mother's own collection."

Fiona's eyes lit up again at the thought that at last she would be wearing some of the McNairs' priceless jewels.

Craig opened the blue velvet box and tried once again. "No, my darling, that won't fit either. Meanwhile, darling, you can wear the Luckenbooth brooch." He reached for the box which contained it and commenced to pin it on her. "This too is a seal of our engagement and, like the ring, it also contains priceless jewels."

"I know, my darling, but I would rather wear my ring." She pushed her bottom lip forward in fury.

"Well, my dear," said her mother, "Craig will get it fixed as soon as he can."

'Well,' she thought, 'at least I can write to Emma and tell her the good news.'

"Now," said Bruce, "a toast to my dear son and soon-to-be daughter, Craig and Fiona."

Then her father decided that he wished another toast. They all stood up again as Craig and Fiona sat gazing into each other's eyes. "To my lovely daughter and the son of my lifelong friend: God bless them both with lots of happiness, good health and, of course, lots of sons and daughters."

Craig stood up to thank them all for their good wishes and sat down again, a little bewildered by it all.

"When," said Margot, "can we expect the engagement to be made known in the village?"

Lady Cleveland was most anxiously waiting to learn the date so that it could be published in all the London and Scottish papers. She was most anxious to tell all her family and friends in London the news so they could start to prepare for the great occasion of the wedding, which would follow Fiona's season in London next year – two things for which she had waited for so long, since the war had made it impossible.

Her sister Emma's daughters, Olga and Victoria, had not as yet even got an understanding with any young men, in spite of them living in London, and here she was, in the far north of Scotland, with her lovely daughter almost married and settled in the wealthiest family. She sighed happily at the thought of it all.

"As for the public announcement," said Bruce, "I think we will let Craig and Fiona decide that for themselves – maybe at the ball. Now, dear friends, I shall put all the jewellery away. I am sure this happy pair will wish to be alone, and I know Elena is most anxious to get on with making all the arrangements for the future."

Fiona looked up to see Elena's eyes fixed on her with disapproval. Of the two sisters, she disliked Elena the most.

'She didn't want us to get betrothed,' she said to herself, 'but it is too late now, my dear aunt.' She returned Elena's look of displeasure. 'And when I am mistress of this house I shall keep your disapproving look in mind.'

"Come, Fiona – we will have a stroll in the garden whilst the rest discuss future events," said Craig.

As they sauntered in the garden several minutes elapsed before either spoke.

"You are very quiet, my darling," said Fiona. "Are you angry with me for wanting to get betrothed in front of all our friends?"

"Yes, a little," he replied. "I should have preferred us to be alone and chosen my own moment."

"But, my darling," she said with a pout, "we have had lovely moments alone and you let them go by."

"Yes, I did," he replied, "but please try to understand, my darling, I have only recently got home to my father after the war."

'Oh, that war! I am tired of hearing about it,' she thought to herself as Craig continued.

"Even now I sometimes feel I am back there amongst all its horror."

Elena knew this only too well. Sometimes, as he awoke from his nightmares, he would find her standing beside him, trying to calm him.

"I also have lots of things to do with my father: all the administration of the estate, and the buying of all the extra land from Margot and her mother. I am now old enough to receive my mother's inheritance, and I will have to travel to see my lawyers. So many things need to be done now I am home – things that only I can do. I shall be away for long periods and I know you won't like it."

"Well, I understand. I know you have to deal with these affairs, but I feel that you could spare some time for me. We need to sort out some things, such as the alterations to the West Wing, before our marriage takes place next year. As you know, it is the London Season just before we marry, and there will not be enough time when we return from London to do all that needs to be done."

"I have also", he continued, "to discuss with Papa about Aunt Harriet and Aunt Elena – whether they will stay at Glencree or whether we find another home for them nearby. As you well know, they gave up their home to look after us when Mama died."

'Oh, bother the aunts – especially Elena!' Fiona inwardly fumed.

"But, my darling," she said, "I didn't mind us not being alone. I thought it was lovely to be betrothed with our parents and friends around us to wish us well."

The sooner it was known amongst a few of their friends, the more secure she felt. She knew that Craig and his father were attached and that Craig would settle more and more into his old routine of fishing, sailing and visiting his friends for days on end – especially the men who had served with him.

'At least when we are married I shall put a stop to it,' she thought. 'In the meantime, I shall just have to be patient during our engagement.'

She would soon be Mistress of Glencree Castle. The title would be Craig's and her sons that followed. All the land, which was expanding so rapidly, would be hers alone.

'I shall just have to let Craig do as he wishes and be patient,' she thought. She sighed in resignation.

Patience was not one of her assets – she whose every whim had always been appeased instantly.

Craig broke in on her thoughts: "So you see, my darling, how occupied I shall be?"

"But, my darling, we are now truly engaged. Doesn't that make you happy?"

"Of course, my darling, if it makes you happier, but I have always thought of us as being betrothed since we were children."

"Yes, I know, my darling, so have I, but I am so much happier now that all our friends know. Soon everyone will know. I love you so much. Please say you are not angry with me," she said, as she tugged his arm.

He turned and pulled her towards him. He held her in a crushing embrace and kissed her passionately.

"No, my darling, I am not angry any longer. Please forgive me," he said, but he smothered her with kisses before she could reply. "I have always loved you, my darling. You are part of everything I hold so very dear: our mountains, lochs and glens. We rode through this countryside together as children, as will our children."

"Yes, yes, my darling."

These were the words she wanted to hear – words of the future, with their children, as she tried to tell him between his kisses.

"Come now, my darling, we must go inside. It is getting chilly and some of our friends will be leaving. I am, as always, going to drive Margot home later on."

They kissed again and again, reluctant to part as they climbed the steps into the house.

CHAPTER 32

After breakfast next morning, Lady Margot told Elizabeth how much she had enjoyed her singing in church.

"Thank you, milady," she replied. "It was such a lovely service. Everything was just beautiful."

"The laird, too, thought your singing was superb, as did all who heard you."

'Fancy the laird noticing such as me,' she thought.

"Now, wasn't the announcement about the ball exciting?"

"Yes," replied Elizabeth. "My brother Roddy is taking me. It is my very first ball."

"How nice for you, my child! It will be a lovely evening. There is nothing quite so exciting as one's very first ball. I still remember mine and it was such a long time ago," she said, and for a moment her thoughts drifted back to the past. "It is such a long time since we had any balls, parties and gatherings. Thank goodness that dreadful, beastly war is over and we can start to have more social life without feeling guilty that we would be better using the time knitting socks for our gallant boys at the front."

At this remark, Elizabeth smiled, knowing Lady Margot could not knit; and the idea of her knitting socks – well!

"Today, Elizabeth, I want you to come up to the attic and help me go through my trunks, but first we must visit Mama. How are you today, Mama dear? I have brought along Elizabeth before we go up to the attic."

Elizabeth bade her good morning and dropped her a little curtsy.

"Very tired. I have not slept at all well."

"Well, Nurse will take you into the morning room and you can rest; then, later in the day, Elizabeth will come and sing for you."

"Did you say you were going up to the attic?" her mother asked.

"Yes, the laird is giving a ball very soon to welcome home all our boys from the war, so I am going to get Elizabeth to help me decide which dress to wear."

"Oh, how nice to be going to balls again! I remember our balls so well – especially my first one – but now I am too old and too tired. Come, Nurse – take me to the morning room."

Elizabeth had looked at Lady Margot as she spoke of the ball and her face saddened.

'Fancy having so many dresses to choose from that she needs me to help her decide; and here am I with not even one. Gosh! I am so unhappy I could cry.'

"Now, come along, Elizabeth," Lady Margot called to her a little impatiently. It will take most of the morning."

Immediately Elizabeth was taken out of her melancholy thoughts. They climbed to what, to Elizabeth, seemed like the stars, before reaching the attic. Her mistress turned the key in the large oak door and it creaked and groaned as she pushed it open. A long, narrow window ran practically the whole length of the room, letting in the early morning sunlight.

Elizabeth stood back for several seconds before entering the room, which seemed to go on for ever, and as she stood inside she thought, 'It must run the whole length of the hall.' She had never noticed these windows before, but she realised they would be hidden behind the low parapet which ran the whole length of the house.

The whole of one wall was filled with huge trunks, all labelled neatly, all of various sizes and dimensions. Never in her life had she seen so many. She remembered her Aunt Ingrid had several, but none as big as these.

"Now, let me see," said Lady Margot. She paused for a moment, looking round, before opening a small drawer in a bureau in the corner. "I have all the contents listed in my notebook." She took a large hard-backed notebook and started to turn the pages. "Thank goodness there is enough light. It is just as well we chose this morning, Elizabeth."

"Yes, milady," she said, still gazing around in awe.

Lady Margot, still looking through the pages of her book, suddenly exclaimed: "Ah, that is the one I must look into first." She rummaged amongst a bunch of keys she withdrew from her pocket and undid the lock of the largest black trunk. The huge lock was difficult to prise open, but at last, with a loud snap, the catch lifted and they both lifted the heavy creaking lid.

Lady Margot handed layer after layer of tissue paper to Elizabeth and told her to lay them on the large table near the window. She did as she was bid and watched as Lady Margot unwrapped long white sheets and brought out the first of the dresses – a bright-red cocktail dress covered with a fringe of silver beads.

Elizabeth gave a gasp of delight. Never in her life had she seen anything so brilliant. Lady Margot held it up to view it more closely.

"Very colourful!" she exclaimed, "but a little too bright for the occasion. I must have a long gown for such an important ball as this one," she muttered to herself. "Just lay it flat on top of the tissue paper, Elizabeth."

Elizabeth took the dress from her and arranged it as prettily as she could before returning to await the next. Several dresses appeared in various colours but the same style.

"No, these won't do, but lay them beside the others. They all need an airing. Now the other trunks – the locks are just as difficult and the lids are just as heavy to lift. Really," she gasped, "I should have got Charles to come up before us and undo all these trunks, but it is too late now. We will manage, won't we Elizabeth?" She looked at her and smiled. "Yes, we are managing quite well." She was eager to see the rest of the trunks' contents. "Ah, these are the ones, I think."

Once more, layers and layers of paper and white cotton covers were placed on the table.

"Now here is one of my favourite ones – this white one with the long flowing skirt and billowing net, edged with silver."

Elizabeth gave another gasp of excitement as she held it up, and Lady Margot looked at her in surprise.

'Why, of course – the dear girl has never seen anything like them before,' she thought to herself.

She brought out two more, identical in style but of different colours.

"As you see, Elizabeth, they all have matching gloves and shoes." She unwrapped several of the small packages containing them, and held them up for her to see. "There are also the evening purses and combs, but they are in another trunk."

"Oh, milady," she declared, "they are all truly magnificent – so pretty, all of them. I could look at them all day."

"Well, there are lots more to see of Mama's, and also my daughter's, but we won't have time today. Ah, here is another one of my favourites."

She lifted out a bright-green one edged with gold lamé and held it against herself as she shook out a few of the creases. The gold-edged pleats fell from the waist.

Several times Elizabeth gave out gasps of ecstasy as she gazed at each one. She hardly believed that so many beautiful dresses could exist, but here they were, one after the other. Lady Margot tried first one and then another against herself and looked questioningly at her reflection in the long mirror on the wall. Then she passed each one to Elizabeth to put on the long rail, so she could get a better view of them as they hung there.

"Put the white sheet on the rail first," she instructed. "Oh, I cannot decide!" she exclaimed, and she pulled another white one with a beautiful red sash from another trunk. She put the long sash over her shoulder and her thoughts drifted back to bygone days as she spoke: "Can you see, Elizabeth, all the dainty silver flowers around the border? They were all hand done by the durzi in India. The durzi is the tailor, and he trains all his children from quite an early age to sew by hand and, of course, by machine. They all sit on the floor as they work. I often used to go to the bazaar as a child with Mama and my ayah and watch them. It was so fascinating – such happy times." She sighed again. "I am longing to return and see my daughter and granddaughters, but", she sighed, "I shall have to wait till Mama is well again – however long that is. Now, Elizabeth, here are the pretty shoes to match each dress, all made by the Chinese."

"Oh, milady, how beautiful they are!" Elizabeth's eyes lit up with excitement.

"Yes, child, but alas! they won't fit me now. Neither will the dresses."

She looked more and more perplexed as she gazed at all the laid-out dresses.

Elizabeth handed back the shoes a little reluctantly. Her face grew sad as she watched them being wrapped and carefully stored away. Such lovely things: dresses, slippers, bangles, coronets, gloves, ribbons and laces. Why had Lady Margot got such lovely things, and she hadn't got anything to go to the ball in? The more she looked at them the more full of longing she became. 'No ball gown for me! It's just not fair,' she thought, biting her lip in disappointment.

But Lady Margot had not noticed Elizabeth's sad face. She rummaged deeper and deeper in the trunk, more and more layers of fine muslin being handed to Elizabeth.

"At last!" she exclaimed excitedly as she pulled out silk saris, all shimmering with silver-and-gold-thread borders.

Elizabeth held her breath before gasping: "Milady, milady, I have never seen such lovely things."

Lady Margot smiled at her exuberance. Never had she heard such exclamations of delight.

Elizabeth grew more and more astounded as Lady Margot unrolled them before handing them to her after viewing them critically against herself. She tried one after another, still undecided, tut-tutting to herself as she did so.

Elizabeth, in her excitement, kept dropping them. She was almost too afraid to handle them, which made her mistress tut-tut more. In fact, she was getting a little exasperated with Elizabeth.

'But how can I show my displeasure at the child? She has never seen such things before.'

Elizabeth was becoming sadder. Her face clouded with longing as Lady Margot viewed herself in the long mirror with lengths of sari thrown over her shoulder. It was then, as she glanced in the mirror, that she noticed Elizabeth's face. Never before had she noticed how exquisite her eyes were – full of longing and ecstasy. As she studied her, Lady Margot noticed Elizabeth's eyes were filled with a deep sadness too.

'But of course – how thoughtless of me! This poor child has evidently not got a dress for the ball. She said it was her first ball and her brother would be taking her. How ever could she afford a new dress on the salary I pay her.'

She averted her eyes quickly.

"I must decide soon, Elizabeth."

"I do so like the green one edged with gold, milady," she ventured.

"I do also, so that is the one. Now we must pack them all away, but I am reluctant to do so. They all hold such memories for me: I travelled all over India with my father and late husband, who was a missionary." Lady Margot kept up the conversation as they put the dresses away. "Before we go I will show you some photographs." She went to the bureau and brought out a box full of albums all labelled with the years. "Come over here, child, near the window and share these wonderful views with me."

Elizabeth sat down beside her, thinking, 'I would rather continue looking at all those lovely dresses.' However, she looked intently at the photographs as Lady Margot, in between deep sighs, kept exclaiming, "Such memories, such memories!" Then there was a long silence.

Elizabeth, waiting for her to continue, glanced shyly up at her and noticed a faraway look in her eyes. Never before had she seen her look so sad and forlorn. She was quite at a loss as to what to say.

"This is a picture of me as a young girl with Mama and Papa. He was in the army. Such happy times I had with all my friends! Most of them are still there. This is Davinia, my daughter, who was born out there. Her husband, Stephen, is a judge in the high court in the city. He also was born out there. His parents have a large tea plantation in the hills. It is so beautiful there. I am just longing to go back. Papa is buried out there, as is my late husband. Mama couldn't settle after that and returned here."

She was silent as her mind went back to her days in India. Her silence seemed so precious to her that Elizabeth sat looking at her, not wanting to break in on her thoughts.

At last Lady Margot spoke: "Now, my child, what was I saying? Never mind, I have forgotten." She turned another page of her album. "This is a picture of my husband and me on our wedding day."

"Oh, milady, what a beautiful bride and such a lovely gown!"

Her mind returned to all the lovely gowns she had seen, now all locked away.

"These are of my son and daughter, but my dear son died of fever shortly after his sixth birthday." She hurried past the painful memory and turned to the next page. "This is my daughter's wedding. I keep only one picture of them downstairs. The rest are here in my box of memories. I have not shared them with anyone for a long time." She sighed again as she closed the book. "Now, my child," she said in a much lighter tone of voice, "these are some of the lovely sights taken on our travels. This is the Taj Mahal – so beautiful, especially by moonlight – and this is the Golden Temple, and these are the mountains."

"Milady, how high they are! I thought our Scottish mountains were high, but these . . ." She was spellbound.

"Yes, you have to see them to appreciate them. They are the highest in the world." She closed the book. "Those days are far gone, but the memories are still as precious as ever."

"I shall never see them, milady, as I shall never leave my beloved Scottish mountains or my lovely Scotland. I have got Papa and Mama, and now my dear Roddy is back."

"Now," said Lady Margot as she rose to put the albums away, "Elizabeth, please put the last of the muslin over the saris in that trunk and the others in the one over there that we forgot."

"Yes, milady. I had quite forgotten the ones on the rail."

Lady Margot watched her closely as she folded each one along its original folds and placed them carefully between the layers of tissue paper and fine linen. A plan was going through her mind: 'I must help this child with a gown for the ball. Yes, yes,' she told herself, 'that's the answer. I wonder if it will make her a little happier?' "Now I remember!" she suddenly exclaimed.

Elizabeth looked up with alarm.

"What, milady? Have I put them away in the wrong order? I am so sorry if so."

"No, no, my child, I have another trunk – quite a special one I had forgotten about. Come – it's over there." She hastened to the far corner.

'Oh, not another!' Elizabeth sighed. 'I am so tired.'

She helped to lift the heavy lid and watched as Lady Margot removed layer after layer of tissue paper and withdrew the most beautiful dress of them all. There seemed no end to the floating yards of blue voile decorated with silver along the bottom, edging the cap sleeves and round the neck.

She looked at it spellbound as it was laid on the long table and her mistress delved deeper inside the trunk, brought out more paper and unwrapped elbow-length mittens, a Dorothy bag, silver hair combs, a fan, a narrow coronet and matching blue slippers.

"In this dress," she declared, as she held it up, watching the utter amazement on Elizabeth's face, "what a picture she was. It was her very first ball at the residency."

'Well,' thought Elizabeth, 'I don't know anything about the residency, but this is the most exquisite dress I have ever seen.'

Lady Margot continued after a long pause (which she made purposely to watch Elizabeth's reaction): "Davinia was about your age, but a little taller. I think it should fit you. She only wore it for that occasion as the next day we left for another mission station. We left it behind and my cousin very kindly brought it here and put it with my other precious treasures. I am sure it will fit you, so it, and everything else that goes with it, is yours. How you would have enjoyed the ball that night – so many interesting people to meet."

Once again Lady Margot was lost in reverie, but Elizabeth wasn't listening. Lady Margot had said they were all for her. Her mind was in a whirl as she tried to take it all in.

"It might be a little too long for you," Lady Margot continued.

"Milady," she ventured, "you did say the dress was for me?" Her voice rose in delight and astonishment.

"Yes, of course, my child." Elizabeth had reacted as she guessed she would. "Now let me try it against you." Elizabeth stood still as they both gazed in the mirror. "Yes, as I thought – too long! But Miss Grant can alter it for you. Now try the slippers."

Elizabeth hung on to the side of the long table as she slid into them.

"Yes, milady, they fit. They're a bit loose, but I will put a sock inside."

"The dress matches your eyes – such a lovely shade of blue," she said as she saw they were almost filled with tears of joy. "Now hurry, child – take them to your room whilst I put my other things away."

Elizabeth laid the dress carefully over her arm as Lady Margot put the accessories in a small bag, along with two sachets of lavender.

"Now don't be too long – we still have a lot to do."

"I will be back soon, milady," she called, as she sped from the room and down the flights of steps, hurriedly in case Lady Margot changed her mind. She leapt up the stairs to her room like a young gazelle and laid everything on her bed. 'How kind Lady Margot is,' she told herself over and over again, her eyes sparkling with happiness. Then, for a moment, she stood still, a look of consternation on her face. What would her mother and father and Roddy think? 'I do hope Mama won't think that I asked Lady Margot for them,' she thought; then she reassured herself: 'No, Mama knows I would never do such a thing. I know Emma will be delighted for me. I bet none of the girls from the academy, and those upstart daughters of Mrs Crawford – her precious jewels, as she calls them – will have a lovelier dress than mine. Now I must hurry.' She caressed the dress once more before reluctantly closing the door. 'I don't want those playful pups having a tug of war with my lovely slippers.'

"Now," said Lady Margot, "we will take these to my room before we start our letters. I still have several to sign before you go to the village. I shall be going to Glencree Castle later on."

Suddenly, the lunch bell rang.

"My goodness, Elizabeth, it's one o'clock already. How quickly time has flown! Get away as soon as you can after lunch and call on Miss Grant. Ask her to come to see me as soon as she can."

CHAPTER 33

Later that afternoon, Elizabeth walked down to the village to post the letters and call in to the dressmaker's shop.

Miss Grant greeted her warmly. "Now, I can guess what has brought you in here. Emma has only just left and Mrs Crawford and her three lovely daughters,

Pearl, Ruby and Sapphire, were here this morning."

'Trust her to be in first with her three precious jewels,' thought Elizabeth. 'I am sorry to be thinking such ungracious thoughts about them.' She knew her parents would be most displeased with her if they ever knew. 'But', she told herself, as if trying to excuse herself, 'they and their precious mother should be a little more gracious to me. It's not my fault her precious jewels cannot sing like I can.'

"They are all having new dresses for the ball, so I am going to be very busy. Such pretty materials they have chosen. They will look really beautiful in them when they are finished. Now, Elizabeth, what about your new dress for the ball?"

"Well," she declared, "I won't be able to have a new dress made, but if you could shorten the one I am having, I will bring it in next time I come."

"Yes, my dear, I will most certainly shorten it for you."

"Thank you," she replied. "My mistress would like you to call to see her as soon as you can about her dress."

"Tell Lady Margot I shall be up as soon as possible."

As she left the shop, Elizabeth met Emma coming out of the library.

"Emma, Emma," she called excitedly, "I have got a new dress for the ball."

"So have I!" Emma exclaimed, just as excited as she. "Mama has said I can have one as it is my first ball. Now tell me about yours, Elizabeth."

"Well," she started excitedly. Then she hesitated for a moment.

Emma glanced at her out of the corner of her eye.

"Well," she continued, "Lady Margot has given me a ball gown, but it will need shortening, so I have just called into the shop and Miss Grant is going to do it for me."

"How wonderful!" Emma exclaimed.

"Now, Emma, promise me you won't tell another soul. I don't think Lady Margot would like my telling anyone, but you are my only confidante and I know I can tell you. I am so thrilled about it I could cry with joy."

"Oh, I am so happy for you, my dearest friend. Of course, you know I would never betray any confidences."

"Now I must really hurry back."

"So must I," Emma replied.

They set off together up the long country lane, and parted at the crossroad leading to the vicarage, with their usual parting words: "I will see you at choir practice."

Elizabeth sat down to tea with Lady Margot, and gave her the message from Miss Grant. She knew Lady Margot would be going up to Glencree Castle to visit, especially to tell Lady Elena the latest news she had had from her daughter regarding the missions. Elizabeth was most anxious for her to leave, as she wanted to get back to her room.

After the meal she saw Lady Margot safely into her carriage.

"Here are your books, milady," she said, and she put them on the seat beside her.

"Thank you, my dear. I really cannot manage without you. I almost went without them. Now go and relieve Nurse, and sing and play for Mama for a while. Nurse will come in later and put her to bed. You retire to your room then, my dear. You have had a busy day and a long walk from the village. Flora will attend to me on my return."

"Thank you, milady. Goodbye," she called as she watched her out of sight.

The small dogs, just returning from their afternoon walk with Charles, rushed up to her with leaps and bounds and she gathered them in her arms.

"And where have you left Charles today, you mischievous pair?" she said.

She looked up to see him coming panting along.

"My, my, Elizabeth, how they do run on so! They fair leave me breathless with the tricks they play on me, running hither and thither. I never know where they are going to pop up next."

He wiped the sweat from his forehead with his already damp handkerchief.

"Well, now you can rest. Their supper will be ready. I must hurry to sing for Lady Roxburgh."

"What a day I have had with Lady Roxburgh!" Nurse exclaimed as soon as she saw Elizabeth in the hallway.

"Well, I will go and sing to her whilst you rest for a while."

"Thank you, Elizabeth. I will return about eight o'clock," she said, and she wended her way up the broad staircase.

"What would you like me to sing for you tonight, milady?" Elizabeth asked.

"Oh, anything, my dear – some of my usual old Scottish melodies. I love to hear you play and sing so beautifully, my child."

It wasn't long before Elizabeth noticed that her mistress was falling asleep. She was glad when Nurse opened the door. She made a hasty retreat. The evening had seemed to drag.

She hastened to her room, up the stairs two at a time. She slipped up several in her haste, banging her shin bone.

"Drat the steps!" she exclaimed as she hurried across the landing to her room and locked the door behind her with a look of sheer satisfaction. "I will not be disturbed now. No one is going to come in and see my new dress."

She gazed at it rapturously, still not quite believing that everything laid out on the bed was hers. She had waited for this moment all day and could hardly contain herself in her excitement.

"How lucky I am, to be sure! No one will have as lovely a dress as mine."

She slipped the combs into her hair and pulled on the gloves. They fitted her perfectly. Then she pulled on the matching slippers.

"Just a little too big, but I will make them fit perfectly before the dance," she said, talking out loud to herself all the time.

She pulled off the gloves and took the combs out of her hair and fingered them lovingly.

"I must fix my hair properly before I use those."

She hastily pulled off her dress and flung it on the back of a nearby chair.

"Oh, how I hate that old black dress! These dull colours don't suit me at all," she said as she stood there in her petticoat, viewing her dress ruefully. "I must ask Mama to make me a new petticoat of the finest linen she can find. This one is too old and the material is far too thick."

She slipped the beautiful blue dress over her head and slid her arms into the pretty cap sleeves, which came just above her elbows. She tried in vain to fasten all the small buttons at the back.

"Well, I shall just have to get someone to help me on the night," she told herself, "but not tonight – tonight is just for me. Oh, drat!" she kept exclaiming as she struggled. "Just the top four I cannot manage, but at least I have got it on."

She fitted it neatly into her waist.

"It just fits me there perfectly. It is just a little too long, but I will ask Emma to see how much it needs shortening before I take it to the shop."

She brushed her hair behind her ears, slid in the combs and brushed a short fringe over her eyes.

"Yes, I think this is the way I shall wear it, but Emma will know best."

She set a great deal of store by Emma's opinions, whatever they were discussing. She pulled on the long silver lamé gloves and put the Dorothy bag over her arm. Then she put on the silver coronet with the pretty droplets, and pulled on the bracelet above her elbow. She stood before the full-length mirror and viewed herself. She picked up the silver-edged fan and waved it to and fro as elegantly as she knew how.

"There is, I believe," she said aloud to herself, "a special language of the fan. I wonder what it is." She sighed. "Maybe Emma knows. I will ask her. I won't need it for this ball, as Roddy is taking me, but it will be nice to know for future balls – and future balls I have every intention of attending, even though at present I have only got this one ball gown."

The light from her bedside paraffin lamp reflected in the mirror. An aura surrounded her, with the sheen on her golden hair and the silver of the combs and coronet; the silver edging on the frill round her neck and cap sleeves against the clouds of misty blue of the volumes of flimsy voile of the dress looked like a host of silver stars in a misty blue sky. Her bright, sparkling blue eyes danced with radiance, becoming brighter and brighter as she gazed at herself.

"How lucky I am! And how kind Lady Margot is to give me such a dress as this! I feel just like a fairy princess. No other girl could possibly be as lucky as I am."

She half closed her eyes and started to sway from side to side, swinging out her arms as she hummed the tune of 'The Blue Danube'. She started to waltz round and round the room, faster and faster. She was like a feather on the breeze, completely oblivious to her surroundings.

Suddenly, one of her slippers flew off and she stumbled headlong into the corner of the room, knocking over the tall plant stand. The tall aspidistra went hurtling to the floor, and the large pot broke in two, scattering the soil across the floor. The shocked wisp of a fairy dancer hastily gathered herself up.

"Oh, my lovely, lovely dress!" she cried in alarm. "I do hope it's not ruined by the soil."

She hastily straightened it out and looked to see how much damage, if any, she had done.

'No, it seems all right,' she thought with relief.

The broken plant pot and stand had not as yet crossed her mind – only her dress mattered.

Just then, a knock on her door aroused her from her concern.

"Elizabeth, Elizabeth, whatever has happened? Are you all right? I heard such a lot of jumping around and then a loud crash."

'Fancy her saying I was jumping around when I was dancing! Could she not tell the difference?' Elizabeth thought. She was quite peeved at the thought of it.

"Yes, yes, Flora. I was only practising a dance for the ball and I knocked over

163

the plant stand. I shall see Lady Margot in the morning about it. Charles will be able to mend the stand and repot the plant."

'Well, I hope he can,' she told herself. She had no intention of opening the door. 'Oh, I wish she would go.'

"All right, then, if you are not hurt . . ."

"No, I am not hurt, thank you, Flora."

"But please be a little quieter: Lady Roxburgh has retired."

"I am so sorry." In her excitement she had forgotten the old lady.

"I cannot think what has come over you. You are usually so quiet."

"I will be, I promise. Goodnight, Flora." She hoped that saying goodnight would encourage Flora to go. It had the desired effect.

"Goodnight, Elizabeth."

She waited patiently to hear Flora go downstairs. She hastily took off her slipper and looked around for the offending one.

"Come here, you nuisance," she said with a pout. She put the slippers to one side near the bag and gloves. "I will most certainly have to take them to the shoe shop for insoles to be fitted before I dance again."

Before finally taking off the dress, she looked once again in the mirror.

'Well, I am still sure', she told herself, 'none of the snobby girls from the academy or Mrs Crawford's precious jewels will have as pretty a dress as Elizabeth Dawn Angeline Ingrid Anderson, although I do say so myself.'

She put the rest of the things away along with the two lavender bags on the hanger. She brushed the dress once more.

'How lovely it will smell!' she thought, and she reluctantly closed the door of the wardrobe.

She hurriedly re-dressed and went to weigh up the damage to the broken plant pot and stand.

'I will take the stand down into the conservatory and bring back the small brush and pan. My word, it's so heavy!'

She gave a gasp of dismay as she picked it up and wended her way to the door, which she opened and closed very softly. She didn't want any more chat with Flora. She sped swiftly down the stairs through the kitchen and into the conservatory, and brought back the small brush and pan. She brushed up as much of the soil as she could, sped off down the steps again into the conservatory, and placed the soil in a bucket.

'My goodness! I never thought the pot held so much soil,' she thought.

On her return, she looked at the plant and decided she couldn't carry it in its broken pot.

'I mustn't disturb the roots more than I have done already. Oh dear, what a pickle I'm in!' She sighed as she struggled to keep it intact. She was pondering what to do next when she saw her wastepaper bin. 'Yes, that will have to do.'

She put the waste paper in a large bag and struggled as best she could to put the plant into the bin. By this time she was quite exhausted.

'Oh, I am so tired, what with all my dancing and now all this.'

She rested back on her heels a little while, mustering up the strength to carry on with the task ahead.

'If only my dear Roddy was here to help me!" she sighed. She glanced at the clock on the shelf and gasped in dismay. "My goodness, how late it is! I must really hurry.'

She gasped at the weight of the plant as she gathered it up. It was almost as tall as herself, and the huge leaves kept waving about in front of her face. She had opened the door beforehand, but she could not close it behind her. She descended the stairs with both hands round the pot and her back resting against the balustrade. She struggled down each step gingerly, stopping now and again to rest.

Unbeknown to her, however, down in the hallway stood Lady Margot, saying goodnight to Craig and Fiona, who had brought her home from the castle.

Fiona, who was facing the staircase, let out a peal of laughter and exclaimed, "Margot, I didn't know you had walking aspidistras in your home!"

"Whatever do you mean?" Lady Margot exclaimed.

She followed Fiona's gaze, as did Craig, who roared with laughter when he saw the waving leaves slowly descending the stairs. Lady Margot, too, laughed at the unexpected sight.

Just then, Elizabeth's face appeared between the waving leaves.

'Only eight more steps to go,' she told herself.

She had run up and down the stairs so often that she knew exactly how many there were. When her eyes alighted on the three of them, gazing up at her with such amusement, she almost dropped the plant.

"My dear Elizabeth," exclaimed Lady Margot, "whatever has happened?"

"I am sorry, Lady Margot," Elizabeth gasped. "I knocked over the plant in my room, and I am taking it to the conservatory."

"But, my dear, Charles would have dealt with it in the morning for you. It is far too heavy for you."

By this time Elizabeth had reached the bottom step.

"Please allow me to assist you, Elizabeth. It is, as Lady Margot said, far too heavy for you."

The smile was gone from Craig's face and he looked at her quite anxiously, but she looked down at him, remembering that only a few moments ago he was laughing almost as much as Fiona still was. She was furious to think that, of all people, this man had seen her in such a state.

"I can manage quite well, Master Craig. The soil will spoil your clothes."

That was the last thought in his head. He looked at her with concern.

"I will take it into the conservatory, Master Craig," she said, more emphatically, and he knew by the tone of her voice that she was quite adamant.

"Very well, then, if you insist, but allow me to open the door."

He did it before she had time to reply. She hurried through and kicked it shut, resting her back against it so that he couldn't follow. She was furious.

'Of all the people to see me in this predicament, it would have to be him. Why couldn't it have been my Roddy instead?' She was nearly crying with sheer anger and exhaustion. She was so hot and tired with the struggle. 'It has quite spoiled my day,' she told herself angrily.

She flung the plant and bin into the corner and yelled at it: "Don't you dare die on me now, after all my hard work and misery."

She opened the door a fraction and waited as she heard Lady Margot bidding Craig and Fiona goodnight. Then she closed it again softly, waiting while her mistress went up the stairs. She heard Lady Margot calling goodnight to Flora as she entered her room, then Elizabeth sped up the stairs as swiftly as she could and flung herself on her bed.

"Oh, what a day, what a day!"

CHAPTER 34

The following morning, Elizabeth found Charles and explained to him about the plant.

"Don't you worry your pretty little head about that, Elizabeth. I will mend the stand; then I will take the plant to the gardener, and soon everything will be as before."

"Thank you so much, Charles. I am sorry I let it fall."

She had no intention of telling him what had happened, but she guessed that Flora would fill in the details. She hurried to the study and was soon joined by Lady Margot.

"After we have finished the correspondence, Elizabeth, you can go to the village and order the books I have listed. Miss Stuart will know which ones I mean. Then you can take your dress to Miss Grant for any alterations and do any other shopping you need. I shall not need you for the rest of the day, but you must, as usual, sing and play for Mama if she wishes. Nurse will let you know. You know how much Mama loves your singing."

"Yes, I love to sing for her."

"Your Aunt Ingrid was a frequent visitor here when she was a girl, so long ago, and we all used to sing round the piano in the evening after dinner. She still kept up her visits to Mama when I had so often to return to India. I always loved going back to India, but I always missed my lovely Scotland so much." She sighed. "You were so lucky to have her for an aunt. She was such a gifted musician and singer too – a gift you have inherited."

"Thank you, milady."

'I wish she would get on with this correspondence,' Elizabeth thought. She had loved her aunt dearly and did not feel up to talking about her.

After lunch she hastened to her room, passing Flora on the stairs.

"My dear," Flora exclaimed, "why the hurry? You must not rush about so. You will be falling again."

But Elizabeth was not heeding her. She was already in her room with the door closed. She put her slippers in a bag. 'I will see what the shoe mender can do with them,' she thought. She reached for her dress and laid it carefully in its tissue paper on the bed. She was most reluctant to part with it even for a short time. 'But it has got to be altered, so that is that. I am so happy. Fancy my having a real ball gown! I can hardly believe it, but it's true. My lovely, lovely dress!'

At last, after folding it to her satisfaction, she hurried down the stairs and into the library to pick up the correspondence. The afternoon was bright and sunny and she hummed a little tune as she went.

'I will post my letters first,' she told herself; 'then I will take my slippers to Mr Macdonald and collect them later in the week; then I will take my dress to Miss Grant. It will only crease more if I go to the library first.'

Squeals of ecstasy were coming from behind one of the fitting-room screens as she entered the dressmaker's.

"Mine is just too beautiful for words, even though it is not yet finished," one voice declared.

"But mine is much prettier with all the lace and ribbons," another replied.

"But mine will be lovelier than either of yours, won't it, Mama?" said another.

"They are all going to look beautiful when they are finished," their mother replied. "You will most certainly be the belles of the ball on the night, don't you think so?"

"Yes, they most certainly will. They have such lovely figures to show the dress off – so tall and graceful."

The three of them cooed with delight, and their mother nodded her head in agreement.

"Now I will leave you for a while to attend to my other customer. I heard the bell go a few moments ago. You can adjust one another's dresses until I return. Then you can let me know if you want any of the trimmings altered."

Their mother looked a little peeved to think that Miss Grant had to go and attend to someone else's dress when her own daughters' were not yet finished.

"Oh, do come in, my dear. Go into this cubicle and put your dress on."

Elizabeth did as she was bid.

"Yes, dear, it needs shortening quite a bit, and the waist needs to be taken in a little also. You are so small and dainty, but rest assured, my dear, it will be a perfect fit when I have altered it."

Elizabeth did not speak as she watched Miss Grant turn up the hem of the dress and place several pins in at the desired length. Then she put in extra pleats at the waist. She stood back to look at it.

"Yes, my dear, that is much more to my liking."

The excitement had died down in the other cubicle, but Elizabeth had recognised their voices.

'It is the Crawford girls and their mother. Why have they gone so silent?' she thought.

The word *altered* had stopped their exclamations of delight at their own beautiful dresses, and they fell silent in order to overhear any more remarks. They looked at one another in disbelief. Their curiosity was excited and they had no intention of missing any further comments on the subject.

"Alterations," they whispered as quietly as they could, and they each leaned forward to get closer to the curtain screening off the cubicle.

"To whom is she speaking?" asked their mother.

"I don't know. I haven't heard her speak yet."

"Well, carry on with your dresses until Miss Grant comes in. Maybe she will tell us."

"Fancy going to a ball in a dress that has to be shortened and the waist altered. It must be second-hand," said Ruby.

They heard the rustle of paper and the dress being hung on the rail. They hastened to open the cubicle curtains, and they peered out.

Elizabeth glanced in dismay as she reappeared and saw the three of them looking at her (in spite of their mother's remonstrations) through the curtains. She hurried past them, with a look of confusion and apprehension as she saw the look of disdain on their faces. But her discomfort lasted only for a fleeting moment.

'Well, it is a beautiful dress anyway, even if it has to be altered to fit me,' she thought.

She held her beautiful head higher as she proceeded to the door. She turned before leaving.

"Miss Grant?"

"Yes, my dear."

"When will my dress be ready?"

"Next week, dear. Call in on Thursday. It should be ready then."

"Thank you, Miss Grant," she called, and hurriedly closed the door.

"It will be ready by Thursday," mimicked Ruby to Sapphire.

"All the alterations will be finished by then," Sapphire mimicked back, and they both started to titter with glee.

"Oh, you two – really!" exclaimed Pearl, easily the most pleasant of the three.

"Now then, where were we?" said Miss Grant as she entered. "Yes, young ladies, I think one more fitting for all of you, then there will only be the trimmings to finish."

"Now, come on, girls," said their mother. "I still have more shopping to do, and we must change your father's library books."

Elizabeth hastened to the library and handed the order to Miss Stuart. She decided to browse through the books for a while. She was so happy about her dress. It had been quite a wrench to even let it out of her sight. 'But it will soon be Thursday,' she told herself. 'Then I can collect it and never let it out of my sight again.'

She was so engrossed in the books and thoughts of her dress that she failed to notice the three Crawford girls and their mother had arrived. But suddenly she heard her name mentioned, and she hid her face in the book she had been idly glancing through. They, however, had spotted her at once and looked at one another in amusement.

"She is probably looking for a book on how to dance properly in time for the ball in her hand-me-down ball gown," exclaimed Ruby. "Imagine, a ball gown with a tuck here and a tuck there for the biggest ball ever held in the castle!"

The three of them let out a shriek of laughter, and their mother tried in vain to shush them into silence, although she was just as amused as they were.

'Thank goodness my lovely girls are not having hand-me-down dresses! That I would never allow,' she told herself. 'I cannot think what her mother is thinking about to allow it.'

Elizabeth heard the girls' remarks, uttered loudly – for her to hear, she was sure. They knew she had never attended dancing classes with Mrs Emmot, the local dancing teacher, as they had.

"Yes," Sapphire reiterated, "she must be looking for a book on how to dance." Another peal of laughter came from them.

'Well, of all the things to think!' she thought. 'Little do they know I was taught on the mainland by a far better teacher than Miss Emmot. What a surprise they will get, to be sure!'

She was getting very angry, but she calmed herself and continued to study the book she was holding. She was anxious to get out as fast as she could. 'But', she told herself, 'I'm not going to run away and give them the satisfaction of knowing that I have heard their remarks.'

Miss Stuart looked up from her desk, a frown on her face.

'Really, I must tell them to be much quieter,' she thought.

She was just going to do so when the door swung open and in walked Craig.

"Now, what may I ask is the cause of all this laughter?" he said, and he looked puzzled as they all looked at one another, not daring to say.

"Why, Mrs Crawford, who are these three lovely girls you are chaperoning?"

She gave him a curtsy. "May I present my three precious jewels: my daughters, Pearl, Ruby and Sapphire."

They curtsied as she spoke. Her silly reference to her precious jewels was a joke to everyone else in the district.

"This is going to be their first ball, so you can imagine how excited they are about it. This, of course, is owing to the dreadful war having lasted so long. What a nuisance it was, to be sure."

"I agree – far too long," he said.

He thought to himself, 'What do they know of war?'

Mrs Crawford still had ideas that one of her precious jewels should be Mistress of Glencree. Of course, she knew of the rumoured engagement of Craig and Lady Fiona. 'But', she told herself, 'there is many a slip betwixt the cup and the lip.'

"You girls have grown into such beautiful ladies whilst I have been away. Truly amazing!"

He was revelling in their evident adoration of him. To them he was like a laughing cavalier. He was quite enjoying the mild flirtation.

Miss Stuart was quite beside herself at the hilarity, but she could hardly rebuke Master Craig, so she continued to grimace her very obvious displeasure. Old Professor Roberts kept raising his head from the old maps he was poring over, and his tut-tuts were getting louder as he gazed at them over his pince-nez.

Craig continued to flirt with each one in turn.

'Well,' he told himself, 'I can indulge myself in these mild flirtations, having been without female company for so long. All is fair game at the moment.'

"Now, you must all save more than one dance for me – promise?"

"Of course they will, Master Craig," their mother replied, highly delighted at his suggestion, "and you must call and have tea with us one afternoon."

"I will."

They were beside themselves with glee.

"But I have so many friends to visit," he continued.

"Well, do come as soon as you can."

He was just going to continue the conversation when he raised his eyes above theirs and was just in time to see Elizabeth, her long golden ringlets swinging down her back, disappearing through the door. He bade them a hasty goodbye and hastened to the door after her, much to their mother's annoyance.

"Well, upon my word!" she exclaimed.

He was just in time to see her climb into the trap beside Emma.

"Oh, Emma, I am so glad to see you," she said. "I thought I might have missed you as I was so long in the library and dressmaker's."

It was their custom to meet in the village if they could, and ride back together.

"Whatever is the matter, Elizabeth? You look so upset." She slowed the horse. "Now rest back quietly, Elizabeth, and tell me what has upset you so. I have never seen you like this before."

Elizabeth related all that had happened in the dressmaker's and library.

"Now, don't you see, Emma, it will be all over the village before the week is out and the girls from the academy will just lap it up. I can imagine their dormitories ringing with laughter and ridicule all night. Lady Margot is sure to get to know, and she will be very angry with me."

Emma noted the sob in her voice.

"Don't worry so, Elizabeth. If Lady Margot mentions it, just say they must have overheard your conversation with Miss Grant as they were in the adjoining cubicle. She will understand. They themselves will be none the wiser, and that will make them angry."

So deep in conversation were they that neither noticed the horseman trying to get abreast of them.

CHAPTER 35

Craig hastened out of the library and raced to where he had tied his horse outside the tailor's shop. He almost fell off in his haste to mount. He paused a moment in thought, suddenly remembering his father's book.

'Oh, bother! I will pick it up another day.'

The three girls and their mother looked at one another in amazement as they followed him out, and watched in fury as they saw his haste to reach the carriage.

"That is Emma and that upstart Elizabeth Anderson sitting beside her," declared Ruby.

"Well, upon my word!" Mrs Crawford said. "Well, girls," she continued, "we shall have to split up that little party. Why is he in such a hurry to speak to them, I wonder? He didn't give me time to arrange a time to take tea with us."

"Oh, Mama," Ruby said, "we were all looking forward to him visiting."

"I don't know what his dear mother would have said about his behaviour," said Mrs Crawford, and she tut-tutted in exasperation. His mother had often called to have tea with her and brought Craig along to play with the girls.

"Now I shall have to wait until the night of the ball to arrange it."

"But, Mama," they chorused, "you must ask him before the ball. We won't know which dances he wants us to save for him."

They all stamped their feet in anger. The thought of missing out on any dances with him was unbearable.

"Well, I shall have to see what I can arrange. Now come – we still have to collect your Papa's book."

Emma's carriage was now out of sight.

Elizabeth looked up, startled, as Craig reined his horse beside them.

"Good afternoon, Misses Elizabeth and Emma. My, my, the village is full of pretty girls today! I shall have to come into the village more often."

'If he includes those three 'jewel' girls," Emma seethed to herself, 'he means *spiteful* girls – jealous also I should think if they have spotted him talking to us.'

"Good afternoon, Master Craig," they both replied.

Emma took command of the conversation, knowing Elizabeth was still too upset to speak, but she noticed that he never took his gaze from Elizabeth's face: "We all have extra shopping to do now things are getting back to normal."

"How are your parents, Elizabeth? Well, I hope. Also your brother, Roddy?"

She felt her face going crimson.

"Yes, Master Craig, they are all well, thank you."

Why did he have to mention Roddy? She was sure there was laughter in his voice as he spoke his name. He gazed at her more intently, but she did not raise her eyes.

"And yourself, Elizabeth – I do hope you are now well?"

'I wish he would go,' she told herself over and over again. 'I am in no mood for conversation, especially his.' Emma was the only one she wished to talk to.

"Yes, I am quite well, Master Craig, thank you," she replied politely.

At last they reached the crossroad.

"Well, young ladies, I must bid you good day. Hasten home before any mist falls." He turned again to give them a final wave.

Emma spurred the horse to go more quickly.

"I will drop you at the hall, Elizabeth. Now, try not to worry about this afternoon," she said, but she knew how difficult it would be for her friend.

"I will try, Emma," Elizabeth said as she dismounted.

'That dratted man! Why had he to come along and spoil our conversation, just when I needed Emma most?'

She was reluctant to let Emma drive away, but she knew Emma must get home before any mist came down.

"I will see you at choir practice," she called to her as she waved her goodbye.

Elizabeth could see the smirky, furtive glances coming her way at the next choir practice from the girls from the academy. Emma saw them too, and she looked at her friend with concern. It was evident that the three precious jewels had lost no time in spreading the news of the conversation they had overheard at the dressmaker's.

Life in the village had been very quiet and sad during the war, but, now it was over, everyone began to enjoy life once more – especially the girls from the academy. They were all hoping for a surfeit of parties and balls now the boys were home. Some of them, quite young when the war began, were now young ladies of sixteen and seventeen, and some a little older were a little perturbed that soon they might be left on the shelf. All of them were anxious to break away from the monotony of studies and the strict discipline. They had grown tired of the nights they had had to spend with the older ladies of the village, knitting socks and gloves and scarves for the boys at the front. Now that time was past, what a time they were all going to have! Almost everyone would be having a 'welcome home' dance or party, and they expected to be invited to them all.

The ball and banquet at Glencree Castle would be the highlight of all, for none of the boys returning had been more eagerly awaited than the young Master of Glencree. Every mother who had a daughter of marriageable age had longed for the day they would meet him at a ball, and now that day was near. They also knew, as it was rumoured, of his engagement to Lady Fiona. That was an understood thing before he left for the front, but since then their daughters had grown into very pretty young ladies. None of them had given up hope that the young master might change his mind when he had cast an eye on them.

None was more hopeful than Mrs Crawford. 'Are not my precious jewels the prettiest girls on the island?' she kept telling herself. 'And if the young master ever does change his mind, I shall make sure that none of them will be out of his line of vision for long, no matter what I have to do to contrive it.'

The rest of the village mothers knew too that they would have their work cut out to try to beat her at her little game – to win his favour for their daughters.

They had already heard from Mrs Crawford's very own lips that Craig had accepted an invitation to have tea with them one afternoon very soon, and he had made it clear to each one of her precious jewels that he would expect them to save more than one dance for him.

As Mrs Crawford told Mrs Bond, who had a very pretty daughter also, "If the young master wishes that, he must have something in mind."

However, Mrs Bond knew only too well, as did the rest of the village, that Mrs Crawford always exaggerated everything.

"Well then," Mrs Bond had replied icily, "we shall just have to wait and see."

CHAPTER 36

The ball had been the only topic of conversation in the village and the scattered cottages since its announcement. The girls from the academy were all agog from morn until night. The dressmaker had had to send to the mainland for her sister, Jeannie, to come and help her finish the dresses in time. No one would be more relieved than they when at last it was over and they could shut the wee shop and get some well-earned rest.

"I shall go to the ball, Jeannie, as soon as I am rested. I must see how my dresses look on all those lovely girls."

Nearly all the men from the village had spent the last few weeks at Glencree Castle, painting the tall gates, putting flares up the long driveway ready for lighting on the night, and hanging lanterns in the trees and indoors under the supervision of one of the finest and oldest decorators in the area. No expense was to be spared, the laird had stated. Wine merchants and food merchants had been much in evidence. Everything just had to be perfect.

"How like old times, Harriet!" Elena exclaimed over and over again. "I already feel ten years younger with the thrill of it all. And my new dress fits perfectly."

Harriet said hers did also, and that was praise indeed. She never got thrilled about anything.

"I shall be glad when all the extra work is finished," she had kept repeating to Elena as the weeks sped by.

Craig and Fiona watched the daily progress. Fiona tried to take over the decorating of the dance hall, deciding what must go here and there, much to Craig's consternation at times.

"My darling, the men are first class. You know Papa would not have it otherwise."

"What is that I hear?" remarked Bruce as he joined them.

"We were just saying how wonderful everything is looking now it is almost finished," remarked Craig.

"Yes, it is more and more like the old days, which we had begun to think would never return. All is now ready, I believe. Extra servants have been arriving for days," Bruce continued.

"Well, my son, I must agree with your aunts that you are looking so much better now. I knew that your cough would soon go and the colour would be back in your cheeks once you were sailing again, riding the hills and valleys and breathing the Highland air. You look splendid in your new tartan. The tailor has done you proud – don't you think so, Fiona?"

"Of course he does. I can hardly wait to see him at the ball in full Highland dress. Harriet and Elena have already seen it, as he asked for their approval, but he says I have to wait until the night of the ball. Don't you think that is most unfair, Papa Bruce?"

"Well, my dear daughter, it is nice to have surprises and I know you won't be disappointed. Now, my children, I must away. Maybe, Craig, you will join me in the wine cellar later?"

"Yes, Papa, I will. I know my darling has lots to do. She will be joining her parents."

CHAPTER 37

At last the night arrived – a fine, clear starlit night. A crescent moon hovered above the turreted old castle. There was a slight nip in the night air.

The lanterns were looped from tree to tree, and, with the tall flares, they lit up the long driveway. Several were hung over the high wrought-iron gates, lighting up the bright gold lettering, 'Glencree Castle'. The lights could be seen for miles around and pointed everyone in the direction of the castle. Brass lamps were agleam in every turret.

Inside was ablaze with lights. Tartan silks were draped on every wall and flowers were everywhere. Purple thistles had been arranged with the green and bluish foliage of the pine forests, gathered early that morning.

A band of pipers, one of several, was playing in the forecourt to the arriving guests. Many of the men wore tartan kilts, and the womenfolk, not to be outdone, had used elements of the clan tartan colours for the ball gowns. Some were dressed all in white with their clan tartans in broad sashes over their shoulders. Almost every clan was represented. The guests mingled in the anterooms, greeting friends they hadn't seen for a long time, their chatter silenced now and again as they partook of the drinks being served. Everyone was very, very happy.

One carriage had already left the vicarage. It contained the vicar and his wife, and Martha and Magnus, who had come over the loch earlier that day and were their guests. Roddy was in the second carriage with Emma, Donald and Charles.

Anthony watched them go. He sat in the gloomy library, assuring them all that he was quite happy being left behind with his books.

"Charles and I will come back for you when we have taken the ladies," Donald called to him. "The laird insists that no one must be left at home."

"Very well, then," Anthony replied.

Very soon they were at Harrison Hall. Roddy leaped out of the carriage and up the steps. He went inside as soon as Charles opened the door.

"Lady Margot has already left," he said.

"I am awaiting Elizabeth," Roddy replied.

"Well, I am sure she will be down in a minute. She has been dancing and singing all day. Flora has been helping her dress after she had seen to Lady Margot."

"Tell me," Roddy enquired: "how is Lady Roxburgh tonight?"

"Not very well, I'm afraid. Lady Margot was reluctant to leave her, but Nurse insisted that she would be all right."

"I am sorry to hear that. I do hope she is better soon."

Just then a door above opened and out Elizabeth rushed.

She spotted Roddy and called out to him: "Roddy, Roddy, I am coming." Then she flounced down the stairs like a dream. "Here I am, Roddy. How do you like my new dress?" she asked, and she twirled round and round in the hall.

"You look really stunning!" he exclaimed.

He stood spellbound. He had had no idea he was going to escort such a dream as this to the dance. He couldn't take his eyes off her. Everything she wore suited her to perfection. The silver coronet glittered in her flaxen hair, which was arranged in cascading ringlets which fell almost to her waist.

"You will be the belle of the ball," he teased.

Emma's feet tapped impatiently on the carriage floor. "Wherever is she? We are late already. Donny, please go and see where she is, and take her this wrap. I forgot to give it to Roddy."

Donald took it from her and leaped up the steps towards the door.

"Here we are," Roddy called to him.

He took the wrap, placed it round Elizabeth's shoulders and assisted her into the carriage.

"I am sorry to keep you all waiting," she said breathlessly. "Emma, how lovely you look in your new gown!"

"So do you. Now come – we must hurry."

The country lanes sped by at an alarming rate. The carriage almost tipped over as it turned too quickly at the crossroad, flinging them almost off their seats. They screamed with laughter as it righted itself. Then they sped on up the long lane to the gates of Glencree Castle, which they could see long before they got there.

Everywhere was like fairyland. None of them had seen anything like it before. Several carriages were ahead of them, but they could not make out the occupants. From the one just ahead they could hear squeals of laughter.

"It sounds like those three precious 'jewel' girls," said Emma disdainfully.

"My dear Emma," replied Charles, "that tone of voice is most unusual for you. I wish you would not refer to them so disparagingly," he admonished.

Emma took no notice. "Does it sound like them, Elizabeth?" she queried.

"Yes, I think so, Emma," she replied meekly.

Emma squeezed her arm as if to reassure her.

"Are you feeling cold, Elizabeth?" Roddy asked, as he felt her tremble.

"No, Roddy, I am quite all right, thank you."

Emma gave her another little squeeze.

"We are nearly there now, Emma," she said, as she tugged her cape a little further round her shoulders.

It wouldn't do for Roddy to know what was really troubling her, but her thoughts had shot back to the day in the dressmaker's shop. Would they still be laughing at her tonight? she wondered. Oh, she couldn't bear it if they were. She had visions of them telling all they knew about her dress. 'Well,' she decided, 'Roddy said my dress was lovely and so it is. I am sure it will be as lovely as theirs.' She gave Emma's arm a little squeeze and a look to reassure her that she was all right. 'I don't care what they think. Mama and Papa are pleased for me, so nothing else matters.'

At last they arrived at the entrance to the castle and their carriage stopped at the steps. Footmen helped them to alight. The entrance hall was filled with gay chatter and rapturous greetings from everyone. Baskets of flowers hung above the doorways and stood on tall pedestals inside. Servants were waiting to take their cloaks and wraps. Music and laughter drifted up from the ballroom below.

Elizabeth stood spellbound at the garlanded hall and stairway. Scottish coats of arms were on display wherever she looked. She was overawed by the vastness of the place. She had thought Harrison Hall was a very large residence, but she had never imagined anything like this.

As they sped along the long gallery towards the main staircase, the fragrance of the flowers took her breath away. Such colour everywhere, and everyone so light-hearted and gay – she just knew it was going to be the most exciting night of her life.

There were tartans everywhere and of every hue. The purple and heather hues of the Scottish countryside contrasted with all the brilliant colours of the ball gowns and the brightly coloured uniforms of the soldiers escorting the beautifully gowned ladies. She noticed she was getting quite a few admiring glances as she passed.

'Surely,' she thought, 'every soldier in Scotland is here tonight. Never have I seen so many tartans.'

She recognised the scarlet of the Camerons and the blue and green of the Black Watch, but she was at a loss regarding most of the others. 'I must ask Roddy to tell me what clans they all are.'

Roddy's voice called to her that they were going to be announced before they went down the steps.

The laird, Lady Harriet and Lady Elena greeted them warmly as Elizabeth curtsied and Roddy bowed.

"Ah, you are the young lady who sang so delightfully in church."

"Yes, sir, I am."

"What a beautiful blue your dress is!" remarked Elena. "It matches the blue of your eyes."

"Thank you, milady."

She could feel her colour rising at the compliment. Elena knew her well from the choir-practice classes and was specially fond of her. Harriet, who never enthused about anyone not connected with the family, gave her a nod of recognition and commenced to greet the next arrival. Elena continued to watch Elizabeth as she descended the stairs, still clinging tightly to Roddy's arm as she went, and gazing all around her at the wonder of it all.

So carried away was she that only Roddy's frantic tugging at her arm, and saying her name over and over again, made her realise that they were almost on the landing between the two flights of stairs, where more presentations were being made.

As he had heard the names Lieutenant Roderick and Elizabeth Anderson announced, Craig's attention was caught by Roddy's name. He glanced up from his conversation with Fiona and her parents and friends.

'Well, well,' he thought, 'this angel always seems to be descending stairs whenever I set eyes on her.' He had thought she was exquisite when he saw her the first time, and when she was in church; now here she was, not in her frilly nightgown, but in a dress fit for a princess. He thought, 'She looks every inch of one,' as she approached. The silver coronet highlighted her hair. She did not notice she was being closely scrutinised as she drew level, but he saw the startled look on her face as he greeted them both warmly. He held her hand several seconds longer than anyone else's.

"Your Roddy, I presume?" he whispered, his dark laughing eyes glinting with delight as her blue eyes met his. The corners of his mouth turned upwards into a gay, mischievous smile.

"Yes, my brother," she stammered, blushing profusely.

'How I wish he would let go of my hand! He is still laughing at my mistaking him for Roddy, so he must still be laughing at me foolishly standing in front of him in my nightgown.' She shuddered.

He noted her shy blush as she dropped her eyes, and he very reluctantly let her hand drop.

Roddy looked at him questioningly, and he nodded as he led her away.

"What did he mean, *your* Roddy?" he asked as they continued down the rest of the stairs.

Craig's eyes continued to watch her, and Fiona glanced back up at him.

"How does he know you? He seems very interested," Roddy asked, but they were both distracted by the next announced guest.

"I don't quite know," she said with a pout. "He must have got me mixed up with someone else. Oh, now I know: he must be thinking I am Roddy Charleston's sister." She hoped she sounded convincing.

"But surely", Roddy continued, "he must have heard us announced as Anderson?"

"Oh, it doesn't matter, surely, Roddy dear!" she exclaimed, her blushes now deepening.

"No, I suppose not," he replied. "Come – I see Emma and the crowd over there. Let us join them."

Craig had weighed Roddy up as they passed. So this was her Roddy. He tried to see the resemblance, but he had to admit that he had been only sitting in the dim light of the oil lamp in the cottage. 'Yes, he is as tall as I am, about my age too, his hair not quite as dark – but of course she wouldn't notice that in the gloom.'

"Craig, dear."

Suddenly he was aware of Fiona as she tugged his arm. She told him that the vicar and his wife and their guests were waiting to greet him. She wondered what had been causing him so much distraction.

Elizabeth was thankful when they reached their circle of friends.

"My, how lovely you look tonight, Elizabeth!" Robin exclaimed. "I claim the first dance. Please say yes, Elizabeth dear," he pleaded.

"You can have the second one," said Roddy. "The first one is mine. I have waited so long to take her to her first dance."

She didn't care who had the first dance; she was anxious to calm herself.

'That man', she told herself, 'seems to want to spoil everything for me. The boys can argue it out amongst themselves.'

"Emma," Roddy called to her, "will you save the second dance for me?"

"Of course, Roddy dear."

She was watching Elizabeth closely and wondered why she was so quiet. 'I do hope she is not still upsetting herself about the dress. It is so beautiful.'

Elizabeth looked up to see Emma looking at her. Immediately she regained her composure and joined in the gay chatter and laughter.

At last the first dance commenced and she waltzed away in Roddy's arms, completely oblivious to everything and everyone around her. Her dream had at last come true. She was at her first ball and in her darling Roddy's arms. Suddenly she was conscious of many admiring glances as they sped round the floor. They stopped for a brief moment to kiss their parents, before speeding off again.

She smiled with delight at the look of dismay on the faces of the three jewels and their mother as they looked at her in disbelief. Elizabeth felt sure Roddy had swept her closer to them as they passed. They were not much to his liking at all.

Margot, who was watching from the balcony above, noticed her at once. 'My, what a pretty picture she looks, to be sure! She is so like my own daughter at her age. I am delighted to see her so happy and gay, and her brother is the perfect partner for her.'

"How lovely our pretty daughter looks tonight, my dear!" Magnus exclaimed.

"Yes, she certainly does, and she is so happy now she is with Roddy. If Ingrid could see them now, she wouldn't believe her eyes. I can hardly believe it myself – to be blessed with such lovely children. The Lord has been so good to us."

"Yes, my dear, He has."

Craig kept casting glances at them over the top of Fiona's head as they danced by. She spoke to him several times, but he wasn't listening. She was getting quite exasperated. She would have been more so if she had realised who was holding his attention. A tug on his arm from her brought him suddenly back to the conversation in hand.

"As I was saying Craig . . . " continued old Colonel Grant.

'War, war, war! How I wish he would shut up about it!' said Craig to himself. 'It is over. Let us forget about it, at least for tonight. Tonight is a celebration night.' He could also see that Fiona was just as tired of his protestations.

"Come, dear, let us dance. Please excuse us, sir."

"By all means, my boy. You young people must make the most of every minute. Go, my children. I shall go and speak with your father."

They waltzed away, Craig on every turn trying to catch sight of Elizabeth. 'Why is she so tiny?' he asked himself repeatedly. 'Every other lady on the floor tonight must be six feet tall.'

Elizabeth was completely overwhelmed and breathless with all the dancing she had done. She had only managed one dance with Roddy. No sooner had one pair of arms released her at the end of the dance, than she was enveloped in another's. The soldiers were all determined to be seen dancing with this dream in blue and silver, this gossamer fairy of the glen.

CHAPTER 38

A roll on the drum caused everyone to come to a standstill and be silent. The master of ceremonies asked that everyone clear the floor as the laird wished to speak.

He stood on the platform. A more splendid figure one would never see than this laird in his full Highland dress. At his side stood Craig, just as resplendent. Next to him were Lady Fiona and her parents and the aunts, Harriet and Elena.

At last he spoke. He thanked them for coming and wished them all a happy evening. "But", he continued, "before we carry on with tonight's enjoyment, I have a very important announcement to make, and that is to make it known to all of you that my very dear son Craig is betrothed to the lovely lady standing beside him – Lady Fiona. She is the lovely daughter of my lifelong friends, General and Lady Cleveland." He took both their hands and those of Craig and Fiona and held them together for a moment. "For us parents it is a precious union of our names and families; for myself and, I know, the General it is a lifelong wish come true. My son Craig, thanks be to the Good Lord, has been spared from the war. The wedding will take place sometime next year, and you are all invited to attend."

At this there was a loud burst of cheering. Then the laird's own piper came on to the platform. He stepped forward and called out, "Our best wishes to Master Craig and Lady Fiona. Three cheers, everyone!"

After the cheers had subsided, Craig stepped forward and thanked everyone for their good wishes. He held on to Fiona's hand. They could all see the Luckenbooth brooch pinned to her dress. Everyone clapped and cheered.

"Now, a kiss to seal the pledge," yelled Craig's closest friend, Captain Ian Fraser.

"Yes, yes," everyone choroused.

Craig drew Fiona to him in a swift embrace and kissed her lightly on the lips.

The girls from the academy were especially excited. Fiona was a frequent visitor to their academy, having attended there before going to a finishing school in Switzerland, from which she had returned sooner than expected as the war clouds began to gather over Europe. She had been determined to see as much of Craig as she could before he enlisted, which she knew he would at the first opportunity.

"How lovely she is and so happy!" exclaimed one of them to her close friend nearby. "The perfect couple! He so tall and handsome."

"Quite the most handsome man on the island!" exclaimed another. "How I wish I could have found such a man!" She sighed.

The younger girls from the academy were at a loss for words, as were their mothers, at the news just announced. Mrs Crawford and her precious jewels could not believe that it was really true.

"But, Mama," Ruby queried, "why is she not wearing a ring?"

"It seems," said her mother, "and I have heard it from very good authority, that it is still in the city. But never you mind, my girl – the brooch she is wearing is a symbol of their true betrothal, just as much as the ring will be."

"How beautiful she looks in that white dress, with Master Craig's tartan on her shoulder!" said Emma.

Elizabeth looked up at them. 'How lovely she is!' she thought. 'And how like my dear Roddy he is! He is a little taller, I think, and has darker hair, and his hair curls carelessly round his ears, whereas Roddy's is very straight. But', she told herself, 'how could I have seen the difference in the dim light?' Once more she was back in the small home, standing before him. She gave a little shudder.

Roddy looked down at her in alarm.

"Are you feeling chilled, Elizabeth?"

"No, Roddy dear, I am quite all right, thank you."

"Are you sure, Elizabeth?" he asked again, with concern.

"No, Roddy dear, I am quite all right, thank you."

Fiona looked up at Craig adoringly, and he kissed her once more.

"You are a lucky blighter," called out one of the officers.

"Yes, I am," Craig agreed, as he looked down at Fiona.

"Are you not going to dance now you are betrothed?" called another.

"Yes, we are!" Craig exclaimed. He gathered Fiona up in his arms and walked down the steps from the platform and on to the floor. He had already given instructions to the musicians what to play.

They waltzed away with eyes only for each other, as if they were the only couple on the floor.

"I do love you so much, my darling," she whispered. "Our marriage next year seems so far away, but now we can prepare for our wedding day and our wonderful life together."

"The time will soon pass, my darling," he replied, "and I love you so much."

"By then I will have been presented and done the season in London. What a wonderful year I have ahead of me – our betrothal announced, my presentation at court, then our marriage!"

"It's just wonderful, my darling," he whispered as he held her closer.

Everyone called out congratulations and good wishes as they passed.

"What an ideal couple they are, to be sure!" exclaimed Miss Grant to Mrs Carruthers. "She is the perfect lady to be the next Mistress of Glencree."

"She most certainly is," was the reply.

At last, their dance over, they rejoined their parents. The laird requested the pipers to play, and announced that there would be a short interval whilst champagne was served.

The next dance, a progressive one, was announced. Roddy's circle of friends were immediately on their feet. Emma with Stuart, Elizabeth with Robin Bainbridge, Roddy with Adeline Derby, Margot Dunbar with Donny, and Madge Bennet with Emma's brother, Charles. Soon the floor was filled with young and not so young, all happily humming the gay tunes. Most of them were now well and truly gay and merry.

"My, my!" exclaimed Mary Simpson to Ruby Crawford as they both stood head to head, noting every couple as they passed. "Ruby," she said with glee, "do look at Lady Margot's maid as she goes by, dressed like a queen."

"So she thinks!" Ruby retorted sarcastically.

"Whoever does she think she is? Wherever did she get that dress and the silver coronet in her hair?"

"It is only someone else's cut-me-down frock she has got on," replied Ruby. "I have not as yet found out whose, but I will soon, you wait and see if I don't."

"But how do you know it was someone else's dress?" Mary queried.

"Well, she was in the dressmaker's one day when we were in for a fitting for our new ball gowns, and we overheard all that Miss Grant, the dressmaker, and she had to say. Miss Grant assured her she could make it fit when it was altered."

"Are you sure? What a laugh, to be sure."

"Yes, the three of us couldn't stop laughing, and Mama got quite angry with us."

Elizabeth noticed them with their heads together as she passed. She saw the smirks on their faces, and realised they were whispering behind their fans.

'It's just like them – jealous that I have danced every dance and they have not. I daresay they are angry that my dress is so much prettier than theirs, even though theirs are new,' she thought.

"Why so preoccupied, Elizabeth?" asked Douglas, who had just taken her from her previous partner.

"I was just thinking what a wonderful time we are all having."

"Yes," he replied, "how long everyone has waited for such a celebration! The end of the war, and now the engagement of Master Craig and Lady Fiona, and lots more to come! Soon it will be the Highland Gathering – just like old times."

Then suddenly his arms released her and he was gone. She looked up to see who her next partner would be, and saw Craig's flashing, laughing eyes looking intensely into her violet-blue ones. So intense was his gaze that she started to tremble and his grip on her waist tightened.

"Are you chilled?" he asked. "I recall you were not well when we met at your father's cottage. I do hope you are now fully recovered, Miss, er, Miss – do you know, I don't yet know your full name?"

'Of course you do,' she thought. 'How much more fun is he going to make of me?'

"My name is Miss Anderson."

"Oh, surely you have other names besides? Take mine, for instance. Have you ever heard all my names?"

"No, Master Craig, I have not." She thought she had heard her mother mention them, but now she was too flustered to think.

"Well then, I shall tell you. Then I shall expect you to tell me yours."

"Why?" she queried. "Is it so important?"

"Yes, it is. I insist on knowing everyone's name. It wouldn't do for me not to know, now, would it? One day I shall be the Earl and laird of Glencree Castle. I shall be responsible for all the people in the district."

'Well, yes,' she said to herself, 'that is so, but I am certain he is only trying to make fun of me.'

"Yes," he continued, "by tonight I shall know everyone's names – especially the girls – and particularly the pretty ones." He noted her blush. "Has anyone ever told you how pretty you are?"

'How I wish he would pass on to the next partner,' she told herself, but, as her head was bent and he so tall, she had not noticed that other intending partners of hers had seen him shake his head as they approached. And, he being Master Craig, they had bid a hasty retreat.

"Well now, your full name if you please?" he insisted.

'Well,' she thought, 'I am not pleased, but what can I do? With anyone else I could have played along with them or even refused and made them guess, but with him I dare not.' He was the laird's son and his every request was practically a command.

He bent his head closer to hers. "I am still waiting," he teased.

"My name is Elizabeth Dawn Angeline Ingrid Anderson, but I am usually only called Elizabeth."

"You have almost as many names as myself. Do you wish to know mine?"

"No, Master Craig."

"Why not call me Craig, as everyone else does?"

"That, Master Craig, I could not possibly do. My parents would not allow it."

'This dance is never-ending,' she thought. 'Surely I should have changed partners by now?'

But the bandsmen knew that as long as the young master was dancing, and seemed to have no intention of leaving the floor, they had to carry on playing.

"Well, maybe some other time I shall tell you my full name."

'Really', she thought, 'I do not wish to know your full name. What possible use could it be to me? You are only keeping up this silly conversation to embarrass me.'

"How strange that your name should be Angeline! When I first saw you on the stairs, I thought I was seeing an angel."

"I would rather forget that night, Master Craig, if you don't mind," she requested politely.

"Just as you wish, Miss Angel."

"My name, sir, is Elizabeth."

"Yes, I know, but I shall always think of you as an angel, so I shall henceforth call you Angel."

"We will be doing the dance wrong if we continue to chatter," she said.

Somehow she must change the subject. She could feel everyone's eyes on her – especially the 'jewel' girls. They were positively fuming, as was their mother. Not one dance had Master Craig had with her lovely daughters.

'Whatever they are thinking, it just serves them right. I just don't care.'

"So we might," he whispered as he pulled her closer and spun her round and round. He was fascinated by the blueness of her black-lashed, exquisite eyes. 'They are the colour of forget-me-nots and she is just like that dainty, dancing, fragile flower which had such depth of meaning in its mere name. She is a gossamer will-o'-the-wisp,' he thought. 'I could lift her up on the lightest froth of a cloud and she would be whisked away, borne on its surface, still only visible to me.' She was also like a frightened fawn, disconcerted at the mere hint of another's presence – so different from Fiona's assuredness. He looked up as he, for a moment, thought of Fiona, but he couldn't see her.

She felt a curious thrill run through her as he spun her round. He felt her tremble and he tightened his grip on her tiny waist a little more. He felt so at peace, so protective towards this dainty, dancing flower in his strong arms.

'If only I dared glance up at him,' she thought. 'If only I could look long enough to weigh him up, to fathom out his always present smile, to judge for myself whether or not he was really amused at my expense.' But she dare not show him that she was even interested in him. She knew he would immediately fix his gaze on hers, and she knew she wouldn't know how to cope with its intensity as he looked into, what seemed to her, her very soul. When Roddy held her in a dance, it wasn't like this. This was something she just couldn't understand. Her puzzled look caught his gaze.

"You look rather puzzled, Miss Angel. Is anything wrong?"

She quickly regained her composure.

"No, not at all, Master Craig." She was annoyed to think he had spotted her in deep thought.

'I cannot seem to keep any thoughts of my own from him,' she thought.

She decided to concentrate on the dance. As they danced he noted her fine porcelain skin, tinted the most delicate pink he had ever seen, turning to deeper and deeper shades as he tantalisingly drew her closer and closer. He felt her tremble and his own heart seemed to stop beating for a fleeting moment at her nearness. He looked down at her and caught her fleeting glance. She dropped her eyes immediately, and the black curve of her lashes reminded him of a fan against her deepening red cheeks. It was as if she had responded to his nearness. Then he laughed gaily at her, to try and allay her fluster.

"What are you thinking of, Miss Angel – Elizabeth?" he corrected himself. "If I may ask."

She hesitated for a moment, unsure of what to say.

"I was just wondering where Roddy was. I cannot see him with so many people here."

'Well, well,' he told himself, 'here I am dancing with this dream girl, who is only thinking of her brother. It is most disconcerting,' he thought. He knew all the girls in the village were longing to be in his arms – especially the three 'jewel' girls, whom he could see out of the corner of his eye, watching his every move, as was Fiona. 'It's strange,' he thought, 'but for a moment I had forgotten all about her.'

Fiona was looking directly at him, evidently very displeased at his lack of attention to her, as was her mother. They had noticed his obvious enjoyment and his devil-may-care attitude.

'But', he told himself, 'I am free and gay and happy as I have never been before.' Was it the drink he had had, or was it the nearness of this angel, who was only looking for her brother?

Elizabeth decided to concentrate on the dance, but as she turned her head, she saw a look of disapproval from several of the ladies from the Church Guild. Craig's closeness to her and his whispering in her ear had not gone unnoticed by the women from the village. 'They no doubt will gossip about it at their next meeting.' Emma had once told her that this was their usual practice, and now she was seeing it for herself.

"You are holding me far too tightly, Master Craig!" she exclaimed. "Everyone is looking at us with disapproval – especially me."

"Everyone?" he replied teasingly. "To me it seems as though we are the only two on the floor." He felt so at peace.

'How opposite these two are!' he thought. 'Fiona is tall, dark, elegant and so assured; and this small fragile wisp of a fairy from the glen looks as though she would fly away at midnight.'

At last, at Bruce's command, the music stopped and they turned to face each other. She curtsied deeply as he bowed. His vivid gaze held hers as she raised her eyes from the floor. He raised her to her feet, and his eyes were still ablaze with laughter and amusement.

'How wonderful everything is!' he thought. 'The war is over, the music, the ball – the whole world seems to be jolly and gay.' He was so happy. Never in his life had he felt so light-hearted and gay. Was it the drink, the gay occasion, or because of this dream angel he had had in his arms?

His smiling face puzzled her. Was he still mocking her? 'He must be. He knows it is my first ball. What is behind his smile?' How she wished she could fathom it out!

He touched her lightly on her arm and led her across the floor. She was most perturbed. Everyone else had returned to their friends. At last they reached Roddy, who was talking to Emma.

"Your very charming sister, I believe?"

'As if he didn't know!' she thought. 'What a tease he is, to be sure!'

"Yes," replied Roddy, quite taken aback as he stood up to receive her.

Craig bowed to her again as he turned to go, and she and the rest of the girls curtsied as he left. All eyes were on him as he walked across the floor, so tall and debonair – such a dashing handsome figure in his full Highland dress – to rejoin Fiona and his father, who were deep in conversation.

Fiona watched him as he approached. She was seething with anger, having seen how interested he had been in the little blonde village maid.

'Well,' she thought to herself, 'I shall certainly see to it that she never dances with him again.'

"Come, Craig darling," she said as he rejoined them, carefully hiding her anger and disapproval as she clung tightly to his arm. "Come – we must go and talk to more of our friends. They will think we have forgotten them."

"Yes, yes, my dear."

"Over there are Lord and Lady Sanders and their daughters, Deirdre and Arabella. I haven't seen you for years. Wherever have you been?"

"Well, we both joined the VAD," said Deirdre. "We went to a hospital in the Midlands and we were fortunate that we were together most of the time."

"I joined them also and I was lucky too," said Fiona. "I was down south, not too far from my aunt and cousins, so I was able to visit them quite often. I was also able to visit the hospital where Craig was when he was wounded."

"Oh, how perfect for you!" Arabella declared.

"But, of course," Fiona continued, "it wasn't for long, as he insisted on returning to his men at the front long before he was well enough. Still, that is my darling Craig all over," she sighed.

"Thank goodness we can all get back to normality now," said Lady Sanders. "This wonderful ball is the start of so many happy events."

"Yes," continued Fiona, "and do remember I want both of you to be bridesmaids, along with my cousins next year."

"Oh, how wonderful that event will be!" Lady Sanders exclaimed.

'How these women chatter on so!' Craig thought to himself. He was getting quite bored with their conversation. His eyes kept wandering to where Elizabeth's crowd were gathered and he could hear their jolly laughter.

"Are you going to make the army your career, Craig?" asked Sir Robert, but Craig wasn't listening. His thoughts were elsewhere.

Fiona tugged his arm impatiently.

"I am so sorry, my dear; I wasn't listening."

"Sir Robert was asking, will you stay in the army?"

"I'm so sorry, Sir Robert. No, there is so much for me to do on the estate; there's so much I have to learn. Being away four years hasn't helped at all and I shall be taking an interest in the new Forestry Commission, which is being set up, the fishing stock and care of the crofts and crofters. There is so much to learn, which will be essential in running an estate as large as this. Now that Papa has bought much more land whilst I have been away, I don't know where it begins and ends."

Bruce had now rejoined them. He placed a loving hand on Craig's shoulder.

"And", continued Craig, "I have seen far too little of dear Papa since I returned. It is quite unthinkable that I should rejoin the army and have to leave him again – quite unthinkable."

"Yes, my son, it is quite unthinkable that you should ever again leave my side and also our beloved Scotland. All our future is now secure since Craig's return. I am the happiest man in Scotland," he said, and he hugged Craig closer.

Bruce nodded to the master of ceremonies to announce the next part of the programme.

"Now, my lords, ladies and gentlemen," he boomed, "the band will entertain us all."

Suddenly, the sliding doors at the far end of the hall opened to reveal a large banqueting hall with tables overflowing with every type of food as far as the eye could see. Wines and whiskies, including the laird's own special blend, were available for everyone's pleasure.

Bruce called out to everyone, "Now, eat, drink and be merry."

Elizabeth stood close to Emma's side and alongside Roddy.

"Gosh!" Roddy exclaimed. "To think what we had to eat during the war – dry biscuits and bully beef, and sometimes nothing else for days and days. I can hardly believe what I am seeing now."

"I know Lady Margot would be pleased to have even a little of this food for her starving people in the missions," said Elizabeth to Emma.

"Are they really starving?" asked Roddy.

"Well, Lady Margot says they are," she replied. "She gets all the news from her daughter. She and Lady Elena work together on their problems."

"Well, this food is not ours to distribute, however worthy the cause," said Roddy, "so let's do as His Lordship bids – eat, drink and be merry. I for one won't be seeing a spread like this ever again."

"Neither shall we," chorused their friends as they sat down to eat, all of them joking and laughing.

At last everyone drifted back to the dance floor. The master of ceremonies announced that the entertainment would recommence with the pipers and the sword dance, followed by the girls from the academy dancing reels and some of the boys joining in.

"I hope I can remember them all," said Roddy to Emma and Elizabeth.

"I have only done a little with you, Elizabeth, since my return."

"Everything will be all right, Roddy," she assured him. "Now be ready to go as soon as it is announced. The others are going too."

At last the girls had changed into their flimsy white reel dresses, with tartan sashes over one shoulder. They proceeded to the centre of the floor, and the men were then called to join them.

"I see", said Emma, "that those three precious jewels of Mrs Crawford's are already there. I wonder who will partner them?"

"Not my dear Roddy," Elizabeth said, "– I hope not anyway."

Everyone else was sitting down, waiting for the dances to start.

"Now, Elizabeth," said Emma, "let's see how many tartans we can recognise as they dance."

"Yes, let's," she replied with glee.

"I will give a big kiss to the one who guesses most!" exclaimed a soldier sitting next to them in a wheelchair. In spite of the loss of both legs, he was as determined as everyone else to join in as much fun as he was able. "Now, come on both of you, one on either side of me, then I can hear you call them out. I have some paper and a pencil, so start now."

"Well," said Elizabeth, "I know Roddy is wearing our tartan."

"And I know that my brothers are wearing ours."

They both laughed, as did the soldier.

"Now, girls, no more tricks! I want the names of the other tartans, if you please."

Elizabeth began: "Stewart, Munro, Macleod, Fraser, Lindsay, Lamont, Grant."

"You are not leaving me any to name, Elizabeth," Emma called to her.

"Go on then," Elizabeth said.

"There's Duncan, Douglas, Montgomery, Maxwell. Oh my! I cannot think of any more at the moment." She pretended to cry plaintively. "No, no, I have to admit, I can't remember."

"They are moving so fast, neither can I," replied Elizabeth.

"Well, that's it, then," the soldier said. "Your time is up. Miss Elizabeth is the winner."

"All right then, I give in," said Emma, laughing gaily.

The soldier bent over to Elizabeth and kissed her lightly on the cheek; she kissed him back.

"There she is again, the hussy," said Mrs Knowell to Mrs Crawford. "She is not satisfied at showing herself up by dancing too close to betrothed Master Craig. She is now kissing a soldier in full view of everyone. Of all the nerve! Never in my born days have I seen such an exhibition."

"How Martha and Magnus came to deserve such a daughter I'll never know. I do hope they have spotted her unseemly behaviour," said Mrs Crawford. "I was glad that she wasn't chosen to dance the reels.

"Aren't our three jewels looking lovely tonight?" she said to her husband, who was standing next to her.

"Yes, my dear. Our daughters are all doing the laird proud tonight, decked out in their lovely dresses and hair ribbons, dancing with the men in their dress tartans."

"They are just like we were when we were young," she sighed.

Craig also had seen Elizabeth kiss the soldier.

'My, my, even I didn't get close enough to her for that,' he told himself.

The drink had made everyone's dancing extra wild and gay. The men, most of them full-time soldiers, were making the most of holding the lovely girls in their arms as they spun them round and round faster and faster. Tonight was, for some of them, their last night before being posted abroad.

Fiona turned to Craig as the dances continued. "Come, my darling – let us go outside for a stroll. It is so hot in here and so crowded, and we haven't been alone all evening."

"Very well, my love, but first get your wrap. It will be chilly outside."

They strolled through the garden, over to the wall overlooking the loch, and Craig was lost in thought as he looked out over the water.

"Are you happy, my darling?" she asked suddenly.

"Why, of course, my dear. Why do you ask?"

"You seem so far away at times – as though you are not here."

"Of course I am happy," he replied. "Why should I not be? I'm here with my betrothed – the girl I adore and love so dearly – and back home with my dear father, safe and sound. I'm back in my beautiful Scotland, with all my friends around me. How could I not be happy? Sometimes I just cannot believe that I am really here, and so happy. What have I done to deserve such happiness? I think of the war, although I try not to do so. The names of the battlefields cross and recross my mind: Ypres, Passchendaele, my men all around me dying, face down in the mud. Some of them should have been here with us tonight. I have so much happiness around me. Tell me dearest, if you can, what had they done to deserve what they had to suffer?"

"Now, Craig, my darling," she replied softly, "you must put all that behind you.

It is finished now. No more wars! People say that was the war to end all wars."

"Yes, they all say that. Let us hope they are right," he replied. "Let us just listen to the piper now."

They both looked up to the parapet, where he was standing outlined against the floodlit castle. Craig listened silently. A faint melancholy enveloped him. As the tune drifted out over the loch, the faint breeze seemed to be wafting it back to him over and over again – 'The Scottish Soldier'. The echo seemed to be whispering to him (not the words of the song, but an extra echo prevailed): 'Remember us, remember us, remember us.'

"I will, I will, I will," he muttered aloud.

"What were you saying, my darling?" Fiona asked. She stood silently watching him. This part of him she knew she would never understand. "Darling, darling," she repeated, her tone sharper and more impatient, "Come, let us go inside. It is getting too chilly. Let us go and dance."

He was jolted out of his reverie at the sound of her voice.

"Yes, yes, of course, my darling. How thoughtless of me! Please forgive me."

He pulled her closer to him and kissed her passionately. She melted into his embrace.

"Never let me go, my darling," she whispered.

"No, I will never let you go, ever. I am home now, never to leave again."

"I was so unhappy whilst you were away. I missed you so much."

"And I you," he whispered between his passionate kisses. "But we are together now, never ever to be separated again."

He pulled her wrap closer round her shoulders.

"I am warmer now we are closer together like this," she sighed. "Like this we will always stay, closer and closer together for ever."

He rained kisses on her hair and mouth, hungry for her nearness. Both were oblivious to everything else, including the piper. The moon's shimmering shaft of light pierced the dark waters of the loch, and the silver ripples sparkled like diamonds.

"We must go back, darling," she whispered.

"Must we, must we?" he sighed. "I want to spend the rest of my life just as we are now, never ever to be parted."

He kissed her once more, and as he pulled her closer to him he pulled her shawl further round her shoulders.

"Yes, we must go back. The guests are ours as well as our parents'."

"You are just in time for the last waltz!" Fiona's mother exclaimed as they appeared.

"Come, dearest," Craig said, "let us take to the floor."

The rest watched as they swept on to the floor, and then others joined in. Mrs Crawford seethed in the corner as she watched Craig.

"So much for the young master's promises!" she fumed.

"Why, what were they, my dear?" her husband asked.

"He promised to have several dances with our daughters, and he hasn't asked one of them all night."

"Well, it's too late now, my dear," he replied, trying to appease her a little. "This is the last waltz."

He knew when he got home he would be hearing about the young master's broken promises for weeks on end.

When the music stopped, they all formed a circle and, try as she might, Mrs Crawford could not manage to get any of her daughters near enough to him to hold hands for the singing of 'Auld Lang Syne'. As it finished, the balloons came cascading down. Then the headmaster of the village school mounted the platform.

Bruce called for everyone to be silent. Then the headmaster thanked the laird for his kindness and expressed thanks on behalf of all present.

"Now, everyone, three cheers for His Lordship and family: Hip hip hurray! Hurray! Hurray!"

Everyone started clapping.

As they wended their way from the hall, the laird and his family shook hands with everyone and wished them all a safe journey home. As they shook hands, Fiona and Elizabeth came face to face.

'How tall and elegant she is,' thought Elizabeth, 'and so beautiful!'

'So this is the poor country maid he couldn't stop looking at. She's frail, pale, timid and so insignificant,' she thought. 'It's just like Craig to take pity on such as her. But I wonder where she got the lovely dress from and the coronet. And what lovely hair and eyes she has! I have to concede that,' she told herself, her head in the air, as she bade her goodnight disdainfully.

Craig held her hand fleetingly, trying not to let his gaze linger.

She glanced shyly up at him as he shook hands with Roddy and their parents and bade them goodnight.

Emma and Stuart were waiting for them in the carriage as Roddy and Elizabeth bade their parents, who were staying with Emma's parents, goodnight.

"We will drop Elizabeth off. Roddy is coming back to stay at the vicarage so he can see more of the boys," Emma said to Stuart.

It was a beautiful clear night as they drove home, laughing and talking.

"Oh, Emma," Elizabeth exclaimed, "hasn't it been exciting? I just know I won't sleep a wink all night."

"Oh yes, you will,' Roddy declared. "You have danced more than anyone else tonight, and you even had a longer dance with the young master than any of the other girls. Did you notice, Emma, the look on the faces of Mrs Crawford and her three precious jewels as the two of them passed them time and time again? I am certain Master Craig was doing it on purpose."

"Well, I did notice," Emma replied, "and I do know what a tease Master Craig can be."

Elizabeth felt herself blushing. She could feel her colour rising. She was thankful that the moon had flitted behind a cloud so that they couldn't see her agitation.

"Roddy, Roddy, my very first ball! It was just like a dream."

"Well, it wasn't a dream," he replied, "it was real. Can you not hear the piper playing farewell? He gets fainter."

Roddy felt her tremble. He tugged her shawl closer round her shoulders.

"Mama and Papa would never forgive me if I let you get another chill. We have seen very little of them tonight."

"Well, they had so many of their friends around them, and Mama does not get as much chance as Papa to talk to them. I daresay she spoke with some tonight she hasn't seen for years."

At last they arrived at Harrison Hall and Roddy helped her alight. After she had bade Stuart goodnight and kissed Emma on the cheeks, Roddy led her up the steps. Charles was waiting for her. Roddy kissed her goodnight. They watched as she waved them goodbye.

"Roddy," she called to him as he was turning the carriage round, "please call tomorrow with Mama and Papa before you sail home."

"I will, I will."

Charles, the butler, waved them off and closed the doors behind her.

CHAPTER 39

After dinner the following evening, Bruce and the General sat discussing the future of their son and daughter over a glass of their favourite whisky, both beaming with delight.

"I am so happy and proud for them!" exclaimed the General. "At last our longed-for wishes are realised by their betrothal and, of course, their marriage, which will join our two names together at last. It is still as we planned, isn't it, Bruce, that Fiona will be known as Lady Fiona Cleveland-McNair?"

"Most certainly, my old friend."

"It means so much to me to know that I shall have grandsons to carry my name into the future.

It had always been a great disappointment to the General that his only son had died soon after he was born. Now his greatest wish had come true: a perfect love match between his darling daughter and the son of his oldest friend.

"And what plans are you two making that are making you both so happy?" asked Craig as he and Fiona joined them.

"We are just talking grandfather talk about the grandsons we shall both delight in," said the General. "What a happy day it will be for the pair of us when our first grandson is born! He will bear both our great names."

"Are you sure it will be a grandson first?" Craig laughed.

"Of course it will," replied his father. "The first two will be boys, then we can have two lovely granddaughters to follow," said Bruce emphatically.

"Well, these fathers of ours seem to have everything settled for us, my darling. Do you mind?" exclaimed Fiona.

"No, not at all, my darling. It will be just as they say," he said, and then he kissed her.

"Well then, let us drink a toast to that," said Lady Cleveland, as she, Harriet and Elena joined them.

"Now your father and I must away to our beds. We are returning home early to prepare for our journey to visit all our relatives so that I can notify them personally of your betrothal. I have so many things to attend to. My, my, what a busy time!"

"But you will enjoy every minute of it," her husband insisted.

"How long do you propose staying here with Craig, Fiona dear? I shall need your help, with so many arrangements to make."

"Well, Mama, Craig and I have a lot to discuss about the plans for the West Wing, and the changes must be to my satisfaction before I leave, but I will join you as soon as I can."

Elena looked at her, thinking, 'Yes, my dear Fiona, they most certainly will be done to your satisfaction – certainly not Craig's, I warrant.' She glanced round at the rest of them, but she alone, it seemed, had noted Fiona's assertiveness. 'Ah well,' she sighed, 'time will tell.'

"I might keep her for ever now she is here," said Craig.

"I know she wouldn't take much persuading," said her father.

"Is it so essential?" asked Craig, looking crestfallen. "This presenting – it is causing a long delay to our marriage."

Her mother gasped in dismay. "But it is the done thing, Craig. All her cousins and friends are going to be presented and have their coming-out balls in the London Season next year. Whatever will she be able to tell her daughters if she has not been presented?" She was almost swooning with the thought of it. "I couldn't possibly face anyone if that happened. Come, dear – we must retire." She fanned herself with her lace-edged handkerchief as they said goodnight.

Next day, Craig and Fiona rode beside their carriage several miles before parting company. Craig had decided to show Fiona as much of the estate as he could.

"It is so vast, Craig darling," she said, after they had been riding for some time. "It seems endless."

The thought pleased her immensely; she thought, 'Soon I shall be mistress of all this. What possessions my sons will have!'

"Well, as you know, Papa has bought all Margot's mother's land, but we haven't time to see it all today. It will take several days. We have ridden far enough for one day."

"Yes, dear, I am rather tired."

They turned their horses for home, stopping now and again as Craig insisted on long conversations with most of the crofters. Fiona grew quite exasperated.

"Craig, darling, when we are married you will be gone for hours and hours. I shall hardly ever see you if you spend so long talking to the crofters."

"But, my darling, you will have to come with me. Mama always accompanied Papa and we shall be expected to attend to the crofters' welfare, as they did."

"But of course I shall – that is, until our children come."

They were both laughed heartily at this remark.

Suddenly, Craig being taller in the saddle than Fiona, reined his horse and bade her be silent. They both sat in silence, and she kept looking up at him as if to ask why. A little figure Craig had spotted in the hedgerow looked up at them.

"Hello there, Merry-Berry. How are all your country friends today?" said Craig. His delight at seeing her knew no bounds.

"All well, Master Craig," she replied.

"You will have heard from all your country friends, no doubt, about our betrothal," he teased.

"I most certainly have."

"And what do you see in the future for us?" he asked.

"Oh, lots of ups and downs, as life's pattern goes on."

"Ah, yes, that is to be expected, Merry-Berry."

"But I see far-off lands for you, Master Craig," she said hesitantly.

"Far-off lands?" he exclaimed incredulously. "You are mistaken this time. I have been to far-off lands and now I am back in my beloved Scotland. There will be no more roaming for me, ever. I have done all the travelling I am going to do.

I shall certainly travel around Scotland and down into England, but that is as far as I shall be going. It is not often you are wrong, Merry-Berry, but you are this time," he laughingly replied.

"That is as might be," she said. A cloud passed over her face and a sad look came in her old crinkled eyes. What she saw no one knew or would ever know from her lips.

Craig watched her closely. "What clouds your face so?" he asked, before she had time to compose her features. "Do you see me dying in some foreign land, and my bones not being buried here in my bonnie Scotland?"

"No, no," she hastened to reassure him. "You will be buried in your beloved Scotland."

"Now, enough of this mad talk," he said gaily. "What else do you see?"

By now the cloud had lifted from her face. "I see a very happy marriage for both of you – and two children, or maybe more. And I see a journey across the water for both of you."

Fiona grew more and more impatient at the delay and what she considered stupid remarks from the old gipsy. She, unlike Craig, set no store by Merry-Berry or her forecasts. To her she was just an old witch.

"England isn't across the water," she told her angrily. "I can tell you that." Her haughty tone of voice was not lost on the old lady, who looked at her knowingly.

"No far-off lands for you, Lady Fiona," she replied emphatically.

"None for me!" rejoined Craig. "Where Fiona goes, I go also, so you are wrong this time, Merry-Berry. I admit it's not often you are, but this time is the exception. I have already been to foreign lands and here I am, back safe and sound. You must be reading into the past, not the future. I bid you good day, Merry-Berry," he said, and she slid silently into the hedgerow.

"Come, Craig," said Fiona, "we have wasted far too much time listening to her prattle. Come – I will race you back."

And off they sped, watched by a pair of wise, crinkled old eyes.

They rested their horses for a while near the stream.

"How can you stand that old gipsy woman?" Fiona exclaimed. "Creeping out of the hedgerows when one least expects her! She used to frighten me to death as a child when I used to come to play hide and seek in the woods. To me she is just an old witch, and I cannot stand the sight of her. I was glad my father never allowed her to put her old caravan on our estate."

"Oh, she is just a dear old lady," Craig replied.

He was especially fond of her. Merry-Berry had been around a long time – since before he was born. Her Romany family many generations ago had been granted permission by the previous lairds of Glencree to live on their estate. She had always been ready to play with him when, as a child, he would creep out of the castle grounds to explore the woods close by. He felt sure he would have been lost time and time again but for her ever watchful eyes. On several occasions he had found himself surrounded by tall, dark undergrowth and a little fear had come over him. Then suddenly and silently she would be there and he would hear her voice saying, "This way, Master Craig, this way."

She was the last of her line and no one knew how old she was. It was doubtful if even she knew. After his mother's death, Craig used to go and lie in the woods with his dog, Flint, by his side. She would sit and talk to him by the hour, of the birds and all the wild country things around him. She knew the names of every flower and leaf. There was not a thing in the forest and hedgerows she didn't know. She belonged to one of the oldest Highland families, and she possessed the gift of second sight and of foretelling the future. From her ancestors she had inherited knowledge of magical medicinal brews, and her expertise was used by all the families in the district, except Fiona's. She could be seen often by the villagers collecting berries or herbs, and sticks fallen from the trees for her fire.

No one else, apart from the laird's family, knew the whereabouts of her actual home. She was always more outdoors than in, and she was more often seen close to the laird's home than anywhere else. Craig was her special favourite.

Her complexion was like rustic amber, and her eyes, like the burning gold of autumn leaves, twinkled in her crinkled, lined face. Only in the very depths of winter was she indoors. Her hands were as gnarled as the old trees of the forests.

"And", continued Fiona, breaking in on his thoughts as he held her close, as their horses chewed the fresh green grass closest to the stream, "I shall certainly see to it that she does not creep out of the hedgerows and frighten my children to death."

"*Our* children," Craig corrected her.

"I shall see", she continued, "that she is sent packing to practise her witchcraft elsewhere when we are married. I just know Papa Bruce will see my point of view when he knows how I feel on the matter."

Craig looked at her askance. "I am just as sure", he replied, "that Papa will not agree to such a step."

"We shall see," she replied haughtily as they remounted.

"Come – I will race you to the harbour," he called to her as they sped away. "I want to show you the new boat Papa has bought me. It's a real beauty." He was anxious to get off the topic of his dear friend, Merry-Berry. "I will let you choose her name if you want to, darling."

"I would love to," she replied, "but you will have to give me time to think about it. I have so many other things to think of."

"Of course, my dear, but don't be too long or else I shall have to name her myself."

"Oh, darling, she is really beautiful. When can we sail in her?' she asked.

"Well, she is not quite ready yet, and I must have more practice in handling her. I have been away from sailing on the loch for so long: I haven't got my sea legs back yet, have I, Larry?"

"Well, you soon will have, Master Craig," replied Larry, his boat keeper. "You used to race when you had your other boat and you will do the same with this one."

"Come, Craig – we must go. I will race you home."

Bruce was awaiting them eagerly on their return. He never liked his son out of his sight for too long.

"Here we are, Papa," Craig called as he arrived, a few seconds before Fiona.

"Here we are, Papa Bruce," she called out breathlessly as Bruce went to help her alight.

"I thought you had got lost in the woods," he called to them.

"Oh, no," Craig said. "Merry-Berry was, as usual, close by to direct us."

"That old witch! I can't stand the sight of her!" Fiona exclaimed with a shudder.

Bruce looked at her with a slight frown on his face, but he decided to let the remark pass. "Oh, you will learn to love her as we do – won't she, my son? This home would not be the same if we thought Merry-Berry was too far away."

"Come – let us go inside. It is getting chilly here," Fiona said. She was getting rather tired of the chatter about the old witch, and she knew, by Bruce's tone of voice, that she would have to tread carefully in any future reference to her.

'But of course it will be a far different matter when I am mistress here,' she told herself reassuringly.

Bruce had watched them arrive, and he thought how lucky he was that all he had wished for all these years was now coming true, but he could not help but wish that his beloved son was not of marriageable age. Then he would have much more of his company. He had felt a deep pang of jealousy as he watched them ride in, laughing gaily. 'How happy they are in each other's company,' he thought. 'Will they ever have room for any thought of me?' His face saddened for a moment. 'I shall never be able to bear it if that is so, but at least they will always be here in the castle with me. I will see Craig daily, and we will ride together over the estate. I am certain Fiona will not want to come with us on every occasion,' he told himself.

"And", Bruce continued when they got inside, "what had Merry-Berry got to say? More wise words, I shouldn't wonder?"

"Well," said Craig, "she said we would both be happily married and we are going to have two children at least."

"Now that is what I call really good news. As you know, my boy, she is always right. How wonderful it will be: my own grandsons to play with!" He chuckled to himself. "What a jolly time for all of us that will be! What a lucky fellow I am! All my dear ones here beside me: no one could wish for more."

Craig broke in on his thoughts: "We are going to change for dinner, Papa. We will join you later."

It had always been a big disappointment to him that he had had no more sons and daughters. Maybe if his darling Isabelle had lived longer there would have been. He glanced up at her picture and sighed. 'No, no,' he told himself, 'I mustn't think of that. The memory of it is too much for me.' The past could never be brought back again, no matter how much he wished it. 'I have my son and, in time, I will have grandsons. I must be satisfied with that.' No amount of sighing or wishing or longing would ever bring Isabelle back.

Craig and Fiona both rushed in on him, holding hands and laughing gaily as always. Harriet entered also.

"The dinner gong has gone. Come – we must away," she said.

"Where is Aunt Elena tonight?" asked Craig.

"She is visiting Margot," Harriet replied. "She will soon be home, but not in time for our after-dinner game of cards. She will stay and have dinner with Margot, and, once those two get talking, there is no telling what time she will arrive back."

"Well, I will play tonight," declared Fiona.

"But you are not keen on cards, my dear," said Harriet.

"Well, I shall be playing more regularly when I am here permanently. I will learn from you, Aunt Harriet."

"Well, we might as well continue tonight as Elena will be away very often now the war is over. She will want to travel to the missions overseas as she did before the war. Also, Fiona, you and I will be on our own quite often when these two men of ours are attending to estate affairs."

"Now, talking of estate affairs, Papa," said Craig, "Fiona and I have decided how we want the West Wing altered, so we can now go ahead and instruct the architects."

"I shall, of course, be here whilst it is being done," Fiona exclaimed. "They must not, on any account, do anything without my personal supervision."

"Everything will be done just as you wish, my darling," Craig agreed. "I shall be tied up with Papa and other estate affairs. I also have to deal with the Forestry Commission people. It is something new – Papa and I have not dealt with them before."

"Yes, my dear Fiona, we have lots to see and discuss," said Bruce.

"Oh," she said with a pout, "I do hope that won't mean you will be neglecting me?"

"No, of course not," said Bruce, "but you must realise, my dear daughter, that the estate is much larger than even Craig realises. There is much more land now than when he went away."

His assertive tone was not lost on Craig, who knew that, even when he was married, Fiona would not be allowed to come between them in anything, especially any matters relating to the running of his estate.

"Well, now all that is settled," said Craig, "we can, Papa, make a start on other things. First, of course, must be the Highland Gathering. It must be extra-gay – lots of music and dancing. We shall, as usual, expect you, Aunt Harriet, to organise the whole affair with Aunt Elena and Margot and the vicar's wife. Papa and I and the ghillies will organise the fishing events, the caber-tossing, etc."

CHAPTER 40

It was some days later that a messenger arrived to tell Fiona that her father had been taken ill and her mother had requested her presence.

"But, darling," exclaimed Craig, when they were alone that evening, "when shall I see you again?"

"I cannot say, but Mama sounds quite worried about Papa's illness. I will write to you as soon as I can, and I will return as soon as possible."

"But, darling, I am going to miss you so much," he whispered. He held her close and kissed her passionately.

"And I you, my darling," she tried to say between breaths.

"Darling, I cannot let you go after all the years we have been apart." He kissed her again and again. At last he released his grasp. "I do understand how concerned you must be about your father, just as I would be about my father. Just tell him to get well soon; then you can come back to me. Come, my darling – you must retire. You have a long journey tomorrow. Goodnight, my darling, my precious one, sleep well," he whispered. He kissed her again before she finally closed the door to her room.

Magnus was waiting at the jetty next morning to row Fiona over to the station. Now, as she was betrothed to a member of the laird's family, the laird's ferryman was at her disposal. Craig assisted her into the boat after kissing her goodbye, and he watched till it was out of sight.

Bruce was relieved to see her go. As much as he loved her, all he really wanted was his son by his side.

Elena, too, was thankful for a different reason: she was tired of Fiona's constant demands for this and that to be done, and for so many things to be altered. Elena had always thought of her as too haughty, and she had not liked her manner any better on this visit. She had behaved as if she was already Mistress of Glencree.

However, as far as Harriet was concerned, Fiona was just perfect. No one else could ever fit the bill as Fiona would as mistress of the house, Harriet kept telling Elena. The union of the two families would be a great delight to her. Fiona's mother had been her closest friend from their schooldays, and through her she had met her husband.

"I am going to miss her almost as much as Craig, I do declare. She is going to be such a perfect partner at cards. She is very good. She and Craig have beaten Bruce and I every night."

"So I noticed," Elena said. "I am so glad it relieves me. I can now concentrate more on my correspondence with Margot."

"But I hope you will be able to spare some time to partner me till Fiona returns," she retorted.

"Well, maybe for a short time, but I have a lot of planning to do for the gathering."

"Well, I too will be kept busy attending to all the arrangements and the alterations to the West Wing, as Fiona has instructed. I know Craig will be too busy with Bruce."

"How did you find Lady Roxburgh last night, Elena?" asked Bruce.

"She's still not too well, but I did not get to see her as she was resting."

"We might see her today," said Craig. "I promised Margot I would visit her soon."

"I am going over there today," said Bruce. "We need to discuss the land and cattle I am buying. She also has some lovely horses for sale. In fact, I have bought her finest one for you, my boy, as a surprise."

"Thank you, Papa. You are so good to me."

They rode off shortly after midday. It was a bright, sunny day with a fresh, cool breeze. Bruce could think of no more idyllic way of spending the time than out riding with his adored son by his side. He stopped now and again to point out the land he would be buying. "This land, my son, will one day be all yours to pass down to the sons that follow you. This will be the heritage, my dear boy, which will be connected with our name and clan for ever."

Craig listened to his father patiently. They paused several times to rest their horses; the estate now reached to the horizon and beyond.

"I have also been thinking, Papa, of this new venture the Forestry Commission are contemplating. It will certainly involve some of our land."

"Yes, my son, we will have to study it very carefully. I have not, as yet, had time to study it. Margot has quite a lot of information about it."

At last, they dismounted at Harrison Hall. Charles, who had seen them ride in, greeted them at the doorway.

"Is Lady Margot at home, Charles?" Bruce asked.

"Yes, Your Lordship, she is down at the stable."

"Good. We will walk round there," said Bruce, "but we will leave our horses here with you, Charles."

"Very well, sir. Shall I go and tell Lady Margot you are here?" he asked.

"No, Charles, she knows I am calling."

"Very good, sir," he replied as he led the horses away to the shade of the trees.

"Hello there, Margot," Bruce called to her. "Show my dear son the lovely mare I have bought for him, and we will look at the rest whilst we are here."

"She is certainly a beauty," Craig declared as soon as he set eyes on her. "What's her name?"

"She has no name as yet. Your dear father snatched her away from me as soon as I brought her home from the sale. I only let her go as she is a present to you."

Craig smiled. He knew how his father could wangle anything he wanted from Margot.

"Well, Craig, my boy, she is all yours," his father said as he handed Craig the reins.

Craig stroked her long, silken mane and the horse responded to him at once.

"Well, I shall call her" – and he paused for a moment – "Flaxen."

"Why that name?" Bruce asked.

"I think it describes her perfectly. Her long silken mane is like shining gold now the sun is on it – don't you think so, Margot?"

"Yes, I think the name is very apt," she replied.

"Well, that is settled, then. I will call in a few days and pick her up. Is Lady Roxburgh well enough to see me today? I haven't seen her since my return."

"Yes, she is slightly better than yesterday. She will be delighted to see you. You will find her in the music room. You haven't forgotten where it is?"

"I will find it. I know you and Papa have a lot to discuss with all the business matters in hand."

As Craig walked up the long, narrow path, he trod carefully over the now overgrown undergrowth and ducked several times under overhanging shrubs.

'What a beautiful garden this used to be! It was always so well tended by so many of the boys, now never to return.' He sighed. He stood in silence, thinking of bygone days.

A famous Scottish tune interrupted his thoughts, and he attentively listened, wondering who was playing so beautifully. He quickened his steps, bounded up the steps and strode along the verandah. The French windows were slightly open and he pushed one slowly and warily, not wishing to startle the old lady. 'Who is playing the piano?' he thought. He pushed aside the long net curtains slightly and he could see Lady Roxburgh rocking herself slowly in time to the music, her eyes closed. She was propped upright with many pillows. A colourful home-made Highland shawl was around her tiny shoulders and another was around her knees. Her silver-grey hair curled from under a snow-white little starched bonnet, the frill almost hiding her face. 'My, how frail and tiny she is!' he thought. The flickering fire caught her in its light.

His eyes strayed to the piano, on top of which stood a silver candlestick on which a dozen candles were still fluttering in the draught from the open window.

Elizabeth looked up, startled, when she saw the candles flicker, and the figure of a man outlined in the evening gloom came slowly into the room and leaned over the piano. She gave a gasp of dismay and stopped playing as her frightened gaze was held by the smiling eyes of Craig.

He put his fingers to his lips, warning her not to make a sound. His gaze wandered round the huge familiar room – a room he knew so well from his childhood days.

"Why have you stopped playing, child? I am not tired yet," Lady Roxburgh called out to her in her small, plaintive voice.

"Nan," he said. "Nan," he said again softly, "it is only me – Craig. Surely you haven't forgotten me?" He went closer and knelt down beside her. He took her tiny hand in his and kissed it lightly.

"Who did you say?" she demanded.

"Craig from Glencree Castle."

"Oh yes, of course I remember you, my boy. Why have you not come to see me for such a long time. You never used to be away so long."

"I was away in France and Belgium fighting in the war."

"Ah yes, now I recall. There should not be any wars in any land. No one ever wins; even the victors lose in the end."

"Yes, it is true," he replied.

'Wise words as always from her lips!' he told himself.

"Now, no more talk of wars! Sit down. Elizabeth can carry on playing for me until I retire in a little while. She sings beautifully. Sing, child."

"What would you like me to sing, milady?" she asked.

"Any of my old favourites," she replied.

"Would you mind, Lady Roxburgh, if she sang one of my favourites? I know it is also one of yours, because you used to ask my mother to play it for you."

"Very well, my son."

He went over to the piano and turned over several pages. "Play and sing this one, Elizabeth."

He stood close beside her, turning the pages one by one, smiling down at her until she had finished singing.

'How I wish he would go!' she told herself. His nearness made her tremble. Why, she did not know.

"That was beautiful, my child. That is enough for now, Elizabeth."

Elizabeth rose as swiftly as she could, dropped them a small curtsy and hastened to the door.

"Tell Nurse I am ready to retire now," Lady Roxburgh called after her.

Craig hastened to open the door for her. She looked at him as she curtsied and thanked him.

'Oh, how I wish he would take that smile off his face!' she thought. She always thought he was laughing at her.

"We are just in time to see you before you retire," said Bruce as he entered the room.

"So, you two have finished talking at last," said Lady Roxburgh as they sat down beside her. "Margot never knows when to stop talking once she starts, but there is, I know, lots to discuss now that you are buying all our land. I am glad to have Margot here to deal with it for me. I am not well enough to be bothered with all these estate details, and I'm far too old," she sighed. "Nurse is here now.

I will bid you all goodnight, but do call and see me again – especially you, young master. You have been away far too long."

"I will, Nan. I promise."

"Do stay and have a drink and stay to dinner," Margot said.

"Another time, thank you, Margot," Bruce replied. "We promised Harriet we would be back for dinner."

Lady Margot watched as they rode away, then Charles closed the door after them.

CHAPTER 41

Craig decided that until Fiona's return he would go to the city with Aunt Elena to visit the office set up to help the disabled men now back from the front. They visited some of the men as well as talking to widows and children of those who had not survived.

Elena worried about his taking their plight so much to heart. He would return to their hotel, where he would spend a long time in deep thought, and sometimes he would get to his feet in sudden anger.

"Aunt Elena, why should these poor bairns have no father? So many! It is unbelievable. It would have been much better if unmarried men, such as I, had been killed, rather than those with children to support. Well, it is up to such as you and me to see that the survivors get the support they so richly deserve. They were told they would return to a land fit for heroes. Let's make sure it is. We need to make sure, Aunt Elena, that we support all those in need, and I will ask my brother officers to help me. I know we won't reach everyone straight away, but eventually the word will spread around the country and those most in need will benefit."

Bruce was not at all pleased when they returned from these visits. Craig was always in deep despair, and Bruce felt that he was spending too much time with Elena discussing plans for the families' welfare. At times he told Craig about his concern.

"My son, is it essential that you spend so much time on these matters? You know how much there is to do on the estate, and now that Fiona is away we could be getting so much done."

"But you don't understand, Papa. I have to do this first."

He would storm out of the room in anger, mount his horse and be away like the wind down the long drive. Flint, as always, would run alongside. Elena and Harriet watched with alarm as Bruce would go to his room and look over the loch for hours.

"Bruce must try to understand", said Elena, "what the war has done to our boy."

"Well, Bruce is right," retorted Harriet: "he should be spending more time with his father on the affairs of the estate, instead of dealing with these other matters. I am certain, Elena," she exclaimed sarcastically, "that if you didn't encourage him the way you do, he would hand the welfare of these families to someone else!"

"Others are helping," Elena replied angrily. "I promised him when he returned

I would assist him, and this I shall always do along with my mission work. I feel sure things will soon be all right." She was trying not to let Harriet see how much her tone of voice and her accusation had upset her.

Bruce would gaze across the loch in deep thought, not understanding his son and his desire to ride alone. Time and time again he would ask him if he could accompany him, but it was always the same answer: "Not today, Papa. I cannot make conversation. Maybe another day."

Bruce would then ride away in another direction, pondering: 'What has the war done to my son? What has it done?' Then Craig would return from his long lonesome ride and beg his father's forgiveness.

The arrangements for the Highland Gathering were now well in hand. Everyone in the village and on the distant crofts was involved, and excitement was growing daily. Fiona was back home with her parents, her father having made a good recovery from his illness. She was often at Glencree Castle attending to the alteration of the West Wing; Bruce was often away in the city, dealing with the transfer of the land and stock of Harrison Hall.

Craig could be seen riding alone, visiting all the old participants of previous gatherings, cajoling them into taking part or helping to arrange events, as there was a lack of younger men.

Craig was sitting, resting his horse beside the loch, reflecting on this thought when he spotted Merry-Berry. He himself had bestowed her nickname on her when he was a child. He recalled his mother's soft laughter as she repeated her correct name to him.

"Her name is Meredith Beresford, my son. We will have to leave it as Merry-Berry. I think, Meredith, my son cannot pronounce your real name correctly."

"No matter, milady. It shall be as the young master wishes."

"Well," he explained to his mother after she left, "she is always so merry and always collecting berries."

"Yes, you are so right, my son, and, as Meredith doesn't mind, it won't matter."

'Dear, dear Mama,' he sighed. 'How I wish she was with us now! How she would have loved to have been involved in all these arrangements!'

"Hello there, Merry-Berry," he called to her. (She had seen him long before he had spotted her.) "How are all your fine fruits on this lovely day?"

"Fine, just fine, Master Craig. Just look at all these lovely berries and herbs I have in my basket." She held it up to him. "Mother Nature is a true provider. She always gives to the birds and animals of the forest and to such as me. As the Good Book says, 'Not a bird shall cleave the air that God does not provide for.' "

"Yes, you are so right. Will you be at the gathering as always?"

"Yes, I will be there with all my herbs."

"And I daresay", he laughed, "all the village girls will be swarming round you as before, all wanting to know their fortunes and asking for love potions."

"Yes, lots more of the girls now grown up will be wanting to know about their futures and their swains, but, more's the pity, alas! many of them will never know a swain with the loss of so many of our young men." She sighed.

"That is true. The war has been an utter waste of young men's lives," he said as he gazed out over the hills in the distance.

A cloud had passed over his previously smiling face and a deep sadness had filled his eyes. Once more his thoughts had winged their way back to the battlefields. Merry-Berry saw that he was lost in a world of his own.

"Master Craig, Master Craig," she called to him after what seemed an eternity. He looked up startled.

"Don't dwell on the past, my son. Nothing that has been done can be undone."

"Yes, you are so right as usual, my friend – so right." He bade her good day, and turned his horse for home, still pondering on the past.

'Here I am, surrounded by all this: the lovely sunny day, the heather-clad hills, the tall pine forests, my mountains and all the birds. Why should such as I have all this beauty to enjoy when my boys over there have nothing – not a leaf on a tree, not a bird on the wing? But I must do as Merry-Berry says and not dwell on the past.'

His father greeted him as he alighted. "How are all the plans getting on?" his father asked.

"Fine, just fine. Everyone is really looking forward to it. How did your visit go?"

"Just fine. Nearly all the transactions of Lady Roxburgh's land are now finalised, but I still have several more visits to make."

CHAPTER 42

The day of the Highland Gathering arrived at last. The night before had been hectic for all who had come from far afield to participate. Tents had been pitched here and there, and some of the soldiers from a nearby camp had been assembling huge marquees and roping off several areas for the various sporting events. A dais had been erected for the Highland dancing and there was a special platform for the laird and his guests. Rows and rows of chairs were already in place. The people from the village and crofts were setting out their stalls.

Emma and Elizabeth were sharing the tea stall with two of the girls from the academy, and they arranged to relieve one another as the day progressed.

"Thank goodness we aren't sharing with those 'jewel' girls," Emma exclaimed.

"I agree," said Elizabeth with a sigh of relief. "I wouldn't enjoy today at all with those three smirking all the time."

"They are on their mother's stall over there."

"My goodness, Emma, I have never seen such a lovely assortment of cakes! And there are still more boxes to open."

"Yes, Mama said the women of the village and crofts had dug out all their oldest recipes, all trying to outdo each other," said Emma. "Our mothers are busy arranging their stall with all the home-made sweets and preserves."

The angling contest had been in progress since early morn and Elizabeth had heard that at this stage her father and Roddy were first and third. "How exciting it all is, Emma! I wish I could go and see."

"Well, we cannot go until relieved, and that won't be for another two hours at least."

"Never mind, Emma. I am so excited to be doing something different today. I get so tired of all that correspondence, and I have to spend nearly every evening singing to Lady Roxburgh. Much as I love singing and playing for her, it does get tiresome at times, but really she is such a dear."

"I haven't seen her for ages. How is her health these days? I must visit her soon," said Emma with concern.

"I do wish you would come over and take tea with me; then we could talk more freely than we can at choir practice."

"Yes, I promise I will visit more often in future – but how is she?"

"Not very well and so frail."

"Now, you two chatterboxes," a sharp, high-pitched voice called to them, "come – we have lots more to do before the day is out and it won't get done if you chatter so much," said Mrs Knowell.

They both looked at her out of the corners of their eyes as she tapped impatiently on the edge of the table. Then she turned to go to speak to Mrs Crawford.

"Now hurry, or I shall take the stall off you."

This remark silenced them. Neither of them could have stood the shame of having to tell their parents that they had been deemed unfit to serve on the tea stall.

"Of all the people to be in charge of our stall, it would have to be that woman. As if we didn't see enough of her at choir practice!"

Emma looked up to make sure Mrs Knowell was out of earshot.

"Now, now, Emma!" quipped Elizabeth. "How unchristian of you – and you the vicar's daughter!"

Both gave a scream of laughter, then both tried to stifle it. They put their hands over their mouths as they spotted Mrs Knowell coming back.

"Now I think we are ready at last," she declared as she proudly rearranged the cakes she herself had made, placing them carefully in the centre of the stall for all to see.

Several people now gathered round waiting to be served, and the cakes fast disappeared as Emma passed them over. Elizabeth handed out cups of tea.

Whilst she was offering a cup of tea to one of the customers, she glanced up to see Master Craig watching her every move with his ever present smile and a mischievous glint in his eyes. How long he had stood there she didn't know. His guests and Fiona were stood some distance away. She was so startled by his intense gaze that she put a cup and saucer into mid-air, instead of into an outstretched hand, and with a loud crash it fell on to the display of cakes put there by none other than Mrs Knowell herself.

Emma let out a peal of laughter. She was such a happy-go-lucky girl and the least thing sent her off into peals of laughter. She tried to help Elizabeth clean up the mess.

"Of all the piles of cakes to land on," she said, still laughing, "it would be hers – and here she comes!"

Elizabeth, hot, flustered and deeply upset, met Mrs Knowell's gaze as she demanded to know what she was thinking about to be so careless.

"It was my fault," Emma declared, still trying not to laugh. "I caught Elizabeth's arm as I was handing over the cakes."

"Very well, then, girls, but do be more careful in future."

"I am so sorry, Mrs Knowell. I certainly will," replied Elizabeth.

"Is everything all right now? No one is scalded, I hope?" remarked Craig, wondering why Elizabeth had been so startled.

"Oh no, Master Craig, all is well. Will you have a cup of tea?" asked Mrs Knowell.

"Yes, I think I will. I will have it from Elizabeth," he said as he saw that Mrs Knowell was getting ready to pour, "if she doesn't mind. Of course, I'd rather she doesn't try to drown me with it, as has been the unfortunate fate of the poor cakes here." He was smiling broadly and Emma once more broke into laughter.

"Very well, then, girls, I will carry on and visit my other stall."

'Good riddance!' thought Emma as she disappeared.

'Trust him to add to my misery!' thought Elizabeth. 'Why doesn't he go away? He is always trying to make me feel foolish. If he hadn't been looking at me, it wouldn't have happened.'

As she poured the tea and handed it to him, her hand was trembling, almost spilling it in the saucer. He held on to it firmly.

"I won't let it fall, Elizabeth."

She was blushing deeply and her face felt hot.

"Do not worry so. Accidents will happen. It doesn't matter."

He turned round to find Fiona beside him. Her look of disdain and disapproval was plain for all to see as she glanced at them.

"Craig," she said in her haughtiest tone, "our tea is being served in the white marquee over there. Surely there is no need to patronise the villagers' stall. Colonel Grant and his wife are waiting for us."

"I will finish my cup of tea first," Craig replied. "That was an excellent cup of tea, Elizabeth and Emma. Is your stall doing well?"

"Yes, very well," Emma replied as he put his cup and saucer down. He bid them good day, and they both curtsied as he left.

"Do hurry, Craig darling," said Fiona, her anger increasing at his obvious interest in the girls of the village. "We are late."

"Oh, that Lady Fiona is so aloof," said Emma, "but have you noticed Elizabeth, Master Craig doesn't take the slightest bit of notice of her when she is like that? He just takes his time. Serves her right, too!"

He turned once more to wave to them. "I have forgotten to pay," he suddenly declared and rushed back to their stall. He called to Fiona: "Just one moment, dear," and he searched frantically in his pocket for small change.

"Oh, there is no charge to you, Master Craig," said Emma.

"But I insist."

At last he found his change and handed it to Elizabeth, who was still blushing profusely.

"We must all support the cause, for our returning soldiers' benefit."

"Here they are at last!" exclaimed Bruce as they entered. "Now we can proceed with our refreshment."

"I'm so sorry to have kept you all waiting," said Craig, "but there is so much to see and everything is going so well."

"Do sit down, Fiona dear. You look so exhausted," said their hostess.

"Yes, I am very tired. Craig spends so long at every stall."

"Well, Aunt Harriet," Craig asked, "how has your effort done? Did all your pretty crockery and other merchandise survive the onslaught?"

"Yes, everything sold in a very short time. I was so pleased."

"And you, Aunt Elena – how did you fare?"

"Well, I was with Becky and Margot collecting gifts for the soldiers' families. I have now got all the names of those still needing our help."

"That's wonderful! I can now get busy tomorrow. All your efforts are so worthwhile."

Elena handed him the list and he looked at it in disbelief.

"I never thought there were so many outstanding. The requests for help are endless, but they will all be dealt with – especially with your help. Really, Aunt Elena, I couldn't possibly do it without you."

He slipped the list into his pocket, sighing deeply. Fiona watched him, wondering when she was going to get some of his attention.

"Now we must all have tea!" exclaimed their hostess. "Then we can all get away to see the other events."

"How is the angling getting on, Papa?" asked Craig. "I haven't managed to get over there yet."

"Fine, just fine," Bruce replied. "Magnus, the ferryman, and Foster, the old ghillie, are having quite a battle. When I left, Magnus was just ahead, but it could have changed by now."

"Come, Papa – we will go and see what is happening now. Are you coming, Fiona?"

"No," she replied, still peeved by his delay at the tea stall. "I will stay and rest. I will stay with Mama, but Papa will join you, I am sure."

"Nothing could keep me away," her father replied. "I only wish I could be alongside them fishing."

"Well, we will fish another day," Bruce retorted. "Come – we will rejoin the ladies later."

CHAPTER 43

With tea finally over, Emma and Elizabeth cleaned their stall and had their own tea. Mrs Knowell, seeing how everything was going so quickly, had put sandwiches and cakes on one side for them.

"I think we have done very well, Elizabeth," Emma declared. "I have never seen so much money."

"Neither have I," Elizabeth replied.

"Yes," remarked Mrs Knowell, overhearing their remarks, "you have done exceedingly well. I am so pleased with you."

"I wonder which stall will have made most money for the cause," Emma said.

"Well, I am sure we won't be far behind the winners, whoever they are."

"May we go now, Mrs Knowell?" Emma asked.

"Yes, girls, you go and join in the fun. You have both worked very hard all day."

"That's praise indeed, coming from her," retorted Emma. "I am surprised she even noticed we were here until you dropped the tea all over her lovely cakes. What a laugh, to be sure!"

"You should not have taken the blame, Emma. It was my fault."

"Well, what does it matter?" Emma replied. "You do worry so, Elizabeth. What were you thinking about to let it happen?"

"Nothing really. I guess I just wasn't paying attention. Come, Emma – let us away."

She wanted to get away from the stall as quickly as possible. They walked over to the other stalls to see their friends.

"Hello there, Marie and Anne," called Emma. "How is everything going?"

"Fine, fine," they both said.

"We are nearly finished," said Marie. "We will join you in a little while."

"We are off to change for dancing now, so don't be too long," said Emma.

"Did you get to see Roddy anywhere, Marie?" Elizabeth called to her.

"Yes," she replied, "he is over there, taking part in the fishing."

"Oh, have we time to go, Emma?" she asked.

"No, no," she replied, "we must change for the Highland dancing. We might have time later."

"I do hope so," she sighed.

They were laughing gaily as they approached the tent.

"Oh, do let's hurry, Emma," said Elizabeth. "Here is Robin heading towards us."

"Well, why shouldn't he?" Emma replied. "He is head over heels in love with you – anyone can see that by the way he looks at you."

"Oh, just because he is my dancing partner doesn't mean he is in love with me."

"How sweet and naive you are, my dear," Emma replied.

With a few long strides he was beside her.

"Good day to both you lovely young ladies. Isn't it a lovely day for the gathering?"

"A delightful day!" replied Emma.

"Do you agree, Elizabeth?"

"Yes, a most delightful day!" she replied.

She found it hard to converse with him. 'Come to think of it,' she told herself, 'I find it difficult to talk with any of the village boys.' She only felt completely at ease with Roddy. 'Robin is such a nice boy, quiet and unassuming, as polite as all of them are. There isn't one of them I truly dislike. Robin is such a wonderful dancer; I love to dance with him.'

He was tall and slim with sandy-coloured hair. He had been anxious to join up, like the rest of the boys on the island, but defective eyesight as the result of a childhood fever had ruled him out. He had helped everyone on their crofts after the other boys had left.

They had now been joined by Stuart, who was practically engaged to Emma. 'I hope they don't leave me to chat to this boy,' she thought. 'I never know what to say.'

"What do you think, Elizabeth?" Stuart said. "Your father has beaten Foster in the fishing contest."

"Oh, hurray!" she exclaimed. "I am so happy for him. How wonderful!"

"And Roddy is third."

At this she clapped her hands with delight. "Oh, I am so happy. Foster will be disappointed, but it is all for the cause."

"Foster has come second, so I am sure he will be pleased," said Stuart.

The tent came into view.

"Now we must reluctantly leave you," Emma said, "but we will meet you at the dais later."

As they departed, the three 'jewel' girls arrived.

"Well, hello, you two," said Ruby. "How did your stall get on? We heard how you, Elizabeth, dropped a cup of tea all over Mrs Knowell's cakes and she was most angry about it all. Our cousin was in the queue and she said it almost scalded Master Craig."

At this remark Elizabeth almost froze with fright. 'Surely not!' she thought. 'If Mama and Papa get to hear of it, they will be very angry with me. How ever can anyone suggest such a thing? They have just made all this up to annoy me,' she told herself.

"Well, accidents can happen to anyone," retorted Emma, seeing the blush and dismay on Elizabeth's face.

The girls knew the jibe had gone home. "Maybe it wasn't an accident at all," one said to another, still revelling in Elizabeth's discomfort.

Emma, quick as ever to protect her friend, said, "Well, maybe one of you will have an accident and trip on the dance floor later." She hastily grabbed Elizabeth's arm and went into the tent.

"We are not dancing tonight, so there!" Ruby retorted.

Emma opened the flap of the tent as they were turning away. "No, I noticed you hadn't been selected. Your dancing evidently isn't good enough," she said, and she hastily closed the tent flap just as Ruby put her tongue out.

"Mama will be very angry with you for that!" exclaimed Pearl angrily.

In the tent they flopped into the chairs.

"Gosh, I must really rest my feet before we dance!" said Elizabeth. "Why do those three 'jewel' girls dislike me so, Emma?"

"It's just jealousy, my dear friend. You are so much prettier and more talented than any of them. That's the reason. Don't let their taunts upset you so. They just love to see you getting upset – more so as all the village boys have set their caps at you instead of them. Not one of them has a beau to call her own. I believe their mother is getting quite exasperated at the fact that not one of her precious jewels is going steady. What a snub it would be for her if no one took any of them off her hands. It would serve them right."

Elizabeth looked up at her and smiled. "How sensibly you deal with things, dear Emma. Really, I just don't know how I could possibly manage without you by my side."

They quickly changed into their dancing attire, helped each other with their hair ribbons and sashes and proceeded towards the stand beside the river, where the fishing contest had just finished.

On the raised platform stood the laird, Craig and the General, who were presenting the prizes. Emma spotted her mother, who was with Martha, and the two girls joined them in the crowd. They were also joined by their partners for the dance, who had been waiting for them to emerge from the tent.

"How exciting it all is, Mama!" exclaimed Elizabeth. "Fancy Papa and Roddy getting prizes."

"Hush, dear!" her mother said. "The laird is going to speak."

But Elizabeth was too excited and kept dancing up and down.

"I do wish, dear," her mother said, "you would stop jumping up and down. People are trying to see what is going on and they cannot whilst you are bobbing up and down."

Craig spotted her at once, his eyes twinkling with laughter at her obvious excitement. As the laird finished speaking and announced the name of the winner, her father stepped forward to receive the cup. Martha, so proud, smiled broadly, but Elizabeth clapped her hands with glee. The three standing beside her smiled at her delight.

The General stepped forward to give Foster his prize, then Roddy's name was called and Elizabeth danced and clapped again.

Craig stepped forward to hand Roddy his prize. "Your sister is delighted, as you can see," he said, and he turned Roddy round to face her.

Roddy held the cup up high to show her and Martha, but Craig's eyes never left Elizabeth's face. She stopped in her delight when she realised he was looking at her. His eyes met hers and she dropped them at once.

'How I wish he would stop staring at me!' she thought. 'I have come to see my darling Roddy, not him.' She felt quite indignant.

"Now we will see the Highland dances," said the laird, and the three of them left the platform amidst prolonged clapping.

Roddy and his father joined the rest of the family, and Elizabeth hugged them both eagerly.

"Oh, Papa and Roddy dear, it's wonderful for us all – isn't it, Mama?"

"Yes it is, my child. Now you must hurry along to the others."

"We must hurry!" exclaimed Robin. He took Elizabeth by the arm as they rushed away.

"It is my fault," she said, "but I wanted to see the prize-giving so much."

"It's all right," he replied. "The others are only just assembling. I can see them from here."

They were quite out of breath when they reached the stand, and Miss Emmot looked at them with annoyance. "Come – we have been waiting for you. Everyone else has been here a long time."

But the group smiled – they knew the laird's party was only just arriving and they could not commence until he gave the word.

At last, at a signal from him, the pipes struck up and they were away. With the skirl of the pipes and a swirl of their tartan kilts, and the girls' swinging dresses, sashes and hair ribbons, it was a sight to behold.

"Papa, isn't it wonderful that things are now back to normal?" Craig said.

"Yes, my son, it is."

Craig's eyes never left Elizabeth as she twirled around in the reels. He noticed the look of admiration on her partner's face and wished he could be so close to her. He couldn't understand this strange fascination she held for him. His feet were tapping in rhythm and Fiona's feet were tapping too.

"How I wish we could join in!" Fiona said.

"Yes, so do I," he murmured in her ear, "but we will have to wait for another time. It is ending now."

The dancers all bowed to the laird's party as they left the dais. Then the laird stood up to thank them all. He said, "Venison is being roasted in the glen nearby. Can everyone make their way there. Later there will be a firework display to end the gathering until next year. Other events will be held in the coming months to raise more funds for our gallant boys' dependants."

A loud cheer went up.

"Craig and Fiona asked me to ask you, instead of giving wedding gifts, to make a donation to the funds for our boys' dependants."

"What a marvellous gesture!" exclaimed Martha to Becky. "You will have quite a big job on hand, my dear. I only wish I was not so far away over the loch – otherwise I could help you more with these efforts."

"Well, I know, Martha dear, that we can sell all the needlework and crochet you have been doing, and that will bring in a large amount for the cause."

"Yes, that is one way I can help."

The people clapped and cheered as the fireworks shot skywards and fell in sparkling cascades over the loch. But to Craig and the other ex-soldiers they brought a shudder – they rekindled too many memories of the front and the Very lights.

At last, the laird's party drove away through the dark night to the castle.

"Oh, Emma," Elizabeth exclaimed, "we did not get a chance to visit the tent of Merry-Berry!"

"Well, never mind. We will visit her next year."

Elizabeth kissed her parents, Roddy and Emma goodbye as she stepped into the carriage of Lady Margot for the journey home.

The following day, the General and Lady Cleveland prepared to leave Glencree Castle.

"Must you go too, my darling?" said Craig, as he watched Fiona preparing to leave.

"Yes, my darling. Now that Papa is well again, I must accompany them down south. We had to leave so many arrangements unfinished when Papa was taken ill, but I will return for a brief spell. Then I will rejoin them for Christmas."

"But will you not spend Christmas with me? It is my first one at home since the war," Craig said, looking crestfallen.

"I know, my darling, but Mama promised so long ago – don't you recall, dear? We always spend Christmas with our relatives in England, Mama's home, and Hogmanay here in Papa's home."

"Yes, yes, now I recall!" He sighed. "But, my darling, I am going to miss you so much." He kissed her passionately before helping her into the carriage.

He stood a long time on the steps as their carriage disappeared, before rejoining his father in the library.

CHAPTER 44

One day, as Craig was returning from visiting the distant crofters, he took the small winding lane to visit the lodge his father had built for him whilst he was away, so that he and his friends could stay there whilst on their shooting expeditions. He had not been to see the place for some weeks, but he assured himself that all would be well.

He had decided, on his last visit, that he would never use it as a shooting lodge, as now the thought of killing anything filled him with horror. He gazed at it lovingly. Everything his father knew he would like was in it; nothing had been spared. A picture of his mother stood on the mantelshelf above the large, open fireplace. A basket of logs was nearby.

He picked up his mother's picture and kissed it fondly. "Dear, dear Mama, how I still miss you!"

He closed the door as he left. Then he mounted his horse and rode across the many glens. Suddenly, in the distance, he spotted a small figure approaching the kissing gate dividing his father's land from Lady Roxburgh's. He and Fiona used to play around the gate as children. Fiona always reached it first and was through it before he could reach her, until, as they grew older, she very wisely let him reach it first.

He was determined to be first today. Elizabeth, as yet, hadn't seen him, so she was quite taken aback when she reached the gate and saw him barring her way. She hesitated and looked up at him questioningly, her lovely blue eyes widening with apprehension, her cheeks now a deeper pink.

"Am I trespassing, sir?" she asked. She was impatient to be on her way.

This was a path she took often on her way back from the village. She loved its flower-strewn hedgerows, and the banks where sometimes she would sit and enjoy the utter peace and beauty of it all. She had never before met anyone using the path. Now and again she had spotted Merry-Berry, but she disappeared so quickly that she had never had time to say good day to her. Lady Margot would be expecting her and she was already late, having been delayed in the village. This tall, impeccably dressed man in his immaculately cut jodhpurs, open silk shirt (in spite of the now cool afternoon breeze), his black wavy hair blowing now and again across his dark, laughing eyes, tapped his riding crop idly across the palm of his hand. He leaned against the gate, his smile increasing at her obvious displeasure.

'Oh, bother!' she thought. 'Why does he taunt me so?'

She repeated, with as much dignity as she could, "Am I trespassing, sir?"

"Yes, you are, Elizabeth. This is my land, and I am sure you are well aware there is a forfeit to be paid if you wish to pass through."

"Yes, sir, I am well aware of the forfeit to be paid, but it is only to be paid by couples who are almost betrothed."

'Oh, bother!' he thought. 'Fancy her springing that one on me! She is quite bright, this little fairy of the glen.'

"Well," he continued, not to be outdone, "we could pretend, until you reach the other side. Then you can be free."

"No, sir, I shall have to return to the village and take the other path home."

"Pray no, Elizabeth. That I cannot allow. You have already walked too far as it is and it is now almost dusk. If I see you walking this way again, you will have to pay the forfeit. Now, you must be getting home."

He stood aside as she passed, but much to her annoyance he followed her and walked beside her, not speaking. He was just so happy to be there.

She felt quite perturbed. 'What if someone should see us?' she thought anxiously.

At the end of the field, a fence barred their way, and a wooden step over the fence was the only way to proceed.

"Allow me, Elizabeth, to assist you over."

"I can manage quite well, Master Craig," she replied.

"Why Master Craig? Why not just Craig, as nearly everyone else calls me?"

She did not answer but started to mount the steps, stumbling in her haste to proceed. He caught her arm and held it firmly as he leapt over the fence before her. Then he bade her proceed as he still clung to her arm. She wished he would let go, but she could hardly shake him off. She thanked him curtly as she touched the ground. She looked up at him, with his dancing eyes and ever present smile.

'How I wish he would stop that stupid grin!' she told herself. In his eyes she saw a flash of something she could not fathom as their eyes met, and she dropped her gaze immediately. She wanted him to go away, but as she tried to pull herself away his grip tightened on her arm and he pulled her closer.

"My angel, why do you pull yourself away from me? How can I be so close to you and yet so far away?" His smile had gone as he spoke.

She looked up at him in dismay. Never in her life had she heard such a question. 'This cannot be,' she told herself. 'Whatever is he thinking about?'

By now, a panic and fury was rising within her – something she had never experienced before. 'I must get away, I must get away,' she told herself over and over again. 'Why won't he let go of my arm?' She looked around her. 'Yes,' she told herself, 'we are now on my mistress's land. He dare not go any further.' Her fury mounted at her delay in getting home.

"You, sir," she said boldly, wondering to herself where she had got her sudden nerve from. "You, sir," she repeated, "are now the trespasser. We are now on Lady Roxburgh's land."

He looked around him. "So we are," he said, with amused laughter. "But there again, Elizabeth, you are mistaken. This land now belongs to my father and so it is mine, as it has been sold by the good lady herself."

She was furious. 'Can I never win with this man?' Every time she thought she held a trump card, however small, he always managed to turn the tables in his favour.

"I am sorry, sir. I did not know."

"But you", he emphasised, "are free to travel over it whenever you wish. However, if I catch you at the kissing gate, you will have to pay the forfeit."

"Thank you, sir, but I shall not trespass on land that is not my mistress's. I shall not come this way in future."

'Damn, damn!' he said to himself. 'I can never get one over on this little one.'

"Why not Craig every time, instead of sir?" he asked. "It would sound so much better from your sweet lips."

"That, sir," she replied, "I cannot and will never say."

At last, the big house came into view.

"I will bid you good day, sir, and thank you for escorting me so far."

"The pleasure, I assure you, Miss Angel Elizabeth, has been all mine."

'Well,' she thought, 'it has not been all mine.'

She dropped him a small curtsy, then turned and ran the rest of the way.

He watched as she entered the tall gates and disappeared out of sight.

"Come on, Flint – we too must return home. We are not visiting Harrison Hall today, but we will return another day soon. Come – Flaxen will be wondering where we have gone."

CHAPTER 45

Bruce was away more and more as the plans for the acquisition of more land from Lady Roxburgh neared completion. There were more and more meetings with their solicitors to attend, but Craig declined to accompany his father.

"You deal with it all, Papa. I cannot bear the thought of spending many hours in offices when I can be riding in the glens."

"Yes, you are so right, my son. The good mountain air will be better for you, but I do miss you by my side."

"And I you, Papa, when I am out riding."

"Well, I hope to join you soon. I don't think there will be many more details to finalise before all the transactions are complete."

Craig accompanied his father to the jetty and saw him safely in the boat, with Magnus as always at the helm. Bruce stopped when he reached the other side of the loch to talk to Martha and Roddy, who now helped more and more with the crofting. Bruce passed the time with Peggoty at the station as he waited for a train to take him to the city. Occasionally he would be accompanied by Margot, as they dealt with her mother's affairs.

In the meantime Craig would be away to the glens, visiting more and more of the crofters, spending long hours with any that were disabled, talking about their welfare.

One day he was returning, having ridden Flaxen pretty hard.

"We will rest here for a while, my pretty mare, and wait for Flint to catch up. Ah, here you are, old friend," he said, as the dog came to heel.

Before alighting he sat looking at the scenery below. 'Oh, what peace and serenity!' he thought. It was after midday, and the sun was still shining in a bright cloudless sky. The mountains in the distance were starting to lose their summer greenness. 'Soon,' he thought, 'the autumn and winter nights will be upon us. Then, Flint, my old friend, spring will be here once more.'

The dog looked up at him as if he understood all he had said.

Craig was quite breathless with the speed he had ridden over hill and dale, calling to the wild animals as he passed. "Fly on, fly on," he called to the birds. They quickly rose and flew away as his approach startled them into flight. And to the deer, as they scampered away, and the sheep, as they scattered, he called, "You are all free – free as the wind. Like myself, you are all free to enjoy and breathe the clean Scottish air."

'I wonder if dear Papa will have returned when I arrive back home,' he said to himself. 'I miss him so, but I am glad he has bought all this land. It is really all mankind's; Papa and I are just its protectors, to safeguard it for generations to come. I shall always be your protector, my lovely, beautiful Scotland – the land your sons fought for.'

Always in his mind were the men who were far away. In his worst nightmares his wartime experiences crossed and recrossed his mind, and he would awake in a cold sweat to find Elena by his side, her soft hand on his forehead, her soft voice whispering in his ear:

"It's all over, dear boy, all over."

"Are you sure, Aunt Elena, are you sure?" he would reply in his half-awake stupor.

Now, resting on the hillside, he could see that at last it was all over. Everything was calm, bright and beautiful. Just as he was going to alight, he saw a wisp of blue he hadn't noticed before.

'What is a wisp of blue doing amongst this wondrous green? I must get a little closer.'

Flaxen, helping herself to some succulent grass nearby, was reluctant to go.

"Come up, boy," he called to Flint. "You can ride for a while. There it is again. Come – we must hasten before it disappears altogether." He knew he had a fair way to go before he reached the glen.

At last he dismounted under a clump of low-lying shrubs.

"I do believe it is Elizabeth herself."

He watched as she walked up the leafy lane with two small dogs playfully barking at her side. She threw a small coloured ball into the distance and the two dogs sped away in pursuit. They brought it back to her to throw again and again.

"I wonder why I haven't seen her taking the dogs for a stroll before." He had often seen Charles along that lane, but never her.

He watched her for several minutes. She reached the turn in the lane, and she called the dogs to her as they turned for home. He could hear her raised gentle voice calling the dogs again and again as they scampered off into the undergrowth in evident enjoyment at disobeying her. As they rejoined her, the three of them ran down the lane.

"I wonder if she takes the dogs for a walk often?" he asked himself. "I wonder, I wonder. What do you think, Flint?"

Flint looked up at him as if to say, "Come – let us away home."

He turned for home, a plan evolving in his mind.

Several days later, he set out once more to ride the glens.

He called to Elena before he left: "Tell Papa I shall be visiting some of the crofters, if he asks about me."

"I will," she replied, "but try not to leave it too late, dear boy. The autumn nights are closing in now, and you know how he worries so once the twilight and mists start falling."

"I won't be late – I promise."

He raced on, his hair blowing wildly in the wind. Flint raced beside him. At last they came to the high rise above the stream and the leafy lane below.

"I wonder if she will come today, Flint," he said, and the dog looked up at him. He had watched her come and go for several afternoons, but today was going to be different, he had decided. "I do hope she comes."

He dismounted and tethered his horse and let it graze. He called Flint to heel and walked to a spot under a large tree, surrounded by smaller shrubs.

"Ah, a perfect view," he decided. From here he could observe anyone coming from the hall.

Sure enough, there she was, taking the old familiar route with the two dogs yelping at her side and running for the ball she threw. Sometimes she pretended to throw the ball high in the air and they would look up at her as if asking, 'Why are you teasing us so?' On and on they came up the narrow, winding lane. At times she was hidden from view by low shrubs, but he could hear her gay laughter at the antics of the dogs. At last they were almost beneath him.

He held tightly to Flint until she threw the ball once more into the distance.

"Go get the ball, Flint, and bring it to me," he said in a hushed voice.

The dog did as he was bid, and Craig crouched back against the tree. He was hidden from view but he could see the three dogs in hot pursuit of the ball.

Elizabeth stood rooted to the spot spellbound. 'The big black dog – where did he come from? Who did he belong to? Where have I see him before?' she pondered. She was furious. She could see him way ahead of her two dogs as he grabbed the ball and ran into the hedgerow. Her two small dogs followed, evidently quite enjoying the fun of hide and seek.

She scrambled up the bank after them, stumbling as she went, her golden hair falling loosely over her shoulders as she did so. While she groped around in the undergrowth, the three dogs watched her from higher up. At last she spotted them all sitting side by side. Flint still held the ball in his mouth. She was hot and exhausted with her efforts. She called the dogs but they paid her no heed. As long as their ball was held captive they were staying close by. As she drew nearer, Flint set off again. The two dogs followed in pursuit.

"Come back, you big black brute, come back!" she cried, but he paid her no heed.

He placed the ball at his master's feet, and Craig picked it up and hid further in the bushes. He told Flint to stay where he was and not to move. The dog was used to obeying and retrieving, so he stayed put.

When Elizabeth spotted him sitting there with no ball visible, she shouted to him, "Where is the ball, you tiresome hound? Where is it?" She was getting more exasperated and angry as she tied her hair back once more.

"Is this what you are looking for, Miss Angel?"

Elizabeth was startled to hear the voice from the bushes as he parted the branches. She looked up to see him laughing gaily.

"I can assure you, Master Craig," she said angrily, "it is no laughing matter. Have you been teaching your dog to steal? It is your dog, I presume?"

"You presume correctly, Elizabeth."

"I was trying to think where I had seen him before," she replied.

"Well, my dear Miss Angel Elizabeth, you will know in future that when you see my big black brute of a dog, as you call him, that I shall not be far away."

"Yes, I will remember in future," she replied tartly.

Her dogs came jumping up by her side. She pushed them down as gently as she could. "Down, down!" she called to them as she tried to brush the soil from her dress and rearrange her hair ribbons.

"Your dogs do not do as you ask," he laughed.

She tried again to make them stay beside her as she tried to calm herself.

"No, they don't. Neither do they steal other dogs' balls!" she exclaimed. "It was just a trick to lure me up here – a pretty clever trick too. Whether it was your brainy idea, or your dog's, I cannot imagine."

Craig looked down at her, still laughing gaily.

"I can assure you, Miss Angel Elizabeth, it was the dog's idea, and his alone – a very clever dog, don't you agree?"

"Yes, a very clever dog," she replied, still with a note of anger in her voice.

"I apologise for my dog," he said.

She doubted it, as he still stood smiling broadly.

"Tell me why you are now taking the dogs for their afternoon walk. Surely Charles always took them before, but I have not seen him out for some time."

"Charles has fallen and sprained his ankle, and Lady Margot has asked me to take them," she replied.

"Yes, I have watched you every day from this very spot."

She was angry with embarrassment as she looked up at him, but she dropped her gaze immediately when she saw the laughter in his eyes.

"Why, may I ask?"

"Just to try to talk to you awhile."

"And you have managed it by a trick."

She was getting more and more angry, but he only continued to laugh at her.

"Well, I could think of no other way, so a trick it had to be."

She continued to brush down her dress.

"Please may I have the ball now?" she said in a tone of voice which surprised her beyond belief, but it only seemed to amuse him all the more.

"Only on one condition," he said: "that you stay and talk with me awhile."

"I must be getting back. Lady Margot will be getting anxious about my long absence; also, it is not fitting that I should be seen talking with you alone like this."

"And why not?" he demanded, the laughter in his voice fading a little.

"Because you are Master Craig and I am only a crofter's daughter, and you are betrothed to Lady Fiona."

She was alarmed at the way she had been addressing him; she suddenly remembered who he was. She always had quick repartee when Roddy was teasing her. 'It's his own fault,' she excused herself, 'but he is Master Craig, so really I should not speak to him in such a manner.' What would her parents say, and Roddy, if they ever found out? And what would Lady Margot say? Her thoughts were in turmoil. 'She might want me to leave my position. What a fix this man always places me in. Why doesn't he go away?' More and more alarming thoughts assailed her.

"You look very thoughtful, Elizabeth. Is anything wrong?" He was concerned at her obvious distress.

'But,' he told himself, 'I might never get another chance to be so close to her and talk with her.'

"No," she replied, "but I must be getting back."

"Surely a few more minutes won't matter. There is so much I want to know about you."

By now they had walked up to where he had tethered his horse.

"And what is it you want to know about me?" she almost demanded. "You must know just about everything. The next laird of Glencree must surely know by now all there is to know about all the local people."

"Well, yes, you are so right. My father knows all there is to know about his tenants, and he will know all about you, but I cannot ask my father any details about you. He would want to know why I am so interested in the prettiest girl in the district. Of course, I shall know all about you later on, but I am an impatient man and I want to know now."

She blushed profusely at his remark about her being pretty, and it did not go unnoticed by him.

'Why is she so shy?' he asked himself. 'I can laugh and joke with all the girls but this one. She is just like a fairy from the glen – so reticent. It is as if at any moment she might hide herself from me in a flower or disappear deep into the forest and I will never see her ever again. No, I must keep her here a little longer.'

Elizabeth was a little surprised at herself. Never before could she recall speaking so curtly to anyone – and, particularly, to such as he. Was it the strangeness of the situation she had found herself in, or her anger at the trick he had played on her, that had unleashed such a brave response from her? 'It must be something,' she told herself. 'Normally, I would hardly be brave enough to say more than "Good day, sir" and drop him a small curtsy.' Nevertheless, here she was, almost equalling his banter with her own.

His voice broke in on her thoughts, so soft and low. She looked up into his laughing eyes and she tried to resist a faint smile.

'What a ridiculous situation this is!' she told herself. 'I am not going to give him the satisfaction of thinking that I am amused. This is an impossible situation he has placed me in. No, I am still too angry with him.'

"You know, you cannot leave here until I say. I have still got the ball, but you can see the dogs are longing to get it back again and be on their way home."

She still noted the banter in his voice. He was still smiling, but there was also something in his voice that told her he was used to being the master and having his own way. He was tapping his riding whip lightly across his thigh – a habit he had picked up from his father.

'Well,' she thought as she watched him, 'whatever it means to him, he has the whip hand at present.'

"Flint," he called, "hold the ball," and he tossed it to him.

The other two dogs gave yelps of delight as they thought the game was on again.

"Stay, boy, and hold the ball."

The dog did as he bid.

Craig reached up to stroke the horse's head and began twisting its mane round and round the whip in long, thin ringlets.

"I wonder what you are thinking at this very moment," he said, and he smiled at Elizabeth.

"I was wondering how much you already know about me."

"Very little," he replied. "My father knows your family very well, and I remember seeing you as a child when I used to cross over the loch with my parents. I can faintly recall seeing, on one or two occasions, a small boy and girl throwing pebbles into the loch, but on later visits they had disappeared so I just thought they were visiting. Why is it I never saw you again until I saw you on the stairs? Surely you are the little girl and your brother was the boy?"

"Yes, that is so," she replied, feeling calmer now and less angry.

He had said he was sorry he let his dog take the ball, and now she felt she had to forgive him. He did look truly sorry, and he had been away in that beastly war for so long. She told herself she wouldn't like any girl to be angry with her Roddy for such a trick, and he might have played the same sort of trick. How alike the two of them were!

"Well," she began, "I was that little girl and Roddy, my brother, was the boy. We did often play beside the loch, throwing pebbles into the water, but we were sent by our parents to live with Aunt Ingrid shortly after her husband died. Mama said we would keep Aunt Ingrid company in her loss, and she was able to provide us with an education. I attended a music academy to learn singing and playing, and I also trained to be a governess. Roddy, who was keen on the army, went to the army training college. He is now helping Papa with the crofting."

"I daresay", Craig replied, "Roddy is sick of the army after the war, as I am."

"Yes, I think so," she replied.

"Tell me; who chose your pretty names? Dawn Angeline interests me most of all."

"That, sir, was my father's choice. He said to Mama when I was born that as dawn had just broken I should always be known as his Dawn Angel. Mama insisted that I have a more suitable name, so she chose Elizabeth and added Aunt Ingrid's name as she was my godmother."

'How I wish he would not keep me talking so! It is getting time for me to return,' she thought to herself, but all he wanted to do was to keep her talking a little while longer.

"Tell me how you came to be at Harrison Hall?"

"Aunt Ingrid and Lady Margot were school friends and, when Aunt Ingrid died suddenly, Lady Margot offered me the job of helping her with her correspondence. Like your Aunt Elena, Lady Margot works for the overseas missions. The war was on and Roddy was away so I was all alone. Lady Margot had returned from India some time previously to be with her mother, who is very ill. I am able to help her by singing and playing for her. I was at home when you first saw me because I had been ill and Lady Margot said that I could stay and await Roddy's return. That, Master Craig, is all I can tell you."

Craig listened to her intently. He watched as she gazed lovingly at the horse and stroked its head so gently.

"She is a lovely horse. What is her name?" she asked.

"Flaxen," he replied almost at once. "She has golden hair like yours."

She looked up startled, and he smiled down at her. He untied the reins from the tree.

"Come – have a little ride on her."

"Oh no, I have never ridden."

"Well, come and try. Just sit on her for a few moments and admire the view." He would not take no for an answer. "Come – I will help you on."

He helped her to sit sideways on the horse's back and gave her the reins.

"Don't let her move off with me!" Elizabeth exclaimed in panic.

"No, she won't move until I tell her – and I am not going to tell her, so you are quite safe."

"I feel a long way from the ground!" she exclaimed. She was growing more alarmed.

"Just hold on to the reins," he said, and he led the horse round and round in the clearing.

"I am sure I am going to fall off," she cried.

"I won't let you fall ever, and I will make you feel safe. I will never let you fall – never."

The tone of his voice frightened her. She knew she should never have agreed to mount the horse, but she had felt compelled to do as he wished.

He sprang up in the saddle behind her and took the reins, holding her hands for a brief moment. A thrill shot through her as his strong arms wrapped around her and his hands held hers. It was the same queer thrill as had shot through her on the night of the dance. He felt her tremble.

"Are you feeling cold, my angel?" he asked.

"Elizabeth is my name," she insisted, almost angrily.

"You will always be Angel to me," he replied.

"Yes, I am feeling cold. The afternoon is getting on. I must be getting home." There was a note of alarm in her voice. "Really, I must go. Please let me down, Master Craig."

"Call me Craig. I insist."

"Well, if you insist, Craig, but only this once." She feared if she refused, he would never let her get off the horse. "Please, I beg of you, let me get down." The panic in her voice increased.

"Forgive me, Miss Angel. Please do not get upset."

He leaped lightly from the horse, reached up and lowered her gently to the ground. He held her tightly to him as her feet touched the ground.

"You are so beautiful, Angel, so beautiful."

Wisps of her golden hair were blowing gently across his face. He moved them slowly away and put them behind her ears. She looked up at him, her large violet-blue eyes widening with the look of a frightened gazelle. She tried not to succumb to the feeling of power and possession he seemed to radiate as he held her close. He was reluctant to let her go. He held her closer and his lips brushed her ears.

"Please, Master Craig!"

"What did I tell you to call me?" he demanded.

"Please release me, Craig," she pleaded.

"Only if you promise I can see you again like this."

"That is impossible and unthinkable. You know that as well as I do."

"But I insist. I must see you again sometime."

"No, no," she replied. "I cannot, I cannot. Please release me." Her pleas grew quite frantic.

'How ever did I get in such a fix as this?' she asked herself.

He released her slightly.

"Charles has hurt his foot, so will you be out walking with the dogs every day?"

"Yes," she replied, not realising what she was saying.

His sudden smile told her too late she had said the wrong thing.

"But it will only be for a short while," she hastened to add. "Sometimes Lady Margot takes them for a stroll, and I shall not come this way again. I will take them into the village."

He knew she meant it. He had not fully released her and she didn't know what else to say to get away.

"I must get back. Lady Margot will be getting quite alarmed at my long absence."

"You can tell her you lost the ball. It will be true to a certain extent," he replied, still smiling.

"Oh, you are impossible," she seethed.

He finally let her go and stood back watching her as she straightened her dress and hair ribbons. She called the dogs to her side and they came at once. Flint rose to his feet to rejoin his master.

"And, you," she said reprovingly, "please don't take the dogs' ball again, you thieving rascal, and don't steal just because your master tells you to."

Craig burst out laughing at the seriousness of her manner as she wagged her finger at Flint. There was a plaintive look on his face, as if he understood every word she was saying as she scolded him.

"It wasn't Flint's fault, but I don't suppose I shall ever be forgiven either," he said, still laughing.

"No, it was quite despicable of you to teach your dog to steal and then let me spend ages looking for it in the bushes. Just look at my dress – all creased and soiled. That reminds me: where is the ball now?"

"Here it is," he said, holding it out to her, but when she closed her fingers over it he gripped the ball tighter and held on to her fingers. "Please say you will see me again, you tormenting angel."

"I cannot, I cannot." The panic in her voice returned.

Before she could say no again, he grasped her to him as though he would never let her go and kissed her passionately.

She held her bruised lips in disbelief as she looked up at him. Anger, as she had never known before, swept over her, and, before she realised it, she had slapped him across the face. Then she turned and fled.

He was taken aback by her attack. He had dropped the ball before he grasped her and the dogs picked it up and chased after her. He leaned back against the tree after picking up his whip and tapped it angrily against his thigh.

"Whatever is happening to me?" he exclaimed. "I am behaving like a cad. It isn't like me to be acting this way. Why, oh why does she cause so much devastation inside of me? I am going crazy."

He remounted his horse and sat looking down the glen. He could still see her running wildly on, the dogs bounding beside her. What was this strange fascination she had? He knew he would never again be as he was before he knew her. He waited.

'I will wait and see her enter the hall safely before I go.'

She ran on and on, headlong through the bracken and the heather. The dogs were hardly able to keep up on their short, sturdy legs. She did not look back to see if he was still on the high rise. Her heart fluttered so fast it alarmed her, and it wasn't just because she was running so fast.

"My goodness!" she exclaimed. "Whatever am I doing in such a state as this? That man – I shall never forgive him. Never! What was I doing to allow such an encounter?"

She was angry and deeply distressed. What if someone had seen her with him – and he betrothed to Lady Fiona? Her flushed cheeks were burning hot with the thought that they might have been seen.

She stopped to rest under a large tree. She felt her cheeks with the back of her hand. They were fiery hot.

'My goodness! I cannot go home like this. Whatever can I do? Whatever can I say with my dress in this state and my hair in tangles and so out of breath? I must calm myself.'

She straightened her dress as best she could and tried to sweep her hair back more tidily. It was then that she spotted a small gap in the hedge close by and the stream beyond.

'It's just wide enough for me to squeeze through,' she told herself. She searched frantically for her handkerchief, and at last she found it. She crawled through the small gap, knelt beside the stream, dipped her small handkerchief in the cold, clear running water and patted her face.

'How lovely and cool!' she thought.

She felt more composed as she patted her hair with the cool water. She had lost one of her ribbons.

'Goodness knows where it is!' she told herself.

The dogs sat beside her. They too were thankful for the rest and cool drink. She stood up and straightened her dress once more.

'I hope I look a little more presentable now,' she said to herself.

She hurried back to the gap and struggled through. Then, to her dismay, she heard the sound of material tearing. She tried to scramble back, but she was well and truly stuck. What she hadn't noticed when she went through before was the barbed wire hidden in the hedgerow which had overgrown it. It was old and rusty. The more she struggled, the more entangled she became and the more she tore her dress.

"Oh, what can I do?" she cried out in anguish, and the dogs, who had been watching her struggle, started to yelp frantically. They knew she was in trouble, and they started to jump up and down.

'I shall be here all night.' It was getting late afternoon. 'No one, I am sure, will come through the glen so late in the day.' She grew more and more distressed until she was almost in tears.

Craig had cantered higher up the hill to get a better view down the glen. He wondered why she had not yet appeared in the opening past the small bridge before the gates of the hall. As he looked and pondered he heard the frantic yelping of the dogs and spotted them jumping up and down near the stream, but he couldn't see anything of Elizabeth.

'What has happened to her?'

He galloped down the hill, jumping all the hedges as if they were not there. Flint raced behind him.

When he came to the gap in the hedge, he saw her lying entangled on the ground. He leapt off his horse and hastily tied it to a tree. Then he ran to her side.

"Are you hurt, my dear Angel?"

"No, I am not," she replied angrily. She was annoyed that it should be him who came to her rescue.

'Why couldn't it have been one of the village boys or Roddy on his way from the vicarage?' She knew that was where Roddy was going after leaving their father earlier in the day.

"If it hadn't been for you," she yelled at him, "this wouldn't have happened."

When he realised she wasn't hurt, he started to laugh.

"Oh, you horrible man, stop laughing at me like a fool." She didn't care who he was at that moment. "Get me unhooked," she pleaded. "It is all your fault. Release me! Get me free!" She was shrieking with rage and embarrassment.

"Now," said Craig, becoming more serious, "stop being so angry and alarmed and ask me like a sweet angel to release you. Otherwise I will go away and leave you here."

"Oh, please, Master Craig."

"What did I tell you to call me?" he exclaimed angrily.

"Please, Craig, do not leave me here," she pleaded. The thought that she had been screaming at him in rage increased her embarrassment. "Please, Craig."

"Say 'dear Craig'," he insisted as he started to disentangle her.

"Dear Craig."

She was growing more and more angry with him. 'He is always mocking me. I don't mean 'dear' at all, but it is the only way I will get free.'

"Now, don't struggle. Keep perfectly still."

After a few seconds, she was unhooked.

"There!" he said as he helped her to her feet. "It is only your pride that is hurt, my dear, but your dress is beyond repair, I'm afraid."

She tried to see the back of her dress as he spoke. She clasped the material together with her hands.

"Are you sure you are not hurt at all?" he enquired more seriously.

"No, thank you. I am not hurt. Thank you for releasing me."

As they both stood up, they noticed through the clearing that on the bridge stood a horse and carriage. The sound of the dogs yelping had caused the choirmaster's wife to stop and investigate, and the beady eyes of Mrs Knowell peered at them.

"That's Elizabeth Anderson with her dress all undone and her hair in disarray, being helped to her feet by none other than the young master of Glencree Castle. He is helping her to fasten her dress at the back." She was staring at them with a look of utter dismay, disbelief and disgust on her face. "It's incredible – just too incredible," she muttered aloud, although only the horse could hear what she had to say.

She cracked her whip at the horse and he started up so quickly that she was almost thrown out of the carriage.

"It would serve her right if she was thrown out!" exclaimed Craig, as she raced off at full speed towards Glencree Castle, no doubt to tell Aunt Harriet all she had seen.

'Now all this will add to my misery,' thought Elizabeth.

Craig walked towards his horse, still watching the carriage, which was disappearing up the lane.

"There's no harm done, Elizabeth. She won't dare say anything. If she does, she will have to answer to me."

"Maybe there's no harm done to you, Master Craig, but what about me? My dress is all torn and my hands are so dirty." She was beside herself with panic.

"My dear one, you do worry so. Wait here – I will clean your hands."

He rushed back to the stream and took from his pocket his snow-white, silk, monogrammed handkerchief. He soaked it thoroughly in the water, taking care not to get himself caught in the wire. Then he washed all the dirt away.

'How gentle he is!' Elizabeth thought. She watched him but avoided his eyes as he looked at her.

"Thank you so much," she whispered.

He wrung his handkerchief as dry as he could and gave it to her.

"I know you won't be satisfied until you have returned it to me all nicely washed and ironed, and that way I shall have the chance to see you again."

"Oh, you are impossible!" She still felt very angry with him in spite of all his help. "Look at the trouble I am in now. Goodness knows what that woman will do!" Once more the panic was evident in her voice.

"I am so sorry, Angel – really I am. It is all my fault, I admit, but, believe me, I only wanted to talk with you awhile."

She looked up at him and held his gaze for a fleeting moment. He felt a tremble pass through her as he held her hand clutching the handkerchief.

"Please say I am forgiven," he pleaded.

"Yes, you are forgiven, just this once. Now I must hurry. I do hope Lady Margot has not been looking for me."

"Shall I see you to the hall?' he asked.

"Oh dear, no, I must go alone. Now where are the dogs?" She looked all round. "Oh, my goodness, they will have run back home! I must go."

'More trouble for me!' she told herself, and she rushed off without another word.

He watched as she ran out of sight over the bridge and through the arched gateway of the hall. He glanced down before moving off and noticed the two leads and a blue hair ribbon, which she had placed beside the stream as she cooled her face. He picked them up.

"I shall return these later, little Angel," he muttered. Then he called Flint and turned for home.

Elizabeth hurried on up the long drive. Her cheeks were still hot with anger and embarrassment at the thought of her torn dress.

'I never seem to be properly dressed in any encounter with that man,' she told herself angrily.

She entered in the back way and spotted Charles with the dogs.

"They ran off as I was looking for their ball."

"I was quite alarmed to see them return without you, Elizabeth. I will put them in their kennel when I have fed them. Have you got their leads?"

For a moment she was stunned. 'Whatever have I done with them?' she asked herself over and over again.

"I cannot think for the moment, Charles. I must have put them down somewhere when I was looking for their ball."

"No matter, Elizabeth. They have others. "

'Well, I haven't time now to go and look for them,' she told herself.

She waited till he had closed the door to the conservatory; then she slipped past the canny Scotsman, up the corridor and past the kitchen.

'If I can only get up the stairs without being seen, I shall be all right,' she thought, but as she started up the stairs she heard the kitchen door creak open.

"Is that you, Elizabeth, I saw flit past my door?" Flora called out to her.

"Yes, Flora."

"Lady Margot has been calling for you."

"I won't be long. I am just going to my room for a moment."

"Well, hurry, dear. You know she doesn't like to be kept waiting."

Elizabeth kept her back to the wall as she sped up the wide, curved staircase and crossed the passage to her room.

'I hope Lady Margot doesn't come out of her room before I get there,' she said to herself.

She closed the door and leaned against it for a few seconds to get her breath. She then tore off the dress and held it up to see the tear. She gasped aloud as she saw the extent of it.

"It would have to be one of my pretty afternoon ones!" she exclaimed angrily. "And to think I have been seen with that man! He seems to be everywhere I turn. I hate him, I hate him! He is so exasperating. I must have looked positively indecent – and for that woman to have seen him trying to fasten my dress! Well, I must hurry. I cannot think about that now."

She hastily slid into another dress. She brushed her hair back and tied it with a ribbon. She could hear Lady Margot calling for her. She hurried down the stairs and knocked timidly on the library door.

"Come in, Elizabeth. I needed you and I was quite anxious at your delay."

"I am sorry, milady. I lost the dogs' ball when I threw it."

"Very well, then, my dear, but don't take them so far next time. They look quite exhausted, poor darlings."

"Very well, milady. I will remember."

"Now, please attend to these letters for me tonight. Then you can post them in the morning. You can have the rest of the day off. You are looking rather tired and flushed. Are you all right?"

"Yes, milady, I am quite all right."

"I shall be away tomorrow as I am going across the loch with Lady Elena to attend the missionary meeting. Our work must start in earnest now. There is so much to catch up on. Also, Mama will not need you tonight. She is not too well and has retired early. Goodnight, Elizabeth. I will be dining tonight at Glencree Castle. You can retire as soon as the letters are finished."

"Goodnight, milady."

After Lady Margot had gone, Elizabeth sat looking out of the window.

"I do hope that Mrs Knowell isn't also dining at the castle, but I daresay that was where she was heading."

Seated at dinner later that night, Mrs Knowell commented, "I thought Lady Fiona would be here tonight. Is she still away?"

"Yes," replied Harriet. "Did I not tell you she was not due back yet?"

She looked up to see Craig glaring at her, as if daring her to say more.

"Why do you ask?" exclaimed Harriet.

"There's no real reason, but I thought I saw her in the glen taking a stroll today." She looked in Craig's direction and she knew her dart had gone home. "But", she exclaimed airily, "I must have been mistaken. It was late afternoon."

"And also," Harriet remarked, "she would not be walking alone in the glen without Craig by her side."

"No, of course not! How silly of me even to think it was she. As I said, it was towards dusk."

"Well now," said Elena, "if you two gentlemen will excuse us, we will retire to the study. We have some things to discuss."

"By all means, ladies. Craig and I also have a lot to discuss, so we will go into the lounge," said Bruce.

CHAPTER 46

Lady Elena's carriage arrived early next morning at Harrison Hall to pick up Margot. They had decided to take the longer route to the station and visit several crofters on their way.

"I have to call in the village first, Elena, and I want Elizabeth to post some important mail for me. Would you mind if she accompanied us so far?"

"Not at all, Margot."

Elizabeth entered the carriage and sat next to her mistress.

"I have told Elizabeth I shall be away for a few days, so, when her father calls today with the supplies, she can go home and see her mother and her brother. I know she misses them a great deal."

To see the delight on Elizabeth's face made her smile. "They will be so pleased, milady. Thank you so much."

"Please give my kind regards to your family," said Elena.

Elizabeth alighted at the post office and said goodbye.

"I shall be back on Saturday evening," Lady Margot called to her.

Elizabeth waved to them both as they drove away.

"What a delightful child she is, to be sure!" said Elena as she waved back to her.

"Her singing is such a delight. Every night she sings for Mama before Mama retires," said Margot. "Ingrid would have been so proud of her, as I am sure her parents are."

"How is your Mama today, Margot?"

"Not too well. I was a little reluctant to leave her, but Nurse assured me she would be all right. Some days she is better than others, but her heart condition and her age are against her. I am thankful I came back from India to be with her, although it was a wrench leaving my daughter – and her expecting her twins. Do you realise, Elena, they are nearly four years old now?"

"My goodness!" Elena exclaimed in disbelief. "How quickly time has flown! But we never expected the war to last so long, did we?"

"We certainly didn't," replied Margot, "but I should never have forgiven myself if I had not returned to Mama whilst she was so ill. Goodness knows when I shall get back to India to see my darling granddaughters and daughter again! It is fortunate that she is able to keep her eye on the mission station for me. She mentioned in her last letter that Stephen was back in charge of it again after his visits to all the other missions. He will have a lot to tell me when I return, but it won't take me too long to pick up the threads. Yes, it will be wonderful to carry on from where we left off."

"I shall certainly look forward to coming over, as I used to do before the war put a stop to all our travels," said Elena.

Elizabeth hurried home from the village as fast as she could to await her father, who duly arrived with the stores. "Oh, Papa, you have come. How wonderful to see you! I miss you all so much."

"I rowed all the way over today," Roddy said, "and I am going to row all the way back. Of course, I am not as good a boatman as Papa."

"You will be in time," she assured him. "Papa, I can come back with you today and stay for a few days as Lady Margot is away in the city."

"How pleased your mother will be!" he replied. "All of us together again after all this time!"

"Roddy rowed all the way home, Mama," she called out to Martha, who was waiting on the shore. "He rows very well – don't you think so, Mama?"

"Yes, he does, but he will never be as good as your father."

"Oh, I will in time, Mama – you wait and see!" Roddy exclaimed indignantly.

"And what has brought our little daughter home today?" Martha asked.

"Well, Lady Margot is away, so I can stay for a few days until she returns."

Craig called to see Lady Roxburgh as soon as he knew that Margot had gone with Elena.

'Why is the house so quiet?' he asked himself as he entered.

Charles, still limping, opened the door.

"Well, Charles, how is your ankle now?"

"Improving daily. I put some of Merry-Berry's lotion on it, and it is much easier now."

"Well, I am indeed pleased to hear it."

"I will go and tell Nurse you are here to see Her Ladyship."

Craig spotted the nurse as she was just leaving Lady Roxburgh's room. She came forward to meet him.

"How is Lady Roxburgh today?"

"Not too well, sir. She is asleep at present. As you probably know, Lady Margot has gone away for a few days. She has allowed Elizabeth to go home for a few days until she returns."

'Damn! Damn!' he exclaimed to himself.

"When do you expect them all back?"

"Elizabeth will be back on Friday. She goes to choir practice on Fridays and she never misses that. Lady Margot will return on Saturday."

"Very well, then. Please tell Lady Roxburgh that I called and that I will call again soon."

"I will, Master Craig."

He bade Charles good day and he was away.

Craig joined his father in the library on his return.

"Anything new happening in the village?" asked Bruce.

"No, not really, Papa. I hear, though, that several of the boys are going to re-enlist in the army. They seemingly cannot settle back on the land, and there is not enough employment anywhere else for them. The depression seems to catch up with everyone sooner or later. At least the war is over, so they will not be going back to fight, but, as they say, the army is all they know."

"I hope not too many of them go," said Bruce. "This fair island of ours has seen enough loss of its young sons, and their departure will cause so much heartache for their families."

"It surely will," agreed Craig.

He sat down after pouring himself a drink. He had stood a long time overlooking the loch.

A thought crossed Bruce's mind as he looked at him. He had thought when he came in that he looked rather dejected.

"I do hope, my son, that you are not thinking of joining them. I know many of your friends will be and I know many of your friends are still in the army."

"No, no, dear Papa, never ever think that. I am here to stay in my beloved homeland for ever. No," he said, "who would look after all this inheritance if I were to leave?"

"Oh, that reminds me," said Bruce: "several letters arrived for you shortly after you left this morning. One is from our solicitor."

"Yes, so it is," said Craig as he sat perusing it. "He wants me to go and see him as soon as possible to discuss Mama's inheritance. I daresay he has been waiting to see if I returned sound in mind and limb after the war," he said sarcastically.

Bruce looked up at him. 'What a strange bitterness the war has left in my dear son.'

"Well, in that case," Craig said, "I may as well go and see him tomorrow. I have nothing else planned, and I can see some of my old comrades at the same time."

"Well," Bruce reminded him, "don't let them talk you into rejoining."

"There's no fear of that, dear Papa," he said as he patted him on the shoulder. "This other letter is from Fiona. She will be coming to stay for a few days next week, but I will be back by then; this other one is from Major Sinclair. He will be in Glasgow, so I shall be able to see him also. I wonder where he is heading for next?"

"The house will seem very silent", remarked Bruce, "without you and Elena."

"Well, I shall be back on Friday at the latest," Craig assured him.

"Now, don't forget to tell Harriet before you leave, my son."

"No, Papa, I won't. What will you do, Papa, whilst I am away?"

"Well, the General will be at home alone until Fiona and her mother return, so I shall ride over for a game of chess with him."

"That's a good idea, Papa. He must be feeling lonely with both his dear ones away."

Craig left early next day. He knew when Magnus would be leaving the village to return home. Sure enough, Magnus spotted him and came to the castle jetty to pick him up.

"Will I be in time for the Glasgow train, Magnus?" he asked.

"Yes, Master Craig, you will," he said after greeting him warmly.

"Are you and your family well?" Craig asked.

"Yes, quite well at present."

"I shall return from Glasgow early on Friday. Will you delay your sail to the village until I return?"

"Very well, sir. Let us hope the weather will be better than when you first arrived back."

"We can only hope," Craig replied with a smile.

Peggoty waved him goodbye as he boarded the train.

Roddy was there to greet him on his return. Craig could see the boat ready to leave as he approached.

"Papa is not too well, Master Craig, so I will be taking the boat across."

"Is it anything serious?" Craig asked.

"No, not really, but if it persists I will call the doctor in. I have another passenger going over with us. I do hope you don't mind?"

"No, not at all. Who is it? Do I know them?"

"It is my sister, Elizabeth. She is returning to Harrison Hall today."

"I shall be only too delighted."

"If you get into the boat, sir, I will tell her we are ready."

As he departed to the cottage, Craig laughed to himself to think how well his plan had turned out – just as he had hoped. He had not seen Elizabeth since that day in the glen.

'I still have the hair ribbon and leads, and she has not returned my handkerchief as yet. I must remind her.'

"Come, Elizabeth – we are waiting," Roddy called to her.

"But I don't wish to leave Papa. He is not well," she pleaded.

"He will be all right," Martha reassured her. "It is only a chill. You have to return. Lady Margot will expect you to be back when she returns."

"Oh yes, I suppose so," she replied petulantly.

She put on her bonnet and coat and picked up her small bag.

"I will carry that," Roddy said as he took the bag from her.

Suddenly she looked up at him. "Roddy, why did you say '*We* are waiting'?"

"Because I have another passenger," he replied.

"Be careful how you go, Roddy," Magnus called out to him.

"Yes, be extra-careful," Martha rejoined. "You have two precious people on board with you."

"I will, Mama dear, I will."

'I wish I knew who it was,' thought Elizabeth.

"Who have we got on board with us, Roddy?"

"Oh, wait and see, little sister, wait and see."

They kissed their parents and proceeded to the jetty.

"I am so sorry to keep you waiting, Master Craig, but you know how long it takes these ladies to get ready."

Elizabeth froze in her tracks as she heard his name, but there was no going back.

"Come, Elizabeth," he called to her as he saw her hesitate, "I will assist you getting aboard." He got up to help her.

"I can manage quite well, thank you, Master Craig," she exclaimed angrily.

Roddy looked at her in amazement.

"I must apologise for my sister's manner and tone of voice, Master Craig. I think leaving Papa ill has upset her."

"She is quite forgiven, Roddy. Think no more of it. Will the boat be steady enough if she sits here beside me?"

"Yes," he replied. "I will stack your cases and the stores for the village at this end."

Martha watched till they sailed away after their final wave. A brisk wind had sprung up and the boat tilted a little from side to side, causing Elizabeth some alarm.

"You are all right, Elizabeth," Roddy reassured her.

"Yes, but you are not as careful as Papa."

"I am just as careful, but not as experienced, you mean. Well, Papa cannot row you over today, and there is nothing I can do about the boat rocking a little in the wind. It has only increased a little since we left home."

"Maybe," suggested Craig, "you would feel safer if I held on to you."

"No, that is not necessary, Master Craig. I feel quite safe."

"I think you should accept Master Craig's help in case the wind rises."

Craig agreed. "I think your brother is quite right," he said, and he proceeded to put his arm round her shoulders. "You will feel much safer now, I'm sure."

She thanked him politely.

'It is better not to arouse Roddy's displeasure,' she thought. Yes, she had to agree, she did feel much safer, but she ignored both men and gazed out over the loch.

"The view is quite spectacular, Elizabeth, don't you think so?"

"Yes, quite, Master Craig," she agreed.

'How I wish he would stop this inane chatter!' she told herself. 'I have, like him, seen it all before.' She looked up to see Roddy looking at her. 'Oh dear,' she told herself, 'I must try not to be so terse.'

"I have seen it several times," she replied. "It is, as you say, spectacular."

"So have I," Craig replied, "but to me it has never looked so lovely as it does now with the sun shining on the distant hills and a golden glow all around."

'He is not even looking at the hills,' she told herself.

Suddenly the boat gave a lurch as Roddy's oar caught one of the submerged rocks, and Elizabeth was flung into Craig's arms. She screamed out in alarm, but he held on to her tightly for several minutes longer than she felt was necessary.

"It is all right, Elizabeth, you are quite safe." His soft, soothing voice was low in her ear.

She had to admit she felt safe with his strong arms around her, but she pulled away from him.

"Roddy, Roddy, it is all your fault," she remonstrated. "Why can't you be more careful?"

"I am so sorry, Sister dear. I will try not to let it happen again."

"Well, I certainly hope so," she replied.

"My apologies, Master Craig," said Roddy.

"Pray do not concern yourself on my behalf. These incidents often happen on the loch. I have done the same thing myself when rowing."

"Well, here we are at last," Craig said as he prepared to leave. "Good day to you, Elizabeth," he called as he ran lightly up the steps.

Roddy followed with his baggage.

"I don't think you were very polite today, Elizabeth. It was so unlike you."

"I am sorry, but I thought we would have a nice trip back, just the two of us, talking like we used to do, and we did not get the chance today."

"But he did allow you to cross with him. He could, if he had wished, have not allowed you to come along, and that would have meant two journeys for me."

Douglas, the old fisherman-cum-handyman, was waiting at the village jetty with the horse and trap.

"How nice to have you back, Elizabeth!" he said as he helped her into the carriage.

Roddy handed her her cases.

"Have you any stores to go to the hall, Roddy?"

"Yes, I will load them up for you."

"Where is your father today?"

"He is not very well – just a chill, I think," said Roddy.

"I do hope he is better soon."

They bade each other goodbye.

"Now, do be more careful, Roddy dear, as you row back. Please watch out for those rocks."

"I will, I will."

"Call and let me know soon how Papa is."

"Yes, I will see you at church on Sunday," he replied.

He waited till the carriage was out of sight before starting for home.

The dogs rushed out to greet her as she alighted from the carriage.

"Hello there, you two rascals. How nice of you to greet me!"

Charles was waiting to take her bags into the house as Douglas unloaded the stores and followed him inside.

"Take them through into the kitchen, Douglas," said Charles. "I will see to Elizabeth first."

"How is Lady Roxburgh today, Charles?"

"Not well at all, but she will be glad to see you back."

She knocked lightly on the lounge door and the nurse opened it.

"How lovely to see you back. Do come in. Her Ladyship is awake."

"There you are, my child. Now I shall start feeling much better. Go and eat first and change. I know you have to hurry to choir practice this afternoon, but you can sing for me tomorrow."

"Thank you, milady, I will," she replied.

She hastened to her room and stood at the window overlooking the loch. She could still see Roddy setting off for home.

'I wonder', she said to herself, 'why that man always turns up everywhere I go. Why did he have to take the same boat as I did? Why do I always get a feeling that he is making fun of me?' Then she pondered more. 'But how wonderful it feels to have his strong arms around me.' The thought of having his strong arms around her filled her with a feeling of excitement she had never known before, but she experienced a feeling of guilt also. She gave a shudder of complete bewilderment. 'Now, I must hurry or I shall be late for choir practice.'

Since Mrs Knowell had seen her that day beside the stream she had not enjoyed choir practice so much as before. The glaring looks of both the choirmaster and his wife told her that he had been fully informed of what his wife had seen.

Much to Emma's amazement, Elizabeth was no longer chosen to sing any solos.

"Papa," she said to her father, "don't you think it strange that Elizabeth has not sung any solos for quite some time?"

"Yes, my child," he replied, "but when I asked the choirmaster why it was, he just replied that it was only right that Mrs Crawford's daughters should be given more practice. So, my dear, I just left it at that."

"Well," she replied, "I suppose that must be the reason, but I know everyone is remarking on it. Even Roddy was asking me about it the other day."

"Well, my dear," her father replied, "if he asks again, you will have to tell him the reason. However, I know everyone is longing to hear her sing again. The choirmaster must decide, as he and his wife are in sole charge of the choir."

"More's the pity!" Emma exclaimed, much to her father's dismay.

"Well, my son," said Bruce as he greeted Craig, "I have missed you so. How did your trip go?"

"Very well, Papa, but I never knew Mama had sold so much of her property down south."

"Yes, yes, my son. She sold it all when her parents died. She said her home was now in Scotland, so the money from the sale was put in trust for you until you reached the age of twenty-one or until you married.

"Tell me: how did you find your army friends?" asked Bruce.

"Well, all my officer friends are doing well. They all got promotion when they signed up for longer service – twenty-one years or more, most of them. We spent a whole day visiting as many men as we could. What poverty, Papa! I just cannot believe it. The poor souls fought for a better future for their children, and they expected to return to a country fit for the heroes they are. Now they find themselves without proper food, clothing or housing and their children are in rags. The men have no hope in their eyes. Jobs are practically non-existent for the ones who are well enough to work, so goodness knows what is going to happen to the maimed, blind and gassed ones. They are pitiful to behold."

"We must all help them!" exclaimed Bruce.

"Yes, I will see Aunt Elena as soon as she returns tomorrow. She is used to looking into all these things, and she will help me to get things moving more quickly. I shall transfer most of the money Mama has left me into a fund for the most needy."

"You do that, my son, and I shall do the same. It is what your dear mother would have wished. What a great help she would have been to us in this situation. She was such a good organiser." He sighed heavily as he thought of her. "But Elena will help you. She knows all the organisations that will be able to help. But I daresay she will want to get on with her mission work with Margot as well. Maybe Fiona will help you also."

"Yes, of course she will," Craig answered, but he was not too sure.

"Now, my son, come and join me in a drink. Try not to dwell on it any more today."

"Where is Aunt Harriet? I haven't seen her since I arrived."

"She was spending the day with Mrs Knowell – something to do with the choir arrangements for harvest, I think."

On hearing the name Mrs Knowell, a thought suddenly struck Craig: 'I haven't heard Elizabeth sing lately in the choir. I do hope that incident by the stream hasn't anything to do with it, but, knowing that old lady, I shouldn't be a bit surprised.'

"Ah, here is Aunt Harriet now!" he exclaimed as the door opened. "Just in time for a wee dram, Aunt."

"Just what I need. My, how that woman chatters on and on! I thought she was never going to stop."

Craig looked at her a little anxiously, but she gave no sign that Mrs Knowell had said anything untoward.

Craig spent a restless night, as he often did after arriving home from visiting his men. He woke often from his nightmare with sweat pouring from him. It was always the same nightmare. He saw them all again in the battlefields. He called out, "Sergeant, how are the men? Where are they?" But when he opened his eyes, there was only an eerie silence around him. He would rise, go to the window and draw back the curtains. Often the moon was visible in a clear sky, as he looked out over the shimmering loch towards the mountains beyond. As if to reassure himself that all was well, and that he was really at home, he would call out aloud: "Yes, all is well. These are my mountains and I am at last home."

His cry would awaken Flint, who always slept outside his door, and his whimpering would awaken Elena in the adjoining room. She had insisted on having the room next to his after his mother died. She would lie quietly for a few moments and, when she heard the curtains being drawn, she would tap lightly on his door.

"Are you all right, my dear boy?"

"Yes, Aunt Elena. I am quite all right, thank you."

Satisfied, she would return to her room, patting Flint on the head as she passed. "Your master is all right, boy. Now settle down. Good boy!"

Flint would let his head flop between his paws as Elena's door closed behind her and he heard his master settle back in bed. Then all would be silent once more.

However, tonight Aunt Elena was not there to tap lightly on his door. He thought how like his mother she was in her concern for him. She had always been there when, as a small boy, he was upset or had been scolded harshly by Aunt Harriet for some boyish prank that she didn't approve of. But tonight there was only the whimpering of Flint – the only other one awake. Tonight he felt more lonely than ever. He got up to open the door and talk to Flint.

"Settle down, boy. Settle down. All is well," he said, and he stroked him fondly.

The dog licked his hand in return, as if to say, "As long as you are by my side, master, all is well."

Craig closed the door, went over to the window and peered out – but not at the mountains as was usual. His eyes wandered towards the hall, just visible now the trees had begun to shed their leaves. 'I wonder if she is sleeping?' he thought, and he recalled the look of surprise on her face as she caught sight of him in the boat. He remembered her closeness when the boat had lurched and he had held her in his arms once more, be it only for a brief moment. Tonight he imagined she was in his arms again, her golden hair blowing across his face. He could still feel her nearness.

'Oh why, oh why does she haunt me so? I must stop thinking of her. I must, I must.'

He felt chilled and realised he had been standing at the open window for far too long. He heard the village church clock strike three o'clock. He closed the window and clambered back into bed, where he lay awake a long time before sleep overcame him.

CHAPTER 47

Fiona was now back from London and staying at Glencree Castle. She chattered non-stop about all she had seen and done on her visit.

"New things are now coming into the shops – things that would be most suitable for the West Wing. I must have them, Craig dear. All my friends are ordering them like mad!" she exclaimed.

"And, my dear," he would reply, "what do you propose we do with all our valuable antiques?"

"They must go elsewhere. The aunts can take them to their new abode when Papa Bruce has found a place suitable for them."

He looked at her, dismayed. "But I am sure Papa would not like them removed from the West Wing. They have been there so long."

"Far too long!" she exclaimed airily. "I said to Mama only the other day that they also should get rid of some of the old-fashioned things now that so many new styles are being made."

"And I suppose she agreed with you."

"Yes, but of course Papa was not too keen. However, he will be when he sees what I am ordering for our home, Craig."

"Well, I don't think Papa will like the idea."

"Of course he will when I explain it to him. It's not as if the antiques were leaving the family. If our sons ever wish to have them back here, they will be able to put them back again when the aunts are no longer here."

"My, my, my dearest one! You are looking far too far ahead."

"Well, I have to do so, as you know, dear. You will just drift along, leaving things as they have been for generations, not caring whether or not things will suit me. But, as I am going to live here for the rest of my life, surely, dear, some concessions can be made to please me?"

"Of course they will be, dear – whatever you wish. Now stop chattering so that I can kiss you. Tomorrow", Craig explained to Fiona, "we are going to visit the crofters."

"But, darling," she exclaimed petulantly, "you know I would rather stay here and make more plans for our home! I shall have to leave soon to go back to London with Mama and Papa for Christmas. I know I shall be back for Hogmanay, but I need my spare time with all our friends here before I leave, as well as making arrangements for the West Wing."

"Oh, my dear, you will have plenty of time before we leave for London – lots of time. You will have to visit the crofters once we are married, so we will go and visit them now. Then you will know who they are."

She knew it would be no use her arguing any more. She knew he would always have his way. She found the visits to the crofters tiring and irksome, but she was pleased to see how happy they were to see her and Craig – especially Craig.

"They will soon get to know you and love you as they did Mama," Craig said. "She just loved visiting every one of them. She knew all their names and their children's names and how old they were. She would make extra visits to them if they were sick. Often she and Aunt Elena would go together."

'Well,' Fiona told herself, 'I shall not spend most of my life visiting them. If Elena wants to do these welfare visits, she can do so. I shall not go. I shall tell her so, too – and also Craig when we are married.' Fiona knew it would be unwise of her to declare her dislike of this visiting until then.

So off they would go, laughing gaily as they rode across the glens, her chatter was non-stop.

Merry-Berry, spotting them, would cast anxious glances after them.

CHAPTER 48

The dark winter nights were approaching fast. Fiona had already left to spend Christmas in London, leaving strict instructions that nothing could be touched or altered in the West Wing whilst she was away.

Elena was not the only one glad to see her go. The maids had criticised her in whispers to each other for weeks.

"I will be glad to see the back of her," Shona said disparagingly.

"Me too," agreed Sarah. "I hate to think how we will be treated when she is mistress here. I hope she brings her own maids with her when that time comes, and I hope they keep their place in the West Wing."

The trees had shed all their summer glory, except the tall evergreen pines standing tall and proud, guarding the glens like tall sentinels. The pink and purple heathers had now faded into a raiment of rusty gold. Life in the village after the Harvest Thanksgiving Service had settled into a quiet, restful peace. The sheep had been brought down to the lower pastures.

Martha, perplexed that Elizabeth had not sung a solo at the Harvest Thanksgiving Service, asked Emma whether or not she was well.

"Oh yes, Mrs Anderson, she is quite well, but it seems the choirmaster and his wife want Mrs Crawford's girls to sing more solos at present."

"I understand," replied Martha, looking a little dejected, "but I would like to have heard her sing. Now the winter nights are almost here, so the weather will not be suitable for me to cross the loch. The journey round the loch is so long and tiring. Is she going to sing any solos for the carol service?"

"Well, she has not been rehearsing any as yet, although the Crawford girls have, but I am sure she will be. I will let you know. If you cannot cross the loch, you can come round the loch and stay overnight at the vicarage. You know you are always welcome."

"Yes, yes, thank you, Emma. I shall wait until I hear from you. But please do not let Elizabeth know I am anxious about her."

"No, I won't."

CHAPTER 49

"Harriet dear," asked Elena one morning, "have you seen my book of carols?"

"You will find it under the pile of harvest hymns in the stool. And that reminds me: I must look for all my old recipes and discuss them with Cook as more stores will have to be brought in. I have not had them out for so long, with the war being on and Craig away. We will have more entertaining to do now that all his friends are visiting more often. It would have been so nice if Fiona could have been with us for his first Christmas at home. She is so good at organising everything. She would have been such a help to me."

"But promises have to be kept," Elena reminded her, smiling complacently.

"Yes, that is so, but she will be back for Hogmanay so it isn't too long to wait."

"It will be our happiest Christmas yet!" exclaimed Elena. "I am so looking forward to it. Such preparations! I have practically forgotten how to start. All the garlands will need to be put up, just as our dear Isabelle would have wished. The tree will have to be decorated. That reminds me: we must find all the things to go on it. How I wish our dear Isabelle could have been here! How perfect everything would have been! The fir trees need to be brought down for the village hall and here and the church. There will be more carol singers this year, now that the boys are back and there are more girls at the academy, so, Harriet, we will need more provisions for when they come carolling. Now, that music! Oh, here it is. I must remember to remind the vicar to announce it on Sunday."

"And what, might I ask, must you remind the vicar of?" asked Craig as he entered the room.

"Just that extra choir practices will be held on Saturday afternoons."

Craig could hardly believe his ears. 'Now', he thought to himself, 'maybe I shall get the chance to see Elizabeth. I must think of a way.' He already knew that on Sundays when Roddy and her parents hadn't come to church Emma would drive her as far as the crossroad. 'Maybe she will do the same on Saturdays after the choir practice,' he thought. 'I could take Mama's flowers to the churchyard then, instead of on Sundays as I do at present. Yes, there will be fewer people about also. Yes, that is what I will do. I know that sometimes Papa will wish to accompany me, but I will attend to that problem when it arises.'

"Are you all right, Craig dear?" Elena asked. "You look in such deep thought now, when only a few minutes ago you bounced breezily into the room."

He had forgotten for a moment that the aunts were still in the room.

"Yes, yes, I am quite all right. I am going to ride out with Papa in a little while. Ah, here he is at last. Come, Papa – we must away. These two are busy planning for Christmas and Hogmanay."

CHAPTER 50

Mrs Knowell had changed Elizabeth's place in the choir stalls. She was making quite sure that she would never be in view of the laird's son again. Apart from her husband, she had told no one of what she had witnessed at the side of the stream, but she felt quite sure that the time would come when she could drop a word in Lady Harriet's ear. Meanwhile, she would see to it that the little hussy sang no more solos, which would have put her in full view of the Laird's Gallery. Her relegation had not gone unnoticed by Craig, and he was most perturbed to think he might have been the cause of it.

Emma was also most put out about it, and she queried it often with her father, even though she knew he never intervened in anything the choirmaster and his wife decided.

"I cannot understand it, Papa."

"Well, my dear, she must think the choir is better balanced that way, although I cannot say that I have noted any difference."

"Neither have I," Emma retorted. "We have always been in those places, and it must be down to Mrs Crawford's scheming that her three precious jewels sing all the solos now."

"Now, now, my dear daughter, that is most unkind and not like you. Tell me: what does Elizabeth say on the matter?"

"Well, like you, she thinks Mrs Knowell might feel that the choir is better balanced. But you know Elizabeth will never ask her. You know how timid she is. She just accepts it. I think I will ask Mrs Knowell the reason for it."

"I wouldn't advise that, my dear Emma. It might make things worse for Elizabeth."

"Yes, it might," she agreed, "but it is most unfair." She proceeded to join the rest of the choir in the hall after bidding her father goodbye.

"Goodbye, my child," he said, looking after her pensively.

Craig stood deep in thought at the side of his mother's grave after he had placed the flowers on it.

"Dear, dear Mama, how I wish you could be with me for my first Christmas at home. If only you could," he sighed, "how perfect everything would be!" Another deep sigh escaped him and he touched her headstone as if the contact made him feel a little closer to her.

He walked slowly away, and called Flint to heel as he mounted his horse to ride to the high rise.

'With any luck,' he told himself, 'I might see Elizabeth today.'

He heard gay chatter and laughter and reined his horse under the trees.

'Yes, there they are. But who is that with her?'

Little did he know that she would be accompanied by Emma, her intended fiancé (Stuart), and Robin, the son of the principal of the young ladies' academy who was madly in love with Elizabeth. He watched as she and Robin alighted from Emma's carriage and waved goodbye as they walked hand in hand down the lane. He felt more and more angry as he heard their gay laughter.

'Now I must think of another way to try to see her, because see her I must. Why? Why does she make me feel like this? I must talk to her. I must.' His depth of feeling for her was getting beyond him. The more he tried to get her out of his mind, the more she seemed to be always there.

He stood leaning heavily against a tree, tapping his riding crop angrily against his jodhpur-clad thighs. Scheme upon scheme raced through his mind. So many possibilities came to mind, but he dismissed them impatiently.

He realised he was feeling chilly as the afternoon was turning to dusk. He cringed madly as he saw Robin take Elizabeth in his arms and kiss her lightly on the cheek. Then she ran off through the gate of Harrison Hall, turning once more to give him a final wave before she disappeared. He watched as Robin went from view.

'He, I believe,' he told himself, 'is due to train for the ministry soon. Yes, I can imagine her as a minister's wife, and I have to admit he is worthy of her.'

He remounted and headed for home, fuming that his well-laid plans had come to naught.

The Christmas preparations were almost complete. For weeks everyone in the village had been hard at work to make the best Christmas since before the war. Almost everyone was having visitors from England, and many would be staying for Hogmanay.

The men had now brought down all the Christmas trees, including one for the church. The choirgirls had spent several evenings decorating it before helping with the one in the village square, to the delight of all the small children who had been allowed to join in.

Elizabeth and Emma joined together to dress the one in the vicarage and at Harrison Hall. They were quite exhausted. Roddy had made several trips over the loch to bring in extra supplies for the village stores and Glencree Castle. He had helped them dress the trees, and to see the sheer delight on his sister's face as he climbed higher and higher to arrange things to her liking was reward enough for him. What a gay hectic time it was for them all!

All the guests were now settled in Glencree Castle. Most had not visited for years – some since the war began and others since Craig's mother had died.

They had now decided that, as this was his first Christmas at home, they just had to come. They all decided to stay for Hogmanay too and they were happy to meet Fiona again. This Hogmanay was to be the start of a very special year for her and Craig. There would be lots of celebrations both at Glencree Castle and at their own homes in England later in the year.

Old Aunt Gertrude kept exclaiming, "Bruce's only son, home and soon to be married! Isabelle's darling son, home at last and spared from that dreadful, dreadful war!"

'How I wish she would stop reminding me of that damn war!' Craig exclaimed to himself.

Elena looked at the aunt in question in exasperation, as she noticed Craig's look of displeasure at her enthusing.

"Come, Craig, help me finish the tree. The old dear", she whispered in his ear, "can go and play cards with Harriet."

Craig had insisted that all the decorations must be just as his mother would have wished: holly and ivy everywhere, and, of course, plenty of mistletoe.

"But of course we will have mistletoe, my dear boy," Elena had playfully replied at his insistence. She wondered whom he might have in mind, as his fiancée was away in England, but she didn't probe further.

Craig had decided that when the girls came from the church carol singing, he and his brother officers could, in all jollity and no one thinking anything untoward, kiss anyone they liked under the mistletoe. He had already decided whom he was going to kiss, and he had purposely put up some mistletoe in the darkest corner he could find.

'A difficult enough job,' he thought: 'Aunt Elena has put lights almost everywhere.'

Harriet was quite relieved to sit down and play cards with the other aunts, her work for Christmas now done. All the provisions and menus she had seen to with Cook, who had been quite overwhelmed with it all. Extra girls had been brought in from the village to help. Now everything was ready.

Dinner was over and all the guests were assembled in the banqueting hall. It was only used on such occasions as this.

Harriet had exclaimed to Elena, "I haven't seen it look as lovely as it does tonight since our dear Isabelle dressed it so." And statements like that from Harriet were praises indeed.

"I helped dress it also," said Craig, looking at her for compliments.

"Of course you did, my dear boy."

"I always helped Mama decorate it."

Craig looked up at the large picture of his mother dressed in a lovely white gown. The family jewels and tiara of rubies and diamonds flashed in the light of the chandeliers.

"See how she looks down at us, Aunt Elena. She is always with us."

He glanced sideways and saw his father gazing longingly up at the picture. A knowing look from Elena told him he had said enough on the subject.

"Well," he said brightly, "I will go and see what mischief my friends are up to."

Bruce, as always, had sat silently gazing at Isabelle's picture for far too long, Elena decided. Although he had many of his friends visiting, he was alone with his thoughts.

"Come, Bruce dear," she called to him, "your friends are all served with coffee and liqueurs in the library. You must join them – but only for a short while, as we will be entertaining the carol singers soon."

"Yes, yes," he replied, "I look forward to them coming so much. How my dear Isabelle adored them! This was her favourite night of the year." He glanced once more at her picture. "Yes, I must go and join my friends. What are you going to do, Craig, and where are you going?" he added as he saw Craig preparing to leave the room.

"I am going to take Flint for his evening stroll before it gets too late, so please excuse me."

"Shall I come with you?" Ivor called to him.

"No, I won't be too long."

"No, don't be too long," Elena called after him. "The snow is falling fast now and the carol singers will be here soon. You know they will still come, hail, rain or snow."

"Yes, I know," he replied. "Now, drink up, fellas, but save me a wee drop for when I return."

"We will," they chorused as he closed the door.

CHAPTER 51

The church carol service had been and gone and, although Martha had not heard from Emma, she had managed to get over the loch for the service.

"Our daughter seems quite well," said Magnus on their return journey. He knew how Martha had worried lately about her.

"Oh yes, she is well enough, but why she is not singing any more solos at church services I cannot understand. Lady Margot assures me she is still singing superbly nearly every night for her mother."

"I spoke to Emma and she says that Elizabeth is not practising extra carol solos, like the Crawford girls are for their visit to Glencree Castle, and you know that is a really special night for the choir."

"Yes, my dear, but do not worry so about it. The choirmaster and his wife know what is best, so we must leave it to them."

The choir had been out several nights during the week prior to Christmas Eve – firstly at the vicarage and then at Harrison Hall – but the main event was always the visit to Glencree Castle. Everyone looked forward to it with glee, and it was a special honour to be selected to sing a solo.

"How I wish", exclaimed Mrs Knowell to her husband, "that I could leave that little hussy Elizabeth out of the choir we are selecting for Glencree Castle."

"That we cannot do, my dear," he replied, "as much as I would like to. I am afraid the laird would query it, and also Lady Elena and even Lady Harriet. No, we will have to include her."

"More's the pity!" exclaimed his wife peevishly. "Mrs Crawford is so pleased that her daughters are to sing the solos when we arrive there, as are the three girls. They have never liked Elizabeth and have always seemed pleased to see her taken down a peg or two."

The three jewels of Mrs Crawford had never ceased telling their father over and over again, as well as everyone else in the village, that they had been specially requested to sing the solos by the laird. Some of the villagers wondered how it came to be so. However, many of them knew that the Crawford family was always one for boasting, so they did not pay too much heed.

At last the night had arrived and the choir were all assembled in their usual places in the procession up to the castle. Emma and Elizabeth were in the third position from the front. Suddenly Elizabeth felt a tap on her shoulder. She turned round to see Mrs Knowell glaring at her.

"Miss Anderson, I want you at the back of the procession."

"But why, Mrs Knowell?" she asked.

"Because I say so."

Mrs Knowell had suddenly realised that if they proceeded as they were, Elizabeth would be in full view of Master Craig, as she would be on the front row when they sang. And that, she had declared to herself, she was not going to have.

Elizabeth dutifully pulled her cloak further round her shoulders and proceeded to the last place; Mrs Knowell told Sarah Readon to proceed to Elizabeth's now vacant space. Sarah smiled as she went. It was, as everyone knew, a more honoured position.

The three 'jewel' girls nudged each other and their friends and tittered softly into the upturned collars of their cloaks. The extra delay caused everyone to stamp their feet and pull their cloaks further round their shoulders as they stood outside the church door.

Emma, who had been talking to Stuart and Robin, was so engrossed in their conversation that none of them noticed what had happened.

"Now, no more talking! Get into line!" exclaimed Mrs Knowell.

Suddenly Emma noticed that Sarah was standing next to her.

"Where has Elizabeth gone?" she demanded.

"Well," Sarah replied meekly, "Mrs Knowell told her to take my place at the back of the column."

"Oh, she did, did she?"

Emma's temper rose as she noticed Mrs Knowell approaching.

"And why, might I ask, has Elizabeth been sent to the back? She has always been with me. It has been our place for all our carol singing this past week. Tell me, why she has been changed tonight of all nights?"

"Don't you dare use that tone of voice with me, Emma. I shall move any one of you any time I like. And you now, Emma, can go and join Miss Anderson at the back."

"Yes, that I shall do," said Emma. She pulled her cloak further round her shoulders and proceeded down the rows.

"You, Miss Lucretia – come to the front in Emma's place."

Elizabeth was quite taken aback to see Emma standing beside her.

"Really, Emma, you should not have made such a fuss and upset Mrs Knowell so."

"I don't care. She is always doing nasty things to you and I won't stand for it. You are so quiet and won't say anything in your own defence."

"Come now, dear," Mr Knowell entreated to his wife, "we really must be going or we are going to arrive late and that has never happened before."

"Proceed forthwith, Stuart and Robin," she commanded. The two of them,

235

who were at the head of the column, had turned round and glared at her with annoyance when they saw that Emma and Elizabeth had been ordered to the rear.

"What has she done that for?" Robin asked Stuart.

"I don't know, but I shall certainly make a point of finding out as soon as I can – if not from Emma, I shall ask the good lady myself," he declared angrily.

"She is anything but a good lady, if you ask me," Robin retorted.

"Now, do as I say, Stuart and Robin, and proceed," ordered Mrs Knowell.

They turned the wicks of their lanterns a little higher as they commenced the long walk to Glencree Castle.

CHAPTER 52

Craig hastily closed the door and called Flint to his side. He ran up the stairs two at a time. Flint ran ahead of him and Craig allowed him into his room. He hastened to the window overlooking the valley and peered down the narrow, dark lane, which was only wide enough for two people to walk side by side. He watched anxiously for a few moments before spotting the swinging lanterns.

"Ah, there they are!"

The group wound their way up the narrow path. They huddled as close as they could to one another as the snow hurtled down. Their lanterns swung to and fro with every step. The bare trees stretched their long eerie branches above them, now covered with a thick layer of snow. The thinner branches were like spidery fingers, ghostlike in the silence and whiteness of the glistening snow.

There seemed to Craig to be more people in the procession than he ever remembered before. 'It must be that I have been away too long,' he told himself as he tried to see more clearly through the frost-covered panes.

'I wonder if I shall see the angel in this crowd. I must find her.'

He hastened to the balcony overlooking the main entrance just as they reached it, and he watched as they formed two semicircles round the huge doorway. Then they commenced to sing the first carol. He heard Jamie drawing the bolts across to let them in.

"They have arrived!" exclaimed Elena. "I do hope Craig gets back soon to help us greet them."

"He will be back, never fear," said Bruce. "This is his first Christmas at home."

Craig watched from the top of the stairway as Jamie guided them into the porch. Then they passed the long marble pillars that led to the main hall. They all put back their snow-covered hoods as they walked along.

'Ah, there she is!' Craig exclaimed to himself as he saw her long flaxen ringlets fall round her exquisite face. He watched as she shook her hood a little further back, then she looked down at her boots.

'Oh, drat! My buttons have come undone, but I haven't time to fasten them now.'

They proceeded up the long corridor. Craig hurried down the stairs and hid behind one of the huge marble pillars, which he knew they would have to pass. He waited for her to draw level, and, as she did so, he tugged sharply at her cloak, almost pulling it off her shoulders.

He spoke to her in a soft voice: "Angel. Angel."

She turned quickly, startled with fright, and she stumbled as he reached out and pulled her into his arms.

"Master Craig, how you startled me!" she said, panic rising in her voice.

"That is just what I intended to do. When can I see you alone?"

"Never, never! You know it is not possible."

"You must make it possible," he demanded.

"I cannot. I cannot. Please release me. I must get back to the choir."

He gently brushed the snowflakes from her hair above her eyes.

"Snowflakes on an angel – my angel," he whispered.

She could feel his grip tightening round her, but she tore herself away and ran to join the others, who were almost out of sight round the bend.

'Oh dear, I do hope Mrs Knowell hasn't missed me,' she said breathlessly to herself as she slid beside Emma.

Emma had kept looking back, wondering what was going on and hoping that Mrs Knowell would not miss Elizabeth. But Mrs Knowell was talking to Jamie at the front of the procession.

"Whatever happened to you, Elizabeth?" asked Emma as she noted her friend's panic. "I thought you must have turned the wrong corner. It is such a vast place." Although she herself had been visiting Glencree Castle since she was a child, she had never failed to wonder at the vastness of the place. "I thought you had got lost. Luckily Mrs Knowell didn't turn round to check that we were all in line."

"It's all right," Elizabeth said. "My boot came undone, so I stopped to rebutton it and it took a little longer than I expected. Even now I have not done up all the buttons."

"Well, never mind them for now. I will fasten them for you later."

They had now all reached the main door of the hall, where they were greeted by Harriet and Elena.

"Do come and take off those wet cloaks!" Elena exclaimed. "Jamie, go and tell Sarah to come and take them to dry."

"Yes, milady," Jamie said as he took several with him.

Craig watched as Elizabeth reached Emma's side; then he raced as fast as he could up the stairs, along the top corridor and down the end flight of stairs to enter the main hall by the end door.

"Ah, Craig, dear boy," said Bruce, "you are just back in time to greet our guests."

"So I see," he replied.

He joined Elena and Harriet as they ushered the choir into the room and bade them all assemble around the organ in the middle of the room. Craig seated himself where he could get a good view of the only one he wished to see.

'I wish Emma would move a little to one side. I cannot see my angel very well,' he mused.

Mrs Knowell commenced to play as her husband raised his baton, and they sang 'The First Noel', then 'Once in Royal David's City' followed by 'Oh Little Town of Bethlehem'. When they stopped for a pause, Craig suddenly leapt to his feet.

"I would like a solo if you please."

"Yes, certainly, Master Craig!" Mrs Knowell exclaimed. "Miss Ruby has been practising specially for such a request."

Ruby smiled at her sister and moved closer to the organ.

"But I am sure Elizabeth could sing it just as well. I have noticed she has not been singing many solos at church services for quite some time now, and I would like to hear her sing again."

"Yes, so would I!" exclaimed Bruce and Elena.

"But, Master Craig," said Mrs Knowell, "Elizabeth has not rehearsed any carols for tonight."

Elizabeth looked at Emma in dismay.

"You can, you can, and it is Master Craig's wish. Go on – stand near the organ and sing," said Emma, and she gave Elizabeth a gentle push.

"But, Emma, you don't understand!"

'If only you did!' she told herself as she ventured forward, quivering like a leaf.

Meanwhile, Mrs Knowell was looking at Master Craig with as much anger as she dared show.

"I am sure, Mrs Knowell," Craig repeated, "that Elizabeth can manage quite well. Certainly no offence is meant to Miss Ruby."

"No, I am sure not," she replied, wondering how on earth she would be able to explain to Mrs Crawford next day that Craig himself had insisted that Elizabeth sang the solo at Glencree Castle instead of one of her precious jewels. She grimaced with dread at the thought of the encounter.

"Which of the carols would you like her to sing?" Mrs Knowell asked in a peeved voice.

Craig thought for several seconds. "Well, it must be my mother's favourite one: 'It Came upon the Midnight Clear'."

"Yes," Bruce agreed, "it was your mother's favourite. When Elizabeth has finished singing, we will all sing it through once again. It is your first Christmas at home, so we will all do as you suggest."

"Now, if you all sit down and rest and Elizabeth stands next to me at the organ, we shall all hear perfectly."

Elizabeth did as she was bid, looking at Emma all the time.

Craig would have liked to accompany her himself, but he had to agree that the lady organist was a much better musician than himself, although he disliked the woman intensely.

Bruce and Elena came alongside while Elizabeth kept her eyes glued to the carol sheet. They all clapped loudly when she had finished.

"Now, do sit down again," said Elena, after they had all sung it through. "I am sure a little refreshment now is called for – don't you think so, Harriet?"

"Yes," she replied, "I have already told the maids to hasten and bring it in."

"Now, Craig, will you and your friends serve the hot punch? Everyone must enjoy every minute of their stay with us," said Elena, "but I must warn all you young ladies about Craig's young officer friends. They have hung some mistletoe around the place and even I don't know where, so be careful where you wander! Craig's friends are very observant, and they will be waiting for some unwary maiden."

The men were laughing gaily as they gave out the punch. They themselves had had more than a wee drop of the famous Scottish drink before their arrival.

The young girls from the academy shrieked with delight when they saw the mistletoe, and the three 'jewel' girls headed in that direction, making sure that they would be seen by Craig. The three were certain that he would seek them out, though Ruby was still smarting at the fact that she had not sung the solo she had been practising for so long.

"Mama will be furious!" she exclaimed.

"Well, it cannot be helped now," said Pearl. "We shall just have to try to catch Craig's eye. I am sure at least one of us can do that. That would please Mama – if only one of us can manage it!"

"Well, I am certainly going to succeed," laughed Ruby. "You just see if I don't. You do recall, Pearl, what Mama has said: he must be referred to as Master Craig and not just Craig, as you have just uttered. That is, unless he expressly requests you to call him Craig."

"Well, Emma calls him Craig, and we know him just as well as she does."

"Well, we must do as Mama wishes. Come – we are wasting time. All the other girls are getting kissed by the officers, and I cannot even see Master Craig as yet. He must be amongst them somewhere." She stood on tiptoe to get a better view, all to no avail.

Elizabeth had kept as close as she could to the organ, which now had been pushed into the corner of the room by Jamie and the other servants. She, too, had noticed where bunches of the mistletoe were hung, but she carefully avoided getting anywhere near them. Emma came to her side, holding a glass of hot toddy.

"Haven't you got a glass, Elizabeth? It's wonderful stuff."

"I will get one later."

"Why are you hiding yourself away, almost behind the organ?"

"No reason really – although Mrs Knowell looks very angry with me every time she glances in my direction."

"Well, it wasn't your fault. You were asked by Craig to sing a solo. He knows you sing much better than that Crawford girl. Just look at the three of them, trying their best to catch his eye."

"I hadn't noticed," Elizabeth replied.

"Well, you won't see anything of the display they are providing, hiding as you are now."

"Nevertheless, I would rather stay here. You go and join Stuart and Robin."

"No, I will stay here with you. They are quite enjoying themselves talking to Lady Elena, and they would not dream of leaving her to join us. After all, they must thank her for our invitation, even though we have had to sing for our supper, as it were."

At this remark, Elizabeth let out a peal of laughter. "Emma, you are so amusing. I just never know what you are going to say next."

"Well," she replied, "if I can say anything to bring a smile to that woebegone face of yours, I will. I just know you are sad because your darling Roddy couldn't join us tonight, as he promised, but maybe he couldn't cross over the loch."

"Well, maybe that is the reason. I do hope Mama and Papa are all right."

"Now, you two young ladies, hiding here!" exclaimed Craig.

He had kept a watch on Elizabeth's every move, and when she let out the peal of laughter he had decided to investigate. He was with his good friend, Captain Ian Fraser. He had skilfully avoided the three jewels, whom he could now see were surrounded by young men.

He had instructed Ian beforehand: "You can kiss the girl on the right; I am going to thank and kiss the little songstress next to her. Don't hurry your kiss, because I am certainly not going to hurry mine."

"Really, Craig!" he replied. "I don't know what your fiancée would say if she knew."

"Well," Craig replied, "I daresay she is kissing someone under the mistletoe this very minute. She has several admirers down south."

"Ah, well, just as you say. The one on the right, you said?"

"I only wish it wasn't in front of all these people," sighed Craig.

"With that look in your eye," Ian exclaimed, "it is probably just as well they are all present!"

"But, my dear friend, it is because of all those hot toddies I've had, plus the wee drams before, that you see this glint in my eye."

"Well, all I can say to that, my dear friend, is have no more, have no more."

"Now, you two young ladies, may we join in the joke that seems to be causing you so much merriment?"

"I am afraid not, Craig," said Emma. She was always quite at home when talking to him, whereas Elizabeth, as usual, blushed profusely and did not reply.

"This is my friend, Captain Ian Fraser; Ian, these two charming ladies are Misses Emma and Elizabeth – always the closest of friends."

They both bobbed a little curtsy as they were introduced. What they hadn't noticed was that, as Emma and Elizabeth curtsied, Craig had beckoned to two officer friends who now stood behind the girls, holding bunches of mistletoe above their heads.

"Now!" said Craig.

He took Elizabeth in his arms and kissed her long and passionately.

Emma laughed gaily when she was released, and she took back her glass of toddy from the officer.

"Thank goodness", she exclaimed, "Christmas only comes once a year or I might get too fond of hot toddies and kisses under the mistletoe – don't you agree, Elizabeth?"

But Elizabeth was still held in Craig's vice-like embrace; as they broke apart, she was too breathless and stunned to speak.

"You have left the poor girl speechless, Craig."

"Well, I am sure Emma will soon be able to coax a few words from her. I am never that lucky with Elizabeth. Now, if you will excuse us, kind ladies, we will let you enjoy your drinks. Ian, please go and get a drink for Elizabeth."

He came back with it and handed it to Craig to give to her.

"Have a very merry Christmas, Elizabeth – and you too, Emma."

They both returned the greetings, Emma still laughing gaily. Elizabeth looked anxiously around the room in case anyone had noticed her discomfort. Craig and Ian had now passed on to the other girls.

"Any preference this time, Craig?"

"No, my friend, you can kiss whom you like."

They parted company, and Fraser headed towards the Crawford girls. He kissed them all lightly on the cheeks, but it was much to their displeasure that they saw Craig pass them by.

"Surely under the mistletoe", pouted Ruby, "it should have been a kiss on the lips, not a mere peck on the cheek. I see that Miss Anderson got more than her share of kisses from Master Craig. I daresay that was because she sang a solo for him," she said, and she stamped her foot in anger.

Elizabeth was glad to see that Mr and Mrs Knowell were in deep conversation with Lady Harriet. She felt more at ease till she saw the look of disdain on the faces of the three precious jewels.

"How I wish we could go, Emma," she sighed.

"Well, we are going now," she replied. "They are getting our cloaks."

Before Robin had time to help her with her cloak, Craig was beside her. "Please allow me," he said as he took it from Robin and put it round her shoulders. "Robin, you can go and help the Crawford girls. They seem to be waiting for someone to assist them."

"Yes, I will," he meekly replied.

"After all, Robin, Elizabeth did sing for me, so I do owe her a small debt of gratitude."

"You are impossible, Craig," said Emma laughingly. "You know Robin cannot bear to be near them."

Craig whispered in Elizabeth's ear as he fastened her cloak: "You sang divinely, my angel. You must sing for me again soon."

"Are you ready, Elizabeth?" Emma called to her. "Mrs Knowell is waiting for us."

"Yes, I am coming."

All the party now assembled in the hall as they bade the choir goodnight, shaking hands with them as they passed.

"How beautifully you sang, my dear Elizabeth!" said Elena.

"Yes, she certainly did," ventured Bruce. "You must sing again for us soon."

"Yes, sir, I will," she said as she curtsied.

"I have never heard a sweeter rendering of that carol."

"Quite, quite!" echoed all the other guests.

'Craig held on to her hand longer than was respectable,' thought Elena, who was watching them as Craig bade her goodbye. 'Maybe it's because he has had too much drink tonight. He is certainly in a very gay mood. But he also may be thanking her for the solo she sang at his request.' She dismissed the thought quickly as Jamie closed the doors of the castle.

As they disappeared from sight down the drive, their lanterns, having been replenished, shone brightly on the crisp snow-covered ground.

CHAPTER 53

Fiona and her parents were now back at Glencree Castle to celebrate Hogmanay. It was already the last day of the old year. The village was holding its annual skating party on the small lochan – the first one since the war was over. Everyone determined that it would be the best one yet, in spite of the fact that so many of the young men were missing.

"The lochan has frozen solid this year," Jamie said to Cook, "so prepare a lot of good food for me and Zan to take down."

"Didn't I always in years gone by?" she exclaimed, rather annoyed at his remark. "Never, ever let it be said", she continued haughtily, "that the laird's cook did not prepare the finest fare at all times."

"No," agreed Jamie, "that will never be said. How lovely it will be for all of us to be beside the lochan as of old – just like old times. You know, Cook, I never realised until now how much we have missed these last few years with the young master away."

"Well, he is back now to stay, thanks be to the Lord."

The party was in full swing when the laird's party arrived. The ice was covered with skaters from far and wide.

"How lovely to see everyone so happy, Bruce!" the General exclaimed.

"Yes," he replied, "we have both spent some wonderful times together doing what they are doing now. The young ladies are positively glowing with beauty as they glide along; the fires all round give their happy faces such a rosy glow. None is more glowing than that of our lovely Fiona – and Craig's also, now she is back. He misses her so when she is not here."

"She misses him too," her father replied. "She is just like a fish out of water without him. They are so perfect together. The year ahead will be the happiest one of their lives and ours."

"Yes, yes," his wife agreed as she stood watching them. "Your son and our daughter will be united at last in marriage. I can hardly wait for the day."

Everyone, it seemed, had brought out all their finest attire. The girls wore long, flowing skirts, fur capes, hats and muffs to ward off the cold until at last they would, with the rest, gather round the long tables beside the roaring log fires. All the bonfires were now well alight, and the tables at the side of the lochan were laid out with a great array of food. Pigs were turning slowly on spits, their savoury aroma exciting everyone's appetite, but not until the laird's piper struck up would anyone be able to appease their hunger.

More of the girls from the academy and their beaux had now arrived, and some boys were waiting to pounce on any unaccompanied young maiden. The 'jewel' girls were there with their parents, and they were waiting anxiously to catch someone's eye – preferably Master Craig's. However, they could see he was skating quite happily with Fiona.

"Come, my darling," he said to her, "we must stop skating for a while and go and give our welcome greetings to the villagers. They are our guests."

"You go, darling. You know them. I will get to know them better when we are married. I will go and join Mama."

He skated off, looking around for Elizabeth as he gave his greetings to all assembled. He noticed Robin standing forlornly beside Emma and Stuart. He skated over to them and spoke to Emma.

"Is Elizabeth not joining your party tonight?" He tried to sound only mildly concerned.

"No, Craig," Emma replied, "she is staying with Lady Roxburgh so that her nurse could come and enjoy the fun."

"How very kind of her!"

Fiona, who had been watching him, was by his side immediately.

"Come, darling," she said, "let us carry on skating. I cannot bear to be away from you."

"No, Fiona, I must first have a word with Margot. I am anxious to know how her mother is. Your mother is beckoning to you," he said, and he skated off, much to her annoyance.

"How is your mother today, Margot?"

"Fairly well," she replied, "so I have brought her nurse with me for a break.

Elizabeth kindly consented to sing and play for her tonight."

"Please wish Lady Roxburgh the compliments of the season. Tell her I will visit her soon – also, give my compliments to Elizabeth."

"I will. You are always welcome; Mama always looks forward to your visits."

The old church clock at last sounded the midnight chimes and everyone greeted each other as its notes died away. They formed a circle round the bonfire and sang 'Auld Lang Syne'. Then the pipers struck up the notes they had all been anxiously waiting for, so they all proceeded to the tables, where hot toddies were being served by Craig and his friends.

At last, the laird's party wished everyone a happy New Year before they drove away, knowing the party would continue throughout the night.

CHAPTER 54

The time came for all the guests to depart from Glencree Castle.

"Never", exclaimed Elena, "have I ever enjoyed such a gathering as much before! It has been so like old times, when Craig was a child and our dearest Isabelle was here. It has been nice to have Fiona here also. To think they are now grown up and this is their wedding year!"

"Yes," agreed Harriet, "by this time next year they will be married, and, no doubt of it, an heir will be on the way, I can hardly wait for the day."

"I too!" exclaimed Bruce, who had overheard their conversation.

Fiona and Craig bade farewell to their many friends and Fiona's relations. The latter demanding that they find time to visit them all when they arrived in London.

"We know it will be a very hectic time for you, but we insist you call on us."

"We have already got a lot of parties lined up for you both," said her cousin Olga. "It is our coming-out season as well as yours. I do believe some commence in May."

"Well, we will be down soon," Fiona called after her as the carriage drove away.

Craig, bidding Captain Fraser farewell, was disturbed to hear that his regiment might be going out to the Middle East or further afield – as yet he was not too sure.

"Let us hope", said Craig, "that you do not go before Fiona and I are married. You did promise to be my best man. Do you remember our conversation on the boat when we left France?"

"I certainly do," he replied. "I shall certainly keep my promise if possible. I shall ask for special leave as soon as I hear the date from you, so keep in touch."

"It will be quite unthinkable, you not being here," rejoined Fiona.

"We are going to miss all of you so much," said Elena. "This house is only just getting used to you all being here again."

"And I", said Harriet, "am just getting used to arranging all my catering. It has been such a joy. Of course, when Fiona is here permanently I shall be able to call on her for help, as she will be able to call on me when she needs me."

The last of the carriages faded into the distance.

Fiona's parents left the following day, and the castle once more settled down to its usual daily routine.

The winter months were speeding by. Fiona was still at Glencree Castle, organising, with Craig, the architects and furnishers, all the changes she was insisting on for the West Wing. At times Craig grew quite exasperated by it all. He longed for more time outdoors, in spite of the chilly days, which were now quickly receding.

One fine day they had planned to ride to the village and visit the crofters on their way, but Fiona decided she was too tired to ride and would travel in the carriage instead.

"Just as you wish, my dear," said Craig, "but I prefer to ride my horse. She needs the exercise."

"Oh, all right, then, ride if you must, but I thought you would have preferred to be with me in the carriage."

"I would normally, my dearest one, but, as I say, today I prefer to ride."

She knew he would not change his mind, no matter how much she pouted.

'I am sick and tired of this fetish he has for visiting the poor and ailing on the estate,' she thought, but she knew she dared not show her dislike for the visits.

At last, the last of the crofters had been seen. Craig and Fiona called into the village for Bruce's ordered books and Fiona's curtain material samples. As they rode towards home, they passed Elizabeth, who was just leaving the post office.

Craig called out to her:

"May we give you a lift, Elizabeth? There is room in the carriage."

"No, thank you, Master Craig," she replied as she bobbed him a small curtsy. "I prefer to walk, and I have the dogs with me so I shall be quite safe."

"Well, don't be too long. It will be dark fairly soon, and also the mists might descend. You are welcome to join us, if you care to."

But her sharp, bright blue eyes did not fail to notice the look of disdain on Lady Fiona's face as he spoke and the way she spread her dress further over the seat she was sitting on. The opposite seat was occupied by the various boxes of materials Fiona had ordered from the milliner and dressmaker.

"No, thank you again, Master Craig. Also the dogs may soil the carriage."

"Just as you wish – maybe another day."

Suddenly his horse reared up and almost threw him. The dogs barked in fright as Fiona, in her fury, cracked her whip across her horse's back and drove away at a furious pace.

"I do hope you are not too alarmed, Elizabeth."

"No, Master Craig, it's quite all right. The dogs will soon be calm again. I will bid you good day."

Furious, Craig raced after the carriage, which was now out of sight. He hastily drew alongside it.

"Really, Fiona," he exclaimed angrily, "that was quite uncalled for!"

"And it was quite uncalled for for you to offer her a seat next to me in my carriage. I certainly don't intend to mix with the people of the village as you do."

"But it is my duty to look after them as the next laird of Glencree Castle."

"Well," she retorted, "it is work you will have to do alone. I shall be far too busy after we are married, as you know, with all the household and family arrangements. I know your mother enjoyed these visits to the crofters, but I don't. To me they are just servants on the estate, and I shall always treat them as such. And that goes for anyone else's servants I meet, such as that one of Lady Margot's."

They rode the rest of the way in silence.

Elena sensed all was not well as she saw Fiona flounce out of the carriage, not waiting for Craig to assist her.

'That madam is up to her peevish tricks again, I daresay,' she thought.

Later that evening, after dinner, Bruce sat in the lounge, at peace with the world. All his loved ones were around him, his favourite drink was in his hand. He sat by the roaring fire so that he could see his darling Isabelle's picture, which he looked at lovingly all the time.

'Yes, I am indeed a very lucky man – but if only my darling could be with us!' he thought. Once again he was lost in his sighs.

Harriet and Elena sat playing cards, but Elena realised there was a silence between Craig and Fiona, and it puzzled her. Craig and Fiona rose from where they were sitting opposite Bruce.

"Come, Fiona – get your wrap and we will take Flint for a short stroll."

"Now don't stay out too long," Harriet called to them as they were leaving. "The evenings are still far too chilly."

"We won't," Craig assured her.

They walked arm in arm as Flint scampered away on his own. Then Fiona freed her arm from his and turned to face him. She was quite perturbed at his silence over dinner and now.

"Kiss me, my darling," she begged. "I am sorry for being so foolish this afternoon. I guess I am jealous of every pretty girl in the village – and more so when you talk to them. Please say you forgive me and tell me you love me."

He looked down into her lovely face and playfully tugged the ribbon from her hair.

"You know I love you," he said, and he kissed her passionately. "I have always loved you and no one else, and I forgive you," he whispered as he smothered her with kisses. "It is rather flattering to me to know that you are so jealous."

"Well, my darling, I do know", she said, "that there are many pretty girls at the academy whose beaux have not returned from the war. I have been so lucky."

He silenced her with a kiss. "Now listen to me, you silly little girl: no one is ever going to take me away from you – never, never. Surely you know that?"

"Of course I do, my darling."

"Well, now, no more talking. I have too much kissing to catch up on, and you will be leaving in a few days' time to attend your cousin's wedding."

"I wish you were coming with me," she sighed as she clung to him.

"I wish I could, but I promised Papa to attend the course on forestry set up by the new Forestry Commission. We will also have several foresters staying here as our guests, so it is impossible for me to accompany you. I will come and join you as soon as I can, and I will let you know as soon as the course has finished. Come – let us join the others inside. It is getting too cold for you here." He called Flint to heel as they went towards the house. He kissed her several times more.

"I am going to miss you so much, my darling," she whispered. "Why can't our wedding be sooner? Then we need never be parted."

"But, dearest," he sighed, "it is your insistence on doing the London Season that is causing the delay."

"Yes, I know, my darling, but I want everything to be so perfect. I just have to do the London Season with my cousins, and I have so much shopping to do for my trousseau now that nearly all the arrangements are complete for the West

Wing. Isn't everything looking lovely there now?"

"Yes, it is, my darling, and it's all due to you. My, what a chatterbox you are, my darling!" he exclaimed. "All I want to do is kiss and kiss you."

CHAPTER 55

Martha looked at her son anxiously. For a few days now she had noticed him in deep thought, and had mentioned the fact to Magnus.

"Why so crestfallen today, my son?"

"Well, Mama, as you know, there is no real job for me, much as I love it here, so I have re-enlisted."

She gave a gasp of dismay, although deep in her mother's heart she had suspected it. She knew it had always been his wish, since he was a small boy, to make the army his career.

"I have discussed it with Papa, and he knows I do not want to follow in his footsteps here. I can always give up the army when he finds the rowing for the laird too difficult, so I would still continue our line of duty to the laird, of which Papa is so proud."

"Well, I am glad to hear that, my son," Martha replied.

"I can't just keep hanging about, helping with sailing over with the stores for the village and Glencree Castle two or three times a week."

"But have you thought about Elizabeth? She will miss your visits to Harrison Hall and seeing you on Sundays when we go to church."

"Yes, I know, Mama, and I don't really know how I am going to begin to tell her."

"If it is really your wish, my son," Martha continued, "Elizabeth will understand. She will want you to be happy – just as you wish happiness for her. At least the war is over, so we won't have that anxiety of not knowing whether or not we shall ever see you again."

"I go later this week."

"So soon, my son!" Magnus exclaimed. He had stood by silently, hoping it wouldn't be for a few more weeks.

"Yes, Papa, it's no good me wasting any more time."

"Roddy, Roddy, my darling Roddy, what a surprise to see you today!"

Elizabeth ran out to meet him with arms outstretched. When Charles had told her he was coming up the drive, she had been arranging flowers in the sitting room.

"What a lovely surprise! Have you no stores today? Why is that?" she queried.

"No, not today, little sister," he said as he unwound her arms from around his neck. "Can we go inside for a moment?" he asked.

"Of course. Wait here a moment whilst I ask Lady Margot if you can wait in the library." She was very alarmed by his serious countenance as she darted off.

"Why, of course, my child. Ask him to come in. Don't leave him standing outside."

"Sit down, Roddy. What is wrong – are Mama and Papa well?"

"Yes, they are well."

"Well, what is it, then?" There was a note of panic in her voice. "It's not like you to look so forlorn and troubled."

"I have come to tell you that I have re-enlisted in the army and I will leave in two days' time."

She looked at him aghast.

"But why, Roddy darling? Why, why?" Her voice trembled as she spoke.

"There is no work for me on the croft. There is barely enough to keep Mama and Papa alive. There is no work I want to do in the whole district. I am tired of searching. I would love to stay close to you and our parents, but, as you know, the army has always been my love. I can help our parents so much more this way. I can send them money."

"But they will miss you so. What about me? I waited so long for you to come back from the war, as did Mama and Papa, and now you are going again."

She started to cry and he put his arms comfortingly around her.

"But there is no war now. I will be quite safe. I can help you all so much more. Mama and Papa need more money now, and, as you know, neither of us can touch our legacy from Aunt Ingrid until we marry. Besides, I haven't found anyone yet I want to marry."

"Neither have I. I know I could marry Robin, but he is going to clerical college for several years and I know he doesn't want to marry before he goes; he told me so, but I know he would marry me if I wished it so."

"No, no, you must not get him to change his plans because of my going away."

"When shall I see you again, Roddy?"

"Not until I get some leave."

"Will that be very long?"

"It could be months, depending on my posting. If it is in England, I shall get home pretty often; on the other hand, I could just get one more leave and then be sent to the Middle East. That would mean I shall be away for a long time."

"The Middle East!" she exclaimed in panic. "That is on the other side of the world."

"Now, don't cry any more. I don't expect I shall go so far away for a few years yet."

Lady Margot paused for a few seconds in the hall as she was passing the door.

'Surely', she thought, 'Elizabeth is not crying? Yes, I do believe she is. I do hope she has not had bad news.'

She tapped lightly on the door.

"Are you all right?" she asked. "Whatever is the matter, my dear child? I do hope your parents are well."

"Yes, they are all right, milady," Roddy replied.

"Well, why all the tears, my child?"

"I have just called to tell her that I have re-enlisted and may not be back for some time."

"Elizabeth is going to miss you a great deal. You have always been so close. Ingrid used to tell me how you looked after her as a little girl."

"That's because I love her so dearly, milady, and she missed our parents so much when we went to live with Aunt Ingrid."

"Have you time to stay for a cup of tea, Roddy?" she asked.

"No, thank you, milady. I have so many other visits to make to my many friends, so if you will excuse me . . . Thank you so much."

"Well, I will leave you to say goodbye to your sister."

Roddy bowed politely as Lady Margot said her goodbye.

"Elizabeth, you walk with him to the gateway."

"Oh, thank you, milady."

They walked arm in arm as Lady Margot watched from the window.

'The poor child is going to miss him so,' she sighed. 'I know, just know, Martha will too, just as I miss my daughter.' She sighed again. 'Now I must go and see how Mama is.'

Elizabeth watched Roddy go over the bridge, and he turned again and again to wave until he was out of sight. Her taking it so badly had upset him more than he realised. 'But then, I am more used to going away than she is. Maybe when Robin knows I have left he will insist on marrying her in spite of his going to college. At least he won't be too far away from her, and if they marry, she won't be so alone.'

He walked quickly on. His first call was at the vicarage to tell Emma and her brothers.

'Emma will help Elizabeth get over my going,' he thought.

Lady Margot was waiting for Elizabeth when she got back.

"Now, come and join me for tea. Tomorrow, when your father comes with the stores, you can return home with him and stay to see Roddy off on the train. I am sure your dear mother will be glad of your company. You must not get so upset, my dear. I am sure he will be home again soon. Now, dry your tears."

"Thank you, milady. You are so very kind to me."

She wiped the last tear away and put her handkerchief in her pocket.

Roddy left the three forlorn figures on the station as his train pulled away from the platform. Their sadness had troubled him greatly as he kissed them all goodbye. How he wished Elizabeth had not wept so!

"I will be back soon, little sister. Look after Mama and Papa for me until I return," he shouted from the window.

Peggoty's arm came around Elizabeth's shoulder.

"I will, I will," she called to Roddy as she wiped away her tears.

"We will be all right, my son," Martha called to him. "Don't you worry."

They watched until the train was out of sight.

"Come now, Elizabeth – your father will take you back now."

"Must I go so soon?"

"Yes, child, Her Ladyship has been very kind to let you stay."

They said their goodbyes to Peggoty, and he closed the little gate after them.

"Now, don't you worry, little girl – your big brother will be home again very soon."

CHAPTER 56

After Fiona left for London, Craig, Elena and Margot had time to spare for the long discussions on the welfare of the men.

"The Special Commission is now appointed," explained Craig. "I am so grateful to you both for helping me and my brother officers. I only wish we could find more work for the more able ones, but it gets more hopeless day by day," he sighed. He gazed a long time over the loch. "This was going to be a land fit for heroes!" he exclaimed angrily as he turned to face them. "Promises, promises – that is all they get. They never get anything better, which they deserve after what they went through. There's no work, so their children starve. Many of them laid down their lives. For what? For what?" He banged his fist angrily on the table.

Elena and Margot looked at each other.

"He's so like his father." Margot was the first to speak, as Craig turned once more to gaze over the loch.

"Did I mention, Elena, that Roddy Anderson has also re-enlisted, for the very same reason? Martha told me after the Sunday service. I could see she and Magnus were very upset at his decision, and Elizabeth – poor child! – was crying at the news."

At the sound of her name, Craig listened intently. Suddenly, he remembered the happy lilt in her voice when she called his name as she descended the stairs, and he recalled her dismay when she realised it wasn't her beloved Roddy sitting beside the fire.

He turned again and banged his fist on the table. "That is another of our island boys leaving. How many more? How many more?" Suddenly, he could see Elizabeth's tear-stained face. "Tears on my angel's face! It's just not fair," he called out loud.

Elena and Margot looked at him anxiously. They knew how deeply he felt for the island and its people. He was so like his dear mother.

"When did he leave, Margot?" Elena asked.

"A week ago. I did allow Elizabeth a few days at home before he left, but she is back now. I know she will miss him dreadfully."

Craig sat down in the big armchair after they left and sipped his whisky slowly. 'I wish I could go and console her,' he thought. 'I must try somehow, but how can I ever get her alone?'

Bruce was spending more time playing chess with the General now that he was at home alone. He had found the time in London with his wife and daughter too tiring after his recent illness.

A few days later, Elena called out to Craig, "I know how busy you are, dear boy, with the people of the Forestry Commission."

"What is it, Aunt?"

"Would you spare the time to drive me over to Margot's? We have now so many plans to make regarding the missions, and there are so many papers needing my signature alongside Margot's."

"Gladly, dear Aunt. It will also give me a chance to visit her mother."

They alighted at Harrison Hall later that day and Charles took them both to the library.

"My dear Elena, how glad I am to see you and to know that we can at last get on with our missionary work! And I'm glad to see you too, Master Craig. Do sit down."

"Now, Mama," Margot continued, "Nurse has the afternoon off. She has gone into the village. I shall be busy in the study with Elena, but Elizabeth will be down directly to sing or read to you."

"Very well, my dear," her mother replied. "You carry on with Elena. I know how much work you both have to do."

'I couldn't wish for more,' thought Craig.

"She will be all right with me, Margot. We have been promising ourselves a long talk for some time now, haven't we, Lady Roxburgh?"

"We certainly have, my dear boy – since before you had to go to that dreadful war."

"Now, no more talk of war!" Elena said as they left the room.

Craig seated himself more comfortably in the huge armchair. Then a gentle knock came on the door.

"Come in, my dear Elizabeth," Lady Roxburgh called in her frail voice.

Elizabeth tripped lightly into the room and closed the door. She bade Lady Roxburgh good evening and curtsied.

"Do you wish me to sing, play or recite for you tonight, milady?" she asked.

She gave a startled gasp as Craig suddenly arose from the deep armchair and came towards her. As usual his laughing dark eyes were searching her violet-blue ones.

"Good evening, Elizabeth," he said, smiling at her obvious fright.

"Good evening, Master Craig," she replied, and she bobbed him a curtsy.

He gripped her sharply by the shoulders as she rose to her feet. The firmness of his grip, and the sudden seriousness she saw in his eyes, she couldn't understand.

Suddenly, he remembered Fiona's words: ". . . anyone's servant, even Lady Margot's".

'Servant!' he exploded inwardly. 'She is no one's servant. I am becoming her slave. Her mere presence has me in turmoil. Why? I just cannot fathom it.'

He suddenly released her. "Well, Lady Roxburgh," he said, "as she sings so beautifully, let her sing for us."

"Just as you wish," she replied. "Just as you wish."

"Come, Elizabeth – I will turn the pages of the music for you."

She sat down, completely shaken and in a state of panic.

"Have you any special preference, milady?" she asked.

"No, my dear. Just sing my old favourites till Nurse returns. She won't be too long."

Craig put his arm gently on her shoulders as he turned the pages. She found it very difficult to sing. She couldn't understand the feeling of ecstasy that ran through her at his nearness. His mere touch set a fire alight in her every nerve as he played with her long golden ringlets. She wanted him to stop, yet she didn't.

"I hear your dear brother has re-enlisted."

At the sound of Roddy's name, he felt her tremble.

"I am so sorry, but I'm sure he will be all right. I know how much you will miss him, but I do hope he will be back soon on leave to visit you."

"Now, Craig," milady's voice rang out, "I thought you wanted to hear her sing. Well, so do I. How can she sing if you keep chattering so?"

"Yes, yes, of course. I apologise to you and Elizabeth."

A knock on the door heralded the arrival of Lady Roxburgh's nurse.

"Good evening, milady, Master Craig." She curtsied. "Is milady ready to rest, Elizabeth?"

"Yes, of course I am ready," Lady Roxburgh replied, before Elizabeth, who had stood up, had time to reply. "I get tired so soon these days, Craig. You must excuse me, and you must come as often as you can to see this very tired old lady."

"I will, I will," he promised as he went to open the door.

He closed it after them and stood with his back to it. Then he lost no time in demanding that Elizabeth come to his side.

"You are now my prisoner. Come here, close to me."

She went slowly up to him, knowing in her heart that she had to do as he said – not only because he was the laird's son but also she felt she had no inner strength to resist him. It was as if a magnet was drawing her closer and closer to him.

As soon as she was within arm's length, he pulled her close and kissed her passionately.

"I love you, my angel," he said. "I love you. Say you care for me. Say it! Say it!"

But she was silent.

"I know you care for me. I know it."

His dark, penetrating eyes looked into hers for an answer, but none came. All he could see was a look of dismay and disbelief.

'Whatever is happening to me?' she thought.

"What is happening to us?" she exclaimed. "What is happening?"

"I love you, my angel," he kept repeating over and over again, as he rained kisses on her lips and cheeks. Then he buried his face in her hair.

"But it cannot be," she protested. "It cannot be. Please release me."

He did as she asked, reluctantly.

"No, you are right: it cannot be. But it is the truth, and *that* can be, however impossible. Come – let us sit down at the card table for a while, but first let me straighten your beautiful hair that I have disarranged." He tied back her hair with the ribbon. "I still have a blue ribbon of yours. I found it by the stream. I will return it one day. I also have the dogs' leads."

'So that is where they are,' she thought.

"I have the handkerchief you loaned me that day," she said. "It is now washed and ironed. Shall I go and get it for you?"

"No, not now. I will leave it for another day. Then I shall have an excuse to call on you again. Come – let us sit down. We can pretend we are playing cards if anyone comes. You do play cards?"

"Yes, I play with Nurse sometimes and I sometimes play with my parents and Roddy when we are together at home."

"Well, we will only pretend today. I only want you near me."

None too soon for Elizabeth, Elena opened the door.

"Has Her Ladyship retired?" she asked.

"Yes, Aunt Elena. Elizabeth kindly consented to join me in a game of cards until we left."

"I thought Mama would have retired by now. She tires so easily. You may go now, Elizabeth," said Margot.

Elizabeth bade them all goodnight and curtsied. She closed the door behind her as she left.

She lay a long time on her bed, gazing into space. Her hand brushed her lips as she recalled his passionate kisses.

'This time I wasn't angry. I am so happy,' she thought. She had returned his kisses, but she excused herself: 'I found it impossible not to do so. It is all so bewildering and so very, very wrong. I know it cannot continue, but what can I do? The more I try to avoid him, the more he seems to be always present. Oh, what a dilemma I am in!' She sighed and glanced at the clock on the wall. 'My goodness, how late it is! I must hurry and change for dinner.'

Soon she heard the first dinner gong ring out.

CHAPTER 57

Fiona had left Glencree Castle to attend her cousin Jane's spring wedding. She was still fuming with indignation because Craig would not accompany her to London. Her mother tut-tutted her displeasure for most of the journey.

Bruce, Craig and the General, accompanied by the officers from the Forestry Commission and the ghillies, enjoyed the early spring days riding the glens and trekking through the tall pine forests. Craig rode alongside the officers in deep, interesting conversation. Bruce and the General trailed behind them, also in deep conversation. The General stopped now and again to view, with pleasure, all the land which Bruce was acquiring from Lady Roxburgh's estate.

"As you realise, my dear friend, all this will belong to our grandsons," said Bruce.

"Yes, my friend, we shall someday all ride across this land together – not many years hence either. I am so looking forward to the day of their wedding," rejoined the General. "Such a celebration cannot come soon enough for me."

The two men hastily rejoined the others.

"I think it is time we returned for lunch. Will you join us?" Bruce asked the officers.

"No, thank you, sir. We have done enough here for today. We still have land to view on the other side of loch."

"Will you join me in a game of chess?" Bruce asked the General after lunch.

"Most gladly."

Craig stood pensively looking out over the loch; then he picked up his riding crop.

"Papa, I am going to keep a promise I made to Lady Roxburgh. I said that I would visit her more often, and, as I am still dressed for riding, I will ride over and see her today."

"Very well, my son. Give her my best wishes."

"Also mine," said the General.

"I will."

Craig was delighted to find when he arrived that Margot had gone to the village. She was then going on to call at the vicarage.

"Lady Roxburgh is resting, but Elizabeth is in the library. Shall I tell her you are here?" asked Charles.

"No, thank you, Charles. I know the way."

Elizabeth, poring over her correspondence, gasped in alarm when Craig dashed in and pulled her to her feet. He crushed her in his embrace as he kissed her.

"Darling, darling angel," he whispered in between his kisses. "I must see you alone. I must. When you take the dogs for a stroll, meet me under our old family oak – you know, the one planted by my ancestors about a hundred years ago. It is the one that the mistletoe grows on. You remember our kisses at the carol service? That mistletoe was from the same old tree."

"Yes, I know where it is," she replied breathlessly.

"Take the small lane to the left, not the one which leads to the vicarage.

Promise me you will always use that one in future. When I can get away, I shall be waiting there. Promise me you will come," he begged.

"I dare not, Master Craig. I dare not see you alone."

"You will come! You will!" he insisted. "You must! Say you will come. I won't release you if you don't promise. Say yes," he demanded. Before she could answer, he began kissing her passionately over and over again. He held her close. "Say yes," he demanded.

"Yes, yes," she replied weakly. His possession of her very soul was too overwhelming to resist. She was swept off her feet by her own ecstasy. She could not explain it, but she knew that whatever he had set his heart on he must have, and she must bow to his will.

"It is all wrong – all wrong," she protested, trying to pull free.

"No, it isn't," he insisted. "You are free to love me and I love you."

"But you are not free to love me."

"I do love you and that will never change."

"It must change," she implored. "You are betrothed to Lady Fiona."

At the mention of Fiona's name, he released his firm grip.

"Whatever happens in the future, nothing will ever stop me loving you," he said as he looked into space. "Yes, my dear, you are so right: I am betrothed.

"Now," he said reluctantly, "I must go and pay my respects to Lady Roxburgh."

He kissed her ardently before rushing to the door.

Elizabeth picked up the correspondence, went into the study and sat down at the bureau. She put the letter on top of the pile of correspondence already there and heaved a sigh of resignation.

"My work will never be finished at this rate. Lady Margot will be wondering what on earth I have been doing all afternoon."

She went to the window and watched as Craig rode away.

"Was that Master Craig I saw, riding away, Elizabeth?" said Margot as she entered the room.

"Yes, I told him you were out, so he decided to visit Lady Roxburgh." She crossed her fingers behind her back, hoping Her Ladyship hadn't noticed her blushes.

Elizabeth noticed Lady Margot's look of displeasure.

"Oh, I do hope he has not tired her out. He is such a chatterbox these days. Come, Elizabeth – we will join Mama for tea."

"Well, Mama," she said as she kissed her on the forehead, "what had that rascal Craig to say today?"

"He was quite jolly and gay as always. What a change there is in him, to be sure, compared to the shy little boy who used to visit us with his parents. I could hardly get a word out of him then. Very strange, very strange!" she muttered.

"Yes," agreed Margot. "Now he is here, there and everywhere, racing like mad over the estate with his hair flying and the neck of his shirt undone as though his freedom is still being threatened. I daresay Bruce doesn't know where he is for two days together, and now, as the estate increases, he will see less and less of him. It will be a good thing when he finally settles down and marries Fiona. I cannot see Fiona ever letting him get too far out of her sight; she is so possessive and won't allow him to go galloping all over the estate as he does now. Bruce will just have to get more ghillies, I'll be bound."

At the sound of Fiona's name, Elizabeth flinched, recalling his kisses. 'Yes, hasten the day,' she thought. 'Then I shall be free to escape from his possession.'

She glanced up to see Lady Margot looking at her.

"Are you all right, Elizabeth? You look rather flushed."

She was aghast to find that her innermost thoughts were so much in evidence. "Yes, milady, I am quite all right, thank you. I have got a little too near the fire I think," she said as she moved away. "I have a few more letters to finish, milady."

"Very well, my dear, go and finish them; then they will be ready for the post tomorrow."

CHAPTER 58

Bruce and Margot had left for Edinburgh. The buying of more and more land was taking up more and more time. Bruce had declared to Margot in confidence one day that he did not wish Craig to be told, till after his marriage, how much land he had acquired from her.

"Your secret is safe with me," she assured him.

"It will be quite a surprise to him and his wife, Fiona, as well as to my old friend the General. What a heritage we shall have to hand on to our grandsons! I am longing so much for the day, Margot, when my first grandson will be born."

"Well Bruce, my dear," she laughed, "it could be a granddaughter, or several granddaughters."

"Oh, how you do love to tease me, my dear Margot. You have never changed from the charming girl of my youth. You have always understood me so well. But now my youth has gone I am preparing for the young ones to follow. I daresay you also, Margot, are longing for the day when you can see your grandchildren."

"Yes, I long for that day," she sighed.

"Is there no chance of them coming to visit you now the war is over? They must be very anxious to see their great-grandmother too?"

"No, it is not possible yet. My daughter and her husband are kept far too busy. Stephen is now a chief judge at the high court and Davinia assists Martin at the missions as much as she can. But", she sighed heavily, "I do long to see my daughter and my granddaughters. They are almost four years old now. However, with Mama's health as it is, I just have to stay. It is a relief to let all the land go to such a dear friend as you, Bruce."

"Well," Bruce declared, "soon all the transactions will be complete and there will be nothing for you to worry about."

"Margot dear, will you and Bruce be staying long in the city?" Lady Roxburgh had asked as they were leaving.

"Only a week, Mama dear."

"Well, I feel better at present, so don't worry about me. I have Nurse and everyone else to look after me."

"Yes, I know you will be all right, Mama dear, otherwise I wouldn't go. Elena has promised to call in very often to see you."

"I shall look forward to that."

Craig lost no time in calling to see Lady Roxburgh. After she had retired for her afternoon nap, when her nurse was resting in her room, he went into the study.

"Now, my angel," he whispered to Elizabeth as he held her close, "there is no reason for you not to come every day. I shall wait every day under the big oak tree near my hunting lodge. Bring the dogs for their usual walk. Say you will come every day," he demanded. Then he kissed her again and again.

"But I will have to finish my work first," she insisted.

"Yes, do that, but I shall be waiting."

He kissed her long and ardently before riding away.

CHAPTER 59

Next day Craig waited at his lodge.

'I know Aunt Harriet will grumble at my not going home,' he thought. 'I forgot to tell her, which won't help matters, but it is too far to go and I much prefer the solitude of my lodge to the vastness of Glencree Castle. How I wish I could spend the rest of my days in these humble surroundings with my precious angel! However, as that cannot be,' he sighed, 'I am going to see her as often as I can.'

He had tied his horse to the tree nearby.

He watched Elizabeth wend her way towards him. He could hear her laughter as she threw a ball for the dogs.

"You stay here now, Flint," he demanded. "No more chasing after their ball!"

He sprang out to clasp her in his arms.

"Darling, darling," he whispered as she clung to him, "I do love you so. Say you love me also."

But he received no answer to his plea.

At last he let her go.

"Come and sit down and rest. You have had a long walk. You are free all this week, I know, so I hope you will meet me here every day. Say you will."

She began to tell him reasons why she couldn't.

"I am not listening to any excuses. I shall be here every day, waiting for you, and you know I will not tolerate being kept waiting by anyone."

"It never can be," she tried to say, but he closed her protesting lips with a passionate kiss. Again and again he kissed her. At last he released her.

She sighed deeply. "Please, Craig," she pleaded, "do not make it harder for me."

"You do love me. I know it! I know it!"

"I shall never say it. I shall never answer," she cried.

She broke away from him and went to tie the dogs under the shade of a tree nearby. "You are getting too hot, my precious pair," she murmured to them.

He joined her under the shade of the tree, and he rested his back against it as he watched her.

"What is that tune you are humming?" she asked. "I am sure I know it, but you are not humming it correctly." She pretended to scold him.

"At the moment, I cannot think of the name of it. I think it is called", he replied, " 'Forget-Me-Not'."

"Ah yes, now I recall it. It is an intermezzo, but I cannot think where it is from," she said with a puzzled frown on her face.

He pulled her close once more. "Don't frown so," he said. "You must always smile for me. Here is a real forget-me-not to match your eyes. You must sing it correctly for me one of these days."

"Yes, of course I will, Your Lordship," she teased.

He ran the tiny flower he had just plucked across her forehead to the level of her wide-open eyes.

"Too, too beautiful! Quite matchless! Exquisite!" he said as he compared the blue of the flower with the blue of her eyes.

His gaze reached the depth of her soul and his lips sealed hers as she tried to utter, "It cannot be, it cannot be." At last she cried out, "It cannot be!" She tried to get away, but his grip only tightened on her fragile frame.

Suddenly, the dogs were by her side, and she cried out in dismay as she looked up at him:

"Someone has untied the dogs!" There was panic in her voice. "We have been seen! We have been seen!"

"Do not get so alarmed, my darling angel. I know who it will be."

"Who? Who?" she demanded.

"It will only be my dear Merry-Berry."

"But it is a gipsy's warning. Don't you see? Don't you realise that?" She hardly knew what she was saying.

"Oh no, my dear one. It is not a warning. She is only letting me know that she is, as always, never far away from me."

Elizabeth wrenched herself free from his grasp and ran down the lane with the dogs yelping after her. 'Yes, yes, I love you,' she thought over and over again as she ran blindly on. 'I love you to distraction. Every minute away from you is agonising torment, and every minute with you is devastating hell and heaven at the same time. How can I ever tell you I love you? You are betrothed to another; that sacred promise, which you have made, I will never be the cause of your breaking, no matter what the cost to me.' She could still hear his pleading, anguished words repeating over and over again and her own voice replying, "It cannot be, it cannot be."

Craig watched her as she ran over the small bridge spanning the stream and through the tall iron gates of Harrison Hall.

He turned to his horse, buried his face in its golden mane and whispered, "Flaxen, what am I going to do? What am I going to do?"

No answer was forthcoming, so he quickly remounted. Flint, by his side, looked up at him anxiously, as if to say, "What ails my master?"

Craig sped away more furiously than ever before. Suddenly, the yelp of Flint reached his ears and halted him in his flight.

"So sorry, Flint, my old friend! I almost forgot you, my so trusting friend."

He reached down and picked Flint up. He cradled the dog in his arms as he set off again at the same mad gallop. 'She does love me – she does, she does, she does. I know it,' he said to himself, but he knew she would never admit it while he was betrothed to Fiona. 'But I can never break off my betrothal to my darling Fiona. It is too unthinkable for words.'

He swept aside his dark curls, now damp with sweat. He was thankful for the cool breeze as he raced on.

'What have I done to deserve such a fate?' he asked himself. He could not break his darling Fiona's heart, but how could he ever live without his darling angel?

Jamie took Craig's horse from him as he hastily dismounted with hardly a word to him.

'That is so unlike my dear young master,' he thought to himself. 'What a state his horse is in! He must have raced like the wind.'

Jamie shook his head in bewilderment, he called the groom to take the horse and watched as Craig ran hastily up the steps into the house.

CHAPTER 60

The next day, Elena decided to make her promised visit to Lady Roxburgh.

"How are you getting on, my dear, whilst Margot is away? I told her I would call in to see you."

"How very kind of you, Elena. It is so nice to see you. Craig calls very often also, and his visits make me feel a lot better."

"So this is where he gets to when we are awaiting him for lunch, and sometimes dinner?"

"Sometimes I tease him when he calls."

"How is that?" Elena queried. "He is usually the one who does the teasing."

"Well," – she smiled as she pondered – "I tell him, 'I think you only come to see such an old woman as me because you like to hear Elizabeth sing to me.' He sits listening to her in such rapture. Of course he denies it. Such a delightful boy!"

"Sometimes", continued Elena, "he isn't in the house more then a few moments before he is tearing off again on his horse, or going off to sail his new boat on the loch. He has not been the same since he came home. It's as if he longs to be free."

"Well, never fear, Elena. When he is married and children arrive, he will stay at home more. There's nothing like small children scampering round the house to make a man feel he must spend most of his time at home. So, Elena, he might as well enjoy his freedom for as long as he can."

"Well, he is certainly enjoying himself. It is, after all, what they fought for. I must be going now that I see you are all right."

"Tell me, Elena, when does Fiona return from visiting her cousins?"

"Very soon now, but I am not sure of the exact day. Of course, she won't be here long before she returns for the London Season and for her presentation at court."

"Oh, how I remember my own presentation, so long ago!" said Lady Roxburgh, and her voice softened. She sighed, leaning further back on her pillows as she drifted back to bygone days. "Yes, yes, such happy days!"

"Yes, they were happy days," Elena agreed. "Harriet and I were presented at the same time as Margot."

"Yes, yes, I recall that time also."

"Then I daresay on her return Fiona will be busy preparing for her wedding. What a wonderful event it will be for all!"

"Yes," agreed Elena, "the villagers are awaiting it with delight. It is the only topic of conversation in the village."

"I just know I shall be well enough to attend."

"Of course you will, my dear. Now I must go. You will be getting overtired if

257

we keep talking." She kissed Lady Roxburgh lightly on the forehead before she left. "I will tell Nurse as I go."

"Come again, Elena, and please ask Craig to bring Fiona to see me. She hasn't been for such a long time."

"I will. Goodbye, my dear." Lady Roxburgh's eyes were already closing as Elena softly closed the door.

CHAPTER 61

Two days later Craig and Elizabeth stood under the large old oak tree. He had gathered, as usual, a bunch of wild flowers for her from the hedgerows.

As he looked down at them, he exclaimed, "This is the only one that matters to me, my darling!"

"Which is it?" she queried.

"This one. It is the only flower that exists for you and me. It is the prettiest and sweetest one of all: the forget-me-not." He plucked them one by one from the bunch and placed them in her hand. "Always remember that, my sweet angel."

Suddenly, he went strangely quiet. She looked up at him perplexed. There was a lost look on his face.

"Why so sad, my dearest one?" she asked.

"It is because I shall not be able to see you again for some time. But here, in the hollow of this tree of ours, look every day as you take your daily walk. In it I shall place a slip of paper. When you see it, come to me at the lodge. The only word I shall write on it will be forget-me-not. Do you understand?"

"Yes, I understand, but really I must not come."

"You must, you must," he demanded. "Say you will."

"I promise, but it isn't right."

Before she could say more he had silenced her with a passionate kiss.

"Come – I will show you the way to my lodge," he said.

He led her by the hand along the narrow paths to where the lodge was hardly visible amongst the dense shrubbery.

"Only the family and possibly Merry-Berry know where it is. I never use it now as a shooting lodge. I made a vow when I returned from the war that never again would I shoot anything. No, never again!" he shuddered.

"Now it is my retreat, where I can come when I am too tired from travelling over the estate. My horse and I often rest here. The door is always open, so if ever you need to come here, you can do so."

"Oh, I am sure I shall never need to come, but thank you, Master Craig."

"What have I demanded you call me?" he exclaimed angrily.

"Craig," she whispered shyly.

"I am not your master – always remember that. You must come to me here when I return from my travels. Look every day for my message. I don't know how long I shall be away."

He ushered her inside, closing the door behind him.

"I thought you said the door was never closed," she said teasingly.

"Well, it will only be closed when we are here, so that we can shut out the rest of the world."

She looked round the room hesitantly; then she went over to the huge log fireplace and picked up the picture of his mother.

"Do you remember Mama?"

"Only a little, when the three of you used to be brought over the loch by my father on your way to the station. That was before Roddy and I went to stay with Aunt Ingrid. Mama tells me how beautiful she was."

"Yes, she was very beautiful." A lost look came to his eyes. "Just too beautiful, my darling – just like you!" He gathered her in his arms and kissed her.

"Please, dear Craig, you know this can never be," she tried to say, but he silenced her with a passionate kiss. He held her as if he never wanted to let her go.

"My darling, I know that I shall always love you and I know that you love me."

"That I cannot say."

"But it is true all the same. Just say it once for me. Say it," he insisted.

She was silent as she looked up at him, but the look in her eyes told him all he wanted to know. She freed herself from his arms.

"What pretty chintz!" she said as she idly played with the curtains.

"Yes, Aunt Elena chose them for me. But how can I be interested in such mundane things as chintz curtains and furnishings when all I can think about is being here with you. What would I give", he sighed, "if only we could spend the rest of our days in this little place! See, I have even got a piano. Come and play for me."

"What shall I play?" she asked.

"Oh, anything." He took the flowers she was still holding and placed some in her hair. "I know: play the piece you said I had got wrong."

"But I haven't played it for so long. I am not too sure of it," she said.

However, it wasn't long before the melody came to her and she played as he stood looking at her. He was completely lost in her beauty and his love for her. She looked up at him as she finished playing. She, too, was lost in the world only the two of them shared.

"I must be returning," she said, and she got up to go.

"Just as you say, my angel." He held her again in a grasp from which she could not, and did not, wish to escape. "Promise, promise", he insisted, "to come again soon."

"I promise."

She could do no other. To his every wish and command she had to submit.

He walked alongside her, leading his horse, as the dogs scampered ahead. The sound of the dogs barking caused Elena to look up from her painting. She often painted in the valley on sunny days. She stood up but could see nothing, yet she was sure they were quite near so she climbed higher up the grassy bank. It was then that she saw them walking side by side. At first she thought Craig must have met her on her way from the village and decided to walk with her to Harrison Hall to see Lady Roxburgh. She knew he often called to see her. However, as they were parting, Craig drew Elizabeth into his arms in a passionate embrace.

Elena gasped with astonishment and put her hand to her mouth in complete bewilderment.

'Oh, what I have just witnessed cannot be true. It cannot – cannot.' She thought. 'My poor, poor Craig! Whatever are you thinking about? Surely you know this is madness?' Then the words of Lady Roxburgh flashed before her. 'So this is the reason for your visiting Harrison Hall so often.'

She watched as Elizabeth turned to give him a final wave before disappearing and she saw Craig blow her a kiss on the wind. He remounted and raced away madly.

Elena slowly returned to where she had left her painting. She put it carefully away in her satchel. "No more painting today," she said with a sigh as she clambered into the trap. She was deeply perplexed. She drove back to Glencree Castle by the longer way, round the loch, to give herself more time for thought, as well as to give Craig more time to return.

What should she say to him? Should she say anything? Should she tell him what she had seen? Her mind was in turmoil. She decided for the time being to do nothing. 'My dear, dear boy, what a problem you have given me! What am I to do? What am I to do?'

CHAPTER 62

Craig searched in vain for a glimpse of Elizabeth the following Sunday at church. As he sat beside his father, Elena was watching him closely out of the corner of her eye.

'Thank goodness Fiona is home at last and he is leaving with Bruce to join her after the service!' She sighed with relief, thankful that Fiona would be home for some time.

'Goodness knows how long it will be before I see my dear angel again,' Craig sighed, as he looked for her in vain.

However, Mrs Knowell had made sure that she would not be seen by the young master of Glencree Castle. She had placed Elizabeth in the second row of the choir, well hidden from view by the taller Crawford girls in front. Emma was still seething at the new placing. Only the thought that it would cause Elizabeth some distress stopped her from demanding an explanation.

Craig looked anxiously around as he drove away with his father. Elena, watching him, was relieved Elizabeth had not appeared.

"Who are you looking for?" exclaimed Harriet when she saw Elena watching everyone coming out of the church.

For a moment, Elena was taken off guard.

"I thought I spotted Martha, but they evidently haven't managed to come over the loch today."

"Why did you specially want to see her today?" Harriet demanded.

"I only wanted to ask her about the things she will be making for the stall later on, but it can wait until another day."

Elena noted that none of the choir had come out of church as Harriet climbed into the trap with her and they started for home.

"Sometimes, Elena, you quite exasperate me with all this voluntary work you get involved in. In the village there are people that ought to do more to help you."

"They cannot do the work I am involved in," Elena retorted.

"I need more help in running Glencree Castle, with more of Craig's friends staying. I am not getting any younger. I shall be glad when he is married and Fiona can take over."

"So shall I be glad when he is safely married to Fiona," Elena said with a sigh.

"Then I will have more time for my missionary work."

Harriet looked at her in exasperation. "Oh, I know nothing else matters to you but your missions. It is the only thing you have ever been interested in."

Margot, sitting opposite them, gave a sigh of resignation. She had known the sisters long enough to know Elena's work would always be a bone of contention between them. Elena was determined to follow her chosen path through life – always happily working for good causes. Nothing else had interested her since she was quite young. However, Harriet, embittered by the death of her young husband in a climbing accident whilst on their honeymoon, grew more and more embittered as time passed, and the limp she had sustained in the fall whilst trying to save him grew more pronounced.

CHAPTER 63

The choir had been told to stay behind after the service.

"I wonder what she wants us for today!" exclaimed Emma. "I don't think we sang anything wrong today, Elizabeth, did we?"

"No, I know we didn't." She was only too thankful that the rest of the choir had to stay also. 'At least', she thought, 'it isn't just me!'

"Now," exclaimed Mrs Knowell, tapping her stick on the desk in the vestry where they were all assembled, "the choirmaster will tell you the plans for the extra practice you will need for the anthems to be sung at the wedding of Master Craig and Lady Fiona. And, I might add," she said with emphasis, "the solos will be sung by Miss Ruby and Miss Pearl Crawford."

A buzz of excitement swept round the room.

"Oh, how pleased Mama will be!" exclaimed Ruby. "It will just serve that upstart Elizabeth Anderson right," she whispered behind her hand, not daring to let Mrs Knowell hear her in case she should get angry and change her mind.

A gasp of disapproval came from the rest of the choir.

"But", exclaimed Emma, not to be outdone, "why cannot there be three solos? Elizabeth sang so beautifully last time for the laird and Master Craig. I know they just loved it as I was there when they told Papa so." She grew more and more indignant.

"Sometimes, Emma," Mrs Knowell exclaimed sarcastically, "I wonder whether it is you or I that runs the choir here. Now, we will get on with the business in hand. Here is Mr Knowell now."

"Well, as it is now getting late we will discuss the extra practices when I have heard from Master Craig which hymns and solos he wants," declared Mr Knowell.

The three 'jewel' girls hastened home as fast as they could.

"Just look at them!" exclaimed Emma. "They cannot wait to tell their mother the bad news."

Elizabeth let out a peal of laughter. "Surely you mean *good* news."

"Well, it might be good news for their mother, but it is certainly bad news for us. Goodness knows what Master Craig will say about it."

Elizabeth sighed to herself. 'Emma, oh Emma, if you only knew! I don't want to sing a solo at his wedding.'

"Emma dear, do not worry so on my behalf. It's quite all right," she said, but she wondered what her mother would think about her not being chosen.

"But, my dear Elizabeth, I do so worry about you. You are such a softy. You let that woman, Mrs Knowell, tread all over you. I will have a word with Mama and Papa about it when I get home."

"Oh, please, Emma, for my sake do not speak to your parents. It would upset me so."

"Oh, very well, then," she replied, "I won't."

Emma and Stuart walked with Elizabeth and Robin and Gregory Burns and Rory Cameron down the long lane – their usual stroll after church. The three boys were all vying for Elizabeth's favours.

"It isn't fair!" Robin exclaimed. "Everyone knows Elizabeth can sing much better than either Pearl or Ruby Crawford. I wonder why they have been chosen? I'm sure if Master Craig was making the choice, he would choose her."

"Oh, it's all right," said Elizabeth, getting a bit exasperated with the topic. (If only they knew!) "I don't expect to sing solo every time a big event is taking place."

"Well, you will certainly sing solo at my wedding," Emma said indignantly.

"And when will that be?" Rory exclaimed, but Emma only blushed and looked up at Stuart.

"Well, she won't be singing solo or in the choir at my wedding," Robin declared.

"Why not?" they all exclaimed in dismay, almost in chorus.

"Because on that day she will be my bride."

"I shall be no one's bride for years to come, so don't waste your time waiting for me," Elizabeth said resignedly.

"Oh, but we will, we will!" the three boys exclaimed. "And, hopefully, one of us will be lucky."

At last they reached the small crossroad and said their goodbyes.

Robin and Elizabeth wended their way to Harrison Hall, and he kissed her lightly on the cheek as they parted.

CHAPTER 64

A few days later Elizabeth was returning from the village after posting some mail. She had been kept very busy after Lady Margot's return as there was such a lot of correspondence to take care of. She was thankful to be on her own, and she decided to take the path that led to the old oak tree. It was the first time she had done so since Craig went away.

She found a huge log to stand on (she was not tall enough to reach inside the hollow of the tree), and she groped around inside the opening. There was no note there.

'Oh, why, oh why have I come?' she asked herself. 'Why? Why? Why?'

She pushed the log to one side and hid it from view. She didn't want anyone else to look inside the hollow, which she thought they might do if she left the log where it was.

She decided to take the path round the loch, and, as she idly strolled along, kicking pebbles into the water, she spotted a small boat coming towards her.

"Hello there, Elizabeth. Wait for us to reach you. I have something exciting to tell you," said Emma, standing up in the boat.

Elizabeth could hear Stuart telling Emma to sit down as she was rocking the boat: "Do sit down, dearest Emma. Elizabeth has seen us. It won't take us long to reach her."

At last, to his relief, Emma sat down, but she continued to wave to Elizabeth. When they reached the shore, Emma leaped out and clasped Elizabeth excitedly.

"Well, my dear Emma, what is causing you so much happiness today?" Elizabeth asked, although she could guess.

"Stuart and I are now engaged. I want you to be my bridesmaid."

"I will, I will. I am so happy for you both," Elizabeth said as she hugged them both. "When is your wedding to be?"

"Not until much later in the year, unfortunately. Papa says he will be far too busy arranging Craig and Fiona's wedding to give our wedding the attention he insists on giving it. Of course, I want it to be done properly too. Will you be able to help me plan my arrangements, Elizabeth?"

Emma's eyes danced with delight.

Elizabeth had never seen her so happy.

"Thank goodness I shall be able to wear a pretty dress again, Emma! I'm so tired of these drab dresses I have to wear."

"We are going to have an engagement party soon, so you can put your pretty dress on for that."

"Now, you two chatterboxes! Come, Emma – we must be going before the mists come down," said Stuart anxiously.

They pulled away from the shore.

"I will let you know more later, Elizabeth," Emma called.

Elizabeth watched them until they were out of sight round the bend in the loch. 'How happy I am for them!' she thought. She sighed a deep sigh. Such happiness as theirs could never be for her, she thought. She stood there for several minutes after they left, taking in the beauty of the loch and the mountains beyond. Her thoughts turned to Craig. 'Oh,' she told herself, 'this daydreaming won't do. I must stop wishing for the impossible.'

She went on her way slowly to Harrison Hall.

CHAPTER 65

Emma's party was a huge success. Without Roddy or Craig there Elizabeth did not enjoy it, though it was not for lack of dancing partners. She could see the looks of jealousy from some of the girls from the academy as she was swept from one pair of arms to another. The three Crawford girls tittered in the corner as she passed by.

'Well, let them titter!' she thought. She guessed it was because she hadn't been chosen to sing at Craig's wedding. If they only knew how glad she was not to have been chosen! No one knew how the thought of it filled her with relief. 'I pray to goodness that they don't both fall ill or I may have to take their place. If that happens, I shall just die, I am sure I shall.' She hoped that the laird, or even Craig himself, didn't request that she sang. 'But then,' she thought, 'what if Fiona's mother asks me to sing and Craig says no? He could hardly give any convincing reason. I will think of some excuse. I will pretend to be ill or something.'

"Why so deep in thought, my dear Elizabeth?" asked Robin. "Sometimes you look so lost in thought that it is as if you are not here. Are you thinking about Roddy?"

"Yes. It is such a long time since I saw him."

"Well, he will be home soon. You know how much I love you. Say you will marry me; then we can announce our engagement too."

"But I do not love you, Robin. You deserve to be loved."

"But I could wait until you change your mind," he pleaded.

"That I will never do, dear Robin. I care for you too much to let you waste your life waiting for me."

"Now, you two," said Bart Curzon, "why all this serious chatter? You are not proposing again, are you, Robin? I have told you Elizabeth is going to marry me."

'How I wish these two would stop their silly banter!' she thought. Here she was, her heart breaking with love for a man she could never have, and these two she could have any time. She was glad when Rory broke in on them.

"Are these two not going to dance with you? If not, let us away."

She noticed the look of spite from the Crawford girls as they danced past. The three of them had decided long ago that if one of them could not catch Master Craig for a husband, then Lord Cameron's son was the next one to be pursued. Their mother had also said that he was the next best catch for one of her precious jewels. Now, here he was, with the girl they detested most in his arms instead of one of them. In fact, he hadn't asked any of them to dance.

"Have you heard from Roddy lately?" Rory asked.

"Yes, he will be home soon on leave, Mama said. Papa told me that he had signed on for twenty years and that soon he will be going to the Middle East."

"You must miss him so, and so must your parents."

"Yes, I looked forward to him staying on the island when he came back from the war, and now he has gone again," she said wistfully.

"Try not to be so sad. He will often come home on leave, and there is no war on now so he will be all right."

Robin dropped Elizabeth off after the dance. As he kissed her goodnight, he begged her to marry him, but she shook her head and simply thanked him for bringing her home. She was thankful to see him drive away.

'Why doesn't he go and ask Ruby Crawford?' she thought. 'She is mad about him, so Emma has told me. That is another reason those sisters dislike me so.'

CHAPTER 66

Elizabeth searched every day in the hollow of the tree. Lady Margot had said she could take the dogs for a walk every day, as Charles said his foot still ached if he walked too far.

"I love walking," she told Lady Margot. "The days are so beautiful."

"Yes, they are and you need the fresh air. You look so pale sometimes; you have me quite concerned."

"I am all right, thank you, milady."

"Well, when we have finished the correspondence in the mornings, you are free to go to the village and then for a walk with the dogs, as long as you are back in the evening to sing and play for Mama before she retires. I know it is not much of a gay life for such a young girl as you, but we will have more dances and parties in the summer. We have to get all the funds we can for our servicemen, as well as some for the missions through the church. As you can see, we have a lot of work to do. You are such a help to me, dear girl. I don't know how I could ever manage without you."

Little did Lady Margot know how much Elizabeth looked forward to her long walks in the afternoons with the dogs, when she could be alone with her thoughts.

Every day she took the small path which led past the old oak tree. Then, one day, as she felt in the hollow, she found a folded sheet of paper. How she had longed for this moment! Now, as she grasped the note, she hardly dared breathe. She withdrew it slowly and held it close. She stepped off the log, which she then sat on as she read the note. She already knew what it would say: 'Forget-me-not'. Craig was back!

'Dare I go to the lodge today?' she asked herself. 'I must go. I must see him.'

She slipped the note in her pocket and hid the log as before. Then she untied the dogs from the nearby tree.

She walked nervously up the small, narrow path towards the lodge and tied the dogs to the shrubs close by, out of the sun. She knocked lightly on the door, but there was no answer. She pushed it open and slowly went inside. Suddenly, it crashed behind her, and in a moment she was in his arms and he was kissing her ardently.

"I thought you would never come. I have been waiting for hours. I have been back almost a week, but I couldn't get away sooner. I have left Fiona talking with Aunt Harriet about the furnishings she wants. I told them I would be out longer and more often now that I have further to travel over the estate. So here I am at last."

"But dearest," she exclaimed, "this cannot go on!"

"It can and it will," he insisted. "I know, my darling angel, it is not kind to you."

"Nor Fiona!" she remarked.

"I know that also, but I will have Fiona for the rest of my life after we are married. I shall only have you for these short spells of time until that day."

"Then, my darling," she said, "we shall have to part. I shall not see you after you are married. In fact, I may marry Robin before you are married."

She saw him wince in despair.

"Oh, I know most of the boys on the island are going crazy to marry you, but you are mine – mine."

"But I cannot be yours."

"I know, my dearest, but you can be mine in my thoughts."

"No, my dear Craig, you must put me out of your thoughts, as I must you."

"But how can that be? You know that can never be," he said. He sighed as he held her face in his hands and looked pleadingly into her eyes.

"But it has to be, it has to be."

He silenced any further protest with a kiss, but she freed herself from his arms.

"I must go now, dearest," she said.

"But now I am back, promise me you will come to the lodge when you can. I will come here every day on my way back from visiting the crofts."

"I promise, but really I shouldn't."

"But you will," he insisted, tightening the grip on her arms, and she knew she just had to obey.

CHAPTER 67

Fiona couldn't understand this dashing debonair Craig. She was with Harriet and Elena in the West Wing, where they had been discussing the material Fiona had chosen.

"I wish he would stay and take more interest in the furnishings," she said, "but all he wants to do is go off every day, wet or fine, to visit the estate and to talk to the villagers and the crofters. He is never here with me. He will certainly not spend his days like this after we are married," she said petulantly.

"But it is his duty," Harriet reminded her. "He has to take an interest in the estate, the crofters and the village."

"Well, he can give that job to the ghillies. After all, that's what they are employed for – to look after the estate and keep Craig informed about how everything is going. My father does not race every day all over our estate, like Craig does."

"But Fiona," Elena said, "my dear, I don't think you realise how extensive our estate is since Bruce bought so much of Margot's mother's land. I don't think even Craig realises how much Bruce has bought for you both."

"Oh, I realise it is for the benefit of our sons, but really he must give up all this riding every day. Riding like a wild man! Breezing in and out! He barely gets back for dinner most days. No, I insist a ghillie must take over. I will have a word with Papa Bruce and see if it cannot be done at once."

"But Craig loves to be free to ride over the glens. He has been like that since he was a child. He takes after his mother in his enthusiasm for visiting the crofters. He always does what his mother would have liked him to do. The people's welfare means so much to him," said Elena.

"Well," declared Fiona, still determined to have the last word, "he does all that, then he chases off to Glasgow to see how all his ex-soldiers are getting on."

"But they too, dear Fiona, need someone to help them."

"Well, you, Aunt Elena, and Margot do a lot for them. That should be enough. I am getting a little tired of it and I shall tell Craig so, but first I will ask Papa Bruce about the extra ghillie. I will go and ask him this very minute."

She flounced swiftly out of the room, slamming the door as she went.

Elena walked over to the window and gazed out over the loch. She recalled the moment she had seen Craig with Elizabeth. 'I do hope he is not still seeing her,' she thought. 'Oh no, that cannot be possible.' She sighed.

"Well, I agree with Fiona. Bruce will have to get more help. Craig must spend more time here, especially when Fiona is here. She hardly sees him," said Harriet.

For a moment, lost in thought, Elena had forgotten that Harriet was still in the room.

"There are so many things still to be completed here, and they have to be done before they marry. As it is, Fiona will be going home again soon to prepare for her trip to London. I know Craig has said he is not too keen on going there. I have never heard the likes of it. He knows she cannot possibly go alone. They will only be away about six to eight weeks," said Harriet.

Suddenly, the door flew open, and Fiona flounced in with a big smile on her face.

"That is all settled, then," she said. "Papa Bruce said he will employ two extra ghillies, and he agreed with me that Craig is spending far too much time travelling alone. It will have to end."

CHAPTER 68

Suddenly, one day, as Elizabeth was setting out for the village, Roddy came bounding up the steps of Harrison Hall.

"Roddy, Roddy, my darling Roddy," she screamed out. "Why didn't you let me know you were home?"

"Because, little sister, I only got home last night. Even Mama and Papa didn't know for sure that I was coming. I wanted to surprise you."

"Tell me: are they both well?"

"Yes, they are fine. Come – I will walk as far as the village with you."

It was whilst they were there that Craig, coming out of the library, spotted them. At first, Craig couldn't make out whom Elizabeth was with. A sudden pang of jealousy swept over him and he rode up to them.

"Good morning, Elizabeth," he said, smiling disarmingly. "It is a lovely day."

"Yes, it is, Master Craig – a truly lovely day."

"Ah, I see your dear brother is home. So it is, as you say, a truly lovely day. How nice to see you again, Roddy!" he said, and he reached down from his horse to shake Roddy's hand.

"I am glad to see you again, Master Craig."

"How long are you home for?"

"Just a week, but I will be here every day to see my dear sister."

Craig glanced at Elizabeth, as Roddy bent down to stroke the two dogs, who were getting a little alarmed at the horse's hoofs dancing too close to them for comfort.

"Where will your next posting be? Have you any idea?" asked Craig.

"The Middle East, I think."

"But, Roddy dear, that is so far away," Elizabeth gasped.

"I know, my dear. That is why I have promised Mama to come and see you every day. Of course, I might not get sent there immediately. I might even manage another short leave before I go."

"Oh, I do hope so," she replied.

"Well, I will bid you both good day," said Craig.

He turned his horse round and shook hands with Roddy before riding away.

"I will see no harm comes to your charming sister whilst you are away," he called back.

"Thank you, sir," replied Roddy. He then asked, "What did he mean by that last remark, I wonder?"

"He says similar things on many occasions. Emma says he feels responsible for all of us," Elizabeth replied, anxious to change the subject. "Emma and Stuart are now engaged. They are to marry later in the year, sometime after Master Craig's wedding, and I am to be Emma's chief bridesmaid."

"How nice for you! When are you and Robin going to get engaged? He has loved you for a long time."

"I don't think I shall ever marry."

"Of course you will, one day. You won't always have Mama and Papa close by, and goodness knows where I will get to in my travels. I should like to hear of you and Robin married and settled. Now, you go and post your mail, then I will walk back with you. I must call on my other friends and get back across the loch before it gets too late."

True to his promise, Roddy was over every day to escort Elizabeth to the village. He sometimes took her along in the trap to visit his many friends, before returning her to Harrison Hall.

Sometimes Craig, on his afternoon rides over the glens, would wave to them as they passed. His heart was longing to be with her. How he longed for her nearness! His feeling of emptiness he dared not admit, even to himself. He had a long talk with his father about the two extra ghillies he was going to appoint.

"But, Papa, we don't need them yet. I can still attend to everything on the estate until I leave for London with Fiona."

"Well, I think we do need them. Fiona is far too much alone; you should be spending more time helping her in the West Wing."

"But, Papa, it is only curtains and fripperies, and Aunt Harriet is helping with those."

"That's as may be, my son. I know Fiona does not like riding as much as you do, or visiting the crofters as much as your dear mother did. I agree, she will have to accompany you after your marriage. It will be her duty to do so, and on that I shall insist, but until then you must spend more time with her here."

"Very well, Papa, if that is your wish, but if I stay here in the morning, I shall need to ride every afternoon. Flaxen needs the exercise as much as I need the fresh Highland air, with my weak chest."

"Yes, I understand, my boy. Choose which part of the day suits you best for your visiting."

"Thank you, Papa."

"My son, I miss our rides, but, with all the extra land on the estate now, it is impossible for us to ride side by side as we used to. Perhaps when we get the extra ghillies, and they have got to know the area we have to cover, we shall be able to ride together, as before."

CHAPTER 69

Roddy came to say his last farewell to all at Harrison Hall, and Lady Margot allowed Elizabeth to ride in the trap with him to the village jetty. They clasped each other tightly as they said their goodbyes. Elizabeth was in tears.

"Now, promise me, dear, you will see as much as you can of Mama and Papa. I will write to them soon, telling them where I am. Promise me you will take care of them whilst I am away and that you will never leave them."

"I promise, Roddy, but you know I would never leave them. Even if I do marry Robin, as you think I should, I shall still be nearby."

"I know he has always loved you and I know, deep down, you must love him also. I am pleased to think that you have given a little more thought to the idea of marrying him."

He kissed her once more as he clambered aboard his boat, and he gave her a final wave before he pulled away.

She tucked away her damp handkerchief in her pocket as she drove back to the hall. Roddy's words were running over and over through her troubled mind. "If I have to go to the Middle East, I might not be home for several years," he had said. She hated the thought that she might not see her darling Roddy for years and years.

'No, it's not possible,' she thought as she reached once again for her handkerchief and searched in vain for a dry patch on which to wipe away her tears.

With Roddy gone, she felt sad and forsaken. Her father rowed across the loch twice a week with supplies to the village, and he always called at Harrison Hall to give her any news. She also saw her parents at church on Sundays. These visits made her realise how alone she would be if anything happened to her parents, but escaping from her loneliness by marrying someone she did not truly love was unthinkable.

After the extra choir practices on Saturday afternoons, she spent the time at the vicarage with Emma, discussing her wedding arrangements and attire. Emma realised that Miss Grant would very soon be commandeered by all and sundry in the village to make their new clothes to attend the wedding celebrations of Master Craig and Lady Fiona.

"So you see, Elizabeth, I am determined to have my dress and yours, and my bridesmaids' dresses, well and truly ready as soon as Craig's wedding is over. Elizabeth, you are not listening to a word I say. Why is there such a faraway look always in your eyes?"

Elizabeth looked up, startled. She fingered the pretty pink voile she had chosen for her dress.

"What gallant knight in shining armour do you keep dreaming of?"

"Well, really, Emma! I was wondering how far away my dear Roddy is now."

If only she could tell her dearest friend what she was really thinking! 'Oh, Emma, if I could really tell you!' she thought.

"Well, your gallant knight in shining armour will turn up one of these days," Emma replied disarmingly, "and it could be Robin in disguise." She laughed.

"Yes, it could be Robin," Elizabeth replied disconsolately.

"What do you think of the anthems we are going to sing for Craig and Fiona's wedding? Papa thinks they are quite nice. Do you think I should have them for my wedding?"

"Yes, I agree they are very nice anthems, but I think you should choose your very own. Lady Fiona, I am sure, would not like you to have the same as she and Master Craig have chosen."

"Yes, you may be right. I know Craig wouldn't mind, but as for Lady Fiona, she will be sure to make a fuss if she ever gets to know. Papa is not too keen on Pearl and Ruby Crawford singing solos at their wedding. He keeps asking me why you are not singing a solo. When I tell him that no one knows why Mr and

Mrs Knowell chose them instead of you, he just tut-tuts and says, 'I cannot understand it.'

"Well," said Elizabeth, anxious to change the subject, "I think they sing them very nicely."

"Oh, Elizabeth, you exasperate me at times. Anyway, you must sing at my wedding, no matter what Mrs Knowell decides. Promise you will."

"Of course I will, my dear Emma."

CHAPTER 70

Later that week, as Bruce was riding through the glen on his way back from Harrison Hall, the rain clouds suddenly burst with such ferocity that he decided to take shelter in the shooting lodge. He spurred his horse into a mad gallop, and when he arrived he leaped off and threw the door open with a crash. He strode into the lodge, shaking his wet cap and cape as he did so.

"Oh, I see, my son," he said as his eyes rested on Craig and the girl clasped in his arms: "you and Fiona got caught in the storm also."

Craig quickly released Elizabeth from his embrace. She had only just arrived and had not had time to take off her hood, but, as Craig released her, it fell on to her shoulders, revealing her long, golden ringlets. She turned and gave a gasp of dismay. When she realised who it was, she started to tremble. Craig held her close as if to protect her from his father's wrath.

"Get home to your work, you village hussy. Get to your work," Bruce roared at her, his face purple with rage.

She struggled free of Craig's grasp, pulled her cloak quickly round her shoulders and fled. Bruce, too shocked for further speech, sank down in the huge armchair.

Craig, torn between the two, quickly decided that his father was less in need. He rushed after Elizabeth and saw her running madly down the lane, the dogs bounding alongside. He drew level and leaped from his horse. He lifted her saturated, exhausted body and the two dogs into the saddle, leaped up behind her and raced to Harrison Hall.

Charles heard the clatter of the horse's hoofs, and he rushed to take the dogs from Craig. Margot came bustling across from the house.

"My dear Craig, whatever is the matter? Is Elizabeth ill?"

"No, I saw her running for here as I left my lodge, and I managed to catch her up."

"Charles, hold on to the dogs."

"Yes, I have them, milady."

Craig lifted Elizabeth carefully off his horse and rushed up the steps.

"Take her to the library, Craig, and put her in the big chair by the fire."

He put her carefully down and brushed her damp ringlets from round her face.

"Now, Craig, you must stay till the storm abates."

"Well, it is not too bad at present," he said as he glanced through the window. "I must get back before it breaks again."

'Any excuse', he thought, 'to get away!'

"Thank you, Craig, for bringing her home. It is so kind of you to go out of your way. You can stay the night, Craig, if you wish."

"Thank you, Margot, but I must hurry home. I promised Fiona I would be back early. I do hope Elizabeth doesn't get a chill," he said, looking at her with concern.

"No, I am sure she will be all right as soon as she has changed into dry clothes. You must get away before the weather changes again."

Margot watched him ride away; then she hurried back to the library.

"My dear child, you are drenched, as are the dogs," she said to Elizabeth. "I told you, my dear, not to go too far on these walks. You would have got back before the storm broke if you had heeded my words."

Elizabeth rubbed her hair with the towel the nurse had brought in.

"Now go, my child, and get out of those wet clothes as soon as you can; then join us for dinner."

"Thank you, milady," Elizabeth replied as she rose to go. "I am so sorry for everything. Will the dogs be all right?" she asked anxiously.

"Yes, Charles is drying them off."

Elizabeth dropped her a little curtsy as she left. She rushed to her room, went over to the window and looked towards the castle.

'Oh, my darling,' she thought, 'this has got to be the end. I cannot ever meet you again. I shall never again feel your arms around me – never, ever again.'

She changed hurriedly, still trembling from the encounter. To be called a hussy by the laird himself! Soon, she felt sure, she would be derided all over the island. Every finger would be pointing at her.

"There she is – the village hussy."

What would her parents and her darling Roddy say if they ever got to know?

CHAPTER 71

Bruce sat for a long time pondering. 'How long has this been going on?' he asked himself, over and over again.

Craig burst into his lodge. He had not noticed his father's horse tethered nearby. He slammed the door to before he realised his father was still sitting where he had left him. Craig had decided to stay for some time at the lodge before returning home.

"Papa, you are still here!" he exclaimed in dismay. "I thought that as the storm has abated you would have returned home."

"Yes, I am still here. I was thinking how very busy Fiona is, making a home for you and your children in the West Wing, while that scheming village hussy is coming here to meet you."

"She is not a hussy, Papa. Do not refer to her in that way again," Craig replied angrily.

"This meeting was not of your doing, my son." In his eyes, his son could do no wrong.

"It is my fault, Papa, not hers."

"She is the cause of all this, my boy. Don't blame yourself."

"I am blaming myself because I am to blame for her being here." He stood looking out of the window, his back to his father.

"I know you are trying to protect her, my son, but I do not accept that you are to blame. You would never stoop to anything that would bring dishonour to our name, like this. No," he said emphatically, "this girl alone is to blame and I forbid you to ever see her again. I won't ask you how long this has been going on. The matter is now closed. Come, my boy – we must get away home."

They rode home in silence. It was the first time they had had cross words and it affected them both deeply. Neither spoke as they dismounted.

Elena, as usual, was the first to greet them. She was always the most anxious if they were delayed, and she had been watching for them from the window upstairs.

"Here you are, saturated by that dreadful storm. I do hope you don't get ill!" she exclaimed as she came rushing down the stairs to greet them in the hall. She noted the strange silence between them at once and a puzzled look crossed her face. "Where are you going, Craig?" she called to him as he raced past her and rushed up the stairs, two at a time.

"To my room to change. Please tell Fiona I will see her at dinner."

"Yes, I will. Now, Bruce, you come near the fire whilst Jamie takes your wet cloak. I will pour you a drink; then you too must go and change. I thought Craig would have joined you in here for a drink before going to his room."

Bruce sat down, drink in hand, and gazed into the fire. Then he gazed up at Isabelle's picture.

"Is Craig back also?" Fiona asked as she entered the room with Harriet.

"Yes," said Elena. "He is just as wet as Bruce. He asked me to tell you he will see you at dinner."

"Oh, very well, then. I shall go and change now. We have had such a busy day, Aunt Harriet, haven't we? I do wish my darling Craig would be a little more interested in our future home. I need his opinion on so many things." She left the room, quite annoyed.

"Bless the day when they are married!" said Harriet. "I cannot make Craig out lately. He seems to get more wild. It's as though he has to be free – as though every moment will be his last. He is never at home to discuss anything with anyone."

Bruce, tired of their chatter, went to his room, and, after changing, he stood for a long time looking out over the loch. He had sat for many hours contemplating his son's devil-may-care attitude. 'He is so much more assured and independent than when he left for the front,' Bruce thought. He could still see in Craig occasional flashes of the mischievous prankster who loved to play tricks on all and sundry, but that side of his character was at odds with his occasional outbursts of bitterness and his wanting to be alone for long spells. Yes, Fiona was right to complain about how little time he spent with her when she was busy in the West Wing. Was this hussy the cause of it all? Yes, more ghillies would be the answer. Only the other day, the head ghillie had mentioned that more help would be needed now that all the extra land had been bought. 'Yes, I will deal with the matter,' he promised himself.

At dinner that night there was the usual chatter. Harriet and Fiona told them all of the progress they were making. Only minor things were now needed. Elena did not fail to see the strange silence between father and son, and she noticed the lack of interest they were showing in the topic being discussed.

'What is bothering them so?' she wondered. 'Craig could be unhappy because Fiona is leaving tomorrow to join her parents travelling to London, but he will be joining her in a few days' time. And Bruce, what is troubling him? Is it the thought that, before the year is out, he will have to take second place in his son's affections?' Whatever it was, she couldn't fathom it. 'I know Craig does not want to go to London,' she thought, 'but it has to be.'

As Craig, Fiona, Harriet and Elena sat playing cards after dinner, the jolly banter between them was much in evidence.

"I do believe, my dear Craig," Elena said, "you have had more than your usual wee dram tonight. Never have I heard you laugh so heartily."

"Yes, dear Aunt, I think you are right as usual."

"Well, he is always happy when we are together," Fiona rejoined, "and tonight is no exception, in spite of my leaving tomorrow. When we return from London, we shall soon be married. I am waiting for my darling to name the actual date. Maybe he is keeping it a surprise for me on our return. You will join me soon, darling, when you have got rid of all these forestry officers and settled all the arrangements for the welfare of your servicemen? Aunt Elena, you will relieve him of the latter duties, which I find so irksome, won't you?"

"Most certainly I will whilst he is away, but I daresay he will want to take up the duties on his return. He knows how busy I shall be with Margot and our correspondence for the overseas missions. I cannot leave it all to Margot."

"Well," said Fiona with a pout, "Craig will just have to get another man to attend to these matters. I don't intend to be left alone whilst he goes visiting."

"Don't worry your beautiful little head, my darling," said Craig. He kissed her hand. "I shall never, ever leave you alone when we are married. I have already got someone to take over most of these duties for me."

"Thank you, my darling. I know you will do anything I wish," she replied, and she kissed him on the cheek. "I will make sure you obey my every wish after our marriage, my darling Craig."

Elena looked at her, knowing only too well what she would try on after they were married. 'But you don't know our dear boy, Fiona,' she thought.

Bruce gazed at them both. "How lucky I shall be to have such a lovely daughter around me – and soon my grandsons! Oh, what a joy that will be for me and Glencree! The great name of McNair will be carried on for evermore. All I wish for will be a reality at last." He sighed with happiness and gazed up at Isabelle's picture. "You will be happy too, my darling, won't you?"

He had forgotten for a moment that he was not alone. The others were all gazing at him.

Elena was the first to speak: "Now it is getting late. We must put the cards away. I daresay, Craig and Fiona, you will be taking Flint for his evening stroll?"

"Craig darling, do you mind if I do not go with you tonight? I have had such a busy day. I am so tired," said Fiona.

He walked with her to the bottom of the stairs and kissed her goodnight. He was glad he would be alone on his evening stroll with Flint. Even his father had not suggested he accompany him.

'How very odd!' thought Elena when she saw Bruce ascend the stairs as Craig disappeared through the hall door. 'It is most unlike them not to go together. I wonder what is wrong?'

Bruce stood looking out over the loch. His thoughts were in turmoil: 'How long has this village hussy been arranging to meet up with Craig in his lodge? It could only have been for a few days' he told himself over and over. 'Craig has been at Fiona's home for some time, and if he had been seeing this hussy before, surely I would have heard about it. Harriet and Elena would have mentioned it.' Bruce knew that, if the villagers had seen anything amiss, it would have been the sole topic in the village and he would certainly have got to know about it. 'No,' he decided, 'it must have only happened on this one occasion. It's just as well I caught her at her little game. It will never happen again – I will make sure of that – but I must make extra sure over the next few weeks as Fiona is leaving tomorrow. I only wish Craig was going down with her instead of having to attend to these forestry plans and discussions. However, he insists on getting the project completed before he goes to see his ex-servicemen before joining Fiona and her parents. I will call in at the lodge every day, and I will make sure she never traps my dear son in her snare ever again.'

Craig flung his cane against the wall and closed his bedroom door. He could hear Flint, who had followed him upstairs and flung himself on the mat outside, whimpering softly, as though he knew how deeply disturbed his master was.

Craig stood a long time, gazing out towards Harrison Hall before flinging himself onto his bed. He lay with his hands under his head as he gazed at the ceiling. 'My poor innocent darling! What am I going to do?' he thought. He could still feel her trembling body in his arms as he tried to shield her from his father's rage. 'She's no hussy. She is the angel I adore. I am the one to blame, not you, my love, not you. How can I ever risk seeing her again and causing her more anguish? But how can I live and not see her again? That is unthinkable. But how? How?' He buried his face in the pillow. 'It is wrong, wrong. I must only think of my dear Fiona – the one I am to marry soon. I love you too, my darling Fiona – but it's not the same, it's not the same.'

CHAPTER 72

Margot was quite dismayed to hear from Nurse about her mother's weakening condition. She decided that the doctor should visit.

The doctor agreed that her mother's condition was getting more serious. He said that she needed a nurse day and night, which he said he would arrange. He also said he would call twice daily.

The villagers were all deeply concerned. Craig told Elena that he would ride over immediately and convey their concern.

"Tell Margot I shall come over every day and attend to all the correspondence with Elizabeth," said Elena.

"Yes, I will," he called as he raced away. He was hoping he would be able to see Elizabeth more often now until he left for London.

"Is Elizabeth in?" he asked Charles as he leapt off his horse.

"Yes, but she has just gone into the garden to gather some flowers for Her Ladyship's room."

She looked up, quite startled, as he approached.

"How is Lady Roxburgh today, Elizabeth?"

"Very weak and ill."

"We are all very concerned to hear the news."

"Yes, it must be very worrying for Lady Margot. Now, if you will excuse me, I must return."

"Yes, I understand, my angel, but when can I see you alone?"

"Never, never, Master Craig."

She straightened the flowers she had plucked and turned to go.

"But I must before I leave. Meet me down at the boathouse. You won't be missed for a few moments. You will not be singing for Lady Roxburgh until she is well. No one uses the boathouse now. I will sail round and wait for you there. You must come before I leave. Say you will. Say it."

"I will try."

He hurried into the hall.

"Ah, there you are Craig. Charles told me you had come. I was with Mama. The doctor is with her now," said Margot.

"We are all very distressed to hear the news. Aunt Elena says she will come every day to help with all the correspondence with Elizabeth."

"That will be a great help. I know you will be leaving soon to join Fiona, but come as often as you can before you leave. Now, I must return to Mama and hear what the doctor has to say. Thank you, dear boy, for calling. Goodbye."

He hung round for several minutes, hoping in vain for another glimpse of Elizabeth. He sighed with disappointment, bade Charles good day and rode away.

CHAPTER 73

Several days later Elizabeth heard Craig's voice outside the library door where she was working with Elena. She felt a thrill at the sound of his voice, but it was torture to be unable to rush into his arms. Only once had she managed to meet him at the boathouse. The path down to it was hopelessly overgrown, but she vowed she would attempt any path, however difficult, to be in his arms again in the few days they had left.

Every moment she waited filled her with a fear she couldn't control – a fear she knew he would disperse the moment she was in his arms. She longed to hear him whispering her name over and over again between his passionate kisses. How safe she felt when she was with him! If only she could stay in his arms for ever!

Several mornings later, as she entered the breakfast room, Lady Margot, who had been up all night, informed her that Lady Roxburgh had died peacefully in her sleep.

"Oh, milady!" she cried. She tried in vain to quell her tears. "I loved her so dearly and I am going to miss her so." She dabbed her eyes. "Such a dear lady!" she murmured.

"Sit down, my dear, " said Margot, putting her hand on Elizabeth's shoulder. "She loved you very dearly, but she has suffered a long time. Now she is at rest."

The church was overflowing at the funeral. Lady Roxburgh had requested that Elizabeth sing her favourite hymn. Elizabeth knew Craig's eyes would be on her – a point not missed by his father – but she never looked up from her hymn book.

CHAPTER 74

Harrison Hall felt very empty. The nurses had departed and life for Elizabeth carried on as before. She was still catching up with the delayed correspondence. Now she was almost always alone, as Lady Margot visited the city with either Bruce or Lady Elena.

After one of these trips with Bruce, Lady Margot suddenly exclaimed one morning, "Soon, Elizabeth, I shall be returning to India. Nearly all my transactions are finalised."

Elizabeth looked at her askance. "India, milady? It is so far away."

"Yes, it is, my dear, but I shall at long last be able to see my daughter and two lovely granddaughters – the darling twin girls. I had to leave India to come to Mama before they were born." She smiled happily in anticipation of seeing them.

"I have spoken to Mrs Murray at the academy and she said she could offer you a position as her secretary when I leave. Would you like that, Elizabeth? I know she is especially fond of you. She hopes that one day you will be part of her family, knowing how fond Robin is of you."

"Yes, milady, I think I should like to be her secretary."

The suddenness of events had taken her aback. Lady Margot noticed her pondering and her slight hesitation.

"It is the only vacant position I know of in the area. I am sure your parents wouldn't like you to move away, especially now Roddy will soon be leaving the country."

"Yes, yes, milady, I couldn't possibly go far away. I am sure I shall be quite all right at the academy. Thank you, milady. I am sure my parents and Roddy will be very pleased for me to accept."

CHAPTER 75

"Yes, yes, my angel," her father declared when he heard the proposition. "How kind of Her Ladyship to suggest it! She is always so considerate. You must thank her for us, my angel, until your mother and I can see her to express our thanks in person."

'Well,' she thought, 'I shall still be near my darling, although I know I shan't be able to speak to him after his marriage. That I shall never do; I shall never meet him alone again.'

She went to the academy with Lady Margot, and she was shown her accommodation and the office where she would be working.

'I shall be able to see more of Emma, as she attends here. How lovely!' she thought. Then another thought crossed her mind: 'I shall also see more of those despicable 'jewel' girls.' She pulled a wry face as she thought of them. The afternoon at the dressmaker's came to mind. 'Well, I shall just avoid them as much as possible.'

(Many of the girls would have gone to finishing schools in Switzerland, but, owing to the war, their parents had refused to let them go. Mrs Murray therefore employed an extra teacher to teach the girls the fine arts of the finishing schools.)

Robin was, as expected, thrilled at the idea of Elizabeth working at the academy, although he knew he would be away most of the time, studying to be a cleric. However, the girl he loved would always be at home, waiting to greet him on his return.

CHAPTER 76

"Now, my dear sisters, Harriet and Elena!" exclaimed Bruce one day.

They both knew that when he used both their names in that tone of voice he had something exciting to tell them. What could it be? Their puzzled expressions as they looked at each other made him smile.

"Well now," he began, "how would you both like to live at Harrison Hall after Craig and Fiona are married? I have decided to purchase it from Margot for you. It will be somewhere quiet for both of you, as soon the castle will be filled with happy, noisy, laughing children and you won't get much peace. I know you made a great sacrifice when you gave up the lovely home you shared to take care of Craig and myself when our darling Isabelle died. In this way I can make it up to you. All Margot's property will be mine, and all the details will be completed before she sails for India, immediately after the wedding."

"Oh, it is a wonderful idea!" said Elena, "but I do hope, Harriet dear, you won't be too lonely when I go on my travels."

"No, of course I won't. You won't be going for quite a few years yet, and by then I expect Craig's children will call to see me. I will have plenty to do around the hall. It has become so neglected since Lady Roxburgh lost interest due to her ill health. Of course, Margot has been too busy with all her own plans. Besides, we will still be near the village and all the people we know."

"I have always thought of it as my second home," Elena enthused. "It is a lovely idea, Bruce."

They all agreed and Elena hugged Bruce warmly.

"Thank you, dear brother," Harriet said. As soon as Fiona has got used to everything at Glencree, we will move."

CHAPTER 77

Lady Margot's extended stay settling matters in the city gave Elizabeth more time to go to the boathouse than she had dared hope. What a thrill she felt as she watched Craig tie up his boat and rush into her arms! The thought of his father or anyone else seeing them filled her with fear and she trembled uncontrollably.

"It is all right, my precious one. I am determined to see you in spite of my father, so don't be so afraid."

"But, my darling," she whispered, "after you are married I shall never see you alone again."

"We must not waste time talking about that. Our time together is too precious," he said, and he kissed her again and again before she could reply.

He was delighted when she told him about her position at the academy.

"Well, at least", he declared, "I shall know you are not far away from me. Will you marry Robin one day?"

"Yes, I daresay I will," she replied.

He winced and hugged her closer. "But he will never love you as I love you," he said with a sigh; "and you will never love him as you love me. I know you do love me, in spite of your silence. I am leaving for London very soon, my darling angel. How am I ever going to live without seeing you for so long? I shall just die," he said. He kissed her and hugged her so tightly she could hardly breathe. "Promise me you will meet me here when I return. Promise, promise," he demanded.

"But, my darling, I might not be here. I shall be at the academy."

"Oh, drat!" he exclaimed angrily, kicking some pebbles in frustration. "Well, I will leave a note in the old oak tree – the one we call our own. You will surely be going for some walks. When you find my note, come to me at the lodge. Papa will be too busy to come visiting again. Never fear, my love."

"But I do fear, my love, and I shall only come until you are marry, then never, ever again." She sighed.

He smothered her with kisses.

"Why does the world have to be so cruel to us," he said. "Why? Why?"

CHAPTER 78

It was the afternoon before Craig left for London. He and Elizabeth spent their last few moments together in the boathouse.

"How I wish I didn't have to go to London. It always overpowers me. I feel so hemmed in I cannot breathe, but I will be back as soon as I can."

"Dearest," she whispered, "it is going to seem like a lifetime."

"But I must go now, my darling," he whispered. "I have so much to do before I leave. Everyone will be wondering where I am, and they worry more than ever if I am sailing on the loch."

"Charles, is your mistress at home?" asked Bruce as he alighted from his horse.

"No, sir, she has gone to the village."

"Well, I will await her return."

"Will you wait inside, sir? I will get some tea prepared for you."

"No, Charles, it is too nice a day to be indoors. I will go down to the stables eventually, but first I will stroll in the garden."

He wandered slowly down the narrow path that led to the small rise and gazed out to the mountains in the distance. It was a view he never tired of.

'To think that one day my grandsons will also see this!' he thought. 'What a heritage for them! What a lucky man I am to be able to give it all to them!' He waved his arm around as if he was already showing them. He was so lost in thought that he had forgotten he was alone. 'I am so used to my dear son Craig being with me,' he thought. 'I wonder where he is this afternoon – probably visiting more of his friends before he leaves.'

As he turned to go, a movement near the old boathouse, just below, caught his eye. He raised his glasses and became speechless with rage when he saw Craig and Elizabeth in a passionate embrace. He watched as Craig climbed into his boat, which was moored close by. Craig blew Elizabeth a kiss, which she returned as he sailed away.

Bruce leaned against a tree, partially hidden by shrubs. He grew more and more furious with every moment. He watched as Elizabeth scrambled up the small winding path, passed within a few feet of him and went into the house. He stayed where he was for a long time, trying to contain his anger, his cheeks a fiery red with rage.

"She has dared to defy me!" he repeated angrily, over and over again. "How dare she!" He had never had anyone defy him like this before. "Thank goodness Craig is leaving tomorrow! I will make sure this village hussy sees him no more. I shall tell my son what I have witnessed today when he returns from London. So this was the reason he was spending time sailing. Now I know why he hasn't been riding as much as before. That little hussy must have contrived all this, taking advantage of the fact that Margot is away." He struck his cane again and again against his thigh before walking slowly into the house.

Elizabeth ran swiftly to her room. She was glad that Lady Margot had not yet returned. She flung open her window and leaned out as far as she could, hoping to catch sight of Craig before he rounded the bend towards Glencree.

CHAPTER 79

Bruce was sitting in the lounge when Margot arrived.

"My dear Bruce, how delightful to see you! Almost everything is settled about the deeds of the house. I am so glad Harriet and Elena have decided to live here. I shall book my sailing ticket for India as soon as Fiona and Craig are married."

"I am going to miss you a great deal, Margot, when you go," he said sadly.

"And I you, Bruce. We have known each other since childhood."

"Have you decided what to do with the servants?"

"Well, Cook is retiring and the maids have got fresh positions in the village, but they would be only too willing to come back here if Harriet and Elena wish them to."

"And what is going to happen to your companion?"

She looked at him questioningly. "I have got her a position at the academy, helping Mrs Murray with her correspondence. Why do you ask?"

He did not reply. "I would have thought", he said at last, "that she could have found something better in the city, with her experience."

'So the little hussy has wheedled a position at the academy,' he thought, seething inwardly.

Margot watched him with a puzzled look on her face. "Well, she would certainly do very well if she went, but I thought that as her brother will soon be leaving for overseas, and may be away for some years, it would be kinder to her parents to give her the chance to stay close to them."

"You are always thinking of others, Margot. You're always so considerate. That is one thing I have always admired you for."

"But you are the same, dear Bruce, where our people are concerned. Why all this questioning, Bruce?"

"Well, I am very perturbed as I have just seen your companion and Craig coming out of your boathouse."

"Well, she often goes for a walk by the loch. Are you sure it was Craig and not Robin Murray? I know they are hoping to marry one day."

"I know my own son," he shouted angrily. Up to that moment he had remained calm.

"Bruce! Bruce!" she exclaimed, shocked by his anger. "Bruce, there is no need for that tone of voice with me."

She was feeling very tired from her long journey and she sat down wearily.

"My dear Margot, please forgive me, but this is not the first time that I have seen them together."

"Well, she is often out walking. I am sure that if they met it was by mere chance."

"Well, I don't think so." His voice rose again in anger. "Forgive me again, dear Margot. I can see you are very tired after your journey. I will call and see you another day. Goodbye, my dear."

Margot could see he was deeply troubled as he rode away.

CHAPTER 80

"You are strangely quiet, my son, this morning," Bruce said as they all sat at breakfast next day. "I would have thought you would be joyful and excited at the thought of going to join your sweetheart, Fiona," Bruce said with emphasis.

Craig looked up at him, but decided not to comment on his father's emphasis of Fiona's name.

"Yes, Papa," he replied, "I am more than delighted to be joining Fiona."

Elena looked up at them. She sensed there was something not quite right in this conversation, but, although she thought about it for several minutes, she could not quite place what it was. It was not like these two to behave so puzzlingly. Their every thought and action was normally like an open book to her. She looked at Harriet, but she was talking to Shona so she had not noticed anything amiss. 'Ah well,' Elena thought, 'maybe I am imagining things.'

"I was thinking of the fact that I shall be spending so much time in London, away from my lovely mountains," Craig continued.

"Yes, that explains it," said Bruce. "Well then, my boy, are you ready? I told Jamie to see that the carriage was here for 9 a.m."

At that moment Jamie knocked and entered the room.

Craig kissed the aunts and his father hugged him close.

"I am going to miss you so much my boy," he said.

"And I you, Papa."

With a final wave, Craig was away down the drive, deep in thought most of the way.

'It will be six weeks before I see my angel again. Six long, long weeks!' he sighed.

"Stop the carriage, Zan, at Harrison Hall. I want to say goodbye to Lady Margot."

As they drew up outside, he leaped from the carriage and Charles came out to meet him.

"Is Her Ladyship in, Charles?"

"No, Master Craig, she has taken the dogs for a stroll, but she won't be long. Elizabeth is in the library if you want to wait. Shall I tell her you are here?"

"No, thank you. I will go to her."

He raced along the hall and into the library, closing the door behind him. She was sitting at her desk, and she looked up in alarm as he rushed to her side. He gathered her in his arms.

"Craig dearest, you should not have come."

"I could not go without trying to see you again, my darling. I love you so. Just tell me once that you love me."

She shook her head. "That I can never say. Never!"

"But I know that you do, so that will sustain me whilst I am away."

Craig kissed her passionately and she tried to free herself from his embrace, but he clung to her more tightly. Just then the curtains of the open French windows parted and Lady Margot appeared. She had come round the garden path and had not seen his carriage. She was aghast.

"Go to your room at once, Elizabeth," she demanded. "Craig," she exclaimed, as the door closed after her, "whatever is the meaning of this?"

"Oh, you wouldn't understand. It is all my fault. Please do not blame Elizabeth. I called to say goodbye to you before I left for London. Please forgive me for taking advantage of your absence to kiss Elizabeth goodbye also."

"I will try to understand, my boy, but you know this fondness you have for her cannot go on."

"Yes, I know. My God, how I know!" Craig's knuckles were white as he gripped the chair. "I beg of you, please do not let my father know about this. Please – I beg of you," he pleaded. "Please promise you will not mention to anyone what you saw today. It is all my fault."

"All right, my boy, your secret is safe with me. You will soon forget all this when you see your lovely Fiona. You will marry her and you will be together for always; this little flirtation will pass as though it had never happened."

"Yes, maybe you are right. You so often are."

"Now, you have a long journey ahead. Will you have some tea before you leave?"

"No, thank you, Margot. Goodbye."

He went outside and leaped into the carriage. Margot watched until he was out of sight.

'There's another one in troubled thought,' she said to herself, as she recalled watching his father ride away the day before. She went back into the library and called for some tea. She recalled the day when Craig had carried Elizabeth in after the storm. 'Had they been together then?' she wondered. 'And how often have they been together since? Poor, poor Elizabeth!' Margot knew the girl would not have pursued this course on her own. She was not that sort of girl. She knew Craig could be persistent, determined to have his own way. The poor child would not stand a chance of rejecting his advances. 'It cannot go on and he knows it. When he is married, it will all be over, thank goodness.' Then a small doubt crossed her mind: 'What if Craig, in his determined way, would not let it be over?' She knew Elizabeth would make no move, but she was not sure about

Craig. He was like his father: always determined to have his own way. She put the thought out of her mind. It was unthinkable.

She called Elizabeth to the library.

"Come – we have a lot of work to do and lots of matters to settle before you take up your other post. I shall not concern myself with what happened today. I shall treat it as though it never happened."

Elizabeth was blushing with embarrassment. "Thank you, milady. I am so sorry."

"Now, let us get on with our work. I shall not leave for India until after the wedding, so we have quite some time yet."

CHAPTER 81

Bruce watched as Craig drove out of sight, then wended his way to his room and stood at the window overlooking the loch.

Elena watched Bruce go slowly up the stairs and she was struck by the unhappiness on his face.

'How he will miss his boy! It will be many weeks before he sees him again. He has never liked him being out of his sight. It is not good, as I know, this longing he always has for him. How I wish our dearest Isabelle could have been spared to share his life! Ah well!' She sighed. 'Soon Craig and Fiona will be married; then all will be well. Hasten the day!'

A plan was going round and round in Bruce's mind.

"Yes, yes!" he exclaimed, over and over again. Then he muttered, "Of course – that is the answer. Tomorrow I will ride over and tell Margot what I have decided."

Bruce woke next morning after a restless night. He knew only too well that if he forbade Craig to see this girl, he would still continue to see her. He knew his son would abhor disobeying him, but he also knew he would still contrive some way to meet her. His son was so like himself. Hadn't he been the same when he married after only a few weeks of courtship? He had had no father to forbid him, but his sisters had begged him time and time again to wait a little longer before marrying.

"Bruce dear, why not have a longer engagement?" Elena had begged of him. She was the one he always took most notice of, but this time her pleas were to no avail. He was determined to go ahead. He had listened to no one, and he knew Craig would not heed anyone either – even himself. It was possible he would go on seeing her even after he married Fiona. If this scheming hussy continued with her tricks, he would fall prey to her insistence and meet her somewhere. Neither he nor Fiona could be with him all the time. Another way to put an end to the situation had to be found and he was certain his proposed plan would work.

He alighted swiftly from his horse when he arrived at Harrison Hall. He hurried up the steps with only a brief nod to Charles and the groom as they came to greet him.

"Good morning, sir," they both said as they doffed their caps to him, but he hardly looked in their direction.

'That's unusual,' they thought. He usually had a few joking things to say to them, but not today.

"Is Lady Margot in?" he demanded brusquely.

"Yes, sir, she is in the library. Shall I tell her you are here?"

He didn't reply. He rushed into the house, followed by Charles, and the groom took his horse.

'What', thought Charles, 'could be troubling the dear laird and Master Craig?'

He quickly showed Bruce into the library, where he took up a position with his back to the huge marble fireplace, tapping his cane angrily against his thigh.

"Bruce dear," exclaimed Margot as he entered, "what brings you here so early? Do be seated, Bruce dear. You make me feel quite anxious standing there." She was so familiar with his habit of tapping his riding crop against his thigh that she knew it did not augur well.

"I would rather stand," said Bruce.

He walked over to the window overlooking the loch.

"Very well, then, if you prefer – but why such a troubled look on this bright sunny day?" she asked. With her woman's intuition she guessed that he wished to continue the conversation they had had previously.

"Elena tells me that your plans are almost completed for your trip to India," he began.

"Yes, we have had lots of discussions as all our missions out there are in need of a lot of help and new equipment. However, as you know, she has been busy helping to raise money for Craig's Ex-Servicemen's Association. Now it is well under way, and he has got more help from other quarters, so she can spare more of her time for our mission service."

"Yes, yes, I understand all that," said Bruce, becoming impatient at the trend of the conversation.

'I have come to discuss far more serious things than this mission chatter,' he thought, fuming inwardly.

She could see he was not really listening.

"I have now only my sailing ticket and actual date of departure to arrange, but I am waiting to know the date of the wedding."

"Yes, yes, I understand all that."

She looked at him questioningly. What was going on in his mind? She knew he was deeply troubled.

"Would you make it two tickets when you sail, Margot?"

"Two?" she exclaimed incredulously. "Has Elena expressed a wish to accompany me? I would be most glad if that is so. I know she is most anxious to start visiting our missions, but I have told her I will write to her as soon as I have visited them all; then I can give her all the details."

'How these women prattle on so!' thought Bruce. He was growing more and more agitated, tapping his cane more and more impatiently against his thigh.

"I was only talking to Elena recently and she didn't mention anything about wanting to go so soon."

"No, it is not Elena that I want to book another passage for," he replied angrily.

"Bruce, please do not use that tone of voice when speaking to me," Lady Margot demanded. Now she too was getting quite angry. "Who is it, then, you want another passage for?" She raised her eyes questioningly.

"For this companion of yours – Miss Anderson, I believe her name is."

'He knows her name well enough,' she thought.

"I want you to take her with you as your companion when you leave."

She looked at him, aghast at his suggestion. "But she is so frail – I don't think she could stand the climate."

"Oh, I am sure she could," he replied impatiently. "She is no more frail than you were when you lived there. Of course she will be all right," he insisted.

"But you forget, Bruce, I was with my parents. This child will have to leave her parents behind. She needs to consider them even more now that her brother is going overseas. That is the main reason she did not wish to leave this area."

"I doubt if that was the reason," he replied sarcastically. "It was because she would still be able to see my son if she stayed here. I know what that little hussy's game is."

"I can assure you, Bruce, she is not a bit like that."

"Are you, then, suggesting, Margot," he said coldly, "that my son would carry on this affair if she wasn't doing all in her power to ensnare him? My dear Margot, you are more blind than I anticipated."

Lady Margot's anger was mounting. "I can assure you, Bruce," she said, "I am not as blind as you think."

Bruce saw how angry Margot was getting but he was still adamant. "Are you insinuating that my son is making all the play in this affair?"

She changed the run of conversation hurriedly, knowing she would get nowhere with him in this mood: "Elizabeth has accepted this good situation at the academy. The principal has agreed that she can start as soon as I can spare her."

"But, Margot," he said, "I could have her appointment cancelled; then there would be no position open to her in the area." He was getting more angry and agitated.

"Surely, Bruce, you wouldn't do such a thing?" she replied angrily.

"Yes, I would. Yes, I would," he insisted, his voice rising higher.

Once again, she reminded him of his tone of voice.

"I am sorry, Margot, but I am certain she will continue to see my son as long as she is in the area. Can't you see my difficulty? I cannot allow this sort of thing to continue. As well you know, Craig has not named the date of the wedding. All the arrangements need to be completed and yet he insists he will not be rushed into finally naming the date. Fiona and her parents are beside themselves with anguish. I am sure that as long as this hussy stays in the area he will continue to delay. I just know he will. My only hope is that she leaves as soon as possible – within the next few weeks, whilst he is away in London."

"But, Bruce, if I agree to your plan, I will miss their wedding, and I promised them both I would not leave before then."

"As I see it," Bruce replied, "you will not leave for a long time yet if you, like us, are waiting for Craig to finally name the date. Besides, I know how anxious you are to see your daughter again."

"Yes, I am anxious, but I also like to keep the promises I make."

"Well, you could tell anyone who asks that you have had news of your daughter's illness."

'He thinks of everything!' Margot thought.

"But what if she refuses to leave her parents?" she said.

"I also have a plan to cover that situation," he said, matter-of-factly.

"Might I ask what that might be?" she queried.

"I would rather not say until I know her reaction. It is a plan I would rather not contemplate; but if there is no other way out, I shall not hesitate to use it. Is she here now?" he asked.

"No, she is down in the village."

"Well then," he concluded, "no more can be done at present. However, I want you to approach this girl and let me know her reply as soon as possible. We have not much time."

"But, Bruce, do you realise the burden you are placing on my shoulders in making me a part of this scheme?"

"Margot, only you and I will know I have approached you. Just make it clear to her that you would, after all, like her to accompany you. Make the offer sound exciting. Tell her it is a chance for her to travel and see India for herself – a chance she will never get again."

"But, Bruce, what if she didn't settle or became ill? I wouldn't want to compel her to stay in a situation where she is unhappy."

"Well, in that case you could let her return to her parents after a couple of years. I will pay all her expenses both ways. Don't you see, my dear Margot, by then Craig and Fiona will be married and a son and heir will, certainly have been born by then." His tone was less brusque than before. He came a little closer to her and held her hands in his. "Can't you see, my dear Margot, what this would mean to me? When Craig has a son – an heir for Glencree and the clan of McNair – the plan will be complete, Margot." He looked at her with a look of complete satisfaction. "The plan, Margot, will be complete," he repeated. "Don't you see?"

"Yes, I do see, Bruce." Her tone of voice and her expression did not show or return his obvious joy. "Yes, I do see," she repeated.

Her obvious displeasure stung him deeply.

"Nothing matters to you, Bruce, except a grandson and heir for Glencree and the clan of McNair. You don't care what the cost may be to this poor girl's happiness and health, and you don't care whether or not her parents are deprived of seeing her, perhaps for two years, which you say is the least possible time before her eventual return. Do you expect me to share your joy and delight at your plan and their sacrifice? She means as much to them as Craig does to you."

"I doubt it," he said cynically. His expression had changed again and his voice had once more taken on a brusque tone.

She dropped her hands from his and walked over to the window, deeply hurt that he showed so little concern for the happiness and family life of others. She would love to have Elizabeth with her – the thought had crossed her mind more than once – but not for one moment would she wish to take her away from her parents. But Bruce had no sympathy with Elizabeth's family. Not he! Hadn't she known him all her life? She knew before she made her last remark what his response would be.

"No, nothing matters to me more than Craig and Fiona's wedding and a grandson and heir for Glencree next year. Nothing! Nothing!"

He was getting quite red in the face again with anger and frustration. He thought that, of all people, Margot would understand, but she was blatantly telling him to understand the other person's feelings. 'How dare she? How dare she?' he thought.

"No, nothing else matters to me one jot. Nothing! Nothing, I tell you!" He banged his fist on the table, and the priceless vase on it almost toppled over.

She looked at him angrily but did not speak.

"I am sorry, my dear Margot. Please forgive me. I did not intend to get so angry and distress you so." He had not expected her opposition to his plan. His voice softened again and once more he took her hands. "Just ask the girl, Margot. Just ask. She may rather like the thought of travelling abroad – especially with you. It would only be for two years."

"All right, Bruce, I will ask her and let you know her answer as soon as I can."

"Thank you, dear. You know how much this means to me."

He kissed her hand lightly and bade her goodbye.

'The encounter has not been as easy as I contemplated,' he thought, 'but I am certain the girl will accept Margot's offer.'

CHAPTER 82

Margot sat down after he left. She was still angry at his attitude and annoyed with him for leaving her with such a distressing problem.

She called for some tea, and Flora looked at her strangely as she brought it in. The raised voices had perplexed the servants deeply. Charles, the most deeply upset, had said to Cook, "Never have I heard the like of it before. I tell you, Flora, I hope I never hear the like of it again."

'Yes,' Margot thought as she sat drinking her tea, 'I know Craig and Bruce only too well.' She knew Craig would not heed his father. The saying 'like father, like son' was very apt where those two were concerned. She knew it was essential to Bruce that nothing interfered with the wedding of Craig and Fiona, and she also knew he was frustrated that Craig would not name the day. Elena had only recently remarked how difficult it made the catering and other arrangements, and she had said that neither she nor Harriet understood the reason why.

Was it true, then, that Elizabeth was the reason? Lady Margot could think of nothing else that could explain it. Elena also said that the General and Lady Cleveland were getting more and more annoyed at what to them seemed like flimsy excuses: that he needed to spend a little more time with his father; that he was getting to know the extent of the estate, with all the extra land they had bought; that he had to attend to the matters affecting his men and their welfare. He said he had made a promise to them and his brother officers, and he would not be deterred from honouring that promise, although Elena had assured him that everything was now in order.

As it was, his closest friend, who was to have been his best man, had now been posted overseas. Margot also knew that Fiona would not have spent so long in London on her previous visit there if Craig had decided on the date. She, too, was getting more and more angry at the delay.

Margot thought on all these things, and her thoughts turned back again and again to Elizabeth. 'Could he be delaying the wedding because of his desire to see Elizabeth? It must be that.' She knew that Bruce, as benefactor of the academy, could, and would, have her turned out. She got up and wandered over to the window. 'Yes, I shall have to give this problem some thought,' she said to herself.

CHAPTER 83

Later that afternoon, when the day's work was finished, Margot asked Elizabeth to stay for tea as she had something very important to discuss with her.

Elizabeth sat silent as Lady Margot unfolded the plan. Margot could see by her expression how anxious and upset Elizabeth was becoming.

"But, milady, I must consider my parents. For myself, I should love to come with you." She knew in her heart that was not really true; never would she go willingly anywhere which would take her away from her darling Craig, although she had made a vow that once he was married she would never again meet him in secret. "No, milady," she said after deep thought, "as much as I shall miss you, as you have always been so very kind to me, I cannot accept your very kind offer."

"Well, my child, as much as I would love to have you with me, I also know what the wrench would be for you leaving your parents, particularly now that Roddy is away. However, my dear, I must explain plainly why I think you should consider coming with me, in spite of the sacrifice of not seeing your parents. It would only be for two years; then you could return if you wished. Today I was visited by the laird of Glencree."

At this, Elizabeth began to tremble.

"I am sure you know that he is very displeased that Master Craig has been seeing you. He has seen for himself on two occasions."

Elizabeth racked her brain, trying to puzzle out when the second time could have been, but she could not think of either the time or the place.

"His Lordship realises that it is only a minor infatuation Master Craig has for you, and he is sure that it will soon pass, but he also feels that if you accept this offer to accompany me, it will leave the way clear for Master Craig to marry Lady Fiona without further delay."

Elizabeth looked at Lady Margot in amazement. Surely what she was stating was not true: that she or the laird could be thinking of her in that way.

"But, milady," she exclaimed in disbelief, "surely His Lordship does not think that I would in any way interfere with Lady Fiona's wedding plans? It is well known in the village that Lady Fiona wanted to be presented at court and do the London Season before her marriage."

"Yes, my child, and if the war had not lasted so long, they would have been married long ago. But the fact remains – and it is annoying His Lordship very much – that Master Craig will not name the day of his marriage. His Lordship believes that your leaving here will ease the situation."

"But, milady," Elizabeth insisted, "I feel sure that I am not the cause of the young master's decision." After a few moments' further thought, Elizabeth exclaimed, "Milady, could His Lordship force me to go?"

"I am sure, my dear child, he has nothing like that in mind. No, he could not force you to go, so do not worry, my dear," she reassured Elizabeth, having noted the tremble in her voice.

"I have spent very little time with my parents, and neither has Roddy, but now that Roddy has gone away I should prefer to stay near them."

"Yes, dear, I know how much time you spent with your Aunt Ingrid, owing to no fault of your parents. However, will you think it over and discuss it with your parents? When next your father comes with the stores, which is tomorrow, I believe, you may go back with him for a few days."

"Thank you, milady."

CHAPTER 84

A few nights later, as Martha, Magnus and Elizabeth sat round the fire after supper, Elizabeth broached the subject.

"Are you quite sure, my child?" her mother said when Elizabeth told her of Lady Margot's offer. "We would not like to prevent you going, my dear, if it is your wish – much as we would miss you. It would give you a chance to visit another country."

"No, Mama," Elizabeth replied emphatically, "I have quite made up my mind. I could never, ever dream of leaving you and Papa, even for two years. Now that my darling Roddy is going abroad soon – and goodness knows when we will see him again! – it is my place to be here near you. I promised him that I would take care of you, as he is now so far away."

"But if you would like to go, my angel . . ." her father said. (She knew that he used that name for her when he most craved her company.)

"No, I have quite made up my mind," she said, to which both her parents gave a deep sigh of relief, which she quickly noted.

'Yes, I have made the right decision,' she thought. 'They do not wish me to accept.'

"But you must thank Her Ladyship for her kind offer, all the same," her mother said, "and we will thank her when we see her after church on Sunday."

CHAPTER 85

On her return, Elizabeth told Lady Margot of her decision. "My parents would not stand in my way if I wished to go, milady, but I told them quite emphatically that I would never leave them – especially now that Roddy is going so far away. If ever one of them was left on their own, there would be no one they could turn to except me. It is my duty to stay close by. So you see, milady, I cannot possibly go."

"I fully understand, my dear," Lady Margot replied.

"My parents asked me to thank you for giving me the opportunity, but when they next see you they will thank you themselves."

Margot looked at her resignedly and sighed. 'Now, how do I tell Bruce?' she thought.

"Now, my dear," she said, "do not worry any more about it. I fully understand your difficulty. Much as I would like to have you with me, I shall explain to the laird that I fully understand your reason."

At the mere mention of the laird, Elizabeth felt a faint tremor of fright rush through her. 'I do hope he won't be too angry about my decision,' she thought.

'But then,' she told herself bravely, 'I have to look after my parents – it is only right. Besides, Roddy would expect it of me.'

"Now, we have still a lot of work to get through. I must get it done before I leave. I have only got to book my sailing date; all else is settled. You carry on to the study, my dear, and do the rest of the correspondence before you go to the village."

Elizabeth hurried out after dropping Lady Margot a little curtsy. "Thank you again, milady, for being so kind and understanding."

She sat down at her desk in the study and pondered several minutes as to what the laird might say to Lady Margot. 'I do hope he too will understand that I cannot leave my parents all alone. I just cannot leave them.'

CHAPTER 86

Bruce was quite elated as he left Glencree that morning on his way to Harrison Hall.

'I just know everything is going to work out all right. I just know it,' he thought.

He alighted and gave the groom and Charles a very bright greeting.

"Is Lady Margot in, Charles?"

"Yes, sir. I will tell her you have arrived. She is in the lounge."

"I know the way, Charles."

He ran up the steps and into the lounge to greet her.

"Good morning, my dear Margot," he said. "What a lovely, bright sunny morning it is! Don't you agree?"

"Indeed I do. One couldn't get a lovelier morning than this, with the sun shining on our lovely loch and mountains above. It is a beautiful morning, to be sure."

He kissed her lightly on the cheek before seating himself in the large armchair.

"Well, my dear," he said, "what good news have you got for me this bright, lovely morning? Tell me, what is the girl's decision?"

"Her decision won't please you, I am sure, but it is one I agree with. She feels that her duty is to her parents, now that her brother is going away. She feels she must stay here to be close to them in case they need her."

"So, she has refused. She has once again defied me. This I will not tolerate." He leaped out of the chair and stormed over to the window, seething with anger. Then he turned to face Margot, who was looking at him askance. "And you, Margot, say you agree with her decision. Can't you see how cunning she is, this – this hussy? That – that is not the real reason she doesn't want to go away. It is because, if she goes away, she will not be able to see my son." His fury grew more and more evident as he spoke. "She is, as I have said before, Margot, a scheming hussy."

Margot looked at him. She was always a match for him – she knew him too well – and she was not afraid of speaking plainly to him.

"I can assure you, Bruce, she is not the hussy you say. Do not ever again refer to her in that way under my roof. I believe her when she says she has to consider her parents. They would not stand in her way if she desired to go, but she rightly feels it is her duty to stay near them."

"And I repeat, Margot," he said, raising his voice in anger, "they are not the reason for her wanting to stay. Why can't you see it too? I can see, Margot, that I cannot convince you of her real motives, so I have no alternative but to implement my other plan. Much as I dislike doing so, I shall go ahead."

She could see by his anger that he meant it.

Elizabeth could hear the raised voices. 'Whatever is wrong? I do hope it hasn't anything to do with my decision to stay,' she thought.

"Where is the girl now?" he demanded.

"In the study."

"Please tell her I wish to speak with her."

"I hope you are not going to be too harsh on the dear child."

"Please do as I ask, Margot." He was getting more and more angry, although he tried not to show it. After all, he was a guest in her house and he was involving her in something she deplored. He tried to moderate his tone of voice.

"His Lordship wishes to speak with me!" exclaimed Elizabeth in alarm when Lady Margot asked her to follow her to the lounge.

"Now, don't be so alarmed, dear. Everything will be all right." Lady Margot was trying to calm Elizabeth's fears.

She followed meekly. The door closed behind her.

"Good morning, sir," she said as she curtsied.

"Sit down, dear," said Margot.

She looked up at the tall, imposing figure of the laird of Glencree. Inwardly she was trembling. 'How stern he looks!' she thought. 'In temperament he's not a bit like my darling, gentle Craig.'

Bruce looked at her. He could not help being struck by the fragile beauty of this golden-haired slip of a girl. She was so like his own adored wife in her frailty. He dismissed the thought at once. There was no room for such thoughts, he decided, with so much at stake. He stood with his back to the large fireplace and began tapping his silver-knobbed cane in the palm of his hand.

'How like Craig!' she thought.

He greeted her with extreme politeness, like the perfect gentleman he was, but she sensed a mounting anger beneath his polite greeting. She tried to steel herself to resist his imposing his will on her. She had already told Lady Margot of her decision. Surely she had told him. Was he waiting to hear it from her own mouth? Her fear and apprehension increased.

"It seems, Miss Anderson," he boomed, a note of anger evident in his tone, "that you have decided not to accept the offer made to you the other day by Lady Margot."

"Yes, sir, that is so." Her voice was almost a whisper owing to her fright.

"Speak up, girl," he demanded.

"Yes, sir," she replied more loudly.

"Why, may I ask?"

"Because", she answered, more frightened than before, "I feel I cannot leave my parents. My brother is now going overseas and I am the only one able to help them. Also, I will have a good position at the academy when Lady Margot leaves."

"So I gather!" he exclaimed angrily. "That is as might be, but it still allows you to see my son at every opportunity you can, and will, contrive. You know he is betrothed to Lady Fiona, and yet you have the audacity to continue to see him. In spite of my forbidding you ever to see him again, you still continued."

'So he must have seen us again,' she thought, 'or that nosy Mrs Knowell has said something to him.' Her mind was in a whirl.

"Well then, Miss Anderson," his voice boomed again, "you leave me no alternative but to inform you that if you do not accept the offer made by Lady Margot to accompany her to India for a period of two years—" For a moment his voice faltered.

"Your offer, not mine, Bruce," Margot reminded him: "yours alone, Bruce."

He regained his composure. "I shall. . .", he continued.

'Rather reluctantly!' thought Margot.

". . . be forced to evict your parents from their cottage."

The word *evict* stung her to the depths of her soul. She flinched, and he knew that his dart had gone home as he had intended. Margot gasped with dismay at his ultimatum. She noticed that Elizabeth's hands were trembling, and she was filled with a deep sense of pity for her. She also felt remorseful that she had allowed herself to become involved in this so distasteful plan. Elizabeth looked up at her in deep despair.

Lady Margot looked at her. She nodded gently and resignedly as if to convey to her, "I am sorry, my child, there is no other way."

'Eviction! Eviction!' The thought kept going over and over in her mind. No, surely this always so kind and just laird they all loved so dearly, whose only thoughts were for the happiness and welfare of his people, would not do this to her parents. She had been told so often by her aunt of the evictions of long ago. 'Surely he could not mean what he had said! Surely it was all a dream!'

The laird's voice droned on: "There is no other course open to me. Two things I demand of you Miss Anderson. You are not listening to me, Miss Anderson," he fumed. "I will not tolerate this impertinence." He banged his fist on the table as Margot looked at him angrily.

Elizabeth, startled, looked up at him. "I beg your pardon, sir," she said, "but I am listening."

"I will repeat: two things I demand of you. One is never to see or speak to my son ever again, and the other is that you sail with Lady Margot to India as soon as possible – certainly before my son returns from London. Do you agree?"

"Yes, yes, sir, I agree. "

"Well then, all is settled. Lady Margot will make all the plans. You may go."

She rose unsteadily to her feet, inwardly trembling. Once before she had seen his anger: when he had found her in the lodge with Craig. She curtsied to them both before closing the door; then she wended her way to the study.

Margot watched Elizabeth helplessly as she left the room. She looked angrily at Bruce.

"You know, Bruce," she said, "I disapprove strongly of this threat that you have made to her. Also, have you forgotten", she said emphatically, "about the Act – the Crofters' Holding Act? Her parents could sue if they wished."

"But I know they would never resort to that against me. I doubt if they even know of it – such simple folk as they are."

"Elizabeth is a well-educated girl and she will surely know of it. There is also her brother."

"Well, my dear Margot," he replied coldly, "her brother is many, many miles away and the girl herself will never dare disobey me ever again."

"Well then, I don't know what to say," she said dejectedly as she sat down. "Are you sure this is the only way to settle the date of Craig's wedding? Are you sure that Elizabeth is the reason for Craig's not naming the date?"

"I am sure. She has already disobeyed me once, so I have no other way out. Will you please see that you both leave for India before he returns. I will explain to them when they return that you had to join your daughter sooner than expected due to her illness, and I'll tell them that you expressed your regrets."

"You seem to have thought of everything as usual, Bruce," Lady Margot retorted angrily.

"I have to do what is best for my son. I will pay all the girl's expenses – whatever it takes." He turned to go. "Goodbye, my dear Margot. I am sorry to have to part from you in this way."

He hastened away, called to Charles and the groom for his horse, and rode hastily away.

It's most unusual for the laird to be so brusque, they both agreed.

"And in such haste too!" said Charles as he turned to go inside, very perplexed.

Bruce rode home at a furious pace. He had done what he intended. All would be well when his son returned. He would be bothered no more by that hussy. He was distressed that his dear friend, Margot, had not seen his point of view. He knew that Craig and Fiona would be most unhappy at Margot's not attending their wedding, and he knew also that Harriet and Elena would be puzzled, as would Craig and Fiona, at her so sudden departure. It had to be this way. Margot would have to excuse herself with a story about her daughter's illness, but he didn't relish the idea that he would have to join in the deceit to make it, if possible, a little easier for Margot. Harriet, he knew, would just shrug her shoulders and dismiss it immediately from her mind. She and Margot had never been the best of friends, owing to the fact that in their earlier years it was Margot who got Elena so interested in missionary work. After that, Elena had been constantly on her travels, and Harriet had been left without Elena's companionship.

Elena, however, he knew would insist on every minute detail from him. When he ventured to impart the news, he would have to pretend to be more shocked than any of them. 'I know Margot will go along with that excuse to protect the girl and also to hide the fact that I have threatened to evict the girl's parents. No one must ever get to know of it,' he thought. 'No doubt, in years to come, Elena will get to know the truth, but then it will be too late for anyone to do anything about it. I shall be able to stand her wrath once Craig and Fiona are married and I have got my dearest wish: an heir to the McNair clan. That is the only thing that matters to me. I will never let anything get in the way of that. Damnation to the girl! The problem she has caused me is detestable,' he fumed.

After Bruce had dismounted, the groom bade him good day, but he received no reply. The groom looked at the sweating horse in dismay. He had never seen his master ride his horse so hard.

Bruce hastened to his room, passing Elena in the hall with barely a nod. She watched as he raced upstairs.

'Whatever has upset him today, I wonder? Something must be drastically wrong. Maybe he is just missing his son – but he has only been gone a few days. Ah well,' she thought, 'he will, no doubt, tell me in due course.'

Bruce slammed his door shut and Elena looked at Jamie, who had just joined her. She was too perplexed to speak.

CHAPTER 87

Some time later Margot rejoined Elizabeth.

"I am so sorry, dear, that this has happened. I shall always care for you as if you were my own daughter." It hurt her deeply to see Elizabeth so distressed.

"I know that, milady. You have always been so kind to me."

"When next your father calls, you may return with him for a few days."

"I would love that, milady," she whispered.

"Then we shall have to go to the city and get all your clothes for the tropics. It is so hot there. You will need a complete new wardrobe. His Lordship is providing all the money, so you have no worries regarding that."

She could see Elizabeth wasn't listening.

"Just finish what you are doing, my dear, and go for a walk by the loch. The fresh air will do you good."

Margot watched Elizabeth wend her way down the path to the loch.

'Poor child! I pray she keeps well whilst we are there. Two years will soon pass. I shall make sure she is happy, and I know Davinia will help me all she can. Elizabeth will just love the children. Yes, yes,' she told herself, 'I cannot wait to see them myself, but my heart aches for Elizabeth. It isn't fair – it just isn't fair.'

CHAPTER 88

Elizabeth walked slowly by the loch and stopped to sit on a huge boulder near the boathouse. Tears trickled down her face as she gazed at the spot where she and Craig had last met. She could still feel Craig's strong arms around her and his hungry, burning lips. Oh, to never ever see him again! What had she done to deserve this fate? This was the price she had to pay for loving him to distraction. To never see him again! The words seared into her brain over and over again.

'To leave my darling parents too! How ever am I going to tell them and my darling Roddy? Whatever will he say? To leave behind my lovely loch, hills and glens for two years. It will seem like a lifetime. When I return, I know I shall see my parents again, but when shall I ever see Roddy? When? When? I know also that I shall have to stay away from Glencree. His Lordship will see that I never get employment in the area. And dear Robin – I wish I could love him the way he deserves to be loved. If only I could love him the way I love my darling Craig! But I know I shall never love anyone as I do him. To never see him again is more than I can bear, but bear it I must. He must never know why I took this decision. It must be my secret and Lady Margot's for ever. I cannot cause any more strife between the laird and his son. It will be hard for Mama and Papa too, after I promised them (and I promised Roddy) I would never leave them. I love them all dearly.'

She had already written to tell Roddy that she had been offered, and had accepted, a good position at the academy, and she knew he would be pleased that she would see more of Robin. She had also told him she would not feel so alone after Lady Margot had left for India. How could she now write and tell him that she had decided, after all, not to accept the position and, instead, she would be going to India with her mistress? What would he say? What would he think of her? 'What reason can I give when I see him again – whenever that might be? I dare not tell him the truth. What if he decides to leave the army, which he loves so much, to come home to Mama and Papa because I have left them?'

The more she tried to stem the flow of tears, the more they flowed. Her handkerchief was now so wet that it was of no use. 'Oh, if I think any more today, I shall go mad.' She dried her eyes as best she could. It wouldn't do for the servants to see that she had been crying. She knew Lady Margot would understand, but no one else would. She hurried back to her rooms to wash her face.

She joined Lady Margot for dinner, but she hardly ate anything and she excused herself to retire early. All she wanted was to be alone.

Lady Margot sighed as she wished Elizabeth goodnight. She too had hardly eaten anything.

"Goodness me!" exclaimed Cook. "Is no one eating in this house? I have never known Lady Margot not to eat – but then," she sighed "she has been so upset since she had those angry words with His Lordship."

CHAPTER 89

Elizabeth lay tossing and turning as she tried to sleep. She was restless and sad. The word eviction was seared in her brain – eviction of her parents from their humble cottage by the loch they all loved so dearly. 'I cannot let that happen. I just won't let it happen,' she thought. She knew what she had to do. Her mind went back to the time she had heard the word first spoken. Since then it had always been spoken in a hushed whisper and always with a sense of sorrow and foreboding. She had asked her Aunt Ingrid when she was quite young, "What does it mean, Aunt?" but her aunt had tried to evade the question. However, she had persisted, and, at last, her aunt sat her down on the small pouffe at her feet to explain it all to her.

Long ago, the poor crofters could be forced off the land at a moment's notice by the tacksman who looked after the laird's land, or even the laird himself. No reason was usually given. Perhaps the land was needed for sheep, but sometimes it was simply the whim of the laird, as was the case with the Earl of Glencree, and Elizabeth's parents.

The people would have to leave, though often they had nowhere to go. In many cases they sold their meagre possessions to travel abroad to start new lives. Most of them had to borrow money and clothes from anyone who could help them. The starving, raggedy children were pitiful to see. Her aunt had told her of a road called Destitution Road, because it was the road taken by the poor crofters when they were evicted.

Then Elizabeth suddenly remembered hearing that in 1886 a law had been passed. 'What was it?' she asked herself, thumping her head in anguish. 'What was it?' Suddenly, it came to her: the Crofters' Holding Act. This Act gave the crofters security of tenure of their land. Her aunt had told her, that most of the evicted crofters in remote parts of Scotland never got to know of it. In those days very few working people could read, and news travelled very slowly.

'Well, what use is this Act to me?' Elizabeth asked herself. 'I cannot go to the law about the laird without this affair becoming known to everyone. It is because of my love for Craig that this is happening to my parents. If I pursue this, it will cause more trouble between Craig and his father. No, no, it is of no use to me,' she sobbed. 'Well, at least I can return in two years. Many of the evicted crofters – poor souls! – were never to return.'

CHAPTER 90

Night after night Elizabeth would have the same nightmare: her parents, their backs bent low under the weight of their last few possessions, trundling up Destitution Road. She could hear her mother's voice pleading not to be sent away, Elizabeth, trembling with fear, found herself gripping the sheets when she awoke, but it was only that dreadful dream again. It was all a dream.

She went over to the window, from where she could see the tall outline of the turrets of the castle outlined in the brilliant moonlight. The extinguished lights reminded her that her darling was not at home and she must be away before his return. She could see the small cottages in the village and on the hillside, conspicuous in the moonlight. Everything was quiet and still. 'Everyone must be sleeping except me,' she thought, but Lady Margot was awake. She had heard, once again, the rattle as Elizabeth drew back the heavy curtains.

'Poor child, poor child!' Lady Margot thought. 'What a sacrifice she has to make! But I will make her as happy as I can. Now we really must get some sleep. We both have so much to do.'

The chimes of the old church clock striking two made Elizabeth realise how late it was. She shuddered in the chill night air and clambered wearily into bed. 'I will speak to Emma,' she said to herself. 'She will understand. I cannot let Mama and Papa suffer because of me. I will have to go.' She buried her face in her pillow as tears filled her eyes. 'I will speak to Emma in the morning.'

CHAPTER 91

"Elizabeth dear, why so sad today?" Emma asked at choir practice next day.

"I cannot say at the moment," Elizabeth whispered.

She looked up to see the choirmaster looking at them with disdain.

Emma was perplexed. 'Never have I seen her so distressed,' she thought.

At last they could be alone together.

"What has happened, Elizabeth?" she exclaimed as they sat on the form in the vicarage garden, where they often went when they were free.

Emma listened carefully to everything Elizabeth had to say, hardly believing what she was hearing.

"Please, Emma, you are the only one I can turn to in my dilemma. I cannot manage this problem alone any longer. The laird must never know I have told you, so, Emma, please promise me never to tell anyone – not even Craig, if he should ever ask. Mama, Papa and Roddy must never get to know the real reason either. I have to write to Roddy soon, and I will say that I have changed my mind and am going with Lady Margot. I shall have to tell my parents soon too. Please, Emma dearest, I have no other way, but do not ever let them know of my dilemma."

"You have my promise, my dearest friend, but surely our dear laird could not be so cruel. It is quite beyond my comprehension."

"Well, he will not be happy until I am off the island and on my way to India. Then he says Craig will state a date for his marriage. I love my darling Craig and I cannot bear to be the cause of any more discord between him and his father. The laird told me I have already been the cause of a lot of anguish to him, Emma, I cannot stand any more."

"But your poor parents – whatever are they going to say and do? And Roddy – what is he going to say when he gets your letter?"

"I just don't know, Emma. I dare not think about it. There are so many problems I have to sort out. How shall I explain to Robin and his mother, who so kindly offered me the position at the academy?"

She held her head in anguish and Emma put a comforting arm round her shoulders.

"Very soon, Lady Margot and I will go to the city to get our sailing tickets and to get my clothes for the tropics."

Emma looked at her in amazement. "When will you have to go?" she asked, almost in a panic.

"On the first available boat in a few weeks' time – certainly before Craig and Fiona return from London."

"So Lady Margot will miss Craig's wedding and you will miss mine. It isn't fair."

"Yes, Lady Margot is most upset about it. She promised them she wouldn't leave till after their marriage. How wonderful for you, Emma, to be able to marry the man you love and to stay here with your parents in our lovely land! On the other hand, I," she said wistfully, "because I love Craig, must forfeit everything – the man I love, my parents and my dearest Roddy. Goodness knows when I shall ever see him again. There was a chance I would see him when he came home on leave, but not now. I shall be too far away from home. I shall miss the friends I have here (and you most of all, dear Emma), the church and the choir. I don't envy you, my dearest Emma, but I would love us to share our lives together here, bring up our children together and remain friends through life." She sighed longingly again and again as her thoughts ran away with her. "To leave everything I love so dearly is going to break my heart."

"Have you told Craig of your love for him?" Emma asked.

"No, no, no! Can't you see, I dare not tell him."

"Has he told you of his love for you?"

"Yes, yes, over and over again. Every time I see him, he begs me to tell him of my love for him, but that I shall never do. This is Craig's rightful place as heir to Glencree and his clan. He has to hand all this on to his sons and heirs, and his father would never hear of him marrying such as me. Also, he is betrothed to Lady Fiona. Even though I know he loves me, I cannot let him break his engagement. As everyone knows, he was practically married to her, but the war intervened. When I am gone, he will not be so tormented. He will settle down and name the date of his marriage, which, his father has told me, he hasn't done up until now because of me. All will be well between father and son when I have finally gone.

"Dearest Emma, how I have chatted on so. Please forgive me. I needed someone to talk to and I only have you. I couldn't cope any more. The laird forbade me to tell anyone, but I didn't promise him."

"My dear Elizabeth, you are being so brave. I am glad you are able to talk to me. Your secret is safe for ever with me. If only I could help in some way, it would make me so happy."

"Thank you, Emma, but there is nothing you or anyone else can do. I cannot bear to think about it. Will you write to me, Emma dear?"

"Of course I will – every week, dear, I promise."

"But, dear Emma, please, I beg of you, do not mention Craig's or Fiona's name."

"If that is your wish, my dear friend, I will not."

"Ah, there you are, you two chatterboxes," called Robin as he approached. "I might have known you were tucked away somewhere, but at last I have found you. I have hunted everywhere. It is too chilly to be sitting out here. Why do you both look so glum? Has the choirmaster or his wife been telling you off again for chattering when you should have been singing? They will not let Elizabeth sing solos as it is; if you keep getting in their bad books, who will we get? Those meddlesome 'jewel' girls. They are just itching to take Elizabeth's place permanently."

Emma squeezed Elizabeth's hand. No words were needed between them.

'How near the truth he is!' they both thought.

"Come, Elizabeth – I will walk you to Harrison Hall. It is now getting late and Lady Margot will be wondering where you are."

CHAPTER 92

"Mama, Papa," Elizabeth called to them after morning service. She bade a hasty goodbye to Emma and Stuart and Robin, who were standing in the doorway of the church. Robin attempted to run after her as she pursued them, but Emma held his arm.

"Don't go, Robin," she said. "She has private things to discuss with them."

"Very well, I will wait until another day. I was only going to ask her the same old question." He sighed. "However, I daresay I would get the same old answer," he continued dejectedly.

Emma looked at him wistfully, knowing that he would. She turned with a heavy heart and watched Elizabeth approaching her parents. 'If only I could help her!' she thought.

"What is it, my child?" her mother asked, noticing Elizabeth's obvious agitation.

"Mama," she began, hardly knowing how to tell her, "I have been thinking again about that offer to go to India with Lady Margot." She tried desperately to seem light-hearted and carefree. "I have decided to accept as it might be the only chance I shall ever get to travel overseas."

'At last', she thought, 'I have got the most important statement out. I hope I can manage the rest.' She was getting more flustered and agitated.

Her mother looked at her in disbelief. "But, my child," she exclaimed, "you have just accepted that good position at the academy!"

"I know, Mama."

She looked up at her father, hoping for a sign of his approval, but he was looking at her reproachfully.

"But, Mama, it will only be for two years, or maybe less – until Lady Margot has had time to train another companion. She would like me to help her grandchildren with their music. I would dearly love that." She was trying all she knew to sound happy about it all. Inwardly she was quaking with despair and fright.

"But, my child," her mother said anxiously, "it is so hot there. I don't think you could stand the climate."

"But, Mama, Lady Margot was younger than I am when she first went there and she told me she was all right in the heat."

'Well,' she thought, 'Lady Margot didn't actually say that, but she must have been all right.'

"I will be all right, Mama. Don't worry so."

Magnus looked at her, not knowing what to make of her sudden change of mind. 'This is so unlike my angel,' he thought. 'She was so adamant before that she would never leave us.'

"But why the sudden change of mind, my angel?" he asked.

She looked at him, perplexed. Never before had she been in such a dilemma. She couldn't tell them the truth, but neither could she answer her father's query truthfully.

"Never mind, my child," he said, noting with concern her obvious hesitation. "If you really want to go, we will not stand in your way. As you say, it might not even be for two years, so return, my angel, as soon as you can."

"I will, Papa. I will, I promise."

At last they reached the jetty and Elizabeth helped her mother into the boat.

"Lady Margot says I can come and stay with you for a few days before we sail."

"When will you sail?" her mother asked.

"I am not sure yet, Mama, but Lady Margot has been most anxious to leave soon, ever since she heard of her daughter's ill health."

"Oh yes, to be sure," Martha replied. "I had quite forgotten she had had that sad news."

At last the boat pulled away and she waved to them as they set off for home. She was thankful that at last they knew she would be leaving. She walked slowly back beside the loch, throwing pebbles into it.

'There's no need to hurry,' she thought. 'There will only be Charles awaiting me.'

She pondered the situation sadly, knowing her parents would never agree to her making this sacrifice for them if they knew the truth. She knew her father would try to find other work, but she doubted whether he could find another job, even if he moved away from Glencree. The depression was hitting young and old alike. Wasn't that why her darling Roddy had to go away?

As he rowed back, Magnus pondered long on her change of mind. 'It's so unlike my angel to be so enthusiastic about leaving us,' he thought.

"Husband dear," called out Martha in alarm, "mind the rocks! You are not rowing as carefully on this trip. I know your thoughts are on our dear daughter, as are mine."

"Did Elizabeth say she was writing to explain to Roddy?" Magnus asked.

"Yes, and she said she hoped he would understand."

"So do I, so do I," Magnus replied; "but I don't think he will."

"Well, we will have to wait and see," sighed Martha.

"I will write to him soon," said Magnus sadly.

CHAPTER 93

Elizabeth opened her small bureau drawer and took out Roddy's last letter. In it he told her that he was still listed for overseas service, but would be due some leave before his departure.

I miss you all very much, but I can help our parents more financially by re-enlisting. I beg of you, dear sister, see as much of them as you can. I am so pleased about your appointment at the academy. Take good care of them after I sail – but I know you will always do that. I will write again soon.
> Always, your loving brother,
> Roddy

She laid it in front of her, sighing deeply. She had replied by return, promising to do as he had asked. How could she now write and tell him she was doing no such thing and that instead she also would be sailing away? Hour after hour she pored over the problem, her tears flowing as she tried to explain.

My dearest Roddy,
> Lady Margot has asked me to accompany her to India to help her with her correspondence. I shall only be away two years, but it might be less. I feel that, as Lady Margot has always been so kind to me, I really ought to help her out until she has found someone else. Mama and Papa are pleased that I have this opportunity to see a little more of the world. I hate the thought of leaving them but they understand, as I hope you will.
> The reason Lady Margot is leaving so soon is that she has received news of her daughter's ill health. She is allowing me to spend some time at home before we sail. I hope you can be home at the same time. I shall miss you all very much. I hope you will get posted to India whilst I am still there.
> By the time you receive this letter, I might have left. I am not sure when we sail.
> Missing you, as always, your ever loving sister,
> Elizabeth

She dried her eyes before putting the letter in the envelope. Then she sealed it with a kiss. 'I do hope he understands and forgives me,' she thought, 'but I don't suppose he ever will.'

She walked slowly to the village next day, wishing that the letter she was clutching so tightly didn't need to be posted. She also had some of Lady Margot's letters to post, and she dropped those into the post box first. Then she gave a deep, deep sigh as she finally posted the one to Roddy. As she turned away, she shuddered to think what he would think of her.

CHAPTER 94

"You are lucky today, Roddy!" exclaimed his friend as he handed him his mail: "Two today. I can tell from your face one is from a girl."

"Yes, you are right, but it is not what you think. It is from my sister – my very special girl. No other girl means as much to me."

"You won't say that, my friend, after you have met the girl you will fall in love with and marry."

"No, I guess you are right; but until the right one turns up, Elizabeth is my only sweetheart, next to my mother."

His friend looked at him with concern: as Roddy read the letter from Elizabeth, his happy expression changed to one of disbelief and mounting anger.

"Is she all right?" the friend asked, with concern.

"Yes, yes. Please excuse me," he said as he hastily left the room to go to his quarters. He sat on his bed to steady himself as he read and reread her letter. All he could think of was her decision to leave for India very soon with Lady Margot. Leave! Leave! How could she leave after promising she would always stay with them?

'It's not like her to do such a thing. Whatever can have come over her?' His anger mounted. For him to be angry with Elizabeth was unprecedented. Never in his life had he felt such fury.

He folded the letter and put it in his pocket. Then he hurriedly opened his father's letter, and he was reminded by the tone of it how much his parents were going to miss Elizabeth.

> Mama has not been too well lately, and I can only think that this is because our darling angel is going so far away. I know this news will distress you. We hope Elizabeth does not find the climate too hot. We explained the dangers to her, but she assured us she would be all right. We trust the Good Lord will protect her. She is so fragile, and she is precious to us.

'All the more reason why she should not be going!' Roddy fumed. 'Lady Margot is used to that heat.'

> I hope you are well, my son. I will write again soon and let you know how Mama is.
>> God bless you and keep you safe.
>> Your loving Mama and Papa

He put the letter in his pocket beside the other. He paced the room, pondering: 'I will never forgive her for making Mama so ill by pursuing her selfish desire to see the world. To go so far away when she had that position at the academy! For the first time in my life, I cannot understand her. It is so unlike her!' he exclaimed bitterly. He scratched his head in bewilderment, took her letter and read it over and over again. 'If Mama and Papa have accepted it, I shall have to do likewise,' he thought. 'I will reply at once.'

He sat down, not knowing how to begin.

CHAPTER 95

Lady Margot and Elizabeth were both relieved to get back to Harrison Hall after their visit to the city for the selection of clothes for the tropics and the arrangement of their passage.

'What hustle and bustle!' Elizabeth thought, 'I shall never be at peace again.'

"My word! My word!" exclaimed Charles as he unloaded the carriage on their return. "Such a lot of cases and trunks!" he declared as he stood scratching his head in bewilderment.

A deep sadness was settling on all of them as the time for their departure was drawing nearer.

"There are more trunks to come from the city containing other things I have ordered which are not wanted on the voyage. Now, when they arrive, Charles, you must see that the address is painted on all of them," said Lady Margot.

"Yes, milady," he replied solemnly. "I will get Gordon from the village to come and attend to them."

"We shall have left by then," she added.

"How long is it before you leave us, milady?" he asked with a sigh.

"About fourteen days," she replied, "so, you see, we will all be very busy."

"We are all going to miss you so much, milady," he said as he pottered to and fro with the cases.

"Yes, and we will miss all of you." She sighed. "Now, no more chatter! We will take tea now. After tea, Elizabeth, you can take the dogs for their stroll. The fresh air will do you good."

"Yes, milady."

Elizabeth was more than thankful to get away from it all. She was getting more depressed each day.

"Next time your father calls, Elizabeth, you can return with him for a few days. In the meantime, I shall be visiting more of my friends. I shall not be able to see them all. It's most annoying, but it cannot be helped."

CHAPTER 96

A few days later, Elizabeth returned home with her father, but although she was glad to be home, she felt more depressed than ever.

"You must play and sing for us every day whilst you are with us," her mother insisted. "It is going to be such a long time before we hear you again – you do realise that, my dear?" her mother said with a sigh.

"Yes, I shall sing all yours and Papa's favourites," she replied meekly. "Have you heard from darling Roddy, Mama?"

"No, not as yet," her father replied. "Maybe we will before you go."

"I haven't heard either," she said, dreading his reply. "After I go back to the hall, Mama, I shall visit Aunt Ingrid's grave before I leave."

"Maybe you should wait for a day when I can come with you, dear."

"No, no, Mama, I would rather go alone."

Her mother looked at her in surprise. It was not like her daughter to be so abrupt and insistent. Somehow she couldn't fathom her out. It was so unlike her. 'Maybe it is just the thought of leaving us that is the cause. Yes, I am sure that must be the reason,' she thought sadly.

"Thank you for your kind offer to accompany me, but I would rather go alone, Mama dear."

"Well, just as you wish, my child, but don't get too upset." Martha knew how badly Elizabeth had taken her aunt's death.

"No, I won't. I will be all right. I won't stay too long – I promise."

CHAPTER 97

Now back at Harrison Hall, after the tearful parting from her parents, Elizabeth went into the village to call at the florists to get the flowers for her aunt's grave before proceeding to the church to say a last farewell.

"Dear Aunt, how I wish you were here to tell me what to do. I loved you so much and you were always near to help me in any dilemma I had. I have needed you so much lately."

She knew what her aunt would have said. She never would have approved of her seeing Craig, and she would have arranged for Elizabeth to leave the area. She would have known that Elizabeth's parents would object, and they would have wanted to know the reason for her decision, but her aunt would have made some plausible excuse for the move. Elizabeth's parents must never ever get to know why it had to be.

Elizabeth arranged the flowers and her tears started to flow.

"Dear Aunt," she whispered, "how I have missed you and your wise talks." She wiped away another tear. "Now, this will never do," she told herself. She stood there for several more minutes before wending her way back to Harrison Hall.

The sight of all the boxes and trunks lined up in the hallway gave her quite a start.

"Now," declared Lady Margot, "we must fill up the trunks with things not wanted on the voyage, such as all your books and music and your other family things. We must keep them safe for when we are settled in. The laird has very kindly consented to let us cross the loch from his private jetty to save us the longer trip from the village jetty."

'Well,' thought Elizabeth, 'it's just as well. I couldn't stand the thought of all my friends from the choir and village coming to see me off. I am sure those smarmy 'jewel' girls would take a special delight in seeing the back of me. I daresay, the laird will want to see me go as he will then be sure I have left.'

Lady Margot looked at Elizabeth as if she knew her thoughts.

"Harriet and Elena will come to see us off. Apparently the laird is confined to his room with a chill."

'How fortunate for him,' Elizabeth thought. 'However, I daresay he will be watching from his room overlooking the loch to make sure I am on that boat.'

CHAPTER 98

Elizabeth found the parting from Emma particularly hard, as Emma did. As they exchanged their parting gifts, they were both in tears.

"Will you write to me often, Emma?" she pleaded.

"Of course I will, my dearest friend."

The news had finally got around that Elizabeth was going to India with Lady Margot and not to the academy.

"Why, that is better still," said Ruby: "she will be far away."

Their mother agreed when she heard the news. Her precious daughters danced around the room with delight.

"Good riddance, too!" she said. "She always had too many airs and graces, ever since Master Craig danced with her at the ball." She blamed Elizabeth entirely for the fact that Craig had not asked for even one dance with any of her precious jewels – and after he had promised, too.

CHAPTER 99

'Mrs Knowell announced Elizabeth's leaving at the choir practice with a certain amount of glee,' thought Emma.

"She doesn't seem to be sorry that you are leaving the choir and going so far away from all your friends, Elizabeth."

"If you only knew the reason, my dear Emma, you would understand." She sighed. Elizabeth had been surprised that Mrs Knowell had managed to keep to herself for so long what she had seen at the side of the stream.

"Those Crawford girls are just as bad. Just look at them gloating. Now they think they will be chosen every time to sing the solos. Well, they won't sing any at my wedding. I shall make that quite clear to Mama and Papa," said Emma. "Just look at them smirking, Elizabeth. They think they can't be seen behind their music sheets."

"That means," continued Mrs Knowell, "that Pearl and Ruby will be singing all the solos from now on."

"Oh, I cannot wait to tell Mama!" Ruby exclaimed.

The 'jewel' girls hastened off as soon as they could after the class was dismissed, but the rest of the class came to say goodbye and wish Elizabeth a safe journey.

"How I wish I was coming too!" said Clare Armstrong. "It sounds so exciting."

'Well,' Elizabeth thought, 'I wish you were going in my place.'

However, she just smiled sweetly back at her and said, "Yes, it is exciting. I am quite looking forward to it."

Mrs Knowell wished her goodbye, but her look of 'good riddance!' was unmistakeable.

Her husband was a little more gracious: he told her how much the choir would miss her singing, before he was hastily pulled away by his wife.

Elizabeth wiped away a tear as she bade the rest of them farewell. "I am going to miss you all so much," she said.

"Will you write to us?" several of them chorused. "We will miss your singing so much."

One of them whispered to Emma, "And to think we will now have to put up with those other two instead."

"Emma, will you write and explain to Robin? I just cannot write to him," said Elizabeth sadly.

"Yes, I will, although I daresay his mother will have told him you are now not going to the academy."

"Oh yes, I had quite forgotten."

Emma and Stuart said their goodbyes after they walked with her to Harrison Hall.

CHAPTER 100

"Well, Elizabeth, this will be the last afternoon you will be taking our two little dears for their afternoon stroll, so off you go," said Lady Margot.

"Now, come on, you two little rascals," Elizabeth called to them as she reached for their ball. "No getting up to any mischief today!" She pretended to scold them as they hastened to get away.

"We have not heard Elizabeth singing so much since all this packing has been going on," Cook said to Charles as they watched her go.

"No, it's a different home altogether since Lady Roxburgh died. And now they are going away. I wonder if we will ever see Lady Margot again?" said Charles with a sigh. "It will be nice to have Lady Harriet and Lady Elena here, Cook – don't you think so?" he asked.

"Well, I shall only be staying for a little while until they get settled in," she replied, "but I am not too sure about Lady Harriet. Lady Elena is more to my liking, but she will no doubt be going over to visit the Indian missions fairly often. I expect she will bring back plenty of news."

Elizabeth walked slowly on in a deeply pensive mood. The dogs happily chased after the ball when she threw it.

"Don't walk too far, my dear," Lady Margot had called to her as she was leaving. "We have so many last little things to do."

"I won't," Elizabeth promised.

'But,' she thought, 'I am going past our tree – our secret tree.'

She had not brought any paper or pencil with her.

"Drat!" she exclaimed. "However, I dare not leave any message. Someone might find it."

When she reached the tree, she scrambled around in the undergrowth for the small log, then she knelt down and gathered a few of their favourite flowers: forget-me-nots.

'Thank goodness I have my blue ribbons on today,' she thought.

She hastily dragged one from her hair and tied the bunch together.

"I hope, my darling," she whispered, "that one day you will find them." She sighed, wiping away a tear.

'He will, he will,' Merry-Berry whispered to herself as she watched

Elizabeth from the nearby hedgerow.

"A letter for you, Elizabeth!" exclaimed Charles on her return.

He was most surprised that she did not hastily take it from him with the same joy as she had in the past.

"Thank you, Charles," she said, and she ran upstairs to her room, clasping it tightly to her heart. She dreaded opening it but, at last, she slit it open with the letter opener Roddy had sent her as a present. She sat down on her bed and her tears blurred the angry words as she read them.

Roddy said he felt she did not owe Lady Margot anything, so she needn't feel duty-bound to accept her offer.

> Mama and Papa should have been your only consideration [he wrote]. I cannot understand why you accepted this so-called opportunity at all – even for a week, never mind two years. Words fail me. I shall write more at length later.
>   Your deeply distressed brother,
>   Roddy

Elizabeth put the letter away in her box of possessions and she dried her eyes. She locked the box and put the key in her pocket.

"It's not fair", she said, "that I have to lose the love of my dear Roddy too. Aren't I losing enough as it is?"

Never had she known him to be so angry with her. Ah, yes, just once, she recalled, when she had almost fallen in the loch – but that was a different anger. Then he was frightened for her safety. This was anger at her deserting Mama and Papa when they needed her. 'But I am unhappy too,' she thought. 'Can Roddy not see that? I won't show the letter to Mama or Papa. It will make them too sad', she decided, 'to think that the two children they both adore so much are parting on such angry terms.' She lay on her bed, buried her face in the pillow and sobbed. 'Oh, how much more can I take?' she thought.

After a while she rose and washed and changed. 'Now I must go to dinner,' she said to herself. 'I mustn't let Lady Margot see that I have been crying. She, too, is upset about leaving so soon.'

Bruce had called on Margot a few days before to bid her farewell and to apologise for her departure before Craig's wedding.

CHAPTER 101

The morning of their departure dawned clear and bright. Neither Elizabeth nor Lady Margot had slept well. The staff were in tears as they watched Charles help them both into the trap. Some of their luggage had already gone ahead. Lady Margot, followed by Elizabeth, gave the dogs their final hug. They were constantly yelping and jumping into the carriage.

"Take great care of them, Charles. They are so precious."

"I will, I will, Elizabeth, never fear."

"I shall call in and see them, Lady Margot, when I return."

"Yes, do that, my dear. They should still be here unless they fret too much."

"Oh, I hope not, milady." Elizabeth sighed as with a final wave, their carriage pulled away.

Lady Margot gazed once more on her lovely home. She was still quite furious at the rush of everything.

'Goodness knows how many of my friends I have missed saying farewell to! To think', she thought, 'that all this is because of Bruce and this scheme of his. I shall never, ever forgive him. Never! Everyone has been calling to ask about my daughter's ill health. It is quite unforgivable of him.'

Elizabeth sat quietly. She glanced up at Lady Margot as if reading her thoughts.

"Now, don't go worrying your pretty little head. I had to leave all this sometime. Maybe I am leaving it sooner than I wished, but never mind, it's just as well. Parting from one's loved ones and home and country is never easy." She patted Elizabeth's arm, trying to reassure her that it was not her fault.

Magnus rowed sadly over the loch that morning and waited at the foot of the steps of the jetty with a heavy heart. Margot told Elizabeth to go and join him, and, as she bid Lady Harriet and Lady Elena goodbye with a little curtsy, Elizabeth thought she saw something strange in Lady Elena's manner. It was something she couldn't quite fathom. 'Anyway,' she thought, 'she has always been very nice to me.' She hurried down the jetty steps and her father stretched out his hand to steady her into the boat. In the meantime, the three ladies chatted on. Elena was doing most of the talking.

"Now, Margot, you must get news to me as soon as you can of how our missions are faring after our long absence. I hope to come and see for myself in a year or two." (This remark did not please Harriet too well.)

Harriet and Elena watched as Jamie and Magnus helped Lady Margot into the boat. Then it started to pull away.

"I do hope Elizabeth keeps well. It was quite a big decision for her to make – and it is so kind of her to go and help Margot. I do hope she doesn't find the heat too trying. She is so small and fragile."

"Oh, Elena, how you do go on about that girl! Margot and her daughter have stood up to it perfectly all their lives."

"Yes, I agree, but they had all their family with them. This child has no one."

"Well, she has chosen to go!" exclaimed Harriet, getting quite exasperated. "Why all the sympathy for her?"

"I don't know. Somehow I thought she looked as though she didn't really want to go – but she will be such a help to Margot."

"I suppose", continued Harriet sarcastically, "that you will, as soon as you can get away, restart your visits to the overseas missions, and I shall be left to look after Bruce and the household all by myself, as well as Harrison Hall."

"But you know as well as I do that Fiona and Craig will be here with Bruce most of the time and we will be at Margot's old home. You needn't be lonely – all your friends can visit. Besides, I won't be going for a couple of years yet, and by then Craig's children will be calling over with Craig. You know, Craig won't stay cooped up in Glencree Castle; he will be out every day with the children."

"Come, let's go inside," said Harriet peevishly. "Margot is now out of sight."

Elizabeth looked up at the castle windows as they left the jetty. She knew Bruce would be watching.

Bruce watched from his window as their boat proceeded. He was thankful they had gone at last. "She's finally away and out of my sight," he murmured aloud. He could hardly believe that at last it was so. "Now, when Craig returns we can all settle down to more normal things. The wedding date will be fixed and the ceremony will be over in a few months from now. All being well, a son and heir for Glencree will come in a year's time. Oh, what joy, to be sure!"

He had promised Margot that Martha and Magnus would always be well cared for, that money would be available for Elizabeth's return in two years' time, and that a position would be found for her on the other side of the loch. Margot had thanked him, but their parting was not that of old friends, which he very much regretted.

"It is all that girl's fault," he declared angrily, "but now she has gone for good, all will be well."

He sat down in his large easy chair, quite pleased with how things had turned out.

CHAPTER 102

Martha was waiting on the other side of the loch, and she helped Margot ashore.

"Do come inside for a while," she said. "You have time for some tea before the train comes." She hastened to the kitchen after telling Margot to sit down and make herself comfortable.

'How kind and humble these people are! How I hate to be party to all that is happening.' Margot looked at Elizabeth sadly. She could see that she was anxious to join her mother. "You go, my child. Your mother will want to see you for as long as possible. I shall be quite all right here."

Elizabeth needed no more telling. She hurried to the kitchen, clasped her mother tightly and kissed her. "Darling Mama," she said, "I am going to miss you and Papa too – so very much."

"And we are going to miss you also, our darling child."

They wept on one another's shoulders.

"Now, this won't do!" exclaimed Martha, as she wiped her own and daughter's tears away on her apron. "I must make the tea and you must hurry back to Lady Margot. She is our guest."

Margot ate the small scone Martha offered, but Elizabeth refused.

"Well, take some with you for your journey."

"Very well, Mama," Elizabeth replied, as her mother wrapped a few in a clean cloth.

"Come now," exclaimed Magnus, "we must be getting to the station. Peggoty is here to help carry your cases."

Elizabeth kept at her father's side as they approached the station. Martha and Lady Margot followed.

"I know this is a very sad time for you, but I promise you, Martha, I will take great care of Elizabeth, just as if she were my own daughter."

"I know you will, milady. I don't think we could trust her with anyone else. She is so precious to us."

"And I promise I will send her back as soon as possible. I know she has told you it may be about two years, but it might be sooner. Her return fare is ready whenever she needs it."

"Oh, thank you, milady. I know she will not leave you until she is satisfied that you have sufficient help."

The extra luggage which they needed on their journey had been taken over to the station by Magnus on several journeys during the days before. It had been stored at the station by Peggoty to await the train for their departure. Lady Margot, Martha and Elizabeth now stood in a small group watching it being loaded into the guard's van. Peggoty, Magnus and the guard made sure that each item was loaded safely. Peggoty hobbled forth, presented Lady Margot with the list and assured her that it was all aboard.

"Thank you, Peggoty. I am going to miss all your kindness to me, but I hope to see you all again sometime."

"Yes, milady," he replied. "It has always been a great pleasure for me to assist you. I shall miss seeing you. Please give my kind regards to Miss Davinia."

"I will. I know she will remember you. Goodbye," she said.

He doffed his cap and Lady Margot shook hands with the three of them. Magnus assisted her into the carriage and placed her hand luggage on the rack above with Elizabeth's beside it. The sight of Elizabeth saying goodbye to her parents touched Lady Margot deeply as she leaned back in her seat. Elizabeth, holding back tears, hugged them as if she would never let go. She kissed them in turn, over and over again. Then she released them reluctantly and turned to kiss Peggoty goodbye.

"Come, my dear," her mistress called.

"Yes, milady." She hurried into the carriage. "I won't be away too long," she called as she stood at the open window:

"Milady, milady," she called, pointing to a small hillock.

"What is it, my dear?"

"It is Merry-Berry, milady."

Lady Margot stood up to get a better view. "Yes, my dear," she said.

They waved her a farewell as the train pulled away. Elizabeth leaned out as far as she could till the station and the hillock had disappeared from view.

The words of her father rang in her ears: "God be with you, my precious dawn angel. Hurry back to us. Hurry back."

"Both of our children are now away," said Martha sadly as she sat in the rocking chair weeping bitterly later that night.

Magnus put his arm round her shoulders and tried to comfort her. "Maybe Roddy will get some leave before he finally sails. I will write and tell him she has left. I know he will be upset, but he will have to accept it as we have done."

"I only wish he could have seen her before she left," Martha sobbed.

CHAPTER 103

Elizabeth's heart sank as they approached the quay. Never in her life had she imagined such a huge ship, or such a hustle and bustle of people everywhere. Porters were stacking cases and trunks of every size and shape onto their trolleys and rushing them to the ship's side to be loaded.

"My, my," she sighed, "what a lot of people going aboard – and soldiers too –

all going to India. I wish my darling Roddy was here." She searched in vain, but he was not amongst them.

She was transported out of her turmoil of thoughts by the shrill voice of Lady Margot. Busy with her list of her trunks and cases, she was walking beside the porter and his trolley, making sure that he was going in the right direction.

"Come, child – hurry to that porter over there and tell him to follow us as we will need more help with our luggage."

Elizabeth did as she was bid. She sped off as fast as she could and tapped him lightly on the arm.

"Yes, pretty missy, and what help can I give you?"

"Please, sir, we need more help with our luggage. Will you please follow me?"

They came to where Lady Margot was standing with the other porter. She was busy counting the cases and ticking them off her list one by one. She was guarding them like some old terrier guarding a precious bone.

"All correct, thank goodness!" she exclaimed. The porter in charge of them breathed a sigh of relief.

'Woe betide anyone', he thought, 'who dares touch this woman's luggage without her permission.'

Elizabeth and the extra porter had arrived out of breath.

"Ah, there you are, my good man," said Lady Margot. "Now, what is your number?"

She hastily jotted it down in her notebook when he turned his shoulder towards her and pointed to where his number was displayed.

"It's just in case we get separated, Elizabeth."

'The devil himself couldn't separate her from her luggage and these porters,' thought Elizabeth. She noted already that Lady Margot had lost the calm countenance of a lady of the manor. There was a note of authority in her voice that Elizabeth hadn't noticed before, as she issued orders to the porters. She gathered up a couple of the smaller cases and followed hastily after Lady Margot, who kept ahead, calling to the porters.

"To the ship, to the ship," she instructed, as she kept glancing round to make sure the porters were following.

At last she was satisfied that all was aboard. She rewarded the porters well and bade them good day. As she and Elizabeth stepped aboard, a member of the crew took their hand luggage and directed them to their cabins.

Elizabeth followed the steward with disbelief: the way to their cabins seemed to her to be endless. At last they arrived. Lady Margot made sure everything was to her liking in her cabin and Elizabeth's, which was next to hers.

"Come, my child – we shall be in our cabins long enough. Come – we will go on deck until we cast off. It is always so thrilling." She glanced at Elizabeth's face and realised she had said the wrong thing. "Time will soon pass, my dear. You are so young. Time will go quickly for you. Try to be happy, my dear. You can stay in your cabin if you wish."

"No, milady, I will do as you suggest. The fresh air will do me good."

Suddenly, Lady Margot recognised some old friends of hers, and she introduced them to Elizabeth. They were returning to India to join their families on the tea plantations.

"I will join you later, Elizabeth," she said, turning to go with her friends.

"I must say you are very lucky, Margot, to have so pretty and so charming a companion."

"Yes, I am lucky," she replied. "The poor child has never left her home before. She is leaving everyone she holds dear behind. I have to take special care of her, so I won't leave her too long on her own."

CHAPTER 104

Elizabeth was thankful to be alone. The ropes tying the ship to her mooring were finally untied, and the people on the shore all exchanged their final waves with their loved ones aboard.

"There's no one to give me a final wave of farewell," Elizabeth sighed. She had begged her parents not to come to the ship. "Let me say my goodbye on the station, Papa," she had said.

"Just as you wish, my angel, just as you wish. Partings from loved ones are always sorrowful, no matter where they take place," he had replied.

She felt the lurch of the ship as it drew away from the quay and her lonely heart lurched with it. She was near to tears. She leaned over the side as it drew further and further away; the gulf between ship and shore grew wider and wider.

'How deep and black and empty everything looks,' she thought. 'It is as if my anchor, too, has been pulled away – away from the safety and comfort of all those I love so dearly. I know I shall see Mama and Papa again, and my darling Roddy also some day, but to never, ever see my darling Craig! How can I go on living? I must not think about it.'

Lady Margot joined her, and they both stood a long time gazing into the water. The evening chill had set in.

"Come, my dear – we will see no more land now as we are out in the open sea. You will see your parents again as soon as possible. The time will soon pass. There will be so much to see and do and enjoy, such as holidays up in the beautiful hills, and balls and tea parties nearly every day. You will be surprised how quickly time flies," she said, but she knew Elizabeth wasn't listening.

Elizabeth, still deep in thought, whispered to herself Craig's name over and over again. 'I shall never see my darling again, even when I do come back,' she thought. She shivered as the cold sea breeze ruffled her hair. Never before had she felt such desolation.

"Come, Elizabeth – come, dear. We must go below. You will get a chill if you stay here any longer. We are to join the Captain at his table for dinner."

'Oh, bother! Just when I wanted to be alone,' Elizabeth thought. She sighed. Lady Margot put a shawl round her shoulders. 'How good she is to me. I must try to be happy for her sake.'

"Yes, I am coming, milady," she said, and she gave a last sad look at the stream of foam following the ship. However, she still clung to the rail, her tiny hands were clenched round it so tightly that her knuckles turned white. She sank her head in the folds of the shawl.

The firm pressure of Lady Margot's hand on her arm, and her soft, gentle voice only seemed to make her feel more lost and alone as they turned to go below.

CHAPTER 105

Emma was quite desolate after Elizabeth's departure. Her mother was at a loss as to what to do to help her overcome her grief. Her father was also concerned. He came upon her sitting on the seat in the garden where she and Elizabeth had often sat chatting.

"Ah, here you are!" he exclaimed. "Are you not reading today?"

"No, Papa, I cannot get interested in my books at all."

"It was quite a sudden decision of Lady Margot to take Elizabeth with her," he said. "I cannot understand it, especially as Elizabeth had been offered the position at the academy." He sat pondering for a while. He, too, was most perturbed by Emma's lack of interest in anything since her departure.

"Yes it was. I miss her dreadfully," she replied sadly.

"The church choir is missing her too. She has such a beautiful voice. We shall never be able to replace it. I know Mrs Crawford's girls sing nicely, but they're not a match for Elizabeth," he said with a sigh.

"Oh, Papa, must we keep on talking of her going?" Emma said almost angrily.

"No, no, my child, not if it upsets you. I shall not mention it again."

"Tell me, Papa: have you any news of Lady Fiona's wedding yet? I cannot make any plans of my own until they are married. Elizabeth has now gone and she was to be my chief bridesmaid. Her dress is still hanging in my wardrobe. Oh, it isn't fair!" She was almost in tears.

Her father looked at her anxiously. Never had he seen his usually so happy-go-lucky daughter so sad and despondent.

'I think there is more than settling her wedding date worrying my dear child. I wonder what it can be?'

"Come, my child – let us go into the quietness of the church and say a prayer for Elizabeth's safe journey and her happiness in the future."

She rose and linked her father's arm in hers as they wended their way. Her mother watched from the window. Yes, her father always knew what would be best for her.

'When she has said a little prayer she will feel much better,' Becky thought.

She turned to finish her baking, hoping now that all would be well with her beloved daughter.

CHAPTER 106

The London Season was now in full swing and the presentation at court of Fiona and her two cousins, Olga and Victoria, was over at last, much to Craig's delight.

The weeks before had bored him to distraction. He had sat beside Fiona's mother and her sister, Maud, in the lounge as day after day the seamstress had arrived with boxes of dresses for their perusal. Fiona, as always, was determined to outshine her cousins.

"I think I will have the taffeta one!" she exclaimed.

"Why?" her cousins asked.

"Well, when I walk, my train will rustle and everyone will turn round to see who is passing."

"Really, Fiona," said Olga, "you never change! You always want to be noticed."

Her visits as a child had always irked her cousins. Whenever she returned from shopping with her mother, she would spend hours preening herself in front of the long mirror, demanding their total attention and asking for their approval of how she looked in the clothes she had purchased

The look from Victoria told her sister that she was in total agreement with her comment.

"Or should I wear the gown of lace?" Fiona continued. "Or maybe the fine Georgette? Or the pure silk? Or the satin one? Then I will shimmer like silver under the chandeliers."

"Oh, do hurry, Fiona dear, and make up your mind," her mother demanded at long last. "Your cousins have to decide on their dresses also." Their mother and the seamstress, like Olga and Victoria, were almost stamping their feet with annoyance.

"I know, Mama dear. Now, let me see." She pondered yet again.

"I think you should have the satin one," said Olga impatiently. "You are so much taller than we are. You can carry it off much better than either of us."

"Yes, I will do as you suggest, Olga. As you say, I will look more dignified, being so much taller. What do you think, Craig dear?" She looked at him as he gazed out of the window.

He turned. "Yes, dear, have the satin," he replied, trying to show some interest.

They all breathed a sigh of relief.

"I shall have the gown of lace," said Olga.

"And I shall have the taffeta one," added Victoria. Their mothers and the seamstress repacked the dresses in tissue paper and breathed a sigh of relief.

"Now we only need to choose their gloves, tiaras and plumes for their hair," said Maud.

"I must have new ones, Mama," demanded Fiona. "Yours are far too old."

"And mine are also," said Maud.

"Well, you must all have new ones. Let us hope they are still available. Everything has been in such short supply due to that dreadful war."

Craig glanced up angrily.

"Now," declared Fiona's mother, "you must all practise your curtsies."

They did so.

"Yes, you are all perfect – don't you think so, Craig?"

"Craig, my darling, don't you think so?" Fiona called.

"It couldn't be more perfect, my love," he replied without enthusiasm.

Fiona was quite annoyed to see he was still gazing out of the window as he spoke.

CHAPTER 107

Craig hated the London Season. He was thankful that every day that passed brought him a day nearer to going home. He had to admit that he had enjoyed the racing, concerts and theatres, but the endless parties had bored him immensely. He tried not to show it for Fiona's sake.

His most enjoyable hours had been spent with his officer friends, telling them of the progress of the help he had obtained for their men.

Tonight, a ball was being given for the coming of age of Victoria. The celebration had been delayed because of the war, but now the house was decorated for this special occasion. Up till now, the building had been used as a convalescent home for the wounded. Craig, himself, had been nursed here, and he was thankful for the care he had received. Now only one or two officers remained in a wing of the house.

'I don't seem to be able to get away from Aunt Maud and the inane chatter of her two daughters, but I suppose I should be grateful to her as tonight she has invited so many of my friends.'

Fiona, Olga and Victoria were deep in conversation with other debutantes.

'They're all enthusing about their presentations, I daresay,' he thought.

Fiona, now and again, flashed him a smile. She knew he was getting tired of the London Season, and the few angry words they had had previously had made him more so. She had insisted that she would need to come to London quite often to see her cousins and friends and do more shopping.

"I know I can shop in Edinburgh or Glasgow, but it is more fun shopping with my cousins," she said.

"Well, if you must, you must, my dear," Craig replied, not too readily, "but I won't be able to accompany you, dear, on every visit. When I do come, I will have to see my officer friends to put them in the picture as to how our men are faring up north."

"Oh, you and your army friends!" she exclaimed in anger. "You know I cannot go to any function here unaccompanied," she said, stamping her feet in frustration.

"Well, see my friends I shall," he replied adamantly.

'Well,' she thought, 'I shall certainly change all that after we are married. I shall not be thwarted in any of my plans.'

"Anyway," he continued, "I will not be able to spare much time now that the estate is so large."

"Now, my darling, don't make excuses for not coming," she replied in a more conciliatory tone of voice. "Surely the extra ghillies that Papa Bruce has promised can deal with all that?"

"But you know, Fiona," he replied angrily, "I like to attend to things myself."

"I know you do, my darling, but, dearest, you need to get away from the estates for a while. You must stop riding hour after hour alone in the glens." She was trying to not show her resentment. "I am sure that if Mama and Papa can come on several visits a year, you can manage the same for me after our marriage."

"But, as I have said, Fiona," – he too was trying not to spoil the evening's pleasure – "my darling, Papa and I have a much larger estate to manage now."

At that, she thought it wisest to let the matter drop. 'But', she thought, 'I shall insist every time that he accompanies me. After all, it is only because I shall be married to my darling Craig that living in the Highlands for the rest of my life will be bearable. Well, I won't concern myself any more with these affairs. Time is going far too quickly for me. It's too wonderful.'

She hugged his arm.

"Now, my darling," she said. "We won't discuss it any more. We are here to enjoy ourselves – especially tonight."

"Well, my dearest, you seem to be enjoying every minute of tonight." He gallantly returned her smile; then she turned to her friends to continue her conversation.

CHAPTER 108

"Fiona dear," Olga demanded, "whenever is your wedding going to be? We are all eager to come to Scotland to help you prepare for your great day. Why the delay? Surely it is time you and Craig decided on the date."

At this, Fiona's face clouded with annoyance for a moment.

"Soon, very soon," she replied, "but my darling Craig says he has to finish some silly forestry course."

"Well, at least he could let you announce the date. We cannot make any other plans whilst we wait," said Victoria, a little peeved. She had been hoping to join her friends for a holiday abroad.

"No, he has said", reiterated Fiona, "that until he has finished the course he won't consider a definite date; then he can give our wedding plans all the attention they will demand." She pouted peevishly. "I cannot even wear my engagement ring as yet. It isn't ready, so I have to be content with my Luckenbooth brooch."

"Well," enthused Victoria as she admired it, "it is certainly a lovely one. I wish I had one of those." She sighed. "What do you mean, Fiona, your engagement ring isn't ready yet?"

"Well, it was a little too small and so Papa Bruce had to take it to the family jewellers to be altered. He has been too busy with the affairs of the estate to deal with it, so it will have to wait until I return."

"Oh, what a shame!" several of them chorused.

"I also thought", continued Fiona, "that Papa Bruce would have allowed me to wear the remaining set of jewels for my presentation, but – would you believe it? – Craig would not allow it. He insisted that they could only be given to me on our wedding day. However, now I realise he was right, although I was angry at the time. They are the gift of his father to his new daughter-in-law, so it is right that we should wait until the wedding. Another few weeks won't matter."

"I daresay", remarked Victoria, "he would not like the idea of such precious jewels leaving Scotland."

"No, I don't suppose he would," agreed Fiona, "but in any case I have such lovely jewellery of my own." (She had left no one in any doubt as to what jewellery she owned. Not a day passed when she had not flaunted a different set.) "I tell you, my dear friends and cousins," she continued, "I have none to match those I shall wear on my wedding day. Oh, I am so longing for that day."

"And so are we," said Olga, sighing with anticipation.

CHAPTER 109

Craig was quite content to stand and watch all that was going on around him. Somehow he didn't feel he was part of it. He glanced down at the two old dears – Maud and her sister – listening to their incessant chatter about the past. His thoughts were far away. He longed for the peace of the mountains and glens; he found the city hot and depressive. He longed for the chill mountain air blowing on his face and through his hair, and to see the purple heather on the hillside. He sighed longingly as he watched the dancers spinning round and listened to their gay laughter.

"Isn't this too exciting for words?" declared Maud to her sister. "It makes me feel seventeen all over again. But this is so austere. It's such a pity the war has caused it to be so – not a bit like our old extravagance."

"Ah well, Maud, the war is now over. We can forget all about it!" she exclaimed exuberantly as they both fanned themselves furiously.

"Yes, I agree. It's such a pity we have to have this austerity for our daughters' presentation. It doesn't seem right that this ball had to be held here. The hall is far too small for such an occasion as this. However, everyone agrees, sister dear, that our girls look beautiful in their dresses, in spite of the austerity."

They raised their heads to view their daughters, and Craig looked at them with contempt.

'Forget it, forget it! You can never please such proud peacocks as these, with all their stupid talk of shimmering dresses, parasols, osprey feathers and coronets. War, war, war! Is that all the war meant to these ostriches with their heads in the sand? Have my gallant men died for useless trivialities such as these?' Craig's anger rose almost uncontrollably. He turned to go.

"Craig dear, don't you agree how wonderful all this is in spite of the austerity?" He shook Lady Cleveland's hand off angrily and raced through the open French windows, into the garden.

"Well, never to my life!" Maud said with a pout. "Whatever is wrong with him? I have never seen him behave like this before."

Fiona came running up just as he was disappearing, and she raced after him, but he was gone from view. She had seen the angry way he had shaken off her mother's hand, but she did not stop to ask her mother the reason. She knew he was tiring of the London Season and wanted to get back to his father. 'Well,' she thought, 'he just has to get over this father fixation he has. I shall certainly see that he does once we are married. It is no reason to be rude to Mama.'

She raced down the steps into the garden, calling his name.

He stood, leaning against the tree beside the ornamental pond, his mood still angry. 'I must leave all this and get back to my mountains and my dear father,' he thought. 'He will be missing me, just as I am missing him. This is too long for me to be away. I must get back. I will go tomorrow. I will not waste another day here.'

He heard Fiona calling his name, but he was in no mood to answer her. What was causing this strange strangulation of his being? Was it the confines of the city, the crowds, the gay, silly parties? He felt as though he were in a trap – a vice he couldn't escape from. These silly young people seemed to have forgotten the once jolly young boys, once like themselves, that were now no more through no fault of their own. They had given their all for such as these. I shall never forget. Never! Never!

'Oh, my head's in a whirl,' he thought. 'I must get back to my mountains to see the salmon leaping and the deer running free. I must have the peace and serenity of it all. Oh, what else is drawing me back?' Was it all this? His father or his wild mountains? Was that what was really drawing him back all the time he had been away? Was it the real reason he was anxious to return?

No. He hardly dared to think it, but it was the flaxen-haired beauty, his angel, his fairy of the glen. He missed her as much as his father, his home and his beloved Scotland.

"Oh, there you are, my darling!" exclaimed Fiona. "I am quite out of breath with running here and there, calling out to you. Did you not hear me? Why did you leave so suddenly? You seemed angry. Are you angry with me, my darling? I know I do chatter on so when I am with the girls. It is such a gay, jolly party. Are you not enjoying it?"

"I was, but I am tired of this constant round of festivities. I am returning to Scotland tomorrow," he said emphatically.

"But you can't, my darling. I haven't finished shopping for my trousseau yet."

"Well, you can stay with your cousins and return later. I have already been away far too long from the estate."

"And your dear papa?" she said sarcastically. "I sometimes think that he means more to you than I do." She knew instantly that she had said the wrong thing. "Oh, my darling, I am so sorry. Please say I am forgiven." She wound her arms swiftly round his neck. "Please forgive me. Kiss me and say you love me."

He looked down into her lovely eyes, now filled with remorse, and he gathered her to him and kissed her passionately. "Of course I forgive you. I do love you," he whispered as he buried his face in her hair.

He felt her soft yielding body against his, stilling the anger he had felt a short time ago. He kissed her again and again.

She was eager for possession of him.

"I love you so," she murmured over and over again as she returned his kisses. "When can we marry and really belong to each other?"

"We will decide that when we both get back to Scotland," he said.

"Oh," she pouted, "why can't we decide now? Then we can tell all our friends who are here. They all keep asking."

"Very well, then, dear, if it means so much to you. What date do you want it to be?"

"On my birthday."

"Very well, then, my darling, it shall be so."

"Come – we will go inside and make the announcement to Papa and Mama."

The announcement was greeted with great joy and delight. Everyone gathered round them.

"At last! At last!" her mother exclaimed. "Now we can get it proclaimed in the English and Scottish papers. The date has been delayed for far too long. There are so many arrangements to make for such a wedding as our daughter's – don't you think so, Maud?"

"Indeed I do, I know how long it will take. Very soon I hope to be making wedding arrangements for Olga and Victoria, but as yet they have to find a suitable man." She sighed.

Craig left next morning as he had vowed. Fiona and her mother entreated him to stay, but their pleas fell on deaf ears. Fiona bade him goodbye at the station.

"I shall be home in a few weeks, my darling," she said. "I have so much shopping to do."

"Well, hurry, my love," he called to her after kissing her goodbye. "I shall be eagerly awaiting your return."

She watched the train out of sight.

CHAPTER 110

Craig found the journey long and tiring. 'It seems almost as long as it did when I returned from France,' he thought. He had decided to stay overnight in Glasgow, to see the officers in charge of the welfare of the men and to tell them about the friends he had met in London.

When he arrived at Glencree Station, he leaped off the train like a schoolboy and took several deep breaths. "Oh, it's so good to be home," he said. "Hello there, Peggoty," he called, as he hurried towards the old stationmaster.

"Home once again, Master Craig!" he called to him.

"Yes, soon my roving days will be over and I will be here to stay."

"Has Miss Fiona not travelled with you?" Peggoty asked as he looked into the carriage.

"No, she is staying in London for a few more weeks," he said. Then he waved goodbye and raced over to the side of the loch, where he found Magnus just arriving with the boat.

"Good day to you, Master Craig. Jump in the boat. I will soon have you home."

"Thank you, Magnus. I am sure you must be tired after all your rowing."

"I'm never too tired to row you home, Master Craig."

"How I have missed the loch and my mountains whilst I have been in London! Everywhere was so crowded. I longed for the peace of my homeland. How fresh and exhilarating everything is! I will never go away again, except for short sojourns to the city with Miss Fiona, when I suppose I shall have to be a dutiful husband and take her shopping." He laughed as he spoke.

He thought Magnus rather quiet, and he nearly remarked on it, but then he thought, 'Maybe it is my own exuberance that makes him seem so subdued.'

"How is my father, Magnus?" he asked

"He was quite well the last time I saw him. He is visiting Edinburgh at present."

"Oh, I see. Tell me, how is your dear wife, Martha?"

"Not too well at the moment, Master Craig, but she will no doubt feel better if Roddy can manage some leave before he departs for the Middle East."

Craig wanted to ask about Elizabeth, but he decided against it.

"Well," he continued, "I too hope Roddy gets home soon. I know only too well what it means to be away, and the Middle East is a long way from home."

"It is, to be sure Master Craig." Magnus looked pensively ahead as he rowed. He seemed not to want further conversation.

Craig thought, 'I have never seen him look so sad and forlorn.'

"Well, here we are. You're home once more."

"Thank you and goodbye, Magnus. Please give Martha my good wishes. I hope she is better soon." With a final wave, he leaped up the jetty steps.

CHAPTER 111

"I am home, Aunt Elena," Craig called as he raced inside. (She was always the first one he called to.)

She came hurrying out of the lounge at the sound of his voice.

"Well, upon my word, Craig dear, your father did not expect you back for another two weeks at least. He is visiting the city. I think he has taken the ring to be altered. Why is Fiona not with you?"

"She wanted to stay and do more shopping for her trousseau. She said she had to make so many plans with her cousins now that the date of our wedding has been decided."

"So, you have finally decided on the date, then? Your father will be so pleased – as I am too."

"Well, Fiona was getting so upset about there being no definite date, so we decided on her birthday, later this year. We were able to tell many of our friends, as they were present at a ball we attended."

"Oh, tell me," she said: "how did the London Season go for them? I remember Harriet's and Margot's and mine so well – as if it was yesterday. What a glorious time it was for us all!" She sighed.

"It went very well, but I missed home."

"Now, come and eat. You must be famished after your long journey."

"Where is Aunt Harriet now?"

"Visiting Mrs Knowell," Elena replied. "She will be home soon."

At the sound of that name, Craig felt a pang of anxiety, but he soon dismissed it.

"Call me early in the morning, Jamie, and tell Zan to saddle my horse."

"Very good, Master Craig," Jamie replied.

Elena remembered Harriet's prediction that as soon as Craig came home he would be away riding the glens. "He will never change," she had said.

Jamie and Elena both bade him goodnight; then he raced up the stairs with Flint at his heels. He went straight to the window and looked out to Harrison Hall.

'There's no light in her room: I wonder why? She must be singing, as she usually does after dinner. I will see her tomorrow. But why should I want to see her, now that I have fixed the date for my marriage to the girl I adore? But I must see her, I must – as often as I can before I marry! I must! I must! Why? Why cannot I ever get her out of my mind?'

Her blue eyes were dancing before him as he tried to sleep.

CHAPTER 112

Craig was already awake when Jamie called him next morning. "It's a bonnie day, to be sure, Master Craig. I daresay you will be out riding all day?"

"I certainly will, and I will be away as soon as I can."

He put on the silk shirt and jodhpurs that Jamie had laid out for him, and, with Flint on his lap, he was away down the bannister, singing a gay Scottish tune as he went.

Sarah, the maid, watched him descend and waited for the landing.

"My, my, Master Craig! It's so good to have you home again. This house is not the same when you are away. Are you all right?" she asked as he picked himself up, laughing gaily as he did so.

"Are you all right, Flint?" he teasingly called out to his dog.

He needn't have asked. The dog was jumping up and down with glee. His master was home, and that was all he cared about.

Elena came down the stairs as he was leaving. She called out to him: "What time will you be back?"

"For dinner, I promise."

"It is your favourite tonight, so don't be late."

"I won't."

He took his silver-knobbed whip from the hook on the wall and raced outside. He stood for a few moments inhaling deeply the good mountain air as Zan brought his horse. With a shake of his whip, he wished Elena and the servants goodbye; then he was away like the wind. He was almost out of sight before they had turned their backs.

"He does miss his mountains when he has been away," said Zan.

"Yes," replied Jamie, "it's as if he thinks that one day they won't be there, though we all know they always will be."

They both nodded in agreement.

Craig rode on. He opened the two top buttons of his shirt to let the bracing mountain air envelop him. His hair blew wildly across his forehead, and now and again he brushed it aside. He was free again – back home again where he belonged. He raced on and on.

"Soon I shall see my dearest angel, Flaxen," he said with a laugh.

The horse pricked up her ears at the sound of her name and Craig tugged one of her ears gently. He stopped to rest his horse on the high rise and lifted Flint down to race amongst the heather. He rolled up his sleeves to his elbows. His natural tan from being in the open air had faded while he was in London.

He looked towards Harrison Hall and stood perplexed. Why was Elizabeth's window closed? 'Maybe the gales have been blowing recently,' he thought.

He remounted and called Flint to heel. "Come on up, then, if you prefer," he said.

Flint leaped into his arms. "You are becoming a lazy rebel in your old age," he said as he tucked the dog lovingly in front of him.

He raced on, but suddenly he felt his horse stumble.

"Now, now, Flaxen, what is it?" he questioned. He alighted and checked each hoof. "Ah, a lost shoe. Well, we will call at the smithy – it isn't too far. Come down, Flint; you can have some exercise too."

He lifted Flint from the saddle, and the dog raced off, bounding amongst the shrubs. Craig walked slowly on ahead.

'I will be able to collect my new saddle at the same time,' he mused.

CHAPTER 113

"Hello there, Master Craig. It's good to see you back again. Have you come to collect your new saddle?" Donny, the old blacksmith, called to him as he approached.

"Well, I will take it if it is ready, but my horse has thrown a shoe."

"Yes, your saddle is ready. I will get it as soon as I have shod your horse."

Craig watched him intently as he picked up the horse's hoof and placed it between his knees. There were beads of sweat on his brow, but he had a smile on his weather-beaten face. His grey old head was bent low; his old leather brat clung to his knees. Over the years Craig had watched this dear old man at his work many times, and he had never ceased to marvel at his dexterity. When he was a child, his parents had brought him here to have his first pony shod and his initials engraved on his saddle.

He wandered into the saddlery, where the smell of fine leather filled his nostrils. He looked at the row of saddles hanging there, and he spotted two side by side with initials carved on them. He traced his fingers round each initial slowly. There was a puzzled look on his face as he tried to work out whose they might be. At last his curiosity got the better of him.

"Donny."

"Yes, Master Craig," he called.

He put the horse's hoof to the floor, straightened up and wiped the sweat from his brow.

"Your horse is ready."

"Whose are the initials on these saddles?"

Donny walked over to him.

"I cannot place anyone on the island with these initials."

"No, you might find it hard to guess those, Master Craig."

Craig looked at him, more puzzled than ever.

"Those are for the daughter and son-in-law of Lady Margot. You will remember her daughter – Davinia?"

"Yes, I remember. She used to visit her late grandmother when they came home from India. So," he exclaimed, "they are going all that way! How wonderful your work is! You are a real craftsman," he said, patting Donny on the shoulder.

"Yes, they are being collected by Charles in a few days, to be packed away, ready for shipping with some other larger items of Lady Margot's."

"Yes," replied Craig, "I daresay she is getting them sorted out before she sails."

"But Her Ladyship has already gone, and, to everyone's surprise, she has taken Miss Anderson with her. Apparently, she wanted Miss Anderson to help her with her correspondence."

"Gone!" The word was like a dagger turning in his heart. "Gone?" he asked again in disbelief. He gave a startled gasp.

"I will get your saddle now," Donny said, but Craig wasn't listening.

He snatched his reins from the stable boy and galloped off, clearing the first hedge with feet to spare. He raced along like wildfire, leaving the boy still looking at his hands, where a few moments before his reins had been. Old Mac, who had just ridden up, wished him good day, but Craig had not time to reply.

"Whatever has upset the young master so, Donny?" he asked.

Donny came into view from the saddlery, scratching his head in bewilderment as they gazed after him.

"Just look at the speed he is going. He will come a cropper for sure," said Mac. "And look at poor Flint trying to catch up."

"Well," replied Donny, "anyone else going at that speed would come a cropper, but not the young master."

They watched till he was out of sight.

Craig rode on, jumping everything in his path. His hair blew across his eyes, and he brushed it aside angrily, time and time again. He undid another button of his shirt to allow more cool air to reach his feverish body.

He spoke aloud, as if to Flaxen: "It cannot be true. It cannot! Flaxen, Flaxen, please tell me it isn't true."

If Flaxen could have spoken, she would have answered, "It is true, it is true."

He who had always had everything that life could offer, whose every whim and wish was granted by all around him, had been denied the only thing that to him was worth living for: the sight of his angel. How could he go on living? He knew that after he was married he would not be able to contact her in any way, but at least she would be around. She would be in the choir at church, or in the village. To never see her again was unthinkable.

'I wonder if that was why Magnus was so quiet and Martha was not well. It could also be', he thought, 'the reason that her window was closed.' His usual mischievous smile had gone and his dancing, piercing eyes were now narrowed to slits with fury and frustration that this, if it were true, could have happened to him. Never before had he felt like this. Never more than kisses had passed between them, but it was as if they were bound together by some invisible thread. He had felt it for so long, and no matter how he tried he could not shake it off. No, she couldn't have gone. It was not possible that he would never see her again. 'Donny must not have heard aright,' he thought. 'Yes, that's it.'

CHAPTER 114

The ride to Harrison Hall seemed to take longer than usual, in spite of his haste.

"Hurry, Flaxen, hurry," he called angrily. It was unlike him to speak harshly like that, and in any case he knew that his horse was straining every muscle as she took the ditches and hedges in her stride. 'She is like the White Horse of Yore,' Craig thought. 'She seems to have wings.'

Flaxen sped across the stream, showering them both with the icy water from the distant mountains.

"Sorry, Flaxen," he whispered as he stroked her mane. "I know you cannot go any faster."

At last Harrison Hall came into view. Craig slackened off, reined to a halt and sat pensively, pondering for a few moments as he tried to disentangle his thoughts.

'No, it won't do for me to be seen riding at this pace and arriving in such a frantic state,' he thought. 'The villagers' tongues wag busily enough. I cannot afford them food for thought and gossip.' Very little excitement happened in their isolated community and in their humdrum but happy lives.

If ever word got out that the young master of Glencree had ridden up the drive of Harrison Hall with hair flying, shirt undone, sleeves rolled up high, his horse panting ready to drop, not to mention the haste with which he had left the smithy after the smith had said that the young miss had left with Lady Margot, the news would cause everyone in the district to tut-tut non-stop.

'Oh, let them talk and think what they like,' he thought angrily. 'No, no, I must not give this impression.' He knew only one other would have seen him race by, and her lips would be sealed for ever. 'No one must ever know of my feelings for my angel, particularly not Fiona or my father. I must make this visit look very casual.'

He swept his hair to one side as best he could, unrolled his sleeves and rebuttoned his shirt. He alighted from his horse and tied her to a low bush to rest awhile. Feeling calmer, and with his horse breathing more easily, he sat down on the cool, green grass and pulled from the pocket of his jodhpurs a cube of sugar. Flaxen nuzzled his ear.

"All right, girl, I haven't forgotten," he said as he handed the sugar to the horse. Craig spoke softly and rubbed her nose gently. "You have earned it today, my friend. I know you could not go any faster. We must be very calm. I know you miss her too."

Flaxen shook her head as if she understood.

Suddenly, Craig remembered Flint: 'I wonder if he is following or if he has gone home,' he thought.

He was annoyed to notice that he had lost one of the buttons from his shirt.

"Drat!" he exclaimed in annoyance as he tucked in his shirt.

He remounted and cantered slowly up the long drive, as outwardly calm and composed as on any of his other visits. He was almost at the steps when the old handyman saw him.

"Good day, sir," he said, but Craig hardly noticed him.

He bade him a polite good day, dismounted and handed him the reins.

He walked slowly up the steps and tapped the door softly.

No answer came.

'I hope someone is in,' he thought as he knocked more loudly and tapped his foot impatiently.

After a short pause, the door opened and Charles looked at him, startled.

"Oh, do come in, Master Craig. We have not had any visitors for so long. How nice to see you!"

But Craig wasn't listening. He strode past Charles into the hallway.

"Is Lady Margot in?" he asked.

"No, Master Craig. She has already left for India, and she has taken Elizabeth with her. Of course, you have been away so you wouldn't know."

The hallway was cluttered up with several large crates and huge black tin trunks on which was written in large, white letters:

> Lady M. Emslie,
> C/O Head Mission,
> Madras,
> India.
> (Not Wanted on Voyage)

"As you see, sir, I am still packing the trunks for Her Ladyship. The ones of Elizabeth are finished."

Craig glanced down at them, and the sight of her name struck him speechless with anger. He read and reread it over and over again:

> Miss E. D. A. Anderson,
> C/O Head Mission,
> Madras,
> India.
> (Not Wanted on Voyage)

What voyage? She couldn't go on any voyage without him. He had known that Margot would be returning to India after the war if her mother was well enough to leave, but she had said she wouldn't leave until after his wedding. 'I wonder why she has not stayed even for that,' he thought. 'She promised Fiona and me, and it isn't like Margot to break her word.' Margot's going, he decided, did not matter to him one iota – but to take his angel with her! He looked up to see Charles looking at him uneasily.

"Why did Her Ladyship leave so soon, Charles?" he asked as casually as he could. "And when did they leave?"

"Well, Her Ladyship had news of her daughter's ill health and, although she didn't think it was too serious, she suddenly decided to go and take Elizabeth with her. Elizabeth at first seemed very reluctant to go; then suddenly she was all excited at the prospect and couldn't wait to get away. It fair puzzled Cook and me and everyone in the village. Her parents apparently fell in with her wishes quite readily when she said she would like to go. It was so strange, especially as she knew her brother was due to go away soon and she had already accepted the position at the academy. Robin's mother was fair put out at her change of mind, and Robin was nearly distracted when he heard."

'Oh, Robin be damned!' he thought angrily. 'So, it must have been owing to her departure that Magnus was so quiet yesterday.'

"When did they leave?" he repeated.

"They sailed two weeks ago, Master Craig."

'All this going on and me at all those silly, stupid parties!' he thought. He was trying not to show his great distress as Charles was still looking at him with concern. 'She knows I would never let her go and leave her parents.' He stood as in a trance and stared into space. 'To never hear her voice ever again – no more singing – or hear her whispering his name as only she could!' He looked down again at the tin trunks and her name seared into his brain. 'To never again kiss her adorable angelic lips and never again gaze into her adorable, forget-me-not-blue eyes! The tree, the tree – she must have left me a message in the tree.'

He thanked Charles and hurried away, grabbing his reins from the old gardener with barely an acknowledgement.

Cook, who had heard him talking and was going to ask him to stay for some tea, was only just in time to see him ride swiftly away. The three watched him in dismay.

"Well, upon my word!" exclaimed Cook as they returned inside and Charles closed the door.

CHAPTER 115

Craig hastily dismounted when he reached the tree. He reached inside, but no crackle of paper could he hear. "Drat! Drat!" he shouted, stamping his foot in frustration.

'She should have left me a note,' he thought. 'Maybe she did and someone found it. No, no, that couldn't be. No one else knows of our secret tree – only one other, and she would never touch anything that didn't belong to her.'

Craig reached lower into the tree and pulled out a long blue ribbon, one end of which was wrapped round a bunch of dying forget-me-nots. He hugged it close and whispered Elizabeth's name over and over again.

'Of course this was all she could leave for me,' he thought. 'Of course she dare not leave me a note in case anyone found it and used it against her.' But no one else knew that forget-me-nots were a symbol of their love, apart from Merry-Berry.

Flint was waiting for him when he arrived home.

"I was getting most anxious," said Elena. "When Flint came back alone I thought you must have had an accident."

"No, Aunt Elena; as you see, I am safe and sound."

"Well, don't be long, my boy. Your dinner will be getting cold. Harriet and I have eaten."

He bent down to pat Flint on the head.

"I am so sorry, my old friend. I forgot for a moment you were not with me," he said.

He raced up to his room, and Flint raced after him. He put the blue ribbon and dead flowers in his secret drawer and hurriedly changed for dinner. He was thankful to be alone with his thoughts as he tried to do justice to his favourite meal, but he found he had no appetite.

He called to both the aunts as they sat playing cards in the lounge: "I am retiring early tonight. Goodnight, my dears."

"Very well. Goodnight," they called.

"I wonder why he didn't join us. He usually likes a game of cards after dinner," said Harriet.

"I daresay he is tired after his long journey yesterday, and he has ridden hard today to fill his lungs with our bracing mountain air. He will be missing his father also," said Elena.

"Well, he will have to make the most of his father's company before he is married. Fiona is so possessive and I think that may cause trouble sooner or later, as will his chasing over the glens by himself."

Elena nodded in agreement.

CHAPTER 116

Bruce was ecstatic on his return from the city to find Craig had returned and the date of his wedding had been finally decided.

"Did you remember, Papa, to take the ring to be altered?" Craig asked.

"No, my son. I am sorry – I completely forgot. I have had so much work to do, arranging Margot's property, since she had to leave in such a hurry."

"Yes, I was most shocked to hear that she had already left for India. Why was it so, Papa?"

Bruce looked at him with a feeling of trepidation, wondering if Craig would mention the fact that Margot's companion had left with her. But, as no mention was forthcoming, he hastily said, "Margot received news of her daughter's ill health and decided to hurry away. She was most upset to have to forgo attending your wedding, and she asked me to wish you and Fiona every happiness for the future."

"How kind of her! We are both going to miss her." He sighed. "It won't be the same without Margot. She has always been such an important friend."

"Yes, we have all missed her greatly since she left. I wish she could have stayed, but it was not to be."

Craig and Bruce were riding side by side. Bruce was determined to have his son all to himself before Fiona arrived back from London.

"Think, my son, of all this land we have got to hand on to our heirs. Soon we will be riding along with your first son, just as when I first rode over the glens with you. I wonder, Craig, if you and your sons will love one another as much as we do."

"I hope so, Papa. I know I shall certainly love them as much as you love me."

Bruce smiled graciously. At last, all was going well. He had, he decided, done the right thing.

"Well, my boy, I only hope you have more sons than I did. If only we hadn't lost your darling mother so young. Maybe then there would be three or four of us riding as we are now. Such fun and laughter we could have shared – but alas! it was not to be. You are aware, my son, how much your marriage, and the sons that will surely follow, will mean to me. Our heritage and clan will be secure."

But Craig wasn't listening as his father's voice droned on and on. Somehow, he didn't feel interested. He gazed into the distance, and Bruce became aware that Craig was not paying any attention to him.

'Maybe the boy is thinking about his forthcoming wedding,' he told himself, 'or maybe he is thinking we shall not be able to be so much a part of each other's lives afterwards.' He glanced at Craig and noted his faraway look.

"I know you and Fiona will have your own apartments," he said, "but we will be able to spend some time together as we are now, my son. In a year's time, there may be – nay, will surely be – an heir for Glencree. Just think, my son, what rejoicing there will be – just as there was when you were born. All the villagers and crofters were so delighted."

He sat lost in reverie as they dismounted on the high rise to rest their horses and view all the land.

"You don't know what it means to me, my dear boy," he added, "to know that after I have gone all this will pass to you and your sons."

But Craig's thoughts were miles away. Yes, he would be here, but this was nothing to him without his angel to share it with him. She was now so far away. 'To think I shall never see her again!' The thought and anguish was getting more than he could bear. 'But I must forget – I must!'

"What are you thinking about, my son? Your thoughts seem miles away."

"I was thinking about all you have been talking about, Papa. Look – it is drawing dusk and we must return."

They remounted and turned for home, each in silence with his own thoughts.

CHAPTER 117

Elizabeth was getting more despondent as the days passed. The increasing warmth, brighter sunshine and bluer skies filled everyone else with increasing joy.

She was, as usual, leaning over the side of the ship looking into the clear blue water below when Lady Margot's voice broke in on her thoughts. A flying fish in the distance brought a faint smile to her sad face.

"Well, my dear, we arrive in Port Said tomorrow so we are well on our way. This journey is getting very tedious." Lady Margot sighed deeply.

Elizabeth agreed silently. Each day seemed like a year. She was sick and tired of looking at the same old sea and sky, the same people every day, the same old topic after dinner every night (all the wonderful things they were going to do once they arrived in India now the dreadful war was over).

"I shall be so glad to get off this ship. I can't wait to see my darling daughter and my two little granddaughters." Lady Margot sighed with happiness at the thought of them.

'My dear Lady Margot,' Elizabeth thought, 'you don't know what it means to me to not see my dear parents for two long years. And goodness knows when I shall see my brother Roddy! And I may never, ever see my darling Craig again.' She sighed deeply, trying hard to hold back her tears.

"I wonder how many of my old friends are still in India and how my missions have been whilst I have been away. I also wonder if anything has changed much. I doubt it; things never do in India. It probably won't be so crowded with troops now the war is over." Her voice droned on and on as Elizabeth listened attentively, but she had to admit she was getting pretty bored at the sound of Lady Margot's voice.

"I must visit my missions as soon as I can and let Lady Elena know as soon as possible what state they are in. I know she will be waiting anxiously for news."

Elizabeth gave a start as she heard Elena's name and Margot noted her startled reaction. 'How foolish of me!' she thought, 'I must really be more careful in future, but letters will have to go to that address and I don't know how I can avoid upsetting the poor child. I shall have to find her other duties to do apart from seeing to my correspondence. I know the children will keep her rather busy, so as soon as I can I will get another secretary. I cannot keep reminding the poor child of all she has left behind and the sacrifices she has made. I am so angry with Bruce for putting me in this deplorable position.' A deep frown crossed her brow.

Elizabeth looked up at her. She wondered why Lady Margot had suddenly gone so quiet and why she was frowning. Suddenly, Lady Margot's mood changed dramatically. In a moment she was bubbling over with joy at the thought of all her loved ones waiting for her. Elizabeth tried in vain to catch some of Lady Margot's joy and happy enthusiasm.

'I wish I wasn't on this dratted ship so far from home and all I love – especially my darling, darling Craig. I wonder if he knows I have left. Oh, my precious, precious darling, how I miss you and my dear friend Emma!' Elizabeth's thoughts raced on and on. Lady Margot and others aboard will have loved ones waiting to greet them with open arms. I have no one waiting for me.' She sighed. Suddenly, she felt an anger she had never known before. 'I shall insist', she told herself boldly, 'that I return to my loved ones in two years, as the laird promised. Then I shall have kept my promise and the laird can keep his, but I know I shall never see my darling Craig ever again.' Her head span at the thought. 'I'll never, ever see him again. How am I going to live without him?'

Lady Margot watched Elizabeth for several minutes without intruding on her thoughts. Then she touched her lightly on her arm.

"Come, my dear," she said, "we must go below."

CHAPTER 118

"Well, my dear Elizabeth, we can go ashore when we dock. The ship is staying two days whilst it restocks with more supplies. Some of the passengers are leaving and I daresay some new passengers will be coming aboard. Come, my dear – we will go and see from the main deck all that is going on. You will find it all so fascinating and intriguing. I just love it."

'Oh, will she never stop prattling on?' thought Elizabeth. 'I know I shan't like it one little bit.'

"This is only the Middle East," Margot continued.

The ship slowed to a halt. Elizabeth watched, fascinated, as the small crafts of the native merchants came alongside. The merchants were hold up all their wares and shouting up the prices, and the passengers were calling back, offering lower prices. She laughed gaily as baskets on ropes were flung down from the ship and filled with goods of every kind, including handmade jewellery and leatherwork. Lady Margot, who was beside her, assured her that haggling was normal in Middle Eastern countries, as it was in India also.

"Come, Elizabeth – there is a party going ashore and we are joining them to visit some pyramids and mosques and the bazaar. Maybe we will see some real Bedouins. Of course, we won't see everything in one day. How exciting it all is my child. Come – we must hurry."

They were both glad to be at last on dry land, and Elizabeth had to admit there were many strange and wonderful things to see. She followed Lady Margot closely, and the hustle and bustle everywhere filled her with dismay. Some women, were dressed in black burkhas, which covered them from head to foot with only their eyes showing. She noticed how quickly their eyes darted here, there and everywhere, and some looked at her with a mysterious, questioning gaze before going on their way.

The men gave her a questioning look of a different kind – a look that she was unfamiliar with. It was as if they had never seen anyone quite like her before.

"It is because of your long golden hair, which is showing below your hat. It is not the custom in these countries for a woman to show her hair," Lady Margot explained.

"Is that so, milady? Then that must be the reason why they are covered so."

"Yes, it is."

Elizabeth stood looking at all the pretty things for sale, and Lady Margot chided her for her delay.

"Come, my child – we must not stand too long in one place. We must keep up with the rest of the party. We can soon get lost. Also someone might want to buy us."

"Buy us!" Elizabeth exclaimed incredulously. "Buy us?" She gave a gasp of disbelief.

"Well, you especially. You are so young and beautiful, but they would have second thoughts about me," she said wryly. She looked at the girl by her side, who was looking back at her in disbelief.

"Oh, milady, you must be joking."

"I can assure you, my dear innocent child, that I am not joking. Someone would pay quite a price for you, but, as for me, well, they would probably prefer a camel instead."

Elizabeth shuddered at the thought of it. "My, my, what queer customs they have, to be sure!" she said. "Fancy trying to buy people!" She wafted the flies from her face. "Never have I seen so many flies. There are easily a hundred or more per person," she said. "And what heat, to be sure! I feel sorry for those poor women wrapped up in all those clothes. They must be very hot to say the least."

She was thankful for her pretty summer dress and brimmed straw hat and the shade of her parasol, which Lady Margot had bought from a vendor as soon as she saw it.

"That we must have!" she exclaimed.

Even so, Elizabeth was very hot and tired.

"We will not be able to visit the casbah," Lady Margot said as they walked on.

"Why not?" Elizabeth asked as she furiously waved her fan (another purchase Lady Margot had insisted on) to ward off the flies and cool herself.

"Well, it is old and the streets are so narrow. The roofs actually touch one another – so the men who have been there state. Not many tourists venture down there."

"How dark and gloomy it must be! It must be rather frightening, I should think," said Elizabeth with a shudder.

"Yes, it is. It is not the sort of place a woman would wish to go, I shouldn't think. Come – we just have time for you to have a ride on a camel, my dear."

Elizabeth found no lack of helpers among the crowd of sightseers from the ship to assist her to mount one of the camels. She stumbled as she walked back to the ship and Lady Margot noticed how pale and lethargic she had become.

"I fear this heat is a little too much for you, dear. We won't join the party going ashore tomorrow. We will stay and rest on board, although there is still a lot to see."

'I would give all these wonderful sights', thought Elizabeth, 'for one glimpse of the cool, green, beloved mountains and glens of home.'

She spent the next day watching new passengers coming aboard. What a lot of soldiers there were! 'How I wish my dear Roddy was amongst them,' she thought, but she searched for him in vain. 'I wonder where he is and when I shall see him again.'

CHAPTER 119

At last, the ship pulled away from the quay on the final stage of its journey. Lady Margot had found several old friends returning to India and the rest of the journey was friendly and gay. There were dances every night, and on several evenings Her Ladyship asked Elizabeth to sing.

Elizabeth was very pleased to note the happiness it brought to everyone – especially to the soldiers. It was as if she was singing to Roddy, as of old. 'Oh, if only one of them could be Roddy!' she told herself with a sigh, but on second thoughts she decided it was better that he wasn't there. How could she explain to him why she was aboard, having broken her promise to all of them? 'I had no option but to break my word,' she thought.

Several of the soldiers tried to break down her barrier of reticence, but to no avail. It was their greatest delight to hold her in their arms as they danced. She was always extremely courteous and chatted gaily as they danced, but when it was over she withdrew into her own secret, silent world. Sigh after sigh escaped her lips as her thoughts lingered on what could never be.

Margot never ceased to introduce her to young men of good standing. One of them was especially smitten by her. She often noticed him watching her, and they chatted together for a great deal of the journey. One could see he was madly in love with her, but Lady Margot could tell by Elizabeth's demeanour that her heart and thoughts were far away.

'If only I could get her to forget all that she has sacrificed!' she thought. 'Her pain will ease in time, but it is too soon yet.'

CHAPTER 120

Elizabeth became more and more despondent and afraid as she thought of the strange country which was to be her new home. 'I shall be quite lost in those vast new surroundings,' she thought, and she shuddered time and time again as she thought of it. 'There will be no one to turn to but Lady Margot. I know she will never fail me, but I want darling Mama and Papa and Roddy around. Alas, it cannot be!' She sighed sadly. If only her darling Craig was near to comfort her and laugh away her fears and to hold her tenderly in his arms. 'How can I live without you, my darling?' She thought she could still hear his voice as the waves pounded the side of the ship. Tears fell slowly from her eyes. Her gaze lingered on the still waters below and she shivered in the chilly night air. Once more she had escaped from the gay party aboard.

"Ah, there you are!" exclaimed Captain Carlton MacVey excitedly as he came down the companionway and rushed to her side. "I have been looking for you everywhere."

She lifted her head but still gazed out to sea.

"Come, my dear – these tropical nights can get very chilly. You really must come indoors. Her Ladyship wanted to come looking for you, but I told her I would find you. So here I am, your ever devoted slave."

She turned to face him. "It is very kind of you to be so concerned about me, but, as you see, I am quite safe."

He lifted up her face to his. "Why so sad, my pretty one?" he said. He looked longingly into her sad blue eyes. "I do love you so, my dearest one. Please say that we could at least be closer friends."

"No, I am sorry, that is not possible."

She turned to go, but he held her lightly by the arms and looked at her crestfallen. "Come," he said, "we will tell Lady Margot you are safe."

CHAPTER 121

Emma greeted her father on the cobbled driveway and dismounted from her horse. He was saying farewell to Craig and Fiona. She gave a wave to Craig and he turned to wave back, but Fiona stared straight ahead until their carriage turned into the lane and disappeared from view.

"Well, my dear Papa, what is the final date for their wedding? The village is agog with excitement now they know Lady Fiona is back, but not knowing the exact date is causing no end of speculation. I know it will be in all the papers, but you know how long it takes for news to reach us. Mrs Macdonald, the florist, is most anxious to get the freshest flowers to decorate the church – as well as everywhere else, I shouldn't wonder. Miss Grant is waiting impatiently for Magnus to deliver her orders for all her materials, cottons and ribbons to complete all the dresses for the events that follow the wedding. Magnus must be tired out with all the extra journeys he is having to make. As you know, Papa, the celebrations will go on for a long time. That is what Mrs Knowell says happened after the laird was married."

"Did she, now?" her father rejoined, noticing her serious expression. "Well, you know as well as I do that there is very little goes on in the village that she doesn't get to hear about."

They both laughed heartily.

"I agree, Papa. Her name should be Mrs Know-All, not Knowell."

"Now, now, my dear daughter, you mustn't make such statements!" He smiled and tugged her plaits.

"Now, about that date, Papa," she said, tugging his arm.

"You could always wheedle any information out of me, you little vixen. It is to be on Lady Fiona's birthday – the third Saturday of next month. They came to inform me that I will only be *assisting* at the wedding ceremony." He sighed.

Emma looked at him in dismay. "Why? Why?" she exclaimed indignantly.

"Because Lady Fiona wants her uncle from England, Bishop Kendry, to marry them."

"I daresay the laird and Master Craig are not too pleased about it."

"No, they don't seem to be," replied her father, "but, as Master Craig said, the bride's every wish must be granted on her wedding day."

"Well, of all the injustice! It's just not fair," Emma replied, and she stamped her foot in anger.

"It's all right, my child. Don't take on so. It is Lady Fiona's wish."

"Yes, yes, Papa. You will have to do all the preparations and Bishop Kendry will just appear on the day of the wedding. Oh, it's just not fair."

"Now, now, my dear!" her father admonished. He was getting quite perturbed at her increasing anger. He knew she had no great liking for Lady Fiona. "This is no way for a daughter of mine to behave."

"Well, at least", she panted, "when Lady Fiona is married, I shall be able to arrange my own wedding. Her wanting to do the London Season has delayed my wedding too. As it is, my best friend, Elizabeth, has left and so she cannot be my bridesmaid."

Her father looked at her sadly. He knew she was trying to cope with two disappointments.

"I don't know what the villagers will say when they get to know," she said. "I suppose also we will have to do more practising for the anthems just because he is present. Mrs Knowell will insist on that just to show off the choir." She stamped her foot again as she loosened her saddle. "I will join you inside, Papa, when I have put my horse away," she told him.

"Very well, my child."

CHAPTER 122

Emma was surprised one Sunday afternoon when Craig arrived at the room used as a Sunday school by the children. She had taken over Elizabeth's class until another of the girls from the academy came to relieve her. All the children stood up politely as he entered.

"You may go now, children. That is all for today. Is Lady Fiona not with you?" she asked as she closed the door after them. "I know you both came to see Papa the other day."

"No," he replied, "she has now returned home to prepare for our wedding. It is not about our wedding that I have come." He hesitated for a moment.

She looked at him apprehensively, and a sudden fear deep within her caused her to sit down beside him.

"Well, what is it, my dear Craig?" she said.

"Will you please tell me Elizabeth's full address in India and, also, why she left so suddenly? You must know – you are her closest friend."

It was the question she had feared. How was she going to answer him without lying? Her heart missed a beat as she weighed him up. He looked at her for a long time and he knew by her hesitancy that she was reluctant to answer him.

'She must know something,' he thought.

"Well, I know that Lady Margot begged her to go with her to assist her. She had to hasten away shortly after you left for London because of her daughter's ill health."

'Well,' she thought, 'he can verify that if he doubts me.'

"Elizabeth was most reluctant to go at first because of leaving her parents," she continued, "but Lady Margot must have pleaded with her. She told Elizabeth she could return in two years if she wished. By that time she would be able to find another companion to help her with the correspondence. Elizabeth must have decided that two years would not be too long after all."

"Oh, I see," he replied, rather dejectedly. "Do you know where they are residing?"

"No, Craig, I do not. I don't think Elizabeth knew exactly. They plan to visit so many missions and she didn't know which one they would finally reside at."

"Yes – yes, I see. I had quite forgotten about the missions. Aunt Elena was waiting for news of those." A plan was going through his mind as he spoke.

"Elizabeth said she would write to me as soon as she could, but I don't expect any news for several months," said Emma. "That is all I can tell you."

"Thank you, Emma dear. I am sure you are missing her too."

"Yes, I am She was to have been a bridesmaid at my wedding later in the year."

"She will be sorry to miss your wedding," he said, noting her sadness. "Goodbye, Emma. I will see you in the village sometime."

"Yes, yes. We are all looking forward to your wedding. There is so much joy and it is mounting daily."

She watched as he sped away. 'Surely, he is not going to write to her!' she thought. 'My dear friend has suffered enough. He has just got to forget her.'

'Of course,' he thought, 'how foolish of me! The address is on the boxes.' He turned his horse towards Harrison Hall, and when he arrived he dismounted quickly and raced up the steps.

"Charles! Charles!" he called.

"Yes, Master Craig. It is a pleasure to see you again so soon."

"Charles, can you remember the address where Her Ladyship is staying? I know it was on the boxes. I would like to keep in touch with her."

"No, Master Craig. I am sorry. The boxes left some days ago. It was only a temporary address for the boxes. Ralph, the painter, has now gone to the mainland to do some work there so I cannot ask him if he remembers. I cannot recall it. I am so sorry."

Craig stamped his foot impatiently. 'These country people!' he thought. 'They cannot remember anything of note.'

"We are now getting ready for Lady Harriet and Lady Elena to settle in here after your wedding."

"Yes, yes, I understand you are very busy. Never mind. Thank you. Good day."

Charles watched as Craig raced away.

Now there was only Aunt Elena and he dare not ask her. He rode on over the familiar paths they had strolled. He dismounted and tied Flaxen to a tree; then he sat down with Flint by his side. As he lay back on the grass, the dog nuzzled his ear.

"Well, old pal, we won't have many more lonesome rides, just the three of us. I will be too tied up with wedding plans and arranging the household. How are you going to like your new mistress?"

Flint looked up at him. Craig realised that Fiona was not too keen on him; she resented his love for his master and Craig's passionate love of him.

"Don't worry, old fella," said Craig. "You will always be with me."

Flint looked at him as though he understood, and he settled into a contented snooze.

Craig's thoughts were far away as he gazed at the deep-blue sky above. 'My angel, my angel, where are you? Why are you so far away from me? Come back, my angel, come back.' He knew it was not to be. 'How can I ever go on living? Never to see her again! How? How?' He lowered his eyes and ran his hands through the cool green grass. His eyes came to rest on a patch of blue-mauve flowers.

At first he thought they were forget-me-nots. Then he looked more closely at them. He plucked one, held it closer to his eyes and pondered for several minutes as he tried to think of its name. "I thought I knew the names of all the flowers that grow here," he said, "but I cannot think of yours. What is your name, little flower?" he asked as he twisted it round and round.

Flint stirred in his sleep, opened one eye and looked at his master, but he didn't know either.

"You are no help," Craig said as he tugged Flint's ear playfully.

Suddenly, a soft voice called out to him from the hedgerow: "It is called heart's-ease, Master Craig. It is the wild pansy."

"Heart's-ease, you say, Merry-Berry! Not for me, Merry-Berry, not for me!" He sighed. He raised his head and turned to where the voice came from.

Flint stirred again and reassured himself that his master was safe.

"Not for me, not for me!" Craig repeated. He sighed, twisting the small flower between his fingers. Then he rose and went over to the hedgerow where Merry-Berry crouched.

She stood up to greet him. She looked at him sadly, then up at the sky. He followed her gaze.

"What do you see, Merry-Berry – you that know all?"

"A storm is brewing, Master Craig – a heavy storm." She turned to go, gathering her shawl further round her shoulders. "Good day, Master Craig. Good day."

"Good day. Thank you for naming the flower for me," he said, but she had gone as silently as she had come.

CHAPTER 124

The following day, whilst Bruce was away in the city, Craig waited till Harriet had left to go and visit Mrs Knowell; then he watched as Elena loaded her easel and paints and set off in the small trap.

Craig had decided that now was his opportunity to search Elena's room for the address he longed for, much as he abhorred the idea of going through her things.

'To think I have come down to this,' he thought. As he searched he was careful to leave everything as before. 'So much paperwork, Aunt Elena! I had no idea you were doing so much for my men, and there's so much correspondence for the missions too. Addresses, addresses – they are endless, but not one says where Margot will finally be.' He sighed again and again. 'The address in Madras seems to be the most likely one. I know she is first going to her daughter's and the mission cannot be far away from there.'

He hastily copied all the addresses down and underlined the one in Madras. He hurried to his room, thankful that no one had seen him.

'I am sure my friend will know of it,' he said to himself as he locked it away in his drawer. 'I feel nearer to my angel now.'

CHAPTER 125

Craig was thankful that his father was making so many visits to the city, and that the aunts, in between their preparations for the wedding, made frequent visits to Harrison Hall to get things there more to their liking.

Craig declined all his father's requests to accompany him. Bruce was frustrated because he felt that Craig should fully understand all the business he was transacting for his future.

"I understand, Papa," Craig proclaimed, "but I still need to have a lot of meetings with the Forestry Commission, and I want the arrangements all completed before I marry."

"Very well, my son," Bruce replied sadly.

Every day he took Flint and rode his horse beside the loch. Flint was always close on his heels, and often looked up at him, puzzled by his master's sadness. Their previous walks beside the loch had always been such fun. Craig would throw pebbles in the water, always laughing heartily when Flint found them and put them down at his feet. But not now, not now! He would now fling them too far and with such anger. Flint couldn't understand what was wrong.

Sometimes, as they returned by the lanes, they saw Charles out with the small dogs. Then Craig would lean against the large oak tree, just gazing toward the mountains in the distance. On other days, Craig wended his way to the small churchyard with flowers to put on his mother's tomb. Sometimes he stood deep in thought, as though silently speaking to her or awaiting an answer.

Often, when no one was about, Craig would spend hours in his mother's room, looking out over the loch. It had been left exactly as she left it on that sad day so long ago. His father's orders were that her favourite flowers should always be beside her picture. Craig would look at her picture sadly, picking it up and whispering, "Goodbye, sweetest of mothers," before closing the door softly as he left.

Elena would often look at him, perplexed, as he wandered aimlessly around, 'He's not a bit like a man about to be married,' she thought. 'Whatever is troubling the boy?' But she could find no answer. 'Unless – unless – no, no, it couldn't be.'

CHAPTER 126

"Papa! Papa!" Craig called out to him one morning as he was mounting his horse.

"What is it, my son?"

"I have a serious matter to discuss with you."

He stood, tapping his foot nervously against the step, as his father looked at him apprehensively.

"Can it not wait until my return, dear boy? I have so many plans to complete. Your wedding is only a few days away."

"No, Papa, it cannot wait," Craig replied pensively. "It is about the wedding I wish to speak."

"Very well, my son."

Bruce dismounted and followed his son into the library.

"Well, my son, what is this serious matter that cannot wait?"

"Papa," – he hesitated as Bruce looked at him with concern – "there is not going to be a wedding." He sighed deeply, waiting for his father's onslaught, but none came.

"But, my son," he said softly, "it is natural for a groom to feel like that before his wedding day – although, I must add, I was blissfully happy. How could I not be when I was, like you are now, going to marry the most beautiful girl in the world? Fiona has loved you since you were children, as you have loved her. It is only nerves, my son. You will feel differently very soon. I know how much we mean to each other. I doubt if any other father and son could ever be so close. I know how resentful you feel, as I do, if anyone comes between us. We will still be under the same roof, so we can still spend a lot of time together;

that is one reason I have employed more ghillies."

"Oh, Papa, Papa, how hard you make it for me!" He sighed and stood silently looking over the loch as his father continued:

"I know you will always want to be with your wife, but when the children come we will all be together – one big happy family. All that we have planned over the years, since you and Fiona were knee-high, will be accomplished. Fiona's parents, Harriet and Elena are only a ride away. Soon we will hear the news of an heir – why, it could be just a year from now. Just think, my son: a new heir for Glencree, and a new chief of the clan. Oh, what rejoicing there will be! It will be just as it was when you were born. I can see it all now."

For a moment he was lost in reverie, but Craig wished he could close his ears to it all as he gazed sadly out over the loch.

"Can you imagine, my son, what it means to me to know that, after I have gone, you and your sons will carry on our proud name and heritage?"

Suddenly, he noticed Craig wasn't listening. He still stood facing the loch with doubts clouding his mind. 'How can I do this to the one I love so dearly and who expects so much from me?' Craig asked himself.

At last, Craig turned to face his father. Never had he thought the day would ever come when he would have to oppose his father's wishes, but now he had to tell him of the choice he had made.

"Papa, Papa, I beg of you, please listen to me."

Bruce looked at him, alarmed at his insistence.

"Papa, Papa, let me make it clear to you: I am now *not* – I repeat, *not* – going to marry Fiona. I don't want to hurt either of you, but I am going to marry the only one I really love."

He turned again to look over the loch, not wishing to see the hurt on his father's face.

"Not going to marry Fiona? What are you saying? Face me when I am speaking to you."

Craig turned reluctantly. He had never seen such a look on his father's face since that dreadful night so long ago when the one they both loved so dearly had been found face down in the loch. How he wished he could spare his father this heartache!

His father looked at him in dismay and shock and anger, as though he hadn't heard a word he'd said.

"Papa, Papa," Craig called to him softly, "do you understand what I said?"

"Yes, I understand," he suddenly raved. "Who is this girl you are going to marry and bring back here to Glencree?"

Never before had Craig seen such anger. 'How I wish I could have written to him instead, and not seen him in such anguish!' he thought.

CHAPTER 127

The moment Craig had dreaded for weeks had arrived and he knew he must face it head on.

His father fumed at him again: "You will *not* – I repeat, will *not* – marry anyone else but Fiona. She is rightfully the next Mistress of Glencree. Is that clear? I shall not accept any heirs to our heritage and clan from anyone else."

"Then," said Craig defiantly, his thoughts still a tangle of despair and sorrow and love for the father he adored, "then", he repeated "there will be no heir to Glencree from me."

"No heir to Glencree!" his father spluttered, his face turning from red to almost purple. "You don't know what you are saying, my boy." He tried to take it all in.

"Well," continued Craig, "there would have been no heir to Glencree if I had been killed in the war, so as far as I can see there is no difference."

"No difference!" His father's wrath was now getting out of control. "No difference!" he roared. "At least the clan, our name, our heritage, would have died with honour on the battlefield, in the defence of our country. No difference, you say! The course you are contemplating is one of dishonour. For a McNair to go back on his word is unheard of. It must never happen as long as we bear this great name of ours."

"I am –" Craig continued, looking at his father in defiance, "I am going to India to bring back the girl I love."

Then suddenly his father exploded in a fury that Craig had never imagined him capable of. At last Bruce had suddenly realised that all his well-laid plans had came to naught. He crashed his fist down on the table.

"You will never bring that hussy here to darken the doors of Glencree. Never! Never! If you go to India, you will stay there and never, ever set foot here again. That is my ultimatum to you, my son. I shall disinherit you of our title and heritage."

"Well, Papa, if it has to be that way, so be it." Craig stamped his foot in anger. He saw his father's colour rising more and more as he stood in silence and despair.

"Have you understood my ultimatum, my boy?" Bruce banged his fist again on the table. "Are you listening?"

Elena was just going to enter the room when she heard their raised voices. She gasped in dismay when she heard the ultimatum each was laying down to the other.

'Surely', she thought, as she stood spellbound, 'what I am hearing isn't so.' She turned from the door and sank down on a chair in the hall. 'Never in this house have I ever heard the like. Surely I must be dreaming!'

Suddenly the door opened and Craig rushed past and up the stairs without noticing her. She heard his door slam.

She stood up, pondering what to do for the best. She knew it would be no use going to talk to Bruce in his present rage, so she slowly mounted the stairs to her room, patting Flint on the head as she passed.

CHAPTER 128

After Craig left the room, Bruce poured himself a full glass of whisky and flung himself into his chair. He was still shaking with fury at Craig's decision. He sat gazing into the fire, muttering aloud: "After all I did to make the girl go away! I risked the loss of my friendship with Margot. That he should now follow her! It can't be true – it can't be." He poured himself another whisky. "He ought to change his mind in the morning when my terms strike home," he fumed, "but I know my son. Yes, how I know my son!" He knew only too well that Craig had inherited his own streak of stubbornness and pride. "I'd rather he had died on the battlefield than bring such shame to this house."

He stood up to gaze at Isabelle's picture. She also, he thought, had not a hint of a smile today. He thought he saw a tear.

"My darling, my darling, what am I to do if he goes?" The pleading in his voice, was now almost a whisper after his rage. "Only you, my darling – only you could change his mind. What am I to do, my love?"

He sat down again and gazed into the fire.

Craig stood leaning against his door, distressed at his father's ultimatum. Then he moved to gaze out over the loch. His birthright, his heritage and the clan should come before anything else, he knew only too well. His love for his father and Fiona told him he must stay, but his passionate love for his angel told him he must go.

Craig spent the rest of the day in his room. The solitude was just what his tangled thoughts needed as he paced the floor and gazed over the loch – the loch he loved so much. As the night drew closer, the sky seemed to be more foreboding. Only a shaft of moonlight penetrated its darkness. "The moon looks lost in despair, just as I am," he said with a sigh.

There was no shaft of light to penetrate his thoughts and hopes; instead the words of his father seared into his troubled mind.

Jamie's knock on his door earlier in the day had broken his trend of thought for a brief moment.

"What is it, Jamie?" he called, knowing his knock so well.

"Lady Elena has sent you some food and says you must eat."

"Thank you, Jamie, but tell Aunt Elena I am not hungry. Please take it away and do not disturb me again."

"Very well, Master Craig." Jamie sighed; then he turned and slowly descended the stairs.

"Oh, why", Craig fumed, "did this have to be the outcome? How could it be true?" To never return to this house, his home, his heritage ever again! The Clan McNair would never be passed on to his sons. Surely his father couldn't have meant all he had said? But he knew his father – how he knew him! Hadn't he, himself, inherited so many of his father's traits?

He recalled his father's rage, in which he'd roared the same threat over and over again: "This family's name will die with me – all the titles, the heritage. You will never be the Chief of the Clan; you will never use the name McNair ever again. What name you choose henceforth will be of no concern to this house."

'Surely my father cannot have meant all this?' he thought. 'I am his only son and I should be the next laird and Earl of Glencree and Chief of the Clan. He cannot disinherit me like this and cut me off from my heritage.'

But the look on his father's face and the tone of his voice had made Craig tremble. He knew that once his father had made a decision it was final. No matter at what cost to him, his Scottish pride would never let him retract one word of it.

"Well, so be it, Papa," he said with a sigh. "I too have made my final decision."

CHAPTER 129

'Maybe soon', Elena thought, 'Craig will see the futility of it all and do as his father wishes. Surely Craig realises he has too much to lose.' She had noted the change in Craig since he found out that Elizabeth had gone, but surely he knew that the feelings he had for her were nothing more than a passing fancy.

Elena woke with a start. She had only been sleeping in short, restless spasms, but now she heard the rattle of curtain rings from his room. After a few moments of contemplation, she rose. 'I must go to my troubled boy,' she thought. 'This is the time he needs me most.'

She paused outside his door. A slight whimper from Flint greeted her.

"It's all right, boy, it's all right," she said, patting him on the head. "You go to sleep."

He snuggled down once more. She knocked hesitantly.

After a brief pause, he answered: "Come in, Aunt Elena," but he did not turn from the window as she entered. A stream of moonlight through the open curtains was the only light. Craig stood silhouetted in its brilliance.

"My dear boy," she whispered, "it is so late. How did you know it was I?"

"Because you, dearest Aunt Elena, are the only one who understands me – you, who filled my dear mother's place as much as it could be filled." He sighed. "Tell me, dear Aunt, what Mama would have expected of me." He still gazed out of the window, as if anxious not to face her.

She went and put her hand on his shoulder. "You already know, my boy, what she would expect of you: that you do what your dear father wishes."

"What am I to do, dear Aunt? What am I to do?" he replied in anguish.

"Only you, dear boy, can answer that – only you." She sighed.

She knew both sides of him so well. The gentle side of his nature, which he had inherited from his mother, told him quietly to stay, no matter what the cost to his own happiness. It urged him to consider his father, his heritage, his name and the clan of McNair, and, above all else, the promise to his betrothed Fiona, which could not be broken. Then the other side of him – the wild impetuous streak he had inherited from his father – told him to do only as he wished.

"Only you, my dear boy, can decide," said Elena. "You know only too well what your duty is to your father and the family honour. You must defend it at all costs. You are an only son, my boy, an only son."

"Yes, more's the pity!" he protested angrily. "At least if Papa had other sons, then the family heritage could be carried on through them; but, Aunt Elena, can you imagine no Earl McNair, no laird of Glencree Castle, no male line to carry on after Papa, no McNair as Chief of the Clan?"

"No, my boy, it is beyond my comprehension. It cannot happen, it cannot happen. You know that as well as I do."

She wished she could have been less emphatic about it, but she had to make clear to him the gravity of his decision.

"Yes, yes, I know. Can you understand why I cannot sleep restfully ever again?"

"Neither will your father if you don't marry Fiona," she reminded him.

"I know, I know," he said, and he wrung his hands in anguish. "And what of

Fiona?" he asked. "My head is in a whirl, thinking of her, of all she has meant to me and still does. I will always be saddened if I hurt her by my decision not to go ahead with our marriage."

"Your mind is finally made up, then?"

"Yes, it is final, Aunt Elena. I can only think of Elizabeth. I cannot live without her. I must go to her."

"Think again, my dear boy," she pleaded, "before you take this so serious step. This hurt of yours will pass – this feeling of wanting to go to her."

"No, no, it never will. I know that only too well. I have died inside since she left. Much as I love Fiona, it is not the same love as I have for Elizabeth. I must go to her."

The old village clock struck three o'clock.

"I must go now," said Elena. "Try to get some rest, if you can. You can think about it again tomorrow."

"It will be the same tomorrow," he replied. "All the tomorrows will be the same. Where and when is tomorrow?" he replied. "Even now it is today, and we await another tomorrow."

She put her arm round his shoulder. "Goodnight, dear boy," she said. "Try to rest."

"Yes, dearest Aunt, I will try to do as you say. I cannot think any more just now. Goodnight. Thank you for coming."

He saw her to the door and closed it softly after her. He stood a long time overlooking the loch in utter despair. His head swam with mingled thoughts, but his uppermost thought was of his father's ultimatum: "You will never ever set foot here again."

'Oh, no, surely my father did not mean what he said!' he thought. 'Surely I am dreaming all this! How can I go? How can I not go? I cannot live without my angel. I must go. I am going. I must stay. I must go. I cannot think any more now.'

He drew the heavy curtains and turned from the window.

Elena, listening for them, breathed a sigh of relief. 'I do hope my dear boy decides to stay,' she told herself with a sigh.

He lay down, knowing sleep would be impossible. 'I will ask Aunt Elena in the morning for Margot's address,' he thought. 'She doesn't know that I already have it. I will tell her I am going soon.'

CHAPTER 130

Next day, to escape his father's wrath, Craig left the house early, before anyone else was about. He got his horse from the stable and raced hard over the glens. He came to a halt underneath the tree near the church. He tied Flaxen and Flint to a small bough.

"You stay, Flint," he ordered, as the dog strained to join him.

He wended his way to the small gate of the churchyard and stood beside his mother's tomb.

"Forgive me, Mama, but I have to do this. I hope Papa will understand and forgive me. Would you have understood and forgiven me? I am sure you would."

He touched the stone lovingly, then wended his way, head bent, up the little path and into the cool shade of the church. There, lit only by the morning sunlight streaming through the stained-glass window behind the altar, he knelt to pray.

It was there that Emma, on her way to look for her father in the vestry, came upon him. She stood silently as she watched his anguished face gradually soften and become more peaceful as he prayed. She knew he was reaching out to the heavenly Father for consolation. To see Craig, who was usually always wildly happy, laughing and teasing, now in this sad, sombre mood brought home to her how troubled he must be. But what was troubling him so? Surely by now he had resigned himself to Elizabeth's departure! His marriage was now only a few days away. She sighed.

He rose to his feet and gave a start as he caught sight of her. He went up to her and clasped both her hands in his, as if for support. He looked straight into her eyes.

"Dearest, dearest Emma," he said, "thank goodness you are here! I want to tell you my news."

"What news, Craig dear?" she exclaimed, a look of perplexity on her face as she saw him tremble with emotion.

"I am leaving in the morning."

"Leaving? Leaving?" she gasped. "Please explain."

"I am leaving here to go to India to join Elizabeth." For a moment his face lit up.

Emma began to tremble as she spoke: "But your father and Fiona!" She clung to him tightly as she tried to grasp the meaning of his words.

She said to herself, 'Oh, the consequences of all this! It just isn't possible.'

"But Craig dear, you know it is too late. This cannot be."

"It is not too late and it can be," he replied emphatically. "I have finally made up my mind."

"Who else knows about this?" she asked.

"Only Papa and Aunt Elena and now you. I shall tell Aunt Harriet tonight. I know Aunt Elena will understand, but Aunt Harriet is another matter."

"And Fiona? And Fiona?" Emma exclaimed, unable to accept all she was hearing. She gazed at him in dismay. "And Fiona?" she repeated.

He looked at her sadly, a note of deep distress in his voice. "I know she will never understand, or ever forgive me, or even accept it," he said. "My poor, dearest, dearest Fiona! I am deeply ashamed to have to hurt her so. She does not deserve all the unhappiness this will cause her. I will write to her tonight to explain. I cannot face her and see her unhappiness – I just cannot. I know it is cowardly, but it is the only way for me. I know it's cruel and unkind, but if you only knew, Emma, the agony and torment I am in! I have spent nights pacing my room, unable to sleep. One moment my thoughts are of my dearest Fiona; then my thoughts are only of my darling Elizabeth. I always, always come back to Elizabeth."

"But", said Emma, "Elizabeth might not agree to marry you when you see her."

"I will make her marry me. I shall follow her until she does."

They both rose to their feet as they heard footsteps approaching. Craig looked at her anxiously.

"Ah, there you are, my dear Emma!" her father exclaimed. "Your mother said you were looking for me. Ah, Master Craig too, I see! I daresay you are asking Emma where you will be standing on your wedding day. There's no need to worry, my boy – everything will be just perfect. You chose the right person to assist you with any problems which may be causing you concern, my dear boy. Emma knows the wedding procedure as well as I do, so do not worry, my boy."

He busied himself with his prayer books, while Emma and Craig stood watching him.

"Now," Craig whispered to her, "not a word to anyone until I have finally gone! Promise me, promise me."

"I do, I do." The look in her eyes pleading for him to stay was lost on him.

"I will bid you good day, sir," Craig said as he shook the Reverend Corwell by the hand.

"Good day, dear boy."

As Emma said goodbye to him at the door she was almost in tears. He kissed her lightly on the cheeks.

"I will give your love to Elizabeth," he said, and he was gone.

Emma walked slowly back to rejoin her father, who was still checking his prayer books.

"I must say, the young master looks rather sad and forlorn. He hardly has the face of a man who is to be a happy groom in a few days' time. No, his is not a happy face at all."

Emma thought, 'Whatever will dear Papa think when he hears? I know he will be very angry.'

"Well, my dear, what did you wish to see me about?"

"Oh, it is not important, Papa. It can wait until another time."

She was thankful for the interruption by the organist, coming to practise, and she hurried away into the garden. She sat on the seat where only a few weeks before she had sat with Elizabeth as she told her of her difficulty. 'Now Craig has been faced with a dilemma. How will it all end?' she wondered. 'So many people are going to be so distressed. And my poor friend Elizabeth? Whatever will she do? She gave up all she held dear here to avoid what is now happening. It has all been to no avail – all to no avail.' She wiped a tear from her eye and went back towards the house. 'I must on no account let Mama or Papa know that I am deeply distressed,' she thought.

CHAPTER 131

Craig rode back slowly. He felt more at peace with himself now that he had spoken with Emma. 'I am sorry to have left her with such a worry,' he thought. 'Maybe she also will forgive me one day, but I at least know she understands.'

Harriet greeted Craig coldly as he entered the lounge. She had watched him from her bedroom window as he rode up the long drive, and she had hastened to the lounge to speak to him.

"Well," she demanded as he sat down, exhausted after his long ride. "This cannot be – you know that."

"It can be, and it is what I am going to do. So, Papa has told you. Well, I was going to tell you myself, but, as you now know, there is nothing more to be said on the matter." His anger matched hers. "I shall be leaving in the morning."

At this she gave a gasp of dismay. "Does Fiona know about your desertion?" she demanded.

"No, not as yet," he replied angrily. "I will write to her tonight. "

"You – you can sit there and tell me that she does not know!" she shouted. She was flabbergasted and speechless with rage – and Harriet speechless was something to behold. At last she regained some of her breath. "How dare you leave your father and your heritage? You are the only son and heir – you cannot do this," she declared. "I daresay that scheming hussy has been writing to you secretly, begging you to join her."

At this, he rose to his feet in a towering rage. "Don't you ever accuse her of such a thing, and don't ever again refer to her as 'that hussy'," he said. "Don't ever again mention her name. I am leaving in the morning, and that is final."

He hastened out of the room and almost knocked Jamie off his feet as he raced up the stairs. Flint as always was close on his heels.

Jamie turned to watch him go and sadly shook his head.

Bruce came to join Harriet in the lounge when he heard the door slam. She was sitting where Craig had left her, with bewilderment on her face.

"Does he really mean it, Bruce dear?" she asked.

"Yes, he does, and I also mean it. After all, the arrangements I made with Margot were to no avail, as you see."

Harriet looked at him, amazed. "Are you telling me that Margot was a party to all this intrigue?" she asked.

"Oh, not in the way that you might be thinking; not for one moment would she ever engage in anything that wasn't correct. Just bide awhile and I will tell you."

"So, that is the real reason that Margot hastened away – to avoid all this. As you say, it has been to no avail."

"Yes. Craig does mean what he says, and I meant what I said in the terms I laid down to him. However, as you see, it is not making the slightest bit of difference. I have disinherited him and also his sons – if he ever has any. He will never inherit my name or titles. After he leaves Glencree, he will never set foot here again."

"Oh, surely not! It will mean no laird or Earl of Glencree and no Chief of the Clan." She sank wearily back in her chair, too distressed to speak.

"Well, he knows all that, but do you think he cares? Not one jot! All he cares about is getting away to join that hussy. Now, don't ever speak of it again."

He stormed out of the room and slammed the door. Then he slowly wended his way up the stairs, stopping to whisper to Isabelle's picture:

"What am I going to do, my darling, without both of you?" he said.

Craig sat down at his desk and reached for his pen and ink.

'Well,' he thought, 'this is the last time I shall use this family crested paper.'

He stared at it for a long time, and as he traced his finger round the family crest he thought of all it meant to him. He started to write, but tore up page after page and threw them one by one into the blazing fire.

At last he had finished. What he had written he hardly knew. He cared deeply for Fiona and it upset him that he should hurt her so. He went to the window and looked down at the loch.

'I am leaving you, and you too, my heather-clad moors and pine-covered mountains.' He thought. 'You will be in my heart for ever. You are my mountains,' he sighed.

He called for Jamie, who was so full of emotion that he was almost unable to speak.

"Jamie, in the morning I want you to give this letter to a messenger to take to Lady Fiona. I will hand it to you before I finally leave."

"Finally, Master Craig?" asked Jamie with a tear in his eye. He was choked with sadness and despair.

"Yes, finally, Jamie. I have no other way. I will call you when I am ready. Goodnight, my dear, dear Jamie. You have always been such a dear friend to me."

"Goodnight, Master Craig," he whispered as Craig closed the door.

CHAPTER 132

Craig had hardly slept. He was up at dawn, gazing over the loch. Elena also spent a troubled night, and when she heard the rattle of his curtains she went to speak to him.

"Will you not change your mind, dear boy?" she said with a sigh. "How I have prayed that you would!"

"It's no use, Aunt; nothing will make me change my mind. Have you got Margot's address for me?"

"Yes, dear boy. She will, I feel sure, be at her daughter's home for some time, but she didn't know her final destination."

"Never mind, dear Aunt, I shall find her. Do write to me and let me know how Papa and everyone else is."

"Yes, I will, and I will visit you when I come to India to visit the missions."

"Oh, hasten that day!" He sighed as he clasped her to him.

Tears trickled down her face. "Goodbye, dear boy," she said. "I will come to the jetty later. I am glad you decided to wear your tartan."

After she left, he finished packing his small bag, which was sufficient for his immediate needs. He had arranged to stay in the city with a friend, who was leaving with him. He gave a final look round his room and sighed. "I will only take Mama's picture – nothing else to remind me of this dear home which has been my whole life. Now I must go."

He looked at the old clock that had ticked away all the moments of his life since his birth. He sighed heavily when he heard Jamie's knock.

"Come in, Jamie. Now, my dearest friend, do this last thing for me: give this letter to the messenger for Lady Fiona and tell him to take great care of it, but don't give it to him till I have left."

"Master Craig, please, I beg of you, do not leave your father and us," Jamie pleaded as he helped him on with his coat.

"I must, Jamie, I must."

Jamie took the letter from him and placed it in his inner pocket. He wiped a tear from his eye as Craig hugged him in a final embrace.

Elena watched from the door of her room as Craig raced down the stairs. He paused for a moment to look at the huge painting of the 1st Earl of Glencree. "We will be no more after my father," he whispered to the portrait.

He stopped to lovingly touch his mother's picture and he thought he saw a tear in her eyes.

Flint raced down after him. Where was his master going? For days he had known something was troubling him.

"Aunt Elena, will you put his lead on when you come to the jetty?"

"Yes, we will follow you shortly," she called as she leaned over the bannister. "Stay, Flint! Stay!"

Craig raced out along the jetty and down the steps into his boat as Bruce, Elena and Jamie followed.

CHAPTER 133

Bruce, still unbelieving, stood close beside Elena. She tried to take his arm to comfort him but he shook her off. He was livid with rage. Harriet had refused to see Craig leave.

'Surely', Bruce thought, 'this cannot be happening to me!' It couldn't be. It couldn't. But there he was, and his only son and heir was going to sail away, never to return.

Elena looked at him. Suddenly, he seemed to have become an old man. His back was bent in despair as he watched Craig reaching for his oars. Then he straightened up to his full height, his fiery Scottish blood and stubborn pride had returned. The early morning sun caught the silver buckles on his shoes; his black hair blew in the stiff breeze.

"You will never set foot on this shore ever again – ever again, do you hear?" It was as if he hoped, by this final threat, to turn Craig back from his course.

Craig looked up at him with a sad, lost look in his eyes. "Goodbye, dear Papa, goodbye," he said; then his voice trailed away on the breeze.

Bruce looked at him, now more in anguish than anger, calling his name: "Come home, Craig, come home."

Elena wiped a tear from her eyes as she waved him a last farewell. She recalled the last time they had all stood on this very spot, awaiting his return home.

"Please come back, my dear boy. Please come back," she whispered silently into her saturated lace-edged handkerchief.

Jamie stood close beside her with tears streaming down his face as he waved his last farewell.

Suddenly Craig heard the pipes playing a lament and he saw Rory Ritchie on the bank. For a moment he hesitated as if to turn back, but instead he sighed heavily and pulled harder on his oars.

Bruce watched him with straining eyes until he was out of sight.

"I little thought when I bought him that boat that it would take him away from me for ever," he said.

Suddenly, a plaintive howl came from Flint. He leaped off the edge of the jetty, and swam madly towards the boat.

"Come back!" Elena shouted. "Flint, come back!" but he paid no heed.

Craig heard Elena's cry and stopped rowing.

"Oh, my poor darling Flint!" he exclaimed.

He watched until the dog reached the boat; then he dragged him aboard. Flint shook himself furiously, drenching him through.

"My poor, dear friend! How am I going to live without you too? But I cannot take you with me, much as I love you. You belong here, as I do – here in the glens and hills. Stay and take care of Papa for me," he said, but the dog, not heeding, snuggled up closer to him and looked up at him with his large, sad brown eyes, as if saying, "Why cannot you take me with you?"

Craig hugged him close, then told him to lie down. He picked up his oars and rowed away from home.

Bruce strained his eyes further, still disbelieving, then he turned silently and raced back to his room. He gazed out of the window, but he could see nothing but the great expanse of the loch. He shook his fist at it, roaring in anger: "Why, why, why have you to take everything from me that I love?"

Jamie stayed a long time after Craig was out of sight; then, when he finally accepted that he wasn't going to return, he wended his way to join the rest of the staff in the kitchen. They had all stood silently beside the loch in the shrubbery as they watched him sail away.

"Tell us, Jamie," said Cook between her sobs, "that what we have just seen isn't true – that our dear young master hasn't really left for good. It cannot be true. It cannot," she kept repeating. Everything had happened so fast, and none of them could comprehend it.

"Yes, it is true – more's the pity!" exclaimed Jamie, wiping away his tears. "Heaven help us all now!"

Cook touched him on the shoulder. "Come, Jamie – sit down and have some tea."

He sat down wearily.

They all knew how worried Bruce had been after Craig had left for the front, in fear that he might never return, and Cook and Jamie remembered well how Bruce was after Isabelle died. They recalled his long walks over the glens and hills, not speaking to anyone, when he went without food for days on end.

"Now", cried Cook, "it will happen again. How ever is he going to manage without Master Craig? How will we manage without him? This won't be a home now – just a house. We have had it filled with such laughter and happiness since his return."

She wiped away more tears with the corner of her apron.

"That will never be again! Never again!" said Jamie with a sigh as he left the room, leaving all the other servants to sorrow in their own way.

CHAPTER 134

Elena stood a long time on the jetty gazing out over the loch, deep in thought. Craig was no longer in sight. She wandered slowly back to the house and joined Harriet in the lounge, where she sank wearily into the large chair overlooking the loch and dried her eyes. Harriet looked at her with disdain.

"Well, I suppose he is well on his way now," she said. "How he could do this terrible thing to his father – and he, the only son and heir – I will never understand."

"Yes, he is away," Elena replied sadly.

"It's all that girl's fault. She must have written to him to join her out there.

After all Bruce did to persuade Margot to take her with her, with the promise of the good position she offered her, even then she has refused to oblige Margot. No, no, she was determined to ruin everything. She was only interested in becoming the next Mistress of Glencree by meeting Craig on the sly whenever she could. I know her type. She is nothing but a hussy of the worst possible kind – just a brazen hussy," she fumed.

"She is nothing of the kind," Elena retorted angrily.

"She even thought that, by taking the position at the academy instead of taking up Margot's offer, she would be free to meet Craig whenever she wanted, but Bruce was wise to her little game. He saw them together before Craig left for London. It was only when Bruce threatened her with the eviction of her parents from their cottage that she finally consented to leave. Otherwise she would still be here making her mischief."

Elena turned, looking at her sister in dismay. Her hands gripped the arms of the chair in disbelief.

"Did Bruce tell you this?" she asked.

"Yes, and I supported him. He didn't tell you as he knew you would have told Craig; he knew Craig would not allow him to carry out such a threat to her parents."

"Do you mean that Bruce forced the child away on those terms?" she cried incredulously.

"Yes, he did, and rightly so," Harriet declared.

"But the poor child has had to sacrifice all for her parents. Do they know about this?"

"No, Bruce forbade her to tell anyone. No, of course they don't know," she retorted. "If they had known, they would never have let her go. Oh no, if they thought for one moment that their daughter could have become the next Mistress of Glencree, do you think they would have let her go? Oh no, not them. This would have been a chance for all of them to settle comfortably in Glencree, along with that brother of hers. He only rejoined the army because he couldn't find work here to suit his high ideals. I can just imagine his lording it over everyone at Glencree, including us."

Elena stood up, fuming with rage, and faced her sister.

"How could you ever think such evil thoughts of such kind people? They would never ever allow their daughter to come between Craig and Fiona. In fact, they would have sent her away, no matter at what cost to themselves. I know them better than you do, and I know Martha and Magnus would not be capable of scheming like that for themselves."

"Oh, given half a chance they would," Harriet continued, determined not to be outdone in this argument. "If they could have their daughter as the Mistress of Glencree, of course they would," she retorted. "I doubt, my dear Elena, whether you know them half as well as you think."

Elena, still blazing with anger, stood silent. 'Oh, I have suffered enough for one day. I cannot stand any more,' she thought, and she rushed from the room slamming the door as she went. Tears streamed down her face. The maid, still with tears in her eyes, came from the kitchen and watched as Elena sped swiftly up the stairs to her room.

CHAPTER 135

Craig rowed on and on, his mind in a whirl. "All this is not really happening to me, is it, Flint, old friend? Why couldn't Papa have understood? I was sure he would understand. All this need not have happened, and I need not have been disinherited like this, or forced to leave all I love behind for ever – even you, my dearest pal. There will be no more long walks beside the loch we love so well or through the glens – not for me anyway. You will still be able to enjoy them, my friend."

Flint looked up at him with sad eyes, knowing his beloved master was once more leaving him. He snuggled up closer to him. Craig dropped an oar to cuddle him.

"I know, I know," he said. "I am going to miss you more than I can say. Now, sit down, boy."

The dog did as he was bid.

"I will never make progress at this rate," Craig said.

He rowed on, dejected and weary. His lack of food and sleep over the past few days was now telling on him.

He dragged the boat up the shaley bank of the loch, called Flint to heel and tied him outside the cottage door. He knocked several times.

Martha and Magnus looked at each other in trepidation. For anyone to be knocking on their door was most unusual.

"Maybe it is Roddy, teasing us. Maybe he has got some leave, as he was hoping. Oh, I do hope so!" Martha exclaimed with glee. "Do open the door for him, Magnus."

CHAPTER 136

Magnus opened the door and gasped in dismay; then he told Craig to enter.

Craig stood leaning against the door as he had done that night on his return from the front. Martha looked up at him aghast. Never since that night had she seen him looking so weary and dishevelled – he who always looked so immaculate in his bearing.

She dropped him a small curtsy as she bade him sit down. She watched in anguish as he buried his face in his hands at the table. She wanted to console him, but she looked up at Magnus, at a loss for words to comfort him.

'Oh, if only his dear mother was here,' she thought.

"I am indeed sorry to call on you like this," he said when he raised his head.

"But, Master Craig, it is always an honour for us to receive you – any time, night or day," said Martha. "You look fair done in. Is anything wrong?"

He gratefully accepted the cup of tea she offered him.

"How can we help you, Master Craig?" Magnus asked. "You have only to say the word and whatever you wish will be done."

"I know that, my dear friends, but no one can help me."

Martha and Magnus looked at each other in utter bewilderment.

"I have left my father for good," he said sadly.

At this, they gave a gasp of dismay.

"I have also left my home, and my heritage, which I should rightly hand on to my sons, will be no more, owing to the action I am now taking."

"Whatever are you saying, my dear boy?" Martha exclaimed in disbelief. "This surely cannot be true?"

"It is true, my dear Martha. I wish it were not so, but it is."

"But, surely, whatever it is can only be a small rift between your father and yourself. It will soon heal."

"This will never heal. My father has said as much. Never! Never!" he exclaimed in despair.

"Never is a long time, my son," she replied as she put her hand on his shoulder. "Where are you going to live?"

"I am going to India to join your daughter, Elizabeth, and I wish to marry her."

It was Martha's turn to sit down. She felt her knees weaken and she clasped her hand to her heart in deep distress.

"You cannot mean this, my dear boy," she cried out, looking up at Magnus, who was too bewildered for words.

Craig explained all that had happened between his father and himself and what he proposed to do. He was calmer now that he saw the effect of his decision on them. That their darling daughter had been the cause of this rift between himself, his father and his betrothed, Lady Fiona, was beyond their comprehension.

"You must on no account blame Elizabeth," he said, trying to ease their evident shock and displeasure. "She knew I loved her, but never once did she ever say that she loved me. It is all my fault and mine alone."

He sat silently gazing into the fire.

'Now,' thought Martha, 'the wrath of the laird will be on us.' Tears filled her eyes. 'What shall happen to us now?'

Magnus looked at her; he read her thoughts.

Craig looked up and saw the anxiety in their eyes.

"I have Aunt Elena's promise that Papa will do nothing to harm you. She has assured me that she will take care of you. Please do not worry about anything. Just carry on serving my father as before."

"We will always do that, Master Craig, as long as the laird allows us."

"He will, Magnus, never fear. He knows it is my fault."

Martha rose to her feet. "Will you have more tea?" she asked, trying not to think of what might happen to them, in spite of the young master's assurance.

"No, thank you, Martha. I must get to the station." (He could hear Flint's plaintive whimper.)

"Shall I accompany you to the station? Shall I take your bag?" Magnus asked.

"Yes, please. I have not much to carry as all my things are already in the city."

Martha and Magnus looked at each other as Magnus picked up his bag.

'So this is why she went,' Martha thought, 'not for her own happiness, but to prevent all that was now happening. Well, her going has been to no avail.' She sat down in deep distress.

"My poor wee child! What is to become of us all?" She shook her head in sorrow and disbelief.

Craig raised himself to his full height and looked towards the stairs. Now there was no golden-haired angel coming down, calling, "Roddy, Roddy." He kissed Martha goodbye and wiped away the tears from her face.

"I will give Elizabeth your love," he said. "Do not think ill of her or me."

But Martha's tears still flowed as she pleaded with him to return to his father.

"No, it cannot be," Craig replied. He held her hands in his, as he wished her goodbye.

She followed him to the open door, where he bent down to give Flint a final hug and pat on the head. Flint strained at his leash when he realised his master was going without him.

Magnus followed him to the small gate of the station.

"Tell me, Master Craig, does our daughter know you are joining her?" he asked.

"No, Magnus, I do not wish her, or anyone else, to know. It will only distress her. I will take great care of her and we will return when my father understands – as I am sure he will in time. Please take Flint home to my father."

"I will, Master Craig." Magnus held on to his hand a long time as he wished him goodbye; then he opened the small gate of the station to let him through and handed him his bag. He then closed the gate after him with a sad, longing look in his eye, wishing that things could be different.

CHAPTER 137

The creak of the gate caused Peggoty to look up from where he was preparing his lamps for the night. He was surprised to see Craig approaching and Magnus leaning over the gate.

"Good day, Master Craig," he said jovially.

Then saw the look of sadness on Craig's face. He took his bag from him.

"Are you going for long, Master Craig?" he asked.

"Yes, for good, Peggoty."

Peggoty looked up at him, expecting to see a smile on his face – he was always one for a joke, the young master. But not today! There was, instead, a deep sadness on his countenance and his reply to Peggoty's 'good day' was a rather feeble one.

"How long will the train be?" Craig asked.

"It is due now," he replied, and a few minutes later this was confirmed by the roar of the engine as it chugged into the station.

Craig turned, glanced all around him and waved Magnus farewell. Peggoty helped him into the train and handed him his bag.

'Is it really true that he is going away for good?' Peggoty asked himself. 'No, that cannot be, but I have never seen the young master look like this before.'

As he was about to close the door, a small, wizened figure appeared and called to him: "Master Craig, Master Craig."

For a moment his face lit up, and he stepped back down on to the platform. He knew somehow his going would have become known to her. 'She always knows my every move,' he thought. 'She's always watching over me. How I am going to miss her!'

Merry-Berry gave him a loving look and noted the sadness in his eyes.

"You were so right, Merry-Berry, so right. You told me I would travel far away and I didn't believe you, but I should have known. You are always right."

"Don't worry, Master Craig. You will return one day, never fear."

"If you say I shall return, then it will be so," he replied. "That has given me fresh heart." A faint smile broke over his face.

"Never fear, my son. Your bones will rest here in your beloved mountains and glens. One day you will come home. Here is something you must keep with you always."

She handed him the smallest bottle he had ever seen in a small knotted handkerchief.

"What is it?" he asked.

"It is water from the loch and soil from your homeland. I repeat, Master Craig: you will return home one day."

She clasped her hand over his as he took the bottle from her.

"I thank you for those kind words. Take care of my father for me."

"I will, I will." Tears were falling down her old weather-beaten face as she turned to go.

He climbed back into the train and he waved Peggoty and Magnus a last goodbye. He watched as Merry-Berry bent down to pick up some pegs that had fallen from her shawl before she disappeared through the hedge.

She watched until the train was out of sight.

"You will return to your home soil, my boy. You will," she called after him, but her words were lost on the mountain breeze.

Magnus turned to go, and Peggoty called to him, "Is it true what the young master has said?"

"Yes, sadly it is true. I can say no more. Good day."

Peggoty returned to his lamps, muttering to himself, "Whatever will become of us if it is so?"

CHAPTER 138

Craig flung himself onto a seat and put his baggage on the opposite one. "Well, at last I am away," he said with a sigh. He was restless and unhappy. He stood up to look out of the window and stared out at the receding mountains and glens as long as he could bear.

"Farewell my beloved mountains and glens," he said. "I will return to you all one day."

He sat down again.

'Oh why, oh why has my decision to go away hurt so many people – particularly my dear father and my darling Fiona,' he thought. 'How I hate hurting her like this. And I have hurt her parents too, though they have always treated me as if I were their son. Now I must forget all this and think only of my darling angel.'

He put his head in his hands in anguish as the consequences of his love for Elizabeth turned over and over in his tormented thoughts.

His friend, Graham Stewart, was waiting for him as he alighted from the train. He took Craig's baggage and weighed up his sad expression.

"We have two days before we sail," he said.

"Well, I have not much to do," replied Craig. "I have everything settled regarding the sale of my property and inheritance from my mother, but I must see as many of my men as I can before I leave."

CHAPTER 139

Magnus sadly wended his way back to the cottage. He could hear the frantic whine of Flint as he approached. Magnus patted him on the head and took him inside.

"The poor fellow must be hungry," he said, but no amount of Martha's coaxing could get him to eat or drink. He slunk into the corner, still whimpering.

Magnus comforted Martha as much as he could, although his own heart was deeply troubled.

"We must write to our dear son and tell him what Master Craig has done, but first I must do as Master Craig has said and take the dog back."

Elena was watching from the window, and she saw Magnus approaching with Flint. She went down to the jetty to meet them.

"Lady Elena, what can we do to help the poor master in this terrible ordeal?"

"Nothing my dear Magnus – nothing at all. Tell Martha not to worry about the laird: I shall be taking care of everything for you. What has happened is not your daughter's fault. You must never ever blame her."

Flint whined by her side and she patted him on the head to try to comfort him.

"Thank you, Magnus, for bringing him back. How he is going to behave now his master has gone, I just can't imagine. They were so attached and he is now so old. Tell me, how was Master Craig when he left you?"

"Very, very sad, milady. I went as far as the station gate, but he wished me to go no further. Peggoty, as you can guess, was, like us, completely bewildered. We cannot yet believe that we will not see the young master again. Is it true that Sir Bruce has forbidden the young master to ever return?"

"Yes – never to return," she replied as she wiped away a tear.

Magnus shook his head in disbelief.

"Merry-Berry was the last person to speak to him, milady," he said.

"Yes, I daresay," she sighed. "She would not let his going pass unnoticed."

"She handed him something just before the train pulled out."

"Yes, I expect it was a keepsake of some kind or something to safeguard him. She has always watched over him since he was born. It would please him to see her." She turned to go. "Good day, Magnus. Thank you – and do tell Martha not to worry."

He stood for a little while watching them; then he turned to get back in his boat.

CHAPTER 140

Preparations were well in hand at Ravenswood Hall for the wedding of Fiona. Her relations were expected any day. Fiona was expecting Craig to call that day. Her maid, drawing the heavy damask curtains, peered out of the window when she noticed a rider approaching.

"Craig is late arriving this morning!" exclaimed Fiona's mother as she entered her room to discuss more details with her daughter as she was dressing. "He did say he would be calling today, didn't he dear?"

351

"Yes, Mama, he did. He said it would be his last call before we marry."

"How exciting it is after waiting so long! Everyone is so thrilled at this great occasion. They will never see the likes of it again – my daughter's marriage to the next Earl of Glencree." She sat down, enthusing with happiness at the thought.

"Yes, Craig is very late," Fiona said with a pout as she looked at the small watch which hung round her neck. "I wonder what has delayed him this time – the army and crofters' problems again, I daresay. Honestly, Mama, the time he gives to their every problem and to the estates! I certainly won't tolerate it when we are married. Papa Bruce has employed extra staff to do the work so I cannot understand why Craig has to take so much on himself." She stamped her foot in anger.

"The maid passed me outside your door as I was entering. She said there was a rider approaching, but it didn't look like Master Craig."

"I daresay", said Fiona impatiently, "it is one of Craig's servants with a message of apology for his delay."

A knock on the door interrupted her.

"Come in," she called angrily.

The maid entered with a letter on a small silver tray. "A letter for you, Lady Fiona," she said. "The messenger said he had been told not to wait for a reply."

"Oh, very well, tell him to go."

The maid dropped Fiona and her mother a curtsy; then she left and closed the door.

Fiona opened the letter impatiently. "Yes, just as I thought: it has the Glencree crest on it." She pouted to her mother, who sat waiting to hear what the letter contained as Fiona hastily unfolded it. "It will be just another excuse for his delay, I suppose, Mama," she said.

"Well, my dear, what does it say?"

Fiona gasped in dismay and her mother glanced up at her with concern. Fiona clutched her face in anguish and the letter dropped from her grasp. She collapsed in a listless, crumpled heap at her mother's feet. Her face was ashen with shock.

"What is it, my child?" Lady Cleveland gasped, as she knelt beside her daughter. She picked up the letter and began to read:

My dearest Fiona,

When this letter reaches you I shall be far away, never to return. It grieves me deeply to know how much this news will distress you. I pray that you will find it in your heart to one day forgive me for what I have done and also for not coming to see you before I left. That was something I could not do, as I could not bear to see the hurt in your eyes.

I know also what distress my going will cause your dear parents, who have always treated me so kindly. To them I send my deepest and sincere apologies, and I beg their forgiveness.

I shall always think of you with deep affection.

Goodbye.

Craig

When she had read the letter, she rang the bell for the maid and told her: "Stay with Lady Fiona until I return and put a shawl over her."

"Yes, milady."

Lady Cleveland hurried out, calling the General to hurry to Fiona's room.

He rushed in and was aghast to see Fiona lying crumpled on the floor. The maid was wondering what she could do to help in the crisis.

"Don't stand there gaping girl," said the General. "Go and bring the other maids."

"Yes, sir," she stammered as she fled from the room.

He rushed to his wife's side as she collapsed in a chair. The crested letter, now creased, had floated to her feet.

"Whatever is it, my dear? Whatever is it?" he asked, but she was too shocked to answer him.

She pointed to the letter at her feet.

He bent down and picked it up. His anger mounted and his face turned from bright red to purple with rage as he read the letter.

"Oh, my poor, poor darling Fiona!" he gasped. "I shall ride over to Glencree as soon as Doctor McTavish has been."

With the help of the maids, the General laid Fiona on her bed; then they led her mother to her room to lie down.

CHAPTER 141

It was later that day when the General left for Glencree. His face was still purple with rage, and his wife and daughter were still confined to their rooms in deep shock.

Elena knew when she saw the messenger leave that morning for Ravenswood Hall that the General would arrive later that day. From her bedroom window she saw him coming. She had spent the day there after her confrontation with Harriet, and she hurried down to meet him as he dismounted.

"What is the meaning of this, Elena?" he demanded as he strode into the hall, still clutching the crumpled letter in his hand. "This cannot be true, it cannot be!" he roared.

Elena looked at him pityingly, nonplussed.

"Where is the scoundrel? I will certainly tell him what I think of him. Where is he?"

The sudden opening of the lounge door stopped his tirade. He stared open-mouthed at the sight that met his eyes. In the frame of the doorway stood an old man, sickly pale, his shoulders shrunken. His once dark hair seemed to have turned grey overnight.

'Surely', General Cleveland thought, as he gazed at him in disbelief, 'this is not my old friend who, when I last saw him, was so dashing, so bright and vigorous!' Bruce's presence was always so compelling, but it seemed to the General that he had changed almost beyond recognition.

Suddenly, Bruce spoke, his voice trembling with rage and despair: "You cannot tell him what a scoundrel he is. He has gone away from Scotland for ever. I have seen to that. He will never ever return to this house or these shores."

"Oh, no, my dear friend, surely you don't mean he has left for good?"

"Yes, he left this morning. He is sailing for India, never to return."

"To India? Why India?"

"He is going to that girl and he says he is going to marry her," Bruce roared in rage.

"Which girl?" the General exclaimed in disbelief.

"That hussy – that companion of Margot's – that Anderson hussy."

Both men looked at each other, almost unable to believe it.

Elena stood quietly beside them as they confronted each other. She cringed as Bruce hurled the abuse. 'The poor child!' she thought. 'All this is not her fault.' She kept silent, looking from one of the men to the other. 'Poor, dear Fiona also – and her parents! They don't deserve all this. Harriet and I must visit them soon.' She sighed.

"Do you mean Magnus's daughter?" said the General. "But that cannot be. Craig is betrothed to my daughter, who is now prostrate with grief and confined to her bed – as is my wife. Well, I tell you this, my old friend: if any permanent harm comes to my daughter through your son's callousness, I too shall make sure that he never again sets foot on these shores. I bid you good day."

He turned and walked swiftly out through the hall, slamming the huge doors of Glencree Castle behind him. Jamie, standing in the drive, looked at him, dumbfounded, as he watched him go.

"Come, Bruce," said Elena. "Come and sit down in the lounge. You have had enough sadness to bear."

He shook her hand off furiously.

"I am all right. Leave me alone," he said.

He turned into the room and slammed the door.

Bruce went over to the fireplace, where the embers were dying low in the grate. He looked up at the face of his wife.

"My darling, what am I to do now both of you are gone? What am I to do?" he said.

He sat down wearily and closed his eyes as if to shut out the horrors of the day.

CHAPTER 142

Mrs Knowell was first to hear the news. She was sorting out the anthems and hymns for the wedding ceremony, making sure they were on hand and in their correct order for her husband, when she overheard Lady Elena talking to the vicar. He had been making sure everything was in order for the Bishop, who was due any day. The Reverend Corwell had been in the church for most of every day for the past week.

"There you are!" Elena called to him. "Becky told me I would find you here."

"Good morning, Lady Elena. It is always a great pleasure to see you. Do come and sit down. You look rather tired and pale. I will tell Becky to make some tea when we go into the vicarage."

She sat down opposite him in the little study he had next to the vestry, the door of which was slightly ajar. She told him the full story, and, as she finished, her tears once again started to flow.

"There, there, my dear!" he said, rising from his chair and putting his arm on her shoulder. "Surely the laird does not mean all he has said. Master Craig, I feel sure, will learn the folly of it all and return in time for the wedding."

"No, no, he will not. He has already left for India and Bruce has forbidden him to ever return. I had to come and tell you before anyone else gets to know, because you will have to cancel all the arrangements for the wedding."

"That I will do. I'll contact the Bishop straight away. Now, you must come with me and talk to Becky for a while until you are feeling better."

As soon as she heard their footsteps fading away, Mrs Knowell hurried to the small vestry window and watched till they were out of sight. She put on her bonnet, then piled up the hymn books and anthem sheets and put them away.

"Well, we won't be needing these," she said. "I must hurry and tell everyone I know, but first I will call on Mrs Crawford and tell her that this afternoon's sewing circle will be earlier than planned. I have some very important news to convey to everyone."

CHAPTER 143

Mrs Knowell sat with the village ladies that same afternoon, presiding over the meeting. She related all she had heard Lady Elena tell the vicar that morning. They all received the news with gasps of dismay.

"You mean everything is cancelled?" said one after another. They looked at one another with open mouths.

"There will be no young master now at Glencree to follow in his father's footsteps – no heir to the title. It is unthinkable. What shall we do when something happens to the laird?" exclaimed Mrs Crawford.

"That scheming hussy of a girl is to blame for all this," said Mrs Knowell. "Did I ever tell you, Mrs Crawford—?" She was about to whisper something to her confidentially, but she suddenly realised that it need no longer be a secret. Now she could let everyone know what a hussy Elizabeth was. She voiced her tale loud and clear, so that even deaf Miss Dorcas, sitting close by, could hear.

"Yes," she said, "I saw her myself with the young master by the side of the stream with the back of her dress undone to the waist."

She waited for the response, and noted with satisfaction the disgust registering on most of their faces. They gasped with dismay and disbelief that any young lady could behave so brazenly.

At last Mrs Knowell had got it off her chest.

"How I managed to keep silent all this time, I shall never know," she said, "but I had to protect the young master. However, now it doesn't matter. I was so shocked at the time. Even now I can hardly believe it, but I saw it with my very own eyes. It is just as well that you all know her now for what she is. And to think of having her in my choir and teaching our children in Sunday school!"

She was pleased to see that most of the ladies shared her outrage. They tut-tutted to one another as they aired their opinions for the rest of the afternoon.

Emma, sitting on the back row, listened silently. She looked at her mother occasionally, her anger and despair mounting.

Mrs Knowell glanced at her and continued: "That poor Martha and Magnus should beget such a hussy for a daughter is beyond my comprehension."

"And mine also," one after another agreed.

Emma hastened out of the room, after excusing herself on the pretext of having a more pressing appointment. She ran to her room, and flung herself on her bed.

"I cannot stand any more," she sobbed as she buried her head in the pillow.

Mrs Knowell glanced after Emma as she left.

"That hussy must have encouraged the young master to do what he has done," she said. "He never would have left his father otherwise. He has always been a perfect gentleman. Goodness knows what his poor mother would have thought had she been spared."

Silence came only as tea was being drunk. Mrs Crawford thought to herself as she sipped her tea, 'I would not have minded one of my precious jewels being compromised in such a way if it would have led to her marrying the heir of Glencree. I just know the laird would have accepted one of my girls as the next Mistress of Glencree.'

"I just know", Mrs Crawford proudly boasted to her husband later that evening, "that the laird would have accepted one of our daughters had Master Craig not been promised to Lady Fiona."

"Yes, yes, my dear," he replied. He knew better than to disagree.

"To think the opportunity has been denied them for ever!" She tut-tutted more angrily. "My girls will never get over it."

The girls in the choir and from the academy tried all they knew to get the full tale from Emma whenever they met her. The 'jewel' girls were especially keen to get her to denounce Elizabeth, and her silence on the matter annoyed them more than ever.

CHAPTER 144

Craig's plans were complete; all his men had been visited. He told them that his Aunt Elena would visit them regularly and she would keep him informed as to their welfare. Money would be provided for their fund. He bade them all a sad farewell.

At last he was beside the quay. He looked up at the huge ship, which would take him away from the land he loved.

'Little did I think that I would ever sail away again,' he thought with a sigh. 'Yes, Merry-Berry was right as usual.'

"Come, Craig," Graham called to him from halfway up the gangplank. "Why are you lingering so? We are already late."

"Very well," he sighed, "I am coming."

Craig followed his friend reluctantly aboard. He looked out over the side of the ship at the swirling water below, his thoughts still in a turmoil of sadness and despair. His love for his father and Fiona overwhelmed him, and he knew he would miss his precious mountains and glens. Their beauty and splendour was engraved on his heart for ever.

'I know Merry-Berry's words will come true,' he thought. Didn't they always? She had said he would return one day, before his father passed on. 'I just know it will come true. I just know.'

The lurch of the ship and the thud of the rope as it landed on the deck jolted him back to the last time he had been on a ship. The thought of his men far away came flooding back. His friend, by his side, had been watching him closely. Graham felt a deep sympathy for him.

"Come, Craig – we must go below. There is nothing left to see – only the coastline."

Craig turned to him. "Yes, only the coastline of home fading away!" he said.

CHAPTER 145

Lady Fiona and her mother left for London shortly after they were visited by Harriet and Elena. Both aunts found their conversation with the heartbroken Fiona and her mother very difficult. Both were deeply distressed, and they were relieved when it was time for them to depart. Neither spoke on their journey back to Glencree, having left a message that Bruce would be calling soon to see the General.

The General greeted Bruce frostily, although he realised he was not responsible for Craig's decision.

"I have decided to make arrangements when I reach London to put Ravenswood Hall up for sale," he said. "I shall be leaving here within the next few days and as I have much to do before I leave I must ask you not to detain me too long. I am sorry that such old friends as we are have to part under a cloud. It is a regrettable and shameful state of affairs."

"No, my friend," Bruce agreed, "my son's shameful treatment of dear Fiona I also cannot condone. That is all I can say, so I will take my leave."

The General offered his hand on parting, and Bruce took it gratefully. They wished each other well.

CHAPTER 146

Only the preparations in the village for Emma's wedding gave the saddened villagers and crofters a measure of happiness after the departure of their beloved Craig.

"Gone for ever!" they had exclaimed, over and over again. "No, no, it cannot be true," but they all saw their beloved laird out once again on his lonely walks in the glens every day with his dogs. Not a day passed when someone did not see his saddened countenance as he passed them by. They received only a nod from him as they wished him good day and doffed their caps or dropped him a curtsy.

"It's as if he had lost his wife all over again," they whispered to one another in the village.

Martha and Magnus were glared at in church, and many parishioners passed them by without speaking. Others wished them a polite good day, then went on their way, but some stood muttering to one another after Martha and Magnus passed them on their way to the loch.

"Their daughter is the cause of our dear laird's unhappiness," said one. "How could they let her do such a thing?"

Mrs Crawford had, as usual, most to say in condemnation. She was still smarting at the thought that Craig hadn't chosen one of her precious jewels – but then, many of the other mothers thought likewise.

Only the vicar and his family and Lady Elena greeted Martha and Magnus like old friends, but their friendliness was frowned on by the village gossips – especially Mrs Crawford.

"Fancy Lady Elena treating the Andersons as if nothing had happened to our dear laird and his son. What about the heritage? Master Craig was the next Chief of the Clan, but Her Ladyship doesn't seem concerned."

"And poor Emma!" said Mrs Carruthers. "All her wedding plans will have to be altered because of that hussy Elizabeth's departure. She will have to choose another chief bridesmaid to attend her at her wedding. It's such a shame!"

Emma threw herself as heartily as she could into the arrangements for her wedding day. Everyone from the village and crofts was invited. Her special friends from the academy spent the day before arranging all the flowers in church with her. The Crawford girls fumed that they had not been included. They heard from Mrs Knowell that they were not requested to sing at the ceremony.

"Don't be disappointed, my dears," their mother said, trying to console them. "It is not as important as Master Craig and Fiona's wedding," she declared disdainfully.

CHAPTER 147

Emma's wedding day dawned. It was a bright, sunny autumn day. Her father's friend, from the cathedral in the city, performed the ceremony. Martha and Magnus were honoured guests, and they sat with Becky.

"How beautiful she is!" Martha whispered to her husband as Emma came down the aisle.

"But she would have been so much happier with Elizabeth by her side."

"Yes," Martha agreed, "but it was not to be."

Emma had decided against her mother's wishes not to fill Elizabeth's place in spite of having many friends in the academy. She only had three small bridesmaids, who were chosen from her Sunday-school class.

Harriet and Elena sat side by side on the other side of Becky. Elena was beaming all over her face with delight at it all, but Harriet was taking very little interest. She was annoyed to find that Martha and Magnus were such honoured guests, sitting so near to her. Bruce had declined the invitation on the pretext of having pressing matters to deal with on the estate. Mrs Crawford tut-tutted with indignation that the Andersons were treated with special favour, and that they had been invited to spend the night at the vicarage.

When the wedding was over, a dismal emptiness descended on the village. A sombre gloom settled, especially on Glencree Castle. Gone was the happy, joyous laughter of Craig and his friends. All the lights in the turrets had been extinguished as Bruce decreed. Jamie had tried in vain to quell his tears as he put them out one by one.

"Whatever is going to happen to us all now?" he repeated over and over again to any of the household staff within listening distance.

CHAPTER 148

Bruce, as usual, went for his daily long walk through the glens with his dog, Sabre. Flint, as always, trailed behind, searching in vain in the hedgerows for his beloved master.

"Well, there is now only one thing to be done," declared Harriet as she sat playing cards with Elena: "Bruce will have to marry again. He is still a very handsome, virile man, not yet fifty, and there are scores of young women, any one of whom would make an excellent Mistress of Glencree. Then we could still take up residence at Harrison Hall."

Elena looked at her askance. "Well," she said, "I would rather you tell him than I do."

"Oh, I shall certainly tell him in due course. As yet it is too soon, but he will have to do his duty to the clan and the heritage and the name of McNair. It cannot just pass away and be lost for ever like a bubble on the breeze."

"How I wish", sighed Elena as she gazed up at the large picture of Isabelle, "that more sons had been born. If only she could have been spared!"

"Well, it was not to be, so it is no good sighing and wishing," said Harriet angrily. "There is no other way. Bruce will just have to marry again."

"That will never be!" Bruce exploded in anger. They had failed to hear him enter the room.

He came and stood in front of the fireplace and banged his fist on the table, scattering the playing cards.

"I shall never, never marry again. How dare you suggest such a thing? My title, the 11th Earl of Glencree, the Chief of the Clan McNair, will die with me."

He left and slammed the door.

Harriet and Elena looked up at Isabelle's picture resignedly. Both wiped away tears, knowing that Bruce's decision was final.

CHAPTER 149

Elizabeth viewed the land coming into view with increasing apprehension, but she had to admit that the brilliant sun shining on the white buildings, causing them to glisten like pearls, was certainly a beautiful sight. Lady Margot came to join her.

"Oh, how I have longed for this familiar sight! It's like coming home," she said with a sigh.

At last the ship was at anchor. The quayside swarmed with people all dressed in a glorious array of colour, such as Elizabeth had never seen before.

"Is everywhere in India so crowded, milady?" she asked.

"Well, certainly in places like this and in the cities, but it is less so in the villages. Now, let me see", she said as she leaned over the side of the ship, "if I can see any of my family." Suddenly, she cried out with delight. "Yes, yes, I can see my daughter and Stephen, her husband, and my two adorable little granddaughters. Oh, oh, how adorable they look! See, Elizabeth, they have spotted me." She began waving frantically, calling out their names.

'They will never hear her above all this tumult,' Elizabeth thought. She sighed, feeling more alone than ever. 'There's not a soul waiting for me in all the crowd below,' she said to herself. She was almost on the verge of tears.

Captain MacVey, standing beside her, had been watching her for several minutes. She looked up as she sensed his nearness.

"You're not waving, Elizabeth. Have you no one waiting to greet you?" he asked.

"No," she sighed.

"Neither have I. Just think: all those people below and no one waiting for us! However, I am luckier than you, I think, my dear: I shall soon be joining my parents."

"Yes, you are lucky. All my loved ones are in Scotland."

He noted her deep sigh and a sad, lost look in her eyes as she turned to face him. 'Why, why', he thought, 'is this lovely slip of a girl so sad? If only she belonged to me! I could make her so happy.'

She noted his questioning look, and she decided she didn't want him asking too many awkward questions, so she added hastily, "But I shall be returning to Scotland in two years' time."

"Oh, just a short stay! You will find time passes very quickly here, especially once the party season starts, when they all return from the hills. Of course, life is one continuous party up there. I do hope you get a chance to go."

'Well, they are not my hills of home,' she thought sadly.

CHAPTER 150

Elizabeth looked around and noted that Her Ladyship was saying goodbye to all her friends.

"Please say I can call on you when I return to Madras very soon?" a young man asked Elizabeth.

"I am sorry, but I might not be staying here; besides, if I stay, I'd rather you didn't call on me."

He was at a loss for words. Never before had any girl refused his permission to visit her.

"Well, I will call anyway, in case you change your mind," he said.

"I'm sorry but I will not change my mind."

"I see Lady Margot is approaching, so goodbye for now," he said.

He kissed her hand lightly before speeding down the gangway; he gave her a final wave when he reached the bottom.

"Now, come, my child – we cannot delay," said Margot. "See, the children are waving to you. Aren't they adorable? Now wave back dear. They are your family now."

Elizabeth waved back, thinking, 'My family? They are not my family.'

CHAPTER 151

The hustle and bustle of the heaving mass of people below filled Elizabeth with dread as she gazed despondently over the side of the ship.

"Now, come, my dear," said Lady Margot, "We must hurry ashore. Just get your hand luggage. Stephen and Martin will see to the rest when it is unloaded. Oh, I am so glad to see my old friend, Martin, has found time to come and meet me. He is standing next to Stephen."

"Yes, I see him, milady. I see them all clearly now. The children do look adorable."

She followed Lady Margot quickly down to where they were waiting and stood to one side as Davinia rushed into her mother's arms.

"I have missed you so much, Mama," she said.

"And I you, my darling."

Both had tears streaming from their eyes.

"I have missed all of you," said Lady Margot, "especially my two adorable little grandchildren. How pretty they look in their flowered dresses!" She bent down to kiss them in turn; then she gazed at them, trying in vain to decide which was Clare and which was Astrid. "Stephen, how well you are looking!" she declared as they embraced.

"Well, Mama, we are all well," said Davinia. "We have been in the hills for weeks."

"Dear, dear Martin, I little thought you would be here to greet me."

"How could I not come to meet you, my dear friend?" he replied as they clasped hands lovingly and gazed into each other's eyes. "My dear, dear Margot, I have missed you so much."

"Well, we are all together now. Now, everyone, I want you to meet Elizabeth Anderson, who sings most divinely. She sang every night for your dear grandmother."

"Yes, so you told me in every letter you wrote. Poor Grandmama! How I wish she could have come back with you to see the children."

"Well, it was not to be," sighed Margot.

"We were all so glad that you were able to return to be with her for her last few years, although we missed you so," declared Stephen.

"Well, now I am back to stay for good. Tell me, Martin: how are all the missions getting on in your care?"

"Now, Mama, you will have plenty of time to discuss all the details about the missions later," said Davinia.

Elizabeth stood demurely by. She was bewildered. She watched the twins dance around in a little game, but she didn't know which was which, although they had stood in front of her and introduced each other.

'I must find out how to tell which is which very soon,' she thought.

CHAPTER 152

"Now, children," Stephen demanded, "just keep still a few minutes and come here and tell your grandmother your names."

"I am Clare," one said, as she gave Margot a little curtsy.

"I am Astrid," said the other, curtsying likewise.

Margot looked at them closely as she shook their hands. "No, it is as you said, Davinia: it is impossible for me to tell them apart. Both have your green eyes and red hair."

"Well," replied Clare, never the one to be stuck for something to say, "no one can." She spoke boldly, standing with her hands on her hips. "We play such tricks on all our friends and our ayah."

"Well, Clare plays more tricks than I do," replied Astrid coyly.

"Oh, and what kind of tricks?" asked Margot.

"Well, we swop the dresses that our ayah gives us. We don't always like the ones she has chosen. And we swop hair ribbons when we have different-coloured ones," laughed Clare, reliving the prank.

"My, my, you are a bright, talkative child!" remarked Margot. "In my young days, little children were seen but not heard. Is she always so precocious, Davinia?"

"Yes, I'm afraid so, Mama. Astrid is much more reserved."

"Well," Margot continued, "you must not play any tricks on your poor old grandmother." She playfully tugged Clare's plaits as she spoke.

"Yes," agreed Stephen, "she is certainly the ringleader when there is any mischief to be done."

"Now, we mustn't leave Elizabeth looking so lost and forlorn. Come, children," said Davinia. She had been watching Elizabeth for some time.

'How sad she seems!' she thought. 'I must get Mama to tell me more about her later.'

The children were at Elizabeth's side, and she turned to look at them more closely.

'I must see if I can spot any difference between them,' she thought. 'Ah, now I see that Clare has a small black mole above her right eye. I am sure they will never guess how I am able to tell them apart.'

"We are all delighted, Elizabeth, that you are going to be part of our family," said Davinia, "although Mama says you are only going to be with us for two years."

"Yes, that is so," Elizabeth replied demurely.

"Well, we will make your stay as happy as we can," Stephen replied.

"Thank you. I am sure I will be very happy with you."

Margot looked at her, knowing that, despite her words, Elizabeth's heart was breaking.

Martin hailed their tongas and they prepared to leave the quayside.

CHAPTER 153

They climbed into the tongas, which took them to the station, where they entered their reserved compartments.

"It isn't too far now, my dear," Lady Margot assured Elizabeth.

Elizabeth gazed out, fascinated, but she grew quite alarmed when she saw small children running beside the train, calling for money.

"Do the children always run along beside the train, milady?"

"Yes. I see, Davinia, nothing has changed since I left."

"Nothing ever seems to change, so you will soon feel as though you have never been away," said Martin.

"Papa, Papa," cried Clare, "please may I have some annas to throw to the children?"

"I gave you some to throw to them when we came. Do you think I am made of money? Very well, then, I shall get no peace from you until I do," Stephen said when he saw the corners of her little mouth start to pout.

"May I have some also?" implored Astrid.

"But really, Stephen, you should not encourage them," Margot chided. "They run the risk of being killed."

"Well, they will always do it, no matter how concerned we are, Mama."

"Hurry, Papa, hurry!" shouted Clare.

"All right, my dear child, don't get so excited."

He lowered the window and the twins rushed to throw out their annas. Elizabeth gazed fascinated as the urchins gathered them up and salaamed. The twins waved to them as the train rushed on.

Soon the family were clambering off the train and into another tonga, much to Elizabeth's consternation.

'Oh, is there no end to all this travelling? I am so tired of it all,' she thought. She fanned herself furiously, finding the heat unbearable.

Margot was watching her closely. "We won't be too long now, my dear," she said. She was concerned by Elizabeth's pallor. She looked exhausted.

The twins asked if they might sit next to her.

"Yes, you may," Margot agreed, "but don't do too much talking. Elizabeth is very tired."

"We won't, Grandmama – we promise."

Astrid looked at Clare with an assertive glance as if to tell her, "Now do as Grandmama says."

Elizabeth smiled at her seriousness, but she had to admit their chatter was exhausting and she was glad Lady Margot had asked them to refrain.

They were travelling now in the countryside. Large bungalows came into view. At last they turned up a long driveway and stopped outside a very large pink bungalow.

CHAPTER 154

"We have prepared your bungalow, Mama. Ours has been closed since we went to the hills, but we just had to return to meet you. We will return to the hills shortly. Well, it is much better for us and, as you have said, the children like it too. They like to play with the children from the mission."

"Well, there won't be many more all-play days. They will be going to the kindergarten when we return," said Stephen.

"But I don't want to go to the kindergarten," wailed Clare sulkily. She had decided she had been quiet for too long.

"Well, school it will have to be."

"I think I shall quite like it, Papa," Astrid replied.

"Oh, you would," Clare replied angrily as she rushed up the verandah steps.

"Clare, come back this minute!" Stephen demanded.

Slowly she returned and stood by the tonga as the rest of them alighted.

CHAPTER 155

Elizabeth looked in awe at the size of the abode, thinking, 'It's almost as large as Harrison Hall. What a dear place that was! I wish I was there now.' She sighed. 'Then I could see—' She stopped suddenly in the middle of her faraway thoughts. 'No, no, I must never ever think of that place again.'

She looked in amazement as lots of children and adults approached, carrying garlands of flowers, which they placed round their necks – especially Lady Margot's. Her head was almost invisible by the time they had finished. Surely, all the villagers from miles around must have come to greet them, from the eldest to the youngest. After placing their garlands, the people stood with their hands together. Margot salaamed in reply, almost in tears.

"Is this usual, Stephen?" asked Elizabeth, her breath almost taken away with astonishment.

"Yes, especially as she has been away so long. They have given you a special greeting because you are a welcome stranger."

"They have all missed Mama so much – almost as much as we have," said Davinia.

When the last one had departed, the family entered the house to be greeted with more garlands from the household staff. The delight at Lady Margot's return was so much in evidence.

"Now we must rest," said Margot, sitting down wearily on a seat on the verandah. She was thinking, especially of Elizabeth, but she was at that moment being reluctantly taken all around the house by the twins.

"No, no, children!" Davinia called. "Elizabeth is very tired. You can show her round tomorrow."

Clare stamped her foot and started to sulk. She looked pleadingly at her father.

"*Tomorrow*, Mama said, young lady, and tomorrow she means."

Clare still looked up at him, but she knew when he used that tone of voice that she had to obey. On most occasions, though, she could wheedle anything out of him.

CHAPTER 156

Elizabeth sat wearily down on the wicker chair on the verandah and watched as Lady Margot rose to wave to the children from the mission. As they wended their way back home, Lady Margot sank happily, but wearily, down beside her.

"Oh, how I have missed their cheerful happy faces and innocent childish laughter!" she said. "I know you are going to be very happy when you get to know them, Elizabeth."

"I am sure I shall, milady," Elizabeth replied.

'I am glad something will make me happy,' she said to herself.

A bearer had already brought Lady Margot her favourite lemon tea – ice-cold with a slice of lemon on top.

"Bearer, bring one for Elizabeth, please," said Lady Margot.

"Yes, memsahib."

She smiled as she heard the bearer's reply. "It is such a long time since I was addressed so," she said. "It is so nice to be back." She watched Elizabeth, as she sipped her tea. "Do you like it?" she asked.

"Yes, milady, it is most refreshing."

"My word, Davinia, how difficult it is to tell these two apart!" said Margot as they sat on the verandah after dinner. (The children were allowed to stay up later than usual on this special occasion.)

"Well," said Stephen, "the talkative one is Clare." He smiled lovingly at them as he spoke. "The ayah is at the door now. Away to bed, you two."

"Oh, must we, Papa?" wailed Clare.

"See what I mean, Mama?" rejoined Davinia. "Now, kiss everyone goodnight." They did as they were bid, giving Elizabeth a special, long hug.

"Will you be able to play with us tomorrow?" Clare asked.

"Yes, of course," Elizabeth replied, revelling in their embrace.

CHAPTER 157

Lady Margot wanted to write home next day, and Elizabeth helped her with her correspondence. Then she joined the children under the shade of the old banyan tree. As she read to them, the bearers constantly supplied them with iced drinks. Then the children amused themselves by trying to teach Elizabeth some of the few Indian words they knew. The ayah, sitting close by under the shade of another tree, smiled at their efforts.

"Will you play some music every night and sing after dinner?" Clare asked.

"Yes, of course," Elizabeth replied.

"Not every night!" Davinia said, as she overheard. "Now, come inside out of the heat. Elizabeth is going to get exhausted."

"Very well, Mama," Astrid replied.

"Grandmama said we could all go with her to see the sisters and children in the mission," said Astrid.

"That will be very nice," said Elizabeth.

"Oh, must we, Mama?" grumbled Clare. "I would much rather play with Ian."

"You go with Grandmama – and no more grumbling, Clare!"

"Very well, Mama, but you know I don't like it as much as Astrid does."

Clare dragged her feet as she followed the others to the mission.

Elizabeth gazed anxiously round at all the sick children in the hospital.

"Will they get better, milady?" she asked with concern.

"Yes, my dear. It is quite surprising how quickly some of them recover. Come now, children – we must go now. You have packing to do."

CHAPTER 158

Elizabeth watched sadly as Davinia, Stephen and the children prepared to return to complete their holiday in the hill station.

"Grandmama, can you and Elizabeth come with us?" asked Astrid.

"Not yet, my child. We will join you soon, when we have completed some of our work at the mission."

"Now you must remember, Elizabeth, to always shake your shoes before you put them on in case a scorpion has crawled inside. They sting very badly."

"I will, but how shall I know they are scorpions?" she asked.

"Well, my dear, they are much bigger than any spiders you will have ever seen and their tails are curled over their backs. That is where the sting is. Call a bearer if you are worried."

"I will, I will," she said with a shudder.

Davinia put her arm around her. "I don't want to frighten you, my dear," she said, "but I must warn you to be careful."

"Thank you."

The thought petrified her. 'How much more have I to put up with in this dratted country?' she thought. 'I am already hearing things in my sleep.'

"Now, Elizabeth, you must remember not to go out without your hat or topee with a veil over your face. This is especially important as your skin is so fair and delicate. Also, take your salt daily; because of the heat you will lose important minerals through sweat," said Stephen.

"Very well. I will remember."

"I will remind her every day," said Margot as they said their goodbye on the station platform. "We will follow you soon, children." Margot could see they were reluctant to leave her and Elizabeth behind. "Now children, don't forget to remember the poor and sick children in the mission hospital in your prayers," she said.

"No, we won't forget them, Grandmama," called Astrid. She was always more concerned than Clare about the mission children. Clare sometimes remembered, but her mind was usually too full of play.

"Clare is not a bit ladylike," her father often remarked to Davinia.

"Well, it is nice that each has her own distinct personality, although I admit it can be a little trying at times."

Both children leaned out of one of the train windows till they were out of sight.

CHAPTER 159

Elizabeth missed the twins more than she anticipated. They had helped to ease her heartache. The heat added to her exhaustion and listlessness. 'Two years of this!' she exclaimed. 'Oh, hasten the day when it is over!'

Elizabeth spent the mornings helping her mistress with her correspondence. A sigh always escaped her when she addressed the letters to Lady Elena McNair, Glencree Castle, Scotland. That address was guaranteed to carry her thoughts far away. Sometimes she and Lady Margot visited the mission school to make lists of equipment they needed.

Elizabeth's afternoons were free. What she enjoyed most, though, was helping the sisters in the hospital. At first, the sight of so many sick children alarmed her, but they always greeted her with a smile and called her by name, no matter how ill they were.

CHAPTER 160

One day, she was called upon to relieve Sister Augustina, who had been called away urgently to visit a sick child in the village. Elizabeth was asked to stay beside the bedside of one of the children and change the compresses on his head until Sister Frances, in another wing, was free to relieve her.

She watched the child anxiously. As he turned and twisted he mumbled incoherently and threw off his sheets. She fanned him furiously as he kept mumbling, "So hot, so hot!" in spite of the cold compresses.

"The room is getting hotter, I'm sure," she gasped as she wiped her forehead. She looked up at the ceiling. "Why is the punkah so slow? It's almost stopped!" she exclaimed angrily. She rushed to the corner of the room where the punkah wallah sat cross-legged with a string attached to the fan from his big toe. Elizabeth prodded the sole of his foot with her sandal, and he woke with a start. He immediately started to pull the string as fast as he could. "*Juldi, juldi!* Quickly, quickly!" she hissed, giving him another gentle reminder with the toe of her sandal.

"Yes, yes, missy memsahib. *Juldi, juldi!*"

She hastened back to the child and quickly changed the compress; then she sighed heavily as she wiped the sweat from her forehead. The room was still too hot. She glanced towards the darkened window and door, both of which were covered with a framework of plaited grass (*khas-khas tatty*), which had to be always kept wet to cool and moisten the air. She rose to inspect them.

"It's just as I thought," she fumed.

She dashed outside, almost falling over the punkah wallah in her haste.

"You lazy, lazy boy," she shouted at the small chokra boy, who was blissfully asleep against the verandah pillar.

She had taken the bowl to get more cold water, but now she flung the remainder in his face. Then she tugged at his frayed cotton shirt and pulled him to his feet.

"Wet the *khas-khas! Juldi, juldi!*"

The startled boy reached hurriedly for his bucket and ladle.

"Yes, yes, missy memsahib. *Juldi, juldi!* Get quickly, missy memsahib," he said as he hastened to the large tank for his supply.

"I will get your annas stopped – you see if I don't."

"No, missy memsahib. No get annas stopped," he implored. "No stop annas, missy memsahib." He was startled at her anger.

"Well, carry on with your work."

The boy quickly got hold of his pan and dipped it in the bucket of water. "One, two, three – fling! One, two, three – fling!" It was a little chant he had been taught, and it helped him to concentrate.

"Now, don't you dare fall asleep again! And get some more cold water in your bucket."

"Yes, missy memsahib. I get more water. I go no more sleep. Please, missy memsahib, no get annas stopped."

"Very well, then," she replied.

She filled her bowl with cold water, hastened back inside and dampened another cloth to put on the sick child's forehead. She felt his fevered brow and sighed.

'I do hope Sister Frances comes soon, or Sister Augustina gets back from the village,' she thought. She was getting quite anxious. At last the boy opened his eyes and looked at her.

"It is so hot, so hot!" he murmured weakly. Then he drifted off again, trying to sleep.

CHAPTER 161

She could hear the boy outside repeating over and over again, "One, two, three – fling! One, two, three – fling!" The incantation rang in her ears, but she was glad of the sound as it relieved the silence of the afternoon. The only other sound was the swish of the punkah as it moved to and fro above her head. The punkah wallah had redoubled his effort after he heard Elizabeth telling the chokra boy he would get his annas stopped.

It was the only bit of English the chokra boy really understood. Some English soldiers had taught it to him and told him he must never forget it. One, to pick up his pan; two, to get it full of water; and three, to fling it at the *khas-khas tatty* as he rocked to and fro on his heels.

As she listened to him, her expression softened. She found it hard to have to be angry with him. 'He must do his work,' she reminded herself. 'This room has got to be kept cool.' Once again she wiped her brow and her arms. 'Oh, this heat!' she thought. 'How ever am I going to manage two years of this?' she sighed.

Lady Margot's voice broke in on her thoughts. She had been watching her from the door for several minutes, and she heard her sigh with exhaustion.

'The poor child!' she thought. 'I do hope she doesn't go down with heat exhaustion.'

"Well, my dear, how is the child now?" she asked.

"A little cooler, but still feverish, Lady Margot. I do hope he gets well soon."

"Oh, I am sure he will. And you, my dear – how are you?"

"Very, very hot, milady, but as long as the child is all right that is all that matters."

"Well, here comes Sister Augustina back from the village. She too looks near to exhaustion. And now Sister Frances is here also."

Elizabeth sighed with relief.

"Thank you, Elizabeth. You have been a great help," said Sister Frances. "I will relieve you now. Sister Augustina can go and rest. As you see, dear, our work is never done, but at least now we have you and Lady Margot to assist us."

"I have to tell you, Sister, we will be leaving tomorrow to rejoin my family in the hills for the next few weeks," said Lady Margot. "I shall, of course, be visiting the missions up there, but I will let you know when we are returning."

CHAPTER 162

Once again, Elizabeth's fears returned as they entered the station next day.

'I am sick of travelling, but it will be worth it to get out of this heat,' she thought. She sighed as she hurried along the platform. She hesitated a moment when she felt a tug on her skirt. She glanced round.

"Baksheesh, baksheesh!" a small voice piped up.

She couldn't understand him, but a sharp word from Lady Margot caused him to let go of Elizabeth's skirt.

Martin, who was following close behind, pushed a few coins into the boy's outstretched hand.

"Now, away, boy! Away!" he said. "You must not take any notice of these little beggars, Elizabeth, no matter how beguilingly they look at you." He had noticed the look of pity on her face as she looked at the beggar child. "They will never let you get away unless you are firm with them."

She looked around with dismay and fright at the sight of the milling crowd of people. Some were fast asleep on the platform as if it were their permanent abode. Others sat cross-legged, huddled in small groups, deep in conversation. However, most were hurrying to catch their trains. Where were they all going? Why did they sleep here? Had they no homes? When a train rushed in, people swarmed frantically into the carriages, and others, much to her horror and consternation, clambered on top. Meanwhile, those who were asleep remained completely unconscious of all that was going on around them.

"My goodness, milady!" Elizabeth cried in alarm. "Are they going to travel like that? Surely some will fall off."

"Yes, they surely will, my dear. It often happens, but they still persist. They never change."

The coolies were staggering under the weight of the luggage they carried as they raced towards the carriages. 'How ever do they manage it?' she thought, a puzzled look on her face. 'I wouldn't believe it', she decided, 'if I wasn't seeing it with my own eyes.'

The water carriers and food sellers called out their wares as they raced from carriage to carriage, but Elizabeth didn't understand a word. She marvelled at how soon Lady Margot had regained her knowledge of the language.

'Well,' she thought, 'I shan't be here long enough to worry about learning it. I shall be going home.'

"Here we are, Elizabeth. Climb aboard." Martin assisted Elizabeth and Lady Margot and placed their hand luggage on the rack above. "My compartment is next to yours, so I shall be handy if you need me. I am sharing with Major Sanders so I have put my luggage with his. We will join you for most of the journey. How fortunate for me that he is leaving so late for the hills this year!"

"Yes," said the Major as he joined them, "this will be my last visit to the hills. I am returning to England in due course, as is Judge Evans, so I am hoping we can sail together. Do you think you will ever return to Britain, Martin?"

"No, I don't think so. I have just been reunited with my dear Margot and we have so much work to do here." He pondered for a moment. "I still have some relatives in Scotland, and so has Margot, but I cannot see us ever returning for good."

"It is so much cooler travelling later in the day, and we shall wake more refreshed after the night's journey," said Margot as Elizabeth fanned herself and gazed out of the window.

"It is a long journey, my dear, so I hope you have brought a good book to read; if not, there are so many sights to see. I think you will find much to interest you on the journey."

"Yes, milady, I'm sure it will be very interesting," she said, not really caring one way or the other.

At the next stop the men bade them goodnight and went to their compartment.

CHAPTER 163

Elizabeth woke to the sun streaming in through the carriage window. Lady Margot was already up.

"Dawn broke several hours ago, Elizabeth. Did you see it?"

"Yes, milady, it was really beautiful."

"Did you not sleep very well, my child?" she asked, looking at Elizabeth with concern.

"No, not really, milady. I kept wondering how much further we had to travel."

"Well, it won't be long before our station. I daresay you are wondering what awaits you?"

"Yes, I am a little."

"Well, it is much cooler and greener than the countryside around Madras. It is similar to the Lowlands back home."

She noticed Elizabeth start and a faraway look came in her eyes.

'Dear me,' Lady Margot thought, 'I really must watch my tongue.'

"When we arrive, the children will be there to meet us."

"Oh yes, it will be lovely to see them again."

They felt the train slowing down and Margot peered out of the window. She said good morning to Major Sanders, who was also looking out. "Just as I thought: we are going to stop for breakfast." Margot said. "Martin will book it for us. I expect we shall stop for about two hours."

They alighted from the train with the help of Martin and the Major and entered a large restaurant. Each table was beautifully laid with a white tablecloth and a centre posy of flowers. All the bearers in their immaculate dress stood waiting to serve them with a full English breakfast.

At last they were back aboard the train, but only Martin joined the ladies in their compartment. Elizabeth watched fascinated from the window, marvelling at the hustle and bustle on the station. Vendors were calling out their wares, which were laid on trays, either in their hands or on their heads. Tea, fruit and lemon juice were offered to the passengers, and breakfast trays were hurriedly collected from those who had had their meals brought to them from the restaurant. The rush and bustle took Elizabeth's breath away.

'I will never get used to it,' she thought. 'How ever am I going to stand it for two years? I cannot even stand it now.'

"Why so pensive, Elizabeth?" Martin asked. "It must all seem very strange to you."

"Yes, very, Martin."

"You will soon get used to it," he concluded.

'I just know I won't,' she thought emphatically.

"Ah, here comes the Major now. I was wondering what was keeping him. The train is ready to go."

CHAPTER 164

The Major was hurrying along the platform.

"We still have a few more minutes, so I won't board yet, Martin," he called out.

"This is your first visit to India, Elizabeth, I hear."

"Yes, sir, it is."

"You will soon get used to it, although I believe you are only staying for two years."

"Yes, that is so," she replied.

"Ah well, you cannot hope to get to know a country such as this in so short a time. I have been here years and don't yet know it."

"Nor I," replied Martin, "and I have spent most of my life here."

"Boy, boy," the Major called to a passing vendor, "come here, please. I must buy these two lovely ladies a garland of flowers before we leave."

Suddenly Elizabeth found a long garland of jasmine hung round her neck as she leaned out of the window. The Major kissed her hand. She looked down at him and smiled her thanks; then she buried her face in the fragrant blooms.

"Lady Margot must be used to all this, but I can tell by your expression you are a little bewildered," the Major said.

Elizabeth had to agree with him. "Oh, they are really beautiful and the perfume is so exquisite," she said.

"It is, my dear," agreed Margot.

Elizabeth arranged her garland more to her satisfaction and thanked the Major profusely. "Now you really must come aboard and make yourself comfortable," she said.

Elizabeth was still looking out of the window, and she noticed that goods were still being sold through carriage windows as the train started to pull away. Several vendors shouted after it.

"Why are they shouting so loudly, milady?" asked Elizabeth.

"Oh, it happens all the time. They haven't had time to get their money before the train pulled away."

"Oh, what a shame!" Elizabeth exclaimed. "I do feel sorry for them."

"They never learn," Lady Margot retorted, "they never learn."

They eventually arrived at the hill station.

"Here we have to change trains. Special arrangements are needed for going up the hills. As you can see, there are two engines – one at the front and one at the rear of the train," said Margot. "Come – we will go and find our compartment.

The men will get the coolies to change our luggage over. Can you feel the cooler air now that we are in the hills? Look how many lovely flowers and lovely coloured birds there are."

"Yes, milady, it is all very interesting," Elizabeth replied, but her mind was only thinking of how much further the train was taking her from home and all those she loved.

"Over there are the tea plantations; now can you smell the eucalyptus trees?"

"Yes, milady, they smell lovely and fresh on this breeze."

'But oh, for the smell of the heather instead – the sweet, sweet smell of the heather!' she thought with a sigh.

CHAPTER 165

The children ran to greet them as they alighted from the train, their beaming smiles showing delight at their long-awaited arrival. Elizabeth grasped their hands as they wended their way to the waiting tonga.

"May we ride with Elizabeth, Mama?" Astrid asked.

"Yes, if you are both good and don't talk too much. She must be tired."

"We won't, Mama," they promised.

They climbed aboard, chattering all the time.

"And what have you been doing all the time you have been here?" asked Elizabeth.

"We have been to lots of lovely parties – nearly every day," said Clare.

"My, so many!" exclaimed Elizabeth, hardly able to believe it.

"Mama took us to the college where she used to go as a girl, and she said we might go there when we are older," said Astrid gleefully. "I just loved it."

"Oh, you would," retorted Clare. "Well, I am not going to leave Mama and Papa and go all that way to college. I shall stay with them – so there!" she exclaimed, putting her tongue out at Astrid.

"Now, Clare!" remonstrated Elizabeth. "That is not very ladylike."

"Well, I don't want to go to college so far from home."

"Well, never mind that for now. You have a long time yet to grow up."

"Oh, I nearly forgot," said Astrid: "we have a fancy-dress party soon. Will you please come and play for us, Elizabeth?"

"Yes, I most certainly will!" she exclaimed joyfully. "What will you two dress up as – or is it a secret?"

"Well, we may go as Jack and Jill," said Astrid disconsolately.

"And I suppose, Clare, you want to be Jack?"

"Yes, I do. Mama thinks I should go as Little Bo-Peep and Astrid should go as Red Riding Hood. But I don't want to be Bo-Peep," she said, screwing up her tiny nose.

"Well, we shall have to see when the time comes," said Elizabeth, not wishing to be drawn into the argument.

A few days later, after much arguing, Clare as usual won the day and went as Jack. Astrid decided that, as she was still going to be dressed as Jill in a very pretty dress, Clare could have her wish. Everyone was delighted with Elizabeth.

She played and sang each nursery rhyme as the children paraded round the room. It was the first time she had really enjoyed herself since she left Scotland.

CHAPTER 166

The visitors that called daily greeted Margot like a long-lost sister.

'She seems to know just about everyone,' thought Elizabeth.

Every night there was a party or dance to attend. She was quite bewildered by it all.

"Do many people from the city come here in the summer, milady?"

"Well, some of the luckier ones live here all the time, but those who have other work to do, like Martin and I, or officers in the government, such as Stephen, who works in the law courts, come here only for the summer. We are all anxious to escape the punishing heat of the city, which, as you have seen, can be almost beyond belief."

"Yes, I was very glad to get away. I must say, it is very pleasant up here."

"Here, in our free time, we can attend all the races and balls. There are always lots of concerts too. Oh, such a lot goes on! It just takes your breath away. It is so nice after the rest of the year's hard work. Martin and I also have missions up here, but it is much more pleasant to work in this area than in the city. There is a lovely flower show every year but we have missed it this year. At some of the grand dinners, the rajahs from the Indian States are invited. Occasionally they are greeted by a salute of guns. We might see them one night. They are a magnificent sight in all their finery. In the olden days, they arrived on their elephants, which were decorated as much as themselves."

"Yes, they must have looked really wonderful," agreed Elizabeth, but she was thinking that the snow-capped mountains of her bonnie Scotland were much more magnificent than anything India could offer.

CHAPTER 167

At the dances they attended, all the men wanted to dance with Elizabeth and she found it quite exhausting. As soon as she sat down to rest, another man would be bowing graciously before her, begging for the next dance. All were taken aback by the sheer beauty of her long golden hair and the blue eyes that smiled so graciously at them.

'Oh,' she thought, 'there is only one pair of arms I want to be in.'

Margot often insisted Elizabeth sing at most events. "They will just love to hear you, so do not be afraid," she said. "Just sing as we know you can. I know it will seem very strange with so many important people present, but you will feel all right once you begin."

She did thrill them. They all praised the sweetness and demureness of this small wisp of a girl.

"I really think, Mama," said Davinia one night when Elizabeth had just finished singing and was accepting her applause with a bow, "that we shall be losing our little Highland lassie to one of these swains before we get back to the city. She is really quite devastating, to be sure. Everyone keeps asking where we got her from? is she attached? is she staying long? and can they call on her when we return?"

"It would please me so much", said Margot, "if she decided to let one swain win her heart. I am hoping that will happen. Then at last I can cease my anxiety over her and I shall know that she has found real happiness at last. I really hope she loses the sad longing-for-home look she always has."

"Well, she certainly seems happy enough with Judge Barnes's son, Rory. I don't think I have ever seen her smile so much before, and they do seem right for each other. He is the right age too," agreed Davinia.

"Well," said Margot, "we will have to wait and see if anything develops when we return, which unfortunately we will be doing very soon. How lucky everyone is who can stay here permanently – such as the tea planters. However, we have our own work to do, and I am anxious to be back with my mission in the city. They need us so."

CHAPTER 168

The monsoon season had passed by the time they returned.

"How lovely and green everything is now – and so much cooler!" exclaimed Elizabeth.

As usual the family was greeted ecstatically by the household servants and children from the mission.

"Now," said Stephen the next night after dinner, as he stood up, "I have a lovely surprise for everyone."

"Oh, do tell us quickly, Papa," said Clare (always the first one to find her tongue at any little sight or sound of anything out of the ordinary). "I just love surprises."

"I do too," echoed Astrid.

"Well, it's for all of us," their father continued. "I am now going to propose a toast to Margot and Martin, who are now engaged and will be marrying in a few weeks."

"Does that mean that we shall have a grandfather and a grandmother?" Clare said excitedly. "We already have a mother and father."

"Yes, my dear child, it will mean just that, so here is a toast to two of the nicest people we know."

"But we have no wine to drink!" exclaimed Clare in a panic.

"Well, you cannot have wine, my dears," their mother explained.

Clare's bottom lip pouted as usual.

"Bearer!" called Stephen.

"Yes, sahib?"

"Bring some lemonade for Clare and Astrid before tears start to spoil this very happy occasion."

At last the toast was drunk and everyone rose from their seats to kiss Margot.

Martin shook hands with everyone and thanked them all for their good wishes.

"Well," said Davinia, "we all knew that it would happen one day."

"Oh, milady, I am so happy for you and Martin. I know you both will be very happy," said Elizabeth.

"Thank you, my dear Elizabeth."

Margot and Martin clasped her close; then Margot watched her closely as she sat down. She whispered to Martin, "How I wish she could find someone soon! She deserves much more happiness in her young life."

"I agree, dear. Maybe Rory will be the answer sooner than we think." Martin replied.

However, Margot knew simply by looking at Elizabeth that it would be a long time before she forgot the one so far away.

'Now,' thought Elizabeth, 'I am really on my own, in spite of all these lovely people who think of me as a daughter. I shall have to grin and bear it until I return home to Mama and Papa; then, when I do go home, my darling Roddy will be far away. Whenever am I going to see him again?'

CHAPTER 169

"Now," said Stephen, looking lovingly at his daughters, "it is back to the office for me, and these two sprites are going to the kindergarten."

"Oh, must we, Papa? I know I shall just hate it," said Clare, her bottom lip drooping.

"I think I shall like it," said Astrid, sounding a little unsure.

"Well, just be thankful you are not being sent to a boarding school like some of your friends."

Clare shuddered at this last remark. "I should really hate that, Papa. You will never send us away to those schools, will you, Papa?" she said, almost in tears. "Oh, I shall miss my friends when they go," she added wistfully.

"Well, you can't have it both ways, my child," he said as he playfully twisted her long curls round his finger. "I don't suppose your friends like it very much either, but their fathers in the army move about so much that there is no alternative. Your friend Sarah is one example. You are lucky I work in the city. Of course, many of those who go to schools in England or Scotland can visit their grandparents, so there are advantages as well as disadvantages."

The twins looked at their father, not quite believing him.

"Have we got any grandparents in Scotland?" they both asked, almost together.

"No, my dears, not now, but I have an old aunt in Scotland and so has your grandmother."

"Oh, you mean the one she calls Agatha!" exclaimed Astrid.

"Yes, that is the one – a very strict old lady, I believe," Stephen said.

"Oh, goody! Goody!" replied Clare as she danced round the room. "That means we will always stay here with you."

"Now, that is enough chatter for one day. The ayah is here, so say your goodnight and don't forget your prayers," said Davinia.

Elizabeth had to admit that time was passing very quickly. Her mornings were busy with correspondence, and in the afternoons she met the twins from school.

Over afternoon tea they chattered constantly about all they had been doing. Then came their music lessons. Already Astrid was showing great promise with both her singing and playing, but Clare was restless and eager to play with her friends. To her, music lessons were a chore, and she longed to finish them as soon as she could.

CHAPTER 170

The arrival of winter heralded constant parties and balls. Rory escorted Elizabeth to every event, frequently begging her to marry him before he departed for England early in the New Year to further his studies in law.

"No, I shall never marry," she told him.

"Well, I shall keep on asking until you say yes."

"That will never be. I shall never ever marry" – a statement he could never fathom.

'Anyway,' she decided, 'if I ever decide to marry, it would only be to someone who would take me home – not someone who wanted to live here for the rest of his life. The very thought of it fills me with dread. No, I shall return home to my parents, as I promised. However, it is nice to think that, of all the young girls Rory could have, I am the only one he wanted.' She was always in great demand at social events for her playing and singing. 'How proud and pleased Aunt Ingrid would have been – and, of course, Mama and Papa!' A tear slid down her face as she thought of them. She had received only one short note from her father since she left. He had told her they were both well and that Roddy had not yet gone abroad. It had been written shortly after that sad night, so long ago, when she left home. 'I feel as though I have been away from them for more than two years already,' she thought. She quickly dried her eyes. 'I must not let Lady Margot see I have been crying.'

Margot and Martin were married quietly in the small mission church a few weeks later. The twins for once were dressed exactly alike in pretty pink dresses, with flowers in their hair. They each carried a small basket of flowers. Their mother had thought that one large basket carried by them both would have looked prettier, but Clare, as usual, demanded her own, so that was that.

CHAPTER 171

To Craig the days were endless. He gazed deep into the water as the ship sailed on. He still could hardly believe all that had happened. Graham often stood beside him in silence watching his despondency. He was aware of Craig's reason for sailing to India, but he was puzzled as to why leaving his father and his homeland to join the woman he loved should be causing him so much heartache. He sometimes sensed that Craig resented his presence, so he would slip silently away.

The thought of Merry-Berry's prediction gladdened Craig's heart and reassured him. She had never before promised or told him anything that had not come to pass. She had told him he would be going far away over the water and now he was. He had laughed it away, but, as always, she was right.

'Now all I must think of is finding my darling angel,' he thought, 'but where will she be? I only know she will be travelling with Margot to the missions.' He sighed with despair. 'It might be weeks or months before I locate her, but find her I shall. How I wish this journey was over!'

"Have you decided, Craig," Graham asked one evening, "what you are going to do eventually. I do hope you will accept my offer and join me in partnership in my tea plantation in the hills. You will love it up there. Why, it will be almost as if you were back in the Highlands."

"Oh, my dear friend," he replied, "how little you know of me and my love for the Highlands! Thank you for the offer, Graham, I shall certainly consider it seriously and, of course, I will visit you as often as I can. Aunt Elena mentioned that Margot has quite a few connections in Madras; I shall first try to contact her through the Indian Civil Service."

CHAPTER 172

During the long days Craig had nothing to do but think of his angel. The dances held every evening irked him more and more, so night after night he slipped away to be on his own.

This was something the scheming mothers aboard couldn't understand. They persistently tried to interest him in their daughters, vying with one another to be the first to exclaim. "My daughter has won him!" The daughters pursued him on every conceivable occasion, much to his annoyance. The knowledge that he was an earl's only son added to their persistence, but he remained aloof. However, he was always extremely courteous as he daily bade them good morning and good night.

CHAPTER 173

"At last," he exclaimed: "land in sight! Soon I shall have my angel in my arms. I pray she is still at Margot's home." He stood transfixed as he gazed at the hectic scene on the quay.

'This must have frightened my darling to death,' he thought.

Graham broke in on his thoughts as they leaned over the ship's rail: "Here is the address where I shall be staying in the city before I travel to the hills. Please come if you don't find Lady Margot at home."

"Thank you, Graham, I will."

"Also, here is my address at the plantation. Please consider my offer. It will always be open. Goodbye, Craig. I hope all goes according to plan. This tonga will take you to the station. It is only a short ride."

"I am sure I will find my way, Graham. Goodbye."

Graham watched him out of sight before entering his tonga.

CHAPTER 174

It was the night of the Governor's Ball at the residency.

"Do hurry, Martin dear. It is getting very late."

"I will be down in a few minutes, Margot," he called as she hurried down the stairs.

"Memsahib! Memsahib!" the bearer called agitatedly as he waited below.

"Whatever is the matter, bearer?" she demanded.

"There is a young sahib at the door insisting on seeing you."

"Tell him it is not possible tonight. Tell him to come back in the morning. We are late for the ball as it is."

"But he insists, memsahib, that you must see him tonight."

"Insists? Indeed? The very idea! Surely it is my husband he wishes to see?"

"No, memsahib, he said he must speak with you. He said it is most urgent."

"Very well, then, show him into the library and tell him I will see him in a few moments."

"Very well, memsahib."

The bearer hurried away when he saw Lady Margot's evident displeasure at the delay. The ayah was standing close by, alarmed at Margot's tone of voice. It was so unlike her to raise her voice.

"Bring my evening wrap at once, Ayah."

"At once, memsahib," she said, rushing away to do her bidding.

The bearer ushered Craig into the lounge and bade him be seated in the big chair by the fire. Craig looked around nervously, wondering if at last he would get to see the one he longed for. As he waited, he tapped his fingers impatiently on the arm of the chair.

"It is most annoying that the caller has not even presented his card – and tonight of all nights!" Lady Margot muttered as she fastened her evening cape round her shoulders.

She entered the library and the bearer closed the door behind her. Craig rose to greet her, but at first, not recognising him, she shrank back. He rushed towards Margot, who almost collapsed as he uttered her name.

"Margot, Margot, please forgive me for startling you so and for calling on you like this. I only arrived this morning, so I could not let you know."

At last she became more composed. She sat down.

"Do sit down, Craig, and tell me what you are doing here at all," she said. "I thought you would still be on your honeymoon."

"My marriage never happened, Margot. It could never be." He looked anxiously round several times, Margot noted, as he spoke.

CHAPTER 175

"Where is she, dear Margot? Please tell me. I cannot live without seeing her."

"But your father, and your dear Fiona!" She was aghast at the thought of all the consequences of his presence.

"I am never going back and I will never marry Fiona. I am going to marry

Elizabeth. Please tell me where I can find her. I will go crazy if I don't." He came and knelt beside Margot. He took both her now chilled hands in his as he looked up at her imploringly.

'He's just like his father', she recalled, 'when he begged me to take the girl away. Now here is his son begging me to tell him where to find her. Oh, why, oh why, have I always to be in such a predicament because of this son and his father?' When she saw the pleading in his eyes she knew she had to accede to his plea.

"Well, Craig, dear boy," she said, "I will tell you only if you promise not to communicate with her until I give you the word."

"Yes, of course, I promise, Margot, but please tell me that I shall see her tonight."

"Yes, I can promise you that."

Martin entered the room, calling Margot's name. "Come, my dear," he said, "we are late." He stopped in alarm as they both stood up. "Do I know this young man, my dear?"

"This young man is Craig McNair, son and heir of the 11th Earl of Glencree."

"Not any more, Margot. Papa has now disinherited me and stripped me of my name and title. We can discuss all that again in a few days. Then I will tell you all you wish to know."

"Where are you staying, Craig?" Margot asked.

"With the friend I travelled with from Scotland. He has a place in the city."

"But you must stay here with us," Margot insisted. "Give me the name and address of your friend and I will send the bearer with a message."

"Margot, I don't know how to thank you enough for all your kindness."

"Forget it, my dear boy," Martin said. "Now, we must all hurry."

"You will come as our guest, but I will ask that your name not be announced," said Margot. "You must hurry and change into evening dress. I will get my bearers to take all your luggage to the guest room."

CHAPTER 176

"Elizabeth is singing and playing for the governor's guests tonight, and, Craig dear, she mustn't know you are here until she has finished her recital."

"I promise, I promise." He knew it would be the hardest thing for him to bear to see her and not be near her, but he gave his word.

Margot looked at him as they travelled. She noted his eager anticipation. 'Poor boy!' she thought. 'He has given up so much to be with her. Poor Bruce!' she thought. 'Poor, poor Bruce! What agony he must be suffering!' Her mind wandered back to all that had gone before.

"Elizabeth is staying with my daughter, Davinia, and her husband and their twin girls. She is their governess, and she helps me with my correspondence whilst the children are at the kindergarten. They will already have left for the ball," she said, but she could see he wasn't listening.

CHAPTER 177

"Mama, you are so late. What has kept you? And who is this? His face seems familiar," exclaimed Davinia as soon as she saw them.

"Yes, you have met before, but not for many years," continued Margot. "It is Master Craig, whom you haven't seen since you were children. But we cannot talk now. Where is Elizabeth?"

"She is just starting to play and sing. You have arrived just in time."

The five of them stood in a small alcove, purposely chosen by Margot, just beneath a dimmed wall light. Elizabeth looked anxiously round several times as she was singing, but she could not see them. Craig stood leaning against a marble pillar, his eyes half closed, as her sweet voice rang out. There was a drink in his hand, but he hardly touched it. His thoughts were only of her. He could only just see the top of her head above the throng of people standing behind the seated governor and his wife and other high officials.

"Oh, how I wish she had finished singing, Margot!" he said with a sigh.

"Well, she has to give a piano recital, but then she will be free for the rest of the evening."

He was tapping his foot in time to the music she was playing, but it was more with impatience than musical appreciation. "Can I have her the rest of the evening, Margot?"

"Well, there is another young man over there – can you see him? He too is anxiously waiting for her recital to finish."

"Another man, Margot?" he exclaimed incredulously. "Surely she hasn't got betrothed to someone else?" He was panic-stricken and his voice shook with emotion. "How foolish of me, Margot, to be so presumptuous as to think that no other swain would love her and want to marry her."

"My dear boy, I must admit she has had quite a difficult task but she hasn't accepted any of them as suitors – though I have wished it since our arrival. Now hush, dear boy!" she whispered to him, as his voice had risen in panic. "We are being looked at very disapprovingly by other guests."

'Oh, bother!' he thought as he glanced around, but he did as she bid.

Margot noted the many admiring glances that came their way as they entered the room, and she saw several of the matronly mothers eyeing him up. No doubt they were asking one another where he had come from. They would insist on being introduced to him as soon as possible if they decided he would be a good catch for their daughters.

"The young man over there", Margot told Craig in a whisper, "asks Elizabeth every time he sees her to become his wife."

"Are you sure she has not accepted, Margot, without you knowing?"

"Yes, I am sure. I would be the first person she would confide in."

He breathed a sigh of relief.

CHAPTER 178

When Elizabeth finished her recital she stood up to take her applause and turned to curtsy to the governor and his wife. Everyone was enthralled. They applauded her madly. She stood up, smiling at everyone, and looked around. She spotted Lady Margot and Davinia, who had eased themselves out of the alcove and were now in the full glow of the light. Then her gaze became transfixed on the tall, handsome man by their side. She wondered if this was part of the dream that haunted her every night. It couldn't be her darling Craig – it just couldn't be! But now she could see him more closely. He was trying to reach her, but he was getting hemmed in by people hoping to be introduced.

She could also see Rory in the crowd, heading straight for her. She made her escape through the open verandah doors down the steps into the flower-bedecked gazebo in the garden.

Craig watched her every move as he excused himself time and time again.

Elizabeth leaned heavily against the cool marble pillars. She was gasping, taking in deep breaths of the scented blossom-laden evening air.

'Oh, it cannot be true, it cannot,' she thought. 'I must be dreaming.' The dream she was always dreaming was one in which she saw Craig again. 'Surely fate cannot be so cruel!' she thought. 'Haven't I suffered enough?'

But suddenly his strong arms were around her and he was whispering, "My angel, my angel." She was not dreaming. No more breath was possible. He kissed her hungrily time and time again as tears streamed down her lovely face. He released her and wiped them away.

"Don't speak, my darling angel," he whispered, "just let me hold you close. Never again shall we be parted. We are going to be married straight away."

She felt limp and weak as his passionate kisses fell on her lips. She tried to call his name, but he made speech impossible.

"I wish we could be married tonight," he whispered.

The presence of Margot by his side caused him to release her.

"Come, my dears," she said, "we must bid goodnight to the guests of honour."

"Yes, of course, Margot," Craig replied, and he led both of them to where the governor and his wife were sitting.

Once more they complimented Elizabeth on her playing and singing. "You must play and sing for us again sometime," said the governor's wife.

"I will, at your pleasure," she replied as she curtsied to them.

"May I present to you", said Margot, "Craig McNair, who only arrived today."

Craig bowed to them as he was introduced.

Rory, standing in the doorway, watched in dismay. Who was this tall, dark stranger Elizabeth was with? Rory had never seen him before, but now he saw the way Elizabeth looked up at him as they crossed the floor. He disappeared into the night, knowing he had lost her for ever.

CHAPTER 179

The next few weeks were hectic and full of happiness. Stephen and Martin made the preparations for the wedding, which Craig had requested must take place as soon as the banns were read and his domicile completed.

Clare and Astrid could talk of nothing else but the wedding and the dresses they would be wearing. Elizabeth decided to leave the choice of colour to them. The durzi (dressmaker) called daily with patterns and rolls of materials. The girls' constant change of mind about style and colour perplexed him more each time he came.

At last their mother had had enough of their constant wrangling. "Well, my two darlings, as it is so near Christmas, how about red velvet trimmed with white swansdown with muffs to match?" she suggested.

Clare, after much thought on the matter, agreed that Mama's choice was just perfect, and Elizabeth was only too delighted to agree with Davinia's choice. She and Davinia made several trips to the city, and finally she chose a dress of white velvet, also trimmed with swansdown.

Elizabeth wanted to wear the coronet Lady Margot had given her, but Craig insisted she must wear the family coronet which he had brought with him. His only disappointment, as he admitted to Margot, was that the ring was missing, and, much to his sorrow, she would never be able to wear it.

"I'm afraid, Margot," he sighed, "the family jeweller was given instructions by my father that only he could collect it."

"Well, that is your father, as you know, Craig."

"Yes, Margot, I know him only too well. Anyway, Elizabeth will be mine, and that he can never deny me."

Their wedding day dawned. There was a chill in the air, but the winter sun shone brilliantly. The twins preceded Elizabeth down the aisle, scattering rose petals specially sent by Margot's friends in the hills. The twins stood demurely just behind her as she joined Craig at the altar.

Craig, standing beside Stephen, turned to face her. He thought she had never looked more beautiful. She clung to Martin's arm nervously, but she was trembling with happiness.

Craig held her possessively as they stood in the doorway after the ceremony.

"Now you are mine, my darling. No one will ever take you away from me."

Girls from the mission and the village thronged around them, piling garlands round their necks. They put bracelets of pretty glass on Elizabeth's wrists.

"Thank you, thank you," she enthused repeatedly as they salaamed and gave her their good wishes.

Craig and Elizabeth were both relieved to escape to the bungalow for a few precious minutes alone.

"Now, my darling," said Craig, "I can give you the marriage jewellery of bracelets and necklace to match the coronet. Only the ring is missing, my love. I don't suppose we shall ever see it. Papa will never let it leave Glencree – more's the pity!" He sighed. "But you, my darling, are more precious to me than any jewels."

He slipped the glass bracelets from her wrists and replaced them with the priceless ones. She looked down at them in awe, speechless in amazement at their beauty. She looked shyly up at him, knowing that their love was more priceless than any gem.

He placed the necklace round her neck and kissed her passionately as she turned to face him. She fingered the jewels lightly.

"They are so beautiful, my darling," she said. "Are you sure I am worthy of them?"

He kissed her again and again; then he grasped her shoulder, tilted her face and looked deep into her eyes.

"Don't ever ask me that again or I shall get very angry with you. It is the only thing that will make me angry. You, my darling, are more than worthy of our family jewels. To me, my love, you are more precious than the Crown Jewels."

"Come, my darling," she whispered, "everyone is waiting for us."

Everyone greeted them with confetti and rose petals when they reappeared. The wedding guests gazed in admiration at the rubies and diamonds glinting in the brilliant sunlight.

A few days later they left for their honeymoon: a grand tour of India.

As they prepared to leave, the twins had still not yet got over the enthralling event of a few days ago.

"Will it be long before we see you again, Elizabeth?" Astrid asked plaintively.

"Yes, my dear, but you must both keep up your practising. I shall be able to tell when I return."

Astrid assured her that she would do as requested, but the look on Clare's face told Elizabeth that there would be no practising except when her parents insisted.

"We will join you in the hills sometime in the summer," said Craig.

"I will rent you a bungalow near us," said Martin.

"Keep us informed of the day of your arrival," called Margot.

As they drove away, she wiped a tear of happiness from her eye. Next to her own family, no one was more precious to her than these two.

CHAPTER 180

Margot sat down that night and wrote to Elena, telling her that at last Craig and Elizabeth were married.

'I knew from the happiness on their faces, that it had to be,' she wrote, 'in spite of all the anguish it must cause you all – especially Bruce.'

She found it a difficult letter to write, and so she kept it as short as possible, promising Elena she would write more later.

The next day she wrote to Martha and Magnus.

Martha and Magnus sighed deeply as they sat idly gazing into the blazing peat fire. They both wished, as they read of the marriage, that it wasn't so. They were still waiting for news of Roddy, who, as yet, had not gone abroad.

"Goodness knows", sighed Martha as she wiped away her tears, "when we shall see our two dear children again!"

"There, there, my dear!" said Magnus comfortingly, putting his arm round her bent shoulders. "I am sure Master Craig will send her home for a holiday, even if he cannot come."

"Do you think so, my dear?" she said, drying her eyes. "I wonder", she pondered, "how the laird will react. He will surely have got the news by now. How I wish it wasn't our dear daughter who had caused him so much sorrow!"

"But it wasn't our daughter's fault. Master Craig decided to follow her. We shall have to be content that they are both well and happy."

"Yes, I suppose you are right, my dear. We must now write to our dear son."

Elena was gazing as usual from her bedroom window down the long drive. It was time for Robbie to come, and sure enough he was now approaching. She hurried down to greet him and hurried back upstairs to read her letter. She was surprised it was so small as usually Margot's letters were quite bulky. She hurried to the window to catch the brighter light.

'Well, at last it has happened. I do so hope they will be happy – I am sure they will be. Now I must tell Bruce and Harriet – but when?'

She knew she could handle Harriet in any encounter – but Bruce? She gave a little shudder at the thought. She put the letter in her pocket to await a suitable time.

Harriet, unbeknown to her, had seen the delivery of mail and wondered about its contents. Elena usually mentioned any news whenever she received her mail. After dinner that night, Harriet decided to speak: "Was there much news in the post today?"

Elena looked up, startled. She had planned to wait until Bruce had had his tot of whisky, which she thought might make the news easier for him to take.

Bruce looked at both of them without really seeing them. They were both deeply saddened to see the change in him since Craig's departure.

"Well, was there any news of any interest in the post?" he queried.

Elena fumbled nervously for the letter in her pocket. "Yes, there was a letter from Margot. It is of interest, but you won't really want to hear what she has to say."

"Well, go on, then, woman!" he exclaimed angrily.

"It says Craig and Elizabeth were married today. He has also taken a sept name, but she has not stated what it is. Probably in her next letter she will tell us."

"I have no wish to know," Bruce exclaimed angrily.

He rose from the table, left the room and slammed the door behind him. He had always thought, even at this late stage, that somehow Craig would see the folly of his ways and return. Now it was too late – all had gone.

"So Craig has finally got what he wanted, and that little hussy has also. If they only knew the suffering they have caused our dear Bruce!" Harriet said before she too left the room.

Jamie, coming to stoke the fire, looked after her, alarmed.

"It is all right, Jamie. Master Craig is now married to Elizabeth," Elena said, and she hurried away.

Jamie sighed as he stoked the fire; then he hurried to the kitchen to tell the news to the other staff.

Cook gasped in dismay. "Well, that's the end of the laird now," she sighed. "He will never get over it."

"Neither will Lady Harriet. I think Lady Elena is more accepting of his marriage. I know she never really liked Lady Fiona. Anyway, don't any of you", Jamie said, glancing at Marie and Sarah, who were standing with mouths open at the news, "tell one word of this to anyone. It will be village gossip soon enough. How poor Magnus and Martha are taking the news I just don't know."

"They will hardly dare come into the village," said Cook with a sigh. "Anyhow, we can only wish that our young master will be happy."

CHAPTER 181

Craig and Elizabeth never tired of the delights on their travels. The magnificence of the Himalayas filled them with awe.

"My darling," she whispered as they stood clasped in each other's arms, "I remember now the photographs Lady Margot showed me a long time ago when we were in the attic at Harrison Hall. I never for one moment thought that one day I should be so close to these mountains."

She glanced up at Craig, whose thoughts were far away.

"Yes, my darling," he said eventually, "they are not the mountains of home, but they are really superb. We will see our mountains one day, my darling, I promise." He hugged her close in the chill mountain air. "I just know we will. Merry-Berry promised I would return, and you know she is always right."

"Yes, I know, my darling. Did she also mention that I would return?"

"But you know, my darling, I will never return without you." He kissed her tenderly as if to dispel her fears.

It was now the late spring of 1921. Craig and Elizabeth's last call was to visit the Taj Mahal. Both stood gazing in speechless wonder at its magnificence under the moonlit sky, neither speaking. They were alone apart from a shoeless bearer standing close by. The marble glistened as the shafts of moonlight were reflected by the semi-precious stones with which it was adorned.

"Shah Jahan's love for his wife was not as great as my love for you, my darling," he whispered. "Come – we will return to it tomorrow and see the inside, but we will have to take off our shoes before we enter."

They thought it looked even more spectacular when they visited next day. The splendour of the interior struck them forcibly as they viewed it in silence.

"What a monument to a great love, my darling!" Craig whispered as they emerged into the brilliant sunlight.

They walked slowly past the fountains and gardens lost in wonder.

They were greeted with outstretched arms on their arrival at the hill station. The twins hugged Elizabeth as if they would never let her out of their sight ever again.

"Oh, how we have missed you, Elizabeth!" exclaimed Astrid. "Please don't go away for so long again," she pleaded.

"I will try not to," she laughed.

"I have done as I promised and kept up my practising – haven't I, Mama?"

"Yes, my child, you have been very good," answered Davinia.

"I did a little too!" exclaimed Clare, determined not to be outdone.

"Well, it was only a little," her mother replied. "Now, no more chatter! I expect Elizabeth and Craig are very tired after their journey."

"Yes, I am rather," said Elizabeth as she sank down in the nearest chair.

"You must stay here for a few days to rest before moving into the nearby bungalow. It is yours for as long as you wish. Maybe you will consider buying it later, Craig. The owner has now left for good," said Margot.

"That will be wonderful. Everything has been just too wonderful for words. I still feel as though I am dreaming a wonderful dream. I am afraid of waking," said Elizabeth.

"Well, we will be here for some time before we return to the city," said Davinia.

"But why have we to return?" Clare asked with a pout.

"School, of course!" her mother replied.

"Whatever is to become of that child? I don't know!" said Margot. "She thinks life should be one long holiday, but when she is older I think she will like being at school."

"I doubt it," Clare's father rejoined.

"Today I am going with Martin and Stephen to the tea plantation to see Graham. The journey will tire you, my darling. You still look very pale and tired," said Craig. "Margot is going to the mission, but you will be all right here with Davinia and the children, my darling?"

"Yes, my dear, I shall be quite all right."

Craig came bounding in on his return and she could tell that he had something exciting to tell her.

"My darling, I have bought a partnership in Graham's tea plantation."

"Oh, darling!" she exclaimed. "Does that mean we will have to stay up here permanently? I shall miss the children so much."

"No, of course not, my love. Our home will be in the city, where my work is. This will be something for me to do when we come to the hills in the summer, along with any office work I bring with me. Graham lives permanently on the plantation. Don't you agree it is wonderful news?"

"Yes it is. I am so happy for you. You will be out riding in the open air in the hills around the plantation. It will be almost like being at home."

"Well, not quite, my darling, but it will be the next best thing. Darling, you look so pale and tired. Are you well?"

"Yes, my darling, I am perfectly well. I also have some good news. Now sit here beside me. We are going to have a baby, and I just know it will be a boy."

Craig was speechless with happiness for a few seconds. "My darling, my precious, precious darling, how wonderful! Have you told anyone else yet?" he asked.

"No, but I think Davinia may suspect it. She mentioned that I was far too pale and not looking at all well."

On hearing Elizabeth's news, Margot and Davinia decided to return to their city home sooner than they normally did. "It will save us from being in too much of a crush," said Davinia, "as everyone stops here till the last possible minute."

Clare, on hearing the news of their early return, sulked as usual. "Will we have to return to school sooner also?" she grumbled.

"No, of course not, silly!" exclaimed Astrid. "We can call and see the sick children in the missionary hospital. That's what we can do, can't we, Grandmama?"

"Yes, of course, my dears."

A letter for each of them was awaiting them on their return. Craig watched Elizabeth as she opened hers eagerly. She gave a gasp of delight as she read it.

"My darling," she said, "it is from Emma. She is expecting a baby in September. Isn't it exciting? Do you realise, my darling," she said as she looked up at him, "both our sons will be born in the same year."

"My darling, how you dream so! How do you know they will be boys?"

"I just know it, my darling. Are you not opening your letter, my darling?"

"Well, I will now that I have heard your good news. Let us hope the news in mine makes us happy also.

"No, it is not good news, my darling," he said.

He sighed heavily and sat down. Elizabeth could tell by the catch in his throat that the letter troubled him greatly. She came and sat beside him.

"What is it, my darling?" She said, nervously, knowing that any sadness for him was hers also.

He did not answer for several seconds. As he gazed into the distance she became more alarmed.

"Do tell me, my love," she implored.

"My dear dog, Flint, has passed away. It seems he just pined too much after I left. I feared he might die as he was so old, but at least now he is resting peacefully."

"Such a darling he was!" Elizabeth sighed. "I loved him dearly."

They held each other in a sad embrace.

CHAPTER 182

Elizabeth was happy to be finally in her own home. To her it seemed like a palace. Every room was vast, with high ceilings and small windows to keep out the heat. The walls were painted white. They both appreciated the help they received from Davinia in its furnishing. Also, she and Stephen knew where to go to find dependable bearers, ayahs and other servants who were well versed in the English language. The outside of the house was painted a delicate shade of pink. There was a wide verandah with white-painted pillars, and at the foot of each pillar was a flowering plant.

After Craig had left for the city, Elizabeth was at a loss as to what to do. She spent hours on the verandah watching the mali tend the garden, and she was thankful when Davinia called. Sometimes they both walked over to the mission to visit Margot and see the children, but they always went in the morning to avoid the heat of the day. In the afternoon she rested until the joyful chatter of the twins and their ayah heralded that it was time for their music lesson.

Astrid was always the first to show Elizabeth how much she had progressed since her last visit. She would sit down at the piano and play scales off by heart. Clare always sat on the verandah, not taking the slightest bit of interest and pouting when her turn came to play. She made mistake after mistake, in spite of Elizabeth's best efforts to teach her. She felt at times that some of Clare's mistakes were intentional, but she was determined that she would learn in the end.

Elizabeth's only real happiness came when the wide gates were flung open by the mali and Craig's tonga dashed through. Craig would leap out and embrace her as soon as he arrived on the top of the verandah steps. More often than not he took the reins from the tonga wallah to hasten the horses. He knew it wasn't the correct thing to do, but he didn't care. He always did as he wished.

Craig had offers of several positions outside the city, but he would not accept any that took him further away from Elizabeth's side. In the end he accepted a position in a bank close by, although he found being confined to an office irksome.

They were both glad that the army barracks were near, and many of his army friends encouraged him to become a member of the polo club. His prowess and daredevil riding amazed them all. Only Elizabeth and Margot knew what it meant to him to be riding so recklessly: it was as if he was back home, riding the glens, as free as the wind.

Craig insisted that the durzi embroider his family crest purple and green (the colour of the thistle and the glens) on everything in the house, including all the bearers' apparel (puggarees and tartan cummerbunds). Aunt Elena sent him the tartan, unbeknown to anyone at Glencree, in a parcel addressed to Margot as if it were something for the missions.

One day, as he leapt out of the tonga, Craig shouted, "Darling, darling, see what I bought today."

"Whatever is it, my love?"

He hastily but carefully unwrapped the parcel he was carrying. "See, my darling, it is a large brass oil lamp I bought in the bazaar."

He put it carefully on the table.

"Bearer, please fill it with oil and light it."

The boy did as Craig asked. Craig then turned the wick up as high as he dared.

"See, my darling," he said, "it is almost like the one in your old home."

Almost at once he wished he hadn't spoken as he noticed the sad, lost look in her eyes, which were now lit up by the light. He held her close and kissed her. "Just think, my darling," he said, "but for that light I might never have seen you."

"Well, I was looking for my dear Roddy, if you recall. I wonder if I shall ever see him again?" she sighed.

CHAPTER 183

To the burra memsahibs the tall, dark, handsome man in their midst was something of a mystery. At first they knew little more than that he had married the lovely golden-haired Elizabeth Anderson, who was governess and music teacher to the children of the high court judge as well as part-time secretary to Lady Margot Emslie. Later they found out that he was an earl's son and that his father had disinherited him because of his marriage, and this knowledge added spice to their afternoon gossip.

They were all anxious to get an invitation to his house so that they could find out more details of this epic story. They wanted to know how a simple village girl (which they believed her to be), had managed to become the wife of such a noble gentleman; why had following this woman to India and marrying her so displeased his father that he had disinherited him?

But they never got the invitations and their own invitations were never accepted, so their curiosity was never satisfied. They often tried to wangle information from either Margot or Davinia, but it was never forthcoming, much to their annoyance.

The Colonel's wife presided at every afternoon tea party. She considered herself of prime importance as the conveyor of any choice topics for discussion at these gatherings, though many of the ladies attending them would gladly excuse themselves from being there if they dared.

"I did hear", she announced disdainfully as the Captain's wife, Mrs Rowan, arrived late and seated herself comfortably at the bottom of the table, "that Master Craig (as he was known) was engaged to a certain Lady Fiona Cleveland and he deserted her two days prior to their wedding. I don't know how any man, especially a titled one, could do such a despicable thing and turn his back on his title and heritage to follow and marry a mere servant girl, as she was back home." She tut-tutted into the lace-edged handkerchief she was wafting like a fan. "I have to admit she is very beautiful and her singing is quite divine, but it still does not alter the fact that she is only a servant. I am only disappointed that he is not an officer in my husband's regiment, in which case I'm sure I could enlighten you further."

"How ever did she get to know so much about him?" hissed Mrs Rowan to Mrs Crawford, who was sitting next to her.

"Apparently," whispered her confidante, "she has a relative in London who told her that his engagement to the Lady Fiona was announced in the London papers. Then lo and behold! read later that the proposed wedding would not take place. That is about all she knows, no matter how she pokes and pries. I believe inwardly she is seething that they keep themselves to themselves. I am glad she can't get to know any more."

"So am I," Mrs Rowan agreed. "Thank goodness tea has arrived! Soon we will be able to get away."

CHAPTER 184

Roddy wrote to Elizabeth and wished her well, but he gave no return address. His letter was still very curt, perhaps, it seemed to her, because he still blamed her for the laird's son breaking his engagement. Magnus had explained to him that Elizabeth was not to blame. However, as Martha's health improved Roddy had begun to feel a little more kindly towards Elizabeth.

"If Roddy comes," said Craig, "as I am certain he will, I shall tell him that you were not to blame in any way for my decision. I know you will both then be the happy, loving brother and sister you always were."

"Thank you, my darling," she whispered. "I love you so."

Elizabeth now had the birth of her baby to look forward to. The twins called to see her often, even when it was not a day for their music lesson. Astrid had continued to make very good progress, but Clare only came to music lessons as she could never bear to be parted from Astrid. The two girls were as different as it was possible to be. She loved them dearly, as if they were her own children.

Now and again she visited the mission to see the children, and they always greeted her with open arms. Margot had now got another assistant and Davinia helped as often as she could. They, too, were anxiously awaiting the birth of Elizabeth's baby.

"I wonder", exclaimed Margot to Davinia one day, "if it will be a boy or a girl?"

"Well, we won't have to wait much longer."

"I do hope she keeps well," Margot said with a sigh. "I do worry so about her, especially as her mother is so far away."

The heavy monsoon rains had finally ceased and the air was hot, dry and humid. Elizabeth sighed heavily. She wiped the perspiration from her brow, in spite of fanning herself furiously.

Margot and Craig had tried in vain to persuade her to return to the hills until after her baby was born, but she refused. "I must stay here with you, my darling Craig, and you cannot leave the office after having been away so long."

"The air would be cooler, my darling. Margot will stay with you."

"I know it is very kind of Margot to offer, but our baby must be born here with you by my side, dear."

"Very well, my angel," he replied, knowing that no further argument would change her mind.

Elizabeth was sitting in the deep bamboo chair on the verandah, thinking of the cool mountain air back home, longing for her mother's presence.

"Not too long to go!" she sighed, as she gazed out into the dark night. "Then I shall have my darling son, and the days will be cooler – for which I shall be thankful."

She watched as the chokidar (nightwatchman) wended his way up the path. He stopped at the bottom of the verandah steps to bid Elizabeth good evening.

"Salaam, memsahib."

"Salaam," she replied. "How is your family?"

"Well, memsahib, well."

He turned to go and, as he glanced at her, a look of terror crossed his face.

She glanced at him, petrified by the terror in his gaze. She rose slightly out of her chair.

"Don't move, memsahib don't move," he said, the fear in his voice rising.

She began to tremble. Her hands clasped the arms of her chair, and beads of perspiration ran down her terror-stricken face.

"Whatever is it, bearer?" she asked as she saw him approaching from the room. "Tell me, tell me!" She tried to scream out but was paralysed with fright.

The chokidar kept repeating, "Don't move memsahib, don't move," and the bearer whispered the same.

Elizabeth realised that their behaviour could only mean some terrible danger, so she did as she was bid.

The two men stood looking above her head, ready for action. They had seen a huge cobra fast asleep along the top of the bamboo rail behind her. It was hardly visible within the folds of curtain, but they knew it could waken suddenly at the slightest noise or movement in its vicinity. Elizabeth watched the chokidar anxiously as he moved silently and cautiously up the verandah steps. He eased himself round to the right. He raised the long *lahti* (stick) which he always carried, then, with lightning speed and a furious swipe and lunge, he struck the cobra behind its head.

The rail and curtain came crashing down, enveloping Elizabeth. She screamed out as she tried to free herself.

Craig, who had been busy in his study, reached for his gun from the drawer when he heard the terrible crash and Elizabeth's scream of terror. He cocked the gun and dashed out, almost falling headlong over the writhing snake and curtain. He fired several shots at it as he regained his balance, although it was already almost dead from the chokidar's blow. The servant still held his *lahti* poised for another swift strike if it moved.

"My darling! My precious, precious darling!" he exclaimed as he raised her up. "Thank goodness you are safe! Well done, boys! Well done!"

She tried to rise to her feet, and Craig was just in time to catch her as she fainted. He picked her up in his arms and laid her gently on her bed. Her ayah was hovering nearby. Craig told the bearer to call Davinia and then to go for Lady Margot and the doctor.

Davinia arrived quite breathless in her haste. Stephen was with her. The bearer had already told them of the episode with the snake.

"How is she now, Craig?" Davinia asked. "I have told the bearer to call the doctor."

"Thank you so much. She has come round now from her faint."

Davinia sat on the side of her bed holding her hand.

"You are all right now, Elizabeth," she said. "Just rest and keep calm." She hoped that this trauma would not hurry the birth of Elizabeth's child. "Mama will be here soon, and so will the doctor."

"Thank you, thank you," Elizabeth replied weakly, "but I shall be all right now."

"Come, Craig," said Stephen, "we must join the boys and bury the snake before its mate comes to search for it. You know they always stay together."

"Yes, I don't think it will be too far away. We must try to find it and frighten it away from the house."

Craig hurried back into the house after a long search.

"Are you sure you are all right, my darling?" he asked as he bent down to kiss her. "How I wish I could take you away from all these things that scare you so."

"Yes, yes, I am quite all right my love."

"Poor darling!" he said. "Now I must go and rejoin Stephen. Davinia will stay with you till we return."

Several other bearers had joined Stephen.

"The boys tell me they think they know where the snakes are," Stephen said. "They have seen them many times before, but never so close to the house. The boys will try to kill its mate in case it strikes anyone."

Elizabeth lay silent, her thoughts far away. 'How I wish I could be far away from all the dust, heat and danger of this strange land. Oh, it can never be, never be, never be!' she thought. She gave a deep sigh. 'Fortunately, I have my darling's love to sustain me. How I wish we could both go back to Glencree with its keen, bracing air, the heather-clad hills and the cool green glens. I hate this eternal brownness everywhere. It only becomes green for a short while when the monsoon comes.'

The monsoon, so welcome when it comes, brings a terror of its own. Elizabeth shuddered violently as she thought of the closeness of the snake, which had taken refuge in the verandah.

"Are you all right, Elizabeth?" said Davinia as she rose from her chair close by.

"Yes, I am all right. Thank you for staying with me."

"Well, here is Craig back again so I will wish you goodnight."

Davinia kissed Elizabeth lightly on the forehead before she left.

"How is she now, Davinia?" asked Stephen.

"She is resting. I have just bidden her goodnight."

"Well I won't disturb her," he replied. "We have not seen anything of the other snake, but the boys are used to these things. They are well protected and they will carry on. Craig was anxious to get back to Elizabeth."

Craig thanked them as they drove away.

The doctor arrived and assured Craig that everything was all right. "She certainly had a lucky escape," he said as he departed.

Craig sat on her bed, twisting her damp golden hair into ringlets.

"This accursed place!" he exclaimed angrily. "Why can't we go home?"

She put her fingers over his lips as he spoke. "We cannot have everything we want in this life," she said, "but we have each other, my love, and soon we shall have our son."

"You seem sure it will be a son," he said as he kissed her repeatedly.

"Yes, a son that looks just like his father."

"And I would like a girl that looks just like her mother. I don't suppose we could have twins?"

"Well," she replied laughingly, "we might not get one of each."

"No, that is true."

"Now, what is this I hear about one of each?" said Margot as she entered the room. They were so engrossed in each other that they had not heard her knock at the half-open door and ask if she could come in. "My dear," she said, as she sat on the other side of the bed, "I am glad to see you are getting over that terrible fright."

"Yes, I am all right now, thank you, Margot."

Margot went and sat in the wicker chair and looked at Elizabeth anxiously. 'The poor dear! All this to contend with!' she thought. She knew Elizabeth was not like Davinia or herself: they could take anything this strange country could throw at them. They had accepted its extremes many years ago. To them it was home, but this child would never be rid of the terror it held for her, no matter how long she lived there. 'If only I had not had to bring her here to suffer all this,' she thought.

She gave Craig and Elizabeth no inkling of what she was thinking as she chatted on, giving them the latest news about her missions. "Now, my dears," she said, "I must bid you goodnight."

"Shall I see you home?" said Craig.

"No, my son, you must stay here. I hear Martin on the verandah. I told him to follow me."

Craig followed them to their waiting tonga and helped them inside.

"How kind of you to come, Margot," he said. "You are always near, like a guardian angel."

"Well, my boy, I promised Elena and also Elizabeth's parents that I would always be close at hand if you needed me."

CHAPTER 185

Emma sent a letter in that September to tell Craig and Elizabeth of the birth of her son. His name was Nicholas Andrew David Roberts.

"My darling, I told you Emma would have a son," said Elizabeth as Craig charged up the verandah steps to greet her.

"Yes, my dear, as always you were right." He tried to stifle her excited exclamations with kisses, but he found it impossible.

"Now we have only to await our own son, which you are so sure we will have."

"I just know, my darling, we will have a son. Emma and I had an agreement: if I wished for a son for her, she would wish for one for me."

"Well, my dear, we shall just have to wait and see." He silenced any further comment with a kiss.

Margot settled herself in Craig's home when she knew the birth was imminent. Davinia called daily to see all was well. She knew how Margot worried about Elizabeth with her mother so far away.

It was mid-December when their son was born.

"My darling angel, a son, a son, just as you said! Our own precious boy!"

"You see, my darling, I was right after all," she said, smiling weakly. He sat beside her, kissing her tenderly and looking at her adoringly. He could hardly believe that she had come safely through.

"You are always right, my darling. Thank you for this so precious gift," he said as Margot took the baby lovingly from Elizabeth and placed him in his father's arms.

"He is adorable – so like you, Craig, when you were born. He has the same dark hair – just adorable!" Margot said as she repeatedly touched the baby's cheek.

"You will have him growing up quite conceited, Margot, if you keep saying that," Craig teasingly remonstrated.

Margot was so relieved that Elizabeth was well and the baby was healthy.

"I shall write to your mother and father tonight, Elizabeth, to give them the glad tidings," she said.

"Thank you, Margot. Tell them I shall write very soon."

"Margot," said Craig, "will you and Martin be his godparents?"

"Of course, my dears, if that is your wish."

They both smiled and nodded their heads.

"Well, my dears, I will leave you to enjoy your precious little boy and go and tell Davinia and the children the news."

"Thank you, thank you, Margot," Craig said as he saw her into the tonga and waved her goodbye.

"Well, my son," Craig said as he cradled his boy in his arms and curled his tiny finger round his own, "you don't know it yet, but there is a chance you will one day be the 13th Earl of Glencree and also Chief of the Clan McNair."

Elizabeth watched him intently, noticing the longing look in his eyes.

"Will he ever be able to claim his title and heritage, my darling?" she asked.

"There's no reason for his grandfather to deny him just because of me," he said with a heavy sigh.

"And me," she reminded him sadly, "and also —" She pondered dejectedly for a few moments as she stared into space.

"Also what, my darling?" Craig looked at her with concern.

"I hope that he is not made to suffer the unhappiness you have known because of me." She sighed as she lay weakly back on her pillow.

"Because of you, my darling?" he exclaimed in dismay.

He carefully put their son in his silk-lined crib; then he raised Elizabeth and cradled her in his arms as he kissed her hair, her cheeks and lips.

"My precious angel, my adored one, I haven't suffered. Suffering would be not having you by my side – not having you always. Remember that, my love. Losing my heritage is nothing compared to not having you."

He laid her gently back on her pillow and wiped away a tear.

"Is our son to have any of the family names?" she queried hesitantly.

"Of course, my love – all of them. He is not going to be denied them, no matter what else he has to forgo. He will be called Lindsay, after my great-grandfather; Bruce, after my father; Craig, after me; and Roderick, after the brother you love so much."

"Oh, thank you, my darling, thank you." She wondered if Roddy would be as pleased as she was, but she dismissed the thought.

"One day, my love," Craig said, "our son will go back and claim the heritage which rightfully belongs to him and all the sons that follow. I know Papa will relent one day." He looked at her and she smiled wanly at him. "I know my father will send for me one day, and he will say, 'Come home, my son. Come home and bring your family with you.'

Next day the twins could hardly contain their excitement as they rushed into the house, both chattering gaily. It was the first baby they had encountered at such close quarters. Margot and Davinia bade them be a little quieter before they entered Elizabeth's room; then they both hurried to her bedside, each with a posy, and kissed her.

"Please may I hold him?" they both chorused, almost at once. "May we?"

"Yes, yes," said Margot, "if you are both very careful."

"Oh, we will be, we will be," said Astrid.

"Now who is going to be first?" said Elizabeth, as she gently lifted Lindsay out of his crib.

Both of them argued as to who should be first.

"I am the eldest, Mama," said Clare.

"Only by about four minutes!" their mother replied.

"And I have held the babies in the mission," she continued.

"So have I!" exclaimed Astrid.

"Now stop this arguing, or else Elizabeth will not let either of you hold him."

Astrid agreed rather reluctantly to let Clare hold him first – after all, she was the eldest, and consequently she had priority.

They had decided that Lindsay was the most beautiful baby they had ever seen, and they watched as Elizabeth placed him back in the crib.

"When can we have a baby brother?" asked Astrid.

Elizabeth, Margot and Davinia looked at each other and smiled.

"Oh, maybe one of these days," said Davinia, looking at Elizabeth as much as to say, 'I have quite enough with these two!' "Come, we must go and let Elizabeth rest," she added.

With a final peep at Lindsay and a kiss for Elizabeth, they said their goodbyes.

CHAPTER 186

Martha and Magnus were too delighted for words when they received the letter from Margot to say that Elizabeth was safely delivered of a son and that she was very well and would write to them herself in a few days.

"I wonder how the laird will receive the news?" said Martha as they both sat by the fire peering at the letter. "I do so hope he relents now and lets Master Craig return home with his wife and wee son."

"I have my doubts about that," said Magnus. "He was so set on having Lady Fiona as the mother of his grandchildren and the heirs to Glencree, I doubt whether he will consider our darling angel worthy of that honour. I still feel sure he will never forgive Master Craig for what he did."

"Well then, it is too late," said Martha. "The wee bairn is born and nothing can change that. Lady Margot did say she would see that our dear daughter would be returned to us in two years, and I know she will keep her word."

Magnus looked at her sadly. "But have you forgotten, my dear," he said, "our dear angel is now married. Unless the young master decides to return to some other part of Scotland, I doubt if we shall see our angel for a long time."

"Well, we shall just have to wait and see. I long for the day when she returns with her lovely bairn," Martha said sadly.

"Yes, hasten the day!" said Magnus.

Elena opened the letter from Margot with trembling hands. She had known the birth was due very soon and had looked longingly every day for the letter. Jamie stood close by and he saw the smile on her face.

"I must find Miss Harriet at once," she said. "Have you seen her?"

"I last saw her entering the dining room," Jamie replied, anxious to hear the news.

"Well, Bruce is in there also so I will tell them both the news – but I don't know how Bruce will take it." She grimaced and gave a shudder, remembering how he had taken the news of Craig's marriage.

"Well, what is it now?" demanded Bruce when he noted the letter in Margot's hand. He was just finishing his breakfast; Harriet was just rising from the table.

"I see you are first to get the mail again," Harriet said resentfully. She had never forgiven Elena for being so much on Craig's side when he left. She knew with one glance at the letter in Margot's handwriting that it would be news concerning Craig. Neither she nor Bruce had been told of his expected baby.

Elena had known that happy news for months, and how she had managed to keep the news to herself for so long she never knew. But now a son had been born and they had to be told.

Elena decided to ignore Harriet's remark. She sat down at the table, and, although silently quaking with apprehension, she smiled graciously as she unfolded the letter.

"Yes, it is wonderful news I have to tell you this morning," she said.

Bruce looked up at her impatiently as Harriet stood close by with her arms folded.

"Well, what is it Elena?" Bruce demanded. "I haven't got all day. I have a lot to attend to on the estate."

"Well," she said hesitantly, "you my dear brother, Bruce, are now a grandfather and you, my dear sister, Harriet, are now the great-aunt of a lovely baby boy: Lindsay Bruce Craig Roderick McNair. He has already been registered with those names."

She heard the gasp of dismay from Harriet, but Elena was watching Bruce and she saw his tanned complexion change to a vivid purple with rage. He stood up to his full height and crashed his fist down on the table. The crockery jumped and came crashing down.

Jamie, who had just entered the room, heard Elena's announcement. A delighted smile crossed his face. Bruce glared at him in his anger.

"Get out! Get out, you smiling old fool! Get out I say," he roared.

Jamie needed no second telling. He looked at Elena and beat a hasty retreat.

"How dare he! How dare he! I have forbidden him to ever use the family name. Now he has the audacity to give it to his son without my consent," Bruce stormed.

"But," Elena persisted, "you would never have granted his son – your *grandson* – ", she said emphatically, "permission to use the family name. That is why he has done it without telling you first. You cannot really deny the child his birthright. Don't you see, Bruce," she said gently, trying to appease him in his fury, "don't you see, you have a grandson who can be your heir: one day he may become the Earl of Glencree and Chief of the Clan."

"That he will never be," Bruce roared at her. "How many times have I to tell you? The title will die with me." He stood banging his fist repeatedly on the table.

"Bruce, dear," Elena pleaded, "please do not be so hasty. I feel sure in time you will change your mind."

"That I will never do. Never!" He sat down exhausted.

"I agree with Bruce," said Harriet, up till then quite speechless with rage herself. "No one – I repeat, no one – is entitled to the family name and title without Bruce's sanction, especially now that the boy's father is no longer a member of the McNair clan. And that child with that scheming hussy, his mother . . . Never! Never! If she thinks that this is the way for her to get this family's title and heritage for her son, she will find she is sadly mistaken. For them to tag my brother's name on to his other names . . . Well!" She spluttered with rage at the mere thought of it. "I know Craig would not have made that decision. It has been done on her insistence – I just know it."

"I am sure it was nothing of the sort!" exclaimed Elena, looking at her sister in anger. "It would have been Craig's wish. I am certain, but I will say no more on the matter," she added before she hastened out of the room.

Jamie, who had stayed in the hall, watched her ascend the stairs and go to her room. He hastened to tell Cook and the rest of the staff.

"Oh, how wonderful!" exclaimed Cook. "I hope the master is pleased."

"Well, Sir Bruce is very displeased, so don't any of you dare offer any congratulations. You will have to pretend you don't know."

Cook wiped away a tear with a corner of her large white apron. "My poor wee boy, Master Craig! Whenever is it all going to end? Whatever would his poor mother have said – his father treating her boy so?"

CHAPTER 187

Craig sat restfully under the huge banyan tree; Elizabeth was opposite him, cradling their son. It was spring and the weather was getting warmer each day. This was the part of the year they both liked best. It was not too hot, but they had brilliant sunshine all day.

Craig reached up to fondle the long trailing roots, which almost reached the ground from the huge branches above. "Oh, great tree, how happy you are in your gentle simplicity! Your roots never stray too far away from the precious trunk that bears you – not like us poor humans."

A bearer stood watching him before breaking in on his thoughts: "A letter for you, sahib."

"From home, I see!" Craig said as he reached for it.

"Yes, sahib, from home."

The bearer knew Craig's thoughts were always of home and that he would never be truly happy until he was back there with the memsahib.

"Thank you, boy. That is all."

Elizabeth watched him anxiously as he read and reread the letter.

"What does it say, my love? You look so pensive; is it sad news?"

"Part of it is, my love. Aunt Elena says a lot of the men are out of work. Their poverty is terrible, there are no prospects for them, some have been tramping miles looking for work. They have insufficient food and clothing for their children."

What had happened to the wonderful land fit for heroes they had all been promised when they returned from the battlefields? Was this their reward for their gallant fight? After all they had gone through for their motherland, the survivors were still suffering. The dependants of those that had been left behind in that 'corner of a foreign field that is for ever England' were not properly provided for. Craig glanced towards his son, cradled in his mother's arms, and he sat in silent meditation for several minutes with a sad frown on his handsome face.

"Now, my darling, you must try not to let it upset you so," said Elizabeth. "What else does Elena say?"

"She says that the ex-servicemen's club is now a reality and she sees all the men as often as she can. My cheques are reaching them safely – it's a relief to know that. If only I could go and see them for myself!" He sighed and continued: "She saw your parents in church and they had quite a long chat about our baby son. She also says Emma's son is doing well."

"Yes, Emma did mention that when she wrote to me," Elizabeth replied.

"Elena also says she longs for the day when she can visit us. She doesn't think it will be too long now."

"That's wonderful news, my darling. I do hope it is very very soon."

"So do I. Then I can ask her how my father and Aunt Harriet took the news of our son's birth – not very well, I guess. Elena has made no comment about their reaction in her letter."

Margot called later that day, full of joy and enthusiasm.

"I have had a letter from Elena," she announced. "She hopes to visit us soon to see the missions. I can hardly wait to see her. I see you also have heard from her," she said, indicating the letter, which lay on a small table.

"Yes, hasten the day!" Craig replied. "Tell her when next you write not to visit until the cooler weather comes and we are back from the hills."

"Yes, I will," Margot replied. She planted a kiss on their son's forehead. "We can arrange his christening for then, also, don't you think?"

"Yes, Margot, we can. It is just as well we delayed it. It can take place at the little mission church where we were married. Would you like that, my darling?"

"Of course, my love. That would be ideal."

CHAPTER 188

The summer of 1922 saw them all once more in the hill station. From their bungalow they could see, in the far distance, high mountains, which were always covered in snow. They glistened in the brilliant sunshine. Craig spent many hours gazing at them, wishing they were the mountains of home.

"I wonder if I ever shall see them again?" he said.

He was unaware he had spoken aloud or that Elizabeth had entered the room, but she came and slid her arms through his.

"I just know, my darling, that your father will send for you," she said. "Then the mountains you will see in the distance will be the mountains of home."

"I hope so, my darling." He sighed.

"Now, come, my love – no more daydreaming today! The mali is waiting to discuss your plans for the garden," she told him.

"Good. That will keep me occupied in between my visits to the plantation. You can help me plan and Lindsay can watch us."

"I daresay, my love, when he is older you will allow him to play in any part of the garden."

"Yes, that will be so. I am planning it just for him."

The days when they visited the plantation were always filled with delight. Astrid and Clare often accompanied them, and the two girls felt very grown-up as they acted as mothers to Lindsay. Their constant chatter, questions and laughter filled the days.

"I think, Stephen," said Davinia one day, "we have lost our darling daughters to Craig and Elizabeth. They refer to Lindsay as if he were their personal property."

"Well, as long as they are all happy together, and don't make a nuisance of themselves, I don't mind at all."

Elizabeth, carrying Lindsay, with the twins alongside, often wandered through the tea plantation. Elizabeth admired the babies carried on the backs of their mothers as they picked the tea leaves.

Margot and Martin, who were often away visiting the missions, thought on their return that they were wasting valuable time with the constant round of going to parties, watching polo matches and endlessly chattering with friends. They decided to return early to their city mission. The children, most upset to see them leave, pleaded with them not to go as they waved them goodbye. As the train pulled away, their mother soon dried their tears by reassuring them that they would soon see Margot and Martin again.

Davinia was always busy planning tea or dinner parties or preparing to go to one of the many balls which were held nearly every night. The children's great delight was to see their mother dressed in a beautiful evening gown as she came to wish them goodnight. The twins spent these nights with Craig and Elizabeth, who would never leave their baby son.

"Oh, Astrid," Clare exclaimed one night after their mother had left. "How I wish I was old enough to go to a ball!" She sighed.

"Well," declared Astrid, getting a little tired of Clare's constant wishing and sighing, "you will just have to be satisfied with going to the dancing classes we attend – so there!"

"Oh, you sound like an old grandmother," Clare retorted indignantly. "When I am older and can go, I shall go to a ball every night – so there!" She put her tongue out at Astrid playfully. "And", she continued, "I shall go with the most handsome man I find – so there!"

"Well, how do you know that the most handsome man will want to take you to a ball?" retorted Astrid in her most matronly manner.

"I just know he will – so there!" She did a little twirl around the room as if to prove to her sister that it couldn't possibly be otherwise. "So there!" she repeated. She was just putting her tongue out again when Elizabeth entered the room.

"Miss Clare," she reprimanded sharply, "that is no way for a lady to behave. Apologise to your sister at once."

"Yes, Elizabeth," she said with a pout, angry that she had been seen. "I am truly sorry, Astrid." However, as if to excuse her unladylike behaviour, she concluded with, "But, Elizabeth, I am not yet a lady; I am only a little girl."

"Well," replied Elizabeth as she tried to hide a smile, "all little girls should behave in a ladylike manner. Come now, little girls, it is time for your music lesson." She smiled openly at the look of disdain on Clare's face.

"Oh, Elizabeth," she sighed, always anxious to delay her piano lesson, "I am so longing to grow up and go to all the balls like Mama." She sighed again. "Did you go to balls in Scotland? Grandmama says there are balls held there."

"Yes, but not as many as here," she replied. "Yes, I used to go." She sighed and gazed out to the hills in the distance, recalling that wonderful night of her first dance with her darling Roddy. 'Dear, dear Roddy, where are you? Shall I ever see you again?' she wondered. That was where she also felt for the first time her darling Craig's arms around her.

"Well, children," she declared as her thoughts turned back to them (they were both looking at her in wonder), "it is no good us all daydreaming like this about balls. We have music lessons to do before you retire."

They followed her out of the room. Clare, as usual dragged her feet.

CHAPTER 189

Craig felt exhausted as he rode home after a hard-fought polo match. He was sweating profusely but he felt chilled and he frequently shivered. He spurred his horse faster. "I must get home soon, but today it seems twice as far," he said. He felt himself falling forward on to his horse's head, but he pulled himself up with a jerk. He tried to pull his thoughts together.

"Oh, what I would give for some of my beloved Scottish breezes and mountain air, rather than this choking dry air!" he muttered aloud.

Damodar had been waiting patiently for him and he heard the clatter of Craig's horse's hoofs before anyone else. He had thought the previous day that Craig did not look too well, but he held his tongue. He rushed to help him dismount when he saw him sway in his saddle. At any other time, Craig leaped off like a young gazelle.

"Munilal," Damodar called, "hurry and take the sahib's horse away."

Craig swayed back and forth in Damodar's arms.

"Come, sahib – hold on to me," Damodar said.

"No, boy, I am all right. I don't want to alarm the memsahib."

He helped Craig up the steps of the verandah to the open French window, where he leaned heavily against the bougainvillea-covered wall.

"Go inside, sahib, master sahib," he pleaded.

"No, no, leave me awhile but stay close."

"Very well, sahib."

Damodar moved a few steps away, and stood watching Craig with concern.

Craig gazed intently into the room where Elizabeth sat cradling their son, singing a soft lullaby, one of their favourites: 'Golden Slumbers Kiss Your Eyes'. He watched her as she rocked to and fro, kissing their son as she sang. Surely no artist could capture such serenity on a mother's face! He sighed.

The bearer touched Craig's arm again when he saw him swaying. "Go inside, please, sahib. Please, sahib!" he implored.

"No, not yet, boy. Soon Lindsay will be asleep and the memsahib will put him in his cot. I will wait till then." He could hear the melody fading away, but his legs were getting weaker. His head swam and his shivering increased. "I am not going to miss one moment of this," he said, but his vision grew blurred, he stumbled against the door and then he fell headlong into the room and lay in a crumpled heap at Elizabeth's feet.

Elizabeth looked up as she heard him crash through the door, and she screamed with alarm as she saw him falling towards her.

"My darling! My darling!" she cried. "Ayah, Ayah, take the baby."

The ayah moved quickly towards her.

"Damodar, what is the matter with him?" she sobbed.

"He has the fever, memsahib. He will be all right in a little while. The boy will help me get him to bed. Another can run for the doctor sahib and also the burra memsahib."

"Yes, yes, tell them to hurry."

"They will, memsahib. They will."

"Oh, this eternal heat! This is to blame for his weakness. Why doesn't a cool breeze ever blow, like it does at home?" she muttered angrily. "He will never be well until he goes home. That wretched old man! Why? Why can't he send for him to come home like any loving father would?"

She sat on his bed and put a cold compress on his forehead. She rose as the doctor entered.

The bearer and the ayah tried to console her as they waited for the doctor to finish examining Craig. When Davinia arrived, she thanked them and bade them leave.

"I will take care of the memsahib now," she said. "Bearer, make some tea, please."

"What is it, Doctor?" Elizabeth sobbed.

"It is malaria, my dear, but he will be all right in a little while."

"Are you sure? Are you sure?"

"Yes, my dear, I am sure."

Elizabeth looked at him still disbelieving. "Are you sure, Doctor? Are you sure he will get well? Please say he will," she implored.

"My dear, my dear, I assure you he will get well, but he will need expert nursing. I will send a nurse along to help you. In the meantime, keep a cool compress on his forehead and keep the room cool and dark. This climate does not suit him – or you, my dear," he added as he looked at her.

"I know, I know," she sighed.

"Is there any chance of you returning to Scotland when he is well enough to travel?" he asked.

Elizabeth shook her head sadly and wiped a tear from her eye.

"Well, try not to worry, my dear." He placed a comforting hand on her shoulder. "I will call back later," he said.

"Will these attacks keep occurring?" she asked.

"Yes, my dear, I'm afraid they will, but he is a strong young man; he will soon be all right. Now you must get some rest also, my dear."

Davinia joined Elizabeth as she wished the doctor goodbye.

Later Davinia prepared to leave. She looked at Elizabeth with concern. "Are you sure you will be all right, dear?" she asked.

"Yes, thank you, Davinia. Thank you for coming."

"Now, you must send the bearer for me if there is any change in Craig's condition. Here comes the nurse. Now you must rest, Elizabeth, or else you will be ill. I will call every day. It's a pity Mama had to return to the city so early."

She kissed Elizabeth lightly on the cheeks as she left.

CHAPTER 190

Weeks passed before Craig was well enough to attempt to walk. The doctor was quite pleased with his progress. "I told you he would soon be well again. He is a very determined young man. Soon he will be well enough to travel to the city, but it would suit you all better to stay in the hills where it is cooler."

"Oh, he won't hear of it," replied Elizabeth with a sigh. "He wants to return to the office."

"Well, he must take care," the doctor reiterated.

At last the day came when they could return to the city. Craig stood looking out of the window towards the mountains. He thought they were mocking him as he gazed out longingly.

"Yes, yes, mock me, you mighty mountains," he said. "One day I shall return to my mountains – you wait and see!"

Elizabeth sat with Lindsay on her knee, watching him with concern.

"You won't forget to take us when you return, my love?" she said.

He rushed to her side. "I will never go anywhere without you, my darling angel, and our adorable son." He bent down and kissed her and stroked Lindsay's head. "You, my son, will see Scotland one day. You will have your very own piper – the finest in the land – in accordance with our family tradition." He returned to the window to have another look at the mountains.

"Come, my darling," Elizabeth said eventually," we must go. Davinia, Stephen and the children left some time ago as the children had to return to school."

Craig laughed heartily. "Yes, yes," he said. "I wondered why it had been so quiet lately."

One day, when Craig and Elizabeth were shopping in the city, Elizabeth went into a dress shop for some silk for a new dress.

"I will walk on a little, dearest," Craig called to her.

"Very well, dear, I shall await you in the tonga," she replied.

He stood watching the silversmiths at work, marvelling at the beautiful intricate patterns they wrought. He was always on the lookout for something special as a surprise gift for her. Suddenly, he heard an exclamation of surprise; then someone called his name. He looked up to see an old friend of his army days racing forward to greet him. Suddenly, Craig was clasped in a vice-like grip.

"Craig! Craig, my old friend!"

They embraced each other like long-lost brothers. Both were breathless with surprise.

At last, Ian released Craig and said, "Well, of all the people to meet out here! I cannot believe it."

"Well, it is true, Ian, I assure you."

"I thought you would have been well and truly settled at home with your father. You used to talk and dream of nothing else but your father and your dearest Fiona – your fiancée and your forthcoming marriage. I remember her well. I was going to be best man at your wedding, but unfortunately I was posted away."

Craig let him chatter on. He was not surprised Ian was so surprised to see him there.

"How come you are in India? Are you here on a visit?" Ian asked.

"I am now settled here," Craig replied. "I have been here for a couple of years."

"Settled here!" Ian exclaimed incredulously. "That I cannot believe. You were so keen to get home to your father. I could never imagine you, of all people, ever leaving your beloved Scotland – and you, the only son and heir to the earldom! Really, Craig, the sight of you here leaves me quite speechless."

"That I doubt," laughed Craig. "You have hardly paused for breath since we met." As he spoke he glanced along the street to the waiting tonga.

"By the way, how is your father?"

"Well, it is a long story – too long to explain now."

"Now, you must come and join me for a drink in the mess straight away; then we can talk more of old times."

"Yes, I will," Craig replied, but he hesitated for a moment.

"Are you too busy, Craig? Please don't say that."

"No, but first I want you to meet my wife. She is waiting for me to join her in the tonga. We were about to go home."

"Yes, I have met her before. It will be nice to see her again."

They walked to the waiting tonga.

"Elizabeth dear," said Craig, "I want you to meet an old friend of mine from my wartime years. He has recently been posted to India."

"Oh, how lucky for you, dearest! That's just what you need: an old friend from home to talk to," Elizabeth said as she stepped down from the tonga to greet him.

Ian was speechless with surprise. He shook her hand and gazed into the most beautiful blue eyes he had ever seen. Her long golden hair peeped from under her wide-brimmed straw bonnet.

Craig noted Ian's puzzled expression as he tried in vain to think. 'Have I been mistaken?' Ian asked himself. 'Surely the fiancée I was introduced to in Scotland had dark hair? I must have been dreaming.' He noticed them both looking at him.

"Dearest, I have been invited to join Ian in the officers' mess for a drink."

"Will you not join us also?" Ian exclaimed. "Please say you will."

"No, thank you, not this time. I must get back to our son," she replied, although she knew he would be perfectly all right with his ayah and Davinia and the twins. "Please come and join us for dinner some evening," she said as she wished him goodbye.

"Thank you. I will."

She wanted Craig to have this long chat with his friend without her presence.

"Now, dearest," said Craig, "as you have finished all your shopping and don't wish to join us at the mess, take the tonga home. Bearer, see that the memsahib gets safely home."

"Yes, sahib," he replied as they sped away.

Suddenly, Ian recalled the night at Christmas and the incident with the mistletoe. So that was where he had seen Elizabeth before!

"Now, tell me all your news, old chap," Craig exclaimed when they were both seated in the large comfortable chairs in the mess.

"Well, as you know, I always intended to make the army my life. I am always on the move, which I like. But now, seeing you here, I hope I shall stay for quite a long time."

"So do I," Craig replied.

"Now, what about you? Tell me how you come to be settled in India – you of all people. I must say, old fella, you seem to be prospering, but you don't look too well."

"No, I am recuperating from an attack of malaria."

"Oh, my dear chap, I do hope you don't get any more attacks. It fairly takes some getting over. I know – I have had it myself."

"Well," said Craig with a laugh, "we usually did identical things, if you recall. Well," Craig continued, "it is a long story."

Ian listened intently as Craig related what had happened. He did not interrupt, but pondered on his friend's words.

"Yes," Craig said, "Papa has forbidden me to use the family name and denied me my heritage. He has totally disinherited me."

"And what about your son's heritage?"

"He has also been disowned, but I have given him the family name in spite of my father."

"But how are you managing, my friend?"

"Well, I have the legacy my mother left me and I sold all the property left to me by her parents. I also part-own a tea plantation in the hills, so I am quite well off financially, but" – Craig faltered and Ian did not fail to notice the longing in his voice as he spoke – "I shall go home one day. I know Papa will relent and send for me and my family. Now, I really must get home and see if my wife has arrived safely. You must come and join us for dinner one day and bring several of your friends with you. I shall get my wife to sing for you."

"Yes, I will come. I remember her singing – so delightful!"

Ian watched Craig with sad eyes until his tonga was out of sight.

Craig felt much better as he rode home. Elizabeth was awaiting his return.

As they sat on the verandah, she asked, "Did your friend mention if any more units were arriving?"

He knew she was hoping for news of Roddy.

"Well, my darling," he answered, "he did say there were a lot of troop movements going on. I asked him if he knew any of the regiments that might be posted here, but he had heard nothing."

"I do wish I knew where Roddy was. He could be anywhere." She sighed.

"Never mind, my darling angel," Craig said as he leaned forward to kiss her. "I am sure one day you will get word of him. Now we must kiss our son goodnight and retire."

CHAPTER 191

Elena decided to go to India to visit the missions, and she was very eager to see the baby. She was still very angry at the way Bruce had reacted to the news of his grandson's birth.

"You would think, Jamie," she confided to him one day, "that the Earl would have been pleased at the news."

Jamie looked at her resignedly, but he didn't reply. To Elena he was not just a servant of the household, but someone she could trust and talk over her troubles with. She felt now that he was the only one she could confide in.

Harriet had been mostly silent since Craig's departure. She blamed Elena for encouraging him. Elena could not recall how, if ever, she had encouraged him. 'Perhaps Harriet is upset because of my friendship with Margot,' she thought. 'Well, that is as maybe. Now I am going to see them all, come what may.'

She called into the shipping office in Glasgow on one of her monthly sojourns there. She had satisfied herself that all was going well for the ex-servicemen on the estate and now she was determined to delay no longer. She felt happier than she had done for years as she looked and relooked at her sailing ticket. But now she had to break the news to Bruce and Harriet – it was something she was not looking forward to, but it had to be done.

Just after breakfast one sunny morning she broke the news to them: she said that she would be leaving in a week's time.

They both looked at her in amazement.

"And I suppose that your decision to visit the missions at this time is really an excuse to visit *your* new great-nephew," Harriet said sourly with emphasis on the *your*.

"He is *your* great-nephew also," Elena rejoined hastily.

"Never!" Harriet replied haughtily.

"Well, it's as good a time as any. I had intended going some time; I shall be gone within the week."

Bruce glared at her angrily and hurriedly left the room without speaking. Silence pervaded the house for the rest of the time. Jamie told the rest of the staff what the trouble was all about, and he bade no one speak of it.

Elena decided to speak to Bruce alone one evening when Harriet had retired to her room. She spent the evening playing the piano, as soon as Harriet left she stopped playing. Bruce was, as usual, sitting in his favourite chair, gazing into the log fire and glancing frequently up at Isabelle's picture. He had become more and more distanced from everything going on around him since he rode in from viewing the estate.

As she looked at him, she could not help but feel his depth of despair and his longing for his wife and son. Surely, now that he had a grandson, he ought to try to heal the rift in his family. Surely, he would not keep this bitterness in his heart for ever.

She sat for ages, leafing through pages of music, wanting to talk to him but wondering how to start. The silence between them was broken for a brief moment when Jamie entered with more logs for the fire and to draw the curtains against the chill evening. When he left, he closed the door behind him and Elena rose and stood beside Bruce.

"I shall be leaving in the morning, Bruce," she said.

His gaze never left the burning logs.

After a few moments he spoke: "Well, what is it you want, Elena? I suppose you want me to give you a message to tell him to come home. Well, if so, you are wasting your time. You have heard my views about that: it will never be."

"No," she replied, "I want to ask if I might take the ring. It is rightfully Elizabeth's as she is now Craig's wife and the mother of his son."

"She has no right to be the mother of his son. Fiona was rightfully the mother of his sons. It was planned so all their lives – ever since they were children. The General and I had looked forward to the sharing of *our* grandchildren and Craig knew that. All was well until that village hussy set her sights on him," he raved.

Elena held her breath at his reference to 'that hussy'. He uttered the words with such vehemence. Never had she ever been able to make him think of Elizabeth in a kinder light.

"Poor child! Poor child!" she sighed, time and time again.

She put her hand on his shoulder, but he shook it off angrily. "Dear, dear Bruce," she said, and her voice was as gentle and soft as his was loud and angry, "try not to be so bitter. Even the best-laid plans don't always turn out as we wish. Fiona has gone now with her kin down south. There is no one else to wear the ring."

"No! No! No!" he roared at her as he banged his fist on the table.

"It will do no good lying in the safe either," she persisted. "Neither Harriet nor I will ever wear it. It could be passed on to Lindsay's wife when he eventually marries; then it will stay in the family for evermore, as it should. Lindsay carries the family name in spite of your denying it to Craig."

"How many times, woman," he roared, "have I told you never to mention his name in this house? There is nothing more to say on the matter."

She stood silently for a few more seconds. "Well," she said softly as she glanced up at Isabelle's picture, "I am certain Isabelle would have wished her to have it."

Bruce gave a start and she knew her dart had gone home. It was not like her to use this method, but if there was anything she could use that might help to change his mind, she would use it, no matter how unpleasant. "Well," she continued, "if that is all you have to say on the matter, I will bid you goodnight. I will call in the morning to bid you farewell."

Bruce sat for a long time after she had left, gazing into the face of Isabelle. He sighed heavily.

"What should I do, my darling one?" he said aloud. "If only you were here to help me." He looked at her as if waiting for a reply. Deep down within him, he knew that what Elena said was true, and he thought he saw in Isabelle's eyes, as the candles in the crystal holders flickered slightly, a faint smile of agreement.

He rose reluctantly to his feet and went to the safe. He removed the ring carefully from the deep velvet cushion in its box. He gazed at it lovingly, dreaming of the days when it adorned the hand of his adored Isabelle. At last, with a sigh, he replaced it and closed the lid. He stood for several more seconds pondering his next step.

At last he closed the safe door and took the box over to the fireplace. He looked up at Isabelle's picture again.

"Yes," he said, "it is what you would have wished, my darling."

He reached for a large envelope from his bureau and slowly sealed the ring inside before placing it in his pocket. Then he bade Isabelle goodnight and closed the door behind him as he left.

Jamie, standing silently in the hall, saw him pass and bade him goodnight, but Bruce made no reply. He was lost in thought as he slowly mounted the stairs. Jamie sighed deeply as he watched him out of sight.

Next morning, Elena came to wish Bruce goodbye, and she kissed him on the cheek. She had said her goodbyes to the staff earlier.

As she pulled the door to behind her, he called her back. He was gazing out over the loch.

"It is on the table," he said. "Take it and go."

A smile of happiness crossed her face and she threw a knowing glance at Isabelle.

Jamie was waiting at the jetty. He had already handed her hand luggage to Magnus, who then helped her into the boat.

Harriet watched her go from an upstairs window. She had bid her goodbye and wished her a safe journey after a peck on the cheek, which Elena felt had been given very grudgingly. Elena guessed that, as yet, Harriet did not know that

Bruce had given her the ring. 'If she knew,' Elena thought, 'I daresay I would not have got even a goodbye. Goodness knows how she will react when she finds out!'

Martha was waiting for Elena on the other side of the loch. As she alighted from the boat, Martha welcomed her with a small curtsy.

"I shall stay a little while, Martha, until my train arrives," Elena said. "I came early to have a little time with you." She could tell by the sad longing look on Martha and Magnus's faces that they wished they were going with her.

"Will you take these presents for them?" Martha asked. "I have knitted some clothes for the baby and a thick jersey for Master Craig. Elizabeth mentioned that he had had a chill, so I thought this jersey would keep him warm in the winter."

"I am sure it will – and he will be so pleased. It is so beautifully knitted too. Is it a skill you acquired during your days in the Orkneys?"

"Yes, milady. Now, do have some tea and scones before your journey."

They both escorted Elena to the station, still with that longing look in their eyes.

"Please give our dear daughter our love and tell her we long for the day of her return with her darling wee son," said Martha. A tear fell as she spoke. "Tell me, milady, why did our daughter do this terrible thing? How did she come to be the cause of the young master deserting Lady Fiona on the eve of her wedding?"

Martha had found it more and more difficult to attend church on Sundays. During the ladies' meetings and in the village shops she had felt all eyes on her. She heard the niggly twitterings of conversation as she passed people in the street, and she knew she was the subject of their gossip.

"Do not worry so, Martha dear!" exclaimed Elena as she touched her reassuringly on the arm. "Craig would have done what he did no matter where Elizabeth went. It was not her fault. They are both very happy and that is all that matters. I shall give the baby a kiss from you both. They will all come back one day – you'll see."

She was mounting the steps of the train when out of the shrubs nearby darted the swarthy figure of Merry-Berry.

"Give this to the baby, please, Lady Elena. Tell him to keep it with him always. It is his good-luck charm," she said, and she disappeared as quickly as she had come.

"I will, I will," Elena called after her. "Tell me, Magnus, have you any news of your son?"

"Yes," declared Magnus, "he will be coming home in a few days."

"Now, Martha," Elena said, "that is something for you to look forward to. I shall tell Elizabeth as soon as I see her."

Peggoty at last got the parcels and Elena's extra luggage aboard the train, and he stood watching with Martha and Magnus until it was out of sight. Martha's handkerchief was wet with tears.

Magnus guided her back to their cottage.

"Come, my dear," he said. "Our son will soon be home."

CHAPTER 192

Roddy arrived home a few days later. Martha had everything prepared.

"I am always ready for your homecoming, my son," she declared when he remarked on it. "I only wish our darling angel was here to welcome you also." She sighed. "We miss her so," she said. Then she wiped away a tear.

"Well, I think they will come home very soon," Roddy ventured. "I am sure our good laird will one day change his mind. He spoke in haste and I am sure he will not disown them for ever. What do you think, Papa?"

"I don't know, my son, but Lady Elena was here the other day and she sounded sure that one day the laird would send for him. That is all we can wish for, and I hope that it won't be too long before it happens."

Roddy made several trips across the loch with his father. He often took over the rowing.

"How I wish I could row as well as you, Papa!" he said. "You know where every rock is."

"Well, my son, I have done it for so many years now."

Roddy noticed that the villagers, who had in the past greeted him so warmly, now turned away as he approached. One day he visited the vicarage, and he was delighted to find Emma there.

"Tell me, Emma," he asked as he helped her into her carriage, "why is everyone so distant? Why do they turn away when I approach? I have noticed it also with Papa."

"Well, dear Roddy, everyone still blames Elizabeth for Master Craig deserting Lady Fiona and for the laird disowning him when he followed her to India."

"Are they the same with Mama?"

"Yes, I'm afraid so. It is most unfair. It was not Elizabeth's fault, so please, Roddy, do not ever blame her. She avoided the young master whenever she could, and she was even willing to leave all of us to get away from him. It broke her heart to go with Lady Margot, but she wanted to clear the way for his marriage to Lady Fiona. However, as you know, Craig was determined to go to her, no matter what the cost."

"How I wish he hadn't!" Roddy exclaimed sadly, looking very downcast. "How I wish he hadn't! It has caused so much hurt to so many people."

"But it is done now," Emma replied, "and it cannot be undone. Tell me, Roddy," she asked, anxious to change the subject which she knew was causing him so much distress: "have you any idea where you will be posted when you return?"

"Well, judging by the length of my leave, I daresay it will be somewhere in the Middle East – somewhere I cannot get home from too often. I hoped to stay nearby for Mama and Papa's sake, especially now that Elizabeth is so far away, but that is what comes of choosing an army career."

She touched his arm reassuringly. "Try not to worry too much about them," she said. "My family and I will help them all we can."

"Yes, I know, dearest Emma. Mama and Papa have said how very kind you have been. Thank you so much." He kissed her on the cheek and he bade her take care as she drove away.

Far too soon the train pulled out of the station, taking Roddy away.

"I will write as soon as I can," he called to his parents as he waved them goodbye.

Martha was trying very hard not to show her deep sadness at his departure.

"We seem to be always waving people goodbye, don't we, dear?" she said to Magnus as they returned to their now very lonely cottage and closed the door.

CHAPTER 193

The news of Elena's visit filled Craig and Elizabeth with such happiness. They could hardly wait for her arrival, and they ticked the days off one by one on the calendar. Margot too was overjoyed.

"Isn't it just too wonderful?" she said. "All I have waited and prayed for so long, and now she is on her way. They are all so happy at the mission. Every day they ask me, 'How much longer before Lady Elena comes?' Many of the older servants remember her still. However," Margot insisted, "I am not going to come over and stay the evening she arrives, although I will certainly come to meet her at the docks. That evening is yours and yours alone, but I shall call early the next day."

"Fancy her leaving us alone the first evening Elena comes! How sweet of her!" said Elizabeth. "It wouldn't matter if she came too. We could all have dinner together."

Craig, knowing Margot so well, understood the reason for her decision. "Well, that is just like her," he said. "I cannot imagine what our life would be like without her."

"Nor I," rejoined Elizabeth.

Elena was not surprised to see so many reminders of Glencree Castle in Craig and Elizabeth's home. She waved a temporary goodbye to Margot and took off the garlands of greeting which the servants had placed around her neck.

"Now let me hold this very precious baby of yours," she said. "He's so much like you were, Craig dear, when you were born."

"Well, like me, he has a beautiful mother – don't you agree Aunt Elena?"

"Yes, that is so. I do hope all the lovely things his grandmother has made for him fit him."

"Oh, I just know they will!" exclaimed Elizabeth as she fondly unfolded them. "How beautiful they are!" She pressed them lovingly against her cheek as if to bring her dear mother closer.

"Tell me, milady—" began Elizabeth.

"Now, now none of that, my child! I am Aunt Elena to you as well as to Craig."

"Oh, thank you – how kind of you!" she replied.

"Not at all! You are now Craig's wife."

"Tell me, Aunt Elena," she began hesitantly: "how are my mother and father?"

"They are both well – missing you, of course, as we miss Craig. They told me your brother was expected home very soon. They send you their love and ask me to kiss their grandson for them." She placed two long kisses on his forehead. "Your mother also sent these lovely jerseys for both of you, and yes, I almost forgot, Merry-Berry sent this lucky charm for Lindsay. You must make sure he always keeps it with him."

"Of course we will," said Craig. "I daresay she carved this leaf using wood from the old McNair oak tree. She did one for me, but I carelessly lost it in the loch one day when I was fishing. Fancy her still thinking of us!"

"She will always do that, my boy," said Elena.

She noticed him thoughtfully thinking of days gone by. For quite a few moments he was silent as his thoughts wandered back to his childhood, playing and riding in the glens. He recalled how Merry-Berry would suddenly appear from out of the hedgerow to make sure he was safe.

As they sat on the verandah later that evening, Craig said, "Tell me: how is Aunt Harriet? You have not mentioned her name since you came."

"Frankly, I am quite worried about her, my dear boy. You know how independent she is: she has always done too much work herself in Glencree, even though extra help could always be got from the village. It is far too much for her, but she won't listen when I tell her to get more help."

"I don't suppose she was too pleased when you told her you were coming to visit us," said Craig.

"My goodness no! I told her I was not going to delay my visit any longer, and therefore she has to have help from the village. I do wish she would not work so hard. It does worry me."

"Why does she do it, do you think?" asked Craig. He looked pensively at her.

"I think it is because she missed having her own home after her husband was killed. She was so looking forward to it, but it was not to be." Elena sighed. "She always was cut out for marriage, whereas I have had the missions. The only thing I ever wanted was my own mission – but that was not to be either."

"Yes," said Craig, "you both gave up so much to look after Papa and me when dear Mama died."

"Yes, my dear boy, but you and Bruce were our only concern."

Elena had been wondering when he would get round to mentioning his father. She had decided not to be the first to mention him.

"So, do you think Aunt Harriet will be all right while you are away?" Craig asked.

"Well, I made sure the extra servants were employed before I left and I saw that they understood their duties. I reminded Harriet that she is not as strong as she used to be, and – do you know? – she actually accepted that I was right. She said she was glad of the extra help."

"Poor Aunt Harriet! She must really be feeling her age, then. Thank goodness she agreed! Tell me: how is Papa?"

This was the question Craig had wanted to ask ever since Elena's arrival.

"He is quite well, but of course he was not very pleased when he knew I was coming. However, he gave me this." She fumbled in her large handbag.

Craig and Elizabeth looked at each other in amazement that Bruce had actually sent them a gift.

"What is it, Aunt?" asked Craig. "You are making it seem very mysterious. Please don't keep us in suspense."

At last Elena found what she was searching for. She placed her bag by her side and unravelled what seemed to them to be reams of tissue paper. At last she uncovered the jewel box. She gave no hint of how reluctantly Bruce had parted with it.

Craig gave a gasp of delight and dismay.

"Really, Aunt Elena, I cannot believe it," he said.

"Well, do so, my boy, because it is true."

"Whatever is it, my darling?" Elizabeth asked, her eyes widening in wonder.

"It is, my darling, the ruby ring my mother always wore, and it is for you as the wife of the heir of Glencree. I always hoped that one day you would wear it, but I never dreamed it would be as soon as this."

"Fortunately," continued Elena, "the jewellers did not have time to alter it before Bruce sent for it. It was only when he came to put it in the safe that he found you had taken the rest."

"I daresay he was furious," smiled Craig. "He didn't know that I had a duplicate key made with the sole intention of bringing the jewels, which rightfully were mine, to give to my wife."

"Yes, he was furious, and he spoke to no one civilly for weeks."

"Well, now, my darling, the whole set is complete. Let me try the ring." He took it carefully out of its velvet-lined box as Elena held it open.

"Come, my darling," he said as he slipped it on her finger and kissed her adoringly.

"See, Aunt Elena, how well it fits! It was meant for her all the time."

"Yes, my son," said Elena, "and no one is more worthy than this lovely girl by your side." She closed the lid and handed him the box.

"Tell me, Aunt Elena: do you think Papa will ever give his blessing to our marriage and let us return home with our son?"

"No, my boy, I don't think he ever will, but you will go back one day and take your rightful place as Earl of Glencree."

"Yes, Aunt, I can imagine that, and I pray that it will be so. Merry-Berry told me I would return one day, but it will only be when my father has died." He sighed. "I want to see him again. I miss him so much; sometimes I feel as though my heart will break with longing."

"Yes, and his may also," she replied, "but he will never tell anyone how unhappy he is. Apart from you, I have been closest to him since your dear mother died and I know what he has gone through to make his sacrifice."

"But what of my sacrifice and the sacrifice of my poor darling angel? No one has sacrificed or suffered as much as she. Tell me: Aunt Elena, did you know of the terms Papa laid down?"

"No, my dear boy, not until it was too late for me to intervene on Elizabeth's behalf. Harriet knew," she added.

"And, of course," exclaimed Craig angrily, "she would agree with Papa wholeheartedly!"

"Yes, I'm afraid so."

Craig bit his lip angrily. "If only I had known all this was going on whilst I was away cavorting uselessly round London!"

"Now, no more talk tonight, Craig dear," said Elizabeth as she entered the room. She had excused herself earlier to let them be alone. "I am sure Aunt Elena is weary after all her travel."

"Yes, to be sure, dearest Aunt. Please forgive me. Come and see our lovely sleeping son before you retire."

"He's so like you, my dear boy. Tomorrow I must visit Margot for a few days. Then we will be away visiting the missions."

"Well, I hope Margot doesn't keep you away too long," Craig said. "When we heard of your visit we delayed our son's christening, so we will arrange the ceremony for as soon as you return. We would like you to be his godmother."

"Well, Margot says these missions aren't too far away. She plans to be back before Christmas."

CHAPTER 194

Some weeks later, as they were seated on the verandah having breakfast, a bearer came in with the mail and handed it to Craig. Craig riffled through the letters before stopping to peruse one more closely. He murmured a little: "Mm, mm."

Elizabeth looked up at him. "Anything of special interest, my darling?" she asked.

"Well, this one might interest you."

She reached over to take it from him and let out a squeal of delight as she recognised the writing. The bearer, who was just serving Craig's breakfast, almost dropped some of it in his lap.

"My dear!" exclaimed Craig as she dropped her fork with a clatter on her plate in her eagerness to open her letter.

"Bearer, Bearer, where is the letter opener?" she exclaimed. "Quickly, quickly, Bearer!"

"Yes, memsahib." He had learned from experience that a letter opener should be kept on the breakfast table at all times. How the boy who had laid the table had come to forget today was a mystery to him. He thought he had taught the boy so well. He sighed a sigh of resignation and tut-tutted as he hurried away. The English people made a fuss about a letter from home, and the Scots were almost as bad, he decided. He scratched his head, deeply puzzled, and he finally decided there was no difference between the two nations in this respect.

By the time he returned with the letter opener, the envelope was in shreds. In her haste to get to its contents, she had simply ripped it apart. She let out another squeal of delight as she read the letter.

"What is it now, my precious one?" Craig called to her. He knew it was no good proceeding to read his own mail when Elizabeth was this excited. Despite his question, he had guessed who the letter was from.

"My darling, listen to this!" Elizabeth exclaimed.

"I am listening, my dear. Whatever is all the excitement about?"

"Darling, darling, it's from Roddy. He has landed in Bombay. He says he is being posted to Madras any day and will be coming to visit us. Are you listening, my darling?"

"Of course, my darling. I have put down my own important mail to hear what you have to say." (His own mail did not matter a jot as long as she was happy.) "My dear angel, do get your breath back before you read any more. Does he mention when he might arrive?"

"No, but I hope it's soon; then he will be in time for the Christmas festivities. Luckily, we have delayed Lindsay's christening, so he can be present as well as Aunt Elena. Just think, my darling, how wonderful it will be."

She sprang up and danced round the room, much to the consternation of the bearer, who stood near the curtained doorway. Then Elizabeth rushed behind Craig's chair and clasped her arms round his neck, covering his head with kisses.

"My darling, you must not do all this in front of the servants," he said as he tried to disentangle her arms from round his neck.

Elizabeth kept repeating, "Roddy's coming! My darling Roddy's coming!"

'How like a fairy of the glen she still is,' he thought as he bade her sit down and calm herself.

"Now, my darling," he said, "I must leave for the office. I am already late."

She waved him away more happily than she had ever done before. "Hurry back, my darling," she called.

Preparations had been in full swing since the news came. Now it was the day of Roddy's arrival. Elizabeth tapped her feet impatiently as they waited for the train to arrive and, when he stepped off the train, he clasped her so tightly that Craig thought he would break every bone in her small, frail frame.

"My darling, darling sister!" he kept repeating as he kissed her over and over again. "You haven't changed one bit." At last he held her at arm's length. "You're still as pretty as ever," he said.

"But, Roddy, my darling, you have changed so much I hardly recognised you."

Tears of joy streamed down her face, and he tenderly wiped them away with his handkerchief.

"Now, now, my dear," he said, "this is not the time for tears – even if they are tears of joy."

Craig watched them in silence, remembering the last time he had seen Roddy in their beloved homeland. He was so delighted to see him and Elizabeth reunited at last.

Eventually Roddy released her, and he reached out to Craig. They clasped each other like two newly found brothers.

Craig was the first to speak: "My, how well you look, Roddy! The flush from the bracing Scottish air is still on your cheeks."

Roddy looked at Craig, thinking, 'My goodness, how pale you are!'

"I must say," said Roddy with concern, "Craig, you do look pale. Are you all right?"

"Yes, I am fine."

"Mama told me you had not been too well of late."

"Oh, it was just a bout of malaria, but it is now gone."

Elizabeth took the baby off the ayah. "See, Roddy – your very own nephew," she said proudly.

"My, how like his father he is!" Roddy exclaimed. "He is a bonnie lad, to be sure." He held Lindsay for a few moments before handing him back.

"Come now," said Craig, "we must away home."

Elizabeth sat between them, her arms linked in theirs. Craig had not seen her so happy since the birth of their son.

'Thank goodness she has at last got someone from home to talk to!' he thought. She had never stopped since his arrival.

After dinner, the talk was non-stop as Craig and Elizabeth tried to get information about home.

"I have some presents to give you, Elizabeth," Roddy said eventually. "Mama has sent you this lovely brooch you always loved and a bracelet of Celtic stones. For you, Craig, there is a dirk with your initials engraved. I always hoped that one day I would be posted to India, as most troops are. I had the engraving done at the smithy at home. Everyone was so pleased that I might be able to visit you one day. They all send their love and best wishes," he added, although he knew that that was not really true.

"How is Emma?" Elizabeth asked.

"She is fine, and so is her bonnie wee lad."

"Oh, how I would love to see her and everyone else at home!" Elizabeth sighed, and Roddy noticed the wistful look on her face and the falter in her voice.

"You will one day, my darling – I promise you," said Craig.

Roddy looked at Craig as he spoke and he inferred from Craig's dejected expression that he doubted his own words. Roddy recalled, as he looked pensively at Craig, that one day, as he sailed over the loch with his father, he had caught a glimpse of the laird striding over the glens. Magnus told him then that the laird was seen every day walking on his own with a dog by his side, speaking to no one, just as he did after his wife had drowned. 'Well,' thought Roddy, 'I shall not be the one to convey such a thing to him, and I certainly won't mention what the villagers say about my dear sister. The laird should forgive his son and ask him to return home.'

"You look in deep thought, my dear Roddy," said Elizabeth.

"Yes, my dear, I was thinking how wonderful it is that we are together at last."

CHAPTER 195

A few days later, Roddy was playing with the two constant visitors, Clare and Astrid. He was swinging them in turn on the garden swing when suddenly they heard the mali calling to them:

"Missy, Missy, Sister tonga is coming. Come quickly."

"Whoever is she?" asked Roddy, looking at them very perplexed.

"It is Sister Christina. Come – we must hurry or she will be gone. She made us both well when we had the fever. We wave to her every time she passes. Come – hurry, Uncle Roddy! She is going to the hospital on duty," said Astrid.

'I am not too sure I want to meet this so-called sister,' he thought. 'She is probably some type of old battleaxe. I have met so many during my tours of duty.'

At the insistence of the girls, he allowed himself to be tugged along. They told him repeatedly to hurry.

"Well, if I must, I must," he said.

The mali opened the gate and they scurried through. Sister Christina alighted from the tonga.

"You are both keeping well, I hope?" she said.

"Yes, Sister, thank you," said Clare – always the first to speak. "We want you to meet our Uncle Roddy, who has come all the way from Scotland to visit us. He is not really our uncle, but he lets us call him that – don't you?"

"Yes, I do," he replied.

Roddy and Sister Christina smiled at each other, his glance lingering on this slim, beautiful slip of a girl, dressed all in white. Her snow-white nurse's cap sat like a bridal veil on her lovely dark hair; her large grey-flecked eyes were almost as lovely as his sister's.

Her eyes held his as he introduced himself. He was spellbound by her beauty and he suddenly realised that he had held her hand far too long, for which he hastily apologised.

'Never', he told himself, 'have I met anyone who has sent such a thrill through me.' He held her gaze steadily, unable to take his eyes off her.

At last she spoke, rather shaken at the intensity of his gaze: "Well, children, I must be going or else I shall be late. Goodbye."

She ran hurriedly to where the tonga man stood patiently waiting for her. Roddy watched as she settled herself once more in the tonga.

"Please, Uncle Roddy," begged Astrid, "come a little way into the road with us to wave her goodbye – otherwise we are not allowed."

"Very well, then!" he exclaimed. "It will be a good excuse for me to see her for a little longer."

"Quickly!" Sister Christina called to the man.

He cracked his whip above the horse's back, and, as it leaped forward, she was jolted heavily back in her seat. Roddy watched as she raised herself to her full stature and straightened her cloak and cap.

She turned once more and called to them, "I will see you again soon."

'Yes, and I will see you again soon,' thought Roddy as they watched her out of sight.

Although he looked out for her for several days, she did not pass. Then, one morning, when he was out early talking to the mali near the gate, he saw her tonga approaching. He opened the gate quickly and called out to her. She hadn't noticed him at first and she looked, startled, when she heard her name. She had had a very busy night on night duty, and she was deep in thought with her eyes closed against the early morning sun. She blushed profusely when she saw Roddy.

"Good morning, Roddy. It's a nice day."

"A very nice day!" he replied, a radiant smile lighting up his face.

"Goodbye," she called, and, with a wave of her hand, she was gone.

"My, my, you are an early riser, Roddy!" exclaimed Craig when he saw him sitting a little disconsolately on the verandah. "I thought you would be resting longer. I am going into the city now. Can I drop you anywhere?"

"Yes, if you would, please – at the barracks. I want to see if any new orders have come for me to move on."

"I hope not!" exclaimed Craig. "You have not been here long."

"It will be just my luck to get posted away before Christmas," Roddy said with a sigh.

"Oh dear, don't say that, Roddy," said Elizabeth as she entered the room. "We want you to spend Christmas with us."

"I want to be here with you," he replied.

He thought, 'I also want to be here to see more of a certain beautiful goddess whom I already adore.'

"Well, just as I thought!" Roddy exclaimed to Elizabeth on his return. "I have only a few more days with you before I leave."

Elizabeth bit her lip in disappointment. She was almost in tears.

"It is only a training course of about a month; then I shall be back again."

"But, Roddy dear," she sighed, "that means you will not be here for Christmas or Hogmanay. Oh, it's not fair!" She pouted. "I was so looking forward to our spending Christmas and Hogmanay together."

"But that is the army, my sweet: here one day and gone the next."

"Well, it is still not fair." She tried to smile through her disappointment.

"If I am lucky," he said as he held her close, "I might just get back in time for Burns Night."

"Oh, do try, Roddy dear, do try. We will have such a wonderful dance and celebration."

"You bet I shall try!"

For the next few days, both morning and evening, he was watching and waiting at the gate for his 'dream girl', as he called her.

Sometimes in the evening, as she was hurrying to get on duty, she would call out in passing: "Goodnight, Roddy."

"Goodnight, Christina," he would reply before he blew a kiss after her.

However, in the mornings she would stop a few moments longer to talk with him.

One morning he told her, "I shall not be here to see you go by."

"Oh, why is that?" she asked. "It has made my journey so pleasant, night and morning, knowing that you would be waiting to greet me."

"I have looked forward to it too. I wanted to ask you to have dinner with me one evening, but you always galloped away before I found the nerve to ask you."

"And now?" she queried. "And now?"

"The army has decided to move me on."

He was pleased to see that she seemed a little crestfallen. 'But she can't be more disappointed than I am,' he thought.

"Well, that is the army, as well you know," he said.

"Yes, I know only too well," she replied.

She looked more crestfallen than before, but her face broke into a smile when he continued: "I shall only be away for about a month. Please say you will come to dinner on my return?"

"Yes, of course," she replied. "I shall be on day duty then, so I shall be free in the evenings."

"That will be wonderful!" he exclaimed, hardly able to believe his luck. "I might", he said daringly, "try to commandeer you for every evening when I return."

She laughed. "Well, I won't promise," she said.

"Of course," he said hesitantly, "I understand that anyone as beautiful as yourself must have many friends to escort you every time you wish to go out, but please, I beg of you, save some evenings for me."

"Yes," she replied. "I will, unless I get posted before you return." She smiled again as she saw that he looked crestfallen.

"Oh, if they dare, I shall demand to be posted to wherever they send you."

She held out her hand in farewell and he was reluctant to let her go as he kissed it lightly.

"That is just to comfort me whilst I am away," he said.

She smiled shyly at him as she waved goodbye; then the tonga galloped off and he watched it out of sight.

"Why so sad, my darling Roddy?" exclaimed Elizabeth as he entered the house. "I know: it is that lovely sister from the hospital. You wait for her night and morning."

"Yes, I am going to miss you both so much whilst I am away."

"Well, when you return you must invite her to dinner; then you can really get acquainted. We are hoping you don't get posted before Lindsay's christening. We have delayed it until Aunt Elena returns with Margot from visiting the missions. She had only just left here when you arrived, and they will return soon," said Elizabeth. "Roddy, do try to be here; then you can be his godfather."

"I expect to be here for that event, but I know I shall be leaving a few days before Christmas."

CHAPTER 196

Lindsay's christening celebrations were going according to plan. Elena was delighted to see Roddy.

'Is it fate', she thought, 'that Craig and Elizabeth have a relation from both sides of their family present at this event?'

"I am so glad, Roddy, for Elizabeth's sake, that you have not been posted away before today's celebration," Elena said.

"Yes, milady, it is such a lovely get-together for us all – something I am sure none of us would have ever thought possible."

"Well now, everybody," said Craig as he stood up, "now is the time to drink a toast to our darling son, and also to have a farewell drink with our dear Roddy, who leaves us tomorrow."

"To think, Margot," said Elena as they sat talking, "that I should be able to be present at the christening of the next Earl of Glencree after all the unhappiness we suffered after our dear Craig left home!"

She was careful not to let their conversation be overheard. They sat in a corner of the room, whilst everyone else was admiring Lindsay. The twins, as always, were deciding whose turn it was to hold him next.

"Do you think Bruce will ever recognise Craig as his heir?" Margot asked.

"Well, the title is rightfully his. Bruce will have to acknowledge him as such in spite of all his talk of the title dying with him. As long as Craig or this child outlives him, the title cannot die with him, and well he knows it."

Davinia stood up. "Now, children, it is getting late," she said. "Say goodnight to everyone."

"But, Mama, we are not tired. Can't we stay a little longer?" said Clare with a pout.

"No. Lindsay is tired so kiss him goodnight."

Lindsay resisted all their hugs and kisses.

"What a lovely day, my darling!" said Craig after they had all departed.

Elizabeth was quite disconsolate after Roddy's departure, but the knowledge that he might be back for Burns Night lifted her spirits. She busied herself preparing for Lindsay's first Christmas in spite of him being too young to understand what it was all about.

Craig was so happy and thrilled to have Elena at last in his own home, and they both tried to recapture a little of the atmosphere of Christmas at Glencree. No expense was spared on decorations. The twins came specially to dress a tree for Lindsay after they had done their own.

"Lindsay, do look at the pretty lights!" they kept exclaiming, but both grew quite exasperated when he chose to look anywhere but at the tree.

The twins were the first to visit the house on Christmas morning on their way to church.

"We were far too tired after the party we attended last night to go to midnight service," said Clare.

"So Mama said we had to get up specially early today to call in and wish you the compliments of the season and to give Lindsay the present we have made for him," added Astrid.

"We made them ourselves – one mitten each," said Clare proudly.

"Well," said Astrid, as if to apologise for Clare's outburst, "Grandmama and Aunt Elena did help us quite a lot."

"No," exclaimed Clare, "they only helped us a little bit!"

"No, they didn't," said Astrid, "they helped you a lot and only helped me a little bit."

Elizabeth and Craig tried not to smile.

"Well, let us see what is the cause of this difference of opinion between you two ladies," said Craig.

The twins watched as he unwrapped the gift.

"Well, they are really lovely," said Elizabeth. "Shall we see if they fit Lindsay?"

"Oh yes," they chorused.

"You put the one on you made and I will do the other one," said Clare.

Lindsay, the centre of all the attention, waved his fists about, resisting all their efforts, much to their consternation. They all laughed gaily. At last the mittens were on and both girls stepped back to admire their handiwork.

"Yes, they are a perfect fit," said Elizabeth. "He will need them in the cold weather, won't he, Craig?" She held Lindsay's hands up for Craig to see.

"I agree: they are a perfect fit. He is a very lucky baby to have two good friends like you. Now, you must hurry or you will be late for the service. Call on your way back."

"We will," said Astrid as they departed.

"I wonder what our presents will be?" said Clare.

"Oh, you mustn't think of getting a present in return. Christmas is a time for giving presents," said Astrid emphatically.

"But someone must give us presents sometime," retorted Clare, "otherwise we will never get any presents." She sighed sulkily.

"Now come, Missy Clare and Missy Astrid," said their ayah, who was taking them to church. "*Juldi, juldi!* Quickly!"

They sped along as fast as they could. When they arrived, the ayah bade them enter the church and she sat under a large banyan tree to await their return.

CHAPTER 197

The New Year was ushered in with the Hogmanay Ball, but all Elizabeth was waiting for was news from Roddy of the date of his return. Suddenly, the night before Burns Night, he arrived at the door.

"Darling Roddy!" she exclaimed as he entered. "I thought you wouldn't arrive in time."

"I told you I would, so here I am. I am not to report to barracks for three more days, so I can spend them with you."

"We have got your ticket for the ball," said Craig. "There are lots of lovely young ladies who will be looking for an escort, so you will not be short of a partner."

But Roddy only wanted to know one thing: would the one he was longing to see be there? He had thought of her constantly whilst he was away and he had longed for the day he would see her again. She had told him that she would attend the ball on Burns Night if she could, so he couldn't wait to get there.

The next evening he stood in the lounge waiting for Elizabeth and Craig to join him. He was getting a little impatient at the delay. Suddenly the door swung open, and he gasped in surprise and laughed with delight as Elizabeth greeted him with a kiss.

"My, my, how beautiful you look, my darling sister!"

Suddenly he remembered where he had last seen her looking like that: it was way back in Harrison Hall on the night of her very first dance. She had purposely dressed as she was on that night in the lovely pale-blue gown Lady Margot had given her, with all the accessories to match. She twirled around several times.

"I have put it on specially tonight for your homecoming," she said. "How do I look?"

"Too beautiful to describe, my dear!"

"And you, Roddy, look so handsome in your new captain's dress uniform. Did you put it on especially for me, or are you hoping to see Sister Christina?"

"Ah, my dear sister, how well you know me! We could never keep our thoughts secret from each other, could we? You and I will make a most handsome couple. As we take to the floor it will remind me so much of when I took you to your very first dance," said Roddy.

"You won't forget to save me a dance," said Craig to Elizabeth as he entered.

"Of course not, my darling!" she exclaimed.

"I will let Roddy have the first dance with you," Craig said. "Then he will have to find his own pretty girl for the rest of the evening. Come – we must be leaving."

The large hall was decorated with tartans and the pipe band was playing Scottish melodies to everyone's delight as they entered. All the guests mingled freely. Craig, Elizabeth and Roddy stood for several minutes framed in the doorway on their arrival as they looked around for Margot's party.

"Perhaps they haven't arrived as yet," murmured Craig.

"Well, I am sure they won't be too long," added Elizabeth.

Roddy looked pensively round the room, and then turned towards the far corner, where he could see a crowd of officers. The Colonel's wife was sitting with several of her friends in a special place she always insisted on, from which she could weigh up everyone as they arrived. She did not fail to notice Craig and Elizabeth. But who, she wondered, was the handsome young soldier standing so proudly beside them?

'I must invite him to the parties I give,' she thought. 'I must get the Colonel to introduce him to all our friends.'

"Who is that young captain standing beside Craig?" she asked the friend next to her.

"He, my dear, is Elizabeth's brother. He has recently been posted here."

"Why is it", she exclaimed petulantly, "that I am always the last to get any news of any new arrivals?"

'Well, as he is only related to Elizabeth it is of no consequence,' she decided; 'if he was related to Craig, well, he would certainly be worth my further interest.'

The room was filling up as Craig, Roddy and Elizabeth proceeded to a corner to await Margot's party. They sat watching the dancers as they danced by. All the men wore their tartan full dress; the women wore their long, flowing white dresses with silk scarves over their shoulders in their own or their husbands' tartan.

"Come, my darling sister – let us take to the floor," said Roddy. "May I, Craig?" he laughed as he took her in his arms.

"Well, just this one dance. That is all I will allow," Craig replied.

Craig stood and watched as Roddy waltzed away with her. It was as if he was back in Glencree on the first night he had seen them together. Once again he was back in the hills – those faraway hills of home, which he could never erase from his mind. As he stood, leaning against the huge marble pillar, he only had eyes for his darling angel. She glided past, smiling happily up at Roddy. 'Never', he thought 'has she ever lost that look of a fairy of the glen.' The lovely Scottish melodies floating up to him did nothing to gladden his countenance.

Roddy hugged her close. "This is almost like being at home," he said.

"Yes, almost," Elizabeth sighed.

"It is a night I shall never forget – like the night Master Craig—"

"Now, you must never let him hear you use that title when you speak of him." She placed her fingers over his lips. "It makes him very angry," she said.

"All right, I will remember," he replied as he twirled her round and round, holding her very protectively, "but it does not alter the fact, my dear, that deep down within us both we know he will always be that. Nothing can change it. Tonight reminds me of the night he stole your heart away. Tell me, little sister: are you happy?"

"Yes, of course. I couldn't be happier."

He looked down at her with concern. "And Craig also?" he asked.

"Of course. Why do you ask?"

"Well, he is standing there looking lost to the world. I have never seen him so sad."

Craig noticed their look of concern, and he smiled and waved to them as they passed.

'I have such a lot to be thankful for,' he sighed. 'My darling angel, my baby son and my dear Aunt Elena are here. If only – if only I still had my father's love, I would be the happiest man in the world, but maybe it is too much to ask of life. I wonder how they are spending Burns Night at home. What a happy night it always was! How gay and jolly it could have been with my angel and baby son and father! But it cannot be, it cannot be.'

"Why is he so sad, Elizabeth?"

"He will be thinking of home. I daresay seeing us dancing has reminded him of the night he first saw us together. I must go to him. He does, as you say, Roddy, look very sad."

'Tonight is Burns Night – a time to be gay, not sad. I must snap out of it,' Craig thought as he saw them approaching.

Roddy greeted him gaily. "Your very charming wife, I believe," he said.

Craig looked at him, puzzled for a fleeting moment, then he started to laugh when he remembered the night at Glencree when he had handed Elizabeth back to Roddy after the dance, with the words, 'Your very charming sister, I believe.'

"How happy they all look together, Davinia," said Margot. "I hope Roddy can stay for some time before he gets posted again."

"I hope so too. They are certainly enjoying tonight."

Roddy looked eagerly round the room and, when he spotted Christina, he suddenly exclaimed, "Please excuse me! I think I see someone I know. Elizabeth, will you sing for me tonight?"

"Of course I will."

She could see he was eager to get away.

Craig and Elizabeth were joined by Margot, Elena, Martin, Davinia and Stephen.

"Oh, you have just missed Roddy. He has spotted someone he knows," said Craig as they watched him wend his way to the far corner of the ballroom.

Christina was standing among the small circle of officers she had arrived with. They were all chatting gaily. Roddy excused himself as he joined them.

"Good evening, Christina," he said. "May I have the pleasure of this dance?"

She gasped when she heard his voice. She was obviously delighted to see him.

"Yes, you may," she replied shyly as she looked up at him, "but first I wish you to meet my friends."

They eyed him up and down, hardly acknowledging him as he was introduced. He felt their resentment.

"This is Captain Roddy Anderson. He has just returned from Delhi," Christina said gaily.

Roddy could see they were not interested where he had come from.

'Yes, I timed it well – just in time for tonight's celebration,' he thought as he and Christina sped away.

One of the officers Christina had come with watched them in dismay.

"My, he's got a nerve!" he exploded angrily to his friends. "I have not had time to ask her to dance and here is this fellow barging in." He stamped his foot in annoyance.

"Well!" exclaimed his closest friend. "As the saying goes, he who dares wins!"

Little did the officer know he would not get the chance to dance with Christina all night.

Elizabeth and Craig watched as they danced past, but Christina and Roddy were too engrossed in each other to see anyone else.

"I sense romance in the air," said Elizabeth.

"My, how quickly you surmise things, my dear!" Craig replied.

"Well, I know my Roddy pretty well, in spite of not seeing him for so long."

"He must be feeling the same as I did when I fell in love with you, my darling, but he will never love Christina as I love you. They certainly both look very happy."

CHAPTER 198

Burns Night was always an excuse, if ever any was needed, for a celebration at the club. The master of ceremonies stood up to announce that before they heard the delightful singing of Elizabeth, Major MacNaughton would give his yearly recitation:

"He has, I think, had his fair ration of whisky to put him in the right mood, and we all know that, in spite of having a wee dram in excess, not one word of it will he say wrong. So up you come, Major. You may begin." He hauled the pretending-to-be-reluctant major on to the dais as the pipes burst forth to introduce him.

"First," the Major said as he held his empty glass aloft, "this must be filled – as must your own."

There was an immediate clinking of bottles against glasses as everyone did his bidding.

"Are you all ready?"

"Yes," came the loud chorus.

"Now," he yelled at them, "none of you is to touch a drop until I have said the last line of my recitation."

"And when will that be?" said one, who evidently wasn't a Scot.

"Hush, you Sassenach!" someone hissed at him.

"Well, now that we have quietened the Sassenach, I will begin. Gentlemen," he called in a loud voice as he held his drink high, " 'The Tartan':

> "Here's to it
> The fighting sheen of it
> The yellow and green of it
> The white and blue of it
> The swing, the hue of it
> The dark, the red of it
> Every thread of it."

His voice softened a little as he continued. The crowd of guests gazed in silence at him.

> "The fair have sighed for it
> The brave have died for it
> Foremen sought for it
> Heroes fought for it
> Honour the name of it
> Drink to the fame of it –
> The Tartan."

A loud shout of "The Tartan!" shook the air as they all drained their glasses. They clapped the Major as he rejoined his friends.

"Well, I never!" exclaimed Elena as she glanced excitedly around. "I have never seen a gathering quite like this before. We always had a gay jolly crowd at Glencree on Burns Night, but never one like this." She saw Craig looking at her, and she realised she had mentioned the home he could never return to. She bit her tongue in anger at her own thoughtlessness.

Margot was quick to remedy the situation. "Well, my dear Elena," she said, "it is like this every year. Ah, here comes Roddy with Sister Christina."

Christina smiled happily at everyone as she was introduced.

"Shall we all join in the dancing?" said Craig as he gathered Elizabeth in his arms.

Roddy and Christina followed them back to the dance floor.

"How divinely they all dance!" said Margot. "How they remind me of my youth!"

"Mine also!" agreed Davinia.

They looked up to see Craig returning, and all three looked at him with concern.

"Are you quite well?" Elena asked.

"Yes, dear Aunt. Don't worry. I just tire easily."

"Well, if you will excuse us," said Margot, "there are some old friends over there I wish Elena to meet."

At last the dance ended and Roddy and Christina rejoined Craig and Elizabeth. Their love and happiness shone for all to see.

"We will sit this one out and have a little chat and a drink to celebrate," said Roddy. "I have asked Christina to marry me and she has accepted."

"Oh, how wonderful!" exclaimed Elizabeth. "My dearest Roddy! I just know you will both be as happy as we are – won't they, my darling?" she added, looking at Craig.

"Of course, my dear," he replied.

He shook Roddy by the hand and kissed Christina lightly on the cheek.

"Now I shall sing a love song specially for you," Elizabeth said.

With that, Craig led her to the dais and stood beside her. He asked the piper to stop.

"Listen carefully, everyone," he announced: "We have something very special to tell you after Elizabeth has sung this love song." He then asked the pianist to play 'My Love Is Like a Red Red Rose.'

Margot and Elena looked at Craig in surprise, wondering what on earth he could be going to tell everyone.

"Whatever can it be, Elena?" exclaimed Margot. "It is most unlike Craig not to tell us first."

"I cannot think what it can be," said Elena.

When Elizabeth finished singing, the conductor tapped his baton for silence. Then everyone gazed at Craig. A perplexed frown crossed the face of the Colonel's wife as she stared at him.

"Well, I never!" she exploded.

She and her circle of ladies were usually the first to know what was going on in the area, but now an announcement was going to be made about something they had no inkling of. She looked at her friends for an explanation, but they all shook their heads in bewilderment.

Silence prevailed at last.

Craig glanced towards Roddy and Christina. "My dear friends," he said, "it gives me very great pleasure to announce that Elizabeth's brother, Roddy, has become engaged to a lady you all know very well – the lovely Sister Christina. I ask you all to raise your glasses and drink to the happy pair. Come, Christina and Roddy, and stand beside me so that everyone can congratulate you."

There was a hum of astonishment. Some of the guests clapped or raised their glasses as Roddy and Christina walked towards the dais. Roddy helped Christina up the steps and held her tightly round the waist as everyone filed past them to offer their congratulations. Everyone eyed him up and down. Some of the burra memsahibs caused him to blush furiously as they tried to find out how this could have happened under their very noses without them getting an inkling of it until now.

Some of the other officers, especially the one who had escorted Christina to the ball, glared at Roddy angrily. Roddy felt that if duelling had still been allowed, he would have been called out to settle the matter.

Craig continued: "Not many of you know Captain Anderson, as he has only been in India a short time. He only returned last night from Delhi, but you will all be able get to know him as he will be stationed here for a while. You will all be invited to their wedding, which, I believe, will be very soon."

At last the congratulations were over and the next dance was announced, but many of the officers were still in a state of shock. They stood talking in a corner of the dance floor, glancing in Roddy's direction, furious that they had all been done out of escorting Christina (as they usually did) to every party they attended. To think that this stranger could just walk into the club and take one of *their* girls! Girls were few and far between – usually one girl to ten swains – and this fellow, not in the country more than a few weeks, had waltzed off with one of their most beautiful and desirable ones.

Captain Gordon stamped his feet in anger. "To think", he exclaimed angrily to his friend, "I was going to propose to Christina myself tonight!"

"Well, my friend, the lucky young captain seems to have guessed your intention. He is looking straight at you as if to say, 'Well, you are just too late, my friend.' "

"Now, my friends," exclaimed the master of ceremonies, who stood in all his tartan splendour on the dais, "will you all take your partners into the banqueting hall for our Burns Night supper. We will begin as always with Robbie Burns' Grace:

> "Some hae meat and canna eat
> And some wad eat that want it,
> But we hae meat and we can eat
> Sae let the Lord be thankit.

"Now fill your glasses and remain standing to herald in the haggis."

The piper duly proceeded round the long tables as the chef carried the haggis aloft for all to admire.

"Now eat, drink and be merry, my friends," the master of ceremonies boomed, "but before you start we will have the toast to the Immortal Memory of the poet."

A chorus of "Robbie Burns, Robbie Burns," greeted this announcement. There was a chinking of many glasses, followed by gay banter and laughter.

"What fun this is, Margot!" laughed Elena. "It's just like being back in Glencree."

"Yes, I remember those occasions well," Margot rejoined.

Elena looked steadfastly across at Craig and was pleased to see he was laughing jovially with Elizabeth, Roddy and Christina. She sighed happily.

The burra memsahibs were still inwardly seething – especially the Colonel's wife – at the thought of Christina's romance happening under their very noses without any of them getting an inkling of it. The Colonel's wife questioned each of the ladies, but they assured her that they had no prior knowledge of the announcement of Sister Christina's engagement.

"And to a newcomer to the station!" she kept muttering to all who would lend her an ear.

Many of the guests glared at Roddy with disdain, but he had eyes for no one but his betrothed.

"Oh, what a heavenly night, my darling Roddy!" Christina exclaimed as they all joined hands to sing 'Auld Lang Syne'.

CHAPTER 199

"Oh, Mama, another wedding!" exclaimed Clare. "That is three weddings we will have been to. Did Christina say we could be her bridesmaids, Mama?" she repeatedly queried.

"Yes, my dear, she did," Davinia replied resignedly, knowing yet again what arguments there would be between them as to the colour of dresses. Christina had already told Davinia they could be dressed in whatever colour they wished.

"How I wish Christina had decided!" she exclaimed.

The girls could talk of nothing else and the durzi could hardly keep pace as they constantly changed their minds. "How lovely it is to have so many pretty new dresses!" said Clare. Nothing else pleased her more than to dress up in something new, and they knew Davinia had been to the city for pretty materials.

Their mother reminded them often to concentrate more on their school work. Astrid did as her mother wished, but Clare put down her school books and gazed into space, dreaming of pretty dresses. In the end her mother threatened that if Clare neglected her school books she would have to tell Christina that alas! she could not be her bridesmaid and she would have to look elsewhere.

"Oh, Mama, you wouldn't do that!" Clare pleaded, and for a short while the threat did the trick.

"Just fancy, Craig darling, Roddy and Christina being married at the same church as ourselves!"

"Yes, my angel, it is quite amazing. How strange fate is sometimes!"

"I just know", she said, "they will be as happy as we are."

On the day of the wedding, the sun shone brilliantly. The crowds were far in excess of the previous weddings. Most of Roddy's regiment and Christina's friends came – as many as could be spared from their duties at the mission. The reception was held in the sisters' mess. The local children and the ones from the mission were given a special tea by Margot and Davinia after they met the happy couple out of church and garlanded them with flowers.

"I suppose," said the Colonel's wife to her friends after Roddy and Christina left on their honeymoon, "they are going to Kashmir to see the Taj."

Her sarcasm was not lost on the friends standing close by.

"Why is she so peeved?" said Mrs Davies, a major's wife, to Mrs Carstairs.

"Because she wasn't the first to hear of their engagement and subsequent wedding, and he has only been in India a few months. It is really beyond her comprehension."

"She is such a busybody. I am so pleased they were able to escape her prying."

"Well, they are away now. I wish them every happiness."

"So do I," replied Mrs Davies as they drifted away.

"What a lovely, lovely day!" sighed Clare twirling round her room in her pretty yellow dress. "I only hope my marriage is just like theirs."

"I hope mine is too," agreed Astrid as she sat sedately pondering on the day. "I have never seen so many people at a wedding before."

"But we also had a lot of people at our wedding," said their mother as she came to bid them goodnight. "Didn't we, dear?" she added, turning to her husband, who had joined her.

"We certainly did, my dear. You looked so beautiful. What a happy day it was!" He kissed and hugged her.

"Well," said Clare indignantly, with hand on hip, "why were we not invited to your wedding?" She looked up at them questioningly.

Their parents exchanged a wry smile as they kissed the girls goodnight.

Their mother whispered to them, "We had to marry first before you were born."

She beat a hasty retreat from the room before Clare responded with her usual, "Why? Why? How? How?"

"The statements our dear Clare comes out with! Really!" exclaimed her father. "I don't like to imagine how she will behave when she gets older! If only she was more ladylike, like Astrid! But I am afraid she never will be. On second thoughts, Davinia, my dear, she is just perfect as she is."

Davinia agreed before she kissed him goodnight.

CHAPTER 200

"How quiet everything is now they have left. I miss Roddy so much," sighed Elizabeth.

"I know you do, my darling, but they will be back in a few weeks," said Craig as he kissed her tenderly.

"I know, my darling, but then we will be preparing to go to the hills and Roddy will have taken nearly all his leave. He might not be able to come and see us and it will be months before we return." She sighed.

Craig held her close. "Well, you will always have me, my love, but you must remember, my darling, Roddy now has Christina and he will want to be with her. They are lucky, as when they return they will be able to get married quarters. As you know, my dear, Roddy will often get posted away and Christina will not be able to accompany him, so they will want to spend all their time together."

"Yes, I know that, my love," she replied, staring pensively into space.

She pondered Craig's last few words: "Roddy now has Christina." For the first time in her life she was not the only girl in his life.

"All the same," she sighed, "I shall just long for the day I see them again."

Roddy's letter telling Martha and Magnus of his marriage filled them both with dismay. They sat beside the blazing fire reading it over and over again.

"He only arrived in India a short time ago and now he has met someone and is married," said Martha. She sat pondering, looking into the flickering flames, lost to the world.

"My dear, our son is not a child. I am sure he will have thought well and long before taking this step," Magnus said.

"I do hope", she replied, still not convinced by Magnus's reply, "that it doesn't mean that both our children will stay in India for ever."

"He sounds very happy, my dear, so we must be thankful for that." He put his arm comfortingly round her shoulders as she shed a little tear. He was still holding the letter.

"What else does he say, Magnus?"

"He says that he will write again soon. He hopes to stay as close as he can to Elizabeth, who is well and very happy. Their son is beautiful and she longs for the day when she can bring him to see us. He says, 'You will adore my beautiful wife, Christina. She cannot wait for the day she meets you as she has no parents of her own.' He also sends us all his love."

CHAPTER 201

Elena made her last visit to the missions and the day for her departure for home drew near. She spent the last few days with Craig and Elizabeth, and, to her delight, Lindsay would now walk to her if she held out her arms. These were the happiest days of her stay. She picked Lindsay up and cradled him for a long time in her arms. Her thoughts were far away in Glencree. She wondered if ever he would see the beautiful land of his father, and if he would ever claim his rightful heritage. She sighed longingly as she gazed at him. Craig, watching her and hearing her sigh, knew the thoughts which were flowing through her mind.

Although Elena was delighted to see them all so happy, her heart ached to leave them. As she waved to them from the ship, Craig's heart almost broke. He watched the ship taking her away until he could see her no more.

"How quickly time has flown, Margot," said Craig. "I cannot believe that she has been here so long."

"Well, visiting the missions has taken up quite a lot of her time," said Margot. "Maybe when she comes again, as I am sure she will, she will not need to visit so many. As I am here all the time, I can take care of them with Martin."

Magnus heard from Jamie one day, as he was delivering goods to the castle, that Lady Elena was expected home the next day. He and Martha were the first to greet her as she stepped off the train, but she had noted, as the train came to a halt, the fleeting figure of Merry-Berry disappearing into the hedgerow.

'I wonder how she knew I would be arriving today?' Elena thought. 'It's uncanny – but then, it has always been so.'

She looked up to see Martha greeting her with a smile and a curtsy, and

Magnus with a nod of his head as he doffed his cap. Then he went to help Peggoty get her luggage from the rear of the train.

"Come, milady, I have prepared some refreshment for you," Martha said.

"Yes, Martha, thank you. I will stay awhile and give you all the news."

She related to them about Roddy's wedding and the lovely daughter-in-law they had, but she could see that Martha was more anxious for news of Elizabeth and Craig.

"They are both very well and very happy. You have a beautiful grandson, and – do you know, Martha? – he actually walked to me before I came away."

"How I would love to see him!" Martha said with a sigh. "Please tell us, milady: will the laird ever forgive our dear daughter and young Master Craig and allow them to return and bring their lovely bairn to see us? Will he? Will he?" Martha implored.

"I don't ever think so, Martha. Maybe he will when he knows of the lovely grandson he has, but I doubt it."

Martha looked at her sadly. "Tell me," she said: "does our daughter sing as sweetly as ever?"

"Yes, she certainly does, and she also teaches music. Lady Margot's lovely twin granddaughters are her constant companions and they just adore Lindsay. Now I must be getting home before the mists come down, but first I must give you the presents they sent."

She drew out of her small case some small silver filigree figures for Martha and several carved pipes for Magnus.

"They are really beautiful!" Martha exclaimed.

She stood a long time at the side of the loch after Elena and Magnus departed.

Only Jamie was there to greet Elena as she stepped from the ferryboat with Magnus following behind with her luggage. Harriet was watching from an upstairs window, and she came to meet her in the hall with a chilly welcoming peck on the cheek.

Elena was the first to speak: "Tell me, Harriet," she asked: "how is Bruce?"

"Oh, just as you left him," she said as she followed Elena into the lounge. "He's more angry and morose if anything."

"Is there no sign yet of forgiveness for Craig?"

"No, none at all. He seems more determined now than ever, in spite of Craig's son, that the title will die with him."

"How stupid he is!" said Elena. "He has such a lovely grandson who is entitled to his heritage."

"Well," began Harriet, beside herself with curiosity, although not wanting to seem so, "put the luggage down there, Jamie, and get Lady Elena some tea."

He did as she bade, very ungraciously. He, too, was most anxious to know how the young master and his son were. 'I will have to wait, I suppose,' he thought.

"Lady Elena will tell me as soon as she can," he muttered as he hurried to the kitchen.

"Now, tell me about the baby. Who does he look like?" asked Harriet.

"Well," began Elena, "he has jet-black hair and dark-brown eyes, like his father and Bruce. However, I have studied his features a good deal and I see more of a look of our dear Isabelle in his ready smile and friendly nature."

"Never! Never!" Bruce's voice boomed behind her. "Never!" He crashed his cane on the table and the crockery rattled.

Both Elena and Harriet had been so engrossed in their conversation that they did not hear Bruce enter the room. They jumped to their feet with fright.

"So, you are back, then, from seeing that no-good scoundrel and his hussy, and you, Elena, dare to say that I am stupid."

'So, he must have been listening all the time,' she thought.

"You dare to say that their brat looks like my darling Isabelle. Never! Never!" He banged his cane again on the table.

Elena faced him, her back as straight as a ramrod. "Yes, I am back and I do say again and again that your grandson does feature our dearest Isabelle," she declared. "I shall always say it, because it is true, no matter what you say or think. I only hope he grows up like Isabelle, with her lovely spirit of gentleness, kindness and forgiveness, rather than like you, you bitter old man."

She knew her dart had gone home as he sank wearily into his chair, but she paid him no heed. She gathered up her small bag and went to her room, ignoring Harriet, who was still standing speechless.

Harriet rang for the maid to take away the tea tray; then she too went to her room. In a mood like this, Bruce was best left alone.

Martha watched till the boat was out of sight; then she turned slowly and wended her way to the cottage. She sat gazing into the fire with tears streaming down her face. She quickly dried her eyes when she heard Magnus's heavy footsteps on the shaley path.

Magnus could see how bitterly she had wept as she fingered the filigree gifts over and over. He put his arm round her shoulders to comfort her.

"To think," she sighed, "if the young master hadn't followed our dear daughter, she would now be home with us. Two years have passed. I'd rather Lady Elena had brought her back instead of these gifts – as beautiful as they are."

"Well, it was not to be, my dear. Maybe when the laird forgives his son they will return home. Just think, my dear: we have a lovely grandson of our very own; we will just have to wait a little longer."

"Yes, maybe." She sighed as she wiped away a tear.

CHAPTER 202

Elena's trips into the village were a constant delight to her. She could talk of nothing else but the baby to the villagers, who were all eager for news. She also enjoyed her visits to see Emma and her son, and she compared the two children.

"How nice it would be, milady, if I could see him! If only they could all come home! We would have so much to talk about, and we could watch them grow up together – especially as they are so close together in age."

"Yes, it would be nice," Elena replied.

"Do you think the laird will ever change his mind now that he has a grandson?"

"No, never," she replied sadly.

Emma often sighed as the villagers compared her son with what they expected Craig's son to look like. Some of them were still angry that Craig had deserted his intended bride, Fiona. Craig's son should have been hers. The 'jewel' girls never ceased to complain to Emma when they met that it was so. They felt she must have been party to it somehow, as she and Elizabeth were such great friends.

However much they quizzed her, no matter what roundabout way they tried, the secret of why Elizabeth had gone away so hurriedly with Lady Margot was safe from their prying.

The summer trip to the hills was now much happier, although Elizabeth missed Roddy. Lindsay and the twins spent long hours playing together under the shade of the huge banyan. The jacaranda and bougainvillea flowers were out in all their splendour. The air felt fresh and cool after the heat of the city.

Craig spent most of his days on the tea plantation. He was also making plans for expansion and he was exploring the possibility of buying some adjacent land, whose owner was returning soon to England.

On other days he played polo at the club. Although Elizabeth missed him when he was away all day, it made her happy to see that he was almost as happy as if he was back home. She would sigh now and again. When he was with the children, the fresh bloom returned to his face.

In the evenings, Margot and Martin, back from visiting their missions, would sit with them on the verandah, and they would tell one another how they had spent their day.

Davinia and Stephen, spent most of their days visiting their friends, playing tennis, going for picnics by the lakeside and enjoying the many parties and balls. Their days always began with horse riding (the twins were now able to ride with them).

All too soon it was time to return to the city. Clare, as always, was the most reluctant to go. She was always inventing more reasons for staying. "But my pony is going to miss me and I am going to miss him; just another day or two, Papa," she pleaded, but she was always given the same reply:

"You must go back to school, young miss, and I must go back to the office. Your pony will be here next time we come."

"Well, Papa, your office will always be there too," Clare replied petulantly, "so you needn't hurry back so soon."

Her mother smiled. Clare would always have the last word.

Roddy and Christina met them on their return. The news of their baby, which was expected in December, filled Elizabeth with happiness.

"Oh, I do hope it is a Christmas Day baby!" exclaimed Elizabeth. "Have you told Mama and Papa yet?"

"No," said Roddy, "we wished to tell you first."

"Well, we must write tonight."

"Well, that is the good news, my dear Elizabeth."

She looked up at him alarmed. "What is it, Roddy dear?" she asked.

"Roddy is being posted up north and I am going with him," said Christina.

"But that means you won't be near us when the baby is born," said Elizabeth sadly.

"Well, we will come and see you as soon as we can," replied Roddy.

It was with great delight that Martha and Magnus received the news that their second grandson was born on Christmas Day.

"What is his name, Martha?" Magnus demanded, as she read and reread the letter. "Hurry and tell me, please," he begged.

"All right then, give me time. His name is Ruaridh Magnus. How wonderful!" said Martha. "At last we have a grandson we can really get to know. No laird can dictate when he can come home to visit us. I pray that it will be soon." She sighed, then continued: "Roddy says they are calling him Ruardy for short."

Magnus sat down in front of the fire beside Martha, smoking his pipe. He reached out to her and clasped her hand in his.

"Roddy also says that as soon as Christina is well enough to travel they will go to see Elizabeth and Craig. They will stay with them for the christening. Fancy, Magnus – both our children married and our grandchildren christened at the same church – and so far away!" She sighed. "How I wish they could have been born and christened at our lovely church here in Scotland."

"Well, that will never be now," said Magnus. "I daresay it will be years before Roddy comes home with the bairn."

"It will be something to look forward to. How I shall long for that day," said Martha as she gripped Magnus's hand in a comforting clasp. "Roddy says they will have to return before long to his posting in the north. He thinks he will be there for about two years. He says they are going to miss Elizabeth, Craig and Lindsay."

January 1924 saw the christening of Ruaridh Magnus Anderson.

CHAPTER 203

"Two years is a long time, Roddy," murmured Elizabeth as they all stood on the platform before the train pulled away.

"Well, dearest sister, I might not have to stay so long, but we never know in the army, as you realise. If I can, I shall try my best to get posted back here."

"I do hope you can be. Goodbye, Christina. Maybe you can come with Ruardy even if Roddy can't get away."

"Maybe, Elizabeth dear. I will try."

Craig cuddled Elizabeth as the train raced out of sight.

"Come, my darling," he said, "it might not be too long before they return. Maybe we can visit them."

"Yes, yes, I hadn't thought of that."

"We will see how our plans go."

The twins ran excitedly into the house to tell Elizabeth the good news.

"We are going on holiday to England to see Papa's aunts first. Then we will go to London, and we might see the King and Queen," said Clare hopefully. "Then we will go to Scotland to see Aunt Agatha – a cousin of our grandmother."

"How long will you be away?" Elizabeth asked.

"About a year or more, Papa thinks. Isn't it wonderful?" said Astrid, always finding it difficult to get a word in once Clare had started any kind of conversation.

"It certainly is," replied Elizabeth. "I only wish we could be coming with you."

"Well, why can't you?" Clare retorted. "Your parents live in Scotland too."

"Well, maybe we will go one day," Elizabeth replied rather wistfully.

"Go where?" said Craig as he entered the room.

"To see your father in Glencree Castle, and Elizabeth's parents, who live beside the loch," said Clare.

"Grandmama said you will be going one day, so why can't you come with us?" said Astrid, looking puzzled. "We can all go together. I am sure Lindsay would love to come on the big ship with us, wouldn't you?"

But Lindsay, playing with his toys, didn't hear them.

Craig and Elizabeth exchanged glances over their heads.

"Well," Craig replied, "we cannot all go at once and leave your poor grandparents alone, now can we?" He was anxious to get off the subject.

"No, I guess not," replied Clare.

"You will have to get in more practising before you leave," said Elizabeth, changing the topic, as she glanced at Craig.

"But we didn't come to practise," said Clare, making it clear she now had more important things to do. "We have got to have some new clothes made by the durzi."

"Well, he isn't coming today," said Astrid. "You go and play with Lindsay until I have had my lesson."

"When do they leave?" asked Craig as soon as they had gone.

"At the end of the month. I am going to miss them so. I knew they were going some time this year, but I didn't expect it to be quite so soon."

"Well, Stephen has to attend to some property business, I believe, and his annual leave is long overdue," said Craig.

"Little do the twins know," said Elizabeth, "that Davinia and Stephen will be looking at boarding schools whilst they are there. I do hope they don't decide to leave them there when they return to India. I know that is Margot and Martin's hope also."

Tears were flowing freely as they said their final goodbyes.

"Hurry back soon," Margot called to them.

"We will, Grandmama, we will," they chorused as they wiped away their tears.

"I daresay", said Margot, "that Astrid's tears will last longer at our parting than Clare's. I reckon Clare will know everyone on the ship before it has gone many miles."

"Yes, I think you are right, my dear," Martin replied.

"To think," said Elizabeth, "they will not be coming up in the hills with us this year – and Roddy and Christina are away also."

"It will be very lonely without them," said Margot.

Elizabeth found the days seemed long after they left. Only the company of Lindsay, and lessons with the other children, helped her to pass the time away. Frequently she would go down to the mission to help Margot, leaving Lindsay in the care of his ayah.

"Margot," asked Elizabeth one day as they sat on the verandah, "do you really think they will leave the girls behind when they return to India?"

"I hope not, but it is difficult to know for sure. Stephen and Davinia want the best possible education for them, and, as you know, they get very lax in their speech here mixing with the servants."

"Yes, I have already noticed that Lindsay speaks as his ayah does in spite of my corrections," replied Elizabeth.

"There are such excellent boarding schools in England," said Margot. "There's one not far from Stephen's aunt's, so at least they could go and stay with her at end of term. Then there is one in Scotland, not far from my cousin Agatha's. In fact, both your dear Aunt Ingrid and I went there."

"Yes, Aunt Ingrid often spoke of it to me." Elizabeth tried not to let Margot see how the mention of her aunt's name had made her long for those happy days she had spent with her as a girl. "It was a pretty strict school, I believe," she said.

"Yes, it most certainly was. It was lucky for your aunt that she had such a flair for music; she was able to transfer to the academy of music."

"Yes, that was why she insisted I went there also."

"It was the right place for you, Elizabeth. Your talent was too good to be wasted."

They both looked up as the garden gates rattled, heralding a visitor.

"Ah, here comes your lovely boy back from the kindergarten with his ayah," said Margot. "What a handsome boy he is! He looks more like his father every day. At first, as a baby, he looked a lot like Isabelle – especially when he smiled."

"Craig thought so too," replied Elizabeth, "but I never saw Isabelle close to as I recall."

"She was a most beautiful lady and such a dear friend of mine. It is such a pity she died so young and never saw her lovely grandson." Margot sighed.

"Well," declared Elizabeth sadly, "she would not have seen him anyway as things are."

"My dear, things would have been far different if she had lived. This boy would have been born at home, where all the Earls of Glencree have been born. The heritage is rightfully his, no matter what his grumpy old grandfather says."

Margot picked Lindsay up and kissed him when he ran to greet her.

"It was nice to have Elena here for his christening, Margot," said Elizabeth. "I hope she can visit again soon."

"If all is well at home, I expect she will come back before too long. I must be going soon," said Margot putting Lindsay down as she prepared to leave.

"Now, say goodbye to Aunt Margot."

"Salaam, memsahib," Lindsay said, clasping his hands together and bowing his head.

Elizabeth and Margot looked at each other aghast.

"No, no, Lindsay!" exclaimed Elizabeth in amazement. "You must say, 'Goodbye, Aunt Margot,' and shake her hand."

"Yes, Mama. Goodbye, Aunt Margot," he said, holding out his chubby hand. She clasped it lovingly and kissed him and his mother.

"See what I mean about education, Elizabeth?" she said.

"I certainly do."

"It is just as well Lindsay has started at the kindergarten," said Margot.

"Now, what is all this talk about education?" asked Martin as he came up the verandah steps with Craig.

"We were just discussing whether or not the children will be coming back with their parents," said Margot.

"I think they will," said Craig, "especially if Clare has any say in the matter. I cannot see her wishing to stay in any boarding school, either here or in England."

"Now, Elizabeth," said Martin, "how about a song for us before we go?"

"Of course. Any preference?"

"No, how about some of our Scottish melodies?"

Craig sat with Lindsay on his knee, and he playfully tried to make his son sing along with them.

"Now we must really say our goodbye," said Margot later as they got up to go.

CHAPTER 204

Craig was still contemplating buying the land adjacent to the tea plantation. He was away with Martin most days viewing it and getting to know more about management.

Elizabeth, after taking Lindsay to the kindergarten, would often go visiting the missions with Margot or she took long strolls with Davinia through the lovely wooded countryside. She often sighed and wished the hills in the distance were the hills of home, but no amount of wishing would make it so.

"You look very thoughtful this afternoon," said Margot to Elizabeth as she joined her on the verandah for tea after visiting the missions.

"Yes, I am trying to persuade Craig to give up the idea of owning his own plantation. I think it might prove too much for him."

"I agree," said Margot. "It will take up all his time when he comes to the hills, and he needs to rest after the heat of the city. Of course, you could stay permanently up here if he did decide to buy it, and that would benefit your health as well as his."

"Oh no, he wouldn't hear of it. He would miss seeing his friends at the bank, polo club and barracks, and I would miss the twins too much, as well as my other pupils. Also, we would only see you and Martin when you came up here in the summer. No, the way it is now is ideal. If only I can persuade him!" said Elizabeth with a sigh.

The matter was settled for them later that day when Craig returned with Martin.

"Well, I cannot get the land, after all, my darling. The fellow is not now going to England for another few years."

Elizabeth looked at Margot with a sigh of relief.

"Thank goodness for that!" said Margot. "You need all the rest you can get when you leave the city."

"Are you very disappointed, dear?" asked Elizabeth.

"No, not really. I already find it tiring riding round the plantation, and I have only been doing it for a few weeks."

"I am glad he has got that bee out of his bonnet," said Martin in a whisper to Margot as they left.

Margot hurriedly opened the letter from Scotland and scanned the pages as quickly as she could for news of the twins.

"Oh, that daughter of mine!" she called exasperatedly to Martin.

"Whatever is the matter, my dear?" he exclaimed as he came into the room.

He watched her amusingly as she hurriedly leafed over the pages.

"She is deliberately holding back until last the news I want to hear most." Suddenly, Margot let out a cry of delight. "Martin dear," she said, "they are going to bring the children back with them. It seems they both got so distressed at the thought of being left behind that she and Stephen decided they could not go ahead with it. The twins have met several girls who are full-time boarders, and some of them simply loved it, but they themselves didn't like the idea of being away from their parents for so long. Some of their friends simply love it."

"Well," exclaimed Martin, "I daresay many of them are glad to get away from their parents' clutches, and, also, they may not have spent as much time with their parents as our children have."

"Yes," agreed Margot, "your dear girls have always been with you. It is understandable they would get distressed. Davinia goes on to say that it will be spring next year when they arrive. Now we must go and tell Elizabeth."

Elizabeth's happiness knew no bounds when she heard the good news. "Oh how happy it makes me, Margot," she said. "I have missed them so much, and so has Lindsay."

They were all sitting on the verandah, Lindsay nestling in Craig's arms.

"I hope we never have to send our darling son away to boarding school," Elizabeth said as she glanced at him.

"No, our son will not be going to any boarding school, either here or abroad," said Craig. He sighed.

Suddenly he saw again his father raging at Aunt Harriet:

"How many times have I to tell you, Harriet: my son will never leave my side, and that is final."

Margot looked at Craig. She remembered Elena's concern at the rows Harriet and Bruce frequently had about his education.

"Well, the wee laddie is far too young yet, so none of us need worry for a long time," she said. "Now we must go."

CHAPTER 205

The twins were delighted at the news that they were going home. They had found nothing to their liking, apart from their trip to London, and they longed to get away from the clutches of stern Great-Aunt Agatha, who they thought was the strangest old lady they had ever seen.

"Why does she wear those horrible long black dresses down to her ankles?" asked Clare. "She looks like a witch."

"Now, don't you ever say such a thing again," replied her startled, angry mother. "Your father would be extremely angry with you if he heard you."

"Well, she does," Clare repeated to Astrid very quietly after her mother had left the room.

"Yes, she does to me too," agreed Astrid. "How glad I shall be to get home to Grandmama! Mama said that they have to wear long clothes because of the terrible cold up in the Highlands. They don't get the hot sun like we do in India."

"Well, it has been too cold for me," said Clare. "Thank goodness Mama and Papa aren't leaving us behind with her."

"Yes, I am thankful for that," replied Astrid. "I should be very unhappy."

At last they were sailing away. Life on board suited Clare immensely. Every day was an adventure: more entertainment, more friends. "There are such a lot of children of our age on board, Mama," Clare kept exclaiming.

"Yes, most of them are going to India for the first time with their soldier fathers. They will find it very hot," replied Davinia.

When the dances were held, Clare was up for each one. She couldn't stop telling Astrid, "Oh, it's all so thrilling! I wish it could go on for ever."

Astrid was more keen on quietly reading her books. "Well, it can't go on for ever," she said. "You have done no studying since we came aboard. Mama and Papa will be very angry when they find out."

"Well, they won't find out if you don't tell them," Clare retorted.

She again glanced in the mirror to fix her ribbons before venturing out once more. Her parents had met many old friends returning to India, and they were occupied most of the day, talking about business; in the evenings they played cards. The freedom Clare was now enjoying suited her immensely. She was always the first to raise her hand to participate in all the games, and she would attend the parties of other children on board whenever they were held.

When the ship stopped at Port Said for a few days, Astrid insisted on her father taking her ashore to see the pyramids.

"Well, I shall stay on board and play deck quoits with my friends," said Clare.

"Oh no, you won't," insisted her father. "Now is a good opportunity to learn something about the Middle East at first hand. Not many people get the opportunity to see the pyramids like this. You are coming along."

"Why? Just because Astrid wants to see them I have to go also. Why? Why?"

"Because I say so," Stephen replied.

Clare followed the others meekly ashore. She sulkily pulled the brim of her hat and veil lower over her face. Davinia had insisted they wear broad-brimmed hats to keep out the harsh rays of the sun.

"Keep close to me both of you," their father insisted. "Don't go wandering away."

"Why?" exclaimed Clare tersely.

"Because you might get stolen."

"Stolen?" she exclaimed in dismay.

"Yes, they are always on the lookout for pretty girls about your age – especially naughty ones like you," her father added, with a sly glance at Davinia, who was walking beside him.

Astrid had already got a booklet on the pyramids and she was perusing it with great interest, but Clare was more interested in the fine silks her mother was viewing. Clare knew her father was not too pleased with her for showing no interest whatsoever in anything that would benefit her education. At most times she could twist him round her little finger, but she also knew that when he was angry she must obey.

"That child is only interested in ribbons, pretty frocks and parties!" he exclaimed exasperatedly to Davinia when they got back to the ship. "I don't know what will become of her when she gets older. My mind would be a lot easier if she were more like Astrid."

"Well, we have to accept that she never will be," Davinia rejoined.

"There was only one nice thing about it," Clare declared resentfully.

"Oh, and what was that?" asked Astrid.

"The ride on the camel, of course – oh, and also the pretty fan and parasol Mama bought for us."

"Yes, I liked those as well, but I thought it was all very fascinating. I should like to have stayed longer."

"Oh, you would," Clare retorted. It was not often they raised their voices at each other, but all Clare wanted to do was to attend the next dance or party.

Davinia and Stephen had to admit that they were glad to be going back to the warmer climate and all the sunshine. The weather in Britain was just as cold and wet as they remembered it on previous visits.

At last the ship drew into Madras. They peered over the side, and Clare was the first to spot Martin, Margot, Elizabeth and Craig with Lindsay perched on his shoulder.

Lindsay called out to them gleefully when Craig pointed them out, and the girls shouted his name above the tumult.

At last they were ashore and greeting each other.

"How good it is to be back!" exclaimed Davinia. "We have missed you all so much."

"We have missed you too. My word, how tall the girls have grown!" said Margot. "It seems like years and years you have been away, my darlings."

"It seems like that to us also!" exclaimed Clare. "Are you really glad Mama and Papa didn't leave us behind?"

"Yes, of course, my dear. Why do you ask?"

"Well, Aunt Agatha told Mama that she thought we ought to stay as it would be better for our education."

"Was that so, Davinia?"

"Yes, she thought the girls lacked decorum – especially Clare."

"What does she mean by decorum?" Clare stuttered.

"She means you should act in a more ladylike way," said Margot.

"Well, how can I act like a lady when I am only a child?" she said with a pout.

Margot looked at Davinia as if to say, "She is back!"

Clare looked up at her grandmother with her hands on her hips. "I am only a child," she said. "Isn't that so, Grandmama?"

"Yes, that is so, my child."

CHAPTER 206

The children from the mission greeted them gaily with garlands, and next day a surprise party, organised by Elizabeth, was held for them and all their school friends.

That same evening, Lindsay and Margot, Martin, Craig and Elizabeth sat on the verandah while Davinia, Stephen and the twins told them about their trip.

"I am so glad to be back here amongst you and all our friends," said Davinia. "I have spent so long here that this seems like my home now."

Craig looked at her with a wry smile. "I wish I could say the same," he said with a sigh.

Margot looked at him sadly. 'I too wish you felt more at home, my boy,' she thought, but she knew only too well how much Craig and Elizabeth longed to go back home.

"Well it will soon be back to work for me," said Stephen. "I am so glad to be home. It was so tiring travelling round to see my relatives. And it will soon be back to school for you two little girls. You will have a lot to catch up on."

Clare pulled a face. "But we are not little girls any longer, Papa. Why, we are almost ten years old now – or had you forgotten?" she retorted. She stood in her usual pose, a personification of indignation, as if she thought that the point she was making had not been fully understood by one and all.

"Oh, I know, my dear Clare," her father replied, just as emphatically, "that you can't wait to grow up, but don't be in too much of a hurry. There's often a lot of problems for children when they grow up, especially for impetuous little girls like you, and those years will be upon us poor parents all too soon." He looked across at his wife and whispered loudly, "When will we be able to get the last word with this precocious child of ours?"

Clare still stood, wondering what the words *impetuous* and *precocious* meant, a worried look on her face.

"Well, growing up can't come too soon for me," she announced. "I am just longing to go to all the parties and balls, aren't you, Astrid?"

"No, not really," Astrid replied. "I shall just wait until the time comes."

Clare gave her a look of resignation. "Well, I will grow up into a young lady by myself," she said.

Their parents smiled above their heads.

"Well, children," said Elizabeth, "the ayah is here. It is long past your bedtime." They bade everyone goodnight.

"How different they are!" exclaimed their mother. "Sometimes it is almost impossible to believe they are twins. They are so different in everything but looks."

"Well," replied Stephen, "maybe as they grow older their ideas will grow more like each other's."

"I doubt it," Davinia replied.

"I doubt it too," said Margot.

Eventually, she and Martin bade them goodnight. Elizabeth and Craig had departed a little earlier in the evening.

CHAPTER 207

The sight of Roddy's letter as always filled Elizabeth with delight. Craig watched her over the top of the letter he had been reading. He suddenly saw her joy turn to dismay and sadness.

"What is it, my dearest one? Bad news?"

"Well, it makes me glad and sad. Roddy and the family will be calling on us soon, as he is going home on a long furlough. He has to attend a special course. How I wish we could go home on a long holiday!" She sighed heavily as she replaced the letter slowly back in the envelope.

"We will one day, my dearest one. Haven't I always promised you?"

He put down the letter he was holding and came round the table to join her. He put his arms round her thin shoulders and kissed her lightly on her hair.

"We will go one day my darling, I promise," he said. "Now, come – let us go and see our son before I go to the office."

Elizabeth stood on the verandah steps holding Lindsay by the hand as she watched Craig climb into the tonga.

"Goodbye, my precious two," he called.

As he sped away he was deep in thought. As always, he was reluctant to leave them, but more so today after the news Elizabeth had received.

She read and reread the letter with Lindsay looking up at her. "It will be nice to have Uncle Roddy and Aunt Christina and Ruardy back again," he said. "They have been away for a long time."

"Yes, my son," she replied, "it will be nice, but they will only be staying a short time; then they will be away for a long, long time."

"How long can you stay, Roddy dear?" she asked when he came bounding through the door to greet her a few weeks later.

"Only three days; then we catch the boat for home. How I wish, my darling sister, that you could come too!"

"Oh, it would be wonderful if we could all be going together – one big happy family," said Christina.

"Well, no more talk like that!" Craig exclaimed. "We too will go home one day, you mark my words." He saw the hurt, longing look in his wife's eyes and sadly thought, 'Oh, my darling, if only I could make it so.'

Suddenly Lindsay and Ruardy came shrieking into the room, both trying to be first with the news.

"Well, what is it my darlings?" exclaimed Elizabeth.

"The monkey man is here! The monkey man is here!" said Lindsay, out of breath in his excitement. "Can he stay, Mama? Please say he can stay."

"Very well, then, he can stay this time as Ruardy won't see him where he is going."

"But where is he going?" Lindsay demanded, stamping his foot in annoyance. "He has only just come. Why does he have to keep going away?"

"Because Uncle Roddy is a soldier, and he has to go where the army sends him," said Craig. "Now he has been told to go to Scotland."

"Well, Papa, why can't you be a soldier? Then we could go to Scotland with Uncle Roddy. Then I could see Grandpapa who lives beside the loch and Grandfather who lives in the big castle. Why, why, Papa? You are always telling Mama we will go one day. Why can't I go with Ruardy?" he cried, stamping his foot again in anger and frustration.

Craig and Elizabeth looked at each other disconsolately.

"One day we will go," said Elizabeth, trying to appease him. "Come now – I thought you wanted to see the monkey man. If we don't hurry, he will be gone."

"Come – we will all go!" exclaimed Craig, anxious to get off the topic of home.

They all hurried outside to watch the little monkey, dressed like a little doll, do his tricks to his master's bidding.

All too soon the time came for Roddy and his family to depart. Roddy hugged Elizabeth for a long time as Craig watched in despair. Tears started to roll down her cheeks.

"Now, don't cry, my dear," Roddy whispered in her ear. "We will be back soon."

"Give Mama and Papa a big kiss for me," she pleaded.

"I will, I will."

"If you see anyone I know," said Craig, "remember me to them."

"I will," replied Roddy.

Craig knew Roddy would be seeing a lot of people he knew.

"Give Emma my love and tell her to write often," said Elizabeth.

They watched them longingly as they waved their farewell from the ship. Elizabeth's small, white, wet handkerchief was limp as she waved back.

"Come back soon, Ruardy," called Lindsay.

"I will, I will," he shouted, his voice trailing on the wind.

"Come, my angel," Craig called to Elizabeth, who still gazed out to sea.

He helped her and Lindsay into the tonga and seated himself beside her. The sight of her tear-stained face upset him deeply.

Often he had asked himself whether he was right to come and join her in India. If he hadn't, she would now be home with her parents, not stuck in this strange foreign land. He asked the tonga wallah to hasten his pace as they headed home.

CHAPTER 208

Roddy alighted from the train, and, after helping Christina and Ruardy to alight, he swept his mother into his arms. He hugged his father as Martha hugged her new daughter-in-law and looked at her proudly. Ruardy hung back, hiding behind his mother's skirt. Roddy lifted him up.

"Here is your grandmother and grandfather. Give them both a kiss, Ruardy."

They all headed towards the cottage.

"Come, my son," said Magnus, "we will show Ruardy the boats before we go inside."

"One day", Roddy told him, "we will sail over the loch in Grandpapa's boat."

"Soon, soon!" Ruardy replied.

"I see you still have Craig's boat here!" Roddy exclaimed.

"Yes," replied Magnus. "I offered to row it back for the laird but he told me to burn it. That I could not do; I have disobeyed his instructions and kept it concealed. One day I know Master Craig will come home with our darling angel and their son, and then I will proudly sail them all over in his boat to their rightful place at Glencree Castle. Tell me, Roddy, how is my darling angel? I would give the world just to see her."

Roddy noted the heavy sigh as he spoke her name.

"She is quite well, as is their son Lindsay," he said. "It is Craig I am more concerned about. He still has attacks of malaria – not quite as severe as his first one, but they are a worry all the same."

They sat a long time after supper. Martha, as always, had cooked his favourite dishes. Roddy was glad to be back and enjoying his mother's home-cooking.

"We have a cook in India, Mama, but he cannot cook any of my favourite dishes like you can."

"Well now," said Martha as they sat round the blazing fire after Ruardy had been tucked up in bed, "tell me about my other grandson."

"He is a beautiful boy," said Christina. "He grows more like his father every day."

"Oh, how I wish they could be here with us so that we could all be together – one big happy family!" said Martha with a sigh. "Do you think it ever will happen, Roddy?" she asked sadly.

"I doubt it very much, Mama, unless the laird calls him home. Lady Elena, when she visited India, said that Craig's father did not show any sign of relenting."

"More's the pity!" said Martha. "We will have to wait patiently to see our dear daughter, but I must say we have another charming daughter, with whom to share our love, and our wee boy upstairs."

"Do you ever see the laird?" asked Roddy one day as they were sailing over the loch to take supplies to the village and castle.

"No, only Jamie comes to the jetty to collect the supplies. It's as if the laird does not wish to see anyone or let anyone into the castle. None of his shooting friends come from England as they used to do in the old days."

"Why is he such a bitter old man?" Roddy exclaimed angrily. "Our Elizabeth is as suitable as anyone else to be Mistress of Glencree."

"Not in the laird's eyes," replied Magnus. "Master Craig should have married the girl he was betrothed to: the Lady Fiona. It had been expected since they were children, and it was wrong of him to desert her practically on the eve of her wedding day. No, it wasn't right and the laird still blames our darling angel for it all."

"What happened to Lady Fiona, Papa?"

"The General sold all the land and house and they went to live in England. I heard talk in the village not long after that she had married some lord or other."

At last they were at the jetty unloading the supplies. Jamie greeted Roddy with open arms.

"Tell me," he asked excitedly: "how is the young master and his son? I don't suppose we shall ever see them again at Glencree."

"They are fine. Lindsay is a bonnie boy; he looks just like his father, but there is also a resemblance to his lovely grandmother – God rest her soul."

"Has Master Craig recovered from his malaria?" asked Jamie anxiously.

"Well, he was quite all right when I left," replied Roddy.

"Will you be long at home, Roddy?"

"Another few weeks, then I am off to England for a special course for a few months. I shall be leaving my wife and son here with Mama and Papa till I return."

"Well, Magnus, maybe you will bring them over to the village sometimes?" asked Jamie

"Yes, I will. We must be away now, Jamie."

With a final wave Roddy and Magnus were off round the bend to the village.

CHAPTER 209

Emma turned round when she heard her name being called, and she saw Roddy hastening towards her. He kissed her lightly on the cheeks. "Dear, dear Roddy," she exclaimed, "after all this time! How many years is it since you went away?"

"It seems ages. I can't really remember, it seems so long ago. And this must be your son, Nicholas – almost the same age as Elizabeth's son," he said as he bent down to ruffle his hair.

"Yes. Tell me, Roddy: how is she?"

"She is well and happy, but of course, longing to return, as does everyone who roams from our bonnie Scotland."

"She could come to the mainland with Craig and her son to reside."

"Oh no, she won't hear of it. She says that if Craig cannot come to Glencree Castle, they will not come at all. She is quite adamant about it."

"What a pity!" Emma sighed. "It would have been so nice to be able to visit them."

Nicholas was jumping up and down with impatience.

"As you see, Roddy, he is a typical boy: he cannot bear to be still for a minute. Tell me: have you time to come to the vicarage with me?"

Roddy looked at Magnus.

"Yes, you go, son," his father said. "I will manage the rest of the supplies, but be at the jetty in good time."

"I will, Papa."

Roddy helped Emma into her carriage and sat beside her. Nicholas looked up at him questioningly.

"Now, what other news of village life is there? Elizabeth will be anxious to hear all the gossip when I return," said Roddy.

"Well, the second precious jewel of Mr and Mrs Crawford got married a few weeks ago," Emma said with a smile.

At this Roddy let out a peal of laughter. "I often wondered when she would get her precious jewels off her hands," he said. "Oh, that woman! I don't suppose she ever got over the shock of my dear sister marrying the man she had earmarked for one of her daughters."

"No, I don't think she ever will either," Emma replied with a laugh. "I think the last one will get left on the shelf; I don't see anyone interested in her up to now."

"That will be Ruby, I dare guess."

"Yes, you guess right."

"She always was the most spiteful one of the three," Roddy rejoined.

The clatter of the carriage wheels on the cobble courtyard of the vicarage caused Tony, Emma's brother, to glance up from the book he was reading.

"Mama, Papa," he called, "Emma is here with Nicholas."

Try as he might, he could not identify the man sitting beside her, who had now alighted and was helping Emma and Nicholas out of the carriage.

"See who I met in the village today," she said as her parents ran out to greet them.

"Is it dear Roddy", her mother exclaimed, "after all this time?"

She kissed him fondly as Roddy shook hands with Emma's father.

"Well, I do declare! Come inside," said Mrs Corwell.

"Tell me: how are the boys?" Roddy asked.

"Well, two are married and live away, but Tony is here with us."

As they entered the library, Roddy glanced towards the window where Tony was sitting in his wheelchair, looking much older than his years. Suddenly he recalled all the suffering of the war years. Always there was someone somewhere to remind them. He rushed over to greet him at a loss for words, but Tony was obviously delighted to see him, and the grip of his hand, as Roddy sat down opposite him, soon put him at his ease. Before long they were laughing gaily as they talked of old times.

The vicar excused himself and took Nicholas for a walk, and the two ladies went to make tea.

"Tell me," asked Roddy when they were alone: "is there any help coming your way?"

"Yes, yes, we get lots of help from the ex-servicemen's association in Glasgow, through the kindness of Lady Elena. She often calls to see me and the other boys in the village, and we all meet as often as we can. It was something she promised to do for Master Craig before he went away. Tell me, Roddy: how is he and Elizabeth? I hear they have a son."

"Yes, that is so. They are very happy, but of course they miss their bonnie Scotland – as anyone does who is away from it for long."

Roddy, anxious to get off the topic of Craig, asked, "What about the work situation? From what I hear, it's not too good."

"No, it's not good at all – very grim, in fact. There have been strikes, hunger marches, and poverty worse than before – if that is possible." He sighed. "Every day seems worse than the day before. You did the right thing re-enlisting, Roddy."

"Yes," he replied, "my only regret is that it takes me away from my home and all those I love."

"Well, I would have done the same if I had been fit enough."

"Now, no more talk of bad times!" his mother demanded as she entered with Emma. "Roddy is having tea before he rejoins his father."

"How time has flown!" Roddy exclaimed when he glanced at the clock. Then he bade them farewell.

"I will come with you to the jetty. The fresh air will do me good," said Tony.

Roddy lifted him into the trap beside Emma.

"We won't be long, Mama," Emma called as they sped away.

Ruardy danced for joy when he saw the boat returning. He had spent quite some time beside the loch with his mother, throwing pebbles in the water awaiting their return.

"Papa, will you take me for a sail next time you go?" he said when they arrived.

"Yes, my son, or maybe Grandpapa will take you. He can row much better than I can."

CHAPTER 210

Elizabeth waited daily for Roddy's return. His last letter had said they hoped to be returning soon. At last she got the letter she was waiting for, telling her that he would be stationed in Madras for a short while after they arrived.

"Is Ruardy coming too?" asked Lindsay when he caught the joy in his mother's voice as she read the letter out to Craig.

"Yes, my son. I can hardly wait for the day," she replied.

Craig, Elizabeth and Lindsay were on the quay waving madly to attract their attention. At last they were ashore. Elizabeth cried with happiness at their return. She held tightly to Roddy's arm on the journey home. "Now, tell me all the news of Mama and Papa."

"Give me time to get in the house, my dear," Roddy laughed. "Really, Elizabeth, you still get as excited as a little girl."

"We will all eat first," said Craig; "then my angel might have calmed down a little."

The two children played excitedly with the ayah until they heard Roddy announce that he had some presents for all. Lindsay came quietly to his father's side as he watched Roddy lift the lid of his suitcase.

"More woollies to keep me warm, I daresay!" said Craig.

"And more lace to edge my pillowslips!" Elizabeth laughed.

"There is also some woven tweed for both of you."

"How wonderful to think Mama is still weaving and spinning!" said Elizabeth.

"I have also got a surprise for you, Craig," said Roddy: "lots more tartan from your Aunt Elena."

"What has she sent for me?" exclaimed Lindsay, almost in tears as he stood watching the grown-ups admiring their presents.

"Grandpapa has made you a lovely boat," said Roddy, handing him a parcel.

Lindsay unravelled all the paper very carefully.

"Oh, it's beautiful! See, Papa – don't you think so too?"

"Yes, my son, I do." He held his breath as he gazed at it in disbelief; Roddy was watching him closely.

"Why, it is a replica of my boat back home, Roddy!" he exclaimed in wonder. "It even has the name on it too. Has Magnus still got my boat, then?"

"Yes, and it is well hidden and protected. It seems your father said he didn't want to see it again and told Papa to burn it, but he decided it was too lovely a boat to burn, so he disobeyed the laird."

"I am glad he did!" Craig exclaimed. "It will be there for when I return."

"It certainly will," Roddy said. "Papa said his proudest day will be when he takes you home in it."

"Yes, hasten the day!" sighed Craig. "It is really wonderful what a craftsman Magnus is!" he kept exclaiming as he admired the boat.

"But, Papa," Lindsay kept reminding him, "Grandpapa made the boat for me. May I have it, please?"

"Yes, of course, my son."

"We will be able to sail them together on the loch when we go home," Lindsay replied.

"How did Magnus know her name?"

"Papa told me he found a slip of paper on the steering gear with the name *Angeline*. He guessed that you had chosen that name but had not had time to have it painted on."

"Well, Roddy, I did have time, but I did not dare put it on in case Papa asked me about it and got angry. I am glad Magnus found it and put it on this replica for my son." Craig handed it back to Lindsay. "You must take great care of it," he said.

"I will, I will."

"I have a boat too," said Ruardy as he searched amongst the luggage. "See, Uncle Craig – Grandpapa made this one for me."

Craig took it from him and admired it as he looked at it closely.

"My, my, it is a lovely boat. Now we will all be able to sail our boats on the loch."

Elizabeth stood silently looking on, wondering when that happy day might be.

"Tell me, Roddy," she said: "what news is there of everyone else back home? Did you see Emma?"

"Yes, I did. She has a lovely boy about as tall as Lindsay, and she and all her family send you their love. She said that the youngest precious jewel of Mr and Mrs Crawford married recently, but she thinks the one that is left would never get married."

"I daresay that is Ruby," said Elizabeth with a smile.

"Yes, that is so."

Craig looked up and laughed when he heard them discussing the precious jewels.

"Well, her mother won't rest until she has got that last jewel off her hands. I wonder who the poor, unfortunate man will be," said Craig.

Roddy and Elizabeth smiled at his comments.

Christina stood nearby with a puzzled expression.

"My dear Christina," said Roddy, "you would have to live for years in the village to get to know all about the lady in question. But it is not important now. We are all better off away from her and her mother's sharp-edged tongue."

They looked up to see the ayah standing at the door.

"Come, boys," said Elizabeth, "it is well past your bedtime. Say goodnight and don't forget your prayers."

"No, Mama, we won't. Can Ruardy's bed be in my room?" Lindsay asked.

"Yes, my son," she replied, and she bade the ayah do as he requested. "You and Roddy can stay on the verandah if you still want to chat," she said to Craig, "but it is getting late and he and Christina have had a long journey. Christina may want to retire. She can tell me tomorrow all I want to know. I will bid you goodnight."

Craig and Roddy talked a long time after they left.

"Tell me, Roddy: how is the old country?" asked Craig. "Is it really as bad as I read in the papers? And the ex-servicemen – how are they faring?"

"Well, the ones I visited told me they were getting help. Lady Elena visits them often."

"I am so glad. I must send her more money. I only wish I was nearer so I could do more for them."

"There is little work for any of the men. Hunger marches and strikes have

445

been held. It is pitiful to see," said Roddy.

"It is unbelievable," said Craig, deeply depressed, "to think of all the sacrifices that were made, and this is all they have got in return!"

They both sat for a long time, silently contemplating this appalling situation before they bade each other goodnight.

CHAPTER 211

Elizabeth and Christina were like sisters and their sons grew up to be like brothers. Elizabeth had never been happier since her arrival in India, now that she had so many of her family around her.

Roddy, still on extended leave, was able to play polo with Craig. All of them were later able to go to the hills, though Roddy stayed only for a short time before he returned alone to the city. Christina was sad to see him leave, but he insisted that they all remain in the hills until the last possible moment. On their return to the city, the news of Roddy's imminent posting to a faraway station saddened them all.

"So far away!" sighed Christina.

"Yes, my dear, and it is a long posting, so Ruardy will have to come with us."

"But, my dear Roddy," said Christina after much thought, "Ruardy has only just settled in the school with Lindsay. We can't take him away now. The boys are so attached that it will break his heart. All his friends are here, and he cannot possibly go to a boarding school. He is far too young."

"No, he is certainly not going to a boarding school. There may be a need for that when he is older, but even then I shall not wish it," said Roddy with a sigh.

Christina stood biting her lip in perplexity as she pondered. Elizabeth entered the room.

"Why so sad, the pair of you?" she asked gaily, but her manner changed quickly when she saw that Christina was on the verge of tears.

Christina explained their dilemma.

"Well, let him stay here with us at least till the end of term until you see what the school situation is," she suggested.

So it was agreed.

Ruardy fretted and cried for days after his parents left, and Elizabeth wondered if she had done the right thing by suggesting he stay. Lindsay, so full of fun and games, always found some new adventure for him and his friends, so Ruardy soon dried his tears. Astrid and Clare were always on hand for games, but Clare preferred to play with older boys.

"Well, you go and play with them," Astrid retorted angrily, "I shall play with Lindsay and Ruardy."

"Cheerio, then! I'm away."

Soon Ruardy was learning to play the piano. He also stood daily beside Lindsay as he practised.

"He has a wonderful ear for music and is doing very well!" Elizabeth exclaimed to Craig. "His parents will be very pleased."

"Well, it is all owing to you, my dear," said Craig.

Elizabeth was excited to hear from Roddy that they would be returning soon.

"It's so good to have you back again," said Elizabeth when they arrived. "We have good news to convey: we are expecting another baby early next year."

"Oh, my dear, dear Elizabeth, we are so happy for you!" said Christina.

Elizabeth noticed the look of concern on Roddy's face.

"My dear Roddy," she said, "I shall be perfectly all right. Don't worry so."

"Very well, my dear, I will try not to."

"We cannot stay too long. All the arrangements have been made at Ruardy's new school. He will only be a day pupil until he is a little older," said Christina.

"Well, that is good news, although we are going to miss him dreadfully when you leave," said Elizabeth with a sigh.

Lindsay and Ruardy ran excitedly into the house from school. Ruardy was crying with happiness as his mother gathered him in her arms.

"You have come back, Mama," he said.

"Yes, my son, we will be taking you back with us."

"Can Lindsay come too?"

"Not this time, my son."

Ruardy's bottom lip dropped in disappointment.

"Now, now, my son! Lindsay can come next year," said Roddy. "I believe you are making good progress with your music. Now, come and play for us."

"Yes, Papa."

Christina and Roddy exchanged looks of satisfaction as he played. When he had finished, Roddy patted him fondly and the others clapped. He clambered off the stool.

"It is a pity we have to leave when he is doing so well," said Christina.

"Have you really to take him back with you? Lindsay is so fond of him. He will be quite lost when you go," ventured Elizabeth.

"Yes, yes, Elizabeth dear, especially now you are pregnant again, I cannot leave you with two rascals like these to contend with, no matter how good the ayah is."

"Please let me know in good time when baby is due. I want to be here with you," said Christina, looking at Elizabeth with concern.

"I should love that, if you are sure it won't inconvenience you."

"My dear, of course not."

"I hope Elizabeth will keep well," sighed Roddy. "I worry so much about her."

They were on their way to Roddy's new posting.

"She will be all right." Christina tried to ease his troubled mind.

"But she is so frail, and this climate, as you see, does not suit her. If only she could return home to be with Mama."

"I daresay she wishes that also, but she will never return unless Craig can return to Glencree. That peevish old father of his is, seemingly, never going to change his mind in spite of having a lovely grandson. I shall come and stay as long as she needs me."

Ruardy, restless in Roddy's arms, whimpered, "Is it much further, Papa? I am so tired."

"No, my son, we are almost there."

Lindsay fretted and fumed for days after they left. "Why is Ruardy always going away and seeing new places? Why can't Uncle Roddy get a job like Papa," he demanded, stamping his feet. "Then he could stay here with me."

"Well, my son, Aunt Christina will be returning soon, and maybe she will bring Ruardy with her."

"I hope she does," he sighed.

CHAPTER 212

In February the following year a beautiful baby girl arrived to make Craig's and Elizabeth's joy complete. Christina arrived the following day.

"My dear Elizabeth, I am so sorry I was not here at her birth as I expected."

"Well," said Craig, "you are here now. She arrived earlier than expected."

"Where is Ruardy?" Lindsay demanded as soon as he saw Christina.

"He is at school. Roddy and his ayah are taking care of him. I promise I will bring him next time I come."

Lindsay's excitement at the arrival of his baby sister eased his disappointment.

"Come and see my baby," he said, taking her by the hand as soon as she took off her coat. "Ruardy hasn't got a new baby sister has he?"

"No, my son, you are a very lucky boy."

Christina was glad to see Margot was with Elizabeth. Craig cradled the baby in his arms, lost in admiration.

"See, Christina," he said as she bent over to peer at the baby. "Isn't she just too beautiful and perfect? She's just like her beautiful mother – look at her eyes! Don't you think so?"

Margot and Christina smiled at Elizabeth who was resting back on her pillow.

"Well, I must admit," said Margot, "they are not the same blue as her mother's, and they're not as dark as Craig's; they're somewhere in between. It's hard to say whose eyes they are most like."

They peered closer.

"They are violet," said Craig, "just like the heather."

The women exchanged glances and smiled.

"These men!" Margot sighed. She knew that if Craig said her eyes were violet they were violet and nothing or no one would change his mind. 'How like his father he is,' she thought.

"As they are violet, like the heather of home, that is what she will be called. Do you agree my darling?" Craig called to Elizabeth, who sat up in bed watching the delight on all their faces.

"Yes, I agree."

"Agreed, my son?" Craig said to Lindsay, who stood beside the bed.

"Yes, Papa, it's a lovely name," he replied.

"That is settled then. Heather Isabelle Angeline Margot Martha McNair. Now no one is left out. Christina and Margot can be her godmothers and Roddy can be her godfather."

"Well, now all that is decided," said Elizabeth, "maybe you will hand her over to Christina so that she can have a proper look at her god-daughter."

"By all means," Craig said as he handed her over.

"Now come, Lindsay – we will go and leave the ladies to take care of your little sister. We will go and buy your mother some flowers."

Martha and Magnus's happiness knew no bounds when they received news from Roddy about their new granddaughter. Martha was delighted when she read the names.

"Fancy Master Craig insisting she should have my name as well as his mother's! What an honour, to be sure! How I wish we could see them all! I wonder if our dear laird could find it in his heart to ask them to return." She sighed.

"Well, he might one day," replied Magnus doubtfully as he continued to read on. "They are all well, Roddy says, so we must be thankful for that and hope the laird changes his mind."

Elena still made sure she was first to get the mail. She waited daily for the sight of Lawrie plodding up the long drive. As she sat one morning at breakfast with Bruce and Harriet, reading the letter she had just received, Harriet watched her cunningly out of the corner of her eye. Bruce was lost in thought in his lonely little world.

Suddenly Elena's face broke into a gleeful smile and she gave a gasp of delight. "Oh, the Good Lord be praised!" she exclaimed. "Thank goodness they are both well!" She clasped the letter to her bosom in ecstasy. Harriet was now more interested, though she viewed Elena with disdain.

"Well, dear brother, Bruce," Elena declared excitedly, "you are now the grandfather of a lovely baby girl. They have named her Heather Isabelle—"

Before she could mention the rest of the names, Bruce leaped up from the table in his usual frantic rage when he heard the name Isabelle.

"It's just as well they have preceded it with another name. There is only one Isabelle in this family, though she is no longer with us," he raged.

"More's the pity!" exclaimed Elena. "She would have loved to have her granddaughter named after her. Also, she would have demanded that they all come home to Glencree where they belong. She would have forgiven her son a long time ago."

"How many more times have I to tell you, Elena? I have no son, now or ever."
He stalked out, banging the door behind him.

Harriet had carried on eating her breakfast as the tirade continued. At last she spoke, her tone as usual was peeved and contemptuous.

"So," she exclaimed angrily, "I suppose you will go to visit them on the pretence of visiting the missions?"

"Yes, I most certainly will go. As soon as it is possible I shall be away."

Harriet looked at her angrily. "And who do you think is going to help me look after things here?" she said. "I am not as young or as strong as I used to be."

"Well, I may soon be too old to travel the long distances with Margot to the missions," retorted Elena; "therefore I must go whilst I am still able."

Elena had thought for some time that Harriet did not seem well.

"We shall have to employ more help from the village, as we did last time, but this time", she added firmly, "they will stay even when I return. I have told you repeatedly, Harriet, that you cannot carry on trying to do everything with so little help. This place is too vast. You must take heed of what I suggest. As you know, I have my work to do visiting the ex-servicemen in the village and the city."

"Yes," replied Harriet bitterly as she faced Elena, "that is work Craig should be doing instead of rushing so far away to marry that hussy."

Elena chose to ignore Harriet's contemptuous reference to Elizabeth.

"I have to link up with Margot's correspondence and get any help she needs for the overseas missions." She shrugged her shoulders, adding quite emphatically, "I have quite enough to do, so I will arrange for extra help at Glencree Castle when next I go to the village."

As she hastened out of the room, she thought, 'Little does Harriet know that I do more visiting than I need just to get away from Glencree Castle – her sharp tongue and Bruce's morbid silences and sudden rages.' When she reached her room, she gazed out from her window over the loch towards Magnus's cottage. 'I know Heather's grandparents will be delighted at the news,' she thought. 'If only Bruce and Harriet could be, what a happy house this would be!'

CHAPTER 213

Lindsay boasted to everyone he met about the beautiful baby sister he had.

"I wonder if he will love his sister as much as Roddy does you," said Craig to Elizabeth when they overheard his boast.

"I hope so; then I shall know she will always have a big brother to take care of her if ever we have to leave her in his care later – although I cannot see us ever going anywhere without our children."

The twins were now more grown-up and more motherly. Whenever they called they did their best to free Heather from her brother's control. When they took her for a walk in the park in her pram, he insisted they must walk with the ayah.

"No, we are too old to walk with an ayah. We would look silly."

"Well," he retorted angrily, "I am too old to walk with an ayah so I too will look silly."

"Very well," said Astrid trying to avoid an argument. "Come Clare – we will walk on either side of her pram."

Lindsay tried to push the ayah away and take hold of the handle.

"No, no, baba sahib," she said firmly, "I must hold the handle. Memsahib says so."

"Very well, if Mama says so," he said as he reluctantly let go. He grumbled sulkily as he trailed behind, kicking up the dust.

Elena, although glad to be leaving for India, still felt a sadness as she bade Harriet and Bruce farewell. No good wishes were forthcoming for anyone, apart from a simple greeting to be conveyed to Margot from Harriet.

'It's as if no other member of the family exists,' Elena thought with a sigh as she clambered into the boat Magnus was steadying.

Jamie, as always, waved her sadly away.

She was thankful her sea journey was at an end. She greeted Craig's family, who were waiting patiently for her on the quayside.

"Is Margot not here?" she asked, looking around.

"We will see her at home. She didn't get back from the mission in time," said Craig.

"My, my, Lindsay, what a big boy you have become since I saw you last!" Elena looked him up and down as she held him at arm's length. He tried to wriggle free when she hugged him. He felt he was getting far too old to be fussed over.

'How like his father at his age!' she thought as she released him.

"Come and see my new sister," he almost demanded when they reached home. He almost pulled her from the tonga in his impatience.

Margot was holding Heather when they arrived.

"Aunt Margot, please show Aunt Elena my new baby sister," said Lindsay.

"Isn't she adorable, Elena?" exclaimed Margot when she saw the look of admiration in Elena's eyes.

"Yes, she's a real beauty, just like her beautiful grandmother, Isabelle," said Elena. "And her other grandmother, Martha, and, of course, her lovely mother, Elizabeth," she added.

The three women stood gazing at Heather, who waved her chubby arms around.

"Well, that just about includes everyone but me," said Craig as he entered the room. "I did have something to do with her beauty," he said jokingly. "Don't you agree, Aunt Elena?"

"Only in a small way, my dear Craig. Lindsay has your likeness, and he is growing more like you as he gets older. This lovely girl is Elizabeth all over again."

"Yes, I agree she is like her beautiful mother."

Craig sat on the verandah a few nights later holding Heather and talking to Elena. "Did Papa say anything about her being named after Mama?"

"He was his usual surly self. He said it was just as well Isabelle wasn't her first name – not that he could have done anything about it if it was. Heather is a lovely name, and it must remind you so much of home." She sighed as she looked at his saddened countenance.

"He still has no forgiveness, even now he has grandchildren," Craig said. "I hoped they would have softened his heart a little towards us."

"Well, that hasn't happened as yet, my dear boy. Whether he will ever relent we shall have to wait and see."

"Yes, maybe in time he will wait to see his grandchildren, even if he won't see me. Maybe one day they will see Glencree in all its glory. That is my wish for them." He sighed deeply.

Elena reached out and clutched his hand. There was complete understanding between them.

"Well, my dear boy," she said, "I must retire and rise early for my visit to the missions with Margot and Martin."

They were all sad as they waved them off on the train next day.

"I do hope they are not away long. We want to see as much as we can of Elena before she sails for home," said Craig sadly as the train disappeared in the distance.

CHAPTER 214

Many weeks passed before their return. Elena found the trip very tiring.

"You must have a long rest now," said Elizabeth, looking at her with some concern.

Later, they sat on the verandah watching the children. "My, how quickly time flies!" said Elena. "The children are growing up so fast. What are you going to do about Lindsay's higher education, Craig? He will soon be too old for his present school."

"He will be all right for a year or two yet, but we keep putting off discussing it time and time again, don't we, dear?" he said, looking across at Elizabeth.

"I daresay," continued Elena, "he will want to go when his friends go."

"Yes, I am afraid so, but it is a time we both dread," said Elizabeth with a sigh. Elena studied Lindsay closely as the days passed. She noticed how determined he was, so like his father and grandfather. Often there was a lost look on his face, as if he were puzzling about things far away. He asked her question after question about the big castle she had come from and his grandfather who lived there.

"Why doesn't he come and see us, like you do, and why cannot we go and see him?" he demanded one day. "Ruardy has been to see grandfather and grandmother who live beside the loch. Why? Why?"

Craig would quickly turn the conversation whenever this subject reared its head.

"Now, my son, you go along now," he said. "Aunt Elena is very tired."

"Very well, Papa," Lindsay replied before he hurried from the room, waving as he went.

"He will have to be told one day, Craig."

"Yes, when he is older and can fully understand." Craig sighed.

"Well, I don't think that time is too far away," said Elena.

They all agreed there was something of Bruce in him: his straight, ramrod stance as he stressed a point; his direct gaze into another person's eyes as he waited for an explanation or an answer to his incessant questioning; also his devil-may-care attitude to anything dangerous, especially if there was fun in it as well as an element of risk. This quality caused much alarm to those responsible for him. They tried to warn him of dangers, but he was afraid of nothing and no one and gave little thought to any repercussions which might follow. He was so wilful and mischievous that he was a torment to all around. He was always the instigator of mischief.

"How hot and humid it is!" sighed Elena as she fanned herself furiously.

"Yes, dear Aunt, it is always like this before the monsoon breaks," said Craig.

They were all seated on the verandah. The low, heavy, threatening clouds had hung over them for days with still no sign of the rain. Lindsay was sitting alongside them with his friend Karl; both were listless and complaining.

"Munilal," called Lindsay.

"Yes, sahib," said the servant as he handed Lindsay another glass of iced lemon juice.

"How much longer, Munilal?"

"How much longer what, sahib?" he queried, knowing full well what Lindsay meant. "Not long now, sahib, not long." He smiled.

"But you told us that some days ago," rejoined Karl, "and still the rain hasn't come. When? When, Munilal?"

"Bearer, please bring everyone more cold drinks," said Craig.

"Yes, sahib," Munilal replied as he hurried away.

"I have never drunk so much in all my life," said Elena. "No amount seems to quench my thirst."

The bearer returned with more ice, and he put some in each glass. He was not surprised when Lindsay held out his hand for more.

Suddenly Karl let out a shriek of dismay: "Oh, you terror, Lindsay!"

Elena looked up, startled. She looked at Lindsay disapprovingly, then smiled.

"Whatever is the matter?" exclaimed Elizabeth as she rushed on to the verandah. "Lindsay," she demanded, "will you never stop being such a torment. He is just like his father – always up to some prank."

"It is only ice, Mama. Karl was complaining about the heat so I put some down his back to cool him off."

"Wait till I catch you unawares, my friend," Karl retorted.

He ran into the garden to escape from Lindsay, but his friend followed him, meaning to do more mischief. Suddenly Lindsay yelled out as a huge raindrop fell down his neck. At first he thought Karl was retaliating, but then a torrent of rain fell, drenching them in seconds. They both dragged off their shirts and started to do a Highland fling, shouting, "Och aye! Och aye!" The rain by now was splashing to their knees.

Elena, Elizabeth and Craig, holding Heather by the hand, stood on the steps laughing gaily. They were soon wet through.

"Me go too!" cried Heather. "Me go too!" she demanded.

Lindsay grabbed her and danced her round and round.

"Now that is enough, Lindsay," said Craig. "Come in at once and change your clothes."

"Very well, Papa," said Lindsay. "Heather, you go to the ayah." (The ayah had been standing watching them.)

"Come, missy baba," the ayah said as she reached to pick Heather up.

"Well, Aunt Elena, how did you like my Highland fling?" asked Lindsay.

"It was very good, my fine young man," she replied as she hugged him and looked into his laughing eyes. "But", she smilingly remonstrated, "you must not let anyone in Scotland see you doing it like that, must he, Craig?"

"Certainly not. He has a lot to learn."

"I hope the heavy rain does not cause too many floods this year," sighed Elizabeth. "It always leaves so many people homeless and so many children are orphaned."

"How dreadful it is for them to suffer so!" sighed Elena. "Margot has often said how much busier the missions are when the orphans arrive. That is why it is so important that the missions carry on."

Lindsay rushed to the bearer.

"You were right, Munilal," he said.

"Yes, Lindsay, sahib, I told you the rains would come soon."

"Come, my son – we must all go and change for dinner," said Elizabeth.

"But, Mama," Lindsay cried, "it is so much cooler in the rain."

"I know, my son, but you must come inside now."

"Very well, Mama. Goodbye, Karl."

CHAPTER 215

As they sat having coffee on the verandah after dinner, Elena on opening her evening bag, gave a gasp of dismay.

"Oh, my dears, how forgetful of me! I had completely forgotten it."

Craig and Elizabeth looked at her with amazement as she pulled out a thick envelope and withdrew a photograph.

"It is a photograph of your father," she said. "It was taken on his birthday, but he doesn't know I had this extra copy made for you."

Craig stared at it in disbelief.

"How white his hair is now and how sad he looks!" he exclaimed. He couldn't help but feel a twinge of pity as he stared at the picture.

"Yes," said Elena, "his smile left him the day your mother died. It returned when you came back from the war, but alas! It went never to return after you left."

"Poor Papa! Why can't he accept things as they are and take us back as a family? Then all would be well," he said sadly. "He couldn't help but fall in love with his beautiful granddaughter and he would be so proud of his grandson."

"Well, my dear boy," Elena said sadly, "I am afraid that may never happen, more's the pity! He grows more bitter every day."

Craig sighed deeply.

"Will you keep it, Craig dear," she asked tentatively, "or should I take it back?"

"No, no, I will keep it. My children must be told about their grandfather in Glencree. I don't want them to grow up feeling too badly about him. Maybe one day he will send for us. I just long for that day. Do you think it ever will happen?"

"Maybe, in time, my dear boy, maybe in time." Elena sighed as she recalled his raging tirades.

Suddenly Craig rose to his feet.

"Excuse me," he said. "I must get some cool air now the rains have come." The photograph had disturbed him greatly.

Elizabeth watched him sadly as he left the room. Lindsay, who was sitting reading a book, looked up as his father departed.

"Where is Papa going, and why does he look so sad?" he asked with a puzzled look on his usually happy face.

"Only into the garden, my son," said Elizabeth.

"Shall I go to keep him company?"

"No, not just now, Lindsay."

He looked at his mother questioningly, and he was just going to ask her why when Elena called to him.

"Come here, my son, and look at this photo. It is of your grandfather."

"Oh, the one who lives in the big castle in Scotland?"

"Yes."

Lindsay studied it for a long time. He looked in awe at the tall, handsome, grey-haired man in full Highland dress.

"His tartan is just like Papa's and mine," he exclaimed in disbelief.

"Well, of course, my son: it is your clan tartan."

"He also has a dagger down his sock, just like Papa."

"Of course, my son, but the correct name for the dagger, as you call it, is a skean-dhu."

"My, that is a strange name! Why has he such a stern face? Why isn't he smiling? Mama says we must always smile; then people will smile back; then everyone is happy."

"You have a very wise mother. Smile we must."

"I don't like that beard and moustache either," he said with a frown, "but I think I should like to see him soon. Can we, Mama?"

"Well, not soon, but maybe one day." She sighed.

"But Ruardy has seen my other grandparents, so why can't I?" he demanded, stamping his foot in frustration.

Elizabeth looked at Elena. She was at a loss for words.

"Now, you go to bed, my son. It is late."

"Very well, Mama."

He kissed them both and bade them goodnight.

"I will retire also, Elizabeth," said Elena.

She rose to go, and kissed Elizabeth before she left.

"Goodnight, my dear," Elizabeth said. "I will go and see if Craig is all right."

She joined him in the garden, where he stood gazing into the night. She slipped her arm through his and he put his arms round her and pulled her close.

"Try, my darling, not to think too harshly of your father," she said. "He will send for us one day, you'll see."

"Well, my darling," he replied, "if you have hope, I must have hope also." He turned her towards him and kissed her tenderly. "Now come, my love – it is too cold in this night air since the rains came."

"Yes, my dear. Everyone else has now retired, and we too must bid goodnight to the night."

CHAPTER 216

Elena was most distressed on her return from the missions to find Craig very ill again with malaria. The house was so silent, whereas before it had always rang with laughter. The bearers, who always walked so softly and stealthily, were extra-silent. They constantly put their fingers to their lips to remind the children to be quiet. Davinia called daily to see what help she could give.

"We have just returned in time," Elena remarked to Margot. "As you know, dear, I was considering returning home after this trip, but I cannot possibly go now. I will write to Harriet and tell her I have been delayed. She won't be pleased, but I won't tell her the reason."

The ayah began taking longer walks home after meeting Heather from the kindergarten, but Lindsay rushed home as fast as he could from school. He was eager to reach his father. The two were almost inseparable, and they were growing closer day by day.

Elizabeth, near to distraction, sat by Craig's side as his nurses came and went. The bearer asked her often, "Can I get anything for the sahib?"

Elizabeth shook her head. "No, thank you, Damodar. The sahib might want something and you may not understand."

"I can call you, memsahib, if the sahib needs you."

"The sahib always needs me. I will stay."

Elena often scolded Elizabeth for not eating and resting enough, but to no avail.

"No, dear Aunt Elena," she said. "Please just see if the children are all right."

Elena shook her head in despair as she sat looking at Elizabeth and Craig.

One day Craig called out in his delirium, "Papa, Papa, Mama is in the water! She is in the water!" The cries were those of a child, faint and weak. Then there was a strange foreboding silence, followed by a cry louder than before. "The guns! The guns! Will they never stop? Sergeant, Sergeant, where are my men? Where are my men? For God's sake, answer me!" He screamed, then there was silence. He grasped the bedclothes, wet with sweat. Now and again he opened his eyes and stared at Elizabeth. He did not know her, but he called her name softly: "Angel, my darling angel, where are you?"

Elizabeth grasped his hand firmly.

"I am here, my darling," she said. "I am always here."

Lindsay crept silently to her side and she took his hand in hers.

"How is Papa today, Mama?" he whispered.

"He is getting better every day, my son."

"When will he be well enough to come and play and go fishing again?"

"Very soon now, very soon. Now go and play."

She turned to watch him go and saw the ayah standing at the door with Heather.

"Papa, Papa," Heather called to him.

He turned his head and raised his hand to her.

"Come, my darling, come," he said feebly.

Elizabeth lifted her up to sit on the side of his bed, just as Elena entered the room.

"Now the worst is over. Every day he will be better than the day before," she said.

"Dear Aunt Elena!" Craig exclaimed, "I thought you would have been back home."

"No, my dear boy, I decided to stay until you were well again," Elena replied.

"How long has he been having these attacks, Elizabeth?" asked Elena one day as Craig, now almost fully recovered, sat on the verandah out of earshot.

"For several years now. Some of them are very slight, but this latest attack was one of the worst. Each one seems to leave him so much weaker."

"It is this climate, dear. It doesn't suit either of you." Elena looked at Craig as he sat holding Heather. "How I wish Bruce would send for all of you!" she said with a sigh.

CHAPTER 217

"There's a letter for you, Aunt Elena," said Elizabeth as she handed an envelope to her one morning at breakfast.

"It is from Harriet," said Elena. "I wonder what she has to say. It is not often she writes to me when I am staying with you."

Craig noticed a look of disbelief and anxiety cross her face as she read the letter.

"My dears," she exclaimed, "I must return at once! It is Bruce."

"Father's not dead, is he?" Craig called out in alarm.

"No, no, my boy, but he has suffered a stroke. He is now over the worst, but he is paralysed down one side."

"Oh no!" exclaimed Craig in disbelief. "Surely that cannot be."

" 'And now,' Harriet continues, 'he will have to spend the rest of his life in a wheelchair.' "

Craig and Elena looked at each other in consternation.

"What is it, dear?" exclaimed Elizabeth on hearing their cries of dismay.

"It is Papa. He's had a stroke. It would have been better if he had died. He will never get used to being in a wheelchair for the rest of his life," said Craig. "Poor, poor, Papa!" Craig sighed heavily.

" 'I suggested', Harriet goes on to say, 'that, as now he cannot manage the estate, he could send for Craig, but he is more adamant than ever – if that were possible.' "

Elena looked at Craig, as if to say, "I will get him to change his mind when I return – you wait and see, my boy."

"Well, Papa knows I will never return, no matter what the circumstances, until he accepts my wife, and that he will never do," Craig said.

"We will see, my boy. Now, I must get ready to return."

When she received the news from Elena, Margot said "I am not surprised he hasn't relented. I remember his tirades and fist-banging, and his furious reaction whenever anything or anyone caused him displeasure. I will get Stephen to sort out your travel arrangements for you, Elena."

"Thank you, Margot. That will be such a help. Now I must hasten back to Craig. He is taking it rather badly and he is still not fully fit."

"Will we ever see you over here again?" Craig asked her as she prepared to leave.

"I don't think so, my dear boy, especially with all the extra work Harriet and I will have looking after your father. If only he wasn't so proud and headstrong! If only he would admit he needs your help! If only he would accept you back as his son – his rightful heir. It is your rightful place, Glencree." She sighed. "You would soon regain your health if you were back once more amongst the mountains and glens, with the cool, fresh mountain air in your lungs, instead of this terrible dust and heat."

"Never mind, Aunt Elena! You have always done your utmost to make Papa see sense, but perhaps it is not to be," he answered sadly as he gazed out of the window at Lindsay and Heather playing ball with Elizabeth.

Elena fastened the last clasp on her case, came over to him, put her arms round his shoulders and ruffled his hair.

"It will happen one day, my dear boy. It will – you wait and see."

"I hope so, Aunt Elena." He sighed as he reached up to clasp her arm. "You know how I long for that day."

"As do we all at Glencree."

They said their goodbyes at the quayside with heavy hearts, and Elena clung to them a long time.

Lindsay, as usual, was almost crying as he called after her, "Please take us with you. Please! You know Papa wants to come home. Why can't we come? Why? Why?"

Elizabeth sprang to his side. "There, there, my son! We will go one day – you will see."

Elena kissed Margot and Davinia and the twins goodbye.

"Write as soon as you can, Elena," said Margot.

"And you also, Margot," Elena replied. "Please write often of Craig and the family. I can see he is still not well."

"I will, I will," she called as Elena boarded the ship.

They waved until the ship was out of sight.

CHAPTER 218

Astrid and Clare were as physically alike as ever. Both were tall and slender, their copper-red hair was worn in long plaits under their school hats; their green eyes viewed the grown-up world with a wonder reserved for pretty young girls entering womanhood. Astrid viewed it with a seriousness beyond her young years; but Clare's green eyes flashed mischief. Her glance darted here, there and everywhere to avoid missing a single occasion where fun and frolic could abound.

"Mama, Mama," Clare cried excitedly one day. She rushed ahead of Astrid into her mother's outstretched arms as she greeted them from their weekly boarding school. Stephen had insisted on them being weekly boarders, much to Clare's chagrin.

"Why weekly, Papa?" she asked. "It's not too far away. We could be day pupils."

"I said weekly boarders, my girl, and that is final," Stephen said.

With a toss of her copper plaits, Clare went to sulk in her room.

Davinia and Stephen decided it was for the best so that the girls would not feel it too much of a wrench when the time came for them to go to a finishing school abroad.

"Clare", Stephen declared time and time again, "will certainly need a finishing school. She has to learn more about decorum before she comes of age."

"Of course," Davinia added, "she most certainly will need to know how to behave when she is presented at court and attends the London Season. I know it is a long way off but time passes so quickly." She sighed.

"Why all the excitement, Clare?" Davinia asked as she walked arm in arm with both girls up the steps of the verandah at the end of another boring week at school for Clare. "Come and sit down and tell me what all the excitement is about, Clare."

Astrid sat down and asked the bearer to bring them iced lime juice. She sipped hers slowly. Davinia looked at Clare with dismay as she picked up a light bamboo chair and waltzed along the verandah humming a tune. Was it 'The Blue Danube' or was it 'The Tales from the Vienna Woods'? Neither her mother or Astrid could be sure.

"Oh, do come and sit down, my child," Davinia said.

"But, Mama, I am not a child," she was quick to remind her.

"Well, whatever you are, dear daughter, tell me what all this excitement is about."

"Well, Mama," explained Astrid, "there is going to be a dance at school and, as we are now old enough, we can attend. As you see, it has quite gone to Clare's head."

"The boys from the boys' college are invited too," said Clare with delight.

"Well, you will be well chaperoned," declared their mother, "so I daresay your father will let you attend."

At this remark, Clare stopped dancing. Not for a moment had she given a thought to them being chaperoned. She pulled a wry face in disbelief (making sure her mother didn't see her) and flopped into the chair next to Astrid.

"You seem to have suddenly lost all your enthusiasm, my child. Why so quiet?"

"Well, I was just thinking, Mama: will we be able to have new ball gowns, as it is our very first dance."

"Of course, my child. I will tell the durzi to call tomorrow. Tonight we will spend the evening looking through the latest magazines, which have just arrived."

"Oh, do let us see them, Mama!" Clare exclaimed gleefully.

"Not now. You must first go along to your music lesson with Elizabeth and, on your way back, call and see Grandmama. She, too, will have received her catalogues, so bring them with you. Tomorrow we can go to the bazaar and choose the material. There will be some lovely sari lengths to choose from."

Clare was worse than ever at her music lesson.

"Why are your thoughts wandering so, Clare?" Elizabeth reprimanded her in disbelief at the mistakes she was making.

"Well, I am so sorry to be so inattentive tonight, but I am too excited for words. We are going to our very first dance at school, and Mama has said we can have new ball gowns. Tomorrow we are going to choose the material."

"How wonderful for you! And how pretty you will look!" Suddenly, Elizabeth's thoughts were back at Glencree in the small dressmaker's shop where she had her own very first ball gown altered. She shuddered as she remembered the mocking voices of the 'jewel' girls: "Fancy! Fancy! A second-hand cut-me-down dress for a first ball gown." She could still hear their shrieks of laughter.

"Do you remember your first ball gown, Elizabeth?" asked Astrid, breaking in on her thoughts.

"Yes, dear, but it is so long ago that I have almost forgotten it."

To think that her Davinia's altered dress was her first ball gown!

The twins bade Elizabeth goodbye and raced off to their grandmother's to pick up the catalogues.

They could hardly wait for dinner to finish that night. Their mother had never tut-tutted as much; she vetoed design after design suggested by Clare. In the past, the two girls had always had identical dresses, but this time Clare was determined to be different.

"Mama, for my very first ball gown I am not going to have one like Astrid. I am grown-up now, and I want my own design."

"Well," exclaimed her exasperated mother, "Clare, you now have to choose one out of the four I have ticked off! The rest are most unsuitable. They are far too revealing." She bade the twins goodnight and went to join their father on the verandah.

"Goodnight, Papa and Mama," the twins called as they wended their way to their room.

"Too revealing! Too, too revealing!" Clare exclaimed in mock displeasure. "When I get older, I shall have the most daring and revealing dress I can find. Just you wait and see if I don't. How can young men get interested in us if they can't see what we look like?" she exclaimed peevishly as she studied and restudied the four designs her mother had ticked off. "I don't like any of these!" she exclaimed, and she threw the book to the foot of her bed.

Astrid looked at her in dismay. "I like the second one in the magazine – and anyway, I don't want young men staring at me."

"Well, I do," said Clare, "and when I am older I shall make sure they do."

"Oh, go to sleep," Astrid demanded. "Go to sleep."

The durzi arrived at last with their finished dresses.

Clare's was a brilliant green with deep bands of silver braid round the hem and on each frill. She had had the décolleté neckline cut as low as she dared, but her mother had made the durzi put an extra frill round it. Clare decided she would take the frill off once they were back in college, but this information she wisely kept to herself. She knew she could always tack it back on if the need arose.

Astrid had settled for white, almost the same design as Clare's but trimmed with small green bows and with a much higher neckline. Their dolly bags, gloves and shoes (handmade by a Chinese shoemaker) all matched to perfection.

They paraded proudly in front of their parents in their dresses before finally packing them ready to return to college.

Their father gave a sigh as they left the next day.

"How beautiful they looked in their dresses, Stephen!" said Davinia.

"Yes, my dear, they did," he replied. " I guess this is when our worries really commence – especially with Clare. She is so self-willed and rebellious. She will always need more chaperoning than dear Astrid."

"Yes, and they are growing up so quickly," Davinia said with a sigh.

At last their dresses were hanging in their wardrobes in their shared room at college. Clare could talk of nothing else but the forthcoming ball. She paid no heed to her lessons, and her teachers were quite exasperated by her inattention.

CHAPTER 219

At last the day of the dance dawned and Clare was more excited than ever. Each lesson during the day had seemed to her more tedious than the last. When she leaned over her desk to speak to Gabrielle Saunders, the maths mistress decided she had had enough of her inattention; she had already warned her once.

"Maybe you know the answer to my last question, Miss Stewart!" she exclaimed angrily.

At the sound of her name, Clare looked up startled, as did Astrid.

"Not you, Astrid, I am referring to Clare. Tonight you will stay behind when the others have left and write out a hundred times, 'I, Miss Clare Stewart, must not talk in class'."

Clare looked at the teacher in dismay, as did Astrid and the rest of the class. "She will miss the dance," whispered Phoebe Montgomery to Maud Barlow, who was sitting next to her.

"Maybe, Phoebe, you would like to keep her company?" Miss Cowburn, the mistress, called to her.

"No, no, Miss," Phoebe replied in alarm.

"Then be silent, girl, or you will. The class is now dismissed except for Miss Clare Stewart."

Clare watched in anger as one by one the other girls left the room. Astrid was reluctant to leave her sister.

"Hurry along, Astrid," Miss Cowburn called to her as she hesitated at the classroom door.

Miss Cowburn made sure that Clare stayed behind; then she pulled the door to as she went.

Clare bit her lip in anger and frustration. She was almost on the verge of tears with disappointment as she looked at the closed door. She took a page of notepaper from the pile the mistress had left on her desk, dipped her pen angrily in the inkwell and started to write. A huge blot fell on the page.

As she sat scribbling away she suddenly decided she had had enough.

"I am not going to sit here any longer writing these stupid lines," she declared. She put her pen back in the ridge of the desk and sat planning what to do. "I am not going to sit here while everyone else is getting ready for the dance. I am not, I am not!" she fumed. Then her face lit up as a plan evolved in her mind. "Yes, yes, that's what I'll do," she muttered aloud. She hastily reached for another sheet of paper and dipped her pen hurriedly in the ink. She scraped off the excess ink and started to write.

Just then the door opened and Miss Cowburn peered in on her way from the teachers' common room. She viewed the bent head of Clare with satisfaction.

"I shall expect those hundred lines on my desk in the morning, Miss Stewart," she said before she closed the door.

Clare looked up from the paper and glared disdainfully after Miss Cowburn's disappearing figure. She put out her tongue as her footsteps disappeared down the corridor.

"I am going to the dance and I am going to get ready this very minute," she declared. She rose to her feet, put her pen in the ridge of the desk and glanced at the paper. On it she had written, 'You, Miss Cowburn, can write the hundred lines yourself, you old cow. I am NOT coming back to your school ever again.'

She hastened towards the door, anxious to get to her room before Miss Cowburn returned. She peered out and, seeing no one around, closed the door behind her and raced off down the long corridor. She ran across the quadrangle, then glanced furtively up and down before running across the huge lawn into the shadows of the Residents Hall. She raced up the long winding staircase, threw open the door of her room and flung herself on Astrid's bed exhausted. She slipped off her shoes, and at the same time she called out to Astrid: "Are you nearly ready?"

"Yes," Astrid replied from the small anteroom. "My word, how quickly you have done your lines tonight!"

"Well, I am getting to be a past master at them. I do more than anyone else in this school."

"Even so, you have never done them as quickly as this before. Did Miss Cowburn reduce them, knowing you were going to the ball?"

"No, she did not, the mean old cow!" Clare exclaimed angrily.

"Clare dear, you must not say such things. You know Mama and Papa wouldn't like it."

"Well, that is what she is, in my opinion," Clare said with a pout. "I am not going to stay in this school any longer."

"Oh, of course you are. You are just feeling angry at present. You will feel much better in the morning – especially after the dance," said Astrid.

Suddenly a thought struck Clare: "Do you think Miss Cowburn will be at the dance?" she asked anxiously.

"No, of course not. You know how old-fashioned she is. She doesn't approve of these dances being held – did you not know that? Why do you ask?"

"Oh, no reason. I just know I shall enjoy it much more if she is not there." Not for one moment did she consider letting Astrid know what she had done.

"Now, hurry and bathe and change into your lovely new ball gown or we will be late," said Astrid as she looked at her watch. "Oh, drat! It looks as though we shall be late."

Clare hurriedly did as Astrid suggested.

"How do I look?" she asked as she stood in front of the mirror.

"Lovely, lovely! Now come – we must hurry."

Astrid looked Clare up and down again and noticed the alteration she had made to her dress.

"Your dress looks too low at the front," she said. "What have you done to it?"

"Oh, that! I took off that silly extra frill that Mama made the durzi put on."

"But Mama will be very angry if she ever finds out," said Astrid.

"Well, she won't ever find out unless you tell her. I shall tack it back on again after tonight," she said carelessly as she picked up her gloves and dolly bag and followed Astrid from the room.

CHAPTER 220

The dance was in full swing as they arrived. Clare looked furtively round the room, thankful to see that, of all the teachers that were chaperoning them, the one she dreaded to meet was not there.

"Thanks be to God!" she exclaimed.

"I am so glad to see you," said Phoebe. "I'm so glad you finished your lines in time."

"Thank you, Phoebe," Clare replied, and she hastened away before any further conversation on the matter could ensue.

"And where might you be hastening, Miss Clare?" exclaimed a voice behind her. "Please may I have the pleasure of this dance?"

"Oh, it's you, Roy. How nice of you to ask me!"

Of all the boys at the adjoining college, she liked Roy the best. She guessed he had been waiting for her to arrive. It was evident by the number of the boys who asked her to dance that she was the belle of the ball – and she knew it. As she danced by the raised dais, on which sat the principal of the school along with one or two teachers, she could feel all their eyes on her.

"Was that Miss Clare Stewart that passed?" said the principal to the teacher standing next to her.

"Yes, it most certainly was, and she is flirting with all the boys as usual."

"That dress has such a low décolleté. It's disgraceful – utterly. Most distasteful!" She kept repeating these words, and the rest of the assembled group agreed with every word and every tut-tut she uttered. She peered glaringly over the top of her pince-nez as Clare passed, time and time again, with a different partner for each dance. "And she is the daughter of a judge in the high court. Her mother should be quite ashamed of herself – allowing her daughter to appear so in public! Whatever is to become of a girl whose mother allows such conduct?"

"Her twin sister is just the opposite, as you can see," said Miss Shaw, a teacher who knew their mother well. "Astrid is sitting quietly in the corner in deep conversation with Roland Seddon, no doubt discussing art and music, which I know they are both very fond of. Her dress is most becoming; it has a higher neckline. I just cannot understand it."

Once again Clare was in the arms of Roy Liddell. She snuggled up close to him as he whispered in her ear.

"We could go outside for a breath of fresh air if we could escape the watchful eyes of all our chaperones," he whispered.

"Well, I dare if you dare," Clare replied, her eyes lighting up with mischief.

"Right then. I will wait for you under the trellis of the bougainvillea. Don't be long," he said.

"I won't."

She sped away towards the ladies room and glanced round several times as she proceeded down the long corridor. Then she slipped out through the side door and ran across the lawn. The chokidar was patrolling the grounds, and he looked up in alarm as she came towards him, but he had seen the young sahib's lighted cigarette as he stood under the trellis and he knew where she was heading.

"Roy, Roy," she gasped as she fell into his arms.

For the first time in her life, she felt a young man's strong arms around her and his light, but firm and passionate kiss on her lips. She responded, perhaps too willingly. Suddenly she felt his lips travelling down to the bare skin of – now she realised – her too low neckline. His arms gripped her waist tighter. 'Mama was right as always,' she thought as she tried to pull away from him.

"Clare, darling," he whispered as he slackened his hold, "I am sorry to behave so badly but I do love you and I may not see you when I leave college tomorrow. I am sailing soon for England to go to university."

She gave a sigh of disappointment. "But I shall be able to see you before you leave, won't I?" she asked.

"Maybe, but I live a long way from your home so I might only be able to write to you."

"Well, I don't suppose Papa would allow me to see you as I am so young, but he might allow me to write to you."

"Well, that would be something." He sighed as he kissed her again and again.

Suddenly she panicked as she thought of her father's wrath if he ever found out about her being kissed.

"Come, we must return," Clare said, and she pulled herself from his increasingly passionate embrace and ran as fast as she could back to the hall.

Roy was dismayed at this sudden change from her apparent desire to be kissed passionately. He leaned against the rose-covered archway and lit a cigarette. He saw the shaft of light from the hall disappear as she closed the door behind her, and he knew she had reached it safely.

"Ah, well," he said with a sigh, "there will be another day."

Clare rushed into the ladies' room quite breathless.

"Thank goodness, no one is here," she gasped. She bent down on the pretext of fastening her slipper, in case anyone entered and remarked on the blush on her cheeks. She hurried to the mirror and tidied her hair; then she tried to tug her décolleté neckline a little higher, but to no avail.

'How stupid I am!' she thought. 'Why did I do this to my lovely dress? I must fix it as soon as I can. I only hope Mama never finds out.'

She hastened quickly to Astrid's side. She was still in deep conversation with Roland Seddon.

"Wherever have you been?" Astrid demanded, after she had excused herself from her friend. "I have been looking for you. The boys kept coming to me asking where you were, as you had promised all of them dances."

"Well," she replied, hoping she sounded convincing, "I was too hot and tired with all the dancing, so I went outside for some fresh air. I was only just outside the door so I was quite safe."

"Well, you still look rather flushed. Miss Cowburn kept looking in my direction – I don't know why."

"So the old cow did come to the dance after all!" exclaimed Clare. "Well, she wouldn't know whether it was you or me. Now it is the last waltz and I have saved that for Roy," she said as she danced away in his arms.

Astrid took the floor with Roland – her conversational beau of the evening.

The dance was held in the main hall of the girls' college, and they were hastily chaperoned back to their rooms under the eagle eyes of the mistresses, after they had bid their partners goodnight.

Clare lay awake revelling in the memory of her first kisses. Her mind wandered back over the night's thrill – his strong arms around her and his kisses travelling down her neck towards her bosom. She knew she was developing well for her age – as was her sister – but she had to admit that, in spite of the thrill, she had been a little scared.

'It's just as well I ran away from him when I did,' she thought. Her thoughts shot back to earlier that evening and she wondered what the morning might bring. She dared not try to retrieve the paper she had left for Miss Cowburn. Besides, everywhere would be locked. 'I know I cannot face that woman,' she thought. Suddenly her thoughts were in a panic. 'I must run away, but where?' she asked herself.

She knew she dare not drop off to sleep, so she crept silently out of bed and put some of her clothes into the valise under her bed. She hesitated and held her breath as Astrid turned over, but she did not waken.

The dance was always held on the evening before the last day of term. The next day, everyone – including the girls who only went home at the end of term – would be leaving to catch their trains.

'I must get away before the first ones leave,' Clare thought.

Many of the girls had tongas ordered to arrive early, so Clare crept out and hailed the first one of these. "Hurry driver," she ordered.

"To the station, missy memsahib?" he asked in his broken English.

"No, I will tell you when I wish to alight. Make for the high court."

He looked at her with a puzzled frown on his face. 'It is so unlike a missy memsahib to be out alone,' he thought.

She tipped him generously and he salaamed her gratefully as she rushed away. Then he headed back to the college.

Thankfully no one was about the streets as yet, apart from an odd servant going to work. They all gave her curious looks but passed silently on.

Clare hastened towards home as fast as she could and entered the compound.

'Fortunately for me I am well hidden by these shrubs,' she thought.

She made her way to the servants' quarters and dashed into her ayah's room. The ayah was already astir and she screamed out when she saw Clare in the doorway. Clare put her fingers to her lips and bade her be quiet, but her ayah was in such a panic that she kept on beseeching her: "Missy baba Clare, Missy baba Clare, go home. Go home."

"No, I cannot go home yet. I must hide here with you," insisted Clare.

"No, no, Missy baba. Burra sahib will get very angry with me if he finds you here."

"No, he won't. I will tell him it's my fault."

"But, Missy Clare, he will come here looking for you. He knows how much I love you and Missy Astrid."

"Be quiet, woman!" Clare demanded. "No one will know I am here if you don't tell anyone."

She sat down on the small stool as the ayah cowered in a corner.

"Don't be afraid, Ayah. Try to get me a glass of milk without anyone seeing you, but water will do if the bearer is about. Be careful you are not caught."

The ayah crept out. She wended her way to the kitchen, thankful that no one else was astir. She pulled her sari closer about her and filled a tumbler with water. She decided she dare not risk the milk – the head bearer would be able to tell.

"Thank you, Ayah," said Clare gratefully. "Now hurry and put the tumbler back before the bearer finds out."

CHAPTER 221

Miss Cowburn stood transfixed as she read the message Clare had left on her desk. She stamped her foot in anger.

"I will speak to this madam at once," she fumed. She called for her servant to go and fetch Miss Clare Stewart to her at once.

"Well, where is she?" she demanded when the servant returned.

"She is not in her room and her closet is empty. Miss Astrid is crying because she doesn't know where she is. She said she wasn't there when she woke up."

"I will go to her room at once," Miss Cowburn declared, and she proceeded up the stairs. "Now then, Miss Stewart," she said when she arrived, "what is all this nonsense about? Where is Miss Clare?"

"She has run away and it is all your fault," Astrid sobbed. "She has! She has, and it is all your fault. Here is the note she left for me. I only found it a few moments ago."

"Where will she have gone?" demanded Miss Cowburn, even more angry after Astrid's outburst.

"I don't know," wailed Astrid. "She wouldn't dare go home."

"Well, that is where we are going first," Miss Cowburn said emphatically.

The rest of the girls were twittering amongst themselves in one another's rooms as most of them tried to finish their packing. Several peeked out of their rooms when they heard the heavy tread of Miss Cowburn. They all asked the same questions: "What is wrong? Where is Clare? Why is Astrid crying?" No one knew the answers but they all hoped they would get to know before they left.

"Come now, Astrid – we will go to see the principal. Meanwhile, a bearer can collect your things. Now, Bearer, take Miss Astrid's cases and call for a tonga."

The girls strained their necks from the windows and watched Miss Cowburn and Astrid clamber inside a tonga and speed away at a gallop.

"Now we will never know what's happened," moaned Phoebe to Celia Carstares.

"We will have to wait till we return next term," Celia said crossly.

Miss Cowburn sat stiffly and silently as they drove along. She was inwardly seething with anger at the note Clare had dared to leave on her desk.

'I shall certainly show her parents the note and tell them in no uncertain terms that, as the principal agrees, under no circumstances will Miss Clare be allowed back next term. However, my first concern must be to find the girl. It is not safe for young girls to be out alone,' she thought. If anything should happen to Clare it would reflect badly on the college. The girls in their care were normally chaperoned at all times. Their parents demanded it.

At last the tonga drew up outside the door and Davinia was most alarmed to see only Astrid and the teacher alight. She bade Miss Cowburn sit down.

"Astrid, go to your room at once," she said; then she told the bearer to serve tea.

She sat quietly but very alarmed as Miss Cowburn related the details.

"I shall leave this note she left me for your perusal," said Miss Cowburn as she got up to go. "If we hear anything at college about Miss Clare's whereabouts, we will let you know immediately."

"As we will you," Davinia replied. She was almost speechless with shock as she bade Miss Cowburn goodbye. She sat down for a few moments and tried to think where Clare might be. Then she hurried over to Margot.

"No, Davinia, she is not here. Try Elizabeth – you know how fond she is of her. Meanwhile, I will phone for Stephen to return home at once."

Elizabeth and Davinia conducted a thorough search of the house, and they asked the servants if they had seen anything of Miss Clare during the morning, but no one had seen her.

Davinia was beside herself with anxiety.

"My poor darling child! Wherever can she be?" she sobbed.

"Come," said Elizabeth, "maybe she has now arrived home."

Margot, Elizabeth and Davinia wended their way back to Davinia's house and waited until they heard Stephen arrive.

"Is there still no sign of her?" he asked as he rushed on to the verandah.

"No, not as yet," said Margot as she and Elizabeth prepared to leave. "Let us know the minute you hear news of her."

"Yes, of course, Margot," replied Stephen.

He sat down and read the note with dismay.

"I am not surprised she has run away, or that the college will not accept her back next term," he said angrily. Then he suddenly shot out of his chair. "I think I know where to find her," he said.

He bounded out of the house and raced down to the ayah's quarters, calling the bearer to accompany him.

The ayah was still beseeching Clare to return home, and Clare was still refusing.

"Your father will come here looking for you," the ayah said. "He knows how much I have loved you and Missy Astrid since you were born."

Suddenly they heard his heavy step approaching, and they heard him call the bearer.

The ayah rushed to cower in the corner when she heard Stephen ask the bearer to bring her out. The bearer called her name and told her in their native language to come out at once as the master sahib wished to speak to her.

She crept out reluctantly, pulling her sari over her face as she faced him, cringing with fear. Her large, dark eyes were almost popping out of her head. Stephen could tell by her silence and her frightened look that he was on the right track.

"Have you seen Miss Clare today?"

She made no answer.

"Answer me, woman," he demanded.

She tried to speak but words wouldn't come.

"I know you are one of the people she would run to, as she has always come to you after being chastised," he angrily continued. "Miss Clare must be found at once. If she is here, as I know she is, you must bring her out to me. Do you understand me, woman?"

Clare, listening inside, stood petrified. She had never heard her father speak so angrily before. He kept on and on at the ayah, getting more and more angry. At last, she could not stand her ayah's distress any longer, so she came out of the small room and faced her father.

"I am sorry, Ayah," she said. "Please forgive me for all the trouble I have caused you."

The ayah nodded her head and disappeared quickly into her room.

"Now, you go home," he ordered Clare, and he turned and followed her.

Her mother breathed a sigh of relief when she saw Clare, but she did not attempt to greet her.

Clare glanced at the table and saw the letter she had written. She started to tremble. The consequences of her conduct were at last dawning on her.

"Now, go to your room." Her father's voice boomed behind her. "I will deal with you in the morning."

"Where is Astrid, Mama?" Clare asked.

"In her room. She's too upset to eat or talk to anyone, so do not disturb her."

"Please, Mama, may I have a snack before I go?"

"No, you may not!" her father exclaimed. "You can go straight to your room this instant."

"But she won't have eaten all day," her mother said.

"Well, that is her own fault," he stormed. "Well, my girl," he boomed, "what have you to say for yourself? The principal will have only Astrid back next term – not you."

Clare looked at her father anxiously, and she gasped. Where would she go all by herself? She and Astrid had never been separated before. She pondered on her fate for a moment; then her courage returned.

"Well," she replied defiantly, "that woman has always hated me, and I don't care if she won't have me back at her stupid school."

"Well, maybe, my girl, you would like to be sent to Aunt Agatha in Scotland to continue your education." He knew that if anything would upset her defiance, it would be that statement. "I shall have no hesitation in sending you alone and leaving Astrid to finish her education here."

He saw her face go pale and her eyes started to fill with tears.

"Oh, Papa, you cannot do that. It isn't fair. You know Astrid cannot bear to be parted from me, nor I from her." She thought that if she made him realise that their separation would also punish Astrid, he might be a little more lenient.

"Well, my girl," he declared, quite unmoved by her plea not to be separated from her sister, "you leave me no alternative: I shall write to her today. You may go now."

He opened the drawer of his desk and took out a sheet of paper as she slowly turned and closed the door behind her.

Later, when she told Astrid what their father proposed to do, she was speechless with dismay.

"Oh, I must go and talk to Papa before he sends the letter," Astrid said. She hastened to the library and knocked timidly on the door.

"Come in!" her father called.

She held back for a moment, frightened at his tone of voice. Never before had she heard him so angry.

In his heart he knew who it was. She came and stood beside him.

"Papa, Papa," she pleaded, "please don't send Clare away. She was only talking in class, and Miss Cowburn had no right to make her stay behind and write all those lines and so make her miss the dance."

"No right? No right?" he exploded. "She had every right. Clare is not a child any longer – as she keeps reminding your mother and me – so she must act like the grown-up young lady she thinks she is."

"Please, Papa!" Astrid pleaded.

Of both his daughters, Astrid was the one that could touch his heart the most, and she knew it. "Please, Papa!"

She could see by his expression that she was not winning him over as she usually could.

"I shall run away also." She tried to threaten him. "I cannot live without Clare – you know that, Papa," she pleaded.

"Well, you might like to go with her to Aunt Agatha's."

Astrid gave a gasp of dismay. Her pleas had fallen on deaf ears. Her father knew how she hated it when they had visited Aunt Agatha, so she had not anticipated his suggestion that she could accompany Clare. 'Oh, how wrong I have been!' she thought.

Her father knew that this was the last thing she wanted. He sat looking at the sheet of paper before him, twisting his pen idly.

"Well, I will talk it over with your mother," he said. "Now, go and leave me in peace."

"Thank you, Papa," Astrid replied.

She noted before she turned to go from the room that he had closed his writing case and laid down his pen.

'Well,' she quickly surmised, 'I don't think he will be writing to her today.'

At dinner that evening they all ate very little and made no conversation.

As Stephen rose from the table he said, "I will see you both in the library."

Astrid and Clare rose and followed him meekly.

"Your mother and I had a long discussion this afternoon about your future education," he said, "and we have decided you both will . . . "

They waited with bated breath.

"Will what, Papa?" said Clare, anxious to learn their fate.

"You will both be sent . . . "

"He is purposely going slowly," she whispered to Astrid – a remark their father pretended not to hear. "Why doesn't he say it and have done with it?" Clare whispered to Astrid again as her anxiety grew.

"I have no alternative . . . " he continued even more slowly, "after the consultation with your dear mother, who, as you know, has been most distressed about this disgraceful escapade of yours, Clare . . . "

"Yes, Papa. I am deeply sorry for all the distress I have caused you and Mama and Astrid." Her head was bent with shame.

" . . . than to send you both away," he said resignedly.

They both looked at him in alarm.

He paused again. " . . . to the young ladies' boarding college in the hills. Your grandmama knows of one near one of the missions. Mama will be writing to the principal in a day or two."

The twins looked at each other with a sigh of relief.

'The Good Lord be praised! Not Aunt Agatha's!' thought Clare.

"It means you will only be home at the end of each term – not every weekend as you are now. I know your mother is going to miss you a great deal, as I am, but there is no other way."

"Oh, thank you, Papa!" exclaimed Clare. "Thank you, Papa!"

"Now go," he said, less brusquely, as he stood up to bid them goodnight.

They both flung their arms around him and kissed him on the cheek.

"Now go and say goodnight to your mother," he said.

"Goodnight, Papa," they called with their hands clasped together.

They rushed to their mother's side as she sat on the verandah looking out into the dark night.

"I am so sorry, Mama," said Clare, "for all the distress I have caused you and Papa."

"Well, it is all over now, my child," she answered. "You have learnt a very valuable lesson. You now understand what unpleasant consequences can follow such acts."

"Yes, Mama. I promise I will not do anything so foolish again."

Davinia kissed them both goodnight, noting the silence of Astrid, who she knew would miss home more than Clare.

They left, not exactly in high spirits, and went slowly to Astrid's room. Clare flung herself on to the bed.

"Well, it won't be too bad, and most of our friends will be coming next year."

"But some will have gone to England before we return, and we won't see them again," said Astrid, who started to weep silently into her handkerchief. "I am going to miss so many of my friends and Mama and Papa and Grandmama and Elizabeth and my music lessons, and I know I shall miss discussing music with Roland."

"Well, you will have music at the college where we are going."

"I know, I know," she cried, "but it won't be the same."

"Well, most of them will still be here when we return at the end of term," said Clare, trying to ease her sister's distress. At last she could see the significance of what she had done. She put a comforting arm round Astrid's shoulder. "I am so sorry, Astrid darling. Please say you forgive me."

Astrid bit her lip and tried to stem her tears.

"Of course I forgive you, Clare dear," she said. "We would be going somewhere at the end of next year anyway. We are just going that bit sooner and without our friends."

"Well, it is almost a year and a half sooner," Clare agreed.

Suddenly she remembered Roy – she wouldn't see him again either. He would be gone before they returned from their first term.

'I must see him,' she thought. 'I must think of a way to see him. That is another problem I have to overcome. Oh, why is life so complicated?' She sighed.

"I don't think I will bother growing up, after all," she said disconsolately as she sobbed into her pillow. "Oh, how I hate that Miss Cowburn – the old cow! It is because of her that I have got all these woes – the old cow!" she exclaimed angrily.

"Clare dear, don't let Mama hear you say things like that or we might still be sent to Aunt Agatha," Astrid said with a shudder.

The time for their departure arrived far too soon. Their farewell party was over. They stood forlornly on the platform as the train rushed in, and they climbed aboard to join other girls accompanied by a mistress.

Davinia cried into her handkerchief, repeating over and over again, "My two precious little girls!" and Stephen tried to comfort her and wondered if, after all, he had been a little too severe. The twins were weeping too, but he once again put on a stiff upper lip and called out to them as the train was pulling away, "Now, be good both of you – especially you Clare."

"Yes, we will."

"Yes, Papa, I will, I will," shouted Clare to reassure her parents.

When their train was out of sight, their mother broke into another flood of tears.

"Don't worry, my dear," said Stephen. "They will get there quite safely. Judge Lansdowne and his wife are travelling to their destination and the college will send an escort for them."

"I know. I know all that, my dear Stephen, but I shall miss them so. I have never been without them before."

"I know just how you feel, Davinia," said Margot, trying to comfort her. "I had to face a similar parting when you went away. Granted, you were a little older, but the girls will be well chaperoned, so don't worry, my dear."

Craig, Elizabeth, Lindsay and Heather were there too. Craig watched a long time after the train had gone. Suddenly Lindsay's hand was in his, and he looked down at him.

"Papa, why does everyone have to keep going away?" said Lindsay.

"Well, my son, one day you will have to go away too, to college and university to get your degrees. All boys and girls have to go away when they are older."

"Well, I don't want any degrees if it means I have to leave you and Mama and Heather."

"Well, it is a long way off yet, my son. Come – the others have all left now."

CHAPTER 222

Lindsay and his friends were growing up fast. Already some of his friends had been sent away to boarding colleges in the hills, and they were only home at the end of term. Their parents had sent them as soon as they could be admitted, hoping to curb their high spirits. However, Craig was reluctant to let Lindsay join them.

"You may go in a year or two, my son," he said. "You still have friends at the school where you are now. Your other friends will soon be home for the Christmas holiday."

"Yes," replied Lindsay, "I can hardly wait for them to arrive."

"Yes, I know you are impatient to see them again, my son. I hope that none of you get up to any of your old tricks; I don't suppose your friends from the hill colleges will have lost any of their old zest for mischief, in spite of their higher education."

"Well, they are all so young and full of life. It is understandable," said Elizabeth, who was sitting quietly beside them.

"I am glad Lindsay has so many friends. I alas! had hardly any," said Craig, "as my father would not allow me to go to boarding school."

"Why was that, Papa?"

"Well, he was very lonely when my dear mother died, and he wanted me beside him every minute of the day. I had a private tutor, which meant I could accompany my father on rides over the hills and glens when my lessons were over. I missed my friends, who went away to further their education, but I won't deny that to you, my son. Nevertheless, I dread the day you go, as I know your dear mother does."

Elizabeth looked up and smiled at them, nodding her head in agreement. "Yes, my son," she agreed, "it will come far too soon for us. As your father says, you may be able to join your friends at college late next year. We will see."

It was just before Christmas and Lindsay and his friends were plotting how they would spend their time.

"Well, we can go and sing and play carols to all we know. That will make a perfect start to the festive season," said Rory Wilde – a name which described him aptly and which he always lived up to.

They went out on several evenings, singing carols. Some dressed as Father Christmas, some as pirates and some as swashbuckling heroes. Their costumes were borrowed from the local repertory company. Their pockets bulged with the money they had been given, which they planned to donate to the mission.

Everyone they visited marvelled at their music. They invited the boys inside their homes for refreshments, but they always declined, saying they had to return home soon and that they had more calls to make. Not for one moment did they dare let it be known how they managed to play such delightful music.

It was the night before Christmas Eve and, for the last time, they went on their rounds, singing and playing carols. The last call of the evening was the home of Margot and Martin.

While they were singing, Stephen called to collect Clare and Astrid from Margot's house. He stopped for several minutes on the path to the house and listened intently to the boys' rendering. 'I must invite them inside for a warm drink before they return home,' he thought as he approached.

"Which one of you is playing the accompaniment to your singing tonight?" he asked.

"Lindsay is playing tonight," the others chorused. They all seemed reluctant to take the credit.

"Well, you played superbly, my boy. You have got your mother's gift for music. Now, you must come inside and play for us."

"Well, thank you, Judge Stewart, but we ought to be getting home soon. It is our last night and we have to hand in our collection at the mission," said Lindsay.

"Well, fortunately the Reverend Martin is here this evening so you can hand it to him."

The boys could not escape from the invitation. Stephen was looking at them with a puzzled expression. He could see no instruments. Lindsay felt his penetrating gaze and fidgeted uneasily. Suddenly the door opened and Davinia stood there.

"Do please come in," she begged. "We have enjoyed your music so much."

As Lindsay reached out to shake her hand, the cape he had over his suit fell to the floor and revealed a small gramophone strapped to his chest.

"Well, upon my word!" Stephen exploded in mirth. "Now, just watch me, Davinia," he said.

He proceeded to turn the handle and a lovely rendering of a carol burst forth, much to Lindsay's consternation.

"Well, sir," he said meekly, "I can see we are well and truly caught out by no other than the Judge himself."

"Yes, you are, my boys, but never mind this time! You must promise me that next year you will sing the carols yourselves."

"We promise," they chorused.

"Now, come inside and we will have a hot drink together. The girls are here from college and I know they will enjoy your company."

Clare greeted the boys enthusiastically and bade them sit next to her and Astrid. She asked the bearer to bring them some hot blackcurrant cordial.

"It is so nice to be home and to see you all again," said Clare. "The parties will be much more exciting now that we are all growing up, don't you agree, Astrid?"

"Well, I shall enjoy some, I daresay."

"Tell me, Lindsay, have you seen Roland Seddon? I have to return some sheet music to him," said Astrid.

"Well, I know he is back from college, but I haven't seen him."

"Well, I daresay I shall see him at one of the parties," she replied.

"Now, come, girls – it is getting late. We can see the boys home as we go," said Stephen.

"Here is the money we have collected for the mission, Reverend Martin," Lindsay said.

"My word, that is a good amount! You have worked very hard."

Stephen looked at the boys and smiled; then they all departed into the night.

CHAPTER 223

Much to Clare's delight, life was a constant round of parties and dances.

"You know, Astrid," she declared one day as they were preparing for another, "I don't mind growing up, after all. It is getting to be more exciting every day. I shall just hate it when we have to return to college." She pulled a long face at herself in the mirror. "Do hurry, Astrid, or we shall be late. It's so nice to meet all our old friends again."

"You mean meeting all your old boyfriends again," said Astrid knowingly. "Tell me, where did Roy Liddell get to? I haven't seen him around."

Clare blushed furiously as she thought of his passionate kisses the last time she had seen him and the way his hands had gripped her tiny waist. Oh, what a thrill it was! 'Does Astrid know where I was that night?' she wondered.

"He left for university in England shortly after we left for college," she replied. "He won't be back for years – if ever. I am not going to wait for him to return when there are so many other boys around just longing to escort me to dances. I know you are only interested in your Roland, but to me he is such a bore. All he wants to do is sit and talk about music."

"Well, I like him and I know he likes me. I am not interested in any of the other boys who spend their time ogling us."

"Well, I enjoy being ogled," said Clare. "Now do hurry – we are late."

Clare went dancing down the stairs, humming a favourite tune; Astrid following her resignedly at a more leisurely pace.

"Another new dress, I see," remarked Margot, who sat with Davinia in the lounge.

The twins stood in front of them waiting for their comments.

"Yes, you both look very pretty," said Davinia. "Now hurry – your tonga is waiting. Your father will escort you home." She did not miss seeing the pout of annoyance on Clare's face at her last remark.

"I am sure they will never settle back at school after all this gaiety – parties and dances and social visits to all their friends," remarked Davinia after the girls had left.

All their friends were anxious to know how they were liking the college, but Clare, as usual, put it in its worst possible light.

"I think Astrid is getting a little tired of the social merry-go-round," said Margot.

"Apart from their looks, they are so different."

"Yes, I agree," replied Davinia. "I just know Astrid would rather be back at college with her books and music. Thank goodness there is now only the Burns Night Ball; then they will be away."

"Their father is already complaining about the cost of all the new dresses they have had, and now Clare is trying to wheedle the cost of another one for Burns Night," said Davinia.

"I just know she will get one, and she will insist on Astrid having one also," said Margot with a smile. "They are young for such a short while. I remember how you used to be – and I myself – at their age."

"Only the other day they both went to a party in the afternoon and Clare requested permission to attend another one in the evening. Astrid, of course, didn't wish to go, but Clare insisted she could go alone. I agreed. I said, 'As long as you are well chaperoned it will be quite all right,' and what do you think she replied, Mama?"

"Well, something not quite the thing, I shouldn't wonder, knowing Clare as I do," said Margot.

"She said, in her most grown-up manner, her hand on her hip, as always, 'But, Mama, this is the twenties, not the Victorian era – did you not realise that?' "

"Well, that reply does not surprise me in the least," said Margot with a smile. "Besides, Clare is quite adept at losing any chaperone."

"Yes," agreed Davinia, "that is what I am afraid of. I could safely send Astrid and not worry about her being chaperoned – but my Clare!" She sighed despairingly. "I shall be more than glad when she is back in college; then she can be properly chaperoned by the mistresses there. I never thought I should see the day when I would be thankful they were back at college, but they are growing up so quickly it frightens me. My two little girls!" She tut-tutted.

"They are so pretty," said Margot.

"If only Clare was more demure and ladylike, like Astrid, I should not worry so, but Clare is always so indignant if her fun and freedom are curtailed."

"But they are young for such a short time. It is understandable," said Margot.

"Yes, I guess you are right, but it is a worry all the same. Thank goodness the Burns Night Ball is the last one before they return! Everyone we know will be there, so she won't get up to any mischief – hopefully."

CHAPTER 224

The Burns Night Ball – the ball of the year – was always something special, particularly for anyone with a spot of Scottish blood in them, and everyone came from miles around to join in the frantic fun.

"I see," remarked Margot when she and Martin called to pick up Davinia and Stephen, and she saw her two granddaughters, "I see you have wangled another new dress from your father."

"Yes, they have," Stephen said as he came into the room. "At least I shall be spared some expense when they return to college."

Clare playfully pulled a face at him before she kissed him.

"Oh, Papa," she said, "we haven't cost you much – have we, Astrid?"

"Well, we certainly won't need any more new dresses for a long time," Astrid replied.

"We will certainly need some for next winter's balls. We cannot wear this year's again. Whatever would our friends think?" Clare retorted.

In Craig's home there was just as much excitement. Heather was determined she was not going to sleep until she had seen her mother in her new ball gown.

"Well, here I am, my darling!" Elizabeth exclaimed as she entered the room. Her long white crinoline dress of pure Indian silk billowed around her like a cloud as she twirled round and round to amuse her small daughter. The tartan sash across her shoulder was a bright contrast.

Heather clapped her hands with glee.

"That is the tartan sash Aunt Elena brought you, isn't it, Mama?" asked Lindsay as he entered. "My, you look so beautiful!"

"Yes, it is the tartan, my son." She clasped him to her and kissed him lightly on the cheeks. "My, my, how tall you seem to be getting!" she said as she tipped back on her heels.

"My angel, how do you think I look in my new tartan?" demanded Craig as he entered. "Hasn't the tailor made it up superbly?" He twirled round and round, to the delight of Heather, who was still clapping her hands excitedly.

"It is you, my darling, that makes it look superb," Elizabeth agreed as she scanned him from top to toe. He was still as handsome, she thought, as the first night she had seen him in full tartan at Glencree, but he was so much thinner. She sighed. "Don't you think he looks splendid, my son?"

"I do," said Heather as her father leaned over to kiss her goodnight.

"You will be the most handsome couple, as always," said Lindsay with pride. "Papa, please show me again the new skean-dhu Aunt Elena brought. Will I have a skean-dhu one day?"

"You will, my son. I shall get you your very own with your initials carved on it." He withdrew the small knife from his sock, then replaced it carefully.

"How old were you, Papa, before Grandpapa bought you your first one?" he queried.

"I was just a little older than you are now," said Craig. 'Oh, why does he keep reminding me of my father?' he thought with a sigh.

"Come, my darling – we must be going. Carry on with your studies, my son, and take care of Heather with the ayah; and you, my darling Heather, will you be good for the ayah?"

"I will. I will, Papa," she replied.

Her mother pulled her bedclothes a little higher. "Yes, be good for the ayah," she said. "It is your birthday soon so I shall expect a good report from the ayah when we return. Now go to sleep." Elizabeth bent down and kissed Heather goodnight.

"Mama," she whispered, "please show me the pretty ring again that Aunt Elena brought you."

Her mother held out her hand and Heather stroked the ring lovingly.

"Will it be mine one day," she asked excitedly, "like Papa's skean-dhu will be Lindsay's?"

"No, my darling, not this one. Papa and I will buy you your very own ring when you are a little older."

"But why not this one? I love it so."

"I know, my darling, but this one is special. Strictly speaking it should only be worn by the Mistress of Glencree Castle. Now, we must go and you must go to sleep. See that she does, Ayah."

"Yes, memsahib."

"Just about everyone is here now," said Margot to Davinia when Craig and Elizabeth arrived.

"I see the twins are already on the dance floor," said Elizabeth as she watched them dance by.

The twins waved a welcome to them all.

"They have not stopped dancing since we arrived," said Margot. "Oh, to be young again!" She sighed, remembering her own young days.

"How handsome and distinguished Craig looks tonight, and Elizabeth as always is the loveliest lady on the floor! How happy they are!" said Davinia, all heads turning to watch them as they danced by.

CHAPTER 225

After they left, Heather lay quietly thinking, then she suddenly sat up looking perplexed.

"Ayah, Ayah," she called softly.

"What is it, Missy baba?" the ayah said as she hurried to Heather's side.

"I want to see which dress I shall be wearing for my birthday party."

The ayah opened the doors of her huge wardrobe, which was full to overflowing with pretty dresses. The ayah lifted her favourite one out first. It was all white with frills from the waist down. She held it up for her inspection.

"Yes, I think I shall wear that one – no, I think the pink one."

The pink one was held up for her approval and the ayah put the white one away while Heather sat, still puzzling, her chin cupped in her tiny hands.

"No, Ayah, I think I will wear my yellow one."

"Yes, Missy baba," the ayah said as she put the others back and held up her yellow one, which had little white bows dotted here and there on the skirt and bodice.

"No, Ayah, I think I shall wear my blue one."

She watched amused as the ayah put the others away. Then she clambered out of bed, much to her ayah's consternation.

"Missy baba, the memsahib will get very angry if she knows you are out of bed. Get back at once," she said quietly, not wishing to disturb Lindsay. "Lindsay Sahib – he too will get angry with me."

"No, he won't. Please, Ayah, lift all my dresses out again. I really don't know which one to choose."

She stood, hand on hip, as the ayah lifted them all out again. Secretly, Heather was enjoying this little charade. She took one off the ayah, held it in front of herself and danced round the bedroom as if she was at a ball.

"Soon, Ayah, I shall be going to the balls like Mama, won't I?" she said.

"Yes, Missy, you will, but now you must get into bed."

Heather handed the dress back to the ayah, who still showed little sign of impatience with her whimsical charge.

"Ayah," she said with her hand on her hip again.

"What, my child?"

"I don't really know which one to wear, really I don't. I think I should have had a new one for my birthday, don't you, Ayah?"

The ayah looked at her. "But Missy baba has so many and we have no more room," she said.

"Well," she replied indignantly, "I shall tell Mama to send some to the mission. I should have a new one for my birthday party." She pouted. "All my friends had one for theirs, and I know I am not going to get one as the durzi hasn't been. I have always had one before. Why not now?" Another frown of annoyance crossed her brow.

"But Missy baba, you don't need another one so soon." The ayah could see she was getting nowhere in this argument.

"Ayah," she begged, "please pull them all out again. I still haven't chosen one."

"You'd best let the memsahib choose one for you, Missy," the ayah said, trying to cajole her into letting the matter drop.

"No, Ayah," Heather said emphatically. "Please bring my ribbons too. I shall need to choose."

The ayah opened a large drawer containing ribbons and lace and brought out ones to match the dress Heather was holding up in front of herself as she gazed into the mirror.

They were both smiling at their little game when the door opened and in came Lindsay to see if Heather was asleep.

"Now, Heather, what is all this? A mannequin parade when you should be asleep! You know, Ayah, it is well past her bedtime."

The ayah looked at him sheepishly.

"Now, Heather, get back to bed this instant," he demanded.

She clambered back, looking very crestfallen.

"But I still don't know which dress to wear for my birthday party," she said as she watched the ayah putting her dresses and ribbons away.

"Well, you will have to wait and let Mama decide," Lindsay replied sharply.

"I should have a new one," she wailed pathetically.

"Well, I know the durzi has not brought any new materials to show Mama, so you cannot be having one."

At that, Heather pouted. "Why? why?" she demanded. "She has always got me one before." Her tears started to fall fast and furious.

Lindsay could never bear to see her cry. "Well," he declared after thinking deeply, wondering if he dared do what he was contemplating, "well, if you promise to keep it a secret . . . "

"Yes, yes, I will," she agreed, drying her eyes with the back of her hand, although she did not know to what she was agreeing.

"I will show my present to you. It has come all the way over the sea from Scotland," said Lindsay.

At this her tears stopped immediately and her eyes became wide open with anticipation.

"What is it, what is it, my darling Lindsay?" she asked eagerly. She crossed her heart as if to stress her promise to keep the secret.

"I am only going to show it to you as I shall be away early on your birthday, so I shall not see you open your presents."

"But why? Why? You have always seen me open them before," she said.

"I will be back later in the day, so I won't miss your party," he replied. He was as delighted as she when he saw the anticipated look of joy on her face. "Now, you mustn't tell Mama or Papa that you have seen it – nor you, Ayah."

"No, no, sahib, Missy baba and I will not tell."

They both put their fingers to their lips as if to reassure him. He could be sure of the ayah, but of his baby sister he had his doubts. However, he knew the ayah would persuade Heather to keep silent in spite of her excitement. Heather once more crossed her heart as she remade her promise. By now, she was fighting to keep awake. Heather and the ayah waited patiently for his return.

He came back carrying a long, stout box and Heather's eyes opened wider. Sleep once more took second place. He sat beside her on the bed as she untied the pink ribbon, lifted the lid and removed layer after layer of tissue paper to reveal the prettiest red dress she had ever seen. It was edged with fine white lace round the neck and sleeves.

"Ayah, Ayah," she called, "please help me to hold it up."

The ayah did as she was bid.

"Oh, Missy baba, it is the prettiest dress you have ever had," the ayah said. This was something she said about every dress Heather had, but this time it was true.

"Now I must take it back," said Lindsay as he put the lid on. "You cannot see it again until your birthday. Now you must go to sleep before Mama and Papa return. Have you said your prayers?"

She nodded her head.

"Goodnight," he said, and he kissed her on the cheek before leaving. "Now, Ayah, she must go to sleep. She has had enough excitement for one night."

The ayah nodded her head as he closed the door. She plumped up Heather's pillow and tucked the bedclothes round her shoulders.

"Will I look as pretty as Mama in my new dress?" she whispered. "Didn't Mama look pretty tonight?"

"Yes, dear, now go to sleep," the ayah said. She knew it would mean trouble for her if her mistress came home and found her charge still awake.

She looked round the room, making sure all was in order, before turning the paraffin light a little lower. Then she went to the small room adjoining, where she slept on the floor just inside her door. She was always within calling distance of her charge.

Heather was too excited to sleep. She tossed and turned, only settling for a moment or two in a light, restless slumber. Her arms one minute were under the covers; the next they were flailing around restlessly. The ayah returned several times; each time she made sure Heather was settled before leaving; and each time, after the ayah had left, her arms started to flail around and she tossed and turned on her pillow.

Suddenly, out of the snow-white pillowslip, having been disturbed by Heather's constant movement, crept a large scorpion. As it crept along her coverlet, Heather's arms flailed again and the scorpion, thinking it was being attacked, lashed out with its long up-curved tail and stung her on the arm.

Heather woke with a piercing scream as the pain shot through her. "Mama! Papa! Ayah!" she screamed.

The ayah returned to the room in time to see the scorpion as it sped across the bed. She almost fainted with terror. She screamed, "Lindsay Sahib! Lindsay Sahib!"

Suddenly, he was beside her.

"Ayah, Ayah, what is the matter?" He shook her roughly by the arm. "Tell me, woman, tell me," he demanded.

He looked to where she was pointing.

"I was only away a minute, sahib," she sobbed. "It must have been in baba's pillow. It was crawling across her bed."

"What was it, woman?" he stormed.

"A scorpion, a scorpion!" she screamed.

He gathered Heather up in his arms. Her face had turned ashen-grey. She was still screaming, "Mama! Papa! Ayah!"

By now the bearers were in the room.

"Find the scorpion! Find it!" Lindsay yelled at them. "And you, Munilal, go and get doctor sahib. *Juldi, juldi*. Lindsay's here, darling Heather, Mama will soon be here. Ayah, bring a cold-water compress to bring down the swelling."

"Yes, sahib," she sobbed as she hurried away.

The bearers hurried in to inform him that they had killed the scorpion.

"Well, search around and see if there are any more lurking about."

"Yes, sahib."

Munilal hailed the first tonga in sight. "Doctor sahib, *juldi, juldi*," he ordered.

The tonga wallah raced away and Munilal leaped out as he reached the doctor's house. He knocked repeatedly on the door and, when it opened, he repeated his request.

"Doctor sahib not in. He is at the ball," he was told.

Munilal rushed back to the waiting tonga. The tonga wallah cracked his whip over the horse.

"Faster, faster," Munilal screamed at him.

At last he reached his destination. He leaped up the steps, calling "Doctor sahib" when he spotted the doctor on the verandah. Several of the house bearers tried to prevent him coming any further as the tonga wallah was running after him calling, "Annas, annas!"

"Later, later," Munilal called to him.

At last he reached the doctor's side and told his tale. The doctor ordered another tonga and told the present tonga wallah to wait. He then hurried inside the hall, followed by Munilal.

"Margot," he called when he spotted her, "where are Craig and Elizabeth?"

"Dancing," she replied, looking at him apprehensively, wondering what was wrong.

Craig and Elizabeth were oblivious of everyone else in the room. Craig was whispering words of love as he held Elizabeth close. Suddenly he noticed Margot trying to attract his attention, and he saw Munilal by her side looking desperately towards him. Then he saw the doctor trying to reach him through the crowded room. Elizabeth felt his firm grip slacken. She looked up at him and the perturbed look on his face filled her with alarm.

"What is it, my darling?" She tried to follow his gaze, but she was too tiny to see over the crowd.

"Come, my dear," said Craig.

He caught her by the arm and elbowed his way towards the doctor. She gave a gasp of dismay when she saw the doctor bearing down on them. Craig was having a difficult time trying to get through the crowd; the other revellers tried to restrain them from leaving, not knowing the cause of their wanting to depart. At last all three reached Margot's side. She had told Munilal to go and await them outside.

When the doctor uttered the name Heather and the word scorpion, Craig rushed towards the door. Elizabeth felt a cloak being put around her shoulders and heard Margot's voice saying, "I will come with you." Her tears started to flow as she trembled with fright.

"No, Margot," she said, "there is no need to spoil your evening."

"My evening is already spoiled", she replied, "when I know that something is troubling you."

Craig and the doctor and Munilal clambered quickly into the tonga and Craig snatched the reins. He set the horse off at a gallop. Martin helped Margot and Elizabeth into the other tonga and they too headed for Craig's house.

Lindsay lay beside Heather stroking her hair. She was damp with sweat as she tossed and turned, delirious with fright and pain. She constantly called, "Mama! Papa! Lindsay! Ayah!"

"I am here, darling, I am here," said Lindsay gently.

'Surely Mama and Papa and the doctor should be here by now!' he thought.

Suddenly they were all by his side. The doctor bent over Heather, frowning with deep concern; Craig and Elizabeth were sick with apprehension.

"I will give her an injection to ease her pain," the doctor said, "and I will stay the night in case anything untoward happens. She is a strong, healthy child, and I am sure she will overcome any ill effects, so try not to worry, Elizabeth." He put his hand on her shoulder as she sat wringing her hands.

Craig sat on the verandah with the doctor a little later.

"Children have been known to die from such a sting," Craig commented, still very perturbed.

"I know, my son – that is why I want to stay with her for the time being. I have sent a bearer home to tell my family where they can contact me."

The doctor left later next day. He assured them that all would be well, but nevertheless he agreed to call in twice daily, and he insisted that they send for him if they noted any change for the worse.

"We will, we will. Thank you so much," said Craig.

He saw the doctor out, then hurried back to Elizabeth's side.

Every day Elizabeth and the ayah sat by Heather's bedside. Craig rushed home from the office to sit with her in the evenings.

"Now hurry and get well, my darling," he said; "then we can all go on holiday – wherever you choose."

"Oh, yes, Papa, that would be wonderful. Can we go and see Grandpapa who lives in the big castle?"

Craig and Elizabeth glanced at each other. Heather was asking the impossible.

"Not yet, my darling," Craig replied; "maybe soon. We will have to wait until Grandpapa writes to us. You will be well enough to go to the kindergarten after you have had a holiday," he said anxious to get off the subject of his father.

"I know where we will go," exclaimed Elizabeth.

"Where? Where?" Heather asked eagerly.

"We will go and visit Uncle Roddy."

"Oh yes, yes!" she exclaimed. "Can Lindsay come too?"

"No, not this time. He has to go to college."

"Not the one far away?" she asked anxiously.

"No, not just yet."

Suddenly she screeched with excitement. "Mama, before we go on holiday, can I have my birthday party?"

"Of course, my darling. Why, we will start this very minute and write out all your invitations."

Heather clapped her hands with glee.

Christina's reply to Elizabeth's letter stated that Roddy was away; she asked Elizabeth to delay their holiday for the time being. Heather's disappointment at the news was soon dispelled as her belated birthday party commenced.

CHAPTER 226

The twins called in several times to see Heather before they left. Their mother breathed a sigh of relief that at last Clare would be under proper supervision. Astrid was anxious to go, but Clare, as usual, grumbled as she packed her things. The only thing she smiled about was the thought of the good fun she had had over the holiday.

"We'll have no more parties or dances or boyfriends until we come home again. I am sick of college!" she kept exclaiming as she slung another dress into her case.

"Missy memsahib," exclaimed the ayah as she came into the room to assist them to pack, "all your dresses will get creased. I will straighten them for you."

"Leave them, Ayah!" their mother exclaimed as she entered. "Clare can pack them all again properly."

Clare pouted angrily, but she did as her mother bade her. Then she closed the lid with a slam.

"You will have time to call in and see Elizabeth and Craig and Heather again before you leave. Mama is coming to the station with us," said Davinia.

The following morning they kissed their father goodbye before he left for the office.

"Now, be good, Clare. I don't want any bad reports. You have had good ones up to now," he said.

"Yes, Papa, I promise," she called as they watched him out of sight.

"Why didn't Papa tell Astrid to be good, Mama?" she said peevishly.

"Because it is always you who gets into mischief, my child," her mother said. Then she kissed her. "Here is Mama now. We must be away."

CHAPTER 227

"Come now, Heather darling," her mother called as they went back onto the verandah to finish breakfast, "the ayah is waiting to take you to the kindergarten."

It was Heather's first day back after her illness and she was most anxious to see all her friends again.

"Will she be all right, Craig dear?" Elizabeth asked anxiously as they watched her go.

"Yes, my dear, she is quite well. Now, try not to worry. We have had enough to worry about lately. She is fit and well now." He turned her to face him and kissed her. "My darling little worrying angel!" he said.

Lindsay's friends too were preparing to return to their various colleges, and the street vendors were more anxious than anyone else to see them go. Whilst they were all at home, hardly a day passed when these poor vendors escaped from their pranks. As they wended their way from the bazaar with their wares on a tray on their heads, they might suddenly find the tray lifted into mid-air by two mischievous youths, one on either side of him on their cycles. They would career down the road, carrying the tray between them and laughing gaily, with the vendor in hot pursuit, swearing at them in his native language and shaking his fist furiously.

"Sahibs, sahibs!" the vendor would exclaim, although he knew he would find his goods intact on someone's garden wall.

Lindsay was often one of the culprits. He was always ill at ease for days on end at home when his friends had gone.

"Can you not come with us to college, Lindsay?" they repeatedly asked. "We shall miss you so."

"And I shall miss you," he answered, but he always had to tell them the same thing: "I will join you next term if my father agrees."

The time was fast approaching when Craig knew he had to make the final decision about Lindsay's higher education. More and more of his friends had left, and he knew Lindsay was affected by the taunting of the local boys: "Cissy boy! Cissy boy! Mama's boy! Who can't leave his mama and his ayah? Cissy boy!" Children could be so cruel in their taunts. He hated to see his son suffer such indignity, as much as he wanted him by his side every day.

For days on end Craig was silent and thoughtful. Even Heather's non-stop chatter and laughter could not tempt a smile from him. Elizabeth found him, time and time again, gazing out of the library window, idly watching the malis at work.

"Well now, my darling," she said as she laid her head on his arm and put her hand in his, "what is troubling you today?"

"Oh, the same old thoughts, my darling. If only – if only I hadn't to send him so far away," Craig replied.

"I know, my darling. I feel the same. Now most of his friends have gone, their parents have had to make the same decision and sacrifice as we are facing."

"But don't you see, my dear," he insisted sadly, "it is not the same sacrifice for them? Most of them, like Ruardy, have fathers who are in the army. They have grown used to being separated for long periods. They are not as close to their fathers as Lindsay is to me. We are as close as my father and I were." He tried to catch the sigh in his voice before it escaped.

Elizabeth was unable to say anything to ease his longing for home or solve his dilemma regarding Lindsay.

"No other father could possibly be as close to his son as I am to Lindsay. I am going to miss him so. I cannot bear the thought of it. Now I understand how my father felt when he had to face the same decision – but of course it was worse for him. He had already lost Mama and only had his sisters to ease his loneliness."

"Yes, but I am always beside you, darling," said Elizabeth. She hugged him closer and he put his hand over hers.

"Yes, my darling, I always have you," he said.

She looked up at him and saw that he was looking down at her with his usual adoration.

"Yes, yes, my darling angel," he continued, "I have always got you by my side."

"Always! Always and for ever!" she replied.

He bent down to kiss her; then he released her, gazed into her captivating eyes and whispered, "I love you so, my darling."

"And I you, but this is not solving the problem of our son's education."

"No, you are so right, my dear," he said.

Suddenly, they heard the crash of a cycle and they both hurried to the window. Munilal tried valiantly to catch the cycle before it hit the floor, and Lindsay laughed as he said, "Too slow again, Munilal! You will never be quick enough to catch it before it hits the ground."

"Ah, sahib, one day I will, you'll see."

They both laughed as the bearer propped the cycle up.

Lindsay rushed into the room when he spotted his parents watching him.

"Why all the rush and excitement, my son?" Elizabeth exclaimed.

"Mama, Papa," he said breathlessly, "the results of my final exams are here. See! See!" He held out the long brown envelope to his father. "It says, Papa," he announced, "that I have passed the top grades for college. Please say I can go."

Craig looked at his wife with a deep sigh of resignation. She nodded her head. He knew he had lost.

"Yes, my son, you may go," he replied reluctantly.

"Oh, thank you, Papa!" Lindsay exclaimed, and he kissed them both on the cheeks before he rushed out as eagerly as he had rushed in. He was unaware as yet of what the parting from them would mean. To him it was just another of life's adventures to be grasped with both hands.

"Well, at least he will be able to see Ruardy, who is in the junior section, so he will have someone there he already knows," said Elizabeth, trying to ease Craig's heartache.

"It will be the first of many partings. I shall always be glad when he is home again."

He watched from the window as Lindsay remounted his cycle.

"I am going to tell all my friends, Papa, that I am going with them," Lindsay called.

"Now I must go and explain to Heather", said Elizabeth, "why Lindsay is so excited." She had seen Heather follow in Lindsay's wake with her ayah close on her heels. "She is going to miss him so much."

"But no one is going to miss him as much as me – no one!" said Craig.

'He's so like his father,' Elizabeth thought. 'He's always thinking of his son – always his son.' She sighed as she left the room.

"But, Mama, I won't ever see him if he goes away. Please tell Papa not to let him go, Mama, please. I don't want Lindsay to go away."

"He will be home at Christmas, and in the summer he will come with us to the hills and the plantation. Then we will all be together with Aunt Margot and Davinia and Astrid and Clare," said her mother, hoping to pacify Heather, who sat rocking her in the large rocking chair on the verandah. However, she could see that no explanation was going to satisfy her small daughter, who was now crying.

"I will have no one to give me a ride on the cycle or rock me on my rocking horse," she sobbed.

"Well, Papa will get you a small cycle of your own and he will rock you on your rocking horse," Elizabeth said.

"But he doesn't rock me fast like Lindsay does. Please, Mama, don't let Papa send Lindsay away."

"Well, Lindsay has to go to his new college now he is a big boy. You will soon be going to a new kindergarten, and you will make lots of new friends."

"But I don't want any new friends; I only want Lindsay. Please tell Papa I only want Lindsay." She snuggled up closer to her mother.

'Dear me,' thought Elizabeth, 'this is as bad as trying to console Craig!'

Craig watched in anguish as the big black trunk arrived. The local painter sat and painted Lindsay's full name and destination on it. It brought back to Craig the memory of the trunks in Margot's home so long ago. Now his son was leaving him. "Why has life to be so cruel – all these partings!" He sighed.

The next few weeks were a hectic bustle as new school equipment arrived, including gym and sports clothes, books and more books.

Craig watched silently. 'I wonder if I would have liked boarding school?' he thought.

Lindsay was bounding round the house and gardens like a young gazelle, without a care in the world.

One day, as time for his departure was drawing near, Lindsay was riding round the garden when he spotted his father watching him from a window. He went to talk to him.

"Why are you so sad, Papa?" he asked. "Are you not pleased for me, passing the entrance exam to the best college in the land?"

"Of course I am, my son. No father could be more proud. I am more than pleased."

"But you have looked so sad lately. Why? Why?"

"Because, my son, it means you are going away from me, and that is something I haven't got used to yet. I will miss you so much." He put his hand on his son's shoulder as they both gazed out of the window.

"I shall miss you also, Papa." At last it was dawning on him that he was going far away from his family and all he held dear. "But if I study hard, Papa, I shall pass out for the university here. Then I shall once again be near you all."

"Yes, my son, I know you will work hard and be a credit to your dear mother and me. Have you decided yet what you want to be later in life?"

"Well, maybe a judge at the high court like Stephen, or a soldier in the army like Uncle Roddy."

He saw his father wince.

"I think you will prefer law to the army," Craig said hurriedly.

"Well, I am interested in languages, and in the army I might get to travel and see the world."

"Well, time will tell," his father remarked resignedly.

The day for parting came and tears fell fast and furious from Heather as Lindsay kissed her goodbye and told her to be a big, brave girl for Mama and Papa. He told her to look after them until his return. He hated to see her tears. His mother also wiped away a tear, but when he glanced at his father's face only a lost, sad expression could he see.

He clung to his father tightly. "I will try to be a credit to you, Papa," he said.

"I know you will, my son. Now go and join your friends on the train. It is due to leave any minute now," Craig replied.

Lindsay kissed his mother and sister once more before hastening towards the train.

"Come back soon, Lindsay," Heather called as the train started to pull away.

"Give our love to Ruardy when you see him, and write often," his mother called.

"I will, I will. Goodbye, Papa."

"Goodbye, my son."

CHAPTER 228

Astrid was happy to be back once more amongst her new friends. As the year progressed, her attitude contrasted more and more sharply with that of Clare, who found every subject a bore. Clare's inattention in every lesson was perceived by her teachers.

"I don't know whatever is to become of that girl!" Miss Andrews exclaimed repeatedly to her friend, Miss Marsh. "To think they are twins! I have never known such opposites. I cannot think how they can come from the same parents." She tut-tutted. "Clare seems so disinterested in every subject when in class, yet in exams she is only a few marks behind her sister. Astrid, however, is always poring studiously over her books. She is top of the school in music."

"Maybe next year Clare will settle and improve. After all, they only left home recently. We must make some allowance for Clare's youthful exuberance," replied Miss Marsh, who was always ready to give her pupils a little leeway.

"Well, she better had or I can see her going before the principal before many more terms are over," replied Miss Andrews crossly.

"Thank goodness Christmas term is almost here! It is the one I think we all look forward to the most," said Miss Marsh.

"It certainly is," Miss Andrews agreed.

No one could be more eager than Clare that soon the term would end and Christmas would be upon them.

"I can't wait to get home and out of this horrible old uniform and into some pretty ball gowns. The holiday will end all too soon and then we will have to come back here." She shuddered at the thought.

"Well, it is better than being sent to live with Aunt Agatha," retorted Astrid.

"Just think, Astrid: if we hadn't been sent here, I might have been engaged to Roy by now, even though he has gone away. He told me he loved me at the school dance and he knew I loved him. He would surely have asked Papa for my hand in marriage before he set off for England. But what did Papa do?" she exclaimed angrily. "He just hurried me away before I had a chance to see him again. Now he has left and I may never see him again." She sighed.

"Well, I had to leave Roland, don't forget," said Astrid.

"Yes, but he will be waiting for you. No doubt, he will be on the platform when we arrive. I have no boyfriend now waiting for me," she fumed.

"Well, you will soon have several if last Christmas is anything to go by," retorted Astrid. She was getting a little tired of Clare's constant complaining at having no beaux. "Have you finished your packing yet, Clare?"

"Yes, almost," she replied as she flung another garment into her suitcase. "I have only my satchel with my books in for the journey to pack – and, of course, my hatbox in which to carry some holly and mistletoe for Mama and Grandmama."

"Well, I will bring some in my hatbox for Elizabeth. Our teachers say we can finish lessons early tomorrow and go to collect some," said Astrid.

CHAPTER 229

The time for leaving arrived. All the girls gabbled away with excitement as they headed towards the station.

"Do hurry, Clare," Astrid called to her. "Everyone is waiting for us."

"Well, I am hurrying," said Clare sharply, "but I cannot close my hatbox. It keeps flying undone and my holly falls out."

"Well, I told you not to get so much, but you would insist," said Astrid. "Sometimes, Clare, you are quite impossible."

They proceeded on to the platform to wait for the train. It arrived. The reserved coaches were clearly marked, and the girls assembled in twos ready to board.

"Now hurry along, girls!" the teacher called to them. "Hurry along!"

Clare, in her usual high spirits hurried far too quickly, without paying any attention to where she was going. She tripped and fell. Her hatbox flew open, scattering the holly far and wide.

"Oh, bother!" she cried. "Well, I am not going without it."

She hastily got to her feet and started to pick it up, grumbling all the time at its prickliness as it scratched her hands. A large bunch of holly wrapped itself round the ankles of a tall Indian Army officer cadet, who was waiting to board a train for Kashmir. He bent down to disentangle the prickly bunch from his socks, wondering where on earth it had come from. At that moment he spotted a red-haired schoolgirl with two plaits down her back, tied with ribbon. Her school hat, which had fallen off, was being brushed by Astrid.

"Oh, come on and leave the rest," Astrid called to her. "We will get into trouble if we don't hurry."

"No, you hurry on, Astrid. It was all your fault anyway. If you hadn't called to me to hurry I wouldn't have tripped."

She was just going to close the lid when she spotted another large clump and made a hasty grab for it. Too late she saw the pair of highly polished shoes. The officer's hand touched Clare's as he freed it, and she looked up to see the most handsome man she had ever seen smiling down at her. His perfect white teeth were in sharp contrast to his dusky skin, jet-black moustache and the most devilish dark eyes she had ever seen. For a moment she felt her knees go weak as he held out the bunch of holly to her.

"Miss Holly, I presume," he said in the most perfect English. "You seem to have mislaid your Christmas greenery," he said good-humouredly.

She knew she should have been extremely coy and demure, as befitted a young lady, but instead she burst out laughing as she took the branch from him.

"I am so sorry. I do hope it has not torn your clothes," she said.

"Not at all! I am glad because it has given me a chance to speak to you, which, as you know, I could never have done otherwise." He laughed with her as she tried to get the holly back in her hatbox and then struggled to fasten the lid. "I am afraid you have too much holly in there, young lady. Please tell me your name," he said softly.

"We haven't been properly introduced, sir," she hastily replied.

"I hope I will see you when you return from your holiday. I am at the officers' academy, not far away."

"No, no, that's impossible," she said, suddenly feeling afraid.

"I will make it possible," he said in a tone of voice which told her he would if she wished it so.

The rest of the girls had hurried on at the teacher's command. Astrid stood waiting impatiently for Clare a little distance away. She was getting more and more annoyed and fearful for her sister.

'Why doesn't she hurry? Whatever is she talking about?' she thought.

She looked up to see Miss Andrews bearing down on them. She passed Astrid and headed for Clare.

"Clare, go at once to the train. Whatever will your parents think of you talking to a stranger?" She glared defiantly at the officer as Clare hurriedly departed towards the train.

"It was my fault entirely. It was — " he started to explain.

"Good day, sir," said Miss Andrews, and she turned on her heels and hurried to the train.

'So, the young lady is called Clare,' he mused as he watched her being hustled into the carriage. 'I must see her again. I must and I shall,' he thought. 'The girls all look similar in their uniforms and their hats and plaits, but I shall never forget which one is Clare.'

Miss Marsh joined Miss Andrews in their reserved carriage.

"I have never met such a troublesome girl. The very idea! Whatever would her parents say about that little encounter? I have a good mind to put it in my report for the principal," said Miss Andrews. "That sort of conduct gives the school a bad name." She sat in the corner tut-tutting.

"Oh, don't do that, Miss Andrews," said Miss Marsh. "After all, it is end of term and she is such a high-spirited girl. I am sure she will settle down next term."

"Well, she better had," Miss Andrews replied as the train pulled away.

Clare hurried to the window. She could just see the officer's head above the rest of the people on the platform.

"Oh, what a thrilling encounter!" she exclaimed as she sat down next to Astrid and flung her hat and school satchel on the luggage rack above their heads.

She carefully put her case with the holly in next to her, thinking of the light touch of his hand on hers as he helped her fasten the catch.

"Oh, what a thrilling encounter, Astrid!" she repeated, but her sister looked at her as though she was quite loopy.

"Honestly, Clare! Sometimes you are quite impossible," Astrid replied. She sighed as she gazed out of the window.

"I just know what those two teachers will be saying about me: 'Whatever would her parents think of us to allow such a thing to happen?' " mocked Clare.

The journey was long and tiring, and the girls were all glad when the train stopped at a station. They had time to spare to shop for small gifts for their parents and friends before, at last, they were away on the final leg of their journey. Clare was the first back in the carriage. Miss Andrews glared at her as she shepherded the other girls on board.

"Why are you so quiet on this trip, Clare? You are usually so full of fun," said Betsy. "I wish I had stayed in the other carriage with Meg. You have hardly spoken."

"I wish you had stayed in the other carriage with Meg. I am sick of your chatter. You have never hushed up once since we got on the train," Clare said quarrelsomely.

The rest of the girls looked at each other incredulously and Astrid looked at Clare with alarm. She had to admit that Clare's silence was most unusual, as was her ill-humoured outburst.

Betsy put her hand in front of her mouth as she whispered to Astrid, out of earshot of Clare. She was quite unperturbed by Clare's outburst.

"I bet she has fallen in love with that officer who picked up her holly; I bet that's it!" she exclaimed with glee.

Astrid gave her a sharp dig in the ribs and glanced at Clare sitting gazing idly through the window.

'Yes, she must be thinking of him,' Astrid thought. 'She has never been so quiet before. Well, she will soon forget him when she is back home with the boys we know and she starts going to dances again.'

Clare was oblivious to all of them. She continued to gaze through the window, lost in thought. Never before had a glance and the touch of a hand affected her so much. Was this the Eastern magic she had heard so much about? She could still feel the magnetism of his gaze and his closeness. Somehow she had felt riveted to the spot. 'Oh, it can't be that,' she thought. 'Oh, why am I thinking of him so much?' She could still hear his silky, soft voice thrilling and teasing her as he handed back her holly – and he had spoken in such perfect English too. He must be from a very high caste. Was the saying true, she suddenly asked herself: 'East is East and West is West and never the twain shall meet'? The thought came into her mind that she might never ever see him again.

'That's impossible,' she told herself. 'I will see him again. I must! I must!'

CHAPTER 230

Clare found the social whirl that Christmas at home rather boring. No one could understand her.

"How quiet and ladylike she has become!" exclaimed Margot to Davinia one evening as they sat talking after dinner. "She's not a bit like her old self. At last she is growing up to be the type of young lady we always wanted her to be."

"It was, after all, a good idea to send her away as we did," Stephen said as he sat quietly drinking his whisky. "Our dear little Astrid too seems much preoccupied. I wonder why? It must suit them both up there."

But Astrid was growing more and more concerned as she noted Clare's constant daydreaming.

One day, as they were preparing to go to yet another dance, Clare exclaimed aloud, "How this place bores me! I can't wait to get back to college."

Astrid could scarcely believe her ears. Clare bored with the dances? On previous occasions she could never have her fill, and yet now she wished she was back at college. 'No,' she thought, 'this is not the same Clare as of old.'

"Clare looks highly delighted to be going back to college. I am so glad she has settled down. According to her school report, she has not received any bad marks against her for misconduct," her father remarked before he, Davinia and Margot saw the twins off on the train.

"And whilst she has been home she has been less eager to go to all the dances than before," said Davinia.

"I thought Astrid seemed rather quiet this Christmas. I do hope she is not fretting too much at being away from home," said Margot. "I was anxious about you sometimes, Davinia, as sometimes the separation seemed too much for you."

"The girls have each other, Mama, but I think Astrid misses her constant companion, Roland, when she is away."

The twins leaned out of the window of the train to wave their parents goodbye.

"Now be good, my dears – especially you, Clare. Don't get up to any mischief," said Stephen.

"No, I won't, Papa," she replied with a huge grin on her face.

"I am concerned about Astrid, Davinia," Margot said. "I have never seen such a woebegone look on her face before."

"Oh, you are imagining things, Mama," replied Davinia.

"Well, they are finally away. We shall have to see what the next term brings," said Stephen.

'Clare is as chatty and jolly as ever – perhaps even more so, if anything,' Astrid thought. As the journey progressed she noticed that Clare seemed increasingly eager to arrive at their destination.

Clare saw him the moment the train pulled in. She grabbed Astrid's arm.

"He's here! He's here!" she whispered excitedly.

"Who, for heaven's sake?" said Astrid, pretending not to understand.

"Sh - sh - sh! I don't want anyone to notice him or hear us," Clare said anxiously.

At the far end of the platform stood the tall, handsome captain.

'Well,' Astrid thought, 'he certainly is very handsome. I wonder how he knew we would be arriving today. He must have bribed the stationmaster. He will tell anyone anything for a few annas. I was hoping they might have posted that officer far away by the time we returned. No such luck!' She could see the enthusiasm Clare was showing at the mere sight of him, and it was filling her with panic.

Clare stood a long time on the step of the carriage before alighting. She made sure she was the last to get off the train. She stood gazing at him and his eyes never left her face. She purposely left her hat off so that he might spot her red hair.

"Come along at once, Clare. Whatever are you staring at? Put on your hat this very minute," said Miss Andrews.

"Oh, bother!" Clare thought. "Now I cannot see him. That woman has already started picking on me."

In the following days Clare could think of nothing else but the young officer.

"Oh, Astrid, I wonder when I shall be able to speak to him," she said every day.

"Probably never!" Astrid replied. "Stop wasting time thinking of him."

"Oh, don't say that, Astrid. I shall just die if I don't see and speak to him soon."

"Really, Clare, you are quite mad. You know Papa would never allow such a thing, so stop getting so thrilled about something you know can never be."

"But I love him, I love him. I do, I do. Don't you understand, Astrid?"

"How can you possibly love someone you have only said hello to? It is too impossible for words," replied Astrid impatiently.

"I knew with that first glance. Just one glance and I knew," she enthused. She pirouetted round the room before climbing into bed, still exclaiming her love.

"Oh, for goodness' sake go to sleep!" said Astrid impatiently. "Every night since we got back you have kept me talking into the small hours – and you know the penalty for that if we get caught. We have our exams coming up soon and you know how much studying we have to do. We daren't go home with bad reports or else we will get sent to live with Aunt Agatha."

Astrid knew that if anything would silence Clare, it was that good lady's name.

CHAPTER 231

One day, as they were cycling to the bazaar with the rest of the class and a chaperone teacher, Clare had to stop when a small chokra ran out in front of her bicycle. She little knew at the time that the boy had done it on purpose.

"Missy memsahib, Missy memsahib," he hissed as he picked himself up off the road, "take, take." He held out a small note to her.

She grasped it quickly and the boy hurried off. In a moment he was lost in the crowd.

"Quick, quick!" called out Astrid in alarm. "Here comes Miss Andrews in the tonga. If she sees you have taken something off a native boy she will be very angry, and she will stop our visits to the bazaar."

Clare wasn't listening. "Come into the silk shop with me," she said. "I need some more silks for my embroidery."

"You know very well", exclaimed Astrid impatiently, "that you don't need anything of the sort."

"Oh, don't be such a sop!" said Clare angrily.

Astrid looked at her in dismay. "I am not a sop. Don't ever call me one again," she replied.

"Oh, very well. I am sorry. Please come with me. I just have to read this note. I can't wait another minute."

In a moment she was inside the shop, reading the note. Astrid was speechless.

The shopkeeper asked, "What do the Missy memsahibs wish to buy?" He could see that one of them did not wish to buy anything.

"Well," Astrid began, "I wish to see some silks for sewing."

"Very nice silks," he declared as he arrayed them on his counter.

Clare was not taking a bit of notice.

'Well, I shall have to buy something,' thought Astrid.

"Will this shade do, Clare?" she asked, holding a skein up, but she might just as well have saved her breath.

Clare had clasped the note to her heart.

"He loves me, he loves me," she whispered.

"Those will be two annas, Missy memsahib."

"Thank you."

They both stumbled out of the shop into the sunshine, and both gasped with dismay when they saw the waiting tonga outside the door.

"Now, girls, what have you been buying?" the haughty voice of the teacher called to them. She had seen the cycles outside and she had decided to wait and see to whom they belonged.

"Only some silks for our embroidery," they both chorused as Astrid undid the wrapping to prove it.

"Very well, then. We must all keep together now. The rest of the girls have been waiting."

"Well, what does the Sheik of Araby have to say?" asked Astrid later.

"He says that he loves me and must see me. He wants me to meet him near the tennis courts tomorrow night. Will you come and play, Astrid, and watch out for me?"

Astrid looked at Clare disdainfully, hardly believing what she was saying.

"Oh, please," Clare begged, "just this once."

"Oh, very well," Astrid replied, "but only this once."

Knowing her sister as she did, she suspected that 'just this once' would mean very, very often; her heart sank at the mere thought of it.

They both sauntered down with the crowd who were going to play tennis next evening.

"I daresay", said Meg, "that you two will be partnering each other."

"Yes, we will," Clare was quick to reply, "and we won't be available to join you in a foursome later as we have to get back to study."

"Very well, then," Meg replied. "I won't look for you. Cheerio. Enjoy your game."

"We will," Astrid replied.

As the teachers did not chaperone them in their free time on the school premises, Clare knew she was safe.

"When we have had one or two games, suddenly I shall go missing," said Clare, "but don't get alarmed or raise the alarm. I won't be long. Just mingle with the others. They won't know whether it's you or me. If they ask where your sister is, tell them I have gone back to the college building."

This wasn't the first time Clare had used this ruse to puzzle any inquisitors when she wanted something done secretly.

"You seem to have thought of everything as usual," said Astrid resignedly. But she found she was speaking to herself, as Clare had already disappeared through the bushes surrounding the courts.

The officer half hidden by shrubs, watched as Clare hurried through the garden. Suddenly she saw him.

"I thought you would never come," he exclaimed softly in her ear.

He gathered her in his eager arms as though he would never, ever let her go again.

"I will have to be very careful," she said breathlessly, between his kisses. "I must not be seen out here or my sister and I will get expelled."

He silenced her with another breathless kiss. Never in her young life had she ever been kissed like this before. Roy's embrace had suddenly become a faded memory. Just a mere peck from boys back home, when she had attended the dances, had sometimes sent her into a seventh heaven, and she would think about it for days. Never had she been held so close to a heart beating as passionately as her own.

'Surely,' she thought, 'it is not my heart beating so?'

His words of love and desire thrilled her and she was filled with a desire and love for him she couldn't grasp, or understand.

"I love you, Miss Holly, I love you," he said. "I have thought of nothing else but you since I saw you disappear from view on that accursed train."

"My name is Clare," she reminded him.

"Well, I prefer Holly, and that is what I am going to call you because I wouldn't have met you but for the holly."

"I don't even know your name!" She suddenly realised, with a gasp of dismay, that she had been kissing an almost total stranger.

"Well, my name is too long for you to remember now, but I will tell you one day. For now, call me Victor."

They both laughed as they saw the significance.

"I watched for you for weeks before I spotted you both with the other girls in the bazaar."

"But how did you know me from my sister?"

"Ah, that is known only to me – call it my magical Eastern sense. I shall always know you."

"Well, I must say you are pretty sure of yourself. Most people cannot tell us apart."

"Oh, I admit she is lovely, but you have a beam of radiance that she hasn't got, because you, Miss Holly, are in love with me as I am with you. Tell me it's true. Tell me, tell me," he insisted.

"Yes, it is true," she said breathlessly, between his kisses. Then she asked, "Do you mean to say you were in the bazaar watching us that day?"

"Yes, but I dared not make myself known to you with that ogre of a teacher watching you all so closely. Therefore, I gave a note to the first chokra I saw and asked him to hand it to you. But don't let us waste time on useless chatter. All I want to do is kiss you."

"Please, Victor, I must go. I have already been away too long. Astrid will be getting alarmed."

"Very well, then. I shall wait for you here every night. I know you come to play tennis. Our military academy is not far away."

He held her tightly, but she tried, time and time again, to free herself.

"I will try to come," she said between his kisses.

"Say you will come," he demanded. "Say it."

She felt the strength of him as he spoke, and she knew she could not but obey his every wish.

"Very well, then, I will come. Now I must go."

By this time, darkness was falling and the girls had already left the tennis courts.

"Clare," Astrid said, "I thought you would never come. We are the last to leave. The girls kept turning round to see if I was following."

"Well, here I am," Clare said jauntily, although she felt guilty about leaving her sister to face the questioning stares of the other girls. "I told you I wouldn't be long. Anyway, I have promised to come every night; we must come to play tennis every night, and I shall slip away as I did tonight."

"But Clare, you know you mustn't do that. Someone might see you," she cried in alarm.

"No one can see us near the stream. We will be out of sight among all the trees and bushes."

"But we have to study, and you know on study nights we have to be together in the library."

"Yes, I know. I shall slip out after studies when it's dark, then no one will see me."

"But, Clare, you mustn't see him again," Astrid pleaded.

"I must and I will," she replied. She danced into the room they shared and flung her racket into the corner and herself onto the bed.

"Oh, what ecstasy being in love is, Astrid!" she exclaimed. "I adore him, adore him."

"You won't adore it when you get caught and we both get expelled!" Astrid exclaimed angrily, but Clare was not listening.

One evening, Victor was escorting Clare back, and, as they crossed the small path round the tennis courts, they realised that they had not noticed a tonga approaching. Clare gave a gasp of dismay when she saw who the occupant was. It was the principal. As it drew level, she ordered the tonga wallah to stop.

"Now, you, Clare, will report to my office in the morning, and you, sir, are trespassing on college property. I shall report this incident to your commanding officer. Now, you, Clare, get in here beside me; you can go to your room the minute we arrive at the college."

She did as the principal ordered. Victor bowed to them, bade them both goodnight, turned on his heel and walked smartly away. He watched from among the trees as the tonga drove away, still smarting from the principal's rebuke, but anguished at the thought of what might await his precious Holly.

'When will I ever see her again?' he wondered. 'I will see her again somehow.'

Clare, her heart sinking, sat looking into space as the tonga drove on.

'Oh, silly me!' she thought. 'I had forgotten she always goes to the evening service on Sundays at the little Anglican church. Oh, why didn't I remember – I could have got to my room before she returned. Why? Why?'

At last she dismounted and bade the principal a polite goodnight before she raced to her room.

She flung herself on her bed and buried her face in the pillow. Astrid, who was sitting at the mirror brushing her hair, turned round to face her.

"Now, don't tell me: he has either told you he doesn't want to see you again or you have been caught. I can guess: you have been caught."

"Yes, yes," Clare cried out, "by none other than the principal herself."

Astrid was speechless with shock. She sat gazing at her sister.

"I knew this would happen!" she exclaimed angrily.

"Why can't she go to the morning service on Sunday like everyone else?" Clare raged. "There she was, right in our path. We couldn't escape anywhere. Now I have to see her in the morning and Victor is going to get into trouble as she will report him to his commanding officer," she wailed, burying her face in her pillow to stifle the sound of her sobbing.

"Well, so he should. It's all his fault," said Astrid angrily.

"Victor's not worried for himself, but he will be very worried about what might happen to us," she sobbed uncontrollably.

"Well, we know what will happen to us," declared Astrid angrily, for once unmoved by Clare's tears.

Clare raised her head, tears streaming down her face.

"Yes, my dear Astrid, I know," she said. "It is all my fault and I am so sorry for your sake. I know I will get expelled, and we may even be separated. Maybe Papa will only send me away to live with Aunt Agatha, and the principal will let you stay on here." She gave another convulsive wail at the thought of going to Aunt Agatha by herself, and buried her head in the pillow again.

"How could I possibly stay here when you have brought me all this shame?" said Astrid, now almost in tears. "I cannot think any more tonight. I am too upset. Goodnight." She clambered into bed and covered her head with the sheet.

Clare lay tossing and turning long after Astrid was asleep.

'Yes, yes, that's what I will do,' she thought.

She sat up and dried her eyes as she planned her next move.

The next day, Victor watched from his window overlooking the main doors of the academy as the principal, dressed all in black, alighted from her tonga and entered the building. He watched until she left a little later.

He had reported the incident to his commanding officer, who was outraged, and he had been warned not to let it ever occur again. He was threatened with expulsion from the academy, or, at least, he would be reported to his father, the maharajah who financed the academy. Neither of which did Victor relish as he had, for his father's sake, to finish the senior officers' course so that he could take over command of his father's own corps of guards. He didn't wish to face his father's wrath.

The principal was assured that the officer in question had been severely reprimanded and that such an incident would never occur again.

The principal severely reprimanded Clare. She was given extra study hours and forbidden to make any trips outdoors. The principal informed her that she had written to her father requesting his presence immediately.

Astrid listened with bated breath to Clare on her return from the principal's office.

"Oh, Clare, whatever will Papa say when he gets here?" she said.

"I don't know," Clare replied, "but at least we shall see him and maybe he will ask the principal not to be too angry with me." She sighed, knowing full well that this was wishful thinking on her part.

CHAPTER 232

Stephen sat down leisurely to read his morning mail after breakfast a few days later. He glanced uneasily at Davinia, who was sitting opposite him as she read the morning paper. He was disturbed to see the college headed notepaper, and he became more and more agitated and angry as he read on. Suddenly, with an exclamation of anger, he rose to his feet.

"Whatever is it my dear?" Davinia exclaimed in alarm, putting down her paper.

"This, my dear, is a letter from the principal of the college asking me to go to see her at once concerning a misdemeanour by our daughter, Clare. It may mean her expulsion, but she would like me to go and see her before she makes a decision. Davinia, whilst I am away, please write to Aunt Agatha and tell her the girls will be coming to stay with her. They must continue their education in Scotland before going on to their finishing school."

"Very well, dear," Davinia sighed meekly. "What has Clare done to warrant such a decision, dear?"

"She's been consorting with an Indian officer cadet from the nearby academy."

"Oh, dear, no! Whatever is she thinking about to do something so wilful. She must have known it was wrong. Our poor, sweet Astrid must be nearly out of her mind with anguish." She sat down, deeply distressed.

"I shall call and see this young man whilst I am there. I wish we had sent the girls to Scotland before."

His anger increased as his bearer helped him pack. The bearer wondered why his sahib was packing and why he was in such a rage. At last Stephen was ready to leave.

"I can ill afford to spare so much time away from my duties at court. It will take me two days to get there and two days to attend to the matter and two days to bring them back. Now, Davinia, you must make all the arrangements for their departure whilst I am away."

Davinia knew it would be no use her making excuses for them on the basis of their being so young. Stephen's mind was made up. She sat down to write the letter she had always dreaded. 'I won't finish it until he returns,' she thought. She put her pen and paper away, hoping that perhaps it might not need sent after all. A sad smile – the first smile since the letter came – crossed her face. 'I shall go and visit Mama and Elizabeth and ask them what they think of the situation,' she decided.

CHAPTER 233

The principal greeted Stephen cordially, for which he was thankful after his long journey. He listened attentively to her complaint.

"As it is the first lapse of college rules, and only one of your daughters is involved, I have decided to let them both stay until the end of term. Their exams are imminent, and it is not fair to upset Miss Astrid's education, as she has done no wrong. But you do understand, sir, that they cannot return when our new term starts. We have to make it clear to our other pupils that we shall not allow them to encourage the young men from the academy."

"I fully understand, madam, and I am more than grateful that you are allowing them to stay for the present. It is most kind of you. I intend to call at the military academy before I return home. Would you be so kind as to give me the name of the young officer cadet concerned?"

"By all means," she said.

She hastily wrote it down and handed it to him.

"I should like to see my daughters before I leave," Stephen said.

"Certainly. You may see them in the adjoining room."

He followed her, and she bade him be seated.

"I will send a tutor to bring them to you," she said. "I shall now bid you good day, sir."

"Good day, madam. Thank you again," he said. He rose to his feet as she left the room.

The twins were crestfallen as they faced their father.

"The principal is very kindly letting you both stay until the end of term because of your exams, but she will not allow you to return next term."

Clare's mind raced on and on. 'Not return!' she thought. 'Shall I never see my beloved ever again? No, no, that cannot be. I must see him again. I must. I must.'

She heard her father's voice droning on: "I will call to see this young man before I return home, and I shall forbid him to see or speak to either of you again."

'Not to see or speak with him again before I leave for good? That's not possible. I shall die,' thought Clare. 'I shall just die. I cannot live without him, and I know he feels the same way about me. I will see him again. I don't care what Papa says. I will. I will.'

Clare was looking at her father, like one in a dream, as his voice droned on and on: "I don't know how your poor mother is going to cope with all this worry. She is too distraught for words. And what will Elizabeth and Craig think of your behaviour, Clare? What will your grandmother feel when all our friends get to know you have been expelled from college because of your association with an Indian Army officer? I dread to think."

Astrid sat with her hands clasped as though in prayer. She was deeply distressed by it all as she listened carefully to her father's every word – but not Clare.

'What do I care what our friends think?' she thought. 'I shall see my darling again. I shall. I shall. As soon as Papa has returned home, I will run away. Yes, that is what I will do. Yes, that is the answer. I will see Victor straight away. He will know where we can go.'

"Are you listening to me, my girl?"

Clare was startled for a moment when she realised her father was addressing her.

"Yes, yes, of course I am listening, Papa." A sudden blush came to her cheeks.

"You will not – I repeat, not – see or speak to this young man ever again. Is that clear?" He raised his voice and looked directly at Clare. "Now, I don't want any more trouble from you, Clare."

"Yes, Papa, it is quite clear."

He stood up to leave and kissed them both before he left the room.

The rest of the girls raced to their rooms during their midday break and watched eagerly from their windows. They were all agog with excitement. It was the first time anything so scandalous had happened in the school.

"Why hasn't she been expelled?" they asked one another.

They had seen Clare's father arrive, but he had left the school without her. It was expected that Clare, at least, would be expelled.

Later, they quizzed Clare and Astrid, but no amount of quizzing could satisfy their curiosity fully.

CHAPTER 234

Davinia and Margot were waiting anxiously for Stephen's return, and they were relieved when they saw that the girls were not with him. At last he related to them the outcome of his visit.

"They will not be allowed to return next term," he said. "Did you post that letter to Aunt Agatha, Davinia?"

"Well, I partly wrote it; then I decided to await your return before posting it."

"I also thought that was the best thing to do," said Margot in Davinia's defence.

"Well, it must be finished and posted tomorrow. I will go as soon as I can to get their sailing tickets. The girls must be sent away before Clare gets up to any more mischief," he said angrily. "Now I am going to rest. I have had a long journey."

The two women sat looking at each other after he had left the room.

"Poor Astrid! Why is Clare so precocious and wilful?" said Davinia with a sigh.

Extra study hours were imposed on both girls: on Clare because of her bringing disrepute on the college, and on Astrid because she aided her sister in the escapade. Astrid was always poring over her books as the exams drew closer, but Clare's mind was in a whirl. She wondered what her father could have said to Victor, and when she would be able to see him again.

'I know he will be still waiting for me every night,' she thought.

Frequently the teacher in charge of them called out to her to pay attention, but Clare paid her no heed.

'How can I meet him? How? How?' she wondered. 'The exams are coming to a close and soon term will be finished. If only these teachers were not watching me so closely!' she thought angrily. 'I will see him tonight. I will.'

She waited until the teacher's back was turned, then she slipped Astrid a note, which read, 'When we leave class tonight, I am going for a few minutes. I won't be long. Please cover for me.'

Astrid quickly put it between the pages of her notebook and looked at her sister angrily.

When they were dismissed, they both dawdled along the corridor, deep in conversation.

"Please don't go, Clare," Astrid pleaded in vain.

"But I must. I must," she replied.

As quick as a flash she slipped out through a side door. Astrid hastened to their room, locked the door and flung herself onto the bed. She hid her face in the pillow and sobbed in despair.

'Oh, what if the principal should come here before she gets back?' Astrid thought, her panic getting worse every minute. 'I won't put the light on; then they will think we are in the music room.' She lay there, hardly daring to breathe.

Clare ran as fast as she could, dodging behind anything that would hide her if she heard voices or the sound of someone coming. At last she was behind the bushes near the tennis courts and she felt Victor's strong arms embracing her. She was quite breathless. He released her for a brief moment to declare his love, over and over again, and to whisper her name.

"Did you see my father?" she gasped. "What did he say to you?"

"Well, of course he was very, very angry. He forbade me to see or speak to you ever again, which I had to agree to – otherwise, he said, he would return to the college and take you back home with him that very day. I had to agree to those terms, knowing I could never keep them, so here we are." He kissed her passionately.

"We can run away!" she exclaimed breathlessly. "Please think of something, my darling," she implored.

"I already have. I have thought of nothing else. We will go to my houseboat in Kashmir. It's my very own. No one will find us there."

"Oh yes, darling, let's go when term ends. I will try to make Astrid understand. It has to be. It's the only way," Clare said.

"I am also leaving the academy. I have not told them yet – and, on second thoughts, I won't tell them in case they notify my father. He – like your father – will be very angry. Now, my darling, I must let you go. I dare not let you get into any more trouble. I will wait here every night. Come if you can." He kissed her again passionately before he reluctantly let her go.

"I will, I will."

All was quiet as she hurried back. She was thankful to get to her room without being seen. Astrid let her in after she gave their secret knock.

"Clare, Clare, I cannot stand all this. I wish Papa had taken us home with him." She was almost in tears.

For a moment, Clare felt remorse as she looked at her sister's unhappy face.

"Darling, darling Astrid, I am so sorry to cause you so much distress." She put her arms around her sister. "Please try to be happy for me. We are going to go away at the end of term."

"Run away!" Astrid exclaimed angrily. "Have you both gone completely mad?" She held her head in anguish. "You must be mad to even think of such a thing."

"Well, Victor has got it all planned. He has his own houseboat in Kashmir, so I shall be quite safe. There will be no need for anyone to worry about me. Astrid darling, help me. It is the only way," she implored. "I shall never leave him – never, never!"

"But you will forget him, Clare, when we get home."

"I am not going home. Cannot you understand? I am not going home with you. Can't you see? It will help you also, as Papa won't send you to live with Aunt Agatha by yourself. Before long, Victor and I will be married."

"Married!" cried Astrid, almost speechless with shock. "But that cannot be! He is not of the same religion. It won't work out."

"Of course it will. Love always finds a way, they say. We love each other too much. Nothing else matters."

"But, I tell you, Clare, it will never work out – never, never."

"Oh Astrid, you are such a scary-pot! Wait till you fall in love as Victor and I have. Then you'll see. Nothing is going to stand in my way," she declared defiantly. "I am going to marry him and that is that." She casually plonked herself on her bed, as if she didn't have a care in the world.

"Papa will forbid it. You will never get Mama and Papa's blessing, and it will mean I shall not be your bridesmaid as we always promised each other. Please, Clare, it doesn't bear thinking about."

"Well, don't think about it," Clare said curtly. "Just help me to think things out by the end of term."

Astrid was realising that reasoning with Clare was useless.

"How shall we know where you are in Kashmir?" she asked. She was hoping that if Clare told her, she could notify her father in time and he could prevent her reaching the houseboat.

"I will ask Victor for the address and leave it with you just before you leave on the train for home."

"You seem to have thought things out very clearly without my help up to now," said Astrid a little bitterly. "Have you thought how difficult it will be for me when I reach home?"

"Yes, my dear sister, I worry about it all the time. But, Astrid, can't you see: I just have to go with him. I couldn't bear to be sent away to live with Aunt Agatha. She is so strict – just like Papa. I will just die if I get sent back there, and I know Papa would send me there alone. Please, Astrid, just help me to make some Indian clothes. We will all go to the bazaar again tomorrow so we can go back to the silk shop and I will buy material for a sari and a yashmak and some bangles. I will keep myself covered as much as I can when I leave."

"And what about your green eyes?" Astrid queried, getting a little more interested. She thought, 'If I am going to help, I might as well do the job properly.' She could see Clare was not going to change her mind, and she knew they would not be coming back to the college. Therefore, she wouldn't have to face their friends and listen to all their sinister giggling all next term. 'Besides,' she reasoned, 'I also know Papa will find her before she gets too far away.'

"Well," said Clare, still determined to have the last word, "some of the women in Kashmir have grey eyes and quite fair skins."

"I know that," said Astrid resignedly, "but what about your red hair?"

"Well, I will just keep my head covered, silly; if I put plenty of mascara on, no one will take too much notice of me."

"Where are you going to get mascara from? You know we are not allowed to use make-up of any kind – so there!" said Astrid.

"Oh, Meg will give me some. She acts in all the school plays. I will tell her I want to experiment with some just for fun. If I hide behind my sunglasses as often as I can, and also keep my eyes down like Indian women do, I will be all right until we reach the houseboat."

"As always, you have thought about everything. I do wish you would change your mind. It frightens me so," said Astrid, shuddering at the mere thought of it all.

"Don't be so scared, Astrid. I am going through with it. I will tell you the whole plan later."

CHAPTER 235

The next day, they all went to the bazaar under the watchful eye of two of the teachers.

"Now, you girls must all keep in groups and you must all be back here within the hour. No one must wander away," one of the teachers stressed.

"Very well, Miss Marsh," they chorused.

"And where might you be going, Clare and Astrid?" she asked when she saw them heading off in the opposite direction to the other girls.

"We are just going to get some matching silks for our embroidery. They might not have them again," replied Clare.

The teacher hesitated for a moment as if considering whether or not to go with them, and they looked at each other askance, praying deep down that she would decide against it. Miss Marsh had had strict instructions not to let these two out of sight.

"Well, I see the shop is not too far away, so go along," she said.

The twins were thankful that just then Miss Henry came to speak to Miss Marsh, and she nodded her approval for them to proceed.

The little man was surprised to see them again. He unrolled his bolts of silks and other fabrics, and the girls enthused over the pretty bangles as they tried on one after another. Astrid often glanced fearfully towards the door as Clare made her choices.

'What', the shopkeeper thought, 'do the English Missy memsahibs want with bangles and lengths of fine silk?' Their constant whispering to each other puzzled him, but he thought, 'I can never understand these memsahibs.'

"I wish", said Clare behind her hand, "that I could buy a burka – then I should be well hidden from view."

"Oh, don't be silly, Clare," Astrid said sharply. "We will be lucky to get away with these few yards of materials in our satchels. Goodness knows what will happen to us if a teacher wants to see what we have bought."

"Well, I will keep some silks handy; then if she asks, I can show her my satchel and you can walk on ahead. Then she won't bother us any more," said Clare.

Clare had just paid for her things and hastily put them away when Miss Marsh appeared at the door.

"Have you got what you came for, girls? We are all waiting."

"Yes, Miss," said Astrid thankfully.

That night, as she met Victor, Clare told him all her plans in between his passionate kisses.

"My darling Holly has thought of everything," he said, "but how can I kiss you if I have to keep answering all your questions?"

"Do you think it will work?" she asked nervously.

"I don't see why not. Anyway, I shall be doing all the talking, so you need have no fear on that account."

"I shall not fear anything when I am with you."

"No, my darling; I shall always see that no harm comes to you."

"Now, I must go," she sighed.

He gave her another long, lingering kiss before she left.

Some days later, Clare dressed in her Indian outfit and looked at herself in the mirror.

"Do you think I shall pass for an Indian lady, sister dear?" she asked.

"I cannot think of anything any more. I am feeling more and more sick at the thought of it as time passes."

"It will be all right, Astrid – you'll see. Everything will work out perfectly."

Astrid shrugged her shoulders resignedly. "Did you manage to convince Meg about the make-up, Clare?"

"Yes, I told her I wanted to use it for our end-of-term masquerade dance and – would you believe it? – she swallowed it all. It took me all my effort to keep from laughing at her serious face."

"Now, take everything off before someone comes," groaned Astrid. She held on to her stomach, expecting any minute to be sick with nerves.

"I have the address in Kashmir, but you must promise me you won't tell Mama or Papa or anyone else."

"I promise – but I wish you would change your mind."

"Please don't worry. I will write to them as soon as I can. I will give it to you as you board the train, so don't lose it or give it to anyone. Now promise."

"Yes, I promise," she replied resignedly, "but I know Papa will demand it. I just know." She held her head in anguish.

"Well," Clare replied defiantly, "we will be married by then. I will belong to Victor, so Papa will not be able to make me return."

"Mama and Papa will be so angry with me," wailed Astrid as she hid her face in her pillow.

CHAPTER 236

It was the end of term and everyone was excited about the approaching masquerade dance.

"We are going as Maid Marion and Robin Hood," declared Clare, "and for once I am going to be the girl, Maid Marion. When I slip away for a few minutes to tell Victor the time we shall be leaving on the train, being dressed as a woman I'm less likely to be missed. There will be so many of the others dressed in long dresses that my absence will, I hope, go unnoticed. Dear Astrid, please don't stand around looking like a lost sheep or else people will start asking you, as Robin Hood, where is your Maid Marion? Go to the cloakroom for a while."

Astrid looked at her askance. "Well, don't you be away long," she said. "I am not going to spend all evening in the cloakroom. I am hoping to do some dancing." Her fear of what the future held in store was making her more nervous by the minute.

At last they were ready to go. As soon as they entered the dance hall, Meg approached them. "I know which of you is which tonight as Maid Marion has the make-up on and it was Clare who was going to practise with the little I gave her. Did you manage all right, Clare?"

"Yes, thank you, Meg. Does it look all right?"

"Yes, it suits you. You look so beautiful tonight in that dress. I expected Astrid to come as the lady tonight as you are always such a tomboy, Clare."

"Well, we thought it would be nice to be different tonight, didn't we, Astrid?"

"Yes, we did," said Astrid, prompted by Clare's dig in her side.

"Well, I will see you both later," said Meg as she slipped away.

Clare's eyes followed her.

"The silly chump!" she exclaimed. "Fancy asking if I managed the make-up all right! Now, Astrid, at eight o'clock, I shall disappear, so you do likewise."

"But what if I am dancing, Clare?"

"Well, go as soon as you have finished the dance, but I am going at eight."

"Oh, very well, then," said Astrid. "I will watch the time."

Clare felt like Cinderella as she waited impatiently for the clock in the hall to strike eight.

Victor had promised to come as close to the school dance hall as he dared, and she had not gone many yards before she was in his arms. He threw a fine Kashmir silk shawl around her shoulders.

"I knew you would feel chilled coming out of the hot dance hall, and I knew you wouldn't risk being seen putting your cloak on."

"What a dearest darling you are, my love!" she exclaimed between his passionate kisses, as he held her close. "How did you manage to get so close to the college?"

"Well, the nightwatchman did try to bar my way, but I spoke to him in his language and he let me pass."

"Oh, you are so wonderful!" Clare exclaimed breathlessly. "It seems you will not let anyone or anything stop you doing whatever you wish."

"Well, I wish you would stop talking," he replied before he kissed her again and again. "You know you must return in a few moments, and yet here you are wasting all our time. Now, tell me: when are you leaving?"

"The day after tomorrow, on the usual train. I shall be disguised as a very smart Indian lady, so watch out for me."

"I would know you in the midst of a hundred very smart Indian ladies, my precious Holly, so I will soon find you. I shall be dressed in my uniform. I haven't notified the military academy that I am leaving. I shall tell them later that my father needs me at home. We can discuss that later. I have all our plans made. All you have to do, darling, is not to be on that train with your sister. I know it won't be easy for you to get away."

"But I am getting away with you, my darling, and that is all that matters. It is upsetting my sister, but she knows it has to be this way."

Suddenly she thought of Astrid, probably still waiting idly in the cloakroom in the dance hall. She gave a gasp of dismay.

"Now, Victor, I must go," she said. "I will meet you as planned."

He kissed her passionately before she could escape.

"I will escort you as close to the door as I dare," he said. "Then I will know you are safe."

Astrid, hid herself in one of the toilet cubicles whenever she heard someone coming. She looked at her watch impatiently as the minutes passed by. It was 8.30 and Clare was not yet back. 'As if I haven't enough to worry about when she leaves!' she thought, her panic rising.

Suddenly, she heard her name being called softly: "Astrid, come – there's no one here at the moment."

"About time too, Clare!" she said angrily. "Look at the time."

"I didn't think I had been so long. I couldn't see my watch in the dark."

"Oh, any excuse!" exclaimed Astrid impatiently. "Now, I suppose we had better slink back. I am sure someone will have noticed our absence."

"Oh, don't be such a scary-pot. Come – you go down one side of the room and I will go down the other. Just mingle with any group you see. No one knows which of us is which, in spite of our costumes," Clare said.

She slipped out of the room, and Astrid followed her a few seconds later.

Astrid tagged on to the crowd where Meg was, and she began chatting away as if nothing was amiss. Clare hastened down the opposite side of the room and bumped straight into Miss Andrews.

'Just my luck!' she thought.

"Are you all right, Miss Stewart?" Miss Andrews asked, using Clare's surname as she didn't know which of the twins she was addressing. It always annoyed her immensely when she found, as she often did, that she was addressing the wrong one. "You look rather flushed and dishevelled. Are you sure you are well?"

"Yes, Miss Andrews, I am quite well, but I am finding the room rather warm," Clare said.

"Well, don't go outside to cool off, will you?"

"No, Miss, I won't," Clare replied, suddenly feeling a strange panic. 'Has she seen something?' she thought.

"I see your sister over there with Meg. I daresay you are anxious to join them," said Miss Andrews.

"Yes, Miss."

"Well, off you go and enjoy yourselves as it will be your last dance."

'Well, if that remark had come from Miss Marsh, I am sure she would have meant it kindly,' Clare thought 'but coming from that acid drop, I suspect it is no such thing. She is certainly glad we are not coming back. Well, I am glad too,' she told herself as she hastened away after bidding Miss Andrews goodnight.

CHAPTER 237

The next day they spent packing and each seeing the principal in turn for their exam results and conduct reports. Clare had already seen Astrid's excellent exam results and good-conduct remarks. She knocked apprehensively on the principal's door. 'What will this acid drop say to me?' she thought as she stood waiting.

"Come in," the principal called. She glared at Clare over the top of her rimless spectacles as she entered. "I left your report till last," she said as she handed it to her. "You have done rather better than I thought, but, of course, not nearly as well as your sister. All your class reports mention your inattention. Can you explain why?"

"No, Miss," answered Clare.

'Why does she keep on?' she thought angrily. 'She is dying to tell me it's all Victor's fault.'

"You may go," said the principal. "You will note that I have not mentioned why you cannot return to my college. Your parents have been informed, and your father did tell me that both of you would be going to Scotland to finish your education. I wish you well for the future."

"Thank you, Miss," Clare said. She turned towards the door as hastily as she could. "Who wants to return to your old college anyway? I don't!" she hissed under her breath.

"Did you say something, Clare?"

"No, Miss," Clare answered, closing the door none too softly.

The principal tut-tutted her displeasure.

The mention of her education in Scotland shook Clare rigid. The steps she had planned so carefully and light-heartedly with Victor were now beginning to take on a seriousness she had not contemplated. 'Well,' she thought, gritting her teeth, 'I am not changing my mind for anyone.'

She skipped hurriedly past the common room, where all the other girls were laughing and talking gaily as they compared their reports.

"Will Clare be coming in with hers?" asked Meg.

"No, I don't think so," Astrid replied. "She hasn't yet started to pack."

"Neither have I," Meg rejoined.

"Now, I must hurry, Meg," said Astrid. "Excuse me – we have a lot to do."

Astrid found that Clare had almost finished her packing.

"I daresay you have just thrown everything in your trunk as usual," said Astrid.

"Yes, I have – and good riddance! I won't need anything in there ever again. Now I have only my hand luggage. The bearers will collect our trunks early in the morning, the head girl said."

"Well, I had better hurry," said Astrid as she laid everything folded very neatly in her trunk and turned the key in the lock. "You had better give me the key to your trunk, Clare."

"Yes, catch!" said Clare as she whizzed the key across the room. "How glad I am to be getting rid of that old acid drop's uniform! In future I shall only dress in the finest silk saris, Victor says," she said as she pirouetted round the room.

Astrid watched her for several minutes as she packed her hand luggage. "I am sick of hearing about Victor," she said.

"Well, you won't hear his name again for a while after tomorrow, dear sister," Clare replied as she climbed into bed. "Thank goodness I shall have a decent bed to sleep in! I am sick of these old bunks and this old college and that old high-and-mighty principal. How Grandmama ever came to recommend this place to Papa I will never know," she exploded.

She clambered out of bed and sat on Astrid's bed; she held her sister's hand as she looked at her sadly.

"Dear, sweet Astrid," she said, "we will see each other again – maybe in a few years, maybe sooner. I know Papa won't send you to Scotland alone. I will write to you every week."

Astrid sat up and stared at her wide-eyed. "At last, Clare, you seem to be realising what all this is about," she said. "This is our last night together. We have never been away from each other before, even when we had the fever and we went to hospital. Please change your mind and come home with me," she pleaded tearfully.

"I cannot, I cannot, my precious sister. That I cannot do, even for you. I just have to go to Victor. Now, you won't forget the plan we have discussed, will you? I know it won't be easy for you on the journey or when you get home, but Mama and Papa will understand when they know how happy I am going to be. I will write to them as soon as I can."

She related the plan again to Astrid as she sat on her bed: "When we get to the station, I will hurry to the ladies' waiting room and leave my hand luggage in there except for my satchel. No one ever uses it so it will be quite safe. Then I will join you again. No one will notice I haven't got my hand luggage. We will keep side by side, very close, just in case. Then the teacher will tick our names off as we both get on the train. I will pile our satchels and topcoats over the top of your hand luggage and everyone will assume there are two lots of hand luggage on the rack. As always, we will only have two junior scholars with us. They won't be too talkative to us seniors, so they won't ask any awkward questions."

"What if the head girl, Sadie, comes to check after you get off?" asked Astrid fearfully.

"Well, tell her I have gone to Meg's compartment. In any case, bossy Sadie will have to hurry to her own compartment before the train leaves. I won't leave our compartment until the last possible moment, so really she won't have time to come checking – I hope not, anyway," she said as an afterthought.

"My goodness!" Astrid exclaimed. "You certainly have Papa's way of working things out – so precise and perfect. You never cease to amaze me. No wonder he wants you to go into law!"

"Well, I have no intention of following in his footsteps," Clare replied. "Now, listen very carefully, Astrid. It must be very clear in your mind as I won't have time to repeat any details tomorrow."

"Oh, I am getting quite sick at the thought of tomorrow," Astrid replied.

"Don't be such a scaredy-cat. Just be outwardly calm and inwardly excited, like I am," said Clare.

"But I am not like you, Clare. I just cannot do the things you do."

"Well, maybe it is just as well. I don't think Mama and Papa could cope with another like me," Clare said, laughing gaily.

"It's nothing to laugh about," said Astrid with a pout, thinking of their parents and what awaited her if this hair-raising scheme of Clare's went through – as, knowing Clare as she did, it certainly would. "I'm so scared, Clare," she said.

They both looked anxiously at each other as a knock on the door silenced their conversation.

"It's only me," said Meg.

They bade her enter.

"We are taking snacks tomorrow," Meg said, "including drinks. We will have one long stop in which we can get out of the train for a hot meal, but that will be late tomorrow afternoon. Sadie came to tell us in the common room, but you had just left so I told her I would call and tell you. Now, I must hurry. I see you have both finished packing and I have yet to start. Goodnight."

"Thank you, Meg. Goodnight."

"Gosh! She gave me quite a start. I thought it was that old witch, the principal, telling me I had to sit with her in her compartment," said Clare with a sigh of relief.

"Clare," said Astrid in alarm, "what if the teacher does a roll-call when we get to the meal station? She does sometimes."

"Well, I shall be far away by then, and she won't be able to do anything about it. There was no roll-call last time we travelled home, so stop worrying and go to sleep. Goodnight."

"Goodnight," Astrid replied disconsolately, knowing that she wouldn't get to sleep.

"Clare," Astrid called out a few minutes later.

"What is it now, Astrid? You know we have to get some sleep. We both have long journeys tomorrow."

"Yes, we have," Astrid rejoined, "in opposite directions, that is why I cannot get to sleep. What if the other girls think it strange that we are not together when we arrive at the station for our meal. What shall I tell them?"

"Oh, tell them anything you can think of. Tell them I am talking to our other friends. If anyone gets too inquisitive, tell her to mind her own business. They are juniors; they are not entitled to question us."

By now Clare was getting quite exasperated at Astrid's apprehension and she herself was getting more nervous. However, she cleared her mind immediately.

"Now go to sleep," she said.

CHAPTER 238

The day of their departure dawned clear and sunny. All the girls were agog with excitement. Shrieks of girlish laughter and chatter filled the station, which, as always, was filled to capacity with people dressed in every colour imaginable.

"It's just like bedlam as usual," remarked Miss Marsh.

She tried to tell the girls above the noise to keep in orderly lines ready to board the train when it arrived. All their main trunks had to be loaded on first. She knew they would take ages getting aboard.

Clare waited until she saw the train approaching the station. She knew that its arrival would cause the teachers more worry and apprehension regarding their charges – especially the juniors. Clare spied her chance, hurried to the ladies' waiting room and hastily put her hand luggage under one of the large easy chairs. She was thankful that the large frill of the one she chose reached almost to the floor, and she was relieved that no one else was in the room.

She hastily sped back to where Miss Andrews was checking everyone was present. Astrid had already informed the teacher that her sister had just slipped to the ladies' room.

"Why did she leave it so late? She knew the train was coming in," Miss Andrews exclaimed angrily. Then she saw Clare panting along the platform. "You are last again as usual, Miss Stewart. Your sister has already got in the compartment."

"Thank you, Miss. Sorry, Miss," Clare replied.

In her haste she tripped and fell. She picked herself up and brushed her uniform down.

"You must be more careful, my girl," said Miss Andrews as Clare straightened her hat. "We don't want to have to tell your parents that one of their daughters had to be left behind in hospital, now, do we?"

"No, Miss."

"Where is your hand luggage?"

"My sister has it," Clare replied.

Crossing her fingers, she rushed to join Astrid.

"Thank goodness – only four berths, Astrid! That means there's less for us to worry about. Here come the juniors, and here are our two," said Clare as she leaned out of the window.

"I notice you say 'for us to worry about' when you know full well you won't be here to worry about anything," said Astrid.

"I am sorry, Astrid," said Clare as she hastily slung their satchels, Astrid's hand luggage, their top coats and hats on top of the luggage rack.

They helped the juniors inside and all introduced themselves. Miss Andrews peered into their carriage and beamed with pleasure to see Clare assisting the juniors with their luggage – as Clare intended she should.

'It's about time that girl made herself useful,' Miss Andrews thought.

She proceeded down the platform, checking the other compartments with Sadie, the head girl.

Astrid and Clare stood at the open window and watched them both enter the train. Clare stretched her neck further, looking at the milling crowd on the platform. 'Thank goodness!' she thought. 'I shall soon get lost in this crowd.'

She squeezed Astrid's arm affectionately in farewell. Then she exclaimed loudly, "Oh, I forgot: I left my meal box with Meg. I must go and get it."

She opened the carriage door and was gone, her plaits blowing in the wind. Astrid gazed after her, almost in tears.

"Do hurry back, Clare, before the train starts," she called, not so loudly that Clare would hear her but loudly enough to be sure the junior girls did. Suddenly, she felt sick as she felt the lurch of the train as it started to move. "Now", she exclaimed angrily, "she will have to stay with Meg until the train stops."

The two juniors looked at her askance.

"Will there be room for her in Meg's compartment?" asked Monica Selby.

"Oh, yes, we went earlier to talk to Meg and there is only herself and two juniors with her, so Clare will be quite all right." Astrid hoped that she wasn't telling a serious lie. She stood with her fingers crossed. "How she came to put her meal box down in there I'll never know," she added. She looked sideways at them as she spoke. They seemed satisfied with her answer.

She looked out of the window and saw the door of the ladies' waiting room open. A sari-clad figure looked in her direction, raised one arm to her and disappeared in the crowd.

'Oh, if only it could have been different!' she sighed. 'I do hope Victor is waiting for her.' Inwardly she was quaking. She sat down as she felt her legs go weak.

'Well,' she thought, 'two days before I reach home! I wish I was there already. I don't know what I will say to Mama – and as for Papa!' She gave a shudder at the mere thought of it, and she gazed silently out of the window.

CHAPTER 239

Clare hurried along the platform with her eyes down. She pulled her scarf lower over her head, obscuring most of her face, but no one gave her a second glance and gradually she began to feel more at ease. At last she saw Victor looking for her as the departing train disappeared from sight. She reached his side and gave a little laugh as she tugged his arm.

"Are you looking for me?"

"Well, well, my little crown jewel, I hardly recognised you. I thought you had changed your mind and that I had lost you for ever. Now, you should not be seen tugging my arm. It's not done. Just keep close behind me as we board our train for Kashmir. It is already in the station and my compartment is reserved, so we won't be disturbed."

He stood to one side as she leaped on the train. Then he quickly locked the door and pulled down the blinds. She sat facing him, her face still hidden. Her large green eyes, now a little frightened at her escapade, peeped at him. He gazed at her sympathetically.

'My poor darling!' he thought. 'How frightened she looks! Soon I shall allay all her fears. Now she is mine and mine alone.'

As soon as the train pulled away, he leaped to her side and kissed her passionately.

"I am going to kiss you all the way to Kashmir and only stop when we are at the stations," he said. "My darling, you must not speak if anyone approaches. Leave the talking to me. I don't want anyone to suspect anything, so keep your face covered."

"But I don't like my face covered," Clare said pleadingly.

"I know, my darling, but you must until I say it's safe. There are always lots of English people travelling to their houseboats in Kashmir, and they wouldn't approve if they saw an English girl in the company of an Indian officer. In the same way, my people would not approve if they saw me in the company of an English girl. If we do not wish to be discovered, we have to be very careful."

CHAPTER 240

The train chugged on throughout the night. The juniors, after their prepared snack and warm drink, had clambered into their overhead bunks without a care in the world. Astrid, unable to eat or sleep, tossed restlessly throughout the night. She dreaded what the morrow would bring, but her main worry was that Clare had not found Victor waiting.

'Oh, how did I get into this awful situation?' she angrily exclaimed to herself. She almost spoke aloud, but, just remembered in time that one of the juniors might be awake and hear her.

The next day at last the train drew to a halt.

"This is our meal station," Astrid called to the juniors as they hurried from the bathroom. "Now we have two hours here before the train restarts, so follow the rest of your form to the station dining room. The meal will be waiting for you. I am going to see my friends, so cheerio for now."

After they left, Astrid sat pensively in the carriage wondering what to do for the best. Suddenly, Meg's face appeared at the window. "Aren't you coming, Astrid? Where is Clare?"

"I don't know. She skipped off the train. You know how restless and impetuous she is. She cannot wait or keep still for long."

'Well, that is true,' Astrid thought: 'I don't know where she has gone.'

"Well, come – let us go for our meal. She will be around somewhere," said Meg.

'That's what you think!' Astrid thought.

They both drifted off to the station restaurant. When the juniors had finished their meal they headed back to the train under the watchful eyes of the teachers. Suddenly, Astrid saw Sadie Westbury making a beeline straight for her.

"Astrid, I just wanted to ask you—"

Astrid coloured up with fright, and Sadie and Meg looked at her questioningly.

"You look so flushed," said Sadie. "Are you well? You haven't got a fever, have you?"

"No, I am quite all right."

"I just wanted to know if you and Clare will be in our tennis squad next term. You are both such excellent players. I know you used to practise every night before we left, and we do want to win the tennis tournament again this year, don't we, Meg?"

"Yes, we certainly do, and we will be sure of winning it with Clare and Astrid in the team."

"Yes, of course we will," replied Astrid, hardly realising what she was saying.

"I will tell Clare you agreed. I will look out for her so that I can confirm it," said Sadie as she went on her way, pencil and paper in her hand.

The senior girls were now all in the station restaurant; Astrid was sitting opposite Meg. She looked anxiously round. She could see Sadie looking for Clare. Eventually, she approached Astrid again.

"I cannot see Clare. Have you any idea where she might be? She is usually with you. When did you last see her, Astrid?"

"Some time ago. She has more friends than I have; she must be with one of them."

"But all the seniors are here," Sadie insisted.

She went on her way looking puzzled. Meg looked anxiously at Astrid after she left.

"Astrid dear," she said, "you look so upset and on edge. Are you in any kind of trouble?"

"In a way, yes, Meg. Clare is not with us on the train. She has run away."

"Run away!" Meg gasped in dismay. "When?" She clasped her hand to her mouth.

"Just before the train left. She has gone to that friend she met from the military academy close to our college. Meg, please don't say anything."

"No, of course I won't, but how are you going to explain her disappearance to your parents?"

"I wish I knew." She sighed as she sat twirling her fork around in her fingers.

"Well, try to eat something," Meg begged of her. "You are going to need all the strength you can get. I see Sadie is still looking for her. She never gives up, that one. She is now going to have a word with the principal."

They watched as Sadie and the principal walked back to the train together. The rest of the teachers followed with the other girls.

The principal sat in her compartment tucking in to her favourite chocolates.

"Well, Sadie, if you think a check on the senior pupils is necessary, go along with Miss Andrews. She knows all the girls so well. We still have plenty of time before the train departs."

"Yes, Miss," Sadie replied before she left the compartment.

Miss Andrews and Sadie checked each compartment and compared their lists.

"No, it's just as I thought," said Sadie: "Clare is not on the train, Miss."

"As if she has not disgraced the school enough!" said Miss Andrews. "As you know, as head girl, anything told to you is in strict confidence."

"Yes, of course, Miss Andrews," replied Sadie, wondering what news she was going to hear.

"Neither of the Stewart girls is allowed back next term. Now, we must go and report to the principal."

Sadie was aghast at the news. 'That vixen Astrid told me she and Clare would be in our tennis squad,' she thought. 'What lies she has told!' She was fuming.

Miss Andrews collected Miss Lawrenson from another compartment. She knew she would need moral support when she relayed the devastating news to the principal.

"You may go to your compartment now, Sadie. You are to be complimented on your observation of the girls. I will see that the principal gets to know of it."

"Thank you, Miss Andrews," Sadie said.

Inwardly she was fuming. She wanted to hear what the principal would say to Astrid. 'Now I will never get to know,' she thought.

"What is wrong, Sadie?" asked her three senior companions as she sat down.

Sadie related the news that Clare was not on the train.

"I bet she has run away with that officer she was seeing on the sly," said Josie Allerton. "She thinks no one saw her, but I did several times, even after her father came to see the principal. Why they never got expelled then I'll never know." Josie was rather peeved that the officer in question had not given her a second glance.

Astrid sat idly pretending to read her book. She noted the two juniors whispering together.

"Is it usual, Astrid," said one eventually, "for a check of everyone to be done?"

"On some journeys home," she replied. 'And this would be one of them!' she thought angrily.

"Well, I do hope no one is missing on this journey," said Carrie, the bolder one of the two, "otherwise the train might not move off until she is found."

"I hope so too," the other junior rejoined. "I am most anxious to get home."

The two teachers entered the compartment of their principal with trepidation. Neither of them was keen to impart the news.

"Well, I presume all is correct," the principal said as she helped herself to the last chocolate.

"No, madam, I regret to say", replied Miss Andrews, the more senior of the two, "that one of the Stewart twins is not on the train."

The principal spluttered in disbelief. "What are you saying?" She almost choked on the chocolate in her mouth. "Not on the train?" Her voice had risen to a crescendo of disbelief. She spluttered and reached for her handkerchief. She was almost swooning with shock. "Go and bring the one on the train to me immediately," she ordered.

Miss Andrews hastened away while Miss Lawrenson waved the smelling salts out of her small Dorothy bag under the principal's nose.

Suddenly, the door of Astrid's compartment swung open.

"Please come with me at once, Miss Stewart," Miss Andrews demanded.

Astrid almost dropped her book with fright. She got up and placed it on her seat, then followed glumly behind as they proceeded along the platform to the principal's compartment. The rest of the girls gazed at her from the windows.

"Well?" the principal snapped at her. (At this stage she did not know which of the twins she was addressing.) "Would you tell me where your sister is?"

"She has run away. She got off the train before it left our school station. She has gone to join Victor. They are on their way to Kashmir now, I think."

"You think! You think!" the principal exploded, her face now almost purple with rage and anxiety.

The two teachers tried to calm her: one fanned her furiously and the other still waved the smelling salts to and fro. The principal buried her head in her hands.

"You see what you and your sister's stupidity has done!" exclaimed Miss Andrews.

"I am so sorry," said Astrid, now petrified with shock and shame.

"And so you should be! Sit down in the corner there and don't dare move," Miss Lawrenson said angrily.

Astrid sat down and gazed out of the window, not daring to look in the principal's direction as she became more and more hysterical. The train had started on its way.

"Whatever will become of her? Whatever shall I tell her parents?" She looked in anguish at the other two teachers for an answer, but none was forthcoming. "To think she would do a thing like this after I gave her a second chance! I should have expelled her the day her father arrived. And to think you, Astrid, would condone such a scheme! What will the other pupils think? And what will their parents think of me and my college for allowing such a thing to happen to one of the girls? They might all decide to withdraw their daughters from the college. Oh, what a disgrace! I shall never get over it. Why," she exclaimed more hysterically, "she might get sold into slavery if that young man isn't genuine." She was becoming more and more inconsolable.

At the mention of slavery, Astrid looked at the principal in panic. She suddenly recalled reading some time ago of young girls being sold into harems. Hadn't her father told her about that when they visited Egypt? 'Oh, my goodness! What have I done to let Clare go through with this mad, mad scheme?' she thought. 'I should have sent a wire to Papa or told someone at the station.'

Suddenly she was terrified. She had never felt so alone before. Her gay, jolly, daredevil, madcap, darling Clare had always been with her, and now Astrid was horrified to think that ill might befall her. How could she ever face her parents – dear, sweet, sweet Mama and dear Papa? She dare not contemplate what he would say or do. The effect of Clare's disappearance on the principal gave Astrid a slight inkling of how her parents would receive the news. They and Grandmama and all their other friends would be beside themselves. Her thoughts tumbled over and over. She was at a loss to know how to cope with this awful situation. Of all the madcap things Clare had done, this was the worst.

'I should have stopped her, I should have!' she thought. 'But then, maybe when they understand how much Clare and Victor are in love, they will accept it. It would have been nicer for Clare to have been married at home; then I could have been her bridesmaid and Papa could have given her away – but then, Papa would not give her away to Victor. He is not of our faith. That is why she had to run away to be married. Oh, I feel so sick. If only I had told someone before the train left! If only! If only! At least it would only have meant a severe reprimand from the principal. As they were not returning to her college next term it wouldn't have mattered. But this – this—!'

"Who will be waiting to meet you off the train, my girl?" the principal's voice boomed at her.

"Only Mama," she replied meekly.

"I should have preferred to speak with your father, but as it is I shall have to explain to your mother that one of her daughters has been left behind and I have no idea where she is."

At the thought of it, off she went again in another swoon. The two teachers tried to bring her round to face the ordeal ahead.

"You ought to be ashamed of yourself, girl," said Miss Lawrenson, "for causing the principal so much distress. Have you nothing to say to excuse your participation in this madness?"

"No, Miss," Astrid whispered, barely finding strength to speak.

"Never mind!" said the principal in between gasps for air. "She will have enough explaining to do when she gets home. Let us hope her sister is found very soon. Goodness knows what might befall her!"

Astrid bent her head to hide her face in her blouse. She felt faint and sick.

CHAPTER 241

At last they arrived at the station. Astrid alighted. She could see her mother looking happily out for them, and she waved gleefully when she spotted Astrid. Then a look of consternation crossed her smiling face as she could see no sign of Clare. Astrid almost fell into her mother's arms, tears streaming down her face. Whether or not they were tears of joy, relief, sadness or anxiety Astrid herself couldn't tell. Her mother's arms clasped her more tightly, and as she looked at her daughter perplexed.

"Why the tears, my child?" she asked. "Maybe Papa will let you return next term if the principal reconsiders her decision. It was Clare's fault, and she was very foolish, but I am sure the principal will change her mind when she sees how upset you are by it all. Here she comes now. By the way, where is Clare? Still talking to all her friends, I daresay!"

"Oh, Mama, how you do go on," Astrid said between her sobs. She shrank further into her mother's embrace when she saw the principal approaching. "I am crying, Mama, because Clare is not with me."

"Whatever do you mean, not with you? Where is she?" Davinia said.

"She left the train at the school station and she has run away with Victor – the officer."

Her mother grasped her throat in disbelief as the principal faced her.

"I think we had all better go into the ladies' waiting room," said the principal. "This is a meal stop for the girls, so they will be going to the restaurant."

She grasped Astrid's mother by the arm and led her into the waiting room. Astrid followed meekly behind.

"Let us hope we are not disturbed," said the principal, as Astrid closed the door.

Astrid and Davinia sat silently as the principal related all that Astrid had told her of the incident. Her mother looked at her daughter in anger and dismay.

"Whatever will your father say? Really, I dread to think!"

Davinia sank further back in the big easy chair. She reached for her handkerchief and dabbed her eyes.

"There was nothing I could do," exclaimed the principal over and over again in panic.

"Please, madam, do not blame or distress yourself. My daughters are old enough to realise what wrong they have done. Thank you for seeing Astrid safely home. You have all the other pupils to take care of. I will write and let you know the minute we get news of Clare's whereabouts."

"Yes, please do. Here is my home address."

"Now, madam, you must really go and get some refreshment before you proceed on your journey. We will stay here until the train leaves."

Davinia and Astrid both stood up to say goodbye as the principal left.

The station restaurant was full with laughter and chatter. By now, everyone knew the truth.

"Oh, it is all so thrilling and exciting," said Meg, glad she had been first to hear the news. "A real romance at last in the school! Only Clare would have the nerve to do such a thing. I feel so sorry for Astrid, though, having to face all the problems when she gets home to her father."

"Well, it serves her right. She is as bad as Clare. She must have helped Clare get away, and she told me lies about the tennis," said Sadie. "What about bringing disgrace to the school? I am glad the principal is not letting them back next term."

She tried to draw her words back, but it was too late.

"So you have known all along, Miss Smarty Pants, that they had been expelled," said Meg angrily.

She was just going to continue her tirade when the principal walked in and sat down at her specially reserved small table. The teachers rose en masse and bade the girls return to the train.

"Miss Andrews," the principal called to her, "please come here one moment."

"Yes, madam?"

"Make sure everyone is on the train. I cannot face any more parents today."

"Yes, madam, I will make sure," she replied.

She had made sure Clare was on the train when it left the school station, but somehow the girl had managed to escape. Miss Andrews couldn't fathom how.

A bearer stood anxiously waiting to take the principal's order, but all she could manage was a sandwich and a cup of tea. This amazed the bearer. He remembered serving her in the past, and she had always ordered several courses.

Eventually she rose and hurried to the train, and soon it was chuffing away out of sight.

'Well,' thought Astrid, 'that's the last time I shall see all my school friends and I have not had a chance to say goodbye. To think I helped Clare carry out this scheme of hers!'

At last Astrid and her mother rose to their feet. She took her mother's arm. She could feel her trembling as they wended their way to the tonga, which was waiting outside the station. Astrid was silent all the way home as she listened sadly to her mother's exclamations: "Whatever will become of her? Wherever can she be? Whatever will your father say?" Tears of anxiety streamed down Davinia's face, and Astrid hardly dared to look at her.

'Poor, poor Mama and Papa! What have we done to you – you who we love so dearly? How could we be so stupid?' she thought. 'Well, how could *I* be so stupid as to let Clare proceed with such a mad scheme? But Clare was so much in love, and they say love is blind. Well, Clare was blind to all these consequences, but she should have realised.' Her thoughts tumbled profusely as she tried to find some excuse for their stupidity, but she found none.

Her mother retired to her room as soon as they reached home. The bearer scratched his head in consternation. Always in the past it had been such a happy time when the girls came home, but now there was no joy at all.

"Where is Missy Clare?" the ayah whispered to him.

"I don't know. The memsahib is sending a bearer to get the sahib from the office."

"Ayah?" called Astrid.

"Yes, Missy memsahib?" she replied, hoping to be let in on the secret of Clare's non-arrival.

"Where is Grandmama?"

"At the mission. She come very soon."

"Thank goodness!" sighed Astrid. "I won't have to experience her wrath for a while."

The ayah brought Astrid a light snack but she hardly touched it. Her mother ate nothing at all. She had gone to lie on her bed, leaving word not to be disturbed. Astrid she sat silently on the verandah.

Stephen gazed in alarm at the bearer when he arrived with the note, and he gave a gasp of dismay when he read its contents: 'Clare is missing. Please come home.'

"Cancel all my appointments until further notice," he told his secretary. "Bearer, call me a tonga as you leave."

Stephen leaped out of the tonga on reaching home and bade Astrid go into his study. Then he raced into his wife's bedroom. He came out very angry and Astrid shrank back in the huge armchair as he stood before her.

"I shall not go into any further details of this sordid affair until your sister is back here," he said. He was speechless with rage as he sat down at his desk and reached for his pen and writing paper. "Now, my girl, if you will give me the address of where this bounder has taken Clare, I will get on to the police straight away. I presume you have it with you?"

"No, Papa," Astrid said between her sobs, "Clare decided not to give it to me as she didn't want anyone to find her."

He stood up threateningly, and for a moment Astrid thought he was going to strike her.

"Do you mean to sit there and tell me you have no idea where she has gone?" he roared at the top of his voice.

The servants listening on the verandah scattered in all directions and looked at one another in dismay. Never had they heard their master raise his voice so angrily before – even when Clare had run away from school. "Has she run away again?" they whispered to one another.

"No, Papa." Astrid wiped away her tears as she tried to speak. "She told me she was going to a houseboat in Kashmir."

"But there are hundreds of those on almost as many lakes. Well, I shall have to call at his academy, and that will mean more of a delay," he declared angrily. "Well, at least I shall get to know where his father's residence is – that is, if his father has a residence, which I doubt. I should have got the address last time I was there and written and told his father, then all this might have been avoided. Now, go to your room and – don't dare to disturb your mother."

"Very well, Papa. I am truly sorry," Astrid said between her sobs as she closed the door.

CHAPTER 242

Craig and Elizabeth were shocked at the news, but they were relieved that Margot and Martin were at the mission, only a few miles away. Margot and Martin came as soon as they read the note Stephen had sent by the bearer. Davinia fell into her mother's arms as soon as she arrived.

"Oh, Mama, whatever shall we do? What will become of my child?" she sobbed. Margot led her back to her bedroom.

"Now, you must rest, my dear. Try not to get so distraught. Clare is not a child; she should have known better than to do such a thing." Inwardly Margot was fuming, but she was determined to try to allay Davinia's fears. "Stephen is making arrangements to travel immediately, and Craig has very kindly offered to accompany him. In the meantime, Martin will take care of everything here."

Margot decided not to chastise Astrid. She knew by her tears and silence that she was suffering enough, and she knew she could have done nothing to stop Clare once that little madam had made up her mind.

After the men left, Elizabeth visited the house daily, after leaving Heather at the kindergarten.

"Any news today, Margot?" she asked one day.

"No," Margot replied sadly. "The men have been gone almost a week. Davinia is distraught, neither eating nor sleeping. I hope we get news soon," she sighed.

"Is Astrid in her room?"

"Yes, she stays there all day reading. She's not eating and I really don't know what to do."

"I will go and talk to her, and I'll take her to meet Heather. Maybe she will come home with me and carry on with her music."

"Yes, yes, I think that will do her good. I will go to sit with Davinia," said Margot.

Elizabeth knocked softly on Astrid's door.

"Come in," Astrid called meekly, and a moment later she fell into Elizabeth's arms, sobbing bitterly. "It is all my fault, Elizabeth, all my fault."

"No, no, my dear, it is not your fault. Clare knew full well what she was doing. She is not a child and she must accept responsibility for her actions. Now dry your tears. I'm sure she will be found very soon. Come home with me and take up your music. On the way we will pick up Heather from the kindergarten."

"Yes, I should like that, but I am so afraid Clare might get sold into a harem."

Elizabeth tried to make light of her fears. "Well, I pity the rest of the women in the harem if Clare arrives," she said. "She would wreck the place within minutes if they tried to keep her there against her will."

Astrid dried her eyes and managed a wry smile.

"Elizabeth," she said, "I am sure Victor would not let that happen to her. He loves her too much. I know he wants to marry her, as she does him. I am convinced of that."

Elizabeth sighed. "But, Astrid dear," she said, "their ways are not our ways. They look at life differently. Clare is under age by our laws, but she isn't by theirs."

Astrid and Elizabeth bade their farewells to Margot and Davinia before leaving.

"Will you let me know the minute you get news?" Elizabeth asked.

"Of course, my dear," Margot said.

CHAPTER 243

Clare, in spite of Victor's nearness throughout the journey, had the feeling of being all alone. She had never ever felt so alone before. She thought of Astrid. She too had never been alone. 'Is she feeling as lonely as I am?' Clare wondered. 'Have they found out yet that I am missing? What will the principal say to her dear, sweet Astrid when she found out? Dear, dear Astrid, I am going to miss you so – and dear, sweet Mama and Papa.'

At last she was realising what misery and anxiety her family might go through when Astrid reached home. If only she could have done it some other way! What of Grandmama? She would be furious. And Elizabeth and Craig? What would they think of her? Surely they, of all people, would understand? Yes, of course they would. Wasn't theirs such a love as hers and Victor's?

"I am too tired to think any more!" she exclaimed. She leaned back with a sigh.

Victor watched her apprehensively.

"Why so sad, my beautiful one?" he asked as he gathered her close and kissed her. "Are you regretting what we have done?"

"No, no, my darling," she hastened to reassure him.

The train was now standing at a station, but she did not gaze out at the teeming crowd. She did as Victor insisted and kept her face covered. He locked the door as he left to order their meal to be served in their carriage. Suddenly, he returned, followed by the bearers. She pulled her scarf around her as she watched them prepare the table. When they left, Victor locked the door and pulled down the blinds.

"Now come, my darling – and please, my darling, do not look so sad." He hugged her close and kissed her passionately. "We will soon arrive home and we will be so happy, just the two of us. We will live happily for ever. Don't you think so, my darling? Please say yes." He tilted her face and gazed lovingly into her eyes. "Say you will be happy, my darling," he begged.

"Yes, yes, my darling," she whispered as she gazed lovingly into his eyes. "I was wondering how my dear Astrid will explain my action to Mama and Papa," she stammered pensively. "I should not have done it this way."

He hugged her close. "But, my darling, there was no other way," he said. "You would have been sent to Scotland, and I wouldn't have seen you ever again. That I couldn't bear."

"Nor I, my darling," she whispered between his passionate kisses, locked in his comforting embrace. "They will understand when they realise how happy I am. I will write to them later."

"Now come," he said, "let us eat and don't worry any more."

She glanced at the beautifully laid table. "I am glad you have sent the bearers away. Now I can wait on you, my master," she said playfully.

"Well, just this once, if it is your wish." He smiled at her teasingly, and she popped a sweetmeat in his mouth.

Suddenly, the train gave a lurch and she fell into his arms.

"Victor, Victor," she pleaded as she looked into his adoring eyes, "don't let anyone take me away from you, will you?"

"No, my darling, I shall never let you go. No one will ever find us where we are going. I have not as yet told my parents I have left the academy." Victor too now realised he would have some explaining to do.

Clare looked at him. "Will they be very angry?" she asked.

"Yes, they will. I have not finished the senior officers' course at the academy, and my father insists that I must graduate so that I can take command of his own corps of guards. But I don't care about that any more. I only know that I love you and nothing else matters. Nothing in the world will ever change that. Ah, I see," he said as he glanced through the window, "that at last we are at our destination."

They alighted from the train and he bade the station porters load their luggage into a tonga. Victor did not fail to notice the questioning look on the bearer's face as he asked, "Is this all, sahib?"

"Yes, that is all." He knew the bearer would have expected more trunks and cases, as was usual when people came to reside on the houseboat for many months.

After a long drive beside the lake, they arrived at Victor's houseboat. Clare glanced up at it apprehensively as she alighted.

"So this is now my home, Victor," she said.

"Our home, my love," he reminded her as he helped her on board.

The bearers and a maid greeted them with salaams and placed garlands of flowers round their necks. Victor saw how exhausted Clare was.

"Now, no talking tonight, my darling," he said as he led her to the door of her bedroom. "You will find your maid inside. She speaks a little English."

He opened the door and Clare gave a gasp of delight as she stepped inside. The decor was the most beautiful she had ever seen. The walls were draped in mauve and pink satin damask, as was the ceiling. The pink satin bedcover and pillows were edged with silver tassels. She gazed in awe as she met her maid, who bowed her head and put her hands together in a salaam.

"Salaam," Clare replied a little shyly, nodding her head in acknowledgement, her usual bouncy greeting failing her for the first time in her life.

Victor turned to go.

"I will visit you later, my precious one," he said as he closed the door.

Clare looked down at her travel-stained sari, then across the room at her hand luggage. She had no change of clothing. The maid eyed her up and down, as if puzzled by Clare's apparel.

'Well, I have been travelling in nothing else,' she reminded herself. 'I will ask Victor to get me some new saris tomorrow.'

She yawned wearily and sank down in the nearest chair.

"Your scented bath is ready, memsahib," said the maid.

"Thank you. Please bring my meal when I have finished bathing."

"Yes, memsahib."

Victor stood a long time looking out over the beautiful, still lake to the mountains in the distance. The water glistened with the reflection of the moonlight. His thoughts mulled over the events of the past few days. Everything had happened so quickly. His thoughts dwelt again and again on the displeasure and anger his parents would show when they found out he had left the academy. 'Well' he thought, 'I have got the girl of my dreams and I am going to marry her, no matter what our parents say.'

He caught sight of the maid standing in the doorway.

"What is it?" he asked.

"The memsahib is asking for you, Raja sahib."

"Tell the memsahib I will see her directly," he said without turning.

She salaamed as she silently slid away.

Sometime later he entered the bedroom where Clare was sleeping. Only the tall candles and the streaming moonlight through the small window lit the room. He moved slowly and silently to her bed and looked adoringly at her as she lay fast asleep. Her long Titian-red hair, now unplaited, was strewn around her pillow. Her white cotton nightgown was in sharp contrast to the deep-pink silver-edged pillows and coverlet.

"My adorable little schoolgirl!" he said softly. A quizzical smile crossed his countenance. "In her school-regulation nightgown!" He looked longingly at her in her exhausted sleep. He longed to hold and caress her, and his passionate love for her almost overwhelmed him, but his desire for her well-being was his chief concern, and he decided to let her rest.

"For all the nights and days henceforth you will be all mine, my darling," he whispered. "I shall dress you in the finest silks and satins, such as you have never seen." He bent down and kissed her lightly on the cheek. "Sleep well, my darling," he whispered.

She stirred but did not waken.

He turned to leave. "Stay close to the memsahib," he commanded the maid curtly as he passed her sitting outside Clare's door.

She stood up and salaamed to him. Then she watched him go to his room before settling down once more on her rug.

518

CHAPTER 244

Clare woke next morning and pondered as she rubbed her eyes. She felt as though everything that had happened had been a dream, but now Victor was kissing her forehead and whispering in her ear: "Wake up, my Princess Holly of the West. We are together and will be for evermore."

"Are we really, my darling?" she tried to say between his kisses.

"Yes, I am sure, my darling. You belong to me now." He raised her up and kissed her. "Now look over there." He pointed to the large chaise-longue, which was now draped with several colourful saris, all sparkling with silver and gold threads and edged with broad bands of gold and silver.

She gave a gasp of delight. "Oh, Victor, they are so beautiful! Which shall I choose?"

"You, my darling, will only wear the one I choose," he said emphatically.

"But why, Victor? I have always chosen which colour of dress I wish to wear," said Clare.

"Because, my precious one, I am your master now. This is the one I have chosen for you to wear this morning." He walked nonchalantly over to the chaise-longue and picked up a turquoise one edged with silver. He laid it on the bed beside her.

She picked it up and caressed it lovingly. "It is just too beautiful," she said.

"Now I will go whilst the maid prepares your bath. Then we will breakfast on the verandah." He kissed her again before leaving.

The maid entered at his command. "Salaam, memsahib," she said. "I will prepare your bath. Here is your robe."

"Thank you."

Clare clambered from the satin sheets and into the robe.

Much later, after several attempts to dress, she called "Maid, maid, please help me with my sari. I really don't know how to put it on."

"Soon you will know, memsahib," she said with a shy smile.

She sat at the dressing table as the maid brushed and plaited her hair.

"You have beautiful hair colour, memsahib," she said as she fastened the ends with two silver tassels.

Clare stood up and viewed herself in the full-length mirror. "My, what a transformation from that old school uniform! I do look like a young lady, don't I?"

"A very pretty young lady," the maid said as she stood back in admiration. "Now go and join the Raja sahib for breakfast."

Clare looked at her. "Why do you call him the Raja sahib?"

"Because he is a raja."

Victor rose to greet her and eyed her from top to toe. "I see the silver sandals fit you," he said. "See how well I know you. You look divine, my darling. Come – sit down and eat. Today I am going to take you for a sail on the lake."

"Victor, the maid called you the Raja sahib. Why is that?"

"Because that is my title, but you can just call me Victor."

"But you are dressed like a raja."

"I always dress like this when I am away from the academy."

"You look like a fairy-tale prince I used to read about when I was small."

"Well, my princess, this is no fairy tale. We are very real. Come – I shall show you the rest of our home."

Each room took her breath away. Never had she seen any to match them. They wandered from room to room, each one decorated in a different colour scheme. All the drapings were of the finest silks, satins, lace and damask, but the crimson damask and gold of the sitting room delighted her the most.

"This, my darling, will be our home for ever," Victor said.

"It's a dream of a home," she said softly. "I know we are going to be so happy here."

He kissed her ardently after he closed the door. "It was given to me by my parents when I came of age," he said. "No one is allowed on board without my permission – not even my parents."

"Not even your parents?" she exclaimed incredulously.

"No, so you see, my darling, we are quite safe from prying eyes."

"But what about the servants?" she asked. "Will they not say they have seen me on board? Then my father might get to know where I am and come and take me away. Victor, please, please, don't let anyone take me away from you."

"No, no, my darling. The servants will not speak. Have no fear. No more worrying!" He held her tightly as he kissed her passionately. "Come – we will go for the sail I promised you," he said.

He helped her into the small boat drawn alongside. Its colourful tasselled awning protected them from the sun. Clare lay back, relaxed and happy, as she trailed her fingers in the lake. There were water lilies of every hue, and Victor pointed out all the different-coloured birds to her. He hailed a small merchant boat and ordered it to follow them back to the houseboat.

"Flowers for the memsahib," cried the merchant.

After Clare had chosen the ones she wanted he ordered the bearer to take them and place them in water till she had time to arrange them.

Victor hailed another small boat. "Now, my love, I will choose more saris for you," he said.

Clare watched the merchant unravel each one.

"But why can't I choose them?" she asked plaintively.

"Because, my pretty Holly, I might not like the colour you choose. As I am now your master," he said playfully, but with a definite note of authority in his voice, "I shall choose the ones you wear."

"Well," she said demurely, "I hope you are going to choose the white one with the gold border, because that is the one I want."

"Yes, my darling, I shall get two. Now, I must buy some cashmere shawls as it gets quite cool in the evening. I have also bought you some gold bangles. You can have six for each wrist."

"Oh, Victor, can I? How good you are to me!" she said, stretching out her arms to him.

"No, no, my pretty one, you cannot wear them till tonight," Victor said.

"But", she replied with a pout, "you know how I love pretty jewellery. Why are you tantalising me so?"

He dismissed the boatmen.

"They will be yours tonight, my dearest one – not before," he said.

"Wear the red sari for dinner," he said as he led her to her room, where her maid was waiting.

"I thought you said the white one," the maid whispered to Victor as he was leaving.

"That is for later."

A puzzled look crossed Clare's face. 'Later, why later?' she thought.

After their candlelight dinner they strolled outside and leaned out to watch the silver moon and the ripples on the water. Faint music was drifting towards them from another boat in the distance. Victor placed a shawl round her shoulders.

"Now, come, my darling – the night air is getting chilled," he said.

He led her past the bedroom she had occupied the previous night.

"Not in there, tonight, my darling!" he said as he led her into his own room, which she had not seen before. He had dismissed the maid and other servants as soon as they finished dinner. "We shall not be disturbed now until I ring in the morning," he said as he locked the door and kissed her.

She gazed round the room, which was lit only by candles in gold candlesticks. The walls were draped with damask satin of royal blue with an arabesque design in gold, which caught the flickering light of the tall candles. The ceiling was draped in paler blue satin. The huge bedcovers were in satin of dark royal blue and the pillows were edged with gold tassels.

"Well, my darling, do you like our bedroom?"

"Yes, my darling, it's like a small palace. I am so happy to be here with you."

"Now, my darling, I want you to go into the small anteroom," he said as he led her to the door. "You must put on the white raiment you find there. I too am going to change into something more comfortable. Don't be long. I shall be waiting."

"I won't," she whispered as he kissed her.

The anteroom was more brilliantly lit. She walked over to the long chaise-longue, on which was draped the white raiment. She held it aloft and gazed at it in amazement. Victor had ordered the durzi to make the two saris into one dress. The gold borders fell down each side; the sides were left open; the opening for the neck was left very low. Beside it lay a length of gold satin to wear as a cummerbund. She hurriedly changed into it and tied the satin round her waist. It fitted her to perfection. She gazed at herself in the long wall mirror. She undid her long braids and let her hair fall down almost to her waist.

'I look like a Greek goddess,' she thought as she rejoined Victor.

He couldn't conceal his look of admiration as he gazed at her in the flickering light of the candles.

"How beautiful you are, my darling!" he exclaimed as she approached.

She gazed at him spellbound. He was standing tall and proud, attired in cream-coloured satin trousers and a fitted coat. Its mandarin collar was studded with rubies and emeralds. The coat was hand-embroidered with exotic birds of every hue.

She had always thought him to be the most handsome man she had ever seen, but attired like this he took her breath away. He looked every inch a prince of the East. His white teeth and narrow black moustache were in sharp contrast against his bronzed features. He flashed her his most mischievous smile, and she smiled shyly back at him. His tantalising eyes gave no clue to what he was thinking.

Suddenly, he swept her into his arms and smothered her with passionate kisses that filled her with an ecstasy she never imagined possible. She hungered for more as she rested in his arms. He picked her up and laid her gently on the bed.

"I love – love you, my darling," he gasped breathlessly. "Tonight and for ever you will be mine and mine alone."

Frenziedly he tore the golden sash from her waist and, for a brief moment, she felt the rubies and emeralds on his jacket brush against her bare breasts. From then on she felt only the overwhelming pressure of his bareness. He smothered her with his passionate ardour until all sense of reality for her ceased. His long, bronzed, slender fingers contrasted sharply with her pearly-white skin. His tenderness as he caressed her voluptuous young body filled her with an ecstasy beyond her wildest fanciful imaginings. Both of them were lost in the fulfilment of their love.

"My *maranee* [great queen], my *maranee*, only mine!" he said breathlessly.

"I love you so, my darling Victor – my darling Prince of the East. Never, never let anyone take me away from you."

"Never, never, my darling," he whispered as he stroked her hair from her forehead and kissed her.

CHAPTER 245

Clare woke next morning to the bright sunlight shining through the small window. Victor was sitting on the bed beside her, attired in a royal-blue robe. He gazed down at her with adoration.

"Wake up my beautiful *maranee*," he whispered as he kissed her. "Now you are my *maranee* I am going to fill your arms with gold bangles," he said, and, as he kissed her hands, he slipped six on each of her wrists.

She fondled them lovingly as she gazed at them in wonder.

"They are so beautiful, my darling," she said as she returned his kisses.

"These bangles tell you that you now belong to me – only to me. Later, I will buy you diamond-studded ones."

"My darling, you are so good to me." She sighed. "Am I now really married to you, my darling?"

"You are, my *maranee*. I have possessed you, so you are mine. Now no more doubt. I am sending in your maid to attend to your every wish." He kissed her again before leaving.

She heard the maid filling her bath. 'Surely,' she thought, 'I must have dreamt all that happened last night.' However, she could see the white gold-bordered raiment flung carelessly at the foot of the bed and the long golden sash lying on the floor and the bangles on her wrists. 'No, it wasn't a dream. At last I really belong to my darling Victor. I am the happiest girl in the world.'

"Your bath is ready, memsahib," the maid said as she laid a silk robe beside her.

"Thank you."

'Never before,' she thought, 'have I ever felt so naked as I do now that I am dressed only in gold bangles,' she admired them as she slipped on the robe.

Every night was a love-filled dream from which she never wished to awaken. One minute he was kissing her tenderly, and the next so passionately she could hardly breathe. He was like a wild tiger in his possession, as he hungered more and more for her nearness. Every moment he declared his love. She was so swept up in his love and tenderness and passion that time did not exist for her.

In the afternoons they walked beside the Shalimar, where they would sit by the hour quoting poetry. Sometimes he would sing softly or hum a little tune.

"Please sing my favourite. Please, please, Victor," she pleaded as she looked adoringly into his eyes. They only had eyes for each other.

"But the one you want, my love, is so sad. Which one is it, my adored one?"

"You know which it is. Why do you tease me so?" she said.

"Well, my love, if I don't tease you, I shall be tempted to kiss you, and that I cannot do here."

"Well, sing my song; then you won't be tempted," she teased.

He began to hum 'Pale Hands I Love Beside The Shalimar'. "It is too sad, my love," he said, "a story of a love that couldn't be."

"It is a great love, like ours, but, unlike the song, ours will last for ever," Clare said. "It will stay for ever, won't it, my darling?"

"Of course, my love."

"I will just die if it doesn't," she said with a sigh.

"Well, my love, I shall never be sat here alone underneath these trees, singing, 'Pale Hands I Love, Where Are You Now?' because you will always be here with me."

"Listen, my darling; music and laughter. It is coming nearer. Is it a wedding?"

"Yes, my love."

"Oh, do let us have a closer look," she demanded excitedly.

"Very well, my darling."

He pulled her to her feet, laughing with her at her excitement.

"Come – we must get further under the tree," he said. He was always conscious of the need to avoid being too conspicuous.

A crowd of dancers came first and then a noisy band playing whatever tune they could think of. Then a beautifully decorated horse came into view. Its rider, the groom, was decked out in the most beautiful-coloured regalia she had ever seen. He was a tall, dark, slender man in long, flowing robes of red and gold, with a length of gold-edged veiling over his face. The children of the village danced alongside.

"Now, heavenly Victor, I wish that man were you coming to claim me for your bride."

"So do I, my darling, but I would be more magnificently dressed."

"How I wish it were so," she sighed.

She turned to face him, her eyes lit up with the thought of it. Her love for him sparkled in her eyes, and the closeness of their bodies sent his heart pounding and his pulse racing.

"My darling, I love you so much," he whispered.

If he had dared, he would have gathered her in his arms. Her gay laughter and exclamation of delight as the wedding passed had caused several people to glance their way. He dared not risk staying longer.

"Come, my darling – we must go. The afternoon is late," he said.

Now and again, she had noticed a flicker of concern cross his face. Silently she prayed that no one would notice her. He always wanted to see her long, red hair floating round her face in the wind, but the thought of her being seen by the residents on the other houseboats caused him disquiet.

'Soon', he thought, 'she will be seen and recognised. She is so beautiful.' He sighed. 'Ah well, I shall cross that bridge when I come to it. This is my country and I shall do as I wish. No one is going to take her away from me.'

Every morning they gazed out to the snow-covered mountains in the distance as they waited for the small merchant boats to draw up alongside. Most were shaped like Italian gondolas, their tasselled awnings blowing in the gentle breeze. They all brought their wares for Clare's approval, and her every wish was granted.

'How lucky I am to be loved so much!' she thought. A faint flicker of misgiving pricked her as she thought of her loved ones at home. 'Surely they will know I am all right! It's not as if I have left the country.'

"Now, my *maranee*, with the little-girl-lost look clouding her pretty eyes, what is worrying you? Write home, my love, if it is worrying you so; then they will know no harm has befallen you. Tell them you now belong to me," Victor said.

"I know, Victor, I belong to you," she replied, "but couldn't we be married officially? Then no one could take me away from you."

"We can, my darling, as soon as everything can be arranged, but at present we have to lie low. There is also the question of my religion, which, my darling, you will have to accept."

"But, I will, my darling – you surely realise that."

"Also, my darling, you will need your parents' consent as you are under age by English law. Now, don't worry any more; you belong to me and that is all that matters. Come – let us go for our sail."

He helped her into the boat and they went for a leisurely sail amongst the colourful water lilies. Every day they enjoyed the same idyllic existence. On their return, the flower seller would be waiting, and Victor would fill Clare's arms with more flowers than she could hold.

She was in a dream world from which she never wanted to awaken. Her love for him was to her like a drug which she could never have enough of. Never in her wildest dreams had she ever imagined love would be like this.

CHAPTER 246

Stephen and Craig arrived at last at the military academy. Stephen was still fuming at the delay this break in their journey had caused.

The commanding officer bade them sit down, and he listened attentively to what Stephen had to say. He was aghast to think that Victor had seduced a young schoolgirl from the nearby ladies' college – especially after his warning.

"The young officer in question is one of the sons of the Maharajah of Jahvizkhan," said the commanding officer. "All his sons, after their education in England, have been sent here to train as officers. He is the only brother who has not been obedient and studious."

"Yes, yes, my dear fellow," declared Stephen with impatience, "I am not concerned as to what the Maharajah's son has or has not done with his time in your academy. Please just give me the address where he will have taken her."

"Well, I can only give you his father's address. I am sure you will find your daughter in safe hands."

He proceeded to copy out the address, and Stephen looked at it in dismay.

"But this is about two days' journey from here!" he exclaimed angrily.

"I am so sorry that I cannot help you further in this matter, but if you would care to rest overnight, you are welcome."

"Thank you kindly, sir, but we must head back to the station and get the first train."

The commanding officer bade them goodbye and watched till their tonga was out of sight. He tut-tutted angrily to himself, deprecating the discredit the young officer had brought to the academy.

"I shall have the principal of the ladies' college to answer to when she returns from vacation!" he angrily exclaimed as he slammed the door of his study and sat down to record the event.

"That's just our luck, Craig," said Stephen as they seated themselves on the train for the start of their journey to the isolated principality of Jahvizkhan, which lies at the foot of the Himalayas. "Surely some English people will have spotted them heading in this direction and informed the authorities. They couldn't have travelled far without someone getting suspicious," fumed Stephen.

"He will have kept her well hidden. It is, after all, his country, and he will know everything there is to know about the land and the art of concealment," said Craig.

"Yes," Stephen agreed, "he probably made her dress in a burka. With her red hair and green eyes it won't be easy to keep her hidden. As she is – or thinks she is – so much in love with him, she will follow him blindly on and on."

At last they reached their destination. They both looked in awe at the huge marble palace glinting in the bright sunlight. The palace guards forbade them entrance until word came back from their commanding officer. At last Stephen and Craig were escorted up the long driveway and shown into a flower-bedecked anteroom to await their summons to the Maharajah's presence.

"Pray be seated," said the Maharajah as he greeted them warmly.

He listened intently to Stephen, who he could see was extremely agitated and annoyed.

"So, it seems my son has left the academy." The Maharajah himself now looked very angry. "And he has eloped with your young daughter."

"Yes, my daughter had been studying at the ladies' college close by, but she was expelled when it was discovered that your son had been meeting her in secret. I visited his academy and left strict instructions with his commanding officer that your son should not see my daughter again.

"A fortnight has now elapsed with no news of her. I had to break my journey and call at the military academy to find out where he lived, as my daughter did not give her sister an address. For obvious reasons, she did not wish to be found. I believe they must be here," he declared angrily.

"My dear sir, I can assure you they are not here. You can rest assured that I would have notified the British authorities immediately, as I am sure your daughter would not have been here without your consent."

Stephen rose to his feet in dismay and anger. "Not here? Not here?" he said. "Then tell me, man, where can she be? I shall hold your son personally responsible if any harm has come to her."

"Pray calm yourself, my dear friend," said the Maharajah. "I understand your worry and concern. I have daughters of my own. I can assure you, my son would not allow any harm to come to her. Now, come and accept my hospitality. Stay here as my guests. I will send my younger son at once to Victor's houseboat. I am certain that is where they will be."

"I should like to go with him and bring back my daughter."

"I do not think that would be wise. My son would not allow you on his boat, but he will have to obey the instructions I send. He will return with her."

"Are you sure of that, sir?"

"Yes, quite sure, so have the hospitality of my home until then."

"What do you think, Craig?" Stephen asked.

Craig could see that the long, tiring journey had told on his strength.

"I think it will be the wisest thing to do, if we cannot hurry things by going," he answered.

"Oh, very well, then," Stephen reluctantly replied, "but I will not wait too long."

"It will only take a couple of days," the Maharajah assured him.

"Another two days, Craig! Davinia will be bereft with anxiety."

'And so will Astrid,' Craig thought. 'They have never been so long apart before.'

CHAPTER 247

"Bearer, Bearer, who is that calling my name?" Victor queried. The bearer leaned over the side of the boat and saw the princely figure of a tall, dark-haired, handsome young man. He looked at him curiously and he knew, by the man's appearance and bearing, that he was someone of importance.

"One moment, Raja sahib," he said.

He hastened away and approached Victor, who was idly lounging on the deck, reluctant to move away from Clare's side.

"What is it, my darling?" she asked, looking at him questioningly.

"What I have been dreading has occurred. My brother, Kassim, has come. He has a message from my father. Now go, my darling, into your room. I wish to speak to him alone."

She rose with a look of panic on her face and did as he asked.

"Bid my brother come aboard, bearer, and tell cook to prepare a meal for him."

"Yes, Raja sahib," said the bearer. He hastened away.

The two brothers greeted each other affectionately.

"Well, my dear Kassim," said Victor, "what message have you from Father?"

"You have to return with me at once. The young memsahib's father has arrived to take her home."

"I daresay they are both stamping their feet with rage?"

"They are, and I wouldn't like to be in your shoes when you meet them face-to-face."

"Well, I have already had one encounter with her father," Victor said with a wry smile, "and I know I won't enjoy the one with Father, but it has to be. Now go and eat whilst I attend to things here."

He went into Clare's room and closed the door softly behind him.

"Father bids me to return at once with you," he said.

She rushed into his arms. "My darling, it means my father has come to take me away from you," she said.

"Yes, I am afraid so, my darling."

"But we cannot go. I love you and you love me and we belong here."

"I know, my love, but our dream is ending – just as I feared it might one day." He held her closely and kissed her and saw the pleading in her eyes. "Oh, my darling," he whispered, "if only we could stay here for ever! But I must do as my father bids."

"You could refuse, Victor. I don't always do as my father bids!" she exclaimed petulantly, willing him to do likewise.

"I am afraid, my darling, my father is not as tolerant as yours. I must do as my father bids. I know your father will not allow you to stay – you are too young."

"I could wait till I was older; then we could marry. I shall tell my father that I shall run away again when I am older and come to you. Don't you see, my darling," she implored him, "they will send me to Scotland as soon as I get home and I shall never see you again. I couldn't bear that."

"Neither could I, my darling, but we will have to do as my father and your father wish. Maybe he won't send you away when he sees how much we love each other." He sighed. "Now, my darling, you must go and prepare for the journey, and I must do likewise."

He held her tightly and kissed her as if he would never let her go. He guessed it would be their last kiss.

Clare salaamed to her maid and said goodbye. Victor rewarded her and the other servants for their services, and asked the head bearer to care for the houseboat until he returned. When that would be he did not know.

Victor and Clare travelled back together, and Kassim followed in another tonga.

Their arrival at the palace caused quite a stir. The guards ran to open the gates as they saw them approach. Clare gasped as she rode up the long driveway. Never had she imagined, in spite of knowing that Victor belonged to a very high-caste family, that he actually lived in a palace such as this. It was beyond her comprehension.

Victor helped her alight from the tonga as Kassim hurried on ahead to tell his father they had arrived.

The bearer salaamed to them as they proceeded towards the steps. "The memsahib's father is in the anteroom, Raja sahib," he said, and he escorted them to the door.

Clare was nervous and afraid as she followed closely behind Victor. The moment she dreaded was upon her. Her father rushed to greet her, almost in tears with relief to see her safe. Craig stood some distance away, breathing a sigh of relief.

'Now I can get back to my angel,' he thought. 'I will send word as soon as we reach the station.'

"Thank God you are safe, my child!" said Stephen.

"I am not a child, Papa," Clare replied.

"Whatever possessed you to run away?" he asked.

"It was all my fault, sir," said Victor apologetically. "It was my idea."

"Well, sir," exclaimed Stephen angrily, "I do not admire your methods of abducting my daughter. You knew she was under age. Fortunately for you, sir, she is now safely back with us. Do you not realise the anxiety you have caused?"

"I do understand, sir, and I am sorry it has caused you so much distress."

"He is not to blame, Papa," Clare interrupted. "It was my idea. I will not let you blame him."

"Well, it is all over now. We will return home at once."

"But I cannot go, Papa. I love him and he loves me." Clare stood looking from one to the other. Victor avoided her tear-dimmed eyes as she continued to beg her father to let her stay.

"We must hurry and get away," he said. "Your dear mother was in a state of collapse when we left a fortnight ago. I dread to think how I shall find her on our return."

Suddenly, the door of the anteroom opened and the Maharajah walked in. Victor bowed to him. Kassim, who was following him, closed the door. The Raja bade Victor stand to one side while he greeted Clare. She bowed her head and salaamed to him in greeting.

"Well, my dear child, I am so glad you are reunited with your father. Now you must return home." He noted that her gaze was fixed on Victor's face as he spoke. She edged nearer to Victor, hoping that they wouldn't be separated in this way.

"But we love each other so, Papa. I cannot go with you," she said pleadingly as she turned to face him.

Victor and Stephen looked at each other, then Victor stood silently aside and looked out of the window. He listened to Clare's pleading.

At last the Raja took Clare by the hand and looked into her tear-dimmed eyes.

"It is better that you go, my child," he said. "Our ways are not your ways. You would miss your way of life and your family and friends too much. At the moment, you don't see it that way, but you will as you get older."

She looked across at Victor, who was still gazing out of the window. He knew he would have to face his father's wrath as soon as Clare left, and he knew he was powerless to prevent her leaving.

"My younger son, Kassim, will escort you safely to the station," the Maharajah said.

They salaamed their farewells and Clare bowed her head in respect to him.

Victor turned from the window and bowed slightly to them. For a fleeting moment, he held Clare's gaze. She tried to protest, but then she turned to go. Never before had he seen such a look of despair or pleading in anyone's eyes.

Suddenly, he shot to her side and snatched her from her father's grasp. He ran with her down the long, marble corridor and out into the garden. Her father cried out in alarm.

"Let them say their goodbyes, Stephen," Craig implored him. Only he understood what these final moments together meant to them.

"Come here and sit down, my friend," the Raja called to Stephen.

He rang for the bearer.

"Bearer, bring some tea and refreshments for my guests."

The bearer slid silently away.

"Kassim, go and tell your brother to return the girl to her father at once."

"Yes, Father," he replied, and he hastened off in the direction they had gone.

Kassim was quite annoyed with his brother, and he grew more angry as he searched the garden frantically.

"How much more running about have I to do after this elder brother of mine?"

he fumed. "I have been at my father's beck and call all my life."

Whenever his father said, "Go find your brother and tell him to come to me at once," Kassim would know which of his four brothers his father meant.

'If I had been old enough,' he thought, 'he would no doubt have sent me to the military academy, just to keep an eye on him. Why he couldn't be like my other brothers I shall never understand.'

Victor was always the most impetuous, daring and disobedient one. He had always stretched his father's patience beyond endurance. 'Let us hope that this present escapade will be his last,' Kassim thought, 'but I doubt if it will be. Now, where can they be?'

Victor could hear Kassim calling his name, but he paid no heed. He and Clare were locked in each other's arms, oblivious to all their surroundings. Clare was sobbing bitterly on his shoulder and he was covering her eyes and lips with kisses.

"Please, my beloved," she pleaded, "do not let them take me away from you. I shall just die."

"I shall die too, my darling. I shall die also," he whispered, "but we must do as our fathers bid and be parted for ever. Inside my heart, dearest one, you will live with me for ever."

"And you will live in my heart too," she sobbed, as she clung to him tightly.

He kissed her passionately, in between his muttering.

"Why, why has it to be so?" he exclaimed. "Why has cruel fate given us so short a time together when our love is so great? Why must we be parted for ever? Think of me, darling," he whispered, "when you hear our song: 'Pale Hands I Love Beside The Shalimar'. Little did we know, my darling, that it would be such a sad parting for us also."

At last, the green bowery leaves parted and Kassim stood there, his eyes blazing.

"Father bids you return Miss Clare to her father at once," he said, and he turned on his heel and left.

Victor kissed her again and again; then he took his initialled silk handkerchief from his pocket, dried her eyes, folded it neatly and placed it in her hand.

"Always keep it close to you, my love," he said. " I shall always be thinking of you." He reached for a rose and broke the thorns off one by one. "Keep this also close to your heart. A rose from Kashmir and Shalimar. Our love story is as great as any yet told. Now, come, my love – we must go."

Victor bowed courteously to Clare's father as he laid her hand in his.

"Good day, sir," he said. "I regret causing you so much concern."

He turned quickly away to avoid her eyes. Her eyes followed him as he left the room. Clare turned to the Maharajah with head bent and hands together.

"Salaam, Your Highness. Thank you for your kindness," she said. Then she wished him goodbye.

He took her clasped hands and held them for a brief moment.

"Salaam, my child. Kassim will escort you to the station. Salaam, my friends," he said, and he turned to follow Victor.

"Thank you for your hospitality!" Stephen exclaimed as they turned to go.

At last they were on their way. As soon as the tonga arrived at the station, Craig leapt out to send a telegram from the telegraph office nearby. Kassim waited till they were all seated on the train before returning home.

Stephen clutched his daughter close. She buried her face in his chest and he stroked her hair.

"There, there, my child!" he said. "Do not upset yourself so. This is for the best. The first love is always the most difficult one to part from."

"I shall never, never part from him in my heart. I just know I won't," she sobbed.

"No, my child, you never will. He will always be there. Only time will ease your heartache, my child – only time."

By now, all Stephen's anger had gone. Now she was his little girl once more, safely back in his arms. He glanced uneasily at the gold bangles on her wrists and wondered when the best time would be to tell her she must take them off. 'Later, later,' he thought. 'Davinia must deal with the matter,' he decided.

Craig sat watching her. He understood her sadness at the loss of her loved one. Hadn't he gone through the same heartache before he was able to follow his darling angel? His love for her had meant the sacrifice of the love of his father and his beloved homeland. He sighed as he thought of it all again; then his heart lightened as he thought that soon he would be seeing his darling angel and their daughter, Heather.

CHAPTER 248

Astrid waited anxiously every day for news. Her mother was still too upset to leave her room. Only the daily visits of Elizabeth and Heather brightened her day, Elizabeth became more anxious as the days slipped by. Never before had she been parted from her beloved Craig for as long as this. Was he well? Had his fever returned? Stephen, with all his own worry and anxiety, had not let them know how his search for Clare was progressing.

Margot, too, became more alarmed. She insisted that Astrid come to the mission for long periods every day to help, but she often sent her back to the house to see if any news had come.

All their friends called often for news, partly out of concern for Clare, but many of them were also hungry for gossip to discuss at their afternoon tea parties and during after-dinner conversations. They were anxious to be first to relate any sordid details that might be forthcoming. Margot and Elizabeth purposely refused every invitation, knowing full well that the conversation would eventually turn to Clare's disappearance. Nothing had ever caused so much excitement in their humdrum lives as this scandal had.

As Mrs Vermont remarked one day to all seated at the afternoon tea party, "Whatever do you think of the audacity of the young girl? She was always wild and unruly, but to think a judge's daughter would do such a thing as to run away with an Indian Army officer! I have been told by my sister, who knows the principal of the college she attended," (and the principal had told her sister in the strictest confidence) "that he was—" Suddenly she stopped in mid-conversation, reluctant to say more.

"That he was . . .? What were you going to say, Mabel?" the woman next to her asked. The group were determined that nothing about this affair would be omitted. They leaned over the table, awaiting the conclusion of the tale Mrs Vermont had started to relate.

"Well, it seems", she whispered, "that he is the son of a Raja."

"Oh, my goodness!" exclaimed the Colonel's wife. "That could cause complications if they marry. Poor Davinia! She's still too ill to see anyone. She doesn't deserve such a daughter. The other daughter is such a well-behaved young lady; it's hard to believe they are sisters."

"Really, it's beyond belief!" exclaimed another.

CHAPTER 249

Astrid was the first to spot the boy with the telegram. She saw him one day as she returned to the house from the mission. She raced up the path after him.

"Boy, boy, please give the telegram to me," she demanded.

"I was instructed to give it only to the burra memsahib," the boy said.

"Well, I will take it to my mother. I will sign your book."

She scribbled her name as fast as she could, and he handed her the telegram. Then he rode off on his cycle.

"Mama, Mama," Astrid called as she rushed into her mother's room.

"What is it, my child? You know how ill with anxiety I am. I cannot stand anyone shouting or disturbing me. I am far too distressed."

Astrid sat hurriedly on her mother's bed.

"Mama, it is the telegram at last from Papa. I will open it for you, Mama," she said breathlessly.

"Well, hurry, child, and tell me what it says."

"It says: 'Clare safe. Am returning with her immediately. Stephen.' "

"Oh thanks be to God! He has answered my prayers."

Tears of relief fell down Davinia's cheeks. Astrid put her arms around her to comfort her.

"Now go and tell Grandmama and Elizabeth and leave me to my prayers," Davinia said.

Astrid watched as her mother knelt beside her bed.

"I will kneel with you, Mama," she said. "We will pray together."

When she heard her name being called, Margot looked up from the small group of children she was talking to. She saw Astrid running to meet her and she knew it could only mean one thing. She bade the children go and play, and she hastened towards her granddaughter.

"Here is the telegram, Grandmama. Clare is safe and they are on their way home."

Margot hugged her close, and they both shed tears of joy.

"Now I have to tell Elizabeth," said Astrid, and off she sped.

Margot hastened to the bungalow and greeted her daughter.

"Come – we will have tea on the verandah," said Davinia.

"I am so glad she is safe. I suppose now the twins will be sent to live with their Aunt Agatha," said Margot.

"They surely will. Their father will not change his mind this time," Davinia replied. "I will write this evening to Aunt Agatha to prepare her for Stephen's letter. What I shall do without my two darling daughters, I just don't know. I found it so hard when they went up to the academy, and now this escapade these last few weeks has made me feel so ill. Do you remember, Mama, what Aunt Agatha's words were to me when we visited her when the girls were small?"

"No, I can't remember for the moment. Agatha is always quoting words of wisdom. What was it she said?"

"Well, she was referring to the two girls – especially Clare, who was creating a fuss because we were thinking of leaving them there to carry on their education. She said, 'My dear Davinia, when they are small they make your arms ache, and when they grow up they make your heart ache.' This saying of hers has been true – especially of Clare."

"You always knew, Davinia, that Clare would grow up to be a wilful young lady," said Margot.

"Yes, Mama, I knew, but at least she will be well chaperoned by Aunt Agatha."

"Yes, Clare will find her wings well and truly clipped," rejoined Margot.

Davinia, Astrid and Margot waited eagerly on the verandah for the tonga to arrive. It had seemed a long day and Davinia was pacing up and down.

"Do sit down, dear," Margot insisted. "They will soon be here."

Clare leaped out of the tonga before it stopped and flung herself in her mother's arms. She wept uncontrollably – partly with relief that at last she was seeing her dear mother again, but mainly with sorrow that her beloved Victor was not with her.

"There, there, my dear child!" her mother said, trying, in vain, to console her.

"I am so sorry, Mama, for causing you so much distress. Oh, I cannot see him ever again and I love him so!"

"You will get over it eventually, my dear child. I know it will be hard for you, but it has to be."

Clare put her arms round Astrid and Margot in turn.

"Forgive me, please, for upsetting you all so," she said, still sobbing.

"It's all right now, my child," Margot whispered to her. "You are safely home; all is forgiven. Now come – we must all eat. Dinner is ready. Astrid, go and ask Elizabeth and Craig to come and join us. Now you, Clare, go and bathe and change after your long journey. Your father is changed already."

Stephen had asked his bearer to prepare his bath as soon as he had said his farewell to Craig. Then Craig had continued home in the tonga, not wishing to be part of this arrival-home scene. He had been away from his darling angel far too long.

Clare did as her mother said, but she did not even glance at her father. She knew that now he was home he would be making plans for their departure to Scotland.

"I suppose you know we are both being sent to live with Aunt Agatha in the furthest and loneliest parts of the Highlands. You saw what it was like when last we visited. How can Papa ever think of sending us there? We don't know anyone there except Aunt Agatha. It is all your fault," Astrid exclaimed angrily to Clare, who was idly gazing out of the window.

"Yes, I know it's my fault and I am sorry, but surely Papa could have found us another aunt to go to instead of that old witch up in the Highlands," said Clare indignantly. "I am so sorry. Please forgive me, sister dear."

"No, I don't think I shall ever forgive you," replied Astrid as she reached for her case, ready to start packing. "We have to leave all our friends here and the ones we knew at the academy, I didn't even get to say goodbye to them. Maybe you don't care, but I did care that the principal would not have us back. Now we have to leave Mama and Papa and Grandmama and Elizabeth. And what about my music lessons! And I have to leave Roland behind because of you."

"Well, we will soon find new friends when we go to finishing school later on, I suppose," said Clare. "Anyway, I am tired of schooling and I know I will hate finishing school. You can go if you wish, Astrid, but I shall tell Papa I am not going – so there."

Astrid looked at Clare askance, hardly able to believe her ears.

"Oh, haven't you caused us enough trouble already?" she exclaimed angrily. "Poor Mama has been so ill and distraught and Papa has been made the laughing stock of the high court. Your escapade has been the favourite topic of conversation at every gathering since it happened."

"Oh, I daresay," she replied nonchalantly, trying hard to play down her escapade. "Those with most to say probably wish they were in my place. None of them have experienced such love as I have known," she fumed haughtily. "You just don't understand, my dear Astrid." She spoke now in a voice much quieter and more subdued. A tear sprang to her eye. "I cannot bear to leave India and my beloved Victor. I just want to stay and rejoin him."

"Well, you know you can't," said Astrid. "His father, like ours, will not permit it. We have to leave and there is nothing you can do about it. Also, Mama will only allow us to have a small gathering of friends when we leave."

"Not even a farewell party and dance?" exclaimed Clare with dismay.

"Mama and Papa say no. We have to depart as quickly and quietly as we can. So here is your case: start packing," retorted Astrid. "Papa has already got our sailing tickets."

Next morning Clare was summoned to her father's study by her mother, who followed her in.

"What is it, Papa?" she asked, inwardly quaking. She now realised that all her arguments would be to no avail with her father.

"Your mother wishes to speak to you concerning the bangles you are wearing. They have to come off!"

"Off, Papa?" she replied, and she looked at her mother appealingly.

"Yes, my child. You must take them off at once," she said. "You should never have accepted them."

"But I promised Victor I would always wear them," she said. Her tears started to flow. "You made me give Victor up, Papa; now you want me to give up the bangles." There was a note of defiance in her voice, in spite of her tears.

"Give the bangles to your father at once," her mother said angrily.

Clare looked at her beseechingly. Never had she heard her mother speak so angrily before. She knew she had to obey.

"Surely I could keep one, Mama?" she pleaded.

"No, no!" her father demanded.

Her parents watched her take them off one by one, very reluctantly. At last she had them all in the palm of her hand.

"Now, what am I supposed to do with them?" she asked. There was still a note of defiance in her voice.

"You must take them at once to Grandmama for the mission funds. Now off you go."

Davinia and Stephen watched her enter the mission hall.

"Grandmama," she called.

Margot, busy dressing a small wound on one of the children, looked up when she heard her name.

"Oh, it's you, my child," she said. "How kind of you to come and visit the mission! It is a long time since you visited the children."

"Well, I have just called to give you these for the mission funds," she said. She left the bangles on the table and hurried away.

Margot looked after her a little sorrowfully. She was not too eager to accept these gifts, given so ungraciously, but, after a moment's contemplation, she decided that the mission needed all the money it could get. The bangles were of solid gold, and they would pay for a great deal of help for the poor.

'Tears, tears, tears!' thought Margot as she helped the girls with their packing.

She had offered to help so that she could spend some time with her two darling granddaughters before they left. There were tears from Davinia as her daughters' departure time drew closer; tears from Astrid because she had to leave so many of her childhood friends behind and would miss her music lessons with Elizabeth; and tears and tantrums from Clare, knowing that she would never again see her beloved Victor. Clare often went to visit Elizabeth – not for music lessons: it was just that she needed a shoulder to cry on from someone who understood her unhappiness.

"I know his address, Elizabeth," she told her one day. "Do you think I should write to him and tell him to come to Scotland and take me away from Aunt Agatha? I know he would if he knew how unhappy I was and that I still loved him."

"No, no, my dear child. Please don't contemplate such a thing. He dare not disobey his father, and neither should you. You will make many new friends as you grow older and you will fall in love again."

"I won't, I won't! I just know I won't."

Elizabeth looked at her sadly.

"No, maybe you won't, my child," she said, contemplating her and Craig's undying love for each other.

Elizabeth watched Clare saunter slowly back home.

More and more tears were shed as the twins said their goodbyes on the quay.

"Now, you will be good girls, won't you – especially you, Clare?" her father enjoined.

"Well, if we aren't, Aunt Agatha won't be long in letting you know," Clare said flippantly. "Maybe, Astrid, if I misbehave often enough she will send us back home again. It might be worth a try, Astrid, don't you think?" she whispered.

"That's wishful thinking on your part," Astrid replied, looking at her angrily.

"Where will you ever get the money to return? Aunt Agatha certainly won't give it to you, in spite of her riches, and Papa won't send it."

"The ship seems to be fully loaded," said Stephen. "Now it is time for you to get aboard, my darlings," he said as he hugged them.

'How I am going to miss them,' he thought, ' – even devilish Clare, for all the heartache she has caused us all. Well, it is for the best.'

Their mother held them a long time before releasing them to dry her eyes once more.

"Be good on the journey," she said. "My friend, Mrs Roberts, has very kindly offered to take you all the way and see you settled with Aunt Agatha. You must write to me the day you arrive."

"I will, Mama, I promise," said Astrid.

"Goodbye, Grandmama," they said. They hugged her and they kissed her. "Goodbye Elizabeth and Craig." They bent down to give Heather a final hug.

"Will I not see you for a long time?" Heather asked between her tears.

"Well, you will have grown into a big girl, I daresay, before you see us again, but we will both write to you, won't we, Clare?" said Astrid.

"Of course we will," Clare replied.

The twins waved sadly as they stood looking over the side of the ship. Their mother was being comforted by their father as she waved back to them with her small tear-soaked handkerchief. Elizabeth wished with all her heart that she could go with her family in their place. Craig looked down at her sadly, knowing her innermost thoughts, and he clasped her closer.

"When will we ever be able to go on that big ship, Papa?" asked Heather as she looked up at him.

"Soon – maybe soon." His voice faltered with emotion.

Margot looked across at Craig as he spoke. She knew their longing only too well.

"Maybe, little Heather," she exclaimed as brightly as she could, "we will all go on the big ship one day."

"Really? I hope so. I hope it will be very soon, Grandmama," she said as she slipped her tiny hand in hers. "Don't you, Mama?" she added.

"Yes, darling. Now look – the big ship is moving."

They watched sadly as it drew further away. The two girls were only faint figures in the distance when they turned away.

CHAPTER 250

Davinia waited eagerly every day for mail from Scotland, and she gave a cry of joy when it arrived. The girls' letters were enclosed with the one from Aunt Agatha. She read their letters first, and she was pleased to know that they had had a good journey and were well.

Agatha's letter was more forthright. Astrid had settled very well and was continuing with her music, but Clare was sullen and uncooperative. She was constantly complaining that her father should have let her marry her Victor. Astrid became more and more angry with her, but to no avail.

I too find it quite a trial [she wrote]. Maybe when they settle in the finishing school that Stephen recommended, then Clare will find more interest in living. When she makes more friends she will hopefully forget this Victor. I expect to get news soon of their acceptance into the finishing school.

    Love as always,
      Agatha

Over dinner that night, Davinia, Stephen, Margot and Martin all agreed that once the girls entered the finishing school all would be well, but Stephen's glance at Davinia conveyed his concern. Would Clare ever settle down?

CHAPTER 251

Elizabeth and Craig were delighted to hear from Christina that she was expecting a baby early in the summer and that all was well, but they decided not to visit her and Roddy till after the baby was born.

"Well dear," Elizabeth announced to Craig, "we shall go and visit them instead of going to the hills with Margot. Margot will be disappointed, but I know she will understand."

"Of course I understand, my dear Elizabeth," Margot said when Elizabeth told her. "We will miss you, but it is only right that you wish to be with Christina at such a time. It will be nice for you to be all together. I daresay we will have left for the hills before you go."

Margot, Martin, Davinia and Stephen had already left for the hills when Elizabeth received a letter from Roddy. Craig watched her delight suddenly change to dismay as she read it. He hastily put down his cup of tea and rushed to her side.

"What does it say, my dear?" he asked.

"He wants us to visit as soon as possible," Elizabeth replied. "He is being posted to the North West Frontier and will be away for some time. He doesn't want Christina to be alone when the baby is born."

"Of course she mustn't be alone," said Craig. "We will go immediately. I will get a telegram away to them and make our travel arrangements at the same time. I will tell Damodar and his wife to accompany us. The rest of the bearers can stay here."

They were all prepared for leaving, but Craig had a shock on opening his mail one morning.

He exclaimed angrily, "Oh, bother."

"What is it, my darling?" Elizabeth asked.

"I will have to stay behind and attend this conference. Drat them! They have changed the date. It wasn't scheduled to take place till the end of the year."

Elizabeth looked at him apprehensively. "Can't you miss it, dear?" she suggested.

He sighed deeply and tapped the letter on his fingers in deep contemplation. "No, no, my angel, it is imperative I attend," he said. "It means, my darling, that

I shall not be able to accompany you and Heather. Your plans must go ahead. You cannot delay, in case Roddy has already left."

"I hope he hasn't. I want to see him so much. I know Christina will be well taken care of by the army, but it's not like having one's family close at hand. I must go at once."

He saw the anxiety on her face. He knew she would never overcome her fear of travelling, even when he was with her.

"I shall be all right, my dear, with Heather," she said. "There will surely be lots of people travelling to the hill station for the summer."

"Well," he sighed, "this conference will delay me; then I shall wait for Lindsay to return from college and join you later. It's a pity Ruardy moved to another college, otherwise he could have travelled with us. Now I must hurry, dear." He kissed them both. "I won't be too long."

A few days later, Craig settled them in their first-class, self-contained train compartment with all their luggage. Damodar and his wife, the ayah, were in another carriage further along the train. Craig gave the bearer strict instructions about their care.

"Yes, sahib," Damodar kept reassuring him, "the memsahib and Missy baba will be quite safe."

Craig knew both Damodar and the ayah would protect them with their lives if need be.

"You must go to the Major sahib in the next compartment if you need anything for them," Craig reminded him. He had already been assured by Major Travis (who was accompanied by his wife) that Elizabeth would be well taken care of, and Craig had thanked them profusely.

"My darling, how you do worry so! We will be all right," Elizabeth kept repeating.

"I know, my angel, but I shan't be happy till I am by your side again."

"Craig, my darling, are you sure you will be all right?" she asked him. Strangely, she was filled with foreboding and she didn't know why. "Don't go catching cold or getting another attack of malaria whilst I am gone, will you?" she asked with concern.

"Now it is you who is worrying," he said. He smiled at her reassuringly. "The bearer will look after me well. I will join you as soon as Lindsay returns, so don't worry so, my precious."

"But I do, I do. I cannot bear the thought of leaving you behind. Hurry and join me. I am so longing to see Lindsay. Do take care, both of you."

He kissed her passionately, and she clung to him, hating to let him go. He kissed Heather, who was so excited about the journey. She was constantly gazing around her.

"Now, my precious, you must look after Mama until I come," he said.

"Yes, yes, Papa. I am a big girl now."

"Yes, you are, precious one, but don't grow up too quickly or else Papa will have no precious little girl," he said.

"But, Papa, you will always have me as your precious little girl."

"Yes, my darling, and you will always have me."

He picked her up and kissed her; then he sat her down in the carriage once more. She had insisted on him showing her where her ayah was on the train. She hugged her doll closer.

"How soon shall we see Aunt Christina, Papa?" she asked.

"Oh, you have quite a few sleeps on the train before you see her. Come, my angel, the train will be moving any minute now." He bent down and whispered his love as he kissed her goodbye.

Then he leaped down from the carriage and made sure he had secured the door handle. Elizabeth clung to his hand through the window as the train started to move.

"Hurry, my love. I cannot bear to be parted from you," she said.

Heather, finally realising they were leaving her father behind, started to cry. She pressed her tear-stained face against the window pane as he disappeared from view.

"When shall we see Papa again?" she sobbed.

Her mother dried her eyes and cradled her in her arms.

"Very, very soon, my darling. As soon as Lindsay comes from college. Then they will join us at Aunt Christina's."

"Will we be able to meet them at the station when they arrive?"

"Of course, my darling. Soon we will be able to see Aunt Christina and her new baby when it arrives."

"Will I be able to hold it? I hope it is a little girl like me; then we can play dolls together."

"Oh, I am sure it will be; then Ruardy will have a little sister."

Heather dried her eyes and gazed out of the window. She waved to all the children along the trackside.

Elizabeth and Heather found it a tiresome journey over the next two days. Only the long breaks at the stations relieved the monotony. The Major and his wife joined them in the station restaurants. Then the ayah took Heather for a walk along the platform, closely followed by the three as they too were eager to stretch their legs before rejoining the train. The bearer made sure all was well as he wended his way back with the ayah to their carriage. The Major made sure that Elizabeth and Heather were all right before he rejoined his wife.

CHAPTER 252

They were met at the station by Mrs Muir, a friend of Christina's, and they clambered into a waiting tonga. The bearer and his wife followed in another tonga with all their luggage. They waved goodbye to the Major and his wife.

"Tell me, Mrs Muir, how is Christina?"

"She is fine. The baby is due any time, but Roddy left three days ago."

"I did so want to see him," she replied, a look of disappointment crossing her face.

Christina was anxiously waiting for them on the steps of her abode. Christina and Elizabeth greeted each other like long-lost sisters, and Elizabeth could see the relief on her face at their safe arrival.

"I was so looking forward to seeing my darling Roddy," Elizabeth said sadly.

"And he was very eager to see you. He did all he could to delay his departure,

but to no avail. He thinks he will be away for only a few weeks; he will pick up Ruardy from college on his way back."

"Are they both well? I am so longing to see them."

"Yes, they are fine. Ruardy is doing very well in his education, in spite of changing schools so often. We are determined not to send him away to Scotland; the time he is away at these boarding schools is long enough. We feel so lost when he has to return there after the holidays."

"It will be like old times again when they return. Craig and Lindsay will be here and also the new baby," said Christina. "Oh, I am so looking forward to it. And how is my lovely little girl?" she said, bending down to kiss Heather.

"I am not a little girl any longer," Heather said proudly. She stood up to her full height. "I have taken care of Mama all the way, just as Papa said I should," she added.

"Well, you have certainly done a very good job. Your father will be very proud of you when he comes. How grown-up you have become since last I saw you!"

They all sat on the verandah and Christina ordered the bearer to bring tea. She told him to make sure that the memsahib's bearer and ayah were shown where to stay.

"Please, Aunt Christina, don't send my ayah away," Heather pleaded.

"She won't be far away," her mother assured her.

"We were thinking of renting a bungalow near you, Christina, during our stay here," Elizabeth said.

"But there is sufficient room here, as you see. This house is far too big for us as it is. I know Lindsay and Ruardy will want to share a room. They will have so much to talk about," declared Christina.

"Oh, that will be lovely, if you are sure we won't be in the way," replied Elizabeth.

"How could you possibly be in the way? It's just as well your darling brother isn't here to hear your remark. He would be so cross with you."

A week passed before Elizabeth received a telegram from Craig saying he would be joining them in a few days.

Christina's time was near. Elizabeth told the ayah to take Heather to see Mrs Muir, as she herself accompanied Christina to the hospital. She was relieved to know that Christina would be staying in hospital until the baby was born.

"Well, I am relieved to know that you're in safe hands," she said. "I will visit you again tomorrow, and I will send a telegram to Roddy as soon as baby is born."

Heather ran to meet Elizabeth as soon as she alighted from the tonga.

"It is all right, Ayah, the memsahib will be staying in the hospital," Elizabeth said.

"But why has Aunty Christina gone to the hospital?" queried Heather.

"She has gone to wait for the baby to arrive in a few days," Elizabeth replied.

She sat down on the verandah, exhausted by the heat of the day. It was now the month of May, and each day was hotter than the day before. She sat with Heather on her knee, and she asked the bearer to bring iced lemon for them.

"Yes, memsahib," he replied.

He hurried away. The ayah sat cross-legged on the ground at the foot of the verandah steps.

Mrs Muir joined them for dinner later that evening and Elizabeth listened eagerly to the story of her life in India, where she had been born. Her husband had been posted away with Roddy.

"There is always so much trouble on the North West Frontier," she said. "One never knows when it will flair up. Maybe they won't be away long."

"I hope not for Christina's sake. I am so longing to see Roddy too," Elizabeth said with a sigh.

"Now you must call me whenever you need me. The bearers know where our bungalow is," Mrs Muir called as she left.

"Thank you. I will," Elizabeth replied gratefully.

She felt lonely and desolate after Mrs Muir had gone. "How I wish my darling Craig was here!" she sighed.

"Mama, Mama," Heather called to her.

"What is it, my precious one?" she answered as she crept to her bedside.

"I am so lonely and frightened without Papa. Can I come and sleep in your bed tonight?"

"Yes, of course, my little girl, but I thought you said you were a big girl now."

"Well, I am getting a big girl, but I am still afraid without Papa, and it's so dark."

"Well, I will get the ayah to light another lamp in our room until you go to sleep."

Elizabeth felt extremely nervous without Craig. She had not been able to shake off the feeling of foreboding she had since she left him, but now he was on his way and she prayed all would be well.

"Mama, Mama," Heather called, "can I sleep with you every night until Papa comes?"

"Of course, my darling." She hugged her close. "Papa and Lindsay are on their way. Now go to sleep, my darling. All will be well."

Elizabeth found sleep impossible. She longed for Craig and Lindsay's arrival. Suddenly she was startled by a rumbling and the ayah rushed into the room.

"Memsahib, memsahib!" she shouted hysterically. The room was shaking and dust was falling around her. The ayah called, "Hurry, memsahib, hurry!"

Heather woke, screaming in fear, so Elizabeth wrapped her in a blanket. The ayah grabbed two more blankets, and they rushed outside. Roofs, trees and walls were falling all around them; buildings were swaying and crashing down. The ground opened up in huge crevasses as they stumbled on, not knowing where they were going.

"Mama, Mama, what is it?" Heather screamed.

Elizabeth was trying to keep calm for Heather's sake. She stumbled several times. The ayah was crying beside her. People ran hither and thither, crying out as they searched the still-falling debris for children and relatives.

Elizabeth looked around but couldn't see anything she recognised.

"Ayah, Ayah," she screamed, "where can we go?"

"Me not know, memsahib."

They stumbled on and on through the dust-laden rubble. Through the darkness they could hear incessant rumblings, cries of "The city's on fire," and cries from the wounded, trapped under the piles of rubble.

CHAPTER 253

"Papa, this journey is so long. I am longing to see Mama and Heather. Is it much further?"

"I don't know my son, but I don't think we have much further to go."

"I hope not," Lindsay sighed as he gazed through the window. "Will Uncle Roddy have got back from his posting, Papa?"

"I am not sure, my son. Let us hope so for Aunt Christina's sake."

"We seem to be slowing down, but I cannot see any station. Everyone seems to be looking through their windows, Papa."

Craig rose to do likewise. Another train had come to a halt beside theirs and the two drivers had descended from their engines to talk to each other. They were talking excitedly, and the other driver was gesticulating wildly with his arms in the direction they were heading. Eventually the other train proceeded on its way.

"What is happening and why the delay?" asked one of the passengers.

The driver came down the train to convey the news to those on board.

"We cannot proceed any further," he said. "There has been a terrible earthquake during the night. The city is in ruins."

Craig froze to the spot for a second in disbelief. Then he dropped into his seat.

"What is it, Papa? What is the man saying?" asked Lindsay.

"Come, my son!"

Craig hastily dragged Lindsay out of the carriage, raced across the lines and up the grassy bank to the road which led to the stricken city. Craig was almost knocked down by several tongas full to overflowing with petrified people. Lindsay raced after him.

"What about our luggage, Papa?" he called.

"There's no time to bother about that," Craig replied.

He hastily grabbed the reins of the next tonga, which contained only the driver. He brought the terrified horse to a standstill.

"Turn back! Turn back!" he demanded.

He took the whip off the driver.

"No, sahib. No go back. The city is on fire."

"Turn back! Turn back!" Craig demanded again.

The man protested wildly.

"Then get out of my way!" Craig said. He pushed the driver off. "Come, Lindsay – hurry, hurry!"

Lindsay stood looking at the scene before him. Never had he seen his father in such a rage and frenzy.

"Get aboard Lindsay," Craig roared. "Don't just stand there!"

He dragged Lindsay in beside him, and he turned the frightened horse round.

The tonga wallah called after him: "Sahib, sahib, my tonga, my tonga!"

"Well get in, then," said Craig. "You can have it back later." The tonga wallah hung on to the side of it as Craig raced off, avoiding other tongas coming towards him by a hair's breadth. The rugged road became increasingly obstructed with fallen trees and fleeing people. Devastation was all around them as they approached the area they were was heading for.

"Will Mama be all right?" Lindsay asked in alarm.

"I don't know, my son, I don't know," Craig said, trying not to show the alarm he felt.

Several times Lindsay and the tonga wallah were flung to the floor as the tonga rocked wildly to and fro. Never in its life had the horse run as fast. It galloped, frantic with fear, while Craig cracked his whip over its head time and time again.

"My God, what a catastrophe!" Craig kept exclaiming.

He was sweating with fear and panic. He could see troops trying to clear the rubble as they searched for survivors.

"How much further, Papa?" Lindsay shouted.

"It's just ahead somewhere. All of the landmarks have been destroyed."

Suddenly their way was barred by a soldier.

"Nothing else can proceed along this road," the soldier said. "It is blocked all the way. More tremors are expected."

Craig saw the soldiers digging everywhere. He leaped out, pulling Lindsay with him. "This is where my wife and daughter were living. Do you know where they might be?" he asked.

"As you see, sir, everywhere is down in this area. We don't know how many people got out safely. We are still searching every inch."

As Craig looked around, he suddenly saw his bearer, Damodar, huddled in a corner against a broken wall, cowering in fear, too shocked to move. Craig raced over the piles of rubble to him. Lindsay was close on his heels.

"Where is the memsahib and Missy baba?" he yelled, as he pulled Damodar to his feet.

"With the ayah," Damodar replied. He pointed frantically to a pile of rubble and he covered his face with his hands.

"Well, come, man," Craig yelled, "help me find them. Help me get them out." Craig tore frantically at the rubble. "Where are you my angel and darling child?" he shouted, his voice almost at screaming pitch. "Darling angel, where are you?"

The bearer followed close at hand whilst Lindsay searched further along the pile of rubble. They too frantically called their names. The bearer knew that his wife, Heather's ayah, would never leave the Missy baba's side. If the child was buried, his wife would be buried also. He hurried his search.

"Oh, I pray to God they are safe!" burst out Craig.

Lindsay was almost sick with dread. He struggled with brick after brick, but to no avail.

Suddenly the bearer screamed out, "They are here, sahib, sahib!"

Craig almost fell as he hastened to where the bearer was kneeling. They could see the ayah's hand clutching Heather's tiny hand. Round Heather's wrist they could see her thistle bracelet. Nearby was her favourite doll. Craig frantically tore at each boulder as he tried to free them. Lindsay did the same close by. Suddenly Lindsay saw the ring, shining out to him despite the thick dust.

"Papa, Papa," he screamed, "here is Mama. Papa she is dead, she is dead."

The soldiers picked up the ayah and they took Heather from Craig. Tears poured down his face as he raced to Lindsay's side and tore frantically at the rubble.

"Let us help you, sir," said one of the soldiers, but he pushed them all aside as he struggled to free her.

"Darling angel, darling angel," he kept crying.

"Oh Papa, Papa," Lindsay screamed hysterically, "what can we do? What can we do?"

At last Craig had freed her. He sat, cradling her in his arms. Lindsay knelt beside him until one of the soldiers took hold of him and led him to the waiting tonga.

"Come, son – we will wait for your father. Come, sir – we will take her to the hospital, where we are taking all casualties. Fortunately the hospital is still standing."

"Show me what transport you have and I will carry her to it," Craig said.

"We have managed to get some army transport as near here as we can. You can take her in that with the little girl. There are more casualties in there, but you and your son can accompany them."

"Please see that my bearer, with his wife, keeps close to us on the journey," said Craig.

"Very well, sir."

"Oh, Mama, Mama," cried Lindsay, as he hugged her to him on the journey.

Craig clung on to the three of them. Suddenly, as he looked at his son, who was sobbing bitterly, his head buried in her hair, his mind shot back to the loch. He heard himself as a child sobbing, as Lindsay was now, as he kept repeating, "Mama, Mama! Papa, Papa, what can we do?" Lindsay looked at his father in anguish, the tears streaming down his dusty face.

Craig in his own anguish could not answer. His thoughts were a jumble of that day's events and those of yesteryear. 'Why, why', he thought, 'has my darling son's mother to die, like mine, so tragically? My own darling wife, angel, to die as my father's did! It cannot be true. It cannot be. Such fate!'

Mrs Muir, whose house had escaped the devastation, followed in another tonga and hastened to Craig and Lindsay's side as they reached the hospital. She introduced herself.

"Is there anything I can do for you?" she asked.

"Would you take care of my son for a short while?" Craig replied. "I want to see if I can get any news of Christina. Please don't let anyone move my wife or children whilst I am away."

She nodded her head in agreement.

After several enquiries, Craig at last found the ward where Christina was. The Sister informed him that she had lost the baby owing to shock and that she was very ill.

"You may see her for a few moments," she said. She looked anxiously at his torn clothing and dusty face. "Come and tidy up. I will get someone to bring you some soap and water. We must not let her see you in this distraught state."

Craig sat down reluctantly. He was anxious to see her, but he decided not to tell her of all that had happened that day until she was stronger.

He stood by her bed and saw how deathly pale she was. Her eyes were closed as if to block out the despair. He was determined to be extra brave, but she knew he had bad news as soon as she opened her eyes and saw him standing there, so overwrought with sorrow that he could not speak.

"Where is Lindsay?" she whispered.

"I have left him with Mrs Muir and the bearer. He is all right."

Craig knelt by her bed, and he broke down, sobbing bitterly. He told her everything. She reached out and stroked his hair. She knew he would never be the same again. "Elizabeth and Heather?" she cried in disbelief, as tears ran down her face.

He nodded silently, and she turned her face into the pillow, numb with grief. He pressed her hand lightly.

"My dear Christina," he said, "you are so ill and you have enough of your own sorrow in losing your baby. Just get well as soon as you can. Roddy will arrive soon." At last he raised his head.

"What are you going to do now, my dearest Craig?" she asked.

"I will await Roddy's return," he said. "He is already on his way with Ruardy, I have been told. Then I will take them home with me for the funerals."

"I will stay beside Christina," Mrs Muir told Craig when he came back from visiting her friend.

"Thank you so much," he replied. "I wish to stay with my son and wife and daughter until Roddy returns."

CHAPTER 254

The devastation that met Roddy's eyes as he entered what was left of the city filled him with dismay. He raced towards the hospital, thankful that Christina was safe but distraught at the news of the loss of the baby.

"Any news of my sister and her daughter, Mrs Muir?" he asked.

She looked at him and in her face he read all she was going to say.

"It's the worst possible news, my dear Roddy," she told him. "You'll find her husband and son with them at the place they are receiving all the dead and wounded. So many are coming in all the time."

After several enquiries he found them. Craig was refusing to be parted from his dead wife and daughter. Both men clasped each other in their grief, which was too deep for words. Roddy looked at Lindsay, who seemed to have aged ten years since last he saw him. He hugged him close, and the boy's streaming tears fell unashamedly on to Roddy's tunic. Roddy searched in his pocket and handed him his large white handkerchief.

"You cry, my son, you cry," he said.

"What are we going to do, Uncle Roddy, without Mama and Heather? What are we going to do?" Roddy could only hug him closer. He had no answer for him.

"I have sent a telegram to Margot," Craig said, "asking her to notify Aunt Elena. I told her to convey the news to Martha and Magnus. When I have time, I will write to them personally."

"Thank you, Craig," Roddy replied. "How I shall ever be able to write and tell Mama and Papa I just don't know." He was still reeling with utter shock and bewilderment at all that had happened in such a short time.

"Roddy?" asked Craig next day, "would you please arrange through the army, if you can, for me to take Elizabeth and Heather home with me as soon as I can. I have spoken to my bearer and he wants to stay here a little longer. He needs to see to his wife's last resting place. Will you assist him? Then he can come home as soon as he is able."

"Yes, Craig, I will see to everything. Mrs Muir is staying with Christina whilst I see about our accommodation for when she is well enough to leave hospital."

"I pray that it will be soon," replied Craig, almost too stricken with grief to make himself heard.

Roddy went with them to the station and watched in despair as his darling sister's coffin was put on one seat and Heather's tiny coffin on another.

'Surely all this isn't happening! It can't be,' he thought as he watched Craig, now a broken man, climb into the carriage. Lindsay, his eyes still streaming with tears, was hardly able to see the carriage step. He almost fell as he followed his father.

"I will come and see you as soon as Christina is well enough to travel," said Roddy.

"Yes, do that Roddy, and bring Ruardy with you. As you see, Lindsay is still in deep shock. He has hardly spoken since their bodies were found, and seeing Ruardy will help him, I'm sure."

Roddy looked at Craig anxiously. "Are you sure you are well enough to travel?" he asked. "I wish I could accompany you."

"My dear Roddy, thank you. We are all right; don't worry about us. You have a sick wife and grief of your own."

Roddy hugged them both again. He took a last lingering look at where Elizabeth and Heather lay, and, putting his fingers to his lips, he touched both their coffins in a last sad farewell.

He watched as the train pulled away. Craig stood at the window, waving him goodbye. He waved back, knowing that that was the last contact he would have with the darling little sister he adored.

"How dear Mama and Papa are going to take the news, I just don't know," he said with a sigh.

Throughout the journey, Craig cradled his son in his arms.

Lindsay constantly called, "Papa, Papa."

Craig had sent another telegram to Margot, telling her when their train would arrive, and she was there, dressed in black, looking pale and dazed with shock. Martin and Davinia supported her, one on either side, as Stephen hurried anxiously towards the special carriage. He greeted Craig and Lindsay as they stepped down.

"I have arranged with the funeral parlour and a hearse is waiting outside. While they transfer the coffins, come and join Margot in the waiting room."

Margot hugged them both. No words were spoken in their sorrow.

They proceeded to the station exit, where they watched as the coffins were borne away. Craig, Martin and Stephen followed the hearse in another car.

Lindsay watched sadly, still too dazed by events to grasp what was happening.

"Come, my boy," said Margot as she cradled him in her arms, "we are going home. Your father will be back soon."

He reluctantly clambered in the tonga beside Davinia, and she put her arm round his shoulder as Margot bade the driver to drive on.

A few days later, Elizabeth and Heather were laid to rest in their bronze-and-copper coffins in the special vault, now surrounded by flowers, in the small churchyard beside the mission.

Craig stood with head bowed, his hand resting on his son's shoulder. Margot stood next to him, stricken with grief. She laid her hand on Craig's arm, her thoughts in a whirl as she recalled the funeral of Isabelle. In her mind's eye she saw father and son together in their grief.

"Margot, Margot," Craig said when he felt the pressure of her hand on his arm, "you are always here when I need you most. Always, Margot!"

He swayed slightly, much to Lindsay's alarm. Martin, who had been watching him closely, caught him before he fell. Craig called out, "Angel, angel, darling angel, why are you leaving me?"

All the mourners left the graveside. Margot wended her way with Lindsay and Davinia; Martin and Stephen supported Craig, who was reluctant to leave.

"Come," said Martin, "everyone has left now," and they turned sadly away.

CHAPTER 255

Elena was busy in the library. She was finding the work almost too much for her since Harriet was now confined to her bed. The extra help with more servants had not greatly eased her workload. She looked at the large grandfather clock as the doorbell rang. 'Now, who could that be at this time of day?' she wondered.

Jamie, on opening the door, was surprised to see Lawrie.

"Good morning, Lawrie. What has brought you here so early?" he asked.

"Good morning, Jamie. I have a telegram addressed to Lady Elena."

Jamie looked at the postman apprehensively as he took it from him. They bade each other good day, and Jamie closed the door.

"What is it, Jamie?" Elena called.

"A telegram, milady."

She looked at him a little bewildered. "Good news, I hope," she said. She sat down in the big chair overlooking the loch. "Tell Shona or Marie to bring my morning tea."

"Very well, milady."

Although he was longing to know the telegram's contents, he hurried out.

"How I hate these things," she sighed, "whether good news or bad!" She opened it slowly as Shona poured her tea, and when the maid had left she read it with a mixture of disbelief and despair.

'Elizabeth and Heather killed. Please inform Martha and Magnus immediately. Letter following. Margot.'

She ran to the door in panic.

"Jamie! Jamie!" she called.

He, as always, was hovering near her.

"Yes, milady?"

"Tell Zan to bring the carriage round at once. I am going to see Martha and Magnus."

"Where to, Lady Elena?" Zan asked.

"To the cottage of Magnus and Martha. I know it is a long way round the loch, but I cannot wait for Magnus to come with the boat. He will no doubt have already been to the village and returned."

Zan looked anxiously at her sad face, and he wondered at her haste as she urged him to go faster.

"Wait for me, Zan," she said when they arrived. "I don't want Magnus to have the trouble of rowing me back."

"Very well, Lady Elena," he replied as he helped her to alight.

He led her to the door of the cottage and then returned alone to the carriage.

Magnus and Martha were both sitting by the fire, and Magnus hurried to the door at the sound of the knock. 'Whoever can it be?' he thought.

He gave a gasp of surprise when he opened the door and saw Elena standing there. He bade her enter, and Martha rose from her chair and dropped her a little curtsy.

"Pray do sit down," said Elena. "I am the bearer of some distressing news for you, Martha."

They both watched apprehensively as she pulled the telegram from her pocket. At the sight of it, Martha clutched Magnus's hand tightly and the colour drained from her face. Then Elena read out its contents.

Elena sat with them a long time trying to console them.

"I will call again as soon as I can," she said eventually.

"Will you and Zan have some refreshment before you leave?" asked Martha bravely.

"No, thank you, dear. I will get back before the mist comes down."

Martha and Magnus sat a long time weeping together after Elena left.

"Whatever could have happened to them? Surely it cannot be? My darling angel cannot be dead, she cannot be," sobbed Magnus. He leaned his head on Martha's shoulder. "Surely Master Craig and Roddy will write soon and tell us it isn't true."

"Well, Roddy will write soon, I know, but it must be so. Poor Master Craig and darling Lindsay! Their grief, like ours, will be too much to bear," said Martha, patting his shoulder, trying to ease his sorrow, though her own heart was broken.

Elena told Bruce and Harriet the sad news, but Harriet made no comment.

"I will wait and hear what Margot has to say when she writes," said Bruce.

Elena watched impatiently from her bedroom every morning for Margot's letter to arrive, and she ran to the door as soon as she saw Lawrie coming up the drive.

When the letter eventually came, she sat down in the library and opened it with trembling hands. Then she read and reread every detail of that fateful day.

Bruce was sitting in his chair overlooking the loch, as he did every morning.

"Well," he boomed, "what has Margot got to say?"

Elena started to read it, but he banged his cane on the table and turned to face her. She almost dropped the letter with fright.

"All I am interested in is what has happened to Craig and Lindsay?" he said. Never, at any time, would he refer to them as his son and grandson. "I am only interested in them. I am not interested in anyone else."

"They are safe. They were not in Quetta at the time," Elena said, trembling with apprehension.

"Thanks be to God!" he exclaimed. "It's a pity about the child," he said condescendingly after a few minutes' contemplation.

Elena glanced at him resignedly. 'How can he be so totally dispassionate about such a tragedy?' she thought.

"Have you no thought for how Craig is suffering from the loss of his wife and child?" she demanded.

"No, I have not," he bellowed. "If he had married Fiona, as he should have, they would not have been in India. Never mind Quetta and the earthquake!" he bellowed again, as he crashed his fist on the table. "Craig is responsible for the death of his wife, whom he never should have married anyway. And the same goes for his daughter. Their deaths are on his head alone. It's just as well she did not take Lindsay up there with her, or he would be dead also," he said bitterly.

"Is that all you have to say, Bruce?"

"Yes, it is. Now the matter is closed. Don't mention them again, do you understand?"

"Yes, Bruce," Elena said with a deep, heartfelt sigh.

'Is there never going to be an end to all this bitterness?' she thought. Never had she hated Bruce as much as she did just then.

She tried to sound calm, in spite of the fury inside her, as she tentatively asked again, "So you have no message of sympathy for your son when I reply?"

"How many more times have I to tell you, Elena? I have no son. His rightful place was by my side here as the next Chief of the Clan, not over there in a foreign country with that hussy."

Elena closed her eyes in anguish and fury at his words. He turned his chair back to overlook the loch, as if to dismiss her. She knew further conversation was impossible, so she turned to leave the room. She had always loved Glencree Castle dearly, but now she hated it more every day.

"Well, I will go and read the letter to Harriet," she said.

"Well, she won't have any more sympathy either, so you will be wasting time with her also," he snapped.

Elena hastily left the room, and only the thought of Harriet ill in her room above stopped her slamming the door in her fury and anguish. She passed Jamie, who, as always, was waiting for any news of his beloved Craig.

"Is Master Craig all right – and Master Lindsay?"

"Yes, they are all right."

She looked at his sad face. 'If only Bruce could love Craig as much as this man does!' she thought with a sigh.

"Oh, the Good Lord be praised!" Jamie murmured. "But Miss Elizabeth and the darling wee bairn?" He pulled his snow-white handkerchief from his pocket and dabbed his tear-filled eyes.

Elena could not bear to see him so distressed and listen to his faltering words. Her own heart was breaking.

"I must now go to Lady Harriet," she said.

"Please, Lady Elena, send our condolences to Master Craig from all of us."

"I will, I will."

Harriet's heart condition now meant she was confined more and more to her bed. She bade Elena enter and listened attentively as she read Margot's letter. At last Elena put the letter in her pocket with a sigh.

"Poor, poor Craig! Our poor boy!" Harriet exclaimed as she lay back on her pillow, gazing out towards the loch. "What he must be going through! But he should have been here with us. This is his rightful place, not there in India. If he had stayed here, none of them would have been in the earthquake."

'Oh,' thought Elena, 'this is the same kind of talk as from Bruce. I might have known she wouldn't understand. They are so much alike.'

"She should have refused to marry him when he arrived there," Harriet continued. "Then he would have returned and married Fiona as he should have done, and *she* would by now be back with her parents. But as it was – no, she was determined to marry Craig. She thought she would be the next Mistress of Glencree, but now see what it has got her," she said vindictively.

"Oh, Harriet," Elena pleaded, "please don't speak of her so. Think of what poor Martha and Magnus must be going through."

"Well, to my way of thinking, they encouraged her. They have brought this misery and heartache on themselves. Send my condolences to Craig when you write. Now go, and don't trouble me any more. I am far too ill."

Elena softly closed her door as she left. She reached for her handkerchief to stem her tears as she went to her room.

Martha and Magnus waited anxiously for news from Roddy, and at last a letter came. Martha knew, by its length, that Roddy must have found writing it a difficult task. Magnus fumbled time and time again in getting his spectacles from his jacket pocket. He was reluctant to read the painful words.

"What does it say, dear?" Martha asked him between her sighs.

Magnus read it out to her:

Elizabeth had come to Quetta to be with Christina as it was nearly time for the baby to be born. I had been posted to the North West Frontier to help deal with some disturbance there. A junior officer had been taken ill, and there was no one else available, so I had to go at once. I could not wait until Elizabeth's arrival, so I did not get a chance to see her. The earthquake occurred in the early hours of the morning after Christina was admitted to hospital, otherwise she would have been killed also. Christina lost our baby girl owing to shock; otherwise we are both well, as is Ruardy. I cannot say any more at present, but I will write again as soon as I am able.

Our love to you both.
God bless.
Roddy

PS: We are going to visit Craig and Lindsay as soon as Christina is well enough to travel.

Everywhere Elena and Magnus went they could see the sadness that overwhelmed the community. All their friends and neighbours asked them to convey their condolences to Master Craig and Lindsay. Elena often hurried away, though she tried not to be impolite in her haste, and Magnus did the same. He told them he had to hurry back to Martha, who was inconsolable.

"Well," said Mrs Knowell to Mrs Crawford one day at the ladies' sewing circle, trying (not very hard) to show some concern about what had happened to one of her former choirgirls, "if it had to be, it had to be."

"Well, I agree with that sentiment entirely," said Mrs Crawford. "As my Ruby said the other day as we all sat discussing the event in the parlour, 'well, she would insist on marrying him, and this is what she has got.' I must say, I agree with all my Ruby said."

"And what else had she to say?" exclaimed Emma, who had sat all afternoon, her head bent over her sewing, getting more and more angry. She looked Mrs Crawford in the eye. "What else did your precious Ruby have to say?" she demanded angrily.

Mrs Crawford looked at her aghast. For a moment she had forgotten how close Elizabeth and Emma had been. She looked sheepishly around the room, hoping that one of the other ladies would come to her rescue. She stammered for a few seconds, wondering how she could put what she had to say in as kind a light as possible. She wanted to spare her precious Ruby the fury of Emma's tongue when next they met.

"Well, all she said was" – and she hesitated again – "that now Miss Elizabeth Anderson would not ever become the next Mistress of Glencree. That is all she said."

Emma doubted if that was all she had said, but she decided not to pursue the conversation any further. She picked up her sewing and hurried from the room.

"Well, I never!" exclaimed Mrs Knowell.

"Hand in glove always, those two were, if you ask me," responded Mrs Crawford, not to be outdone by Mrs Knowell's exclamation.

Emma was distraught with grief. She spent hours in the garden of her parents' home, sitting on the small garden seat she and Elizabeth had often shared. It was there one afternoon that her father came and sat beside her.

"Come, my child – this sorrowing will not bring your dear friend back. I know how lonely you are with Nicholas away at college. Would you like me to hold a special memorial service for them?"

"Yes, Papa, that would be nice," she said listlessly. "Mama and I can arrange the flowers."

"I will go and see Lady Elena right away." He kissed her tenderly as he left.

Elena was only too happy to agree with the Reverend Corwell's plan for the service.

"The vicar is arranging a memorial service for Elizabeth and your granddaughter next Sunday, Bruce. Will you be attending?" she asked, although she knew what his answer would be.

"No, I will not be attending. You may go and represent the family now that Harriet is too ill to perform that task," he replied.

Elena met Martha and Magnus at the village jetty and drove them to church in her small carriage. The villagers all offered their condolences when they saw them. Elena took Martha and Magnus into the Laird's Gallery for the service to spare them some of the unkind stares she knew would be their lot from certain members of the village community. As she suspected, Mrs Crawford and her three precious jewels were constantly nodding, nudging and whispering to each other. 'At least,' she thought, 'they have attended the service.'

Emma, who was watching them, doubted whether they were motivated by any kind concern for Martha and Magnus, but she suspected that they were hoping for something to gossip about for many weeks ahead.

Mrs Knowell, Elena noted, gave Martha and Magnus a look of disapproval when she saw them sitting beside her in the Laird's Gallery.

After the service they all bade their farewells to the vicar and Becky (his wife). Emma and her husband accompanied Martha and Magnus to the jetty and watched till they were out of sight. Emma stood there gazing a long time across the loch.

"Come, my dear," Stuart called, "Lady Elena is waiting and we must bid her farewell before she leaves."

"You know, my dear . . ." said Magnus sadly as he rowed slowly back. Up to then, neither had spoken.

"What, my dear?" Martha replied.

"I could see my darling angel so clearly beside the flowers in the church. It was as if she was outlined against the stained-glass window as she used to be when she sang her solos in that same spot."

"Yes, I too felt her presence all through the service. It was such a nice service!" She sighed as she put her handkerchief away once more.

CHAPTER 256

Craig sat holding the letter Elena had written, reading and rereading it.

'How kind of the vicar to hold a memorial service for my darling angel and Heather!' he thought. 'I am so glad Magnus and Martha felt up to the service. How dreadful they must be feeling!' Although Elena had not mentioned his father's reaction to the tragic happenings, he could guess what he might have said.

'Perhaps Papa is right to condemn me,' he thought with a sigh. 'It is my fault my darling angel was here in the first place. If I hadn't followed her here, she would be safe at home with her parents. I should have married Fiona – but how could I, loving my angel as I do? I would have been as I am now: living, but dead inside. Only our darling son keeps me alive now. No, no, I could have taken no other course.'

Martha and Magnus's letter soon followed.

'How forgiving they are!' he thought. 'If only my father could be likewise! At least he could have gone to the service for his little granddaughter!' For a moment he felt a pang of bitterness towards his father. 'Even in death, my darling little girl is not spared the wrath of that bitter old man, her grandfather. He didn't deserve her, nor the fine grandson he has,' he fumed as he wiped away tears of anger and anguish from his sad eyes.

Several other letters of condolence followed, including ones from the twins to both Craig and Lindsay, but the one that touched him most was from Emma.

'Dear, dear Emma!' he thought with a sigh. 'They were such close friends!' He could feel, in her letter, her deep distress. 'My poor, poor, darling angel! What a lot of loyal friends she had to leave behind!' Emma promised to keep in touch with him. He sighed deeply as he put her letter with the others.

Night after night, Craig and Lindsay sat on the verandah after dinner, hardly speaking. The dinner was hardly ever eaten. Damodar took away each course, beside himself with his own grief and concern for them. He could see how they were suffering as daily he went about his work. There was no laughter now that Elizabeth was gone, and he missed the squeals of delight from the little Missy baba, who used to play so happily with his wife, the ayah. He missed them all so much.

"The sahibs must eat something," he would say to the cook.

"In a little more time, a little more time," the cook replied.

Damodar would stand silently beside Craig, long after Lindsay had bade his father goodnight.

"Go, Damodar; I shall be all right. Goodnight," said Craig.

"Goodnight, sahib."

Craig gazing out into the still, dark night, would, night after night, often hear Lindsay scream out in his nightmares: "Papa, Mama is here with Heather under the stones. Come quickly, Papa! What can we do?"

Craig, out of his chair in an instant, would race to his side, and Lindsay would wake in a sweat to find his father clutching him tightly.

"It's all right, my son. Papa is here beside you, where I will always be," he said as he laid him back on his pillow. "You go to sleep, my son."

Later he left his son's side and went back to his own room, passing his ever dutiful bearer just outside Lindsay's door.

"Is the young sahib all right now, sahib?" said Damodar.

"Yes, he is sleeping now," Craig replied.

"Papa," Lindsay said some weeks later, "I have decided not to return to the boarding school. I have had a long talk with the principal of the college here and he has accepted me for next term. He says I can sit my exams for the university. From now on I want to always be at home with you."

"I would like that, my son, but you will miss all the new friends you have made."

"Well, they can still visit me any time they wish. You are my dearest friend, Papa: I need no other. I want to be at your side, as Mama would wish."

"There is no one else I would rather have near me, my son, but you are young and must be with friends of your own age."

"No, Papa, I have made up my mind. Nothing is ever going to separate us. There is now just the two of us and we must take care of each other."

"Yes, yes, that is so, my son," Craig said with a sigh. Suddenly in his mind's eye he was back at Glencree. He could hear himself saying to his father the same thing: "Nothing is ever going to separate us again, Papa."

And he could hear his father's reply: "No, nothing ever again, my son."

Lindsay looked at his father sadly, as Craig, lost in his memories of bygone days, was oblivious to everyone and everything about him.

"Papa, Papa, you are not listening to me," he said.

"Yes, I am, my son, I am. If it is your wish, it will be so."

CHAPTER 257

Craig was more than delighted to receive Roddy's letter telling him they would be arriving to spend the Christmas season with them. Lindsay gave a loud 'whoopee!' on hearing the news when he arrived home from college. His father was more than happy to hear his outburst of joy – his first show of delight since their return home from the catastrophe.

Now, he thought, Lindsay will begin to laugh more often, and maybe his dreadful nightmares will become less frequent. His constant wish to be left alone had caused great concern to Margot and Davinia, who were constantly trying to help him over the loss of his mother and adored baby sister.

Martin and Stephen constantly tried to get Craig interested once again in living. For far too long he had shunned all links with his friends from the officers' club and the polo team, even though he knew the team was most keen to get their finest player back on the turf.

His answer was always the same: "Not now, not now. Maybe later, but not now."

Hour after hour he would sit on the verandah staring into space. Only the sound of Lindsay's voice, hailing him as he sped through the wrought-iron gate or as his cycle crashed to the ground before the bearer had time to catch it, brought him out of his sad reverie.

Roddy and Christina were deeply shocked to see the change in Craig and Lindsay, but they made no comment as they greeted them joyfully at the station.

"My word, Lindsay, how tall you are growing!" exclaimed Roddy as he hugged him.

"Well, Uncle Roddy, I shall soon be fourteen. You are in time for my birthday."

"My, how quickly time flies!" said Christina. "It only seems like yesterday you were a small boy."

"As was Ruardy!" said Craig as he hugged him. "He will soon be as tall as Lindsay."

"Come, Ruardy," said Lindsay, "clamber in the tonga with me and we will race our father's tonga home."

They sped off, almost knocking down a sacred cow.

"Gosh, that was a close shave!" Ruardy declared. "You are still as reckless as I remember, Lindsay."

They glanced back to see their parents' tonga in the distance.

"They will be well and truly beaten," Ruardy laughed.

"We beat you, we beat you!" they shouted from the verandah steps, laughing heartily as Craig's tonga pulled up.

"Papa," Lindsay called, "can you pay our tonga wallah? We haven't any money."

"Of course you have," laughed Christina. "You two are just rogues."

"Oh, very well, but only this time." Craig pretended to remonstrate.

The constant round of parties and visits to and from their friends helped to make the time as happy as possible, but they all found it difficult at times. Lindsay's outbursts of laughter now and again, as he and Ruardy got up to their pranks, brought many a smile to Craig's wan face. Roddy, however, often looked at him with deep concern.

"When are you due back, Roddy?" Craig asked one day.

"Well, we cannot stay for Burns Night unfortunately," he sighed.

"Oh, Papa, why not?" Ruardy demanded crossly.

"Because, my son, I have to report back."

"We have always got to be moving around, Mama. Why can't Papa get a job in the city?"

"Because your father is a regular soldier. It's his career."

"It would be so nice if you were back at the barracks here," said Craig. "Then we could have all enjoyed Burns Night as of old."

"I think my next posting will be further away up in the north. Then I hope to get some home leave."

The time for their departure arrived far too soon. They all wished they could stay longer. Roddy hugged Lindsay as if he would never let him go – as if his nearness helped him to feel the presence of his darling sister. He had noticed during his stay how like Elizabeth he was in so many ways.

"You are growing into a fine young man, my dear Lindsay. Take special care of your father. He needs you so."

"Yes, Uncle Roddy, I know how much he needs me and I will always take great care of him and never ever leave him."

"Try to visit us again soon," Craig called as they boarded the train.

"We will, we will," Ruardy replied.

Craig, his hand resting on Lindsay's shoulder, watched sadly as the train pulled away. As Roddy leaned from the window, Craig recalled the night when his darling angel had mistaken him for her dear, dear Roddy.

"That was so long ago, so long ago," he murmured as the train disappeared from view.

"What were you saying, Papa?" Lindsay asked.

"Nothing really, my son – just a few thoughts of long ago."

Craig refused all invitations to attend the Burns Night celebration – the night he had always enjoyed more than any other.

Margot was beside herself with concern.

"Davinia," she said one day, "really I don't know what to do about Craig. I do hope he soon recaptures some of his zest for living." She sighed.

"It will take him a long time, Mama – many, many years. Maybe it will never happen."

"Well, I am glad to see Lindsay is taking more interest in things around him. Ruardy has done wonders for him. I hope they can return soon. Craig has promised me he will take Lindsay to the hills and visit the plantation this summer."

"Well, that will do them both good," said Davinia.

CHAPTER 258

Elena found each day more and more difficult, in spite of the extra help from the village. Harriet's condition worsened and Bruce's rages became more frantic. However, in spite of all this, she was determined to carry on with her work for Craig and also for the missions.

She spent many hours talking with Emma, who was now helping her with her mission correspondence so that she could attend to the ex-servicemen's affairs for Craig. She wrote to him often to tell him about their welfare.

'I should be doing all that work on their behalf, Aunt Elena,' he thought as he read her letter.

"Do you hear often from Master Craig?" Emma asked Elena one day.

"Well, not as often as I would like, but Margot gives me news of him, so I know about his loss of interest in living. Only Lindsay, who is at college nearby, keeps him going. Margot says he visits Elizabeth and Heather's grave every day, always taking fresh flowers from his garden. Lindsay, it seems, will soon be going to the university, which fortunately is not too far away either."

"Thank goodness for that!" sighed Emma.

"How I wish", said Elena, "Craig would give up his work and go and live permanently in the hills! The doctor says it would strengthen his weak chest and lessen his recurring attacks of fever. Margot has begged him time and time again, but he will not leave the grave. How I wish I was nearer, to comfort our dear boy, but it can never be." She sighed.

Some months later, Elena, in her room, heard Shona call out to her:

"Lady Elena, Lady Elena, please hurry!"

Elena hastened to the door and out into the corridor. Shona was hastening towards her from Harriet's room.

"It's Lady Harriet," she said. "I have just taken her breakfast in, but she looks so poorly."

"Well, send Zan to bring the doctor at once."

"Yes, milady," Shona said as she hurried away.

Elena stood beside Harriet's bed. Already it was too late.

"Dear, dear Harriet, I am going to miss you so," she said.

She knelt beside her sister, holding her snow-white hand in hers as she wept and prayed.

Harriet was buried quietly in the family vault. Bruce, in his wheelchair, was a pathetic figure as he sat with Elena, Becky, and Emma and her husband. Harriet had left instructions that she wanted no fuss or large gathering, and so it was.

Elena found the castle more and more lonely, desolate and sombre after Harriet had gone. It depressed her deeply. Bruce became more morose as the days passed. He sat for long hours overlooking the loch, only showing some interest when his tacksman came to tell him how everything was on the estate. The tacksman himself, Elena thought, dreaded the daily encounter with his master and was glad to get away back to his work on the estate. Bruce raged at him at every meeting.

How Elena longed for the days long gone! If only she could hear once more Craig's youthful laughter and enjoy his gay pranks with all his friends around him! If only Bruce had sent for them to come home, how happy they would have all been! Even Bruce, she felt, could not but be happy with such happy, jolly children around him as Lindsay and Heather were. 'That darling cherub of a child! To have been killed alongside her beautiful mother! To this day, I cannot believe it happened,' she thought sadly.

Many times she could be seen on the battlements of the castle, her thoughts far away, oblivious to all the beautiful scenery around her.

Jamie often crept up the long winding staircase when the maids told him, "Milady is weeping again." He pretended to polish the large brass lamps, to let her know she was not alone. Then, on hearing an angry tirade from Bruce, she would hastily dry her eyes and hasten to do his bidding.

CHAPTER 259

Craig opened the letter from Elena. How glad he always was to receive news from her! However, his moment of delight turned to sadness as he read and reread the account of Harriet's passing.

'She often spoke so lovingly of you,' the letter said.

'It is no good, Aunt Elena, you trying to soften the blow,' Craig thought. 'I know Aunt Harriet too well and I can guess how she spoke of me and my darling angel: with such bitterness. But I forgive her. She always did her best for me when Papa and I needed you both so much.' He folded the letter slowly after looking at it again and again.

"Another chapter closed!" he murmured aloud.

He looked up to see Margot approaching.

"I see you also have the distressing news from home," he said.

"Yes, my dear Craig, I have," she replied.

They both sat silently, their thoughts winging their way back to bygone days.

"The work in the castle and on the estate, and coping with the illness of your father, must be more than Elena can manage," Margot said eventually. "Emma is now relieving her of all the correspondence I send her regarding the missions, so that leaves her free to attend to the needs of the ex-servicemen, which is so dear to her heart and yours, Craig."

"Yes, yes, I should be there to take all this work of the estates off her shoulders, but, as things are, it can never be." He sighed.

"Oh, I am sure in time your father will cease to be so angry. He will beg you and Lindsay to go home."

"I doubt it, Margot," Craig said sadly. "He is far too proud to admit he needs me, and I know he will never accept my darling angel's son as a future heir to Glencree. He had set his heart on Fiona giving me a son. I promised him I would marry Fiona."

"Well, it was not to be," said Margot, with a note of anger in her voice, "and he should now send for you and Lindsay to be where you both belong."

"Please, Margot," Craig sighed, "say no more on this topic. We have all said enough on this matter."

"I also received another letter from home," Margot said.

"Well, tell me what other news you have from bonnie Scotland." He tried to put a lilt of happiness in his voice.

"Well, Agatha says the twins are quite beautiful young ladies."

"Well, they were always that. Tell me: how old are they now?"

"They will be coming of age this year. It is the year for their coming-out, so I suppose they will be looking forward to doing the London Season. It is such an exciting time!" she exclaimed as she sat reminiscing about her own youth.

Suddenly, Craig's thoughts went winging back to the London Season he had had to endure. He recalled all the distress his precious angel was going through at the time.

Margot looked up at him and, knowing him so well, she knew what he was thinking.

"It's incredible how quickly time has flown, Margot. It seems like only yesterday when the twins were just tiny tots with coloured ribbons in their hair – just like my own little girl," he said sadly as he gazed into space.

"Davinia and Stephen are now preparing to go to Scotland to be with them, but they will be returning in the autumn." Margot sighed deeply. "I shall miss them so much when they go."

Craig looked at her apprehensively, noticing her deep sigh.

"Are you thinking of joining them, Margot?" he asked.

"No, my dear boy, there is too much to do here and Martin would not hear of it. Nevertheless, I should dearly love to be with my two darling granddaughters at this special time in their young lives. It is such an honour to be accepted for presentation at court. It is such a happy, fulfilling time," she said with a smile. She had noted the panic in Craig's voice when he thought she might be leaving. She hurriedly changed the subject: "I hear Lindsay has done extremely well in his entrance exams for the university."

"He certainly has!" Craig exclaimed proudly. "Even his grandfather would have to acknowledge that. Martha and Magnus are very proud, and Elena is always most anxious to hear of his progress.

"It seems he has an exceptional gift for languages, so he is going to pursue that interest. He will take Oriental studies and Egyptian mythology and archaeology. There are enough ancient sites in India to keep him occupied for years."

Margot rose to go and ruffled his hair.

"I am so pleased, Craig, that he is doing so well," she said. "Tell him so when he comes home. Well, I have talked too much for too long; Martin will be wondering what has become of me."

Craig rose and walked with her to her tonga. After he had kissed her goodbye, he said, "Do come and join us for dinner when you can."

"We will very soon," she replied.

Margot looked up in surprise when she saw Davinia rushing up the garden path a few days later.

"Whatever is it, Davinia?" Margot exclaimed. She bade Davinia sit down and asked the bearer to bring tea at once.

"Yes, memsahib," the bearer replied, not too eager to rush away, hoping to hear some news.

"There's not something wrong with the girls, I hope," Margot said, looking at her daughter anxiously. She glanced at the letter Davinia was clutching tightly in her hand.

"Aunt Agatha has written again, begging us to come as soon as we can and to stay if possible."

"But why? Why?" Margot asked.

"It is Clare again." She sighed deeply. "Aunt Agatha had assumed that both Clare and Astrid would be delighted to be presented at court. Now Clare says she will do the London Season and attend all the parties and balls, but she says she will not be presented at court with Astrid." Davinia swooned back in her chair. "I dread to think what state Agatha is in," she said. "I am so angry with Clare."

Margot, too shocked to speak for several minutes, put her hand to her head in despair. "But my dear Davinia," she said, "it is like ignoring a royal request."

"I know it is, Mama," Davinia replied. "Agatha goes on to say that Clare insists she is going to marry a man that Agatha thoroughly disapproves of, and she says we most certainly will disapprove of him too. Clare angrily told her that she is almost twenty-one years old, so before long she will be able to please herself and no one will be able to prevent her from doing anything she wants."

"Stephen has gone to the office to ask for leave and he is going to book our sailing tickets. We are going soon."

Margot looked at her.

"That child! Whatever is going to become of her?" she said. "I agree that your returning soon is the only way to stop her, but I am going to miss you so much." She sighed.

"And I you, Mama. Stephen has sent a telegram to tell Agatha to put a stop to Clare's plans."

Craig was surprised a few days later to see Margot hastening up the garden path. He rose and greeted her at the top of the verandah steps. He looked at her with concern.

"You look so sad today, Margot," he said. "Not bad news from home, I hope?"

"No, not from *your* home."

She sat down thankfully as Craig bade the bearer bring them iced tea.

"Yes, sahib," the bearer replied.

"Now, what is troubling you so, Margot. Can I be of any help?"

"No, my dear boy, but thank you all the same. Davinia has heard again from Agatha." She related all that Agatha had said. "Davinia and Stephen have decided to stay in Scotland for good. Clare is a constant worry and Agatha can't cope any longer. Astrid is, as always, content to keep to her music. She hopes eventually to gain a place at the music academy.

"But Clare," – she sighed, again and again – "but Clare is quite adamant about not being presented at court. She insists, however, on doing the London Season and attending all the parties and balls." Margot managed a wry smile. "Well, that is Clare all over." She sank back in her chair, quite despondent.

"Well, I certainly remember well the chase Stephen and I had to Kashmir after her so long ago," he said with a sigh.

"I hope", said Margot, deeply concerned, "that she does not elope with the young man before they arrive."

"Well, I shall be more than sorry to see Stephen and Davinia go. I do hope, Margot," he said, "that you and Martin do not decide to go too."

"No, no, my dear boy. As I have said before, we have too much work to do."

She looked at Craig sadly. His face was so pale and thin. How could she ever think of leaving him with just Lindsay? Hadn't she known him since the day he was born? 'Well, who knows?' she thought. 'Perhaps his father will decide to send for him. Then perhaps Martin and I will decide to rejoin my family in Britain. Until that time comes, I will never forsake Craig and his son.'

A few weeks later, Margot stood forlornly, strongly supported by Martin, with Craig and Lindsay at her side. They all gazed out to sea as the ship carried Davinia and Stephen away from the shore of India for ever.

During the previous weeks they had all been so busy, packing and labelling crates and boxes and endless trunks with all their precious possessions. They were loath to leave anything behind. The farewells to their servants had upset them more than leaving their many friends. The servants were, in many ways, like family, many of them having been with them for most of their lives.

Davinia had been daily in tears as she thought of their parting. She begged

Margot to take special care of them and let her know how each of them was faring. Stephen had made arrangements for the longest-serving ones to receive monthly a small pension for life.

Margot could hardly bring herself to believe it was all happening, but now the final farewells had been said, and she had waved a last farewell.

"Come, my dear," Martin begged, "we must be getting home."

She turned sadly towards him, and they walked away.

Craig, standing with Lindsay, stared at the ship until it was only a speck in the distance.

"Another chapter has closed," he murmured.

"What did you say, Papa?"

"I was just thinking aloud, my son. Life is like a book, except that one lives each chapter instead of reading it. Now the time has come to start another chapter. Come – we must away."

"Now they have finally gone," said Margot. She sighed as she sat, a lonely figure on her verandah, gazing into space.

"Come now," said Martin as he came up the steps and sat down beside her, "this will never do."

"No, I know, my dear. It most certainly will not. We still have far too much work to do, but I miss them so. It was bad enough when the girls left, but now that Davinia has gone I feel so alone."

"Well, I will always be by your side, my dear," he said as he held her outstretched hand.

"I know that, my dear," she sighed.

"Well," said Martin, trying to cheer her up, "maybe next year we can get some home leave. It is long overdue. It will be our year for seeing all the family again."

Margot's face suddenly brightened. "Yes, it will be nice to see once again all the places I knew as a child, to feel the chill mountain air on my cheeks, to see the heather and the pine trees, the lochs and the mountains." Suddenly, lost in thought, she was back there once more. "My bonnie, bonnie Scotland! How ever did I ever come to leave you?" she said.

She did not see Craig approaching up the steps, and she was startled when his voice broke in on her thoughts.

"Do come and sit down, my dear friend," said Martin.

"I thought you might be feeling a bit low, Margot, so how about you both joining Lindsay and me for dinner? There will be just the four of us."

"Yes, we will be delighted," said Martin, "but first join us in a drink."

Craig sat down and looked sadly at Margot's face. 'I just know how she is feeling. Everyone she loves most has now gone,' he thought.

"I daresay you and Martin will be off to another mission station in a day or two, so we too will be all alone," he said.

Margot looked at him sadly. He had spoken in such a melancholy tone of voice. She knew that as long as he was here, so alone, with only Lindsay to ease his heartache, she would never take home leave. Martin would understand, but Craig must never know.

Martin watched Margot as she opened her letter from Davinia.

"It seems, my dear," Margot said at last, as she put the letter down, "that Clare will be presented at court with Astrid after all. I am so thankful for Davinia's sake. Stephen has insisted that he will not allow her to take part in the London Season or marry the young man of her choice unless she acquiesces to his demands."

"It would be so nice for you to visit them for their coming of age and the London Season. You could also see the young man she wants to marry," Martin said. "Our home leave is due. I could arrange everything and we could be away before the end of the month. I will go tomorrow and arrange our sailing."

"Oh, that would be lovely!" Margot exclaimed, "I would love to be there with them at this time in their young lives." Then, suddenly, she thought of Craig. The memory of his pale, sad face came to her mind.

"No, no, my dear!" she hastily exclaimed. "Much as I would love to go, we have more important work to do here. No, I wouldn't dream of it."

He looked at her sadly. "But it is such a milestone in the girls' lives," he said. "I really think you ought to go. Besides, both of us could do with the rest."

"Well, maybe we can go next year for Clare's wedding, if she still desires to marry the young man. In the meantime, we must carry on with our work and plan for next year or the year after to take our home leave."

"Very well, then, my dear," Martin said. "Just as you wish. But I am going to insist that we get more help in visiting the missions. You must rest more. The long journeys are getting too much for you."

"Yes, I realise that. It will be nice for me to rest here at this mission. The correspondence is getting far too much. Elena only remarked on it in her last letter. She said she couldn't possibly manage if Emma didn't help her."

Margot was overjoyed to get a letter from Davinia telling her all about the twins' presentation at court and the exciting time they had at all the coming-out parties they had attended.

Clare, as you can imagine, Mama, was too excited for words. I know Astrid will write to you at length and tell you all about it, but she has been focusing on being accepted at the music academy in London so I daresay her letter will be more on that topic.

Clare too has promised to write. I will leave you to guess what topic she will dwell most on. I must add that Stephen and I totally disapprove of the young man she was hoping to marry, but now her interest is well and truly on another man, whom she met at one of the balls. The young man in question has already asked Stephen for her hand. We both approve of him, but we have insisted that they wait six months before an official engagement is announced.

The young man lives in London, in the hub of the city, so that will suit Clare. As you know, we have decided to move near London to be near Astrid. We will, of course, often visit Scotland. I think Aunt Agatha will be more than relieved to see the back of the twins – especially Clare.

I do wish, Mama, that you would take the home leave which is due to you and Martin. You both need the rest and change. In any case, you must come for Clare's wedding, whenever that takes place.

We are all longing to see you.

Love,
    Davinia

CHAPTER 260

Margot was not at all surprised to receive news of Clare's engagement as the New Year was heralded in. Davinia begged Margot to attend the wedding in the summer.

"Well," Martin exclaimed when she put the letter down, "of course we must go! There is nothing to stop us. Write at once and tell Davinia we will come."

"Yes, dear. I will write soon and tell her."

"Now, don't you dare change your mind," Martin said emphatically. "The new missionary workers are arriving soon, so I must go. I have a lot to do before they arrive."

Margot sat a long time in contemplation on the verandah. She knew that she must go and that no one would be more delighted than Craig that at last she and Martin would get the long-overdue home leave and the consequent rest which she so badly needed.

A few days later, she went to visit him.

"My dear, dear Margot, I am so delighted for you. When will you be leaving?" Craig said when she told him of her decision.

"Sometime soon," she replied.

"Will you be returning?" he asked, trying hard not to show his eagerness for an affirmative reply.

"Yes, yes, of course," she assured him, almost as soon as he had spoken. "In spite of the new missionary workers, we still have a lot to do. Will you be going to the hills this year with Lindsay?"

"I may go," he said indecisively, looking away from her towards the small church in the distance. "How can I go so far away and leave my two darlings, Margot? How can I?"

"My dear Craig," she replied, "this heat is not good for you. You would be better off in the hills. You cannot keep this up without injuring your health further, and it is not good for Lindsay. I believe Roddy has been posted to a hill station. Why not join him and Christina this year whilst we are away? The mission sisters will take your flowers to the grave daily. Think it over, my boy. It would be Elizabeth's wish."

His little-boy-lost look did not escape her keen appraisal. Hadn't she, along with Elena and Harriet, helped to fill his dear mother's place?

"Think it over, Craig dear," she said, patting his arm.

"Yes, Margot, I will. Now, to change the subject, Margot, tell me about this talk of Indian independence. You and Martin hear so much more about it than I do, owing to the travelling you do."

"Well, as you know, it has been talked about for years and years. They say the British must quit India. I'm sure it will come to pass, but not for many years yet. Why do you ask?" She looked at him questioningly.

"Well, I was wondering about the future," Craig replied. "What will you and Martin do if India gains independence?"

"Well, we shall go home," she said. Suddenly she wished she could take the statement back.

"Yes, *you* can go home," he sighed, "but that's something I cannot do."

"Oh, surely your father will send for you and Lindsay when that happens. I just know he will."

"I wish, for Lindsay's sake, he would, but I doubt it. Anyway, I will never go and leave my two darlings here alone. I shall stay with them always. I will be buried here with them." Suddenly, he laughed.

Margot looked at him with concern.

"Do you know why I am laughing, Margot?" he asked.

"No," she replied, looking puzzled.

"Well, I have just thought of home – as I do so often – and, suddenly, who do you think I thought of?"

Again the puzzled look appeared on her face. "No, tell me," she said.

"Why, Merry-Berry, of course. She told me once that my bones will never rest in a foreign land. Can't you see how wrong she will be?"

"Well, if she is wrong," Margot replied a little angrily, "it will be the first thing she has been wrong about. You must always be optimistic. I know your father will send for you," she said.

"I know it, Margot: Merry-Berry is wrong. I just know it."

CHAPTER 261

Margot sailed away, happy in the knowledge that already Craig and Lindsay were in the hills with Roddy and Christina. Now she felt she could enjoy her stay in England and attend Clare's wedding. Then, whilst Martin spent time at Aunt Agatha's, she would visit Glencree Castle to stay with Elena.

Roddy had begged Craig time and time again to come and visit them in the hills. Now Roddy and Christina both had to admit they were glad to see, after a few weeks in the fresh country air, his colour and general health improve greatly. His interest in life revived. He, Roddy, Lindsay and Ruardy would trek off daily to the woods, climbing or fishing.

Lindsay was now a fine, strapping, handsome youth and Ruardy, almost identical in build, looked like his younger brother. Often people remarked on their likeness to each other. Their interests were the same, as were their views of the world in general. Often their conversation turned to the unrest in India, which was progressively getting to be the topic of everyone's conversation.

"Where will you go, Ruardy, when we have to quit India – the place of our birth and the only home we have known?" asked Lindsay one day as they sat side by side fishing in one of the many streams. They were alone as Roddy and Craig had gone to watch a polo match.

"Well, Papa has said we will stay with our grandparents, who live beside the loch in Scotland. My grandfather is getting older, and Papa says he will have to take over the job of ferrying supplies to Glencree Castle and the village."

"I wish I could be in that boat when Uncle Roddy rows to Glencree," said Lindsay with a sigh, "but that will never happen until Grandpapa Bruce sends for Papa and me. Papa says that will never happen."

"What will you do and where will you go?" asked Ruardy. He already knew that Craig and his son had been disowned by Craig's father.

"We will have to stay here. Papa still owns part of the tea plantation in the hills. I daresay his partner will leave, and, if so, Papa will buy him out. That will be something for my future after I have travelled the world doing my archaeology. I think, in years to come, if he can be persuaded to leave the house in the city, Papa might spend longer in the hills. It would certainly benefit his health. Maybe one day he will feel he can leave my mother and Heather for a longer spell each summer. Maybe Uncle Roddy will be able to persuade him. I hope so." Lindsay sighed as he idly tugged some grass. Then he gazed into space.

"Yes, Papa surely will," replied Ruardy, "but in a few years he will be retiring from the army. He has always said he will not settle in India."

Lindsay looked at him in dismay. "That will mean we will never see each other again once you leave," he said. "That will just leave Papa and me. Well, there is nothing we can do about it," he said resignedly, as he tugged more and more at the grass beside him. "Come, Ruardy – let's return home. Our fathers will certainly laugh at the catches we haven't got today."

They both managed a wry smile as they gathered up their fishing lines.

CHAPTER 262

Margot's joy at being with her family again brought her to tears as they greeted her off the ship. The twins, now taller than herself, held each of her arms as if they would never let her go ever again. They talked incessantly: Clare of her forthcoming wedding in London; Astrid of her acceptance at the music academy and her future career in music.

"You know, Grandmama," said Astrid, "I have decided I am not going to marry ever. I hope to travel the world with the orchestra if I am selected. The Professor has told Papa that I am progressing so well that I am assured of a place eventually."

"My dear child, I am so pleased. Now, Davinia," Margot asked as soon as they reached their abode, "tell me: has Elena replied to your invitation? Is she able to attend the wedding?"

"Yes, Mama. She will be spending a few days with us and then she hopes you will return with her. She is getting a nurse to look after Bruce."

"Poor nurse!" replied Margot. "She will be keenly awaiting Elena's return. Maybe Bruce will appreciate Elena a little more whilst she is away."

"Never a more radiant bride went to the altar," Margot declared to Davinia after the bride and groom had departed on their honeymoon.

Stephen, sitting quietly in the corner drinking his first peaceful tot of whisky since Clare had become a young lady, agreed most heartily. Margot, Davinia, Elena and Martin had quite forgotten he was there as they sat discussing the events of the day. Astrid had retired early, after her stressful day of attending to Clare's every whim. She was thankful that at last her darling harum-scarum sister was now the harum-scarum wife of Lord Nicholas Joseph Royston Waugh. Now she could get on with her own life.

A few weeks later, Martin, Margot, Stephen and Elena headed north to Scotland.

"Will you stay with us a little while when you return from Scotland, before you sail back to India?" asked Astrid before she kissed her grandmother goodbye.

"Yes, my child, I will."

Elena had told Martha and Magnus that Margot would be visiting Glencree and staying for some time in the summer, so they were not surprised to see the Glencree carriage waiting on the small lane leading to the station one day. Zan, the driver, had gone to talk to Peggoty in the station.

Margot had pondered long on the journey as to what to say to them. She was afraid they blamed her for taking Elizabeth with her to India. Elena frequently put a reassuring hand on her arm as if guessing her thoughts.

Stephen and Martin helped the ladies alight and wished them goodbye. Then they rejoined the train, which was continuing to the north.

Margot gazed a long time at the loch and mountains with a lump in her throat and a tear in her eye. She quickly wiped away the tear before Elena's keen eye spotted it.

"Now, Peggoty, help Zan load the carriage," Elena said. "Margot and I are going to call on Martha and Magnus."

"Yes, ma'am," they both replied.

Martha and Magnus came to meet them when they saw them approaching. Magnus raised his cap and Martha dropped a little curtsy. Margot held Martha in a long embrace. They were almost in tears.

"Well," said Martha, embarrassed at the show of affection, "do come and sit down awhile whilst I prepare tea. You must be thirsty after such a long journey."

"Thank you, Martha, but we cannot stay too long. I will come and spend an afternoon with you sometime soon," said Margot.

"How kind of you, milady! I shall look forward to that. Tell me, milady," she said shyly, "tell me: how is Master Craig and our wee grandson?"

"Well, he is not so wee now, Martha. He's a fine, strapping young man and a most handsome one too."

"How I wish we could see him and his dear father!" she said with a sigh.

Margot looked at her sadly as she slowly sipped her tea.

"How I wish, Martha, I had not been compelled to take your lovely daughter away!" she exclaimed.

Martha looked towards Elena.

"Now don't you go upsetting yourself, milady," she replied. "I know she went of her own free will, but I wish the young master had not followed her. He should have remained here with his father, who needed him so much." She hesitated as she looked sadly at Margot and Elena. "I wish we could have seen her once more and also our lovely granddaughter, but it was not to be." She sighed, but then she quickly composed herself. "Are you sure you would not like more tea?" she asked.

"No, thank you, Martha," said Elena, eager to get Margot away from this stressful conversation. "We must get away round the loch before the mist comes down."

Martha and Magnus went with them to the now loaded carriage and watched as it sped away. Magnus put his arm round Martha's shoulder as they went back inside and closed the door of their cottage.

Bruce retired early, before Elena and Margot arrived that evening.

"Does Bruce often not have dinner with you, Elena?" Margot asked, surprised.

"Yes, very often, but I thought tonight he might have made an exception, knowing you were coming," Elena said in exasperation.

"Never mind!" Margot exclaimed, trying to save Elena from her obvious embarrassment. "I will meet him after breakfast in the morning."

Margot spent a long time gazing out over the loch. She could still see the rooftops of her old home. Bruce had resold it after Craig's departure, as Harriet and Elena had decided to stay at Glencree Castle instead of moving into it as planned.

She spent a restless night going over and over the events of all those years long ago.

CHAPTER 263

Margot was shocked almost beyond comprehension when she entered the library next morning and came face-to-face with Bruce. In her mind's eye, she had still imagined him as he was when last she saw him, although she knew he was now in a wheelchair, so she was taken aback by the sight of this old, old man. His hair was now grey instead of jet-black; his back was bent, whereas it had formerly been so straight. He held his wizened old hand out to her in greeting.

However, his voice was as strong as ever. He boomed out, in a rasping, ungracious voice, "Well, sit down, woman. So, you have returned safely, I see. I hope you are well. And Davinia? Is she well also?"

"Yes, she is quite well, Bruce, as I am also. How are you?"

"I am, as you see me, a useless cripple," he replied bitterly, "but I am grateful for Elena's help, and, of course, Jamie's. I attend to the affairs of the estate every day, although I cannot travel as of old. I am told by Elena that you will soon be returning to India."

"Yes, Bruce. I will only be here for a few days before rejoining my relatives up north."

"Very well, then. I shall not see you again before you leave. Goodbye."

She watched as he pulled the long bell pull over the fireplace and wheeled himself towards the door. Jamie arrived immediately, and he closed the door as they left.

Margot sat down and looked up at the picture of Isabelle above the fireplace. She was almost unable to believe what had just happened. She knew Bruce was an embittered man, but she couldn't understand his attitude towards her. Was he blaming her for Craig going to India? Or did he feel so guilty for making her a part of the sad affair that he could not now hold any kind of friendly feeling towards her. It was clear he didn't wish to involve himself in any further polite conversation with her!

She glanced again at Isabelle's picture and whispered softly to her: "Dear, dear Isabelle, whatever has become of this once so dear friend of mine? Why should he treat me so?" She leaned back in the chair and closed her eyes in deep contemplation.

"Well, my dear Margot, I see Bruce is away for his morning visit round the estate with Jamie and the ghillie. He can't have spent much time talking with you. I should have thought you two would have been talking for hours about old times. You were always such good companions," said Elena when she came into the room. She looked anxiously at Margot as she spoke. "Are you all right, Margot dear? You look rather pale. You are probably still tired after your long journey yesterday. Sarah will be along directly with our mid-morning tea. You will feel better soon."

"No, Elena," she replied sadly, "it is not the long journey. Bruce hardly spoke, and when he did he was rather abrupt and very unfriendly. He stated that he would not see me again before I left."

"Well, that is Bruce these days, Margot."

Sarah's knock on the door came as a welcome relief to both of them.

"Well," said Elena, "tomorrow we will go into the village. Everyone is longing to see you."

Margot's visit to the village and the greeting she got from all her old friends more than made up for the disappointment of the very brief conversation she had had with Bruce. They all clamoured round her to ask about Master Craig and Lindsay, and they enthused over the photographs Margot showed them.

Margot was delighted that Elena had asked Martha and Magnus to join them, along with Becky and Emma, in the Laird's Gallery for morning service the following Sunday in the family church.

As she gazed towards the altar, she could see beside the magnificent arrangement of flowers a vision of Elizabeth. She imagined her singing as she used to do. For a moment or two Margot was still standing when the rest of the congregation had sat down. Only the tug on her arm by Elena brought her back to reality.

"Are you all right?" Elena whispered to her as Emma looked at her sadly.

"Yes, my dears, I am quite all right."

After the service, Becky and Emma had arranged, in the church hall, several long tables loaded with home-made cakes. There was also a large tea urn, from which Emma was graciously pouring tea. As the choirmaster's wife approached with a small tray of cakes in her hand, Emma's mind shot back to the day of the Highland games, when Elizabeth had looked after the stall of home-made cakes with her. She recalled that this woman now approaching had reacted disapprovingly when Elizabeth had almost scalded Craig.

She sighed heavily as she thought of Elizabeth. 'How I wish she was here with me now!' she thought.

"Now, Emma, watch where you are pouring the tea!" Mrs Knowell exclaimed in a harsh voice.

"Oh, I am so sorry. I'm afraid I was daydreaming."

Emma looked up to see Mrs Crawford and Ruby, the only unmarried precious jewel, heading towards Margot. 'No doubt she hopes to glean some information from her about Master Craig,' she thought. 'Not if I can help it.'

"Mary, Mary," she hissed, "take over the tea urn from me, please. There are only one or two waiting to be served now."

"Very well, Emma."

Emma made a beeline for the space between Margot and Ruby and her mother.

"Ruby dear," she called to her.

"Yes, Emma?"

"Will you help me with the children next week at choir practice?"

"Yes, of course, if you wish."

Her mother now looked angrily at Emma, whose interruption had disrupted her plan. She watched helplessly as Margot, Elena, Martha and Magnus said their farewells to everyone and disappeared through the door. Emma hurried to join them.

"Just when I wanted to speak to Margot!" exclaimed Mrs Crawford. "Why did Emma need to ask you that? She knows you always help her with the children," she said peevishly. "Now I don't suppose I will get a chance to speak to Margot before she returns home. Come, Ruby – nearly everyone has gone."

CHAPTER 264

A few days later Margot and Elena were shopping in the village. Margot was idly gazing into the bakery-shop window, waiting for Elena, who had popped into the library to get Bruce's books.

"Mama, Mama!" exclaimed Ruby, as she and her mother came out of the library, "there is Lady Margot."

"Well now, Lady Margot," said Mrs Crawford charmingly as they approached her.

"Just Margot, if you don't mind. I do so prefer it," she replied.

"Very well, Margot, just as you wish. I was most anxious to speak to you after the morning service but you left before I had a chance."

Margot looked at her slightly disdainfully. She knew full well what Mrs Crawford wanted to discuss.

"What is it you wish to speak to me about?" she asked.

"Tell me, Margot: how are Master Craig and Lindsay? I believe Lindsay is a very handsome boy, just like his father. What a dreadful thing to happen to Martha's daughter and grand—"

She didn't finish her sentence.

Margot glared at her angrily. "To Master Craig's wife, you mean, and his daughter," Margot snapped.

"Well, yes, of course," Mrs Crawford stammered, rather taken aback at the tone of Margot's reply. She was still determined to glean as much information as she could, so she took no notice of Margot's obvious displeasure. "Will they be returning home in the near future?" she asked. Her mind was on the fact that her daughter, Ruby, was still unattached, and she had never given up hope that the last of her daughters might still be the next Mistress of Glencree Castle.

Before Margot could reply, Elena rejoined her.

"How nice to see you both again," she said, "but we must bid you good day. Zan is here with the carriage and we must hurry home. Good day to you." She took hold of Margot's arm and Zan helped them both into the carriage.

"Goodbye," Margot called as they sped away.

"Now I don't suppose I will ever get to know," Mrs Crawford fumed. "Now, Ruby, you must at every opportunity quiz Emma and find out all you can. I know she hears from Master Craig frequently." She looked at Ruby, who was drawing circles in the dust with her foot. "Are you listening to me, my girl?"

"Yes, of course, Mama," she replied meekly. They watched until Elena's carriage was out of sight.

Margot's visit ended far too soon for Elena and all her other friends. Bruce did as he said he would, and he never wished her farewell.

The afternoon she spent with Martha and Magnus had caused her both happiness and sadness. They had been delighted to see the photos and hear the tales she had related of their daughter and her family. She was glad they bore no ill will towards Craig.

She wished them goodbye on the station; then the train left for the north, where Margot rejoined Martin and Stephen for a short while. Then they all returned to spend their last few days with Davinia before leaving for India.

"Mama dear, you really ought to be thinking of coming back for good," Davinia said. "You are not as young as you were, your workload is getting no lighter and there is also so much unrest now in India."

"I know, my dear Davinia," she replied, "but my work for the missions is not yet finished. Before I make any decision to return for good, I will need to be sure the missionary work is in good hands. That may take a few years, but I promise I will try to curtail my visits to the missions now that the other missionaries are taking on more work."

'How strange!' thought Davinia as she watched the ship leaving the dock. 'I have often waved goodbye to family members who were leaving India, but now Mama is sailing *to* India. I wonder when I shall see her again.'

"Could you not have persuaded her and Martin to stay for good, Mama?" sobbed Astrid as she waved her small, wet handkerchief.

"I am sure you could have, Mama," rejoined Clare, now back from her honeymoon.

"Now, girls, you know very well that once your grandmother has made up her mind to do something no power on earth will make her change her mind. All we can hope is that she will come back to us soon," said Stephen.

CHAPTER 265

Margot and Martin were both delighted to see Craig and Lindsay waiting on the quayside on their arrival. They were relieved that Craig was looking well after his stay in the hills with Roddy. Margot had worried incessantly about his health whilst she had been away.

"Well, my dear Craig, how are you feeling now?" she asked.

"So much better, Margot, thank you," he replied.

"Well, if you come with us to the hills every year," said Martin, "you will soon regain your full strength."

"Yes, I will come, I promise. The mission took great care of my darlings' grave whilst I was away, so I shall be able to go with an easier mind in future. Now, you must join us for dinner and tell me how everything was at home."

"How was my father?" asked Craig as they sat on the verandah later that evening.

Not for one moment would Margot let Craig see the deep distress she still felt at Bruce's disregard of her.

"He is quite well, but, as you can imagine, rather embittered at being confined to a wheelchair. He manages to attend to matters concerning the estate. He would be mighty proud of this lovely grandson here if he saw him," she said, looking admiringly at Lindsay, who was sitting beside her. "You are growing more like your grandfather every day," she told him.

"Well, I hope I am only like him in looks and nothing else," he said with a tinge of bitterness in his voice. "I hope I grow up with my grandmother's and mother's kinder natures, and I wish to be more like my father, rather than like that selfish old man."

"How about another drink before we leave?" exclaimed Martin, keen to change the subject.

"Yes, of course," said Craig. "Bearer, bring more drinks for everyone, please."

"Yes, sahib."

After their drinks Craig said, "You must be tired after your long journey we can talk another time about those at home."

They bade one another goodnight and their tonga drove away.

A few days later Margot and Craig sat alone on the verandah, and Margot related all the events that had taken place whilst she was in Britain.

"Tell me," Craig said: "how is Aunt Elena coping with the loss of Aunt Harriet, and with Papa being as he is?"

"Well, she has extra helpers in from the village. Emma visits every day to help with correspondence. I managed to spend some time with Martha and Magnus. They were delighted with the photographs you sent. I went with Elena to visit the home for the ex-servicemen, and all is going well."

"Thank God for that!" Craig exclaimed. "Everyone is able to help them except me," he added bitterly.

"Well, you help financially, dear Craig. Don't persecute yourself so," she said, patting his arm to reassure him.

"Yes, I realise that, Margot," he said, sighing deeply, "but I should be at home helping with all the work. Aunt Elena requires my help so much."

"Yes, yes, my boy, I understand how you feel. I feel sure your father will swallow his pride and send for you and Lindsay to return before very long."

"Well, even if he does, I shall never leave my two darlings out here all alone."

She looked at him despairingly as she rose to go.

"Tell me, how is the news in India now?" she asked.

"Well, the same old chant for the British to quit India is heard more often now."

"Well, we shall have to see what the future brings," Margot said hopefully. "In the meantime, Craig dear, I must away and visit my missions and get back in time for Christmas. You must join us for Christmas and Hogmanay. I insist."

"Thank you, Margot. We will be delighted."

He waved her off reluctantly.

Craig was surprised next day to receive a letter from Roddy. He pondered for several minutes, reluctant to open it, as if he expected it to contain bad news.

The bearer watched him keenly as he handed him a letter opener.

'This is very short,' he thought, as he unfolded it.

Dear Craig,

Returning to Britain. We will break our journey to spend a few days with you before we sail. We will arrive Friday of this week. We'll give you all the news when we see you.

Love,

Roddy, Christina and Ruardy

Craig sighed deeply as he put it in his pocket.

"Bad news, sahib?" asked Damodar, looking at Craig with concern.

"Yes, Damodar. Prepare the rooms for Captain Roddy and his wife and son."

"Yes, sahib," Damodar replied before he hurried away.

Craig and Lindsay were delighted to see Roddy and his family. As they stepped from the train, Roddy was startled to see how tall Lindsay had grown. 'Such a handsome boy too,' he thought. 'He's so like his father before the tragedy that made him an old man overnight. He's got his father's dignified, upright stance, which was also that of his grandfather, Bruce.' Roddy soon dismissed the fleeting thought of that bitter old man. He noted that Lindsay also had his father's habit of brushing a wayward curl from his forehead. His jet-black, wavy hair was brushed back in waves. 'How sad his eyes are still,' Roddy thought. 'At one time they were always filled with such gaiety. He has such assurance, though. He looks as if he takes everything in his stride. I expect he is a tower of strength to his father.'

Roddy also saw in Lindsay something of his beloved sister: his ready smile, always present but without her shyness. His affectionate hug was so reminiscent of the way Elizabeth had always greeted him. For a moment, a lump came in his throat as he thought of her, but he quickly brushed his sad thoughts away as he noted Craig looking at him.

"How quickly our sons are growing up! They are both so tall," Roddy said as Craig hugged Ruardy. "It can only mean that we are growing into two old men, now that our sons are such fine young men."

Both of them looked at their sons admiringly.

Christina stood silently watching them greet one another. Craig turned suddenly to hug her.

"Dear, dear Christina, I am so pleased to see you looking so well," he said. "You must forgive us proud fathers going on so about our sons."

"It is a failing of fathers, this adoration of their sons," she replied. "They sometimes forget, I think, that their mothers adore them just as much."

"Yes, you are so right, Christina. Now, we must get away home. You must be tired after such a long journey."

CHAPTER 266

"I am delighted at your promotion to Major, Roddy," said Craig as they sat alone on the verandah after dinner one day. "Elizabeth would have been so proud of you."

"This should have been just home leave for us, but I shall be staying in Britain for good," Roddy said. He had been reluctant to tell Craig this news. "We were told to pack all our belongings for transportation to Britain before we left, and we had to inform Ruardy's college. I shall be taking some important courses at the military headquarters in England, so I shall have to leave Christina and Ruardy at Papa's home until I get settled. Ruardy, I know, is anxious to get into the military academy when he is older."

Roddy took a draught of his whisky when he finished his discourse; he looked across at Craig.

Craig looked into space for a long time after Roddy had finished speaking. "It is doubtful if we will ever see you again," he said with a sigh.

"Well, Craig, as you know, we are always on the move so I could get posted back here in a few years' time."

"I do hope so," Craig replied, trying not to show how deeply disturbed he was at Roddy's news. "It will be so nice for you to see your parents again. How are they?"

"Quite well, and, of course, they are most eager to see us after all these years."

"Yes, I would love to see my father again too," Craig replied sadly.

"You will one day, Craig, I feel sure."

"I wish I felt so sure, Roddy," Craig answered dejectedly, "and I know Lindsay would dearly love to meet him."

Roddy now felt nothing but pity for Craig. He watched him gazing into space as if oblivious of his presence. At one time he had felt nothing but bitterness towards him for following Elizabeth out to India.

'If only he had stayed with his father and married Fiona, as he should have done, my darling Elizabeth would have been safely back home with our parents where she belonged, alive and well. She would not have died under a pile of earthquake rubble with her daughter.' He gave a shudder as he relived it all again. 'But how can I be angry,' he thought, 'when I look at this broken man? He loved her so dearly, and his love has cost him so much. I know I would have done the same for Christina.'

Christina now rejoined them. They could hear the jolly laughter of the two boys as they returned from their short stroll.

"I daresay, Lindsay," Roddy said, laughing gaily, "you and Ruardy have been flirting with all your girlfriends."

"Well, I must admit Lindsay has quite a string of them out there," said Ruardy, "but it isn't worth my while getting serious with anyone as we are here for such a short time."

"Well, it is getting late," said Christina. "We must retire."

"I must visit Elizabeth's grave before we leave, Craig," said Roddy.

"We can all go tomorrow," replied Craig. "I will tell the mali to gather some flowers."

Craig and Roddy stood side by side as Lindsay, Christina and Ruardy placed the flowers on the grave. Christina spent some time arranging them to her liking before kneeling down to say a silent prayer. After a while Roddy raised her to her feet and wiped the tears from her eyes. Then she walked on ahead with Lindsay and Ruardy, their arms around her shoulders.

Craig and Roddy stood for several minutes in silence, each alone in his own grief, before turning and following the others. Craig closed the creaking gate behind them, and they salaamed to the mali, who stood close by watching them sadly.

"Salaam, sahibs, salaam," he murmured as he put his hands together and bowed his head.

Their departure day arrived. They were sad to be leaving. Craig, Roddy and Christina drove to the quay in one tonga; Lindsay and Ruardy followed behind, loath to part. There was a special brotherly love between them.

"Do you think you will ever return to India, Ruardy?" Lindsay asked him.

"We might. We all love it here, but Papa will soon finish his army career and he has always said he would like to return home to Scotland."

They waved to several girls Lindsay knew, who laughed gaily and waved back as they passed.

"Ruardy," said Lindsay teasingly, "it's a pity you aren't staying. I think you would make quite a few conquests before long."

"Maybe, maybe, but I am a little too young, don't you think? Anyway, as I am leaving I shall have to leave all my admirers to you. Will you ever come to Scotland, Lindsay?" he asked.

"I doubt it," Lindsay replied. "My father is forbidden to return to Glencree, and he will not hear of us going anywhere else. Besides, he will never leave Mama and Heather alone here," he said sadly.

It was almost time to board the ship, so they said their farewells.

"Give my love to your dear parents and Aunt Elena when you see her," said Craig.

"Do you have any message for your father if I see him?" Roddy asked Craig.

"I doubt if he will welcome any greeting from me. Give Emma my fondest regards – and, of course, anyone else I know. If you see Merry-Berry, which I doubt, tell her I am well."

"She will be hard to find," said Roddy with a laugh.

"I think she might search you out, Roddy, if she thinks you might have a message from me."

"Merry-Berry?" said Lindsay, looking puzzled. "Who is she?"

"Just a very kind old lady neither of us will ever see again," said Craig.

Craig hugged Roddy and Ruardy closely as they said goodbye; he kissed Christina lightly on both cheeks.

"Now, you, dear, take care of yourself," he said.

"And you also, Craig dear," she replied.

He tried to quell the tears in his eyes and the falter in his voice.

"Please give our love to Margot and Martin," Christina said. "We are sorry they are away at the missions."

"Goodbye, dear, dear Ruardy," said Lindsay sadly. "Give my grandparents a big hug and kiss for me."

"I will, I will," he called back as he raced after his parents up the gangplank.

"Tell Aunt Elena to write to me more often, when you see her, Roddy."

"I will, I will."

They waved their last farewells.

Craig didn't move till the ship was nearly out of sight.

"If only we could be going with them to see my father too," he said with a sigh, his heart almost breaking at yet another parting.

He felt a tug on his arm.

"Come, Papa – I have called the tonga," said Lindsay.

CHAPTER 267

Martha and Magnus waited impatiently at Glencree Station for the train's arrival. Roddy leaped out to greet them before the train stopped. He gathered them in his arms, and their tears of happiness flowed.

"Mama, Papa, it's good to be home," Roddy said.

Christina and Ruardy, standing close by, wept with them. Ruardy, the first to recover his composure, rushed to his grandmother's side. He took a handkerchief from his pocket and wiped her eyes. "Don't cry any more, Grandmama. Papa will be home for some time now. We are staying for a few years – maybe even for good."

"We shall have to wait and see, my boy." Martha sighed between her tears, and she continued to dab her eyes. She hugged him close. Then, holding him at arm's length, she gazed at him from head to toe in admiration.

"My word, my boy, how tall you are! Quite a young man!"

"Yes, I shall soon be a fully grown man," he replied with an air of assurance. "I am nearly as tall as Papa."

"My boy, my boy," said Magnus, "don't hasten your youth away. Enjoy it. It will pass all too soon."

"Far too soon!" rejoined Christina as she hugged Martha close.

Peggoty, busy stacking their luggage, stopped for a moment to wipe a tear from his eye. "Is this all your luggage, Roddy?" he asked as he closed the carriage door, anxious to get the train away.

"Yes, thank you, Peggoty."

Roddy rushed over to greet him. "It's so good to be home. I almost forgot you and the luggage. I'm sorry," he said.

"That's all right, my boy. I am so glad to see you back."

He waved the train away and closed the gate after them. Roddy turned to give him a wave.

"Please stack the rest of the luggage, Peggoty. Ruardy and I will pick it up tomorrow."

"I will. Goodbye."

They retired late that night, after talking of how Craig and Lindsay were coping after the terrible loss of Elizabeth and Heather. Magnus constantly wiped tears from his eyes, and Martha comforted him as she patted him on the arm.

"Our darling angel is now sleeping peacefully with our other little angel," she said. "We must weep no more, husband dear, weep no more." She wiped away a tear. "Come – we must retire."

Next day, Roddy visited the vicarage to thank the vicar for the special service he had held. He was delighted to find Lady Elena and Emma there when he arrived.

They all sat quietly in the lounge as Roddy related the tragic event. Emma became very distressed, so Elena rose and comforted her. She nodded to Roddy, indicating that it would be better to change the subject. Becky also wiped tears away.

Eventually, Emma rose and wiped her eyes.

"I will make tea," she said. "Then we shall all feel better."

"Tell me, Roddy, how is Craig now?" asked Elena. "Is he ill? His letters to me are full of despair. I am so concerned about him."

Roddy sat for several minutes in deep contemplation before replying. "To tell you the truth, milady," he said, "he is a broken man. He has a wonderful son. Lindsay is such a fine boy and such a comfort to him. They both asked me to convey their love to you." He turned to Becky. "He also wished me to convey to the Reverend his very deep gratitude for the service he held for them."

Becky nodded her head and smiled sadly.

Emma was now more composed as she served the tea.

"Now I must go," said Elena, rising from her chair. "Now, Roddy dear, I expect you and your family will be attending church on Sunday?"

"Of course, milady."

"Well, I want you all to join me in the Laird's Gallery."

Roddy looked a little surprised. "Yes, of course, milady," he said.

"In the meantime, all my love to you all! Goodbye."

Roddy helped her into the carriage. She held his hand a long time before waving them all a sad farewell. They waved till she was out of sight.

Roddy put his arms round Becky and Emma and led them back inside. Emma wept bitterly on his shoulder.

"There, there, dearest Emma!" he said as he dried her eyes. "Elizabeth would not like to see you cry."

"But, Roddy, I never thought when she went away that I would never see her again. I always hoped that she would return after Lady Margot had trained another assistant. Even when Master Craig went to join her, I still hoped she would return."

"Well, dear, we all knew that once Master Craig made up his mind to marry her, she couldn't refuse," Roddy replied. "They were too much in love. Now I must depart." He kissed them both on the cheek. "I will see you all on Sunday," he said.

He was eager to get away. The visit had depressed him deeply, but he put on a brave smile as he waved them farewell.

"Emma, tell the boys I will see them often now I am home," he said.

"I will," she called after him.

CHAPTER 268

The following Sunday, Mrs Crawford and her three precious jewels, and Sapphire's and Pearl's daughters, watched in dismay as the Anderson family took their seats next to Lady Elena in the Laird's Gallery. Alongside them sat Becky, Emma and Stuart. Nicholas, home from university, sat next to Ruardy.

The two granddaughters of Mrs Crawford stared at the two handsome boys, but the stares were returned with indifference. Their gazes became fixed on the girls from the academy, who were seated on the opposite side of the church. Both boys wanted the service to end so that they could discuss young men's topics.

"How Lady Elena could stoop to invite them to join her in the Laird's Gallery is beyond me," Mrs Crawford hissed behind her gloved hand to her daughters. "I wonder what His Lordship would say if he ever found out. I shall most certainly mention it to him if I ever get the chance. I shall also ask Mrs Knowell for her opinion. Maybe she could mention it to him when she visits Glencree Castle."

Several of the congregation turned round and glared at her, but she ignored them.

"And that Roddy's wife sits there as if she is the lady of the manor," she continued.

"Do be quiet, woman," Mr Crawford murmured quietly. He looked disarmingly around at the congregation.

She decided to heed him, and she reluctantly joined in the hymn.

Emma, looking down, had not failed to notice the disdainful looks of Mrs Crawford and her daughters, nor the looks of disapproval from others of the congregation in the direction of the Crawfords' pew. Emma cast an uneasy look at Martha, who was quietly listening to the sermon.

'Thank goodness', she sighed, 'Martha has not noticed anything.'

However, the event had not gone unnoticed by Her Ladyship, who, Emma noticed, had looked down at the Crawfords with very obvious displeasure.

Nicholas and Ruardy hastened out of church when they saw the granddaughters of Mrs Crawford heading their way.

"Come, Ruardy – let's catch up with the family. They are bidding goodbye to Lady Elena. We certainly don't want to be waylaid by the daughters of the 'jewel' girls."

"The 'jewel' girls?" Ruardy queried. "How come they are called that?"

"It's a long story. I will explain another time."

They both assisted Lady Elena into her carriage and watched till it was out of sight. They were all pleased to see that Mrs Crawford's family had hastened away.

Emma was delighted to see how warmly Martha's family was greeted by so many of the villagers. She wished them farewell and they headed back to the jetty.

CHAPTER 269

Roddy's posting to his course down south arrived far too soon.

"Oh. darling," Christina exclaimed, "that means you won't be back for Christmas!"

"Never mind! I shall be home for Hogmanay, which is much more to my liking."

Soon Roddy was bidding them goodbye on the station.

Christina linked her arm protectively in Martha's, and Magnus and Ruardy followed as they wended their way to the cottage.

"How empty it feels without him!" said Martha as she sat wearily in the old rocking chair.

"Well, the time will soon pass," said Christina, trying to hide her own loss. "I will make some tea, Mama, whilst you rest. Then I will see how Ruardy is getting on with his packing. He will be away in a few days, off to the college."

"Thank goodness he has not yet been accepted at the military academy; otherwise he too would have to go far away down south," said Magnus with a sigh.

Roddy was unable to get home for Hogmanay, but he was home for Burns Night in late January of 1939. The celebrations were held in the village hall.

Roddy, Christina and Ruardy had been invited to stay with Emma and Stuart, much to Nicholas's delight. Martha and Magnus were invited to stay at the vicarage.

Nicholas and Ruardy arrived at the hall earlier than their parents and soon they were surrounded by most of the young damsels from the academy, all laughing gaily, oblivious to anyone else. Nicholas was pleased to note that as yet the daughters of the 'jewel' girls had not yet arrived.

"Hang on to your partner," he whispered to Ruardy; "then the daughters of the 'jewel' girls will not be able to monopolise us as soon as they arrive."

"You seem to have had lots of encounters with them in the past," commented Ruardy. "Are they not nice to know?"

"They are far too possessive for my liking." He glanced round the room. "Ah, I see our parents have arrived. We will join them later," he said.

Roddy and Christina glanced round the room, looking for Ruardy. They soon spotted him, resplendent in his new Anderson tartan. He was with Nicholas in the middle of a group of girls from the academy.

"Ruardy, I see," commented Roddy, "is certainly making up for lost time now that he is not at a boys-only college. I have never seen him surrounded by so many young ladies."

"They are both fine boys – head and shoulders above the rest of the boys," said Christina with pride.

"Yes," agreed Emma, "Nicholas knows all the girls so well, so he will have introduced Ruardy to all of them."

"How I wish dear Lindsay could have been here to enjoy this Burns Night with them," sighed Christina.

"Well, let's hope he will be here one day, hopefully soon," rejoined Emma.

Ruardy glanced at his parents. "Come, Shona, I want you to meet my parents," he said. He turned to a pretty girl who had just linked arms with him. "Excuse us please," he said. Then he freed his other arm from a rather possessive girl who was reluctant to let go. She looked after them angrily as they departed.

"Mama, Papa, I want you to meet Shona," he declared.

"Delighted!" said Shona, as they all shook hands.

"I believe you have already met Nicholas's parents," he said.

"Yes, we have met," she replied shyly.

Suddenly, the band struck up for the first dance to begin. Everyone took to the floor, all in gay, jolly mood. There was food and drink in plenty. Little did they know that this would be the last Burns Night they would celebrate with such gay abandon as they danced and laughed, all in high spirits, into the night.

A few days later, Roddy waved them all farewell again at the station. They wended their way back to the cottage.

As they sat later that evening by the roaring peat fire, Christina could see a small tear on Martha's face.

"To think, Mama," she said, as she poured the tea and handed it to her, "if Ruardy is accepted at the military academy later this year, he too will be leaving us!" She sighed.

"I daresay," sighed Martha. "Partings! So many partings!"

CHAPTER 270

As the year of 1939 sped on, the whole world viewed with alarm the events on the Continent. A madman was on the march. Menacing threats were increasing daily to the small countries surrounding Germany. By March, Czechoslovakia had been invaded; Danzig, in Poland, threatened to be next. Germany and Italy had signed a military pact with each other. In April, Britain, France and Poland signed a Mutual Assistance Pact. Both Britain and France warned Germany that if Poland was attacked, it would mean war.

Craig and his friends sat for long hours after dinner, discussing the latest news. Craig sat long after they had left, gazing into space, pondering on each new development. He relived once more the horror of the mud-filled trenches and the suffering of his men. He remembered the relief when it was all over. Surely it could not happen again! It didn't seem possible that all this would lead the world into another war.

He recalled the night of his homecoming, when he first saw his darling angel, as she crept down the stairs in an aura of candlelight, her hair floating round her beautiful face like a silver cloud.

"Angel, my angel, why have you left me all alone like this?" he murmured.

He opened his eyes to see Lindsay gazing at him from the top of the verandah steps. On returning from visiting his friends, Lindsay had stood for several minutes listening to his father's murmuring. He wished he could help him.

'Poor, poor Papa!' he thought.

Craig gazed at him lovingly and held out his hand. Lindsay knelt down beside him and clung to his outstretched hand.

"You are not alone, Papa," he said. "I am here, always at your side. Nothing will ever separate us. Never fear – I will always be here."

"Not always, my son, not always," Craig sighed. He ruffled Lindsay's hair and gazed into his steadfast eyes.

"I will, Papa," Lindsay replied, "just as we have always promised – just the two of us."

'How strange!' thought Craig, as his mind went back to the promise he had made to his own father.

He remembered his father's reply: "Yes, my son, just the two of us."

Once more he was lost in reverie as Lindsay looked at him sadly.

"Come, Papa – we must retire. The bearers need to go home, and you know they won't go until we dismiss them. We tend to forget."

"So we do, my son, so we do." He looked at Lindsay again. "You are so like your dear mother: always thinking of others." He ruffled his hair again. "Thank you, bearers. Goodnight," he called.

"Salaam, sahibs, salaam," they replied.

They watched as Lindsay linked his arm in his father's and led him indoors.

As the months passed there was no respite from the depressing news from the Continent. The threats to Poland continued and Britain reiterated her pledge to defend her if she was attacked.

Later that year, the Military Training (Conscription) Act received the royal assent. Mobilisation papers were prepared. Craig's friends from the barracks called almost daily to bid him farewell.

'Roddy must have known of the gravity of the situation when he was called back home from India,' thought Craig as he sat on the verandah pondering over the military build-up.

'Will the Continent never find peace?' he wondered.

He was delighted one morning to see Margot hastening up his garden path with a beaming smile on her face.

"My, my, Margot!" he exclaimed as he greeted her. "What good news have you brought this lovely day? Whatever it is, it will be a joy to hear compared with this never-ending gloomy news from abroad." He pulled a chair closer to his. "Do sit down, dear. You look quite exhausted. Damodar, bring tea, please."

"Yes, sahib," Damodar replied, but he was in no great hurry to depart. He wanted to hear the memsahib's good news.

Craig noticed his hesitation. "Bearer, I said tea, please."

"Very well, sahib."

They both smiled as he departed.

Craig looked up to see Martin at the top of the steps. There was a smile of happiness on his face too.

"Well, tell me your good news," Craig said. "It must be very important to bring such glowing smiles to you both. Ah, here is the tea."

The bearer placed the tea tray on the small table.

"Shall I pour, sahib?" he asked.

"No, Damodar, I will pour," said Margot.

They all smiled as he reluctantly departed.

Margot withdrew a letter from her pocket.

"Davinia has written to say that Clare was safely delivered of twin girls, named Judith and Rosalind. They are all well," she declared.

"That is wonderful news indeed!"

"Let us hope", said Martin, "that neither of them grows up to be as naughty as their mother – but only time will tell." He laughed aloud as he leaned back in his chair, musing on Clare's past antics.

"What a journey we had, Craig! All the way to Kashmir to stop her marrying!"

"Yes, I remember," said Craig, laughing with him. "What else does she have to say, Margot?" He noticed that she was still eager to read on.

"She says Astrid has now passed all her exams in music and hopes to go on tour very soon. Astrid has also joined the Red Cross, and she has been helping in the local hospital."

"Well, she always did like helping in the mission hospital," said Martin.

"How proud my darling Elizabeth would have been, Margot, that she has done so well in music," Craig said with a sigh.

CHAPTER 271

In England that summer, the people whose yearly jaunts to the Continent were a must were now full of nervous apprehension. Events across Europe were moving forward with a speed no one could grasp. Hitler, defying the threat from France and Britain, invaded Poland. It meant war.

On Friday, 1 September, the news flashed across the world: 'Germany Invades Poland'. The Anglo-French ultimatum to Germany to withdraw its troops was rejected.

In Britain, the National Service Act was passed, and conscription for men aged from nineteen to forty-one was introduced. The news that everyone hoped they would never hear again was announced at 11.15 a.m., on Sunday, 3 September 1939: 'Britain is at war with Germany.' By 12 October 1939, the British Expeditionary Force was already fighting in France and Belgium.

Craig, like everyone else, sat by his radio throughout the day, ordering fresh tea constantly. When he heard the fateful message coming from London – 'This country is at war with Germany', the cup he had been holding crashed to the floor.

Damodar dashed to his side. "Are you all right, sahib?" he asked as he bent down to pick up the broken pieces.

"Great Britain is now at war with Germany, Damodar. God knows what will happen before it all ends." He sank back in his chair and covered his face with his hands as Damodar crept silently away, too perturbed at the effect the news had had on his master to venture any comment of his own. "No, no, surely not again!" Craig kept on muttering.

Martin came rushing up the steps.

"Craig, Craig, have you heard the news?" He saw Craig slumped in his chair, his head clasped in his hands. "Yes, I can see you have," he said. He slumped in the chair next to Craig. "Australia, New Zealand and British India will also be involved, I daresay. The King is going to broadcast to the Empire."

Suddenly Craig screamed in alarm: "Oh, my God, Martin! Will my son be called up?"

"I shouldn't think so, Craig," he replied, looking at him sadly, trying to allay his fears. He placed his hand on Craig's shoulder. "Craig, don't take on so," he said. "The war will no doubt be over soon."

"But, Martin, they said that about the last war," Craig raged. "They said it would be 'over by Christmas' – but they never said which Christmas. By the way things sound, many a Christmas will pass before this war is over. Four long years the Great War lasted, and the men are still suffering. God spare the world from such a war happening again!" He covered his face as if by doing so the crisis would all go away.

They looked up to see Margot standing near the door. As she approached, Craig thought he had never seen her looking so sad. He stood up to welcome her.

"Sit down, Margot," he said, and he called to the bearer to bring more tea.

Margot felt a little more composed after she drank her tea.

"This is dreadful news, to be sure," she sighed. "When will it end? Davinia's last letter to me was full of reproach at my not giving up the missions and going to live with them. It is ironic to think that during the last war I was marooned in Scotland because of Mama's illness and she and the children were here. Now here I am marooned in India. Goodness knows when we will get home now. Davinia begs us to return as soon as hostilities cease." She saw Craig's anxious look in her direction, but she pretended not to notice. "Of course, I have written and told her I cannot leave until our mission work is done," she said.

"Come, dear – it is getting late!" Martin exclaimed. "Goodnight, Craig. Try not to worry."

Craig waved them sadly away. He sauntered back to his seat, rested his head on the small table and fell asleep.

Damodar stood silently, close beside him. Lindsay came back from visiting his friends, looked at his father with concern and looked up at the bearer.

"What is the matter, Damodar?" he asked. "Is Papa not well?"

Craig woke at the sound of Lindsay's voice and looked at him.

"Are you all right, Papa?" Lindsay said. "Speak to me."

"Yes, I am all right, my son."

"Don't upset yourself about today's news, Papa. It won't be as bad as you think."

"It will be my son, it will be. The world is going mad. Mad!" he shouted.

Damodar rushed back into the room.

"Are you all right, sahib?" he asked.

"Yes, Damodar, I'm all right. Pour me a double whisky."

Damodar looked at him with consternation and hesitated.

"But, sahib, it is not good for you," he said.

"I know, Damodar, but bring me one just the same."

"Bring me one also," Lindsay called.

Dinner was served. Lindsay relished his, but hardly a morsel passed Craig's lips.

"The doctor says you must keep up your strength, Papa, and eat more," Lindsay said.

"I know, my son. Maybe tomorrow I will."

"It's always tomorrow with you, Papa," Lindsay admonished.

They rose and bade each other goodnight.

Craig had a sleepless night; Lindsay soon descended into the sleep of the carefree young.

CHAPTER 272

As the war news reached every abode, the village of Glencree was shaken to its foundations. All the families feared the call-up of their menfolk.

Lawrie, sitting in his old rocking chair, sighed deeply, wondering when his weary unhappy journeys delivering the dreaded small buff envelopes would begin.

Elena called a special meeting of the Ladies' Sewing Circle, where she suggested that everything knitted from then on should be for the troops. She begged the villagers to unravel unwanted woollen garments to provide wool for socks, scarves, gloves and balaclavas. She appealed for old knitting patterns so that the girls in the village and at the academy could join in the effort. She arranged for Magnus to call weekly at Glencree to collect some of the wool she had collected on her travels round the village. Using this supply, Martha and Christina were able to work from home on the other side of the loch.

"How I wish, Emma," she declared one day, "that we were not so isolated! Then we could take in some of the evacuee children from the cities. It will be so much safer for them here."

Later Elena realised that isolated parts of Scotland weren't as safe as she thought: on 13 November 1939, the first bombs to be dropped on British soil fell on the Shetlands.

"Fortunately," she related later, to the Ladies' Sewing Circle, "there were no casualties. Only one rabbit was killed, I believe."

Dive-bombers also attacked ships in the Firth of Forth and Rosyth. The ladies shuddered at the nearness of it all. The bombs were getting too close for comfort, they agreed as they sat knitting furiously.

The war news became more grave daily. Everyone now realised that this war, like the last, would not be over quickly.

By early May 1940 the Germans had invaded Holland, Belgium and Luxembourg. They swept on towards France, in spite of the stubborn resistance they encountered along the way from the British Expeditionary Force.

The evacuation of as many people as possible from the Continent became a priority as the blitzkrieg by Germany continued relentlessly across Europe towards the English Channel.

By early June, every small ship had been commandeered to evacuate the troops to England. On 4 June, the Germans captured Dunkirk: by 14 June, they had occupied Paris.

Italy had by then declared war on Britain and France; Canada declared war on Italy. On 11 June, Australia, New Zealand and South Africa declared war on Italy.

As the days, weeks and months sped on, the Battle of Britain continued unabated, and bombs rained on British cities.

CHAPTER 273

Craig became more and more alarmed as time passed.

Shortly after their return from the hills, in the late summer of 1940, Craig, dozing on the verandah one late afternoon, was startled by a wild whoop. He heard Lindsay's voice and the sound of his cycle crashing to the floor, followed by his laughter. He heard Lindsay rebuke Munilal for not breaking its fall and Munilal's reply: "Sorry, sahib."

"You are not sorry one bit," Lindsay laughed in reply.

"Papa! Papa!" he called excitedly.

Craig opened his eyes to see his tall son, bronzed from their recent visit to the hills, framed in the doorway, a wide smile on his handsome face.

"Now, now, my son, why all the haste and excitement? What wild schemes have you and your friends thought up now?" he asked when he saw Lindsay's friends mounting the verandah steps close on his heels.

"Papa," he exclaimed breathlessly, "I and my friends have enlisted. We rode to the recruiting office after we finished our studies early."

The look of dismay on his father's face stopped his gleeful utterance.

"Sit down, boys," Lindsay said. "Bearer, please bring whisky for me and my friends."

"Yes, sahib," Damodar replied. Before he hastened away, he looked from Craig to Lindsay in consternation.

"Will you join us, Papa?" Lindsay asked.

"Indeed I will not!" Craig fumed angrily. "You and your friends may think of this as a celebration, but, mark my words, you will all rue this day."

Damodar handed out the glasses of whisky and hastened away. He had no wish to witness the hullabaloo which he knew was brewing.

Lindsay's friends saw the look of anguish on Craig's face, and they looked askance at one another as they sheepishly sipped their whisky. Suddenly, Craig rose to his feet.

"You fools! You young fools!" he remonstrated. "Do you realise what you have done? You have thrown your university education away! And for what? For what?" he demanded.

Lindsay drained his glass and stood to face his father.

"But, Papa," he said, "we must fight to defend our freedom and that of all mankind. We can't let everyone else do it for us, whilst we sit at our desks as though nothing is happening on the other side of the world."

Craig stared at him, his eyes blazing with fury.

"Well, I, alongside my men, fought for the freedom of all mankind in the last war. That was supposed to end all wars. What did it gain? All their suffering was in vain. The war was futile, as this one will be. Already far too many men have been killed or maimed. "You young men think that by joining in the fray you will help to win the war. Perhaps you are all afraid that the war will be over before you have a chance to become heroes."

"But, Papa, we were told we would only be in non-combatant units," replied Lindsay, his voice now more subdued.

He looked at his father, and Craig looked from one young man to another. He sighed.

"Well, my dear young chaps," he said, "if you think you will stay in non-combatant units the way this war is going, you are sadly mistaken. You mark my words."

He sat down dejectedly.

"Bearer, bring me whisky," he called.

"Yes, sahib," replied Damodar, and he hastily sped away.

Lindsay looked at his father sadly; he had to admit he was far more clear-sighted than he or his friends were. What his father had always dreaded was now staring him full in the face, and Lindsay was sorry that he himself was causing his father such anguish.

"Well, Papa, I shall in any case be due for call-up after my nineteenth birthday this year. I would rather be a volunteer than a conscript. Papa, please try to understand," he said, but, seeing his father taking it so badly, he knew further excuses would be to no avail. He looked at his friends resignedly and shook his head.

"I think we had better go, chaps," said Ross Fairfax, and they all stood up to leave.

"Won't you stay to dinner?" asked Lindsay.

"Not today, thank you, Lindsay. We have not as yet broken the news of our enlistment to our parents."

The effect of Lindsay's news on his father had given them all a severe jolt. How would their own parents react?

Craig and Lindsay saw them to the door and bade them goodbye. Then Lindsay excused himself and rushed to his room. Craig returned slowly to his chair on the verandah, where he sipped his whisky in deep contemplation.

Martin and Margot joined them later for dinner, and immediately Margot sensed that all was not well between father and son. The silences between them puzzled her. Now and again she glanced from one to the other, then across to Martin, but a shrug of his shoulders told her he had no answer.

Later, as they sat on the verandah, Margot could not stand it any longer.

"What is troubling you, Craig dear?" she asked, touching his arm lightly. "I know the war news is troubling you greatly, as it does us all."

Craig looked into the dark night as if he were not listening. He made no reply.

At last Lindsay spoke: "Well, Aunt Margot," – a name he had always used – "I enlisted today," he announced.

A deep silence ensued, during which she glanced from Martin to Craig.

"My dear boy, how could you?" she said at last. "You know what your poor father and his men had to endure in the last war. You do realise he will be all alone when you leave! Of course, we will always be near."

"Oh, he doesn't care whether I am alone or not. He and his friends are all going to be great war heroes, dead or alive," Craig exclaimed bitterly.

"Now, Papa, that is most unfair," said Lindsay. "Have you forgotten that you joined up as you thought it was your duty? I feel I must do likewise."

"My father was not left alone, as I shall be. His sisters were with him. I cannot impose on my dear friends all the time. Your place is here with me until such time as you are called up."

"I have told you, Papa, we have only joined a non-combatant unit; I doubt if we will ever leave the country. That means I shall be home quite often."

"Well," Craig replied bitterly in a tone of voice none had heard before, "we shall have to wait and see."

Margot looked uneasily at Martin as Lindsay rose to his feet.

"May I be excused, Papa?" Lindsay said. "I can see this conversation is never going to resolve anything."

He stood several minutes waiting for his father's reply, but Craig remained silent, gazing into space.

"Please excuse me, Aunt Margot and Martin," Lindsay said as he prepared to leave.

They nodded their consent as he bid them goodnight.

"Goodnight, Papa," he added.

Margot patted Craig on the arm. "He is deeply troubled, Craig dear. He is torn between what he feels is his duty and his love for you. Don't make it harder for him. He is so young. Try to let him go with your blessing. It will be much easier for you both."

Martin looked at Craig sadly.

"We do understand what a wrench it will be for both of you," he said. "He feels it is his duty, and I believe you will one day be proud he volunteered and didn't wait to be conscripted. I know, being the fine young fellow he is, that if he didn't do what he thinks is right he would find it hard to live with for the rest of his life."

"Yes, you are right, Martin," Craig replied. "Oh, why has there to be these damned wars? When is man going to live in peace with his fellow man? That is God's wish for us all, but man has yet to learn to live without conflict."

Martin and Margot rose to go, and Craig rose with them. He saw them to the door.

"Goodnight and God bless you both," said Margot as she kissed him on the cheek. "We will come over again in a day or two."

"Yes, do," said Craig. "And stay for dinner. We don't know how many more dinners we will have together before Lindsay goes." The words caught in his throat as he spoke.

He watched them down the long driveway till they were out of sight; then he bade Munilal lock up for the night, and he headed for his bedroom.

"How Craig is ever going to get used to being alone when Lindsay finally goes, I just don't know!" Margot exclaimed with a deep sigh on their way home. "Poor Craig! How he must dread that day!"

Martin patted her arm reassuringly. "Well, deep down, Craig must be very proud of him, but I know he will miss him terribly. If only lovely Elizabeth and Heather could have been spared to be with him! They could have supported one another through this difficult time."

"Well, it was not to be," Margot sighed. "We will all have to rally round after he has gone and see that Craig is not left alone too long. We should be able to help with all our friends here. So many of Craig's friends are being called away every week, so he's bound to feel isolated," said Margot. "I know how badly his father took it when Craig himself enlisted in the last war. Harriet and Elena were unable to console him."

"Well, my dear, we will have to face that when the time comes," Martin replied, as he assisted Margot up the steps on reaching home.

CHAPTER 274

The long buff-coloured envelope arrived a few days later. Damodar handed it to Craig, not smiling as he did so. He knew it boded ill. Craig flung it back to him.

"It is for Lindsay," he said. "Take it to him." He dismissed Damodar angrily.

Damodar hurried away to Lindsay's room.

So, it had come – the day he had dreaded. Craig sank back in his chair, his head in his hands in utter disbelief.

Lindsay sat down to study the letter's contents. Eventually, he rose to join his father. Lindsay looked at him apprehensively.

"Here is my form, Papa. Will you please sign it for me? I am sorry you feel so bitter, Papa, but it is my duty to go."

"Duty, duty! Yes, yes, I suppose everyone must once again do their duty," Craig replied sarcastically. "Go and bring my pen from my bureau."

"Yes, Papa," he replied meekly.

As Lindsay reached for the pen, he saw the picture of his grandfather. 'I hate you, you bitter old man,' he thought. 'You are the cause of all my father's unhappiness and his unwillingness to let me go.' He stood glaring at the picture in anger for several minutes.

"Lindsay, bring my pen at once," Craig demanded impatiently.

He hastily scrawled his signature.

"Now, take the form out of my sight," he said.

"Thank you, Papa. I will post it tomorrow."

One after another, the long buff-coloured envelopes arrived, telling Lindsay to report for interviews and a medical test. Then there was a lull until the one Craig dreaded the most arrived. He tried to put on a brave face, knowing the final parting was not far off. Both of them were taking breakfast when the call-up came.

Lindsay looked at his father as he took the envelope from the bearer, but Craig pretended not to notice. Lindsay ripped the envelope apart and studied carefully the official slip it contained.

"Well, my son, what does it say?" Craig asked breezily, trying for Lindsay's sake not to show how deeply it affected him.

"It says I am to report to Balwar. That is only 500 miles away. I told you, Papa, I wouldn't be going too far away. I shall be home often."

"All right, my son," – he sighed deeply – "I have accepted your going. I did the same thing myself. I also knew it would upset my father, but, with our proud military history on the side of both your grandfathers, you could only do likewise. Tell me, when do you report?"

"A week today, Papa."

"My, my! As soon as that?" Craig said resignedly.

Lindsay rose from the table and stood beside his father. He laid his hand on his shoulder.

"You know I love you very dearly, Papa," he said. "This would not have been my chosen profession if things had been different in the world. I would have been a teacher of languages at the university. Then we would have been together always, fishing and sailing up in the hills as we always have."

Craig patted his arm affectionately. "Yes, I know, my son," he replied. "I understand. It's just that I am going to miss you so much."

"And I you, Papa. Will you please excuse me now, Papa? I wish to see if Ross or any other of my friends has received his posting yet."

"You go, my son. I will be all right."

"Thank you, Papa. I won't be long."

Craig rose from the table and watched Lindsay from the window. He smiled as Lindsay leaped on to his cycle, which Munilal held out to him, both of them muttering their usual jokes to each other.

Munilal joined Damodar on the verandah steps as Lindsay sped away.

"Poor young sahib! I wonder what will become of him? I pray to Allah he does not have to go far, for the sahib's sake. I hope this dreadful war will soon be over," said Munilal.

Damodar rejoined Craig in the dining room.

"Well, that is the first step to the unknown future for Lindsay," he said with a sigh. He sat down deep in thought.

"Yes, sahib," Damodar replied, his head bent, as he hurried to clear the breakfast things away.

Lindsay was delighted to find that Ross also had to report to Balwar. Their other friends had not yet received their postings.

A week later, they said their farewells to their many girlfriends, who stood forlornly by the wayside and waved to the two young men as they passed on their way to the station.

All too soon, the guard called for them to board the train. Craig clung to Lindsay as if to never let him go.

"Go now, my son, go now," he whispered.

Lindsay hugged Margot fondly and whispered in her ear: "Will you let me know how Papa is keeping?"

"Yes, my son, I will. Do not worry," she replied.

He shook hands with Martin and Ross's parents and finally they climbed aboard. Both hung from the window as the train pulled away. Craig strained his neck till they were out of sight.

"I wonder what we will have to do first?" said Ross as he flung his case on the luggage rack.

"Just get our kit sorted out I expect," said Lindsay, not in the mood for any kind of conversation.

"Oh, it is all so exciting. Maybe we will get to travel later on. I hope so. I need a change from studying law, don't you agree, Lindsay?"

"I suppose so," he replied glumly.

He sat in the corner, gazing out of the window, trying to take his mind off his father's sad face.

"Are you wishing you hadn't enlisted, Lindsay?"

"No, not really. It is just the thought of Papa being so alone."

"Well, I know my parents are going to visit him often."

"Yes, it is very kind of them – and of all our other friends."

"Won't you join us for dinner, Craig?" asked Margot as he alighted from their tonga on reaching home.

"No, thank you, Margot – not tonight. Tonight I wish to be alone."

"But it is not good for you to be alone – especially tonight," she insisted.

"I know, I know, but I have got to get used to it so I might as well start tonight."

"Well, goodnight dear. Come round when you wish," Margot said.

"I will. Thank you. Goodnight," Craig replied.

He sat night after night on the verandah, gazing into the still, dark night. Damodar hovered close by, getting more and more perturbed at how much whisky Craig was drinking. Every night he looked for a long time at a photograph of his family, which he kept beside his bed. He ate very little.

Damodar, Munilal and the cook were concerned. They discussed with one another what they could do to help. Night after night they talked of this once so happy home and their distress at seeing their dear sahib like this.

"I will tell the burra memsahib," said Damodar.

"I am glad you told me, Damodar. I will deal with it. But don't let the sahib know," Margot insisted.

"No, memsahib," Damodar replied, salaaming his thanks with relief.

He returned to tell the others.

Daily they watched as Craig wended his way to the small churchyard close by, taking a small posy of flowers.

CHAPTER 275

Long letters arrived from Lindsay telling of his progress. He had passed all the exams with top marks, and the language tutor had complimented him most highly on his fluency.

'I will call and tell my tutor at college how I am getting on, when I come home on leave in two days' time,' he wrote.

'That's all I want to hear, my son,' Craig thought.

"Hasten the day, Damodar!" he said.

"Yes, sahib," Damodar replied.

"Please prepare Lindsay's room. He will be home soon."

Craig could not contain his excitement as he rushed over to tell Margot.

"Well, when he comes, you must come over for dinner as often as you can. Martin is due home from the missions today," she said.

"We will, we will. Thank you, Margot."

He kissed her on the cheeks before he left, and he put his precious letter safely back in his pocket before he drove away.

Craig rose early. Damodar hovered nearby, making sure everything needed was on hand.

"Hail a tonga for the sahib," Damodar demanded.

"Yes, right away," Munilal replied as he hastened away.

As soon as it arrived, Craig leaped aboard, telling the driver to hurry.

"But, sahib," Damodar called after him in consternation, "sahib, sahib, you have not taken breakfast, and it will be a long time before you return."

"I know, I know," Craig called back. "I'm not hungry. I will eat when Lindsay arrives."

Damodar and Munilal, standing beside the cook on the top step of the verandah, all shook their heads as Craig disappeared from view.

"You must prepare all Lindsay sahib's favourite meals, cook," Damodar demanded.

"I know, I know. I am off to the bazaar now."

"Here is the list and money," said Damodar. "Don't be long."

"I won't. I know the young sahib doesn't like to be kept waiting."

Craig could hardly contain his happiness as he commanded the tonga wallah: "Hurry, hurry, boy," he shouted as they raced to the station.

His only fear was that Lindsay would be sent abroad when this leave expired. 'Well, I won't think about it for the time being,' he told himself.

He tapped his foot impatiently as he waited on the platform. Suddenly, the train rushed in and, as the first carriage door opened, he guessed who would come bounding out. He was not disappointed.

'He has arrived exactly like I did', he recalled, 'so long ago.'

"Papa, Papa, it's so good to be home," Lindsay cried as he rushed into Craig's outstretched arms.

"My son, it's good to have you home. I am so proud of you. Come – our tonga is waiting. My, my, how fit you are!" he said, holding Lindsay at arm's length.

"Well, they make us train very hard every day for any eventuality, but I am going to rest now."

They linked arms with each other possessively and hurried to the waiting tonga.

"There are such a lot of troops on the move. All the trains are full, Papa," Lindsay said.

"Well, there are not many of our friends here any more. Some of them were called away so suddenly that there was no time for a farewell party. There is hardly time for a goodbye sometimes. Things are looking more serious every day – but this is cheerless talk. We had better be silent."

"Well, Papa, we will pretend there is no war on whilst I am home," Lindsay said.

"Rightly so, my son, rightly so!"

The bearers and the cook and all their families were waiting to greet Lindsay with garlands of flowers. He laughingly took some and placed them round his father's neck; then he returned their salaams before dashing up the verandah steps and flinging his cap and kitbag on the nearest chair. Margot, who had just arrived, came up the steps with Craig.

"Welcome home, my dear boy, welcome home," she said. "We have arranged several parties for you and your friends as soon as you are rested."

"Thank you. Thank you, Aunt Margot," he replied. Then he kissed and embraced her.

"Sit down and have a drink to refresh yourself," Craig said. "Bearer – tea please."

"I can't stay long today," Margot said after a while. She rose to leave. Before she hurried away, she said, "I will let you know in good time about the parties, Lindsay."

"Very well, Aunt Margot. Thank you," he replied as he stood beside Craig to wave her goodbye.

"Have you seen Sylvia recently, Papa?"

"No, she hasn't called," Craig replied as he glanced at Lindsay.

Craig certainly didn't want him to spend too much time with his friends. He wanted him all to himself.

"Don't worry, Papa," Lindsay exclaimed, guessing his father's thoughts; "I shall be spending all my leave with you."

'I am no better than my own father – selfish and possessive,' Craig thought as he looked at his son.

"No, my son, you must see your friends as often as you wish. By the way, when does Ross arrive home?"

"Soon. He had to attend another course. Tomorrow, Papa, I must take flowers for Mama and Heather."

CHAPTER 276

Margot's parties and dances were not a great success. Lindsay found most of them rather tiring. He only attended them out of courtesy, and he excused himself early to play chess or cards with his father. They were often joined by Margot and Martin.

On Lindsay's last night at home, Craig could see he was anxious to visit his friends before he left.

"You go and visit your friends," he said. "Don't worry about me. I shall just sit here until you return."

"Yes, Papa. I want to see some of them before they join up. They are all very eager to join up before the war ends."

Craig sighed. "Wars, wars!" he exclaimed. "Why do you young people speak of war so lightly? All of you treat it as though it was some great party."

"But, Papa, they don't want to be labelled as cowards by their friends. They want to be part of it. Besides, we are all sure this war will be over soon."

Craig looked at him, a faint smile on his face.

"Oh, the innocence of youth!" he said. "Don't you and your friends count on it, my son. They said – whoever *they* were – the last war would be over quickly, but it lasted four long years."

"But, Papa, this one won't last long – you'll see."

"Now, you go and enjoy the time you have left."

"I won't be long, Papa," Lindsay called as he raced away.

Lindsay collected his friends one by one, and they gathered at their favourite restaurant to eat, drink and be merry. Soon they were laughing and joking, all now in high spirits.

"Come, brothers in arms," said Ross gaily, "I want a last look at the town before I leave."

They agreed as one.

"We will have to borrow some transport," someone said. "A truck will do. We cannot get very far on our cycles."

"Good idea! A truck passes close by our house every night about this time. It will be due to leave the barracks about now," said Garth Austin.

"Come on, then," said Ross. "We will waylay it on some pretext. You are good at that sort of thing, Lindsay – always game for a lark. See what you can do."

They hastened off to the cover of a tree-lined road close by.

"Here it comes!" yelled Garth. "We haven't much time."

As the truck slowed down to take the corner, Lindsay pretended to fall off his cycle. He made sure the bicycle landed in its path, but he rolled to one side. As planned, the truck stopped just in time with a screech of brakes. Two Indian men leaped out.

Lindsay lay prostrate, not moving. The men leaned over him, quarrelling as to what was to be done. They waved their arms about wildly in their perplexity. Suddenly, the rest of Lindsay's friends pounced. Lindsay got to his feet, dusting himself down.

"Nay, sahibs," the men protested, as their arms were tied behind their backs. "It was not our fault, sahibs."

Their protestations were cut short as they were gagged, and then they were lifted unceremoniously into the back of the truck along with the cycles.

"They are not hurt, are they, Ross?" Lindsay asked apprehensively.

"No, just stunned at the speed of it all – as we are," he laughed. "I really think", he said as he looked at them more closely, "they seem to be asleep. Don't you also think so, Philip?"

"Yes," the young man replied, "I'm sure they are," he said, although he could see their frightened eyes watching their every move.

"Asleep?" exclaimed Lindsay incredulously. "That will never do. A court martial for them, without a doubt!"

They all laughed as they sang a lullaby.

"Where shall we go first, Ross?" asked Lindsay with a twinkle in his eye.

"Well, I think we should call on our good friend, Fergus Keir. We won't stop. We'll just go round to his house and give him a scare. He will think the army has come for him at last. He is such a softy that he will probably wet himself with fright."

Fergus's acquaintances had never forgiven him for declaring, "I am not joining up before I need to. I shall wait till the army sends for me."

"Well," said Lindsay with a laugh, "he will get a fright tonight when we call."

The young men were drinking merrily.

"We'd better not give any to these two," Ross said. "We wouldn't like them to be kicked out of the army for being drunk in charge of a truck."

Lindsay drove the truck swiftly up the driveway of the Keir residence. The chokidar patrolling the grounds jumped for his life out of their way. He shouted and waved his *lahti* (stick) at them as they roared past. Suddenly, a light lit up on the verandah. They increased their speed as they approached the house. Suddenly, to their dismay, too late they realised that the top of the truck would not clear the portico.

"Duck, everyone and cover your heads!" yelled Lindsay.

Clumps of concrete, flowers and hanging baskets came raining down on them. Two of them had the forethought to fling themselves on top of the two Indians.

They sped on, increasing their speed, not stopping to assess the damage. Ross turned to see a very irate crowd – Fergus, his mother, two bearers and the chokidar – shaking their fists at them as they shot out of sight. Down the unlit road they careered. Suddenly, they realised they were approaching locked gates, going too fast to halt. They crashed through and came to a halt in a pond.

"My God, Lindsay! Can you not drive better than that?" Ross exclaimed, laughing, as he, along with the rest, clambered out of the water.

They dragged the two Indians from the back and laid them on the ground; then they untied their feet and ordered them to climb in the front of the truck.

"Are you sure they are all right, Ross?" Lindsay asked.

"They seem to be. Let's hurry and get out of sight."

They retrieved their cycles from the rubble in the truck, and Ross and Lindsay waited until the others were out of sight before they took the gags off the men, untied their hands and bolted as quickly as they could.

"Fortunately for us," exclaimed Ross, "it's dark!"

A little further along the road, their friends were waiting, all viewing their bent cycles ruefully.

"I think we will just about get home on these," said Ross. "Let's away – but split up. I can hear another army truck coming." (The incident in the Keir driveway had been duly reported.)

"Lindsay and I will be away tomorrow," said Ross. "You others must lie low for a while and hope no one finds you out. No real harm has been done."

"More damage is being done daily to army trucks in the war," they agreed.

They said their goodbyes and sped away. Their night on the town was over.

Damodar was waiting for Lindsay anxiously when he arrived home on his rickety cycle.

"Sahib, sahib, what has happened to your cycle?" Damodar asked with concern.

"Just a slight mishap! Don't say anything to Papa."

"No, sahib. I will get it mended before the burra sahib finds out," Damodar replied, and he hurried away with it to the back of the house.

He returned to find Lindsay brushing down his damp clothes.

"Did you get hurt, sahib?"

"No, Damodar," Lindsay replied.

"Your father is waiting for you, sahib."

"He is still up, then?"

"Yes, he wouldn't retire until you came."

Lindsay, looking crestfallen, raced up the steps and stood for several minutes looking at his father asleep in his chair. He was filled with remorse that he had left him alone for so long. He kissed him lightly on the forehead. His father stirred.

"Is it you, my son? Now, no saying you are sorry! If you have spent a happy evening with your friends, that makes me happy also."

"No, Papa, I should have spent it with you," Lindsay said regretfully.

Craig scrutinised him as Lindsay helped him to his feet.

"You look a little dishevelled and your suit is wet and dirty," he said. "What happened?"

"I had a little friendly tussle with my friends. We went too near the fountain and I had the misfortune to fall in," Lindsay replied.

"You are not hurt?"

"No, Papa. I soon scrambled out with the help of my friends."

"Now, I think it's time we retired."

They linked arms and wished the bearers goodnight.

"Goodnight. Salaam, sahibs," they replied.

CHAPTER 277

Next day, Margot watched Craig sadly as he stood watching Lindsay's train speeding away in the distance. If only she knew what to say or do to ease his heartache!

"Will you join us for the rest of the day, Craig?" she asked as light-heartedly as she could as she took his arm.

"No, no, Margot. It is so kind of you to think of me, as always." He sighed, and he patted her hand on his arm. "You are such a dear friend, but I want to spend the day alone."

"Well, come and see us as often as you wish."

"I will, I will. Thank you," he called after her as she walked away.

He returned to the lonely, desolate house reluctantly, and both bearers came to greet him. Only the patter of their bare feet broke the silence. Both of them watched him as he sank lethargically into his favourite seat on the verandah and flung his topee on the peg of the hatstand.

The bearers were always amazed at his accuracy; never had they seen him miss. Craig had always performed the same trick to hang his hat on the deer antlers in Glencree Castle.

"Bring me a double whisky, please, Munilal," he said.

"Yes, sahib," Munilal replied, frowning deeply.

He disappeared into the dining room, where Damodar watched as he poured it into an the engraved crystal glass and added some soda water.

"It is too early for the sahib to be drinking," he said angrily.

"I know, but it is the sahib's wish."

Munilal carried the solitary glass on the silver tray to his dejected master.

"Thank you," Craig replied listlessly as he took the glass from him. "I must celebrate my son's nineteenth birthday alone."

Craig spent a restless night. Lately his dreaded nightmares had returned. He screamed out several times: "Sergeant, Sergeant, where are my men? How many men have I now, Sergeant?"

Only a deathly silence followed.

"Answer me, answer me, damn you!"

Beads of sweat poured down his face, but he awoke to find Damodar by his side, cloth in hand, to wipe his fevered brow.

"It's all right, sahib," Damodar said. "All is well. It's only one of your dreams again."

"Yes, how silly of me! Thank you. Go now – I shall be all right."

During most of the days following Lindsay's departure, Craig wandered aimlessly round the house. In the evenings he sat at his bureau writing to Lindsay, hardly knowing what to say. Now and then he would pick up his father's picture and talk to it.

"Now I know, Papa, what loneliness means, and I understand what anguish you must have felt when I left you. Forgive me, Papa but I could do no other."

His thoughts wandered back to his youth, when he too had sailed away to war. He remembered his family and friends waving to him from the jetty. 'Such a fine strapping youth, I was then,' he thought. 'Now look at me: not fit enough to be of any use to the war effort. Well, they have my son – what more can I give?'

One evening, after a game of solitaire, he rose with impatience and wandered over to the piano to play some of his favourite Scottish melodies. He gazed at Elizabeth's picture. She seemed to be smiling down at him.

Suddenly he closed the lid with a crash as despair overcame him.

"Damodar!"

"Yes, sahib?"

"Bring my whisky, please."

"But, sahib!" Damodar exclaimed, looking at him as a father to his son.

"Yes, yes, I know it is my third one this evening."

"Very well, sahib," he said, disapproval and concern for his master showing clearly on his countenance.

Craig sat on the verandah dreaming of bygone days. As he gazed out into the dark night, often he thought he could see Elizabeth once more dancing along like a will-o'-the-wisp through the glens of home, and it seemed as though he had only to reach out and he could touch her. 'Now, I have no darling angel, and no darling, mischievous Heather, laughing gaily as she teases me,' he thought. 'Well, Lindsay will be home again soon, I know he will.' He sighed.

Daily Craig visited the graveyard – a place of solitude for his tormented mind. Its garden was always filled with flowers as the seasons changed. He often sat for hours under the shade of the huge banyan tree, watching the mali at work; then he would saunter round the graves to read over and over again the inscriptions, until he knew many of them by heart.

The one he spent most time pondering over was that of an old soldier. 'A Scottish Soldier: Sergeant Major Fergus McTavish' was its only inscription. 'Evidently he died without kin,' thought Craig. It always brought a lump to his throat. 'Perhaps his heart, like mine, longed to be home in our beloved Scotland, but now his bones rest here.'

"Yes, you're like me," he whispered: "my bones too will never rest in my beloved Scotland."

Often he pondered on Merry-Berry's last words. How could she have made such a prediction when his father was as adamant as ever?

"She is wrong this time," he said with a sigh.

Dusk was falling before he wended his way home. He bade the mali goodbye.

"Salaam, sahib," said the old man as he rose to his feet, hands clasped in prayer.

Craig closed the old creaking gate. He always vowed he would fix that gate one day.

The sudden arrival of Lindsay on a few days' leave dispelled his loneliness, but there was a strange silence about his son he couldn't fathom. It was a sign that he had left his carefree boyhood behind.

As they parted once again, Lindsay pleaded: "Papa, please go to the hills with Margot, I beg of you."

"Yes, I think I will, my son."

Lindsay's departure left Craig with a deeper feeling of loss. He did as he promised, but he felt his loneliness more in the hills than at home, and he returned early, much to Margot's concern.

CHAPTER 278

Lindsay was bitterly disappointed to be sailing away from India without seeing his father again.

"Well, we are all in the same boat," his friends remarked with a laugh as they scrambled aboard.

Ross and Lindsay stood leaning over the side of the ship. They had been sailing for several days.

"I wonder where we are heading, Lindsay," said Ross.

"By the position of the sun, I know we are heading west."

"I hope we shall see some action!" Ross exclaimed. "I am sick of all this inactivity."

"So am I," agreed Lindsay.

Lindsay spent many hours every day gazing over the side of the ship, oblivious of his companions around him. He was often deep in thought about his father, worrying constantly about his health. He hoped that the war would soon be over, and he promised himself that there would be no more roving once he returned.

"Ross, your friend Lindsay is certainly the strong, dark, silent type. Whatever does he think about all the time he is gazing at the sea?" someone asked one day.

"I daresay he is thinking about all the lovely girls he left behind," said Ross light-heartedly. "I don't advise you to intrude on him," he continued warningly.

"No, I won't. I have heard he has rather a fiery temper at times."

"Yes, that is so."

At last they disembarked. They piled into waiting trucks and set out along a long, dusty desert road.

"There seems no end to this road, Ross," said Lindsay wearily after they had been travelling for hours. "I am gasping for a drink."

"So am I," Ross agreed. "Our friends are also parched."

"What wouldn't I give, Ross, to be sitting in the garden at home in the shade of the old banyan tree, calling for the bearer to bring us iced lemon!"

"So would I," Ross agreed. "Bearer, iced lemon, if you please!" he called playfully.

"Right away, sahib," replied Lindsay.

"Less joking, mate! Aren't we all thirsty enough without you rubbing it in?" said one of the others.

"I'm so sorry, my friends," replied Ross apologetically.

"I wonder how much of this desert dust we will have to endure before this war is over, Ross?"

"Quite a bit, I should think," Ross muttered with a sigh.

Little were they to know how much desert sand would blow into their eyes and parched mouths before that day came.

Many more thirsty miles passed before they reached their tented abode in the desert.

"Well, Ross, this seems to be it: not exactly the Ritz. Let's hope there is a drink somewhere," Lindsay said as they alighted from the truck.

They settled into the transit camp but it was not many days before they were all posted to various units. They sadly wished one another farewell. Lindsay and Ross were delighted to learn that they would be going together.

"We're still in a non-combatant unit, worst luck," Ross said angrily.

"Well, it might not be for too long, the way things are going."

"I should think they will be wanting us all in the battle ranks before long," replied Lindsay.

"There is certainly a lot of action on, and I hope we are part of it soon," said Ross.

CHAPTER 279

Craig waited daily for the mail to arrive. Then, one day, his patience was rewarded. He hurried to meet the mail boy as he came up the drive. He ripped the envelope open hurriedly and gasped.

"Just what I have dreaded!" he exclaimed.

It was heavily censored. He almost fell as he staggered up the verandah steps to his chair.

"Sahib, sahib," called Damodar in alarm, "are you ill, sahib? Shall I bring doctor, sahib?"

"No, Damodar, I shall be all right," Craig replied. "Just bring some tea."

Damodar returned with the tea and stood at Craig's elbow looking at him with concern. At last, after sipping his tea slowly for some time, Craig spoke.

"Well, Damodar, Lindsay is now abroad somewhere – where, I do not know." He sighed as he slipped the letter back in his pocket.

He looked up to see Margot at the door. She looked at him sadly.

"Read this, Margot," he said, and he pulled the letter from his pocket and handed it to her with a sigh. "Damn the war! Why has man to make war? It is not God's wish!" he exclaimed angrily.

Margot read the letter and handed it back.

"Well, my dear Craig," she said, "let us hope it is all over soon." She sighed.

"He is now overseas. He must be in danger, Margot. Do you think I will ever see him again?"

She pulled her chair closer to his and placed her arm round his shoulders.

"Of course you will, Craig dear," she replied. "Try not to worry. I will call again tomorrow."

He rose and kissed her lightly on the cheeks as she prepared to leave.

"What a blessing you are to me, Margot," he said. "I really couldn't manage without you. I always knew how much my dear mother and aunts loved you."

He helped her into the tonga and watched as she sped away.

Martin greeted her on her arrival home.

"Well, my dear," he said, "how is Craig now?"

She sat down wearily.

"He does worry me so, dear," she replied. "He is only just keeping alive. He barely eats or sleeps. He spends his whole time worrying what might happen to Lindsay. Time and time again I reassure him that Lindsay will be all right, but I don't think he hears me. When I write to Lindsay, I reassure the dear boy that his father is well, but I know he is not."

"Well, my dear, you cannot do more," Martin assured her. "I only wish we *could* do more for him."

"He would be so much better in health if he would stay in the hills, but he won't hear of it. I don't know what more we can do." She sighed.

Lindsay wrote as often as he could, but he was unable to give a hint as to where he was or even say if he was in danger. Craig replied as light-heartedly as he could, disguising his desperate loneliness and anxiety. Night after night he sat on the verandah rereading Lindsay's letters and his favourite poems. He sometimes read the same one over and over again:

> If ye break faith with us who die
> We shall not sleep, though poppies grow
> In Flanders Fields.

Well, it had happened. They had broken faith with the fallen.

"How many more fallen will there be before this war ends?" Craig exclaimed loudly.

He rested his head in his hands in despair.

Damodar broke in on his reverie: "Are you all right, sahib? It is very late."

"So it is, so it is," he sighed. "I am sorry, Damodar. You go – I will be all right."

"No, sahib, I will stay till you retire."

Craig got up to go.

"Thank you, Damodar. Thank you. Goodnight," he said.

"Goodnight. Salaam, sahib," Damodar replied.

CHAPTER 280

Some weeks later Ross hurried to tell Lindsay that headquarters was selecting men for special assignments.

"Are you interested, Lindsay?" he said.

"I should say I am – anything to get away from this tedious job I am doing now."

They both passed the selection for places with flying colours. Their knowledge of languages had stood them in good stead. A few days later, they said farewell to their comrades and proceeded to a special training school. They both excelled in all their courses, and their fluency in the local dialects impressed all who heard them. They were also skilled in the art of self-defence, which they had learned during their childhood from their many Indian friends.

Every project was a thrilling adventure, and Lindsay could hardly wait to put into practice all he had learned about map-reading, explosives, booby-traps, sabotage and the art of killing silently. The preparations for his future assignments proceeded, and night after night he and Ross discussed all they were being taught. Both were anxious to be part of the action as soon as possible.

They did not have to wait long. They smiled at each other as the instructor told them their assignment: "You will both be covering the same area, but you will be hundreds of miles apart. You might not meet for the rest of the duration."

They both looked at the instructor with a look of resignation on their faces.

"You will have your own code names, and you will be supplied with all the necessary equipment – including clothing and transport."

They both looked at each other as they recalled their last escapade at home.

"You are familiar with our ciphers and codes. You may enter the bazaars or any other areas which are normally out of bounds to troops. You have to obey local customs at all times. Your task is to mix with the natives and listen out for any talk of sabotage. You are, I know, familiar with all the local currency."

They were assigned to their allocated posts in the desert, having been told that their paths were unlikely to cross, even if they got leave, which was doubtful.

"Well, that's a cheerful thought, Ross!" Lindsay exclaimed. "Oh well – all in the cause of duty!"

They both laughed.

"Well, I will always be on the lookout for you," Ross said. "If an old beggar creeps up beside you and whispers, 'Who is Sylvia and who ditched us in the pond?' guess who it will be?"

"I will reply, 'Who took the roof off the portico?' " replied Lindsay. "The answer will be, 'We did.' "

They shook hands before they mounted their motorbikes, and they then rode a short way side by side before parting. They had been warned that they would be met from time to time by other intelligence officers in disguise, who would pass on their reports to headquarters. They needed no extra warning that their lives would be in constant danger.

CHAPTER 281

Lindsay settled into his small desert outpost and made it as comfortable as he could. As he scanned the expanse of the desert with his binoculars, he often thought of his father and hummed the tunes his mother used to sing. Sometimes he thought he could hear her singing in the stillness of the desert night.

'How beautiful she was!' he thought. 'If only they could have returned to Glencree Castle! I know Papa will never be happy until he returns to his dear homeland. These are just dreams! Just dreams!' he reminded himself. 'That bitter old grandfather of mine has no intentions of making anyone's dreams come true.'

One night, Lindsay was suddenly jolted out of his reverie by a voice on his walkie-talkie informing him of suspected spies and saboteurs heading his way.

"Well, I shall be ready for them, no matter when they appear," he replied and he thanked the unknown voice, using his code name.

Over the next few days he carefully scrutinised each visa and passport handed to him, weighing each person up very closely. All the travellers explained that they were on their way to a holy shrine – a ruse much used by spies and saboteurs.

His interest focused on a man accompanied by women in purdah. The man explained to Lindsay that the women would be visiting relations while he was at the shrine: he knew Lindsay would be aware that women were not allowed in the holy shrine.

Lindsay looked them up and down, noticing, as he handed back their documents, that their hands were far too big to be those of a woman, that they were usually eager to get past him, and that they glanced shiftily and muttered incoherently to their fellow-travellers. He decided to make them wait longer while he conversed on his walkie-talkie to headquarters. He noticed their discomfort at the delay.

He was given instructions to let them pass, but arrangements were made to detain them at the next checkpoint, which was guarded by more men. As he bade them pass through, he noticed their smirks of satisfaction.

He was thankful when it was time for him to escort the long convoys of lorries, taking supplies to the Russian battle areas along the long, dusty roads, through the hills and mountains which he had come to know by heart.

After listing the number of each lorry he would head the column. Then, when they were well on their way, he would signal to the first lorry driver to carry on whilst he doubled back to recheck each lorry's number. He found that very often one or two were missing. As he raced along the line, he would instruct the other lorries to proceed. Then he would go back to investigate the disappearance. All too often, telltale tyre marks would tell him only too clearly what their fate had been. The drivers, through exhaustion, had fallen asleep and driven over the edge of the ravine. All their vital supplies were lost.

Sighing at the loss of more lives, Lindsay would reluctantly draw a thin red line through the truck number on his list. Then he would race back to head his column through the long, winding, dangerous terrain to its destination.

After these long, weary journeys, he was thankful to return to his lonely outpost. His relief counterpart was always more than thankful for his safe return.

"Has anything happened whilst I have been away?" he asked after another gruelling mission.

"Well, I have just received news there are more enemy agents heading in this direction. Their mission is to destroy the oil pipelines, so we will have to be more vigilant than ever, if that is possible."

"Well," remarked Lindsay, "a pair of eyes in the back of my head might help."

"That's certainly what we all need. Be extra-careful, Lindsay. We lost two of our best men last week."

"Ross wasn't one of them, was he?" he asked with concern.

"No, Ross is working at headquarters at present. Well, I must get on my way. How you tolerate this isolated post amazes us all, and yet you always seem so eager to return here. It's the worst posting we have."

"Well, someone has to do the job, and it might as well be me."

They both laughed.

Later they shook hands on parting.

"Cheerio, Lindsay. I will give your regards to Ross."

'Now to await my furtive friends,' Lindsay thought. 'Well, I shall be ready for them.'

Lindsay had been in many skirmishes. He knew he had to match his skill against that of the enemy in order to survive. He had let the previous group through his post, only for them to be picked up at the next checkpoint by armed guards, and he suspected that, as a result, enemy agents would be sent to get rid of him and his post. He laid his plans carefully.

He moved his bed under the window and placed an effigy he had made of himself at the table where he wrote his daily reports. The table was in the middle of the room opposite the window.

He spent several nights sleeping on the floor under his bed before he heard the sound of a truck speeding towards his post. He lit a candle, placed it on the table and bent the head of his effigy towards the book. Then he dived under his bed.

He was none too soon. A hail of bullets tore the effigy to pieces and the window was smashed into hundreds of splinters, which fell on his bed. The truck, without lights, raced off into the desert.

Lindsay waited for several minutes before easing his stiff, aching body to its feet. "Well, old fella," he said ruefully, as he viewed the remains of the effigy, "there's not much of you left. I shall have to make another one."

The saboteurs were furious to learn a few days later that Lindsay was still alive.

He reported the incident to headquarters and was instructed to take any action he deemed necessary to protect his life.

He was determined to do just that. He knew that another attempt on his life would be made very soon, and he hoped that once again his informant would pass on the enemy's plans to him. 'I shall be ready when they come,' he thought, 'whenever that might be.'

He decided to keep a vigil every night, even though it would mean very little sleep. He assumed they would come in a truck again, in which case he would see their lights across the desert long before the sound of their truck was heard. He guessed they would speed up and put out their lights before reaching his abode.

He lay on his mattress on top of his flat roof, wrapped in several blankets to keep out the chill of the desert night as he waited, scanning the distant horizon with his binoculars. He guessed which direction they would come from.

Soon his patience was rewarded. Two pinpoints of light appeared.

'Well, I am ready for you tonight,' he thought.

Suspecting that they would try to demolish his abode with hand grenades, he had spent several nights digging a deep hole in the soft sand opposite. Then he had concealed the hole with shrubs. He hastened into it and waited. He would need split-second timing to achieve his aim. He was thankful for the moonlit night.

He heard a voice shout an Arabic command. Then he saw a figure rise up in the truck and another one shout and raise his arm.

Suddenly, he put his emergency light on them, blinding them. He hurled his grenades straight at the truck, which was thrown onto its side by the impact. He hurled another two grenades. The petrol tank exploded and bodies flew through the air. Burning debris was scattered everywhere.

Lindsay waited for some time before venturing out. He listened, but all was silent. He summoned aid from headquarters. Whilst waiting for them to arrive, he went over to each body in turn and kicked it over, his gun at the ready.

"It was not my turn to die tonight, you desert dogs, but yours," he said.

He was delighted to see Ross in the relief party.

"Sorry, Lindsay, I couldn't get back-up to you in time," Ross said.

"It doesn't matter, Ross. I was ready for them. This lot won't trouble me any more, but there will always be others. We just have to make sure we remain one step ahead of them."

"Well, jump in my Jeep. We will get your report to headquarters. The military police will clear up this mess and make their own report. They will bring a relief with them, so you can stay with us for a day or two."

"Right you are! Let's away," Lindsay replied gratefully.

CHAPTER 282

Throughout 1941, the war news worsened as the German army advanced into Russia. The desert war around Tobruk consisted of a succession of advances and retreats by the British and German armies. There was little respite for the fighting forces, who also had to contend with sandstorms and flies and the cold of the desert nights.

Then, before the year had ended, more devastating news came. On Sunday, 7 December 1941, Japan attacked Pearl Harbor and destroyed the US Pacific Fleet. The Japanese were at war with America and the British Commonwealth.

Craig spent the day with Margot and Martin, as he often did, after morning service in the small mission chapel. They all looked at each other in disbelief.

Craig was the first to speak: "Now it has become a truly global war, my friends. Now it has reached the Far East." A look of sheer dejection crossed his countenance.

"Who knows where it will all end, or when or what is to become of mankind!" said Margot sadly.

Martin, who had sat in deep contemplation, said, "Why, India herself could be invaded, as could distant Australia."

"And here we are, Martin, sitting safely whilst all around the world is going mad," said Margot. "Martin and I, at our age and in my poor state of health, can do nothing but sit idly by and watch and listen."

CHAPTER 283

Elena sat at the breakfast table relating to Bruce the previous day's news of the attack by Japan. He sat, as usual, gazing into space. She could never tell whether he had not heard her or just did not *want* to hear.

"Emma's son, Nicholas, has enlisted," Elena continued, "as have most of the boys from the village. They all went before they were conscripted. It was very gallant of them all, don't you think so, Bruce?"

Only a stony silence ensued.

"Lindsay also enlisted long before he needed to. I think he was very brave."

She watched Bruce as he moved away from the table to sit in his chair by the large fire. She sat patiently waiting for some comment from him, and she didn't have to wait too long.

"Well, so he should! And now his father is all alone, like I was. Now Craig knows how it feels to be deserted by his son," he retorted bitterly.

"I think he is more alone than you are, Bruce. At least I am here. He has only got Margot close to him."

She saw Bruce wince as she mentioned Margot's name. Memories came flooding back to him of his demand to her that she take the girl to India.

'It was all to no avail,' he thought, seething inwardly.

"Well, it serves him right! He knew it was his duty to be here with me. Don't talk to me any more about him or his kin," he shouted angrily, banging his fist on the small table.

Elena could see that no further talk was possible.

"Well, I must hurry. The ladies are coming early today," she said as she looked at the clock.

"You must stop all those confounded ladies coming here, talking all the time and whatever else they do. Their constant chatter gets on my nerves."

"I doubt if you can hear them!" Elena exclaimed angrily.

"You must take them all to the vicarage," he demanded.

"I will do no such thing," she said angrily. "The vicarage has been taken over by the Red Cross, and the village hall, which we used to use, has been commandeered by the local Home Guard. They use it twenty-four hours a day, seven days a week. So, my dear Bruce, the ladies have to come here. We have plenty of room," she said emphatically. "I am also thinking of converting the West Wing into a hospital for convalescent servicemen. It will be most suitable. It will be wonderful to have some young people in Glencree Castle again. We have had none since—" She was just in time to stop herself from saying, "since our dear Craig was driven away".

"You will do no such thing!" Bruce boomed. He again banged his fist on the table.

"Well, I shall as soon as I get word. I want to provide those poor, wounded boys with somewhere to rest their war-weary selves. We have such ideal surroundings here, where they can relax and enjoy themselves and get back to health."

"You will do no such thing!" he raved.

"You wait and see. It is our duty to do everything we can to help the war effort." She bounced out of the room and banged the door behind her.

Martha, Magnus and Christina toiled all day in the fields to grow food for the village, as they had done since rationing became acute. In the evenings Martha and Christina sat by the fire, their knitting needles flying, as the finished socks, scarves, gloves and balaclavas piled up beside them. From time to time they were delivered to Lady Elena and the Ladies' Sewing Circle, who parcelled them up and sent them off to be distributed to servicemen.

One evening the cottage door suddenly flew open and in rushed Ruardy. Christina caught her breath. She hurriedly put down her knitting. She lived in dread of what she felt sure he was going to say. She knew he was not happy in the course he had started at the agricultural college. As the war news had worsened, he felt his father would expect more of him.

"Mama, I have enlisted," he announced. "I shall continue my course when the war is over."

Christina, trying to hide her dismay and worry, got up and clasped him tightly.

"Well, my son," she said, "if it is your wish! Now go and change whilst I prepare supper."

Ruardy kissed Martha fondly. "Still knitting, I see. I hope you knit some for me," he said lightly as he playfully hugged her.

"Yes, my son, some will be for you – more's the pity!"

He looked up to see his grandfather looking at him fondly.

"Well, my boy," he said, "you are away to do your duty. When do you have to report?"

"A fortnight from now, Grandpapa, I shall be away. I hope to get into my father's regiment, with any luck, but I don't know whether or not I shall meet up with him during the war. I may not see him till the war is over. I shall have to wait and see. Now I must wash before supper."

Later that night, as they all sat round the fire, Ruardy sprang another surprise on them.

"Mama, before I leave, I am going to propose to Shona," he announced. "As soon as I return, we can marry and settle down. We can live in a little cottage in the village until I finish my forestry course."

"You seem to have your life well mapped out, my son," Christina said. "Let us hope the war finishes very soon and that it all comes true. I cannot think of a nicer person than Shona to be my daughter-in-law."

"Oh, thank you, Mama. I knew you would give us your blessing." Ruardy kissed them all and wished them goodnight. "Call me early, Grandpapa. I want to go to the village to see Shona," he called as he raced upstairs.

"Very well, my son," Magnus replied.

"What a night of surprises!" said Martha. "Everything seems to be moving so fast! It fair takes my breath away. All that's left of the fire is dying embers. It too is telling us it's time to say goodnight."

Magnus and Ruardy crossed the loch early the next morning. They waved goodbye to Christina and Martha, who watched them till they were out of sight.

Ruardy swept Shona into his arms as soon as she opened the small cottage door.

"Darling Ruardy, what a lovely surprise!" she exclaimed. "Mama, Ruardy is here."

"Well, bring him inside, my dear," called her mother.

He sat down.

"Well, Shona, I have given up my course at college till after the war. I have enlisted."

He saw her catch her breath.

"Well, I am sure the war won't last much longer," he said.

"Don't you believe that, my son," said Shona's father as he entered. "Things are looking more grave every day. Nearly all the boys in the village are away now."

"Yes, I realise that," said Ruardy solemnly. "Can I see you alone, sir, for a few minutes?" he asked.

"Yes, my boy, follow me."

They strolled into the small garden.

"Well, my son, what do you wish to speak to me about?" he asked, half guessing what Ruardy wished to say.

"I wish to ask for Shona's hand in marriage. I want to marry on my return from the war – or maybe sooner if I can get leave before I go abroad."

"Yes, my boy, I couldn't wish my daughter to be in any better care than yours, so go and ask her now."

Ruardy and Shona excused themselves and went for a stroll beside the loch.

"Darling, I am so happy," she said, "but I am going to miss you terribly when you leave."

"I know, my darling, and I shall miss you. Tomorrow we will go to the city to buy a ring; then you will have something to remind you of how much I love you."

All too soon, Ruardy was standing at the station on his way to join his regiment. His arms were round his beloved Shona. Martha and Christina were happy for them, but sad that they would soon lose him. Magnus stood beside Peggoty, awaiting the train, wishing it would never arrive.

"Well, here is the train, dead on time for a change," said Peggoty.

"Why couldn't it have been late, as it usually is?" sighed Magnus. "Come, my son – it is time to go."

"Now, Shona, my darling," Ruardy whispered as he clung desperately to her, "prepare for our wedding whilst I am away. We shall marry on my next leave, whenever it is. How little time I have in which to plan things!"

"Yes, my darling, I will be ready. I will get Emma to assist me," she said tearfully as she reached for her handkerchief. He took it from her and dried her eyes.

"I must go now, my darling," he said. "Now, smile for me. I cannot bear to see you weep."

He kissed her lips and her ring. He took her by the hand and they rejoined his mother and grandparents.

Christina hugged him close. "Now, write as soon as you can," she said. She cupped his face in her hands as she kissed him. "Hurry back to us, my darling."

He hugged and kissed his grandparents in turn. "How I am going to miss you all," he stammered as he tried to hide the tears he felt were not far away. "Take care of all our dear ladies, Grandpapa, until Papa and I return."

"I will, my son, I will. Now hurry, my boy – the train is ready to pull away."

Ruardy flung his luggage into the carriage and hurriedly grabbed Shona for a final kiss before jumping aboard. The engine driver had already sounded the hooter, anxious (yet not too anxious) to part him from his loved ones. To him it was by now a too familiar situation and he hated being part of it.

At last the train was away. Ruardy leaned out till they were all out of sight. Then he sat dejectedly beside his luggage. After a while he flung it on the rack.

When they arrived back at the cottage, Christina and Martha wept in each other's arms. Shona, the first to compose herself, led them to the two large chairs by the fire.

"Now, both of you sit down whilst I make some tea," she said.

"Thank you, my dear child," said Martha.

Shona disappeared into the kitchen. Martha once again wept bitterly as she dabbed her eyes.

Christina rose, sat on the arm of Martha's chair and put her arms round her.

"There, there, Mama!" she said. "Don't upset yourself so. Maybe the war will be over soon; then they will all come home."

Magnus looked at her resignedly. He knew that she knew that the war would not be over soon.

"My loved ones are always saying goodbye," said Martha as she put her handkerchief away.

"Well, I am here with you, Mama, and here comes our sweet Shona with the tea. We will all feel much better now."

CHAPTER 284

In the summer of 1942, Martin, Margot and Craig decided to forgo their summer trip to the hills. Margot looked wonderingly at Craig when he made his decision to do likewise.

"Do you realise, dear, that the heat here is very detrimental to your health?" she said.

"Yes, Margot, as you and the doctor keep telling me; but I feel, as you do, that I have a duty to the troops now stationed here. Most are recovering from their terrible experiences in Burma.

"I am, like you, going to open my home for all to come and go as they please. Their company will do me good and make up for any discomfort I feel due to the heat. I only hope that Lindsay is able to get some respite wherever he is, but I fear that may not be possible for him," he said.

More often than not, Margot and Martin joined the servicemen at Craig's house. Their chatter of the homes they had not seen for such a long time, and the appreciation they expressed at their welcome, was enough to gladden Craig's heart. The heat, which troubled him greatly, was, he thought, a small price to pay. He said he felt quite well, but Margot had her doubts.

Craig's greatest joy was when officers from the barracks came to spend an evening with him. These officers, new to the area, had been on active service in the Far East and were now on overdue leave. They appreciated the warm, friendly hospitality of Craig's home.

On one of these evenings, several of them were assembled at Craig's. They were all waiting for another officer to join them.

"He is late. I hope he hasn't got lost. He has only just arrived at the barracks. I did tell him how to get here," said Captain Brooks.

Just then a tonga stopped outside, and they were all surprised to hear a very heated argument between the officer and the tonga wallah. Craig rose from his chair in alarm and hastened to investigate. He was just in time to see the tonga pulling away at a furious rate. The officer, whose name was James Parton, called exclamations of anger after it as it went.

"He is moving pretty fast," said Craig as he reached Parton's side.

"Yes, he'd better. He probably thinks that if he doesn't get the hell out of here, I will take back the fare I have given him."

"Well, come inside and join us in a drink."

"Yes, thank you," he said as he accepted his drink from the bearer. "I am furious. That fellow was out to rob me. That's why he has beaten a hasty retreat."

"Now, tell me all about it," said Craig. "Maybe I can help, so that next time you won't have this problem. I cannot understand your difficulty. The tonga wallahs are usually very honest."

"Well, he wasn't," Parton ranted angrily. "I gave him four rupees."

Craig and the others looked perturbed.

"He kept on saying, 'Eight annas, sahib, eight, sahib', over and over again. I will 'eight annas' him if he ever crosses my path again!"

He stood with his arms raised, mimicking the tonga wallah, before sitting down to take another sip of his whisky.

He continued, muttering under his breath, "So I told him, 'You are not getting eight; you are only getting four.' The damn cheek of him!" Parton was getting more hysterical. "Eight! Imagine! So I told him, 'Get the hell out of here.' "

By now Craig and the other officers were almost hysterical with laughter. Even the bearer, standing close by, was having difficulty in controlling his smile.

"I'm telling you," Parton said, looking aggrievedly first at one and then at another, "it's no laughing matter."

"But it is, it is," said Craig, trying to control his laughter. "The poor fellow was trying to tell you that you had given him too much when you gave him four rupees. Eight annas is only half a rupee."

"Well, I'll be damned!" Parton exclaimed. He joined in the roar of laughter. "I take back all I have said about him and his kind," he said.

"Now, James," Craig said later that night, as he drove away with the others. "Remember, eight annas is half a rupee."

"I won't forget, Craig. Goodnight," he said.

"Goodnight, Craig," said Captain Brooks. "We will see he gets it right. Thank you."

Craig sat for a long time on the verandah after they had gone.

'Never can I remember enjoying a laugh so much as this evening,' he thought. Suddenly, his face saddened as he thought of Lindsay. 'I wonder how he is and what danger he is in. How I wish he was coming home!' He tapped the small table with his fingers in tired resignation. 'But as things are, as things are—'

He looked up to see Damodar looking at him.

"You go, Damodar," he said. "I will lock up when I retire. Salaam."

"Salaam, Sahib. Goodnight, sahib," Damodar replied.

CHAPTER 285

Lindsay knew, as did everyone else, that now the war was worldwide many more Christmases would pass before anyone saw his home or his loved ones again.

'How I long to see my father!' he thought. 'The only way to leave the battlefields is to be so badly wounded that you cannot fight, but I have no wish to go home like that.'

In spite of the dangers, Lindsay was glad he had been transferred to this special unit. He enjoyed the thrill of not knowing what danger might befall him next, and there was an added thrill and sense of satisfaction when he had overcome his fears and won through.

His assignments took him away over the desert for weeks at a time. He travelled through the villages, into the bazaars and sometimes the casbahs, and among the tents of the Bedouins, gleaning any information he could about any enemy activity. His whereabouts was at times unknown, even to his headquarters.

The tricks of the spies and saboteurs kept him constantly alert. They were, of course, trying not to be caught, but he was determined to catch them. He had to admit it was a relief to get called back to his lonely outpost and to link up again with headquarters.

After one of these trips, after many hours riding along the dusty road on his way back to headquarters (riding as he always did at top speed), he rounded a corner too fast and ran into a tight mass of sheep and goats. They were being driven back to their small village. They and their two minders scattered in all directions. Lindsay and his motorbike landed in the ditch with several goats on top of him.

He gathered himself up, cursing furiously in English and Arabic.

The small boy came towards him to retrieve his goats.

Lindsay furiously brushed the dust from his tunic and raged at the boy in

Arabic. Then, seeing how young he was, and how helpful he was trying to be, he was filled with remorse. He patted the boy on the shoulder.

"I'm so sorry, my boy," he said in Arabic. "I will help you collect your goats."

However, before he could do so, he suddenly heard a shrill tinkling laugh coming from the bushes nearby. His temper rose again. Someone had the audacity to be laughing at his downfall.

He snatched the bush aside angrily, but his anger was swiftly quelled when he came face-to-face with the loveliest pair of laughing dark eyes he had ever seen. They were fringed with long eyelashes, which the girl lowered as he stared at her. Her hair, which she hastily covered with some ragged, filmy cloth, which had fallen on to her shoulders, was as blue-black as a raven's plumage. However, her eyes spoke volumes about how amusing she had found his downfall.

As he looked at her and gathered up his motorbike, he too saw the funny side of his predicament and burst into laughter. He hadn't laughed for a long time.

'How good it is to laugh!' he thought.

Then, just as suddenly, his laughter ceased as he saw a look of fear in her eyes. Her brother, young though he was, looked at Lindsay angrily as he handed him his cap.

Lindsay thanked him in his native tongue and examined his motorbike. He straightened the handlebars, readjusted the lights and found his satchel. He thanked God that the motorbike was otherwise undamaged and the satchel was safe.

He remounted, bidding the boy good day in Arabic. Then, without another glance at the girl, he rode away. He stopped a little further along the road, and turned to watch as the girl helped her brother to gather together the scattered sheep and goats. He felt guilty at not helping them, but he knew his presence was not wanted – at least, not by the boy.

He realised with horror the delay this mishap had caused him, but, before he sped on, he was relieved to see them on their way to their village.

It was growing dark and he had a long way to go.

When he arrived, he hastily jumped off his motorbike and gave it to the transport sergeant who was waiting for him.

"Where the hell have you been?" he demanded. "The Captain is stamping his feet in yonder office."

"You know better than to question where I have been or what I have been doing," Lindsay said curtly.

"All right, all right, keep your curly hair on! What the hell have you been doing with this bike? I hope you don't need it again tonight, because it won't be mended in time."

"Well, if I do need another one tonight, Sergeant, you will just have to find me one," Lindsay replied as he hastened up the office steps.

"I'm glad to see you safely back," said the Captain. "I was wondering if the enemy had waylaid you."

"No, sir, I went head over heels into a flock of sheep and goats – but no harm done! The only damage is a bent motorcycle, which the transport sergeant assures me he would mend tonight if I needed it." Lindsay smiled broadly as he spoke.

The Captain looked up at him and smiled back. "I doubt it, knowing our transport sergeant. Thank goodness the papers you carried are safe!" he said as he took them from him. "You will not be needed again tonight, Sergeant. You are also due three days' leave. Report to me on your return – unless, of course, you hear anything on your travels. As you well know, you are never off duty."

"Yes, sir." He saluted the Captain as he bade him goodnight.

Lindsay was thankful to reach the mess and to see the letters from his father and Margot. He read his father's letter first, and he was thankful to hear that he was well; however, Margot's letter gave him cause for concern. He read that his father had had another attack of malaria, but was now over it and much improved.

'Thank goodness for that! It's just like Papa not to mention it!' he thought.

He laid the letters side by side in his bedside locker and was soon fast asleep.

Lindsay was glad to get away early before the heat of the day. In the nearby small town he was able to mix with other troops on leave for a brief respite from the desert war.

His first call was at the military hospital, where he found Philip, who had hurried to join up with Ross and himself. Philip had not passed the exams for the special course, so he was still in the non-combatant unit.

"Have you seen anything of Ross lately?" Lindsay asked.

"Well, he called in a couple of months ago. I daresay he will, like you, turn up again out of the blue one day."

Philip escorted him round the ward.

"I don't think there is anyone here at present whom you might know," he said.

"Well, as you know, Philip, my visits here are not just to see you. Ross and I always have to be on the lookout for anyone or anything suspicious. Many enemy agents are posing as allied servicemen."

Posing as a welfare visitor, Lindsay sauntered round the ward. He listened to the conversations of recuperating soldiers, who sat playing cards, draughts, dominoes or chess. He moved slowly on, pausing whenever his suspicions were aroused. He spoke in Arabic, enquiring about the soldiers' welfare, at the same time looking directly at them for any sign of unease.

One patient glanced idly up at him and said, "Don't speak to me in that bloody lingo, mate."

"I'm glad to see you are getting better, soldier," Lindsay replied as he passed on.

It distressed him deeply to see so many fine young men suffering. Many were severely wounded. Some were limbless, some were blind.

"I daresay you are, like the rest of us, longing for the day when you can return home to your loved ones," Lindsay said to one of them.

"Yes," he replied. "Why did we bloody well have to come in the first place?" he exclaimed, rising wearily from his chair on his only leg.

"Well, I hope you all get home soon. Good day," Lindsay said.

"No day is a bloody good day in this neck of the woods," a disgruntled voice yelled after him. "The only good day we shall have is when we arrive back home."

"Yes, Blighty will do for me. The sooner the better," several yelled.

Lindsay and Philip bade them goodbye.

"I am free this evening, Lindsay. We will go into town together," Philip suggested.

"Shall we watch the belly dancers, Philip?" Lindsay laughed heartily as he spoke.

"Would you like to watch them?" Philip asked.

"Well, I might take a quick glance from time to time, but my real reason for going there is not to see them but to watch for any undesirables among the spectators."

"Well, I must say," replied Philip, "I was mighty disappointed I didn't get through the course with you and Ross; but now I realise what you have to do, I am much happier where I am. Of course, I don't know how long I will stay here – no one knows where they will be from one day to the next."

They parted later that evening.

Next day, Lindsay sat at a small table in one of the outside cafés. All around him sat troops, most of them laughing and joking with their comrades. The ones he was most interested in were sitting at the small table nearest to him. He could hear their conversation: all of them were talking of home.

He ordered another cup of coffee from the waiter in order to prolong his stay. Suddenly, one of the soldiers leaned forward to tell his friends what he intended to do on reaching home.

"I am going to spend days and days just walking my dogs beside the loch at Glencree."

Lindsay, speechless with amazement, looked at the tall, fair-haired, handsome young soldier.

'He's about my age,' Lindsay thought. 'I wonder who he is. I did hear him say Glencree – I am sure of it.'

He waited till they rose to go.

"Excuse me, soldier, can you spare me a moment?" he said.

"Me, Sergeant?" the one he was addressing queried.

"Yes, please sit down and join me in a cup of coffee, if you have time."

"Yes, I have time." He sat down, after calling to his friends as they left, "I will join you in a few moments." He looked at Lindsay questioningly.

"Well, you know where to find us. We will walk on," one of the other men said.

"Forgive my intrusion," said Lindsay, "but I overheard your conversation."

The soldier looked at him apprehensively. "I can assure you, Sergeant, it wasn't careless talk," he said.

"No, my friend, it was just that I thought I heard you mention Glencree."

"Yes, that's right. It is near Glencree Castle, owned by the Earl of Glencree. Why, do you know of it, Sergeant?" he asked excitedly. "I don't recall ever seeing you at Glencree."

"No, I have never been there, and I don't suppose I ever will."

The soldier noted a touch of bitterness in Lindsay's reply.

"Well, you will no doubt have heard of me," Lindsay said enigmatically.

The soldier looked at him questioningly as Lindsay pondered long.

"My grandfather," he said at last, "is the selfsame Earl of Glencree. My father's name is Craig and my mother's name was Elizabeth."

"Your name is Lindsay," the soldier replied in amazement. "My name is Nicholas and my mother's name is Emma – your mother's best friend. She is still deeply distressed at your mother's death. It was so tragic." He sighed deeply.

"Let us not dwell on the past – it is far too painful for me. I am so delighted to meet up with you at last. I have known of you all my life, Nicholas."

"And I you, Lindsay. How delighted my parents and, of course, Lady Elena will be when I write and tell them of our meeting!"

"Yes, I must tell my father also. I shall write tonight. I know Aunt Margot will also be delighted."

"I met Lady Margot when she stayed at Glencree Castle after she attended the wedding of her granddaughter, Clare, a few years ago now."

"Did you see much of Great Aunt Elena?"

"I used to see her every Sunday at church, before I left to go to university. I also saw her many times when I was on embarkation leave."

"Was she well?" asked Lindsay with concern.

"She was quite well when I saw her, but my mother says she finds her brother, Bruce, quite a handful at times. My mother, as I suppose you know, sees Lady Elena every day. She helps her with the correspondence for the missions whilst Lady Elena deals with other matters and visits some of the ex-servicemen."

"Yes, ex-servicemen from the last war! Now we are in the middle of an even worse war. I thought when it started that it would be over by the first Christmas, and now we are heading for our third one," Lindsay said bitterly.

"Well, I also thought that," replied Nicholas.

"Will you be on leave much longer?"

"No, I am due back tomorrow. What regiment are you in, Lindsay?"

"That I cannot say." He rose to go. "I hope we meet again soon," he said. "If not, maybe you will come and visit us in India with your parents when this wretched war is over. I know my father would dearly love to see you all."

"We would like nothing better."

"Let us hope it ends soon. Tell me, Nicholas: did you see much of Roddy and Ruardy?"

"Roddy was away most of the time, but Ruardy and I are great friends. We used to take long walks by the loch with our dogs, but then I enlisted and, as you see, here I am."

"I can't tell you, Nicholas, how much meeting you has meant to me. It is a pity we cannot talk longer."

They looked solemnly at each other as they clasped hands in farewell.

"Nicholas, when you get home, will you visit my grandparents by the loch and give them my love?"

"Of course I will." Then, after a moment's pause, he looked sadly at Lindsay and added, "That is, if I ever get home."

"Never doubt that, Nicholas. That hope is the only thing that keeps many of us going."

Lindsay watched as Nicholas rejoined his friends. He turned once more to wave Lindsay farewell.

Lindsay sat down and ordered more coffee, unable to believe that, of all the people he could meet, it was someone who knew his grandfathers.

CHAPTER 286

"Craig dear," Margot called, as she flopped exhausted on the chair in the garden under the shade of the banyan tree.

"What is it, Margot?" Craig exclaimed as he joined her from his seat on the verandah. He looked at her with concern and called to the bearer to bring them both iced lime juice.

"We are going to the hills this summer. Please come with us. We have done as much as we can to give the troops some home comforts, but neither Martin nor I could stand another summer in this heat. You, my dear boy, are looking all washed out."

Craig thought for a few moments.

"Yes, Margot," he said. "As you say, I am washed out. I will come with you. I must be fit and well when Lindsay returns."

"That you must, or else he will think we have not been looking after you."

"No, dear, he would never think that. He knows only too well that I might have died but for your care. I will make arrangements for the nuns from the mission to see that flowers go daily to the grave, and I'll ask them to post my mail on."

After a few weeks in the hills on his plantation, Margot was pleased to see Craig looking more robust. The colour returned to his wan face. Often she and Martin accompanied him on his rounds. The children of the tea pickers ran to greet them as they alighted from the tonga, and they laughed gaily as they placed garlands of flowers round their necks.

Margot never failed to notice the look of longing on his face as he picked up the children. He playfully tugged the long plaits of some of the girls, then made them all stand in line and gave a sweet to each one. They watched as the children scampered back to their mothers.

Craig was more than delighted, on returning one day from the plantation, to find a letter from Lindsay. After reading it, he could hardly contain his excitement.

"Margot, Margot," he called, as he raced over to find them, "what do you think? Lindsay has met up with Nicholas. Apparently all were well when Nicholas left home. He sends his love to you."

"Well, fancy their meeting in a war situation! What a strange world it is, to be sure! I daresay most of the boys in Glencree have joined up," said Margot.

"Yes, Ruardy has now enlisted. Here, read it, Margot."

She took the letter from him and ordered the bearer to bring tea. Eventually, she handed it back.

"There's no mention of when he might get any leave," she said.

"No, the censors would not allow him to say even if he knew. He might get respite leave, but not home leave," Craig said sadly as he put the letter in his pocket.

"Surely, the war cannot last much longer," Margot said with a sigh.

"At least another year, I should think," Martin said.

Margot noted the look of distress on Craig's face.

"Well, at least every day is a step nearer to its ending," she said. "Now let's enjoy the good news we have had today and finish our tea."

CHAPTER 287

The war continued. The Allied armies continued to move forward in 1944, and an Allied landing on the Continent was widely expected. When? That was the question. Would it really be this year?

None was more interested than Craig. As he sat listening to his radio one day, suddenly the news everyone was waiting for was announced: D-Day – the Allied invasion of Europe had begun in Normandy.

"At last, at last!" Craig exclaimed as he banged his fist on the table in glee.

Damodar rushed in.

"Sahib, sahib."

"Shush, Damodar! Shush!"

A big smile crossed Damodar's face. "The invasion has come at last. War will be over soon. Bring me whisky. I want to celebrate," said Craig.

Damodar rushed away and brought back the bottle and a glass on a tray. He placed it in front of Craig.

"Sahib, sahib, do not drink whole bottle," said Damodar with a big smile across his placid face.

"No, I won't drink the whole bottle – not just yet."

"Will war be over soon in Far East also?"

"Hopefully," replied Craig, trying to speak between gulps of whisky. "Now I must see if Margot has heard the news."

He took another gulp and rushed off.

"Margot, Margot," he called as he raced up her garden path, where the mali was watering the plants. Never had the mali seen Craig so excited.

"Whatever is it, Craig?" Margot said as she rushed to greet him. For a moment she thought he had had bad news about Lindsay.

"Good news, Margot: the invasion of Normandy by the Allies. Maybe the war will soon be over and my son will be coming home."

He grabbed her round her waist and waltzed round and round.

"Stop, stop, my dear boy! I am getting quite dizzy. Come – let us rest under the banyan tree. Boy, please bring iced water."

Craig told Margot that he would complete his visits to his plantation and then leave it all in charge of his friend. As the war news was getting better, and the Allies were progressing closer and closer to the boundaries of Germany, he felt he should now return home to the city.

Margot and Martin decided to return also. Their visits to the missions in the hills had been completed, so Martin made preparations for their departures.

A week before their intended departure, Craig woke with a severe headache. He felt chilled and he was shaking. His teeth were chattering. He rang his bedside bell with some effort.

At once Damodar was beside him, looking at him with alarm.

"Please bring me a warm drink and more blankets, Damodar," he asked.

"Yes, sahib. Anything else?"

"No, I will soon be all right when I get warm."

Damodar brought the warm drink and left the room. He closed the bedroom door reluctantly and crouched just outside.

Craig lay back on his pillow after taking a little of the warm drink.

'Not this damn fever again!' he thought. 'Just when I am going home!'

He tugged his blankets higher and reached again for his drink. As soon as he grasped it, it crashed to the floor. He dropped back on his pillow exhausted, then looked up to see Damodar.

"Shall I get the memsahib and doctor, sahib?" he asked anxiously.

"No, Damodar, I don't want to disturb the memsahib. Get my tablets and another warm drink. I shall be all right by the morning."

Next morning, as soon as Margot got the bearer's message, she told Martin to call the doctor and rushed over to see Craig.

She watched as the doctor examined him; there was a look of concern on his face. She followed him apprehensively on to the verandah.

"He has had these recurring attacks of malaria before," she told the doctor.

"This one may be more serious than any he has had before," the doctor replied. "His lungs are very congested. Has he had lung trouble before?"

"Well, I know he was in a gas attack for a short while during the last war."

"Well, that is now catching up with him, and the heat of this country is making it worse. This climate does not suit everyone."

He sighed as he looked at Margot's troubled face. He tapped his stethoscope on the palm of his hand.

"He is showing signs of delirium and his heart is very weak. Has he any next of kin?" He spoke quietly as they slowly walked on.

"He has only a son, but he is away in the war somewhere. I doubt if they would let him come home."

"Well, it is worth a try. Go ahead and make enquiries. In the meantime, I will send a nurse from the mission hospital to help you."

"Thank you, Doctor."

"I shall be calling twice a day, but send for me any time if his condition worsens."

"Martin, please go to the telegraph office and send a telegram to Lindsay."

He looked at her, alarmed. "Is it so serious?" he asked.

"I'm afraid so. We can only hope the army will let him come home, but there is always a lot of red tape involved in situations like this. They will probably want to send someone to ascertain that his father is seriously ill."

Margot sat beside Craig as he tossed and turned. She looked at him lovingly. The healthy colour she had noticed in his face only a few days before was now gone. Now only a deathly pallor remained.

He opened his eyes, reached out to her and mumbled something.

"What is it, Craig dear?"

He raised his hand a little and tried to point to the table near his bed.

She looked around. What could it be?

Damodar, standing silently in the corner, watching his every move, moved to where Margot was sitting.

"Sahib wants the memsahib's picture, memsahib."

Margot gave it to him and he raised it to his feverish eyes.

"Angel, where are you?" he whispered.

The picture fell from his weakened grasp. Margot put it closer to him on the table.

"His fever has subsided a little now and he is more rational," said the doctor a few weeks later.

"Will it last?" Margot asked as they walked along the verandah.

"It is difficult to say at this stage. He seems to have the will and desire to get well for his son's return. We will have to wait and see."

"Doctor, I should like to sit up for a short while," said Craig the next day.

"Well, if you feel up to it, you may – but only for about ten minutes at first."

"I will do as the doctor orders," Craig replied, smiling wanly. "Margot, please tell Damodar to move my bed closer to the window. Then I can see the mountains more clearly."

A few days later, Margot stood beside Craig's bed as they gazed out.

"Aren't the mountains magnificent, Margot?"

"Yes, dear, they are."

"But they are not our mountains," he sighed.

"No, dear, but we will all see the Highlands again one day, you'll see."

"No, Margot; you will, but I won't. When you see Papa, tell him I am sorry to have caused him so much pain and sorrow when I left – but I couldn't live without my angel, you know that, Margot." He looked up at her and grasped her hand as if to make sure she understood.

She nodded her head. "I know Bruce will send for you both as soon as Lindsay returns from the war," she said.

"Damn the war!" he exclaimed angrily. "That's why I haven't seen Lindsay for so long." He looked up at her again. "He will soon be home, won't he?" he asked.

"Yes, but you are talking too much. Now you are feeling a little better, I am going home for a wee while. A nurse from the mission will come to stay."

"Do I know her?"

"It is Sister Grant. She is one of the nurses who has been helping to look after you recently."

Craig thought for a little while. "Yes, now I remember," he said. "I also met her at the mission."

"I will see you in the morning. Goodnight, dear."

"Goodnight, Margot. Thank you."

Margot met Sister Grant on the verandah, just taking off her cape.

"Good evening, Sister. Master Craig feels better today."

"I am so pleased."

"Now, send one of the boys if you need me."

Sister Grant nodded her head and wished Margot goodnight.

She greeted Craig gaily. "How are you feeling tonight?" she asked. Her soft Scottish lilt reminded him of his aunts.

"I am not feeling as well as I was this morning. I feel hot."

She looked at him, noticing the beads of sweat on his forehead. Her calm, efficient manner as she read the thermometer belied her concern. Another relapse! It took several shakes of her wrist to reduce the thermometer to normal. She readjusted his pillows, turning them over.

"That feels cooler, Sister."

"You have been overdoing it, my boy. Now, here is your tablet and a little iced water. You will soon feel better."

"Yes, I will soon be better," he mumbled. "My son is coming home soon."

He gulped the water eagerly.

"Yes, he will be home soon. Now you must sleep."

Next day, after the doctor examined Craig, he took Margot to one side.

"I shall have to admit him to the main hospital, Margot," he said.

"I am not going to hospital," Craig protested loudly when he heard. He reached out to her. "Margot," he pleaded, "do not send me away from you. You are all I have now."

He sank back on his pillow.

"No, my dear boy, I shall stay with you, as you wish."

Daily his spells of delirium increased.

"Angel, angel, I can hear you singing. Where are you?"

Margot sat beside him, wiping his feverish brow; her soft, soothing voice only eased his mind for a few moments. Again, all the thoughts of his childhood and the men he had left on the battlefield came crowding in on him. He screamed out frantically, "Papa, Papa, Mama is in the water!" His voice sounded like that of a child in his weakness and delirium. "Flint! Good dog! Come here, boy."

Margot was now joined by Martin. They looked down at Craig, and Martin shook his head.

'What can we do to ease this poor boy's heartache?' he thought.

"Heather, come to Papa, darling girl." Craig stretched out his arms as if to receive her. "Where are you? Don't play hide and seek today. Papa is so tired, so tired."

Suddenly, a clap of thunder was heard. Craig struggled to get out of bed and both Martin and Margot tried to restrain him. Another thunder clap made him wince in anguish. He clutched his head.

"Sergeant, Sergeant, where are my men? Why don't you answer me? You damn fool, answer me," he shouted. "Lindsay, where are you? I have not seen you for a long time. Come and see me soon."

"Any news yet from the army, Margot?" Martin asked.

She shook her head.

A few days later, an officer called to ascertain Craig's condition.

"Is there any chance of his son returning home?" Margot asked as they sat taking tea on the verandah.

"It is not for me to say, madam. I have to report on my visit today; then word will be sent to his headquarters."

"It is only the thought of seeing his son that keeps him going," said Martin.

"I understand. That is very often the case," the officer replied sadly.

He rose to go, and he shook them by the hand. "Rest assured I shall do all I can to hasten his son's return," he said reassuringly.

"Thank you so much," Margot said as she wiped away a tear.

The doctor patted her comfortingly on the arm as they watched the officer out of sight.

The doctor prepared to leave. "Call me, no matter what the hour, Margot, if his condition worsens. You too, dear, must rest more. Craig will sleep now he's had his medicine."

"I cannot rest till Lindsay comes. Hasten the day!" She sighed. "Sister, I am going home to rest for a while. Send the boy for me as soon as Craig wakes."

"Yes, Margot," she replied. "You are worn out."

Craig tossed and turned, muttering his anxious thoughts: "Are you there, Aunt Elena and Harriet? Why are you so far away? Lindsay, where are you? Ah, now I remember. You had to go to war; you had to do your duty. Why did you leave me alone? You know I don't like being alone." He sighed. He dazedly opened his eyes and rubbed his parched lips. "Water, water!"

The Sister went to tell Damodar to bring it. She sent Munilal for Lady Margot; then she stood near the door waiting for the jug of iced water.

Craig flung back the bedclothes, staggered to the window and opened it wide. The icy chill of the mountains rushed in on him. "Where is my piper?" he shouted. "Are ye no there, laddie?" He glanced up at the snow-clad mountain tops silhouetted against the golden moonlit sky. "No, no, you are not my mountains. Not mine! Why do you play such tricks on me? Why? Why?"

Sister Grant put down the jug of water, and she and Damodar rushed across the room. The chokidar patrolling the garden raced to the window.

"Sahib, sahib, close the window," the chokidar called. He rushed away to find a bearer.

Sister Grant and Damodar tried in vain to prise Craig's fingers from the window sill. He resisted them frantically.

"See, boy, there are my pipers. I knew they would come over the mountains and down the glen. Can you see them, boy?"

"Yes, I see them, sahib. Come to bed. The wind is too cold."

"No, boy, I want to see and hear my pipers. See, here they come, their kilts swinging in the breeze. There is my tartan leading them. Come on, laddies – I am waiting for you."

Suddenly his grip loosened and he fell backwards into their arms. They crashed to the floor, just as Margot and Martin, with the doctor close on their heels, rushed to their aid. Margot helped Sister Grant to her feet.

"Are you hurt?" she asked.

"No, I must hurry and cover him with a blanket." The Sister was almost in tears in her anguish.

It took them several minutes to get him back to bed.

"Bearers, go and make some tea. We will be staying the rest of the night."

Damodar looked anxiously at the doctor and Margot as he went. "Will my sahib be all right?" he asked. He was distraught.

"Yes, he will be all right. Don't worry," Margot reassured him.

He took his leave, after a last look at Craig, who now lay ashen-faced and exhausted on his pillow.

Craig opened his eyes and reached out for Margot's hand.

"Hello, dear, dear Margot. You are always near when I need you. Has Lindsay come?" he asked.

"Not yet, but I am sure he won't be long," Margot replied.

"Maybe tomorrow, Margot," he sighed. "Always tomorrow! Where is tomorrow, Margot?"

She looked up at Martin, as if appealing to him for the answer, but he shook his head.

"You know, Margot . . ." Craig murmured as she bent closer.

"What, my son?"

" . . . Merry-Berry told me one day in the woods that my bones would rest in my bonnie Scotland, but I know that will not be so. I am going to rest here with my two darlings when my time comes, so Merry-Berry will be wrong for the first time ever. Margot," he whispered again.

"What is it?" she replied, leaning closer to him.

"Please give Lindsay the water and soil of home she gave me," he implored.

She patted his arm. "He will be here soon, dear. Then you can give it to him yourself."

"I am so cold, Margot. Please take this compress off my head."

She glanced at the doctor, alarmed, as she removed it. The unruly lock, which always fell across his forehead, now lay saturated with beads of sweat. She stroked it back.

Suddenly, he sat bolt upright and looked towards the window as a shaft of early morning sun rose above the mountains.

"See, angel," he said, "the sun is shining for us today. I knew you would come. Sing for me, my love. It's such a long time since I heard you. Shush, everyone! Can't you hear her singing?"

A radiance came over his face as he listened intently. He raised himself higher on his pillow.

Margot tried to restrain him.

"Craig dear," she said, "you must lie back and rest."

He pushed her arms away.

Then it was as if the singing he had heard had suddenly ceased. He reached out, calling Elizabeth's name. He could see her now as she was on the first night he had seen her, coming down the stairs. The sunlight was catching her long golden hair as she turned to go.

They watched as Craig gazed into the distance, a smile on his face as he reached out to her. Then there was a sudden panic in his voice as he cried out, "Angel, angel, wait for me! Don't leave me again. Wait! Wait! I am coming." He slumped back into Margot's arms with the word 'angel' on his lips.

Margot rested him back on his pillow and he gripped her arm as his eyes closed. His grip slackened and his arm fell to his side. His other hand, she noticed for the first time, was tightly clenched. She leaned over, and unclasped it to find a damp blue-velvet ribbon. She looked at the bearer.

"The sahib always has it close, memsahib – always," he said.

"You are with your angel now, my son," Margot said as she kissed him on his forehead.

She rose to join Martin at the window. Tears were streaming down her face. The doctor and Sister Grant were now by Craig's side. Martin put his arm round her shoulders, and they gazed out, numb with grief.

"Why couldn't they have been his mountains? Why? Why? That is where he should have been – not here in this foreign land. You know, Martin, for a long time I have seen him looking longingly at Lindsay's picture as if he knew he might never see him again. If only he had been spared to see him," she said between her sobs. "Why couldn't Bruce have sent for him long ago? How am I going to tell the boy and also Elena?"

"Don't try to answer all those questions now, dear. Come and sit down. I will tell the bearer to bring tea."

He went over to the bedside and gazed down at Craig's anguished face. He held Craig's hand. "Goodbye, dear friend. We will take care of Lindsay." He looked at the doctor. "I will take my wife home now. We can do no more. We will take Craig back with us to the city as soon as possible."

"Very well," the doctor replied. "I will deal with all the details. It is a sad day for us all."

Margot turned to the distraught bearers before leaving. "When the mission sisters have left, close up the house and prepare to leave with us."

They nodded as they stood silently, their heads bent and hands clasped in silent prayer.

"Yes, memsahib," Damodar managed at last.

Next day Martin walked sadly to the telegraph office to send the distressing news to Elena. He also telephoned the officer who had called on them, and told him of Craig's death. He asked the officer to notify Lindsay.

"Yes, I most certainly will," the officer replied. "Please accept my very deep condolences on your great loss."

"Thank you, sir. Will you give him this message: 'Lindsay, your dear father passed away peacefully yesterday. We were with him. Letter following. Signed, Margot and Martin.' "

He hurried back to Margot. Their bearers were preparing to leave, all moving silently and swiftly. Margot and Martin sat on the verandah holding hands as they watched all the hurry and bustle going on around them.

"We will leave tomorrow. All is completed," the doctor said.

"I will write the letters as soon as I arrive home," Margot said sadly. "My poor boy! What a shock it will be for him! How I wish he could have been home with his father! And my poor Elena!" She dried her eyes once more.

"Come, dearest – we must retire. We have a long journey tomorrow," Martin said.

Craig was buried, as he had requested, quietly in the vault beside his angel and child.

The mali stood silently behind a shrub, his head bowed, his hands clasped. He watched as the mourners passed through the small gate Craig had always used. Margot had instructed him that fresh flowers must be placed daily on the grave.

Martin turned to close the small creaking gate. He suddenly remembered Craig's words: "One day I will oil this creaking gate."

Martin watched Margot anxiously as she tore up letter after letter. She found it easier to write to Elena, although Martin could see the task depressed her deeply.

The letter to Lindsay she found almost impossible. The telegram would have reached him by now. She imagined his deep distress as she gazed into the distance, pen poised, not a word forthcoming as to how to begin.

"Would you like me to write to Lindsay?" Martin suggested.

"No, thank you, Martin. It is something I must do."

"Well, dear, don't write a long letter tonight. You are far too distressed. Explain how you feel and that you will write more at length later."

"Yes, dear, I will do as you say. Please check these few lines after I have finished and seal and post them tomorrow."

Her eyes filled with tears as she wrote.

"Now I must retire," she said eventually.

She stumbled, almost falling as she proceeded to her room with the help of Martin and her maid.

Next morning Margot sat on the verandah, having said farewell to Martin on his way to the mission, and to post her letters. Her mind was in a whirl of thoughts of long ago.

Now, everything associated with the past – even her own home – filled her with a deep depression. She thought of the home she had loved. It had always been filled with such happiness. She thought of her daughter as a child and the twins. "How I miss them all so!" she sighed. Then she thought of Elizabeth and Craig and their lovely children.

"Now all that has gone," she sobbed. "I do hope Martin gets home early from the mission."

The voice of the bearer woke her from her reverie: "Here is your tea, memsahib."

"Thank you, bearer."

Later that day, they mounted the steps of the verandah of Craig's home. Damodar stood silently at the entrance, as if too overcome with sorrow to speak.

"Bearer, make some tea, please," said Margot as she sank down, almost dumb with shock and grief. Her thoughts were of all the happiness she had known in this once happy home.

"Damodar?"

"Yes, memsahib."

He approached her silently with a questioning look on his face.

"The house must be kept always as your master wished. Everything must be covered up with the sheets I wish you to collect from my home. Meanwhile, I shall employ you and Munilal until Lindsay arrives home. The mali will stay and tend the garden as usual. I will need flowers for the grave."

"Very good, memsahib." The relief on his face was plain to see, now that he knew his job was safe. "When will Lindsay sahib come home, memsahib?"

"That we don't know. I will let you know the minute I hear."

Martin rose to his feet. "Come, my dear," he said, "our work isn't yet done." He helped her to her feet. "We still have more letters to write."

"Bearer, here is the key. Make sure everything is locked before you leave. Come daily to check all is well," said Margot.

"Yes, memsahib."

He and Munilal and the mali stood side by side on the garden path. They salaamed as Martin and Margot wended their way home.

CHAPTER 288

Lindsay was surprised to see the motorbike approaching. He hurried from his lookout as his friend Ross leaped from it. "What news have you brought today? News of our demob?"

"No such luck! It seems that will be quite some time yet. I have brought you a message telling you to report to headquarters immediately. I have to stay at your post till you return."

"Another assignment, I suppose! But you are as able as I – why me?"

"I don't know. It says urgent, so you had better get moving."

With a wave of his hand, he was away. Ross watched him out of sight.

Lindsay mounted the steps and entered the CO's office with some trepidation.

"Good morning, Sergeant McNair. Please sit down."

"Thank you, sir."

He looked at his colonel questioningly. This was not the usual procedure when sent for. A sudden foreboding assailed him.

"I am sorry, but I have sad news for you. This telegram arrived last night."

Lindsay took it from the Colonel, trying hard not to show his feelings.

The Colonel watched closely as Lindsay read and reread it, seeming not to grasp its meaning. Lindsay sat silent, too stunned to speak.

"Thank you, sir," he said eventually.

"I should write immediately to your mother and family. Take the day off to deal with it."

"Thank you, sir. I have no mother, and now I have no family." He sighed.

The Colonel looked at him, as a father would look at a son. "Have you no one to deal with the arrangements?" he asked.

"Yes, sir. My father will have been buried by now, judging by the length of time this has taken to reach me." His underlying anger, evident in the tone of his voice, was not lost on his officer.

"I have very good friends who will have dealt with everything that I should have been at home to deal with. They will soon be writing to me, as it states here." He reread the telegram again before putting it into his pocket.

The Colonel rose. "Please accept my deepest condolences on the loss of your father," he said. "We have all been away from home and our loved ones for far too long."

They shook hands. The Colonel was at a loss to find anything more to say to ease Lindsay's loss. Lindsay turned on his heel after saluting him.

"Come and see me in the morning," the Colonel called after him.

"Yes, sir."

He stumbled down the steps, ignoring a greeting from one of his friends. He entered the billet they all used when called to headquarters, and he flung himself on his bed. He buried his head in the pillow. Several of his friends came in and spoke to him, but he ignored them.

"I will play him a lullaby," laughed Sergeant Grant as he picked up his mouth organ.

"He's asleep already," replied his friend.

"It can't be bad on these so-called special assignments. I wish they would send me on some. Anyway, we had better get a move on. We are late already. We aren't allowed to sleep on our job."

They both hastened to the door.

Sergeant Grant popped his head back inside. "Nighty-night! Sleep tight," he quipped.

Lindsay raised his head. He reached for an army boot, which was protruding from under the bed next to him, and flung it with all his might at the now closing door.

A few days later Sergeant Grant apologised to Lindsay and expressed his sorrow. The Colonel had told Lindsay to take more leave and await the letter he was expecting from Margot.

When it arrived, he spent days lying on his bed, reading it again and again. He wrote back immediately, thanking her for all she and Martin had done. He had no idea when he would be home. It could be quite some time yet.

> I might be able to let you know [he wrote]. On the other hand, I might just turn up. Things are so uncertain. Now Papa will never see his beloved Scotland again. It's all the fault of that bitter old man in Glencree. Forgive this brief letter. I will write at length later.
>> Yours as ever,
>> Lindsay

He was now anxious to get back to his post. In spite of its isolation, it was where he longed to be. The other men in his unit abhorred it. His colonel offered him a post at headquarters, but he declined.

"You ought to be with company at such a time," the Colonel said, "but, as you wish! You may return tomorrow. Tell your relief to report to me on his return."

"I will, sir."

Ross was more than pleased to see Lindsay, but most distressed to hear his sad news.

"Now, just as the war is going in our favour, my father has died," Lindsay said bitterly.

CHAPTER 289

Elena saw Lawrie hurrying up the long drive as she gazed from her bedroom window. For days she had felt an unease she couldn't fathom. Her thoughts of late had all been with Craig, but now, as she noticed the small envelope in Lawrie's hand, her first thought was of Lindsay. Her mind was in turmoil. 'It's not time for mail; it must be a telegram.' A cry of anguish escaped from her panic-stricken lips.

She fled downstairs, uttering, "Craig, Craig! Lindsay, Lindsay!"

She almost knocked Marie over in her blind panic. Marie recovered her balance.

"Milady, you should not hurry so," she said. "You might fall. We don't want two of you in wheelchairs."

Elena paid her no heed. She raced towards the door, flinging it open as Lawrie, hand in air, was about to ring the bell.

"Good morning, milady. A telegram for you!" He held it out nervously to her.

"Thank you, Lawrie. Good day."

He doffed his cap as he turned to go. "Good day, milady," he said.

She stood with her back to the door. Jamie rushed to her side when he heard the door close.

"What is it, milady?" he asked. He held his breath in anguish as he noted the telegram.

She opened it with trembling hands and unfolded it.

She whispered the fateful words over and over again: "Craig died Sunday. Lindsay notified. Letter following. Love, Margot."

She gasped for breath as her tears streamed forth. Reaching for her handkerchief, she fell in a crumpled heap at Jamie's feet. Marie and Jamie eased her into the big chair nearby, and Marie rubbed the life back into her white, frozen hands. Both servants looked at each other, at a loss as to what to do or say.

Elena tried to compose herself. She held the telegram close to her heart.

"Our darling boy is dead," she said. "Our darling Craig, Jamie! Whatever shall we do, Jamie? What shall we do? I must go and tell Bruce."

She stood up and dried her eyes.

"We will make some tea, milady."

The huge oak door seemed twice as forbidding as it ever did before. She steeled herself before knocking. The door had, over the years, become more and more a barrier between her and Bruce. Since Harriet's death they had been flung closer in everything but polite conversation. She had sensed, over the years, that he longed to ask her about Craig and Lindsay, but the wound in his heart was cut deeper than a ravine. His stubborn pride would never let him utter their names. Now it was too late to tell Craig that all was forgiven and it was too late to ask him to return home, although a letter had been sent recently telling him just that.

"Oh, I do hope it reached him in time," Elena sighed as she stood at the door. She had recently had dreams and premonitions that something bad would happen to Craig, and she guessed that Bruce might have had them also. He and Craig were very much a part of each other.

She had been more than surprised when Bruce had called her into the library one day and asked her for pen and paper and Craig's address. As she watched his pathetic effort at writing, she sighed heavily, her mind travelling back to how fit and strong he used to be. Why had he suddenly felt he had to write to the son he had banished? No matter how long she puzzled over it, she could not fathom it out. An answer was never forthcoming. She had let him struggle with his feeble effort, a strange look of resigned finality on his face. She also detected a faint smile of satisfaction. Perhaps he had found a peace he hadn't known since Craig's departure.

"Seal and post it for me, Elena," he had said. "You know how I am fixed in this useless state of mine."

"Yes, Bruce, I am going into the village today," she had replied.

'The sooner I can get it away, the better,' she thought. Still puzzling at this change in him, she suddenly recalled that, a few nights earlier, she had been awakened by his cries. She had rushed to his bedside and found him bathed in sweat, crying out for Isabelle and Craig – Craig, whose name he had never uttered since his banishment.

She had never felt happier as she rode with Jamie to the village later, smiling at everyone she encountered, wanting to tell everyone that at last Bruce had forgiven his son and that he would soon be home. Craig's pride was like his father's, but she knew he would come home.

"He must, he must," she had prayed.

"Now this, now this!" she exclaimed.

She sighed, dried her eyes again, straightened her hair and dress and put her handkerchief in her pocket. She turned the heavy knob of the door and eased it open, calling his name softly.

"Bruce dear," she said.

"Well, what is it now?" he bellowed. "You know I don't like to be disturbed."

Since being confined to his chair, he had spent his days near the fire, looking up at Isabelle's picture. For the past few weeks, Elena had been perturbed at his spending all day looking out over the loch, leaning out as far as he was able as if looking for someone.

This was as he was now. His back was to the door so he did not see the anguish on her face or notice her nervously stumbling across the room towards him. She held the telegram behind her back as if subconsciously she wanted to keep the news from him a little longer. If only she could spare him the pain and sorrow! She picked up his woollen shawl and put it round his shoulders.

"The air is getting very chilled, Bruce."

"Stop fussing, woman! I am all right. Just leave me to my thoughts. Tell me, Elena: do you think my letter will have reached him yet? What do you think he will say, that boy of mine? He will do as I ask and come home, Elena. I just know he will. I know my son. We know our dear boy, don't we, Elena? Why do you not answer me?"

He turned round to face her, and he caught sight of the paper in her hand.

"It is my reply from Craig. Give it to me, Elena."

She offered it to him and watched as he struggled to unfold it.

"You undo it, Elena," he said. "You know I cannot manage with only one good hand."

"It is not a letter, Bruce. It is a telegram."

"I know. He wants to tell me as soon as possible. That's why he has sent a telegram!" Bruce exclaimed excitedly.

She watched as he tried to discern its message, his eyes dimmed with the years.

"You read it, Elena," he said.

Her voice faltered as she spoke.

With a moan of anguish and despair, his head dropped on to his chest in disbelief.

"It cannot be true, Elena," he said. "Tell me it isn't true."

He took it from her and tried to read it through his tear-dimmed eyes; then he let it flutter to the floor.

"I will make you some tea," she said sadly.

"No, I don't want anything, except to be left alone. Now go."

He turned to face the loch again.

She dried her eyes once more as she closed the door.

Jamie, standing in the hall with the tray of tea, looked at her sadly. "Tell me it's not true, milady: my wee bonnie lad dead?"

"Yes, Jamie, our boy is no more. Craig will never be here with us ever again. Sir Bruce does not want tea or to be disturbed. Tell Zan to bring the carriage. I must go to see Martha and Magnus, also Emma."

As she sped towards the village, she spotted Merry-Berry disappearing through the hedgerow and she recalled another memory. She had heard the servants talking one day. Several of them had seen Merry-Berry closer to the castle than they had ever seen her before.

"I haven't seen her this close since Master Craig went away," she heard Cook exclaim.

'Well, she always knew things before they happened,' thought Elena.

Bruce, in his distress, demanded to be taken every day to Isabelle's grave, no matter what the weather, as if he felt guilty about what he had done to her son.

"Please, forgive me, my darling," he whispered. "Now he is with you."

CHAPTER 290

Lindsay, back at his desert outpost, felt more and more alone. He spent every night looking at the black Eastern night. The brilliant stars were the only light in his dark mood of sadness, despair and anger at events.

"Damn the bloody wars and all who cause them," he seethed. "They are the reason I had to leave my father for so long. To think I told him it would be over by Christmas when I enlisted! Ah, ah, what a laugh!" Suddenly he was laughing uncontrollably; then he sank into his chair sobbing hysterically.

How long he sat there he neither knew nor cared, but eventually he eased himself to his feet, cramped and stiff with cold. He refilled his paraffin lamp and held his hands over it as it sprang into a blaze. He rubbed some warmth into them and waited impatiently for the warmth to seep through to the rest of his body. Then he heated some water for his coffee. He drank it hurriedly as he hastened to his lookout post.

Dawn was breaking, and the rays of the golden sun helped to subdue his dark, sombre thoughts. As he scanned the horizon with his binoculars, a slight movement to his left caught his eye.

'Yes, here they come,' he thought.

He could set his watch by the time they always appeared daily, night and morning, over the crest of the sand dunes. The women and girls from the nearby village were on their way to the well. They carried pitchers on their heads. Their bare feet trod the cool sand and rough rocks. Their black, loose, raggedy garments covered them from head to foot. They passed his post with heads held high, walking like queens. He could hear their laughter as they passed. The one he trained his glasses on was a tall, slender waif, who carried her pitcher more regally than the rest. She was the same little waif who had laughed at his downfall when he fell off his cycle so long ago. Her flimsy raiment, blown by the desert breeze against her frail, slender frame, outlined every curve of her beautiful young body.

For months he had watched, and gradually he had fallen in love with her. It was torture to him that she would never know. How he longed to take her in his arms and tell her that he loved her! How he craved to take her away from all the squalor and infernal desert dust, to dress her in silks and satins and lace. What a queen she would look! He sighed longingly and blew her a kiss as she passed, but the gesture was lost on the desert breeze.

'Good morning, my desert queen,' he thought silently.

She, of course, was unaware of his silent adoration.

His friends often wondered why, of all the available posts, he only wanted to be sent to this one. They all detested it.

"Why, for goodness' sake?" they would exclaim.

"Well, as I love you all so much, I like to do all of you a favour," he would reply, laughing. "I feel as free as the wind there."

"It's a mighty damn chilly wind, and you are welcome to it," one of them said. "I will always be willing to do your spell of duty at headquarters when it's due."

"So will I," several others chorused.

That year, 1945, would see the end of the war. Already the Allies were in Germany, and an end was almost in sight in the Far East. Japan would soon be defeated. Everyone's thoughts now turned to how soon they could go home.

'Home, home, why should I go home? To whom and to what? How can I pick up where I left off? Besides, if I go, I shall never see my desert queen ever again.' Once more his sombre thoughts had returned.

Often, on their return from the well, she would be a step or two behind the others. She would glance shyly up at his lookout post, as if something was willing her to glance in his direction. Their gazes, attracted like magnets, met for a brief second; then she would swiftly lower her head, pull her veil higher and hurry on.

One morning, he, as usual, watched the women filling their pitchers. She, as always, was the last, trailing behind on their return.

Suddenly, she stumbled and fell, and her pitcher broke into pieces. Her head struck a huge boulder. She lay motionless and he could see the blood streaming over her face. The women ahead were singing, laughing and talking, unaware of her fall.

He hesitated, remembering his strict instructions; then, flinging caution to the wind, he raced across the sand and bent over her. His only concern was for her.

One of the women suddenly turned and saw her lying in the sand.

"Kechi! Kechi!" she screamed in alarm, as did the others. They watched in horror as Lindsay picked her up and ran to the shelter of some date trees close by, where he disappeared from view.

The women sped as fast as they could back to the village.

"Come – we must tell Kechi's father!" the eldest exclaimed.

Lindsay laid her gently in the cool shade and tried to stem the blood from her head with his handkerchief. His efforts were to no avail. He snatched his neckerchief from his neck and raced back to the well, muttering impatiently as he wound up the bucket. He saturated the cloth and raced back to the girl. Very gently, he bathed the cut on her head and lowered her veil to wipe the blood from her eyes. He ran again to the well to re-soak the cloth. Again he bathed her face with the cool water.

Her jet-black lashes flickered several times, and her almond-shaped eyes opened narrowly, but she perceived nothing. At last, opening her eyes wider, she looked up at him and smiled a timid smile as she recognised him. Then, suddenly, fear, like that of a hunted gazelle, flashed across her face. Lindsay felt her tremble as she reached for her veil.

"My veil! My veil!" she screamed in terror. "You should not have removed it."

She tried to rise to her feet but stumbled again and again. At last she fell in a crumpled heap in his arms as he tried to break her fall. She struggled to resist his help. Gradually he realised that he himself was causing her distress.

'What a fool I have been!' he thought. 'How could I have been so stupid? But what else could I have done?'

"You cannot walk," he said. "You have broken your ankle."

"I must! I must!" she screamed. "I must get to my village."

'I know what will be waiting for me when I get to her village,' Lindsay thought.

She collapsed once again as she struggled, and this time she fainted with the shock of the pain in her head and foot.

He gathered her swiftly in his arms and hurried towards the village. As he drew nearer the village, he saw several men approaching.

"Here comes the reception committee," he muttered.

Her father and uncle stepped forward. The fury on their faces told him he was in great danger, but he stood his ground.

"Put her down!" her father demanded, but Lindsay paid no heed.

Then her uncle came threateningly close to him, waving his stick in his face, the venom in his voice increasing with every word.

"Put her down! Put her down! You know the penalty for touching our women. You will be killed." His swarthy face was now livid. "You will be killed!"

For a moment, Lindsay thought he would be killed there and then, but he stood defiant as he held her out to her father. She had recovered enough to try to free herself from his arms, but her father declined to help her.

"She must walk," he said.

"She cannot walk; her ankle is broken," Lindsay said, his fury now matching theirs. "Assist her, I say."

He stood holding her out to them.

"She is defiled. We will not assist her," her father replied.

They recoiled from her as she reached out to them. She struggled from Lindsay's grasp and tried to stand, but she fell again and the blood started to flow from her head. She dabbed it frequently with her own headdress. Lindsay grabbed her with one hand to support her.

"Assist her," he repeated, but no one moved. He withdrew his revolver from his holster and pointed it at the rest of the villagers. "Return to your village," he demanded.

They turned and fled.

When they were out of sight, he pointed the gun at her father and uncle.

"You will assist her or I shall shoot you where you stand and bury you both here."

They knew by his menacing attitude that he would do as he said.

They approached with fear and fury in their eyes and grabbed her roughly by the arms. She leaned heavily towards her father, the blood still pouring down her face. She shook her uncle's arm off as she tried to stem the flow. She had always hated him. Lindsay followed them all the way to the village, before returning to his post.

He notified headquarters to send him a relief so that he could report in.

His colonel's face as he related the events turned from a pale shade of tan to pink, red and purple with disbelief.

"You picked up the girl?" he raged. "Damn you! That was contrary to all instructions."

"I had no choice, sir. Her ankle was broken."

"Well, that's as maybe, but there will be serious repercussions for her and you. You will stay here on leave due to you, and you will have to wear a disguise. Be careful where you wander. Be on your guard and report to me daily. Your post was due to close soon. Go now. I will send Sergeant Fairfax to your post till then. He is in the bazaar somewhere. Find him and tell him to report to me."

"Yes, sir," Lindsay answered, before he turned and beat a hasty retreat to the door.

Ross was enjoying his long overdue leave. He wandered through the bazaar, trying to decide what presents to buy for when the happy day came to go home.

"Get out of my way, beggar," he demanded. He tried time and time again to shake off a beggar who tugged repeatedly at his clothing. "Begone, I say." He became more and more angry.

The beggar drew level with him and whispered, "Who is Sylvia? Who ditched you in the fountain in the park?"

Without looking to right or left, he replied, "Who took the roof off the portico?"

"We did!" they both exclaimed.

"You have to report immediately to the Colonel. I will see you there later."

"Begone, beggar!" Ross exclaimed angrily as he hurried him away.

Later Lindsay joined Ross in the barracks.

"I hate that post of yours!" Ross exclaimed angrily. "I am supposed to be on leave." He was hastily packing his things. "You might have waited till your post was closed before you asked for your leave. I expected more consideration from you, Lindsay."

Lindsay watched him in silence.

"Did the Colonel not tell you why I left my post?" he asked eventually.

"No, he didn't. He just told me to be extra-vigilant."

"Well, I will tell you. . . . "

When he finished speaking, Ross shook him by the hand.

"Do be careful, Ross," Lindsay said. "You might get mistaken for me."

"I will be careful. No one is going to get me after all we have been through. And you be careful too, friend. If I get to hear any news about the girl, I will let you know."

"Thanks, Ross."

"Any news of the girl, Colonel?" Lindsay asked tentatively on his next visit.

"No, not yet. Fancy you, of all my men, putting me in this predicament! I too am anxious for news of the girl. Let's hope for your sake they just send her to another village. They might kill her – it has happened before." He dismissed Lindsay impatiently.

Lindsay closed the door. The Colonel's last remark had filled him with dread.

He spent the following days touring the city and bazaars in disguise, watching and waiting to see if he was being followed. He spent hours watching craftsmen at work, and he grew tired of hearing the monotonous tones of the muezzin calling the faithful to prayer. In the past he had relished the persistent smells of the spicy traditional cooking after his spells in the desert, but now everything nauseated him. As he tired of each scene in turn, he wandered in the desert, trying to glean any information from wandering Bedouins.

His troubled mind drifted back to the lovely brown eyes of the one who was never far from his thoughts. His love for her burned in his soul as hot as the blistering sand, and the chill of his concern for her safety was as cold as the desert night.

Often he would sit in the walled garden on the outskirts of the city and sit under the shady trees, reciting lines from his favourite poem over and over again:

The Rubáiyát of Omar Khayyám

Awake! for Morning in the Bowl of Night
Has flung the Stone that puts the Stars to Flight:
And Lo! the Hunter of the East has caught
The Sultan's Turret in a Noose of Light. . . .

Into this Universe, and Why not knowing,
Nor whence, like Water willy-nilly flowing:
And out of it, as Wind along the Waste,
I know not Whither, willy-nilly blowing. . . .

The Moving Finger writes; and, having writ,
Moves on: nor all your Piety nor Wit
Shall lure it back to cancel half a Line,
Nor all thy Tears wash out a Word of it. . . .

Yesterday This Day's Madness did prepare;
To-morrow's Silence, Triumph, or Despair:
Drink! for you know not whence you came, nor why:
Drink! for you know not why you go, nor where. . . .

CHAPTER 291

It was one of those days. Lindsay was tired of inactivity and concerned for Ross's safety. He sat in deep contemplation of the events that were causing him so much anguish. 'What has happened to my darling of the desert? Will I ever get to know?' he asked himself. He thought of some lines from the Rubáiyát of Omar Khayyám poem. 'One seems to fit me,' he thought, 'for I am willy-nilly blowing.' He also pondered on the line, Drink! for you know not why you go, nor where. 'Well,' he decided, 'I know where I'm going: to hell, with this sitting about idly dreaming.' He sighed deeply as he rose to leave. 'Drink, that's what I need,' he thought.

It was already dusk when he changed into his dress uniform.

'Tonight I am not going to hide behind a beggar's garb,' he thought. 'If they want to get me, I shall be ready for them. Tonight I am going to enjoy myself like everyone else.' However, he knew that his gaiety would be false.

He entered the dimly lit, smoky hall and flung the beaded curtain aside impatiently. He gazed steadfastly round. Through the haze he could see several of his friends, but he remained standing just inside the door. He made no move to join them. They were all celebrating the end of the war. All were now relaxing, awaiting the call for home.

Several beckoned him to join them, but he paid them no heed. Tonight there was no need for furtive messages to be flashed between them – messages with meanings known only to a few of them. They were always alert for any danger, and they guessed by Lindsay's demeanour that he must be in danger. His safety was the concern of them all.

"Why is he on leave and why has Ross had to cancel his?" Corporal Gray whispered to the friend by his side. "I know his father's death has been a big shock to him, but surely that's not the reason?"

"Ah, well, it's not for us to question why," the friend replied.

Lindsay leaned back against a pillar, drinking the iced lime juice he had ordered.

The bearer looked at him questioningly. 'Why is the soldier not drinking, like the others, in celebration?' he wondered.

Lindsay watched the dancing girls idly. Tonight they gave him no pleasure. One he knew well came dancing towards him, flashing her dark eyes and swishing her hips round and round in her spangled skirt.

'I only want one pair of dark eyes dancing before me,' he thought. 'Shall I ever see them again? Where are you now, my princess of the desert?'

He was not to wait long for the answer.

He suddenly sensed someone too close for comfort. He glanced sidewards, but didn't turn his head as he moved to one side. Then he heard the question, "Who is Sylvia?" He knew this was a message from Ross. He stood rooted to the spot, without changing his manner or expression, as he waited for the message.

The messenger, dressed in the robes of a well-to-do Arab, whispered softly, "The girl is dead. They have killed her."

"Who killed her?" Lindsay whispered back, his anger mounting.

"Her uncle."

The messenger went as swiftly as he had come.

Lindsay leaned more heavily against the pillar, thankful for its support. 'No, no, it cannot be!' he thought. 'Why? Why? She was innocent of any crime, as was I. Why did she have to die for my stupidity? Why?' He could visualise her terror.

Suddenly, one of his friends rose from the table.

"Are you all right, Lindsay?" he asked. "We saw one of Ross's messengers approach you. Is anything wrong?"

"No, nothing that you can help me put right," he said curtly.

"Well, come and join us. The war is over; everyone is celebrating."

"No, no, leave me alone," he replied, and he dashed out into the dark night.

"I have never seen such a change in him," said his friend as he rejoined the others. "I don't suppose he feels like celebrating his going home, now that he has no one to return to – not like us chaps. Let's have another drink. I don't think we can aid our friend. He will be safe if Ross's men are watching him."

Lindsay raced back to the Colonel's office.

"Come in." The Colonel looked up from the report he was writing. "Yes, it's true. I feared this would be the outcome. The matter has been taken out of my hands by Higher Authority. I'm afraid the matter is closed. You may go now."

"Yes, sir."

Lindsay saluted and stumbled down the steps towards the billet. He flung himself on his bed, utter dejection assailing him.

"My, you are back early!" commented Sergeant Grant. "Why aren't you celebrating with your friends?"

"Mind your own damn business! Get out and celebrate yourself."

"That is where I am going. Goodnight." He glanced at Lindsay perplexed.

The door slammed.

Lindsay buried his face in the pillow. Bitter sobs racked his body.

"These aren't people; they are murderers! Murderers!" He spoke the words aloud in mounting vehemence. "All of them!" He tossed and turned, smoking one cigarette (which he abhorred) after another, stubbing them out viciously after smoking an inch or two. "Murderers! Murderers!" he seethed.

One by one, the other occupants returned from their revelling. All were very jolly and some were a little tipsy.

"My, we are early to bed!" quipped Sergeant Morris. "Are the girls in town not entertaining enough for you?"

"They were for us," the others chorused as they laughingly got ready to retire.

"Shut up, all of you, you big-mouthed rats!" Lindsay yelled.

Soon silence reigned. He had waited all evening for *this*!

Later the heavy snoring of Taffy Carr drove him to distraction. He passed their beds on pretext of slipping to the toilet, and on his way back he quickly snatched up a boot.

He lay awake for what to him seemed like hours. Sleep was beyond him. His fury mounted. Suddenly, in his anger, he threw the boot in the direction of the snorer. It landed with a loud thud. There was a sudden shout of pain.

"What smart bugger threw that?" one yelled.

He was answered by a chorus of, "Not me, not me!"

"Well, it's going back to its owner, whoever that is."

He flung the boot back across the room, and another cry of pain was heard as it struck another soldier.

"I will keep this bugger," the soldier yelled, "and, whoever is looking for it tomorrow – God help him."

At last all was silent once more, but Lindsay lay awake in torment. He was going over and over a plan in his mind. He imagined he could hear her calling out to him, "Save me! Save me!"

'I cannot save you, my love, but my revenge will be sweet. I will avenge you, my lovely flower of the desert, never fear.'

He pulled on his thick jersey and crept out into the night. The bitter cold took his breath away. He raced round the back of the hut when he heard the sound of an approaching Jeep, and the flash of the headlights made him leap into a nearby alcove. He was just in time. He watched as the Jeep came to a standstill and his colonel leaped out.

'Evidently he's been celebrating also. Everyone is happy but me,' he thought bitterly.

"I won't need the Jeep any more tonight, driver," he heard the Colonel say.

"Very good, sir. Goodnight," replied the driver.

Lindsay waited till they both disappeared.

'Well, Colonel, if you don't need your Jeep tonight, I do,' he said to himself as he clambered aboard.

He headed towards the gate barrier. The sentry looked at him suspiciously.

"What is the purpose of your journey at this time of night?"

"You know better than to question my movements," Lindsay replied.

"Oh, it's you, Sergeant. I am sorry, I didn't recognise you. I thought it was some thief, sloping off with the Colonel's Jeep."

He let Lindsay through the barrier, thinking it was not like him to be so abrupt. 'Well, the ending of the war's putting all our nerves on edge. He usually jokes about these trips he takes in the middle of the night.' The sentry watched as Lindsay turned into the road, and then he closed the barrier.

Lindsay drove like a madman, mile after mile. Eventually he put out his lights. The brilliant moonlight and clear starry night gave him all the light he needed. He knew every mile of the road. 'I hope there's enough petrol in this thing,' he thought.

He came to the small area of trees, stopped and jumped out. 'I hope Ross hasn't heard the sound of the Jeep,' he told himself.

He gazed round, recalling his brief encounter with the girl. His thoughts were only of her and the terror she must have endured before she died. He checked his gun and his knife, which he tucked more firmly down his sock. 'I am in enough trouble already; no one must know I have been here tonight,' he said to himself. He took the keys of the Jeep and hid them under a date palm. He raced along the sand to the village and entered the hut of the uncle, which he knew because of the many searches he had done looking for saboteurs.

He hesitated. The children stirred in their sleep but no one else moved. He put his hand over the man's mouth and dragged him to his feet. His wife woke with a start and screamed out his name. To Lindsay's horror, he realised he had hold of the younger brother of the man he wanted.

"Where is he?" he demanded.

"Who?" the bewildered man exclaimed in terror.

"Shehi, the elder?"

"He is not here."

"You liar! I shall search every hut till I find him."

He dragged the helpless man with him, keeping the gun at his head. He kicked in every door and looked at every male occupant. He was sorry to see the fear on the women's faces, but he screamed at them, "Never forget Kechi! Never forget Kechi!"

In spite of saying it in their own language, they did not understand.

His fury mounted as he continued his futile search. He herded the men along to the headman's hut. The headman had heard the commotion, and he calmly awaited Lindsay's arrival.

"Where is the uncle of Kechi – the one who killed her? Tell me, or some of you will die."

They looked at one another. Now they knew why Lindsay had come.

At last, the headman spoke: "The woman was defiled by you. Her uncle had to do what was right."

Lindsay smiled sardonically. "Where is he?" he raged. He was anxious to get the night over.

The headman, wondering what to do for the best, was playing for time. He had seen one of the elders near the door whisper to one of the boys, who then disappeared into the night.

"Take our fastest camel and go to the barracks. Go like the wind." These were the boy's instructions.

"Our ways are not your ways," the headman said. "We must do as we must."

"You are all murderers of an innocent woman. Where is he?" he kept demanding. "I shall stay till you tell me where he is, even if I have to blow this man's head off." He clutched the uncle's luckless brother more firmly. The others made a move towards him and he threatened them with his revolver. "Don't move, any of you, or I will shoot the lot of you."

"I do not know where he is. I am not my brother's keeper," said the headman.

"You are lying. You know everything. If you don't tell me, I shall set the village on fire."

The headman looked at him, alarmed. He knew that in his anger Lindsay might do just that. He continued to play for time.

"He is not in the village, but he should arrive soon," he said. "Let his brother go. We can sit down till he returns."

Lindsay sat down and made his hostage sit at his feet. He kept his gun pointing at the rest.

The boy raced like the wind, singing a ditty to the camel to make it move faster. At last he reached the camp, slid off its back and tied it to the barrier. He crawled under the bottom rail and raced to the dimly lit office ahead.

The sentry scratched his head in disbelief when, on hearing the rattle of the barrier and the grunt of the camel, he came out to investigate. He glanced round and saw the boy entering the duty officer's office. He raced up to him just as the boy was about to speak.

"He must have slid under the barrier, Captain. He has left his camel tied to it," the sentry said.

"Well, I'll be damned!" he exclaimed. He could see the boy was frantic to speak to him. "I will deal with him. You go back to your post."

"Right, sir."

The boy blurted out his story while the officer looked at him in amazement. They had always had such good relations with the small villages scattered across the desert – especially this one. "The bloody fool! Whoever he is, whatever is he thinking about? I shall have to wake the Colonel. Come with me, boy."

The Colonel was still up when the Captain knocked on his door.

"What has happened that you disturb me at this hour of the morning, Captain?" he said. "I have not, as yet, got to my bed."

He glanced at the boy at the Captain's side.

"I doubt, Colonel, if you will see your bed tonight after you hear the boy's story. . . ."

"Well, as you speak their language, you deal with it. I have a pretty good idea who the soldier is," he said at last.

"Who, sir?"

"It's Sergeant McNair. Only he would do something like this."

"But I saw him in the casbah not long ago."

"Well, you must have been dreaming," the Colonel retorted angrily. "Get the nearest border guards to get over there and hold him till we arrive. Send the boy back. Take my Jeep and two MPs. I will go and see the headman in the morning."

The Captain returned to report that the Jeep had gone.

"Gone?" the Colonel spluttered. "Send the guard to me at once. Well, tell the MPs to bring their Jeep – and hurry! Why did you allow my Jeep to leave the premises without my consent?" he yelled at the sentry.

"Sir, I did query it but the driver told me I had no right to question him on assignments."

"All right, go back to your post." The Colonel sat down. "That's just like McNair: the perfect answer every time. As if he isn't in enough trouble! It's because of him I am working so late, damn him!"

Lindsay pricked up his ears when he heard a motorbike approaching.

"Damn! Damn!" he said.

The headman gave a sardonic smirk. "I will tell you where the man you seek is," he said.

"Where? Tell me, and be quick about it."

"He is on the other side of the river, and he won't be back tonight."

Ross rushed into the room, revolver at the ready. "Lindsay, what the hell are you doing here?" he exclaimed. "I have orders to hold you till the MPs arrive."

"It's a long story, Ross. I will tell you in good time."

"Hand me your revolver." Ross turned to the headman. "Your people can return to their huts. There will be no further trouble."

Lindsay stood with his arms folded, cursing his luck.

"Why all this, Lindsay, when we are nearly due home?" Ross asked.

They heard the roar of a Jeep outside and three men hurried in. The Captain had informed the MPs that the incident was an intelligence matter and was not to be discussed with anyone.

"Sergeant McNair, you get into the Jeep whilst I speak with the headman," he said. "I will join you in a few minutes, and then we must pick up the other Jeep."

Lindsay clambered on to the back seat with one of the MPs as the other took the driving seat. Ross stayed alongside until the officer bade him go.

"I will see you in headquarters tomorrow, Lindsay. Goodnight," said Ross.

"Goodnight, Ross. I look forward to that."

The Captain apologised to the headman. "The Colonel will come and visit you in the morning," he added. "I assure you, there will be no more trouble from the young soldier."

The old man nodded his head in acceptance as the Captain bade him farewell.

"Where did you leave the Colonel's Jeep, Sergeant McNair?"

"Under the date palms."

"Drop me there, driver, and I will follow you."

The Captain left the Jeep, and the MPs escorted Lindsay back to camp. When they arrived, the Colonel looked Lindsay up and down in anger.

"I don't want your explanation tonight," he said. "I have had enough for one night. I will get your report when I have seen the headman in the morning. Put him in solitary, Captain, for his own safety."

Lindsay flung himself on the hard straw palliasse of his cell. He went over the events of the night. 'You murderer! I will get you yet,' he said to himself. 'I know you take your boat across the river every other night; one night you will find me waiting. Why? Why', he pondered as sleep evaded him, 'have my loved ones to die so tragically? My grandmother drowned in a loch, my mother was crushed under a pile of rubble in an earthquake, and now my only love has been murdered.'

He buried his head in his hands.

CHAPTER 292

"What is he doing in solitary?" several of his friends remarked when they heard the news. "Solitary!" they exclaimed. "He surely doesn't deserve that. Whatever he has done can't be that bad."

From his cell window he watched them climb into the trucks next day and leave for home.

"Good luck, lads," he yelled to them. "Watch those bumps on that dusty road." He stood on his bed as he waved them off.

"We will. Good luck! We might see you at a reunion."

Lindsay was called to the office two days later. He was glad to see Ross sitting on the form outside.

"I have given my account of events to the Colonel," Ross said. "I am going back to the post. It is being closed. Then I shall be back here till demob."

"Thank God I shall see more of you, then," Lindsay replied, "but whether or not I get my demob to go home with you remains to be seen."

The Captain ordered Lindsay inside. He stood to attention in front of the three senior officers.

"We have studied your case, Sergeant McNair. The headman has accepted the Colonel's apologies, and we believe that, on your part, you were motivated to carry out an act of kindness to the girl. However, by their laws, you defiled the girl by touching her and removing her veil. Fortunately for you, the headman is a reasonable man. If you will pay for all the damage to the village huts, the matter is closed as far as he is concerned. We, as the investigating body, have taken into account your long, loyal service and the troubled state of your mind, as well as the fact that you have lost your only remaining relative during your absence from home. Under the circumstances, no more will be said on the matter. These events would normally be dealt with by a court martial, but the war is over and you have served your country well. Also you were a young volunteer. Your debt to the village will be taken out of your accumulated pay and you will be kept in solitary confinement for your own safety until your departure for home in about a week's time. You know how unpredictable these people are. Have you anything to say in your defence before you go?"

Lindsay was still fuming at the failure of his mission. He realised now that if he had killed the man, he would be facing a murder charge and would not be going home for years – if ever.

The officers sat waiting as he gazed into space.

"Yes, I have something to say before I go," he replied angrily. "I want you to know that I am not sorry. I would do the same again. A court martial would not worry me one iota. I am as sick as everyone else of this damn country and the damn war. All the best years of my life have gone – wasted in this godforsaken country, protecting the local people. Some of them have been helping the enemy all along. I hardly consider our effort to have been worthwhile."

"Sergeant, Sergeant," the most senior officer said, trying to allay some of Lindsay's anger, "you know as well as we do that we had to protect the oilfields and the supplies of oil to our troops. You did your duty better than most."

"I know, sir. I don't owe anyone any more of myself."

"Now, Sergeant," the Colonel said, "you, like the rest of us, have to readjust your life. You may go."

Lindsay saluted before he went.

"There is a very bitter young man," the Colonel remarked as the door closed behind him. "I shall be glad when he is out of the country."

'Solitary? Well, that's what I need. I have a plan to prepare.' Lindsay thought.

The two occupants of adjoining cells were only in for one night. They had been caught having a roustabout in the town – celebrating their departure for home too well. For most of the soldiers, every night was party night. There were sing-songs and concert parties for those who had yet to finish their schedules before they too departed for home.

'All this activity suits me fine,' Lindsay thought. He reckoned up the nights as he lay on his bed. 'Yes, the night of the last concert will suit me fine if all goes well for me.'

He was thankful that Ross had been assigned to headquarters. After his post closed, he had special instructions to guard Lindsay till they were safely out of the country.

Every morning Lindsay watched through his cell window as more and more of the men climbed into the trucks and moved off for demob and home. Several called to say farewell, although most only remembered him as a shadowy figure who flitted in and out of camp at night. He had been nicknamed the Silent Sheik of the Desert.

Lindsay knew his plan had to work perfectly. He grew more impatient, and he worried that he might be sent home before he could carry it out.

"Ross, please get my revolver and knife," he said one day.

"You must be joking."

"No, I'm not. How do I know who might attack me in here when you lot are at the concert?"

"Well, they might let you come to the concert if I guard you well."

"I will refuse that invitation. I am tired and want to rest."

"Are you not well?"

"No, I have a stomach upset. It will pass in a day or two. The MO has given me medicine."

"Very well, I will get what you need, but don't let anyone find them on you or we will both be in trouble."

"Well, don't get caught, Ross."

"Everyone is very busy with the arrival of the concert party, fixing up the stage and dressing rooms. I can wander anywhere at will. I will bring them tonight."

"What time is the concert starting tomorrow night?"

"About 7 p.m."

Lindsay felt more secure with his revolver and knife. Several times during the day he made excuses to go to the latrine on the pretext of being sick.

"Are you sure you will be well enough to travel in a day or two?" asked Ross.

"Of course, old fella. Stop worrying about me."

"Tony will be your guard tonight. I am going to have my last night on the town. I will tell him to leave your cell door open. As you say, you have nowhere to run – only the latrine," he said with a laugh.

"Be off with you", said Lindsay, "before I crack your skull. Have a good time tonight. Sorry I can't be with you."

"So am I, old fella. Never mind, we will make up for it when we get home. Cheerio."

Tony wished him good evening. "Are you sure you do not wish to go to the concert? The Colonel has given you permission," he said.

"No, thanks. I would only have to keep running out. I am tired. I have been up most nights with this damn stomach upset so don't disturb me once I get to sleep," Lindsay replied.

"I won't, Sergeant. Goodnight."

CHAPTER 293

When darkness fell, Lindsay made it look as though there was a sleeping figure in his bed. He put his keys in the heel of his boot, his knife down his sock, and his revolver in his pocket. 'Thank God they left my clothing intact!' he thought. 'Now to find my motorbike! It should still be full of petrol.'

He unlocked the motorbike compound and wheeled his motorbike round the back of the buildings. He waited till the guard went in to answer the phone, then he sped headlong under the window and barrier and out on to the road, not daring to start the motor till he was well away. He looked up at the sky: another moonlit night and a few scudding clouds. 'They will serve me well,' he thought.

He raced flat out till he reached the date palms. There he hid his bike. He glanced around, thinking of Kechi, his heart as heavy as lead, his wrath knowing no bounds.

'Why? Why, my love, did I have to be the cause of your death? Well, I will avenge you,' he said to himself.

He rushed to his secret hiding place on the hilly ridge amongst the rocks, where he found his Arab disguise.

"Thank God, it is still intact!" he exclaimed.

He pondered for a few seconds before he put the stain on his face. 'God knows who I will meet,' he thought.

Suddenly, he heard a babble of Arab voices near the well.

'God is with me tonight,' he thought. 'I might borrow one of their camels.'

He slid across the sand and watched as the Arabs settled round their fire of camel dung, wrapping their clothing about them. Soon an eerie silence prevailed.

He knew this Bedouin tribe well. He had sat with them round their fires. He knew he could join them, as he had done in the past when gleaning information about enemy movements, but tonight he didn't want conversation. His time was precious. The last ferry over the river was due soon. He listened to the grunts and groans of the camels as one of the men hobbled them for the night. Soon all the men were asleep.

'They are a bit too close to the camels for comfort,' thought Lindsay.

He slid stealthily closer and lay still beside the nearest camel. The stench of the camels made him feel sick. He was tired, weary and thirsty. He made up his mind to free a camel and hobble the others together so securely that they could not be undone quickly. If he was caught, it was likely that he would be shot or have his head chopped off.

He muttered softly in Arabic to the camel as he untied it.

It rose to its feet as he retied the others.

The nearest Bedouin stirred in his sleep as if sensing all was not well. Lindsay crept behind him and punched him silently into oblivion. He looked warily around as he led the camel away. Not a soul stirred. At last he mounted and sped away over the high sand dunes to the small landing stage.

He looked at his watch with his small torch. 'All's well, so far,' he thought.

He could see a small dhow approaching and hear the babble of voices. He quickly dismounted, tied the camel to a small shrub and lay in wait. He watched as the village men salaamed to one another and drifted off to their villages. Then he spotted Kechi's uncle, tying up his dhow.

'That's the last salaam you will ever see, you murderer,' Lindsay said to himself. He could still picture the look of terror on Kechi's face as her father and uncle approached them.

The old man gathered up his few belongings.

'You won't need those where you are going,' Lindsay thought grimly, his anger now uncontrollable.

The old man hurried towards Lindsay down the path beside the river.

Lindsay rubbed the stain off his face. 'I want this murderer to recognise me,' he thought.

He waited till the man drew level, then he sprang out to confront him.

Kechi's uncle gave a gasp of dismay as Lindsay grabbed him by the throat, but his look turned to one of terror when he recognised the young soldier and saw the glint of the knife now at his throat.

"Yes, old man, it's me. Did you really think I would let you get away with her murder?"

"She was defiled by you," he hissed.

"And you are defiled by her murder."

"The military will get to know of this attack on me," he said.

"You, old man, will not live to tell them."

"I will be missed by my village and they will come to look for me." In spite of his show of bravado, Lindsay could feel the old man trembling with fear.

"You will be caught," the old man said.

"Your body will never be found. Besides, the military don't know I am here. Why did you kill her? She did no wrong."

"It is our custom."

"You and your damn customs! Killing a defenceless woman! You big, brave man of the East! Come – you are wasting my time."

The old man fell silent for a moment. He knew no amount of pleading would appease this angry young man.

"She had to die. I had to kill her," he hissed angrily.

These were the words Lindsay had waited for. His eyes flashed murderously. He said, *"Y Ibn Elkalb!"* (Son of a dog, among Arabs a deadly insult.)

The old man recoiled in fear. "It had to be! It had to be!" he gasped. His voice was barely audible as the clothing round his throat was pulled tighter, choking him. "Sahib," he croaked, "I do not want to die."

"Neither did she."

"Spare me! Spare me!" He was on his knees, gasping in anguish.

"You didn't spare her," Lindsay raged as he pulled him to his feet.

"Mercy, mercy!" he croaked, his voice a plaintive wail.

"Did you show her any mercy, you big, brave warrior?"

The terror in the man's voice caused Lindsay to experience a sudden stab of compunction. His thoughts went back to the gentle upbringing he'd had and his sweet, sweet, gentle mother. What had this war done to him and others like him? Well, he had killed in war. This was his own private war. Her frightened eyes were before him now, and he repeated her name: 'Kechi, Kechi, my darling desert queen,' like a record going round and round in his tormented mind.

"Spare me! Spare me!" the uncle cried, but his pleas were lost in an anguished moan as the knife plunged into him.

He sank to the ground at Lindsay's feet.

"You plead in vain for mercy, you murderer. The earth is well rid of you." The dead man finally fell on his side. Lindsay, his fury unabated, kicked him over the edge of the path into the fast-flowing river.

"She is avenged!" he shouted, flinging the knife after the body.

He raced back to the camel and rode it back to the Bedouin camp. All was as silent as when he left. He tied the camel to the others, concealed his Arab disguise and ran with his bike across the sand and on to the road. He ran as fast as he could until he was out of earshot. He scrubbed at his face, finally throwing away the grubby cloth. He was feeling clean and free once more.

He roared off without lights and shut down the engine as he neared camp. He dismounted, hoping that no one had heard the rattle of his bike. He crept back and laid it against the others. 'No one's likely to notice that it's not locked to the rest. Anyway, it's just too bad if they do,' he thought. The party, following the concert, was in full swing. He slipped back to his bunk, exhausted.

Next morning, the guard caught sight of him as he emerged from the latrine.

"Ah, you're finally awake at last," he said. "You know, you never moved at all in your bed for most of last night."

"Fancy that now!" said Lindsay, laughing.

'I moved more than you think, chum,' he said to himself.

"Well, I must be much better," he added. "It's my first night without the runs."

"The concert was good. You would have enjoyed it."

"I enjoyed my sleep better," Lindsay smirked.

CHAPTER 294

Ross rushed in on him early next day.

"Come on – get up, you lazy sod. Our names are on the list for demob. The Colonel says you are in my custody until you are out of the country, so hurry and get packed."

'None too soon!' Lindsay thought as he followed Ross to the barrack block.

They spent the day packing up their few belongings and saying farewell to all their friends. The Colonel shook them warmly by the hand, wished them all good luck and thanked them for their loyal service.

"I think the Colonel is glad to see the back of me," Lindsay remarked to Ross as they left his office.

"Well, he will be glad to get home too. Here are the trucks. Let's get aboard."

Frantic shouting was going on around them: names, ranks and answers of "Coming, Sergeant."

"Well, get aboard. If you don't want to go, I'll go in your place."

"That you won't," yelled several.

At last the back of the truck was fastened. There was a lurch forward and they were away, down the long, dusty road. Lindsay was oblivious to all the gay chatter and sing-song around him. Ross looked at him several times but left him alone with his thoughts.

"Thank God it is the last time down this road!" Lindsay said at last.

"Yes, it's a damn sight more potholed than when we came after all the war traffic over the years," said Ross.

Lindsay's thoughts were far away as he gazed over the desert. 'Goodbye, my desert queen. I would rather have stayed here with you,' he said to himself.

The men began singing the song 'Home Sweet Home'.

"We will be home much sooner than those of our pals who have to sail to Blighty. I believe we are going by air," said Ross. "It will be nice to get home and see all my family again." Suddenly, he realised what he had said. "I am sorry, my friend. Please forgive me," he added.

"Don't worry, my dear friend. I should feel like you if things were different. It is not your fault my homecoming will be less joyful than yours. Will you look me up sometime?"

"Of course. Little did we think, when we left university to join up, as we thought, for about six months, that it would be almost six years." He sighed heavily. Six years! For what?

"Hey, what do you think, lads? They are going to give us a suit each on demob."

"Great! I will choose the most expensive one I can find."

"So will I," several chorused. "A new suit!" they exclaimed in glee.

Lindsay listened to them expressing their delight on hearing the news. Suddenly, he started laughing uncontrollably. For several minutes he rocked back and forth on the rickety bench, almost falling off. His friends looked at him as if he had a touch of the sun, but his laughter was full of bitterness, anger, the futility of it all. Suddenly, he got to his feet, swaying along with the truck.

"They are going to give us a suit," he shouted. "You bloody fools! What have we given them? Years and years of our bloody lives are gone never to return. Some men are lost and gone for ever. Just look at some of the men in this convoy: blind, legless, armless. Think of our comrades who are killed and buried in the desert. What good is a bloody suit to them?" He waved his arms across the desert as he spoke.

"Sit down, Sergeant," the Captain ordered. He knew only too well what the men had gone through and how they felt about going home. "Taffy, how about some music to pass away the time?" he said.

"Right, sir." He pulled out his mouth organ. "What do you want, lads?"

" 'When the Lights Go on Again' and the one our fathers used to sing: 'Take Me Back to Dear Old Blighty'. "

The playing, singing and humming floated out over the other trucks and the desert.

Lindsay sat down, deep in silent remorse at his outburst.

At last they arrived at the dispersal station.

"Hurray! Hurray!" they yelled. "About time too!"

"Now, keep your seats," ordered the Captain.

He jumped down to greet the transport officer. The men became more and more restive at the delay.

"Did someone say they were giving us a suit?" said Private Barnes. "Well, they can have my bloody suit."

He started to take his uniform off, much to everyone's amusement. He was nearly half undressed when the officer came back.

"Stop fooling about and put your uniform back on," he ordered.

The men didn't wait for the tailgate of the truck to be let down. They jumped out and raced towards the canteen.

"Tea up!" was the chant from everyone.

Now all they wanted to know was what time they were leaving for home. All their papers were complete; all their armaments were handed in. Only their Blighty details were of any interest to them. They were all laughing and singing the songs dearest to their hearts. Songs they had sung over the years, such as 'Show Me the Way to Go Home', now had real meaning at last.

"Surely," remarked Ross to Lindsay, "this must be one of the happiest places on earth."

"I am sure it is," Lindsay replied. "I hope they sail soon."

"We fly in the morning, so we had better say our farewells tonight," Ross said.

Lindsay wished he could feel the happiness of his fellow-travellers as they approached the plane. Ross was brimming over with mirth and laughter. He hoped but failed to bring even a slight smile to Lindsay's face as one by one the men raced up the steps to the plane.

Lindsay hesitated at the foot of the steps. It was as if the desert was calling him back. He could still hear Kechi's name on the breeze. Should he go? Should he stay? 'There's no one waiting at home for me,' he thought. 'Why go?' He glanced back. A long, lingering sigh escaped him.

The Corporal behind him gave him a push.

"What the bloody hell is wrong with you, man?" he exclaimed angrily. "Don't tell me you want to stay in this bloody place? We want to go, even if you don't."

Then Lindsay knew he must cut for ever the silent tie that was holding him back.

"Sure I want to go," he said.

He kicked the last of the sand off his boots, and he raced up the steps to join Ross. The others followed close on his heels.

"Not one grain of this bloody sand am I taking home with me!" exclaimed Taffy Carr, as he viciously kicked every step to the top.

"Hurray! Hurray!" they shouted as the plane finally lifted into the air. "All is now quiet on the desert front."

Lindsay sank back in his seat and closed his eyes against the sight of the desert fast disappearing below. Each of them was thinking of what he would do when he reached that heaven called home. Most of them were thinking of the loving parents and families waiting to greet them.

"Yes, I too want to be home," Lindsay sighed, "but no one will be waiting for me."

Lindsay opened his eyes when he felt a nudge in his ribs.

"At last we are on home soil," Ross yelled. "Thanks be to God!"

"Now to get the train for home," Lindsay said wearily.

They all bade their pals goodbye, after promising to try to meet at a reunion.

"I am not going in your direction, Lindsay, but I will keep in touch," said Ross. He shook Lindsay's hand and patted him on the shoulder. He looked at his friend sadly, not knowing what else to say before he disappeared.

Lindsay flung his kitbag in the corner when he entered the train for home. He was thankful to be alone with his thoughts at last. After a hearty meal, which was brought to his carriage, he fell into a deep sleep.

He awoke, startled, to the sound of an old, familiar cry. The train came to a standstill. He leaped up and put his head out of the window.

"Tahsa char-garumi garum."

The sound was like music to his ears.

"Here, boy!"

"Very nice hot tea, sahib."

"I am sure it is, boy," he said as he took the cup from him. "Keep the change, boy."

"Thank you, sahib. Salaam, sahib."

Lindsay gulped the welcome tea and undid the carriage door. Suddenly, the railway porters pounced.

"Luggage, sahib? Luggage, sahib?"

"Yes, boy, just my bag."

He hurried after the porter as he raced along the platform, going around the small groups of people sitting cross-legged, all deeply engrossed in conversation. He nodded to several other soldiers on their way home. 'Nothing has changed,' he said to himself. He managed a wry smile. 'I don't suppose it ever will,' he thought.

Soon his bag was in the tonga the porter had commandeered, after pushing everyone else out of the way. He salaamed to Lindsay several times, and Lindsay put several rupees in his outstretched grubby palm. He settled back after giving the tonga wallah his directions.

The familiar cries of the beggars rang in his ears:

"Baksheesh, sahib! Baksheesh, sahib!"

The colourful garb of the people was a delight to his tired eyes after the drabness of the desert.

'Yes,' he thought. 'I am home among the people I know and love so well.'

He stood up several times as familiar sights came into view, such as the university he had promised he would return to ('Now I feel too old,' he thought) and the residence of Mrs Keir and her son. He smiled as he recalled the night they took the roof off her portico. 'I wonder if she has had it fixed yet, and if she ever found out who the culprits were,' he thought. 'That was so long ago, so long ago.' He sighed.

A lump came into his throat as the sight of his home amongst the trees came into view. He dismounted as the tonga wallah placed his bag against the closed wrought-iron gates.

"Thank you, sahib," he said as he accepted the huge fare. "Salaam, sahib."

Lindsay tried to turn the handle of the gate, but it was locked. Then the full realisation that there was no one at home hit him forcibly. A feeling of anger assailed him.

"The damn war! It has robbed me of the time I should have spent with my father. I am sick and weary!" he exclaimed.

He tried the handle again to no avail, then gave the gate a vicious kick. The gold-painted monogram on top rattled. He peered through but could see nothing.

Suddenly, a small chokra boy who had been sleeping under the big banyan tree sprang up in alarm, as though he had been shot. He rushed to the gate and peered at Lindsay in alarm.

"Get the mali and open the gate," Lindsay demanded.

"Yes, sahib. Yes, sahib."

The boy scampered away, but the mali, who had heard the rattle of the gate, put a stop to the boy's flight.

He peered through, unlocked the gate and cried, "Sahib, sahib!" There was a look of relief and disbelief on his face. "Lindsay Sahib!" He sent the boy to the house. "Hurry! Tell Damodar, Lindsay Sahib home."

The servants' children, when they saw who had arrived, came running with garlands of flowers. Lindsay laughed gaily and knelt down so that they could put them round his neck. He went slowly up the long driveway, viewing all before him; the children were dancing and laughing as they escorted him.

"The gardens are lovely, mali. Everything is as my parents would have wished."

The mali grinned with pleasure. "Of course, sahib," he said.

Damodar had delayed long enough to change into his best snow-white garments with the silver Scottish thistle emblem of his master in his turban and his tartan cummerbund fastened smartly round his waist. He came running out to greet Lindsay. "Sahib, sahib, Lindsay Sahib!" He almost fell at Lindsay's feet in his delight at seeing him again.

"All right, Damodar, I am home now."

They reached the door at the top of the steps.

"Where is the key, Damodar?" asked Lindsay.

"Here, sahib." Damodar commenced opening the door.

"No, Damodar, give me the key," said Lindsay. He looked at it lovingly. "Oh, how I have longed for this day – the day I would hold the key to home once again."

Damodar looked at him, puzzled. He stood pondering. "It is the right key, sahib."

"Yes, Damodar; I know it only too well."

He turned it slowly as if to relish the precious moment longer before entering. He flung his kitbag in the corner of the verandah and his cap on the hatstand.

Damodar quickly uncovered the seat his father had always sat in, and Lindsay sank wearily into it. He glanced around. Everything else was covered with white dust sheets. The house seemed to be haunted by ghosts from the past.

"Well, at last I am home, but what is a home with no one here?" He sighed. A deep depression assailed him. He rose to his feet and walked slowly into the adjoining rooms. Damodar wanted to follow him, but Lindsay said, "I want to be alone. Make a fire in the study. Everywhere smells damp."

"Shall I make tea, sahib?"

"No, not yet."

He closed the door and leaned against it. Then he took the garlands off his neck and laid them gently on the bed. A feeling of sadness and loneliness brought him almost to tears. He walked over to the tall dresser and picked up the picture of his family. He gazed at it for several minutes before laying it down. "Everything is the same as it was the last night I was here," he said with a sigh.

He went into the nursery and stood rocking the rocking horse to and fro, running his fingers through its mane. He imagined he could hear Heather's gay laughter when he rocked it faster. He picked up her favourite doll from the chair and buried his face in its blonde curls. All his grief at her death returned. He wiped away a tear. He sighed heavily as he idly glanced through one of her picture books.

"All I have been through is nothing – nothing compared to this emptiness everywhere," he said. "I have survived the war for nothing."

As soon as he had closed the door, Damodar sent Munilal post haste for Margot.

She heard the crash of Munilal's cycle as it hit the ground outside her verandah.

"Whatever is happening, Bearer?" she called in alarm, but Munilal did not give her bearer time to explain. He hastened up the steps to her side.

"Memsahib, memsahib, Lindsay Sahib come," he said.

"Thank you. You return," said Martin, who had looked up from reading his paper. "Bearer, bring a tonga quickly."

"Yes, sahib," the bearer replied before he hastened away.

Margot rose unsteadily to her feet; the colour had drained from her face. "That poor boy! He has come home and there is no one to greet him. I must go at once."

"Shall I come with you, dear?"

"No, my dear. It's best I see him alone. Come for me later."

Damodar greeted her as she alighted from the tonga.

"Where is Lindsay now?" she asked.

"He is wandering through all the rooms, memsahib."

"Very well, I will find him."

She stood hidden by a tall plant as she saw him wend his way into his father's study. He opened the writing desk and spotted a letter lying on the blotter. He picked it up, a puzzled look on his face, not recognising the frail, scribbly writing.

He murmured, "Damodar, when did this letter arrive?"

Damodar looked up from the fire he was lighting and looked at Lindsay sadly.

"It came the day the burra sahib died, sahib," he said.

Lindsay slit it open and read, almost disbelievingly; then he started to laugh hysterically. Fury built up inside him.

Damodar looked up at him, then glanced at Margot, who now stood at the door.

She put her finger to her lips, bidding him be silent.

"Leave me, Damodar," Lindsay said.

He went over to the fireplace as a strange chill had come over him. He had picked up his grandfather's photo from the writing desk, and now he placed it in front of him on the mantelpiece and shouted at it. "You! You! You were the cause of so much of my father's misery throughout his life. You! You want him to come home. Well, you are too damned late. Too damned late, just as I am! You bitter, hateful old man! I hate you. I shall hate you till I die." He flung the photo crashing into the fire and rested his head on his arms. "Yes, old man, you deserve to burn for all the anguish you have caused in our lives."

He watched till the last corner of the photograph was consumed and the silver frame had turned black. He kicked it further into the flames and heard it snap in two. He raised his head and saw, through the large mirror, Margot framed in the doorway.

She bade Damodar make tea and went over to Lindsay. He wept uncontrollably on her shoulder as she greeted him.

"You cry, my son, she said. "You will feel a little better for it."

He picked up the photo of his parents and Heather. Heather was sitting on her father's knee, laughing.

"All three are gone, Margot," he whispered as he dried his eyes. "What am I going to do without my dear father, Margot? Why had I to be so far away in another land when he needed me so much? What was I doing there, Margot? I need him so much."

A look of sadness and despair was her only answer.

"Come and sit down, dear boy," she said. "Damodar has brought tea – and here comes Martin, just in time," she said with an assumed gaiety in her voice.

Lindsay stood up to greet him. Martin gripped his hand tightly and hugged him in a warm embrace.

"Home at last, my son!" said Martin. "Are you well?"

"Yes, quite well. And you?"

"Yes, better now the war is over – even more so now that you are home."

"I am glad you are here, Martin. I will read you the letter Grandfather sent."

"Are you sure you feel up to it now, Lindsay?" asked Margot.

"Yes, Margot, I feel a little better now, thank you. He begins, *My dear son, please come home. Come back to me and your heritage. I am getting old and I do not wish to go to my grave without your forgiveness.* Note, Margot, he doesn't say, 'Come home, my son; I forgive you.' He is selfish to the last. My father must forgive him."

Lindsay stood up as he read the letter. Martin looked at Margot, not knowing whether or not to make any comment, but she shook her head so he decided to remain silent.

Lindsay finished his reading of the letter, and he addressed Margot and Martin: "You know, my father went to his grave without his forgiveness, so my grandfather can also die unforgiven," he said bitterly. "This letter did not reach my father in time; I do not know what his answer would have been. I am going to ignore it. I shall never forgive him."

Margot rose and held Lindsay close. She knew, for all his bitterness and his air of defiance, that he was deeply troubled. "Try, dear boy, not to make any decision tonight," she said. "Come and join us for dinner."

"No, thank you, Margot, not tonight. I need to be alone."

"Well, join us tomorrow," she suggested as they prepared to leave.

"Yes, I will. Thank you. Goodnight," he replied, staring into the fire.

After Martin and Margot had left, he called Damodar.

"Yes, sahib."

"Tell the mali to bring fresh flowers in the morning. I will go to visit the grave."

"Yes, sahib," Damodar replied sadly. "Sahib, shall I tell Cook to prepare dinner?"

"No, I'm not hungry. Bring me whisky, please."

"But, Lindsay Sahib, you must eat," Damodar said gravely.

"Tomorrow, Damodar. Go now and dismiss the other servants. I want to be alone."

"Salaam, sahib."

"Goodnight, Damodar."

Lindsay wended his way to the verandah, where he sat down wearily in his father's favourite chair and gazed out on the starry night. He traced his fingers round the family crest on the glass he was holding.

"Yes, I am really home," he said.

CHAPTER 295

The mali looked up in alarm when he heard the creak of the old, rusty gate – the gate the late burra sahib had used. He watched as the tall figure emerged, closing the gate behind him. He sprang with fright behind a large flowering shrub to watch what was to him a strange apparition. His eyesight was now failing. Was it the great burra sahib? He raised himself a little higher as he watched.

Lindsay stood for a moment, as if to compose himself, before proceeding. He read the inscription on the marble tombstone. For a moment he wondered why his father's name was missing. Yes, he remembered, Margot had said she would leave his father's inscription until he came home.

The mali stood up. "It is Lindsay Sahib returned!" he exclaimed. "Allah be praised!"

He pattered barefoot across the grass towards Lindsay. Lindsay had picked up the large vase, and he was looking for somewhere to put the dead flowers when he saw the mali approaching.

"Fresh water and a clean vase, please," he said.

"Yes, sahib," replied the mali, and he pottered away.

Lindsay knelt down and traced the engraving with his fingers. He let out a deep sigh from the depths of his soul.

"All I had and loved is now so close," he said. His memories of bygone days flooded back. "Dear Papa, how can I face this loneliness without you?"

The mali broke in on his thoughts, handing him the vase full of water.

"Thank you," said Lindsay.

"Welcome home, sahib. Allah's blessing be with you."

Lindsay acknowledged his salaam and the mali departed.

Margot, not finding him at home, knew where he had gone. She stood for several minutes outside the gate, watching him.

'What can I say to him?' she wondered.

The moment she had dreaded had come. She opened the gate. Only the mali heard its age-old creak. For several minutes she stood beside Lindsay. He was silent, as if unaware of her presence. At last he looked at her.

"Thank you for coming, Margot," he said. "I am so glad you were with him at the end. Did he ask for me?"

"Yes, he called your name."

"I should have been with him, Margot. It didn't occur to me that I would never see him again. When I was away I often longed to be home with him again."

"Come, dear boy – it was not to be. It is getting late. Come home with me now." She tugged his arm.

"Yes, thank you, Margot. I don't wish to be alone tonight."

He closed the creaking gate and bade the mali good day.

Day after day, Lindsay wandered aimlessly round the garden. His thoughts were all of yesteryear. This garden had always been full of laughter. In his youth, he had sat with his friends under the colourful bougainvillea tree loaded with bright-red blossoms, but now most of those friends were back in England or lost in the war. Sylvia, he heard, had married and moved away.

Margot and Martin were frequent visitors.

"Have you thought of what you want to do now you are home?" asked Martin one day.

"Well, I have thought about it, but I have no training apart from how to kill people. That will look fine on an application form," he replied sarcastically. "At least I have my health, such as it is. Some poor devils have returned limbless or blind. Others are dead and buried in the desert."

Margot and Martin looked at each other in despair.

"But, my dear boy, you must try to put this bitterness behind you," Margot said.

Every night they sat on the verandah discussing the news of the day and how everyone was coping with the after-effects of the war.

"Tell me, Martin," asked Lindsay: "what is happening here? There seems to be such an air of uncertainty everywhere."

"Yes, there is, my boy," Martin replied. "As you know, India has been promised her independence at the earliest possible date. That statement was made last year, but it is the cause of uncertainty everywhere. The politicians can't settle their differences. The Muslims and Sikhs want their own states, separate from the Hindus."

"Yes, I recall Papa often talking of independence one day coming to pass. It will certainly be a big upheaval when it comes."

"It will. All we can do is wait for it to happen," said Margot.

"Will you and Martin be returning to Scotland then?" asked Lindsay, trying not to show his concern.

"Most probably, but first we have two more years of our mission work. We will wait till then before we decide," Margot said, hoping to allay his apprehension.

"It will be a big wrench for lots of people who have known no other country but this," he said with a sigh.

"When you are rested, dear boy, you will have to think of your future. Your father would have wished it so."

"Yes, Margot, you are so right. Tell me, Martin: is Mr Powell, who took care of Papa's affairs, still in business?"

"Yes, he also looks after our affairs."

"When next you visit him, would you ask him to come and see me? Then we can go over all Papa's papers. Maybe he can find some suitable work for me."

"Before you decide on any work," Margot suggested, "why not come to the hills with us?"

"I would love to, thank you, Margot, as soon as I have spoken to Mr Powell."

After the years he had spent swallowing the desert dust, Lindsay found the fresh air and greenness of the plantation exhilarating. He met up with several old friends, who had come back from the war and were trying to pick up the threads of their lives. The social whirl was in full swing, but Lindsay turned down every invitation. He preferred to be alone.

Margot worried about him constantly. "He is so like his father, preferring to be alone," she said one day. "How I wish he would give the slightest encouragement to the girls here! They are all swooning at his feet. He's the most eligible bachelor here, and so handsome, but he is too absorbed in the plantation." She sighed.

"Well, that's as maybe," said Martin. "He told me the other day he wanted to return to the city. He says he wants to see if Mr Powell has any news for him."

"But I know", said Margot, "that he wants to get back home to be near his loved ones, just as his father did."

"Yes, I think you are right, my dear."

Lindsay was loath to leave the peace of the plantation and the green hills, but he felt drawn back to the city. He made a promise to his friends resident there that he would return the following year.

On his return to the city, he was delighted to find several letters awaiting him. He could hardly contain his excitement that at last a letter had come from Roddy. His grandparents, Roddy himself and Christina were quite well, but Ruardy had been invalided out of the army after losing an eye in a skirmish. He had married Shona, the girl he had left behind, and they now had a son, Ian Lindsay, aged two years old.

"How nice of Ruardy to think of me!" Lindsay exclaimed. "It's a pity I shall never have the joy of meeting my namesake."

The letter continued:

All were delighted, as was Emma, that you met her son, Nicholas, whilst you were serving in the Middle East. You will also be pleased to know he has returned home practically unscathed. Lucky fellow indeed, to come out of that campaign all in one piece!

All send their love.

Write soon,

Roddy

"How close I feel to them all now!" Lindsay said with a sigh as he sat down to read the letter from Elena.

It was as he expected: his grandfather was pleading for his return to claim his heritage as his heir – a heritage his father had been denied. Elena pleaded that his grandfather was now old and infirm and his eyesight was failing. She said he would dearly love to make up for all the unhappiness he had caused them all.

Lindsay decided to reply at once. He went to his father's study, contemplating how to begin.

> Dear Aunt Elena,
>   I have just returned from the hills with Margot and Martin, hence my delay in replying to your very welcome letter. As to my grandfather's request, he will never be able to make up to me for all the unhappiness he caused Mama and Papa, also myself: the lifelong distress of my father, who never again saw his homeland, and the anguish of my dear mother, who was made to feel she was the cause of it.
>   My dear mother was more than worthy of being a McNair and the next Mistress of Glencree. If my grandfather had accepted this, he would have had all his family by his side now that he is old and sick.
>   Dearest Aunt, much as I would love to see *you* again, I will never come to Scotland.
>   I have received a letter from Roddy. If you see them, please tell them I will write soon. Also, give my best wishes to Emma's son, Nicholas.
>   Always,
>   Your loving Lindsay

Lindsay accepted a position in the office with Mr Powell, but he found it irksome and depressing. He wanted something more active and demanding.

He confided in Martin: "I have considered going to stay in the hills permanently, but I would be too far away from my loved ones and the only home I have known."

"I understand, my boy," Martin replied. "I will keep a lookout for something more worthwhile. I realise you have no qualifications, as you enlisted before finishing your degrees."

"Yes, that is why Papa was so angry. I realise it all now it's too late."

CHAPTER 296

The winter of 1946/7 dragged on. Invitations to parties and balls for Hogmanay and Burns Night continued to fall on Lindsay's desk, but he politely refused them all, unless Margot made a special plea. However, she had to admit that they were not the gay events of yesteryear. Fewer and fewer of their old friends remained as the exodus for England, or another country, continued.

India's independence was assured. The question was not if it would be announced, but when. It became more and more imperative that decisions regarding the future be taken seriously: 1947 was to be the decisive year.

Margot and Martin sat for long hours on their verandah contemplating.

"But how can we go home and leave Lindsay?" Margot said as they sat discussing their decision. "It is certainly a dilemma for us, Martin; he is so adamant about not going to Scotland."

"Well, I don't know what we can do," Martin replied.

"Now that the situation is changing so dramatically here, maybe if I keep writing to Elena, telling her to keep imploring him to leave for Scotland, in time he will decide to come with us."

"Well, it might work, dear," Martin replied.

Debate after debate was held, regarding the future of India, but no satisfactory solution was reached. The partition of the country was inevitable. India was split into two states: India for the Hindus and Pakistan for the Muslims.

In 1947, Lindsay's visit to the hills was marred by civil unrest. Owing to partition, hundreds of refugees were moving. Hindus living in Pakistan travelled to India; Muslims living in India were on the move to Pakistan. Severe fighting broke out between the rival factions.

On 15 August 1947, India and Pakistan were freed from colonial rule.

"Thank goodness we are in the hills!" exclaimed Margot, as she sat with Martin, Lindsay and several friends after dinner that night. "There will be crowds of people celebrating in the towns."

"Well, it is what they have wanted for so long," said Martin. "Now they have got it. Much as I have loved living in India, I now look forward to the day I return home. By then, all our work here will have been handed over."

"Certainly more people will go than stay," replied Margot. She looked at Lindsay, who, she thought, for once was giving the matter some thought.

"When do you think you will be leaving, Margot?" asked her friend, Clara. "We ourselves will definitely be gone by Christmas."

"Possibly next year," said Margot. "We will see how the mission situation is." She continued to look at Lindsay as she spoke. He had a disconcertingly sad look on his face.

"And you, dear boy," Clara said, addressing Lindsay, "when are you thinking of leaving?"

"I am not leaving," he replied emphatically. "This is the only country I know. Having been born here, I intend to stay. Now, if you will excuse me, I do not wish to discuss my intentions further. I will bid you all goodnight."

"My, my!" exclaimed Clara. "The young man is very cut up about my remark. Many of us were born here, but there is this pressure in the country for us to quit India. Why is he turning a deaf ear to it all? We are only too glad to be turning our backs on it, aren't we, dear?" she said, addressing her husband.

"Yes, my dear, we are. Now, dear friends, we must bid you goodnight on this so momentous day."

"Before you go," said Martin, "let us drink a toast and wish both countries well."

"Agreed, agreed!" They clinked their glasses together. "India and Pakistan!"

Lindsay sat for a long time on the verandah staring into the moonlit night. His mind was in a whirl. He thought of Margot and Martin returning to Scotland for good, and the unrest in the country he loved – all these people killing one another. Yes, he had heard the cries of "Quit India" too, but he never thought the slogan applied to himself. Now he realised it did. He knew they could all stay if they wished, but life for them could never be the same after independence. He put his hand to his head in anguish.

'I cannot think about it any more tonight,' he said to himself. 'I will think about it tomorrow.'

On their return to the city, they found everywhere strangely quiet. Most of their friends had gone or were in the process of packing all their household goods. Already, some empty houses had been taken over and Indian families had moved in. There was also constant movements of troops leaving the barracks.

"We will have no one to protect us," said Margot with deep apprehension. "Some British people have been attacked," she whispered to Martin, "so I have heard."

"Well, we won't be attacked," he said, trying to allay her now constant fear.

"Well, Martin, we will have to make some plans about returning home."

"Yes, dear, as soon as I make arrangements regarding the handover of our missions."

"All our life's work to end like this! I am going to miss it all so much." She sighed.

"Well, I am sure the new missionaries will carry on splendidly," said Martin.

"Yes, that will be a great consolation." She sighed again.

"My dear, have you any idea what Lindsay is going to do?"

"No, he is moody and silent. I don't think he knows what to do. I have written again to Elena, asking her to try to persuade him to return with us," Margot said.

"Well, my dear, we can do no more," replied Martin.

One day Lindsay decided to go to the bazaar. He asked Damodar to order a tonga, but Damodar looked at him askance.

"Sahib, sahib, do not go to bazaar, sahib," Damodar replied. "Lots of men make trouble for you, sahib." He looked at Lindsay pleadingly, shaking his head.

"But, Damodar, I have gone to the bazaar ever since I was a child. No harm will come to me."

As Lindsay drove away, Damodar watched him with a worried look on his face.

"Where to, sahib?" asked the tonga wallah.

"The bazaar."

"But, sahib, many men fighting in bazaar."

"Yes, so I hear. Muslim fighting Hindu; Hindu fighting Muslim. It has been going on a long time and will continue. They won't attack me."

He felt the nervousness of the driver as they drove further and further into the bazaar. Then he saw the slogan scrawled in large white letters across the walls: 'Quit India British'. People began to gather in groups, pointing towards the tonga. He saw the look of fear in the tonga wallah's eyes and the panic in his voice as he turned to him.

"Sahib, no go further, sahib," he said.

The now hostile crowd started to move forward, and they began to chant as they surged towards him: "Quit India! Quit India!"

"Turn back, boy," Lindsay yelled, realising the life of the driver was at risk.

As they turned, the tonga almost tipped on its side in their haste. The crowd rushed them, battering the tonga sides till it almost reeled over. The horse's nostrils quivered with fear as it raced away.

"My, that was close!"

"Yes, sahib. You no go again, sahib."

They were almost home before the tonga slowed to a more leisurely pace. The incident had confirmed what everyone had been saying for months; it brought home to Lindsay the reason everyone was packing up.

The tonga wallah thanked him profusely for his very generous tip.

Lindsay alighted quickly, glad to be home. Damodar was anxiously awaiting him.

"I should have heeded your warning, Damodar," Lindsay said. "I shall not go again."

He sat down, weary and sad, hardly able to believe what had occurred.

"Tea, sahib?"

"Thank you. You always have the right cure," said Lindsay.

He related the incident to Margot later that day.

"I certainly don't want another encounter like that," he said. "I wasn't afraid, but it was such a shock to me to see that the people I have loved all my life now think of me as their enemy."

"Well, my dear boy, it will be like that for some time to come."

"Yes, I suppose so, Margot. I am glad they have got their independence at last – but to think of us as their enemy! Really, Margot, I cannot grasp the fact."

"Well, neither can we, dear. It will take time before the hostility dies down."

"I must go now, Margot. Goodnight," said Lindsay.

"Maybe", said Margot to Martin later that day, "Lindsay might consider coming home with us after such a scare. He will never adjust to the changes that are coming. However, we mustn't rush him in any way. The decision to come to Scotland must be his and his alone. We have all our loving family waiting to greet us. I am sure Elena will greet him with open arms, as will Martha and Magnus and Roddy and his family, but as for Bruce's welcome . . . Well, that remains to be seen."

"Let us hope, dear, he will eventually change his mind," Martin replied.

A letter arrived from Roddy later that week, asking Lindsay to consider coming to Scotland in the light of the news he had read of the unrest in India.

> Things will never be the same ever again [he wrote]. The way of life that we knew has gone for ever. Mama and Papa have sat night after night, discussing the probability of you coming to see them. It is as your dear mother would wish, they feel sure.

"These dear, dear people!" Lindsay exclaimed. "As they say, it would have been my mother's wish for me to visit them. I should consider them also. They are not young now."

He pondered long on the letter that night as he sat staring into space. He spent a restless, sleepless night, and, when morning came, he still did not know what to do.

A letter arrived from Elena, and there was also one from his grandfather, asking him once more to come home. He looked again and again at his grandfather's almost indecipherable scrawl, which seemed imbued with the pathos of his longing for Lindsay's homecoming. In Aunt Elena's letter she urged him to try to forgive his grandfather before his demise.

'Well,' he thought, 'maybe I should put all this bitterness behind me. I will go to Margot. I think she will agree.' As he sat pondering, he suddenly felt a tranquillity he had not felt before.

Margot was looking down the garden as she sat on the verandah. She watched as Lindsay came up the path with a jaunty stride. The letter was in his hand.

"Margot, Margot," he exclaimed breathlessly, "another letter has arrived from Aunt Elena and my grandfather! I have decided to go with you when you return."

"Well, sit down, my dear boy, and tell me all about it. Boy, bring us tea, please."

She listened attentively to all Lindsay had to say as she sipped her tea slowly. 'Thanks be to God! My prayers have been answered,' she thought with a sigh.

"I am going to reply right away," said Lindsay.

"Yes, do, Lindsay," Margot replied.

'The sooner that letter is on its way, the happier I shall be,' she thought. 'It solves all our problems.'

"But, Margot, I should really first go to the hills and arrange the sale of my plantation," Lindsay continued.

"No, no, Lindsay, please leave it all to Mr Powell. It is not safe to travel on the trains at present. The mood of the people is so uncertain, as you saw in the bazaar. There have been massacres on the trains. Mr Powell is already in the hills, and he told Martin the other day that he intends to stay there until things are more settled."

"Very well, I will get a letter to him right away."

"What else does Elena say in her letter?" Margot asked as she noticed Lindsay looking at the letter with concern.

"She says, 'Your grandfather knows you are not married, but he is sure you will soon find an eligible lady very soon after your arrival'." Lindsay looked pensively at Margot.

She looked at him with a smile before replying. 'That's Bruce all over,' she thought: 'already thinking of the birth of a son to carry on his lineage. However, the fact that he has written shows that he now realises the folly of his ways; he must be aware of how much he has thrown away in his lifetime.'

"Well, my dear boy," she said, "you and you alone must decide on whom you will marry and when. Don't heed your grandfather on that matter."

"No, Margot, I certainly won't. Margot," he said, after further deep thought, "I shall go only if I can take my mother and father and Heather with me. As you know, Papa always wanted to be buried in the family vault."

"Of course, of course," she replied. She looked at him sadly as she pondered. "I am not certain of the procedure involved, but I'm sure Martin will help to arrange everything."

"I shall charter special transport and travel with them," Lindsay said.

"Yes," she replied, "we can go on ahead and make all the arrangements for when you arrive."

"Am I doing the right thing, Margot?"

"Yes, my boy. Now, in the meantime, write to Elena and your grandfather – and don't forget your other grandparents."

"No, I will write to them later. Now I must go. I will see you again soon.

Goodnight, Margot. I really don't know what I should do without you."

She sat a long time after he left. At last, all that she had hoped and prayed for was being realised.

Lindsay lay awake most of the night after he had posted the letter home. 'This is my home, the only one I have known,' he thought. 'What do I know of that land across the sea which drew my parents so, and which it broke their hearts to leave. Soon I shall see it all for myself: the lovely mountains and glens. I shall smell and see the bonnie purple heather, after which my darling little sister was named to remind Papa over and over again of what he craved: to see his home by the loch. Soon I shall see the magnificent castle on the hill. It was rightfully part of my father's heritage, but he was so cruelly banished. Now, the heritage shall be restored to me, to pass on to my sons and heirs. One day I shall become the Earl of Glencree and Chief of the Clan and I shall devote my life to the service and protection of the people of Glencree.'

His father had never ceased to tell him the name he bore was his by right. "You must carry it with pride, my son," he said.

"I couldn't."

"But you must. I know your grandfather will send for you one day."

'Well,' thought Lindsay, 'now he has sent for me and I am going home to claim my heritage. I wonder what he is like. I shall try not to be too apprehensive. Aunt Elena will be there, and I know she will support me. Once I get there, there will be no turning back. Tomorrow I must write to my grandparents by the loch. These I know I shall be much happier with.'

CHAPTER 297

Every day, Elena became more and more despondent. She watched Jamie sorting the letters after Lawrie had been, but he always shook his head when he saw her peering over the bannister on her way downstairs.

Then, one bright sunny morning, Jamie called excitedly, "Lady Elena, Master Lindsay's letter has come."

She almost stumbled down the last few steps in her haste.

"Give it to me, Jamie." She glanced at it in disbelief. "It's addressed to his grandfather, Jamie. The Good Lord be praised!

"Bruce, Bruce," she cried as she rushed into the lounge.

"Elena, Elena, don't startle me so. What is it?"

"Lindsay's letter has come. Do open it quickly."

"No, you open it. You know how I fumble. Read it for me."

She sat down opposite him, her hands trembling as she tore it open. She began to read it to herself, and she exclaimed, "Bruce dear, he is coming home! Our boy is coming home at last."

"Are you sure you have read it aright?" Bruce was now trembling with anticipation. "When? When, Elena?"

"He cannot give us a date as yet. He will write again nearer the time."

She read on silently to herself.

"Well, what else does my grandson say?" Bruce demanded impatiently.

"He says—" She hesitated and looked up at him.

"Well?" he demanded.

"He says he wishes to bring his mother and father and sister to take their rightful places in the family vault, but if this request is refused, he will not return."

For a few moments Bruce sat in deep contemplation. Elena watched him intently. 'I pray to God he will acquiesce,' she thought.

Today there was no sudden raging thump on the table.

"Of course he must bring them," Bruce said at last. "Isn't it all I have wished for all these years, Elena – for my son to come home? If only I had told him so, Elena – if only! Why didn't I tell him so, Elena?" he said sadly as he gazed over the loch.

"Because of your stupid pride, Bruce. That is all that kept you apart."

"Yes, that is all."

He sank back in his chair, unable to speak as the tears rolled down his cheeks.

"Margot and Martin are coming with him."

"So, Margot is coming also?" he whispered, remembering the angry words they had exchanged so long ago. He sighed. "Is that all, Elena?" he asked.

"Yes, I will write to him today, telling him all will be ready for his arrival."

"Very well. Now leave me."

She hastened towards the door. "I must tell the rest of the household," she said.

She closed the door softly behind her.

Jamie, hovering in the hall, was beside himself with joy. "Our boy is coming home at last," he said, with tears of joy running down his cheeks.

"Well," said Cook, "I shall make him all the dishes his father loved. It will be just like having Master Craig with us again."

"Yes," said Elena, "we must all be ready for his arrival."

"When will that be, milady?" asked Jamie.

"I am not sure. Lindsay has several business matters to finalise first, but I will let you know in good time."

She hastened to her room and gazed out over the loch. 'He will have written to Martha also,' she thought. 'What a wonderful homecoming it will be for him! He will be as welcome as when our dear Craig came back from the war!'

"Mama, Mama," said Roddy excitedly, as he recognised the letter from Lindsay. "It's a letter from your grandson, Lindsay."

"Open it and read it to me. My eyes aren't as good as they used to be."

"It is only a very short letter, Mama." He sat down, unfolded it and began to read.

"What does it say, my son?" Martha asked, wondering, owing to his silence, if it might be bad news.

"He is coming home. His grandfather at Glencree Castle has sent for him, and Lindsay has written to say he will be coming. He is bringing Craig and . . . " His voice faltered.

"What is it, my son?" Martha said, looking at him, alarmed.

"He is also bringing our darling Elizabeth and Heather, if the laird agrees to inter them in the family vault. He has got to agree," said Roddy adamantly.

"Well, we will have to wait and see," said Martha, sighing.

The following day, Lady Elena's carriage drew up outside Martha's cottage, just as Magnus, Roddy, Ruardy and Christina were clambering out of the boat on their return from the village. Roddy hastened to help Lady Elena alight.

"Come – Mama is inside," he said.

Martha dropped Elena a little curtsy and bade her sit down.

"Martha," she said as she patted her hand affectionately, "have you heard the good news from Lindsay?"

"Yes, it is good news, to be sure. Tell me, Lady Elena: has the laird agreed that Lindsay can bring home our dear daughter and little granddaughter?"

"Yes, Martha, they are all coming home."

"Thanks be to God!" said Roddy as he hugged his father, who, since the news, had been overwhelmed almost to speechlessness.

"It's true, Papa. Our Elizabeth, your dawn angel, is coming home to us."

Christina knelt at Martha's feet and wiped the tears from the old lady's eyes. "Don't cry, Mama dear," she said. "Elizabeth and Heather will be home where they belong."

Martha looked at Elena. "Lady Elena," she said, "please forgive me. My tears are tears of happiness as well as sorrow."

"There is nothing to forgive, Martha," Elena replied. "I, like you, wished so long for things to be different, but it was not to be."

"Will you take tea with us?" said Christina as she rose to her feet.

"I will gladly. Then I must get home."

"It is a long way round the loch, Lady Elena. Shall I dismiss Zan? I will row you home."

"Yes, do, Roddy, please," Elena said gratefully.

Elena now spent her days singing and laughing, as did all the household. In the evenings, she and Bruce sat in the lounge in front of the fire. He often looked up at Isabelle's picture and smiled. Now and again he nodded his head as if he was talking to her. Elena had not seen him smile since Craig had left home. Sometimes she sat at the piano and played Bruce's favourite Scottish melodies while he tapped along with them on the arm of his chair.

"There are none so fine as our Scottish tunes, Elena," he said happily.

She looked up and smiled at him, nodding her head in reply. Jamie stopped to listen outside the door before ambling in with his basket of logs.

"Elena?" said Bruce.

"Yes, dear?"

"I have chosen a piper for Lindsay."

"How wonderful! Who's the chosen piper?"

"It's the son of Craig's piper."

"Young Fergus? How time flies! He was such a wee boy when I saw him last."

"Well, he is a bonnie lad now and not so wee. His father brought him round one day when he knew Lindsay was coming home. It was one day when you had gone to the village. We must have a grand ball, as we did before; and next summer we'll have the largest Highland gathering ever."

"Yes, dear," Elena said, nodding, as she played on. "I will get it all arranged in time, Bruce," she said.

"Then, of course," Bruce continued, "there will be his marriage to be arranged.

654

Elena, you must invite all the eligible young ladies of noble birth to visit here. I shall expect a son to be born as soon as possible so that I can be sure the family name will continue. I shall then be the happiest man alive." He leaned back in the chair and closed his eyes, confident that all he was contemplating would come to pass.

Elena closed the piano lid and glanced towards him with a look of exasperation. Already he was making his own plans for the boy. Her fury mounted.

"But, Bruce dear," she said, "we mustn't rush the poor boy. It will take him some time to settle. Everything will be so strange to him. He has to learn to manage the estate and get to know the crofters. He will, I think, wish to do the course on forestry management that his cousin, Ruardy, is doing."

For a moment there was a stifled silence; then suddenly Bruce sat bolt upright and turned to glare at her.

"His cousin who?" he said.

"Ruardy – he's Magnus's grandson, as is Lindsay."

"He is my grandson and he belongs to me," Bruce bellowed as he thumped the arm of the chair in anger. "I will not have him anywhere near that family. Haven't they caused me enough trouble? No, he will be staying here with me. I shall expect you, Elena, to see that he has nothing to do with them."

"I shall do no such thing," Elena replied angrily.

She hastily put the sheets of music away and slammed the lid of the stool. She hastened to the door.

"Goodnight, Bruce," she said. "I will tell Jamie you are ready to retire."

Every time Elena went to the village shopping, or to change Bruce's library books, which she read to him every night, the villagers asked her when Lindsay would arrive. All were eagerly waiting to greet him.

"Soon, soon," she would call to them. "I will let you all know in plenty of time."

"We have so many things planned for his welcome," said Mrs Munro from the general store.

"Is Lady Elena not coming to the Ladies' Sewing Circle today, Emma?" asked Mrs Crawford as she sat down.

"No, she is away in Glasgow visiting the office of the ex-servicemen's charity."

"I wonder when Lindsay McNair will be arriving?" she said, looking at Emma. She continued: "I am so looking forward to his arrival."

"As we all are! I just know he will be as handsome as his dear father," sighed Mrs Dunbar.

"Of course he will," retorted Mrs Crawford. She, as always, was determined to make her voice heard above the rest. "He will most certainly have inherited his father's and grandfather's proud bearing and high breeding," Mrs Crawford continued. She tut-tutted. "But, of course, we have to remember his father did marry beneath him," she said disdainfully.

The rest of the ladies kept their eyes firmly fixed on their sewing, but a few of them signalled their agreement with a tut-tut or a shake of the head.

"His mother was a most gracious lady," said Mrs Carr. "Don't you agree, Emma?"

"I most certainly do; and you, Mrs Crawford, have no right to make such a reference to his mother," she retorted.

Everyone could see Emma's temper rising. Mrs Crawford pretended not to hear her remark.

"Well, we shall have to wait and see," she said.

Her three precious jewels had missed out on marrying Craig, but, ever since she heard the news of Lindsay's coming, she had been planning to make sure her granddaughters would be the first damsels he would encounter when he arrived. She was determined to make sure his interest in them would never waver, if it was the last thing she did.

A few weeks later, Merry-Berry was sitting outside her small caravan. That morning she had gathered some herbs, and now she added them to the infusion she was brewing in a large cauldron which swung to and fro over her blazing log fire. She stopped and listened intently as the sound of the woodsmen's felling came closer. Gathering her shawl round her shoulders, and picking up her stick for support, she struggled to her feet. She was almost bent double with age, but her mind and hearing were still as acute as ever. She was attuned to all the wild creatures of the woods and countryside. Her wizened brown face showed more and more consternation as she listened.

"Why so close?" she muttered.

She wended her way up the narrow shrub-lined path. She drew nearer to the woodsmen and watched in dismay. Suddenly she darted out to confront them.

"Not that tree!" she shouted at them in Gaelic. "Not that tree!"

The men looked up, startled, and stopped their felling.

"It's the old witch of the woods," said one.

They understood what she was saying, but not the reason for her concern.

"Why not this tree, old woman?"

"Fell it not! Fell it not!" she cried. "Go search for another. Ill luck will befall. You'll see. It is the mistletoe-bearing tree."

But it was too late. The tree was almost sawn through. They looked at her in consternation.

"Ill luck will befall. You'll see, you'll see!" She shook her stick at them as she shouted the words.

They, being true men of the glens, lived in fear of gipsy warnings and curses – especially Merry-Berry's. Very few had seen her, but they all knew of her and set store by her words, which had always come true.

The men looked at one another. If she said ill luck would befall, then surely it would, but who would be the one to suffer?

"I hope it's not any of us," they muttered amongst themselves.

They hastily grabbed their saws and fled, as her curses rained down on them.

She looked down at the fallen tree in despair. Tears flowed down her sad face, and she uttered a gipsy prayer.

CHAPTER 298

Margot and Martin sat taking tea on the verandah, enjoying a brief respite from packing. "I shall be glad when we finally leave," she said. She sighed wearily as she leaned back, eyes closed.

"Well, dear, everything is almost finished now," Martin assured her. "The boy is painting the address on the last trunk." As he spoke, he glanced at the boy. "Make sure, boy, you spell the address correctly," he said.

"Yes, sahib. All correct, sahib," the boy replied after he had leaned back to look again at the instructions by his side.

"How was Lindsay getting on with his packing when you called, Margot?" Martin asked.

"He was almost finished. He insists on taking so many of his parents' things. Poor boy! It is such a wrench for him. I hope Bruce greets him kindly; otherwise I don't know what the poor boy will do," she said dejectedly. "Elena is so excited. In her letters she says she cannot wait for his arrival, but Bruce is so unpredictable." She sighed.

Martin leaned over and patted her arm reassuringly.

"Bruce will surely have learned his lesson," he said. "I think all will be well. Don't worry so, my dear."

"I am so glad we are leaving the missions in such good hands," Margot replied. "Pastor Gregory and his family have settled in well. I only wish the country could have been partitioned without all this bloodshed." She sighed as she glanced at the boy, who was now finishing the last word on the trunk. She continued: "If our parents and grandparents could see it all, what would they think?" Another deep sigh escaped her as she pondered, gazing into space.

"Well, there have always been feuds," said Martin, "and I daresay they will continue long after we have gone." He rose, glancing at the boy, who was now gathering up his brushes and his can of white paint. "Finished, boy?" he said

"Yes, sahib. Is it all right, sahib?" He looked up at Martin, who was viewing his work.

"Yes, boy, very good. Well done!"

He handed him his payment, and the boy's face lit up in a beaming grin when he saw the large amount offered.

"Thank you, sahib. Salaam, sahib. Salaam, memsahib."

"Salaam, boy," Margot replied as she watched him go down the steps.

"Boy," Martin called before he cycled away, "call at Lindsay Sahib's and ask when he will need you."

"Very well, sahib."

Damodar crouched beside Lindsay on the verandah. He was fighting hard to hold back his tears. He listened carefully to Lindsay, who sat tapping his pen against his lips, pondering before ticking off each item.

"Papa's full Highland dress, mother's tartan shawl, Heather's favourite doll . . . "

Damodar carefully packed each item.

"All these I am taking with me, Damodar," Lindsay said. "The other items in the large trunks over there are going by sea, and they must be well on the way before I fly out."

"Yes, sahib," Damodar replied dejectedly. "They will be ready, sahib." He didn't really want to know.

Two days later, Lindsay finally locked the two black trunks. He watched as the village painter wrote, as he instructed, the bold lettering on his mother's old trunk.

The words 'Not Wanted On Voyage' were still faintly discernible.

"Paint over it well, boy," Lindsay told him. "The address is now Glencree Castle, Scotland."

"Yes, sahib. I do it all correct, sahib." He sat back on his heels, viewing his handiwork. "See, Sahib."

"Yes, boy," Lindsay replied as he sat looking at it. "The old trunks are going back where they should have gone years ago." He fumed inwardly. Lindsay looked up at Damodar who was watching him intently. "Take these trunks to the shipping office tomorrow, Damodar. Also pick up Martin Sahib's luggage. Transport is arranged."

"Very well, sahib," Damodar replied sadly.

The next few days dragged heavily. Lindsay wandered wearily from room to room through the now almost empty house. A strange silence pervaded the rooms as the servants, in their bare feet, pattered sadly around, dreading the time of Lindsay's final departure.

Earlier, Lindsay had stood with Margot, Martin and Pastor Gregory in the small tree-shaded cemetery as the coffins were taken away. The mali, watching sadly nearby, followed close behind them as they left through the small gate. He salaamed in farewell as the rusty, creaking gate closed.

"You will rest easy now, my sahib," the mali whispered. "You are going home." He stood several minutes with hands clasped, his fingers touching his forehead. "Salaam, my sahib," he said.

Lindsay, having said farewell to Martin and Margot a few days earlier, was happy in the knowledge that soon he would be meeting them again. However, the day of his own departure was almost more than he could bear. He looked out from the verandah steps after he had finally closed the door. Everyone, it seemed, had come to say farewell. They all lined the garden path, waiting to hang their parting garlands round Lindsay's neck.

"Salaam, sahib," each whispered in turn, many with tears in their eyes.

Lindsay's heart was heavy with the thought that he would never see them again.

Damodar was standing tall and proud, as he always did. The tartan cummerbund was still round his waist, and the thistle monogram on his puggaree. Lindsay felt Damodar trembling with emotion as he clung to his hand and clasped him to him.

"Here are the keys, Damodar," he said. "Give them to Mr Powell when he calls. I have arranged with him for a pension to be paid monthly to you and the other household staff."

"Thank you, sahib," he said, but Lindsay knew Damodar hadn't been listening.

Damodar's small son was standing at his side, clinging to his father's attire. He was looking up at Lindsay appealingly. Tears flowed from his large, dark eyes.

Lindsay bent down so that the child could put his proffered garland round his neck when his father ushered him forward.

"Please take me with you, sahib. Please take me with you," the boy pleaded. "I can count, sahib: one, two, three, four, five, six . . ." He hesitated.

Lindsay smiled at his effort and Damodar tried to hush him.

"I know, sahib," the boy stammered, as he suddenly remembered: "Sebern, sahib."

"Yes, my little Chiko, seven it is." Lindsay's voice was choked with held-back tears. He held the child's hand and looked into his sad eyes. "Your mother couldn't spare such a fine young man," he said.

He handed the boy back to her, ruffling his jet-black hair as he reluctantly released his hand. The numerous garlands were not the only things choking him as he hurried to the gate. He closed it quickly after him.

"Put the bolt across, Damodar," he said.

"Yes, sahib. Salaam, sahib," Damodar replied.

Lindsay climbed into the waiting tonga, with a last glance at his once so happy home. The small chokra boy's hand reached out to him through the gate as he sped away.

CHAPTER 299

At last Lindsay's long journey was almost over. He was delighted to see Margot and Martin and one of the twins waiting at the railway station in London to greet him.

"My, what a journey!" he exclaimed as he hugged them. "Well, I know this beautiful young lady is one of the twins, but I'm blowed if I can tell which one."

"It is Astrid," said Margot proudly as she hugged her close. "Clare is in Scotland with the twins and Davinia and Stephen. They had to hurry there, owing to Aunt Agatha's sudden illness."

"I am so sorry to hear that. I should dearly love to have seen them."

"Well," exclaimed Margot, "when next they come to visit us in Scotland, you must come and stay for a holiday!"

"I most certainly will."

"I must now say goodbye, Grandmama," said Astrid. "I am playing in the concert tonight and must hurry to rehearsal. I am sorry not to be able to wait until you board your train for Scotland, Lindsay." After kissing them both goodbye, she turned back to Lindsay. "I do hope it isn't too long before you visit us," she said.

"I shall look forward to it immensely," Margot replied.

"So shall I, dear Astrid," said Lindsay. "Papa often spoke of you and how well you were doing in your musical career. Mama would have been so proud of you."

He held her close and kissed her on both cheeks. Her salty tears brushed his lips.

She turned quickly away. "I must fly," she said. "Goodbye."

Margot looked after her longingly. 'I don't think she can bear to see the coffins of the ones she loved so much,' she thought.

Lindsay watched sadly as the coffins were placed in a special carriage at the end of the train before he joined Margot and Martin in the reserved compartment next to it.

They travelled together to Scotland. Lindsay sat, hour after hour, gazing at the lovely scenery unfolding before him, wishing he could feel less sad. 'How happy my father would have been in my place!' he thought. 'He would not have this feeling of sadness and loneliness as I do.' Lindsay was filled with misgivings at the thought of what might await him. 'If only Papa were coming home with me, alive and well!' he thought. 'Well, I shall be brave, as Papa would expect me to be.' He sighed.

Margot and Martin watched him, neither breaking in on his thoughts.

At last they were over the Border. Lindsay stood up to get a closer view.

"So at last, Margot, I am in the land of my father!" he exclaimed. "So is my father, Margot," he added sadly.

"Yes, my boy, he is on home soil at last," she replied. "They say nothing is lonelier than a Scottish heart when it is away from this lovely land of its birth."

He lowered the window and leaned out.

"It is a lovely land," he said. "I can understand Papa loving it so."

The mountains came into view.

'They are so low,' he thought.

"These mountains are not as high as the ones we have left, Martin," he remarked.

"No, my boy, but they are just as meaningful and beautiful."

"Everywhere is so green – so many shades of green, Margot," Lindsay said. She nodded her head in agreement.

"Margot, Margot," – he called her excitedly to look out with him – "is that heather over yonder?"

"Yes, my boy. You will see lots more soon." She peered out further. "Over there are some tall bluish pines. See how stately they stand."

"And so many grazing sheep! I have never seen so many. They are scattered so far and wide." Already he was feeling that this really was his home. "Yes, Margot, this is my true homeland," he said. "I know I can be truly happy here."

He sat down, overwhelmed by a feeling of contentment.

Margot sighed happily as she looked across at Martin. She felt happier than she had for years.

Suddenly, the train slowed down. Lindsay looked across at Margot and Martin. They both smiled knowingly. As the train stopped, he heard the call, "Glencree, Glencree," which his father had often told him would be the grandest sound he would ever hear. Yes, as usual, his father had been right. 'If only he could hear it also!' he thought with a sigh.

Suddenly, he could hear people calling his name. Roddy and Ruardy were the first to greet him as he stepped down from the train.

Roddy tugged Magnus's arm. "Papa, here is the grandson you have waited so long to see."

"Yes, my son, I have longed for this day."

He reached out to Lindsay with tears in his eyes.

"I too, Grandpapa," Lindsay replied.

He turned to see Martha approaching, holding on to Christina's arm. He reached out to her and looked into her eyes, which reminded him at once of his mother's. Martha's once golden hair had long ago turned to silver. She hugged him as if she would never let him go. Her tears wet his cheeks.

"I am here to stay, Grandmama. Don't cry any more," Lindsay said. He dabbed her cheeks with his handkerchief. "We are all home now."

She nodded her head, unable to speak.

Ruardy ushered Shona and his son forward. "This is my wife, Shona, and wee son, Ian Lindsay," he said.

Lindsay ruffled the child's hair. "I feel I have known you all your life," he said. "What a fine boy you have, Ruardy!"

"Shona, please take our son back to the cottage and prepare a meal," Ruardy said.

"Yes, that's the wisest thing," said Christina. "I will go also." She did not wish to witness the coffins of the ones she loved so dearly being carried from the train.

"You stay with your grandmother, Lindsay," said Roddy.

Lindsay looked at her sadly. "Do you wish to go also, Grandmama?" he said.

"No, my boy. I must see my daughter safely home," she replied as she dried her eyes.

Suddenly, she remembered Margot and hastened to where they stood. They greeted each other like two loving sisters.

"Thank you, Margot, for bringing our dear daughter and granddaughter home," Martha said.

Margot patted her shoulder. "They are all home now, dear, where they belong," she replied.

"Yes, where they belong," replied Martha.

They clung to each other as they waited.

The villagers, who had come over especially to escort their beloved Craig, stood quietly watching Lindsay's welcome. Soon, Roddy, Magnus, Ruardy and Peggoty unloaded the coffins from the train.

"How I wish, Martha, that I could have brought your lovely daughter home unharmed. Not like this, not like this!" Margot sobbed as they watched Elizabeth's coffin pass by.

Martha felt her trembling.

"It was not to be, my dear friend," said Martha, trying to console her, in spite of her own heartbreak. "You were always so kind to her, and she loved you dearly."

"Yes, Martha, I loved her as my own."

Margot and Martin bade them all goodbye, and they reboarded the train. Lindsay and Roddy assisted Margot to her seat, and Martin sat down beside her.

"I will visit you as soon as I can," said Lindsay.

"Come soon, my boy," she replied.

She made a small circle on the steamed-up windowpane, and she watched the villagers wending their way to the loch side. She sighed heavily and murmured, "They're all back home now. I promised Martha that her lovely daughter would be home again in two years. If it only could have been! If only!"

Martin held her in his arms. "Do not distress yourself so, my dear," he said. "They understand it could not be so."

Lindsay stepped back into the carriage and kissed her tear-filled eyes.

"Do not weep any more," he said. "Thank you for being the dearest of godparents. You have always treated me as if I were your own son."

"You are very dear to us," Margot said as she clung to him.

Lindsay shook Martin by the hand once more and stepped down on to the platform. The train was now ready to pull away.

Margot made a larger circle on the glass, but all she could see as she gazed at Lindsay was the face of his lovely mother. She pictured Elizabeth standing almost where Lindsay was standing, kissing her parents goodbye for the last time. She gazed beyond him as she thought of her old home in the glen.

"Well," she sighed, "at last I have brought back Bruce's heir. I can do no more."

She looked back at the station as the train pulled away, and she gave a gasp of surprise as a tiny, swarthy figure emerged from the shrubs nearby. She leaned forward to get a better view.

"What is it, my dear?" asked Martin, a little alarmed.

"You wouldn't understand, my dear," she replied. "It's just a little old lady, very dear to all of us at Glencree. She has gone now," she said when Martin stood up to peer out.

He sat down, thankful that they were at last on the final lap of their journey. He looked at Margot, who was now leaning back with her eyes closed. There was a tear still on her cheek. 'Poor dear! She has gone through so much,' he thought. 'I shall be glad when we reach Davinia and Stephen; then she can rest and put all this behind her.'

The boats were now ready to sail. All were eager to get away before the mist descended. Lindsay stood beside Martha and watched Magnus preparing the flares. The flag had already been hoisted.

"Come, my boy, you must light the flares," Magnus said. "They will tell your grandfather that your father's body is now being brought over. Lady Elena knows you will be spending the night with us."

"Oh, what a pretty sight, Mama!" said Ian, who was held at the window. "Can I not light one, Mama?"

"No, my son, only Lindsay can light those."

Craig's body had been placed in its own boat, which Magnus was determined to row in spite of Roddy's admonitions.

"Very well, then, Papa," he relented, "but you are not as strong now and it is a heavy boat."

"I am strong enough to row over the laird's son, laddie, so don't worry."

"Well, I will join you. Ruardy and Nicholas can row Elizabeth and Heather over. The rest of the villagers can follow."

Lindsay stood watching with a deep ache in his heart. Sorrow was intermingled with happiness that at last his father was on his way. Martha looked at his sad face and held him close.

"Come, my boy," she said, "they will soon be out of sight."

Bruce and Elena had never left the window overlooking the loch all morning. Jamie went back and forth to the edge of the pier, grumbling as time dragged on.

"Bruce, Bruce," Elena called out excitedly, "the flares, the flares! Our boy is on the loch at last. Did you not see them, Bruce?"

"Barely, dear. I cannot see too well now."

"There are Jamie's in reply," she cried.

"Yes, yes, I can see those." He held her hand in a vice-like grip with his one good hand as tears streamed down his face. "Is my son really coming over the loch, Elena?"

"Yes, dear Bruce, our Craig is almost home." She dabbed her eyes frantically as she tried to stem her tears.

Martha turned Lindsay to face the loch before going inside the cottage. "Look yonder, my boy – there they go! The flares! – an answer from your grandfather."

He stood watching as the shower of sparks fell into the loch.

"Is that always done, Grandmama?" he asked.

"Always, my boy," she replied.

He opened the cottage door and led her inside. He closed the door and stood with his back to it, gazing at the swinging lamp and the blazing fire. Never had he seen such a small abode, but it was so welcoming. Martha turned to look at him. She gave a small gasp.

'My, he looks so like his father did as he stood on that very spot so long ago.' She shuddered as she thought of Craig.

"Come, Mama sit down near the fire. You have stood too long in the chill wind," said Christina.

"Yes, do, Grandmama," Lindsay said with concern as he led her to the fireside chair.

"Yes, I will sit here. You, my boy, must sit in the rocking chair your dear father sat in when he was here."

He did as she bade, and he rocked to and fro as he gazed into the fire. 'This is so warm and homely,' he thought. 'I am sure I shall be happier here than in the big castle on the other side of the loch. Oh, I mustn't think this way. I shall have the best of both worlds. I shall spend most of my time here with these grandparents.' A smile crossed his face. Suddenly another thought struck him: 'Oh no, my grandfather would surely not try to prevent me spending my time here.' Lindsay was filled with apprehension.

He noticed the three women looking at him in consternation. Martha was the first to speak.

"You know, my boy," she said, "your father first saw your mother from that very chair and by the light of this lamp."

"Is that so, Grandmama? I know he always called her his angel. That was his first impression of her, and it was how he always thought of her."

"Yes," said Christina, "she certainly was an angel."

"Come – you must eat, my boy," said Martha.

She rose and went into the kitchen. Before long she placed a bowl of steaming broth in front of him.

"This is Scotch broth, such as your father had when he arrived," she told him.

Lindsay sat at the table, taking in the savoury smell of the broth.

"It smells delightful," he said. "It is making me feel so hungry."

He watched, fascinated, as Christina and Shona placed more food on the table. He looked up at them.

"Thank you all for your welcome," he said. "It is so nice to be home at last."

"Now, Ian," said Shona to her son, who had watched Lindsay with interest throughout the meal, "say goodnight to Lindsay."

"Must I, Mama?" he said with a pout.

"Yes, my son, you have only been allowed up longer than usual tonight to welcome him."

Lindsay ruffled Ian's hair as he clambered down from his chair.

"Goodnight, little fellow," Lindsay said. "I will come soon and help you throw pebbles in the loch."

"Will you? Will you?" Ian exclaimed with glee. "Will you come soon?"

"I will, I promise."

"Ian, do come to bed," said Shona. She was already halfway up the stairs.

"I'm coming, Mama."

He rushed to kiss them all goodnight; then they all watched him fondly as he scampered after her, his tiny feet pattering across the creaking floorboards.

CHAPTER 300

A mist was slowly descending as the three boats drew alongside the jetty. The villagers waited in small huddled groups. Two pipers played a lament, the black ribbons on their pipes and bonnets flicking across their faces. The slight breeze wafted the flag into some sort of welcome.

Elena stood between Becky and her husband. Emma, her husband and her brothers were close by. Jamie, his back ramrod-straight as he tried to keep a stiff upper lip, stood close to a group of clan elders.

"Did Sir Bruce not wish to come, milady?" asked Emma as she looked at Elena sadly.

"No, Emma, he had, as usual, an excuse."

Elena wiped her tears away, and Emma looked at her father sadly.

'He won't welcome home his son even now,' the vicar thought. He bowed his head in despair.

All three coffins were now draped in the mourning tartan of the clan. The pipers continued playing the lament as they wended their way to the castle. Jamie hastened ahead and opened the huge oak doors. The villagers dispersed when they saw the coffins safely home.

Inside, the household staff stood with bowed heads, dropping little curtsies as the procession passed into the library. The curtains of the castle were drawn against the darkening day.

Magnus, Roddy and Ruardy took their leave.

"We will return with Lindsay tomorrow, milady," Magnus said.

They bowed their heads in farewell to Bruce, who stood close by with his arm resting along the mantelpiece.

The clan elders had placed the coffins on three waiting pedestals. The two pipers stood several minutes in silence before taking their leave.

"I will bring Fergus tomorrow when I return, milord," said Rory Ritchie. Bruce nodded his head in reply.

Bruce and Elena stood side by side as the vicar and Becky bade them goodbye.

"We will return tomorrow to greet Lindsay," said the Reverend Corwell. Bruce nodded his farewell.

Becky kissed Elena, whose head was bent in grief.

"Master Craig is home now, my dear friend," Becky said. "He is where he has always longed to be. Today has been a sad day, but tomorrow will be a happy day for us all."

"Yes, it will," Elena replied. "We must all look forward to tomorrow." She dried her eyes.

Jamie closed the door after them, and the castle was left shrouded in its silent grief.

After the others had left, Bruce and Elena sat beside the blazing fire. Bruce's arm rested on Craig's coffin.

"Is my son really home, Elena?" he said.

"Yes, Bruce dear."

"Thanks be to God!" he murmured as he wiped a tear from his eye. He looked up at Isabelle's picture. "See, my darling, our dear son is home." He managed a weak smile, and he thought he could see her smile of acknowledgement.

Jamie's knock broke in on his contemplation.

"Come in, Jamie," Elena called.

"Shall I bring more logs, milady?" he asked tearfully.

"Yes, Jamie, we must keep a good fire going."

Bruce ran his fingers round the engraved plaque on the coffin lid. "Forgive me, my son, forgive me," he said.

Later, Elena touched him lightly, and for once he did not shake her off. She had always been near to comfort him, and she was here now when he needed her most. "Come Bruce," she whispered softly, "you must retire and rest."

"No, Elena, you go and rest. I will stay here with my son."

She knew it would be no good arguing with him. She bent and kissed him goodnight.

"I will stay with the master," said Jamie as he stoked up the fire.

"Thank you, Jamie. Are all the lamps lit? We must be ready for Lindsay's arrival tomorrow."

"Yes, milady."

She wended her way slowly to her room, wiping her tears away repeatedly. "Why had our dear boy to come home like this? Why? Why?" she murmured as she closed the door and went over to the window. In the distance, across the loch, she could discern Martha's cottage outlined in the moonlight. "Welcome home, dear Lindsay – the next Earl of Glencree. Your heritage awaits you."

She drew her curtains, but she knew sleep would evade her as she slumped wearily on to her bed.

CHAPTER 301

After their meal finished, the women and Lindsay sat talking by the fire until the three men returned. They were all sad and reluctant to talk.

"I'm glad you got back before the mist came down," said Shona.

"Yes, the breeze sprang up again, but it is quite a clear night now," said Ruardy.

"Yes, we should get a fine day tomorrow," said Magnus.

Shona and Christina placed the men's suppers before them. Though hungry, they ate reluctantly, their thoughts far away.

Lindsay watched them in silence. He moved his chair to one side to let more warmth reach them, and Roddy noticed his kind gesture.

'He's so like his sweet mother,' Roddy thought.

"We must make an early start in the morning, Lindsay," he said. "Your grandfather will be waiting impatiently."

Lindsay looked at him pensively. "Is my father safely home, Roddy?" he asked.

"Yes, safely home."

"Thanks be to God! At last!" he murmured as he sat rocking to and fro, gazing into the blazing fire.

Martha rose to her feet.

"Come, my boy – you must retire," she said. "You have had a long journey."

She started up the stairs, and he rose to follow, wishing them all goodnight. Christina lit him a candle.

"Sleep well, dear boy," she said.

"I'll try."

The candlelight outlined his weary figure as he went step by step up the steep staircase. The creaking floorboards accompanied his tread.

Martha opened the door of the small room.

"This, my boy, is the room your father had," she said. "From the window you can see the lights in the turrets of Glencree Castle."

She pulled back the curtain, watching him closely as he gazed out with a thoughtful look on his face.

'I hope the morrow brings him the happiness he so richly deserves,' she thought with a sigh.

"The lights are very clear, Grandmama," Lindsay said. "Are they always lit at night?"

"No, my boy, they were lit on your father's return from the war and again tonight, now he is home. They will stay lit until you are home." She turned to go. "Rest easy, my boy. Goodnight."

"Tell me, Grandmama," Lindsay said, the thought still troubling him: "do you think my grandfather will let me visit you often?"

"Oh, I am sure he will," she replied. "Don't be worrying your young head about that. Goodnight."

She closed the door softly behind her.

'Oh, I doubt it very much, my boy,' she thought with a sigh.

Lindsay stood for a long time, still gazing over the loch, pondering. 'I wonder if he will?' he thought. 'I am sure he cannot be as nice as this grandfather.'

He heard several softly spoken goodnights, and at last the house became silent. He blew out his candle and lay a long time, sleep evading him.

"This was dear Mama's home," he murmured. As he gazed idly round the moonlit room, his eye was repeatedly drawn to a picture on the wall opposite. The more he tried not to look at it, the more it seemed to beckon him. He tossed and turned to no avail. Suddenly, he sat bolt upright and relit the candle. He clambered out of bed to view the picture more closely. He raised his candle and gave a gasp of surprise.

"It is my beautiful mother!" he exclaimed. "Dear, dear Mama, how I miss you!" he whispered as he touched it.

She was dressed in a lovely blue coat and bonnet, trimmed with fur. Two small dogs stood at her feet, looking up at her and the ball she was ready to throw. There was a lovely playful smile on her face.

He lowered the light and saw his father's signature across the bottom. 'I wonder how it got here?' he asked himself. He pondered for some time before remembering. 'This must be the picture Papa was asking Aunt Elena about so many years ago.' He recalled the conversation he had overheard as the two sat on the verandah one night. Bruce had said that everything in Craig's room at the castle had to be destroyed. Craig had been angry when Elena told him this, but she had calmed him down and assured him that she had kept all his things herself. 'She must have given this picture to my grandparents,' he thought. 'Well, I shall ask her tomorrow.' He tenderly touched the picture again before clambering back into bed and putting out his candle.

He snuggled further down in the so comfortable bed. 'Well, tomorrow I shall be home,' he thought. 'I wonder what else the day will hold for me.'

CHAPTER 302

Lindsay woke with a start as he heard Martha calling his name. A shaft of bright sunlight lit up the room. For a moment he wondered where he was.

"Here is your tea, Lindsay," she said as she entered.

She went to the window and peered out, shading her eyes against the sun.

"I can see the flag flying at the jetty," she said. "Magnus will hoist a flag here when you set sail." She turned to go. "Now hurry and drink your tea. Roddy will bring you water to wash with directly."

"Where is Ruardy?"

"He is loading the boat with your trunks and the rest of your things."

Roddy greeted Lindsay joyfully. He tipped his water into the large bowl on the dressing table.

"Mama has re-pressed the clothes you wished to greet your grandfather in," he said as laid them neatly over the back of the chair. "Now, don't be too long. We mustn't keep your grandfather waiting."

"I won't, Roddy," Lindsay replied as Roddy left and closed the door behind him.

'My goodness!' he thought. 'Everyone seems to hold him in such awe. I wish I could stay here with these grandparents.' He sighed.

"Good morning, everyone. How do I look?" he exclaimed as he stood halfway up the stairs. "Do you think my grandfather will approve?"

Martha, Magnus, Roddy and Christina looked at him in amazement. It could have been his father standing there in his full tartan. The crisp, snow-white lace jabot at his throat was in startling contrast to his tanned features and dark eyes.

"Splendid, my boy, just splendid!" said Magnus. "Your parents would have been so proud of you."

"As your grandfather will be," said Martha.

"I want him to be proud of me for Papa's sake." Lindsay said. He pondered silently for a few moments before descending.

"Now, come and eat, my boy, before you leave," said Martha.

She looked at him sadly as he sat down. 'How proud our darling angel would have been to see him sitting here!' she thought.

They all wended their way to the loch. Lindsay hoisted the flag and lit the flares, and Ian screamed with delight as the sparks fell into the water. He picked up a handful of pebbles and handed them to Lindsay.

"Throw in the water, please," he said, looking up at Lindsay.

"Very well, my boy. I did promise. Come and help me."

They both laughed gaily as they spun the pebbles across the loch. Ian danced up and down with delight when Lindsay let his pebble fall short.

"He's so like you were in days gone by, Roddy," said Martha, smiling wistfully. "Come now, Ian – Lindsay has to go in the boat."

"Me go in the boat! Me go in the boat!" Ian cried as he stamped his foot.

"No, not today. Papa will take you another day," said Shona.

He came reluctantly to her side, still grumbling.

"Hurry now, Lindsay," Roddy exclaimed, getting a little perturbed at the delay. "Papa insists on rowing you over in your father's boat."

"Of course I do, laddie. Didn't I always row the laird and the young master over?" he retorted indignantly.

"But you are not as strong now. You rowed yesterday, and, in any case, this boat is heavier. Unfortunately, there is no room for me today with Lindsay's boxes."

"I will be all right, Roddy. You follow with Ruardy. There are more stores to take," said Magnus.

"I should like Grandpapa to row me over. Are you sure it will not be too much for you, Grandpapa?" said Lindsay, looking at him with concern.

"Very well, then," Roddy replied, noting his father's indignant glare.

Lindsay turned to say his farewells, and he noticed a small, frail, wizened old lady watching him from the shrubs close by. "Who is that old lady, Grandmama?" he asked.

Before Martha could reply, Merry-Berry approached and touched him.

"I know who you are!" he exclaimed. "You are Merry-Berry. How kind of you to come and greet me! Papa often spoke of you. He told me that if ever I came home and saw you, I must give you this."

From his coat pocket he pulled out a frayed, still-knotted, spotted red kerchief. The soil of his homeland and the small bottle of water from the loch were still wrapped in it.

She looked at Lindsay intently as he handed it to her. She reached out to him. Her tanned, scrawny fingers closed over his.

"You keep it, my boy," she said.

There was a look of sadness on her face. She held his gaze for several seconds, muttering a Gaelic blessing, and then she turned to go.

He stared after her with a puzzled look on his face. She turned and gave him a final wave; then she gathered her shawl round her thin shoulders and disappeared into the hedgerow.

'She is a nice old lady,' he thought, 'as Papa said.' He turned to Martha. "What did she say, Grandmama?" he asked. "I couldn't understand her."

"It was a Gaelic blessing, my son. You will soon learn Gaelic."

"Yes," he replied, "I will get Merry-Berry to teach me."

"Come, my boy," said Magnus, "do hurry."

"Yes, Grandpapa." He rushed to get in the boat. "Thank you, Ruardy, for packing all my things aboard," he said.

Roddy came alongside to help Magnus aboard.

"Yes, everything is aboard, Lindsay, so seat yourself down," he said. He was getting perturbed at the delay.

Lindsay leaped out of the boat and hurriedly kissed Martha.

"I will return soon, Grandmama," he said. He kissed Christina and Shona lightly on the cheeks and bent down to kiss Ian. "I will come soon and throw pebbles in the loch with you again."

"Don't be long," Ian replied.

"No, I promise." There was a look of consternation on Roddy's face as he clambered back into the boat. He sat in deep contemplation as he gazed ahead. Magnus glanced at him now and again as he rowed silently on.

'I wonder what is troubling him so,' Magnus thought.

'How strange it feels!' thought Lindsay, as he turned to give a final wave to Martha before the boat rounded the bend. 'My mother's mother is waving me off; my father's father is beckoning me on!'

He reached for his binoculars and gazed into the distant hills.

"Are those bonfires lit for my homecoming, Grandpapa?" he asked.

"Yes, my boy."

"My, what a lot of customs I have to learn!"

"That is so, my boy."

CHAPTER 303

Elena woke early from her restless night. 'Now, no tears of sadness today; only tears of joy!' she reminded herself.

She hastened downstairs and met Jamie coming from the library.

"How is Sir Bruce now, Jamie?" she asked.

"He has not slept all night. He kept calling for Master Craig. I have just given him some tea. Now he wants to be dressed in his full tartan."

She opened the door slowly and bade Bruce good morning, but he did not reply. "Come, Bruce – we will take breakfast in the dining room," she said.

"You go, Elena. I will eat when Craig comes."

She looked at him sadly. His thoughts were still only of Craig. Already he had forgotten that Craig had arrived the night before, his coffin draped in its mourning tartan, his piper at his head. 'Well, I won't remind him just yet,' she thought as she hurried away.

"Is Sir Bruce ready, Jamie?"

"Yes, milady."

"Come, Bruce – we must get you in your wheelchair. We are going to the jetty to await Lindsay, your grandson."

"Is it today, Elena?" he asked, surprised.

"Yes, we must hurry."

"The flares have gone up and the flags are flying," said Jamie excitedly.

They hurried towards the jetty, where the villagers were all waiting. Elena could see the bonfires in the distance.

"Oh, what a happy day this is, Bruce!" Elena said as she and Jamie busied themselves making Bruce comfortable in his chair.

"Stop fussing, woman!" Bruce exclaimed impatiently. "Put my chair close to the flag. I want to see the boat as soon as it comes in sight. Is his piper on the bank?"

"Yes, both are there, sir," replied Jamie reassuringly. "They will play him ashore."

"Good morning, everyone. We are blessed with a lovely day," said Elena.

"We are!" exclaimed Becky as Elena went to greet her.

There was hardly room for everyone to stand. More and more villagers arrived, and, after greeting Bruce and Elena happily, they huddled up close to one another.

"I am so looking forward to his arrival," Nicholas remarked to his father. "Then we can both walk our dogs together beside the loch."

"I am sure you will be inseparable," remarked Emma.

Lindsay was humming his mother's favourite tunes most of the way as he restlessly waited for the end of the journey. Now and again he broke into song, much to Magnus's amusement.

"You don't sing them as well as your mother did, my boy," he said.

"No, I'm afraid not, Grandpapa. No one could sing them as delightfully as she did." He sighed.

They both sat silently as if they could hear Elizabeth's lovely voice floating out to them. Suddenly, Lindsay rose to his feet and gazed into the distance through his father's old binoculars.

"Everywhere is so beautiful, Grandpapa," he said.

"Please sit down, Lindsay."

"Yes, Grandpapa."

Roddy, watching their boat anxiously, exclaimed to Ruardy, "That is the second time Papa has told him to sit down! He doesn't seem to realise it unsteadies the boat."

"He's just like his father: always reaching out to the beyond. He will be remembering all his father spoke of, I know. We both sat for many hours listening to him talking of his lovely homeland," said Ruardy.

"Well, he is now nearly home," replied Roddy. "He will have the rest of his life to see all his father spoke of."

"I am so glad he decided to come home," said Ruardy. "We have so much to talk about and do together. I hope his grandfather allows him to do the forestry course his father was going to do."

"Well, we can only wait and see," replied Roddy, still watching the boat ahead with concern.

"This is a lovely boat of my father's, Grandpapa," said Lindsay. "I am so glad you didn't destroy it."

"You must never tell your grandfather of its existence. He will never let you keep it, and he will be mighty angry with me for disobeying him," said Magnus warningly.

"Never fear! I shall never say."

Ahead they could see Glencree Castle in all its splendour. The brilliant sun made it look like something out of a fairy tale.

'How magnificent!' Lindsay thought. 'It is all my father said it was. Oh, why did he have to leave such beauty as this?' His face saddened as his mind wandered back.

Once again, he rose to his feet.

"I can see the flag and all the people on the jetty," he said.

"Do sit down, my boy," Magnus implored.

"I'm so sorry, Grandpapa. I forgot."

Magnus shook his head in mock reproach. Roddy tut-tutted his disapproval yet again.

"I can hear bells chiming. Are they for me also?" Lindsay asked.

Magnus nodded in reply.

Suddenly, Lindsay felt he had been here before.

"Now I hear the pipes," he said. "How beautiful they sound over the loch!"

"Yes, that will be old Gordon, your grandfather's piper, and his grandson, Fergus. He is now your very own piper."

"My very own piper?"

"Yes, your very own. They are on the bank over yonder."

Lindsay trained his glasses on them.

"The young piper looks very smart, as does his grandfather."

"Your father's piper will be at his head in Glencree Castle."

"Oh, yes."

Lindsay's joy was suddenly gone. He was wakened out of his sad reverie by the sound of a voice.

"Craig, Craig, my son, my son!"

Lindsay glanced at Magnus, bewildered.

"It is Lindsay, Bruce dear," said Elena.

"It is my son, Craig, I tell you," Bruce replied. "You said he was coming home today. Isn't he a fine boy, my son, Elena?"

"Yes, yes, Bruce, just as you say."

She looked at Emma. Both were at a loss for words. She glanced lovingly down at Bruce. Never had she seen such a glow of happiness on his face or such brilliance in his eyes, which had for so long been dimmed.

"He has been away a long time, hasn't he, Elena?" Bruce said.

"Yes, dear, he has, but he is almost home now." Elena looked at him sadly, her thoughts mingled with regret for all that had gone before.

Lindsay raised his glasses again and focused on the old man in the wheelchair. "It is my grandfather – I just know it. And Aunt Elena is standing beside him. I can make her out now. My grandfather is wearing the tartan, like I am. I can see his bonnet and crest. What a pity he has to stay in his wheelchair!"

"Yes, sadly there will be no more walking, riding or climbing for him. It distresses him so," Magnus replied.

"Well, I shall take him through the glens every day if he so wishes."

"He will enjoy that, my boy."

Magnus looked at him proudly. 'How thoughtful and kind he is – so like his mother!' he thought.

Lindsay sat thoughtfully for several minutes. 'Yes, these are my mountains and I am home. There will be no more tomorrows for us, Papa. We are all home now.'

Jamie handed Bruce his binoculars again. The old man leaned forward, peering excitedly over the loch.

"Elena, Elena, I can see him more clearly now. My son, Craig, is almost home," he said.

"No, dear," she said again. "It is your grandson, Lindsay."

"It isn't, I say," he insisted angrily. "You stupid woman, do you think I do not know my own son? It is Craig. He has come back to me. I knew he would." He sighed contentedly as he peered out.

"Very well, if you say so, Bruce," Elena replied.

She looked at Jamie in despair. "Whatever would he be like when he realised it wasn't Craig?" they seemed to ask each other.

Bruce sat bolt upright and turned to face the villagers. "What a fine figure of a man my son, Craig, is – don't you agree?"

They all nodded their heads in agreement.

"Have you all lost your tongues?" he bellowed angrily.

They shuffled their feet, wondering who would be brave enough to reply. Elena looked from one to the other.

"Yes, milord, your son is a fine-looking man," Mrs Crawford ventured as loudly as she could, from where she stood beside her two granddaughters.

Lindsay raised his glasses again.

"Grandpapa!" he shouted excitedly. "I can see Aunt Elena waving her white handkerchief and my grandfather is waving his bonnet, but he is calling 'Craig, Craig'." Lindsay looked sadly at Magnus. "I do wish he would remember my name, Grandpapa," he said.

"Don't worry, my boy. He will soon get used to you. You will have to be patient. He cannot see too well."

Suddenly, again in his excitement, he stood up and called out to him: "I am home, Grandf—" The cry died on his lips. Too late he remembered Magnus's previous warnings. The boat was caught by the stiffening breeze, and this, combined with Lindsay's sudden movement, caused the boat to overturn.

They were both thrown in the water. Lindsay's head struck a rock, and his trunk and boxes fell on top of him.

There was a frantic cry from Roddy and Ruardy in the following boat. They plunged over the side and swam to help them. Magnus had managed to grasp the side as it keeled over, and he was clinging to the upturned boat. Ruardy reached him, and, with a struggle, managed to right it.

"Get Lindsay! Get the youngster!" Magnus cried frantically.

"Papa has dived in to help him, Grandpapa. You climb in the boat. I will go and assist him."

Bruce had been dabbing his tear-dimmed eyes when Lindsay called to him. Then he had heard Elena's scream of terror and cries of "Lindsay's in the loch. The boat has overturned." She brought her hands to her face in disbelief.

Bruce cried with anguish, "My son, my son!"

Nicholas was the first of the men on the shore to dive in. He was followed by several more as the others watched in horror. Bruce in his distraction tried to stand and reach out to Lindsay, but his chair started to move forward. In their excitement they had forgotten to put the brake on. Elena's hand was resting lightly on his shoulder, and she felt him slip from her grasp. She made a frantic grab for the handle, and Jamie did too, but they were too slow. It tipped headlong into the loch. Several villagers plunged in after it. Emma and Becky rushed to Elena's side, and she collapsed in their arms.

Roddy, with Ruardy and Nicholas's help, got Lindsay's body to the side of the boat. Roddy, glancing in consternation towards the jetty, saw several more men coming to their aid; he also noticed a flurry of activity around the jetty.

Soon Lindsay's lifeless body was hauled into the boat.

"Why are some men swimming under the jetty? It is here we need more assistance!" Magnus exclaimed.

"His Lordship has also fallen into the loch," said one.

Magnus looked at them in disbelief.

"Surely that cannot be!" said Roddy, as he still struggled with Nicholas's help to free Lindsay's mouth of mud and slime.

At last they succeeded. Lindsay started to splutter. The gash on his head was bleeding profusely.

"I thought he was dead," said Nicholas with a sigh of relief.

Ruardy ripped off his wet shirt and tore off several pieces to bandage Lindsay's head.

"No, he isn't dead – thank God! – but his breathing isn't good. We must make haste," said Roddy.

Two of the villagers took the oars and rowed as quickly as they could to the shore. Several pairs of hands reached out to them as they reached the jetty.

"Is the laird all right?" Roddy asked anxiously as he looked at Emma.

She shook her head. She and Becky stood supporting Elena, who reached out to touch Lindsay.

"Is Lindsay all right, Roddy – my poor, poor boy?" Elena asked.

"Yes, he is all right, milady, but we must hurry."

"Jamie, you lead them home. Take Lindsay to his father's room."

"Yes, milady," Jamie replied in a voice distraught with grief.

When news was received of Lindsay's homecoming, Elena had demanded that he have Craig's bedroom, much to Bruce's annoyance. At last he had consented. He felt too old and tired to argue the point. Elena, knowing Bruce would never enter the room, had, with Jamie's help, moved all the things she had saved of Craig's into it.

"It will be just as it was when his father was here," she said to Jamie one day as she stood viewing the room. "Now we only have to put the picture of his grandmother on that wall; then it will be all done. I know Lindsay will love the picture just as much as his father did."

"Yes, I know he will, milady," Jamie replied as he stood back to admire it. "It will be just like having Master Craig home again." He sighed.

"Well, almost!" she replied sadly.

On the morning of his arrival, Jamie had flung the windows wide open to the bracing Scottish air, and the curtains had waved out as if to greet him.

"This is his room, Roddy," said Jamie as the four men mounted the stairs. Jamie rushed ahead to close the windows and prepare his bed. Cook, weeping into her snow-white apron, stood watching with the rest of the household staff beside her, too overwhelmed at events to utter anything but heartbroken sobs.

The doctor and one of the village nurses came to examine him and dress his wounds. The others softly closed the door as they left.

"Jamie, will you stay with Lindsay?" asked Roddy.

"But, Roddy," he sobbed, "Sir Bruce is still in the loch."

Roddy put his arm round Jamie's shoulder.

"Come, then," he said. "We will go to the loch. Nicholas, will you stay?"

"Of course."

As they approached the jetty, they saw the men of the clan carrying Bruce's body, followed by Elena, who was supported by Becky and Emma.

"Roddy, Roddy," Elena cried out, "how is Lindsay? Is he all right?"

"Yes, milady, he seems to be all right."

"Thanks be to God!"

"Is there more we can do for you, milady?"

She clung to his hand. "No, Roddy. Thank you for all you have done," she whispered.

Bruce was placed next to Craig, dressed in his full mourning tartan, by the elders of the clan. His piper stood at his head. Both Craig and Bruce lay in state until all the villagers had come to bid their last farewells.

As they left, they asked in whispers, "How is young Lindsay, Jamie?"

"Not well, not well," was his sad reply.

CHAPTER 304

Elena had sent for Martha to come and sit with her at Lindsay's bedside. Both of them were too numb with shock to weep any more. As he tossed and turned, muttering in delirium, each in turn leaned over him, trying to make out what he was saying. They renewed the cool compresses to his fevered brow.

Often he was back in his childhood, screaming loudly, "Papa, Papa, Mama is here under the stones. Papa, come quickly. Heather is here too. What shall we do, Papa?" His tears flowed as he relived the scene.

Martha, looking in anguish at Elena, covered her face with her hands. At last she could picture only too well how her darling daughter had died. Although her heart was breaking, she clasped Lindsay's hand in hers as she sobbed.

"Don't worry, my boy," she said. "I am here to take care of you."

Elena put her hand over theirs.

"We are all here, dear boy, to take care of you. Just get well for us."

Suddenly, a knock on the door caused them to look up. The nurse, who had been standing close by, went to answer it. Jamie was standing there with Roddy and the elders of the clan.

"Please ask Lady Elena if the elders of the clan can pay their respects to the new Chief of the Clan," Roddy asked.

For a few moments, Elena hesitated, deep in thought. Of course, Lindsay was now the Chief of the Clan, the 12th Earl of Glencree. The title had not died with Bruce, as he always said it would. Surely, Lindsay must get well now to carry on his heritage. She looked up to see Martha and the nurse looking at her questioningly.

"May the elders come in, Lady Elena?" asked Martha.

Elena looked up at the doctor, who stood looking out over the loch. He turned and nodded his head in agreement.

"Come, Martha – we will have a brief respite and take some refreshment," Elena said.

"Only a few moments, gentlemen, please," the doctor said.

They nodded; then they came in and stood silently, three on either side of his bed.

Lindsay's eyes flickered for a brief second as if acknowledging their presence.

They each touched him lightly on the hand and greeted him in Gaelic as Chief of the Clan. The doctor followed them out.

"He is desperately ill – do you understand?"

They nodded and wished him good day.

Elena, on her return, bade the nurse go to the kitchen and partake of some food, "and take a stroll by the loch, dear, for some fresh air," she added.

"Thank you, milady. I will."

"What about you, Doctor?"

"I am quite all right, Lady Elena, thank you."

They continued their silent vigil. Lindsay's delirium now and again increased

Suddenly he cried out, a plaintive wail of despair, "Kechi, Kechi, my precious princess of the desert. Why did you have to die? You, so young and beautiful and innocent!" He cried out more loudly. "She is innocent, I tell you, innocent." He raised his head and reached out, then dropped back on his pillow. "Kechi, Kechi, I love you so," he said.

Elena and Martha looked at each other in despair. 'Who is Kechi?' they wondered.

Martha bent over him and wiped his feverish brow as the doctor came beside them.

"We don't know who he is talking about," said Elena.

The doctor took Lindsay's hand in his and gazed at him. Then he looked kindly at Elena and Martha.

"It's someone he knew a long time ago, I think – maybe during the war. Was he out East?"

"Yes," replied Elena.

The doctor let go of Lindsay's hand.

"Come, ladies," he said, "you must both rest for a while. Nurse is back, and also the extra nurse I sent for is here. I shall stay a little longer."

Days passed, and Lindsay's condition worsened. The villagers called daily, hoping for good news, but they returned to the village with heads bowed. They relayed the news to the others, and some of them stayed to keep a vigil at the gate. Some prayed daily at the church for his recovery.

The woodsmen in the forest still carried on with their felling, always looking tensely at each other when they saw Merry-Berry watching them. They feared her anger. Was this the ill luck she had prophesied would befall?

Margot, after reading the telegram from Elena, sank in her chair, crying, "No, no, it cannot be, it cannot be!"

Martin, reading in the library, heard her cry.

"What is it, my dear?" he asked as he rushed to her side.

Elena was too distressed to answer. She handed him the telegram.

"Oh, how much more tragedy has that family to endure?" he said with a sigh as he sat down beside her. He rubbed her hands to bring them back to life and wrapped a shawl round her shoulders.

"We must go to Elena at once," Margot sobbed. "Martin, send a telegram to Davinia and the girls in London. I cannot face this sorrow alone."

She dried her eyes as Martin placed a cup of tea beside her before leaving. She picked up the telegram and read and reread the fateful message: 'Bruce drowned. Lindsay not expected to recover.'

'My dear, dear boy, whatever has happened to him?' she wondered. 'I pray to God he lives!' She closed her eyes and clasped her hands together.

Daily, as Elena and Martha continued their vigil, Lindsay's delirious rambling persisted.

"Papa, please don't be angry because I enlisted. We all had to do our duty," he cried one day. Then he gave a sudden cry of alarm and clasped his hands to his head. "Duck, lads! Cover your heads! The truck won't clear the portico."

They looked at each other.

"The poor boy's mind never rests, Martha," said Elena as she looked at him sadly.

She placed another cool compress on his fevered brow.

Martha stroked his hand gently and nodded her head in agreement.

"Margot, Margot," he called, "Grandfather wants me to come home. I am coming, Grandfather. I am coming home."

They looked up to see the specialist, who had been sent for, standing at the foot of the bed. Neither had heard him enter the room. He gazed silently down at Lindsay. He had already read the reports of his accident. He asked the nurse to take the two ladies away.

They paced up and down anxiously at the foot of the stairs, awaiting the specialist's verdict. As he came slowly down the stairs, Elena rushed to meet him. Martha stood in the background, looking up at him. She nervously twisted her damp handkerchief round and round her finger.

"Will he get well for us?" Elena asked. "Please say he will get well," she implored.

The specialist clasped both her hands in his as he shook his head. "I only wish I could say yes, my dear," he said. "I am sorry, but I cannot. The blow on his head is far worse than first thought, and his lungs are severely congested."

Elena looked up at him, searching his face for a sign that all would still be well.

"I am so sorry, my dears," he continued. "I regret very much to say, I doubt if he will survive the night."

"No, no," Elena cried, "I cannot lose him also! I have already lost too much."

She reached out to the specialist for support, but she sank in a heap at his feet before he could prevent her fall.

The village doctor arrived at that moment, and he helped the specialist to pick Elena up and place her in a fireside chair. Martha knelt beside her, rubbing her hand as if to give her some of her strength, even though she herself was distracted with grief.

The specialist bade them goodnight, and Jamie closed the door softly behind them. The village doctor returned to Lindsay's room.

A few hours later, there was a knock on the door and Jamie ushered in the doctor. Both women looked at him as he came towards them.

"Lindsay is now sinking fast, Lady Elena," he said. "Do you wish to be with him?"

She nodded, and she rose to her feet. Elena's face was ashen. She stood trembling, pulling her shawl further round her shoulders. Martha did likewise. In spite of the warmth of the log fire, which Jamie had kept blazing all night, an icy chill assailed them.

"Do you feel up to it, Lady Elena?" Martha asked with concern.

"Yes, we must go to our boy."

With Martha and the doctor supporting her, Elena slowly climbed the stairs. The two nurses looked at them sadly as they approached, before making their way to the far corner of the room.

Elena sat beside Lindsay, holding his hand to her lips. She touched his pale cheeks and stroked back the damp black curl on his forehead. Martha knelt beside him, her head bent in prayer. She held his hand, sobbing quietly.

His agitated ramblings had now ceased, but his lips moved as he faintly murmured, "Home, Papa – we are home."

"Come, dears," the doctor whispered as he and one of the nurses raised them to their feet. "He is at rest with those gone before." They kissed Lindsay goodbye and the nurses led them away.

CHAPTER 305

Margot stumbled from the train in her haste to reach Glencree Castle. Only the waiting arms of Roddy prevented her fall.

"Thank you, Roddy," said Martin, as he too helped to steady her.

"Roddy, how is my dear boy? What is the latest news?" Margot asked.

"Not good, Lady Elena. The doctors are still not hopeful of his recovery."

"Will you take some light refreshment after your long journey?" asked Christina.

"No, my dear," Margot replied. "I am most anxious to get to Elena. Where are Martha and Magnus?" she asked as she looked around.

"Mama is staying at Glencree Castle."

"I am so glad Elena has had her company. And Magnus?"

"Papa is recovering well from his fall in the loch when Lindsay had his accident."

"Do wish him a speedy recovery," said Martin. "I see Zan is waiting, so we must hurry."

"Davinia and the girls will be arriving tomorrow," said Margot as they drove away.

"We will make sure they arrive safely at Glencree Castle."

"Thank you, Roddy dear."

The tolling of the church bells told the villagers the news they wished not to hear.

"No, no, it cannot be," they sobbed as they greeted one another. "Not Lindsay also! What is to become of us?"

Merry-Berry trailed her fingers in the loch, then she beat the air with her fists in fury and anguish. Tears streamed down her face.

"The McNair family is finished. Never in all its history has the Castle of Glencree been without a McNair. Now there will be no more tomorrows for them or us," she cried as she wended her way towards the castle gates.

Jamie, on hearing the clatter of horses' hoofs on the cobbled forecourt, raced out to await them. He tried to stem his tears.

Margot alighted from the carriage as the peal of bells rang out. She looked up, startled, and gasped in shock and dismay as she crumpled into Martin's arms.

With Jamie's help he assisted her up the steps and into the lounge.

"Elena, Elena dear, my dear," Margot sobbed as she clung to her, "I am too late."

Elena nodded her head. Margot looked up to see Martha standing forlornly by the large window. She rushed to her side.

"Martha, Martha, it cannot be true!" she exclaimed. "Have we lost our dear boy?"

Martha, tears streaming down her face, could only nod her head in reply. She clasped her hands together in prayer.

"Do sit down, all of you!" Elena exclaimed, trying to be calm. "You brought our boy home, Margot. You could do no more. He is now resting with all his loved ones. For that we must be thankful." She glanced at Jamie, who was standing near the door.

"Jamie, tell Marie to bring refreshments, please," she asked.

"Yes, milady."

Later that day, after waving Martha goodbye, Elena and Margot strolled slowly through the gardens, deep in thought.

"I could not have borne all this without Martha and the thought that soon you would be with me," Elena said.

"My dear Elena, you do not deserve all the sorrow you have had to bear – and so much of it alone."

"Well, I shall have to find more strength when everyone returns home," she replied sadly.

On the following day, Zan was once more waiting near the station for the arrival of the train. Roddy, Christina, Ruardy and Shona talked to Peggoty as they stood on the platform.

"Will it be much longer, Peggoty?" asked Roddy.

"Not long now, Roddy. It's a sorry business to be sure. Lindsay was so young and full of life only a short while ago. Here's the train coming now, Roddy."

The train came to a halt, and Roddy and Christina rushed to meet Davinia, Stephen, Clare and Astrid as they stepped down.

"What a tragedy, to be sure!" exclaimed Davinia.

"We have worse news to greet you with," said Roddy sadly: "Lindsay has died also."

Clare and Astrid, who were talking to Ruardy and Shona, gasped with dismay when they overheard.

"Oh, Ruardy, it cannot be!" exclaimed Astrid as she clung to her mother. "But he was so well when I last saw him," she sobbed.

Clare was sobbing in Christina's arms.

"Come, my dears," said Stephen, "we must get to Glencree Castle as quickly as we can."

"Will you not take tea before you leave?" asked Shona.

"No, thank you, dear," Davinia replied.

Roddy and Ruardy helped them into the carriage and watched as they sped away.

CHAPTER 306

Elena, with Margot and her family, stood in the Great Hall watching in disbelief and despair as, one by one, the coffins emerged from the room where they had lain. Each was covered with the mourning tartan of the clan; each was headed by its own piper. The coffins of Elizabeth and Heather followed a little way behind.

Martha and Magnus and their family stood near the door. They bowed their heads and touched the coffins of their daughter and granddaughter as they passed. Magnus and Roddy supported Martha. Christina, Ruardy and Shona stood beside them. Ian clung to his mother's coat and hid behind her as the coffins approached. He was overawed by the solemnity of the occasion, but Magnus had insisted that he be there to pay his respect to the dead.

Elena stopped to speak to them.

"How are you, Magnus? I do hope you are now fully recovered from your chill. Thank you all so much for trying to save Lindsay, but it was not to be."

Ian, now standing in front of his mother, gazed up at her as she spoke. She glanced down at him and gently patted his head.

"Such a lovely great-grandson you have, Magnus," she said with a sigh.

"Thank you, Lady Elena."

Roddy and Ruardy helped them into the black-draped carriages. Becky, Emma, Stuart and Nicholas were in the last. The servants stood on the steps with bowed heads – all except Jamie, who followed in a carriage alone. He was determined to follow his masters to the end. His head was bowed in a great sorrow, bewildered by the fate that had fallen on this great house.

Down the long winding lane the solemn procession went. The silent thoughts of each mourner were of what might have been.

Suddenly, the hedgerow parted and Merry-Berry peered out. She nodded her head gravely as they passed. Ian gave a whimper of fright at the sight of her. Roddy hugged him close as he tried to hide his face.

"Do not be afraid, my child," Roddy said. "She will not harm you."

Merry-Berry stood there for a long time after they had disappeared from sight. When the great tree was felled, it spelt doom for the Earls of Glencree. She turned back into the hedgerow, and she waved her fist towards the loch in anger and despair.

The elders of the clan, all in mourning tartan, were the first to greet the coffins. The villagers stood close by, still too numb with grief to understand the full significance of what had happened.

Emma glanced slightly disdainfully at a group of women who pushed forward to get a better view as the coffins were carried into the church.

"They're always in front to be first to relate all that is happening to everyone – especially that one." She sighed as she gave Mrs Crawford a withering look.

"I always knew," said Mrs Crawford to her three precious jewels, who were accompanied by their daughters. "I always knew", she repeated scornfully, "that no good would ever come once *she* married into the family. If she had left him alone to marry the one he was betrothed to, none of this would have happened."

"Oh, Mama," said Pearl, "do not speak so of the dead. It is all over now; nothing can be changed."

Her mother shrugged her shoulders, angered by her daughter's reproach.

The final notes of their pipers' lament faded out over the loch as the bodies were finally laid to rest.

Margot and her family bade farewell to all the villagers before departing a few days later. Elena's tears touched them all deeply as they drove away from Glencree Castle.

"I never realised, Grandmama," said Astrid sadly, "how deeply Craig must have loved Elizabeth to sacrifice his heritage for her as he did."

"Yes, few could understand his behaviour at the time, but, as we all know, he couldn't live without her, so it had to be. Zan," she called.

"Yes, milady?" he replied, drawing to a halt.

"I want you to drive to my old home before we reach the station."

They galloped away in silence, the girls eager to see where their grandmother used to live.

"Stop here, Zan, on this high rise," Margot said at last. "We can see it very well from here. Somebody else lives there now, so I won't go closer."

"Well," exclaimed Davinia, "it looks just the same to me. The trees are taller, but I can still see my bedroom window."

"When did you last see it, Mama?" Clare and Astrid chorused.

"A long time ago, when I was quite young. Mama brought me to visit Grandmama, before we left to join Papa in India."

"It was such a lovely home," sighed Margot, lost in reverie.

"Come, dears," said Martin, "we must hurry to catch our train."

Martha and Magnus and their family were waiting for them with worried looks.

"Sorry we are late. We drove to Harrison Hall. It brought back so many memories," said Margot with a sigh.

They hastily said their goodbyes as the train steamed into the station. Margot and Martha both dried their eyes as they waved their final farewells.

"That is the last time we shall see them," said Martha sadly as they wended their way back to the cottage.

Elena stood a long time gazing down the long drive after they disappeared. Jamie watched her sadly.

"Come, milady," he said. "It is too cold to stand out here any longer."

Elena turned and mounted the steps to the castle. They went inside, and Jamie closed the huge oak doors behind them.

CHAPTER 307

In Magnus's cottage, a cloud of sadness prevailed. Coming so soon after the loss of their laird and Master Craig, the loss of their grandson, Lindsay, was more than Martha and Magnus could bear.

"Our darling daughter and granddaughter are buried beside him," said Martha with a sigh as she rested her head on Magnus's shoulder. "Don't you see, Magnus dear, how much we have lost? They were ours. Part of us is laid to rest with them."

"Yes, my dear, I see only too well," Magnus replied, wiping her tears away with his damp handkerchief; "but we cannot change anything," he said sadly as he rose, patting her tenderly on the head. "Don't cry any more, my dear – we have much to do."

Christina and Shona were already packing. Ian watched them curiously. He went and stood beside Martha.

"But, Great-Grandmama, why have we to go away on the big train, and why are you crying again?" he asked as he looked up at her wistfully.

She sat him on her knee.

"Well, my boy," she said, "there is no laird at the big castle now to row over the loch. Great-Grandpapa's work is done, so we have to leave."

"Come, my son," Ruardy called, "Grandpapa is waiting to take us to say goodbye to Lady Elena."

"Yes, Papa."

He ran to Martha and Magnus and tugged them by the hand as he pointed to the loch.

"Papa says come quick. The boat's ready," he said.

"Very well, my boy," said Magnus as he helped Martha to her feet.

Martha and Magnus settled themselves in the boat with Ian sitting between them. Roddy and Ruardy took the oars. Christina and Shona watched them go.

"We must first go to the village," said Martha. "I want to take flowers to the church and also to Lady Elena."

Several times during the journey, Ian rose to his feet, calling out excitedly.

"Look, Great-Grandmama, all the sheep are there," he cried.

"Sit down, Ian," demanded Roddy sternly. "You are rocking the boat."

Ian sat down sulkily and curled up closer to Martha. Tears welled up in his eyes as he looked towards his father. It was not like his grandfather to raise his voice to him.

Since the tragedy, Roddy had viewed with apprehension every trip over, when any of the family were with him. He looked kindly at Ian.

"I shall be glad when we leave this place. It always filled me with happiness, but now there is only bitterness," he said.

Martha knew her son only too well; she knew what he was suffering.

Elena had entreated them to stay, but Magnus had explained to her that Glencree held too many sorrowful memories for them. He was getting too old to row over the loch, and Roddy and Ruardy wished to work with the Forestry Commission further up north. "I wish to go with them," he told her.

"I understand," she replied sadly.

It was a sad farewell to all their friends. Martha's special friends had tears in their eyes. She was thankful she did not meet Mrs Crawford and Mrs Knowell, who, she thought, always looked at her with disdain. They always seemed to be giving her the message, "Begone, all of you. It is because of your daughter that all this ill has befallen us."

When they arrived at the vicarage, they were pleased to find Emma there. She rushed to greet them as the carriage stopped, and she kissed Ian several times before putting him down.

"Come inside. Mama is in. What a sad day for us all, knowing we shall probably never meet again!" she said sadly.

"Yes, it is indeed, my dear Emma," Roddy replied; "but, apart from the tragedy, we all have lovely memories of you all to treasure for ever."

"When do you leave?" Emma asked.

"Tomorrow is our final day," Roddy replied. "I will call again later today with Christina and Shona."

"Well, I will stay until I have said my goodbyes to them."

"Will you stay for tea?" asked Becky as she sat holding Martha's hand.

"No, thank you. We must hurry and say farewell to Lady Elena."

Becky and Martha clung together for a long time after the others had got into the carriage. Both were sobbing as they parted. Emma was also in tears by the time the carriage disappeared from view.

Elena greeted them warmly as Jamie ushered them into the room.

"Do sit down. Jamie, tell Sarah to bring tea," she said.

Jamie hurried away.

"We have brought you these flowers along with our goodbyes," said Martha sadly as she handed them to her.

"They are lovely, Martha, but we cannot say the same about goodbyes, can we?" she replied sadly. "When do you leave, Martha?"

Martha was too distressed to answer.

"We leave tomorrow, Lady Elena," replied Roddy sadly.

"Oh, Roddy," she said as she returned his glance, "we have all lost so much that was dear to us." She sighed.

"Yes, Lady Elena, we have," added Magnus. He found the topic difficult to discuss, but he felt that she wanted to talk and to delay their departure. "Although our loss has been great," he continued, "it has been more so for you. I still have my son, grandson and great-grandson to carry on my name."

"Yes, Magnus, that is so, but that is life. Nothing can alter it now, much as we would wish it otherwise. Now, let there be no more talk of what might have been." She could see that Martha was getting more and more distressed. "Do take more tea before you leave – although I can see Ruardy, your delightful son is eager to leave."

She walked with them to the carriage, where she kissed Martha lightly on both cheeks. Magnus, Roddy and Ruardy bowed their heads as they kissed Elena's hand.

She picked up Ian and cuddled him close. A tear welled up in her eyes as she looked into his. She stroked his hair, as if in him she could see something of what she had lost in her own family. She kissed him, and then she sat him beside Martha in the carriage. She wiped away a tear of farewell as they sped away.

She stood at the doorway for several minutes after they were out of sight.

"Come, milady – let me close the door," said Jamie, who was standing just inside.

She turned to go inside.

"Yes, Jamie," she said, "all the doors are closing one by one."

The next day dawned bright and sunny. Roddy and Ruardy made the last two journeys to the station with the household effects. Peggoty stacked them carefully in one corner to await loading in the train later.

A crisp wind was causing ripples to lap the shores of the loch as Roddy and Ruardy joined Magnus and Ian. Ian busily picked up pebbles while Magnus gazed towards the castle in the distance. Ian gave them all a few pebbles each.

"Throw some pebbles in the water, Great-Grandpapa, please."

"Very well, my boy," Magnus replied.

He spun them into the water.

"I cannot throw them as far as I used to. Ask your father to throw some," Magnus said.

"Very well."

Roddy joined Magnus, and they gazed out, both in deep thought, thinking of bygone days. At last Magnus turned.

"Come, Roddy, my son," he said, "don't dwell on the past any more."

"Yes, I'm coming." He picked up three large pebbles and flung each one as far as he could. "The first one is for you, my darling sister; the next is for you, Craig, who brought her so much joy; and the last one is for you, Lindsay, the last Earl of Glencree and Chief of the Clan. You will be with us all as long as we live."

"Do come, Roddy," Christina called. "Mama and Papa are getting quite chilled."

They watched in silence as Magnus finally locked the door of their small cottage.

"I will leave the key with Peggoty. He can give it to Lady Elena when he goes to the village," Magnus said.

They wended their way slowly to the station.

"Where are we going?" Ian kept crying. "I want to throw pebbles in the loch."

He tugged at his father's hand. Ruardy picked him up.

"We cannot throw any more pebbles in the loch, my son, but there is lots of water where we are going, near Great-Grandpapa's old home up north. See, my son, here comes the big train." Ian dried his eyes.

"I will take him now, Ruardy, whilst you help Roddy and Peggoty," said Shona.

Ian was still whimpering as she tried to console him.

Peggoty gave a blow on his whistle and a forlorn wave of his flag, as the whistle from the engine heralded its departure. All three men reached out from the window to grasp Peggoty's hand in farewell as the train pulled away.

Martha sat silently in the corner. As she took a final glimpse at her home, she wiped away a tear. She hoped to prevent Ian from questioning her as to why she was crying again, but he was looking at the now disappearing loch. He was still despondent because he had been told he would be throwing no more pebbles into it.

Peggoty watched the train of sight. Magnus's head was the last one to withdraw. He was just in time to see Merry-Berry before she slunk back into the shrubbery.

Magnus sat down beside Martha, who was still looking out towards the castle. Roddy watched him closely.

"What are you thinking, Papa?" he asked with concern.

"I was thinking", he said sadly, "that it was my darling dawn angel that took Master Craig away from Glencree, and I was the cause of Lindsay's death. I shall never forgive myself." He sighed.

"Papa, you mustn't blame yourself. It was not your fault," Roddy replied.

"Yes, my son, but you don't understand. I have my heirs; why could it not have been so for the laird of Glencree Castle?"

Martha grasped his hand tightly.

"It was not to be, my dear," she said.

CHAPTER 308

Elena sat, as she had often done since the funeral, in Bruce's chair, gazing into the blazing log fire. In spite of its warmth, a recurring chill kept overwhelming her. She frequently tugged her shawl further round her shoulders, and she glanced now and again at Isabelle's picture. Often she thought she saw a tear seep from the eyes of the portrait, but she put it down to the reflection of the firelight. She rose and ran her fingers along the picture. She caressed Isabelle's fingers.

"Isabelle, my dearest, what am I going to do now? I am so alone without my three boys. What am I to do?"

She gazed into the eyes of the painting and pondered a few moments.

"You seem to be smiling now, dear. Yes, you be happy, my dearest one. They are all with you now. Only I am left to mourn them here, but one day, one day, we will all meet again."

She wiped away her tears, and she sat wearily down.

Jamie's knock on the door broke in on her reverie. "I have brought more logs for the fire, milady," he said as he entered the room.

He put down his heavy basket and stirred the embers. Then he placed a few fresh logs on top.

"Jamie," Elena said listlessly, "the master always liked the blazing firelight. Where has all the light gone from this house, Jamie?"

Jamie rose to his feet, keeping his head low, not answering. His grief was too great for speech.

Elena rose to look over the loch. It was now shimmering in the morning sun, which had once cast a glowing radiance over their happy days. At night the golden moon laid its peaceful light over its waters. Her thoughts winged back to all their childhood days. She remembered them skimming their pebbles, laughing gaily, seeing who could throw them the furthest, watching the ripples as they spread and were broken by another stone falling close by.

Of course, Bruce's always spun the furthest, but he now and again would let one fall short and pretend to be angry with himself for losing.

Then she could see the ever laughing face of Craig doing likewise, his adoring mother laughing with him as she collected his pebbles. Then she pictured him in his first rowing boat, so proud as he called them to watch. She sighed. This lovely loch had, until that fateful day, always brought them so much happiness. Now all was gone, like a sigh on the wind. She sighed again as she wended her way back to her chair. She started at a sudden knock on the door.

"What is it, Jamie?" she asked as he entered.

"It is Lawrie with a letter. Shall I take it?"

"No, Jamie, I will go to him. I want to wish him goodbye."

Lawrie doffed his cap and looked at her sadly. She took the letter from him reluctantly.

'How I hate these long buff envelopes, as I hated the small ones long ago,' she thought. 'None ever contains any good news.'

"Thank you, Lawrie, it will probably be the last letter you bring me, so goodbye."

She held out her hand. He bowed his head low as he held it lightly.

"It is a sad time for us all, Lady Elena," he said. "Goodbye," he whispered as he turned to go.

Jamie closed the door behind him and followed Elena back to the lounge. She sighed deeply as she read the letter. Jamie looked at her, pondering as to its contents. She looked up at him, noticing his look of concern.

'Poor Jamie!' she thought. 'Whatever would I do without him?'

"It is from the trust, Jamie. They say they will be delighted to accept Glencree Castle and all the estate. The castle will be used as a convalescent home for crippled ex-servicemen of both world wars; the estate will be made into a park for the recreation of all the people.

"Bruce planned it all long ago, when he didn't know that Lindsay would be coming home. I know Lindsay would approve of his plan. The solicitor will be here tomorrow for my final signature," she said sadly as she placed the letter on the small table beside her chair. "Rebuild the fire, Jamie; I am feeling quite chilled."

She stood up and gazed at Isabelle's portrait.

"Only you, dear, will be left to watch over it all," she said. "I know it will be something dear to your heart."

"Did you say something, milady?" asked Jamie.

"No, Jamie, I was only thinking out loud."

The next day, Jamie ushered Mr Macrae into the library. Elena listened intently to all he said, showing no sigh of what the ordeal was costing her.

She rang for tea as he finished talking and placed the papers before her. He handed her his pen, which she took from him reluctantly. Trembling with the finality of it all, she scrawled her signature across each page. He gathered them up carefully and placed them in his briefcase.

"There are also the family jewels," she said as she poured his tea. "It is my wish that they be sold and the proceeds sent to the overseas missions."

"Very well, Lady Elena. I shall see that it is done."

She went over to the safe and withdrew all the cases of jewels. She watched as Mr Macrae placed them inside his case. "I will leave them at our bank in the city for safekeeping," he said.

She flinched visibly as she heard the final click of the catch on his briefcase.

She handed him the large bunch of keys to the castle and watched with a heavy heart as he placed them in his pocket.

Elena thought, 'He takes the keys to people's hearts and puts them in his pocket as he would a handkerchief.'

"I will send my key to you later," she said. She was getting anxious for him to leave.

"That will be quite in order, Lady Elena. Please accept my deep condolences on your great loss," he said as he shook her hand on leaving.

CHAPTER 309

Early next day, Elena stood alone at the doorway of the large hall, her head held high as one by one she said farewell to her servants. They were almost too upset to speak as she kissed them on each cheek.

"Goodbye, milady," they said.

All were now going to rejoin their families in the village. For most of them, their whole life had been bound up with the family of Glencree Castle. Tears flowed freely as she watched them enter the carriages and hastily speed away.

Zan, in a carriage alone, drew up opposite her. He alighted and with Jamie's help loaded up her few personal possessions.

"Leave them all at the vicarage, Zan. I will send for them later," she said.

Later that day, Jamie brought her carriage to the front door and dismounted. He entered the hall and watched her sadly as she stood, a lonely figure in black, gazing at all that was dear to her. Her last glance of all was reserved for Isabelle's picture. Then she looked at Jamie.

"Are you sure all the turret lights are out, Jamie?" she asked.

"All out, milady!" he replied with a catch in his throat.

She picked up her hand luggage, and he followed her to the door. She withdrew her key from her pocket, placed it in the lock and pulled the large brass knob, but the door seemed to resist her. A faint frown crossed her brow. Was it her own weakness that was defeating her efforts, she wondered, or was the old home reluctant to let her go? Were the ghosts of the past willing her to stay?

Jamie tried to assist her.

"I can manage, Jamie," she said. "Please hold my bag."

Then, with an extra-hard pull, the door closed. She sighed. Tears streamed down her face as she struggled to turn the key. She dried her eyes, stiffened her tiny back and tried again.

"Shall I try, milady? Shall I try, milady?" Jamie repeated, putting the bag on the step.

She pushed his hand away.

"I must lock it, Jamie," she said.

After several more attempts, she heard the fateful click. She stood back, gazing at it. How could the end of the McNairs be true? This great door had never before been locked.

Jamie picked up her bag, and he kept his eyes on the steps so as to hide his threatening tears. He told himself, 'I must be brave for Lady Elena's sake.'

At last, she walked reluctantly down the steps and entered the carriage. Jamie placed her bag beside her and put her travel rug round her, then he urged the horse into a sharp trot down the long drive. The only goodbye to be said now was to old Dougal who was waiting at the tall gates.

Dougal shook her hand as she leaned out to say goodbye. Tears ran down his weather-beaten face.

"Lock the gate now, Dougal," Elena said.

"But, milady, these gates have never been locked," he stammered between his sobs.

"I know, Dougal, but they must be locked now," she said with a deep broken-hearted sigh.

She turned and watched with a heavy heart as the tall, gold-emblazoned, scrolled gates, with their gold-painted monogram, shuddered closed.

"I am taking the road by the loch, Jamie."

"Very well, milady," he said.

He looked at her questioningly, then urged the horse to proceed down the narrow lane leading to the loch side.

"Stop here, Jamie," Elena ordered.

She gathered her extra shawl round her shoulders and prepared to dismount. Jamie hastily rushed to assist her.

"Why do you wish to stop? Are you not feeling well, milady?"

"I am quite all right, Jamie," she said. "I want to spend a few moments beside the loch."

"Shall I help you down? It is quite steep."

"No, I want to go alone."

She went cautiously down the small, rugged path, the loose pebbles clattering as they slid towards the water's edge.

"Be careful, Lady Elena," he warned as she stumbled several times.

She bent down and trailed her fingers in the icy water. Then she gazed into its depths, seeing her reflection and that of Harriet and Bruce. Her thoughts went back to her childhood. She stood up after several minutes and fumbled in her pocket for the key. Then, after kissing it fondly, she flung it as far as she could. She watched the swirling ripples it made when it hit the water, and she saw in them the faces of Bruce, Craig and Lindsay.

At last the water was still. She reached for her handkerchief and wiped away a tear.

"Why, dear loch, had you to take everything from me? Why? Why?" she cried in anguish.

A rustle of branches close by made her turn, and Merry-Berry came towards her. Elena held out her hands, and the bronzed, wizened old lady gripped them firmly.

"Goodbye. God be with you, Lady Elena," Merry-Berry uttered in Gaelic as she turned to go.

"God be with you. Goodbye, dear friend," Elena replied, also in Gaelic.

She retraced her steps, and Jamie aided her last few strides.

"My, I never realised, Jamie, how steep the banking is. I am quite out of breath. I must be older than I thought."

Back in the carriage, she turned for a last glimpse of the castle, which was now only a faint outline against the evening sky.

"Go, Jamie," she demanded, "as fast as you can."

She shuddered in the chill of the evening and, pulling her shawl further round her shoulders, they disappeared in the Highland mist.

A Lonely Scottish Heart

None lonelier than a Scottish heart
When from his mist-enshrouded mountains he has roamed.
Always the whisper on the wind he hears:
"Come home, my son, come home."

In other's lands and hills and vales
None but his own, his heart enslave.
Always the whisper on the wind he hears:
"Come home, my son, come home."

The sunnier skies, the mountains high,
Only re-echo his soul-lost sighs.
Only the whisper of the wind is nigh:
"Come home, my son, come home.
Come home, my son, come home."

Gone for ever, the sunnier skies;
Gone for ever, the mountains high;
Gone for ever, his soul-lost sighs.
Only the whisper on the wind is nigh:
"You are home, my son, you are home."

No more tomorrows to bide on their way;
No more sorrows to break o'er their day.
Their silent souls traverse land, sea and sky;
Not even the wind is whispering nigh.